at Port Mahon, a handsome

fated

fitted with the   first

C major Quartet   players,

by the rows of little round gilt

mounting & mounting in   chasm of
high rich   the tremendous   deep   silence

te crescendo, pause, & the liberating

s at least some of the audience

n: in the third row, on the left

they happened to be sitting next to

f between twenty and thirty, whose big

a streak of gold to be seen here

waistcoat,
form — the fine blue coat, white/breeches

Royal Navy — and the broad gold-

, while his bright blue eyes, staring

The Complete
Aubrey/Maturin
Novels

The Works of Patrick O'Brian

The sails of a square-rigged ship, hung out to dry in a calm

1	Flying jib	12	Mainsail, or course
2	Jib	13	Maintopsail
3	Fore topmast staysail	14	Main topgallant
4	Fore staysail	15	Mizzen staysail
5	Foresail, or course	16	Mizzen topmast staysail
6	Fore topsail	17	Mizzen topgallant staysail
7	Fore topgallant	18	Mizzen sail
8	Mainstaysail	19	Spanker
9	Maintopmast staysail	20	Mizzen topsail
10	Middle staysail	21	Mizzen topgallant
11	Main topgallant staysail		

Illustration source: Serres, Liber Nauticus.
Courtesy of the Science and Technology Research Center,
The New York Public Library, Astor, Lenox, and Tilden Foundations

PATRICK O'BRIAN

The Complete Aubrey/Maturin Novels

Books 1–4

W. W. NORTON & COMPANY   NEW YORK • LONDON

For information about permission to reproduce selections from
this book, write to Permissions, W. W. Norton & Company, Inc.,
500 Fifth Avenue, New York, NY 10110

Manufacturing by R. R. Donnelley & Sons, Inc.
Production manager: Anna Oler

ISBN 0-393-06011-X (for the set of five volumes)

W. W. Norton & Company, Inc.
500 Fifth Avenue, New York, N.Y. 10110
www.wwnorton.com

W. W. Norton & Company Ltd.
Castle House, 75/76 Wells Street, London W1T 3QT

1 2 3 4 5 6 7 8 9 0

CONTENTS

CONTENTS

Master and
Commander

AUTHOR'S NOTE

When one is writing about the Royal Navy of the eighteenth and early nineteenth centuries it is difficult to avoid understatement; it is difficult to do full justice to one's subject; for so very often the improbable reality outruns fiction. Even an uncommonly warm and industrious imagination could scarcely produce the frail shape of Commodore Nelson leaping from his battered seventy-four-gun *Captain* through the quarter-gallery window of the eighty-gun *San Nicolas*, taking her, and hurrying on across her deck to board the towering *San Josef* of a hundred and twelve guns, so that 'on the deck of a Spanish first-rate, extravagant as the story may seem, did I receive the swords of the vanquished Spaniards; which, as I received, I gave to William Fearney, one of my bargemen, who put them, with the greatest *sang-froid*, under his arm'.

The pages of Beatson, James and the *Naval Chronicle*, the Admiralty papers in the Public Record Office, the biographies in Marshall and O'Byrne are filled with actions that may be a little less spectacular (there was only one Nelson), but that are certainly no less spirited – actions that few men could invent and perhaps none present with total conviction. That is why I have gone straight to the source for the fighting in this book. From the great wealth of brilliantly-fought, baldly-described actions I have picked some I particularly admire; and so when I describe a fight I have log-books, official letters, contemporary accounts or the participants' own memoirs to vouch for every exchange. Yet, on the other hand, I have not felt slavishly bound to precise chronological sequence; and the naval historian will notice, for example, that Sir James Saumarez' action in the Gut of Gibraltar has been postponed until after the grape-harvest, just as he will see that at least one of my *Sophie*'s battles was fought by quite another sloop, though one of exactly the same strength. Indeed, I have taken great liberties; I have seized upon documents, poems, letters; in short, *j'ai pris mon bien là où je l'ai trouvé*, and within a context of general historical accuracy I have changed names, places and minor events to suit my tale.

My point is that the admirable men of those times, the Cochranes, Byrons, Falconers, Seymours, Boscawens and the many less famous sailors from whom I have in some degree compounded my characters, are best celebrated in their own splendid actions rather than in imaginary contests; that authenticity is a jewel; and that the echo of their words has an abiding value.

At this point I should like to acknowledge the advice and assistance I have had from the patient, erudite officials of the Public Record Office and of the National Maritime Museum at Greenwich, as well as the Commanding Officer of HMS *Victory*: no one could have been kinder or more helpful.

P.O'B.

1

THE MUSIC-ROOM in the Governor's House at Port
Mahon, a tall, handsome, pillared octagon, was filled
with the triumphant first movement of Locatelli's C major
quartet. The players, Italians pinned against the far wall by
rows and rows of little round gilt chairs, were playing with
passionate conviction as they mounted towards the penulti-
mate crescendo, towards the tremendous pause and the
deep, liberating final chord. And on the little gilt chairs at
least some of the audience were following the rise with an
equal intensity: there were two in the third row, on the left-
hand side; and they happened to be sitting next to one
another. The listener farther to the left was a man of between
twenty and thirty whose big form overflowed his seat, leaving
only a streak of gilt wood to be seen here and there. He was
wearing his best uniform – the white-lapelled blue coat,
white waistcoat, breeches and stockings of a lieutenant in the
Royal Navy, with the silver medal of the Nile in his button-
hole – and the deep white cuff of his gold-buttoned sleeve
beat the time, while his bright blue eyes, staring from what
would have been a pink-and-white face if it had not been so
deeply tanned, gazed fixedly at the bow of the first violin. The
high note came, the pause, the resolution; and with the resolution the sailor's fist swept firmly down upon his knee. He
leant back in his chair, extinguishing it entirely, sighed happily and turned towards his neighbour with a smile. The
words 'Very finely played, sir, I believe' were formed in his
gullet if not quite in his mouth when he caught the cold and
indeed inimical look and heard the whisper, 'If you really
must beat the measure, sir, let me entreat you to do so in
time, and not half a beat ahead.'

Jack Aubrey's face instantly changed from friendly ingenuous communicative pleasure to an expression of somewhat
baffled hostility: he could not but acknowledge that he *had*

been beating the time; and although he had certainly done so with perfect accuracy, in itself the thing was wrong. His colour mounted; he fixed his neighbour's pale eye for a moment, said, 'I trust . . .', and the opening notes of the slow movement cut him short.

The ruminative 'cello uttered two phrases of its own and then began a dialogue with the viola. Only part of Jack's mind paid attention, for the rest of it was anchored to the man at his side. A covert glance showed that he was a small, dark, white-faced creature in a rusty black coat – a civilian. It was difficult to tell his age, for not only had he that kind of face that does not give anything away, but he was wearing a wig, a grizzled wig, apparently made of wire, and quite devoid of powder: he might have been anything between twenty and sixty. 'About my own age, in fact, however,' thought Jack. 'The ill-looking son of a bitch, to give himself such airs.' With this almost the whole of his attention went back into the music; he found his place in the pattern and followed it through its convolutions and quite charming arabesques to its satisfying, logical conclusion. He did not think of his neighbour again until the end of the movement, and then he avoided looking in his direction.

The minuet set Jack's head wagging with its insistent beat, but he was wholly unconscious of it; and when he felt his hand stirring on his breeches and threatening to take to the air he thrust it under the crook of his knee. It was a witty, agreeable minuet, no more; but it was succeeded by a curiously difficult, almost harsh last movement, a piece that seemed to be on the edge of saying something of the very greatest importance. The volume of sound died away to the single whispering of a fiddle, and the steady hum of low conversation that had never stopped at the back of the room threatened to drown it: a soldier exploded in a stifled guffaw and Jack looked angrily round. Then the rest of the quartet joined the fiddle and all of them worked back to the point from which the statement might arise: it was essential to get straight back into the current, so as the 'cello came in with its predictable and necessary contribution of *pom, pom-pom-pom, poom*, Jack's chin sank upon his breast and in unison with the 'cello he went *pom, pom-pom-pom, poom*. An elbow drove into his ribs and the sound *shshsh* hissed in his ear. He found that his hand was high in the air, beating time; he lowered it, clenched his mouth shut and looked down at his feet until the music was over. He heard the noble conclusion and recognized that it was far beyond the straightforward winding-up that he had foreseen, but he could take no pleasure in it. In the applause and general din his neighbour looked at him, not so much with defiance as with total, heart-felt disapprobation: they did not speak, but sat in rigid awareness of one another while Mrs Harte, the commandant's wife, went through a long and technically difficult piece on her harp. Jack Aubrey looked out of the long, elegant windows into the night: Saturn was rising in the south-south-east, a glowing ball in the Minorcan sky. A nudge, a thrust of that kind, so vicious and deliberate, was very like a blow. Neither his personal temper nor his professional code could patiently suffer an affront: and what affront was graver than a blow?

As it could not for the moment find any outward expression, his anger took on the form of melancholy: he thought of his shipless state, of half and whole promises made to him and broken, and of the many schemes he had built up on visionary foundations. He owed his prize-agent, his man of business, a hundred and twenty pounds; and its interest of fifteen per cent was about to fall due; and his pay was five pounds twelve shillings a month. He thought of men he knew, junior to him but with better luck or better interest, who were now lieutenants in command of brigs or cutters, or who had even been promoted master and commander: and all of them snapping up trabacaloes in the Adriatic, tartans in the Gulf of Lions, xebecs and settees along the whole of the Spanish coast. Glory, professional advancement, prize-money.

The storm of applause told him that the performance was

over, and he beat his palms industriously, stretching his mouth into an expression of rapturous delight. Molly Harte curtseyed and smiled, caught his eye and smiled again; he clapped louder; but she saw that he was either not pleased or that he had not been attending, and her pleasure was sensibly diminished. However, she continued to acknowledge the compliments of her audience with a radiant smile, looking very well in pale blue satin and a great double rope of pearls – pearls from the *Santa Brigida*.

Jack Aubrey and his neighbour in the rusty black coat stood up at the same time, and they looked at one another: Jack let his face return to its expression of cold dislike – the dying remnants of his artificial rapture were peculiarly disagreeable, as they faded – and in a low voice he said, 'My name is Aubrey, sir: I am staying at the Crown.'

'Mine, sir, is Maturin. I am to be found any morning at Joselito's coffee-house. May I beg you to stand aside?'

For a moment Jack felt the strongest inclination to snatch up his little gilt chair and beat the white-faced man down with it; but he gave way with a tolerable show of civility – he had no choice, unless he was to be run into – and shortly afterwards he worked through the crowd of tight-packed blue or red coats with the occasional civilian black as far as the circle round Mrs Harte, called out 'Charming – capital – beautifully played' over heads three deep, waved his hand and left the room. As he went through the hall he exchanged greetings with two other sea-officers, one of them a former messmate in the gun-room of the *Agamemnon*, who said, 'You are looking very hipped, Jack,' and with a tall midshipman, stiff with the sense of occasion and the rigour of his starched, frilled shirt, who had been a youngster in his watch in the *Thunderer*; and lastly he bowed to the commandant's secretary, who returned his bow with a smile, raised eyebrows and a very significant look.

'I wonder what that infamous brute has been up to now,' thought Jack, walking down towards the harbour. As he

walked memories of the secretary's duplicity and of his own
ignoble truckling to that influential personage came into his
mind. A beautiful, newly-coppered, newly-captured little
French privateer had been virtually promised to him: the secretary's brother had appeared from Gibraltar – adieu, kiss my
hand to that command. 'Kiss my arse,' said Jack aloud,
remembering the politic tameness with which he had
received the news, together with the secretary's renewed professions of good will and of unspecified good offices to be
performed in the future. Then he remembered his own conduct that evening, particularly his withdrawing to let the
small man walk by, and his inability to find any remark, any
piece of repartee that would have been both crushing and
well clear of boorishness. He was profoundly dissatisfied with
himself, and with the man in the black coat, and with the service. And with the velvet softness of the April night, and the
choir of nightingales in the orange-trees, and the host of stars
hanging so low as almost to touch the palms.

The Crown, where Jack was staying, had a certain resemblance to its famous namesake in Portsmouth: it had the
same immense gilt and scarlet sign hanging up outside, a
relic of former British occupations, and the house had been
built about 1750 in the purest English taste, with no concessions whatever to the Mediterranean except for the tiles; but
there the likeness stopped. The landlord was from Gibraltar
and the staff was Spanish, or rather Minorcan; the place
smelt of olive oil, sardines and wine; and there was not the
least possibility of a Bakewell tart, an Eccles cake or even a
decent suet pudding. Yet, on the other hand, no English inn
could produce a chambermaid so very like a dusky peach as
Mercedes. She bounced out on to the dim landing, filling it
with vitality and a kind of glow, and she called up the stairs,
'A letter, Teniente: I bring him . . .' A moment later she was at
his side, smiling with innocent delight: but he was only too
clearly aware of what any letter addressed to him might have
in it, and he did not respond with anything more than a

mechanical jocosity and a vague dart at her bosom.

'And Captain Allen come for you,' she added.

'Allen? Allen? What the devil can he want with me?' Captain Allen was a quiet, elderly man; all that Jack knew of him was that he was an American Loyalist and that he was considered very set in his ways – invariably tacked by suddenly putting his helm hard a-lee, and wore a long-skirted waistcoat. 'Oh, the funeral, no doubt,' he said. 'A subscription.'

'Sad, Teniente, sad?' said Mercedes, going away along the corridor. 'Poor Teniente.'

Jack took his candle from the table and went straight to his room. He did not trouble with the letter until he had thrown off his coat and untied his stock; then he looked suspiciously at the outside. He noticed that it was addressed, in a hand he did not know, to *Captain* Aubrey, R.N.: he frowned, said 'Damned fool', and turned the letter over. The black seal had been blurred in the impression, and although he held it close to the candle, directing the light in a slanting manner over its surface, he could not make it out.

'I cannot make it out,' he said. 'But at least it ain't old Hunks. He always seals with a wafer.' Hunks was his agent, his vulture, his creditor.

At length he went so far as to open the letter, which read:

By the Right Honourable Lord Keith, Knight of the Bath, Admiral of the Blue and Commander in Chief of His Majesty's Ships and Vessels employed and to be employed in the Mediterranean, etc., etc., etc.

Whereas Captain Samuel Allen of His Majesty's Sloop *Sophie* is removed to the *Pallas*, Captain James Bradby deceased –

You are hereby required and directed to proceed on board the *Sophie* and take upon you the Charge and Command of Commander of her; willing and requiring all the Officers and Company belonging to the said Sloop to behave themselves in their several Employ-

ments with all due Respect and Obedience to you their
Commander; and you likewise to observe as well the
General Printed Instructions as what Orders and
Directions you may from time to time receive from any
your superior Officer for His Majesty's Service. Hereof
nor you nor any of you may fail as you will answer the
contrary at your Peril.
    And for so doing this shall be your Order.
    Given on board the *Foudroyant*
    at sea, 1st April, 1800.
To John Aubrey, Esqr,
hereby appointed Commander of
His Majesty's Sloop *Sophie*
By command of the Admiral Thos Walker

His eyes took in the whole of this in a single instant, yet his
mind refused either to read or to believe it: his face went red,
and with a curiously harsh, severe expression he obliged himself to spell through it line by line. The second reading ran
faster and faster: and an immense delighted joy came welling
up about his heart. His face grew redder still, and his mouth
widened of itself. He laughed aloud and tapped the letter,
folded it, unfolded it and read it with the closest attention,
having entirely forgotten the beautiful phrasing of the middle
paragraph. For an icy second the bottom of the new world
that had sprung into immensely detailed life seemed to be
about to drop out as his eyes focused upon the unlucky date.
He held the letter up to the light, and there, as firm, comforting and immovable as the rock of Gibraltar, he saw the Admiralty's watermark, the eminently respectable anchor of hope.

He was unable to keep still. Pacing briskly up and down the
room he put on his coat, threw it off again and uttered a
series of disconnected remarks, chuckling as he did so.
'There I was, worrying . . . ha, ha . . . such a neat little brig –
know her well . . . ha, ha . . . should have thought myself the
happiest of men with the command of the sheer-hulk, or the

Vulture slop-ship . . . any ship at all . . . admirable copperplate hand – singular fine paper . . . almost the only quarterdeck brig in the service: charming cabin, no doubt . . . capital weather – so warm . . . ha, ha . . . if only I can get men: that's the great point . . .' He was exceedingly hungry and thirsty: he darted to the bell and pulled it violently, but before the rope had stopped quivering his head was out in the corridor and he was hailing the chambermaid. 'Mercy! Mercy! Oh, there you are, my dear. What can you bring me to eat, manger, mangiare? Pollo? Cold roast pollo? And a bottle of wine, *vino* – two bottles of *vino*. And Mercy, will you come and do something for me? I want you, désirer, to do something for me, eh? Sew on, cosare, a button.'

'Yes, Teniente,' said Mercedes, her eyes rolling in the candlelight and her teeth flashing white.

'Not teniente,' cried Jack, crushing the breath out of her plump, supple body. 'Capitan! Capitano, ha, ha, ha!'

HE WOKE in the morning straight out of a deep, deep sleep: he was fully awake, and even before he opened his eyes he was brimming with the knowledge of his promotion.

'She is not quite a first-rate, of course,' he observed, 'but who on earth wants a blundering great first-rate, with not the slightest chance of an independent cruise? Where is she lying? Beyond the ordnance quay, in the next berth to the *Rattler*. I shall go down directly and have a look at her – waste not a minute. No, no. That would never do – must give them fair warning. No: the first thing I must do is to go and render thanks in the proper quarters and make an appointment with Allen – dear old Allen – I must wish him joy.'

The first thing he did in point of fact was to cross the road to the naval outfitter's and pledge his now elastic credit to the extent of a noble, heavy, massive epaulette, the mark of his present rank – a symbol which the shopman fixed upon his left shoulder at once and upon which they both gazed with great complacency in the long glass, the shopman looking from behind Jack's shoulder with unfeigned pleasure on his face.

As the door closed behind him Jack saw the man in the black coat on the other side of the road, near the coffee-house. The evening flooded back into his mind and he hurried across, calling out, 'Mr – Mr Maturin. Why, there you are, sir. I owe you a thousand apologies, I am afraid. I must have been a sad bore to you last night, and I hope you will forgive me. We sailors hear so little music – are so little used to genteel company – that we grow carried away. I beg your pardon.'

'My dear sir,' cried the man in the black coat, with an odd flush rising in his dead-white face, 'you had every reason to be carried away. I have never heard a better quartetto in my life – such unity, such fire. May I propose a cup of chocolate, or coffee? It would give me great pleasure.'

'You are very good, sir. I should like it of all things. To tell the truth, I was in such a hurry of spirits I forgot my break-fast. I have just been promoted,' he added, with an off-hand laugh.

'Have you indeed? I wish you joy of it with all my heart, sure. Pray walk in.'

At the sight of Mr Maturin the waiter waved his forefinger in that discouraging Mediterranean gesture of negation – an inverted pendulum. Maturin shrugged, said to Jack, 'The posts are wonderfully slow these days,' and to the waiter, speaking in the Catalan of the island, 'Bring us a pot of chocolate, Jep, furiously whipped, and some cream.'

'You speak the Spanish, sir?' said Jack, sitting down and flinging out the skirts of his coat to clear his sword in a wide gesture that filled the low room with blue. 'That must be a splendid thing, to speak the Spanish. I have often tried, and with French and Italian too; but it don't answer. They gener-ally understand me, but when *they* say anything, they speak so quick I am thrown out. The fault is here, I dare say,' he observed, rapping his forehead. 'It was the same with Latin when I was a boy: and how old Pagan used to flog me.' He laughed so heartily at the recollection that the waiter with the chocolate laughed too, and said, 'Fine day, Captain, sir, fine day!'

'Prodigious fine day,' said Jack, gazing upon his rat-like visage with great benevolence. 'Bello soleil, indeed. But,' he added, bending down and peering out of the upper part of the window, 'it would not surprise me if the tramontana were to set in.' Turning to Mr Maturin he said, 'As soon as I was out of bed this morning I noticed that greenish look in the nor-nor-east, and I said to myself, "When the sea-breeze dies away, I should not be surprised if the tramontana were to set in." '

'It is curious that you should find foreign languages difficult, sir,' said Mr Maturin, who had no views to offer on the weather, 'for it seems reasonable to suppose that a good ear for music would accompany a facility for acquiring – that the two would necessarily run together.'

'I am sure you are right, from a philosophical point of view,' said Jack. 'But there it is. Yet it may well be that my musical ear is not so very famous, neither; though indeed I love music dearly. Heaven knows I find it hard enough to pitch upon the true note, right in the middle.'

'You play, sir?'

'I scrape a little, sir. I torment a fiddle from time to time.'

'So do I! So do I! Whenever I have leisure, I make my attempts upon the 'cello.'

'A noble instrument,' said Jack, and they talked about Boccherini, bows and rosin, copyists, the care of strings, with great satisfaction in one another's company until a brutally ugly clock with a lyre-shaped pendulum struck the hour: Jack Aubrey emptied his cup and pushed back his chair. 'You will forgive me, I am sure. I have a whole round of official calls and an interview with my predecessor. But I hope I may count upon the honour, and may I say the pleasure – the great pleasure – of your company for dinner?'

'Most happy,' said Maturin, with a bow.

They were at the door. 'Then may we appoint three o'clock at the Crown?' said Jack. 'We do not keep fashionable hours in the service, and I grow so devilish hungry and peevish by then that you will forgive me, I am sure. We will wet the swab, and when it is handsomely awash, why then perhaps we might try a little music, if that would not be disagreeable to you.'

'Did you see that hoopoe?' cried the man in the black coat.

'What is a hoopoe?' cried Jack, staring about.

'A bird. That cinnamon-coloured bird with barred wings. Upupa epops. There! There, over the roof. There! There!'

'Where? Where? How does it bear?'

'It has gone now. I had been hoping to see a hoopoe ever since I arrived. In the middle of the town! Happy Mahon, to have such denizens. But I beg your pardon. You were speaking of wetting a swab.'

'Oh, yes. It is a cant expression we have in the Navy. The swab is this' – patting his epaulette – 'and when first we ship it, we wet it: that is to say, we drink a bottle or two of wine.'

'Indeed?' said Maturin with a civil inclination of his head. 'A decoration, a badge of rank, I make no doubt? A most elegant ornament, so it is, upon my soul. But, my dear sir, have you not forgot the other one?'

'Well,' said Jack, laughing, 'I dare say I shall put them both on, by and by. Now I will wish you a good day and thank you for the excellent chocolate. I am so happy that you saw your epop.'

The first call Jack had to pay was to the senior captain, the naval commandant of Port Mahon. Captain Harte lived in a big rambling house belonging to one Martinez, a Spanish merchant, and he had an official set of rooms on the far side of the patio. As Jack crossed the open spaces he heard the sound of a harp, deadened to a tinkle by the shutters – they were drawn already against the mounting sun, and already geckoes were hurrying about on the sunlit walls.

Captain Harte was a little man, with a certain resemblance to Lord St Vincent, a resemblance that he did his best to increase by stooping, by being savagely rude to his subordinates and by the practice of Whiggery: whether he disliked Jack because Jack was tall and he was short, or whether he suspected him of carrying on an intrigue with his wife, it was all one – there was a strong antipathy between them, and it was of long standing. His first words were, 'Well, Mr Aubrey, and where the devil have you been? I expected you yesterday afternoon – Allen expected you yesterday afternoon. I was astonished to learn that he had never seen you at all. I wish you joy, of course,' he said without a smile, 'but upon my word you have an odd notion of taking over a command. Allen must be twenty leagues away by now, and every real sailorman in the *Sophie* with him, no doubt, to say nothing of his officers. And as for all the books, vouchers, dockets, and so on, we have had to botch it up as best we could. Precious irregular. Uncommon irregular.'

'*Pallas* has sailed, sir?' cried Jack, aghast.

'Sailed at midnight, sir,' said Captain Harte, with a look of satisfaction. 'The exigencies of the service do not wait upon our pleasure, Mr Aubrey. And I have been obliged to make a draft of what he left for harbour duty.'

'I only heard last night – in fact this morning, between one and two.'

'Indeed? You astonish me. I am amazed. The letter certainly went off in good time. It is the people at your inn who are at fault, no doubt. There is no relying on your foreigner. I give you joy of your command, I am sure, but how you will ever take her to sea with no people to work her out of the harbour I must confess I do not know. Allen took his lieutenant, and his surgeon, and all the promising midshipmen; and I certainly cannot give you a single man fit to set one foot in front of another.'

'Well, sir,' said Jack, 'I suppose I must make the best of

what I have.' It was understandable, of course: any officer who could would get out of a small, slow, old brig into a lucky frigate like the *Pallas*. And by immemorial custom a captain changing ships might take his coxswain and boat's crew as well as certain followers; and if he were not very closely watched he might commit enormities in stretching the definition of either class.

'I can let you have a chaplain,' said the commandant, turning the knife in the wound.

'Can he hand, reef and steer?' asked Jack, determined to show nothing. 'If not, I had rather be excused.'

'Good day to you, then, Mr Aubrey. I will send you your orders this afternoon.'

'Good day, sir. I hope Mrs Harte is at home. I must pay my respects and congratulate her – must thank her for the pleasure she gave us last night.'

'Was you at the Governor's then?' asked Captain Harte, who knew it perfectly well – whose dirty little trick had been based upon knowing it perfectly well. 'If you had not gone a-caterwauling you might have been aboard your own sloop, in an officerlike manner. God strike me down, but it is a pretty state of affairs when a young fellow prefers the company of Italian fiddlers and eunuchs to taking possession of his own first command.'

THE SUN SEEMED a little less brilliant as Jack walked diagonally across the patio to pay his call on Mrs Harte; but it still struck precious warm through his coat, and he ran up the stairs with the charming unaccustomed weight jogging there on his left shoulder. A lieutenant he did not know and the stuffed midshipman of yesterday evening were there before him, for at Port Mahon it was very much the thing to pay a morning call on Mrs Harte; she was sitting by her harp, looking decorative and talking to the lieutenant, but when he came in she jumped up, gave him both hands and cried,

'Captain Aubrey, how happy I am to see you! Many, many congratulations. Come, we must wet the swab. Mr Parker, pray touch the bell.'

'I wish you joy, sir,' said the lieutenant, pleased at the mere sight of what he longed for so. The midshipman hovered, wondering whether he might speak in such august company and then, just as Mrs Harte was beginning the introductions, he roared out, 'Wish you joy, sir,' in a wavering bellow, and blushed.

'Mr Stapleton, third of the *Guerrier*,' said Mrs Harte, with a wave of her hand. 'And Mr Burnet, of the *Isis*. Carmen, bring some Madeira.' She was a fine dashing woman, and without being either pretty or beautiful she gave the impression of being both, mostly from the splendid way she carried her head. She despised her scrub of a husband, who truckled to her; and she had taken to music as a relief from him. But it did not seem that music was enough, for now she poured out a bumper and drank it off with a very practised air.

A little later Mr Stapleton took his leave, and then after five minutes of the weather – delightful, not too hot even at midday – heat tempered by the breeze – north wind a little trying – healthy, however – summer already – preferable to the cold and rain of an English April – warmth in general more agreeable than cold – she said, 'Mr Burnet, I wonder whether I might beg you to be very kind? I left my reticule at the Governor's.'

'How charmingly you played, Molly,' said Jack, when the door had closed.

'Jack, I am so happy you have a ship at last.'

'So am I. I don't think I have ever been so happy in my life. Yesterday I was so peevish and low in my spirits I could have hanged myself, and then I went back to the Crown and there was this letter. Ain't it charming?' They read it together in respectful silence.

'*Answer the contrary at your peril*,' repeated Mrs Harte. 'Jack, I do beg and pray you will not attempt to make prize of neutrals. That Ragusan bark poor Willoughby sent in has not been condemned, and the owners are to sue him.'

'Never fret, dear Molly,' said Jack. 'I shall not be taking any prizes for a great while, I do assure you. This letter was delayed – damned curious delay – and Allen has gone off with all my prime hands; ordered to sea in a tearing hurry before I could see him. And the commandant has made hay of what was left for harbour duty: not a man to spare. We can't work out of harbour, it seems; so I dare say we shall ground upon our own beef-bones before ever we see so much as the smell of a prize.'

'Oh, indeed?' cried Mrs Harte, her colour rising: and at that moment in walked Lady Warren and her brother, a captain in the Marines. 'Dearest Anne,' cried Molly Harte, 'come here at once and help me remedy a very shocking injustice. Here is Captain Aubrey – you know one another?'

'Servant, ma'am,' said Jack, making a particularly deferential leg, for this was an admiral's wife, no less.

'– a most gallant, deserving officer, a thorough-paced Tory, General Aubrey's son, and he is being most abominably used . . .'

THE HEAT HAD INCREASED while he was in the house, and when he came out into the street the air was hot on his face, almost like another element; yet it was not at all choking, not at all sultry, and there was a brilliance in it that took away all oppression. After a couple of turns he reached the tree-lined street that carried the Ciudadela road down to the high-perched square, or rather terrace, that overlooked the quays. He crossed to the shady side, where English houses with sash windows, fanlights and cobbled forecourts stood on unexpectedly good terms with their neighbours, the baroque Jesuit church and the withdrawn Spanish mansions with great stone coats of arms over their doorways.

A party of seamen went by on the other side, some wearing broad striped trousers, some plain sailcloth; some had fine red waistcoats and some ordinary blue jackets; some wore tarpaulin hats, in spite of the heat, some broad straws, and some spotted handkerchiefs tied over their heads; but they all of them had long swinging pigtails and they all had the indefinable air of man-of-war's men. They were Bellerophons, and he looked at them hungrily as they padded by, laughing and roaring out mildly to their friends, English and Spanish. He was approaching the square, and through the fresh green of the very young leaves he could see the *Généreux*'s royals and topgallants twinkling in the sun far over on the other side of the harbour, hanging out to dry. The busy street, the green, and the blue sky over it was enough to make any man's heart rise like a lark, and three-quarters of Jack's soared high. But the remaining part was earthbound, thinking anxiously about his crew. He had been familiar with this nightmare of manning since his earliest days in the Navy, and his first serious wound had been inflicted by a woman in Deal with a flat-iron who thought her man should not be pressed; but he had not expected to meet it quite so early in his command, nor in this form, nor in the Mediterranean.

Now he was in the square, with its noble trees and its great twin staircases winding down to the quay – stairs known to British sailors for a hundred years as Pigtail Steps, the cause of many a broken limb and battered head. He crossed it to the low wall that ran between the stair-heads and looked out over the immense expanse of enclosed water before him, stretching away left-handed to the distant top of the harbour and right-handed past the hospital island miles away to its narrow, castle-guarded mouth. To his left lay the merchantmen: scores and, indeed, hundreds of feluccas, tartans, xebecs, pinks, polacres, polacre-settees, houarios and barca-longas – all the Mediterranean rigs and plenty from the northern seas as well – bean-cods, cats, herring-busses. Opposite him and to his right lay the men-of-war: two ships of the line, both seventy-fours; a pretty twenty-eight gun frigate, the *Niobe*, whose people were painting a vermilion band under the chequered line of her gunports and up over

her delicate transom, in imitation of a Spanish ship her captain had admired; and a number of transports and other vessels; while between them all and the steps up to the quay,
innumerable boats plied to and fro – long-boats, barges from
the ships of the line, launches, cutters, yawls and gigs, right
down to the creeping jolly-boat belonging to the *Tartarus*
bomb-ketch, with her enormous purser weighing it down to a
bare three inches off the water. Still farther to the right the
splendid quay curved away towards the dockyard, the ordnance and victualling wharfs and the quarantine island, hiding many of the other ships: Jack stared and craned with one
foot on the parapet in the hope of catching a glimpse of his
joy; but she was not to be seen. He turned reluctantly away to
the left, for that was where Mr Williams' office lay. Mr
Williams was the Mahon correspondent of Jack's prize-agent
in Gibraltar, the eminently respectable house of Johnstone
and Graham, and his office was the next and most necessary
port of call; for besides feeling that it was ridiculous to have
gold on his shoulder but none to jingle in his pocket, Jack
would presently need ready money for a whole series of grave
and unavoidable expenses – customary gifts, douceurs and
the like, which could not possibly be done on credit.

He walked in with the utmost confidence, as if he had just
won the battle of the Nile in person, and he was very well
received: when their business was over the agent said, 'I suppose you have seen Mr Baldick?'

'The *Sophie*'s lieutenant?'

'Just so.'

'But he has gone with Captain Allen – he is aboard the *Pallas*.'

'There, sir, you are mistaken, if I may say so, in a manner of
speaking. He is in the hospital.'

'You astonish me.'

The agent smiled, raising his shoulders and spreading his
hands in a deprecating gesture: he possessed the true word
and Jack had to be astonished; but the agent begged pardon
for his superiority. 'He came ashore late yesterday afternoon

and was taken to the hospital with a low fever – the little hospital up past the Capuchins, not the one on the island. To tell you the truth' – the agent held the flat of his hand in front of his mouth as a token of secrecy and spoke in a lower tone – 'he and the *Sophie*'s surgeon did not see eye to eye, and the prospect of a cruise under his hands was more than Mr Baldick could abide. He will rejoin at Gib, no doubt, as soon as he is better. And now, Captain,' said the agent, with an unnatural smile and a shifty look, 'I am going to make so bold as to ask you a favour, if I may. Mrs Williams has a young cousin who is with child to go to sea – wants to be a purser later on. He is a quick boy and he writes a good clear hand; he has worked in the office here since Christmas and I know he is clever at figures. So, Captain Aubrey, sir, if you have no one else in mind for your clerk, you would infinitely oblige . . .' The agent's smile came and went, came and went: he was not used to be on the asking side in a favour, not with sea officers, and he found the possibility of a refusal wonderfully unpleasant.

'Why,' said Jack, considering, 'I have no one in mind, to be sure. You answer for him, of course? Well then, I tell you what, Mr Williams, you find me an able seaman to come along with him and I'll take your boy.'

'Are you in earnest, sir?'

'Yes . . . yes, I suppose I am. Yes: certainly.'

'Done, then,' said the agent, holding out his hand. 'You won't regret it, sir, I give you my word.'

'I'm sure of it, Mr Williams. Perhaps I had better have a look at him.'

David Richards was a plain, colourless youth – literally colourless except for some mauve pimples – but there was something touching in his intense, repressed excitement and his desperate eagerness to please. Jack looked at him kindly and said, 'Mr Williams tells me you write a fine clear hand, sir. Should you like to take down a note for me? It is addressed to the master of the *Sophie*. What's the master's name, Mr Williams?'

'Marshall, sir, William Marshall. A prime navigator, I hear.'

'So much the better,' said Jack, remembering his own struggles with the Requisite Tables and the bizarre conclusions he had sometimes reached. 'To Mr William Marshall, then, Master of His Majesty's sloop the *Sophie*. Captain Aubrey presents his compliments to Mr Marshall and will come aboard at about one o'clock in the afternoon. There, that should give them decent warning. Very prettily written, too. You will see that it reaches him?'

'I shall take it myself this minute, sir,' cried the youth, an unhealthy red with pleasure.

'Lord,' said Jack to himself as he walked up to the hospital, gazing about him at the vast spread of severe, open, barren country on either side of the busy sea, 'Lord, what a fine thing it is to play the great man, once in a while.'

'Mr Baldick?' he said. 'My name is Aubrey. Since we were so nearly shipmates I have called in to ask how you do. I hope I see you on the way to recovery, sir?'

'Very kind in you, sir,' cried the lieutenant, a man of fifty whose crimson face was covered with a silvery glinting stubble, although his hair was black, 'more than kind. Thankee, thankee, Captain. I am far better, I am glad to say, now I am out of the clutches of that bloody-minded sawbones. Would you credit it, sir? Thirty-seven years in the service, twenty-nine of them as a commissioned officer, and I am to be treated to the water-cure and a low diet. Ward's pill and Ward's drop are no good – quite exploded, we hear: but they saw me through the West Indies in the last war, when we lost two-thirds of the larboard watch in ten days from the yellow jack. They preserved me from that, sir, to say nothing of scurvy, and sciatica, and rheumatism, and the bloody flux; but they are of no use, we are told. Well, they may say what they please, these jumped-up young fellows from the Surgeons' Hall with the ink scarcely dry on their warrants, but I put my faith on Ward's drop.'

'And in Brother Bung,' remarked Jack privately, for the

place smelt like the spirit-room of a first-rate. 'So the *Sophie* has lost her surgeon,' he said aloud, 'as well as the more valuable members of her crew?'

'No great loss, I do assure you, sir: though, indeed, the ship's company did make great case of him – swore by him and his silly nostrums, the damned set of gabies; and were much distressed at his going off. And how ever you will replace him in the Med I do not know, by the by, such rare birds they are. But he's no great loss, whatever they may say: and a chest of Ward's drop will answer just as well; nay, better. And the carpenter for amputations. May I offer you a glass, sir?' Jack shook his head. 'As for the rest,' the lieutenant went on, 'we really were very moderate. The Pallas has close on her full complement. Captain A only took his nephew and a friend's son and the other Americans, apart from his cox'n and his steward. And his clerk.'

'Many Americans?'

'Oh no, not above half a dozen. All people from his own part – the country up behind Halifax.'

'Well, that's a relief, upon my word. I had been told the brig was stripped.'

'Who told you that, sir?'

'Captain Harte.'

Mr Baldick narrowed his lips and sniffed. He hesitated and took another pull at his mug; but he only said, 'I've known him off and on these thirty years. He is very fond of practising upon people: by way of having a joke, no doubt.' While they contemplated Captain Harte's devious sense of fun, Mr Baldick slowly emptied his mug. 'No,' he said, setting it down, 'we've left you what might be called a very fair crew. A score or two of prime seamen, and a good half of the people real man-of-war's men, which is more than you can say for most line of battle ships nowadays. There are some untoward sods among the other half, but so there are in every ship's company – by the by, Captain A left you a note about one of 'em – Isaac Wilson, ordinary – and at least you have no

damned sea-lawyers aboard. Then there are your standing
officers: right taut old-fashioned sailormen, for the most part.
Watt, the bosun, knows his business as well as any man in
the fleet. And Lamb, the carpenter, is a good, steady fellow,
though maybe a trifle slow and timid. George Day, the gunner
– he's a good man, too, when he's well, but he has a silly way
of dosing himself. And the purser, Ricketts, is well enough,
for a purser. The master's mates, Pullings and young Mowett,
can be trusted with a watch: Pullings passed for a lieutenant
years ago, but he has never been made. And as for the youngsters, we've only left you two, Ricketts' boy and Babbington.
Blockheads, both of them; but not blackguards.'

'What about the master? I hear he is a great navigator.'

'Marshall? Well, so he is.' Again Mr Baldick narrowed his
lips and sniffed. But by now he had drunk a further pint of
grog, and this time he said, 'I don't know what *you* think
about this buggery lark, sir; but *I* think it's unnatural.'

'Why, there is something in what you say, Mr Baldick,' said
Jack. Then, feeling the weight of interrogation still upon him,
he added, 'I don't like it – not my line at all. But I must confess I don't like to see a man hanged for it. The ship's boys, I
suppose?'

Mr Baldick slowly shook his head for some time. 'No,' he
said at last. 'No. I don't say he *does* anything. Not now. But
come, I do not like to speak ill of a man behind his back.'

'The good of the service . . .' said Jack, with a general wave
of his hand; and shortly afterwards he took his leave, for the
lieutenant had come out in a pale sweat; was poorly, lugubrious and intoxicated.

The tramontana had freshened and now it was blowing a
two-reef topsail breeze, rattling the fronds of the palms; the
sky was clear from rim to rim; a short, choppy sea was getting
up outside the harbour, and now there was an edge to the hot
air like salt or wine. He tapped his hat firmly on his head,
filled his lungs and said aloud, 'Dear God, how good it is to
be alive.'

He had timed it well. He would pass by the Crown, make sure that dinner would be suitably splendid, brush his coat and maybe drink a glass of wine: he would not have to pick up his commission, for it had never left him – there it was against his bosom, crackling gently as he breathed.

Walking down at a quarter to one, walking down to the waterside with the Crown behind him, he felt a curious shortness of his breath; and as he sat in the waterman's boat he said nothing but the word 'Sophie', for his heart was beating high, and he had a curious difficulty in swallowing. 'Am I afraid?' he wondered. He sat looking gravely at the pommel of his sword, scarcely aware of the boat's smooth passage down the harbour, among the crowded ships and vessels, until the Sophie's side rose in front of him and the waterman rattled his boathook.

A quick automatic searching look showed him yards exactly squared, the side dressed, ship's boys in white gloves running down with baize-covered side-ropes, the bosun's call poised, winking silver in the sun. Then the boat's motion stopped, there was the faint crunch as it touched the sloop, and he went up the side to the weird screaming of the call. As his foot touched the gangway there was the hoarse order, the clump and crash of the marines presenting arms, and every officer's hat flew off; and as he stepped upon the quarterdeck he raised his own.

The warrant-officers and midshipmen were drawn up in their best uniforms, blue and white on the shining deck, a less rigid group than the scarlet rectangle of the marines. Their eyes were fixed very attentively on their new commander. He looked grave and, indeed, rather stern: after a second's pause in which the boatman's voice could be heard over the side, muttering to himself, he said, 'Mr Marshall, name the officers to me, if you please.'

Each came forward, the purser, the master's mates, the midshipmen, the gunner, the carpenter and the bosun, and each made his bow, intently watched by the crew. Jack said,

'Gentlemen, I am happy to make your acquaintance. Mr Marshall, all hands aft, if you please. As there is no lieutenant I shall read my commission to the ship's company myself.'

There was no need to turn anybody up from below: every man was there, washed and shining, staring hard. Nevertheless, the calls of the bosun and his mates piped *All hands aft* for a good half-minute down the hatchways. The shrilling died away. Jack stepped forward to the break of the quarter-deck and took out his commission. As soon as it appeared there came the order 'Off hats', and he began in a firm but somewhat forced and mechanical voice.

'By the right Honourable Lord Keith . . .'

As he ran through the familiar lines, now so infinitely more full of meaning, his happiness returned, welling up through the gravity of the occasion, and he rolled out the 'Hereof nor you nor any of you may fail as you will answer the contrary at your peril' with a fine relish. Then he folded the paper, nodded to the men and returned it to his pocket. 'Very good,' he said. 'Dismiss the hands and we will take a look at the brig.'

In the hushed ceremonial procession that followed Jack saw exactly what he had expected to see – a vessel ready for inspection, holding her breath in case any of her beautifully trim rigging with its geometrically perfect fakes and perpendicular falls should be disturbed. She bore as much resemblance to her ordinary self as the rigid bosun, sweating in a uniform coat that must have been shaped with an adze, did to the same man in his shirt-sleeves, puddening the topsail yard in a heavy swell; yet there was an essential relationship, and the snowy sweep of the deck, the painful brilliance of the two brass quarter-deck four-pounders, the precision of the cylinders in the cable-tier and the parade-ground neatness of the galley's pots and tubs all had a meaning. Jack had whited too many sepulchres to be easily deceived; and he was pleased with what he saw. He saw and appreciated all he was meant to see. He was blind to the things he was not meant to see – the piece of ham that an officious fo'c'sle cat dragged from behind a bucket, the girls the master's mates had hidden in the sail-room and who would keep peeping out from behind mounds of canvas. He took no notice of the goat abaft the manger, that fixed him with an insulting devilish split-pupilled eye and defecated with intent; nor of the dubious object, not unlike a pudding, that someone in a last-minute panic had wedged beneath the gammoning of the bow-sprit.

Yet his was an eminently professional eye – it had been nominally at sea since he was nine and, in fact, since he was twelve – and it picked up a great many other impressions. The master was not at all what he had expected, but a big, good-looking, capable middle-aged man – the sodden Mr Baldick had probably got the whole thing wrong. The bosun was: his character was written in his rigging – cautious, solid, conscientious, traditional. The purser and the gunner neither here nor there, though indeed the gunner was obviously too ill to do himself justice, and half-way through he quietly vanished. The midshipmen were more presentable than he had expected: brig's and cutter's midshipmen were often a pretty squalid lot. But that child, that youngster Babbington, could not be allowed ashore in those garments: his mother must have counted upon a growth that had not taken place, and he was so extinguished by his hat alone that it would bring discredit to the sloop.

His chief impression was of old-fashionedness: the *Sophie* had something archaic about her, as though she would rather have her bottom hobnailed than coppered, and would rather pay her sides than paint them. Her crew, without being at all elderly – indeed, most of the hands were in their twenties – had an old-fashioned look; some were wearing petticoat-breeches and shoes, a rig that had already grown uncommon when he was a midshipman no bigger than little Babbington. They moved about in an easy, unconstrained manner, he noticed: they seemed decently curious, but not in the least bloody-minded, resentful or cowed.

Yes: old-fashioned. He loved her dearly – had loved her

from the moment his eye first swept along her sweetly curving deck – but calm intelligence told him that she was a slow brig, an old brig and a brig that was very unlikely to make his fortune. She had fought a couple of creditable actions under his predecessor, one against a French twenty-gun ship-rigged privateer from Toulon, and the other in the Gut of Gibraltar, protecting her convoy from a swarm of Algeciras gunboats rowing out in a calm; but as far as he could remember she had never taken a prize of any real value.

They were back at the break of the odd little quarter-deck – it was really more like a poop – and bending his head he stepped into the cabin. Crouching low, he made his way to the lockers beneath the stern-windows that stretched from one side to the other of the after end – an elegant, curving frame for an extraordinarily brilliant, Canaletto view of Port Mahon, all lit with the silent noon-day sun and (seen from this comparative dimness) belonging to a different world. Sitting down with a cautious sideways movement he found he could hold his head up with no difficulty at all – a good eighteen inches to spare – and he said, ' There we are, Mr Marshall. I must congratulate you upon the *Sophie's* appearance. Very trim: very shipshape.' He thought he might go as far as that, so long as he kept his voice quite official, but he was certainly not going to say any more; nor was he going to address the men or announce any indulgence to mark the occasion. He loathed the idea of a 'popular' captain.

'Thank you, sir,' said the master.

'Now I am going ashore. But I shall sleep aboard, of course; so pray be good enough to send a boat for my chest and dunnage. I am at the Crown.'

He sat on for a while, savouring the glory of his day-cabin. It had no guns in it, for the peculiar build of the *Sophie* would have brought their muzzles to within six inches of the surface if there had been, and the two four-pounders that would ordinarily have taken up so much space were immediately over his head; but even so there was not much room, and one table running athwart was all that the cabin would hold, apart from the lockers. Yet it was far more than he had ever owned before, at sea, and he surveyed it with glowing complacency, looking with particular delight at the handsomely mounted inward-sloping windows, all as bright as glass could very well be, seven sets of panes in a noble sweep quite furnishing the room.

It was more than he had ever had, and more than he had ever really hoped for so early in his career; so why was there something as yet undefined beneath his exultation, the *aliquid amari* of his schooldays?

As he rowed back to the shore, pulled by his own boat's crew in white duck and straw hats with *Sophie* embroidered on the ribbon, a solemn midshipman silent beside him in the stern-sheets, he realized the nature of this feeling. He was no longer one of 'us': he was 'they'. Indeed, he was the immediately-present incarnation of 'them'. In his tour of the brig he had been surrounded with deference – a respect different in kind from that accorded to a lieutenant, different in kind from that accorded to a fellow human-being: it had surrounded him like a glass bell, quite shutting him off from the ship's company; and on his leaving the *Sophie* had let out a quiet sigh of relief, the sigh he knew so well: 'Jehovah is no longer with us.'

'It is the price that has to be paid,' he reflected. 'Thank you, Mr Babbington,' he said to the child, and he stood on the steps while the boat backed out and pulled away down the harbour, Mr Babbington piping, 'Give way now, can't you? Don't go to sleep, Simmons, you grog-faced villain.'

'It is the price that has to be paid,' he reflected. 'And by God it's worth it.' As the words formed in his mind so the look of profound happiness, of contained delight, formed once more upon his shining face. Yet as he walked off to his meeting at the Crown – to his meeting with an equal – there was a little greater eagerness in his step than the mere Lieutenant Aubrey would have shown.

2

THEY SAT AT A ROUND table in a bow window that protruded from the back of the inn high above the water, yet so close to it that they had tossed the oyster-shells back into their native element with no more than a flick of the wrist: and from the unloading tartan a hundred and fifty feet below them there arose the mingled scents of Stockholm tar, cordage, sail-cloth and Chian turpentine.

'Allow me to press you to a trifle of this ragoo'd mutton, sir,' said Jack.

'Well, if you insist,' said Stephen Maturin. 'It is so very good.'

'It is one of the things the Crown does well,' said Jack. 'Though it is hardly decent in me to say so. Yet I had ordered duck pie, alamode beef and soused hog's face as well, apart from the kickshaws. No doubt the fellow misunderstood. Heaven knows what is in that dish by you, but it is certainly not hog's face. I said, *visage de porco*, many times over; and he nodded like a China mandarin. It is provoking, you know, when one desires them to prepare five dishes, *cinco platos*, explaining carefully in Spanish, only to find there are but three, and two of those the wrong ones. I am ashamed of having nothing better to offer you, but it was not from want of good will, I do assure you.'

'I have not eaten so well for many a day, nor' – with a bow – 'in such pleasant company, upon my word,' said Stephen Maturin. 'Might it not be that the difficulty arose from your own particular care – from your explaining in Spanish, in Castilian Spanish?'

'Why,' said Jack, filling their glasses and smiling through his wine at the sun, 'it seemed to me that in speaking to Spaniards, it was reasonable to use what Spanish I could muster.'

'You were forgetting, of course, that Catalan is the language they speak in these islands.'

'What is Catalan?'

'Why, the language of Catalonia – of the islands, of the whole of the Mediterranean coast down to Alicante and beyond. Of Barcelona. Of Lerida. All the richest part of the peninsula.'

'You astonish me. I had no notion of it. Another language, sir? But I dare say it is much the same thing – a *putain*, as they say in France?'

'Oh no, nothing of the kind – not like at all. A far finer language. More learned, more literary. Much nearer the Latin. And by the by, I believe the word is *patois*, sir, if you will allow me.'

'*Patois* – just so. Yet I swear the other is a word: I learnt it somewhere,' said Jack. 'But I must not play the scholar with you, sir, I find. Pray, is it very different to the ear, the unlearned ear?'

'As different as Italian and Portuguese. Mutually incomprehensible – they sound entirely unlike. The intonation of each is in an utterly different key. As unlike as Gluck and Mozart. This excellent dish by me, for instance (and I see that they did their best to follow your orders), is *jabalí* in Spanish, whereas in Catalan it is *senglar*.'

'Is it swine's flesh?'

'Wild boar. Allow me . . .'

'You are very good. May I trouble you for the salt? It is capital eating, to be sure; but I should never have guessed it was swine's flesh. What are these well-tasting soft dark things?'

'There you pose me. They are *bolets* in Catalan: but what they are called in English I cannot tell. They probably have no name – no country name, I mean, though the naturalist will always recognize them in the boletus edulis of Linnaeus.'

'How . . .?' began Jack, looking at Stephen Maturin with candid affection. He had eaten two or three pounds of mutton, and the boar on top of the sheep brought out all his benevolence. 'How . . .?' But finding that he was on the edge of questioning a guest he filled up the space with a cough and rang the bell for the waiter, gathering the empty decanters over to his side of the table.

The question was in the air, however, and only a most repulsive or indeed a morose reserve would have ignored it. 'I was brought up in these parts,' observed Stephen Maturin. 'I spent a great part of my young days with my uncle in Barcelona or with my grandmother in the country behind Lerida – indeed, I must have spent more time in Catalonia than I did in Ireland; and when first I went home to attend the university I carried out my mathematical exercises in Catalan, for the figures came more naturally to my mind.'

'So you speak it like a native, sir, I am sure,' said Jack. 'What a capital thing. That is what I call making a good use of one's childhood. I wish I could say as much.'

'No, no,' said Stephen, shaking his head. 'I made a very poor use of my time indeed: I did come to a tolerable acquaintance with the birds – a very rich country in raptores, sir – and the reptiles; but the insects, apart from the lepidoptera, and the plants – what deserts of gross sterile brutish ignorance! It was not until I had been some years in Ireland and had written my little work on the phanerogams of Upper Ossory that I came to understand how monstrously I had wasted my time. A vast tract of country to all intents and purposes untouched since Willughby and Ray passed through towards the end of the last age. The King of Spain invited Linnaeus to come, with liberty of conscience, as no doubt you remember; but he declined: I had had all these unexplored riches at my command, and I had ignored them. Think what Pallas, think what the learned Solander, or the Gmelins, old and young, would have accomplished! That was why I fastened upon the first opportunity that offered and agreed to accompany old Mr Browne: it is true that Minorca is not the mainland, but then, on the other hand, so great an area of calcareous rock has its particular flora, and all that flows from that interesting state.'

'Mr Brown of the dockyard? The naval officer? I know him well,' cried Jack. 'An excellent companion – loves to sing a round – writes a charming little tune.'

'No. My patient died at sea and we buried him up there by St Philip's: poor fellow, he was in the last stages of phthisis. I had hoped to get him here – a change of air and regimen can work wonders in these cases – but when Mr Florey and I opened his body we found so great a . . . In short, we found that his advisers (and they were the best in Dublin) had been altogether too sanguine.'

'You cut him up?' cried Jack, leaning back from his plate.

'Yes: we thought it proper, to satisfy his friends. Though upon my word they seem wonderfully little concerned. It is weeks since I wrote to the only relative I know of, a gentleman in the county Fermanagh, and never a word has come back at all.'

There was a pause. Jack filled their glasses (how the tide went in and out) and observed, 'Had I known you was a surgeon, sir, I do not think I could have resisted the temptation of pressing you.'

'Surgeons are excellent fellows,' said Stephen Maturin with a touch of acerbity. 'And where should we be without them, God forbid: and, indeed, the skill and dispatch and dexterity with which Mr Florey at the hospital here everted Mr Browne's eparterial bronchus would have amazed and delighted you. But I have not the honour of counting myself among them, sir. I am a physician.'

'I beg your pardon: oh dear me, what a sad blunder. But even so, Doctor, even so, I think I should have had you run aboard and kept under hatches till we were at sea. My poor *Sophie* has no surgeon and there is no likelihood of finding her one. Come, sir, cannot I prevail upon you to go to sea? A man-of-war is the very thing for a philosopher, above all in the Mediterranean: there are the birds, the fishes – I could promise you some monstrous strange fishes – the natural phenomena, the meteors, the chance of prize-money. For even Aristotle would have been moved by prize-money. Doubloons, sir: they lie in soft leather sacks, you know, about so big, and they are wonderfully heavy in your hand. Two is all a man can carry.'

He had spoken in a bantering tone, never dreaming of a serious reply, and he was astonished to hear Stephen say, 'But I am in no way qualified to be a naval surgeon. To be sure, I have done a great deal of anatomical dissection, and I am not unacquainted with most of the usual chirurgical operations; but I know nothing of naval hygiene, nothing of the particular maladies of seamen . . .'

'Bless you,' cried Jack, 'never strain at gnats of that kind. Think of what we are usually sent – surgeon's mates, wretched half-grown stunted apprentices that have knocked about an apothecary's shop just long enough for the Navy Office to give them a warrant. They know nothing of surgery, let alone physic; they learn on the poor seamen as they go along, and they hope for an experienced loblolly boy or a beast-leech or a cunning-man or maybe a butcher among the hands – the press brings in all sorts. And when they have picked up a smattering of their trade, off they go into frigates and ships of the line. No, no. We should be delighted to have you – more than delighted. Do, pray, consider of it, if only for a while. I need not say,' he added, with a particularly earnest look, 'how much pleasure it would give me, was we to be shipmates.'

The waiter opened the door, saying, 'Marine,' and immediately behind him appeared the red-coat, bearing a packet. 'Captain Aubrey, sir?' he cried in an outdoor voice. 'Captain Harte's compliment.' He disappeared with a rumble of boots, and Jack observed, 'Those must be my orders.'

'Do not mind me, I beg,' said Stephen. 'You must read them directly.' He took up Jack's fiddle and walked away to the end of the room, where he played a low, whispering scale, over and over again.

The orders were very much what he had expected: they

required him to complete his stores and provisions with the utmost possible dispatch and to convoy twelve sail of merchantmen and transports (named in the margin) to Cagliari. He was to travel at a very great pace, but he was by no means to endanger his masts, yards or sails: he was to shrink from no danger, but on the other hand he was on no account to incur any risk whatsoever. Then, labelled *secret*, the instructions for the private signal – the difference between friend and foe, between good and bad: 'The ship first making the signal is to hoist a red flag at the foretopmast head and a white flag with a pendant over the flag at the main. To be answered with a white flag with a pendant over the flag at the maintopmast head and a blue flag at the foretopmast head. The ship that first made the signal is to fire one gun to windward, which the other is to answer by firing three guns to leeward in slow time.' Lastly, there was a note to say that Lieutenant Dillon had been appointed to the *Sophie*, vice Mr Baldick, and that he would shortly arrive in the *Burford*.

'Here's good news,' said Jack. 'I am to have a capital fellow as my lieutenant: we are only allowed one in the *Sophie*, you know, so it is very important . . . I do not know him personally, but he is an excellent fellow, that I am sure of. He distinguished himself very much in the *Dart*, a hired cutter – set about three French privateers in the Sicily Channel, sank one and took another. Everyone in the fleet talked about it at the time; but his letter was never printed in the Gazette, and he was not promoted. It was infernal bad luck. I wonder at it, for it was not as though he had no interest: Fitzgerald, who knows all about these things, told me he was a nephew, or cousin was it? to a peer whose name I forget. And in any case it was a very creditable thing – dozens of men have got their step for much less. I did, for one.'

'May I ask what you did? I know so little about naval matters.'

'Oh, I simply got knocked on the head, once at the Nile and then again when the *Généreux* took the old *Leander*:

rewards were obliged to be handed out, so I being the only surviving lieutenant, one came my way at last. It took its time, upon my word, but it was very welcome when it came, however slow and undeserved. What do you say to taking tea? And perhaps a piece of muffin? Or should you rather stay with the port?'

'Tea would make me very happy,' said Stephen. 'But tell me,' he said, walking back to the fiddle and tucking it under his chin, 'do not your naval appointments entail great expense, going to London, uniforms, oaths, levees . . .?'

'Oaths? Oh, you refer to the swearing-in. No. That applies only to lieutenants – you go to the Admiralty and they read you a piece about allegiance and supremacy and utterly renouncing the Pope; you feel very solemn and say "to this I swear" and the chap at the high desk says "and that will be half a guinea", which does rather take away from the effect, you know. But it is only commissioned officers – medical men are appointed by a warrant. *You* would not object to taking an oath, however,' he said, smiling; and then feeling that this remark was a little indelicate, a little personal, he went on, 'I was shipmates with a poor fellow once that objected to taking an oath, any oath, on principle. I never could like him – he was for ever touching his face. He was nervous, I believe, and it gave him countenance; but whenever you looked at him there he was with a finger at his mouth, or pressing his cheek, or pulling his chin awry. It is nothing, of course; but when you are penned up with it in the same wardroom it grows tedious, day after day all through a long commission. In the gun-room or the cockpit you can call out "Leave your face alone, for God's sake," but in the wardroom you must bear with it. However, he took to reading in his Bible, and he conceived this notion that he must not take an oath; and when there was that foolish court-martial on poor Bentham he was called as a witness and refused, flatly refused, to be sworn. He told Old Jarvie it was contrary to something in the Gospels. Now that might have washed with

Gambier or Saumarez or someone given to tracts, but not
with Old Jarvie, by God. He was broke, I am sorry to say: I
never could like him – to tell you the truth, he smelt too – but
he was a tolerably good seaman and there was no vice in him.
That is what I mean when I say you would not object to an
oath – *you* are not an enthusiast.'

'No, certainly,' said Stephen. 'I am not an enthusiast. I was
brought up by a philosopher, or perhaps I should say a
philosophe; and some of his philosophy has stuck to me. He
would have called an oath a childish thing – otiose if voluntary and rightly to be evaded or ignored if imposed. For few
people today, even among your tarpaulins, are weak enough
to believe in Earl Godwin's piece of bread.'

There was a long pause while the tea was brought in. 'You
take milk in your tea, Doctor?' asked Jack.

'If you please,' said Stephen. He was obviously deep in
thought: his eyes were fixed upon vacancy and his mouth was
pursed in a silent whistle.

'I wish . . .' said Jack.

'It is always said to be weak, and impolitic, to show oneself
at a disadvantage,' said Stephen, bearing him down. 'But you
speak to me with such candour that I cannot prevent myself
from doing the same. Your offer, your suggestion, tempts me
exceedingly; for apart from those considerations that you so
obligingly mention, and which I reciprocate most heartily, I
am very much at a stand, here in Minorca. The patient I was
to attend until the autumn has died. I had understood him to
be a man of substance – he had a house in Merrion Square –
but when Mr Florey and I looked through his effects before
sealing them we found nothing whatever, neither money nor
letters of credit. His servant decamped, which may explain it:
but his friends do not answer my letters; the war has cut me
off from my little patrimony in Spain; and when I told you,
some time ago, that I had not eaten so well for a great while, I
did not speak figuratively.'

'Oh, what a very shocking thing!' cried Jack. 'I am heartily sorry for your embarrassment, and if the – the res angusta is pressing, I hope you will allow me . . .' His hand was in his breeches pocket, but Stephen Maturin said 'No, no, no,' a dozen times smiling and nodding. 'But you are very good.'

'I am heartily sorry for your embarrassment, Doctor,' repeated Jack, 'and I am almost ashamed to profit by it. But my *Sophie* must have a medical man – apart from anything else, you have no notion of what a hypochondriac your sea-man is: they love to be physicked, and a ship's company without someone to look after them, even the rawest half-grown surgeon's mate, is not a happy ship's company – and then again it is the direct answer to your immediate difficulties. The pay is contemptible for a learned man – five pounds a month – and I am ashamed to mention it; but there is the chance of prize-money, and I believe there are certain perquisites, such as Queen Anne's Gift, and something for every man with the pox. It is stopped out of their pay.'

'Oh, as for money, I am not greatly concerned with that. If the immortal Linnaeus could traverse five thousand miles of Lapland, living upon twenty-five pounds, surely I can . . . But is the thing in itself really feasible? Surely there must be an official appointment? Uniform? Instruments? Drugs, medical necessities?'

'Now that you come to ask me these fine points, it is surprising how little I know,' said Jack, smiling. 'But Lord love you, Doctor, we must not let trifles stand in the way. A warrant from the Navy Office you must have, that I am sure of; but I know the admiral will give you an acting order the minute I ask him – delighted to do so. As for uniform, there is nothing particular for surgeons, though a blue coat is usual. Instruments and so on – there you have me. I believe Apothecaries' Hall sends a chest aboard: Florey will know, or any of the surgeons. But at all events come aboard directly. Come as soon as you like – come tomorrow, say, and we will dine together. Even the acting order will take some little time, so make this voyage as my guest. It will not be comfortable – no elbow-room in a brig, you know – but it will introduce you to naval life; and if you have a saucy landlord, it will dish him instantly. Let me fill your cup. And I am sure you will like it, for it is amazingly philosophical.'

'Certainly,' said Stephen. 'For a philosopher, a student of human nature, what could be better? The subjects of his inquiry shut up together, unable to escape his gaze, their passions heightened by the dangers of war, the hazards of their calling, their isolation from women and their curious, but uniform, diet. And by the glow of patriotic fervour, no doubt.' – with a bow to Jack – 'It is true that for some time past I have taken more interest in the cryptogams than in my fellow-men; but even so, a ship must be a most instructive theatre for an inquiring mind.'

'Prodigiously instructive, I do assure you, Doctor,' said Jack. 'How happy you make me: to have Dillon as the *Sophie*'s lieutenant and a Dublin physician as her surgeon – by the way, you are countrymen, of course. Perhaps you know Mr Dillon?'

'There are so many Dillons,' said Stephen, with a chill settling about his heart. 'What is his Christian name?'

'James,' said Jack, looking at the note.

'No,' said Stephen deliberately. 'I do not remember to have met any James Dillon.'

'MR MARSHALL,' said Jack, 'pass the word for the carpenter, if you please. I have a guest coming aboard: we must do our best to make him comfortable. He is a physician, a great man in the philosophical line.'

'An astronomer, sir?' asked the master eagerly.

'Rather more of a botanist, I take it,' said Jack. 'But I have great hopes that if we make him comfortable he may stay with us as the *Sophie*'s surgeon. Think what a famous thing that would be for the ship's company!'

'Indeed it would, sir. They were right upset when Mr Jackson went off to the *pallas*, and to replace him with a physician would be a great stroke. There's one aboard the flagship and one at Gibraltar, but not another in the whole fleet, not that I know of. They charge a guinea a visit, by land; or so I have heard tell.'

'Even more, Mr Marshall, even more. Is that water aboard?'

'All aboard and stowed, sir, except for the last two casks.'

'There you are, Mr Lamb. I want you to have a look at the bulkhead of my sleeping-cabin and see what you can do to make it a little more roomy for a friend: you may be able to shift it for'ard a good six inches. Yes, Mr Babbington, what is it?'

'If you please, sir, the *Burford* is signalling over the headland.'

'Very good. Now let the purser, the gunner and the bosun know I want to see them.'

From that moment on the captain of the *Sophie* was plunged deep into her accounts – her muster-book, slop-book, tickets, sick-book, complete-book, gunner's, bosun's and carpenter's expenses, supplies and returns, general account of provisions received and returned, and quarterly account of same, together with certificates of the quantity of spirits, wine, cocoa and tea issued, to say nothing of the log, letter and order books – and what with having dined extremely well and not being good with figures at any time, he very soon lost his footing. Most of his dealings were with Ricketts, the purser; and as Jack grew irritable in his confusion it seemed to him that he detected a certain smoothness in the way the purser presented his interminable sums and balances. There were papers here, quittances, acknowledgements and receipts that he was being asked to sign; and he knew very well that he did not understand them all.

'Mr Ricketts,' he said, at the end of a long, easy explanation that conveyed nothing to him at all, 'here in the muster-book, at number 178, is Charles Stephen Ricketts.'

'Yes, sir. My son, sir.'

'Just so. I see that he appeared on November 30th, 1797.

From *Tonnant*, late *Princess Royal*. There is no age by his name.'

'Ah, let me see: Charlie must have been rising twelve by then, sir.'

'He was rated Able Seaman.'

'Yes, sir. Ha, ha!'

It was a perfectly ordinary little everyday fraud; but it was illegal. Jack did not smile. He went on, 'AB to September 20th, 1798, then rated Clerk. And then on November 10th, 1799, he was rated Midshipman.'

'Yes, sir,' said the purser: not only was there that little awkwardness of the eleven-year-old able seaman, but Mr Ricketts' quick ear caught the slight emphasis on the word *rated* and its slightly unusual repetition. The message it conveyed was this: 'I may seem a poor man of business; but if you try any purser's tricks with me, I am athwart your hawse and I can rake you from stem to stern. What is more, one captain's rating can be disrated by another, and if you trouble my sleep, by God, I shall turn your boy before the mast and flog the tender pink skin off his back every day for the rest of the commission.' Jack's head was aching; his eyes were slightly rimmed with red from the port, and there was so clear a hint of latent ferocity in them that the purser took the message very seriously. 'Yes, sir,' he said again. 'Yes. Now here is the list of dockyard tallies: would you like me to explain the different headings in detail, sir?'

'If you please, Mr Ricketts.'

This was Jack's first direct, fully responsible acquaintance with book-keeping, and he did not much relish it. Even a small vessel (and the *Sophie* barely exceeded a hundred and fifty tons) needs a wonderful amount of stores: casks of beef, pork and butter all numbered and signed for, puncheons, butts and half-pieces of rum, hard-tack by the ton from Old Weevil, dried soup with the broad arrow upon it, quite apart from the gunner's powder (mealed, corned and best patent), sponges, worms, matches, priming-irons, wads and shot –

bar, chain, case, langrage, grape or plain round – and the countless objects needed (and so *very* often embezzled) by the bosun – the blocks, the long-tackle, single, double, parrel, quarter-coak, double-coak, flat-side, double thin-coak, single thin-coak, single strap-bound and sister blocks alone made up a whole Lent litany. Here Jack was far more at home, for the difference between a single double-scored and a single-shoulder block was as clear to him as that between night and day, or right and wrong – far clearer, on occasion. But by now his mind, used to grappling with concrete physical problems, was thoroughly tired: he looked wistfully over the dog-eared, tatty books piled up on the curving rim of the lockers out through the cabin windows at the brilliant air and the dancing sea. He passed his hand over his forehead and said, 'We will deal with the rest another time, Mr Ricketts. What a God-damned great heap of paper it is, to be sure: I see that a clerk is a very necessary member of the ship's company. That reminds me, I have appointed a young man – he will be coming aboard today. I am sure you will ease him into his duties, Mr Ricketts. He seems willing and competent, and he is nephew to Mr Williams, the prize-agent. I think it is to the *Sophie*'s advantage that we should be well with the prize-agent, Mr Ricketts?'

'Indeed it is, sir,' said the purser, with deep conviction.

'Now I must go across to the dockyard with the bosun before the evening gun,' said Jack, escaping into the open air. As he set foot upon deck so young Richards came up the larboard side, accompanied by a Negro, well over six feet tall. 'Here is the young man I was telling you about, Mr Ricketts. And this is the seaman you have brought me, Mr Richards? A fine stout fellow he looks, too. What is his name?'

'Alfred King, if you please, sir.'

'Can you hand, reef and steer, King?'

The Negro nodded his round head; there was a fine flash of white across his face and he grunted aloud. Jack frowned, for this was no way to address a captain on his own quarter-deck.

'Come, sir,' he said sharply, 'haven't you got a civil tongue in your head?'

Looking suddenly grey and apprehensive the Negro shook his head. 'If you please, sir,' said the clerk, 'he has no tongue. The Moors cut it out.'

'Oh,' said Jack, taken aback, 'oh. Well, stow him for'ard. I will read him in by and by. Mr Babbington, take Mr Richards below and show him the midshipmen's berth. Come, Mr Watt, we must get to the dockyard before the idle dogs stop work altogether.'

'There is a man to gladden your heart, Mr Watt,' said Jack, as the cutter sped across the harbour. 'I wish I could find another score or so like him. You don't seem very taken with the idea, Mr Watt?'

'Well, sir, I should never say no to a prime seaman, to be sure. And to be sure we could swap some of our landmen (not that we have many left, being as we've been in commission so long, and them as was going to run having run and most of the rest rated ordinary, if not able . . .' The bosun could not find his way out of his parenthesis, and after a staring pause he wound up by saying, 'But as for mere numbers, why no, sir.'

'Not even with the draft for harbour-duties?'

'Why, bless you, sir, they never amounted to half a dozen, and we took good care they was all the hard bargains and right awkward buggers. Beg pardon, sir: the idle men. So as for mere numbers, why no, sir. In a three-watch brig like the *Sophie* it's a puzzle to stow 'em all between-decks as it is: she's a trim, comfortable, home-like little vessel, right enough, but she ain't what you might call roomy.'

Jack made no reply to this; but it confirmed a good many of his impressions, and he reflected upon them until the boat reached the yard.

'Captain Aubrey!' cried Mr Brown, the officer in charge of the yard. 'Let me shake you by the hand, sir, and wish you joy. I am very happy to see you.'

'Thank you, sir; thank you very much indeed.' They shook hands. 'This is the first time I have seen you in your kingdom, sir.'

'Commodious, ain't it?' said the naval officer. 'Rope-walk over there. Sail-loft behind your old *Généreux*. I only wish there were a higher wall around the timber-yard: you would never believe how many flaming thieves there are in this island, that creep over the wall by night and take away my spars: or try to. It is my belief they are sometimes set on it by the captains; but captains or not, I shall crucify the next son of a bitch I find so much as looking at a dog-pawl.'

'It is my belief, Mr Brown, that you will never be really happy until there is not a King's ship left in the Mediterranean and you can walk round your yard mustering a full complement of paint-pots every day of the week, never issuing out so much as a treenail from one year's end to the next.'

'You just listen to me, young man,' said Mr Brown, laying his hand on Jack's sleeve. 'Just you listen to age and experience. Your *good* captain never wants anything from a dockyard. He makes do with what he has. He takes great care of the King's stores: nothing is ever wasted: he pays his bottom with his own slush: he worms his cables deep with twice-laid stuff and serves and parcels them so there is never any fretting in the hawse *anywhere*: he cares for his sails far more than for his own skin, and he never sets his royals – nasty, unnecessary, flash, gimcrack things. And the result is promotion, Mr Aubrey; for we make our report to the Admiralty, as you know, and it carries the greatest possible weight. What made Trotter a post-captain? The fact that he was the most economical master and commander on the station. Some men carried away topmasts two and three times in a year: never Trotter. Take your own good Captain Allen. Never did he come to me with one of those horrible lists as long as his own pennant. And look at him now, in command of as pretty a frigate as you could wish. But why do I tell you all this, Captain Aubrey? I know very well you are not one of these spendthrift, fling-it-down-the-kennel young commanders, not after the care you took bringing in the *Généreux*. Besides, the *Sophie* is perfectly well found in every possible respect. Except conceivably in the article of paint. I might, at great inconvenience to other captains, find you some yellow paint, a very little yellow paint.'

'Why, sir, I should be grateful for a pot or two,' said Jack, his eye ranging carelessly over the spars. 'But what I really came for was to beg the favour of the loan of your duettoes. I am taking a friend on this cruise and he particularly desires to hear your B minor duetto.'

'You shall have them, Captain Aubrey,' said Mr Brown. 'You shall most certainly have them. Mrs Harte is transcribing one for the harp at the present moment, but I shall step round there directly. When do you sail?'

'As soon as I have completed my water and my convoy is assembled.'

'That will be tomorrow evening, if the *Fanny* comes in: and the watering will not take you long. The *Sophie* only carries ten ton. You shall have the book by noon tomorrow, I promise you.'

'I am most obliged, Mr Brown, infinitely obliged. Good night to you, then, and my best respects wait on Mrs Brown and Miss Fanny.'

'CHRIST,' SAID JACK, as the shattering din of the carpenter's hammer prised him from his hold on sleep. He clung to the soft darkness as hard as he could, burying his face in his pillow, for his mind had been racing so that he had not dropped off until six – indeed, it was his appearance on deck at first light, peering at the yards and rigging, that had given rise to the rumour that he was up and about. And this was the reason for the carpenter's untimely zeal, just as it was for the nervous presence of the gun-room steward (the former captain's steward had gone over to the *Pallas*) hovering with what had been Captain Allen's invariable breakfast – a mug of small beer, hominy grits and cold beef.

But there was no sleeping; the echoing crash of the hammer right next to his ear, ludicrously followed by the sound of whispering between the carpenter and his mates, made certain of that. They were in his sleeping-cabin, of course. Jets of pain shot through Jack's head as he lay there. ' 'Vast that bloody hammering,' he called, and almost against his shoulder came the shocked reply, 'Aye aye, sir,' and the tip-toe pittering away.

His voice was hoarse. 'What made me so damned garrulous yesterday?' he said, still lying there in his cot. 'I am as hoarse as a crow, with talking. And what made me launch out in wild invitations? A guest I know nothing about, in a very small brig I have scarcely seen.' He pondered gloomily upon the extreme care that should be taken with shipmates – cheek by jowl – very like marriage – the inconvenience of pragmatic, touchy, assuming companions – incompatible tempers mewed up together in a box. In a box: his manual of seamanship – and how he had conned it as a boy, poring over the impossible equations.

Let the angle YCB, to which the yard is braced up, be called the trim of the sails, and expressed by the symbol b. This is the complement of the angle DCI. Now $CI:ID = rad.:tan. DCI = I:tan. DCI = |: cotan. b.$ Therefore we have finally $|: cotan. b = A^1:B^1:tan.^2x$, and $A^1. cotan. b = B$ 'angent^2, and tan. $^1x = \frac{A}{B} cot$. This equation evidently ascertains the mutual relation between the trim of the sails and the leeway . . .

'It *is* quite evident, is it not, Jacky darling?' said a hopeful voice, and a rather large young woman bent kindly over him (for at this stage in his memory he was only twelve, a stocky little boy, and tall, nubile Queeney sailed high above).

'Why, no, Queeney,' said the infant Jack. 'To tell you the truth, it ain't.'

'Well,' said she, with untiring patience. 'Try to remember

what a cotangent is, and let us begin again. Let us consider
the ship as an oblong box . . .'

For a while he considered the *Sophie* as an oblong box. He
had not seen a great deal of her, but there were two or three
fundamentals that he knew with absolute certainty: one was
that she was under-rigged – she might be well enough close
to the wind, but she would be a slug before it; another was
that his predecessor had been a man of a temper entirely
unlike his own; and another was that the *Sophie*'s people had
come to resemble their captain, a good sound quiet careful
unaggressive commander who never set his royals, as brave as
could be when set upon, but the very opposite of a Sallee
rover. 'Was discipline to be combined with the spirit of a
Sallee rover,' said Jack, 'it would sweep the ocean clean.' And
his mind descending fast to the commonplace dwelt on the
prize-money that would result from sweeping the ocean even
moderately clean.

'That despicable main-yard,' he said. 'And surely to God I
can get a couple of twelve-pounders as chasers. Would her
timbers stand it, though? But whether they can or not, the
box can be made a little more like a fighting vessel – more
like a real man-of-war.'

As his thoughts ranged on so the low cabin brightened
steadily. A fishing-boat passed under the *Sophie*'s stern,
laden with tunny and uttering the harsh roar of a conch; at
almost the same time the sun popped up from behind St
Philip's fort – it did, in fact, pop up, flattened like a sideways
lemon in the morning haze and drawing its bottom free of
the land with a distinct jerk. In little more than a minute the
greyness of the cabin had utterly vanished: the deck-head
was alive with light glancing from the rippling sea; and a single ray, reflected from some unmoving surface on the distant
quay, darted through the cabin windows to light up Jack's
coat and its blazing epaulette. The sun rose within his mind,
obliging his dogged look to broaden into a smile, and he
swung out of his cot.

THE SUN HAD REACHED Dr Maturin ten minutes earlier, for he was a good deal higher up: he, too, stirred and turned away, for he too had slept uneasily. But the brilliance prevailed. He opened his eyes and stared about very stupidly: a moment before he had been so solidly, so warmly and happily in Ireland, with a girl's hand under his arm, that his waking mind could not take in the world he saw. Her touch was still firm upon his arm and even her scent was there: vaguely he picked at the crushed leaves under him – dianthus perfragrans. The scent was reclassified – a flower, and nothing more – and the ghostly contact, the firm print of fingers, vanished. His face reflected the most piercing unhappiness, and his eyes misted over. He had been exceedingly attached; and she was so bound up with that time . . .

He had been quite unprepared for this particular blow, striking under every conceivable kind of armour, and for some minutes he could hardly bear the pain, but sat there blinking in the sun.

'Christ,' he said at last. 'Another day.' With this his face grew more composed. He stood up, beat the white dust from his breeches and took off his coat to shake it. With intense mortification he saw that the piece of meat he had hidden at yesterday's dinner had oozed grease through his handkerchief and his pocket. 'How wonderfully strange,' he thought, 'to be upset by this trifle; yet I am upset.' He sat down and ate the piece of meat (the eye of a mutton chop); and for a moment his mind dwelt on the theory of counter-irritants, Paracelsus, Cardan, Rhazes. He was sitting in the ruined apse of St Damian's chapel high above Port Mahon on the north side, looking down upon the great winding inlet of the harbour and far out beyond it over a vast expanse of sea, a variegated blue with wandering lanes; the flawless sun, a hand's breadth high, rising from the side of Africa. He had taken refuge there some days before, as soon as his landlord began to grow a shade uncivil; he had not waited for a scene, for he was too emotionally worn to put up with any such thing.

Presently, he took notice of the ants that were taking away his crumbs. Tapinoma erraticum. They were walking in a steady two-way stream across the hollow, or dell, of his inverted wig, as it lay there looking very like an abandoned bird's nest, though once it had been as neat a physical bob as had ever been seen in Stephen's Green. They hurried along with their abdomens high, jostling, running into one another: his gaze followed the wearisome little creatures, and while he was watching them a toad was watching him: their eyes met, and he smiled. A splendid toad: a two-pound toad with brilliant tawny eyes. How did he manage to make a living in the sparse thin grass of that stony, sun-beaten landscape, so severe and parched, with no more cover than a few tumbles of pale stone, a few low creeping hook-thorned caper-bushes and a cistus whose name Stephen did not know? Most remarkably severe and parched, for the winter of 1799–1800 had been uncommonly dry, the March rains had failed and now the heat had come very early in the year. Very gently he stretched out his finger and stroked the toad's throat: the toad swelled a little and moved its crossed hands; then sat easy, gazing back.

The sun rose and rose. The night had not been cold at any time, but still the warmth was grateful. Black wheatears that must have a brood not far: one of the smaller eagles in the sky. There was a sloughed snake's skin in the bush where he pissed, and its eye-covers were perfect, startlingly crystalline.

'What am I to think of Captain Aubrey's invitation?' he said aloud, in that great emptiness of light and air – all the more vast for the inhabited patch down there and its movement, and the checkered fields behind, fading into pale dun formless hills. 'Was it merely Jack ashore? Yet he was such a pleasant, ingenuous companion.' He smiled at the recollection. 'Still and all, what weight can be attached to . . .? We had dined extremely well: four bottles, or possibly five. I must not expose myself to an affront.' He turned it over and over, arguing against his hopes, but coming at last to the conclusion that if he could make his coat passably respectable – and the dust does seem to be getting it off, or at least disguising it, he said – he would call on Mr Florey at the hospital and talk to him, in a general way, about the naval surgeon's calling. He brushed the ants from his wig and settled it on his head: then as he walked down towards the edge of the road – the magenta spikes of gladioli in the taller grass – the recollection of that unlucky name stopped him in his stride. How had he come to forget it so entirely in his sleep? How was it possible that the name James Dillon had not presented itself at once to his waking mind?

'Yet it is true there are hundreds of Dillons,' he reflected. 'And a great many of them are called James, of course.'

'*CHRISTE*,' HUMMED James Dillon under his breath, shaving the red-gold bristles off his face in what light could make its way through the scuttle of the *Burford*'s number twelve gunport. '*Christe eleison. Kyrie* . . .' This was less piety in James Dillon than a way of hoping he should not cut himself; for like so many Papists he was somewhat given to blasphemy. The difficulty of the planes under his nose silenced him, however, and when his upper lip was clean he could not hit the note again. In any case, his mind was too busy to be seeking after an elusive neume, for he was about to report to a new captain, a man upon whom his comfort and ease of mind was to depend, to say nothing of his reputation, career and prospects of advancement.

Stroking his shining smoothness, he hurried out into the ward-room and shouted for a marine. 'Just brush the back of my coat, will you, Curtis? My chest is quite ready, and the bread-sack of books is to go with it,' he said. 'Is the captain on deck?'

'Oh no, sir, no,' said the marine. 'Breakfast only just carrying in this moment. Two hard-boiled eggs and one soft.'

The soft-boiled egg was for Miss Smith, to recruit her from her labours of the night, as both the marine and Mr Dillon knew very well; but the marine's knowing look met with a total lack of response. James Dillon's mouth tightened, and for a fleeting moment as he ran up the ladder to the sudden brilliance of the quarter-deck it wore a positively angry expression. Here he greeted the officer of the watch and the *Burford*'s first lieutenant. 'Good morning. Good morning to you. My word, you're very fine,' they said. 'There she lies: just beyond the *Généreux*.'

His eyes ranged over the busy harbour: the light was so nearly horizontal that all the masts and yards assumed a strange importance, and the little skipping waves sent back a blinding sparkle.

'No, no,' they said. 'Over by the sheer-hulk. The felucca has just masked her. There – now do you see her?'

He did indeed. He had been looking far too high and his gaze had swept right over the *Sophie* as she lay there, not much above a cable's length away, very low in the water. He leant both hands on the rail and looked at her with unwinking concentration. After a while he borrowed the telescope from the officer of the watch and did the same again, with a most searching minute scrutiny. He could see the gleam of an epaulette, whose wearer could only be her captain: and her people were as active as bees just about to swarm. He had been prepared for a little brig, but not for quite such a dwarfish vessel as this. Most fourteen-gun sloops were between two hundred and two hundred and fifty tons in burthen: the *Sophie* could scarcely be more than a hundred and fifty.

'I like her little quarter-deck,' said the officer of the watch. 'She was the Spanish *Vencejo*, was she not? And as for being rather low, why, anything you look at close to from a seventy-four looks rather low.'

There were three things that everybody knew about the *Sophie*: one was that unlike almost all other brigs she had a quarter-deck; another was that she had been Spanish; and a third was that she possessed an elm-tree pump on her fo'c'sle, that is to say, a bored-out trunk that communicated directly with the sea and that was used for washing her deck – an insignificant piece of equipment, really, but one so far above her station that no mariner who saw it or heard of this pump ever forgot it.

'Maybe your quarters will be a little cramped,' said the first lieutenant, 'but you will have a quiet, restful time of it, I am sure, convoying the trade up and down the Mediterranean.'

'Well . . .' said James Dillon, unable to find a brisk retort to this possibly well-intentioned kindness. 'Well . . .' he said with a philosophical shrug. 'You'll let me have a boat, sir? I should like to report as early as I can.'

'A boat? God rot my soul,' cried the first lieutenant, 'I shall be asked for the barge, next thing I know. Passengers in the *Burford* wait for a bumboat from shore, Mr Dillon; or else they swim.' He stared at James with cold severity until the quartermaster's chuckle betrayed him; for Mr Coffin was a great wag, a wag even before breakfast.

'DILLON, SIR, REPORTING for duty, if you please,' said James taking off his hat in the brilliant sun and displaying a blaze of dark red hair.

'Welcome aboard, Mr Dillon,' said Jack, touching his own, holding out his hand and looking at him with so intense a desire to know what kind of man he was, that his face had an almost forbidding acuity. 'You would be welcome in any case, but even more so this morning: we have a busy day ahead of us. Masthead, there! Any sign of life on the wharf?'

'Nothing yet, sir.'

'The wind is exactly where I want it,' said Jack, looking for the hundredth time at the rare white clouds sailing evenly across the perfect sky. 'But with this rising glass there is no trusting to it.'

'Your coffee's up, sir,' said the steward.

'Thank you, Killick. What is it, Mr Lamb?'

'I haven't no ring-bolts anywheres near big enough, sir,' said the carpenter. 'But there's a heap on 'em at the yard, I know. May I send over?'

'No, Mr Lamb. Don't you go near that yard, to save your life. Double the clench-bolts you have; set up the forge and fashion a serviceable ring. It won't take you half an hour. Now, Mr Dillon, when you have settled in comfortably below, perhaps you will come and drink a cup of coffee with me and I will tell you what I have in mind.'

James hurried below to the three-cornered booth that he was to live in, whipped out of his reporting uniform into trousers and an old blue coat, reappearing while Jack was still blowing thoughtfully upon his cup. 'Sit down, Mr Dillon, sit down,' he cried. 'Push those papers aside. It's a sad brew, I'm afraid, but at least it is wet, that I can promise you. Sugar?'

'If you please, sir,' said young Ricketts, 'the *Généreux*'s cutter is alongside with the men who were drafted off for harbour-duty.'

'All of 'em?'

'All except two, sir, that have been changed.'

Still holding his coffee-cup, Jack writhed from behind the table and with a twist of his body out through the door. Hooked on to the larboard main-chains there was the *Généreux*'s boat, filled with seamen, looking up, laughing and exchanging witticisms or mere hoots and whistles with their former shipmates. The *Généreux*'s midshipman saluted and said, 'Captain Harte's compliments, sir, and he finds the draft can be spared.'

'God bless your heart, dear Molly,' said Jack: and aloud, 'My compliments and best thanks to Captain Harte. Be so good as to send them aboard.'

They were not much to look at, he reflected, as the whip from the yardarm hoisted up their meagre belongings: three or four were decidedly simple, and two others had that inde-finable air of men of some parts whose cleverness sets them apart from their fellows, but not nearly so far as they imagine. Two of the boobies were quite horribly dirty, and one had managed to exchange his slops for a red garment with remains of tinsel upon it. Still, they all possessed two hands; they could all clap on to a rope; and it would be strange if the bosun and his mates could not induce them to heave.

'Deck,' hailed the midshipman aloft. 'Deck. There is someone moving about on the wharf.'

'Very good, Mr Babbington. You may come down and have your breakfast now. Six hands I thought lost for good,' he said to James Dillon with intense satisfaction, turning back to the cabin. 'They may not be much to look at – indeed, I think we must rig a tub if we are not to have an itchy ship – but they will help us weigh. And I hope to weigh by half-past nine at the latest.' Jack rapped the brass-bound wood of the locker and went on, 'We will ship two long twelves as chase-pieces, if I can get them from Ordnance. But whether or no I am going to take the sloop out while this breeze lasts, to try her paces. We convoy a dozen merchantmen to Cagliari, sailing this evening if they are all here, and we must know how she handles. Yes, Mr . . . Mr . . .?'

'Pullings, sir: master's mate. *Burford*'s long-boat alongside with a draft.'

'A draft for us? How many?'

'Eighteen, sir.' *And rum-looking cullies some of 'em are*, he would have added, if he had dared.

'Do you know anything about them, Mr Dillon?' asked Jack.

'I knew the *Burford* had a good many of the *Charlotte*'s people and some from the receiving ships as drafts for Mahon, sir; but I never heard of any being meant for the *Sophie*.'

Jack was on the point of saying, 'And there I was, worrying about being stripped bare,' but he contented himself with chuckling and wondering why this cornucopia should have poured itself out on him. 'Lady Warren,' came the reply, in a flash of revelation. He laughed again, and said, 'Now I am going across to the wharf, Mr Dillon. Mr Head is a businesslike man and he will tell me whether the guns are to be had or not within half an hour. If they are, I will break out my handkerchief and you can start carrying out the warps directly. What now, Mr Richards?'

'Sir,' said the pale clerk, 'Mr Purser says I should bring you the receipts and letters to sign this time every day, and the fair-copied book to read.'

'Quite right,' said Jack mildly. 'Every ordinary day. Presently you will learn which is ordinary and which is not.' He glanced at his watch. 'Here are the receipts for the men. Show me the rest another time.'

The scene on deck was not unlike Cheapside with road-work going on: two parties under the carpenter and his crew were making ready the places for the hypothetical bow- and stern-chasers, and parcels of assorted landmen and boobies stood about with their baggage, some watching the work with an interested air, offering comments, others gaping vacantly about, gazing into the sky as though they had never seen it before. One or two had even edged on to the holy quarter-deck.

'What in God's name is this infernal confusion?' cried Jack. 'Mr Watt, this is a King's ship, not the Margate hoy. You, sir, get away for'ard.'

For a moment, until his unaffected blaze of indignation galvanized them into activity, the *Sophie*'s warrant officers gazed at him sadly: he caught the words 'all these people . . .'

'I am going ashore,' he went on. 'By the time I come back this deck will present a very different appearance.'

He was still red in the face as he went down into the boat after the midshipman. 'Do they really imagine I shall leave an able-bodied man on shore if I can cram him aboard?' he said to himself. 'Of course, their precious three watches will have to go. And even so, fourteen inches will be hard to find.'

The three-watch system was a humane arrangement that allowed the men to sleep a whole night through from time to time, whereas with two watches four hours was the most they could ever hope for; but on the other hand it did mean that half the men had the whole of the available space to sling their hammocks, since the other half was on deck. 'Eighteen and six is twenty-four,' said Jack, 'and fifty or thereabout, say seventy-five. And of those how many shall I watch?' He worked out this figure in order to multiply it by fourteen, for fourteen inches was the space the regulations allowed for each hammock: and it seemed to him very doubtful whether the *Sophie* possessed anything like that amount of room, whatever her official complement might be. He was still working at it when the midshipman called, 'Unrow. Boat your oars,' and they kissed gently against the wharf.

'Go back to the ship now, Mr Ricketts,' said Jack on an impulse. 'I do not suppose I shall be long, and it may save a few minutes.'

But with the *Burford*'s draft he had missed his chance: other captains were there before him now and he had to wait his turn. He walked up and down in the brilliant morning sun with one whose epaulette matched his own – Middleton, whose greater pull had enabled him to snap up the command of the Vertueuse, the charming French privateer that would have been Jack's had there been any justice in the world. When they had exchanged the naval gossip of the Mediterranean, Jack remarked that he had come for a couple of twelve-pounders.

'Do you think she'll bear them?' asked Middleton.

'I hope so. Your four-pounder is a pitiful thing: though I must confess I feel anxious for her knees.'

'Well, I hope so, too,' said Middleton, shaking his head. 'At all events you have come on the right day: it seems that Head is to be placed under Brown, and he has taken such a spite at it that he is selling off his stock like a fishwife at the end of the fair.'

Jack had already heard something of this development in the long, long squabble between the Ordnance Board and the Navy Board, and he longed to hear more; but at this moment Captain Halliwell came out, smiling all over his face, and Middleton, who had some faint remains of conscience, said,

'You take my turn. I shall be an age, with all my carronades to explain.'

'Good morning, sir,' said Jack. 'I am Aubrey, of the *Sophie*, and I should like to try a couple of long twelves, if you please.'

With no change in his melancholy expression, Mr Head said, 'You know what they weigh?'

'Something in the nature of thirty-three hundredweight, I believe.'

'Thirty-three hundredweight, three pounds, three ounces, three pennyweight. Have a dozen, Captain, if you feel she will bear them.'

'Thank you: two will be plenty,' said Jack, looking sharply to see whether he were being made game of.

'They are yours, then, and upon your own head be it,' said Mr Head with a sigh, making secret marks upon a worn, curling parchment slip. 'Give it to the master-parker and he will troll you out as pretty a pair as ever the heart of man could desire. I have some neat mortars, if you have room.'

'I am extremely obliged to you, Mr Head,' said Jack, laughing with pleasure. 'I wish the rest of the service were run so.'

'So do I, Captain, so do I,' cried Mr Head, his face growing suddenly dark with passion. 'There are some slack-arsed, bloody-minded men – flute-playing, fiddle-scraping, present-seeking, tale-bearing, double-poxed hounds that would keep you waiting about for a month; but I am not one of them. Captain Middleton, sir: carronades for you, I presume?'

In the sunlight once more Jack threw out his signal and, peering among the masts and criss-crossed yards, he saw a figure at the *Sophie*'s masthead bend as though to hail the deck, before disappearing down a backstay, like a bead sliding upon a thread.

Expedition was Mr Head's watchword, but the master-parker of the ordnance wharf did not seem to have heard of it. He showed Jack the two twelve-pounders with great good will. 'As pretty a pair as the heart of man could desire,' he said, stroking their cascabels as Jack signed for them; but after that his mood seemed to change – there were several other captains in front of Jack – fair was fair – turn and turn about – them thirty-sixes were all in the way and would have to be moved first – he was precious short of hands.

The *Sophie* had warped in long ago and she was lying neatly against the dock right under the derricks. There was more noise aboard her than there had been, more noise than was right, even with the relaxed harbour discipline, and he was sure some of the men had managed to get drunk already. Expectant faces – a good deal less expectant now – looked over her side at her captain as he paced up and down, up and down, glancing now at his watch and now at the sky.

'By God,' he cried, clapping his hand to his forehead. 'What a damned fool. I clean forgot the oil.' Turning short in his stride he hurried over to the shed, where a violent squealing showed that the master-parker and his mates were trundling the slides of Middleton's carronades towards the neat line of their barrels. 'Master-parker,' called Jack, 'come and look at my twelve-pounders. I have been in such a hurry all morning that I do believe I forgot to anoint them.' With these words he privately laid down a gold piece upon each touch-hole, and a slow look of approval appeared on the parker's face. 'If my gunner had not been sick, he would have reminded me,' added Jack.

'Well, thankee, sir. It always has been the custom, and I don't like to see the old ways die, I do confess,' said the parker, with some still-unevaporated surliness: but then brightening progressively he said, 'A hurry, you mentioned, Captain? I'll see what we can do.'

Five minutes later the bow-chaser, neatly slung by its train-loops, side-loops, pommelion and muzzle, floated gently over the *Sophie*'s fo'c'sle within half an inch of its ideal resting-place: Jack and the carpenter were on all fours side by side, rather as though they were playing bears, and they were lis-

tening for the sound her beams and timbers would make as
the strain came off the derrick. Jack beckoned with his hand,
calling 'Handsomely, handsomely now.' The *Sophie* was perfectly silent, all her people watching intently, even the tub-
party with their buckets poised, even the human chain who
were tossing the twelve-pound round shot from the shore to
the side and so down to the gunner's mate in the shot-locker.
The gun touched, sat firm: there was a deep, not unhealthy
creaking, and the *Sophie* settled a little by the head. 'Capital,'
said Jack, surveying the gun as it stood there, well within its
chalked-out space. 'Plenty of room all round – great-oceans
of room, upon my word,' he said, backing a step. In his haste
to avoid being trodden down, the gunner's mate behind him
collided with his neighbour, who ran into his, setting off a
chain-reaction in that crowded, roughly triangular space
between the foremast and the stem that resulted in the
maiming of one ship's boy and very nearly in the watery death
of another. 'Where's the bosun? Now, Mr Watt, let me see the
tackles rigged: you want a hard-eye becket on that block.
Where's the breeching?'

'Almost ready, sir,' said the sweating, harassed bosun. 'I'm
working the cunt-splice myself.'

'Well,' said Jack, hurrying off to where the stern-chaser hung
poised above the *Sophie*'s quarter-deck, ready to plunge
through her bottom if gravity could but have its way, 'a simple
thing like a cunt-splice will not take a man-of-war's bosun long,
I believe. Set those men to work, Mr Lamb, if you please: this
is not fiddler's green.' He looked at his watch again. 'Mr
Mowett,' he said, looking at a cheerful young master's mate.
Mr Mowett's cheerful look changed to one of extreme gravity.
'Mr Mowett, do you know Joselito's coffee-house?'

'Yes, sir.'

'Then be so good as to go there and ask for Dr Maturin. My
compliments and I am very much concerned to say we shall
not be back in port by dinner-time; but I will send a boat this
evening at any time he chooses to appoint.'

THEY WERE NOT back in port by dinner-time: it would indeed have been a logical impossibility, since they had not yet left it, but were sweeping majestically through the close-packed craft towards the fairway. One advantage of having a small vessel with a great many hands aboard is that you can execute manoeuvres denied to any ship of the line, and Jack preferred this arduous creeping to being towed or to threading along under sail with a thoroughly uneasy crew, disturbed in all their settled habits and jostling full of strangers.

In the open channel he had himself rowed round the *Sophie*: he considered her from every angle, and at the same time he weighed the advantages and disadvantages of sending all the women ashore. It would be easy to find most of them while the men were at their dinner: not merely the local girls who were there for fun and pocket-money, but also the semi-permanent judies. If he made one sweep now, then another just before their true departure might clear the sloop entirely. He wanted no women aboard. They only caused trouble, and with this fresh influx they would cause even more. On the other hand, there was a certain lack of zeal aboard, a lack of real spring, and he did not mean to turn it into sullenness, particularly that afternoon. Sailors were as conservative as cats, as he knew very well: they would put up with incredible labour and hardship, to say nothing of danger, but it had to be what they were used to or they would grow brutish. She was very low in the water, to be sure: a little by the head and listing a trifle to port. All that extra weight would have been far better below the water-line. But he would have to see how she handled.

'Shall I send the hands to dinner, sir?' asked James Dillon when Jack was aboard again.

'No, Mr Dillon. We must profit by this wind. Once we are past the cape they may go below. Those guns are breeched and frapped?'

'Yes, sir.'

'Then we will make sail. In sweeps. All hands to make sail.'

The bosun sprang his call and hurried away to the fo'c'sle amidst a great rushing of feet and a good deal of bellowing.

'Newcomers below. Silence there.' Another rush of feet. The *Sophie*'s regular crew stood poised in their usual places, in dead silence. A voice on board the *Généreux* a cable's length away could be heard, quite clear and plain, '*Sophie*'s making sail.'

She lay there, rocking gently, out in Mahon harbour, with the shipping on her starboard beam and quarter and the brilliant town beyond it. The breeze a little abaft her larboard beam, a northerly wind, was pushing her stern round a trifle. Jack paused, and as it came just so he cried, 'Away aloft.' The calls repeated the order and instantly the shrouds were dark with passing men, racing up as though on their stairs at home.

'Trice up. Lay out.' The calls again, and the topmen hurried out on the yards. They cast off the gaskets, the lines that held the sails tight furled to the yards; they gathered the canvas under their arms and waited.

'Let fall,' came the order, and with it the howling peep-peep, peep-peep from the bosun and his mates.

'Sheet home. Sheet home. Hoist away. Cheerly there, in the foretop, look alive. T 'garns'l sheets. Hands to the braces. Belay.'

A gentle push from above heeled the *Sophie* over, then another and another, each more delightfully urgent until it was one steady thrust; she was under way, and all along her side there sang a run of living water. Jack and his lieutenant ex-changed a glance: it had not been bad – the foretopgallant-sail had taken its time, because of a misunderstanding as to how *newcomer* should be defined and whether the six restored *Sophie*s were to be considered in that injurious light, which had led to a furious, silent squabble on the yard; and the sheeting-home had been rather spasmodic; but it had not been disgraceful, and they would not have to support the derision of the other men-of-war in the harbour. There had

been moments in the confusion of the morning when each
had dreaded just that thing.

The *Sophie* had spread her wings a little more like an
unhurried dove than an eager hawk, but not so much so that
the expert eyes on shore would dwell upon her with disapprobation; and as for the mere landsmen, their eyes were so sati-
ated with the coming and going of every kind of vessel that
they passed over her departure with glassy indifference.

'FORGIVE ME, SIR,' said Stephen Maturin, touching his
hat to a nautical gentleman on the quay, 'but might I ask
whether you know which is the ship called Sophia?'

'A King's ship, sir?' asked the officer, returning his salute. 'A
man-of-war? There is no ship of that name – but perhaps you
refer to the sloop, sir? The sloop *Sophie*?'

'That may well be the case, sir. No man could easily sur-
pass me in ignorance of naval terms. The vessel I have in
mind is commanded by Captain Aubrey.'

'Just so: the sloop, the fourteen-gun sloop. She lies almost
directly in front of you, sir, in a line with the little white
house on the point.'

'The ship with triangular sails?'

'No. That is a polacre-settee. Somewhat to the left, and farther off.'

'The little small squat merchantman with two masts?'

'Well' – with a laugh – 'she is a trifle low in the water; but
she is a man-of-war, I assure you. And I believe she is about
to make sail. Yes. There go her topsails: sheeted home. They
hoist the yard. To'garns'ls. What's amiss? Ah, there we are.
Not very smartly done, but all's well that ends well, and the
Sophie never was one of your very brisk performers. See, she
gathers way. She will fetch the mouth of the harbour on this
wind without touching a brace.'

'She is sailing away?'

'Indeed she is. She must be running three knots already –
maybe four.'

'I am very much obliged to you, sir,' said Stephen, lifting his hat.

'Servant, sir,' said the officer, lifting his. He looked after Stephen for a while. 'Should I ask him whether he is well? I have left it too late. However, he seems steady enough now.'

Stephen had walked down to the quay to find out whether the *Sophie* could be reached on foot or whether he should have to take a boat to keep his dinner engagement; for his conversation with Mr Florey had persuaded him that not only was the engagement intended to be kept, but that the more general invitation was equally serious – an eminently practicable suggestion, most certainly to be acted upon. How civil, how more than civil, Florey had been: had explained the medical service of the Royal Navy, and taken him to see Mr Edwardes of the Centaur perform quite an interesting amputation, had dismissed his scruples as to lack of purely surgical experience, had lent him Blane on diseases incident to seamen, Hulme's *Libellus de Natura Scorbuti*, Lind's *Effectual Means* and Northcote's *Marine Practice*, and had promised to find him at least the bare essentials in instruments until he should have his allowance and the official chest – 'There are trocars, tenaculums and ball-scoops lying about by the dozen at the hospital, to say nothing of saws and bone-rasps.'

Stephen had allowed his mind to convince itself entirely, and the strength of his emotion at the sight of the *Sophie*, her white sails and her low hull dwindling fast over the shining sea, showed him how much he had come to look forward to the prospect of a new place and new skies, a living, and a closer acquaintance with this friend who was now running fast towards the quarantine island, behind which he would presently vanish.

He walked up through the town with his mind in a curious state; he had suffered so many disappointments recently that it did not seem possible he could bear another. What was more, he had allowed all his defences to disperse – unarm. It was while he was reassembling them and calling out his reserves that his feet carried him past Joselito's coffee-house and voices said, 'There he is – call out – run after him – you will catch him if you run.'

He had not been into the coffee-house that morning because it was a question either of paying for a cup of coffee or of paying for a boat to row him out to the *Sophie*, and he had therefore been unavailable for the midshipman, who now came running along behind him.

'Dr Maturin?' asked young Mowett, and stopped short, quite shocked by the pale glare of reptilian dislike. However, he delivered his message; and he was relieved to find that it was greeted with a far more human look.

'Most kind,' said Stephen. 'What do you imagine would be a convenient time, sir?'

'Oh, I suppose about six o'clock, sir,' said Mowett.

'Then at six o'clock I shall be at the Crown steps,' said Stephen. 'I am very much obliged to you, sir, for your diligence in finding me out.' They parted with a bow apiece, and Stephen said privately, 'I shall go across to the hospital and offer Mr Florey my assistance: he has a compound fracture above the elbow that will call for primary resection of the joint. It is a great while since I felt the grind of bone under my saw,' he added, smiling with anticipation.

CAPE MOLA LAY on their larboard quarter: the troubled blasts and calms caused by the heights and valleys along the great harbour's winding northern shore no longer buffeted them, and with an almost steady tramontana at north by east the *Sophie* was running fast towards Italy under her courses, single-reefed topsails and topgallants.

'Bring her up as close as she will lie,' said Jack. 'How near will she point, Mr Marshall? Six?'

'I doubt she'll do as well as six, sir,' said the master, shaking his head. 'She's a little sullen today, with the extra weight for'ard.'

Jack took the wheel, and as he did so a last gust from the island staggered the sloop, sending white water along her lee rail, plucking Jack's hat from his head and streaming his bright yellow hair away to the south-south-west. The master leapt after the hat, snatched it from the seaman who had rescued it in the hammock-netting and solicitously wiping the cockade with his handkerchief he stood by Jack's side, holding it with both hands.

'Old Sodom and Gomorrah is sweet on Goldilocks,' murmured John Lane, foretopman, to his friend Thomas Gross: Thomas winked his eye and jerked his head, but without any appearance of censure – they were concerned with the phenomenon, not with any moral judgment. 'Well, I hope he don't take it out of us too much, that's all, mate,' he replied.

Jack let her pay off until the flurry was over, and then, as he began to bring her back, his hands strong on the spokes, so he came into direct contact with the living essence of the sloop: the vibration beneath his palm, something between a sound and a flow, came straight up from her rudder, and it joined with the innumerable rhythms, the creak and humming of her hull and rigging. The keen clear wind swept in on his left cheek, and as he bore on the helm so the *Sophie* answered, quicker and more nervous than he had expected. Closer and closer to the wind. They were all staring up and forward: at last, in spite of the fiddle-tight bowline, the foretopgallantsail shivered, and Jack eased off. 'East by north, a half north,' he observed with satisfaction. 'Keep her so,' he said to the timoneer, and gave the order, the long-expected and very welcome order, to pipe to dinner.

Dinner, while the *Sophie*, as close-hauled on the larboard tack as she could be, made her offing into the lonely water where twelve-pound cannon-balls could do no harm and where disaster could pass unnoticed: the miles streamed out behind her, her white path stretching straight and true a little south of west. Jack looked at it from his stern-window with approval: remarkably little leeway; and a good steady hand must be steering, to keep that furrow so perfect in the sea. He was dining in solitary state – a Spartan meal of sodden kid and cabbage, mixed – and it was only when he realized that there was no one to whom he could impart the innumerable observations that came bubbling into his mind that he remembered: this was his first formal meal as a captain. He almost made a jocose remark about it to his steward (for he was in very high spirits, too), but he checked himself. It would not do. 'I shall grow used to it, in time,' he said, and looked again with loving relish at the sea.

THE GUNS WERE NOT a success. Even with only half a cartridge the bow-chaser recoiled so strongly that at the third discharge the carpenter came running up on deck, so pale and perturbed that all discipline went by the board. 'Don't ee do it, sir!' he cried, covering the touch-hole with his hand. 'If you could but see her poor knees – and the spirketting started in five separate places, oh dear, oh dear.' The poor man hurried to the ring-bolts of the breeching. 'There. I knew it. My clench is half drawn in this poor thin old stuff. Why didn't you tell me, Tom?' he cried, gazing reproachfully at his mate.

'I dursen't,' said Tom, hanging his head.

'It won't do, sir,' said the carpenter. 'Not with these here timbers, it won't. Not with this here deck.'

Jack felt his choler rising – it was a ludicrous situation on the overcrowded fo'c'sle, with the carpenter crawling about at his feet in apparent supplication, peering at the seams; and this was no sort of a way to address a captain. But there was no resisting Mr Lamb's total sincerity, particularly as Jack secretly agreed with him. The force of the recoil, all that weight of metal darting back and being brought up with a twang by the breeching was too much, far too much for the *Sophie*. Furthermore, there really was not room to work the ship with the two twelve-pounders and their tackle filling so much of what little space there was. But he was bitterly disappointed: a twelve-pound ball could pierce at five hundred yards: it could send up a shower of lethal splinters, carry away a yard, do great execution. He tossed one up and down in his hand, considering. Whereas at any range a four-pounder . . .

'And was you to fire off t'other one,' said Mr Lamb with desperate courage, still on his hands and knees, 'your wisitor wouldn't have a dry stitch on him: for the seams have opened something cruel.'

William Jevons, carpenter's crew, came up and whispered, 'Foot of water in the well,' in a rumble that could have been heard at the masthead.

The carpenter stood up, put on his hat, touched it and reported, 'There's a foot of water in the well, sir.'

'Very well, Mr Lamb,' said Jack, placidly, 'we'll pump it out again. Mr Day,' he said, turning to the gunner, who had crawled up on deck for the firing of the twelve-pounders (would have crept out of his grave, had he been in it), 'Mr Day, draw and house the guns, if you please. And bosun, man the chain-pump.'

He patted the warm barrel of the twelve-pounder regretfully and walked aft. He was not particularly worried about the water: the *Sophie* had been capering about in a lively way with this short sea coming across, and she would have made a good deal by her natural working. But he was vexed about the chasers, profoundly vexed, and he looked with even greater malignance at the main-yard.

'We shall have to get the topgallants off her presently, Mr Dillon,' he observed, picking up the traverse-board. He consulted it more as a matter of form than anything else, for he knew very well where they were: with some sense that develops in true seamen he was aware of the loom of the land, a dark presence beyond the horizon behind him – behind his right shoulder-blade. They had been beating steadily up into the wind, and the pegs showed almost equal boards – east-north-east followed by west-north-west: they had tacked five times (*Sophie* was not as quick in stays as he could have wished) and worn once; and they had been running at seven knots. These calculations ran their course in his mind, and as soon as he looked for it the answer was ready: 'Keep on this course for half an hour and then put her almost before the wind – two points off. That will bring you home.

'It would be as well to shorten sail now,' he observed. 'We will hold our course for half an hour.' With this he went below, meaning to do something in the way of dealing with the great mass of papers that called for attention: apart from such things as the statements of stores and the pay books there was the *Sophie*'s log, which would tell him something of the past history of the vessel, and her muster-book, which would do the same for her company. He leafed through the pages: '*Sunday, September 22, 1799, winds NW, W, S. course N40W, distance 49 miles, latitude 37°59′ N longitude 9°38′W, Cape St Vincent S27E 64 miles. PM Fresh breezes and squally with rain, made and shortened sail occasionally. AM hard gales, and 4 handed the square mainsail, at 6 saw a strange sail to the southward, at 8 more moderate, reefed the square mainsail and set it, at 9 spoke her. She was a Swedish brig bound to Barcelona in ballast. At noon weather calm, head round the compass.*' Dozens of entries of that kind of duty; and of convoy work. The plain, unspectacular, everyday sort of employment that made up ninety per cent of a service life: or more. '*People variously employed, read the Articles of War . . . convoy in company, in topgallantsails and second reef topsails. At 6 made private signal to two line of battle ships which answered. All sails set, the people employed working up junk . . . tacked occasionally, in third reef maintopsail . . . light airs inclinable to calm . . . scrubbed hammocks. Mustered by divisions, read Articles of War and punished Joseph Wood, Jno. Lakey, Matt. Johnson and Wm. Musgrave with twelve lashes for drunkenness . . . PM calm and hazy weather, at 5 out sweeps and boats to pull off shore at ½ past 6 came to with the stream anchor Cape Mola S6W distance 5 leagues. At ½ past 8 coming on to blow suddenly was obliged to cut the hawser and make sail . . . read the Articles of War and performed Divine Service . . . punished Geo. Sennet with 24 lashes for contempt . . . Fra. Bechell, Robt. Wilkinson and Joseph Wood for drunkenness . . .*'

A good many entries of that kind: a fair amount of flogging, but nothing heavy – none of your hundred-lash sentences. It contradicted his first impression of laxity: he would have to look into it more thoroughly. Then the muster. *Geo. Williams, ordinary seaman, born Bengal, volunteered at Lisbon 24 August 1797, ran 27 March 1798, Lisbon. Fortunato Carneglia, midshipman, 21, born Genoa, discharged 1 June 1797 per order Rear-Admiral Nelson per ticket. Saml. Willsea, able seaman, born Long Island, volunteered Porto 10 October 1797, ran 8 February 1799 at Lisbon from the boat. Patrick Wade, landman, 21, born County Fermanagh, prest 20 November 1796 at Porto Ferraio, discharged 11 November 1799 to Bulldog, per order Captain Darley. Richard Sutton, lieutenant, joined 31 December 1796 per order Commodore Nelson, discharged dead 2 February 1798, killed in action with a French privateer. Richard William Baldick, lieutenant, joined 28 February 1798 per commission from Earl St Vincent, discharged 18 April 1800 to join Pallas per order Lord Keith.* In the column Dead Mens Cloaths there was the sum of £8 10s 6d. against his name: clearly poor Sutton's kit auctioned at the mainmast.

But Jack could not keep his mind to the stiff-ruled column. The brilliant sea, darker blue than the sky, and the white wake across it kept drawing his eyes to the stern-window. In the end he closed the book and indulged himself in the luxury of staring out: if he chose he could go to sleep, he reflected; and he looked around, relishing this splendid privacy, the rarest of commodities at sea. As a lieutenant in the *Leander* and other fair-sized ships he had been able to look out of the ward-room windows, of course; but never alone, never unaccompanied by human presence and activity. It was wonderful: but it so happened that just now he longed for human presence and activity – his mind was too eager and restless to savour the full charm of solitude, although he knew it was there, and as soon as the ting-ting, ting-ting of four bells sounded he was up on deck.

Dillon and the master were standing by the starboard brass

four-pounder, and they were obviously discussing some part
of her rigging visible from that point. As soon as he appeared
they moved over to the larboard side in the traditional way,
leaving him his privileged area of the quarter-deck. This was
the first time it had happened to him: he had not expected it
– had not thought of it – and it gave him a ridiculous thrill of
pleasure. But it also deprived him of a companion, unless he
were to call James Dillon over. He took two or three turns,
looking up at the yards: they were braced as sharp as the
main and foremast shrouds would allow, but they were not as
sharp as they might have been in an ideal world, and he made
a mental note to tell the bosun to set up cross catharpings –
they might gain three or four degrees.

'Mr Dillon,' he said, 'be so good as to bear up and set the
square mainsail. South by west a half south.'

'Aye aye, sir. Double-reefed, sir?'

'No, Mr Dillon, no reef,' said Jack with a smile, and he
resumed his pacing. There were orders all round him, the
trample of feet, the bosun's calls: his eyes took in the whole
of the operation with a curious detachment – curious,
because his heart was beating high.

The *Sophie* paid off smoothly. 'Thus, thus,' cried the master
at the con, and the helmsman steadied her: as she was coming round before the wind the fore-and-aft mainsail vanished
in billowing clouds that quickly subsided into the members of
a long sailcloth parcel, greyish, inanimate; and immediately
afterwards the square mainsail appeared, ballooning and fluttering for a few seconds and then mastered, disciplined and
squared, with its sheets hauled aft. The *Sophie* shot forward,
and by the time Dillon called 'Belay' she had increased her
speed by at least two knots, plunging her head and raising her
stern as though she were surprised at her rider, as well she
might have been. Dillon sent another man to the wheel, in
case a fault in the wind should broach her to. The square
mainsail was as taut as a drum.

'Pass the word for the sailmaker,' said Jack. 'Mr Henry,

could you get me another cloth on to that sail, was you to take a deep goring leach?'

'No, sir,' said the sailmaker positively. 'Not if it was ever so. Not with that yard, sir. Look at all the horrible bunt there is now – more like what you might call a hog's bladder, properly speaking.'

Jack went to the rail and looked sharply at the sea running by, the long curve as it rose after the hollow under the lee-bow: he grunted and returned to his staring at the mainyard, a piece of wood rather more than thirty feet long and tapering from some seven inches in the slings, the middle part, to three at the yard-arms, the extremities.

'More like a cro'jack than a mainyard,' he thought, for the twentieth time since he first set eyes upon it. He watched the yard intently as the force of the wind worked upon it: the *Sophie* was running no faster now, and so there was no longer any easing of the load; the yard plied, and it seemed to Jack that he heard it groan. The *Sophie*'s braces led forward, of course, she being a brig, and the plying was greatest at the yard-arms, which irked him; but there was some degree of bowing all along. He stood there with his hands behind his back, his eyes set upon it; and the other officers on the quarter-deck, Dillon, Marshall, Pullings and young Ricketts stood attentively, not speaking, looking sometimes at their new captain and sometimes at the sail. They were not the only men to wonder, for most of the more experienced hands on the fo'c'sle had joined in this double scrutiny – a gaze up, then a sidelong stare at Jack. It was a strange atmosphere. Now that they were before the wind, or very nearly – that is to say, now that they were going in the same direction as the wind – nearly all the song had gone out of the rigging; the *Sophie*'s long slow pitching (no cross-sea to move her quickly) made little noise; and added to this there was the strained quietness of men murmuring together, not to be heard. But in spite of their care a voice drifted back to the quarter-deck: 'He'll carry all away, if he cracks on so.'

Jack did not hear it: he was quite unconscious of the tension around him, far away in his calculations of the opposing forces – not mathematical calculations by any means, but rather sympathetic; the calculations of a rider with a new horse between his knees and a dark hedge coming.

Presently he went below, and after he had stared out of the stern-window for some time he looked at the chart. Cape Mola would be on their starboard now – they should raise it very soon – and it would add a little greater thrust to the wind by deflecting it along the coast. Very quietly he whistled *Deh vieni*, reflecting, 'If I make a success of this, and if I make a mint of money, several hundred guineas, say, the first thing I shall do after paying-off is to go to Vienna, to the opera.'

James Dillon knocked on the door. 'The wind is increasing, sir,' he said. 'May I hand the mainsail, or reef at least?'

'No, no, Mr Dillon . . . no,' said Jack, smiling. Then reflecting that it was scarcely fair to leave this on his lieutenant's shoulders he added, 'I shall come on deck in two minutes.'

In fact, he was there in less than one, just in time to hear the ominous rending crack. 'Up sheets!' he cried. 'Hands to the jears. Tops'l clewlines. Clap on to the lifts. Lower away cheerly. Look alive, there.'

They looked alive: the yard was small; soon it was on deck, the sail unbent, the yard stripped and everything coiled down.

'Hopelessly sprung in the slings, sir,' said the carpenter sadly. He was having a wretched day of it. 'I could try to fish it, but it would never be answerable, like.'

Jack nodded, without any particular expression. He walked across to the rail, put a foot on to it and hoisted himself up into the first ratlines; the *Sophie* rose on the swell, and there indeed lay Cape Mola, a dark bar three points on the starboard beam. 'I think we must touch up the look-out,' he observed. 'Lay her for the harbour, Mr Dillon, if you please. Boom mainsail and everything she can carry. There is not a minute to lose.'

Forty-five minutes later the *Sophie* picked up her moorings, and before the way was off her the cutter splashed into the water; the sprung yard was already afloat, and the boat set off urgently in the direction of the wharf, towing the yard behind like a streaming tail.

'Well, there's the fleet's own brazen smiling serpent,' remarked bow oar, as Jack ran up the steps. 'Brings the poor old *Sophie* in, first time he ever set foot on her, with barely a yard standing at all, her timbers all crazy and half the ship's company pumping for dear life and every man on deck the livelong day, dear knows, with never a pause for the smell of a pipe. And he runs up them old steps smiling like King George was at the top there to knight him.'

'And short time for dinner, as will never be made up,' said a low voice in the middle of the boat.

'Silence,' cried Mr Babbington, with as much outrage as he could manage.

'Mr Brown,' said Jack, with an earnest look, 'you can do me a very essential service, if you will. I have sprung my main-yard hopelessly, I am concerned to tell you, and yet I must sail this evening – the *Fanny* is in. So I beg you to condemn it and issue me out another in its place. Nay, never look so shocked, my dear sir,' he said, taking Mr Brown's arm and leading him towards the cutter. 'I am bringing you back the twelve-pounders – ordnance being now within your purview, as I understand – because I feared the sloop might be over-burthened.'

'With all my heart,' said Mr Brown, looking at the awful chasm in the yard, held up mutely for his inspection by the cutter's crew. 'But there is not another spar in the yard small enough for you.'

'Come, sir, you are forgetting the *Généreux*. She had three spare foretopgallantyards, as well as a vast mound of other spars; and you would be the first to admit that I have a moral right to one.'

'Well, you may *try* it, if you wish; you may sway it up to let us see what it looks like. But I make no promise.'

'Let my men take it out, sir. I remember just where they are stowed. Mr Babbington, four men. Come along now. Look alive.'

' 'Tis only on trial, remember, Captain Aubrey,' called Mr Brown. 'I will watch you sway it up.'

'Now that is what I call a real spar,' said Mr Lamb, peering lovingly over the side at the yard. 'Never a knot, never a curl: a French spar I dare say: forty-three foot as clean as a whistle. You'll spread a mainsail as a mainsail on that, sir.'

'Yes, yes,' said Jack impatiently. 'Is that hawser brought to the capstan yet?'

'Hawser to, sir,' came the reply, after a moment's pause.

'Then heave away.'

The hawser had been made fast to the middle of the yard and then laid along it almost to its starboard extremity, being tied in half a dozen places from the slings to the yardarm with stoppers – bands of spun yarn; the hawser ran from the yardarm up to the top-block at the masthead and so down through another block on deck and thence to the capstan; so as the capstan turned the yard rose from the water, sloping more and more nearly to the vertical until it came abroad quite upright, steered carefully end-on through the rigging.

'Cut the outer stopper,' said Jack. The spun yard dropped and the yard canted a little, held by the next: as it rose so the other stoppers were out, and when the last went the yard swung square, neatly under the top.

'It will never do, Captain Aubrey,' called Mr Brown, hailing over the quiet evening air through his trumpet. 'It is far too large and will certainly carry away. You must saw off the yardarms and half the third quarter.'

Lying stark and bare like the arms of an immense pair of scales, the yard certainly did look somewhat over-large.

'Hitch on the runners,' said Jack. 'No, farther out. Half way to the second quarter. Surge the hawser and lower away.' The yard came down on deck and the carpenter hurried off for his tools. 'Mr Watt,' said Jack to the bosun. 'Just rig me the brace-pendants, will you?' The bosun opened his mouth, shut it again and bent slowly to his work: anywhere outside Bedlam brace-pendants were rigged after the horses, after the stir-rups, after the yard-tackle pendants (or a thimble for the tackle-hook, if preferred): and none of them, ever, until the stop-cleat, the narrow part for them all to rest upon, had been worked on the sawn-off end and provided with a collar to pre-vent them from drawing in towards the middle. The carpen-ter reappeared with a saw and a rule. 'Have you a plane there, Mr Lamb?' asked Jack. 'Your mate will fetch you a plane. Unship the stuns'l-boom iron and touch up the ends of the stop-cleats, Mr Lamb, if you please.' Lamb, amazed until he grasped what Jack was about, slowly planed the tips of the yard, shaving off wafers until they showed new and white, a round the size of a halfpenny bun. 'That will do,' said Jack. 'Sway her up again, bracing her round easy all the time square with the quay. Mr Dillon, I must go ashore: return the guns to the ordnance-wharf and stand off and on for me in the channel. We must sail before the evening gun. Oh, and Mr Dillon, all the women ashore.'

'All the women without exception, sir?'

'All without their lines. All the trollops. Trollops are capital things in port, but they will not do at sea.' He paused, ran down to his cabin and came back two minutes later, stuffing an envelope into his pocket. 'Yard again,' he cried, dropping into the boat.

'You will be glad you took my advice,' said Mr Brown, receiving him at the steps. 'It would certainly have carried away with the first puff of wind.'

'May I take the duettoes now, sir?' asked Jack, with a certain pang. 'I am just about to fetch the friend I was speaking of – a great musician, sir. You must meet him, when next we are in Mahon: you must allow me to present him to Mrs Brown.'

'Should be honoured – most happy,' said Mr Brown.

'Crown steps now, and give way like heroes,' said Jack, returning at a shambling run with the book: like so many sailors he was rather fat, and he sweated easily on shore. 'Six minutes in hand,' he said, peering at his watch in the twilight as they came in to the landing. 'Why, there you are, Doctor. I do hope you will forgive me for ratting on you this afternoon. Shannahan, Bussell: you two come with me. The others stay in the boat. Mr Ricketts, you had better lie twenty yards off or so, and deliver them from temptation. Will you bear with me, sir, if I make a few purchases? I have had no time to send for anything, not so much as a sheep or a ham or a bottle of wine; so I am afraid it will be junk, salt horse and Old Weevil's wedding cake for most of the voyage, with four-water grog to wet it. However, we can refresh at Cagliari. Should you like the seamen to carry your dunnage down to the boat? By the way,' he added, as they walked along, with the sailors following some way behind, 'before I forget it, it is usual in the service to draw an advance upon one's pay upon appointment; so conceiving you would not choose to appear singular, I put up a few guineas in this envelope.'

'What a humane regulation,' said Stephen, looking pleased. 'Is it often taken advantage of?'

'Invariably,' said Jack. 'It is a universal custom, in the service.'

'In that case,' said Stephen, taking the envelope, 'I shall undoubtedly comply with it: I certainly should not wish to look singular: I am most obliged to you. May I indeed have one of your men? A violoncello is a bulky object: as for the rest there is only a small chest and some books.'

'Then let us meet again at a quarter past the hour at the steps,' said Jack. 'Lose not a moment, I beg, Doctor; for we are extremely pressed. Shannahan, you look after the Doctor and trundle his dunnage along smartly. Bussell, you come along with me.'

As the clock struck the quarter and the note hung up there unresolved, waiting for the half, Jack said, 'Stow the chest in

the fore-sheets. Mr Ricketts, you stow yourself upon the
chest. Doctor, you sit down there and nurse the 'cello. Capital. Shove off. Give way together, and row dry, now.'

They reached the *Sophie*, propelled Stephen and his
belongings up the side – the larboard side, to avoid ceremony
and to make sure they got him aboard: they had too low an
opinion of landmen to allow him to venture upon even the
Sophie's unaspiring height alone – and Jack led him to the
cabin. 'Mind your head,' he said. 'That little den in there is
yours: do what you can to make yourself comfortable, pray,
and forgive my lack of ceremony. I must go on deck.

'Mr Dillon,' he said, 'is all well?'

'All's well, sir. The twelve merchantmen have made their
signal.'

'Very good. Fire a gun for them and make sail, if you please.
I believe we shall just get down the harbour with topgallants,
if this fag-end of a breeze still holds; and then, out of the lee
of the cape, we may make a respectable offing. So make sail;
and by then it will be time to set the watch. A long day, Mr
Dillon?'

'A very long day, sir.'

'At one time I thought it would never come to an end.'

3

TWO BELLS in the morning watch found the *Sophie* sailing steadily eastward along the thirty-ninth parallel with
the wind just abaft her beam; she was heeling no more than
two strakes under her topgallantsails, and she could have set
her royals, if the amorphous heap of merchantmen under her
lee had not determined to travel very slowly until full daylight, no doubt for fear of tripping over the lines of longitude.

The sky was still grey and it was impossible to say whether
it was clear or covered with very high cloud; but the sea itself

already had a nacreous light that belonged more to the day than the darkness, and this light was reflected in the great convexities of the topsails, giving them the lustre of grey pearls.

'Good morning,' said Jack to the marine sentry at the door.

'Good morning, sir,' said the sentry, springing to attention.

'Good morning, Mr Dillon.'

'Good morning, sir,' touching his hat.

Jack took in the state of the weather, the trim of the sails and the likelihood of a fair forenoon; he drew deep gusts of the clean air, after the dense fug of his cabin. He turned to the rail, unencumbered by hammocks at this time of day, and looked at the merchantmen: they were all there, straggling over not too vast an area of sea; and what he had taken for a far stern lantern or an uncommonly big top-light was old Saturn, low on the horizon and tangled in their rigging. To windward now, and he saw a sleepy line of gulls, squabbling languidly over a ripple on the sea – sardines or anchovies or maybe those little spiny mackerel. The sound of the creaking blocks, the gently straining cordage and sailcloth, the angle of the living deck and the curved line of guns in front of him sent such a jet of happiness through his heart that he almost skipped where he stood.

'Mr Dillon,' he said, overcoming a desire to shake his lieutenant by the hand, 'we shall have to muster the ship's company after breakfast and make up our minds how we are to watch and quarter them.'

'Yes, sir: at the moment things are at sixes and sevens, with the new draft unsettled.'

'At least we have plenty of hands – we could fight both sides easily, which is more than any line of battle ship can say. Though I rather fancy we had the tail end of the draft from the *Burford*; it seemed to me there was an unnatural proportion of Lord Mayor's men among them. No old Charlottes, I suppose?'

'Yes, sir, we have one – the fellow with no hair and a red

handkerchief round his neck. He was a foretopman, but he seems quite dazed and stupid still.'

'A sad business,' said Jack shaking his head.

'Yes,' said James Dillon, looking into vacancy and seeing a leaping spring of fire in the still air, a first-rate ablaze from truck to waterline, with eight-hundred men aboard. 'You could hear the flames a mile away and more. And sometimes a sheet of fire would lift off and go up into the air by itself, cracking and waving like a huge flag. It was just such a morning as this: a little later in the day, perhaps.'

'You were there, I collect? Have you any notion of the cause? People talk about an infernal machine taken aboard by an Italian in Boney's pay.'

'From all I heard it was some fool who allowed hay to be stowed on the half-deck, close to the tub with the slow-match for the signal-guns. It went up in a blaze and caught the mainsail at once. It was so sudden they could not come to the clew-garnets.'

'Could you save any of her people?'

'Yes, a few. We picked up two marines and a quarter-gunner, but he was most miserably burnt. There were very few saved, not much above a hundred, I believe. It was not a creditable business, not at all. Many more should have been brought away, but the boats hung back.'

'They were thinking of the *Boyne*, no doubt.'

'Yes. The *Charlotte*'s guns were firing as the heat reached them, and everybody knew the magazine might go up at any minute; but even so . . . All the officers I spoke to said the same thing – there was no getting the boats close in. It was the same with my people. I was in a hired cutter, the *Dart* –'

'Yes, yes, I know you were,' said Jack, smiling significantly.

'– three or four miles down-wind, and we had to sweep to get up. But there was no way of inducing them to pull heartily, rope's end or no. There was not a man or boy who was what you would call shy of gunfire – indeed, they were as well-conducted a set of men as you could wish, for boarding or for carrying a shore-battery, or for anything you please. And the *Charlotte*'s guns were not aimed at us, of course – just going off at random. But no, the whole feeling in the cutter was different; quite unlike action or an ugly night on a lee-shore. And there is little to be done with a thoroughly unwilling crew.'

'No,' said Jack. 'There is no forcing a willing mind.' He was reminded of his conversation with Stephen Maturin, and he added, 'It is a contradiction in terms.' He might have gone on to say that a crew thoroughly upset in its ways, cut short in the article of sleep, and deprived of its trollops, was not the best of weapons either; but he knew that any remark passed on the deck of a vessel seventy-eight feet three inches long was in the nature of a public statement. Apart from anything else, the quartermaster at the con and the helmsman at the wheel were within arm's reach. The quartermaster turned the watch-glass, and as the first grains of sand began their tedious journey back into the half they had just so busily emptied he called 'George,' in a low, night-watch voice, and the marine sentry clumped forward to strike three bells.

By now there was no doubt about the sky: it was pure blue from north to south, with no more than a little violet duskiness lingering in the west.

Jack stepped over to the weather-rail, swung himself into the shrouds and ran up the ratlines. 'This may not look quite dignified, in a captain,' he reflected, pausing under the loom of the top to see just how much more clearance well-bowsed cross-catharpings might give the yard. 'Perhaps I had better go up through the lubber's hole.' Ever since the invention of those platforms some way up the mast called tops, sailors have made it a point of honour to get into them by an odd, devious route – by clinging to the futtock-shrouds, which run from the catharpings near the top of the mast to the futtock-plates at the outer edge of the top: they cling to them and creep like flies, hanging backward about twenty-five degrees from the vertical, until they reach the rim of the top and so

climb upon it, quite ignoring the convenient square hole next
to the mast itself, to which the shrouds lead directly as their
natural culmination – a straight, safe path with easy steps
from the deck to the top. This hole, this lubber's hole, is as
who should say never used, except by those who have never
been to sea or persons of great dignity, and when Jack came
up through it he gave Jan Jackruski, ordinary seaman, so disagreeable a fright that he uttered a thin scream. 'I thought
you were the house-demon,' he said, in Polish.

'What is your name?' said Jack.

'Jackruski, sir. Please: thank you,' said the Pole.

'Watch out carefully, Jackruski,' said Jack, moving easily up
the topmast shrouds. He stopped at the masthead, hooked an
arm through the topgallant shrouds and settled comfortably
in the crosstrees: many an hour had he spent there by way of
punishment in his youth – indeed, when first he used to go
up he had been so small that he could easily sit on the middle
crosstree with his legs dangling, lean forward on his arms
folded over the after tree and go to sleep, firmly wedged in
spite of the wild gyrations of his seat. How he had slept in
those days! He was always sleepy or hungry, or both. And how
perilously high it had seemed. It had been higher, of course,
far higher, in the old *Theseus* – somewhere about a hundred
and fifty feet up: and how it had swung about the sky! He had
been sick once, mast-headed in the old *Theseus*, and his dinner had gone straight up into the air, never to be seen again.
But even so, this was a comfortable height. Eighty-seven feet
less the depth of the kelson – say seventy-five. That gave him
a horizon of ten or eleven miles. He looked over those miles
of sea to windward – perfectly clear. Not a sail, not the slightest break on the tight line of the horizon. The topgallantsail
above him was suddenly golden: then two points on the larboard bow, in the mounting blaze of light, the sun thrust up
its blinding rim. For a prolonged moment Jack alone was sunlit, picked out: then the light reached the topsail, travelled
down it, took in the peak of the boom mainsail and so

reached the deck, flooding it from stem to stern. Tears welled up in his eyes, blurred his vision, overspilt, rolled down his cheeks: they did not use themselves up in lines upon his face but dropped, two, four, six, eight, round drops slanting away through the warm golden air to leeward.

Bending low to look under the topgallantsail he gazed at his charges, the merchantmen: two pinks, two snows, a Baltic cat and the rest barca-longas; all there, and the rearmost was beginning to make sail. Already there was a living warmth in the sun, and a delicious idleness spread through his limbs.

'This will never do,' he said: there were innumerable things to be seen to below. He blew his nose, and with his eyes still fixed on the spar-laden cat he reached out for the weather backstay. His hand curled round it mechanically, with as little thought as if it had been the handle of his own front door, and he slid gently down to the deck, thinking, 'One new land-man to each gun-crew might answer very well.'

Four bells. Mowett heaved the log, waited for the red tag to go astern and called 'Turn.' 'Stop!' cried the quarter-master twenty-eight seconds later, with the little sand-glass close to his eye. Mowett nipped the line almost exactly at the third knot, jerked out the peg and walked across to chalk 'three knots' on the logboard. The quartermaster hurried to the big watch-glass, turned it and called out 'George' in a firm and rounded voice. The marine went for'ard and struck the four bells heartily. A moment later pandemonium broke loose: pandemonium, that is, to the waking Stephen Maturin, who now for the first time in his life heard the unnatural wailing, the strange arbitrary intervals of the bosun and his mates pip-ing 'Up all hammocks'. He heard a rushing of feet and a great terrible voice calling 'All hands, all hands ahoy! Out or down! Out or down! Rouse and bitt! Rise and shine! Show a leg there! Out or down! Here I come, with a sharp knife and a clear conscience!' He heard three muffled dumps as three sleep-sodden landmen were, in fact, cut down: he heard oaths, laughter, the impact of a rope's end as a bosun's mate started a torpid, bewildered hand, and then a far greater trampling as fifty or sixty men rushed up the hatchways with their hammocks, to stow them in the nettings.

On deck the foretopmen had set the elm-tree pump awheezing, while the fo'c'slemen washed the fo'c'sle with the fresh sea-water they pumped, the maintopmen washed the starboard side of the quarter-deck and the quarter-deck men all the rest, grinding away with holystones until the water ran like thin milk from the admixture of minute raspings of wood and caulking, and the boys and the idlers – the people who merely worked all day – heaved at the chain-pumps to clear the night's water out of the bilges, and the gunner's crew cosseted the fourteen four-pounders; but none of this had had the electrifying effect of the racing feet.

'Is it some emergency?' wondered Stephen, working his way with rapid caution out of his hanging cot. 'A battle? Fire? A desperate leak? And are they too much occupied to warn me – have forgotten I am here?' He drew on his breeches as fast as he could and, straightening briskly, he brought his head up against a beam with such force that he staggered and sank on to a locker, cherishing it with both hands.

A voice was speaking to him. 'What did you say?' he asked, peering through a mist of pain.

'I said, "Did you bump your head, sir?" '

'Yes,' said Stephen, looking at his hand: astonishingly it was not covered with blood – there was not even so much as a smear.

'It's these old beams, sir' – in the unusually distinct, didactic voice used at sea for landmen and on land for half-wits – 'You want to take care of them; for – they – are – very – low.' Stephen's look of pure malevolence recalled the steward to a sense of his message and he said, 'Could you fancy a chop or two for breakfast, sir? A neat beefsteak? We killed a bullock at Mahon, and there's some prime steaks.'

'There you are, Doctor,' cried Jack. 'Good morning to you. I trust you slept?'

'Very well indeed, I thank you. These hanging cots are a most capital invention, upon my word.'

'What would you like for breakfast? I smelt the gunroom's bacon on deck and I thought it the finest smell I had ever smelt in my life – Araby left at the post. What do you say to bacon and eggs, and then perhaps a beefsteak to follow? And coffee?'

'You are of my way of thinking entirely,' cried Stephen, who had great leeway to make up in the matter of victuals. 'And conceivably there might be onions, as an antiscorbutic.' The word onions brought the smell of them frying into his nostrils and their peculiarly firm yet unctuous texture to his palate: he swallowed painfully. 'What's afoot?' he exclaimed, for the howling and the wild rushing, as of mad beasts, had broken out again.

'The hands are being piped down to breakfast,' said Jack carelessly. 'Light along that bacon, Killick. And the coffee. I'm clemmed.'

'How I slept,' said Stephen. 'Deep, deep, restorative, roborative sleep – none of your hypnogogues, none of your tinctures of laudanum can equal it. But I am ashamed of my appearance. I slept so late that here I am, barbarously unshaved and nasty, whereas you are as smug as a bridegroom. Forgive me for a moment.

'It was a naval surgeon, a man at Haslar,' he said, coming back, smooth, 'who invented these modern short arterial ligatures: I thought of him just now, as my razor passed within a few lines of my external carotid. When it is rough, surely you must get many shocking incised wounds?'

'Why, no: I can't say we do,' said Jack. 'A matter of use, I suppose. Coffee? What we do get is a most plentiful crop of bursten bellies – what's the learned word? – and pox.'

'Hernia. You surprise me.'

'Hernia: exactly so. Very common. I dare say half the idlers are more or less ruptured: that is why we give them the lighter duties.'

'Well, it is not so very surprising, now that I reflect upon the nature of a mariner's labour. And the nature of his amusements accounts for his pox, of course. I remember to have seen parties of seamen in Mahon, wonderfully elated, dancing and singing with sad drabble-tail pakes. Men from the *Audacious*, I recall, and the *Phaëton*: I do not remember any from the *Sophie*.'

'No. The Sophies were a quiet lot ashore. But in any case they had nothing to be elated about, or with. No prizes and so, of course, no prize-money. It's prize-money alone lets a seaman kick up a dust ashore, for precious little does he see of his pay. What do you say to a beefsteak now, and another pot of coffee?'

'With all my heart.'

'I hope I may have the pleasure of introducing my lieutenant to you at dinner. He appears to be a seamanlike, gentlemanly fellow. He and I have a busy morning ahead of us: we must sort out the crew and set them to their duties – we must watch and quarter them, as we say. And I must find you a servant, as well as one for myself, and a cox'n too. The gunroom cook will do very well.'

'WE WILL MUSTER the ship's company, Mr Dillon, if you please,' said Jack.

'Mr Watt,' said James Dillon. 'All hands to muster.'

The bosun sprung his call, his mates sped below roaring 'All hands', and presently the *Sophie*'s deck between the mainmast and the fo'c'sle was dark with men, all her people, even the cook, wiping his hands on his apron, which he balled up and thrust into his shirt. They stood rather uncertainly, over to port, in the two watches, with the newcomers huddled vaguely between them, looking shabby, mean and bereft.

'All hands for muster, sir, if you please,' said James Dillon, raising his hat.

'Very well, Mr Dillon,' said Jack. 'Carry on.'

Prompted by the purser, the clerk brought forward the muster-book and the *Sophie*'s lieutenant called out the names. 'Charles Stallard.'

'Here sir,' cried Charles Stallard, able seaman, volunteer from the *St Fiorenzo*, entered the *Sophie* 6 May 1795, then aged twenty. No entry under Straggling, none under Venereals, none under Cloaths in Sick Quarters: had remitted ten pounds from abroad: obviously a valuable man. He stepped over to the starboard side.

'Thomas Murphy.'

'Here, sir,' said Thomas Murphy, putting the knuckle of his index finger to his forehead as he moved over to join Stallard – a gesture used by all the men until James Dillon reached Assei and Assou, with never a Christian-name between them: able seamen, born in Bengal, and brought here by what strange winds? And they, in spite of years and years in the Royal Navy, put their hands to their foreheads and thence to their hearts, bending quickly as they did so.

'John Codlin. William Witsover. Thomas Jones. Francis Lacanfra. Joseph Bussell. Abraham Vilheim. James Courser. Peter Peterssen. John Smith. Giuseppe Laleso. William Cozens. Lewis Dupont. Andrew Karouski. Richard Henry . . .' and so the list went on, with only the sick gunner and one Isaac Wilson not answering, until it ended with the newcomers and the boys – eighty-nine souls, counting officers, men, boys and marines.

Then began the reading of the Articles of War, a ceremony that often accompanied divine service and that was so closely associated with it in most minds that the faces of the crew assumed a look of devout blankness at the words, 'for the better regulating of his Majesty's navies, ships of war, and forces by sea, whereon under the good providence of God, the wealth, safety and strength of his kingdom chiefly depend; be it enacted by the King's most excellent Majesty, by and with the advice and consent of the lords spiritual and temporal, and commons, in this present parliament assembled, and by

the authority of the same, that from and after the twenty-fifth
day of December, one thousand seven hundred and forty-
nine, the articles and orders hereinafter following, as well in
time of peace as in time of war, shall be duly observed and
put in execution, in manner hereinafter mentioned', an
expression that they retained throughout, unmoved by 'all flag
officers, and all persons in or belonging to his Majesty's ships
or vessels of war, being guilty of profane oaths, cursings, exe-
crations, drunkenness, uncleanliness, or other scandalous
actions, shall incur such punishment as a court-martial shall
think fit to impose'. Or by the echoing repetition of 'shall suffer death'. 'Every flag-officer, captain and commander in the
fleet who shall not . . . encourage the inferior officers and
men to fight courageously, shall suffer death . . . If any person
in the fleet shall treacherously or cowardly yield or cry for
quarter – being convicted thereof by the sentence of a court-
martial, shall suffer death . . . Every person who through cowardice shall in time of action withdraw or keep back . . . shall
suffer death . . . Every person who through cowardice, negligence or disaffection shall forbear to pursue any enemy,
pirate, or rebel, beaten or flying . . . shall suffer death . . . If
any officer, mariner, soldier or other person in the fleet shall
strike any of his superior officers, draw, or offer to draw, or lift
up any weapon . . . shall suffer death . . . If any person in the
fleet shall commit the unnatural and detestable sin of buggery or sodomy with man or beast, he shall be punished with
death.' Death rang through and through the Articles; and
even where the words were utterly incomprehensible the
death had a fine, comminatory, Leviticus ring, and the crew
took a grave pleasure in it all; it was what they were used to –
it was what they heard the first Sunday in every month and
upon all extraordinary occasions such as this. They found it
comfortable to their spirits, and when the watch below was
dismissed the men looked far more settled.

'Very well,' said Jack, looking round. 'Make signal twenty-
three with two guns to leeward. Mr Marshall, we will set the

main and fore stays'ls, and as soon as you see that pink coming up with the rest of the convoy, set the royals. Mr Watt, let the sailmaker and his party get to work on the square mainsail directly, and send the new hands aft one by one. Where's my clerk? Mr Dillon, let us knock these watch-bills into some kind of a shape. Dr Maturin, allow me to present my officers . . .' This was the first time Stephen and James had come face to face in the *Sophie*, but Stephen had seen that flaming red queue with its black ribbon and he was largely prepared. Even so, the shock of recognition was so great that his face automatically took on a look of veiled aggression and of the coldest reserve. For James Dillon the shock was far greater; in the hurry and business of the preceding twenty-four hours he had not chanced to hear the new surgeon's name; but apart from a slight change of colour he betrayed no particular emotion. 'I wonder,' said Jack to Stephen when the introductions were over, 'whether it would amuse you to look over the sloop while Mr Dillon and I attend to this business, or whether you would prefer to be in the cabin?'

'Nothing would give me greater pleasure than to look over the ship, I am sure,' said Stephen. 'A very elegant complexity of . . .' his voice trailed away.

'Mr Mowett, be so good as to show Dr Maturin everything he would like to see. Carry him into the maintop – it affords quite a visto. You do not mind a little height, my dear sir?'

'Oh no,' said Stephen, looking vaguely about him. 'I do not mind it.'

James Mowett was a tubular young man, getting on for twenty; he was dressed in old sailcoth trousers and a striped Guernsey shirt, a knitted garment that gave him very much the look of a caterpillar; and he had a marlinspike dangling round his neck, for he had meant to take a hand in the making of the new square mainsail. He looked attentively at Stephen to make out what kind of a man he was, and with that mixture of easy grace and friendly deference which comes naturally to so many sailors he made his bow and said,

'Well, sir, where do you choose to start? Shall we go into the top directly? You can see the whole run of the deck from there.'

The whole run of the deck amounted to some ten yards aft and sixteen forward, and it was perfectly visible from where they stood; but Stephen said, 'Let us go up then, by all means. Lead the way, and I will imitate your motions as best I can.'

He watched thoughtfully while Mowett sprang into the ratlines and then, his mind far away, slowly hoisted himself up after him. James Dillon and he had belonged to the United Irishmen, a society that at different times in the last nine years had been an open, public association calling for the emancipation of Presbyterians, dissenters and Catholics and for a representative government of Ireland; a proscribed secret society; an armed body in open rebellion; and a defeated, hunted remnant. The rising had been put down amidst the usual horrors, and in spite of the general pardon the lives of the more important members were in danger. Many had been betrayed – Lord Edward Fitzgerald himself at the very outset – and many had withdrawn, distrusting even their own families, for the events had divided the society and the nation most terribly. Stephen Maturin was not afraid of any vulgar betrayal, nor was he afraid for his skin, because he did not value it: but he had so suffered from the incalculable tensions, rancour and hatreds that arise from the failure of a rebellion that he could not bear any further disappointment, any further hostile, recriminatory confrontation, any fresh example of a friend grown cold, or worse. There had always been very great disagreements within the association; and now, in the ruins of it, it was impossible, once daily contact had been lost, to tell where any man stood.

He was not afraid for his skin, not afraid for himself: but presently his climbing body, now half-way up the shrouds, let him know that for its own part it was in a state of rapidly increasing terror. Forty feet is no very great height, but it seems far more lofty, aerial and precarious when there is nothing but an insubstantial yielding ladder of moving ropes underfoot; and when Stephen was three parts of the way up cries of 'Belay' on deck showed that the staysails were set and their sheets hauled aft. They filled, and the *Sophie* heeled over another strake or two; this coincided with her leeward roll, and the rail passed slowly under Stephen's downward gaze, to be followed by the sea – a wide expanse of glittering water, very far below, and directly underneath. His grip on the ratlines tightened with cataleptic strength and his upward progress ceased: he remained there spreadeagled, while the varying forces of gravity, centrifugal motion, irrational panic and reasonable dread acted upon his motionless, tight-cramped person, now pressing him forward so that the checkered pattern of the shrouds and their crossing ratlines were imprinted on his front, and now plucking him back-wards so that he bellied out like a shirt hung up to dry.

A form slid down the backstay to the left of him: hands closed gently round his ankles, and Mowett's cheerful young voice said, 'Now, sir, on the roll. Clap on to the shrouds – the uprights – and look upwards. Here we go.' His right foot was firmly moved up to the next ratline, his left followed it; and after one more hideous swinging backward lunge in which he closed his eyes and stopped breathing, the lubber's hole received its second visitor of the day. Mowett had darted round by the futtock-shrouds and was there in the top to haul him through.

'This is the maintop, sir,' said Mowett, affecting not to notice Stephen's haggard look. 'The other one over there is the foretop, of course.'

'I am very sensible of your kindness in helping me up,' said Stephen. 'Thank you.'

'Oh, sir,' cried Mowett, 'I beg . . . And that's the mainstays'l they just set, below us. And that's the forestays'l for'ard: you'll never see one, but on a man-of-war.'

'Those triangles? Why are they called staysails?' asked Stephen, speaking somewhat at random.

'Why, sir, because they are rigged on the stays, slide along them like curtains by those rings: we call 'em hanks, at sea. We used to have grommets, but we rigged hanks when we were laying off Cadiz last year, and they answer much better. The stays are those thick ropes that run sloping down, straight for'ard.'

'And their function is to extend these sails: I see.'

'Well, sir, they do extend them, to be sure. But what they are really for is to hold up the masts – to stay them for'ard. To prevent them falling backwards when she pitches.'

'The masts need support, then?' asked Stephen, stepping cautiously across the platform and patting the squared top of the lower mast and the rounded foot of the topmast, two stout parallel columns – close on three feet of wood between them, counting the gap. 'I should scarcely have thought it.'

'Lord, sir, they'd roll themselves overboard, else. The shrouds support them sideways, and the backstays – these here, sir – backwards.'

'I see. I see. Tell me,' said Stephen, to keep the young man talking at any cost, 'tell me, what is the purpose of this platform, and why is the mast doubled at this point? And what is this hammer for?'

'The top, sir? Why, apart from the rigging and getting things up, it comes in handy for the small-arms men in a close action: they can fire down on the enemy's deck and toss stink-pots and grenadoes. And then these futtock-plates at the rim here hold the dead-eyes for the topmast shrouds – the top gives a wide base so that the shrouds have a purchase: the top is a little over ten foot wide. It is the same thing up above. There are the cross-trees, and they spread the topgallant shrouds. You see them, sir? Up there, where the look-out is perched, beyond the topsail yard.'

'You could not explain this maze of ropes and wood and canvas without using sea-terms, I suppose. No, it would not be possible.'

'Using no sea-terms? I should be puzzled to do that, sir; but I will try, if you wish it.'

'No; for it is by those names alone that they are known, in nearly every case, I imagine.' The *Sophie's* tops were furnished with iron stanchions for the hammock-netting that protected their occupants in battle: Stephen sat between two of them, with an arm round each and his legs dangling, he found comfort in this feeling of being firmly anchored to metal, with solid wood under his buttocks. The sun was well up in the sky by now and it threw a brilliant pattern of light and sharp shadow over the white deck below – geometrical lines and curves broken only by the formless mass of the square mainsail that the sailmaker and his men had spread over the fo'c'sle. 'Suppose we were to take that mast,' he said, nodding forward, for Mowett seemed to be afraid of talking too much – afraid of boring and instructing beyond his station, 'and suppose you were to name the principal objects from the bottom to the top.'

'It is the foremast, sir. The bottom we call the lower mast, or just the foremast; it is forty-nine feet long, and it is stepped on the kelson. It is supported by shrouds on either side – three pair of a side – and it is stayed for'ard by the forestay running down to the bowsprit: and the other rope running parallel with the forestay is the preventer-stay, in case it breaks. Then, about a third of the way up the foremast, you see the collar of the mainstay: the mainstay goes from just under here and supports the mainmast below us.'

'So that is a mainstay,' said Stephen, looking at it vaguely. 'I have often heard them mentioned. A stout-looking rope, indeed.'

'Ten-inch, sir,' said Mowett proudly. 'And the preventer-stay is seven. Then comes the forecourse yard, but perhaps I had best finish the masts before I go on to the yards. You see the foretop, the same kind of thing as we are on now? It lies on the trestletrees and crosstrees about five parts of the way up the foremast: and so the remaining length of lower mast runs double with the topmast, just as these two do here. The topmast, do you see, is that second length going upwards, the thinner piece that rises above the top. We sway it up from below and fix it to the lower mast, rather like a marine clapping a bayonet on to his musket: it comes up through the trestletrees, and when it is high enough, so that the hole in the bottom of it is clear, we ram a fid through, banging it home with the top-maul, which is this hammer you were asking about, and we sing out "Launch ho!" and . . .' the explanation ran eagerly on.

'Castlereagh hanging at the one masthead and Fitzgibbon at the other,' thought Stephen, but with only the weariest gleam of spirit.

'. . . and it's stayed for'ard to the bowsprit again: you can just see a corner of the foretopmast stays'l if you crane over this way.'

His voice reached Stephen as a pleasant background against which he tried to arrange his thoughts. Then Stephen was aware of an expectant pause: the words 'foretopmast' and 'crane over' had preceded it.

'Just so,' he said. 'And how long might that topmast be?'

'Thirty-one feet, sir, the same as this one here. Now, just above the foretop you see the collar of the maintopmast stay, which supports this topmast just above us. Then come the topmast trestletrees and crosstrees, where the other lookout is stationed; and then the topgallantmast. It is swayed up and held the same way as the topmast, only naturally its shrouds are slighter; and it is stayed for'ard to the jib-boom – do you see, the spar that runs out beyond the bowsprit? The bowsprit's topmast, as it were. It is twenty-three feet six inches long. The topgallantmast, I mean, not the jib-boom. That is twenty-four.'

'It is a pleasure to hear a man who thoroughly understands his profession. You are very exact, sir.'

'Oh, I hope the captains will say the same, sir,' cried

Mowett. 'When next we put into Gibraltar I am to go for my lieutenant's examination again. Three senior captains sit upon you; and last time a very devilish captain asked me how many fathoms I should need for the main crowfoot, and how long the euphroe was. I could tell him now: it is fifty fathoms of three-quarter-inch line, though you would never credit it, and the euphroe is fourteen inches. I believe I could tell him anything that can even be attempted to be measured, except perhaps for the new mainyard, and I shall measure that with my tape before dinner. Should you like to hear some dimensions, sir?'

'I should like it of all things.'

'Well, sir, the Sophie's keel is fifty-nine feet long; her gundeck seventy-eight foot three inches; and she is ten foot ten inches deep. Her bowsprit is thirty-four foot, and I have told you all the other masts except for the main, which is fifty-six. Her maintopsail yard – the one just above us, sir – is thirty-one foot six inches; the maintopgallant, the one above that, twenty-three foot six; and the royal, up at the top, fifteen foot nine. And the stuns'l booms – but I ought to explain the yards first, sir, ought I not?'

'Perhaps you ought.'

'They are very simple, indeed.'

'I am happy to learn it.'

'On the bowsprit, now, there's a yard across, with the spritsail furled upon it. That's the sprits'l yard, naturally. Then, coming to the foremast, the bottom one is the foreyard and the big square sail set upon it is the fore course; the foretopsail yard crosses above it; then the foretopgallant and the little royal with its sail furled. It is the same with the mainmast, only the mainyard just below us has no sail bent – if it had it would be called the square mainsail, because with this rig you have two mainsails, the square course set on the yard and the boom mainsail there behind us, a fore-and-aft sail set on a gaff above and a boom below. The boom is forty-two feet nine inches long, sir, and ten and a half inches through.'

'Ten and a half inches, indeed?' How absurd it had been to affect not to know James Dillon – and a very childish reaction – the most usual and dangerous of them all.

'Now to finish with the square sails, there are the stuns'ls, sir. We only set them when the wind is well abaft the beam, and they stand outside the leeches – the edges of the square sails – stretched by booms that run out along the yard through boom-irons. You can see them as clear as can be –'

'What is that?'

'The bosun piping hands to make sail. They will be setting the royals. Come over here, sir, if you please, or the topmen will trample you down.'

Stephen was scarcely out of the way before a swarm of young men and boys darted over the edge of the top and raced on grunting up the topmast shrouds.

'Now, sir, when the order comes you will see them let the sail fall, and then the men on deck will haul home the lee sheet first, because the wind blows it over that way and it comes home easy. Then the weather sheet: and as soon as the men are off the yard they will hoist away at the halliards and up she'll go. Here are the sheets, leading through by the block with a patch of white on it: and these are the halliards.'

A few moments later the royals were drawing, the *Sophie* heeled another strake and the hum of the breeze in her rigging rose by half a tone: the men came down less hurriedly than they had mounted; and the *Sophie*'s bell sounded five times.

'Tell me,' said Stephen, preparing to follow them, 'what is a brig?'

'This is a brig, sir; though we call her a sloop.'

'Thank you. And what is a – there is that howling again.'

' 'Tis only the bosun, sir: the square mainsail must be ready, and he desires the men to bend it to the yard.

> O'er the ship the gallant bosun flies
> Like a hoarse mastiff through the storm he cries.

Prompt to direct th'unskilful still appears,
The expert he praises, and the timid cheers.'

'He seems very free with that cane: I wonder they don't knock him down. So you are a poet, sir?' asked Stephen, smiling: he was beginning to feel that he could cope with the situation.

Mowett laughed cheerfully, and said, 'It would be easier this side, sir, with her heeling so. I will just get round a little below you. They say it is a wonderful plan not to look down, sir. Easy now. Easy does it. Handsomely wins the day. There you are, sir, all a-tanto.'

'By God,' said Stephen, dusting his hands. 'I am glad to be down.' He looked up at the top, and down again. 'I should not have thought myself so timid,' he reflected inwardly; and aloud he said, 'Now shall we look downstairs?'

'PERHAPS WE MAY find a cook among this new draft,' said Jack. 'That reminds me – I hope I may have the pleasure of your company to dinner?'

'I should be very happy, sir,' said James Dillon with a bow. They were sitting at the cabin table with the clerk at their side and the *Sophie*'s muster-book, complete-book, description-book and various dockets spread out before them.

'Take care of that pot, Mr Richards,' said Jack, as the *Sophie* gave a skittish lee-lurch in the freshening breeze. 'You had better cork it up and hold the ink-horn in your hand. Mr Ricketts, let us see these men.'

They were a lacklustre band, compared with the regular Sophies. But then the Sophies were at home; the Sophies were all dressed in the elder Mr Ricketts' slops, which gave them a tolerably uniform appearance; and they had been tolerably well fed for the last few years – their food had at least been adequate in bulk. The newcomers, with three exceptions, were quota-men from the inland counties, mostly furnished by the beadle; there were seven ardent spirits from Westmeath who had been taken up in Liverpool for causing an affray, and so little did they know of the world (they had come over for the harvest, no more) that when they were offered the choice between the dampest cells of the common gaol and the Navy, they chose the latter, as the dryer place; and there was a bee-master with a huge lamentable face and a great spade beard whose bees had all died; an out-of-work thatcher; some unmarried fathers; two starving tailors; a quiet lunatic. The most ragged had been given clothes by the receiving-ships, but the others were still in their own worn corduroy or ancient second-hand coats – one countryman still had his smock-frock on. The exceptions were three middle-aged seamen, one a Dane called Christian Pram, the second mate of a Levanter, and the two others Greek sponge fishers whose names were thought to be Apollo and Turbid, pressed in circumstances that remained obscure.

'Capital, capital,' said Jack, rubbing his hands. 'I think we can rate Pram quartermaster right away – we are one quartermaster shy – and the brothers Sponge able as soon as they can understand a little English. As for the rest, all landmen. Now, Mr Richards, as soon as you have finished those descriptions, go along to Mr Marshall and tell him I should like to see him.'

'I think we shall watch almost exactly fifty men, sir,' said James, looking up from his calculation.

'Eight fo'c'sle men, eight foretop – Mr Marshall, come and sit down and let us have the benefit of your lights. We must work out this watch-bill and quarter the men before dinner: there's not a minute to be lost.'

'AND THIS, SIR, is where we live,' said Mowett, advancing his lantern into the midshipmen's berth. 'Pray mind the beam. I must beg your indulgence for the smell: it is probably young Babbington here.'

'Oh, it is not,' cried Babbington, springing up from his book. 'You are *cruel*, Mowett,' he whispered, with seething indignation.

'It is a pretty luxurious berth, sir, as these things go,' said Mowett. 'There is some light from the grating, as you see, and a little air gets down when the hatch-covers are off. I remember in the after-cockpit of the old *Namur* the candles used to go out for want of anything in that line, and we had nothing as odorous as young Babbington.'

'I can well imagine it,' said Stephen, sitting down and peering about him in the shadows. 'How many of you live here?'

'Only three now, sir: we are two midshipmen short. The youngsters sling their hammocks by the breadroom, and they used to mess with the gunner until he took so poorly. Now they come here and eat our food and destroy our books with their great greasy thumbs.'

'You are studying trigonometry, sir?' said Stephen, whose eyes, accustomed to the darkness, could now distinguish an inky triangle.

'Yes, sir, if you please,' said Babbington. 'And I believe I have nearly found out the answer.' (And should have, if that great ox had not come barging in, he added, privately.)

> *'In canvassed berth, profoundly deep in thought,*
> *His busy mind with sines and tangents fraught,*
> *A Mid reclines! In calculation lost,*
> *His efforts still by some intruder crost,'* said Mowett. 'Upon my word and honour, sir, I am rather proud of that.'

'And well you may be,' said Stephen, his eyes dwelling on the little ships drawn all round the triangle. 'And pray, what in sea-language is meant by a ship?'

'She must have three square-rigged masts, sir,' they told him kindly, 'and a bowsprit; and the masts must be in three – lower, top and topgallant – for we never call a polacre a ship.'

'Don't you, though?' said Stephen.

'Oh no, sir,' they cried earnestly, 'nor a cat. Nor a xebec; for although you may *think* xebecs have a bowsprit, it is really only a sorts of woolded boomkin.'

'I shall take particular notice of that,' said Stephen. 'I suppose you grow used to living here,' he observed, rising cautiously to his feet. 'At first it must seem a little confined.'

'Oh, sir,' said Mowett, *'think not meanly of this humble seat,*

Whence spring the guardians of the British fleet!

Revere the sacred spot, however low,

Which formed to martial acts an Hawke! An Howe!'

'Pay no attention to him, sir,' cried Babbington, anxiously. 'He means no disrespect, I do assure you, sir. It is only his disgusting way.'

'Tush, tush,' said Stephen. 'Let us see the rest of the – of the vessel, the conveyance.'

They went for'ard and passed another marine sentry; and groping his way along the dim space between two gratings, Stephen stumbled over something soft that clanked and called out angrily, 'Can't you see where you're a-coming to, you grass-combing bugger?'

'Now then, Wilson, you stow your gob,' cried Mowett. 'That's one of the men in the bilboes – lying in irons,' he explained. 'Never mind him, sir.'

'What is he lying in irons for?'

'For being rude, sir,' said Mowett, with a certain primness.

'Come, now, here's a fair-sized room, although it is so low. For the inferior officers, I take it?'

'No, sir. This is where the hands mess and sleep.'

'And the rest of them downstairs again, I presume.'

'There is no downstairs from here, sir. Below us is the hold, with only a bit of a platform as an orlop.'

'How many men are there?'

'Counting the marines, seventy-seven, sir.'

'Then they cannot all sleep here: it is physically impossible.'

'With respect, sir, they do. Each man has fourteen inches to sling his hammock, and they sling 'em fore and aft: now, the midship beam is twenty-five foot ten, which gives twenty-two places – you can see the numbers written up here.'

'A man cannot lie in fourteen inches.'

'No, sir, not very comfortably. But he can in eight and

twenty; for, do you see, in a two-watch ship at any one time about half the men are on deck for their watch, which leaves all their places free.'

'Even in twenty-eight inches, two foot four, a man must be touching his neighbour.'

'Why, sir, it is tolerably close, to be sure; but it gets them all in out of the weather. We have four ranges, as you see: from the bulkhead to this beam; and so to this one; then to the beam with the lantern hanging in front of it; and the last between that and the for'ard bulkhead, by the galley. The carpenter and the bosun have their cabins up there. The first range and part of the next is for the marines; then come the seamen, three and a half ranges of them. So with an average of twenty hammocks to a row, we get them all in, in spite of the mast.'

'But it must be a continuous carpet of bodies, when even half the men are lying there.'

'Why, so it is, sir.'

'Where are the windows?'

'We have nothing like what you would call windows,' said Mowett, shaking his head. 'There are the hatches and gratings overhead, but of course they are mostly covered up when it blows.'

'And the sick-quarters?'

'We have none of them either, sir, rightly speaking. But sick men have cots slung right up against the for'ard bulkhead on the starboard side, by the galley; and they are indulged in the use of the round-house.'

'What is that?'

'Well, it is not really a round-house, more like a little rowport: not like in a frigate of a ship of the line. But it serves.'

'What for?'

'I hardly know how to explain, sir,' said Mowett, blushing. 'A necessary-house.'

'A jakes? A privy?'

'Just so, sir.'

'But what do the other men do? Have they chamber-pots?'

'Oh no, sir, Heavens above! They go up the hatch there and along to the heads – little places on either side of the stem.'

'Out of doors?'

'Yes, sir.'

'But what happens in inclement weather?'

'They still go to the heads, sir.'

'And they sleep forty or fifty together down here, with no windows? Well, if ever a man with the gaol-fever, or the plague, or the cholera morbus, sets foot in this apartment, God help you all.'

'Amen, sir,' said Mowett, quite aghast at Stephen's immovable, convincing certainty.

'THAT IS AN ENGAGING young fellow,' said Stephen, walking into the cabin.

'Young Mowett? I am happy to hear you say so,' said Jack, who was looking worn and harried. 'Nothing pleasanter than good shipmates. May I offer you a whet? Our seaman's drink, that we call grog – are you acquainted with it? It goes down gratefully enough, at sea. Simpkin, bring us some grog. Damn that fellow – he is as slow as Beelzebub . . . Simpkin! Light along that grog. God rot the flaming son of a bitch. Ah, there you are. I needed that,' he said, putting down his glass. 'Such a tedious damned morning. Each watch has to have just the same proportions of skilled hands in the various stations, and so on. Endless discussion. And,' said he, hitching himself a little closer to Stephen's ear, 'I blundered into one of those unhappy gaffes . . . I picked up the list and read off Flaherty, Lynch, Sullivan, Michael Kelly, Joseph Kelly, Sheridan and Aloysius Burke – those chaps that took the bounty at Liverpool – and I said "More of these damned Irish Papists; at this rate half the starboard watch will be made up of them, and we shall not be able to get by for beads" – meaning it pleasantly, you know. But then I noticed a damned frigid kind of a chill and I said to myself, "Why, Jack, you damned fool, Dil-

lon is from Ireland, and he takes it as a national reflexion."
Whereas I had not meant anything so illiberal as a national
reflexion, of course; only that I hated Papists. So I tried to put
it right by a few well-turned flings against the Pope; but perhaps they were not as clever as I thought, for they did not
seem to answer.'

'And do you hate Papists, so?' asked Stephen.

'Oh, yes: and I hate paper-work. But the Papists are a very
wicked crew, too, you know, with confession and all that,' said
Jack. 'And they tried to blow up Parliament. Lord, how we
used to keep up the Fifth of November. One of my very best
friends – you would not believe how kind – was so upset
when her mother married one that she took to mathematics
and Hebrew directly – aleph, beth – though she was the prettiest girl for miles around – taught me navigation – splendid
headpiece, bless her. She told me quantities of things about
the Papists: I forget it all now, but they are certainly a very
wicked crew. There is no trusting them. Look at the rebellion
they have just had.'

'But my dear sir, the United Irishmen were primarily
Protestants – their leaders were Protestants. Wolfe Tone and
Napper Tandy were Protestants. The Emmets, the O'Con-
nors, Simon Butler, Hamilton Rowan, Lord Edward Fitzgerald were Protestants. And the whole idea of the club was to
unite Protestant and Catholic and Presbyterian Irishmen.
The Protestants it was who took the initiative.'

'Oh? Well, I don't know much about it, as you see – I
thought it was the Papists. I was on the West Indies station at
the time. But after a great deal of this damned paper-work I
am quite ready to hate Papists and Protestants, too, and
Anabaptists and Methodies. And Jews. No – I don't give a
damn. But what really vexes me is that I should have got
across Dillon's hawse like that; as I was saying, there is nothing pleasanter than good shipmates. He has a sad time of it,
doing a first lieutenant's duty *and* keeping a watch – new ship
– new ship's company – new captain – and I particularly

wished to ease him in. Without there is a good understanding between the officers a ship cannot be happy: and a happy ship is your only good fighting ship – you should hear Nelson on that point: and I do assure you it is profoundly true. He will be dining with us, and I should take it very kindly if you would, as it were . . . ah, Mr Dillon, come and join us in a glass of grog.'

Partly for professional reasons and partly because of an entirely natural absence, Stephen had long ago assumed the privilege of silence at table; and now from the shelter of this silence he watched James Dillon with particular attention. It was the same small head, held high; the same dark-red hair, of course, and green eyes; the same fine skin and bad teeth – more were decaying now; the same very well-bred air; and although he was slim and of no more than the average height, he seemed to take up as much room as the fourteen-stone Jack Aubrey. The main difference was that the look of being just about to laugh, or of having discovered a private joke, had quite vanished – wiped out: no trace of it. A typically grave, humourless Irish countenance now. His behaviour was reserved, but perfectly attentive and civil – not the least appearance of sullen resentment.

They ate an acceptable turbot – acceptable when the flour-and-water paste had been scraped off him – and then the steward brought in a ham. It was a ham that could only have come from a hog with a long-borne crippling disease, the sort of ham that is reserved for officers who buy their own provisions; and only a man versed in morbid anatomy could have carved it handsomely. While Jack was struggling with his duties as a host and adjuring the steward 'to clap on to its beakhead' and 'to look alive', James turned to Stephen with a fellow-guest's smile and said, 'Is it not possible that I have already had the pleasure of being in your company, sir? In Dublin, or perhaps at Naas?'

'I do not believe I have had the honour, sir. I am often mistaken for my cousin, of the same name. They tell me there is a striking resemblance, which makes me uneasy, I confess; for he is an ill-looking fellow, with a sly, Castle-informer look on his face. And the character of an informer is more despised in our country than in any other, is it not? Rightly so, in my opinion. Though, indeed, the creatures swarm there.' This was in a conversational tone, loud enough to be heard by his neighbour over Jack's 'Easy, now . . . wish it may not be infernally tough . . . get a purchase on its beam, Killick; never mind thumbs . . .'

'I am entirely of your way of thinking,' said James with complete understanding in his look. 'Will you take a glass of wine with me, sir?'

'With all my heart.'

They pledged one another in the sloe-juice, vinegar and sugar of lead that had been sold to Jack as wine and then turned, the one with professional interest and the other with professional stoicism, to Jack's dismembered ham.

The port was respectable, however, and after the cloth was drawn there was an easier, far more comfortable atmosphere in the cabin.

'Pray tell us about the action in the *Dart*,' said Jack, filling Dillon's glass. 'I have heard so many different accounts . . .'

'Yes, pray do,' said Stephen. 'I should look upon it as a most particular favour.'

'Oh, it was not much of an affair,' said James Dillon. 'Only with a contemptible set of privateers – a squabble among small-craft. I had temporary command of a hired cutter – a one-masted fore-and-aft vessel, sir, of no great size.' Stephen bowed. '– called the *Dart*. She had eight four-pounders, which was very well; but I only had thirteen men and a boy to fight them. However, orders came down to take a King's Messenger and ten thousand pounds in specie to Malta; and Captain Dockray asked me to give his wife and her sister a passage.'

'I remember him as first of the *Thunderer*,' said Jack. 'A dear, good, kind man.'

'So he was,' said James, shaking his head. 'Well, we had a steady tops'l libeccio, made our offing, tacked three or four leagues west of Egadi and stood a little west of south. It came on to blow after sundown, so having the ladies aboard and being short-handed in any case, I thought I should get under the lee of Pantelleria. It moderated in the night and the sea went down, and there I was at half-past four the next morning. I was shaving, as I remember very well, for I nicked my chin.'

'Ha,' said Stephen, with satisfaction.

'– when there was a cry of sail-ho and I hurried up on deck.'

'I'm sure you did,' said Jack, laughing.

'– and there were three French lateen-rigged privateers. It was just light enough to make them out, hull-up already, and presently I recognized the two nearest with my glass. They carried each a brass long six-pounder and four one-pounder swivels in their bows, and we had had a brush with them in the *Euryalus*, when they had the heels of us, of course.'

'How many men in them?'

'Oh, between forty and fifty apiece, sir: and they each had maybe a dozen musketoons or patareroes on their sides. And I made no doubt the third was just such another. They had been haunting the Sicily Channel for some time, lying off Lampione and Lampedusa to refresh. Now they were under my lee, lying thus –' he drew in wine on the table – 'with the wind blowing from the decanter. They could outsail me, close-hauled, and clearly their best plan was to engage me on either side and board.'

'Exactly,' said Jack.

'So taking everything into consideration – my passengers, the King's Messenger, the specie, and the Barbary coast ahead of me if I were to bear up – I thought the right thing to do was to attack them separately while I had the weather-gage and before the two nearest could join forces: the third was still three or four miles away, beating up under all sail. Eight of the cutter's crew were prime seamen, and Captain

Dockray had sent his cox'n along with the ladies, a fine strong fellow named William Brown. We soon cleared for action and treble-shotted the guns. And I must say the ladies behaved with great spirit: rather more than I could have wished. I represented to them that their place was below – in the hold. But Mrs Dockray was not going to be told her duty by any young puppy without so much as an epaulette to his name and did I think a post-captain's wife with nine years' seniority was going to ruin her sprigged muslin in the bilges of my cockleshell? She should tell my aunt – my cousin Ellis – the First Lord of the Admiralty – bring me to a court-martial for cowardice, for temerity, for not knowing my business. She understood discipline and subordination as well as the next woman, or better; and "Come, my dear," says she to Miss Jones, "you ladle out the powder and fill the cartridges, and I will carry them up in my apron." By this time the position was so –' he redrew the plan. 'The nearest privateer two cables' lengths away and to the lee of the other: both of them had been firing for ten minutes with their bow-chasers.'

'How long is a cable?' asked Stephen.

'About two hundred yards, sir,' said James. 'So I put my helm down – she was wonderfully quick in stays – and steered to ram the Frenchman amidships. With the wind on her quarter, the *Dart* covered the distance in little more than a minute, which was as well, since they were peppering us hard. I steered myself until we were within pistol-shot and then ran for'ard to lead the boarders, leaving the tiller to the boy. Unhappily, he misunderstood me and let the privateer shoot too far ahead, and we took her abaft her mizzen, our bowsprit carrying away her larboard mizzen shrouds and a good deal of her poop-rail and stern-works. So instead of boarding we passed under her stern: her mizzen went by the board with the shock, and we flew to the guns and poured in a raking broadside. There were just enough of us to fight four guns, with the King's Messenger and me working one and Brown helping us run it out when he had fired his own. I

luffed up to range along under her lee and get across her
bows, so as to prevent her from manoeuvring; but with that
great spread of canvas they have, you know, the *Dart* was
becalmed for a while, and we exchanged as hot a fire as
quickly as we could keep it up. But at last we forged ahead,
found our wind again and tacked as quickly as we could, right
athwart the Frenchman's stem – quicker, indeed, for we
could only spare two hands to the sheet and our boom came
crack against her foreyard, carrying it away – the falling sail
dowsed her bow-chaser and the swivels. And as we came
round there was our starboard broadside ready, and we fired it
so close that the wads set light to her foresail and the wreckage of the mizzen lying there all over her deck. Then they
called for quarter and struck.'

'Well done, well done!' cried Jack.

'It was high time,' said James, 'for the other privateer had
been coming up fast. By something like a miracle our
bowsprit and boom were still standing, so I told the captain of
the privateer that I should certainly sink him if he attempted
to make sail and bore up directly for his consort. I could not
spare a single hand to take possession, nor the time.'

'Of course not.'

'So here we were approaching on opposite tacks, and they
were firing as the whim took them – everything they had.
When we were fifty yards away I paid off four points to bring
the starboard guns to bear, gave her the broadside, then
luffed up directly and gave her the other, from perhaps
twenty yards. The second was very remarkable, sir. I did not
think four-pounders could have done such execution. We
fired on the down-roll, a trifle later than I should have
thought right, and all four shot struck her on the waterline at
the height of her rise – I saw them go home, all on the same
strake. A moment later her people left their guns – they were
running about and hallooing. Unhappily, Brown had stumbled as our gun recoiled and the carriage had mangled his
foot most cruelly. I bade him go below, but he would have

none of it – would sit there and use a musket – and then he gave a cheer and said the Frenchman was sinking. And so he was: first they were awash, and then they went down, right down, with their sails set.'

'My God!' cried Jack.

'So I stood straight on for the third, all hands knotting and splicing, for our rigging was cut to pieces. But the mast and boom were so wounded – a six-pound ball clean through the mast, and many deep scores – that I dared not carry a press of sail. So I am afraid she ran clean away from us, and there was nothing for it but to beat back to the first privateer. Luckily, they had been busy with their fire all this time, or they might have slipped off. We took six aboard to work our pumps, tossed their dead overboard, battened the rest down, took her in tow, set course for Malta and arrived two days later, which surprised me, for our sails were a collection of holes held together with threads, and our hull not much better.'

'Did you pick up the men from the one that sank?' asked Stephen.

'No, sir,' said James.

'Not corsairs,' said Jack. 'Not with thirteen men and a boy aboard. What were your losses, though?'

'Apart from Brown's foot and a few scratches we had no one wounded, sir, nor a single man killed. It was an astonishing thing: but then we were pretty thin on the ground.'

'And theirs?'

'Thirteen dead, sir. Twenty-nine prisoners.'

'And the privateer you sank?'

'Fifty-six, sir.'

'And the one that got away?'

'Well, forty-eight, or so they told us, sir. But she hardly counts, since we only had a few random shots from her before she grew shy.'

'Well, sir,' said Jack, 'I congratulate you with all my heart. It was a noble piece of work.'

'So do I,' said Stephen. 'So do I. A glass of wine with you, Mr Dillon,' he said, bowing and raising his glass.

'Come,' cried Jack, with a sudden inspiration. 'Let us drink to the renewed success of Irish arms, and confusion to the Pope.'

'The first part ten times over,' said Stephen, laughing. 'But never a drop will I drink to the second, Voltairian though I may be. The poor gentleman has Boney on his hands, and that is confusion enough, in all conscience. Besides, he is a very learned Benedictine.'

'Then confusion to Boney.'

'Confusion to Boney,' they said, and drank their glasses dry.

'You will forgive me, sir, I hope,' said Dillon. 'I relieve the deck in half an hour, and I should like to check the quarter-bill first. I must thank you for a most enjoyable dinner.'

'Lord, what a pretty action that was,' said Jack, when the door was closed. 'A hundred and forty-six to fourteen; or fifteen if you count Mrs Dockray. It is just the kind of thing Nelson might have done – prompt – straight at 'em.'

'You know Lord Nelson, sir?'

'I had the honour of serving under him at the Nile,' said Jack, 'and of dining in his company twice.' His face broke into a smile at the recollection.

'May I beg you to tell me what kind of a man he is?'

'Oh, you would take to him directly, I am sure. He is very slight – frail – I could pick him up (I mean no disrespect) with one hand. But you know he is a very great man directly. There is something in philosophy called an electrical particle, is there not? A charged atom, if you follow me. He spoke to me on each occasion. The first time it was to say, "May I trouble you for the salt, sir?" – I have always said it as close as I can to his way ever since – you may have noticed it. But the second time I was trying to make my neighbour, a soldier, understand our naval tactics – weather-gage, breaking the line, and so on – and in a pause he leant over with such a smile and said, "Never mind manoeuvres, always go at them."

I shall never forget it: never mind manoeuvres – always go at 'em. And at that same dinner he was telling us all how someone had offered him a boat-cloak on a cold night and he had said no, he was quite warm – his zeal for his King and country kept him warm. It sounds absurd, as I tell it, does it not? And was it another man, any other man, you would cry out "oh, what pitiful stuff" and dismiss it as mere enthusiasm; but with him you feel your bosom glow, and – now what in the devil's name is it, Mr Richards? Come in or out, there's a good fellow. Don't stand in the door like a God-damned Lenten cock.'

'Sir,' said the poor clerk, 'you said I might bring you the remaining papers before tea, and your tea is just coming up.'

'Well, well: so I did,' said Jack. 'God, what an infernal heap. Leave them here, Mr Richards. I will see to them before we reach Cagliari.'

'The top ones are those which Captain Allen left to be written fair – they only need to be signed, sir,' said the clerk, backing out.

Jack glanced at the top of the pile, paused, then cried, 'There! There you are. Just so. There's the service for you from clew to earing – the Royal Navy, stock and fluke. You get into a fine flow of patriotic fervour – you are ready to plunge into the thick of the battle – and you are asked to sign this sort of thing.' He passed Stephen the carefully-written sheet.

> His Majesty's Sloop *Sophie*
>   at sea
>
> My Lord,
>   I am to beg you will be pleased to order a Court Martial to be held on Isaac Wilson (seaman) belonging to the Sloop I have the honour to Command for having committed the unnatural Crime of Sodomy on a Goat, in the Goathouse, on the evening of March 16th.
>   I have the Honour to remain, my Lord,

Your Lordship's most obedient very humble servant

The Rt. Hon. Lord Keith, K.B., etc., etc.
Admiral of the Blue.

'It is odd how the law always harps upon the unnaturalness of sodomy,' observed Stephen. 'Though I know at least two judges who are pæderasts; and of course barristers . . . What will happen to him?'

'Oh, he'll be hanged. Run up at the yard-arm, and boats attending from every ship in the fleet.'

'That seems a little extreme.'

'Of course it is. Oh, what an infernal bore – witnesses going over to the flagship by the dozen, days lost . . . The *Sophie* a laughing-stock. Why will they report these things? The goat must be slaughtered – that's but fair – and it shall be served out to the mess that informed on him.'

'Could you not set them both ashore – on separate shores, if you have strong feelings on the moral issue – and sail quietly away?'

'Well,' said Jack, whose anger had died down. 'Perhaps there is something in what you propose. A dish of tea? You take milk, sir?'

'Goat's milk, sir?'

'Why, I suppose it is.'

'Perhaps without milk, then, if you please. You told me, I believe, that the gunner was ailing. Would this be a convenient time for seeing what I can do for him? Pray, which is the gun-room?'

'You would expect to find him there, would you not? But in fact his cabin is elsewhere nowadays. Killick will show you. The gun-room, in a sloop, is where the officers mess.'

IN THE GUN-ROOM itself the master stretched and said to the purser, 'Plenty of elbow-room now, Mr Ricketts.'

'Very true, Mr Marshall,' said the purser. 'We see great

changes these days. And how they will work out I do not know.'

'Oh, I think they may answer well enough,' said Mr Marshall, slowly picking the crumbs off his waistcoat.

'All these capers,' went on the purser, in a low, dubious voice. 'The mainyard. The guns. The drafts he pretended to know nothing about. All these new hands there is not room for. The people at watch and watch. Charlie tells me there is a great deal of murmuring.' He jerked his head towards the men's quarters.

'I dare say there is. I dare say there is. All the old ways changed and all the old messes broken up. And I dare say we may be a little flighty, too, so young and fine with our brand-new epaulette. But if the steady old standing officers back him up, why, then I think it may answer well enough. The carpenter likes him. So does Watt, for he's a good seaman, and that's certain. And Mr Dillon seems to know his profession, too.'

'Maybe. Maybe,' said the purser, who knew the master's enthusiasms of old.

'And then again,' went on Mr Marshall, 'things may be a little more lively under the new proprietor. The men will like that, when they grow used to it; and so will the officers, I am sure. All that is wanted is for the standing officers to back him up, and it will be plain sailing.'

'What?' said the purser, cupping his ear, for Mr Dillon was having the guns moved, and amid the general rumbling thunder that accompanied this operation an occasional louder bang obliterated speech. Incidentally, it was this all-pervasive thunder that made their conversation possible, for in general there could be no such thing as private talk in a vessel twenty-six yards long, inhabited by ninety-one men, whose gun-room had even smaller apartments opening off it, screened by very thin wood and, indeed, sometimes by no more than canvas.

'Plain sailing. I say, if the officers back him up, it will all be plain sailing.'

'Maybe. But if they do not,' went on Mr Ricketts, 'if they do *not*, and if he persists in capers of this kind – which I believe it is his nature so to do – why then, I dare say he will exchange out of the old *Sophie* as quick as Mr Harvey did. For a brig is not a frigate, far less a ship of the line: you are right on top of your people, and they can give you hell or cause you to be broke as easy as kiss my hand.'

'You don't have to tell *me* a brig is not a frigate, nor yet a ship of the line, Mr Ricketts,' said the master.

'Maybe I don't have to tell you a brig is not a frigate, nor yet a ship of the line, Mr Marshall,' said the purser warmly. 'But when you have been at sea as long as I have, Mr Marshall, you will know there is a great deal more than mere seamanship required of a captain. Any damned tarpaulin can manage a ship in a storm,' he went on in a slighting voice, 'and any housewife in breeches can keep the decks clean and the falls just so; but it needs a headpiece' – tapping his own – 'and true bottom and steadiness, as well as conduct, to be the captain of a man-o'-war: and these are qualities not to be found in every Johnny-come-lately – nor in every Jack-lie-by-the-wall, neither,' he added, more or less to himself. 'I don't know, I'm sure.'

4

THE DRUM ROLLED and thundered at the *Sophie's* hatchway. Feet came racing up from below, a desperate rushing sound that made even the tense drum-beat seem more urgent. But apart from the landmen's in the new draft, the men's faces were calm; for this was beating to quarters, an afternoon ritual that many of the crew had performed some two or three thousand times, each running to a particular place by one allotted gun or to a given set of ropes that he knew by heart.

No one could have called this a creditable performance, however. Much had been changed in the *Sophie*'s comfortable old routine; the manning of the guns was different; a score of worried, sheep-like landmen had to be pushed and pulled into something like the right place; and since most of the newcomers could not yet be allowed to do anything more than heave under guidance, the sloop's waist was so crowded that men trampled upon one another's toes.

Ten minutes passed while the *Sophie*'s people seethed about her upper deck and her fighting-tops: Jack stood watching placidly abaft the wheel while Dillon barked orders and the warrant-officers and midshipmen darted furiously about, aware of their captain's gaze and conscious that their anxiety was not improving anything at all. Jack had expected something of a shambles, though not anything quite so unholy as this; but his native good-humour and the delight of feeling even the inept stirring of this machine under his control overcame all other, more righteous, emotions.

'Why do they do this?' asked Stephen, at his elbow. 'Why do they run about so earnestly?'

'The idea is that every man shall know exactly where to go in action – in an emergency,' said Jack. 'It would never do if they had to stand pondering. The gun-teams are there at their stations already, you see; and so are Sergeant Quinn's marines, here. The foc's'le men are all there, as far as I can make out; and I dare say the waisters will be in order presently. A captain to each gun, do you see; and a sponger and boarder next to him – the man with the belt and cutlass; they join the boarding-party; and a sail-trimmer, who leaves the gun if we have to brace the yards round, for example, in action; and a fireman, the one with the bucket – his task is to dash out any fire that may start. Now there is Pullings reporting his division ready to Dillon. We shall not be long now.'

There were plenty of people on the little quarter-deck – the master at the con, the quartermaster at the wheel, the marine sergeant and his small-arms party, the signal midshipman, part of the afterguard, the gun-crews, James Dillon, the clerk, and still others – but Jack and Stephen paced up and down as though they were alone, Jack enveloped in the Olympian majesty of a captain and Stephen caught up within his aura. It was natural enough to Jack, who had known this state of affairs since he was a child, but it was the first time that Stephen had met with it, and it gave him a not altogether disagreeable sensation of waking death: either the absorbed, attentive men on the other side of the glass wall were dead, mere phantasmata, or he was – though in that case it was a strange little death, for although he was used to this sense of isolation, of being a colourless shade in a silent private underworld, he now had a companion, an audible companion.

'. . . your station, for example, would be below, in what we call the cockpit – not that it is a real cockpit, any more than that fo'c'sle is a real fo'c'sle, in the sense of being raised: but we call it the cockpit – with the midshipmen's sea-chests as your operating table and your instruments all ready.'

'Is that where I should live?'

'No, no. We shall fix you up with something better than that. Even when you come under the Articles of War,' said Jack with a smile, 'you will find that we still honour learning; at least to the extent of ten square feet of privacy, and as much fresh air on the quarter-deck as you may choose to breathe in.'

Stephen nodded. 'Tell me,' he said, in a low voice, some moments later. 'Were I under naval discipline, could that fellow have me whipped?' He nodded towards Mr Marshall.

'The master?' cried Jack, with inexpressible amazement.

'Yes,' said Stephen, looking attentively at him, with his head slightly inclined to the left.

'But he is the *master* . . .' said Jack. If Stephen had called the *Sophie*'s stem her stern, or her truck her keel, he would have understood the situation directly; but that Stephen should confuse the chain of command, the relative status of a captain and a master, of a commissioned officer and a war-

rant officer, so subverted the natural order, so undermined
the sempiternal universe, that for a moment his mind could
hardly encompass it. Yet Jack, though no great scholar, no
judge of a hexameter, was tolerably quick, and after gasping
no more than twice he said, 'My dear sir, I believe you have
been led astray by the words *master* and *master and commander* – illogical terms, I must confess. The first is subordinate
to the second. You must allow me to explain our naval ranks
some time. But in any case you will never be flogged – no, no;
you shall not be flogged,' he added, gazing with pure affection, and with something like awe, at so magnificent a
prodigy, at an ignorance so very far beyond anything that even
his wide-ranging mind had yet conceived.

James Dillon broke through the glass wall. 'Hands at quarters, sir, if you please,' he said, raising his three-corner hat.

'Very well, Mr Dillon,' said Jack. 'We will exercise the great
guns.'

A four-pounder may not throw a very great weight of metal,
and it may not be able to pierce two feet of oak half a mile
away, as a thirty-two-pounder can; but it does throw a solid
three-inch cast-iron ball at a thousand feet a second, which is
an ugly thing to receive; and the gun itself is a formidable
machine. Its barrel is six feet long; it weighs twelve hundredweight; it stands on a ponderous oak carriage; and when it is
fired it leaps back as though it were violently alive.

The *Sophie* possessed fourteen of these, seven a side; and
the two aftermost guns on the quarter-deck were gleaming
brass. Each gun had a crew of four and a man or boy to bring
up powder from the magazine. Each group of guns was in
charge of a midshipman or a master's mate – Pullings had the
six forward guns, Ricketts the four in the waist and Babbington the four farthest aft.

'Mr Babbington, where is this gun's powder horn?' asked
Jack coldly.

'I don't know, sir,' stammered Babbington, very red. 'It
seems to have gone astray.'

'Quarter-gunner,' said Jack, 'go to Mr Day – no, to his mate, for he is sick – and get another.' His inspection showed no other obvious shortcomings: but when he had had both broadsides run in and out half a dozen times – that is to say, when the men had been through all the motions short of actually firing the guns – his face grew long and grave. They were quite extraordinarily slow. They had obviously been trained to fire nothing but whole broadsides at once – very little independent firing. They seemed quite happy with easing their guns gently up to the port at the rate of the slowest of them all: and the whole exercise had an artificial, wooden air. It was true that ordinary convoy-duty in a sloop did not give the men any very passionate conviction of the guns' vital reality, but even so . . . 'How I wish I could afford a few barrels of powder,' he thought, with a clear image of the gunner's accounts in his mind: forty-nine half-barrels in all, seven under the *Sophie*'s full allowance; forty-one of them red, large grain, seven of them white, large grain – restored powder of doubtful strength – and one barrel of fine grain for priming. The barrels held forty-five pounds, so the *Sophie* would nearly empty one with each double broadside. 'But even so,' he went on, 'I think we can have a couple of rounds: God knows how long these charges have been lying in the guns. Besides,' he added in a voice within his inner voice – a voice from a far deeper level, 'think of the lovely smell.'

'Very well,' he said aloud. 'Mr Mowett, be so good as to go into my cabin. Sit down by the table-watch and take exact note of the time that elapses between the first and second discharge of each gun. Mr Pullings, we'll start with your division. Number one. Silence, fore and aft.'

Dead silence fell over the *Sophie*. The wind sang evenly in her taut weather-rigging, steady at two points abaft the beam. Number one's crew licked their lips nervously. Their gun was in its ordinary position of rest, bowsed up tight against its port and lashed there – put away, as it were.

'Cast loose your gun.'

They cast loose the tackles that held the gun hard against the side and cut the spun-yarn frapping that clenched the breeching to hold it firmer still. With a gentle squeal of trucks the gun showed that it was free: a man held each side-tackle, or the *Sophie*'s heel (which made the rear-tackle unnecessary) would have brought the gun inboard before the next word of command.

'Level your gun.'

The sponger pushed his handspike under the thick breech of the gun and with a quick heave levered it up, while number one's captain thrust the wooden wedge more than half-way under, bringing the barrel to the horizontal point-blank position.

'Out tompion.'

They let the gun run in fast: the breeching checked its inward course when the muzzle was a foot or so inboard: the sail-trimmer whipped out the carved and painted tompion that plugged it.

'Run out your gun.'

Clapping on to the side-tackles they heaved her up hand over hand, running the carriage hard against the side and coiling the falls, coiling them down in wonderfully neat little fakes.

'Prime.'

The captain took his priming-iron, thrust it down the touch-hole and pierced the flannel cartridge lying within the gun, poured fine powder from his horn into the open vent and on to the pan, bruising it industriously with the nozzle. The sponger put the flat of his hand over the powder to prevent its blowing away, and the fireman slung the horn behind his back.

'Point your gun.' And to this order Jack added, 'As she lies,' since he wished to add no complications of traversing or elevating for range at this stage. Two of the gun's crew were now holding the side tackles: the sponger knelt on one side with his head away from the gun, blowing gently on the smouldering slow-match he had taken from its little tub (for the *Sophie* did not run to flintlocks): the powder-boy stood with the next cartridge in its leather box over on the starboard side directly behind the gun: the captain, holding his vent-bit and sheltering the priming, bent over the gun, staring along its barrel.

'Fire.'

The slow-match whipped across. The captain stubbed it hard down on to the priming. For an infinitesimal spark of time there was a hissing, a flash, and then the gun went off with the round, satisfying bang of a pound and more of hard-rammed powder exploding in a confined space. A stab of crimson flame in the smoke, flying morsels of wad, the gun shooting eight feet backwards under the arched body of its captain and between the members of its crew, the deep twang of the breeching as it brought up the recoil – all these were virtually inseparable in time; and before they were over the next order came.

'Stop your vent,' cried Jack, watching for the flight of the ball as the white smoke raced streaming down to leeward. The captain stabbed his vent-piece into the touch-hole; and the ball sent up a fleeting plume in the choppy sea four hundred yards to windward, then another and another, ducks and drakes for fifty yards before it sank. The crew clapped on to the rear-tackle to hold the gun firmly inboard against the roll.

'Sponge your gun.'

The sponger darted his sheepskin swab into the fireman's bucket, and pushing his face into the narrow space between the muzzle and the side he shot the handle out of the port and thrust the swab down the bore of the gun: he twirled it conscientiously and brought it out, blackened, with a little smoking rag on it.

'Load with cartridge.'

The powder-boy had the tight cloth bag there ready: the sponger entered it and rammed it hard down. The captain, with his priming-iron in the vent to feel for its arrival, cried, 'Home!'

'Shot your gun.'

The ball was there to hand in its garland, and the wad in its cheese; but an unlucky slip sent the ball trundling across the deck towards the fore-hatch, with the anxious captain, sponger and powder-boy following its erratic course. Eventually it joined the cartridge, with the wad rammed down over it, and Jack cried, 'Run out your gun. – Prime. – Point your gun. – Fire. Mr Mowett,' he called, through the cabin skylight, 'what was the interval?'

'Three minutes and three-quarters, sir.'

'Oh dear, oh dear,' said Jack, almost to himself. There were no words in the vocabulary at his command to express his distress. Pullings' division looked apprehensive and ashamed: number three gun-crew had stripped to the waist and had tied their handkerchiefs round their heads against the flash and the thunder: they were spitting on their hands, and Mr Pullings himself was fussing anxiously about with the crows, handspikes and swabs.

'Silence. Cast loose your gun. Level your gun. Out tompion. Run out your gun . . .'

This time it was rather better – just over three minutes. But then they had not dropped their shot and Mr Pullings had helped run up the gun and haul on the rear-tackle, gazing absently into the sky as he did so, to prove that he was not in fact there at all.

As the firing came aft gun by gun, so Jack's melancholy increased. One and three had not been unlucky bands of boobies: this was the *Sophie*'s true average rate of fire. Archaic. Antediluvian. And if there had been any question of aiming, of traversing the guns, heaving them round with crows and handspikes, it would have been even slower. Number five would not fire, damp having got at the powder, and the gun had to be wormed and drawn. That could happen in any ship: but it was a pity that it also occurred twice in the starboard broadside.

The *Sophie* had come up into the wind to fire her starboard guns, out of a certain delicacy about shooting at random into her convoy, and she was lying there, pitching easily with almost no way on her, while the last damp charge was being extracted, when Stephen, feeling that in this lull he might without impropriety address the captain, said to Jack, 'Pray tell me why those ships are so very close together. Are they conversing – rendering one another mutual assistance?' He pointed over the neat wall of hammocks in the quarter-netting: Jack followed his finger and gazed for an unbelieving second at the rearmost vessel in his convoy, the *Dorthe Engelbrechtsdatter*, the Norwegian cat.

'Hands to the braces,' he shouted. 'Port your helm. Flat in for'ard – jump to it. Brail up the mainsail.'

Slowly, then faster and faster with all the wind in her sharp-braced headsails, the *Sophie* paid off. Now the wind was on her port beam: a few moments later she was right before it, and in still another moment she steadied on her course, with the wind three points on her starboard quarter. There had been a good deal of trampling to and fro, with Mr Watt and his mates roaring and piping like fury, but the Sophies were better hands with a sail than a gun, and quite soon Jack could cry, 'Square mains'l. Topmast stuns'ls. Mr Watt, the top-chains and puddening – but I need not tell you what to do, I see.'

'Aye aye, sir,' said the bosun, clanking away aloft, already loaded with the chains that were to prevent the yards falling in action.

'Mowett, run up with a glass and tell me what you see. Mr Dillon, you'll not forget that look-out? We'll have the hide off him tomorrow, if he lives to see it. Mr Lamb, you have your shot-plugs ready?'

'Ready, aye ready, sir,' said the carpenter, smiling, for this was not a serious question.

'Deck!' hailed Mowett, high above the taut, straining canvas. 'Deck! She's an Algerine – a quarter-galley. They've boarded the cat. They have not carried her yet. I think the Norwegians are holding out in their close-quarters.'

'Anything to windward?' called Jack.

In the pause that followed the peevish crackling of pistols could be heard from the Norwegian, struggling faintly up through the streaming of the wind.

'Yes, sir. A sail. A lateen. Hull down in the wind's eye. I can't make her out for sure. Standing east . . . standing due east, I think.'

Jack nodded, looking up and down his two broadsides. He was a big man at any time, but now he seemed to be at least twice his usual size; his eyes were shining in an extraordinary manner, as blue as the sea, and a continuous smile showed a gleam across the lively scarlet of his face. Something of the same change had come over the *Sophie*; with her big new square mainsail and her topsails immensely broadened by the studdingsails at either side of them she, like her master and commander, seemed to have doubled in size as she tore heavily through the sea. 'Well, Mr Dillon,' he cried, 'this is a bit of luck, is it not?'

Stephen, looking at them curiously, saw that the same extraordinary animation had seized upon James Dillon – indeed, the whole crew was filled with a strange ebullience. Close by him the marines were checking the flints of their muskets, and one of them was polishing the buckle of his cross-belt, breathing on it and laughing happily between the carefully-directed breaths.

'Yes, sir,' said James Dillon. 'It could not have fallen more happily.'

'Signal the convoy to haul two points to larboard and to reduce sail. Mr Richards, have you noted the time? You must carefully note the time of everything. But, Dillon, what can the fellow be thinking of? Did he suppose we were engaged? Blind? However, this is not time to . . . We will board, of course, if only the Norwegians can hold out long enough. I hate firing into a galley, in any event. I believe you may have all our pistols and cutlasses served out. Now, Mr Marshall,' he said, turning to the master, who was at his action-station by the wheel, and who was now responsible for sailing the *Sophie*, 'I want you to lay us alongside that damned Moor. You may set the lower-stuns'ls if she will bear them.' At this moment the gunner crept up the ladder. 'Well, Mr Day,' said Jack, 'I am happy to see you on deck. Are you a little better?'

'Much better, sir, I thank you,' said Mr Day, 'thanks to the gentleman' – nodding towards Stephen. 'It worked,' he said, directing his voice towards the taffrail. 'I just thought I'd report as I was in my place, sir.'

'Glad of it – I'm very glad of it. This is a bit of luck, master-gunner, I believe?' said Jack.

'Why, so it is, sir – it worked, Doctor: it worked, sir, like a maiden's dream. – So it is,' said the gunner, looking complacently over the mile or so of sea at the *Dorthe Engelbrechts-datter* and the corsair, at the *Sophie*, with all her guns warm, freshly-loaded, run out, perfectly ready, her crew on tip-toe and her decks cleared for action.

'Here we were exercising,' went on Jack, almost to himself. 'And that impudent dog rowed up-wind on the far side and made a snatch at the cat – what can he be thinking of? – and would be running off with her now if our good doctor had not brought us to our senses.'

'Never was such a doctor, is my belief,' said the gunner. 'Now I fancy I had best get down into my magazine, sir. We've not all that powder filled; and I dare say you'll be calling for a tidy parcel, ha, ha, ha!'

'My dear sir,' said Jack to Stephen, measuring the *Sophie*'s increasing speed and the distance that separated her from the embattled cat – in this state of triply intensified vitality he could perfectly well calculate, talk to Stephen and revolve a thousand shifting variables all at once – 'my dear sir, do you choose to go below or should you rather stay on deck? Perhaps it would divert you to go to into the maintop with a musket, along with the sharpshooters, and have a bang at the villains?'

'No, no, no,' said Stephen. 'I deprecate violence. My part is to heal rather than to kill; or at least to kill with kindly intent. Pray let me take my place, my station, in the cockpit.'

'I hoped you would say that,' said Jack, shaking him by the hand. 'I had not liked to suggest it to my guest, however. It will comfort the men amazingly – all of us, indeed. Mr Ricketts, show Dr Maturin the cockpit. And give the loblolly boy a hand with the chests.'

A sloop with the depth of a mere ten feet ten inches cannot rival a ship of the line for dank airless obscurity below; but the *Sophie* did astonishingly well, and Stephen was obliged to call for another lantern to check and lay out his instruments and the meagre store of bandages, lint, tourniquets and pledgets. He was sitting there with Northcote's *Marine Practice* held close to the light, carefully reading '. . . having divided the skin, order the same assistant to draw it up as much as possible; then cut through the flesh and bones circularly,' when Jack came down. He had put on Hessian boots and his sword, and he was carrying a pair of pistols.

'May I use the room next door?' asked Stephen, adding in Latin, so that he might not be understood by the loblolly boy, 'it might discourage the patients, were they to see me consulting my printed authorities.'

'Certainly, certainly,' cried Jack, riding straight over the Latin. 'Anything you like. I will leave these with you. We shall board, if ever we can come up with them; and then, you know, they may try to board us – there's no telling – these damned Algerines are usually crammed with men. Cut-throat dogs, every one of 'em,' he added, laughing heartily and vanishing into the gloom.

Jack had only been below a very short while, but by the time he returned to the quarter-deck the situation had entirely changed. The Algerines were in command of the cat: she was falling off before the northerly wind; they were setting her crossjack, and it was clear that they hoped to get away with her. The galley lay in its own length away from her, on her starboard quarter: it lay there motionless on its oars,

fourteen great sweeps a side, headed directly towards the
Sophie, with its huge lateen sails brailed up loosely to the
yards – a long, low, slim vessel, longer than the *Sophie* but
much slighter and narrower: obviously very fast and obviously
in enterprising hands. It had a singularly lethal, reptilian air.
Its intention was clearly either to engage the *Sophie* or at
least to delay her until the prize-crew should have run the cat
a mile or so down the wind towards the safety of the coming
night.

The distance was now a little over a quarter of a mile, and
with a smooth continuous flow the relative positions were
perpetually changing: the cat's speed was increasing, and in
four or five minutes she was a cable's length to the leeward of
the galley, which still lay there on its oars.

A fleeting cloud of smoke appeared in the galley's bows, a
ball hummed overhead, at about the level of the topmast
crosstrees, followed in half a heart's beat by the deep boom of
the gun that had fired it. 'Note down the time, Mr Richards,'
said Jack to the pale clerk – the nature of his pallor had
changed and his eyes were starting from his head. Jack hurried forward, just in time to see the flash of the galley's second gun. With an enormous smithy-noise the ball struck the
fluke of the *Sophie*'s best bower anchor, bent it half over and
glanced off into the sea far behind.

'An eighteen-pounder,' observed Jack to the bosun, standing there at his post on the fo'c'sle. 'Maybe even a twenty-
four. Oh, for my long twelves,' he added inwardly. The galley
had no broadside, naturally, but mounted her guns fore and
aft: in his glass Jack could see that the forward battery consisted of two heavy guns, a smaller one and some swivels;
and, of course, the *Sophie* would be exposed to their raking
fire throughout her approach. The swivels were firing now, a
high sharp cracking noise.

Jack returned to the quarter-deck. 'Silence fore and aft,' he
cried through the low, excited murmur. 'Silence. Cast loose
your guns. Level your guns. Out tompions. Run out your guns.

Mr Dillon, they are to be trained as far for'ard as possible. Mr Babbington, tell the gunner the next round will be chain.' An eighteen-pound ball hit the *Sophie*'s side between the larboard number one and three guns, sending in a shower of sharp-edged splintered wood, some pieces two feet long, and heavy: it continued its course along the crowded deck, knocked down a marine and struck against the mainmast, its force almost spent. A dismal 'Oh oh oh' showed that some of the splinters had done their work, and a moment later two seamen hurried by, carrying their mate below, leaving a trail of blood as they went.

'Are those guns trained round?' cried Jack.

'All hard round sir,' came the reply after a gasping pause.

'Starboard broadside first. Fire as they bear. Fire high. Fire for the masts. Right, Mr Marshall, over she goes.'

The *Sophie* yawed forty-five degrees off her course, presenting quarter of her starboard side to the galley, which instantly sent another eighteen-pound ball into it amidships, just above the water-line, its deep resonant impact surprising Stephen Maturin as he put a ligature round William Musgrave's spouting femoral artery, almost making him miss the loop. But now the *Sophie*'s guns were bearing, and the starboard broadside went off on two successive rolls: the sea beyond the galley spat up in white plumes and the *Sophie*'s deck swirled with smoke, acrid, piercing gunpowder smoke. As the seventh gun fired Jack cried, 'Over again,' and the *Sophie*'s head came round for the larboard broadside. The eddying cloud cleared under her lee: Jack saw the galley fire its whole forward battery and leap into motion under the power of its oars to avoid the *Sophie*'s fire. The galley fired high, on the upward roll, and one of its balls severed the maintopmast stay and struck a great lump of wood from the cap. The lump, rebounding from the top, fell on to the gunner's head just as he put it up through the main hatchway.

'Lively with those starboard guns,' cried Jack. 'Helm amidships.' He meant to bring the sloop back on to the port tack, for if he could manage to get in another starboard broadside he would catch the galley as it was moving across from left to right. A muffled roar from number four gun and a terrible shrieking: in his haste the sponger had not fully cleared the gun and now the fresh charge had gone off in his face as he rammed it down. They dragged him clear, re-sponged, re-loaded the gun and ran it up. But the whole manoeuvre had been too slow: the whole starboard battery had been too slow: the galley was round again – it could spin like a top, with all those oars backing water – and it was speeding away to the south-west with the wind on its starboard quarter and its great lateen sails spread on either side – set in hares' ears, as they say. The cat was now standing south-east; it was half a mile away already, and their courses were diverging fast. The yawing had taken a surprising amount of time – had lost a surprising amount of distance.

'Port half a point,' said Jack, standing on the lee-rail and staring very hard at the galley, which was almost directly ahead of the *Sophie*, a little over a hundred yards away, and gaining. 'Topgallant stuns'ls. Mr Dillon, get a gun into the bows, if you please. We still have the twelve-pounder's ring-bolts.'

As far as he could see they had done the galley no harm: firing low would have meant firing straight into benches packed tight with Christian rowers chained to the oars; firing high . . . His head jerked sideways, his hat darted across the deck: a musket-ball from the corsair had nicked his ear. It was perfectly numb under his investigating hand, and it was pouring with blood. He stepped down from the rail, craning his head out sideways to bleed to windward, while his right hand sheltered his precious epaulette from the flow. 'Killick,' he shouted, bending to keep his eyes on the galley under the taut arch of the square mainsail, 'bring me an old coat and another handkerchief.' Throughout his changing he gazed piercingly at the galley, which had fired twice with its single after gun, both shots going a very little wide. 'Lord, they run that twelve-pounder in and out briskly,' he reflected. The top-gallant studdingsails were sheeted home; the Sophie's pace increased; now she was gaining perceptibly. Jack was not the only one to notice this, and a cheer went up from the fo'c'sle, running down the larboard side as the gun-crews heard the news.

'The bow-chaser is ready, sir,' said James Dillon, smiling. 'Are you all right, sir?' he asked, seeing Jack's bloody hand and neck.

'A scratch – nothing at all,' said Jack. 'What do you make of the galley?'

'We're gaining on her, sir,' said Dillon, and although he spoke quietly there was an extraordinarily fierce exultation in his voice. He had been shockingly upset by Stephen's sudden appearance, and although his innumerable present duties had kept him from much consecutive thought, the whole of his mind, apart from its immediate forefront, was filled with unvoiced concern, distress and dark incoherent nightmare shadows: he looked forward to the turmoil on the galley's deck with a wild longing.

'She's spilling her wind,' said Jack. 'Look at that sly villain by the mainsheet. Take my glass.'

'No, sir. Surely not,' said Dillon, angrily clapping the telescope shut.

'Well,' said Jack, 'well . . .' A twelve-pounder ball passed through the Sophie's starboard lower studdingsails – two holes, precisely behind each other, and hummed along four or five feet from them, a visible blur, just skimming the hammocks. 'We could do with one or two of their gunners,' observed Jack. 'Masthead!' he hailed.

'Sir?' came the distant voice.

'What do you make of the sail to windward?'

'Bearing up, sir, bearing up for the head of the convoy.'

Jack nodded. 'Let the captains of the bow guns and the quartergunners serve the chaser. I'll lay her myself.'

'Pring is dead, sir. Another captain?'

'Make it so, Mr Dillon.'

He walked up forward. 'Shall we catch 'un, sir?' asked a grizzled seaman, one of the big boarding-party, with the pleasant friendliness of crisis.

'I hope so, Cundall, I hope so indeed,' said Jack. 'At least we shall have a bang at him.'

'That dog,' he said to himself, staring along the dispartsight at the Algerine's deck. He felt the first beginning of the upward roll under the *Sophie*'s forefoot, snapped the match down on to the touch-hole, heard the hiss and the shattering crash and the shriek of trucks as the gun recoiled.

'Huzzay, huzzay!' roared the men on the fo'c'sle. It was no more than a hole in the galley's mainsail, about half-way up, but it was the first blow they had managed to get home. Three more shots; and they heard one strike something metallic in the galley's stern.

'Carry on, Mr Dillon,' said Jack, straightening. 'Light along my glass, there.'

The sun was so low now that it was difficult to see as he stood balancing to the sea, shading his object-glass with his far hand and concentrating with all his power on two red-turbanned figures behind the galley's stern-chaser. A musketoon-ball struck the *Sophie*'s starboard knighthead and he heard a seaman rip out a string of furious obscenity. 'John Lakey copped it something cruel,' said a low voice close behind him. 'In the ballocks.' The gun went off at his side, but before its smoke hid the galley from him he had made up his mind. The Algerine was, in fact, spilling his wind – starting his sheets so that his sails, apparently full, were not really drawing with their whole force: that was why the poor old fat heavy dirty-bottomed *Sophie*, labouring furiously and on the very edge of carrying everything away, was gaining slightly on the slim, deadly, fine-cut galley. The Algerine was leading him on – could, in fact, run away at any moment. Why? To draw him far to the leeward of the cat, that was why: together with the real possibility of dismasting him, raking him at leisure

(being independent of the wind) and making a prize of the
Sophie as well. To draw him to the leeward of the convoy, too,
so that the sail to windward might snap up half a dozen of
them. He glanced over his left shoulder at the cat. Even if
she were to go about they would still fetch her in one board,
close-hauled, for she was a very slow creature – no topgallants and, of course, no royals – far slower than the *Sophie*.
But in a very little while, on this course and at this pace, he
would never be able to reach her except by beating up, tack
upon tack, with the darkness coming fast. It would not do.
His duty was clear enough: the unwelcome choice, as usual.
And this was the time for decision.

' 'Vast firing,' he said as the gun ran in. 'Starboard broadside: ready, now. Sergeant Quinn, look to the small-arms
men. When we have her dead on the beam, aim for her cabin
abaft the rowers' benches, right low. Fire at the word of command.' As he turned and ran back to the quarter-deck he
caught a look from James Dillon's powder-blackened face, a
look if not of anger or something worse, then at least of bitter
contrariety. 'Hands to the braces,' he called, mentally dismissing that as something for another day. 'Mr Marshall, lay her
for the cat.' He heard the men's groan – a universal exhalation
of disappointment – and said, 'Hard over.'

'We'll catch him unaware and give him something to
remember the *Sophie* by,' he added, to himself, standing
directly behind the starboard brass four-pounder. At this
speed the *Sophie* came round very fast: he crouched, half-
bent, not breathing, all his being focused along the central
gleam of brass and the turning seascape beyond it. The
Sophie turned, turned; the galley's oars started into furious
motion, churning up the sea, but it was too late. A tenth of a
second before he had the galley dead on the beam and just
before the *Sophie* reached the middle of her downward roll
he cried 'Fire!' and the *Sophie*'s broadside went off as crisply
as a ship of the line's, together with every musket aboard. The
smoke cleared and a cheer went up, for there was a gaping

hole in the galley's side and the Moors were running to and fro in disorder and dismay. In his glass Jack could see the stern-chaser dismounted and several bodies lying on the deck: but the miracle had not happened – he had neither knocked her rudder away nor holed her disastrously below the water-line. However, there was no further trouble to be expected from her, he reflected, turning his attention from the galley to the cat.

'WELL, DOCTOR,' he said, appearing in the cockpit, 'how are you getting along?'

'Tolerably well, I thank you. Has the battle begun again?'

'Oh, no. That was only a shot across the cat's bows. The galley is hull-down in the south-south-west and Dillon has just taken a boat across to set the Norwegians free – the Moors have hung out a white shirt and called for quarter. The damned rogues.'

'I am happy to hear it. It is really impossible to sew one's flaps neatly with the jarring of the guns. May I see your ear?'

'It was only a passing flick. How are your patients?'

'I believe I may answer for four or five of them. The man with the terrible incision in his thigh – they tell me it was a splinter of wood: can this be true?'

'Yes, indeed. A great piece of hard sharp-edged oak flying through the air will cut you up amazingly. It often happens.'

'– has responded remarkably well; and I have patched up the poor fellow with the burn. Do you know that the rammer was actually thrust right through between the head of the biceps, just missing the ulnar nerve? But I cannot deal with the gunner down here – not in this light.'

'The gunner? What's amiss with the gunner? I thought you had cured him?'

'So I had. Of the grossest self-induced costiveness it has ever been my privilege to see, caused by a frantic indulgence in Peruvian bark – self-administered Peruvian bark. But this is a depressed cranial fracture, sir, and I must use the trephine: here he lies – you notice the characteristic stertor? – and I think he is safe until the morning. But as soon as the sun is up I must have off the top of his skull with my little saw. You will see the gunner's brain, my dear sir,' he added with a smile. 'Or at least his dura mater.'

'Oh dear, oh dear,' murmured Jack. Deep depression was settling on him – anticlimax – such a bloody little engagement for so little – two good men killed – the gunner almost certainly dead – no man could survive having his brain opened, that stood to reason – and the others might easily die too – they so often did. If it had not been for that damned convoy he might have had the galley – two could play at that game. 'Now what's to do?' he cried, as a clamour broke out on deck.

'They're carrying on very old-fashioned aboard the cat, sir,' said the master as Jack reached the quarter-deck in the twilight. The master came from some far northern part – Orkney, Shetland – and either that or a natural defect in his speech caused him to pronounce *er* as *ar*: a peculiarity that grew more marked in time of stress. 'It looks as though those infernal buggers were cutting their capars again, sir.'

'Put her alongside, Mr Marshall. Boarders, come along with me.'

The *Sophie* braced round her yards to avoid any more damage, backed her fore-topsail and glided evenly along the cat's side. Jack reached out for the main channels on the Norwegian's high side and swung himself up through the wrecked boarding netting, followed by a grim and savage-looking band. Blood on the deck: three bodies: five ashy Moors pressed against the roundhouse bulkhead under the protection of James Dillon: the dumb Negro Alfred King with a boarder's axe in his hand.

'Get those prisoners across,' said Jack. 'Stow them in the forehold. What's to do, Mr Dillon?'

'I can't quite make him out, sir, but I think the prisoners must have attacked King between decks.'

'Is that what happened, King?'

The Negro was still glaring about – his mates held his arms – and his answer might have meant anything.

'Is that what happened, Williams?' asked Jack.

'Don't know, sir,' said Williams, touching his hat and look-ing glassy.

'Is that what happened, Kelly?'

'Don't know, sir,' said Kelly, with a knuckle to his forehead and the same look to a hairsbreadth.

'Where's the cat's master, Mr Dillon?'

'Sir, it seems the Moors tossed them all overboard.'

'Good God,' cried Jack. Yet the thing was not uncommon. An angry noise behind him showed that the news had reached the *Sophie*. 'Mr Marshall,' he called, going to the rail, 'take care of these prisoners, will you? I will not have any foolery.' He looked up and down the deck, up and down the rigging: very little damage. 'You will bring her in to Cagliari, Mr Dillon,' he said in a low voice, quite upset by the savagery of the thing. 'Take what men you need.'

He returned to the *Sophie*, very grave, very grave. Yet he had scarcely reached his own quarter-deck before a minute, discreditable voice within said, 'In that case she's a prize, you know, not just a rescue.' He frowned it down, called for the bosun and began a tour of the brig, deciding the order of the more urgent repairs. She had suffered surprisingly for a short engagement in which not more than fifty shots had been exchanged – she was a floating example of what superior gun-nery could do. The carpenter and two of his crew were over the side in cradles, trying to plug a hole very near the water-line.

'I can't rightly come at 'un, sir,' said Mr Lamb, in answer to Jack's inquiry. 'We'm half drowned, but we can't seem to bang 'un home, not on this tack.'

'We'll put her about for you, then, Mr Lamb. But let me know the minute she's plugged.' He glanced over the darken-ing sea at the cat, now taking her place in the convoy once

more: going about would mean travelling right away from the
cat, and the cat had grown strangely dear to his heart.
'Loaded with spars, Stettin oak, tow, Stockholm tar, cordage,'
continued that inner voice eagerly. 'She might easily fetch
two or three thousand – even four . . .' 'Yes, Mr Watt, certainly,' he said aloud. They climbed into the maintop and
gazed at the injured cap.

'That was the bit that done poor Mr Day's business for
him,' said the bosun.

'So that was it? A devilish great lump indeed. But we must
not give up hope. Dr Maturin is going to – going to do something prodigious clever with a saw, as soon as there is light. He
needs light for it – something uncommonly skilful, I dare say.'

'Oh, yes, I'm sure, sir,' cried the bosun warmly. 'A very
clever gentleman he must be, no question. The men are wonderfully pleased. "How kind," they say, "to saw off Ned Evans'
leg so trim, and to sew up John Lakey's private parts so neat;
as well as all the rest; he being, so to speak, on leave – a visitor, like." '

'It *is* handsome,' said Jack. 'It is very handsome, I agree.
We'll need a kind of gammoning here, Mr Watt, until the carpenter can attend to the cap. Hawsers bowsed as tight as can
be, and God help us if we have to strike topmasts.'

They saw to half a dozen other points and Jack climbed
down, paused to count his convoy – very close and orderly
now after its fright – and went below. As he let himself sink
on to the long cushioned locker he found that he was in the
act of saying 'Carry three,' for his mind was busily working
out three eighths of £3,500 – it had now fixed upon this sum
as the worth of the *Dorthe Engelbrechtsdatter*. For three-
eighths (less one of them for the admiral) was to be his share
of the proceeds. Nor was his the only mind to be busy with
figures, by any means, for every other man on the *Sophie*'s
books was entitled to share – Dillon and the master, an
eighth between them; the surgeon (if the *Sophie* had officially borne one on her books), bosun, carpenter and master's

mates, another eighth; then the midshipmen, the inferior warrant officers and the marine sergeant another eighth, while the rest of the ship's company shared the remaining quarter. And it was wonderful to see how briskly minds not given to abstract thought rattled these figures, these symbols, up and down, coming out with the acting yeoman of the sheets' share correct to the nearest farthing. He reached for a pencil to do the sum properly, felt ashamed, pushed it aside, hesitated, took it up again and wrote the figures very small, diagonally upon the corner of a leaf, thrusting the paper quickly from him at a knock on the door. It was the still-moist carpenter, coming to report the shot-holes plugged, and no more than eighteen inches of water in the well, 'which is less nor half what I expected, with that nasty rough stroke the galley give us, firing from so low down'. He paused, giving Jack an odd, sideways-looking glance.

'Well, that's capital, Mr Lamb,' said Jack, after a moment.

But the carpenter did not stir; he stood there dripping on the painted sailcloth squares, making a little pool at last. Then he burst out, 'Which, if it is true about the cat, and the poor Norwegians dumped overboard – perhaps wounded, too, which makes you right mad, as being mere cruelty – what harm would they do if battened down? Howsoever, the warrant officers of the *Sophie* would wish the gentleman' – jerking his head towards the night-cabin, Stephen Maturin's temporary dwelling-place – 'cut in on their share, fair do's, as a mark of – as an acknowledgement of – his conduct considered very handsome by all hands.'

'If you please, sir,' said Babbington, 'the cat's signalling.'

On the quarter-deck Jack saw that Dillon had run up a motley hoist – obviously all the *Dorthe Engelbrechtsdatter* possessed – stating, among other things, that he had the plague aboard and that he was about to sail.

'Hands to wear ship,' he called. And when the *Sophie* had run down to within a cable's length of the convoy he hailed, 'Cat ahoy!'

'Sir,' came Dillon's voice over the intervening sea, 'you will
be pleased to hear the Norwegians are all safe.'

'What?'

'The – Norwegians – are – all – safe.' The two vessels came
closer. 'They hid in a secret place in the forepeak – in the
forepeak,' went on Dillon.

'Oh, – their forepeak,' muttered the quartermaster at the
wheel; for the *Sophie* was all ears – a very religious hush.

'Full and by!' cried Jack angrily, as the topsails shivered
under the influence of the quartermaster's emotion. 'Keep
her full and by.'

'Full and by it is, sir.'

'And the master says,' continued the distant voice, 'could
we send a surgeon aboard, because one of his men hurt his
toe hurrying down the ladder.'

'Tell the master, from me,' cried Jack, in a voice that
reached almost to Cagliari, his face purple with effort and
furious indignation, 'tell the master that he can take his man's
toe and – with it.'

He stumped below, £875 the poorer, and looking thoroughly sour and disagreeable.

THIS, HOWEVER, was not an expression that his features
wore easily, or for long; and when he stepped into the cutter
to go aboard the admiral in Genoa roads his face was quite
restored to its natural cheerfulness. It was rather grave, of
course, for a visit to the formidable Lord Keith, Admiral of
the Blue and Commander-in-Chief in the Mediterranean,
was no laughing matter. His gravity, as he sat there in the
stern-sheets, very carefully washed, shaved and dressed,
affected his coxswain and the cutter's crew, and they rowed
soberly along, keeping their eyes primly inboard. Yet even so
they were going to reach the flagship too early, and Jack, looking at his watch, desired them to pull round the *Audacious*
and lie on their oars. From here he could see the whole bay,
with five ships of the line and four frigates two or three miles

from the land, and inshore of them a swarm of gunboats and mortar-vessels; they were steadily bombarding the noble city that rose steeply in a sweeping curve at the head of the bay – lying there in a cloud of smoke of their own making, lobbing bombs into the close-packed buildings on the far side of the distant mole. The boats were small in the distance; the houses, churches and palaces were smaller still (though quite distinct in that sweet transparent air), like toys; but the continuous rumbling of the fire, and the deeper reply of the French artillery on shore, was strangely close at hand, real and menacing.

The necessary ten minutes passed; the *Sophie's* cutter approached the flag-ship; and in answer to the hail of Boat ahoy the coxswain answered *Sophie*, meaning that her captain was aboard. Jack went up the side in due form, saluted the quarter-deck, shook hands with Captain Louis and was shown to the admiral's cabin.

He had every reason to be pleased with himself – he had taken his convoy to Cagliari without loss; he had brought up another to Leghorn; and he was here at exactly the appointed time, in spite of calms off Monte Cristo – but for all that he was remarkably nervous, and his mind was so full of Lord Keith that when he saw no admiral in that beautiful great light-filled cabin but only a well-rounded young woman with her back to the window, he gaped like any carp.

'Jacky, dear,' said the young woman, 'how beautiful you are, all dressed up. Let me put your neck-cloth straight, La, Jacky, you look as frightened as if I were a Frenchman.'

'Queeney! Old Queeney!' cried Jack, squeezing her and giving her a most affectionate smacking kiss.

'God damn and blast – a luggit corpis sweenie,' cried a furious Scotch voice, and the admiral walked in from the quarter-gallery. Lord Keith was a tall grey man with a fine leonine head, and his eyes shot blazing sparks of rage.

'This is the young man I told you about, Admiral,' said Queeney, patting poor pale Jack's black stock into place and waving a ring at him. 'I used to give him his bath and take him into my bed when he had bad dreams.'

This might not have been thought the very best possible recommendation to a newly-married admiral of close on sixty, but it seemed to answer. 'Oh,' said the admiral. 'Yes. I was forgetting. Forgive me. I have such a power of captains, and some of them are very mere rakes . . .'

'"AND SOME OF THEM are very mere rakes," says he, piercing me through and through with that damned cold eye of his,' said Jack, filling Stephen's glass and spreading himself comfortably along the locker. 'And I was morally certain that he recognized me from the only three times we were in company – and each time worse than the last. The first was at the Cape, in the old Reso, when I was a midshipman: he was Captain Elphinstone then. He came aboard just two minutes after Captain Douglas had turned me before the mast and said, "What's yon wee snotty bairn a-greeting at?" And Captain Douglas said, "That wretched boy is a perfect young whoremonger; I have turned him before the mast, to learn him his duty."'

'Is that a more convenient place to learn it?' said Stephen.

'Well, it is easier for them to teach you deference,' said Jack, smiling, 'for they can seize you to a grating at the gangway and flog the liver and lights out of you with the cat. It means disrating a midshipman – degrading him, so that he is no longer what we call a young gentleman but a common sailor. He becomes a common sailor; he berths and messes with them; and he can be knocked about by anyone with a cane or a starter in his hand, as well as being flogged. I never thought he would really do it, although he had threatened me with it often enough; for he was a friend of my father's and I thought he had a kindness for me – which indeed he did. But, however, he carried it out, and there I was, turned before the mast: and he kept me there six months before rating me midshipman again. I was grateful to him in the end, because I came to understand the lower deck through and through – they were wonderfully kind to me, on the whole. But at the time I bawled like a calf – wept like any girl, ha, ha, ha.'

'What made him take so decided a step?'

'Oh, it was over a girl, a likely black girl called Sally,' said Jack. 'She came off in a bum-boat and I hid her in the cable-tier. But Captain Douglas and I had disagreed about a good many other things – obedience, mostly, and getting out of bed in the morning, and respect for the schoolmaster (we had a schoolmaster aboard, a drunken sot named Pitt) and a dish of tripe. Then the second time Lord Keith saw me was when I was fifth of the Hannibal and our first lieutenant was that damned fool Carrol – if there's one thing I hate more than being on shore it's being under the orders of a damned fool that is no seaman. He was so offensive, so designedly offensive, over a trivial little point of discipline that I was obliged to ask him whether he would like to meet me elsewhere. That was exactly what he wanted: he ran to the captain and said I had called him out. Captain Newman said it was nonsense, but I must apologize. But I could not do that, for there was nothing to apologize about – I was in the right, you see. So there I was, hauled up in front of half a dozen post-captains and two admirals: Lord Keith was one of the admirals.'

'What happened?'

'Petulance – I was officially reprimanded for petulance. Then the third time – but I will not go into details,' said Jack. 'It is a very curious thing, you know,' he went on, gazing out of the stern window with a look of mild, ingenuous wonder, 'a prodigious curious thing, but there cannot be many men who are both damned fools and no seamen, who reach post rank in the Royal Navy – men with no interest, I mean, of course – and yet it so happens that I have served under no less than two of them. I really thought I was dished that time – career finished, cut down, alas poor Borwick. I spent eight months on shore, as melancholy as that chap in the play, going up to

town whenever I could afford it, which was not often, and
hanging about that damned waiting-room in the Admiralty. I
really thought I should never get to sea again – a half-pay
lieutenant for the rest of my life. If it had not been for my fiddle, and fox-hunting when I could get a horse, I think I
should have hanged myself. That Christmas was the last time
I saw Queeney, I believe, apart from just once in London.'

'Is she an aunt, a cousin?'

'No, no. No connexion at all. But we were almost brought
up together – or rather, *she* almost brought *me* up. I always
remember her as a great girl, not a child at all, though to be
sure there can't be ten years between us. Such a dear, kind
creature. They had Damplow, the next house to ours – they
were almost in our park – and after my mother died I dare say
I spent as much time there as I did at home. More,' he said
reflectively, gazing up at the tell-tale compass overhead. 'You
know Dr Johnson – Dictionary Johnson?'

'Certainly,' cried Stephen, looking strange. 'The most
respec-table, the most amiable of the moderns. I disagree
with all he says, except when he speaks of Ireland, yet I honour him; and for his life of Savage I love him. What is more,
he occupied the most vivid dream I ever had in my life, not a
week ago. How strange that you should mention him today.'

'Yes, ain't it? He was a great friend of theirs, until their
mother ran off and married an Italian, a Papist. Queeney was
wonderfully upset at having a Papist to her father-in-law, as
you may imagine. Not that she ever saw him, however. "Anything but a Papist," says she. "I should rather have had Black
Frank a thousand times, I declare." So we burnt thirteen guys
in a row that year – it must have been '83 or '84 – not long
after the Battle of the Saints. After that they settled at
Damplow more or less for good – the girls, I mean, and their
old she-cousin. Dear Queeney. I believe I spoke of her
before, did I not? She taught me mathematics.'

'I believe you did: a Hebrew scholar, if I do not mistake?'

'Exactly so. Conic sections and the Pentateuch came as

easy as kiss my hand to her. Dear Queeney. I thought she was
to be an old maid, though she was so pretty; for how could
any man make up to a girl that knows Hebrew? It seemed a
sad pity: anyone so sweet-tempered should have a prodigious
great family of children. But, however, here she is married to
the admiral, so it all ends happy . . . yet, you know, he is
amazingly ancient – grey-haired, rising sixty, I dare say. Do
you think, as a physician – I mean, is it possible . . .?'

'*Possibilissima.*'

'Eh?'

'*Possibile è la cosa, e naturale,*' sang Stephen in a harsh,
creaking tone, quite unlike his speaking voice, which was not
disagreeable. '*E se Susanna vuol, possibilissima,*' discordantly,
but near enough to Figaro to be recognized.

'Really? *Really?*' said Jack with intense interest. Then after a
pause for reflexion, 'We might try that as a duetto, improvising . . . She joined him at Leghorn. And there I was, thinking
it was my own merit, recognized at last, and honourable
wounds' – laughing heartily – 'that had won me my promotion. Whereas I make no doubt it was all dear Queeney, do
you see? But I have not told you the best – and this I certainly
owe to her. We are to have a six weeks' cruise down the
French and Spanish coasts, as far as Cape Nao!'

'Aye? Will that be good?'

'Yes, yes! Very good. No more convoy duty, you understand.
No more being tied to a lubberly parcel of sneaking rogues,
merchants creeping up and down the sea. The French and the
Spaniards, their trade, their harbours, their supplies – these
are to be our objects. Lord Keith was very earnest about the
great importance of destroying their commerce. He was very
particular about it indeed – as important as your great fleet
actions, says he; and so very much more profitable. The
admiral took me aside and dwelt upon it at length – he is a
most acute, far-sighted commander; not a Nelson, of course,
but quite out of the ordinary. I am glad Queeney has him.
And we are under no one's orders, which is so delightful. No

bald-pated pantaloon to say "Jack Aubrey, you proceed to Leghorn with these hogs for the fleet", making it quite impossible even to hope for a prize. Prize-money,' he cried, smiling and slapping his thigh; and the marine sentry outside the door, who had been listening intently, wagged his head and smiled too.

'Are you very much attached to money?' asked Stephen.

'I love it passionately,' said Jack, with truth ringing clear in his voice. 'I have always been poor, and I long to be rich.'

'That's right,' said the marine.

'My dear old father was always poor too,' went on Jack. 'But as open-handed as a summer's day. He gave me fifty pounds a year allowance when I was a midshipman, which was uncommon handsome, in those days . . . or would have been, had he ever managed to persuade Mr Hoare to pay it, after the first quarter. Lord, how I suffered in the old Reso – mess bills, laundry, growing out of my uniforms . . . of course I love money. But I think we should be getting under way – there's two bells striking.'

Jack and Stephen were to be the gun-room's guests, to taste the sucking-pig bought at Leghorn. James Dillon was there to bid them welcome, together with the master, the purser and Mowett, as they plunged into the gloom: the gun-room had no stern-windows, no sash-ports, and only a scrap of skylight right forward, for although the peculiarity of the Sophie's construction made for a very comfortable captain's cabin (luxurious, indeed, if only the captain's legs had been sawn off a little above the knee), unencumbered with the usual guns, it meant that the gun-room lay on a lower level than the spardeck and reposed upon a kind of shelf, not unlike an orlop.

Dinner was rather a stiff, formal entertainment to begin with, although it was lit by a splendid Byzantine silver hanging lamp, taken by Dillon out of a Turkish galley, and although it was lubricated by uncommonly good wine, for Dillon was well-to-do, even wealthy, by naval standards. Everyone was unnaturally well behaved: Jack was to give the tone, as he knew very well – it was expected of him, and it was his privilege. But this kind of deference, this attentive listening to every remark of his, required the words he uttered to be worth the attention they excited – a wearing state of affairs for a man accustomed to ordinary human conversation, with its perpetual interruption, contradiction and plain disregard. Here everything he said was right; and presently his spirits began to sink under the burden. Marshall and Purser Ricketts sat mum, saying please and thank you, eating with dreadful precision; young Mowett (a fellow guest) was altogether silent, of course; Dillon worked away at the small talk; but Stephen Maturin was sunk deep in a reverie.

It was the pig that saved this melancholy feast. Impelled by a trip on the part of the steward that coincided with a sudden lurch on the part of the *Sophie*, it left its dish at the door of the gun-room and shot into Mowett's lap. In the subsequent roaring and hullaballoo everyone grew human again, remaining natural long enough for Jack to reach the point he had been looking forward to since the beginning of dinner.

'Well, gentlemen,' he said, after they had drunk the King's health, 'I have news that will please you, I believe; though I must ask Mr Dillon's indulgence for speaking of a service matter at this table. The admiral gives us a cruise on our own down to Cape Nao. And I have prevailed upon Dr Maturin to stay aboard, to sew us up when the violence of the King's enemies happens to tear us apart.'

'Huzzay – well done – hear, hear – topping news – good – hear him,' they cried, all more or less together, and they looked so pleased – there was so much candid friendliness on their faces that Stephen was intensely moved.

'Lord Keith was delighted when I told him,' Jack went on. 'Said he envied us extremely – had no physician in the flag-ship – was *amazed* when I told him of the gunner's brains – called for his spy-glass to look at Mr Day taking the sun on deck – and wrote out the Doctor's order in his own hand, which is something I have never heard of in the service before.'

Nor had anyone there present – the order had to be wetted – three bottles of port, there Killick – bumpers all round – and while Stephen sat looking modestly down at the table, they all stood up, crouching their heads under the beams, and sang.

Huzzay, huzzay, huzzay,
Huzzay, huzzay, huzzay,
Hussay, huzzay, huzzay,
Huzzay.

'There is only one thing I do not care for, however,' he said as the order was passed reverently round the table, 'and that is this foolish insistence upon the word surgeon. "Do hereby appoint you surgeon . . . take upon you the employment of surgeon . . . together with such allowance for wages and vict-uals for yourself as is usual for the surgeon of the said sloop." It is a false description; and a false description is anathema to the philosophic mind.'

'I am sure it is anathema to the philosophic mind,' said James Dillon. 'But the naval mind fairly revels in it, so it does. Take that word sloop, for example.'

'Yes,' said Stephen, narrowing his eyes through the haze of port and trying to remember the definitions he had heard.

'Why, now, a sloop, as you know, is properly a one-masted vessel, with a fore-and-aft rig. But in the Navy a sloop may be ship-rigged – she may have three masts.'

'Or take the Sophie,' cried the master, anxious to bring his crumb of comfort. 'She's rightly a brig, you know, Doctor, with her two masts.' He held up two fingers, in case a land-man might not fully comprehend so great a number. 'But the minute Captain Aubrey sets foot in her, why, she too becomes a sloop; for a brig is a lieutenant's command.'

'Or take me,' said Jack. 'I am called captain, but really I am only a master and commander.'

'Or the place where the men sleep, just for'ard,' said the purser, pointing. 'Rightly speaking, and official, 'tis the gun-deck, though there's never a gun on it. We call it the spardeck – though there's no spars, neither – but some say the gun-deck still, and call the right gun-deck the upper-deck. Or take this brig, which is no true brig at all, not with her square mainsail, but rather a sorts of snow, or a hermaphrodite.'

'No, no, my dear sir,' said James Dillon, 'never let a mere word grieve your heart. We have nominal captain's servants who are, in fact, midshipmen; we have nominal able seamen on our books who are scarcely breeched – they are a thousand miles away and still at school; we swear we have not shifted any backstays, when we shift them continually; and we take many other oaths that nobody believes – no, no, you may call yourself what you please, so long as you do your duty. The Navy speaks in symbols, and you may suit what meaning you choose to the words.'

5

THE FAIR COPY of the *Sophie's* log was written out in David Richards' unusually beautiful copperplate, but in all other respects it was just like every other log-book in the service. Its tone of semi-literate, official, righteous dullness never varied; it spoke of the opening of beef-cask no. 271 and the death of the loblolly-boy in exactly the same voice, and it never deviated into human prose even for the taking of the sloop's first prize.

> *Thursday, June* 28, *winds variable, SE by S, course S50W, distance 63 miles. – Latitude 42°32′N, longitude 4°17′E, Cape Creus S76°W 12 leagues. Moderate breezes and cloudy PM at 7 in first reef topsails. AM d° weather. Exercising the great guns. The people employed occasionally.*
>
> *Friday, June 29, S and Eastward . . . Light airs and clear weather. Exercising the great guns. PM employed worm-*

*ing the cable. AM moderate breezes and clouds, in third
reef maintopsail, bent another foretopsail and close reefed
it, hard gales at 4 handed the square mainsail at 8 more
moderate reefed the square mainsail and set it. At noon
calm. Departed this life Henry Gouges, loblolly-boy. Exercising the great guns.*

*Saturday, June 30, light airs inclinable to calm. Exercised
the great guns. Punished Jno. Shannahan and Thos. Yates
with 12 lashes for drunkenness. Killed a bullock weight
530 lb. Remains of water 3 tons.*

*Sunday, July 1 . . . Mustered the ship's company by divi-
sions read the Articles of War performed Divine Service
and committed the body of Henry Gouges to the deep. At
noon d° weather.*

Ditto weather: but the sun sank towards a livid, purple,
tumescent cloud-bank piled deep on the western horizon,
and it was clear to every seaman aboard that it was not going
to remain ditto much longer. The seamen, sprawling abroad
on the fo'c'sle and combing out their long hair or plaiting it up
again for one another, kindly explained to the landmen that this
long swell from the south and east, this strange sticky heat that
came both from the sky and the glassy surface of the heaving
sea, and this horribly threatening appearance of the sun,
meant that there was to be a coming dissolution of all natural
bonds, an apocalyptic upheaval, a right dirty night ahead. The
sailormen had plenty of time to depress their hearers, already
low in their spirits because of the unnatural death of Henry
Gouges (had said, 'Ha, ha, mates, I am fifty years old this day.
Oh dear,' and had died sitting there, still holding his untasted
grog) — they had plenty of time, for this was Sunday afternoon, when in the course of nature the fo'c'sle was covered
with sailors at their ease, their pigtails undone. Some of the
more gifted had queues they could tuck into their belts; and
now that these ornaments were loosened and combed out,
lank when still wet, or bushy when dry and as yet ungreased,

they gave their owners a strangely awful and foreboding look, like oracles; which added to the landmen's uneasiness.

The seamen laid it on; but with all their efforts they could scarcely exaggerate the event, for the south-easterly gale increased from its first warning blasts at the end of the last dog-watch to a great roaring current of air by the end of the middle watch, a torrent so laden with warm rain that the men at the wheel had to hold their heads down and cup their mouths sideways to breathe. The seas mounted higher and higher: they were not the height of the great Atlantic rollers, but they were steeper, and in a way more wicked; their heads tore off streaming in front of them so as to race through the *Sophie*'s tops, and they were tall enough to becalm her as she lay there a-try, riding it out under a storm staysail. This was something she could do superbly well: she might not be very fast; she might not look very dangerous or high-bred; but with her topgallantmasts struck down on deck, her guns double-breeched and her hatches battened down, leaving only a little screened way to the after-ladder, and with a hundred miles of sea-room under her lee, she lay to as snug and unconcerned as an eider-duck. She was a remarkably dry vessel too, observed Jack, as she climbed the creaming slope of a wave, slipped its roaring top neatly under her bows and travelled smoothly down into the hollow. He stood with an arm round a backstay, wearing a tarpaulin jacket and a pair of calico drawers: his streaming yellow hair, which he wore loose and long as a tribute to Lord Nelson, stood straight out behind him at the top of each wave and sank in the troughs between – a natural anemometer – and he watched the regular, dreamlike procession in the diffused light of the racing moon. With the greatest pleasure he saw that his forecast of her qualities as a sea-boat was fulfilled and, indeed, surpassed. 'She is remarkably dry,' he said to Stephen who, preferring to die in the open, had crept up on deck, had been made fast to a stanchion and who now stood, mute, sodden and appalled, behind him.

'Eh?'

'She – is – remarkably – dry.'

Stephen frowned impatiently: this was no time for trifling.

But the rising sun swallowed up the wind, and by half-past seven the next morning all that was left of the storm was the swell and a line of clouds low over the distant Gulf of Lions in the north-west; the sky was of an unbelievable purity and the air was washed so clean that Stephen could see the colour of the petrel's dangling feet as it pattered across the *Sophie*'s wake some twenty yards behind. 'I remember the *fact* of extreme, prostrating terror,' he said, keeping his eye on the tiny bird, 'but the *inward nature* of the emotion now escapes me.'

The man at the wheel and the quartermaster at the con exchanged a shocked glance.

'It is not unlike the case of a woman in childbirth,' went on Stephen, moving to the taffrail to keep the petrel in view and speaking rather more loudly. The man at the wheel and the quartermaster looked hastily away from one another: this was terrible – anybody might hear. The *Sophie*'s surgeon, the opener (in broad daylight and upon the entranced maindeck) of the gunner's brainpan – *Lazarus* Day, as he was called now – was much prized, but there was no telling how far he might go in impropriety. 'I remember an instance . . .'

'Sail ho!' cried the masthead, to the relief of all upon the *Sophie*'s quarter-deck.

'Where away?'

'To leeward. Two points, three points on the beam. A felucca. In distress – her sheets a-flying.'

The *Sophie* turned, and presently those on deck could see the distant felucca as it rose and fell on the long troubled sea. It made no attempt to fly, none to alter course nor yet to heave to, but stood on with its shreds of sail streaming out on the irregular breaths of the dying wind. Nor did it show any answering colours or reply to the *Sophie*'s hail. There was no one at the tiller, and when they came nearer those with glasses could see the bar move from side to side as the felucca yawed.

'That's a body on deck,' said Babbington, full of glee.

'It will be awkward lowering a boat in this,' remarked Jack, more or less to himself. 'Williams, lay her along, will you? Mr Watts, let some men stand by to boom her off. What do you make of her, Mr Marshall?'

'Why, sir, I take it she's from Tangiers or maybe Tetuan — the west end of the coast, at all events . . .'

'That man in the square hole died of plague,' said Stephen Maturin, clapping his telescope to.

A hush followed this statement and the wind sighed through the weather-shrouds. The distance between the vessels narrowed fast, and now everyone could see a shape wedged in the after-hatchway, with perhaps two more beneath it; an almost naked body among the tangle of gear near the tiller.

'Keep her full,' said Jack. 'Doctor, are you quite sure of what you say? Take my glass.'

Stephen looked through it for a moment and handed it back. 'There is no possible doubt,' he said. 'I will just make up a bag and then I will go across. There may be some survivors.'

The felucca was almost touching now, and a tame genet — a usual creature in Barbary craft, on account of the rats — stood on the rail, looking eagerly up, ready to spring. An elderly Swede named Volgardson, the kindliest of men, threw a swab that knocked it off its balance, and all the men along the side hooted and shrieked to frighten it away.

'Mr Dillon,' said Jack, 'we'll get the starboard tacks aboard.'

At once the *Sophie* sprang to life — bosun's calls shrilling, hands running to their places, general uproar — and in the din Stephen cried, 'I insist upon a boat — I protest . . .'

Jack took him by the elbow and propelled him with affectionate violence into the cabin. 'My dear sir,' he said, 'I am afraid you must not insist, or protest: it is mutiny, you know, and you would be obliged to be hanged. Was you to set foot in that felucca, even if you did not bring back the contagion, we should have to fly the yellow flag at Mahon: and you know what that means. Forty mortal bloody days on the quarantine island and shot if you stray outside the pallisado, that is what. And whether you brought it back or not, half the hands would die of fright.'

'You mean to sail directly away from that ship, giving it no assistance?'

'Yes, sir.'

'Upon your own head, then.'

'Certainly.'

The log took little notice of this incident; it scarcely could have found any appropriate official language for saying that the *Sophie*'s surgeon shook his fist at the *Sophie*'s captain, in any case; and it shuffled the whole thing off with the disingenuous *spoke felucca: and ¼ past 11 tacked,* for it was eager to come to the happiest entry it had made for years (Captain Allen had been an unlucky commander: not only had the *Sophie* been almost entirely confined to convoy-duty in his time, but whenever he did have a cruise the sea had emptied before him – never a prize did he take) . . . *PM moderate and clear, up topgallantmasts, opened pork cask no. 113, partially spoiled. 7 saw strange sail to westward, made sail in chase.*

Westward in this case meant almost directly to the *Sophie*'s lee; and making sail meant spreading virtually everything she possessed – lower, topsail and topgallant studdingsails, royals of course, and even bonnets – for the chase had been made out to be a fair-sized polacre with lateens on her fore and mizzen and square sails on her mainmast, and therefore French or Spanish – almost certainly a good prize if only she could be caught. This was the polacre's view, without a doubt, for she had been lying-to, apparently fishing her storm-damaged mainmast, when they first came in sight of one another; but the *Sophie* had scarcely sheeted home her topgallants before the polacre's head was before the wind and she fleeing with all she could spread in that short notice – a very suspicious polacre, unwilling to be surprised.

The *Sophie*, with her abundance of hands trained in setting sail briskly, ran two miles to the polacre's one in the first quarter of an hour; but once the chase had spread all the canvas it could, their speeds became more nearly even. With the wind two points on her quarter and her big square mainsail at its best advantage, the *Sophie* was still the faster, however, and when they had reached their greatest speed she was running well over seven knots to the polacre's six. But they were still four miles apart, and in three hours' time it would be pitch dark – no moon until half-past two. There was the hope, the very reasonable hope, that the chase would carry something away, for she had certainly had a rough night of it; and many a glass was trained upon her from the *Sophie's* fo'c'sle.

Jack stood there by the starboard knighthead, willing the sloop on with all his might, and feeling that his right arm might not be too great a price for an effective bow-chaser. He stared back at the sails and how they drew, he looked searchingly at the water rising in her bow-wave and sliding fast along her smooth black side; and it appeared to him that with her present trim the after sails were pressing her forefoot down a trifle much – that the extreme press of canvas might be hindering her progress – and he bade them take in the main royal. Rarely had he given an order more reluctantly obeyed, but the log-line proved that he was right: the *Sophie* ran a little easier, a very little faster, with the wind's thrust more forward.

The sun set over the starboard bow, the wind began to back into the north, blowing in gusts, and darkness swept up the sky from behind them: the polacre was still three-quarters of a mile ahead, holding on to her westward course. As the wind came round on to the beam they set staysails and the fore-and-aft mainsail: looking up at the set of the fore-royal and having it braced round more sharply, Jack could see it perfectly well; but when he looked down it was twilight on deck.

Now, with the studdingsails in, the chase – or the ghost of the chase, a pale blur showing now and then on the lifting swell – could be seen from the quarter-deck, and there he took up his stand with his night-glass, staring through the rapidly gathering darkness, giving a low, conversational order from time to time.

Dimmer, dimmer, and then she was gone: suddenly she was quite gone. The quadrant of horizon that had shown that faint but most interesting bobbing paleness was bare heaving sea, with Regulus setting into it.

'Masthead,' he hailed, 'what do you make of her?'

A long pause. 'Nothing, sir. She ain't there.'

Just so. What was he to do now? He wanted to think: he wanted to think there on deck, in the closest possible touch with the situation – with the shifting wind on his face, the glow of the binnacles just at hand and not the least interruption. And this the conventions and the discipline of the service allowed him to do. The blessed inviolability of a captain (so ludicrous at times, such a temptation to silly pomp) wrapped him about, and his mind could run free. At one time he saw Dillon hurry Stephen away: he recorded the fact, but his mind continued its unbroken pursuit of the answer to his problem. The polacre had either altered its course or would do so presently: the question was, where would this new course bring it to by dawn? The answer depended on a great many factors – whether French or Spanish, whether homeward or outward bound, whether cunning or simple and, above all, upon her sailing qualities. He had a very clear notion of them, having followed her every movement with the utmost attention for the last few hours; so building his reasoning (if such an instinctive process could be called by that name) upon these certainties and a fair estimate of the rest, he came to his conclusion. The polacre had worn; she might possibly be lying there under bare poles to escape detection while the *Sophie* passed her in the darkness to the northward; but whether or no, she would presently be making all sail, close-hauled for Agde or Cette, crossing the *Sophie*'s wake and relying on her lateen's power of lying nearer to run her clear to windward and so to safety before daylight. If this was so the *Sophie* must tack directly and work to windward under an easy sail: that should bring the polacre under her lee at first light; for it was likely that they would rely on their fore and mizzen alone – even in the chase they had been favouring their wounded mainmast.

He stepped into the master's cabin, and through narrowed, light-dazzled eyes he checked their position; he checked it again with Dillon's reckoning and went on deck to give his orders.

'Mr Watt,' he said, 'I am going to put her about, and I desire the whole operation shall be carried out in silence. No calls, no starting, no shouts.'

'No calls it is, sir,' said the bosun, and hurried off uttering 'All hands to tack ship,' in a hoarse whisper, wonderfully curious to hear.

The order and its form had a strangely powerful effect: with as much certainty as though it had been a direct revelation, Jack knew that the men were wholly with him; and for a fleeting moment a voice told him that he had better be right, or he would never enjoy this unlimited confidence again.

'Very well, Assou,' he said to the Lascar at the wheel, and smoothly the *Sophie* luffed up.

'Helm's a-lee,' he remarked – the cry usually echoed from one horizon to the other. Then 'Off tacks and sheets'. He heard the bare feet hurrying and the staysail sheets rasping over the stays: he waited, waited, until the wind was one point on her weather bow, and then a little louder, 'Mainsail haul!' She was in stays: and now she was paying off fast. The wind was well round on his other cheek. 'Let go and haul,' he said, and the half-seen waisters hauled on the starboard braces like veteran forecastlemen. The weather bowlines tightened: the *Sophie* gathered way.

Presently she was running east-north-east close-hauled

under reefed topsails, and Jack went below. He did not choose to have anything showing from his stern-windows, and it was not worth shipping the dead-lights, so he walked, bending low, into the gun-room. Here, rather to his surprise, he found Dillon (it was Dillon's watch below, certainly; but in his place Jack would never have left the deck) playing chess with Stephen, while the purser read them pieces from the Gentleman's Magazine, with comments.

'Do not stir, gentlemen,' he cried, as they all sprang up. 'I have just come to beg your hospitality for a while.'

They made him very welcome – hurried about with glasses of wine, sweet biscuits, the most recent Navy List – but he was an intruder: he had upset their quiet sociability, dried up the purser's literary criticism and interrupted the chess as effectually as an Olympian thunderbolt. Stephen messed down here now, of course – his cabin was the little boarded cup-board beyond the hanging lantern – and he already looked as though he belonged to this community: Jack felt obscurely hurt, and after he had talked for a while (a dry, constrained interchange, it seemed to him; so very polite) he went up on deck again. As soon as they saw him looming in the dim glow of the hatchway the master and young Ricketts moved silently over to the larboard side, and Jack resumed his soli-tary pacing from the taffrail to the aftermost deadeye.

At the beginning of the middle watch the sky clouded over, and towards two bells a shower came weeping across, the drops hissing on the binnacles. The moon rose, a faint, lop-sided object scarcely to be made out at all: Jack's stomach was pinched and wrung with hunger, but he paced on and on, looking mechanically out over the leeward darkness at every turn.

Three bells. The quiet voice of the ship's corporal reporting all's well. Four bells. There were so many other possibilities, so many things the chase could have done other than bearing up and then hauling her wind for Cette: hundreds of other things . . .

'What, what's this? Walking about in the rain in your shirt? This is madness,' said Stephen's voice just behind him.

'Hush!' cried Mowett, the officer of the watch, who had failed to intercept him.

'Madness. Think of the night air – the falling damps – the fluxion of the humours. If your duty requires you to walk about in the night air, you must wear a woollen garment. A woollen garment, there, for the captain! I will fetch it myself.'

Five bells, and another soft shower of rain. The relieving of the helm, and the whispered repetition of the course, the routine reports. Six bells, and a hint of thinner darkness in the east. The spell of silence seemed as strong as ever; men tiptoed to trim the yards, and a little before seven bells the look-out coughed, hailing almost apologetically, only just loud enough to be heard. 'Upon deck. Deck, sir. I think him vos there, starboard beam. I think . . .'

Jack stuffed his glass into the pocket of the grego Stephen had brought him, ran up to the masthead, twined himself firmly into the rigging and trained the telescope in the direction of the pointing arm. The first grey forerunners of the dawn were straggling through the drifting showers and low torn cloud to leeward; and there, her lateens faintly gleaming, lay a polacre, not half a mile away. Then the rain had hidden her again, but not before Jack had seen that she was indeed his quarry and that she had lost her maintopmast at the cap.

'You're a capital fellow, Anderssen,' he said, clapping him on the shoulder.

To the concentrated mute inquiry from young Mowett and the whole of the watch on deck he replied with a smile that he tried to keep within bounds and the words, 'She is just under our lee. East by south. You may light up the sloop, Mr Mowett, and show her our force: I don't want her to do anything foolish, such as firing a gun – perhaps hurting some of our people. Let me know when you have laid her aboard.' With this he retired, calling for a light and something hot to drink; and from his cabin he heard Mowett's voice, cracked and squeaking with the excitement of this prodigious command (he would happily have died for Jack), as under his orders the *Sophie* bore up and spread her wings.

Jack leant back against the curved run of the stern-window and let Killick's version of coffee down by gulps into his grateful stomach; and at the same time that its warmth spread through him, so there ran a lively tide of settled, pure, unfevered happiness – a happiness that another commander (remembering his own first prize) might have discerned from the log-entry, although it was not specifically mentioned there: *½ past 10 tacked, 11 in courses, reefed topsail. AM cloudy and rain. ½ past 4 chase observed E by S, distance ½ mile. Bore up and took possession of d°, which proved to be* L'Aimable Louise, *French polacre laden with corn and general merchandise for Cette, of about 200 tons, 6 guns and 19 men. Sent her with an officer and eight men to Mahon.*

'ALLOW ME TO fill your glass,' said Jack, with the utmost benevolence. 'This is rather better than our ordinary, I believe?'

'Better, dear joy, and very, very much stronger – a healthy, roborative beverage,' said Stephen Maturin. ' 'Tis a neat Priorato. Priorato, from behind Tarragona.'

'Neat it is – most uncommon neat. But to go back to the prize: the main reason why I am so very happy about it is that it bloods the men, as one might say; and it gives me room to spread my elbows a little. We have a capital prize agent – is obliged to me – and I am persuaded he will advance us a hundred guineas. I can distribute sixty or seventy to the crew, and buy some powder at last. There could be nothing better for these men than kicking up a dust on shore, and for that they must have money.'

'But will they not run away? You have often spoken of desertion – the great evil of desertion.'

'When they have prize-money due to them and a strong notion of more to come they will not desert. Not in Mahon, at all events. And then again, do you see, they will turn to exercising the great guns with a much better heart – do not suppose I do not know how they have been muttering, for indeed I have driven them precious hard. But now they will feel there is some point in it . . . If I can get some powder (I dare not use up much more of the issue) we will shoot lar-bowlines against starbowlines and watch against watch for a handsome prize; and what with that and what with emula-tion, I don't despair of making our gunnery at least as danger-ous to others as it is to ourselves. And then – God, how sleepy I am – we can set about our cruising in earnest. I have a plan for nightwork, lying close inshore . . . but first I should tell you how I think to divide up our time. A week off Cape Creus, then back to Mahon for stores and water, particularly water. Then the approaches to Barcelona, and coastwise . . . coastwise . . .' He yawned prodigiously: two sleepless nights and a pint of the *Aimable Louise*'s Priorato were bearing him down with an irresistible warm soft delicious weight. 'Where was I? Oh, Barcelona. Then off Tarragona, Valencia . . . Valencia . . . water's the great trouble, of course.' He sat there blinking at the light, musing comfortably; and he heard Stephen's distant voice discoursing upon the coast of Spain – knew it well as far as Denia, could show him many an inter-esting remnant of Phoenician, Greek, Roman, Visigothic, Arabian occupation; the certainty of both kinds of egret in the marshes by Valencia; the odd dialect and bloody nature of the Valencianos; the very real possibility of flamingoes . . .

THE *AIMABLE LOUISE*'s ill wind had stirred up the ship-ping all over the western Mediterranean, driving it far from its intended courses; and not two hours after they had sent their prize away for Mahon, their first fine plump prize, they saw two more vessels, the one a barca-longa heading west and the other a brig to the north, apparently steering due south. The brig was the obvious choice and they set a course to cut her off, keeping closest watch upon her the while: she sailed on placidly enough under courses and topsails, while the *Sophie* set her royals and topgallants and hurried along on the larboard tack with the wind one point free, heeling so that her lee-channels were under the water; and as their courses converged the Sophies were astonished to see that the stranger was extraordinarily like their own vessel, even to the exaggerated steeve of her bowsprit.

'That would be a brig, no doubt,' said Stephen, standing at the rail next to Pullings, a big shy silent master's mate.

'Yes, sir, so she is; and more exactly like us nor ever you would credit, without you seen it. Do you please to look in my spy-glass, sir?' he asked, wiping it on his handkerchief.

'Thank you. An excellent glass – how clear. But I must venture to disagree. That ship, that brig, is a vile yellow, whereas we are black, with a white stripe.'

'Oh, that's nobbut paintwork, sir. Look at her quarterdeck, with its antic little break right aft, just like ourn – you don't see many of such, even in these waters. Look at the steeve of her bowsprit. And she must gauge the same as us, Thames measurement, within ten ton or less. They must have been off of the same draught, out of the same yard. But there are three rows of reefbands in her fore tops'l, so you can see she's only a merchantman, and not a man-of-war like we.'

'Are we going to take her?'

'I doubt that'd be too good to be true, sir: but maybe we shall.'

'The Spanish colours, Mr Babbington,' said Jack; and looking round Stephen saw the yellow and red break out at the peak.

'We are sailing under false colours,' whispered Stephen. 'Is not that very heinous?'

'Eh?'

'Wicked, morally indefensible?'

'Bless you, sir, we always do that, at sea. But we'll show our own at the last minute, you may be sure, before ever we fire a gun. That's justice. Look at him, now – he's throwing out a

Danish waft, and as like as not he's no more a Dane than my grandam.'

But the event proved Thomas Pullings wrong. 'Danish prig *Clomer*, sir,' said her master, an ancient bibulous Dane with pale, red-rimmed eyes, showing Jack his papers in the cabin. 'Captain Ole Bugge. Hides and peeswax from Dripoli to Parcelona.'

'Well, Captain,' said Jack, looking very sharply through the papers – the quite genuine papers – 'I'm sure you will forgive me for troubling you – we have to do it, as you know. Let me offer you a glass of this Priorato; they tell me it is good of its kind.'

'It is better than good, sir,' said the Dane, as the purple tide ran out, 'it is vonderful vine. Captain, may I ask you the favour of your positions?'

'You have come to the right shop for a position, Captain. We have the best navigator in the Mediterranean. Killick, pass the word for Mr Marshall. Mr Marshall, Captain B . . . – the gentleman would like to know what we make our position.'

On deck the Clomers and the Sophies were gazing at one another's vessels with profound satisfaction, as at their own mirror-images: at first the Sophies had felt that the resemblance was something of a liberty on the part of the Danes, but they came round when their own yeoman of the sheets and their own shipmate Anderssen called out over the water to their fellow-countrymen, talking foreign as easy as kiss my hand, to the silent admiration of all beholders.

Jack saw Captain Bugge to the side with particular affability; a case of Priorato was handed down into the Danish boat; and leaning over the rail Jack called after him, 'I will let you know, next time we meet.'

Her captain had not reached the *Clomer* before the *Sophie*'s yards were creaking round, to carry her as close-hauled as she would lie on her new course, north-east by north. 'Mr Watt,' observed Jack, gazing up, 'as soon as we

have a moment to spare we must have cross-catharpings fore
and aft; we are not pointing up as sharp as I could wish.'

'What's afoot?' asked the ship's company, when all sail was
set and drawing just so, with everything on deck coiled down
to Mr Dillon's satisfaction; and it was not long before the
news passed along from the gun-room steward to the purser's
steward and so to his mate, Jack-in-the-dust, who told the
galley and thereby the rest of the brig – the news that the
Dane, having a fellow-feeling for the *Sophie* because of her
resemblance to his own vessel, and being gratified by Jack's
civility, had given word of a Frenchman no great way over the
northern horizon, a deep-laden sloop with a patched mainsail
that was bearing away for Agde.

Tack followed tack as the *Sophie* beat up into the freshening breeze, and on the fifth leg a scrap of white appeared in
the north-north-east, too far and too steady for a distant gull.
It was the French sloop, sure enough: from the Dane's
description of her rig there was no doubt of that after the first
half hour; but her behaviour was so strange that it was impossible to be wholly persuaded of it until she was lying tossing
there under the *Sophie*'s guns and the boats were going to
and fro over the lane of sea, transferring the glum prisoners.
In the first place she had apparently kept no look-out of any
kind, and it was not until no more than a mile of water lay
between them that she noticed her pursuer at all; and even
then she hesitated, wavered, accepted the assurance of the
tricolour flag and then rejected it, flying too slowly and too
late, only to break out ten minutes later in a flurry of signals
of surrender and waving them vehemently at the first warning
shot.

The reasons for her behaviour were clear enough to James
Dillon once he was aboard her, taking possession: the *Citoyen
Durand* was laden with gunpowder – was so crammed with
gunpowder that it overflowed her hold and stood in tarpau-
lined barrels on her deck; and her young master had taken his
wife to sea. She was with child – her first – and the rough

night, the chase and the dread of an explosion had brought on her labour. James was as stout-hearted as the next man, but the continuous groaning just behind the cabin-bulkhead and the awful hoarse, harsh, animal quality of the cries that broke out through the groaning, and their huge volume, terrified him; he gazed at the white-faced, distracted, tear-stained husband with a face as appalled as his.

Leaving Babbington in sole command he hurried back to the *Sophie* and explained the situation. At the word *powder* Jack's face lit up; but at the word *baby* he looked very blank.

'I am afraid the poor woman is dying,' said James.

'Well, I don't know, I'm sure,' said Jack hesitantly; and now that he could put a meaning to the remote, dreadful noise he heard it far more clearly. 'Ask the Doctor to come,' he said to a marine.

Now that the excitement of the chase was over, Stephen was at his usual post by the elm-tree pump, peering down its tube into the sunlit upper layers of the Mediterranean; and when they told him there was a woman in the prize, having a baby, he said, 'Aye? I dare say. I thought I recognized the sound,' and showed every sign of returning to his place.

'Surely you can do something about it?' said Jack.

'I am certain the poor woman is dying,' said James.

Stephen looked at them with his odd expressionless gaze and said, 'I will go across.' He went below, and Jack said, 'Well, that's in good hands, thank God. And you tell me all that deck cargo is powder too?'

'Yes, sir. The whole thing is mad.'

'Mr Day – Mr Day, there. Do you know the French marks, Mr Day?'

'Why, yes, sir. They are much the same as ours, only their best cylinder large grain has a white ring round the red: and their halves weigh but thirty-five pound.'

'How much have you room for, Mr Day?'

The gunner considered. 'Squeezing my bottom tier up tight, I might stow thirty-five or six, sir.'

'Make it so, then, Mr Day. There is a lot of damaged stuff aboard that sloop – I can see it from here – that we shall have to take away to prevent further spoiling. So you had better go across and set your hand upon the best. And we can do with her launch, too. Mr Dillon, we cannot entrust this floating magazine to a midshipman; you will have to take her into Mahon as soon as the powder is across. Take what men you think fit, and be so good as to send Dr Maturin back in her launch – we need one badly. God love us, what a terrible cry! I am truly sorry to inflict this upon you, Dillon, but you see how it is.'

'Just so, sir. I am to take the master of the sloop along with me, I presume? It would be inhuman to move him.'

'Oh, by all means, by all means. The poor fellow. What a – what a pretty kettle of fish.'

The little deadly barrels travelled across the intervening sea, rose up and vanished into the *Sophie*'s maw; so did half a dozen melancholy Frenchmen, with their bags or sea-chests; but the usual festive atmosphere was lacking – the Sophies, even the family men, looked guilty, concerned, apprehensive; the dreadful unremitting shrieks went on and on; and when Stephen appeared at the rail to call out that he must stay aboard, Jack bowed to the obscure justice of this deprivation.

THE *CITOYEN DURAND* ran smoothly through the darkness down towards Minorca, a steady breeze behind her; now that the screaming had stopped Dillon posted a reliable man at the helm, visited the little watch below in the galley and came down into the cabin. Stephen was washing, and the husband, shattered and destroyed, held the towel in his drooping hands.

'I hope . . .' said James.

'Oh, yes: yes,' said Stephen deliberately, looking round at him. 'A perfectly straightforward delivery: just a little long, perhaps; but nothing out of the way. Now, my friend' – to the captain – 'these buckets would be best over the side; and then I recommend you to lie down for a while. Monsieur has a son,' he added.

'My best congratulations, sir,' said James. 'And my best wishes for Madame's prompt recovery.'

'Thank you, sir, thank you,' said the captain, his eyes brimming over again. 'I beg you to take a little something – to make yourselves quite at home.'

This they did, sitting each in a comfortable chair and eating away at the hill of cakes laid up against young hasty's christening in Agde next week; they sat there easily enough, and next door the poor young woman slept at last, her husband holding her hand and her crinkled pink baby snorting at her bosom. It was quiet below, wonderfully quiet and peaceful now; and it was quiet on deck with the following wind easing the sloop along at a steady six knots, and with the rigorous barking precision of a man-of-war reduced to an occasional mild 'How does she lie, Joe?' It was quiet; and in that dimly-lighted box they travelled through the night, cradled by the even swell: after a little while of this silence and this uninterrupted slow rhythmic heave they might have been anywhere on earth – alone in the world – in another world altogether. In the cabin their thoughts were far away, and Stephen for one no longer had any sense of movement to or from any particular point – little sense of motion, still less of the immediate present.

'It is only now,' he said in a low voice, 'that we have the opportunity of speaking to one another. I looked forward to this time with great impatience; and now that it is come, I find that in fact there is little to be said.'

'Perhaps nothing at all,' said James. 'I believe we understand each other perfectly.'

This was quite true; it was quite true as far as the heart of the matter was concerned; but nevertheless they talked all through their remaining hours of harboured privacy.

'I believe the last time I saw you was at Dr Emmet's,' said James, after a long, reflective pause.

'No. It was at Rathfarnham, with Edward Fitzgerald. I was going out by the summerhouse as you and Kenmare came in.'

'Rathfarnham? Yes: yes, of course. I remember now. It was just after the meeting of the Committee. I remember . . . You were intimate with Lord Edward, I believe?'

'We knew one another very well in Spain. In Ireland I saw less and less of him as time went on; he had friends I neither liked nor trusted, and I was always too moderate – far too moderate – for him. Though the dear knows I was full enough of zeal for humanity at large, full enough of republicanism in those days. Do you remember the test?'

'Which one?'

'The test that begins *Are you straight?*'

'*I am.*'

'*How straight?*'

'*As straight as a rush.*'

'*Go on then.*'

'*In truth, in trust, in unity and liberty.*'

'*What have you got in your hand?*'

'*A green bough.*'

'*Where did it first grow?*'

'*In America.*'

'*Where did it bud?*'

'*In France.*'

'*Where are you going to plant it?*'

'Nay, I forget what follows. It was not the test I took, you know. Far from it.'

'No, I am sure it was not. I did, however: the word liberty seemed to me to glow with meaning, in those days. But even then I was sceptical about *unity* – our society made such very strange bedfellows. Priests, deists, atheists and Presbyterians; visionary republicans, Utopists and men who merely disliked the Beresfords. You and your friends were all primarily for emancipation, as I recall.'

'Emancipation and reform. I for one had no notion of any republic; nor had my friends of the Committee, of course.

With Ireland in her present state a republic would quickly become something little better than a democracy. The genius of the country is quite opposed to a republic. A *Catholic* republic! How ludicrous.'

'Is it brandy in that case-bottle?'

'It is.'

'The answer to that last part of the test was *In the crown of Great Britain,* by the way. The glasses are just behind you. I know it was at Rathfarnham,' Stephen went on, 'for I had spent the whole of that afternoon trying to persuade him not to go on with his shatter-brained plans for the rising: I told him I was opposed to violence – always had been – and that even if I were not I should withdraw, were he to persist with such wild, visionary schemes – that they would be his own ruin, Pamela's ruin, the ruin of his cause and the ruin of God knows how many brave, devoted men. He looked at me with that sweet, troubled look, as though he were sorry for me, and he said he had to meet you and Kenmare. He had not understood me at all.'

'Have you any news of Lady Edward – of Pamela?'

'Only that she is in Hamburg and that the family looks after her.'

'She was the most beautiful woman that ever I saw, and the kindest. None so brave.'

'Aye,' thought Stephen, and stared into his brandy. 'That afternoon,' he said, 'I spent more spirit than ever I spent in my life. Even then I no longer cared for any cause or any theory of government on earth; I would not have lifted a finger for any nation's independence, fancied or real; and yet I had to reason with as much ardour as though I were filled with the same enthusiasm as in the first days of the Revolution, when we were all overflowing with virtue and love.'

'Why? Why did you have to speak so?'

'Because I had to convince him that his plans were disastrously foolish, that they were known to the Castle and that he was surrounded by traitors and informers. I reasoned as closely and cogently as ever I could – better than ever I thought I could – and he did not follow me at all. His attention wandered. "Look," says he, "there's a redbreast in that yew by the path." All he knew was that I was opposed to him, so he closed his mind; if, indeed, he was *capable* of following me, which perhaps he was not. Poor Edward! *Straight as a rush*; and so many of them around him were as crooked as men can well be – Reynolds, Corrigan, Davis . . . Oh, it was pitiful.'

'And would you indeed not lift a finger, even for the moderate aims?'

'I would not. With the revolution in France gone to pure loss I was already chilled beyond expression. And now, with what I saw in '98, on both sides, the wicked folly and the wicked brute cruelty, I have had such a sickening of men in masses, and of causes, that I would not cross this room to reform parliament or prevent the union or to bring about the millennium. I speak only for myself, mind – it is my own truth alone – but man as part of a movement or a crowd is indifferent to me. He is inhuman. And I have nothing to do with nations, or nationalism. The only feelings I have – for what they are – are for men as individuals; my loyalties, such as they may be, are to private persons alone.'

'Patriotism will not do?'

'My dear creature, I have done with all debate. But you know as well as I, patriotism is a word; and one that generally comes to mean either *my country, right or wrong,* which is infamous, or *my country is always right,* which is imbecile.'

'Yet you stopped Captain Aubrey playing *Croppies lie down* the other day.'

'Oh, I am not consistent, of course; particularly in little things. Who is? He did not know the meaning of the tune, you know. He has never been in Ireland at all, and he was in the West Indies at the time of the rising.'

'And I was at the Cape, thank God. Was it terrible?'

'Terrible? I cannot, by any possible energy of words,

express to you the blundering, the delay, the murderous confusion and the stupidity of it all. It accomplished nothing; it delayed independence for a hundred years; it sowed hatred and violence; it spawned out a vile race of informers and things like Major Sirr. And, incidentally, it made us the prey of any chance blackmailing informer.' He paused. 'But as for that song, I acted as I did partly because it is disagreeable to me to listen to it and partly because there were several Irish sailors within hearing, and not one of them an Orangeman; and it would be a pity to have them hate him when nothing in the manner of insult was within his mind's reach.'

'You are very fond of him, I believe?'

'Am I? Yes; perhaps I am. I would not call him a gremial friend – I have not known him long enough – but I am very much attached to him. I am sorry that you are not.'

'I am sorry for it too. I came willing to be pleased. I had heard of him as wild and freakish, but a good seaman, and I was very willing to be pleased. But feelings are not to command.'

'No. But it is curious: at least it is curious to me, the midpoint, with esteem – indeed, more than esteem – for both of you. Are there particular lapses you reproach him with? If we were still eighteen I should say "What's wrong with Jack Aubrey?" '

'And perhaps I should reply "Everything, since he has a command and I have not," ' said James, smiling. 'But come, now, I can hardly criticize your friend to your face.'

'Oh, he has faults, sure. I know he is intensely ambitious where his profession is at issue and impatient of any restraint. My concern was to know just what it was that offended you in him. Or is it merely *non amo te, Sabidi*?'

'Perhaps so: it is hard to say. He can be a very agreeable companion, of course, but there are times when he shows that particular beefy arrogant English insensibility . . . and there is certainly one thing that jars on me – his great eagerness for prizes. The sloop's discipline and training is more like that of a starving privateer than a King's ship. When we were chasing that miserable polacre he could not bring himself to leave the deck all night long – anyone would have thought we were after a man-of-war, with some honour at the end of the chase. And this prize here was scarcely clear of the *Sophie* before he was exercising the great guns again, roaring away with both broadsides.'

'Is a privateer a discreditable thing? I ask in pure ignorance.'

'Well, a privateer is there for a different motive altogether. A privateer does not fight for honour, but for gain. It is a mercenary. Profit is its *raison d'être*.'

'May not the exercising of the great guns have a more honourable end in view?'

'Oh, certainly. I may very well be unjust – jealous – wanting in generosity. I beg your pardon if I have offended you. And I willingly confess he is an excellent seaman.'

'Lord, James, we have known one another long enough to tell our minds freely, without any offence. Will you reach me the bottle?'

'Well, then,' said James, 'if I may speak as freely as though I were in an empty room, I will tell you this: I think his encouragement of that fellow Marshall is indecent, not to use a grosser word.'

'Do I follow you, now?'

'You know about the man?'

'What about the man?'

'That he is a paederast?'

'Maybe.'

'I have proof positive. I had it in Cagliari, if it had been necessary. And he is enamoured of Captain Aubrey – toils like a galley-slave – would holystone the quarter-deck if allowed – hounds the men with far more zeal than the bosun – anything for a smile from him.'

Stephen nodded. 'Yes,' he said. 'But surely you do not think Jack Aubrey shares his tastes?'

'No. But I do think he is aware of them and that he encour-
ages the man. Oh, this is a very foul, dirty way of speaking . . .
I go too far. Perhaps I am drunk. We have nearly emptied the
bottle.'

Stephen shrugged. 'No. But you are quite mistaken, you
know. I can assure you, speaking in all sober earnest, that he
has no notion of it. He is not very sharp in some ways; and in
his simple view of the world, paederasts are dangerous only to
powder-monkeys and choir-boys, or to those epicene creatures that are to be found in Mediterranean brothels. I made
a circuitous attempt at enlightening him a little, but he
looked very knowing and said, "Don't tell *me* about rears and
vices; I have been in the Navy all my life." '

'Then surely he must be wanting a little in penetration?'

'James, I trust there was no *mens rea* in that remark?'

'I must go on deck,' said James, looking at his watch. He
came back some time later, having seen the wheel relieved
and having checked their course; he brought a gust of cool
night air with him and sat in silence until it had dispersed in
the gentle lamp-lit warmth. Stephen had opened another
bottle.

'There are times when I am not altogether just,' said James,
reaching for his glass. 'I am too touchy, I know; but sometimes, when you are surrounded with Proddies and you hear
their silly, underbred cant, you fly out. And since you cannot
fly out in one direction, you fly out in another. It is a continual tension, as you ought to know, if anyone.'

Stephen looked at him very attentively, but said nothing.

'You knew I was a Catholic?' said James.

'No,' said Stephen. 'I was aware that some of your family
were, of course; but as for you . . . Do you not find it puts you
in a difficult position?' he asked, hesitantly. 'With that oath . .
. the penal laws . . .?'

'Not in the least,' said James. 'My mind is perfectly at ease,
as far as that is concerned.'

'That is what you think, my poor friend,' said Stephen to

himself, pouring out another glass to hide his expression.

For a moment it seemed that James Dillon might take this further, but he did not: some delicate balance changed, and now the talk ran on and on to friends they had shared and to delightful days they had spent together in what seemed such a very distant past. How many people they had known! How valuable, or amusing, or respectable some of them had been! They talked their second bottle dry, and James went up on deck again.

He came down in half an hour, and as he stepped into the cabin he said, as though he were catching straight on to an interrupted conversation, 'And then, of course, there is that whole question of promotion. I will tell you, just for your secret ear alone and although it sounds odious, that I thought I should be given a command after that affair in the *Dart*; and being passed over does rankle cruelly.' He paused, and then asked, 'Who was it who was said to have earned more by his prick than his practice?'

'Selden. But in this instance I conceive the common gossip is altogether out; as I understand it, this was the ordinary operation of interest. Mark you, I make no claim of outstanding chastity – I merely say that in Jack Aubrey's case the consideration is irrelevant.'

'Well, be that as it may, I look for promotion: like every other sailor I value it very highly, so I tell you in all simplicity; and being under a prize-hunting captain is not the quickest path to it.'

'Well, I know nothing of nautical affairs: but I wonder, I wonder, James, whether it is not too easy for a rich man to despise money – to mistake the real motives . . . To pay too much attention to mere words, and – '

'Surely to God you would never call me rich?'

'I have ridden over your land.'

'It's three-quarters of it mountain, and one quarter bog; and even if they were to pay their rent for the rest it would only be a few hundred a year – barely a thousand.'

'My heart bleeds for you. I have never yet known a man admit that he was either rich or asleep: perhaps the poor man and the wakeful man have some great moral advantage. How does it arise? But to return – surely he is as brave a commander as you could wish, and as likely as any man to lead you to glorious and remarkable actions?'

'Would you guarantee his courage?'

'So here is the true gravamen at last,' thought Stephen, and he said, 'I would not; I do not know him well enough. But I should be astonished, *astonished,* if he were to prove shy. What makes you think he is?'

'I do not say he is. I should be very sorry to say anything against any man's courage without proof. But we should have had that galley. In another twenty minutes we could have boarded and carried her.'

'Oh? I know nothing of these things, and I was downstairs at the time; but I understood that the only prudent thing to do was to turn about, to protect the rest of the convoy.'

'Prudence is a great virtue, of course,' said James.

'Well. And promotion means a great deal to you, so?'

'Of course it does. There never was an officer worth a farthing that did not long to succeed and hoist his flag at last. But I can see in your eye that you think me inconsistent. Understand my position: I want no republic – I stand by settled, established institutions, and by authority so long as it is not tyranny. All I ask is an independent parliament that represents the responsible men of the kingdom and not merely a squalid parcel of place-men and place-seekers. Given that, I am perfectly happy with the English connexion, perfectly happy with the two kingdoms: I can drink the loyal toast without choking, I do assure you.'

'Why are you putting out the lamp?'

James smiled. 'It is dawn,' he said, nodding towards the grey, severe light in the cabin window. 'Shall we go on deck? We may have raised the high land of Minorca by now, or we shall very soon; and I think I can promise you some of those

birds the sailors call shearwaters if we lay her in towards the
cliff of Fornells.'

Yet with one foot on the companion-ladder he turned and
looked into Stephen's face. 'I cannot tell what possessed me
to speak so rancorously,' he said, passing his hand over his
forehead and looking both unhappy and bewildered. 'I do not
think I have ever done so before. Have not expressed myself
well – clumsy, inaccurate, not what I meant nor what I meant
to say. We understood one another better before ever I
opened my mouth.'

6

M R FLOREY the surgeon was a bachelor; he had a large
house high up by Santa Maria's, and with the broad,
easy conscience of an unmarried man he invited Dr Maturin
to stay whenever the *Sophie* should come in for stores or
repairs, putting a room at his disposal for his baggage and his
collections – a room that already housed the hortus siccus
that Mr Cleghorn, surgeon-major to the garrison for close on
thirty years, had gathered in countless dusty volumes.

It was an enchanting house for meditation, backing on to
the very top of Mahon's cliff and overhanging the merchants'
quay at a dizzy height – so high that the noise and business of
the harbour was impersonal, no more than an accompaniment to thought. Stephen's room was at the back, on this cool
northern side looking over the water; and he sat there just
inside the open window with his feet in a basin of water, writing his diary while the swifts (common, pallid and Alpine)
raced shrieking through the torrid, quivering air between him
and the *Sophie*, a toy-like object far down on the other side of
the harbour, tied up to the victualling-wharf.

'So James Dillon is a Catholic,' he wrote in his minute and
secret shorthand. 'He used not to be. That is to say, he was not

a Catholic in the sense that it would have made any marked
difference to his behaviour, or have rendered the taking of an
oath intolerably painful. He was not in any way a religious
man. Has there been some conversion, some Loyolan change?
I hope not. How many crypto-Catholics are there in the service? I should like to ask him; but that would be indiscreet. I
remember Colonel Despard's telling me that in England
Bishop Challoner gave a dozen dispensations a year for the
occasional taking of the sacrament according to the Anglican
rite. Colonel T—, of the Gordon riots, was a Catholic. Did
Despard's remark refer only to the army? I never thought to
ask him at the time. Quaere: is this the cause for James Dillon's agitated state of mind? Yes, I think so. Some strong pressure is certainly at work. What is more, it appears to me that
this is a critical time for him, a lesser climacteric – a time that
will settle him in that particular course he will never leave
again, but will persevere in for the rest of his life. It has often
seemed to me that towards this period (in which we all three
lie, more or less) men strike out their permanent characters;
or have those characters struck into them. Merriment, roaring
high spirits before this: then some chance concatenation, or
some hidden predilection (or rather inherent bias) working
through, and the man is in the road he cannot leave but must
go on, making it deeper and deeper (a groove, or channel),
until he is lost in his mere character – persona – no longer
human, but an accretion of qualities belonging to this character. James Dillon was a delightful being. Now he is closing in.
It is odd – will I say heart-breaking? – how cheerfulness goes:
gaiety of mind, natural free-springing joy. Authority is its great
enemy – the assumption of authority. I know few men over
fifty that seem to me entirely human: virtually none who has
long exercised authority. The senior post-captains here; Admiral Warne. Shrivelled men (shrivelled in essence: not, alas, in
belly). Pomp, an unwholesome diet, a cause of choler, a pleasure paid too late and at too high a price, like lying with a pep-
pered paramour. Yet Ld Nelson, by Jack Aubrey's account, is

as direct and unaffected and amiable a man as could be wished. So, indeed, in most ways is JA himself; though a certain careless arrogancy of power appears at times. His cheerfulness, at all events, is with him still. How long will it last? What woman, political cause, disappointment, wound, disease, untoward child, defeat, what strange surprising accident will take it all away? But I am concerned for James Dillon: he is as mercurial as ever he was – more so – only now it is all ten octaves lower down and in a darker key; and sometimes I am afraid in a black humour he will do himself a mischief. I would give so much to bring him cordially friends with Jack Aubrey. They are so alike in so many ways, and James is made for friendship: when he sees that he is mistaken about JA's conduct, surely he will come round? But will he ever find this out, or is JA to be the focus of his discontent? If so there is little hope; for the discontent, the inner contest, must at times be very severe in a man so humourless (on occasion) and so very exigent upon the point of honour. He is obliged to reconcile the irreconcilable more often than most men; and he is less qualified to do so. And whatever he may say he knows as well as I do that he is in danger of a horrible confrontation: suppose it had been he who took Wolfe Tone in Lough Swilly? What if Emmet persuades the French to invade again? And what if Bonaparte makes friends with the Pope? It is not impossible. But on the other hand, JD is a mercurial creature, and if once, on the upward rise, he comes to love JA as he should, he will not change – never was a more loyal affection. I would give a great deal to bring them friends.'

He sighed and put down his pen. He put it down upon the cover of a jar in which there lay one of the finest asps he had ever seen, thick, venomous, snub-nosed, coiled down in spirits of wine, with its slit-pupilled eye looking at him through the glass. This asp was one of the fruits of the days they spent in Mahon before the *Sophie* came in, a third prize at her tail, a fair-sized Spanish tartan. And next to the asp lay two visible results of the *Sophie*'s activity: a watch and a telescope. The

watch pointed at twenty minutes to the hour, so he picked up
the telescope and focused it upon the sloop. Jack was still
aboard, conspicuous in his best uniform, fussing amidships
with Dillon and the bosun over some point of the upper rigging: they were all pointing upwards, and inclining their persons from side to side in ludicrous unison.

Leaning forward against the rail of the little balcony, he
trained his glass along the quay towards the head of the harbour. Almost at once he saw the familiar scarlet face of
George Pearce, ordinary seaman, thrown back skywards in an
ecstasy of mirth: there was a little group of his shipmates
with him, along by the huddle of one-storeyed wineshops that
stretched out towards the tanneries; and they were passing
their time at playing ducks and drakes on the still water.
These men belonged to the two prize-crews and they had
been allowed to stay ashore, whereas the other Sophies were
still aboard. Both had shared in the first distribution of prize-
money, however; and looking with closer attention at the silvery gleam of the skipping missiles and at the frenzied diving
of the little naked boys out in the noisome shallows, Stephen
saw that they were getting rid of their wealth in the most
compendious manner known to man.

Now a boat was putting off from the *Sophie*, and in his
glass he saw the coxswain nursing Jack's fiddle-case with
stiff, conscious dignity. He leant back, took one foot out of
the water – tepid now – and gazed at it for a while, musing
upon the comparative anatomy of the lower members in the
higher mammals – in horses – in apes – in the Pongo of the
African travellers, or M. de Buffon's Jocko – sportive and gre-
garious in youth, sullen, morose and withdrawn in age.
Which was the true state of the Pongo? 'Who am I,' he
thought, 'to affirm that the gay young ape is not merely the
chrysalis, as it were, the pupa of the grim old solitary? That
the second state is not the natural inevitable culmination –
the Pongo's true condition, alas?'

'I was contemplating on the Pongo,' he said aloud as the

door opened and Jack walked in with a look of eager expectation, carrying a roll of music.

'I am sure you were,' cried Jack. 'A damned creditable thing to be contemplating on, too. Now be a good fellow and take your other foot out of that basin – why on earth did you put it in? – and pull on your stockings, I beg. We have not a moment to lose. No, not blue stockings: we are going on to Mrs Harte's party – to her rout.'

'Must I put on silk stockings?'

'Certainly you must put on silk stockings. And do show a leg, my dear chap: we shall be late, without you spread a little more canvas.'

'You are always in such a hurry,' said Stephen peevishly, groping among his possessions. A Montpellier snake glided out with a dry rustling sound and traversed the room in a series of extraordinarily elegant curves, its head held up some eighteen inches above the ground.

'Oh, oh, oh,' cried Jack, leaping on to a chair. 'A snake!'

'Will these do?' asked Stephen. 'They have a hole in them.'

'Is it poisonous?'

'Extremely so. I dare say it will attack you, directly. I have very little doubt of it. Was I to put the silk stockings over my worsted stockings, sure the hole would not show: but then, I should stifle with heat. Do not you find it uncommonly hot?'

'Oh, it must be two fathoms long. Tell me, is it really poisonous? On your oath now?'

'If you thrust your hand down its throat as far as its back teeth you may meet a little venom; but not otherwise. Malpolon monspessulanus is a very innocent serpent. I think of carrying a dozen aboard, for the rats – ah, if only I had more time, and if it were not for this foolish, illiberal persecution of reptiles . . . What a pitiful figure you do cut upon that chair, to be sure. *Barney, Barney, buck or doe, Has kept me out of Channel Row*,' he sang to the serpent; and, deaf as an adder though it was, it looked happily into his face while he carried it away.

Their first visit was to Mr Brown's, of the dockyard, where, after greetings, introductions and congratulations upon Jack's good fortune, they played the Mozart B flat quartet, hunting it along with great industry and good will, Miss playing a sweet-toned, though weak, viola. They had never played all together before, had never rehearsed this particular work, and the resulting sound was ragged in the extreme; but they took immense pleasure there in the heart of it, and their audience, Mrs Brown and a white cat, sat mildly knitting, perfectly satisfied with the performance.

Jack was in tearing high spirits, but his great respect for music kept him in order throughout the quartet. It was during the collation that followed – a pair of fowls, a glazed tongue, sillabub, flummery and maids of honour – that he began to break out. Being thirsty, he drank off two or three glasses of Sillery without noticing them: and presently his face grew redder and even more cheerful, his voice more decidedly masculine and his laughter more frequent: he gave them a highly-coloured account of Stephen's having sawn the gunner's head off and fixed it on again, better than before; and from time to time his bright blue eye wandered towards Miss's bosom, which the fashion of that year (magnified by the distance from Paris) had covered with no more than a very, very little piece of gauze.

Stephen emerged from his reverie to see Mrs Brown looking grave, Miss looking demurely down at her plate and Mr Brown, who had also drunk a good deal, starting on a story that could not possibly come to good. Mrs Brown made great allowances for officers who had been long at sea, particularly those who had come in from a successful cruise and were disposed to be merry; but she made less for her husband, and she knew this story of old, as well as this somewhat glassy look. 'Come, my dear,' she said to her daughter. 'I think we will leave the gentlemen now.'

MOLLY HARTE'S ROUT was a big, miscellaneous affair, with nearly all the officers, ecclesiastics, civilians, merchants and Minorcan notables – so many of them that she had a great awning spread over Señor Martinez' patio to hold all her guests, while the military band from Fort St Philip played to them from what was ordinarily the commandant's office.

'Allow me to name my friend – my particular friend – and surgeon, Dr Maturin,' said Jack, leading Stephen up to their hostess. 'Mrs Harte.'

'Your servant, ma'am,' said Stephen, making a leg.

'I am very happy to see you here, sir,' said Mrs Harte, instantly prepared to dislike him very much indeed.

'Dr Maturin, Captain Harte,' went on Jack.

'Happy,' said Captain Harte, disliking him already, but for an entirely opposite reason, looking over Stephen's head and holding out two fingers, only a little way in front of his sagging belly. Stephen looked deliberately at them, left them dangling there and silently moved his head in a bow whose civil insolence so exactly matched his welcome that Molly Harte said to herself, 'I shall like that man.' They went on to leave room for others, for the tide was flowing fast – the sea-officers all appeared within seconds of the appointed time.

'Here's Lucky Jack Aubrey,' cried Bennet of the Aurore. 'Upon my word, you young fellows do pretty well for yourselves. I could hardly get into Mahon for the number of your captures. I wish you joy of them, in course; but you must leave something for us old codgers to retire upon, Eh? Eh?'

'Why, sir,' said Jack, laughing and going redder still, 'it is only beginner's luck – it will soon be out, I am sure, and then we shall be sucking our thumbs again.'

There were half a dozen sea-officers round him, contemporaries and seniors; they all congratulated him, some sadly, some a little enviously, but all with that direct good-will Stephen had noticed so often in the Navy; and as they drifted off in a body towards a table with three enormous punch-bowls and a regiment of glasses upon it, Jack told them, in an uninhibited wealth of sea-jargon, exactly how each chase had behaved. They listened silently, with keen attention, nodding their heads at certain points and partially closing their eyes; and Stephen observed to himself that at some levels complete communication between men was possible. After this both he and his attention wandered; holding a glass of arrack-punch, he took up his stand next to an orange-tree, and he stood looking quite happy, gazing now at the uniforms on the one hand and now through the orange-tree on the other, where there were sofas and low chairs with women sitting in them hoping that men would bring them ices and sorbets; and hoping, as far as the sailors on his left were concerned, in vain. They sighed patiently and hoped that their husbands, brothers, fathers, lovers would not get too drunk; and above all that none of them would grow quarrelsome.

Time passed; an eddy in the party's slow rotatory current brought Jack's group nearer the orange-tree, and Stephen heard him say, 'There a hellish great sea running tonight.'

'It's all very well, Aubrey,' said a post-captain, almost immediately afterward. 'But your Sophies used to be a quiet, decent set of men ashore. And now they have two pennies to rub together they kick up bob's a-dying like – well, I don't know. Like a set of mad baboons. They beat the crew of my cousin Oaks's barge cruelly, upon the absurd pretence of having a physician aboard, and so having the right to tie up ahead of a barge belonging to a ship of the line which carries no more than a surgeon – a very absurd pretence. Their two pennies have sent them out of their wits.'

'I am sorry Captain Oak's men were beat, sir,' said Jack, with a decent look of concern. 'But the fact is true. We do have a physician aboard – an amazing hand with a saw or a clyster.' Jack gazed about him in a very benevolent fashion. 'He was with me not a pint or so ago. Opened our gunner's skull, roused out his brains, set them to rights, stuffed them back in again – I could not bear to look, I assure you, gentlemen – bade the armourer take a crown piece, hammer it out thin into a little dome, do you see, or basin, and so clapped it on, screwed it down and sewed up his scalp as neatly as a sailmaker. Now that's what I call real physic – none of your damned pills and delay. Why, there he is . . .'

They greeted him kindly, urged him to drink a glass of punch – another glass of punch – they had all taken a great deal; it was quite wholesome – excellent punch, the very thing for so hot a day. The talk flowed on, with only Stephen and a Captain Nevin remaining a little silent. Stephen noticed a pondering, absorbed look in Captain Nevin's eye – a look very familiar to him – and he was not surprised to be led away behind the orange-tree to be told in a low confidential fluent earnest voice of Captain Nevin's difficulty in digesting even the simplest dishes. Captain Nevin's dyspepsy had puzzled the faculty for years, for *years*, sir; but he was sure it would yield to Stephen's superior powers; he had better give Dr Maturin all the details he could remember, for it was a very singular, interesting case, as Sir John Abel had told him – Stephen knew Sir John? – but to be quite frank (lowering his voice and glancing furtively round) he had to admit there were certain difficulties in – in *evacuation*, too . . . His voice ran on, low and urgent, and Stephen stood with his hands behind his back, his head bowed, his face gravely inclined in a listening attitude. He was not, indeed, inattentive; but his attention was not so wholly taken up that he did not hear Jack cry, 'Oh, yes, yes! The rest of them are certainly coming ashore – they are lining the rail in their shore-going rig, with money in their pockets, their eyes staring out of their heads and their pricks a yard long.' He could scarcely have avoided hearing it, for Jack had a fine carrying voice, and his remark happened to drop into one of those curious silences that occur even in very numerous assemblies.

Stephen regretted the remark; he regretted its effect upon the ladies the other side of the orange-tree, who were standing up and mincing away with many an indignant glance; but how much more did he regret Jack's crimson face, the look of maniac glee in his blazing eyes and his triumphant, 'You needn't hurry, ladies – they won't be allowed off the sloop till the evening gun.'

A determined upsurge of talk drowned any possibility of further observations of this kind, and Captain Nevin was settling down to his colon again when Stephen felt a hand on his arm, and there was Mrs Harte, smiling at Captain Nevin in such a manner that he backed and lost himself behind the punch-bowls.

'Dr Maturin, please take your friend away,' said Molly Harte in a low, urgent tone. 'Tell him his ship is on fire – tell him anything. Only get him away – he will do himself *such* damage.'

Stephen nodded. He lowered his head and walked directly into the group, took Jack by the elbow and said, 'Come, come, come,' in an odd, imperative half-whisper, bowing to those whose conversation he had interrupted. 'There is not a moment to be lost.'

'THE SOONER WE are at sea the better,' muttered Jack Aubrey, looking anxiously into the dim light over against Mahon quay. Was the boat his own launch with the remaining liberty-men, or was it a messenger from the angry, righteous commandant's office, bringing orders that would break off the *Sophie*'s cruise? He was still a little shattered from his night's excess, but the steadier part of his mind assured him from time to time that he had done himself no good, that disciplinary action could be taken against him without any man thinking it unjust or oppressive, and that he was exceedingly averse to any immediate meeting with Captain Harte.

What air was moving came from the westward – an unusual wind, and one that brought all the foul reek of the tanneries drifting wetly across. But it would serve to help the *Sophie* down the long harbour and out to sea. Out to sea, where he could not be betrayed by his own tongue; where Stephen could not get himself into bad odour with authority;

and where that infernal child Babbington did not have to be rescued from aged women of the town. And where James Dillon could not fight a duel. He had only heard a rumour of it, but it was one of those deadly little after-supper garrison affairs that might have cost him his lieutenant – as valuable an officer as he had ever sailed with, for all his starchiness and unpredictability.

The boat reappeared under the stern of the *Aurore*. It was the launch and it was filled with liberty-men: there were still one or two merry souls among them, but on the whole the Sophies who could walk were quite unlike those who had gone ashore – they had no money left, for one thing, and they were grey, drooping and mumchance for another. Those who could not walk were laid in a row with the bodies recovered earlier, and Jack said, 'How is the tally, Mr Ricketts?'

'All aboard, sir,' said the midshipman wearily, 'except for Jessup, cook's mate, who broke his leg falling down Pigtail Stairs, and Sennet, Richards and Chambers, of the foretop, who went off to George Town with some soldiers.'

'Sergeant Quinn?'

But there was no answer to be had from Sergeant Quinn: he could, and did, remain upright, bolt upright, but his only reply was 'Yes, sir' and a salute to everything that was proposed to him.

'All but three of the marines are aboard, sir,' said James privately.

'Thank you, Mr Dillon,' said Jack, looking over towards the town again: a few pale lights were moving against the darkness of the cliff. 'Then I think we shall make sail.'

'Without waiting for the rest of the water, sir?'

'What does it amount to? Two tons, I believe. Yes: we will take that up another time, together with our stragglers. Now, Mr Watt, all hands to unmoor; and let it be done silently, if you please.'

He said this partly because of a cruel darting agony in his head that made the prospect of roaring and bellowing won-

derfully disagreeable and partly because he wished the
Sophie's departure to excite no attention whatsoever. Fortunately she was moored with simple warps fore and aft, so
there would be no slow weighing of anchors, no stamp and go
at the capstan, no acid shrieking of the fiddle; in any case,
the comparatively sober members of the crew were too jaded
for anything but a sour, mute, expeditious casting-off – no
jolly tars, no hearts of oak, no Britons never, never, in this
grey stench of a crapulous dawn. Fortunately, too, he had
seen to the repairs, stores and victualling (apart from that
cursed last voyage of water) before he or anyone else had set
foot on shore; and rarely had he appreciated the reward of
virtue more than when the Sophie's jib filled and her head
came round, pointing eastward to the sea, a wooded,
watered, well-found vessel beginning her journey back to
independence.

An hour later they were in the narrows, with the town and
its evil smells sunk in the haze behind them and the brilliant
open water out in front. The Sophie's bowsprit was pointing
almost exactly at the white blaze on the horizon that showed
the coming of the sun, and the breeze was turning northerly,
freshening as it veered. Some of the night's corpses were in
lumpish motion. Presently a hose-pipe would be turned on to
them, the deck would return to its rightful condition and the
sloop's daily round would begin again.

AN AIR OF surly virtue hung over the Sophie as she made
her tedious, frustrating way south and west towards her cruising-ground through calms, uncertain breezes and headwinds
– winds that grew so perverse once they had made their offing that the little Ayre Island beyond the eastern point of
Minorca hung obstinately on the northern horizon, sometimes larger, sometimes smaller, but always there.

Thursday, and all hands were piped to witness punishment.
The two watches stood on either side of the main-deck, with
the cutter and the launch towing behind to make more room;

the marines were lined up with their usual precision from number three gun aft; and the little quarter-deck was crowded with the officers.

'Mr Ricketts, where is your dirk?' said James Dillon sharply.

'Forgot it, sir. Beg pardon, sir,' whispered the mid-shipman.

'Put it on at once, and don't you presume to come on deck improperly dressed.'

Young Ricketts cast a guilty look at his captain as he darted below, and he read nothing but confirmation on Jack's frowning visage. Indeed, Jack's views were identical with Dillon's: these wretched men were going to be flogged and it was their right to have it done with due ceremony – all hands gravely present, the officers with their gold-laced hats and swords, the drummer there to beat a roll.

Henry Andrews, the ship's corporal, brought up his charges one by one: John Harden, Joseph Bussell, Thomas Cross, Timothy Bryant, Isaac Isaacs, Peter Edwards and John Surel, all accused of drunkenness. No one had anything to say for them: not one had anything to say for himself. 'A dozen apiece,' said Jack. 'And if there were any justice on earth you would have two dozen, Cross. A responsible fellow like you – a gunner's mate – for shame.'

It was the *Sophie*'s custom to flog at the capstan, not at a grating: the men came gloomily forward, slowly stripped off their shirts and adapted themselves to the squat cylinder; and the bosun's mates, John Bell and John Morgan, tied their wrists on the far side, more for the form than anything else. Then John Bell stood clear, swinging his cat easily in his right hand, with his eye on Jack. Jack nodded and said, 'Carry on.'

'One,' said the bosun solemnly, as the nine knotted cords sighed through the air and clapped against the seaman's tense bare back. 'Two. Three. Four . . .'

So it went on; and once again Jack's cold, accustomed eye noticed how cleverly the bosun's mate set the knotted ends lashing against the capstan itself, yet without giving any appearance of favouring his shipmate. 'It's very well,' he reflected, 'but either they are getting into the spirit-room or some son of a bitch has brought a store of liquor aboard. If I could find him, I should have a proper grating rigged, and there would be none of this hocus-pocus.' This amount of drunkenness was more than was right: seven in one day. It was nothing to do with the men's lurid joys ashore, for that was all over – no more than a memory; and as for the paralytic state of the seamen awash in the scuppers as the sloop stood out, that was forgotten too – put down to the easy ways of port, to relaxed harbour discipline, and never held against them. This was something else. Only yesterday he had hesitated about exercising the guns after dinner, because of the number of men he suspected of having had too much: it was so easy for a tipsy fool to get his foot under a recoiling carriage or his face in front of a muzzle. And in the end he had had them merely run in and out, without firing.

Different ships had different traditions about calling out: the old Sophies kept mum, but Edwards (one of the new men) had been drafted from the *King's Fisher*, where they did not, and he uttered a great howling Oh at the first stroke, which so disturbed the young bosun's mate that the next two or three wavered uncertainly in the air.

'Come now, John Bell,' said the bosun reproachfully, not from any sort of malignance towards Edwards, whom he regarded with the placid impartiality of a butcher weighing up a lamb, but because a job of work had to be done proper; and the rest of the flogging did at least give Edwards some excuse for his shattering crescendo. Shattering, that is to say, to poor John Surel, a meagre little quota-man from Exeter, who had never been beaten before and who now added the crime of incontinence to that of drunkenness; but he was flogged, for all that, in great squalor, weeping and roaring most pitifully, as the flustered Bell laid into him hard and fast, to get it over quickly.

'How utterly barbarous this would seem to a spectator that was not habituated to it,' reflected Stephen. 'And how little it

matters to those that are. Though that child does appear concerned.' Babbington was indeed looking a little pale and anxious as the unseemly business came to an end, with the
moaning Surel handed over to his shamefaced messmates
and hurried away.

But how transient was this young gentleman's pallor and
anxiety! Not ten minutes after the swabber had removed all
traces of the scene, Babbington was flying about the upper
rigging in pursuit of Ricketts, with the clerk toiling with laborious, careful delight a great way behind.

'Who is that skylarking?' asked Jack, seeing vague forms
through the thin canvas of the main royal. 'The boys?'

'The young gentlemen, your honour,' said the quarter-master.

'That reminds me,' said Jack. 'I want to see them.'

Not long after this the pallor and the anxiety were back
again, and with good reason. The midshipmen were supposed
to take noon observations to work out the vessel's position,
which they were to write on a piece of paper. These pieces of
paper were called *the young gentlemen's workings* and they
were delivered to the captain by the marine sentry, with the
words, 'The young gentlemen's workings, sir'; to which Captain Allen (an indolent, easy-going man) had been accustomed to reply, '– the young gentlemen's workings', and toss
them out of the window.

Hitherto, Jack had been too busy working up his crew to
pay much attention to the education of his midshipmen, but
he had looked at yesterday's slips and they, with a very suspicious unanimity, had shown the *Sophie* in 39°21´N., which
was fair enough, but also in a longitude that she could only
have reached by cleaving the mountain-range behind Valencia to a depth of thirty-seven miles.

'What do you mean by sending me this nonsense?' he asked
them. It was not really an answerable question; nor were
many of the others that he propounded, and they did not, in
fact, attempt to answer them; but they agreed that they were

not there to amuse themselves, nor for their manly beauty, but rather to learn their professions; that their journals (which they fetched) were neither accurate, full, nor up to date, and that the ship's cat would have written them better; that they would for the future pay the greatest attention to Mr Marshall's observation and reckoning; that they would prick the chart daily with him; and that no man was fit to pass for a lieutenant, let alone bear any command ('May God forgive me,' said Jack, in an internal aside) who could not instantly tell the position of his ship to within a minute – nay, to within thirty seconds. Furthermore, they would show up their journals every Sunday, cleanly and legibly written.

'You *can* write decently, I suppose? Otherwise you must go to school to the clerk.' They hoped so, sir, they were sure; they should do their best. But he did not seem convinced and desired them to sit down on that locker, take those pens and these sheets of paper, to pass him yonder book, which would answer admirably for them to be read to out of from.

This was how it came about that Stephen, pausing in the quietness of his sick-bay to reflect upon the case of the patient whose pulse beat weak and thin beneath his fingers, heard Jack's voice, unnaturally slow, grave and terrible, come wafting down the wind-sail that brought fresh air below. 'The quarterdeck of a man-of-war may justly be considered as a national school for the instruction of a numerous por- tion of our youth; there it is that they acquire a habit of dis- cipline and become instructed in all the interesting minutiae of the service. Punctuality, cleanliness, diligence and dis- patch are regularly inculcated, and such a habit of sobriety and even of self-denial acquired, that cannot fail to prove highly useful. By learning to *obey*, they are also taught how to *command*.

'Well, well, well,' said Stephen to himself, and then turned his mind entirely back to the poor, wasted, hare-lipped creature in the hammock beside him, a recent landman belonging to the starboard watch. 'How old may you be, Cheslin?' he asked.

'Oh, I can't tell you, sir,' said Cheslin with a ghost of impatience in his apathy. 'I reckon I might be about thirty, like.' A long pause. 'I was fifteen when my old father died; and I could count the harvests back, if I put my mind to it. But I can't put my mind to it, sir.'

'No. Listen, Cheslin: you will grow very ill if you do not eat. I will order you some soup, and you must get it down.'

'Thank you, sir, I'm sure. But there's no relish to my meat; and I doubt they would let me have it, any gate.'

'Why did you tell them your calling?'

Cheslin made no reply for a while, but stared dully. 'I dare say I was drunk. 'Tis mortal strong, that grog of theirn. But I never thought they would be so a-dread. Though to be sure the folk over to Carborough and the country beyond, they don't quite like to name it, either.'

At this moment hands were piped to dinner, and the berth-deck, the long space behind the canvas screen that Stephen had had set up to protect the sick-bay a little, was filled with a tumult of hungry men. An orderly tumult, however: each mess of eight men darted to its particular place, hanging tables appeared, dropping instantly from the beams, wooden kids filled with salt pork (another proof that it was Thursday) and peas came from the galley, and the grog, which Mr Pullings had just mixed at the scuttle-butt by the mainmast, was carried religiously below, everyone skipping out of its way, lest a drop should fall.

A lane instantly formed in front of Stephen, and he passed through with smiling faces and kind looks on either side of him; he noticed some of the men whose backs he had oiled earlier that morning looked remarkably cheerful, particularly Edwards, for he, being black, had a smile that flashed far whiter in the gloom; attentive hands tweaked a bench out of his way, and a ship's boy was slewed violently round on his axis and desired 'not to turn his back on the Doctor – where were his fucking manners?' Kind creatures; such good-natured faces; but they were killing Cheslin.

'I HAVE A CURIOUS case in the sick-bay,' he said to James, as they sat digesting figgy-dowdy with the help of a glass of port. 'He is dying of inanition; or will, unless I can stir his torpor.'

'What is his name?'

'Cheslin: he has a hare lip.'

'I know him. A waister – starboard watch – no good to man or beast.'

'Ah? Yet he has been of singular service to men and women, in his time.'

'In what way?'

'He was a sin-eater.'

'Christ.'

'You have spilt your port.'

'Will you tell me about him?' asked James, mopping at the stream of wine.

'Why, it was much the same as with us. When a man died Cheslin would be sent for; there would be a piece of bread on the dead man's breast; he would eat it, taking the sins upon himself. Then they would push a silver piece into his hand and thrust him out of the house, spitting on him and throwing stones as he ran away.'

'I thought it was only a tale, nowadays,' said James.

'No, no. It's common enough, under the silence. But it seems that the seamen look upon it in a more awful light than other people. He let it out and they all turned against him immediately. His mess expelled him; the others will not speak to him, nor allow him to eat or sleep anywhere near them. There is nothing physically wrong with him, yet he will die in about a week unless I can do something.'

'You want to have him seized up at the gangway and given a hundred lashes, Doctor,' called the purser from the cabin where he was casting his accounts. 'When I was in a Guinea-man, between the wars, there was a certain sorts of blacks called Whydaws, or Whydoos, that used to die by the dozen in the Middle Passage, out of mere despair at being taken away from their country and their friends. We used to save a good many by touching them up with a horse-whip in the mornings. But it would be no kindness to preserve that chap, Doctor: the people would only smother him or scrag him or shove him overboard in the end. They will abide a great deal, sailors, but not a Jonah. It's like a white crow – the others peck him to death. Or an albatross. You catch an albatross – it's easy, with a line – and paint a red cross on his bosom, and the others will tear him to pieces before the glass is turned. Many's the good laugh we had with them, off the Cape. But the hands will never let that fellow mess with them, not if the commission lasts for fifty years: ain't that so, Mr Dillon?'

'Never,' said James. 'Why in God's name did he ever come into the Navy? He was a volunteer, not a pressed man.'

'I conceive he was tired of being a white crow,' said Stephen. 'But I will not lose a patient because of sailors' prejudices. He must be put to lie out of reach of their malignance, and if he recovers he shall be my loblolly boy, an isolated employment. So much so, indeed, that the present lad –'

'I beg your pardon, sir, but Captain's compliments and would you like to see something amazingly philosophical?' cried Babbington, darting in like a ball.

After the dimness of the gun-room the white blaze on deck made it almost impossible to see, but through his narrowed eyelids Stephen could distinguish Old Sponge, the taller Greek, standing naked in a pool of water by the starboard hances, dripping still and holding out a piece of copper sheathing with great complacency. On his right stood Jack, his hands behind him and a look of happy triumph on his face: on his left most of the watch, craning and staring. The Greek held the corroded copper sheet out a little farther and, watching Stephen's face intently, he turned it slowly over. On the other side there was a small dark fish with a sucker on the back of its head, clinging fast to the metal.

'A remora!' cried Stephen with all the amazement and delight the Greek and Jack had counted upon, and more. 'A bucket, there! Be gentle with the remora, good Sponge, honest Sponge. Oh, what happiness to see the true remora!'

Old Sponge and Young Sponge had been over the side in this flat calm, scraping away the weed that slowed the *Sophie*'s pace: in the clear water they could be seen creeping along ropes weighed down with nets of shot, holding their breath for two minutes at a time, and sometimes diving right under the keel and coming up the other side from lightness of heart. But it was only now that Old Sponge's accustomed eye had detected their sly common enemy hiding under the garboard-strake. The remora was so strong it had certainly torn the sheathing off, they explained to him; but that was nothing – it was so strong it could hold the sloop motionless, or almost motionless, in a brisk gale! But now they had him – there was an end to his capers now, the dog – and now the *Sophie* would run along like a swan. For a moment Stephen felt inclined to argue, to appeal to their common sense, to point to the nine-inch fish, to the exiguity of its fins; but he was too wise, and too happy, to yield to this temptation, and he jealously carried the bucket down to his cabin, to commune with the remora in peace.

And he was too much of a philosopher to feel much vexation a little later when a pretty breeze reached them, coming in over the rippling sea just abaft the larboard beam, so that the *Sophie* (released from the wicked remora) heeled over in a smooth, steady run that carried her along at seven knots until sunset, when the mast-head cried, 'Land ho! Land on the starboard bow.'

7

THE LAND IN QUESTION was Cape Nao, the southern limit of their cruising ground: it stood up there against the western horizon, a dark certainty, hard in the vagueness along the rim of the sky.

'A very fine landfall, Mr Marshall,' said Jack, coming down from the top, where he had been scrutinizing the cape through his glass. 'The Astronomer Royal could not have done better.'

'Thank you, sir, thank you,' said the master, who had indeed taken a most painstaking series of lunars, as well as the usual observations, to fix the sloop's position. 'Very happy to – approbation –' His vocabulary failed him, and he finished by jerking his head and clasping his hands by way of expression. It was curious to see this burly fellow – a hard-faced, formidable man – moved by a feeling that called for a gentle, graceful outlet; and more than one of the hands exchanged a knowing glance with a shipmate. But Jack had no notion of this whatsoever – he had always attributed Mr Marshall's painstaking, scrupulous navigation and his zeal as an executive officer to natural goodness, to his nautical character; and in any case his mind was now quite taken up with the idea of exercising the guns in the darkness. They were far enough from the land to be unheard, with the wind wafting across; and although there had been a great improvement in the Sophie's gunnery he could not rest easy without some daily approach to perfection. 'Mr Dillon,' he said, 'I could wish the starboard watch to fire against the larboard watch in the darkness. Yes, I know,' he went on, dealing with the objection on his lieutenant's lengthening face, 'but if the exercise is carried on *from* light *into* darkness, even the poorest crews will not get under their guns or fling themselves over the side. So we will make ready a couple of casks, if you please, for the daylight exercise, and another couple, with a lantern, or a flambeau, or something of that kind, for the night.'

Since the first time he had watched a repetition of the exercise (what a great while since it seemed), Stephen had tended to avoid the performance; he disliked the report of the guns, the smell of the powder, the likelihood of painful injury to the men and the certainty of a sky emptied of birds, so he spent his time below, reading with half an ear cocked for the sound of an accident – so easy for something to go wrong, with a briskly-moving gun on a rolling, pitching deck. This evening, however, he came up, ignorant of the approaching din, meaning to go forward to the elm-tree pump – the elm-tree pump, whose head the devoted seamen unshipped for him twice a day – to take advantage of the sloping light as it lit up the under-parts of the brig; and Jack said, 'Why, there you are, Doctor. You have come on deck to see what progress we have made, no doubt. It is a charming sight, is it not, to see the great guns fire? And tonight you will see them in the dark, which is even finer. Lord, you should have seen the Nile! And heard it! How happy you would have been!'

The improvement in the Sophie's fire-power was indeed very striking, even to so unmilitary a spectator as Stephen. Jack had devised a system that was both kind to the sloop's timbers (which really could not bear the shock of a united broadside) and good for emulation and regularity: the leeward gun of the broadside fired first, and the moment it was at its full recoil its neighbour went off – a rolling fire, with the last gun-layer still able to see through the smoke. Jack explained all this as the cutter pulled out into the fading light with the casks aboard. 'Of course,' he added, 'we make our run at no great range – only enough to get in three rounds. How I long for four!'

The gun-crews were stripped to the waist; their heads were tied up in their black silk handkerchiefs; they looked keenly attentive, at home and competent. There was to be a prize, naturally, for any gun that should hit the mark, but a better one for the watch that should fire the faster, without any wild, disqualifying shots.

The cutter was far away astern and to leeward – it always surprised Stephen to see how smoothly-travelling bodies at sea could appear to be almost together at one moment and then, when one looked round, miles apart without any apparent effort or burst of speed – and the cask was bobbing on the waves. The sloop wore and ran evenly down under her topsails to pass at a cable's length to windward of the cask. 'There is little point in being farther,' observed Jack, with his watch in one hand and a piece of chalk in the other. 'We cannot hit hard enough.'

The moments passed. The cask bore broader on the bow. 'Cast loose your guns,' cried James Dillon. Already the smell of slow-match was swirling along the deck. 'Level your guns . . . out tompions . . . run out your guns . . . prime . . . point your guns . . . fire.'

It was like a great hammer hitting stone at half-second intervals, admirably regular: the smoke streamed racing away in a long roll ahead of the brig. It was the larbowlines who had fired, and the starboard watch, craning their necks a-tiptoe upon any point of vantage, watched jealously for the fall of the shot: they pitched too far, thirty yards too far, but they were well grouped. The larboard watch worked with concentrated fury at their guns, swabbing, ramming, heaving in and heaving out: their backs shone and even ran with sweat.

The cask was not quite abeam when the next broadside utterly shattered it. 'Two minutes five,' said Jack, chuckling. Without even pausing to cheer, the larboard watch raced on; the guns ran up, the great hammer repeated its seven-fold stroke, white water sprang up round the shattered staves. The swabs and rammers flashed, the grunting crews slammed the loaded guns up against their ports, heaving them round with tackles and handspikes as far as ever they would go; but the wreckage was too far behind – they just could not get in their fourth broadside.

'Never mind,' called Jack. 'It was very near. Six minutes and ten seconds.' The larboard watch gave a corporate sigh. They had set their hearts on their fourth broadside, and on beating six minutes, as they knew very well the starboard watch would do.

In fact, the starboard watch achieved five minutes and fifty-seven seconds; but on the other hand they did not hit their cask, and in the anonymous dusk there was a good deal of audible criticism of 'unscrupulous grass-combing buggers that blazed away, blind and reckless – anything to win. And powder at eighteen pence the pound.'

The day had given place to night, and Jack observed with profound satisfaction that it made remarkably little difference on deck. The sloop came up into the wind, filled on the other tack and bore away towards the wavering flare on the third tub. The broadsides rapped out one after another, crimson-scarlet tongues stabbing into the smoke; the powder-boys flitted along the deck, down through the dreadnought screens past the sentry to the magazine and back with cartridge; the gun-crews heaved and grunted; the matches glowed: the rhythm hardly changed. 'Six minutes and forty-two seconds,' he announced after the last, peering closely at his watch by the lantern. 'The larboard watch bears the bell away. A not discreditable exercise, Mr Dillon?'

'Far better than I had expected, sir, I confess.'

'Well now, my dear sir,' said Jack to Stephen, 'what do you say to a little music, if your ears are not quite numbed? Is it any good inviting you, Dillon? Mr Marshall has the deck at present, I believe.'

'Thank you, sir, thank you very much. But you know what a sad waste music is on me – pearls before swine.'

'I am really pleased with tonight's exercise,' said Jack, tuning his fiddle. 'Now I feel I can run inshore with a clearer conscience – without risking the poor sloop too much.'

'I am happy you are pleased; and certainly the mariners seemed to ply their pieces with a wonderful dexterity; but you must allow me to insist that that note is not A.'

'Ain't it?' cried Jack anxiously. 'Is this better?'

Stephen nodded, tapped his foot three times, and they dashed away into Mr Brown's Minorcan divertimento.

'Did you notice my bowing in the pump-pump-pump piece?' asked Jack.

'I did indeed. Very sprightly, very agile. I noticed you neither struck the hanging shelf nor yet the lamp. I only grazed the locker once myself.'

'I believe the great thing is not to think of it. Those fellows, rattling their guns in and out, did not think of it. Clapping on to the tackles, sponging, swabbing, ramming – it has grown quite mechanical. I am very pleased with them, particularly three and five of the port broadside. They were the merest parcel of lubbers to begin with, I do assure you.'

'You are wonderfully earnest to make them proficient.'

'Why, yes: there is not a moment to be lost.'

'Well. You do not find this sense of constant hurry oppressive – jading?'

'Lord, no. It is as much part of our life as salt pork – even more so in tide-flow waters. Anything can happen, in five minutes' time, at sea – ha, ha, you should hear Lord Nelson! In this case of gunnery, a single broadside can bring down a mast and so win a fight; and there's no telling, from one hour to the next, when we may have to fire it. There is no telling, at sea.'

How profoundly true. An all-seeing eye, an eye that could pierce the darkness, would have beheld the track of the Spanish frigate *Cacafuego* running down to Carthagena, a track that certainly would have cut the *Sophie*'s if the sloop had not lingered a quarter of an hour to dowse her lighted casks; but as it was the *Cacafuego* passed silently a mile and a half to the westward of the *Sophie*, and neither caught sight of the other. The same eye would have seen a good many other vessels in the neighbourhood of Cape Nao for, as Jack knew very well, everything coming up from Almeria, Alicante or Malaga had to round that headland: it would particularly have noticed a small convoy bound for Valencia under the protection of a letter of marque; and it would have seen that the *Sophie*'s course (if persisted in) would bring her inshore and to the windward of the convoy in the half hour before first light.

'Sir, sir,' piped Babbington into Jack's ear.

'Hush, sweetheart,' murmured his captain, whose dreaming mind was occupied with quite another sex. 'Eh?'

'Mr Dillon says, top lights in the offing, sir.'

'Ha,' said Jack, instantly awake, and ran up on to the grey deck in his nightshirt.

'Good morning, sir,' said James, saluting and offering his night-glass.

'Good morning, Mr Dillon,' said Jack, touching his nightcap in reply and taking the telescope. 'Where away?'

'Right on the beam, sir.'

'By God, you have good eyes,' said Jack, lowering the glass, wiping it and peering again into the shifting sea-haze. 'Two. Three. I think a fourth.'

The *Sophie* was lying there, hove to, with her foretopsail to the mast and her maintopsail almost full, the one counter-balancing the other as she lay right under the dark cliff. The wind – what wind there was – was a puffy, unreliable air from the north-north-west, smelling of the warm hillside; but presently, as the land grew warmer, it would no doubt veer to the north-east or even frankly into the east itself. Jack gripped the shrouds. 'Let us consider the positions from the top,' he said. 'God damn and blast these skirts.'

The light increased; the thinning haze unveiled five vessels in a straggling line, or rather heap; they were all hull-up, and the nearest was no more than a quarter of a mile away. From north to south they ran, first the *Gloire*, a very fast ship-rigged Toulon privateer with twelve eight-pounders, chartered by a wealthy Barcelona merchant named Jaume Mateu to protect his two settees, the *Pardal* and the *Xaloc*, of six guns apiece, the second carrying a valuable (and illegal) cargo of uncustomed quicksilver into the bargain; the *Pardal* lay under the privateer's quarter to leeward; then, almost abreast of the *Pardal* but to windward and only four or five hundred yards from the *Sophie*, the *Santa Lucia*, a Neopolitan snow, a prize belonging to the *Gloire*, filled with disconsolate French royalists taken on their passage to Gibraltar; then came the second settee, the *Xaloc*; and lastly a tartan that had joined the company off Alicante, glad of the protection from Barbary rovers, Minorcan letters of marque and British cruisers. They were all smallish vessels; they all expected danger from the seaward (which was why they kept inshore – an uncomfortable, perilous way of getting along, compared with the long course of the open sea, but one that allowed them to run for the shelter of coastal batteries); and if any of them noticed the *Sophie* in the stronger light they said, 'Why, a little brig, creeping along close to the land: for Denia, no doubt.'

'What do you make of the ship?' asked Jack.

'I cannot count her ports in this light. She seems a little small for one of their eighteen-gun corvettes. But at all events she is of some force; and she is the watch-dog.'

'Yes.' That was certain. She lay there to the windward of the convoy as the wind veered and as they rounded the cape. Jack's mind was beginning to move fast. The flowing series of possibilities ran smoothly before his judgment: he was both the commander of that ship and of this sloop under his feet.

'May I make a suggestion, sir?'

'Yes,' said Jack in a flat voice. 'So long as we do not hold a council of war – they never decide anything.' He had asked Dillon up here as an attention due to him for having detected the convoy; he really did not want to consult him, or any other man, and he hoped Dillon would not break in on his racing ideas with any remarks whatever, however wise. Only one person could deal with this: the *Sophie*'s master and commander.

'Perhaps I should beat to quarters, sir?' said James stiffly, for the hint had been eminently clear.

'You see that slovenly little snow between us and the ship?' said Jack, breaking across him. 'If we gently square our foreyard we shall be within a hundred yards of her in ten minutes, and she will mask us from the ship. D'ye see what I mean?'

'Yes, sir.'

'With the cutter and the launch full of men you can take her before she's aware. You make a noise, and the ship bears up to protect her: he has no way on him to tack – he must wear; and if you put the snow before the wind, I can pass through the gap and rake him once or twice as he goes round, maybe knocking away a spar aboard the settee at the same time. On deck, there,' he called in a slightly louder voice, 'silence on deck. Send those men below' – for the rumour had spread, and men were running up the forward hatchway. 'The boarders away, then – we should be best advised to send all our black men: they are fine lusty fellows, and the Spaniards dread them – the sloop cleared for action with the least possible show and the men ready to fly to their quarters. But all kept below out of sight: all but a dozen. We must look like a merchantman.' He swung over the edge of the top, his night-shirt billowing round his head. 'The frappings may be cut, but no other preparation that can be seen.'

'The hammocks, sir?'

'Yes, by God,' said Jack, pausing. 'We shall have to get them up precious fast, if we are not to fight without 'em – a damned uncomfortable state. But do not let one come on deck until the boarders are away. Surprise is everything.'

Surprise, surprise. Stephen's surprise at being jerked awake with 'Quarters, sir, quarters,' and at finding himself in the midst of an extraordinarily intense muted activity – people hurrying about in almost pitch darkness – not a glim – the gentle clash of weapons secretly handed out – the boarders creeping over the landward side and into the boats by twos and threes – the bosun's mates hissing 'Stand by, stand by for quarters, all hands stand by,' in the nearest possible approach to a whispered shout – warrant officers and petty officers checking their teams, quieting the *Sophie's* fools (she bore a competent share), who urgently wanted to know what? what? and why? Jack's voice calling down into the gloom, 'Mr Ricketts. Mr Babbington.' 'Sir?' 'When I give the word you and the topmen are to go aloft at once: topgallants and courses to be set instantly.' 'Aye aye, sir.'

Surprise. The slow, growing surprise of the sleepy watch aboard the *Santa Lucia*, gazing at this brig as it drifted closer and closer: did it mean to join company? 'She is that Dane who is always plying up and down the coast,' stated Jean Wiseacre. Their sudden total amazement at the sight of two boats coming out from behind the brig and racing across the water. After the first moment's unbelief they did their best: they ran for their muskets, they pulled out their cutlasses and they began to cast loose a gun; but each of the seven men acted for himself, and they had less than a minute to make up their minds; so when the roaring Sophies hooked on at the fore and main chains and came pouring over the side the prize crew met them with no more than one musket-shot, a couple of pistols and a half-hearted clash of swords. A moment later the four liveliest had taken to the rigging, one had darted below and two lay upon the deck.

Dillon kicked open the cabin door, glared at the young privateer's mate along a heavy pistol and said, 'You surrender?'

'Oui, monsieur,' quavered the youth.

'On deck,' said Dillon, jerking his head. 'Murphy, Bussell, Thompson, King, clap on to those hatch-covers. Bear a hand, now. Davies, Chambers, Wood, start the sheets. Andrews, flat in the jib.' He ran to the wheel, heaved a body out of the way and put up the helm. The *Santa Lucia* paid off slowly, then faster and faster. Looking over his shoulder he saw the topgallants break out in the *Sophie*, and in almost the same moment the foresail, mainstaysail and boom mainsail: ducking to peer under the snow's forecourse, he saw the ship ahead of him beginning to wear – to turn before the wind and come back on the other tack to rescue the prize. There was great activity aboard her: there was great activity aboard the three other vessels of the convoy – men racing up and down, shouts, whistles, the distant beating of a drum – but in this gentle breeze, and with so little canvas abroad, they all of them moved with a dream-like slowness, quietly following smooth predestinate curves. Sails were breaking out all over, but still the vessels had no way on them, and because of their slowness he had the strangest impression of silence – a silence broken a moment later as the *Sophie* came shaving past the snow's larboard bow with her colours flying, and gave them a thundering cheer. She alone had a fair bow-wave, and with a spurt of pride James saw that every sail was sheeted home, taut and drawing already. The hammocks were piling up at an incredible speed – he saw two go by the board – and on the quarter-deck, stretching up over the nettings, Jack raised his hat high, calling 'Well done indeed, sir,' as they passed. The boarders cheered their shipmates in return; and as they did so the atmosphere of terrible killing ferocity on the deck of the snow changed entirely. They cheered again, and from within the snow, under the hatches, there came a generalized answering howl.

The *Sophie*, all sails abroad, was running at close on four knots. The *Gloire* had little more than steerage-way, and she was already committed to this wheeling movement – was already engaged upon the gradual curve down-wind that would turn her unprotected stern to the *Sophie's* fire. There was less than a quarter of a mile between them, and the gap was closing fast. But the Frenchman was no fool; Jack saw the ship's mizzen topsail laid to the mast and the main and fore yards squared so that the wind should thrust the stern away to leewards and reverse the movement – for the rudder had no bite at all.

'Too late, my friend, I think,' said Jack. The range was narrowing. Three hundred yards. Two hundred and fifty. 'Edwards,' he said to the captain of the aftermost gun, 'Fire across the settee's bows.' The shot, in fact, went through the settee's foresail. She started her halliards, her sails came down with a run and an agitated figure hurried aft to raise his colours and lower them emphatically. There was no time to attend to the settee, however. 'Luff up,' he said. The *Sophie* came closer to the wind: her foresail shivered once and filled again. The *Gloire* was well within the forward traverse of the guns. 'Thus, thus,' he said, and all along the line he heard the grunt and heave as the guns were heaved round a trifle to keep them bearing. The crews were silent, exactly-placed and tense; the spongers knelt with the lighted matches in their hands, gently blowing to keep them in a glow, facing rigidly inboard; the captains crouched glaring along the barrels at that defenceless stern and quarter.

'Fire.' The word was cut off by the roar; a cloud of smoke hid the sea, and the *Sophie* trembled to her keel. Jack was unconsciously stuffing his shirt into his breeches when he saw that there was something amiss – something wrong with the smoke: a sudden fault in the wind, a sudden gust from the north-east, sent it streaming down astern; and at the same moment the sloop was taken aback, her head pushed round to starboard.

'Hands to the braces,' called Marshall, putting up the helm to bring her back. Back she came, though slowly, and the second broadside roared out: but the gust had pushed the *Gloire's* stern round too, and as the smoke cleared so she replied. In the seconds between Jack had had time to see that her stern and quarter had suffered – cabin windows and little gallery smashed in; that she carried twelve guns; and that her colours were French.

The *Sophie* had lost much of her way, and the *Gloire*, now right back on her original larboard tack, was fast gathering speed; they sailed along on parallel courses, close-hauled to the fitful breeze, the *Sophie* some way behind. They sailed along, hammering one another in an almost continuous din and an unbroken smoke, white, grey-black and lit with darting crimson stabs of fire. On and on: the glass turned, the bell clanged, the smoke lay thick: the convoy vanished astern.

There was nothing to say, nothing to do: the gun-captains had their orders and they were obeying them with splendid fury, firing for the hull, firing as quickly as they could; the midshipmen in charge of the divisions ran up and down the line, bearing a hand, dealing with any beginning of confusion; the powder and shot travelled up from the magazine with perfect regularity; the bosun and his mates roamed gazing up for damage to the rigging; in the tops the sharpshooters' muskets crackled briskly. He stood there reflecting: a little way to his left, scarcely flinching as the balls came whipping in or hulled the sloop (a great rending thump), stood the clerk and Ricketts, the quarter-deck midshipman. A ball burst through the packed hammock-netting, crossed a few feet in front of him, struck an iron netting-crane and lost its force on the hammocks the other side – an eight-pounder, he noticed, as it rolled towards him.

The Frenchman was firing high, as usual, and pretty wild: in the blue, smokeless, peaceful world to windward he saw splashes as much as fifty yards ahead and astern of them – particularly ahead. Ahead: from the flashes that lit the far side of the cloud and from the change of sound it was clear that the *Gloire* was forging ahead. That would not do. 'Mr Marshall,' he said, picking up his speaking-trumpet, 'we will cross under her stern.' As he raised the trumpet there was a tumult and shouting forward – a gun was over on its side: perhaps two. 'Avast firing there,' he called with great force. 'Stand by, the larboard guns.'

The smoke cleared. The *Sophie* began to turn to starboard, moving to cross the enemy's wake and to bring her port broadside to bear on the *Gloire*'s stern, raking her whole length. But the *Gloire* was having none of it: as though warned by an inner voice, her captain had put up his helm within five seconds of the *Sophie*'s doing so, and now, with the smoke clearing again, Jack, standing by the larboard hammocks, saw him at his taffrail, a small trim grizzled man a hundred and fifty yards away, looking fixedly back. The Frenchman reached behind him for a musket, and resting his elbows on the taffrail he very deliberately aimed it at Jack.

The thing was extraordinarily personal: Jack felt an involuntary stiffening of the muscles of his face and chest – a tendency to hold his breath.

'The royals, Mr Marshall,' he said. 'She is drawing away from us.' The gunfire had died away as the guns ceased to bear, and in the lull he heard the musket-shot part almost as if it had been in his ear. In the same second of time Christian Pram, the helmsman, gave a shrill roar and half fell, dragging the wheel over with him, his forearm ploughed open from wrist to elbow. The *Sophie*'s head flew up into the wind, and although Jack and Marshall had the wheel directly, the advantage was gone. The port broadside could only be brought to bear by a further turn that lost still more way; and there was no way to be lost. The *Sophie* was a good two hundred yards behind the Gloire now, on her starboard quarter, and the only hope was to gain speed, to range up and renew the battle. He and the master glanced up simultaneously: everything was set that could be set – the wind was too far forward for the studdingsails.

He stared ahead, watching for the stir aboard the chase, the slight change in her wake, that would mean a coming movement to starboard – the *Gloire* in her turn crossing the *Sophie*'s stem, raking her fore and aft and bearing up to protect the scattered convoy. But he stared in vain. The *Gloire* held on to her course. She had drawn ahead of the *Sophie* even without her royals, but now these were setting: and the breeze was kinder to her, too. As he watched, the tears brimming over his eyelids from the concentration of his gaze against the rays of the sun, a slant of wind laid her over and the water ran creaming under her lee, her wake lengthening away and away. The grey-haired captain fired on pertinaciously, a man beside him passing loaded muskets, and one ball severed a ratline two feet from Jack's head; but they were almost beyond musket-range now, and in any case the indefinable frontier between personal animosity and anonymous warfare had been passed – it did not affect him.

'Mr Marshall,' he said, 'pray edge away until we can salute her. Mr Pullings – Mr Pullings, fire as they bear.'

The *Sophie* turned two, three, four points from her course. The bow gun cracked out, followed in even sequence by the rest of the port broadside. Too eager, alas: they were well pitched up, but the splashes showed twenty and even thirty yards astern. The *Gloire*, more attentive to her safety than her honour, and quite forgetful of her duty to Señor Mateu, the unvindictive *Gloire* did not yaw to reply, but hauled her wind. Being a ship, she could point up closer than the *Sophie*, and she did not scruple to do so, profiting to the utmost by the favour of the breeze. She was plainly running away. Of the next broadside two balls seemed to hit her, and one certainly passed through her mizzen topsail. But the target was diminishing every minute as their courses diverged, and hope diminished with it.

Eight broadsides later Jack stopped the firing. They had knocked her about shrewdly and they had ruined her looks, but they had not cut up her rigging to make her unmanage-able, nor carried away any vital mast or yard. And they had certainly failed to persuade her to come back and fight it out yard-arm to yard-arm. He gazed at the flying *Gloire*, made up his mind and said, 'We will bear away for the cape again, Mr Marshall. South-south-west.'

The *Sophie* was remarkably little wounded. 'Are there any repairs that will not wait half an hour, Mr Watt?' he asked, absently hitching a stray slab-line round a pin.

'No, sir. The sailmaker will be busy for a while; but she sent us no chain nor bar, and she never clawed our rigging, not to say clawed. Poor practice, sir; very poor practice. Not like that wicked little old Turk, and the sharp raps *he* give us.'

'Then we will pipe the hands to breakfast and knot and splice afterwards. Mr Lamb, what damage do you find?'

'Nothing below the water-line, sir. Four right ugly holes amidships and two and four gun-ports well-nigh beat into one: that's the worst. Nothing to what we give her (the sodomite),' he added, under his breath.

Jack went forward to the dismounted gun. A ball from the *Gloire* had shattered the bulwark where the aft ring-bolts were fastened, just as number four was on the recoil. The gun, partly checked on the other side, had slewed round, jamming its run-out neighbour and oversetting. By wonderful good luck the two men who should have been crushed between them were not there – one washing the blood from a graze off his face in the fire-bucket, the other hurrying for more slow-match – and by wonderful good luck the gun had gone over, rather than running murderously about the deck.

'Well, Mr Day,' he said, 'we were in luck one way, if not the other. The gun may go into the bows until Mr Lamb gives us fresh ring-bolts.'

As he walked aft, taking off his coat as he went – the heat was suddenly unbearable – he ran his eye along the south-western horizon. No sign of Cape Nao in the rising haze: not a sail to be seen. He had never noticed the rising of the sun, but there it was, well up into the sky; they must have run a surprising long way. 'By God, I could do with my coffee,' he said, coming abruptly back into a present in which ordinary time flowed steadily once more and appetite mattered. 'But, however,' he reflected, 'I must go below.' This was the ugly side: this was where you saw what happened when a man's face and an iron ball met.

'Captain Aubrey,' said Stephen, clapping his book to the moment he saw Jack in the cockpit. 'I have a grave complaint to make.'

'I am concerned to hear it,' said Jack, peering about in the gloom for what he dreaded to see.

'They have been at my asp. I tell you, sir, they have been at my asp. I stepped into my cabin for a book not three minutes ago, and what did I see? My asp drained – *drained*, I say.'

'Tell me the butcher's bill; then I will attend to your asp.'

'Bah – a few scratches, a man with his forearm moderately scored, a couple of splinters to draw – nothing of conse-quence – mere bandaging. All you will find in the sick-bay is an obstinate gleet with low fever and a reduced inguinal hernia: and that forearm. Now my asp –'

'No dead? No wounded?' cried Jack, his heart leaping up.

'No, no, no. Now my asp –' He had brought it aboard in its spirits of wine; and at some point in very recent time a criminal hand had taken the jar, drunk up all the alcohol and left the asp dry, stranded, parched.

'I am truly sorry for it,' said Jack. 'But will not the fellow die? Must he not have an emetic?'

'He will not: that is what is so vexing. The bloody man, the more than Hun, the sottish rapparee, he will not die. It was the best double-refined spirits of wine.'

'Pray come and breakfast with me in the cabin; a pint of coffee and a well-broiled chop between you and the asp will take away the sting – will appease . . .' In his gaiety of heart, Jack was very near a witticism; he felt it floating there, almost within reach; but somehow it escaped and he confined himself to laughing as cheerfully as Stephen's vexation would with decency allow and observing, 'The damned villain ran clean away from us; and I am afraid we shall have but a tedious time making our way back. I wonder, I *wonder* whether Dillon managed to pick up the settee, or whether she ran for it, too.'

It was a natural curiosity, a curiosity shared by every man aboard the *Sophie,* apart from Stephen; but it was not to be satisfied that forenoon, nor yet for a great while after the sun had crossed the meridian. Towards noon the wind fell to something very near a calm; the newly-bent sails flapped, hanging in flaccid bulges from their yards, and the men working on the tattered set had to be protected by an awning. It was one of those intensely humid days when the air has no nourishment in it, and it was so hot that even with all his restless eagerness to recover his boarders, secure his prize and move on up the coast, Jack could not find it in his heart to order out the sweeps. The men had fought the ship tolerably well (though the guns were still too slow by far) and they had been very active repairing what damage the *Gloire* had inflicted. 'I will let them be at least until the dog-watch,' he reflected.

The heat pressed down upon the sea; the smoke from the galley funnel hung along the deck, together with the smell of grog and the hundredweight or so of salt beef the Sophies had devoured at dinner-time: the regular tang-tang of the bell came at such long intervals that long before the snow was seen it appeared to Jack that this morning's sharp encounter must belong to another age, another life or, indeed (had it not been for a lingering smell of powder in the cushion under his head), to another kind of experience – to a tale he had read. Stretched out on the locker under his stern window, Jack revolved this in his mind, revolved it again more slowly, and again, and so sank far down and away.

He woke suddenly, refreshed, cool and perfectly aware that the *Sophie* had been running easily for a considerable time, with a breeze that leant her over a couple of strakes, bringing her heels higher than his head.

'I am afraid those damned youngsters woke you, sir,' said Mr Marshall with solicitous vexation. 'I sent 'em aloft, but I fear it was too late. Calling out and hallooing like a pack of baboons. Damn their capers.'

Although he was singularly open and truthful, upon the whole, Jack at once replied, 'Oh, I was not asleep.' On deck he glanced up at the two mastheads, where the midshipmen were peering anxiously down to see whether their offence was reported. Meeting his eye, they at once stared away, with a great demonstration of earnest duty, in the direction of the snow and her accompanying settee, rapidly closing with the *Sophie* on the easterly breeze.

'There she is,' said Jack inwardly, with intense satisfaction. 'And he picked up the settee. Good, active fellow – capital seaman.' His heart warmed to Dillon – it would have been so easy to let that second prize slip away while he was making sure of the crew of the snow. Indeed, it must have called for extraordinary exertions on his part to pin the two of them, for the settee would never have respected her surrender for a moment.

'Well done, Mr Dillon,' he cried, as James came aboard, guiding a figure in a tattered, unknown uniform over the side. 'Did she try to run?'

'She *tried*, sir,' said James. 'Allow me to present Captain La Hire, of the French royal artillery.' They took off their hats, bowed and shook hands. La Hire said, 'Appy,' in a low, pénétré tone: and Jack said, 'Domestique, monsieur.'

'The snow was a Neapolitan prize, sir: Captain La Hire was good enough to take command of the French royalist passengers and the Italian seamen, keeping the prize-crew under control while we pulled across to take possession of the settee. I am sorry to say the tartan and the other settee were too far to windward by the time we had secured her, and they have run down the coast – they are lying under the guns of the battery at Almoraira.'

'Ah? We will look into the bay when we have the prisoners across. Many prisoners, Mr Dillon?'

'Only about twenty, sir, since the snow's people are allies. They were on their way to Gibraltar.'

'When were they taken?'

'Oh, she's a fair prize, sir – a good eight days since.'

'So much the better. Tell me, was there any trouble?'

'No, sir. Or very little. We knocked two of the prize-crew on the head, and there was a foolish scuffle aboard the settee – a man pistolled. I hope all was well with you, sir?'

'Yes, yes – no one killed, no serious wounds. She ran away from us too fast to do much damage: sailed four miles to our three, even without her royals. A most prodigious fine sailer.'

Jack had a notion that some fleeting reserve passed across James Dillon's face, or perhaps showed in his voice; but in the hurry of things to be done, prizes to survey, prisoners to be dealt with, he could not tell why it affected him so unpleasantly until some two or three hours later, when the impression was reinforced and at least half defined.

He was in his cabin: spread out on the table was the chart of Cape Nao, with Cape Almoraira and Cape Ifach jutting out from its massive under-side, and the little village of Almoraira at the bottom of the bay between them: on his right sat James, on his left Stephen, and opposite him Mr Marshall.

'. . . what is more,' he was saying, 'the Doctor tells me the Spaniard says that the other settee has a cargo of quicksilver hidden in sacks of flour, so we must handle *her* with great care.'

'Oh, of course,' said James Dillon. Jack looked at him sharply, then down at the chart and at Stephen's drawing: it showed a little bay with a village and a square tower at the bottom of it: a low mole ran twenty or thirty yards out into the sea, turned left-handed for another fifty and ended in a rocky knob, thus enclosing a harbour sheltered from all but the south-west wind. Steep-to cliffs ran from the village right round to the north-east point of the bay. On the other side there was a sandy beach all the way from the tower to the south-west point, where the cliffs reared up again. 'Could the fellow possibly think I am shy?' he thought. 'That I left off chasing because I did not choose to get hurt and hurried back for a prize?' The tower commanded the entrance to the harbour; it stood some twenty yards to the south of the village and the gravel beach, where the fishing-boats were hauled out. 'Now this knob at the end of the jetty,' he said aloud, 'would you say it was ten foot high?'

'Probably more. It is eight or nine years since I was there,' said Stephen, 'so I will not be absolute; but the chapel on it withstands the tall waves in the winter storms.'

'Then it will certainly protect our hull. Now, with the sloop anchored with a spring on her cable so' – running his finger in a line from the battery to the rock and so to the spot – 'she should be tolerably safe. She opens as heavy a fire as she can, playing on the mole and over the tower. The boats from the snow and the settee land at the Doctor's cove' – pointing to a little indentation just round the south-west point – 'and we run as fast as ever we can along the shore and so take the tower from behind. Twenty yards short of it we fire the rocket and you turn your guns well away from the battery, but blaze away without stopping.'

'Me, sir?' cried James.

'Yes, you, sir; I am going ashore.' There was no answering the decision of this statement, and after a pause he went on to the detailed arrangements. 'Let us say ten minutes to run from the cove to the tower, and . . .'

'Allow twenty, if you please,' said Stephen. 'You portly men of a sanguine complexion often die suddenly, from unconsidered exertion in the heat. Apoplexy – congestion.'

'I wish, I *wish* you would not say things like that, Doctor,' said Jack, in a low tone: they all looked at Stephen with some reproach and Jack added, 'Besides, I am not portly.'

'The captain has an uncommon genteel figgar,' said Mr Marshall.

THE CONDITIONS WERE perfect for the attack. The remains of the easterly wind would carry the *Sophie* in, and the breeze that would spring up off the land at about moonrise would carry her into the offing, together with anything they managed to cut out. In his long survey from the masthead, Jack had made out the settee and a number of other vessels moored to the inner wall of the mole, as well as a row of fishing-boats hauled up along the shore: the settee was at the chapel end of the mole, directly opposite the guns of the tower, a hundred yards on the other side of the harbour.

'I may not be perfect,' he reflected, 'but by God I am not shy; and if we cannot bring her out, then by God I shall burn her where she lies.' But these reflexions did not last long. From the deck of the Neapolitan snow he watched the *Sophie* round Cape Almoraira in the three-quarter darkness and stand into the bay, while the two prizes, with the boats in tow, bore away for the point on the other side. With the settee already in the port there was no possibility of surprise for the *Sophie*, and before she anchored she would have to undergo the fire of the battery. If there was to be a surprise it would lie with the boats: the night was almost certainly too dark now for the prizes to be seen crossing outside the bay to land the boats in Stephen's cove beyond the point – 'one of the few I know where the white-bellied swift builds her nest'. Jack watched her going with a tender and extreme anxiety, torn with longing to be in both places at once: the possibilities of hideous failure flooded into his mind – the shore guns (how big were they? Stephen had been unable to tell) hulling the *Sophie* again and again, the heavy shot passing through both sides – the wind falling, or getting up to blow dead on shore – not enough hands left aboard to sweep her out of range – the boats all astray. It was a foolhardy attempt, absurdly rash. 'Silence fore and aft,' he cried harshly. 'Do you want to wake the whole coast?'

He had had no idea how deeply he felt about his sloop: he knew exactly how she would be moving in – the particular creak of her mainyard in its parrel, the whisper of her rudder magnified by the sounding-board of her stern; and the passage across the bay seemed to him intolerably long.

'Sir,' said Pullings. 'I think we have the point on our beam now.'

'You are right, Mr Pullings,' said Jack, studying it through his night-glass. 'See the lights of the village going, one after the other. Port your helm, Algren. Mr Pullings, send a good man into the chains: we should have twenty fathom directly.' He walked to the taffrail and called over dark water, 'Mr Marshall, we are standing in.'

The high black bar of the land, sharp against the less solid darkness of the starry sky: it came nearer and nearer, silently eclipsing Arcturus, then the whole of Corona: eclipsing even Vega, high up in the sky. The regular splash of the lead, the steady chant of the man in the weather chains: 'By the deep nine; by the deep nine; by the mark seven; and a quarter five; a quarter less five . . .'

Ahead lay the pallor of the cove beneath the cliff, and a faint white edge of lapping wave. 'Right,' said Jack, and the snow came up into the wind, her foresail backing like a sentient creature. 'Mr Pullings, your party into the launch.' Fourteen men filed fast by him and silently over the side into the creaking boat: each had his white arm-band on. 'Sergeant Quinn.' The marines followed, muskets faintly gleaming, their boots loud on the deck. Someone was grasping at his stomach. It was Captain La Hire, a volunteer attached to the soldiers, looking for his hand. 'Good lucky,' he said, shaking it.

'Merci very much,' said Jack, adding, 'Mon captain,' over the side; and at that moment a flash lit the sky, followed by the deep thump of a heavy gun.

'Is that cutter alongside?' said Jack, his night-eyes half blinded by the flash.

'Here, sir,' said the voice of his coxswain just beneath him. Jack swung over, dropped down. 'Mr Ricketts, where is the dark lantern?'

'Under my jacket, sir.'

'Show it over the stern. Give way.' The gun spoke again, followed almost immediately by two together: they were trying for the range, that was sure: but it was a damned roaring great note for a gun. A thirty-six pounder? Peering round he could see the four boats behind him, a vague line against the loom of the snow and the settee. Mechanically he patted his pistols and his sword: he had rarely felt more nervous, and his whole being was concentrated in his right ear for the sound of the *Sophie's* broadside.

The cutter was racing through the water, the oars creaking as the men heaved, and the men themselves grunting deep with the effort – ugh, ugh. 'Rowed-off all,' said the coxswain quietly, and a few seconds later the boat shot hissing up the gravel. The men were out and had hauled it up before the launch grounded, followed by the snow's boat with Mowett, the jolly-boat with the bosun and the settee's launch with Marshall.

The little beach was crowded with men. 'The line, Mr Watt?' said Jack.

'There she goes,' said a voice, and seven guns went off, thin and faint behind the cliff.

'Here we are, sir,' cried the bosun, heaving two coils of one-inch line off his shoulder.

Jack seized the end of one, saying, 'Mr Marshall, clap on to yours, and each man to his knot.' As orderly as though they had been mustering by divisions aboard the *Sophie*, the men fell into place. 'Ready? Ready there? Then tear away.'

He set off for the point, where the beach narrowed to a few feet under the cliff, and behind him, fast to the knotted line, ran his half of the landing-party. There was a bubbling furious excitement rising in his chest – the waiting was over – this was the now itself. They came round the point and at once there were blinding fireworks before them and the noise increased tenfold: the tower firing with three, four deep red lances very low over the ground, the *Sophie*, her brailed-up topsails clear in the irregular flashes that lit up the whole sky, hammering away with a fine, busy, rolling fire, playing on the jetty to send stone splinters flying and discourage any attempt at warping the settee ashore. As far as he could judge from this angle, she was in exactly the position they had laid down on the chart, with the dark mass of the chapel rock on her port beam. But the tower was farther than he had expected. Beneath his delight – indeed, his something near a rapture – he could feel his body labouring, his legs heaving him slowly along as his boots sank into the soft sand. He must not, must *not* fall, he thought, after a stumble; and then again at the sound of a man going down on Marshall's rope. He shaded his eyes from the flashes, looked with an unbelievably violent effort away from the battle, ploughed on and on and on, the pounding of his heart almost choking his mind, hardly progressing at all. But now suddenly it was harder ground, and as though he had dropped a ten-stone load he flew along, running, really running. This was packed, noiseless sand, and all along behind him he could hear the hoarse, gasping, catching breath of the landing-party. The battery was hurrying towards them at last, and through the gaps in the parapet he could see busy figures working the Spanish guns. A shot from the *Sophie*, glancing off the chapel rock, howled over their heads; and now an eddy in the breeze brought a choking gust of the tower's powder-smoke.

Was it time for the rocket? The fort was very close – they could hear the voices loud and the rumble of trucks. But the Spaniards were wholly engrossed with answering the *Sophie*'s fire: they could get a little closer, a little closer, closer still. They were all creeping now, by one accord, all clearly visible to one another in the flashes and the general glow. 'The rocket, Bonden,' murmured Jack. 'Mr Watt, the grapnels. Check your arms, all.'

The bosun fixed the three-pronged grapnels to the ropes; the coxswain planted the rockets, struck a spark on to tinder and stood by cherishing it; against the tremendous din of the battery there was a little metallic clicking and the easing of belts; the strong panting lessened.

'Ready?' whispered Jack.

'Ready, sir,' whispered the officers.

He bent. The fuse hissed; and the rocket went away, a red trail and a high blue burst. 'Come on,' he shouted, and his voice was drowned in a great roaring cheer, 'Ooay, ooay!'

Running, running. Dump down into the dry ditch, pistols snapping through the embrasures, men swarming up the ropes on to the parapet, shouting, shouting; a bubbling scream. His coxswain's voice in his ear, 'Give us your fist, mate.' The tearing roughness of stone and there he was, up, whipping his sword out, a pistol in the other hand: but there was no one to fight. The gunners, apart from two on the ground and another kneeling bent over his wound near the great shaded lantern behind the guns, were dropping one by one over the wall and running for the village.

'Johnson! Johnson!' he cried. 'Spike up those guns. Sergeant

Quinn, keep up a rapid fire. Light along those spikes.'

Captain La Hire was beating the locks off the heated twenty-four-pounders with a crowbar. 'Better make leap,' he said. 'Make all leap in the air.'

'Vou savez faire leap in the air?'

'Eh, pardi,' said La Hire with a smile of conviction.

'Mr Marshall, you and all the people are to cut along to the jetty. Marines form at the landward end, sergeant, firing all the time, whether they see anyone or not. Get the settee's head round, Mr Marshall, and her sails loosed. Captain La Hire and I are going to blow up the fort.'

'By GOD,' said Jack, 'I hate an official letter.' His ears were still singing from the enormous bang (a second powder magazine in a vault below the first had falsified Captain La Hire's calculations) and his eyes still swam with yellow shapes from the incandescent leaping half-mile tree of light; his head and neck were horribly painful from all the left-hand half of his long hair having been burnt off – his scalp and face were hideously seared and bruised; on the table in front of him lay four unsatisfactory attempts; and under the *Sophie*'s lee lay the three prizes, urgent to be away for Mahon on the favourable wind, while far behind them the smoke still rose over Almoraira.

'Now just listen to this one, will you,' he said, 'and tell me if it is good grammar and proper language. It begins like the others: *Sophie, at sea; My Lord, I have the honour to acquaint you that pursuant to my orders I proceeded to Cape Nao, where I fell in with a convoy of three sail under the conduct of a French corvetto of twelve guns.* Then I go on to put about the snow – merely touch upon the engagement, with a fling about his *alacrity* – and come to the landing-party. *Upon its appearing that the remainder of the convoy had run under the guns of the Almoraira battery it was determined that they should be attempted to be cut out which was happily accomplished, the battery (a square tower mounting four iron twenty-four-*

pounders) being blown up at twenty-seven minutes after two, the boats having proceeded to the SSW point of the bay. Three tartans that had been hauled up and chained were obliged to be burnt, but the settee was brought out, when she proved to be the Xaloc, *loaded with a valuable cargo of quicksilver concealed in sacks of flour.* Pretty bald, ain't it? However, I go on. *The zeal and activity of Lieutenant Dillon, who took his Majesty's sloop I have the honour to command, in, and kept up an incessant fire on the mole and battery, I am much indebted to. All the officers and men behaved so well that it were insidious to particularize; but I must acknowledge the politeness of Mons. La Hire, of the royal French artillery, who volunteered his services in setting and firing the train to the magazine, and who was somewhat bruised and singed. Enclosed is a list of the killed and wounded: John Hayter, marine, killed; James Nightingale, seaman, and Thomas Thompson, seaman, wounded. I have the honour to be, my Lord* – and so on. What do you think of it?'

'Well, it is somewhat clearer than the last,' said Stephen. 'Though I fancy *invidious* might answer better than *insidious*.'

'Invidious, of course. I knew there was something not quite shipshape there. *Invidious*. A capital word: I dare say you spell it with a V?'

THE *SOPHIE* LAY off San Pedro: she had been extraordinarily busy this last week, and she was rapidly perfecting her technique, staying well over the horizon by day, while the military forces of Spain hurried up and down the coast looking for her, and standing in at night to play Old Harry with the little ports and the coast-wise trade in the hours before dawn. It was a dangerous, highly personal way of carrying on; it called for very careful preparation; it made great and continual demands on luck; and it had been remarkably successful. It also made great demands on the *Sophie*'s people, for when they were in the offing Jack exercised them mercilessly at the guns and James at the still brisker setting of sails. James was as taut an officer as any in the service: he liked a clean ship, action or no action, and there was no cutting-out expedition or dawn skirmishing that did not come back to gleaming decks and resplendent brass. He was *particular*, as they said; but his zeal for trim paintwork, perfectly-drawing sails, squared yards, clear tops and flemished ropes was, in fact, surpassed by his delight in taking the whole frail beautiful edifice into immediate contact with the King's enemies, who might wrench it to pieces, shatter, burn or sink it. The *Sophie*'s people bore up under all this with wonderful spirit, however, a worn, lean and eager crew, filled with precise ideas of what they should do the minute they stepped ashore from the liberty-boat – filled, too, with a tolerably precise notion of the change in relations on the quarter-deck: Dillon's marked respect and attention to the captain since Almoraira, their walking up and down together and their frequent consultations had not passed unnoticed; and, of course, the conversation at the gun-room table, in which the lieutenant spoke in the highest terms of the shore-party's action, had at once been repeated throughout the sloop.

'Unless my adding is out,' said Jack, looking up from his paper, 'we have taken, sunk or burnt twenty-seven times our own weight since the beginning of the cruise; and had they all been together they could have fired forty-two guns at us, counting the swivels. That is what the admiral meant by wringing the Spaniard's lugs; and' – laughing heartily – 'if it puts a couple of thousand guineas in our pockets, why, so much the better.'

'May I come in, sir?' asked the purser, appearing in the open door.

'Good morning, Mr Ricketts. Come in, come in and sit down. Are those today's figures?'

'Yes, sir. You will not be pleased, I am afraid. The second butt in the lower tier was started in the head, and it must have lost close on fifty gallon.'

'Then we must pray for rain, Mr Ricketts,' said Jack. But when the purser had gone he turned sadly to Stephen. 'I should have been perfectly happy but for that damned water: everything delightful – people behaving well, charming cruise, no sickness – if only I had completed our water at Mahon. Even at short allowance we use half a ton a day, what with all these prisoners and in this heat; the meat has to be soaked and the grog has to be mixed, even if we do wash in sea-water.' He had wholly set his heart on lying in the sea-lanes off Barcelona, perhaps the busiest convergency in the Mediterranean: that was to have been the culmination of the cruise. Now he would have to bear away for Minorca, and he was by no means sure of what welcome would be waiting for him there, or what orders; not much of his cruising time was left, and capricious winds or a capricious commandant might swallow it entirely – almost certainly would.

'If it is fresh water you are wanting, I can show you a creek not far from here where you may fill all the barrels you choose.'

'Why did you never tell me?' cried Jack, shaking him by the hand and looking delighted – a disagreeable sight, for the left side of his face, head and neck was still seared a baboonish red and blue, it shone under Stephen's medicated grease, and through the grease rose a new frizz of yellow hair; all this, taken with his deep brown, shaved other cheek, gave him a wicked, degenerate, inverted look.

'You never asked.'

'Undefended? No batteries?'

'Never a house, far less a gun. Yet it was inhabited once, for there are the remains of a Roman villa on the top of the promontory, and you can just make out the road beneath the trees and the undergrowth – cistus and lentisk. No doubt they used the spring: it is quite considerable, and it may, I conceive, have real medicinal qualities. The country people use it in cases of impotence.'

'And can you find it, do you think?'

'Yes,' said Stephen. He sat for a moment with his head down. 'Listen,' he said, 'will you do me a kindness?'

'With all my heart.'

'I have a friend who lives some two or three miles inland: I should like you to land me and pick me up, say, twelve hours later.'

'Very well,' said Jack. It was fair enough. 'Very well,' he said again, looking aside to hide the knowing grin that would spread over his face. 'It is the night you would wish to spend ashore, I presume. We will stand in this evening – you are sure we shall not be surprised?'

'Quite sure.'

'– send the cutter in again a little after sunrise. But what if I am forced off the land? What would you do then?'

'I should present myself the next morning, or the morning after that – a whole series of mornings, if need be. I must go,' he said, getting up at the sound of the bell, the still-feeble bell, that his new loblolly-boy rang to signify that the sick might now assemble. 'I dare not trust that fellow alone with the drugs.' The sin-eater had discovered a malignance towards his shipmates: he had been found grinding creta alba into their gruel, under the persuasion that it was a far more active substance, far more sinister; and if ill-will had been enough, the sick-bay would have been swept clean days ago.

THE CUTTER, followed by the launch, rowed attentively in through the warm darkness, with Dillon and Sergeant Quinn keeping watch on the sides of the high wooded inlet; and when the boats were two hundred yards from the cliff the exhalation of the stone-pines, mixed with the scent of the gum-cistus, met them – it was like breathing another element.

'If you row a little more to the right,' said Stephen, 'you may avoid the rocks where the crayfish live.' In spite of the heat he had his black cloak over his shoulders, and sitting huddled there in the stern-sheets he stared into the narrowing cove with a singular intensity, looking deathly pale.

The stream, in times of spate, had formed a little bar, and

upon this the cutter grounded: everybody leapt out to float it over, and two seamen carried Stephen ashore. They put him down tenderly, well above the high-water mark, adjured him to take care of all them nasty sticks laying about and hurried back for his cloak. Falling and falling, the water had made a basin in the rock at the top of the beach, and here the sailors filled their barrels, while the marines stood guard at the outward extremities.

'What an agreeable dinner it was,' observed Dillon, sitting with Stephen upon a smooth rock, warm through and through, convenient to their hams.

'I have rarely eaten a better,' said Stephen. 'Never at sea.' Jack had acquired a French cook from the *Santa Lucia*, a royalist volunteer, and he was putting on weight like a prize ox. 'You were in a very copious flow of spirits, too.'

'That was clean against the naval etiquette. At a captain's table you speak when you are spoken to, and you agree; it makes for a tolerably dismal entertainment, but that is the custom. And after all, he does represent the King, I suppose. But I felt I should cast etiquette adrift and make a particular exertion – should try to do the civil thing far more than usual. I have not been altogether fair to himself, you know – far from it,' he added, nodding towards the *Sophie*, 'and it was handsome to invite me.'

'He does love a prize. But prize-taking is not his prime concern.'

'Just so. Though in passing I may say not everyone would know it – he does himself injustice. I do not think the men know it, for example. If they were not kept well in check by the steady officers, the bosun and the gunner, and I must admit that fellow Marshall too, I think there would be trouble with them. There may be still: prize-money is heady stuff. From prize-money to breaking bulk and plunder is no great step – there has been some already. And from plunder and drunkenness to breaking out entirely and even to mutiny itself is not a terrible long way further. Mutinies always happen in ships where the discipline is either too lax or too severe.'

'You are mistaken, sure, when you say they do not know him: unlearned men have a wonderful penetration in these matters – have you ever known a village reputation to be wrong? It is a penetration that seems to dissipate, with a little education, somewhat as the ability to remember poetry will go. I have known peasants who could recite two or three thousand verses. But would you indeed say our discipline is relaxed? It surprises me, but then I know so little of naval things.'

'No. What is commonly called discipline is quite strict with us. What I mean is something else – the intermediate terms, they might be called. A commander is obeyed by his officers because he is himself obeying; the thing is not in its essence personal; and so down. If he does not obey, the chain weakens. How grave I am, for all love. It was that poor unlucky soldier at Mahon I was thinking of brought all this morality into my mind. Do you not find it happens very often, that you are as gay as Garrick at dinner and then by supper-time you wonder why God made the world?'

'I do. Where is the connexion with the soldier?'

'It was prize-money we fought over. He said the whole thing was unfair – he was very angry and very poor. But he would have it we sea-officers were in the Navy for that reason alone. I told him he was mistaken, and he told me I lied. We walked to those long gardens at the top end of the quay – I had Jevons of the *Implacable* with me – and it was over in two passes. Poor, stupid, clumsy fellow: he came straight on to my point. What now, Shannahan?'

'Your honour, the casks are full.'

'Bung 'em up tight, then, and we will get 'em down to the water.'

'Goodbye,' said Stephen, standing up.

'We lose you, then?' said James.

'Yes. I am going up before it grows too dark.'

Yet it would have had to be strangely dark for his feet to have missed this path. It wound up, crossing and recrossing the stream, its steps kept open by the odd fisherman after crayfish, the impotent men going to bathe in the pool and by a few other travellers; and his hand reached out of itself for the branch that would help him over a deep place – a branch polished by many hands.

Up and up: and the warm air sighing through the pines. At one point he stepped out on to a bare rock and there, wonderfully far below already, rowed the boats with their train of almost sunken barrels, not unlike the spaced-out eggs of the common toad; then the path ran back under the trees and he did not emerge again until he was on the thyme and the short turf, the rounded top of the promontory jutting out bare from the sea of pines. Apart from a violet haze on the farther hills and a startling band of yellow in the sky, colour had all gone; but he saw white scuts bobbing away, and as he had expected there were the half-seen forms of shadowy nightjars wheeling and darting, turning like ghosts over his head. He sat down by a great stone that said *Non fui non sum non curo*, and gradually the rabbits came back, nearer and nearer, until on the windward side he could indeed hear their quick nibbling in the thyme. He meant to sit there until dawn, and to establish a continuity in his mind, if that could be done: the friend (though existent) was a mere pretext. Silence, darkness and these countless familiar scents and the warmth of the land had become (in their way) as necessary to him as air.

'I THINK WE MAY run in now,' said Jack. 'It will do no harm to be before our time, for I should like to stretch my legs a little. In any case, I should like to see him as early as can be; I am uneasy with him ashore. There are times when I feel he should not be allowed out alone; and then again there are times when I feel he could command a fleet, almost.'

The *Sophie* had been standing off and on, and it was now the end of the middle watch, with James Dillon relieving the master; they might just as well take advantage of having all hands on deck to tack the sloop, observed Jack, wiping the dew off the taffrail and leaning upon it to stare down at the cutter towing astern, clearly visible in the phosphorescence of the milk-warm sea.

'That's where we filled, sir,' said Babbington, pointing up the shadowy beach. 'And if it was not so dark you could see the little sorts of path the Doctor went up from here.'

Jack walked over to stare at the path and to view the basin; he walked stumpily, for he could not come by his land legs right away. The ground would not heave and yield like a deck; but as he paced to and fro in the half-light his body grew more used to the earth's rigidity, and in time his legs carried him with an easier, less rough and jerking action. He reflected upon the nature of the ground, upon the slow and uneven coming of the light – a progression by jerks – upon the agreeable change in his lieutenant since the brush at Almoraira and upon the curious alteration in the master, who was quite sullen at times. Dillon had a pack of hounds at home, thirty-five couple – had had some splendid runs – famous country it must be, and prodigious stout foxes to stand up so long – Jack had a great respect for a man who could show good sport with a pack of hounds. Dillon obviously knew a great deal about hunting, and about horses; yet it was strange he should mind so little about the noise his dogs made, for the cry of a tuneful pack . . .

The *Sophie*'s warning gun jerked him from these placid reflexions. He whipped round, and there was the smoke drifting down her side. A hoist of signals was racing up, but without his glass he would not be able to make out the flags in this light: the sloop came round before the wind, and as though she could feel his perplexity of mind she reverted to the oldest of all signals, her topgallants loose and sheets flying, to say *strange sails in sight*; and she emphasized this with a second gun.

Jack glanced at his watch and with longing into the motionless silent pines: said, 'Lend me your knife, Bonden,' and picked up a big flattish stone. *Regrediar* he scratched on it (a notion of secrecy flitting through his mind), with the time and his initials. He struck it into the top of a little heap, took a last hopeless look into the wood and leapt aboard.

The moment the cutter was alongside the *Sophie*'s yards creaked round, she filled and pointed straight out to sea.

'Men-of-war, sir, I am almost certain,' said James. 'I thought you would wish us to get into the offing.'

'Very right, Mr Dillon,' said Jack. 'Will you lend me your glass?'

At the masthead, with his breath coming back and the light of day broad over the sharp, unmisted sea, he could make them out clearly. Two ships to windward, coming up fast from the south with all sails set: men-of-war for a ten-pound note. English? French? Spanish? There was more wind out there and they must be running a good ten knots. He glanced over his left shoulder, at the landing trending away eastwards out to sea. The *Sophie* would have a devil of a job rounding that cape before they were up with her; yet she must do so, or be shut in. Yes, they were men-of-war. They were hull-up now, and although he could not count the ports they were probably heavy frigates, thirty-six gun frigates: frigates for sure.

If the *Sophie* rounded the cape first she might have a chance: and if she ran through the shoal water between the point and the reef beyond it she would gain half a mile, for no deep-drafted frigate could follow her there.

'We will send the people to their breakfast, Mr Dillon,' he said. 'And then clear for action. If there is to be a dust-up, we might just as well have full bellies for it.'

But there were few bellies that filled themselves heartily aboard the *Sophie* that brilliant morning; a kind of impatient rigidity kept the oatmeal and hard-tack from going down regular and smooth; and even Jack's freshly-roasted, freshly-ground coffee wasted its scent on the quarter-deck as the officers stood very carefully gauging the respective courses,

speeds and likely points of convergence: two frigates to windward, a hostile coast to leeward and the likelihood of being
embayed – it was enough to take the edge off any appetite.

'Deck,' called the look-out from within the pyramid of
tightly-drawing canvas, 'she's breaking out her colours, sir.
Blue ensign.'

'Aye,' said Jack, 'I dare say. Mr Ricketts, reply with the
same.'

Now every glass in the *Sophie* was trained upon the nearer
frigate's foretopgallant for the private signal: for although anyone could heave out a blue ensign, only a King's ship could
show the secret mark of recognition. There it was: a red flag
at the fore, followed a moment later by a white flag and a
pendant at the main, and the faint boom of a windward gun.

All the tension slackened at once. 'Very well,' said Jack.
'Reply and then make our number. Mr Day, three guns to leeward in slow time.'

'She's the *San Fiorenzo*, sir,' said James, helping the flustered midshipman with the signal-book, whose prettily-
coloured pages would race out of control in the freshening
breeze. 'And she is signalling for *Sophie*'s captain.'

'Christ,' said Jack inwardly. The *San Fiorenzo*'s captain was
Sir Harry Neale, who had been first lieutenant of the *Resolution* when Jack was her most junior midshipman, and then
his captain in the *Success*: a great stickler for promptness,
clean-liness, perfection of dress and hierarchy. Jack was
unshaved; what hair he had left was in all directions;
Stephen's bluish grease covered one half of his face. But
there was no help for it. 'Bear up to close her, then,' he said,
and darted into his cabin.

'HERE YOU ARE at last,' said Sir Harry, looking at him with
marked distaste. 'By God, Captain Aubrey, you take your
time.'

The frigate seemed enormous; after the *Sophie* her towering masts might have been those of a first-rate ship of the

line; acres of pale deck stretched away on either hand. He had a ludicrous and at the same time a very painful feeling of being crushed down to a far smaller size, as well as that of being reduced all at once from a position of total authority to one of total subservience.

'I beg pardon, sir,' he said, without expression.

'Well. Come into the cabin. Your appearance don't change much, Aubrey,' he remarked, waving towards a chair. 'However, I am quite glad of the meeting. We are overburdened with prisoners and mean to discharge fifty of 'em into you.'

'I am sorry, sir, truly sorry, not to be able to oblige you, but the sloop is crowded with prisoners already.'

'*Oblige*, did you say? You will oblige me, sir, by obeying orders. Are you aware I am the senior captain here, sir? Besides, I know damned well you have been sending prize-crews into Mahon: these prisoners can occupy their room. Anyhow, you can land them in a few days' time; so let us hear no more of it.'

'But what about my cruise, sir?'

'I am less concerned with your cruise, sir, than with the good of the service. Let the transfer be carried out as quickly as possible, because I have further orders for you. We are sweeping for an American ship, the *John B. Christopher*. She is on her passage from Marseilles to the United States, calling at Barcelona, and we expect to find her between Majorca and the main. Among her passengers she may have two rebels, United Irishmen, the one a Romish priest called Mangan and the other a fellow by the name of Roche, Patrick Roche. They are to be taken off, by force if necessary. They will probably be using French names and have French passports: they speak French. Here is their description: *a middle-sized spare man about forty years old, of a brown complexion and dark brown-coloured hair, but wears a wig; a hooked nose; a sharp chin, grey eyes, and a large mole near his mouth.* That's the parson. T'other is *a tall stout man above six foot high, black hair and blue eyes, about thirty-five, has the little finger of his left hand cut off and walks stiff from a wound in his leg.* You had better take these printed sheets.'

'Mr DILLON, PREPARE to receive twenty-five prisoners from *San Fiorenzo* and twenty-five from *Amelia*,' said Jack. 'And then we are to join in a sweep for some rebels.'

'Rebels?' cried James.

'Yes,' said Jack absently, peering beyond him at the slack foretopsail bowline and breaking off to call out an order. 'Yes. Pray glance at these sheets when you have leisure – leisure, forsooth.'

'Fifty more mouths,' said the purser. 'What do you say to that, Mr Marshall? Three and thirty full allowances. Where in God's name am I supposed to find it all?'

'We shall have to put into Mahon straight away, Mr Ricketts, that's what I say to it, and kiss my hand to the cruise. Fifty is impossible, and that's flat. You never saw two officers look so glum in your life. Fifty!'

'Fifty more of the buggers,' said James Sheehan, 'and all for their own imperial convenience. Jesus, Mary and Joseph.'

'And think of our poor doctor, all alone among them damned trees – why, there might be owls. God damn the service, I say, and the – *San Fiorenzo*, and the bleeding *Amelia*, too.'

'Alone? Don't you think it, mate. But damn the service to hell, just as you say.'

It was in this mood that the *Sophie* stretched away to the north-west, on the outward or right-hand extremity of the sweeping line. The *Amelia* lay half topsails down on her larboard beam and the *San Fiorenzo* the same distance inshore of the Amelia, quite out of sight of the *Sophie* and in the best position for picking up any slow prize that offered. Between them they could oversee sixty miles of the clear-skied Mediterranean; and so they sailed all day long.

It was indeed a long day, full and busy – the fore-hold to clear, the prisoners to stow away and guard (many of them privateer's men, a dangerous crew), three slow-witted heavy merchantmen to scurry after (all neutrals and all unwilling to heave-to; but one did report a ship, thought to be American, fishing her injured foretopmast two days' sail to windward) and the incessant trimming of the sails in the shifting, uncertain, dangerously gusty wind, to keep up with the frigates – the Sophie's very best would only just avoid disgrace. And she was short-handed: Mowett, Pullings and old Alexander, a reliable quartermaster, were away in prizes, together with nearly a third of her best men, so that James Dillon and the master had to keep watch and watch. Tempers ran short, too, and the defaulters' list lengthened as the day wore on.

'I did not think Dillon could be so savage,' thought Jack, as his lieutenant roared up into the foretop, making the weeping Babbington and his reduced band of topmen set the larboard topsail studdingsail afresh for the third time. It was true that the sloop was flying along at a splendid pace (for her); but in a way it was a pity to flog her so, to badger the men – too high a price to pay. However, that was the service, and he certainly must not interfere. His mind returned to its many problems and to worrying about Stephen: it was sheer madness, this rambling about on a hostile shore. And then again he was profoundly dissatisfied with himself for his performance aboard the San Fiorenzo. A gross abuse of authority: he should have dealt with it firmly. Yet there he was, bound hand and foot by the Printed Instructions and the Articles of War. And then again there was the problem of midshipmen. The sloop needed at least two more, a youngster and an oldster; he would ask Dillon if there was any boy he chose to nominate – cousin, nephew, godchild; it was a handsome compliment for a captain to pay his lieutenant, not unusual when they liked one another. As for the oldster, he wanted someone with experience, best of all someone who could be rated master's mate almost at once. His thoughts dwelt upon his coxswain, a fine seaman and captain of the maintop; then they moved on to consider the younger men belonging to the lower deck. He would far, far rather have someone who came in through the hawse-hole, a plain sailor-man like young Pullings, than most of the youths whose families could afford to send them to sea . . . If the Spaniards caught Stephen Maturin they would shoot him for a spy.

It was almost dark by the time the third merchantman had been dealt with, and Jack was shattered with fatigue – red eyes prickling, ears four times too sharp and a feeling like a tight cord round his temples. He had been on deck all day, an anxious day that began two hours before first light, and he went to sleep almost before his head was down. Yet in that brief interval his darkening mind had time for two darts of intuition, the one stating that all was well with Stephen Maturin, the other that with James Dillon it was *not*. 'I had no notion he minded so about the cruise: though no doubt he has grown attached to Maturin too: a strange fellow,' he said, sinking right down.

Down, down, into the perfect sleep of an exhausted healthy well-fed young fattish man – a rosy sleep; yet not so far that he did not wake sharply after a few hours, frowning and uneasy. Low, urgent, quarrelling voices came whispering in through the stern-window: for a moment he thought of a surprise, a boat-attack, boarding in the night; but then his more woken mind recognized them as Dillon's and Marshall's, and he sank back. 'Yet,' said his mind a great while later, and still in sleep, 'how do they both come to be on the quarter-deck at this time of the night, when they are keeping watch and watch? It is not eight bells.' As if to confirm this statement the *Sophie*'s bell struck three times, and from various points all through the sloop came the low answering cries of *all's well*. But it was not. She was not under the same press of sail. What was amiss? He huddled on his dressing-gown and went on deck. Not only had the *Sophie* reduced sail, but her head was pointing east-north-east by east.

'Sir,' said Dillon, stepping forward, 'this is my responsibility entirely. I overruled the master and ordered the helm to be put up. I believe there is a ship on the starboard bow.'

Jack stared into the silvery haze – moonlight and a half-covered sky: the swell had increased. He saw no ship, no light: but that proved nothing. He picked up the traverseboard and looked at the change of course. 'We shall be in with the coast of Majorca directly,' he said, yawning.

'Yes, sir: so I took the liberty of reducing sail.'

It was an extraordinary breach of discipline. But Dillon knew that as well as he did: there was no good purpose to be served in telling him of it publicly.

'Whose watch is it at present?'

'Mine, sir,' said the master. He spoke quietly, but in a voice almost as harsh and unnatural as Dillon's. There were strange currents here; much stronger than any ordinary disagreement about a ship's light.

'Who is aloft?'

'Assei, sir.'

Assei was an intelligent, reliable Lascar. 'Assei, ahoy!'

'Hollo,' the thin pipe from the darkness above.

'What do you see?'

'See nothing, sir. See star, no more.'

But then there would be nothing obvious about such a fleeting glimpse. Dillon was probably right: he would never have done such an extraordinary thing else. Yet this was a damned odd course. 'Are you quite persuaded about your light, Mr Dillon?'

'Fully persuaded, sir – quite happy.'

Happy was the strangest word to hear said in that grating voice. Jack made no reply for some moments; then he altered the course a point and a half to the north and began pacing up and down his habitual walk. By four bells the light was mounting fast from the east, and there indeed was the dark presence of the land on their starboard bow, dim through the vapours that hung over the sea, though the high bowl of the sky was clear, something between blue and darkness. He went below to put on some clothes, and while the shirt was still over his head there was the cry of a sail.

She came sailing out of a brownish band of mist a bare two miles to leeward, and as soon as he had cleared it Jack's glass picked out the fished foretopmast, with no more than a close-reefed topsail on it. Everything was clear: everything was plain: Dillon had been perfectly right, of course. Here was their quarry, though strangely off its natural course; it must have tacked some time ago off Dragon Island, and now it was slowly making its way into the open channel to the south; in an hour or so their disagreeable task would be done, and he knew very well what he would be at by noon.

'Well done, Mr Dillon,' he cried. 'Well done indeed. We could not have fallen in with her better; I should never have believed it, so far to the east of the channel. Show her our colours and give her a gun.'

The *John B. Christopher* was a little shy of what might prove a hungry man-of-war, eager to impress all her English seamen (or anyone else the boarding-party chose to consider English), but she had not the least chance of escape, above all with a wounded topmast and her topgallantmasts struck down on deck; so after a slight flurry of canvas and a tendency to fall off, she backed her topsails, showed the American flag and waited for the *Sophie's* boat.

'You shall go,' said Jack to Dillon, who was still hunched over his telescope, as though absorbed in some point of the American's rigging. 'You speak French better than any of us, now the Doctor is away; and after all you discovered her in this extraordinary place – she is your discovery. Should you like the printed papers again, or shall you . . .' Jack broke off. He had seen a very great deal of drunkenness in the Navy; drunken admirals, post-captains, commanders, drunken ship's boys ten years old, and he had been trundled aboard on a wheelbarrow himself before now; but he disliked it on duty – he disliked it very much indeed, above all at such an hour in the morning. 'Perhaps Mr Marshall had better go,' he said coldly. 'Pass the word for Mr Marshall.'

'Oh, no, sir,' cried Dillon, recovering himself. 'I beg your pardon – it was a momentary – I am perfectly well.' And to be sure, the sweating pallor, the boltered staring look had gone, replaced by an unhealthy flush.

'Well,' said Jack, dubiously, and the next moment James Dillon was calling out very actively for the cutter's crew, hurrying up and down, checking their arms, hammering the flints of his own pistols, as clearly master of himself as possible. With the cutter alongside and ready to push off, he said, 'Perhaps I should beg for those sheets, sir. I will refresh my memory as we pull across.'

Gently backing and filling, the *Sophie* kept on the *John B. Christopher*'s larboard bow, prepared to rake her and cross her stem at the first sign of trouble. But there was none. A few more or less derisive cries of 'Paul Jones' and 'How's King George?' floated across from the *John B. Christopher*'s fo'c'sle, and the grinning gun-crews, standing there ready to blow their cousins to a better world without the least hesitation or the least ill-will, would gladly have replied in kind; but their captain would have none of it – this was an odious task, no time for merriment. At the first call of 'Boston beans' he rapped out, 'Silence, fore and aft. Mr Ricketts, take that man's name.'

Time wore on. In its tub the slow-match burned away, coil by coil. All along the deck attention wandered. A gannet passed overhead, brilliant white, and Jack found himself pondering anxiously about Stephen, forgetful of his duty. The sun rose: the sun rose.

Now at last the boarding-party were at the American's gangway, dropping down into the cutter: and there was Dillon, alone. He was replying civilly to the master and to the passengers at the rail. The *John B. Christopher* was filling – the odd colonial twang of her mate urging the men to 'clap on to that tarnation brace' echoed across the sea – and she was under way southwards. The *Sophie*'s cutter was pulling across the intervening space.

On the way out James had not known what he would do.

All that day, ever since he had heard of the squadron's mission, he had been overwhelmed by a sense of fatality; and now, although he had had hours to think about it, he still did not know what he would do. He moved as though in a nightmare, going up the American's side without the slightest volition of his own; and he had known, of course, that he would find Father Mangan. Although he had done everything possible, short of downright mutiny or sinking the *Sophie*, to avoid it; although he had altered course and shortened sail, blackmailing the master to accomplish it, he had known that he would find him. But what he had not known, what he had never foreseen, was that the priest should threaten to denounce him if he did not turn a blind eye. He had disliked the man the moment recognition flashed between them, but in that very first moment he had made up his mind – there was not the slightest possibility of his playing the constable and taking them off. And then came this threat. For a second he had known with total certainty that it did not affect him in the least, but he had hardly reached another breath before the squalor of the situation became unbearable. He was obliged to make a slow pretence of examining all the other passports aboard before he could bring himself under control. He had known that there was no way out, that whatever course he took would be dishonourable; but he had never imagined that dishonour could be so painful. He was a proud man; Father Mangan's satisfied leer wounded him beyond anything he had yet experienced, and with the pain of the wound there came a cloud of intolerable doubts.

The boat touched the *Sophie*'s side. 'No such passengers aboard, sir,' he reported.

'So much the better,' said Jack cheerfully, raising his hat to the American captain and waving it. 'West a half south, Mr Marshall; and house those guns, if you please.' The exquisite fragrance of coffee drifted up from the after hatchway. 'Dillon, come and breakfast with me,' he said, taking him familiarly by the arm. 'You are still looking most ghastly pale.'

'You must excuse me, sir,' whispered James, disengaging himself with a look of utter hatred. 'I am a little out of order.'

8

'I AM ENTIRELY at a loss, upon my honour; and so I lay the position before you, confiding wholly in your candour . . . I am entirely at a loss: I cannot for the life of me conceive what manner of offence . . . It was not my landing of those monstrously unjust prisoners on Dragon Island (though he certainly disapproved it), for the trouble began before that, quite early in the morning.' Stephen listened gravely, attentively, never interrupting; and very slowly, harking back for details overlooked and forward to straighten his chronology by anticipation, Jack laid before him the history of his relations with James Dillon – good, bad; good, bad – but with this last extraordinary descent not only inexplicable but strangely wounding, because of the real liking that had grown up, in addition to the esteem. Then there was Marshall's unaccountable conduct, too; but that was of much less importance.

With the utmost care, Jack reiterated his arguments about the necessity for having a happy ship if one was to command an efficient fighting machine; he quoted examples of like and contrary cases; and his audience listened and approved. Stephen could not bring his wisdom to the resolution of any of these difficulties, however, nor (as Jack would somewhat ignobly have liked) could he propose his good offices; for he was a merely ideal interlocutor, and his thinking flesh lay thirty leagues to the south and west, across a waste of sea. A rough waste, and a cross sea: after frustrating days of calm, light airs and then a strong south-wester, the wind had backed easterly in the night, and now it was blowing a gale across the waves that had built up during the day, so that the *Sophie* went thumping along under double-reefed topsails and courses, the cross-sea breaking over her weather-bow and soaking the lookout on the fo'c'sle with a grateful spray, heeling James Dillon as he stood on the quarter-deck communing with the Devil and rocking the cot in which Jack silently harangued the darkness.

His was an exceedingly busy life; and yet since he entered an inviolable solitude the moment he passed the sentry at his cabin door, it left him a great deal of time for reflexion. It was not frittered away in very small exchanges, in listening to three-quarters of a scale on a quavering German flute or in sailors' politics. 'I shall speak to him, when we pick him up. I shall speak in the most general way, of the comfort it is to a man to have a confidential friend aboard; and of this singularity in the sailor's life, that one moment he is so on top of his shipmates, all hugger-mugger in the ward-room, that he can hardly breathe, let alone play anything but a jig on the fiddle, and the next he is pitched into a kind of hermit's solitude, something he has never known before.'

In times of stress Jack Aubrey had two main reactions: he either became aggressive or he became amorous; he longed either for the violent catharsis of action or for that of making love. He loved a battle: he loved a wench.

'I quite understand that some commanders take a girl to sea with them,' he reflected. 'Apart from the pleasure, think of the *refuge* of sinking into a warm, lively, affectionate . . .'

Peace. 'I *wish* there were a girl in this cabin,' he added, after a pause.

This disarray, this open, acknowledged incomprehension, were kept solely for his cabin and his ghostly companion; the outward appearance of the *Sophie*'s captain had nothing hesitant about it, and it would have been a singularly acute observer to tell that the nascent friendship between him and his lieutenant had been cut short. The master was such an observer, however, for although Jack's truly hideous appearance when singed and greased had caused a revulsion for a while, at the same time Jack's obvious liking for James Dillon had set up a jealousy that worked in the contrary direction. Furthermore, the master had been threatened in terms that left almost no room for doubt, in very nearly direct terms, and so for an entirely different cause he watched the captain and the lieutenant with painful anxiety.

'Mr Marshall,' said Jack in the darkness, and the poor man jumped as though a pistol had been fired behind him, 'when do you reckon we shall raise the land?'

'In about two hours' time, sir, if this wind holds.'

'Yes: I thought as much,' said Jack, gazing up into the rigging. 'I believe you may shake out a reef now, however; and at any further slackening set the topgallants – crack on all you can. And have me called when land is seen, if you please, Mr Marshall.'

Something less than two hours later he reappeared, to view the remote irregular line on the starboard bow: Spain, with the singular mountain the English called Egg-top Hill in line with the best bower anchor, and their watering bay therefore directly ahead.

'By God, you are a prime navigator, Marshall,' he said, lowering his glass. 'You deserve to be master of the fleet.'

It would take them at least an hour to run in, however, and now that the event was so close at hand, no longer at all theoretical, Jack discovered how anxious he was in fact – how very much the outcome mattered to him.

'Send my coxswain aft, will you?' he said, returning to his cabin after he had taken half a dozen uneasy turns.

Barret Bonden, coxswain and captain of the maintop, was unusually young for his post; a fine open-looking creature, tough without brutality, cheerful, perfectly in his place and, of course, a prime seaman – bred to the sea from childhood. 'Sit down, Bonden,' said Jack, a little consciously, for what he was about to offer was the quarter-deck, no less, and the possibility of advancement to the very pinnacle of the sailor's hierarchy. 'I have been thinking . . . should you like to be rated midshipman?'

'Why, no sir, not at all,' answered Bonden at once, his teeth flashing in the gloom. 'But I thank you very kindly for your good opinion, sir.'

'Oh,' said Jack, taken aback. 'Why not?'

'I ain't got the learning, sir. Why' – laughing cheerfully – it's all I can do to read the watch-list, spelling it out slow; and I'm too old to wear round now. And then, sir, what should I look like, rigged out like an officer? Jack-in-the green: and my old messmates laughing up their sleeves and calling out "What ho, the hawse-hole." '

'Plenty of fine officers began on the lower deck,' said Jack. 'I was on the lower deck myself, once,' he added, regretting the sequence as soon as he had uttered it.

'I know you was, sir,' said Bonden, and his grin flashed again.

'How did you know that?'

'We got a cove in the starboard watch, was shipmates with you, sir, in the old *Reso*, off the Cape.'

'Oh dear, oh dear,' cried Jack inwardly, 'and I never noticed him. So there I was, turning all the women ashore as righteous as Pompous Pilate, and they knew all the time . . . well, well.' And aloud, with a certain stiffness, 'Well, Bonden, think of what I have said. It would be a pity to stand in your own way.'

'If I may make so bold, sir,' said Bonden, getting to his feet and standing there, suddenly constrained, lumpish and embarrassed, 'there's my Aunt Sloper's George – George Lucock, foretopman, larboard watch. He's a right scholar, can write so small you can scarcely see it; younger nor I am, and more soople, sir, oh, far more soople.'

'Lucock?' said Jack dubiously. 'He's only a lad. Was not he flogged last week?'

'Yes, sir: but it was only his gun had won again. And he couldn't hold back from his draught, not in duty to the giver.'

'Well,' said Jack, reflecting that perhaps there might be wiser prizes than a bottle (though none so valued), 'I will keep an eye on him.'

MIDSHIPMEN WERE MUCH in his mind during this
tedious working in. 'Mr Babbington,' he said, suddenly stopping in his up and down. 'Take your hands out of your pockets. When did you last write home?'

Mr Babbington was at an age when almost any question
evokes a guilty response, and this was, in fact, a valid accusa-
tion. He reddened, and said, 'I don't know, sir.'

'Think, sir, think,' said Jack, his good-tempered face clouding unexpectedly. 'What port did you send it from? Mahon?
Leghorn? Genoa? Gibraltar? Well, never mind.' There was no
dark figure to be made out on that distant beach. 'Never
mind. Write a handsome letter. Two pages at least. And send
it in to me with your daily workings tomorrow. Give your
father my compliments and tell him my bankers are Hoares.'
For Jack, like most other captains, managed the youngsters'
parental allowance for them. 'Hoares,' he repeated absently
once or twice, 'my bankers are Hoares,' and a strangled ugly
crowing noise made him turn. Young Ricketts was clinging to
the fall of the main burton-tackle in an attempt to control
himself, but without much success. Jack's cold glare chilled
his mirth, however, and he was able to reply to 'And you, Mr
Ricketts, have you written to your parents recently?' with an
audible 'No, sir' that scarcely quavered at all.

'Then you will do the same: two pages, wrote small, and no
demands for new quadrants, laced hats or hangers,' said Jack;
and something told the midshipman that this was no time to
expostulate, to point out that his loving parent, his only parent, was in daily, even hourly communication with him.
Indeed, this awareness of Jack's state of tension was general
throughout the brig. 'Goldilocks is in a rare old taking about
the Doctor,' they said. 'Watch out for squalls.' And when hammocks were piped up the seamen who had to pass by him to
stow theirs in the starboard quarter-deck netting glanced at
him nervously; one, trying to keep an eye on the quartermaster, and on the break of the deck, and on his captain, all at
the same time, fell flat on his face.

But Goldilocks was not the only one to be anxious, by any manner of means, and when Stephen Maturin was at last seen to walk out of the trees and cross the beach to meet the jolly-boat, a general exclamation of 'There he is!' broke out from waist to fo'c'sle, in defiance of good discipline: 'Huzzay!'

'How very glad I am to see you,' cried Jack, as Stephen groped his way aboard, pushed and pulled by well-meaning hands. 'How are you, my dear sir? Come and breakfast directly – I have held it back on purpose. How do you find yourself? Tolerably spry, I hope? Tolerably spry?'

'I am very well, I thank you,' said Stephen, who indeed looked somewhat less cadaverous, flushed as he was with pleasure at the open friendliness of his welcome. 'I will take a look at my sick-bay and then I will share your bacon with the utmost pleasure. Good morning, Mr Day. Take off your hat, if you please. Very neat, very neat: you do us credit, Mr Day. But no exposure to the sun as yet – I recommend the wearing of a close Welsh wig. Cheslin, good morning to you. You have a good account of our patients, I trust?'

'THAT,' HE SAID, a little greasy from bacon, 'that was a point that exercised my mind a good deal during your absence. Would my loblolly boy pay the men back in their own coin? Would they return to their persecution of him? How quickly could he come by a new identity?'

'Identity?' said Jack, comfortably pouring out more coffee. 'Is not identity something you are born with?'

'The identity I am thinking of is something that hovers between a man and the rest of the world: a mid-point between his view of himself and theirs of him – for each, of course, affects the other continually. A reciprocal fluxion, sir. There is nothing absolute about this identity of mine. Were you, you personally, to spend some days in Spain at present you would find yours change, you know, because of the general opinion there that you are a false harsh brutal murdering villain, an odious man.'

'I dare say they are vexed,' said Jack, smiling. 'And I dare say they call me Beelzebub. But that don't make me Beelzebub.'

'Does it not? Does it not? Ah? Well, however that may be, you have angered, you have stirred up the mercantile interest along the coast to a most prodigious degree. There is a wealthy man by the name of Mateu who is wonderfully incensed against you. The quicksilver belonged to him, and being contraband it was not insured; so did the vessel you cut out at Almoraira; and the cargo of the tartan burnt off Tortosa – half of that was his. He is well with the ministry. He has moved their indolence and they have allowed him and his friends to charter one of their men-of-war . . .'

'Not *charter*, my dear sir: no private person can possibly *charter* a man-of-war, a national vessel, a King's ship, not even in Spain.'

'Oh? Perhaps I use the wrong term: I often use the wrong term in naval matters. However. A ship of force, not only to protect the coasting trade but even more to pursue the *Sophie*, who is perfectly well known now, both by name and by description. This I had from Mateu's own cousin as we danced –'

'You danced?' cried Jack, far more astonished than if Stephen had said 'as we ate our cold roast baby.'

'Certainly I danced. Why would I not dance, pray?'

'Certainly you are to dance – most uncommon graceful, I am sure. I only wondered . . . but did you indeed go about *dancing*?'

'I did. You have not travelled in Catalonia, sir, I believe?'

'Not I.'

'Then I must tell you that on Sunday mornings it is the custom, in that country, for people of all ages and conditions to dance, on coming out of church: so I was dancing with Ramon Mateu i Cadafalch in the square before the cathedral church of Tarragona, where I had gone to hear the Palestrina Missa Brevis. The dance is a particular dance, a round called the sardana; and if you will reach me your fiddle I will play you the air of the one I have in mind. Though you must imagine I am a harsh braying hoboy.' Plays.

'It is a charming melody, to be sure. Somewhat in the Moorish taste, is it not? But upon my word it makes my flesh creep, to think of you rambling about the countryside – in ports – in towns. I had imagined you would have gone to earth, that you would have kept close with your friend, hidden in her room . . . that is to say . . .'

'Yet I had told you, had I not, that I could ride the length and breadth of that country without a question or a moment's uneasiness?'

'So you had. So you had.' Jack reflected for a while. 'And so, of course, if you chose, you could find out what ships and convoys were sailing, when expected, how laden, and so on. Even the galleons themselves, I dare say?'

'Certainly I could,' said Stephen, 'if I chose to play the spy. It is a curious and apparently illogical set of notions, is it not, that makes it right and natural to speak of the *Sophie*'s enemies, yet beyond any question wrong, dishonourable and indecent to speak of her prey?'

'Yes,' said Jack, looking at him wistfully. 'You must give a hare her law, there is no doubt. But what do you tell me about this ship of force? What is her rate? How many guns does she carry? Where does she lie?'

'*Cacafuego* is her name.'

'*Cacafuego*? *Cacafuego*? I have never heard of her. So at least she cannot be a ship of the line. How is she rigged?'

Stephen paused. 'I am ashamed to say I did not ask,' he said. 'But from the satisfaction with which her name was pronounced, I take her to be some prepotent great argosy.'

'Well, we must try to keep out of her way: and since she knows what we look like, we must try to change our appearance. It is wonderful what a coat of paint and a waist-cloth will do, or even an oddly patched jib or a fished topmast – by the way, I suppose they told you in the boat why we were compelled to maroon you?'

'They told me about the frigates and your boarding the American.'

'Yes: and precious stuff it was, too. There were no such people aboard – Dillon searched her for close on an hour. I was just as glad, for I remembered you had told me the United Irishmen were good creatures, on the whole – far better than those other fellows, whose name I forget. Steel boys, white boys, orange boys?'

'United Irishmen? I had understood them to be French. They told me the American ship had been searched for some Frenchmen.'

'They were only pretending to be Frenchmen. That is to say, if they had been there at all, they might have pretended to be French. That is why I sent Dillon, who speaks it so well. But they were not, you see; and in my opinion the whole thing was so much cock. I was just as glad, as I say; but it seemed to upset Dillon most strangely. I suppose he was very eager to take them: or he was very much put out at our cruise being cut short. Ever since then – however, I must not bore you with all that. You heard about the prisoners?'

'That the frigates had been so good as to give you fifty of theirs?'

'Merely for their own convenience! It was not for the good of the service at all. A most shabby, unscrupulous thing!' cried Jack, his eyes starting from his head at the recollection. 'But I dished 'em, though. As soon as we were done with the American we bore away for the *Amelia*, told her we had drawn a blank and made our signal for parting company; and a couple of hours later, the wind serving, we landed every man jack on Dragon Island.'

'Off Majorca?'

'Just so.'

'But is not that wrong? Will you not be reproved – court-martialled?'

Jack winced, and clapping his hand to wood he said, 'Pray

never say that ill-conditioned word. The mere sound of it is enough to spoil the day.'

'But will you not get into trouble?'

'Not if I put into Mahon with a thundering great prize at my tail,' said Jack, laughing. 'For now we may just have time to go and lie off Barcelona, do you see, if the wind is kind – I had quite set my heart upon it. We shall just have time for a quick stroke or two and then we must bear away for Mahon with anything we may have caught, for we certainly cannot spare another prize-crew, with our numbers so reduced. And we certainly cannot stay out much longer, without we eat our boots.'

'Still and all . . .'

'Never look so concerned, dear Doctor. There was no specific order as to where to land them, no order at all; and, of course, I'll square the head-money. Besides, I am covered: all my officers formally agreed that our shortage of water and provisions compelled us to do so – Marshall and Ricketts and even Dillon, although he was so chuff and pope-holy about it all.'

THE *SOPHIE* REEKED of grilled sardines and fresh paint. She lay fifteen miles off Cape Tortosa in a dead calm, wallowing on the oily swell; and the blue smoke of the sardines she had bought out of a night-fishing barca-longa (she had bought the whole catch) still hung sickeningly about her 'tweendecks, her sails and rigging, half an hour after dinner.

The bosun had a large working-party slung over her side, spreading yellow paint over the neat dockyard black and white; the sailmaker and a dozen palm-and-pricket men were busy at a long narrow strip of canvas designed to conceal her warlike character; and her lieutenant was pulling round her in the jolly-boat to judge of the effect. He was alone, except for her surgeon, and he was saying '. . . everything. I did everything in my power to avoid it. *Everything*, breaking all measures. I altered course, I shortened sail – unthinkable in the service – blackmailing the master to do so; and yet in the morning there she lay, two miles away under our lee, where she had no conceivable right to be. Ahoy, Mr Watt! Six inches lower all round.'

'It was just as well. If any other man had gone aboard they might have been taken.'

A pause, and James said, 'He leant over the table, so close I had his stinking breath in my face, and with a hateful yellow look he poured out this ugly stuff. I had already made up my mind, as I said; yet it looked exactly as though I were yielding to a vulgar threat. And two minutes later I was sure I had.'

'But you had not: it is a sick fancy. Indeed, it is not far from morose delectation: take great care of that sin, James, I beg. As for the rest, it is a pity you mind it so. What does it amount to, in the long run?'

'A man would have to be three parts dead not to mind it so; and quite dead to a sense of duty, to say nothing of . . . Mr Watt, that will do very well.'

Stephen sat there, weighing the advantage of saying 'Do not hate Jack Aubrey for it: do not drink so much: do not destroy yourself for what will not last' against the disadvantage of setting off an explosion; for in spite of his apparent calm, James Dillon was on a hair-trigger, in a state of pitiful exacerbation. Stephen could not decide, shrugged, lifting his right hand, palm upwards, in a gesture that meant 'Bah, let it go,' and to himself he observed, 'However, I shall oblige him to take a black draught this evening – that at least I can do – and some comfortable mandragora; and in my diary I shall write "JD, required to play Iscariot either with his right hand or with his left, and hating the necessity (the absolute necessity), concentrates all this hatred upon poor JA, which is a remarkable instance of the human process; for, in fact, JD does not dislike JA at all – far from it." '

'At least,' said James, pulling back to the *Sophie*, 'I do hope that after all this discreditable shuffling we may be taken into action. It has a wonderful way of reconciling a man with himself: and with everybody else, sometimes.'

'What is that fellow in the buff waistcoat doing on the quarterdeck?'

'That is Pram. Captain Aubrey is dressing him as a Danish officer; it is part of our plan of disguise. Do not you remember the yellow waistcoat the master of the *Clomer* wore? It is customary with them.'

'I do not. Tell me, do such things often happen, at sea?'

'Oh, yes. It is a perfectly legitimate *ruse de guerre*. Often we amuse the enemy with false signals too – anything but those of distress. Take great care of the paint, now.'

At this point Stephen fell straight into the sea – into the hollow of the sea between the boat and the side of the sloop as they drew away from one another. He sank at once, rose just as they came together, struck his head between the two and sank again, bubbling. Most of the *Sophie*'s people who could swim leapt into the water, Jack among them; and others ran with boat-hooks, a dolphin-striker, two small grapnels, an ugly barbed hook on a chain; but it was the brothers Sponge that found him, five fathoms down (heavy bones for his size, no fat, lead-soled half-boots) and brought him up, his clothes blacker than usual, his face more white, and he streaming with water, furiously indignant.

It was no epoch-making event, but it was a useful one, since it provided the gun-room with a topic of conversation at a moment when very hard work was needed to maintain the appearance of a civilized community. A good deal of the time James was heavy, inattentive and silent; his eyes were bloodshot from the grog he swallowed, but it seemed neither to cheer nor yet to fuddle him. The master was almost equally withdrawn, and he sat there stealing covert glances at Dillon from time to time. So when they were all at table they went into the subject of swimming quite exhaustively – its rarity among seamen, its advantages (the preservation of life: the pleasure to be derived from it, in suitable climates: the carrying of a line ashore in an emergency), its disadvantages (the prolongation of death-agonies in shipwreck, in falling overboard unseen: flying in the face of nature – had God meant men to swim, etc.), the curious inability of young seals to swim, the use of bladders, the best ways of learning and practising the art of swimming.

'The only right way to swim,' said the purser for the seventh time, 'is to join your hands like you were saying your prayers' – he narrowed his eyes, joined his hands very exactly – 'and shoot them out so –' This time he did strike the bottle, which plunged violently into the solomongundy and thence, deep in thick gravy, into Marshall's lap.

'I knew you would do it,' cried the master, springing about and mopping himself. 'I told you so. I said "Soonar or latar you'll knock down that damned decantar", and you can't swim a stroke – prating like a whoreson ottar. You have wrecked my best nankeen trousars.'

'I didn't go for to do it,' said the purser sullenly; and the evening relapsed into a barbarous gloom.

Indeed, as the *Sophie* beat up, tack upon tack, to the northward, she could not have been described as a very cheerful sloop. In his beautiful little cabin Jack sat reading Steel's Navy List and feeling low, not so much because he had over-eaten again, and not so much because of the great number of men senior to him on the list, as because he was so aware of this feeling aboard. He could not know the precise nature of the complicated miseries inhabiting Dillon and Marshall. He could not tell that three yards from him James Dillon was trying to fend off despair with a series of invocations and a haggard attempt at resignation, while the whole of his mind that was not taken up with increasingly mechanical prayer converted its unhappy turmoil into hatred for the established order, for authority and so for captains, and for all those who, never having had a moment's conflict of duty or honour in their lives, could condemn him out of hand. And although Jack could hear the master's shoes crunching on the deck some inches above his head, he could not possibly divine the particular emotional disturbance and the sickening dread of exposure that filled the poor man's loving heart. But he knew very well that his tight, self-contained world was hopelessly out of tune and he was haunted by the depressing sentiment of failure – of not having succeeded in what he had set out to do. He would very much have liked to ask Stephen Maturin the reasons for this failure; he would very much have liked to talk to him on indifferent subjects and to have played a little music; but he knew that an invitation to the captain's cabin was very like an order, if only because the refusing of it was so extraordinary – that had been borne in upon him very strongly the other morning, when he had been so amazed by Dillon's refusal. Where there was no equality there was no companionship: when a man was obliged to say 'Yes, sir,' his agreement was of no worth even if it happened to be true. He had known these things all his service life; they were perfectly evident; but he had never thought they would apply so fully, and to *him*.

Farther down in the sloop, in the almost deserted midshipmen's berth, the melancholy was even more profound: the youngsters were, in fact, weeping as they sat. Ever since Mowett and Pullings had gone off in prizes these two had been at watch and watch, which meant that neither ever had more than four hours' sleep – hard at that dormouse, lovebed age that so clings to its warm hammock; then again in writing their dutiful letters they had contrived to cover themselves with ink, and had been sharply rebuked for their appearance; what is more, Babbington, unable to think of *anything to put*, had filled his pages with asking after everybody at home and in the village, human beings, dogs, horses, cats, birds, and even the great hall clock, to such an extent that he was now filled with an overwhelming nostalgia. He was also afraid that his hair and teeth were going to fall out and his bones soften, while sores and blotches covered his face and body – the inevitable result of conversing with harlots, as the wise old-experienced clerk Richards had assured him. Young Ricketts' woe had quite another source: his father had been talking of a transfer into a store-ship or a transport, as being safer and far more homelike, and young Ricketts had accepted the prospect of separation with wonderful fortitude; but now it appeared that there was to be no separation – that he, young Ricketts, was to go too, torn from the *Sophie* and the life he loved so passionately. Marshall, seeing him staggering with weariness, had sent him below, and there he sat on his sea-chest, resting his face in his hands at half-past three in the morning, too tired even to creep into his hammock; and the tears oozed between his fingers.

Before the mast there was much less sadness, although there were several men – far more than usual – who looked forward with no pleasure to Thursday morning, when they were to be flogged. Most of the others had nothing positive to be glum about, apart from the hard work and the short commons; yet nevertheless the *Sophie* was already so very much of a community that every man aboard was conscious of something out of joint, something more than their officers' snappishness – what, they could not tell; but it took away from their ordinary genial flow. The gloom on the quarter-deck seeped forward, reaching as far as the goat-house, the manger, and even the hawse-holes themselves.

The *Sophie*, then, considered as an entity, was not at the top of her form as she worked through the night on the dying tramontana; nor yet in the morning, when the northerly weather was followed (as it so often happens in those waters) by wreathing mists from the south-west, very lovely for those who do not have to navigate a vessel through them, close in shore, and the forerunners of a blazing day. But this state was nothing in comparison with the tense alarm, not to say the dejection and even dread, that Stephen discovered when he stepped on to the quarter-deck just at sunrise.

He had been woken by the drum beating to quarters. He had gone directly to the cockpit, and there with Cheslin's help he had arranged his instruments. A bright eager face from the upper regions had announced 'a thundering great

xebec round the cape, right in with the land'. He acknowledged this with mild approval, and after a while he fell to
sharpening his catlin; then he sharpened his lancets and then
his fleam-toothed saw with a little hone that he had bought
for the purpose in Tortosa. Time passed, and the face was
replaced by another, a very much altered pallid face that
delivered the captain's compliments and desired him to come
on deck.

'Good morning, Doctor,' said Jack, and Stephen noticed
that his smile was strained, his eyes hard and wary. 'It looks as
though we had caught a Tartar.' He nodded over the water
towards a long, sharp, strikingly beautiful vessel, bright light
red against the sullen cliffs behind. She lay low in the water
for her size (four times the *Sophie*'s bulk), but a high kind of
flying platform carried out her stern, so that it jutted far over
her counter, while a singular beak-like projection advanced
her prow a good twenty feet beyond her stem. Her main and
mizzen masts bore immense curved double tapering lateen
yards, whose sails were spilling the south-east air to allow
the *Sophie* to come up with her; and even at this distance Stephen noticed that the yards, too, were red. Her starboard broadside, facing the *Sophie*, had no less than sixteen
gunports in it; and her decks were extraordinarily crowded
with men.

'A thirty-two-gun xebec-frigate,' said Jack, 'and she cannot
be anything but Spanish. Her hanging-ports deceived us
entirely – thought she was a merchantman until the last
moment – and nearly all her hands were down below. Mr Dillon, get a few more people out of sight without its showing.
Mr Marshall, three or four men, no more, to shake out the
reef in the fore topsail – they are to do it slowly, like lubbers.
Anderssen, call out something in Danish again and let that
bucket dangle over the side.' In a lower voice to Stephen, 'You
see her, the fox? Those ports opened two minutes ago, quite
hidden by all that bloody paintwork. And although she was
thinking of swaying up her square yards – look at her fore-

mast – she can have that lateen back in a moment, and snap us up directly. We must stand on – no choice – and see whether we can't amuse her. Mr Ricketts, you have the flags ready to hand? Slip off your jacket at once and toss it into the locker. Yes, there she goes.' A gun spoke from the frigate's quarter-deck: the ball skipped across the Sophie's bows, and the Spanish colours appeared, clear of the warning smoke. 'Carry on, Mr Ricketts,' said Jack. The Dannebrog broke out at the Sophie's gaff-end, followed by the yellow quarantine flag at the fore. 'Pram, come up here and wave your arms about. Give orders in Danish. Mr Marshall, heave to awkwardly in half a cable's length. No nearer.'

Closer and closer. Dead silence aboard the Sophie: gabble drifting across from the xebec. Standing just behind Pram, in his shirt sleeves and breeches – no uniform coat – Jack took the wheel. 'Look at all those people,' he said, half to himself and half to Stephen. 'There must be three hundred and more. They will hail us in a couple of minutes. Now, sir, Pram is going to tell them we are a Dane, a few days out of Algiers: I beg you will support him in Spanish, or any other language you see fit, as the opportunity offers.'

The hail came clear over the morning sea. 'What brig?'

'Good and loud, Pram,' said Jack.

'Clomer!' called the quartermaster in the buff waistcoat, and very faintly off the cliffs there came back the cry 'Clomer!' with the same hint of defiance, though so diminished.

'Back the foretopsail slowly, Mr Marshall,' murmured Jack, 'and keep the hands to the braces.' He murmured, for he knew very well that the frigate's officers had their glasses trained on the quarter-deck, and a persuasive fallacy assured him that the glasses would magnify his voice as well.

The way began to come off the brig, and at the same time the close groups aboard the xebec, her gun-crews, began to disperse. For a moment Jack thought it was all over and his heart, hitherto tranquil, began to bound and thump. But no. A boat was putting off.

'Perhaps we shall not be able to avoid this action,' he said. 'Mr Dillon, the guns are double-shotted, I believe?'

'Treble, sir,' said James, and looking at him Stephen saw that look of mad happiness he had known often enough, in former years – the contained look of a fox about to do something utterly insane.

The breeze and the current kept heaving the *Sophie* in towards the frigate, whose crew were going back to their task of changing from a lateen to a square rig: they swarmed thick into the shrouds, looking curiously at the docile brig, which was just about to be boarded by their launch.

'Hail the officer, Pram,' said Jack, and Pram went to the rail. He uttered a loud, seamanlike, emphatic statement in Danish; but very ludicrously in pidgin-Danish. And no recognizable form of Algiers appeared – only the Danish for *Barbary coast*, vainly repeated.

The Spanish bowman was about to hook on when Stephen, speaking a Scandinavian but instantly comprehensible Spanish, called out, 'Have you a surgeon that understands the plague aboard your ship?'

The bowman lowered his hook. The officer said, 'Why?'

'Some of our men were taken poorly at Algiers, and we are afraid. We cannot tell what it is.'

'Back water,' said the Spanish officer to his men. 'Where did you say you had touched?'

'Algiers, Alger, Argel: it was there the men went ashore. Pray what is the plague like? Swellings? Buboes? Will you come and look at them? Pray, sir, take this rope.'

'Back water,' said the officer again. 'And they went ashore at Algiers?'

'Yes. Will you send your surgeon?'

'No. Poor people, God and His Mother preserve you.'

'May we come for medicines? Pray let me come into your boat.'

'No,' said the officer, crossing himself. 'No, no. Keep off, or we shall fire into you. Keep out to sea – the sea will cure them. God be with you, poor people. And a happy voyage to you.' He could be seen ordering the bowman to throw the boathook into the sea, and the launch pulled back fast to the bright-red xebec.

They were within very easy hailing distance now, and a voice from the frigate called out some words in Danish; Pram replied; and then a tall thin figure on the quarter-deck, obviously the captain, asked, had they seen an English sloop-of-war, a brig?

'No,' they said; and as the vessels began to draw away from one another Jack whispered, 'Ask her name.'

'*Cacafuego*,' came the answer over the widening lane of sea. 'A happy voyage.'

'A happy voyage to you.'

'SO THAT IS a frigate,' said Stephen, looking attentively at the *Cacafuego*.

'A *xebec*-frigate,' said Jack. 'Handsomely with those braces, Mr Marshall: no appearance of hurry. A xebec-frigate. A wonderfully curious rig, ain't it? There's nothing faster, I suppose – broad in the beam to carry a vast great press of sail, but with a very narrow floor – but they need a prodigious crew; for, do you see, when she is sailing on a wind, she is a lateen, but when the wind comes fair, right aft or thereabouts, she strikes 'em down on deck and sways up square yards instead, a great deal of labour. She must have three hundred men, at the least. She is changing to her square rig now, which means she is going up the coast. So we must stand to the south – we have had quite enough of her company. Mr Dillon, let us take a look at the chart.'

'Dear Lord,' he said in the cabin, striking his hands together and chuckling, 'I thought we were dished that time – burnt, sunk and destroyed; hanged, drawn and quartered. What a jewel that Doctor is! When he waved the guess-rope and begged them so earnestly to come aboard! I understood him, though he spoke so quick. Ha, ha, ha! Eh? Did not you think it the drollest thing in life?'

'Very droll indeed, sir.'

'*Que vengan*, says he, most piteously, waving the line, and they start back as grave and solemn as a parcel of owls. *Que vengan*! Ha, ha, ha . . . Oh dear. But you don't seem very amused.'

'To tell you the truth, sir, I was so astonished at our sheering off that I have scarcely had time to relish the joke.'

'Why,' said Jack, smiling, 'what would you have had us do? Ram her?'

'I was persuaded that we were about to attack,' said James passionately. 'I was persuaded that was your intention. I was delighted.'

'A fourteen-gun brig against a thirty-two-gun frigate? You are not speaking in earnest?'

'Certainly. When they were hoisting in their launch and half their people were busy in the rigging our broadside and small-arms would have cut them to pieces, and with this breeze we should have been aboard before they had recovered.'

'Oh, come now! And it would scarcely have been a very honourable stroke, either.'

'Perhaps I am no great judge of what is honourable, sir,' said Dillon. 'I speak as a mere fighting man.'

MAHON, AND THE *Sophie* surrounded by her own smoke, firing both broadsides all round and one over in salute to the admiral's flag aboard the *Foudroyant*, whose imposing mass lay just between Pigtail Stairs and the ordnance wharf.

Mahon, and the *Sophie*'s liberty-men stuffing themselves with fresh roast pork and soft-tack, to a state of roaring high spirits, roaring merriment: wine-barrels with flowing taps, a hecatomb of pigs, young ladies flocking from far and near.

Jack sat stiffly in his chair, his hands sweating, his throat parched and rigid. Lord Keith's eyebrows were black with strong silver bristles interspersed, and from beneath them he directed a cold, grey, penetrating gaze across the table. 'So you were driven to it by necessity?' he said.

He was speaking of the prisoners landed on Dragon Island: indeed, the subject had occupied him almost since the beginning of the interview.

'Yes, my lord.'

The admiral did not reply for some time. 'Had you been driven to it by a want of discipline,' he said slowly, 'by a dislike for subordinating your judgment to that of your seniors, I should have been compelled to take a very serious view of the matter. Lady Keith has a great kindness for you, Captain Aubrey, as you know; and myself I should be grieved to see you harm your own prospects; so you will allow me to speak to you very frankly . . .'

Jack had known that it was going to be unpleasant as soon as he had seen the secretary's grave face, but this was far rougher than his worst expectations. The admiral was shockingly well informed; he had all the details – official reprimand for petulance, neglect of orders on stated occasions, reputation for undue independence, for temerity, and even for insubordination, rumours of ill behaviour on shore, drunkenness; and so it ran. The admiral could not see the smallest likelihood of promotion to post rank: though Captain Aubrey should not take that too much to heart – plenty of men never rose even to commander; and the commanders were a very respectable body of men. But could a man be entrusted with a line of battle ship if he were liable to take it into his head to fight a fleet engagement according to his own notions of strategy? No, there was not the least likelihood, unless something very extraordinary took place. Captain Aubrey's record was by no means all that could be wished. Lord Keith spoke steadily, with great justice, great accuracy in his facts and his diction; at first Jack had merely suffered, ashamed and uneasy; but as it went on he felt a glow somewhere about his heart or a little lower, the beginning of that rising jet of furious anger that might take control of him. He bowed his head, for he was certain it would show in his eye.

'Yet on the other hand,' said Lord Keith, 'you do possess one prime quality in a commander. You are lucky. None of my other cruisers has played such havoc with the enemy's trade; none has taken half as many prizes. So when you come back from Alexandria I shall give you another cruise.'

'Thank you, my lord.'

'It will arouse a certain amount of jealousy, a certain amount of criticism; but luck is something that rarely lasts – at least that is my experience – and we should back it while it is with us.'

Jack made his acknowledgements, thanked the admiral not ungracefully for his kindness in giving him advice, sent his duty – his affectionate duty, if he might say so – to Lady Keith, and withdrew. But the fire in his heart was burning so high in spite of the promised cruise that it was all he could do to get his words out smoothly, and there was such a look on his face as he came out that the sentry at the door instantly changed his expression of knowing irony to one of deaf, dumb, unmoving wood.

'If that scrub Harte presumes to use the same tone to me,' said Jack to himself, walking out into the street and crushing a citizen hard against the wall, 'or anything like it, I shall wring his nose off his head, and damn the service.'

'Mercy, my dear,' he roared, stepping into the Crown on his way, 'bring me a glass of vino, there's a good girl, and a copito of aguardiente. God damn all admirals,' he said, letting the young green flowery wine run cool and healing down his throat.

'But he is a topping old admiral, dear Capitano,' said Mercedes, brushing dust off his blue lapels. 'He will give you a cruise when you are coming back from Alexandria.'

Jack cocked a shrewd eye at her, observed 'Mercy querido, if you knew half as much about Spanish sailings as you do about ours, how happy, felix, you would make me', tossed down the burning drop of brandy and called for another glass of wine, that appeasing, honest brew. 'I have an auntie,' said Mercedes, 'that know a great deal.' 'Have you, my dear? Have you indeed?' said Jack. 'You shall tell me about her this evening.' He kissed her absently, tapped his lace hat more firmly on to his new wig and said, 'Now for that scrub.'

But as it happened, Captain Harte received him with more than ordinary civility, congratulated him upon the Almoraira affair – 'that battery was a damned nuisance; hulled the *Pallas* three times and knocked away one of the *Emerald*'s topmasts; should have been dealt with long ago' – and asked him to dinner. 'And bring your surgeon along, will you? My wife particularly desires me to invite him.'

'I am sure he will be very happy, if he is not already bespoke. Mrs Harte is well, I trust? I must pay my respects.'

'Oh, she's very well, I thank you. But it's no use calling on her this morning – she's out riding with Colonel Pitt. How she does it in this heat, I don't know. By the by, you can do me a service, if you will.' Jack looked at him attentively, but did not commit himself. 'My money-man wants to send his son to sea – you have a vacancy for a youngster: it is as simple as that. He is a perfectly respectable fellow, and his wife was at school with Molly. You will see them both at dinner.'

ON HIS KNEES, and with his chin level with the top of the table, Stephen watched the male mantis step cautiously towards the female mantis. She was a fine strapping green specimen, and she stood upright on her four back legs, her front pair dangling devoutly; from time to time a tremor caused her heavy body to oscillate over the thin suspending limbs, and each time the brown male shot back. He advanced lengthways, with his body parallel to the table-top, his long, toothed, predatory front legs stretching out tentatively and his antennae trained forwards: even in this strong light Stephen could see the curious inner glow of his big oval eyes.

The female deliberately turned her head through forty-five degrees, as though looking at him. 'Is this recognition?' asked Stephen, raising his magnifying glass to detect some possible movement in her feelers. 'Consent?'

The brown male certainly thought it was, and in three strides he was upon her; his legs gripped her wing-covers; his antennae found hers and began to stroke them. Apart from a vibratory, well-sprung quiver at the additional weight, she made no apparent response, no resistance; and in a little while the strong orthopterous copulation began. Stephen set his watch and noted down the time in a book, open upon the floor.

Minutes passed. The male shifted his hold a little. The female moved her triangular head, pivoting it slightly from left to right. Through his glass Stephen could see her sideways jaws open and close; then there was a blur of movements so rapid that for all his care and extreme attention he could not follow them, and the male's head was off, clamped there, a detached lemon, under the crook of her green praying arms. She bit into it, and the eye's glow went out; on her back the headless male continued to copulate rather more strongly than before, all his inhibitions having been removed. 'Ah,' said Stephen with intense satisfaction, and noted down the time again.

Ten minutes later the female took off three pieces of her mate's long thorax, above the upper coxal joint, and ate them with every appearance of appetite, dropping crumbs of chitinous shell in front of her. The male copulated on, still firmly anchored by his back legs.

'There you are,' cried Jack. 'I have been waiting for you this quarter of an hour.'

'Oh,' said Stephen, starting up. 'I beg your pardon. I beg your pardon. I know what importance you attach to punctuality – most concerned. I had put my watch back to the beginning of the copulation,' he said, very gently covering the mantis and her dinner with a hollow ventilated box. 'I am with you now.'

'No you aren't,' said Jack. 'Not in those infamous half-boots. Why do you have them soled with lead, anyhow?'

At any other time he would have received a very sharp reply to this, but it was clear to Stephen that he had not spent a pleasant forenoon with the admiral; and all he said, as he changed into his shoes, was, 'You do not need a head, nor even a heart, to be all a female can require.'

'That reminds me,' said Jack, 'have you anything that will keep my wig on? A most ridiculous thing happened as I was crossing the square: there was Dillon on the far side, with a woman on his arm – Governor Wall's sister, I believe – so I returned his salute with particular attention, do you see. I lifted my hat right off my head and the damned wig came with it. You may laugh, and it is damned amusing, of course; but I would have given a fifty-pound note not to have looked ridiculous with him there.'

'Here is a piece of court plaster,' said Stephen. 'Let me double it over and stick it to your head. I am heartily sorry there should be this – constraint, between Dillon and you.'

'So am I,' said Jack, bending for the plaster: then with a sudden burst of confidence – the place being so different, and they on land, with no sort of sea-going relationship – he said, 'I never have been so puzzled what to do in all my life. He practically accused me – I hardly like to name it – of want of conduct, after that *Cacafuego* business. My first impulse was to ask him for an explanation, and for satisfaction, naturally. But then the position is so very particular – it is heads I win tails you lose in such a case; for if I were to sink him, why, there he would be, of course; and if he were to do the same by me, he would be out of the Navy before you could say knife, which would amount to much the same thing, for him.'

'He is passionately attached to the service, sure.'

'And in either case, there is the *Sophie* left in a pitiable state . . . damn the man for a fool. And then again he is the best first lieutenant a man could wish for – taut, but not a slave-driver; a fine seaman; and you never have to give a thought to the daily running of the sloop. I like to think that that was not his meaning.'

'He would certainly never have meant to impugn your courage,' said Stephen.

'Would he not?' asked Jack, gazing into Stephen's face and balancing his wig in his hand. 'Should you like to dine at the Hartes'?' he asked, after a pause. 'I must go, and I should be glad of your company, if you are not engaged.'

'Dinner?' cried Stephen, as though the meal had just been invented. 'Dinner? Oh, yes: charmed – delighted.'

'You don't happen to have a looking-glass, I suppose?' said Jack.

'No. No. But there is one in Mr Florey's room. We can step in on our way downstairs.'

In spite of a candid delight in being fine, in putting on his best uniform and his golden epaulette, Jack had never had the least opinion of his looks, and until this moment he had scarcely thought of them for two minutes together. But now, having gazed long and thoughtfully, he said, 'I suppose I am rather on the hideous side?'

'Yes,' said Stephen. 'Oh yes. Very much so.'

Jack had cut off the rest of his hair when they came into port and had bought this wig to cover his cropped poll; but there was nothing to hide his burnt face which, moreover, had caught the sun in spite of Stephen Maturin's medicated grease, or the tumefaction of his battered brow and eye, which had now reached the yellow stage, with a blue outer ring; so that his left-hand aspect was not unlike that of the great West African mandrill.

When they had finished their business at the prize-agent's house (a gratifying reception – such bows and smiles) they walked up to their dinner. Leaving Stephen contemplating a tree-frog by the patio fountain, Jack saw Molly Harte alone for a moment in the cool anteroom.

'Lord, Jack!' she cried, staring. 'A wig?'

' 'Tis only for the moment,' said Jack, pacing swiftly towards her.

'Take care,' she whispered, getting behind a jasper, onyx and cornelian table, three feet broad, seven and a half feet long, nineteen hundredweight. 'The servants.'

'The summerhouse tonight?' whispered he.

She shook her head and mutely, with great facial expression, said, 'Indisposée.' And then in a low but audible tone, a sensible tone, 'Let me tell you about these people who are coming to dinner, the Ellises. She was of some sort of family, I believe – anyhow, she was at Mrs Capell's school with me. Very much older, of course: quite one of the great girls. And then she married this Mr Ellis, of the City. He is a respectable, well-behaved man, extremely rich and he looks after our money very cleverly. Captain Harte is uncommonly obliged to him, I know; and I have known Laetitia this age; so there is the double whatever you call it – bond? They want their boy to go to sea, so it would give me great pleasure if . . .'

'I would do anything in my power to give you pleasure,' said Jack heavily. The words *our money* had stabbed very deep.

'Dr Maturin, I am so glad you were able to come,' cried Mrs Harte, turning towards the door. 'I have a very learned lady to introduce you to.'

'Indeed, ma'am? I rejoice to hear it. Pray what is she learned in?'

'Oh, in everything,' said Mrs Harte cheerfully; and this, indeed, seemed to be Laetitia's opinion too, for she at once gave Stephen her views on the treatment of cancer and on the conduct of the Allies – prayer, love and Evangelism was the answer, in both cases. She was an odd, doll-like little creature with a wooden face, both shy and extremely self-satisfied, rather alarmingly young; she spoke slowly, with an odd writhing motion of her upper body, staring at her interlocutor's stomach or elbow, so her exposition took some time. Her husband was a tall, moist-eyed, damp-handed man, with a

meek, Evangelical expression, and knock-knees: had it not
been for those knees he would have looked exactly like a butler. 'If that man lives,' reflected Stephen, as Laetitia prattled
on about Plato, 'he will become a miser: but it is more likely
that he will hang himself. Costive; piles; flat feet.'

They sat down ten to dinner, and Stephen found that Mrs
Ellis was his left-hand neighbour. On his right there was a
Miss Wade, a plain, good-natured girl with a splendid
appetite, unhampered by a humid ninety degrees or the calls
of fashion; then came Jack, then Mrs Harte, and on her right
Colonel Pitt. Stephen was engaged in a close discussion of
the comparative merits of the crayfish and the true lobster
with Miss Wade when the insistent voice on his left broke in
so strongly that soon it was impossible to ignore it. 'But I
don't understand – you are a real physician, he tells me, so
how come you to be in the Navy? How come you to be in the
Navy if you are a real doctor?'

'Indigence, ma'am, indigence. For all that clysters is not
gold, on shore. And then, of course, a fervid desire to bleed
for my country.'

'The gentleman is joking, my love,' said her husband across
the table. 'With all these prizes he is a very warm man, as we
say in the City' – nodding and smiling archly.

'Oh,' cried Laetitia, startled. 'He is a wit. I must take care of
him, I declare. But still, you have to look after the common
sailors too, Dr Maturin, not only the midshipmen and officers: that must be very horrid.'

'Why, ma'am,' said Stephen, looking at her curiously: for so
small and Evangelical a woman she had drunk a remarkable
quantity of wine and her face was coming out in blotches.
'Why, ma'am, I cut 'em off pretty short, I assure you. Oil of
cat is my usual dose.'

'Quite right,' said Colonel Pitt, speaking for the first time. 'I
allow no complaints in my regiment.'

'Dr Maturin is admirably strict,' said Jack. 'He often desires
me to have the men flogged, to overcome their torpor and to

open their veins both at the same time. A hundred lashes at
the gangway is worth a stone of brimstone and treacle, we
always say.'

'*There's* discipline,' said Mr Ellis, nodding his head.

Stephen felt the odd bareness on his knee that meant his
napkin had glided to the floor; he dived after it, and in the
hooded tent below he beheld four and twenty legs, six
belonging to the table and eighteen to his temporary messmates. Miss Wade had kicked off her shoes: the woman
opposite him had dropped a little screwed-up handkerchief:
Colonel Pitt's gleaming military boot lay pressed upon Mrs
Harte's right foot, and upon her left – quite a distance from
the right – reposed Jack's scarcely less massive buckled shoe.

Course followed course, indifferent Minorcan food cooked
in English water, indifferent wine doctored with Minorcan
verjuice; and at one point Stephen heard his neighbour say, 'I
hear you have a very high moral tone in your ship.' But in time
Mrs Harte rose and walked, limping slightly, into the drawing-room: the men gathered at the top end of the table, and
the muddy port went round and round and round.

The wine brought Mr Ellis into full bloom at last; the diffidence and the timidity melted away from the mound of
wealth, and he told the company about discipline – order and
discipline were of primordial importance; the family, the disciplined family, was the cornerstone of Christian civilization;
commanding officers were (as he might put it) the fathers of
their numerous families, and their love was shown by their
firmness. Firmness. His friend Bentham, the gentleman that
wrote the *Defence of Usury* (it deserved to be printed in gold),
had invented a whipping machine. Firmness and dread: for
the two great motives in the world were greed and fear, gentlemen. Let them look at the French revolution, the disgraceful rebellion in Ireland, to say nothing – looking archly at
their stony faces – of the unpleasantness at Spithead and the
Nore – all greed, and to be put down by fear.

Mr Ellis was clearly very much at home in Captain Harte's

house, for without having to ask the way he walked to the sideboard, opened the lead-lined door and took out the chamber-pot, and looking over his shoulder he went on without a pause to state that fortunately the lower classes naturally looked up to gentlemen and loved them, in their humble way; only gentlemen were fit to be officers. God had ordered it so, he said, buttoning the flap of his breeches; and as he sat down again at the table he observed that he knew one house where the article was silver — solid silver. The family was a good thing: he would drink a toast to discipline. The rod was a good thing: he would drink a toast to the rod, in *all* its forms. Spare the rod and spoil the child — loveth, chastitheth.

'You must come to us one Thursday morning and see how the bosun's mate loveth our defaulters,' said Jack.

Colonel Pitt, who had been staring heavily at the banker with an undisguised, boorish contempt, broke out into a guffaw and then left, excusing himself on the grounds of regimental business. Jack was about to follow him when Mr Ellis desired him to stay — he begged the favour of a few words.

'I do a certain amount of business for Mrs Jordan, and I have the honour, the great honour, of being presented to the Duke of Clarence,' he began, impressively. 'Have you ever seen him?'

'I am acquainted with His Highness,' said Jack, who had been shipmates with that singularly unattractive hot-headed cold-hearted bullying Hanoverian.

'I ventured to mention *our* Henry and said we hoped to make an officer of him, and he condescended to advise the sending of him to sea. Now, my wife and I have considered it carefully, and we prefer a little boat to a ship of the line, because they are sometimes rather *mixed*, if you understand me, and my wife is very particular — she is a Plantagenet; besides, some of these captains want their young gentlemen to have an allowance of fifty pounds per annum.'

'I always insist that their friends should guarantee my midshipmen at least fifty,' said Jack.

'Oh,' said Mr Ellis, a little dashed. 'Oh. But I dare say a good many of the things can be picked up second-hand. Not that I care about that – at the beginning of the war all of us in the alley sent His Majesty an address saying we should support him with our lives and fortunes. I don't mind fifty quid, or *even more*, so long as the ship is genteel. My wife's old friend Mrs H was telling us about you, sir; and what is more, you are a thorough-going Tory, just like me. And yesterday we caught sight of Lieutenant Dillon, who is Lord Kenmare's nephew, I understand, and has a pretty little estate of his own – seems quite the gentleman. So to put it in a nutshell, sir, if you will take my boy I shall be very much obliged to you. And allow me to add,' he said, with an awkward jocularity, clearly against his own better judgment, 'what with my inside knowledge and experience of the market, you won't regret it. You'll find your advantage, I warrant you, hee, hee!'

'Let us join the ladies,' said Captain Harte, actually blushing for his guest.

'The best thing is to take him to sea for a month or so,' said Jack, standing up. 'Then he can see how he likes the service and whether he is suited for it; and we can speak of it again.'

'I am sorry to have let you in for that,' he said, taking Stephen's arm and guiding him down Pigtail Stairs, where the green lizards darted along the torrid wall. 'I had no notion Molly Harte was capable of giving such a wretched dinner – cannot think what has come over her. Did you remark that soldier?'

'The one in scarlet and gold, with boots?'

'Yes. Now he was a perfect example of what I was saying, that the army is divided into two sorts – the one as kind and gentle as ever you could wish, just like my dear old uncle, and the other heavy, lumpish brutes like that fellow. Quite unlike the Navy. I have seen it again and again, and I still cannot understand it. How do the two sorts live together? I wish he may not be a nuisance to Mrs Harte – she is sometimes very free and unguarded, quite unsuspecting – can be imposed upon.'

'The man whose name I forget, the money-man, was an eminently curious study,' said Stephen.

'Oh, him,' said Jack, with an utter want of interest. 'What do you expect, when a fellow sits thinking about money all day long? And they can never hold their wine, those sorts of people. Harte must be very much in his debt to have him in the house.'

'Oh, he was a dull ignorant superficial darting foolish prating creature in himself, to be sure, but I found him truly fascinating. The pure bourgeois in a state of social ferment. There was that typical costive, haemorrhoidal facies, the knock-knees, the drooping shoulders, the flat feet splayed out, the ill breath, the large staring eyes, the meek complacency; and, of course, you noticed that womanly insistence upon authority and beating once he was thoroughly drunk? I would wager that he is *very nearly* impotent: that would account for the woman's restless garrulity, her desire for predominance, absurdly combined with those girlish ways, and her thinning hair – she will be bald in a year or so.'

'It might be just as well if everybody were impotent,' said Jack sombrely. 'It would save a world of trouble.'

'And having seen the parents I am impatient to see this youth, the fruit of their strangely unattractive loins: will he be a wretched mammothrept? A little corporal? Or will the resiliency of childhood . . .?'

'He will be the usual damned little nuisance, I dare say; but at least we shall know whether there is anything to be made of him by the time we are back from Alexandria. We are not saddled with him for the rest of the commission.'

'Did you say Alexandria?'

'Yes.'

'In Lower Egypt?'

'Yes. Did I not tell you? We are to run an errand to Sir Sidney Smith's squadron before our next cruise. He is watching the French, you know.'

'Alexandria,' said Stephen, stopping in the middle of the

quay. 'O joy. I wonder you did not cry out with delight the moment you saw me. What an indulgent admiral – pater classis – O how I value that worthy man!'

'Why, 'tis no more than a straight run up and down the Mediterranean, about six hundred leagues each way, with precious little chance of seeing a prize either coming or going.'

'I did not think you could have been such an earthling,' cried Stephen. 'For shame. Alexandria is classic ground.'

'So it is,' said Jack, his good nature and pleasure in life flooding back at the sight of Stephen's delight. 'And with any luck I dare say we shall have a sight of the mountains of Candia, too. But come, we must get aboard: if we go on standing here we shall be run down.'

9

'IT IS UNGRATEFUL in me to repine,' he wrote, 'but when I think that I might have paced the burning sands of Libya, filled (as Goldsmith tells us) with serpents of various malignity; that I might have trodden the Canopic shore, have beheld the ibis, the Mareotic grallatores in their myriads, even perhaps the crocodile himself; that I was whirled past the northern coast of Candia, with Mount Ida in sight all day long; that at a given moment Cythera was no more than half an hour away, and yet for all my pleas no halt to be made, no "heaving to"; and when I reflect upon the wonders that lay at so short a distance from our course – the Cyclades, the Peloponnese, great Athens, and yet no deviation allowed, no not for half a day – why, then I am obliged to restrain myself from wishing Jack Aubrey's soul to the devil. Yet on the other hand, when I look over these notes not as a series of unfulfilled potentialities but as the record of positive accomplishment, how many causes have not I for rational exultation! The

Homeric sea (if not the Homeric land); the pelican; the great white shark the seamen so obligingly fished up; the holothurians; euspongia mollissima (the same that Achilles stuffed his helmet with, saith Poggius); the non-descript gull; the turtles! Again, these weeks have been among the most peaceful I have known: they might have been among the happiest, if I had not been so aware that JA and JD might kill one another, in the civillest way in the world, at the next point of land: for it seems these things cannot take place at sea. JA is still deeply wounded about some remarks concerning the *Cacafuego* – feels there is a reflexion upon his courage – cannot bear it – it preys upon him. And JD, though quieter now, is wholly unpredictable: he is full of contained rage and unhappiness that will break out in some way; but I cannot tell what. It is not unlike sitting on a barrel of gunpowder in a busy forge, with sparks flying about (the sparks of my figure being the occasions of offence).'

Indeed, but for this tension, this travelling cloud, it would have been difficult to imagine a pleasanter way of spending the late summer than sailing across the whole width of the Mediterranean as fast as the sloop could fly. She flew a good deal faster now that Jack had hit upon her happiest trim, restowing her hold to bring her by the stern and restoring her masts to the rake her Spanish builders had intended. What is more, the brothers Sponge, with a dozen of the *Sophie*'s swimmers under their instruction, had spent every moment of the long calms in Greek waters (their native element) scraping her bottom; and Stephen could remember an evening when he had sat there in the warm, deepening twilight, watching the sea; it had barely a ruffle on its surface, and yet the *Sophie* picked up enough moving air with her topgallants to draw a long straight whispering furrow across the water, a line brilliant with unearthly phosphorescence, visible for quarter of a mile behind her. Days and nights of unbelievable purity. Nights when the steady Ionian breeze rounded the square mainsail – not a brace to be touched, watch relieving watch – and he and Jack on deck, sawing away, sawing away, lost in their music, until the falling dew untuned their strings. And days when the perfection of dawn was so great, the emptiness so entire, that men were almost afraid to speak.

A voyage whose two ends were out of sight – a voyage sufficient in itself. And on the plain physical side, she was a well-manned sloop, now that her prize-crews were all aboard again: not a great deal of work; a fair sense of urgency; a steady routine day after day; and day after day the exercise with the great guns that knocked the seconds off one by one until the day in 16°31′E., when the larboard watch succeeded in firing three broadsides in exactly five minutes. And, above all, the extraordinarily fine weather and (apart from a languid week or so of calm far to the east, a little after they had left Sir Sidney's squadron) fair winds: so much so that when a moderate Levanter sprang up as soon as their chronic shortage of water made it really necessary to put into Malta, Jack said uneasily, 'It is too good to last. I am afraid we must pay for this, presently.'

He had a very particular wish to make a rapid passage, a strikingly rapid passage that would persuade Lord Keith of his undeviating attention to duty, his reliability; nothing he had ever heard in his adult life had so chilled him (upon reflexion) as the admiral's remarks about post rank. They had been kindly meant; they were totally convincing; they haunted his mind.

'I wonder you should be so concerned over a mere title – a tolerably Byzantine title,' observed Stephen. 'After all, you are called Captain Aubrey now, and you would still only be called Captain Aubrey after that eventual elevation; for no man, as I understand it, ever says "Post-captain So-and-so". Surely it cannot be a peevish desire for symmetry – a longing to wear two epaulettes?'

'That does occupy a great share of my heart, of course, along with eagerness for an extra eighteenpence a day. But you will allow me to point out, sir, that you are mistaken in everything you advance. At present I am called captain only by courtesy – I am dependent upon the courtesy of a parcel of damned scrubs, much as surgeons are by courtesy called Doctor. How should you like it if any cross-grained brute could call you Mr M the moment he chose to be uncivil? Whereas, was I to be made post some day, I should be captain by right; but even so I should only shift my swab from one shoulder to the other. I should not have the right to wear both until I had three years' seniority. No. The reason why every sea-officer in his right wits longs so ardently to be made post is this – once you are over that fence, why, there you are! My dear sir, you are there! What I mean is, that from then onwards all you have to do is to remain alive to be an admiral in time.'

'And that is the summit of human felicity?'

'Of course it is,' cried Jack, staring. 'Does it not seem plain to you?'

'Oh, certainly.'

'Well then,' said Jack, smiling at the prospect, 'well then, up the list you go, once you are there, whether you have a ship or no, all according to seniority, in perfect order – rear-admiral of the blue, rear-admiral of the white, rear-admiral of the red, vice-admiral of the blue, and so on, right up – no damned merit about it, no selection. That's what I like. Up until that point it is interest, or luck, or the approbation of your superiors – a pack of old women, for the most part. You must truckle to them – yes, sir; no, sir; by your leave, sir; your most humble servant . . . Do you smell that mutton? You will dine with me, will you not? I have asked the officer and midshipman of the watch.'

The officer in question happened to be Dillon, and the acting midshipman young Ellis. Jack had very early determined that there should be no evident breach, no barbarous sullen inveteracy, and once a week he invited the officer (and sometimes the midshipman) of the forenoon watch to dinner, whoever he was; and once a week he in turn was invited to dine in the gun-room. Dillon had tacitly acquiesced in this arrangement, and on the surface there was a perfect civility between them – a state of affairs much helped in their daily life by the invariable presence of others.

On this occasion Henry Ellis formed part of their protection. He had proved an ordinary boy, rather pleasant than otherwise: exceedingly timid and modest at first and outrageously made game of by Babbington and Ricketts, but now, having found his place, somewhat given to prating. Not at his captain's table, however: he sat rigid, mute, the tips of his fingers and the rims of his ears bleeding with cleanliness, his elbows pressed to his sides, eating wolf-like gulps of mutton, which he swallowed whole. Jack had always liked the young, and in any case he felt that a guest was entitled to consideration at his table, so having invited Ellis to drink a glass of wine with him, he smiled affably and said, 'You people were reciting some verses in the foretop this morning. Very capital verses, I dare say – Mr Mowett's verses? Mr Mowett turns a pretty line.' So he did. His piece on the bending of the new mainsail was admired throughout the sloop: but most unhappily he had also been inspired to write, as part of a general description:

White as the clouds beneath the blaze of noon
Her bottom through translucent waters shone.

For the time being this couplet had quite destroyed his authority with the youngsters; and it was this couplet they had been reciting in the foretop, hoping thereby to provoke him still further.

'Pray, will you not recite them to us? I am sure the Doctor would like to hear.'

'Oh, yes, pray do,' said Stephen.

The unhappy boy thrust a great lump of mutton into his cheek, turned a nasty yellow and gathered to his heart all the

fortitude he could call upon. He said, 'Yes, sir,' fixed his eyes
upon the stern-window and began,

'*White as the clouds beneath the blaze of noon* Oh God don't
let me die

'*White as the clouds beneath the blaze of noon*

Her b –' His voice quavered, died, revived as a thin desperate ghost and squeaked out '*Her bottom*'; but could do no
more.

'A damned fine verse,' cried Jack, after a very slight pause.
'Edifying too. Dr Maturin, a glass of wine with you?'

Mowett appeared, like a spirit a little late for its cue, and
said, 'I beg your pardon, sir, for interrupting you, but there's a
ship topsails up three points on the starboard bow.'

In all this golden voyage they had seen almost nothing on
the open sea, apart from a few caiques in Greek waters and a
transport on her passage from Sicily to Malta, so when at
length the newcomer had come close enough for her topsails
and a hint of her courses to be seen from the deck, she was
stared at with an even greater intensity than usual. The
Sophie had cleared the Sicilian Channel that morning and
she was steering west-north-west, with Cape Teulada in Sar-
dinia bearing north by east twenty-three leagues, a moderate
breeze at north-east, and only some two hundred and fifty
miles of sea between her and Port Mahon. The stranger
appeared to be steering west-south-west or something south,
as though for Gibraltar or perhaps Oran, and she bore north-
west by north from the sloop. These courses, if persisted in,
would intersect; but at present there was no telling which
would cross the other's wake.

A detached observer would have seen the *Sophie* heel
slightly as all her people gathered along her starboard side,
would have noticed the excited talk die away on the fo'c'sle
and would have smiled to see two-thirds of the crew and all
the officers simultaneously purse their lips as the distant ship
set her topgallants. That meant she was almost certainly a
man-of-war; almost certainly a frigate, if not a ship of the

line. And those topgallants had not been sheeted home in a
very seamanlike way – scarcely as the Royal Navy would have
liked it.

'Make the private signal, Mr Pullings. Mr Marshall, begin
to edge away. Mr Day, stand by for the gun.'

The red flag soared up the foremast in a neat ball and broke
out smartly, streaming forwards, while the white flag and pendant flacked overhead at the main and the single gun fired to
windward.

'Blue ensign, sir,' reported Pullings, glued to his telescope.
'Red pendant at the main. Blue Peter at the fore.'

'Hands to the braces,' called Jack. 'South-west by south a
half south,' he said to the man at the wheel, for that signal
was the answer of six months ago. 'Royals, lower and tops'l
stuns'ls. Mr Dillon, pray let me know what you make of her.'

James hoisted himself into the crosstrees and trained his
glass on the distant ship: as soon as the *Sophie* had steadied
on her new course, bowing the long southern swell, he compensated for her movement with an even pendulum motion
of his far hand and fixed the stranger in the shining round.
The flash of her brass bow-chaser winked at him across the
sea in the afternoon sun. She was a frigate sure enough: he
could not count her gun-ports yet but she was a heavy frigate:
of that there was no doubt. An elegant ship. She, too, was setting her lower studdingsails; and they were having difficulty
in rigging out a boom.

'Sir,' said the midshipman of the maintop as he made his
way down, 'Andrews here thinks she's the *Dédaigneuse*.'

'Look again with my glass,' said Dillon, passing his telescope, the best in the sloop.

'Yes. She's the *Dédaigneuse*,' said the sailor, a middle-aged
man with a greasy red waistcoat over his bare copper-brown
upper half. 'You can see that new-fangled round bow. I was
prisoner aboard of her a matter of three weeks and more: took
out of a collier.'

'What does she carry?'

'Twenty-six eighteen-pounders on the main deck, sir, eighteen long eights on the quarter-deck and fo'c'sle, and a brass long twelve for a bow-chaser. They used to make me polish 'un.'

'She is a frigate, sir, of course,' reported James. 'And Andrews of the maintop, a sensible man, says she is the *Dédaigneuse*. He was a prisoner in her.'

'Well,' said Jack, smiling, 'how fortunate that the evenings are drawing in.' The sun would, in fact, set in about four hours' time; the twilight did not last long in these latitudes; and this was the dark of the moon. The *Dédaigneuse* would have to sail nearly two knots faster than the *Sophie* to catch her, and he did not think there was any likelihood of her doing so – she was heavily armed, but she was no famous sailer like the *Astrée* or the *Pomone*. Nevertheless, he turned the whole of his mind to urging his dear sloop to her very utmost speed. It was possible that he might not manage to slip away in the night – he had taken part in a thirty-two-hour chase over more than two hundred miles of sea on the West Indies station himself – and every yard might count. She had the breeze almost on her larboard quarter at present, not far from her best point of sailing, and she was running a good seven knots; indeed, so briskly had her numerous and well-trained crew set the royals and studdingsails that for the first quarter of an hour she appeared to be gaining on the frigate.

'I wish it may last,' thought Jack, glancing up at the sun through the poor flimsy canvas of the topsail. The prodigious spring rains of the western Mediterranean, the Greek sun and piercing winds had removed every particle of the contractor's dressing as well as most of the body of the stuff, and the bunt and reefs showed poor and baggy: well enough before the wind, but if they were to try a tacking-match with the frigate it could only end in tears – they would never lie so close.

It did not last. Once the frigate's hull felt the full effect of the sails she spread in her leisurely fashion, she made up her loss and began to overhaul the *Sophie*. It was difficult to be

sure of this at first – a far-off triple flash on the horizon with a
hint of darkness beneath at the top of the rise – but in three-
quarters of an hour her hull was visible from the *Sophie*'s
quarter-deck most of the time, and Jack set their old-fashioned spritsail topsail, edging away another half point.

At the taffrail Mowett was explaining the nature of this sail
to Stephen, for the *Sophie* set it flying, with a jack-stay
clinched round the end of the jib-boom, having an iron traveller on it, a curious state of affairs in a man-of-war, of
course; and Jack was standing by the aftermost starboard
four-pounder with his eyes recording every movement aboard
the frigate and his mind taken up with the calculation of the
risks involved in setting the topgallant studdingsails in this
freshening breeze, when there was a confused bellowing forward and the cry of *man overboard*. Almost at the same
moment, Henry Ellis swept by in the smooth curving stream
beneath him, his face straining up out of the water, amazed.
Mowett threw him the fall of the empty davit. Both arms
reached up from the sea to catch the flying line: head went
under – hands missed their hold. Then he was away behind,
bobbing on the wake.

Every face turned to Jack. His expression was terribly hard.
His eyes darted from the boy to the frigate coming up at eight
knots. Ten minutes would lose a mile and more: the havoc of
studdingsails taken aback: the time to get way on her again.
Ninety men endangered. These considerations and many
others, including a knowledge of the extreme intensity of the
eyes directed at him, a recollection of the odious nature of
the parents, the status of the boy as a sort of guest, Molly
Harte's protégé, flew through his racing mind before his
stopped breath had begun to flow again.

'Jolly-boat away,' he said harshly. 'Stand by, fore and aft.
Stand by. Mr Marshall, bring her to.'

The *Sophie* flew up into the wind: the jolly-boat splashed
into the water. Very few orders were called for. The yards
came round, her great spread of canvas shrank in, halliards,

bunt-lines, clew-lines, brails racing through their blocks with scarcely a word; and even in his cold black fury Jack admired the smooth competence of the operation.

Painfully the jolly-boat crept out over the sea to cut the curve of the *Sophie*'s wake again: slowly, slowly. They were peering over the side of the boat, poking about with a boat-hook. Interminably. Now at last they had turned; they were a quarter of the way back; and in his glass Jack saw all the rowers fall violently into the bottom of the boat. Stroke had been pulling so hard that his oar had broken, flinging him backwards.

'Jesus, Mary . . .' muttered Dillon, at his side.

The *Sophie* was on the hover, with some way on her already, as the jolly-boat came alongside and the drowned boy was passed up. 'Dead,' they said. 'Make sail,' said Jack. Again the almost silent manoeuvres followed one another with admirable rapidity. Too much rapidity. She was not yet on her course, she had not reached half her former speed, before there was an ugly rending crack and the foretopgallantyard parted in the slings.

Now the orders flew: looking up from Ellis' wet body, Stephen saw Jack utter three bouts of technicalities to Dillon, who relayed them, elaborated, through his speaking-trumpet to the bosun and the foretopmen as they flew aloft; saw him give a separate set of orders to the carpenter and his crew; calculate the altered forces acting on the sloop and give the helmsman a course accordingly; glance over his shoulder at the frigate and then look down with a sharp attentive glance. 'Is there anything you can do for him? Do you need a hand?'

'His heart has stopped,' said Stephen. 'But I should like to try . . . could he be slung up by the heels on deck? There is no room below.'

'Shannahan. Thomas. Bear a hand. Clap on to the burton-tackle and that spun-yarn. Carry on as the Doctor directs you. Mr Lamb, this fish . . .'

Stephen sent Cheslin for lancets, cigars, the galley bellows; and as the lifeless Henry Ellis rose free of the deck so he swung him forwards two or three times, face down and tongue lolling, and emptied some water out of him. 'Hold him just so,' he said, and bled him behind the ears. 'Mr Ricketts, pray be so good as to light me this cigar.' And what part of the *Sophie*'s crew that was not wholly occupied with the fishing of the sprung yard, the bending of the sail afresh and swaying all up, with the continual trimming of the sails and with furtively peering at the frigate, had the inexpressible gratification of seeing Dr Maturin draw tobacco smoke into the bellows, thrust the nozzle into his patient's nose, and while his assistant held Ellis' mouth and other nostril closed, blow the acrid smoke into his lungs, at the same time swinging his suspended body so that now his bowels pressed upon his diaphragm and now they did not. Gasps, choking, a vigorous plying of the bellows, more smoke, more and steadier gasps, coughing. 'You may cut him down now,' said Stephen to the fascinated seamen. 'It is clear that he was born to be hanged.'

The frigate had covered a great deal of sea in this time, and now her gun-ports could be counted without a glass. She was a heavy frigate – her broadside would throw three hundred pounds of metal as against the *Sophie*'s twenty-eight – but she was deep-laden and even in this moderate wind she was making heavy weather of it. The swell broke regularly under her bows, sending up white water, and she had a labouring air. She was still gaining perceptibly on the *Sophie*. 'But,' said Jack to himself, 'I swear with that crew he will have the royals off her before it is quite dark.' His intent scrutiny of the *Dédaigneuse*'s sailing had convinced him that she had a great many raw hands aboard, if not a new crew altogether – no uncommon thing in French ships. 'He may try a ranging shot before that, however.'

He looked up at the sun. It was still a long way from the horizon. And when he had taken a hundred counted turns from the taffrail to the gun, from the gun to the taffrail, it was still a long way from the horizon, in exactly the same place, shining with idiot good humour between the arched foot of the topsail and the yard, whereas the frigate had moved distinctly closer.

Meanwhile, the daily life of the sloop went on, almost automatically. The hands were piped to supper at the beginning of the first dog-watch; and at two bells, as Mowett was heaving the log James Dillon said, 'Will I beat to quarters, sir?' He spoke a little hesitantly, for he was not sure of Jack's mind: and his eyes were fixed beyond Jack's face at the Dédaigneuse, coming on with a most impressive show of canvas, brilliant in the sun, and her white moustache giving an impression of even greater speed.

'Oh, yes, by all means. Let us hear Mr Mowett's reading; and then by all means beat to quarters.'

'Seven knots four fathoms, sir, if you please,' said Mowett to the lieutenant, who turned, touched his hat and repeated this to the captain.

The drum-roll, the muffled thunder of bare feet on the hollow, echoing deck, and quarters; then the long process of lacing bonnets to the topsails and topgallants; the sending-up of extra preventer-backstays to the topgallant mastheads (for Jack was determined to set more sail by night); a hundred minute variations in the spread, tension and angle of the sails – all this took time; but still the sun took longer, and still the Dédaigneuse came closer, closer, closer. She was carrying far too much sail aloft, and far too much aft: but everything aboard her seemed to be made of steel – she neither carried anything away nor yet (his highest hope of all) broached to, in spite of a couple of wild yawing motions in the last dog-watch that must have made her captain's heart stand still. 'Why does he not haul up the weather skirt of his mainsail and ease her a trifle?' asked Jack. 'The pragmatical dog.'

Everything that could be done aboard the Sophie had been done. The two vessels raced silently across the warm kind sea in the evening sun; and steadily the frigate gained.

'Mr Mowett,' called Jack, pausing at the end of his beat. Mowett came away from the group of officers on the larboard side of the quarter-deck, all gazing very thoughtfully at the *Dédaigneuse*. 'Mr Mowett . . .' he paused. From below, half-heard through the song of the quartering wind and the creak of the rigging, came snatches of a 'cello suite. The young master's mate looked attentive, ready and dutiful, inclining his tube-like form towards his captain in a deferential attitude continually and unconsciously adapted to the long urgent corkscrewing motion of the sloop. 'Mr Mowett, perhaps you would be so kind as to tell me over your piece about the new mainsail. I am very fond of poetry,' he added with a smile, seeing Mowett's look of wary dismay, his tendency to deny everything.

'Well, sir,' said Mowett hesitantly, in a low, human voice; he coughed and then, in quite another, rather severe, tone, said, '*The New Mainsail*', and went on –

> *'The mainsail, by the squall so lately rent,*
> *In streaming pendants flying, is unbent:*
> *With brails refixed, another soon prepared,*
> *Ascending, spreads along beneath the yard.*
> *To each yardarm the head-rope they extend,*
> *And soon their earings and their robans bend.*
> *That task performed, they first the braces slack,*
> *Then to the chesstree drag th'unwilling tack:*
> *And, while the lee clew-garnet's lowered away,*
> *Taut aft the sheet they tally and belay.'*

'Excellent – capital,' cried Jack, clapping him on the shoulder. 'Good enough for the Gentleman's Magazine, upon my honour. Tell me some more.'

Mowett looked modestly down, drew breath and began again, '*Occasional Piece*':

> *'Oh were it mine with sacred Maro's art,*
> *To wake to sympathy the feeling heart,*

Then might I, with unrivalled strains, deplore,
Th'impervious horrors of a leeward shore.'

'Ay, a leeward shore,' murmured Jack, shaking his head; and at this moment he heard the frigate's first ranging shot. The thump of the *Dédaigneuse*'s bow-chaser punctuated Mowett's verse for a hundred and twenty lines, but no fall of shot did they see until the moment the sun's lower limb touched the horizon, when a twelve-pound ball went skipping by twenty yards away along the starboard side of the sloop, just as Mowett reached the unfortunate couplet,

'Transfixed with terror at th'approaching doom
Self-pity in their breasts alone has room.'

and he felt obliged to break off and explain 'that of course, sir, they were only people in the merchant service.'

'Why, that is a consideration, to be sure,' said Jack. 'But now I am afraid I must interrupt you. Pray tell the purser we need three of his largest butts, and rouse them up on to the fo'c'sle. Mr Dillon, Mr Dillon, we will make a raft to carry a stern lantern and three or four smaller ones; and let it be done behind the cover of the forecourse.'

A little before the usual time Jack had the *Sophie*'s great stern-lantern lit, and himself he went into the cabin to see that the stern-windows were as conspicuous as he could wish: and as the twilight deepened they saw lights appear on the frigate too. What is more, they saw her main and mizzen royals disappear. Now, with her royals handed, the *Dédaigneuse* was a black silhouette, sharp against the violet sky; and her bow-chaser spat orange-red every three minutes or so, the stab showing well before the sound reached them.

By the time Venus set over their starboard bow (and the starlight diminished sensibly with her going) the frigate had not fired for half an hour: her position could only be told by her lights, and they were no longer gaining – almost certainly not gaining any more.

'Veer the raft astern,' said Jack, and the awkward contraption came bobbing down the side, fouling the studdingsail booms and everything else it could reach: it carried a spare stern-lantern on a pole the height of the *Sophie*'s taffrail and four smaller lanterns in a line below. 'Where is a handy nimble fellow?' asked Jack. 'Lucock.'

'Sir?'

'I want you to go on to the raft and light each lantern the very moment the same one on board is put out.'

'Aye aye, sir. Light as put out.'

'Take this darky and clap a line round your middle.'

It was a tricky operation, with the sea running and the sloop throwing the water about; and there was always the possibility of some busy fellow with a glass aboard the *Dédaigneuse* picking out a figure acting strangely abaft the *Sophie*'s stern; but presently it was done, and Lucock came over the taffrail on to the darkened quarter-deck.

'Well done,' said Jack softly. 'Cast her off.'

The raft went far astern and he felt the *Sophie* give a skip as she was relieved of its drag. It was a creditable imitation of her lights, although it did bob about too much; and the bosun had rigged a criss-cross of old rope to simulate the casement.

Jack gazed at it for a moment and then said, 'Topgallant stuns'ls.' The topmen vanished upwards, and everyone on deck listened with grave attention, unmoving, glancing at one another. The wind had lessened a trifle, but there was that wounded yard; and in any case such a very great press of canvas . . .

The fresh sails were sheeted home; the extra preventer-back-stays tightened; the rigging's general voice rose a quarter-tone; the *Sophie* moved faster through the sea. The topmen reappeared and stood with their listening shipmates, glancing aft from time to time to watch the dwindling lights. Nothing carried away; the strain eased a little; and suddenly their attention was wholly shifted, for the *Dédaigneuse* had begun to fire again. Again and again and again; and then her lit side appeared as she yawed to give the raft her whole broadside – a very noble sight, a long line of brilliant flashes and a great sullen roar. It did the raft no harm, however, and a low contented chuckle rose from the *Sophie*'s deck. Broadside after broadside – she seemed in quite a passion – and at last the raft's lights went out, all of them at once.

'Does he think we have sunk?' wondered Jack, gazing back at the frigate's distant side. 'Or has he discovered the cheat? Is he at a stand? At all events, I swear he will not expect me to carry straight on.'

It was one thing to swear it, however, and quite another to believe it with the whole of his heart and head, and the rising of the Pleiades found Jack at the masthead with his night-glass swinging steadily from north-north-west to east-north-east; first light still found him there, and even sunrise, although by then it was clear that they had either completely outsailed the frigate or that she had set a new course, easterly or westerly, in pursuit.

'West-north-west is the most likely,' observed Jack, stabbing his bosom with the telescope to close it and narrowing his eyes against the intolerable brilliance of the rising sun. 'That is what I should have done.' He lowered himself heavily, stiffly down through the rigging, stumped into his cabin, sent for the master to work out their present position and closed his eyes for a moment until he should come.

They were within five leagues of Cape Bougaroun in North Africa, it appeared, for they had run over a hundred miles during the chase, many of them in the wrong direction. 'We shall have to haul our wind – what wind there is –' (for it had been backing and dying all through the middle watch) 'and lie as close as ever we can. But even so, kiss my hand to a quick passage.' He leant back and closed his eyes again, thought of saying what a good thing it was that Africa had not moved northwards half a degree during the night, and smiling at the notion went fast asleep.

Mr Marshall offered a few observations that brought no response, then contemplated him for a while and then, with infinite tenderness, eased his feet up on to the locker, cradled him back with a cushion behind his head, rolled up the charts and tiptoed away.

Farewell to a quick passage, indeed. The *Sophie* wished to sail to the north-west. The wind, when it blew, blew *from* the north-west. But for days on end it did nothing whatever, and at last they had to sweep for twelve hours on end to reach Minorca, where they crept up the long harbour with their tongues hanging out, water having been down to quarter-allowance for the past four days.

WHAT IS MORE, they crept down it too, with the launch and cutter towing ahead and the men heaving crossly on the heavy sweeps, while the reek of the tanneries pursued them, spreading by mere penetration in the still and fetid air.

'What a disappointing place that is,' said Jack, looking back from Quarantine Island.

'Do you think so?' said Stephen, who had come aboard with a leg wrapped in sailcloth, quite a fresh leg, a present from Mr Florey. 'It seems to me to have its charms.'

'But then you are much attached to toads,' said Jack. 'Mr Watt, those men are supposed to be heaving at the sweeps, I believe.'

The most recent disappointment or rather vexation – a trifle, but vexing – had been singularly gratuitous. He had given Evans, of the *Aetna* bomb, a lift in his boat, although it was out of his way to thread through all the victuallers and transports of the Malta convoy; and Evans, peering at his epaulette in that underbred way of his, had said, 'Where did you get your swab?'

'At Paunch's.'

'I thought as much. They are nine parts brass at Paunch's, you know: hardly any real bullion at all. It soon shows through.'

Envy and ill-nature. He had heard several remarks of that kind, all prompted by the same pitiful damned motives: for his part he had never felt unkindly towards any man for being given a cruise, nor for being lucky in the way of prizes. Not that he had been so very lucky in the way of prizes either – had made nothing like so much as people thought. Mr Williams had met him with a long face: part of the *San Carlo*'s cargo had not been condemned, having been consigned by a Ragusan Greek under British protection; the admiralty court's expenses had been very high; and really it was scarcely worthwhile sending in some of the smaller vessels, as things were at present. Then the dockyard had made a childish scene about the topgallant yard – a mere stick, most legitimately expended. And the backstays. But above all, Molly Harte had not been there for more than a single afternoon. She had gone to stay with Lady Warren at Ciudadela: a long-standing engagement, she said. He had had no idea of how much it would matter to him, how deeply it would affect his happiness.

A series of disappointments. Mercy and what she had to tell him had been pleasant enough: but that was all. Lord Keith had sailed two days before, saying he wondered Captain Aubrey did not make his number, as Captain Harte was quick to let him know. But Ellis' horrible parents had not yet left the island, and he and Stephen had been obliged to undergo their hospitality – the only occasion in his life he had ever seen a half bottle of small white wine divided between four. Disappointments. The Sophies themselves, indulged with a further advance of prize-money, had behaved badly; quite badly, even by the standards of port behaviour. Four were in prison for rape; four had not been recovered from the stews when the *Sophie* sailed; one had broken his collarbone and a wrist. 'Drunken brutes,' he said, looking at them coldly; and, indeed, many of the waisters at the sweeps were deeply unappetizing at this moment – dirty, mazed still, unshaven; some still in their best shore-going rigs all foul and be-slobbered. A smell of stale smoke, chewed tobacco, sweat and whore-house scent. 'They take no notice of punishment. I shall rate that dumb Negro bosun's mate. King is his name. And rig a proper grating: that will make them mind what they are about.' Disappointments. The bolts of honest number three and four sail-cloth he had ordered and paid for himself had not been delivered. The shops had run out of fiddle strings. His father's letter had spoken in eager, almost enthusiastic, tones of the advantages of remarriage, the great conveniency of a woman to supervise the housekeeping, the desirability of the marriage state, from all points of view, particularly from that of society – society had a call upon a man. Rank was a matter of no importance whatever, said General Aubrey: a woman took rank from her husband; *goodness of heart* was what signified; and good hearts, Jack, and damned fine women, were to be found even in cottage kitchens; the difference between not quite sixty-four and twenty-odd was of *very little importance*. The words 'an old stallion to a young – ' had been crossed out, and an arrow pointing to 'supervising the housekeeping' said 'Very like your first lieutenant, I dare say.'

He glanced across the quarter-deck at his lieutenant, who was showing young Lucock how to hold a sextant and bring the sun down to the horizon. Lucock's entire being showed a restrained but intense delight in understanding this mystery, carefully explained, and (more generally) in his elevation; the sight of him gave the first thrust to shift Jack's black humour, and at the same moment he made up his mind to go south about the island and to call in at Ciudadela – he would see Molly – there was perhaps some little foolish misunderstanding that he would clear away directly – they would pass an exquisite hour together in the high walled garden overlooking the bay.

Out beyond St Philip's a dark line ruled straight across the sea showed a wafting air, the hope of a westerly breeze: after two sweaty hours in the increasing heat they reached it, hoisted in the launch and cutter and prepared to make sail.

'You can run inside Ayre Island,' said Jack.

'South about, sir?' asked the master with surprise, for north round Minorca was the directest course for Barcelona, and the wind would serve.

'Yes, sir,' said Jack sharply.

'South by west,' said the master to the helmsman.

'South by west it is, sir,' he replied, and the headsails filled with a gentle urgency.

The moving air came off the open sea, clean, salt and sharp, pushing all the squalor before it. The *Sophie* heeled just a trifle, with life flowing back into her, and Jack, seeing Stephen coming aft from his elm-tree pump, said, 'My God, it is prime to be at sea again. Don't you feel like a badger in a barrel, on shore?'

'A badger in a barrel?' said Stephen, thinking of badgers he had known. 'I do not.'

They talked, in a quiet, desultory fashion, of badgers, otters, foxes – the pursuit of foxes – instances of amazing cunning, perfidy, endurance, lasting memory in foxes. The pursuit of stags. Of boars. And as they talked so the sloop ranged close along the Minorcan shore.

'I remember eating boar,' said Jack, his good humour quite restored, 'I remember eating a dish of stewed boar, the first time I had the pleasure of dining with you; and you told me what it was. Ha, ha: do you remember that boar?'

'Yes: and I remember we spoke of the Catalan language at the same time, which brings to mind something I had meant to tell you yesterday evening. James Dillon and I walked out beyond Ulla to view the ancient stone monuments – druidical, no doubt – and two peasants called out to one another from a distance, alluding to us. I will relate the conversation. First peasant: Do you see those heretics walking along so pleased with themselves? The red-haired one is descended from Judas Iscariot, no doubt. Second peasant: Wherever the English walk the ewes miscarry and abort; they are all the same; I wish their bowels may gush out. Where are they going? Where do they come from? First peasant: They are going to see the navetta and the taula d'en Xatart: they come from the disguised two-masted vessel opposite Bep Ventura's warehouse. They are sailing at dawn on Tuesday to cruise on the coast from Castellon up to Cape Creus, for six weeks. They have been paying four dollars a score for hogs. I, too, wish their bowels may gush out.'

'He had no great fund of originality, your second peasant,' said Jack, adding in a pensive, wondering tone, 'They do not seem to love the English. And yet, you know, we have protected them most of this past hundred years.'

'It is astonishing, is it not?' said Stephen Maturin. 'But my point was rather to hint that our appearance on the main may not be quite so unexpected as you suppose, perhaps. There is a continual commerce of fishermen and smugglers between this and Majorca. The Spanish governor's table is furnished with our Fornells crayfish, our Xambo butter and Mahon cheese.'

'Yes, I had taken your point, and am much obliged to you for your attention in –'

A dark form drifted from the sombre cliff-face on the starboard beam – an enormous pointed wingspan: as ominous as fate. Stephen gave a swinish grunt, snatched the telescope from under Jack's arm, elbowed him out of the way and squatted at the rail, resting the glass on it and focusing with great intensity.

'A bearded vulture! It is a bearded vulture!' he cried. 'A young bearded vulture.'

'Well,' said Jack instantly – not a second's hesitation – 'I dare say he forgot to shave this morning.' His red face crinkled up, his eyes diminished to a bright blue slit and he slapped his thigh, bending in such a paroxysm of silent mirth, enjoyment and relish that for all the *Sophie*'s strict discipline the man at the wheel could not withstand the infection and burst out in a strangled 'Hoo, hoo, hoo,' instantly suppressed by the quartermaster at the con.

'THERE ARE TIMES,' said James quietly, 'when I understand your partiality for your friend. He derives a greater pleasure from a smaller stream of wit than any man I have ever
known.'

It was the master's watch; the purser was away forward discussing accounts with the bosun; Jack was in his cabin, his
spirits still high, one part of his mind designing a new disguise for the *Sophie* and the other revelling (by anticipation)
in the happy outcome of his evening's interview with Molly
Harte. She would be so surprised to see him at Ciudadela, so
pleased: how happy they would be! Stephen and James were
playing chess in the gun-room: James' furious attack, based
upon the sacrifice of a knight, a bishop and two pawns, had
very nearly reached its culminating point of error, and for a
long placid stretch of time Stephen had been wondering how
he could avoid mating him in three or four moves by any
means less obvious than throwing down the board. He
decided (James minded these things terribly) to sit it out
until the drum beat to quarters, and meanwhile he waved his
queen thoughtfully in the air, humming the Black Joke.

'It seems,' said James, dropping the words into the silence,
'that there may be some danger of peace.' Stephen pursed his
lips and closed one eye. He, too, had heard these rumours in
Port Mahon. 'So I hope to God we may see a touch of real
action before it is too late. I am very curious to know what
you will think of it: most men find it entirely unlike what they
had expected – like love in that. Very disappointing, and yet
you cannot wait to be starting again. It is your move, you
know.'

'I am perfectly aware of it,' said Stephen sharply. He
glanced at James, and he was surprised at the look of naked,
unguarded distress on his face. Time was not doing what
Stephen had expected of it: not by any means. The American
ship was still there on the horizon. 'And would you not say we
had seen any action, then?' he went on.

'These scuffles? I was thinking of something on a rather larger scale.'

'NO, MR WATT,' said the purser, ticking the last item in the private arrangement by which he and the bosun made thirteen and a half per cent on a whole range of stores on the borderland of their respective kingdoms, 'you may say what you please, but this young chap will end up by losing the *Sophie*; and what is more, he will either get us all knocked on the head or taken prisoner. And I've no wish to drag out my days in a French or Spanish prison, let alone be chained to an oar in an Algerine galley, rained upon, sunned upon and sitting there over my own stink. And I don't want my Charlie knocked on the head, either. That's why I'm transferring. It's a profession that has its risks, I grant you, and I'm willing for him to run them. But understand me, Mr Watt: willing for him to run the ordinary risks of the profession, not these. Not capers like that huge bloody great battery; nor lying right inshore by night as though we owned the place; nor watering here there and everywhere, just to stay out a little longer; nor setting about anything you see, regardless of size or number. The main chance is all very well; but we must not only be thinking of the main chance, Mr Watt.'

'Very true, Mr Ricketts,' said the bosun. 'And I can't say I have ever really liked those cross-catharpings. But you're wide of the mark when you say it's all the main chance. Look at this hawser-laid stuff, now: better rope you'll never see. And there's no rogue's yarn in it,' he said, teasing out an end with his marlin-spike. 'Look for yourself. And why is there no rogue's yarn in it, Mr Ricketts? Because it never come off of the King's yard, that's why: Mr Screw-penny Bleeding Commissioner Brown never set eyes on it. Which Goldilocks bought it out of his own pocket, as likewise the paint you're a-sitting on. So there, you mean-souled dough-faced son of a cow-poxed bitch,' he would have added, if he had not been a peaceable, quiet sort of a man, and if the drum had not begun to beat to quarters.

'PASS THE WORD for my cox'n,' said Jack after the drum had beat the retreat. The word passed – cap'n's cox'n, cap'n's cox'n, come on George, show a leg George, at the double George, you're in trouble George, George is going to be cruci- fied, ha, ha, ha – and Barret Bonden appeared. 'Bonden, I want the boat's crew to look their best: washed, shaved, trimmed, straw hats, Guernsey frocks, ribbons.'

'Aye aye, sir,' said Bonden with an impassive face and his heart brimming with inquiry. Shaved? Trimmed? Of a Tues- day? They mustered clean to divisions on Thursdays and Sundays: but to be shaved on Tuesday – on a Tuesday at sea! He hurried off to the ship's barber, and by the time half the cutter's crew were as rosy and smooth as art could make them the answer to his questions appeared. They rounded Cape Dartuch, and Ciudadela came into view on the starboard bow; but instead of sailing steadily north-west the *Sophie* bore up for the town, heaving to in fifteen fathom water with her foretopsail aback a quarter of a mile from the mole.

'Where's Simmons?' asked James, quickly passing the cut- ter's crew in review.

'Reported sick, sir,' said Bonden, and in a lower voice, 'His birthday, sir.'

James nodded. Yet the substitution of Davies was not very clever, for although he was much of a size, and filled the straw hat with *Sophie* embroidered on its ribbon, he was an intense blue-black and could not but be noticed. However, there was no time to do anything about it now, for here was the captain, very fine in his best uniform, best sword and gold-laced hat.

'I do not expect to be more than an hour or so, Mr Dillon,' said Jack, with an odd mixture of conscious stiffness and hid- den excitement; and as the bosun sprung his call he stepped down into the scrubbed and gleaming cutter. Bonden had judged better than James Dillon: the cutter's crew might have been all the colours of the rainbow, or even pied, for all Captain Aubrey cared at this moment.

The sun set in a somewhat troubled sky; the bells of Ciudadela rang for the Angelus and the *Sophie*'s for the last dog watch; the moon rose, very near the full, swimming up gloriously behind Black Point. Hammocks were piped down. The watch changed. Seized by Lucock's passion for navigation, all the midshipmen took observations of the moon as it mounted, and of the fixed stars, one by one. Eight bells, and the middle watch. The lights of Ciudadela all going out.

'Cutter's away, sir,' reported the sentry at last, and ten minutes later Jack came up the side. He was very pale, and in the strong moonlight he looked deathly – black hole for a mouth, hollows for his eyes. 'Are you still on deck, Mr Dillon?' he said, with an attempt at a smile. 'Make sail, if you please: the tail of the sea-breeze will carry us out,' he said, and walked uncertainly into his cabin.

10

'MAIMONIDES HAS an account of a lute-player who, required to perform upon some stated occasion, found that he had entirely forgot not only the piece but the whole art of playing, fingering, everything,' wrote Stephen. 'I have sometimes had a dread of the same thing happening to me; a not irrational dread, since I once experienced a deprivation of a similar nature: coming back to Aghamore when I was a boy, coming back after an eight years' absence, I went to see Bridie Coolan, and she spoke to me in Irish. Her voice was intimately familiar (none more, my own wet-nurse); so were the intonations and even the very words; yet nothing could I understand – her words conveyed no meaning whatever. I was dumbfounded at my loss. What puts me in mind of this is my discovery that I no longer know what my friends feel, intend, or even mean. It is clear that JA met with a severe disappointment in Ciudadela, one that he feels more deeply than I should have supposed possible, in him; and it is clear that JD is still in a state of great unhappiness: but beyond that I know almost nothing – they do not speak and I can no longer look into them. My own testiness does not help, to be sure. I must guard against a strong and increasing tendency to indulge in dogged, sullen conduct – the conduct of vexation (much promoted by want of exercise); but I confess that much as I love them, I could wish them both to the Devil, with their highflown, egocentrical points of honour and their purblind spurring one another on to remarkable exploits that may very well end in unnecessary death. In their death, which is their concern: but also in mine, to say nothing of the rest of the ship's company. A slaughtered crew, a sunken ship, and my collections destroyed – these do not weigh at all against their punctilios. There is a systematic flocci-naucinihili-pilification of all other aspects of existence that angers me. I spend half my time purging them, bleeding them, prescribing low diet and soporifics. They both eat far too much, and drink far too much, especially JD. Sometimes I am afraid they have closed themselves to me because they have agreed upon a meeting next time we come ashore, and they know very well I should stop it. How they vex my very spirit! If *they* had the scrubbing of the decks, the hoisting of the sails, the cleaning of the heads, we should hear little enough of these fine vapourings. I have no patience with them. They are strangely immature for men of their age and their position: though, indeed, it is to be supposed that if they were not, they would not be here – the mature, the ponderate mind does not embark itself upon a man-of-war – is not to be found wandering about the face of the ocean in quest of violence. For all his sensibility (and he played his transcription of *Deh vieni* with a truly exquisite delicacy, just before we reached Ciudadela), JA is in many ways more suited to be a pirate chief in the Caribbean a hundred years ago: and for all his acumen JD is in danger of becoming an enthusiast – a latter-day Loyola, if he is not knocked on the head first, or run through the body. I am much exercised in my mind by that unfortunate conversation . . .'

The *Sophie*, to the astonishment of her people, had not headed for Barcelona after leaving Ciudadela, but west-north-west; and at daybreak, rounding Cape Salou within hail of the shore, she had picked up a richly-laden Spanish coaster of some two hundred tons, mounting (but not firing) six six-pounders – had picked her up from the landward side as neatly as though the rendezvous had been fixed weeks ahead and the Spanish captain had kept his hour to the minute. 'A very profitable commercial venture,' said James, watching the prize disappear in the east, bound with a favourable wind for Port Mahon, while they beat up, tack upon tack, to their northern cruising-ground, one of the busiest sea-lanes in the world. But that (though unhappy in itself) was not the conversation Stephen had in mind.

No. That came later, after dinner, when he was on the quarterdeck with James. They were talking, in an easy, off-hand manner, about differences in national habit – the Spaniards' late hours; the French way of all leaving the table together, men and women, and going directly into the drawing-room; the Irish habit of staying with the wine until one of the guests suggested moving; the English way of leaving this to the host; the remarkable difference in duelling habits.

'Rencounters are most uncommon in England,' observed James.

'Indeed they are,' said Stephen. 'I was astonished, when first I went to London, to find that a man might not go out from one year's end to the other.'

'Yes,' said James. 'Ideas upon matters of honour are altogether different in the two kingdoms. Before now I have given Englishmen provocation that would necessarily have called for a meeting in Ireland, with no result. We should call that remarkably timid; or is shy the word?' He shrugged, and he was about to continue when the cabin skylight in the surface of the quarter-deck opened and Jack's head and massive shoulders appeared. 'I should never have thought so ingenuous a face could look so black and wicked,' thought Stephen.

'Did JD say that on purpose?' he wrote. 'I do not know for sure, though I suspect he did – it would be all of a piece with the remarks he has been making recently, remarks that may be unintentional, merely tactless, but that all tend to present reasonable caution in an odious and, indeed, a contemptible light. I do not know. I should have known once. But all I know now is that when JA is in a rage with his superiors, irked by the subordination of the service, spurred on by his restless, uneasy temperament, or (as at present) lacerated by his mistress' infidelity, he flies to violence as a relief – to action. JD, urged on by entirely different furies, does the same. The difference is that whereas I believe JA merely longs for the shattering noise, immense activity of mind and body, and the all-embracing sense of the present moment, I am very much afraid that JD wants more.' He closed the book and stared at its cover for a long while, far, far away, until a knock recalled him to the *Sophie*.

'Mr Ricketts,' he said, 'what may I do for you?'

'Sir,' said the midshipman, 'the captain says, will you please to come on deck and view the coast?'

'TO THE LEFT of the smoke, southwards, that is the hill of Montjuich, with the great castle; and the projection to the right is Barceloneta,' said Stephen. 'And rising there behind the city you can make out Tibidabo: I saw my first red-footed falcon there, when I was a boy. Then continuing the line from Tibidabo through the cathedral to the sea, there is the Moll de Santa Creu, with the great mercantile port: and to the left of it the basin where the King's ships and the gunboats lie.'

'Many gunboats?' asked Jack.

'I dare say: but I never made it my study.'

Jack nodded, looked keenly round the bay to fix its details in his mind once more and, leaning down, he called, 'Deck? Lower away: handsomely now. Babbington, look alive with that line.'

Stephen rose six inches from his perch at the mast-head, and with his hands folded to prevent their involuntary clutching at passing ropes, yards, blocks, and with the ape-nimble Babbington keeping pace, heaving him in towards the weather backstay, he descended through the dizzy void to the deck, where they let him out of the cocoon in which they had hoisted him aloft; for no one on board had the least opinion of his abilities as a seaman.

He thanked them absently and went below, where the sail-maker's mates were sewing Tom Simmons into his hammock.

'We are just waiting for the shot, sir,' they said; and as they spoke Mr Day appeared, carrying a net of the *Sophie*'s cannonballs.

'I thought I would pay him the attention myself,' said the gunner, arranging them at the young man's feet with a practised hand. 'He was shipmates with me in the *Phoebe*: though always unhealthy, even then,' he added, as a quick afterthought.

'Oh, yes: Tom was never strong,' said one of the sailmaker's mates, cutting the thread on his broken eye-tooth.

These words, and a certain unusual delicacy of regard, were intended to comfort Stephen, who had lost his patient: in spite of all his efforts the four-day coma had deepened to its ultimate point.

'Tell me, Mr Day,' he said, when the sailmakers had gone, 'just how much did he drink? I have asked his friends, but they give evasive answers – indeed, they lie.'

'Of course they do, sir: for it is against the law. How much did he drink? Why, now, Tom was a popular young chap, so I dare say he had the whole allowance, bating maybe a sip or two just to moisten their victuals. That would make it close on a quart.'

'A quart. Well, it is a great deal: but I am surprised it should kill a man. At an admixture of three to one, that amounts to six ounces or so – inebriating, but scarcely lethal.'

'Lord, Doctor,' said the gunner, looking at him with affectionate pity, 'that ain't the mixture. That's the rum.'

'A quart of rum? Of neat rum?' cried Stephen.

'That's right, sir. Each man has his half-pint a day, at twice, so that makes a quart for each mess for dinner and for supper: and that is what the water is added to. Oh dear me,' he said, laughing gently and patting the poor corpse on the deck between them, 'if they was only to get half a pint of three-water grog we should soon have a bloody mutiny on our hands. And quite right, too.'

'Half a pint of spirits a day for every man?' said Stephen, flushing with anger. 'A great tumbler? I shall tell the captain – shall insist upon its being poured over the side.'

'AND SO WE commit his body to the deep,' said Jack, closing the book. Tom Simmons' messmates tilted the grating: there was the sound of sliding canvas, a gentle splash and a long train of bubbles rising up through the clear water.

'Now, Mr Dillon,' he said, with something of the formal tone of his reading still in his voice, 'I think we may carry on with the weapons and the painting.'

The sloop was lying to, well over the horizon from Barcelona; and a little while after Tom Simmons had reached the bottom in four hundred fathoms she was far on her way to becoming a white-painted snow with black topsides, with a horse – a length of cable bowsed rigidly vertical – to stand for the trysail mast of that vessel; while at the same time the grindstone mounted on the fo'c'sle turned steadily, putting a keener edge, a sharper point, on cutlasses, pikes, boarding-axes, marines' bayonets, midshipmen's dirks, officers' swords.

The *Sophie* was as busy as she could well be, but there was a curious gravity with it all: it was natural that a man's messmates should be low after burying him, and even his whole watch (for Tom Simmons had been well liked – would never have had so deadly a birthday present otherwise); but this solemnity affected the whole ship's company and there was none of those odd bursts of song on the fo'c'sle, none of those ritual jokes called out. There was a quiet, brooding atmosphere, not at all angry or sullen, but – Stephen, lying in his cot (he had been up all night with poor Simmons) tried to hit upon the definition – oppressive? – fearful? – vaticinatory? But in spite of all the deeply shocking noise of Mr Day and his party overhauling the shot-lockers, scaling all the balls with any rust or irregularity upon them, and trundling them back down an echoing plane, hundreds and hundreds of four-pound cannon-balls clashing and growling and being beaten, he went to sleep before he could accomplish it.

He woke to the sound of his own name. 'Dr Maturin? No, certainly you may not see Dr Maturin,' said the master's voice in the gun-room. 'You may leave a message with me, and I will tell him at dinner-time, if he wakes up by then.'

'I was to ask him what physic would answer for a slack-going horse,' quavered Ellis, now filled with doubt.

'And who told you to ask him that? That villain Babbington, I swear. For shame, to be such a flat, after all these weeks at sea.'

This particular atmosphere had not reached the midshipmen's berth, then; or if so it had already dissipated. What private lives the young led, he reflected, how very much apart: their happiness how widely independent of circumstance. He was thinking of his own childhood – the then intensity of the present – happiness not then a matter of retrospection nor of undue moment – when the howling of the bosun's pipe for dinner caused his stomach to give a sharp sudden grinding wring and he swung his legs over the side. 'I am grown a naval animal,' he observed.

These were the fat days of the beginning of a cruise; there was still soft tack on the table, and Dillon, standing bowed under the beams to carve a noble saddle of mutton, said. 'You will find the most prodigious transformation when you go on deck. We are no longer a brig, but a snow.'

'With an extra mast,' explained the master, holding up three fingers.

'Indeed?' said Stephen, eagerly passing up his plate. 'Pray, why is this? For speed, for expediency, for comeliness?'

'To amuse the enemy.'

The meal continued with considerations on the art of war, the relative merits of Mahon cheese and Cheshire, and the surprising depth of the Mediterranean only a short way off the land; and once again Stephen noticed the curious skill (the outcome, no doubt, of many years at sea and the tradition of generations of tight-packed mariners) with which even so gross a man as the purser helped to keep the conversation going, smoothing over the dislikes and tensions – with platitudes, quite often, but with flow enough to make the dinner not only easy, but even mildly enjoyable.

'Take care, Doctor,' said the master, steadying him from behind on the companion ladder. 'She's beginning to roll.'

She was indeed, and although the *Sophie*'s deck was only so trifling a height from what might be called her subaqueous gun-room, the motion up there was remarkably greater: Stephen staggered, took hold of a stanchion and gazed about him expectantly.

'Where is your prodigious great transformation?' he cried. 'Where is this third mast, that is to amuse the enemy? Where is the merriment in practising upon a landman, where the wit? Upon my honour, Mr Farcical Comic, any poteen-swilling shoneen off the bog would be more delicate. Are you not sensible it is very wrong?'

'Oh, sir,' cried Mr Marshall, shocked by the sudden extreme ferocity of Stephen's glare, 'upon my word – Mr Dillon, I appeal to you . . .'

'Dear shipmate, joy,' said James, leading Stephen to the horse, that stout rope running parallel to the mainmast and some six inches behind it, 'allow me to assure you that to a seaman's eye this is a mast, a third mast: and presently you will see something very like the old fore-and-aft mainsail set upon it as a trysail, *at the same time as a cro'jack on the yard above our heads*. No seaman afloat would ever take us for a brig.'

'Well,' said Stephen, 'I must believe you. Mr Marshall, I ask your pardon for speaking hastily.'

'Why, sir, you would have to speak more hasty by half to put me out,' said the master, who was aware of Stephen's liking for him and who valued it highly. 'It looks as though they had had a blow away to the south,' he remarked, nodding over the side.

The long swell was setting from the far-off African coast, and although the small surface-waves disguised it, the rise and fall of the horizon showed its long even intervals. Stephen could very well imagine it breaking high against the rocks of the Catalan shore, rushing up the shingle beaches and drawing back with a monstrous grating indraught. 'I hope it does not rain,' he said, for again and again, at the beginning of the fall, he had known this sea swelling up out of calmness to be followed by a south-eastern wind and a low yellow sky, pouring down warm beating rain on the grapes just as they were ready to be picked.

'Sail ho!' called the look-out.

She was a medium-sized tartan, deep in the water, beating up into the fresh easterly breeze, obviously from Barcelona; and she lay two points on their port bow.

'How lucky this did not happen an hour ago,' said James. 'Mr Pullings, my duty to the captain, and there is a strange sail two points on the larboard bow.' Before he had finished speaking Jack was on deck, his pen still in his hand, and a look of hard excitement kindling in his eye.

'Be so kind . . .' he said, handing Stephen the pen, and he ran up to the masthead like a boy. The deck was teeming with sailors clearing away the morning's work, trimming the sails as they surreptitiously changed course to cut the tartan off from the land, and running about with very heavy loads; and after Stephen had been bumped into once or twice and had 'By your leave, sir,' and 'Way there – oh parding, sir' roared into his ear often enough, he walked composedly into the cabin, sat on Jack's locker and reflected upon the nature of a community – its reality – its difference from every one of the individuals composing it – communication within it, how effected.

'Why, there you are,' said Jack returning. 'She is only a tub of a merchantman, I fear. I had hoped for something better.'

'Shall you catch her, do you suppose?'

'Oh, yes, I dare say we shall, even if she goes about this minute. But I had so hoped for a dust-up, as we say. I can't tell you how it stretches your mind – your black draughts and blood-letting are nothing to it. Rhubarb and senna. Tell me, if we are not prevented, shall we have some music this evening?'

'It would give me great pleasure,' said Stephen. Looking at Jack now he could see what his appearance might be when the fire of his youth had gone out: heavy, grey, authoritarian, if not savage and morose.

'Yes,' said Jack, and hesitated as though he were going to say much more. But he did not, and after a moment he went on deck.

The *Sophie* was slipping rapidly through the water, having set no more sail and showing no sort of inclination to close with the tartan – the steady, sober, mercantile course of a snow bound for Barcelona. In half an hour's time they could see that she carried four guns, that she was short-handed (the cook joined in the manoeuvres) and that she had a disagreeably careless, neutral air. However, when the tartan prepared to tack at the southern end of her board, the *Sophie* heaved out her staysails in a flash, set her topgallants and bore up with surprising speed – so surprising to the tartan, indeed, that she missed stays and fell off again on the larboard tack.

At half a mile Mr Day (he dearly loved to point a gun) put a shot across her forefoot, and she lay to with her yard lowered until the *Sophie* ranged alongside and Jack hailed her master to come aboard.

'He was sorry, gentleman, but he could not: if he could, he should with joy, gentleman, but he had burst the bottom of his launch,' he said, through the medium of a quite lovely young woman, presumably Mrs Tartan or the equivalent. 'And in any case he was only a neutral Ragusan, a neutral bound for Ragusa in ballast.' The little dark man beat on his boat to mark the point: and holed it was.

'What tartan?' called Jack again.

'*Pola*,' said the young woman.

He stood, considering: he was in an ugly mood. The two vessels rose and fell. Behind the tartan the land appeared with every upward heave, and to add to his irritation he saw a fishing-boat in the south, running before the wind, with another beyond it – sharp-eyed barca-longas. The Sophies stood silently gazing at the woman: they licked their lips and swallowed.

That tartan was not in ballast – a stupid lie. And he doubted it was Ragusan-built, too. But *Pola* – was that the right name? 'Bring the cutter alongside,' he said. 'Mr Dillon, who have we aboard that speaks Italian? John Baptist is an Italian.'

'And Abram Codpiece, sir – a purser's name.'

'Mr Marshall, take Baptist and Codpiece and satisfy yourself as to that tartan – look at her papers – look into her hold – rummage her cabin if needs be.'

The cutter came alongside, the boat-keeper booming her off from the fresh paint with the utmost care, and the heavily-armed men dropped into her by a line from the main yardarm, far more willing to break their necks or drown than spoil their fine black paint, so fresh and trim.

They pulled across, boarded the tartan: Marshall, Codpiece and John Baptist disappeared into the cabin: there was the sound of a female voice raised high in anger, then a piercing scream. The men on the fo'c'sle began to skip, and turned shining faces to one another.

Marshall reappeared. 'What did you do to that woman?' called Jack.

'Knocked her down, sir,' replied Marshall phlegmatically. 'Tartan's no more a Ragusan than I am. Captain only talks the lingua franca, says Codpiece, no right Italian at all; Missis has a Spanish set of papers in her pinny; hold's full of bales consigned to Genoa.'

'The infamous brute to strike a woman,' said James aloud. 'To think we have to mess with such a fellow.'

'You wait till you're married, Mr Dillon,' said the purser, with a chuckle.

'Very well done, Mr Marshall,' said Jack. 'Very good indeed. How many hands? What are they like?'

'Eight, sir, counting passengers: ugly, froward-looking buggers.'

'Send 'em over, then. Mr Dillon, steady men for the prize-crew, if you please.' As he spoke rain began to fall, and with the first drops came a sound that made every head aboard turn, so that in a moment each man's nose was pointing north-east. It was not thunder. It was gunfire.

'Light along those prisoners,' cried Jack. 'Mr Marshall, keep in company. It will not worry you, looking after the woman?'

'I do not mind it, sir,' said Marshall.

Five minutes later they were under way, running diagonally across the swell through the sweeping rain with a lithe cork-screwing motion. They had the wind on their beam now, and although they had handed the topgallants almost at once, they left the tartan behind in less than half an hour.

Stephen was gazing over the taffrail at the long wake, his mind a thousand miles away, when he became aware of a hand gently plucking at his coat. He turned and saw Mowett smiling at him, and some way beyond Mowett Ellis on his hands and knees being carefully, desperately sick through a small square hole in the bulwark, a scuttle. 'Sir, sir,' said Mowett, 'you are getting wet.'

'Yes,' said Stephen; and after a pause he added, 'It is the rain.'

'That's right, sir,' said Mowett. 'Should not you like to step below, to get out of it? Or may I bring you a tarpaulin jacket?'

'No. No. No. You are very good. No . . .' said Stephen, his attention wandering, and Mowett, having failed in the first part of his mission, went cheerfully on to the second: this was to stop Stephen's whistling, which made the afterguard and quarter-deckmen – the crew in general – so very nervous and uneasy. 'May I tell you something nautical, sir – do you hear the guns again?'

'If you please,' said Stephen, unpursing his lips.

'Well then, sir,' said Mowett, pointing over the grey hissing sea to his right in the general direction of Barcelona, 'that is what we call a lee shore.'

'Ah?' said Stephen, with a certain interest lighting his eye. 'The phenomenon you dislike so much? It is not a mere prejudice – a weak superstitious traditional belief?'

'Oh, no, sir,' cried Mowett, and explained the nature of lee-way, the loss of windward distance in wearing, the impossibility of tacking in a very great wind, the inevitability of leeward drift in the case of being embayed with a full gale blowing dead on short, and the impervious horror of this situation. His explanation was punctuated by the deep boom of gunfire, sometimes a continuous low roaring for half a minute together, sometimes a single sharp report. 'Oh, how I wonder what it is!' he cried, breaking off and craning up on tiptoe.

'You need not be afraid,' said Stephen. 'Soon the wind will blow in the direction of the waves – this often happens towards Michaelmas. If only one could protect the vines with a vast umbrella.'

Mowett was not alone in wondering what it was: the Sophie's captain and lieutenant, each burning for the uproar and the more than human liberation of a battle, stood side by side on the quarterdeck, infinitely remote from one another, all their senses straining towards the north-east. Almost all the other members of the crew were equally intent; and so were those of the *Felipe V*, a seven-gun Spanish privateer.

She came racing up out of the blinding rain, a dark squall a little way abaft the beam on the landward side, making for the sound of battle with all the canvas she could bear. They saw one another at the same moment: the *Felipe* fired, showed her colours, received the *Sophie*'s broadside in reply, grasped her mistake, put up her helm and headed straight back to Barcelona with the strong wind on her larboard quarter and her big lateens bellying out and swaying wildly on the roll.

The *Sophie*'s helm was over within a second of the privateer's: the tompions of the starboard guns were out: cupping hands sheltered the sputtering slow-match and the priming.

'All at her stern,' cried Jack, and the crows and handspikes heaved the guns through five degrees. 'On the roll. Fire as they bear.' He brought the wheel up two spokes and the guns went off three and four. Instantly the privateer yawed as though she meant to board; but then her flapping mizzen came down on deck, she filled again and went off before the wind. A shot had struck the head of her rudder, and without it she could bear no sail aft. They were putting out a sweep to steer with and working furiously at the mizzen-yard. Her two larboard guns fired, one hitting the *Sophie* with the strangest sound. But the sloop's next broadside, a careful, collected fire within pistol-range, together with a volley of musketry, put a stop to all resistance. Just twelve minutes after the first gun fired her colours came down and a fierce, delighted cheer broke out – men clapping one another on the back, shaking hands, laughing.

The rain had stopped and it was drifting westwards in a dense grey swathe, blotting out the port, very much nearer now. 'Take possession of her, Mr Dillon, if you please,' said Jack, looking up at the dog-vane. The wind was veering, as it so often did in these waters after rain, and presently it would be coming from well south of east.

'Any damage, Mr Lamb?' he asked, as the carpenter came up to report.

'Wish you joy of the capture, sir,' said the carpenter. 'No damage, rightly speaking; no struc-tur-al damage; but that one ball made a sad mess in the galley – upset all the coppers and unshipped the smoke-funnel.'

'We will take a look at it presently,' said Jack. 'Mr Pullings, those for'ard guns are not properly secured. What the devil?' he cried. The gun-crews were strangely, even shockingly pied, and horrible imaginations flashed through his mind until he realized that they were covered with wet black paint and with the galley's soot: and now, in the exuberance of their hearts, those farthest forward were daubing their fellows. 'Avast that God-damned – foolery, God rot your – eyes,' he called out in an enormous line-of-battle voice. He rarely swore, apart from an habitual damn or an unmeaning blasphemy, and the men, who in any case had expected him to be far more pleased with the taking of a neat privateer, fell perfectly mute, with nothing more than the rolling of an eye or a wink to convey secret understanding and delight.

'Deck,' hailed Lucock from the top. 'There are gunboats coming out from Barcelona. Six. Eight – nine – eleven behind 'em. Maybe more.'

'Out launch and jolly-boat,' cried Jack. 'Mr Lamb, go across, if you please, and see what can be done to her steering.'

Getting the boats to the yardarms and launching them in this swell was no child's play, but the men were in tearing spirits and they heaved like maniacs – it was as though they had been filled with rum and yet had lost none of their ability. Muffled laughter kept bursting out: it was damped by the cry of a sail to windward – a sail that might place them between two fires – then revived by the news that it was only their own prize, the tartan.

The boats plied to and fro; the glum or surly prisoners made their way down into the fore-hold, their bosoms swollen with personal possessions; the carpenter and his crew could be heard working away with their adzes to make a new tiller; Stephen caught Ellis as he darted by. 'Just when did you stop being sick, sir?' 'Almost the moment the guns began to go, sir,' said Ellis. Stephen nodded. 'I thought as much,' said he. 'I was watching you.'

The first shot sent up a white plume of water topmast high, right between the two vessels. Infernally good practice for a ranging shot, thought Jack, and a damned great heavy ball.

The gunboats were still over a mile away, but they were coming up surprisingly fast, straight into the eye of the wind. Each of the three foremost carried a long thirty-six-pounder and rowed thirty oars. Even at a mile a chance hit from one of these would pierce the *Sophie* through and through. He had to restrain a violent urge to tell the carpenter to hurry. 'If a thirty-six-pound ball does not hasten him, nothing I can say will do so,' he observed, pacing up and down, cocking an eye at the dog-vane and at the gunboats at each turn. All seven of the foremost had tried the range, and now there was a spasmodic firing, most falling short, but some howling right overhead.

'Mr Dillon,' he called over the water, after half a dozen turns, and the splash from a ball plunging into the swell just astern wetted the back of his neck. 'Mr Dillon, we will transfer the rest of the prisoners later, and make sail as soon as you can conveniently do so. Or should you like us to pass you a tow?'

'No, thank you, sir. The tiller will be shipped in two minutes.'

'In the meantime we might as well pepper them, for what it is worth,' reflected Jack, for the now silent Sophies were looking somewhat tense. 'At least the smoke will hide us a little. Mr Pullings, the larboard guns may fire at discretion.'

This was much more agreeable, with the banging, the rumble, the smoke, the immense intent activity; and he smiled to see the earnestness of every man at the brass gun nearest him as they glared out for the fall of their shot. The *Sophie*'s fire stung the gunboats to a great burst of activity, and the dull grey western sea sparkled with their flashes over a front of a quarter of a mile.

Babbington was in front of him, pointing: wheeling about, Jack saw Dillon hailing through the din – the new tiller had been fitted.

'Make sail,' he said: the *Sophie*'s backed foretopsail came round and filled. Speed was called for, and setting all her headsails he took her down with the wind well abaft her beam before hauling up into the north-north-west. This took the sloop nearer to the gunboats and across their front: the larboard guns were firing continuously, the enemies' shots were kicking up the water or passing overhead, and for a moment his spirits rose to a wild pitch of delight at the idea of dashing down among them – they were unwieldy brutes at close quarters. But then he reflected that he had the prizes with him and that Dillon still had a dangerous number of prisoners aboard; and he gave the order to brace the yards up sharp.

The prizes hauled their wind at the same time, and at a smooth five or six knots they ran out to sea. The gunboats followed for half an hour, but as the light faded and the range lengthened to impossibility, one by one they turned and went back to Barcelona.

'I PLAYED THAT very badly,' said Jack, putting down his bow.

'Your heart was not in it,' said Stephen. 'It has been an active day – a fatiguing day. A satisfactory day, however.'

'Why, yes,' said Jack, his face brightening somewhat. 'Yes, certainly. I am most uncommonly delighted.' A pause. 'Do you remember a fellow named Pitt we dined with one day at Mahon?'

'The soldier?'

'Yes. Now, would you call him good-looking – handsome?'

'No. Oh, no.'

'I am happy to hear you say so. I have a great regard for your opinion. Tell me,' he added, after a long pause, 'have you noticed how things return to your mind when you are hipped? It is like old wounds breaking out when you come down with scurvy. Not, indeed, that I have ever for a moment forgotten what Dillon said to me that day: but it has been rankling in my heart, and I have been turning it over this last day or so. I find that I must ask him for an explanation – I should certainly have done so before. I shall do so as soon as we go into port: unless, indeed, the next few days make it unnecessary.'

'Pom, pom, pom, pom,' went Stephen in unison with his 'cello, glancing at Jack: there was an exceedingly serious look on that darkened, heavy face, a kind of red light in his clouded eyes. 'I am coming to believe that laws are the prime cause of unhappiness. It is not merely a case of born under one law, required another to obey – you know the lines: I have no memory for verse. No, sir: it is born under half a dozen, required another fifty to obey. There are parallel sets of laws in different keys that have nothing to do with one another and that are even downright contradictory. You, now – you wish to do something that the Articles of War and (as you explained to me) the rules of generosity forbid, but that your present notion of the moral law and your present notion of the point of honour require. This is but one instance of what is as common as breathing. Buridan's ass died of misery between equidistant mangers, drawn first by one then by the other. Then again, with a slight difference, there are these double loyalties – another great source of torment.'

'Upon my word, I cannot see what you mean by double loyalty. You can only have one King. And a man's heart can only be in one place at a time, unless he is a scrub.'

'What nonsense you do talk, to be sure,' said Stephen. 'What "balls", as you sea-officers say: it is a matter of common observation that a man may be sincerely attached to two women at once – to three, to four, to a very surprising number of women. However,' he said, 'no doubt you know more of these things than I. No: what I had in mind were those wider loyalties, those more general conflicts – the candid American, for example, before the issue became envenomed; the unimpassioned Jacobite in '45; Catholic priests in France today – Frenchmen of many complexions, in and out of France. So much pain; and the more honest the man the worse the pain. But there at least the conflict is direct: it seems to me that the greater mass of confusion and distress must arise from these less evident divergencies – the moral law, the civil, military, common laws, the code of honour, custom, the rules of practical life, of civility, of amorous conversation, gallantry, to say nothing of Christianity for those that practise it. All sometimes, indeed generally, at variance; none ever in an entirely harmonious relation to the rest; and a man is perpetually required to choose one rather than another, perhaps (in his particular case) its contrary. It is as though our strings were each tuned according to a completely separate system – it is as though the poor ass were surrounded by four and twenty mangers.'

'You are an antinomian,' said Jack.

'I am a pragmatist,' said Stephen. 'Come, let us drink up our wine, and I will compound you a dose – requires Nicholai. Perhaps tomorrow you should be let blood: it is three weeks since you was let blood.'

'Well, I will swallow your dose,' said Jack. 'But I tell you what – tomorrow night I shall be in among those gunboats and I shall do the blood-letting. And don't they wish they may relish it.'

THE *SOPHIE*'S ALLOWANCE of fresh water for washing was very small, and she made no allowance of soap at all. Those men who had blackened themselves and one another with paint remained darker than was pleasant; and those who had worked in the wrecked galley, covering themselves with grease and soot from the coppers and the stove, looked, if anything, worse – they had a curiously bestial and savage appearance, worst of all in those that had fair hair.

'The only respectable-looking fellows are the black men,' said Jack. 'They are all still aboard, I believe?'

'Davies went with Mr Mowett in the privateer, sir,' said James, 'but the rest are still with us.'

'Counting the men left in Mahon and the prize-crews, how many are we short at the moment?'

'Thirty-six, sir. We are fifty-four all told.'

'Very good. That gives us elbow-room. Let them have as much sleep as possible, Mr Dillon: we shall stand in at midnight.'

Summer had come back after the rain – a gentle, steady tramontana, warm, clear air, and phosphorescence on the sea. The lights of Barcelona twinkled with uncommon brilliance, and over the middle part of the city floated a luminous cloud: the gunboats guarding the approaches to the port could be made out quite clearly against this background before ever they saw the darkened *Sophie*: they were farther out than usual, and they were obviously on the alert.

'As soon as they start to come for us,' reflected Jack, 'we will set topgallants, steer for the orange light, then haul our wind at the last moment and run between the two on the northern end of the line.' His heart was going with a steady, even beat, a little faster than usual. Stephen had drawn off ten ounces of blood, and he thought he felt much the better for it. At all events his mind was as clear and sharp as he could wish.

The moon's tip appeared above the sea. A gunboat fired: deep, booming note – the voice of an old solitary hound.

'The light, Mr Ellis,' said Jack, and a blue flare soared up, designed to confuse the enemy. It was answered with Spanish signals, hoists of coloured lights, and then another gun, far over to the right. 'Topgallants,' he said. 'Jeffreys, steer for that orange mark.'

This was splendid: the *Sophie* was running in fast, prepared, confident and happy. But the gunboats were not coming on as he had hoped. Now one would spin about and fire, and now another; but on the whole they were falling back. To stir them up the sloop yawed and sent her broadside skipping among them – with some effect, to judge by a distant howl. Yet still the gunboats moved away. 'Damn this,' said Jack. 'They are trying to lead us on. Mr Dillon, trysail and staysails. We'll make a dash for that fellow farthest out.'

The *Sophie* came round fast and brought the wind on to her beam: heeling over so that the silk black water lapped at her port-sills, she raced towards the nearest gunboat. But now the others showed what they could do if they chose: they all faced about in a moment and kept up a continuous raking fire, while the chosen gunboat fled quartering away, keeping the *Sophie*'s unprotected stern towards them. A glancing blow from a thirty-six-pounder made her whole hull ring again; another passed just above head-height the whole length of the deck; two neatly severed backstays fell across Babbington, Pullings and the man at the wheel, knocking them down; a heavy block clattered on to the wheel itself as James leapt for its spokes.

'We'll tack, Mr Dillon,' said Jack; and a few moments later the *Sophie* flew up into the wind.

The men working the sloop moved with the unthinking smoothness of long practice; but seen suddenly picked out by the flashes of the gunboats' fire they seemed to be jerking like so many puppets. Just after the order 'let go and haul' there were six shots in quick succession, and he saw the marines at the mainsheet in a rapid series of galvanic motions – a few inches between each illumination – but throughout they wore exactly the same concentrated diligent expressions of men tallying with all their might.

'Close hauled, sir?' asked James.

'One point free,' said Jack. 'But gently, gently: let us see if we can draw *them* out. Drop the maintopsailyard a couple of feet and slacken away the starboard lift – let us look as though we were winged. Mr Watt, the topgallant backstays are our first care.'

And so they all moved back again across the same miles of sea, the *Sophie* knotting and splicing, the gunboats following and firing steadily, the old left-handed moon climbing with her usual indifference.

There was not much conviction in the pursuit: but even so, a little while after James Dillon had reported the completion of the essential repairs, Jack said, 'If we go about and set all sail like lightning, I believe we can cut those heavy chaps off from the land.'

'All hands about ship,' said James. The bosun started his call, and racing to his post by the maintopsail bowline Isaac Isaacs said to John Lakey, 'We are going to cut those two heavy buggers off from the land,' with intense satisfaction.

So they might have, if an unlucky shot had not struck the *Sophie*'s foretopgallant yard. They saved the sail, but her speed dropped at once and the gunboats pulled away ahead, away and away until they were safe behind their mole.

'Now, Mr Ellis,' said James, as the light of dawn showed just how much the sloop's rigging had suffered in the night, 'here is a most capital opportunity for learning your profession; why, I dare say there is enough to keep you busy until sunset, or even longer, with every variety of splice, knot, service and parcelling you could desire.' He was singularly gay, and from time to time, as he hurried about the deck, he hummed or chanted a sort of song.

There was the swaying up of the new yard, too, some shot-holes to be repaired and the bowsprit to be new gammoned, for the strangest grazing ricochet had cut half the turns without ever touching the wood – something the oldest seamen aboard had never yet beheld, a wonder to be recorded in the log. The *Sophie* lay there unmolested, putting herself to rights all through that sunny gentle day, as busy as a hive, watchful, prepared, bristling with pugnacity. It was a curious atmosphere aboard her: the men knew very well they were going in again very soon, perhaps for some raid on the coast, perhaps for some cutting-out expedition; their mood was affected by many things – by their captures of yesterday and last Tuesday (the consensus was that each man was worth fourteen guineas more than when he sailed); by their captain's continuing gravity; by the strong conviction aboard that he had private intelligence of Spanish sailings; and by the sudden strange merriment or even levity of their lieutenant. He had found Michael and Joseph Kelly, Matthew Johnson and John Melsom busily pilfering aboard the *Felipe V*, between decks, a very serious court-martial offence (although custom winked at the taking of anything above hatches) and one that he particularly abhorred as being 'a damned privateer's trick'; yet he had not reported them. They kept peering at him from behind masts, spars, boats; and so did their guilty messmates, for the Sophies were much given to rapine. The outcome of all these factors was an odd busy restrained quietly cheerful attentiveness, with a note of anxiety in it.

With all hands so busy, Stephen scrupled to go forward to his elm-tree pump, through whose unshipped head he daily observed the wonders of the deep and where his presence was now so usual that he might have been the pump itself for all the restraint he placed upon the men's conversation; but he caught this note and he shared the uneasiness that produced it.

James was in tearing spirits at dinner; he had invited Pullings and Babbington informally, and their presence, together with Marshall's absence, gave the meal something of the air of a festivity, in spite of the purser's brooding silence. Stephen watched him as he joined in the chorus of Babbington's song, thundering out

And this is law, I will maintain
Until my dying day, sir,
That whatsoever king shall reign,
I will be Vicar of Bray, sir

in a steady roar.

'Well done,' he cried, thumping the table. 'Now a glass of wine all round to whet our whistles, and then we must be on deck again, though that is a cursed thing for a host to say. What a relief it is, to be fighting with king's ships again, rather than these damned privateers,' he observed, à propos of nothing, when the young men and the purser had withdrawn.

'What a romantic creature you are, to be sure,' said Stephen. 'A ball fired from a privateer's cannon makes the same hole as a king's.'

'Me, romantic?' cried James with real indignation, an angry light coming into his green eyes.

'Yes, my dear,' said Stephen, taking snuff. 'You will be telling me next about their divine right.'

'Well, at least even you, with your wild enthusiastic levelling notions, will not deny that the King is the sole fount of honour?'

'Not I,' said Stephen. 'Not for a moment.'

'When I was last at home,' said James, filling Stephen's glass, 'we waked old Terence Healy. He had been my grandfather's tenant. And there was a song they sang there has been in the middle part of my mind all day – I cannot quite bring it to the front, to sing it.'

'Was it an Irish song or an English?'

'There were English words as well. One line went

Oh the wild geese a-flying a-flying a-flying,
The wild geese a-swimming upon the grey sea.'

Stephen whistled a bar and then, in his disagreeable crake, he sang

> 'They will never return, for the white horse has scunnered
> Has scunnered has scunnered
> The white horse has scunnered upon the green lea.'

'That's it – that's it. Bless you,' cried James, and walked off, humming the air, to see that the *Sophie* was gathering the utmost of her strength.

She made her way out to sea at sunset, with a great show of farewell for ever and set her course soberly for Minorca; and some time before dawn she ran inshore again, still with the same good breeze a little east of north. But now there was a true autumnal nip in it, and a dampness that brought fungi in beech woods to Stephen's mind; and over the water lay impalpable wafting hazes, some of them a most uncommon brown.

THE *SOPHIE* WAS standing in with her starboard tacks aboard, steering west-north-west; hammocks had been piped up and stowed in the nettings; the smell of coffee and frying bacon mingled together in the eddies that swirled on the weather-side of her taut trysail. Wide on the port bow the brown mist still hid the Llobregat valley and the mouth of the river, but farther up the coast towards the dim city looming there on the horizon, the rising sun had burnt off all but a few patches of haze – those that remained might have been headlands, islands, sandbanks.

'I know, I *know*, those gunboats were trying to lead us into some trap,' said Jack, 'and am with child to know what it was.' Jack was no great hand at dissembling, and Stephen was instantly persuaded that he knew the nature of the trap perfectly well, or at least had a very good notion of what it was likely to be.

The sun worked upon the surface of the water, doing won-

derful things to its colour, raising new mists, dissolving others, sending exquisite patterns of shadow among the taut
lines of the rigging and the pure curves of the sails and down
on to the white deck, now being scrubbed whiter, to the
steady grinding noise of holystones: with a swift yet imper-
ceptible movement it breathed away a blue-grey cape and
revealed a large ship three points on the starboard bow, running southwards under the land. The look-out called that she
was there, but in a matter-of-fact voice, formally, for as the
cloud-bank dissolved she was hull-up from the deck.

'Very well,' said Jack, clasping his glass to after a long stare.
'What do you make of her, Mr Dillon?'

'I rather think she is our old friend, sir,' said James.

'So do I. Set the mainstaysail and haul up to close her.
Swabs aft, dry the deck. And let the hands go to breakfast at
once, Mr Dillon. Should you care to take a cup of coffee with
the Doctor and me? It would be a said shame to waste it.'

'Very happy, sir.'

There was almost no conversation during their breakfast.
Jack said, 'I suppose you would like us to put on silk stockings, Doctor?'

'Why silk stockings, for all love?'

'Oh, everyone says it is easier for the surgeon, if he has to
cut one up.'

'Yes. Yes, certainly. Pray do by all means put on silk stockings.'

No conversation, but there was a remarkable feeling of easy
companionship, and Jack, standing up to put on his uniform
coat, said to James, 'You are certainly right, you know,' as
though they had been talking about the identity of the
stranger throughout the meal.

On deck again he saw that it was so, of course: the vessel
over there was the *Cacafuego*; she had altered course to meet
the *Sophie*, and she was in the act of setting her studdingsails. In his telescope he could see the vermilion gleam of her
side in the sun.

'All hands aft,' he said, and as they waited for the crew to assemble Stephen could see that a smile kept spreading on his face – that he had to make a conscious effort to repress it and look grave.

'Men,' he said, looking over them with pleasure. 'That's the *Cacafuego* to windward, you know. Now some of you were not quite pleased when we let her go without a compliment last time; but now, with our gunnery the best in the fleet, why, it is another thing. So, Mr Dillon, we will clear for action, if you please.'

When he began to speak perhaps half the Sophies were gazing at him with uncomplicated pleasurable excitement; perhaps a quarter looked a little troubled; and the rest had downcast and anxious faces. But the self-possessed happiness radiating from their captain and his lieutenant, and the spontaneous delighted cheer from the first half of the crew, changed this wonderfully; and as they set about clearing the sloop there were not above four or five who looked glum – the others might have been going to the fair.

The *Cacafuego*, square-rigged at present, was running down, turning in a steady westward sweep to get to windward and seaward of the *Sophie*; and the *Sophie* was pointing up close into the wind; so that by the time they were a long half-mile apart she was directly open to a raking broadside from the frigate, the thirty-two-gun frigate.

'The pleasant thing about fighting with the Spaniards, Mr Ellis,' said Jack, smiling at his great round eyes and solemn face, 'is not that they are shy, for they are not, but that they are never, never ready.'

The *Cacafuego* had now almost reached the station that her captain had set his mind upon: she fired a gun and broke out the Spanish colours.

'The American flag, Mr Babbington,' said Jack. 'That will give them something to think about. Note down the time, Mr Richards.'

The distance was lessening very fast now. Second after sec-

ond; not minute after minute. The *Sophie* was pointing astern
of the *Cacafuego*, as though she meant to cut her wake; and
not a gun could the sloop bring to bear. There was a total
silence aboard as every man stood ready for the order to tack
– an order that might not come before the broadside.

'Stand by with the ensign,' said Jack in a low voice: and
louder, 'Right, Mr Dillon.'

'Helm's a-lee,' and the bosun's call sounded almost at the
same moment; the *Sophie* spun on her heel, ran up the English colours, steadied and filled on her new course and ran
close-hauled straight for the Spaniard's side. The *Cacafuego*
fired at once, a crashing broadside that shot over and among
the *Sophie*'s topgallants, making four holes, no more. The
Sophies cheered to a man and stood tense and eager by their
treble-shotted guns.

'Full elevation. Not a shot till we touch,' cried Jack in a
tremendous voice, watching the hen-coops, boxes and lumber tossing overboard from the frigate. Through the smoke he
could see ducks swimming away from one coop, and a panic-
stricken cat on a box. The smell of powder-smoke reached
them, and the dispersing mist. Closer, closer: they would be
becalmed under the Spaniard's lee at the last moment, but
they would have way enough . . . He could see the round
blackness of her guns' mouths now, and as he watched so
they erupted, the flashes brilliant in the smoke and a great
white bank of it hiding the frigate's side. Too high again, he
observed, but there was no room for any particular emotion
as he searched through the faults in the smoke to put the
sloop right up against the frigate's mainchains.

'Hard over,' he shouted; and as the grinding crash came,
'Fire!'

The xebec-frigate was low in the water, but the *Sophie* was
lower still. With her yards locked in the *Cacafuego*'s rigging
she lay there, and her guns were below the level of the
frigate's ports. She fired straight up through the *Cacafuego*'s
deck, and her first broadside, at a six-inch range, did shock-

ing devastation. There was a momentary silence after the
Sophie's cheer, and in that half-second's pause Jack could
hear a confused screaming on the Spaniard's quarter-deck.
Then the Spanish guns spoke again, irregular now, but
immensely loud, firing three feet above his head.

The Sophie's broadside was firing in a splendid roll, one-
two-three-four-five-six-seven, with a half-beat at the end and
a rumbling of the trucks; and in the fourth or fifth pause
James seized his arm and shouted, 'They gave the order to
board.'

'Mr Watt, boom her off,' cried Jack, directing his speaking
trumpet forward. 'Sergeant, stand by.' One of the Cacafuego's
backstays had fallen aboard, fouling the carriage of a gun; he
passed it round a stanchion and as he looked up a swarm of
Spaniards appeared on the Cacafuego's side. The marines and
small-arms men gave them a staggering volley, and they hesitated. The gap was widening as the bosun at the head and
Dillon's party aft thrust on their spars. Amidst a crackling of
pistols some Spaniards tried to jump, some tried to throw
grapnels; some fell in and some fell back. The Sophie's guns,
now ten feet from the frigate's side, struck right into the
midst of the waverers, tore seven most dreadful holes.

The Cacafuego's head had fallen off: she was pointing
nearly south, and the Sophie had all the wind she needed to
range alongside again. Again the thundering din roared and
echoed round the sky, with the Spaniards trying to depress
their guns, trying to fire down with muskets and blindly-held
chance pistols over the side, to kill the gun-crews. Their
efforts were brave enough – one man balanced there to fire
until he had been hit three times – but they seemed totally
disorganized. Twice again they tried to board, and each time
the sloop sheered off, cutting them up with terrible slaughter,
lying off five or ten minutes, battering her upper-works,
before coming in again to tear out her bowels. By now the
guns were so hot that they could scarcely be touched; they
were kicking furiously with every round. The sponges hissed

and charred as they went in, and the guns were growing almost as dangerous to their crews as to their enemies.

And all this time the Spaniards fired on and on, irregularly, spasmodically, but never stopping. The Sophie's maintop had been hit again and again, and now it was coming to pieces – great lumps of timber falling down on deck, stanchions, hammocks. Her foresail yard was held only by its chains. Rigging hung in every direction and the sails had innumerable holes: burning wad was flying aboard all the time and the unengaged starboard crews were running to and fro with their firebuckets. Yet within its confusion the Sophie's deck showed a beautiful pattern of movement – the powder passing up from the magazine and the shot, the gun-crews with their steady heave-crash-heave, a wounded man, a dead man carrying below, his place instantly taken without a word, every man intent, threading the dense smoke – no collisions, no jostling, almost no orders at all.

'We shall be a mere hull presently, however,' reflected Jack: it was unbelievable that no mast or yard had gone yet; but it could not last. Leaning down to Ellis he said in his ear, 'Cut along to the galley. Tell the cook to put all his dirty pans and coppers upside-down. Pullings, Babbington, stop the firing. Boom off, boom off. Back topsails. Mr Dillon, let the starboard watch black their faces in the galley as soon as I have spoken to them. Men, men,' he shouted as the Cacafuego slowly forged ahead, 'we must board and carry her. Now's the time – now or never – now or no quarter – now while she's staggering. Five minutes' hearty and she's ours. Axes and broadswords and away – starbowlines black their faces in the galley and forward with Mr Dillon – the rest aft along of me.'

He darted below. Stephen had four quiet wounded men, two corpses. 'We're boarding her,' said Jack. 'I must have your man – every man-jack aboard. Will you come?'

'I will not,' said Stephen. 'I will steer, if you choose.'

'Do – yes, do. Come on,' cried Jack.

On the littered deck and in the smoke Stephen saw the

towering xebec's poop some twenty yards ahead on the port
bow; the *Sophie*'s crew in two parties, the one blackfaced and
armed racing from the galley and gathering at the head, the
other already aft, lining the rail – the purser pale and glaring,
wild; the gunner blinking from the darkness below; the cook
with his cleaver; Jack-in-the-dust; the ship's barber and his
own loblolly boy were there. Stephen noticed his hare-lip
grinning and he cherishing the curved spike of a boarding-
axe, saying over and over again, 'I'll hit the buggers, I'll hit the
buggers, I'll hit the buggers.' Some of the Spanish guns were
still firing out into the vacancy.

'Braces,' called Jack, and the yards began to come round to
fill the topsails. 'Dear Doctor, you know what to do?' Stephen
nodded, taking over the spokes and feeling the life of the
wheel. The quartermaster stepped away, picked up a cutlass
with a grim look of delight. 'Doctor, what's the Spanish for
fifty more men?'

'Otros cincuenta.'

'Otros cincuenta,' said Jack, looking into his face with a
most affectionate smile. 'Now lay us alongside, I beg.' He
nodded to him again, walked to the bulwark with his
coxswain close behind and hoisted himself up, massive but
lithe, and stood there holding the foremost shroud and swinging his sword, a long heavy cavalry sabre.

Holes and all, the topsails filled: the *Sophie* ranged up:
Stephen put the wheel hard over: the grinding crunch, the
twang of some rope parting, a jerk, and they were fast
together. With an enormous shrieking cheer fore and aft the
Sophies leapt up the frigate's side.

Jack was over the shattered bulwark straight down on to a
hot gun run in and smoking, and its swabber thrust at him
with the pole. He cut sideways at the swabber's head; the
swabber ducked fast and Jack leapt over his bowed shoulder
on to the *Cacafuego*'s deck. 'Come on, come on,' he roared,
and rushed forwards striking furiously at the fleeing gun-crew
and then at the pikes and swords opposing him – there were

hundreds, hundreds of men crowding the deck, he noticed; and all the time he kept roaring 'Come on!'

For some moments the Spaniards gave way, as though amazed, and every one of the *Sophie*'s men and boys came aboard, amidships and over the bow: the Spaniards gave way from abaft the mainmast, backing into the waist; but there they rallied. And now there was hard fighting, now there were cruel blows given and received – a dense mass of struggling men, tripping among the spars, scarcely room to fall, beating, hacking, pistolling one another; and detached fights of two or three men together round the edges, yelling like beasts. In the looser part of the main battle Jack had forced his way some three yards in: he had a soldier in front of him, and as their swords clashed high so a pikeman drove under his right arm, ripping the flesh outside his ribs and pulling out to stab again. Immediately behind him Bonden fired his pistol, blowing off the lower part of Jack's ear and killing the pikeman where he stood. Jack feinted at the soldier, a quick double slash, and brought his sword down on his shoulder with terrible force. The fight surged back: the soldier fell. Jack heaved out his sword, tight in bone, and glanced quickly fore and aft. 'This won't do,' he said.

Forward, under the fo'c'sle, the sheer weight and number of the three hundred Spaniards, now half recovered from their surprise, was pushing the Sophies back, driving a solid wedge between his band and Dillon's in the bows. Dillon must have been held up. The tide might turn at any second now. He leapt on to a gun and with a hail that ripped his throat he roared, 'Dillon, Dillon, the starboard gangway! Thrust for the starboard gangway!' For a fleeting moment, at the edge of his field of vision, he was aware of Stephen far below, on the deck of the *Sophie*, holding her wheel and gazing collectedly upwards. 'Otros cincuenta!' he shouted, for good measure: and as Stephen nodded, calling out something in Spanish, he raced back into the fight, his sword high and his pistol searching.

At this moment there was a frightful shrieking on the
fo'c'sle, a most bitter, furious drive for the head of the gangway, a desperate struggle; something gave, and the dense
mass of Spaniards in the waist turned to see these black faces
rushing at them from behind. A confused milling round the
frigate's bell, cries of every kind, the blackened Sophies
cheering like madmen as they joined their friends, shots, the
clash of arms, a trampling huddled retreat, all the Spaniards
in the waist hampered, crowded in upon, unable to strike.
The few on the quarter-deck ran forward along the larboard
side to try to rally the people, to bring them into some order,
at least to disengage the useless marines.

Jack's opponent, a little seaman, writhed away behind the
capstan, and Jack heaved back out of the press. He looked up
and down the clear run of deck. 'Bonden,' he shouted, plucking his arm, 'Go and strike those colours.'

Bonden ran aft, leaping over the dead Spanish captain.
Jack hallooed and pointed. Hundreds of eyes, glancing or
staring or suddenly looking back, half-comprehending, saw
the *Cacafuego*'s ensign race down – her colours struck.

It was over. ' 'Vast fighting,' cried Jack, and the order ran
round the deck. The Sophies backed away from the packed
mob in the waist and the men there threw down their
weapons, suddenly dispirited, frightened, cold and betrayed.
The senior surviving Spanish officer struggled out of the crowd
in which he had been penned and offered Jack his sword.

'Do you speak English, sir?' asked Jack.

'I understand it, sir,' said the officer.

'The men must go down into the hold, sir, at once,' said
Jack. 'The officers on deck. The men down into the hold.
Down into the hold.'

The Spaniard gave the order: the frigate's crew began to file
down the hatchways. As they went so the dead and wounded
were discovered – a tangled mass amidships, many more forward, single bodies everywhere – and so, too, the true number of the attackers grew clear.

'Quickly, quickly,' cried Jack, and his men urged the prisoners below, herded them fast, for they understood the danger as well as their captain. 'Mr Day, Mr Watt, get a couple of their guns – those carronades – pointing down the hatchways. Load with canister – there's plenty in the garlands aft. Where's Mr Dillon? Pass the word for Mr Dillon.'

The word passed, and no answer came. He was lying there near the starboard gangway, where the most desperate fighting had been, a couple of steps from little Ellis. When Jack picked him up he thought he was only hurt; but turning him he saw the great wound in his heart.

11

H.M. Sloop *Sophie*
off Barcelona

Sir,

I have the honour to acquaint you, that the sloop I have the honour to command, after a mutual chase and a warm action, has captured a Spanish xebec frigate of 32 guns, 22 long twelve-pounders, 8 nines, and 2 heavy carronades, viz. the *Cacafuego*, commanded by Don Martin de Langara, manned by 319 officers, seamen and marines. The disparity of force rendered it necessary to adopt some measure that might prove decisive. I resolved to board, which being accomplished almost without loss, after a violent close engagement the Spanish colours were obliged to be struck. I have, however, to lament the loss of Lieutenant Dillon, who fell at the height of the action, leading his boarding-party, and of Mr Ellis, a supernumerary; while Mr Watt the boatswain and five seamen were severely wounded. To render just praise to the gallant conduct and impetuous attack of Mr Dillon, I am perfectly unequal to.

'I SAW HIM for a while,' Stephen had said, 'I saw him
through that gap where two ports were beaten into one:
they were fighting by the gun, and then when you called out
at the head of those stairs into the waist; and he was in front
– black faces behind him. I saw him pistol a man with a pike,
pass his sword through a fellow who had beaten down the
bosun and come to a redcoat, an officer. After a couple of
quick passes he caught this man's sword on his pistol and
lunged straight into him. But his sword struck on the breast-
bone or a metal plate, and doubled and broke with the thrust:
and with the six inches left he stabbed him faster than you
could see – inconceivable force and rapidity. You would never
believe the happiness on his face. The light on his face!'

> I must be permitted to say, that there could not have
> been greater regularity, nor more cool determined con-
> duct shown by men, than by the crew of the *Sophie*.
> The great exertions and good conduct of Mr Pullings, a
> passed midshipman and acting lieutenant whom I beg
> to recommend to their Lordships' attention, and of the
> boatswain, carpenter, gunner and petty officers, I am
> particularly indebted for.
>
> I have the honour to be, etc.
>
> *Sophie*'s force at commencement of action: 54 offi-
> cers, men, and boys. 14 4-pounders. 3 killed and 8
> wounded.
>
> *Cacafuego*'s force at commencement of action: 274
> officers, seamen and supernumeraries. 45 marines.
> Guns 32.
>
> The captain, boatswain, and 13 men killed; 41
> wounded.

He read it through, changed 'I have the honour' on the first
page to 'I have the pleasure', signed it Jno. Aubrey and
addressed it to M. Harte, Esqr. – not to Lord Keith alas, for
the admiral was at the other end of the Mediterranean, and

everything passed through the hands of the commandant.

It was a passable letter; not very good, for all his efforts and revisions. He was no hand with a pen. Still, it gave the facts – some of them – and apart from being dated 'off Barcelona' in the customary way, whereas it was really being written in Port Mahon the day after his arrival, it contained no falsehood: and he thought he had done everyone justice – had done all the justice he could, at least, for Stephen Maturin had insisted upon being left out. But even if it had been a model of naval eloquence it would still have been utterly inadequate, as every sea-officer reading it would know. For example, it spoke of the engagement as something isolated in time, coolly observed, reasonably fought and clearly remembered, whereas almost everything of real importance was before or after the blaze of fighting; and even in that he could scarcely tell what came first. As to the period after the victory, he was unable to recapture the sequence at all, without the log: it was all a dull blur of incessant labour and extreme anxiety and weariness. Three hundred angry men to be held down by two dozen, who also had to bring the six-hundred-ton prize to Minorca through an ugly sea and some cursed winds; almost all the sloop's standing and running rigging to be set up anew, masts to be fished, yards shifted, fresh sails bent, and the bosun among the badly wounded; that hobbling voyage along the edge of disaster, with precious little help from the sea or the sky. A blur, and a sense of oppression; a feeling more of the *Cacafuego*'s defeat than the *Sophie*'s victory; and exhausted perpetual hurrying, as though that were what life really consisted of. A fog punctuated by a few brilliantly clear scenes.

Pullings, there on the bloody deck of the *Cacafuego*, shouting in his deafened ear that gunboats were coming down from Barcelona; his determination to fire the frigate's undamaged broadside at them; his incredulous relief when he saw them turn at last and dwindle against the threatening horizon – why?

The sound that woke him in the middle watch: a low cry mounting by quarter tones or less and increasing in volume to a howling shriek, then a quick series of spoken or chanted words, the mounting cry again and the shriek – the Irish men of the crew waking James Dillon, stretched there with a cross in his hands and lanterns at his head and his feet.

The burials. The child Ellis in his hammock with the flag sewed over him looked like a little pudding, and now at the recollection his eye clouded again. He had wept, wept, his face streaming with tears as the bodies went over the side and the marines fired their volley.

'Dear Lord,' he thought. 'Dear Lord.' For the re-writing of the letter and this casting back of his mind brought all the sadness flooding up again. It was a sadness that had lasted from the end of the action until the breeze had died on them some miles off Cape Mola and they had fired urgent guns for a pilot and assistance: a sadness that fought a losing battle against invading joy, however. Trying to fix the moment when the joy broke through he looked up, stroking his wounded ear with the feather of his pen; and through the cabin window he saw the tall proof of his victory at her moorings by the yard; her undamaged larboard side was towards the *Sophie*, and the pale water of the autumn day reflected the red and shining gold of her paintwork, as proud and trim as the first day he had seen her.

Perhaps it was when he received the first unbelieving amazed congratulations from Sennet of the *Bellerophon*, whose gig was the first boat to reach him: then there was Butler of the *Naiad* and young Harvey, Tom Widdrington and some midshipmen, together with Marshall and Mowett, almost out of their minds with grief at not having taken part in the action, yet already shining with reflected glory. Their boats took the *Sophie* and her prize in tow; their men relieved the exhausted marines and idlers guarding the prisoners; he felt the accumulated weight of those days and nights come down on him in a soft compelling cloud, and he went to sleep in the midst of their questions. That marvellous sleep, and his waking in the still harbour to be given a quick unsigned note in a double cover from Molly Harte.

Perhaps it was then. The joy, the great swelling delight was certainly in him when he woke. He grieved, of course he grieved, he grieved bitterly for the loss of his shipmates – would have given his right hand to save them – and mixed in his sorrow for Dillon there was a guilt whose cause and nature eluded him; but a serving officer in an active war has an intense rather than a lasting grief. Sober objective reason told him that there had not been many successful single-ship actions between quite such unequal opponents and that unless he did something spectacularly foolish, unless he blew himself as high as the Boyne, the next thing that would reach him from the Admiralty would be the news of his being gazetted – of his being made a post-captain.

With any kind of luck he would be given a frigate: and his mind ran over those glorious high-bred ships – *Emerald, Seahorse, Terpsichore, Phaëton, Sibylle, Sirius,* the lucky *Ethalion, Naiad, Alcmène* and *Triton,* the flying *Thetis. Endymion, San Fiorenzo, Amelia* . . . dozens of them: more than a hundred in commission. Had he any right to a frigate? Not much: a twenty-gun post-ship was more his mark, something just in the sixth rate. Not much right to a frigate. Not much right to set about the *Cacafuego,* either; nor to make love to Molly Harte. Yet he had done so. In the post-chaise, in a bower, in another bower, all night long. Perhaps that was why he was so sleepy now, so apt to doze, blinking comfortably into the future as though it were a sea-coal fire. And perhaps that was why his wounds hurt so. The slash on his left shoulder had opened at the far end. How he had come by it he could not tell; but there it was after the action, and Stephen had sewn it up at the same time he dressed the pike-wound across the front of his chest (one bandage for the two) and clapped a sort of dressing on what was left of his ear.

But dozing would not do. This was the time for riding in

with the tide of flood, for making a dash for a frigate, for seizing fortune while she was in reach, running her aboard. He would write to Queeney at once, and half a dozen letters more that afternoon, before the party – perhaps to his father too, or would the old boy make a cock of it again? He was the worst hand imaginable at plot, intrigue or the management of what tiny amount of interest they had with the grander members of the family – should never have reached the rank of general, by rights. However, the public letter was the first of these things, and Jack got up carefully, smiling still.

This was the first time he had been openly ashore, and early though it was he could not but be conscious of the looks, the murmurs and the pointing that accompanied his passage. He carried his letter into the commandant's office, and the compunction, the stirrings if not of conscience or principle then at least of decency, that had disturbed him on his way up through the town and even more in the anteroom, disappeared with Captain Harte's first words. 'Well, Aubrey,' he said, without getting up, 'we are to congratulate you upon your prodigious good luck again, I collect.'

'You are too kind, sir,' said Jack. 'I have brought you my official letter.'

'Oh, yes,' said Captain Harte, holding it some way off and looking at it with an affectation of carelessness. 'I will forward it, presently. Mr Brown tells me it is perfectly impossible for the yard here to supply half your wants – he seems quite astonished that you should want so much. How the devil did you contrive to get so many spars knocked away? And such a preposterous amount of rigging? Your sweeps destroyed? There are no sweeps here. Are you sure your bosun is not coming it a trifle high? Mr Brown says there is not a frigate on the station, nor even a ship of the line, that has called for half so much cordage.'

'If Mr Brown can tell me how to take a thirty-two gun frigate without having a few spars knocked away I shall be obliged to him.'

'Oh, in these sudden surprise attacks, you know . . . however, all I can say is you will have to go to Malta for most of your requirements. *Northumberland* and *Superb* have made a clean sweep here.' It was so evidently his intention to be ill-natured that his words had little effect; but his next stroke slipped under Jack's guard and stabbed right home. 'Have you written to Ellis' people yet? This sort of thing' – tapping the public letter – 'is easy enough: anyone can do this. But I do not envy you the other. What I shall say myself I don't know . . .' Biting the joint of his thumb he darted a furious look from under his eyebrows, and Jack had a moral certainty that the financial setback, misfortune, disaster, or whatever it was, affected him far more than the debauching of his wife.

Jack had, in fact, written that letter, as well as the others – Dillon's uncle, the seamen's families – and he was thinking of them as he walked across the patio with a sombre look on his face. A figure under the dark gateway stopped, obviously peering at him. All Jack could see in the tunnel through to the street was an outline and the two epaulettes of a senior post-captain or a flag-officer, so although he was ready with his salute his mind was still blank when the other stepped through into the sunlight, hurrying forward with his hand outstretched. 'Captain Aubrey, I do believe? Keats, of the *Superb*. My dear sir, you must allow me to congratulate you with all my heart – a most splendid victory indeed. I have just pulled round your capture in my barge, and I am amazed, sir, *amazed*. Was you very much clawed? May I be of any service – my bosun, carpenter, sailmakers? Would you do me the pleasure of dining aboard, or are you bespoke? I dare say you are – every woman in Mahon will wish to exhibit you. Such a victory!'

'Why, sir, I thank you most heartily,' cried Jack, flushing with undisguised open ingenuous pleasure and returning the pressure of Captain Keats' hand with such vehemence as to cause a dull crepitation, followed by a shattering dart of agony. 'I am infinitely obliged to you, for your kind opinion.

There is none I value more, sir. To tell you the truth, I am
engaged to dine with the Governor and to stay for the concert; but if I might beg the loan of your bosun and a small
party – my people are all most uncommon weary, quite fagged
out – why, I should look upon it as a most welcome, indeed, a
Heaven-sent relief.'

'It shall be done. Most happy,' said Captain Keats. 'Which
way do you go, sir? Up or down?'

'Down, sir. I have appointed to meet a – a person at the
Crown.'

'Then our ways lie together,' said Captain Keats, taking
Jack's arm; and as they crossed the street to walk in the shade
he called out to a friend, 'Tom, come and see who I have in
tow. This is Captain Aubrey of the *Sophie*! You know Captain
Grenville, I am sure?'

'This gives me very great pleasure,' cried the grim, battle-
scarred Grenville, breaking out into a one-eyed smile: he
shook Jack by the hand and instantly asked him to dinner.

Jack had refused five more invitations by the time he and
Keats parted at the Crown: from mouths he respected he had
heard the words 'as neat an action as ever I knew', 'Nelson
will rejoice in this', and 'if there is justice on earth, the frigate
will be bought by Government and Captain Aubrey given
command of her'. He had seen looks of unfeigned respect,
good will and admiration upon the faces of seamen and junior
officers passing in the crowded street; and two commanders
senior to him, unlucky in prizes and known to be jealous, had
hurried across to make their compliments, handsomely and
with good grace.

He walked in, up the stairs to his room, threw off his coat
and sat down. 'This must be what they call the vapours,' he
said, trying to define something happy, tremulous, poignant,
churchlike and not far from tears in his heart and bosom. He
sat there: the feeling lasted, indeed grew stronger; and when
Mercedes darted in he gazed at her with a mild benevolence,
a kind and brotherly look. She darted in, squeezed him pas-

sionately and uttered a flood of Catalan into his ear, ending 'Brave, brave Captain – good, *pretty* and brave.'

'Thank you, thank you, Mercy dear; I am infinitely obliged to you. Tell me,' he said, after a decent pause, trying to shift to an easier position (a plump girl: a good ten stone), 'diga me, would you be a good creature, bona creatura, and fetch me some iced negus? Sangria colda? Thirst, soif, very thirst, I do assure you, my dear.'

'Your auntie was quite right,' he said, putting down the beaded jug and wiping his mouth. 'The Vinaroz ship was there to the minute, and we found the false Ragusan. So here, acqui, aqui is auntie's reward, the recompenso de tua tia, my dear' – pulling a leather purse out of his breeches pocket – 'y aqui' – bringing out a neat sealing-waxed packet – 'is a little regalo para vous, sweetheart.'

'Present?' cried Mercedes, taking it with a sparkling eye, nimbly undoing the silk, tissue-paper, jeweller's cotton, and finding a pretty little diamond cross with a chain. She shrieked, kissed him, darted to the looking-glass, shrieked some more – eek, eek! – and came back with the stone flashing low on her neck. She pulled herself in below and puffed herself out above, like a pouter-pigeon, and lowered her bosom, the diamonds winking in the hollow, down towards him, saying, 'You like him? You like him? You like him?'

Jack's eyes grew less brotherly, oh far less brotherly, his glottis stiffened and his heart began to thump. 'Oh, yes, I like him,' he said, hoarsely.

'Timely, sir, bosun of the *Superb*,' said a tremendous voice at the opening door. 'Oh, beg pardon, sir . . .'

'Not at all, Mr Timely,' said Jack. 'I am very happy to see you.'

'And indeed perhaps it was just as well,' he reflected, landing again at the Rope-Walk stairs, leaving behind him a numerous body of skilful, busy Superbs rattling down the newly set-up shrouds, 'there being so much to do. But what a sweet girl it is . . .' He was now on his way to the Governor's dinner. That, at least, was his intention; but a bemused state of mind, swimming back into the past and onwards into the future, together with a reluctance to seem to parade himself in what the sailors called the High Street, brought him by obscure back ways filled with the smell of new fermenting wine and purple-guttered with the lees, to the Franciscan church at the top of the hill. Here, summoning his wits into the present, he took new bearings; and looking with some anxiety at his watch he paced rapidly along by the armoury, passed the green door of Mr Florey's house with a quick upward glance and headed north-west by north for the Residence.

BEHIND THE GREEN door and some floors up Stephen and Mr Florey were already sat down to a haphazard meal, spread wherever there was room on odd tables and chairs. Ever since coming back from the hospital they had been dissecting a well-preserved dolphin, which lay on a high bench by the window, next to something covered by a sheet.

'Some captains think it the best policy to include every case of bloodshed or temporary incapacity,' said Mr Florey, 'because a long butcher's bill looks well in the Gazette. Others will admit no man that is not virtually dead, because a small number of casualties means a careful commander. I think your list is near the happy mean, though perhaps a trifle cautious – you are looking at it from the point of view of your friend's advancement of course?'

'Just so.'

'Yes . . . Allow me to give you a slice of this cold beef. Pray reach me a sharp knife – beef, above all, must be cut thin, if it is to savour well.'

'There is no edge on this one,' said Stephen. 'Try the catling.' He turned to the dolphin. 'No,' he said, peering under a flipper. 'Where can we have left it? Ah' – lifting the sheet – 'here is another. Such a blade: Swedish steel, no doubt. You began your incision at the Hippocratic point, I see,' he said, raising the sheet a little more, and gazing at the young lady beneath it.

'Perhaps we ought to wash it,' said Mr Florey.

'Oh, a wipe will do,' said Stephen, using a corner of the sheet. 'By the way, what was the cause of death?' he asked, letting the cloth fall back.

'That is a nice point,' said Mr Florey, carving a first slice and carrying it to the griffon vulture tied by the leg in a corner of the room. 'That is a nice point, but I rather incline to believe that the battering did her business before the water. These amiable weaknesses, follies . . . Yes. Your friend's advancement.' Mr Florey paused, gazing at the long straight double-edged catling and waving it solemnly over the joint. 'If you provide a man with horns, he may gore you,' he observed with a detached air, covertly watching to see what effect his remark might have.

'Very true,' said Stephen, tossing the vulture a piece of gristle. 'In general *fenum habent in cornu.* But surely,' he said, smiling at Mr Florey, 'you are not throwing out a generality about cuckolds? Do not you choose to be more specific? Or do you perhaps refer to the young person under the sheet? I know you speak from your excellent heart, and I assure you no degree of frankness can possibly offend.'

'Well,' said Mr Florey, 'the point is, that your young friend – our young friend, I may say, for I have a real regard for him, and look upon this action as reflecting great credit upon the service, upon us all – our young friend has been very indiscreet: so has the lady. You follow me, I believe?'

'Oh, certainly.'

'The husband resents it, and he is in such a position that he may be able to indulge his resentment, unless our friend is very careful – most uncommon cautious. The husband will not ask for a meeting, for that is not his style at all – a pitiful fellow. But he may try to entrap him into some act of disobedience and so bring him to a court-martial. Our friend is famous for his dash, his enterprise and his good luck rather

than for his strict sense of subordination: and some few of
the senior captains here feel a good deal of jealousy and
uneasiness at his success. What is more, he is a Tory, or his
family is; and the husband and the present First Lord are
rabid Whigs, vile ranting dogs of Whigs. Do you follow me,
Dr Maturin?'

I do indeed, sir, and am much obliged to you for your candour in telling me this: it confirms what was in my mind, and
I shall do all I can to make him conscious of the delicacy of
his position. Though upon my word,' he added with a sigh,
'there are times when it seems to me that nothing short of a
radical ablation of the membrum virile would answer, in this
case.'

'That is very generally the peccant part,' said Mr Florey.

CLERK DAVID RICHARDS was also having his dinner; but
he was eating it in the bosom of his family. 'As everyone
knows,' he told the respectful throng, 'the captain's clerk's
position is the most dangerous there is in a man-of-war: he is
up there all the time on the quarter-deck with his slate and
his watch, to take remarks, next to the captain, and all the
small-arms and a good many of the great guns concentrate
their fire upon him. Still, there he must stay, supporting the
captain with his countenance and his advice.'

'Oh, Davy,' cried his aunt, 'and did he ask your advice?'

'Did he ask my advice, ma'am? Ha, ha, upon my sacred
word.'

'Don't swear, Davy dear,' said his aunt automatically. 'It ain't
genteel.'

' "La, Mr Richards bach," says he, when the maintop begins
to tumble about our ears, tearing down through the quarterdeck splinter-netting like so much Berlin wool, "I don't know
what to do. I am quite at a loss, I protest." "There's only one
thing for it, sir," says I. "Board 'em. Board 'em fore and aft,
and I give you my sacred word the frigate's ours in five minutes." Well, ma'am and cousins, I do not like to boast, and I

confess it took us ten minutes; but it was worth it, for it won us as pretty a copper-fastened, new-sheathed xebec frigate as any I have seen. And when I came aft, having dirked the Spanish captain's clerk, Captain Aubrey shook me by the hand, and with tears in his eyes, "Richards," says he, "we ought all to be very grateful to you," says he. "Sir, you are very good," says I, "but I have done nothing but what any taut captain's clerk would do." "Well," says he, " 'tis very well." '
He took a draught of porter and went on, 'I very nearly said to him, "I tell you what, Goldilocks" – for we call him Goldilocks in the service, you know, in much the same way as they call me Hell-fire Davy, or Thundering Richards – "just you rate me midshipman aboard the *Cacafuego* when she's bought by Government, and we'll cry quits." Perhaps I may, tomorrow; for I feel I have the genius of command. She ought to fetch twelve pound ten, thirteen pound a ton, don't you think, sir?' he said to his uncle. 'We did not cut up her hull a great deal.'
'Yes,' said Mr Williams slowly. 'If she was bought in by Government she would fetch that and her stores as much again: Captain A would clear a neat five thou' apart from the head-money; and your share would be, let's see, two hundred and sixty-three, fourteen, two. *If* she was bought by Government.'
'What do you mean, Nunckie, with your *if*?'
'Why, I mean that a *certain person* does the Admiralty buying; and a *certain person* has a lady that is not over-shy; and a *certain person* may cut up horrid rough. O Goldilocks, Goldilocks, wherefore are thou Goldilocks?' asked Mr Williams, to the unspeakable amazement of his nieces. 'If he had attended to business instead of playing Yardo, the parish bull, he . . .'
'It was she as set her bonnet at him!' cried Mrs Williams, who had never yet let her husband finish a sentence since his 'I will' at Trinity Church, Plymouth Dock, in 1782.
'O the minx!' cried her unmarried sister; and the nieces' eyes swung towards her, wider still.

'The hussy,' cried Mrs Thomas. 'My Paquita's cousin was the driver of the shay she came down to the quay in; and you would never credit . . .'

'She should be flogged through the town at the cart's tail, and don't I wish I had the whip.'

'Come, my dear . . .'

'I know what you are thinking, Mr W.,' cried his wife. 'and you are to stop it this minute. The nasty cat; the wretch.'

THE WRETCH'S REPUTATION had indeed suffered, had been much blown upon in recent months, and the Governor's wife received her as coldly as she dared; but Molly Harte's looks had improved almost out of recognition – she had been a fine woman before, and now she was positively beautiful. She and Lady Warren arrived together for the concert, and a small troop of soldiers and sailors had waited outside to meet their carriage: now they were crowding about her, snorting and bristling with aggressive competition, while their wives, sisters and, even, sweethearts sat in dowdy greyish heaps at a distance, mute, and looking with pursed lips at the scarlet dress almost hidden amidst the flocking uniforms.

The men fell back when Jack appeared, and some of them returned to their womenfolk, who asked them whether they did not find Mrs Harte much aged, ill dressed, a perfect frump? Such a pity at her age, poor thing. She must be at least thirty, forty, forty-five. Lace mittens! They had no idea of wearing lace mittens. This strong light was unkind to her; and surely it was very outré to wear all those enormous great pearls?

She *was* something of a whore, thought Jack, looking at her with great approval as she stood there with her head high, perfectly aware of what the women were saying, and defying them: she was something of a whore, but the knowledge spurred his appetite. She was only for the successful; but with the *Cacafuego* moored by the *Sophie* in Mahon harbour, Jack found that perfectly acceptable.

After a few moments of inane conversation – a piece of dissembling which Jack thought he accomplished with particular brilliance, alas – they all surged in a shuffling mob into the music-room, Molly Harte to sit looking beautiful by her harp and the rest to arrange themselves on the little gilt chairs.

'What are we to have?' asked a voice behind him, and turning Jack saw Stephen, powdered, respectable apart from having forgotten his shirt, and eager for the treat.

'Some Boccherini – a 'cello piece – and the Haydn trio that we arranged. And Mrs Harte is going to play the harp. Come and sit by me.'

'Well, I suppose I shall have to,' said Stephen, 'the room being so crowded. Yet I had hoped to enjoy this concert: it is the last we shall hear for some time.'

'Nonsense,' said Jack, taking no notice. 'There is Mrs Brown's party.'

'We shall be on our way to Malta by then. The orders are writing at this moment.'

'The sloop is not nearly ready for sea,' said Jack. 'You must be mistaken.'

Stephen shrugged. 'I have it from the secretary himself.'

'The damned rogue . . .' cried Jack.

'Hush,' said all the people round them; the first violin gave a nod, brought down his bow, and in a moment they were all dashing away, filling the room with a delightful complexity of sound, preparing for the 'cello's meditative song.

'UPON THE WHOLE,' said Stephen, 'Malta is a disappointing place. But at least I did find a very considerable quantity of squills by the sea-shore: these I have conserved in a woven basket.'

'It is,' said Jack. 'Though God knows, apart from poor Pullings, I should not complain. They have fitted us out nobly, apart from the sweeps – nobody could have been more attentive than the Master Attendant – and they entertained us like emperors. Do you suppose one of your squills would be a good thing, in a general way, to set a man up? I feel as low as a gib cat – quite out of order.'

Stephen looked at him attentively, took his pulse, gazed at his tongue, asked squalid questions, examined him. 'Is it a wound going bad?' asked Jack, alarmed by his gravity.

'It is a wound, if you wish,' said Stephen. 'But not from our battle with the *Cacafuego*. Some lady of your acquaintance has been too liberal with her favours, too universally kind.'

'Oh, Lord,' cried Jack, to whom this had never happened before.

'Never mind,' said Stephen, touched by Jack's horror. 'We shall soon have you on your feet again: taken early, there is no great problem. It will do you no harm to keep close, drink nothing but demulcent barley-water and eat gruel, thin gruel – no beef or mutton, no wine or spirits. If what Marshall tells me about the westward passage at this time of the year is true, together with our stop at Palermo, you will certainly be in a state to ruin your health, prospects, reason, features and happiness again by the time we raise Cape Mola.'

He left the cabin with what seemed to Jack an inhuman want of concern and went directly below, where he mixed a draught and a powder from the large stock that he (like all other naval surgeons) kept perpetually at hand. Under the thrust of the gregale, coming in gusts off Delamara Point, the *Sophie*'s lee-lurch slopped out too much by half.

'It is too much by half,' he observed, balancing like a seasoned mariner and pouring the surplus into a twenty-drachm phial. 'But never mind. It will just do for young Babbington.' He corked it, set it on a rail-locked rack, counted its fellows with their labelled necks and returned to the cabin. He knew very well that Jack would act on the ancient seafaring belief that *more is better* and dose himself into Kingdom Come if not closely watched, and he stood there reflecting upon the passage of authority from one to the other in relationships of this kind (or rather of potential authority, for they had never entered into any actual collision) as Jack gasped and retched over his nauseous dose. Ever since Stephen Maturin had grown rich with their first prize he had constantly laid in great quantities of asafetida, castoreum and other substances, to make his medicines more revolting in taste, smell and texture than any others in the fleet; and he found it answered – his hardy patients knew with their entire beings that they were being physicked.

'The Captain's wounds are troubling him,' he said at dinner-time, 'and he will not be able to accept the gun-room's invitation tomorrow. I have confined him to his cabin and to slops.'

'Was he very much cut up?' asked Mr Dalziel respectfully. Mr Dalziel was one of the disappointments of Malta: everybody aboard had hoped that Thomas Pullings would be confirmed lieutenant, but the admiral had sent down his own nominee, a cousin, Mr Dalziel of Auchterbothie and Sodds. He had softened it with a private note promising to 'keep Mr Pullings in mind and to make particular mention of him to the Admiralty', but there it was – Pullings remained a master's mate. He was not 'made' – the first spot on their victory. Mr Dalziel felt it, and he was particularly conciliatory; though, indeed, he had very little need to be, for Pullings was the most unassuming creature on earth, painfully diffident anywhere except on the enemy's deck.

'Yes,' said Stephen, 'he was. Sword, pistol and pike wounds; and probing the deepest I have found a piece of metal, a slug, that he had received at the Battle of the Nile.'

'Enough to trouble any man,' said Mr Dalziel, who through no fault of his own had seen no bloodshed whatever and who suffered from the fact.

'I speak under correction, Doctor,' said the master, 'but surely fretting will open wounds? And he must be fretting something cruel not to be on our cruising-ground, the season growing so late.'

'Ay, to be sure,' said Stephen. And certainly Jack had reason to fret, like everybody else aboard: to be sent to Malta while they had a right to cruise in fine rich waters was very hard, in any case, and it was made all the worse by the persistent rumour of a galleon earmarked by fate and by Jack's private intelligence for the *Sophie* – a galleon, or even galleons, a parcel of galleons, that might at this very moment be creeping along the Spanish coast, and they five hundred miles away.

They were extremely impatient to be back to their cruise, to the thirty-seven days that were owing to them, thirty-seven days of making hay; for although there were many aboard who possessed more guineas than they had ever owned shillings ashore, there was not one who did not ardently long for more. The general reckoning was that the ordinary seaman's share would be close on fifty pounds, and even those who had been blooded, thumped, scorched and battered in the action thought it good pay for a morning's work – more interesting by far than the uncertain shilling a day they might earn at the plough or the loom, by land, or even than the eight pounds a month that hard-pressed merchant captains were said to be offering.

Successful action together, strong driving discipline and a high degree of competence (apart from Mad Willy, *Sophie's* lunatic, and a few other hopeless cases, every man and boy aboard could now hand, reef and steer) had welded them into a remarkably united body, perfectly acquainted with their vessel and her ways. It was just as well, for their new lieutenant was no great seaman, and they got him out of many a sad blunder as the sloop made her way westwards as fast as ever she could, through two shocking gales, through high battering seas and maddening calms, with the *Sophie* wallowing in the great swell, her head all round the compass and the ship's cat as sick as a dog. As fast as ever she could, for not only had all her people a month's mind to be on the enemy's coast again, but all the officers were intensely eager to hear the news from London, the Gazette and the official reaction to their exploit – a post-captain's commission for Jack and perhaps advancement for all the rest.

It was a passage that spoke well for the yard at Malta, as well as for the excellence of her crew, for it was in these same waters that the sixteen-gun sloop *Utile* foundered during their second gale – she broached to going before the wind not twenty miles to the south of them, and all hands perished. But the weather relented on the last day, sending them a fine steady close-reef topsail tramontana: they raised the high land of Minorca in the forenoon, made their number a little after dinner and rounded Cape Mola before the sun was half-way down the sky.

All alive once more, though a little less tanned from his confinement, Jack looked eagerly at the wind-clouds over Mount Toro, with their promise of continuing northerly weather, and he said, 'As soon as we are through the narrows, Mr Dalziel, let us hoist out the boats and begin to get the butts on deck. We shall be able to start watering tonight and be on our way as soon as possible in the morning. There is not a moment to lose. But I see you have hooks to the yards and stays already – very good,' he added with a chuckle, going into his cabin.

This was the first poor Mr Dalziel had heard of it: silent hands that knew Jack's ways far better than he did had fore-seen the order, and the poor man shook his head with what philosophy he could muster. He was in a difficult position, for although he was a respectable, conscientious officer he could not possibly stand any sort of comparison with James Dillon: their former lieutenant was wonderfully present in the mind of the crew that he had helped to form – his dynamic authority, his immense technical ability and his sea-manship grew in their memories.

Jack was thinking of him as the *Sophie* glided up the long harbour, past the familiar creeks and the islands one after another: they were just abreast of the hospital island and he was thinking how much less noise James Dillon used to make when he heard the hail of 'Boat ahoy' on deck and far away the answering cry that meant the approach of a captain. He did not catch the name, but a moment later Babbington, looking alarmed, knocked on his door to announce 'Commandant's barge pulling alongside, sir.'

There was a good deal of plunging about on deck as Dalziel set about trying to do three things at once and as those who should dress the sloop's side tried to make themselves look respectable in a violent hurry. Few captains would have darted from behind an island in this way; few would have worried a vessel about to moor; and most, even in an emergency, would have given them a chance, would have allowed them a few minutes' grace; but not Captain Harte, who came up the side as quickly as he could. The calls twittered and howled; the few properly dressed officers stood rigid, bareheaded; the marines presented arms and one dropped his musket.

'Welcome aboard, sir,' cried Jack, who was in such charity with the present shining world that he could feel pleased to see even this ill-conditioned face, it being familiar. 'I believe this is the first time we have had the honour.'

Captain Harte saluted the quarter-deck with a sketchy motion towards his hat and stared with elaborate disgust at the grubby sideboys, the marines with their crossbelts awry, the heap of water-butts and Mr Dalziel's little fat meek cream-coloured bitch, that had come forward into the only open space, and that there, apologizing to one and all, her ears and whole person drooping, was in the act of making an immeasurable pool.

'Do you usually keep your decks in this state, Captain Aubrey?' he asked. 'By my living bowels, it's more like a Wapping pawnshop than the deck of a King's sloop.'

'Why, no, sir,' said Jack, still in the best humour in the world, for the waxed-canvas Admiralty wrapper under Harte's arm could only be a post-captain's commission addressed to J. A. Aubrey, Esqr., and brought with delightful speed. 'You have caught the *Sophie* in her shift, I am afraid. Will you step into the cabin, sir?'

The crew were tolerably busy as she made her way through the shipping and prepared to moor, but they were used to their sloop and they were used to their anchorage, which was just as well, for a disproportionate amount of their attention was taken up with listening to the voices that came out of the cabin.

'He's coming it the Old Jarvie,' whispered Thomas Jones to William Witsover, with a grin. Indeed, this grin was fairly general abaft the mainmast, where those in earshot quickly gathered that their captain was being blown up. They loved him much, would follow him anywhere; but they were pleasantly amused at the thought of his copping it, his being dressed down, hauled over the coals, taken to task a little.

' "When I give an order I expects it to be punctually obeyed," ' mouthed Robert Jessup in silent pomp to William Agg, quartermaster's mate.

'Silence there,' cried the master, who could not hear.

But presently the grin faded, first on the faces of the brighter men nearest the skylight, then on those within reach of their communicative eyes, meaning gestures and significant grimaces, and so forward. And as the best bower splashed into the sea the whisper ran 'No cruise.'

Captain Harte reappeared on deck. He was seen into his barge with rigid ceremony, in an atmosphere of silent suspicion, much strengthened by the look of stony reserve on Captain Aubrey's face.

The cutter and the launch began watering at once; the jolly-boat carried the purser ashore for stores and the post; bumboats came off with their usual delights; and Mr Watt, together with most of the other Sophies who had survived their wounds, hurried out in the hospital wherry to see what those sods in Malta had done to his rigging.

To these their shipmates cried, 'Do you know what?'

'What, mate?'

'So you don't know what?'

'Tell us, mate.'

'We ain't going to have no more cruise, that's what. – We've
had it, says old Whoreson Prick, we've had our time. – We'm
used it up, going to Malta. – Our thirty-seven days! – We convoy that damned lubberly packet down to Gib, that's what we
do; and thank you kindly for your efforts in the cruising line.
– Cacafuego was not bought in – sold to them bloody Moors
for eighteen-pence and a pound of shit, the swiftest bleeding
xebec that ever swam. – We come back too slow: "Don't you
tell me, sir," says he, "for I knows better." – Nothing in the
Gazette about us, and Old Fart never brought Goldilocks his
step. – They say she weren't regular and her captain had no
commission – all bloody lies. – Oh, if I had his cullions in my
hand, wouldn't I serve him out, just? I'd . . .' At this point they
were cut short by a peremptory message from the quarterdeck, delivered by a bosun's mate with a rope's end; but their
passionate indignation flowed on in what they meant to be
whispers, and if Captain Harte had reappeared at that
moment they might have broken out in mutinous riot and
flung him in the harbour. They were furious for their victory,
furious for themselves and furious for Jack; and they knew
perfectly well that their officers' reproaches were totally
devoid of conviction; the rope's end might have been a wafting handkerchief; and even the newcomer Dalziel was
shocked by their treatment, at least as it was delivered by
rumour, eavesdropping, inference, bumboat talk and the
absence of the lovely Cacafuego.

In fact, their treatment was even shabbier than rumour had
it. The Sophie's commander and her surgeon sat in the cabin
amidst a heap of papers, for Stephen Maturin had been helping with some of the paper work as well as writing returns
and letters of his own, and now it was three in the morning:
the Sophie rocked gently at her moorings, and her tight-
packed crew were snorting the long night through (the rare
joys of harbour-watch). Jack had not gone ashore at all – had
no intention of going ashore; and now the silence, the lack of
real motion, the long sitting with pen and ink seemed to insu-

late them from the world in their illuminated cell; and this made their conversation, which would have been indecent at almost any other time, seem quite ordinary and natural. 'Do you know that fellow Martinez?' asked Jack quietly. 'The man whose house the Hartes have part of?'

'I know *of* him,' said Stephen. 'He is a speculator, a sort of would-be rich man, the left-handed half.'

'Well, he has got the contract for carrying the mails – a damned job, I'm sure – and has bought that pitiful tub the *Ventura* to be the packet. She has never sailed six miles in an hour since she was launched and we are to convoy her to the Rock. Fair enough, you say. Yes, but *we* are to take the sack, put it aboard her when we are just outside the mole and then return back here directly, without landing or communicating with Gibraltar. And I will tell you another thing: he did not forward my official letter by *Superb*, that was going down the Mediterranean two days after we left, nor by *Phoebe*, that was going straight home; and I will lay you any odds you choose to mention that it is here, in this greasy sack. What is more, I know as certainly as if I had read it that his covering letter will be full of this fancied irregularity about the *Caca-fuego*'s command, this quibble over the officer's status. Ugly hints and delay. That is why there was nothing in the Gazette. No promotion, either: that Admiralty wrapper only held his own orders, in case I should insist upon having them in writing.'

'Sure, his motive is obvious to a child. He hopes to provoke you into an outburst. He hopes you will disobey and ruin your career. I do beg you will not be blinded with anger.'

'Oh, I shan't play the fool,' said Jack, with a somewhat dogged smile. 'But as for provoking me, I confess he has succeeded to admiration. I doubt I could so much as finger a scale, my hand trembles so when I think of it,' he said, picking up his fiddle. And while the fiddle was passing through the two feet of air from the locker to the height of his shoulder, purely self-concerned and personal thoughts presented themselves to his mind, scarcely in succession but as a cluster: these weeks and months of precious seniority slipping away – already Douglas of the *Phoebe*, Evans on the West Indies station, and a man he did not know called Raitt had been made; they were in the last Gazette and now they were ahead of him on the immutable list of post-captains; he would be junior to them for ever. Time lost; and these disturbing rumours of peace. And a deep, barely acknowledged suspicion, a dread that the whole thing might have gone wrong: no promotion: Lord Keith's warning truly prophetic. He tucked the fiddle under his chin, tightening his mouth and raising his head as he did so: and the tightening of his mouth was enough to release a flood of emotion. His face reddened, his breath heaved deep, his eyes grew larger and, because of the extreme contraction of their pupils, bluer: his mouth tightened still further, and with it his right hand. *Pupils contract symmetrically to a diameter of about a tenth part of an inch,* noted Stephen on a corner of a page. There was a loud, decided crack, a melancholy confused twanging, and with a ludicrous expression of doubt and wonder and distress, Jack held out his violin, all dislocated and unnatural with its broken neck. 'It snapped,' he cried. 'It snapped.' He fitted the broken ends together with infinite care and held them in place. 'I would not have had it happen for the world,' he said in a low voice. 'I have known this fiddle, man and boy, since I was breeched.'

INDIGNATION AT THE *Sophie*'s treatment was not confined to the sloop, but naturally it was strongest there, and as the crew heaved the capstan round to unmoor they sang a new song, a song that owed nothing whatever to Mr Mowett's chaste muse.

– old Harte, – old Harte,
That red-faced son of a dry French fart.
Hey ho, stamp and go,

Stamp and go, stamp and go,
Hey ho, stamp and go.

The cross-legged fifer on the capstan-head lowered his pipe and sang the quiet solo part:

Says old Harte to his missis
O what do I see?
Bold Sophie's commander
With his fiddle-dee-dee.

Then the deep cross rhythmical bellow again

– old Harte, – old Harte,
That one-eyed son of a blue French fart.

James Dillon would never have allowed it, but Mr Dalziel had no notion of any of the allusions and the song went on and on until the cable was all below in tiers, smelling disagreeably of Mahon ooze, and the *Sophie* was hoisting her jibs and bracing her foretopsailyard round. She dropped down abreast of the Amelia, whom she had not seen since the action with the *Cacafuego*, and all at once Mr Dalziel observed that the frigate's rigging was full of men, all carrying their hats and facing the *Sophie*.

'Mr Babbington,' he said in a low voice, in case he should be mistaken, for he had only seen this happen once before, 'tell the captain, with my duty, that I believe *Amelia* is going to cheer us.'

Jack came blinking on deck as the first cheer roared out, a shattering wave of sound at twenty-five yards' range. Then came the *Amelia*'s bosun's pipe and the next cheer, as precisely timed as her own broadside: and the third. He and his officers stood rigidly with their hats off, and as soon as the last roar had died away over the harbour, echoing back and forth, he called out, 'Three cheers for the *Amelia*!' and the

Sophies, though deep in the working of the sloop, responded like heroes, scarlet with pleasure and the energy needed for huzzaying proper – huge energy, for they knew what was manners. Then the *Amelia*, now far astern, called 'One cheer more,' and so piped down.

It was a handsome compliment, a noble send-off, and it gave great pleasure: but still it did not prevent the Sophies from feeling a strong sense of grievance – it did not prevent them from calling out 'Give us back our thirty-seven days' as a sort of slogan or watchword between decks, and even above hatches when they dared – it did not wholly recall them to their duty, and in the following days and weeks they were more than ordinarily tedious.

The brief interlude in Port Mahon harbour had been exceptionally bad for discipline. One of the results of their fierce contraction into a single defiant ill-used body was that the hierarchy (in its finer shades) had for a time virtually disappeared; and among other things the ship's corporal had let the wounded men returning to their duty bring in bladders and skins full of Spanish brandy, anisette and a colourless liquid said to be gin. A discreditable number of men had succumbed to its influence, among them the captain of the foretop (paralytic) and both bosun's mates. Jack disrated Morgan, promoting the dumb negro Alfred King, according to his former threat – a *dumb* bosun's mate would surely be more terrible, more deterrent; particularly one with such a very powerful arm.

'And, Mr Dalziel,' he said, 'we will rig a proper grating at the gangway at last. They do not give a damn for a flogging at the capstan, and I am going to stop this infernal drunkenness, come what may.'

'Yes, sir,' said the lieutenant: and after a slight pause, 'Wilson and Plimpton have represented to me that it would grieve them very much to be flogged by King.'

'Of course it will grieve them very much. I sincerely hope it *will* grieve them very much. That is why they are to be flogged. They were drunk, were they not?'

'Blind drunk, sir. They said it was their Thanksgiving.'

'What in God's name have they got to be thankful about? And the *Cacafuego* sold to the Algerines.'

'They are from the colonies, sir, and it seems that it is a feast in those parts. However, it is not the flogging they object to, but the colour of the flogger.'

'Bah,' said Jack. 'I'll tell you another man who will be flogged if this goes on,' he said, bending and peering sideways through the cabin window, 'and that is the master of that damned packet. Just give him a gun, Mr Dalziel, will you? Shotted, not too far from his stern, and desire him to keep to his station.'

The wretched packet had had a miserable time of it since leaving Port Mahon. She had expected the *Sophie* to sail straight to Gibraltar, keeping well out in the offing, out of sight of privateers, and certainly out of range of shore batteries. But although the *Sophie* was still no Flying Childers, in spite of all her improvements, she could nevertheless sail two miles for the packet's one, either close-hauled or going large, and she made the most of her superiority to work right down along the coast, peering into every bay and inlet, obliging the packet to keep to the seaward of her, at no great distance and in a very high state of dread.

Hitherto, this eager, terrier-like searching had led to nothing but a few brisk exchanges of fire with guns on shore, for Jack's harsh restrictive orders allowed no chasing and made it almost certain that he should take no prize. But that was an entirely secondary consideration: action was what he was looking for; and at this juncture, he reflected, he would give almost anything for a direct uncomplicated head-on clash with some vessel about his own size.

So thinking he stepped on deck. The breeze off the sea had been fading all the afternoon, and now it was dying in irregular gasps; although the *Sophie* still had it the packet was almost entirely becalmed. To starboard the high brown rocky coast trended away north and south with something of a pro-

trusion, a small cape, a headland with a ruined Moorish castle, on the beam, perhaps a mile away.

'You see that cape?' said Stephen, who was gazing at it with
an open book dangling from his hand, his thumb marking
the place. 'It is Cabo Roig, the seaward limit of Catalan
speech: Orihuela is a little way inland, and after Orihuela
you hear no more Catalan – 'tis Murcia, and the barbarous
jargon of the Andalou. Even in the village round the point
they speak like Morescoes – algarabia, gabble-gabble,
munch, munch.' Though perfectly liberal in all other senses,
Stephen Maturin could not abide a Moor.

'There is a village, is there?' asked Jack, his eyes brightening.

'Well, a hamlet: you will see it presently.' A pause, while the
sloop whispered through the still water and the landscape
imperceptibly revolved. 'Strabo tells us that the ancient Irish
regarded it as an honour to be eaten by their relatives – a
form of burial that kept the soul in the family' he said, waving
the book.

'Mr Mowett, pray be so good as to fetch me my glass. I beg
your pardon, dear Doctor: you were telling me about Strabo.'

'You may say he is no more than Eratosthenes redivivus, or
shall I say new-rigged?'

'Oh, do, by all means. There is a fellow riding hell for
leather along the top of the cliff, under that castle.'

'He is riding to the village.'

'So he is. I see it now, opening behind the rock. I see something else, too,' he added, almost to himself. The sloop glided
steadily on, and steadily the shallow bay turned, showing a
white cluster of houses at the water's edge. There were three
vessels lying at anchor some way out, a quarter of a mile to
the south of the village: two houarios and a pink, merchantmen of no great size, but deeply laden.

Even before the sloop stood in towards them there was
great activity ashore, and every eye aboard that could command a glass could see people running about, boats launch-

ing and pulling industriously for the anchored vessels. Presently men could be seen hurrying to and fro on the merchantmen, and the sound of their vehement discussion came clearly over the evening sea. Then came the rhythmic shouting as they worked at their windlasses, weighing their anchors: they loosed their sails and ran themselves straight on shore.

Jack stared at the land for some time with a hard calculating look in his eye: if no sea were to get up it would be easy to warp the vessels off – easy both for the Spaniards and for him. To be sure, his orders left no room for a cutting-out expedition. Yet the enemy lived on his coastwise trade – roads execrable – mule-trains absurd for anything in bulk – no waggons worth speaking of – Lord Keith had been most emphatic on that point. And it was his duty to take, burn, sink or destroy. The Sophies stared at Jack: they knew very well what was in his mind, but they also had a pretty clear notion of what was in his orders too – this was not a cruise but a piece of strict convoy-work. They stared so hard that the sands of time ran out. Joseph Button, the marine sentry whose function it was to turn the half-hour glass the moment it emptied and to strike the bell, was roused from his contemplation of Captain Aubrey's face by nudges, pinches, muffled cries of 'Joe, Joe, wake up Joe, you fat son of a bitch,' and lastly by Mr Pullings' voice in his ear, 'Button, turn that glass.'

The last tang of the bell died away and Jack said, 'Put her about, Mr Pullings, if you please.'

With a smooth perfection of curve and the familiar, almost unnoticed piping and cries of 'Ready about – helm's a-lee – rise tacks and sheets – mainsail haul,' the Sophie came round, filled and headed back towards the distant packet, still becalmed in a smooth field of violet sea.

She lost the breeze herself when she had run a few miles off the little cape, and she lay there in the twilight and the falling dew, with her sails limp and shapeless.

'Mr Day,' said Jack, 'be so good as to prepare some fire barrels – say half a dozen. Mr Dalziel, unless it comes on to blow I think we may take the boats in at about midnight. Dr Maturin, let us rejoice and be gay.'

Their gaiety consisted of ruling staves and copying a borrowed duet filled with hemidemisemiquavers. 'By God,' said Jack, looking up with red-rimmed streaming eyes after an hour or so, 'I am getting too old for this.' He pressed his hands over his eyes and kept them there for a while: in quite another voice he said, 'I have been thinking about Dillon all day. All day long I have been thinking about him, off and on. You would scarcely credit how much I miss him. When you told me about that classical chap, it brought him so to mind . . . because it was about Irishmen, no doubt; and Dillon was Irish. Though you would never have thought so – never to be seen drunk, almost never called anyone out, spoke like a Christian, the most gentleman-like creature in the world, nothing of the hector at all – oh Christ. My dear fellow, my dear Maturin, I do beg your pardon. I say these damned things . . . I regret it extremely.'

'Ta, ta, ta,' said Stephen, taking snuff and waving his hand from side to side.

Jack pulled the bell, and through the various ship-noises, all muted in this calm, he heard the quick pittering of his steward. 'Killick,' he said, 'bring me a couple of bottles of that Madeira with the yellow seal, and some of Lewis' biscuits. I can't get him to make a decent seed-cake,' he explained to Stephen, 'but these petty fours go down tolerably well and give the wine a relievo. Now this wine,' he said, looking attentively through his glass, 'was given me in Mahon by our agent, and it was bottled the year Eclipse was foaled. I produce it as a sin-offering, conscious of my offence. Your very good health, sir.'

'Yours, my dear. It is a most remarkable ancient wine. Dry, yet unctuous. Prime.'

'I say these damned things,' Jack went on, musing as they drank their bottle, 'and don't quite understand at the time, though I see people looking black as hell, and frowning, and my friends going "Pst, pst", and then I say to myself, "You're brought by the lee again, Jack." Usually I make out what's amiss, given time, but by then it's too late. I am afraid I vexed Dillon often enough, that way' – looking down sadly – 'but, you know, I am not the only one. Do not think I mean to run him down in any way – I only mention it as an instance, that even a very well-bred man can make these blunders some-times, for I am sure he never meant it – but Dillon once hurt me very much, too. He used the word *commercial*, when we were speaking rather warmly about taking prizes. I am sure he did not mean it, any more than I meant any uncivil reflex-ion, just now; but it has always stuck hard in my gullet. That is one of the reasons why I am so happy . . .'

Knock-knock on the door. 'Beg pardon, your honour. Loblolly boy's all in a mother, sir. Young Mr Ricketts has swal-lowed a musket-ball and they can't get it out. Choking to death, sir, if you please.'

'Forgive me,' said Stephen, carefully putting down his glass and covering it with a red spotted handkerchief, a bandanna.

'Is all well – did you manage . . .?' asked Jack five minutes later.

'We may not be able to do all we could wish in physic,' said Stephen with quiet satisfaction, 'but at least we can give an emetic that answers, I believe. You were saying, sir?'

'*Commercial* was the word,' said Jack. 'Commercial. And that is why I am so happy to have this little boat expedition tonight. For although my orders will not allow me to bring 'em off, yet I have to wait for the packet to come up, and there is nothing to prevent me from burning 'em. I lose no time; and the most scrupulous mind could not but say that this is the most uncommercial enterprise imaginable. It is too late, of course – these things always are too late – but it is a great sat-isfaction to me. And how James Dillon would have delighted in it! The very thing for him! You remember him with the boats at Palamos? And at Palafrugell?'

The moon set. The star-filled sky wheeled about its axis, sweeping the Pleiades right up overhead. It was a midwinter sky (though warm and still) before the launch, the cutter and the jolly-boat came alongside and the landing-party dropped down into them, the men in their blue jackets and wearing white armbands. They were five miles from their prey, but already no voice rose much above a whisper – a few smothered laughs and the clink of weapons handing down – and when they paddled off with muffled oars they melted so silently into the darkness that in ten minutes Stephen's straining eyes lost them altogether.

'Do you see them still?' he asked the bosun, lame from his wound and now in charge of the sloop.

'I can just make out the darkie the captain's looking at the compass with,' said Mr Watt. 'A little abaft the cathead.'

'Try my night-glass, sir,' said Lucock, the only midshipman left aboard.

'I wish it were over,' said Stephen.

'So do I, Doctor' said the bosun. 'And I wish I were with them. 'Tis much worse for us left aboard. Those chaps are all together, jolly like, and time goes by like Horndean fair. But here we are, left all thin and few, nothing to do but wait, and the sand chokes in the watch-glass. It will seem years and years before we hear anything of them, sir, as you will surely see.'

Hours, days, weeks, years, centuries. Once there was an ominous clangour high overhead – flamingoes on their way to the Mar Menor, or maybe as far as the marshes of the Guadalquivir: but for the most part it was featureless darkness, almost a denial of time.

The flashes of musketry and the subsequent crackle of firing did not come from the small arc on which his stare had been concentrated, but from well to the right of it. Had the boats gone astray? Run into opposition? Had he been looking in the wrong direction? 'Mr Watt,' he said, 'are they in the right place?'

'Why, no, sir,' said the bosun comfortably. 'And if I know anything of it, the captain is a-leading of 'em astray.'

The crackling went on and on, and in the intervals a faint shouting could be heard. Then to the left there appeared a deep red glow; then a second, and a third; and all at once the third grew enormously, a tongue of flame that leapt up and up and higher still, a most prodigious fountain of light – a whole ship-load of olive-oil ablaze.

'Christ almighty,' murmured the bosun, deep struck with awe. 'Amen,' said one among the silent, staring crew.

The blaze increased: in its light they could see the other fires and their smoke, quite pale; the whole of the bay, the village; the cutter and the launch pulling away from the shore and the jolly-boat crossing to meet them; and all round behind, the brown hills, sharp in light and shade.

At first the column had been perfectly straight, like a cypress; but after the first quarter of an hour its tip began to lean southwards and inland, towards the hills, and the smoke-cloud above to stream away in a long pall, lit from below. The brilliance was if anything greater, and Stephen saw gulls drifting across between the sloop and the land, all heading for the fire. 'It will be attracting every living thing,' he reflected, with anxiety. 'What will be the conduct of the bats?'

Presently the top two-thirds was leaning over strongly, and the *Sophie* began to roll, with the waves slapping up against her larboard side.

Mr Watt broke from his long state of wonder to give the necessary orders, and coming back to the rail he said, 'They will have a hard pull, if this goes on.'

'Could we not bear down and pick them up?' asked Stephen.

'Not with this wind come round three points, and those old shoals off of the headland. No, sir.'

Another group of gulls passed low over the water. 'The flame is attracting every living thing for miles,' said Stephen.

'Never mind, sir,' said the bosun. 'It will be daylight in an hour or two, and they will pay no heed then, no heed at all.'

'It lights up the whole sky,' said Stephen.

It also lit up the deck of the *Formidable*, Captain Lalonde, a beautifully built French eighty-gun ship of the line wearing the flag of Rear-Admiral Linois at the mizzen: she was seven or eight miles off shore, on her way from Toulon to Cadiz, and with her in line ahead sailed the rest of the squadron, the *Indomptable*, eighty, Captain Moncousu, the *Desaix*, seventy-four, Captain Christy-Pallière (a splendid sailer), and the *Muiron*, a thirty-eight gun frigate that had until recently belonged to the Venetian Republic.

'Let us put in and see what is afoot,' said the admiral, a small, dark, round-headed, lively gentleman in red breeches, very much the seaman; and a few moments later the hoists of coloured lanterns ran up. The ships tacked in succession with a quiet efficiency that would have done credit to any navy afloat, for they were largely manned from the Rochefort squadron, and as well as being commanded by efficient professional officers they were filled with prime sailormen.

They ran inshore on the starboard tack with the wind one point free, bringing up the daylight, and when they were first seen from the *Sophie*'s deck they were greeted with joy. The boats had just reached the sloop after a long wearisome pull, and the French men-of-war were not sighted as early as they might have been: but sighted they were, in time, and at once every man forgot his hunger, fatigue, aching arms, and the cold and the wet, for the rumour instantly filled the sloop – 'Our galleons are coming up, hand over fist!' The wealth of the Indies, New Spain and Peru: gold ingots by way of their ballast. Ever since the crew had come to know of Jack's private intelligence about Spanish shipping there had been this persistent rumour of a galleon, and now it was fulfilled.

The splendid flame was still leaping up against the hills, though more palely as dawn broke all along the eastern sky; but in the cheerful animation of putting all to rights, of mak-

ing everything ready for the chase, no one took notice of it
any more – whenever a man could look up from his business
his eyes darted eager, delighted glances over the three or four
miles of sea at the *Desaix*, and at the *Formidable*, now some
considerable way astern of her.

It was difficult to say just when all the delight vanished:
certainly the captain's steward was still reckoning up the cost
of opening a pub on the Hunstanton road when he brought
Jack a cup of coffee on the quarter-deck, heard him say 'A
horrid bad position, Mr Dalziel,' and noticed that the *Sophie*
was no longer standing towards the supposed galleons but
sailing from them as fast as she could possibly go, close-
hauled, with everything she could set, including bonnets and
even drabblers.

By this time the *Desaix* was hull-up – had been for some
time – and so was the *Formidable*: behind the flagship there
showed the topgallants and topsails of the *Indomptable*, and
out to sea, a couple of miles to windward of her, the frigate's
sails nicked the line of the sky. It was a horrid bad position;
but the *Sophie* had the weather-gage, the breeze was uncertain and she might be taken for a merchant brig of no importance – something a busy squadron would not trouble with
for more than an hour or so: they were not in very grave
earnest, concluded Jack, lowering his glass. The behaviour of
the press of men on the *Desaix*'s fo'c'sle, the by no means
extraordinary spread of canvas, and countless indefinable trifles, persuaded him that she had not the air of a ship chasing
in deadly earnest. But even so, how she slipped along! Her
light, high, roomy, elegant round French bows and her beautifully cut, taut, flat sails brought her smoothly over the water,
sailing as sweetly as the *Victory*. And she was well handled:
she might have been running along a path ruled out upon the
sea. He hoped to cross her bows before she had satisfied her
curiosity about the fire on shore and so lead her such a dance
of it that she would give it up – that the admiral would eventually make her signal of recall.

'Upon deck,' called Mowett from the masthead. 'The frigate has taken the packet.'

Jack nodded, sweeping his glass out to the miserable *Ventura* and back beyond the seventy-four to the flagship. He waited: perhaps five minutes. This was the crucial stage. And now signals did indeed break out aboard the *Formidable*, signals with a gun to emphasize them. But they were not signals of recall, alas. The *Desaix* instantly hauled her wind, no longer interested in the shore: her royals appeared, sheeted home and hoisted with a brisk celerity that made Jack round his mouth in a silent whistle. More canvas was appearing aboard the *Formidable* too; and now the *Indomptable* was coming up fast, all sails abroad, sweeping along with a freshening of the breeze.

It was clear that the packet had told what the *Sophie* was. But it was clear, too, that the rising sun was going to make the breeze still more uncertain, and perhaps swallow it up altogether. Jack glanced up at the *Sophie*'s spread: everything was there, of course; and at present everything was drawing in spite of the chancy wind. The master was at the con, Pram, the quartermaster, was at the wheel, getting everything out of her that she was capable of giving, poor fat old sloop. And every man was at his post, ready, silent and attentive: there was nothing for him to say or do; but his eye took in the threadbare, sagging Admiralty canvas, and his heart smote him cruelly for having wasted time – for not having bent his own new topsails, made of decent sailcloth, though unauthorized.

'Mr Watt,' he said, a quarter of an hour later, looking at the glassy patches of calm in the offing, 'stand by to out sweeps.'

A few minutes after this the *Desaix* hoisted her colours and opened with her bow-chasers; and as though the rumbling double crash had stunned the air, so the opulent curves of her sails collapsed, fluttered, swelled momentarily and slackened again. The *Sophie* kept the breeze another ten minutes, but then it died for her too. Before the way was off her – long before – all the sweeps that Malta had allowed her (four short, alas) were out and she was creeping steadily along, five men to each loom, and the long oars bending perilously under the urgent, concentrated heave and thrust, right into what would have been the wind's eye if there had still been any blowing. It was heavy, heavy work: and suddenly Stephen noticed that there was an officer to almost every sweep. He stepped forward to one of the few vacant places, and in forty minutes all the skin was gone from his palms.

'Mr Dalziel, let the starboard watch go to breakfast. Ah, there you are, Mr Ricketts: I believe we may serve out a double allowance of cheese – there will be nothing hot for a while.'

'If I may say so, sir,' said the purser with a pale leer, 'I fancy there will be something uncommon hot, presently.'

The starboard watch, summarily fed, took over the labouring sweeps while their shipmates set to their biscuit, cheese and grog, with a couple of hams from the gun-room – a brief, uneasy meal, for out there the wind was ruffling the sea, and it had chopped round two points. The French ships picked it up first, and it was striking to see how their tall, high-reaching sails sent them running on little more than an air. The *Sophie*'s hard-won advance was wiped out in twenty minutes; and before her sails were drawing the *Desaix* already had a bow-wave, whiskers that could be seen from the quarter-deck. *Sophie*'s sails were drawing now, but this creeping pace would never do.

'In sweeps,' said Jack. 'Mr Day, throw the guns overboard.'

'Aye aye, sir,' said the gunner briskly, but his movements were strangely slow, unnatural and constrained as he sprung the capsquares, like those of a man walking along the edge of a cliff, by will-power alone.

Stephen came on deck again, his hands neatly mittened. He saw the team of the starboard brass quarter-deck four-pounder with crows and handspike in their hands and a common look of anxious, almost frightened concern, waiting for the roll: it came, and they gently urged their gleaming, highly-polished gun overboard – their pretty number fourteen over the side. Its splash coincided exactly with the fountain thrown up not ten yards away by a ball from the *Desaix*'s bow-chaser, and the next gun went overboard with less ceremony. Fourteen splashes at half a ton apiece; then the heavy carriages over the rail after them, leaving the slashed breeching and the unhooked tackles on either side of the gaping ports – a desolation to be seen.

He glanced forward, then astern, and understood the position: he pursed his lips and retired to the taffrail. The lightened *Sophie* gathered speed minute by minute, and as all this weight had gone from well above the water-line she swam more upright – stiffer to the wind.

The first of the *Desaix*'s shot whipped through the topgallantsail, but the next two pitched short. There was still time for manoeuvre – for plenty of manoeuvre. For one thing, reflected Jack, he would be very much surprised if the *Sophie* could not come about twice as quickly as the seventy-four. 'Mr Dalziel,' he said, 'we will go about and back again. Mr Marshall, let her have plenty of way on her.' It would be quite disastrous if the *Sophie* were to miss stays on her second turn: and these light airs were not what she liked – she never gave of her best until there was something of a sea running and at least one reef in her topsails.

'Ready about . . .' The pipe twittered, the sloop luffed up, came into the wind, stayed beautifully and filled on the larboard tack: her bowlines were as taut as harpstrings before the big seventy-four had even begun her turn.

The swing began, however; the *Desaix* was in stays; her yards were coming round; her checkered side began to show; and Jack, seeing the first hint of her broadside in his glass, called out, 'You had better go below, Doctor.' Stephen went, but no farther than the cabin; and there, craning from the stern-window, he saw the *Desaix*'s hull vanish in smoke from stem to stern, perhaps a quarter of a minute after the *Sophie*

had begun her reverse turn. The massive broadside, nine
hundred and twenty-eight pounds of iron, plunged into a
wide area of sea away on the starboard beam and rather short,
all except for the two thirty-six pound balls, which hummed
ominously through the rigging, leaving a trail of limp, dangling cordage. For a moment it seemed that the *Sophie* might
not stay – that she would fall impotently off, lose all her
advantage and expose herself to another such salute, more
exactly aimed. But a sweet puff of air in her backed headsails
pushed her round and there she was on her former tack,
gathering way before the *Desaix*'s heavy yards were firmly
braced – before her first manoeuvre was complete at all.

The sloop had gained perhaps a quarter of a mile. 'But he
will not let me do that again,' reflected Jack.

The *Desaix* was round on the starboard tack again, making
good her loss; and all the while she fired steadily with her
bowchasers, throwing her shot with remarkable accuracy as
the range narrowed, just missing, or else clipping the sails,
compelling the sloop to jig every few minutes, slightly losing
speed each time. The *Formidable* was lying on the other tack
to prevent the *Sophie* slipping through, and the *Indomptable*
was running westwards, to haul her wind in half a mile or so
for the same purpose. The *Sophie*'s pursuers were roughly in
line abreast behind her and coming up fast as she ran sloping
across their front. Already the eighty-gun flagship had yawed
to fire one broadside at no unlikely distance; and the grim
Desaix, making short boards, had done so on each turn. The
bosun and his party were busy knotting, and there were some
sad holes in the sails; but so far nothing essential had been
struck, nor any man wounded.

'Mr Dalziel,' said Jack, 'start the stores over the side, if you
please.'

The hatch-covers came off, the holds emptied into the sea
– barrels of salt beef, barrels of pork, biscuit by the ton, peas,
oatmeal, butter, cheese, vinegar. Powder, shot. They started
their water and pumped it overboard. A twenty-four pounder

hulled the *Sophie* low under the counter, and at once the pumps began gushing sea as well as fresh water.

'See how the carpenter is doing, Mr Ricketts,' said Jack.

'Stores overboard, sir,' reported the lieutenant.

'Very good, Mr Dalziel. Anchors away now, and spars. Keep only the kedge.'

'Mr Lamb says two foot and a half in the well,' said the midshipman, panting. 'But he has a comfortable plug in the shot-hole.'

Jack nodded, glancing back at the French squadron. There was no longer any hope of getting away from them close-hauled. But if he were to bear up, turning quickly and unex-pectedly, he might be able to double back through their line; and then, with this breeze one or two points on her quarter, and with the help of the slight following sea, her lightness and her liveliness, why, she might live to see Gibraltar yet. She was so light now – a cockleshell – she might outrun them before the wind; and with any luck, turning briskly, she would gain a mile before the line-of-battle ships could gather way on the new tack. To be sure, she would have to survive a couple of broadsides as she passed through . . . But it was the only hope; and surprise was everything.

'Mr Dalziel,' he said, 'we will bear up in two minutes' time, set stuns'ls and run between the flagship and the seventy-four. We must do it smartly, before they are aware.' He addressed these words to the lieutenant, but they were instantly understood by all hands, and the topmen hurried to their places, ready to race up and rig out the studdingsail booms. The whole crowded deck was intensely alive, poised. 'Wait . . . wait,' murmured Jack, watching the *Desaix* coming up wide on the starboard beam. She was the one to beware of: she was terribly alert, and he longed to see her beginning to engage in some manoeuvre before he gave the word. To port lay the *Formidable*, overcrowded, no doubt, as flagships always were, and therefore less efficient in an emergency. 'Wait . . . wait,' he said again, his eyes fixed on the *Desaix*. But her steady approach never varied and when he had counted twenty he cried 'Right!'

The wheel span, the buoyant *Sophie* turned like a weather-cock, swinging towards the *Formidable*. The flagship instantly let fly, but her gunnery was not up to the *Desaix*'s, and the hurried broadside lashed the sea where the sloop had been rather than where she was: the *Desaix*'s more deliberate offering was hampered by the fear of ricochets skipping as far as the admiral, and only half a dozen of her balls did any harm – the rest fell short.

The *Sophie* was through the line, not too badly mauled – certainly not disabled; her studdingsails were set and she was running fast, with the wind where she liked it best. The surprise had been complete, and now the two sides were drawing away from one another fast – a mile in the first five minutes. The *Desaix*'s second broadside, delivered at well over a thousand yards, showed the effects of irritation and precipitancy; a splintering crash forward marked the utter destruction of the elm-tree pump, but that was all. The flagship had obviously countermanded her second discharge, and for a while she kept to her course, close-hauled, as though the *Sophie* did not exist.

'We may have done it,' said Jack inwardly, leaning his hands on the taffrail and staring back along the *Sophie*'s lengthening wake. His heart was still beating with the tension of waiting for those broadsides, with the dread of what they might do to his *Sophie*; but now its beat had a different urgency. 'We may have done it,' he said again. Yet the words were scarcely formed in his mind before he saw a signal break out aboard the admiral, and the *Desaix* began to turn into the wind.

The seventy-four came about as nimbly as a frigate: her yards traversed as though by clockwork, and it was clear that everything was tallied and belayed with the perfect regularity of a numerous and thoroughly well trained crew. The *Sophie* had an excellent ship's company too, as attentive to their duty and as highly-skilled as Jack could wish; but nothing that they could do would make her move through the water at more than seven knots with this breeze, whereas in another quarter of an hour the *Desaix* was running at well over eight *without her studdingsails*. She was not going to trouble herself with setting them: when they saw that – when the minutes went by and it was clear that she had not the least intention of setting them – then the Sophies' hearts died within them.

Jack looked up at the sky. It looked down on him, a broad and meaningless expanse, with stray clouds passing over it – the wind would not die away that afternoon: night was still hours and hours away.

How many? He glanced at his watch. Fourteen minutes past ten. 'Mr Dalziel,' he said, 'I am going into my cabin. Call me if anything whatever occurs. Mr Richards, be so good as to tell Dr Maturin I should like to speak to him. And Mr Watt, let me have a couple of fathoms of logline and three or four belaying-pins.'

In his cabin he made a parcel of his lead-covered signal-book and some other secret papers, put the copper belaying-pins into the bag of mail, lashed its neck tight, called for his best coat and put his commission into its inner pocket. The words 'hereof nor you nor any of you may fail as you will answer the contrary at your peril' floated before his mind's eye, wonderfully clear; and Stephen came in. 'There you are, my dear fellow,' said Jack. 'Now, I am afraid that unless something very surprising happens we are going to be taken or sunk in the next half hour.' Stephen said, 'Just so,' and Jack continued, 'So if you have anything you particularly value perhaps it would be wise to entrust it to me.'

'They rob their prisoners, then?' asked Stephen.

'Yes: sometimes. I was stripped to the bone when the *Leander* was taken, and they stole our surgeon's instruments before he could operate on our wounded.'

'I will bring my instruments at once.'

'And your purse.'

'Oh, yes, and my purse.'

Hurrying back on deck, Jack looked astern. He would never have believed the seventy-four could have come up so far. 'Masthead!' he cried. 'What do you see?'

Seven ships of the line just ahead? Half the Mediterranean fleet? 'Nothing, sir,' answered the look-out slowly, after a most conscientious pause.

'Mr Dalziel, should I be knocked on the head, by any chance, these go over the side at the last moment, of course,' he said, tapping the parcel and the bag.

Already the strict pattern of the sloop's behaviour was growing more fluid. The men were quiet and attentive; the watch-glass turned to the minute; four bells in the afternoon watch rang with singular precision but there was a certain amount of movement, unreproved movement up and down the fore-hatch – men putting on their best clothes (two or three waistcoats together, and a shoregoing jacket on top), asking their particular officers to look after money or curious treasures, in the faint hope they might be preserved – Babbington had a carved whale's tooth in his hand, Lucock a Sicilian bull's pizzle. Two men had already managed to get drunk: some wonderfully hidden savings, no doubt.

'Why does he not fire?' thought Jack. The *Desaix*'s bow-chasers had been silent these twenty minutes, though for the last mile or so of their course the *Sophie* had been well within range. Indeed, by now she was in musket-shot, and the people in her bows could easily be told from one another: seamen, marines, officers – one man had a wooden leg. What splendidly cut sails, he reflected, and at the same time the answer to his question came: 'By God, he's going to riddle us with grape.' That was why he had silently closed the range. Jack moved to the side; leaning over the hammock-netting he dropped his packets into the sea and saw them sink.

In the bows of the *Desaix* there was a sudden movement, a response to an order. Jack stepped to the wheel, taking the spokes from the quartermaster's hands and looking back over his left shoulder. He felt the life of the sloop under his fingers: and he saw the *Desaix* begin to yaw. She answered her helm as quickly as a cutter, and in three heartbeats there were her thirty-seven guns coming round to bear. Jack heaved strongly at the wheel. The broadside's roar and the fall of the *Sophie's* maintopgallantmast and foretopsail yard came almost together – in the thunder a hail of blocks, odd lengths of rope, splinters, the tremendous clang of a grape-shot striking the *Sophie's* bell; and then a silence. The greater part of the seventy-four's roundshot had passed a few yards ahead of her stem: the scattering grape-shot had utterly wrecked her sails and rigging – had cut them to pieces. The next broadside must destroy her entirely.

'Clew up,' called Jack, continuing the turn that brought the *Sophie* into the wind. 'Bonden, strike the colours.'

12

THE CABIN OF a ship of the line and the cabin of a sloop of war differ in size, but they have the same delightful curves in common, the same inward-sloping windows; and in the case of the *Desaix* and the *Sophie* a good deal of the same quietly agreeable atmosphere. Jack sat gazing out of the seventy-four's stern-windows, out beyond the handsome gallery to Green Island and Cabrita Point, while Captain Christy-Pallière searched through his portfolio for a drawing he had made when he was last in Bath, a prisoner on parole.

Admiral Linois' orders had required him to join the Franco-Spanish fleet in Cadiz; and he would have carried them out directly if, on reaching the straits, he had not learnt that instead of one or two ships of the line and a frigate Sir James Saumarez had no less than six seventy-fours and an eighty-gun ship watching the combined squadron. This state of affairs called for some reflexion, so here he lay with his ships in Algeciras Bay, under the guns of the great Spanish batteries, over against the Rock of Gibraltar.

Jack was aware of all this – it was obvious, in any case – and as Captain Pallière muttered through his prints and drawings, 'Landsdowne Terrace, another view – Clifton – the Pump Room –' his mind's eye pictured messengers riding at a great pace between Algeciras and Cadiz; for the Spaniards had no semaphore. His bodily eye, however, looked steadily through the window panes at Cabrita Point, the extremity of the bay; and presently it saw the topgallant masts and pendant of a ship moving across, behind the neck of land. He watched it placidly for some two or three seconds before his heart gave a great leap, having recognized the pendant as British before his head had even begun to weigh the matter.

He darted a furtive look at Captain Pallière, who cried, 'Here we are! Laura Place. Number sixteen, Laura Place. This is where my Christy cousins always stay, when they come to Bath. And here, behind this tree – you could see it better, was it not for the tree – is my bedroom window!'

A steward came in and began to lay the table, for Captain Pallière not only possessed English cousins and the English language in something like perfection, but he had solid notions of what made a proper breakfast for a seafaring man: a pair of ducks, a dish of kidneys and a grilled turbot the size of a moderate cartwheel were preparing, as well as the usual ham, eggs, toast, marmalade and coffee. Jack looked at the water-colour as attentively as he could, and said, 'Your bedroom window, sir? You astonish me.'

BREAKFAST WITH Dr Ramis was a very different matter – austere, if not penitential: a bowl of milkless cocoa, a piece of bread with *a very little oil*. 'A *very little oil* cannot do us much harm,' said Dr Ramis, who was a martyr to his liver. He was a severe and meagre, dusty man, with a harsh greyish-yellow face and deep violet rings under his eyes; he did not look capable of any pleasant emotion, yet he had both blushed

and simpered when Stephen, upon being confided to his care
as a prisoner-guest, had cried, 'Not the illustrious Dr Juan
Ramis, the author of the *Specimen Animalium*?' Now they
had just come back from visiting the *Desaix*'s sick-bay, a
sparsely inhabited place, because of Dr Ramis' passion for
curing other people's livers too by a low diet and no wine: it
had a dozen of the usual diseases, a fair amount of pox, the
Sophie's four invalids and the French wounded from the
recent action – three men bitten by Mr Dalziel's little bitch,
whom they had presumed to caress: they were now confined
upon suspicion of hydrophobia. In Stephen's view there was
an error in his colleague's reasoning – a Scotch dog that bit a
French seaman was not therefore and necessarily mad;
though it might, in this particular case, be strangely wanting
in discrimination. He kept this reflexion to himself, however,
and said, 'I have been contemplating on emotion.'

'Emotion,' said Dr Ramis.

'Yes,' said Stephen. 'Emotion, and the *expression* of emotion. Now, in your fifth book, and in part of the sixth, you
treat of emotion as it is shown by the cat, for example, the
bull, the spider – I, too, have remarked the singular intermittent brilliance in the eyes of lycosida: have you ever detected
a glow in those of the mantis?'

'Never, my dear colleague: though Busbequius speaks of it,'
replied Dr Ramis with great complacency.

'But it seems to me that emotion and its expression are
almost the same thing. Let us take your cat: now suppose we
shave her tail, so that it cannot shall I say *perscopate* or bris-
tle; suppose we attach a board to her back, so that it cannot
arch; suppose we then exhibit a displeasing sight – a sportive
dog, for instance. Now, she cannot express her emotions
fully: Quaere: will she feel them fully? She will *feel* them, to
be sure, since we have suppressed only the grossest manifes-
tations; but will she feel them *fully*? Is not the arch, the bot-
tle-brush, an integral part and not merely a potent
reinforcement – though it is that too?'

Dr Ramis inclined his head to one side, narrowed his eyes and lips, and said, 'How can it be measured? It cannot be measured. It is a notion; a most valuable notion, I am sure; but, my dear sir, where is your measurement? It cannot be measured. Science is measurement – no knowledge without measurement.'

'Indeed it can,' cried Stephen eagerly. 'Come, let us take our pulses.' Dr Ramis pulled out his watch, a beautiful Bréguet with a centre seconds hand, and they both sat gravely counting. 'Now, dear colleague, pray be so good as to imagine – to imagine vehemently – that I have taken up your watch and wantonly flung it down; and I for my part will imagine that you are a very wicked fellow. Come, let us simulate the gestures, the expressions of extreme and violent rage.'

Dr Ramis' face took on a tetanic look; his eyes almost vanished; his head reached forward, quivering. Stephen's lips writhed back; he shook his fist and gibbered a little. A servant came in with a jug of hot water (no second bowls of cocoa were allowed).

'Now,' said Stephen Maturin, 'let us take our pulses again.'

'That pilgrim from the English sloop is mad,' the surgeon's servant told the second cook. 'Mad, twisted, tormented. And ours is not much better.'

'I will not say it is conclusive,' said Dr Ramis. 'But it is wonderfully interesting. We must try the addition of harsh reproachful words, cruel flings and bitter taunts, but without any physical motion, which could account for part of the increase. You intend it as a proof per contra of what you advance, I take it? Reversed, inverted, or *arsy-versy*, as you say in English. Most interesting.'

'Is it not?' said Stephen. 'My mind was led into this train of thought by the spectacle of our surrender, and of some others that I have seen. With your far greater experience of naval life, sir, no doubt you have been present at many more of these interesting occasions than I.'

'I imagine so,' said Dr Ramis. 'For example, I myself have had the honour of being your prisoner no less than four times. That,' he said with a smile, 'is one of the reasons why we are so very happy to have you with us. It does not happen quite as often as we could wish. Allow me to help you to another piece of bread – *half* a piece, with a very little garlic? Just a scrape of this wholesome, antiphlogistical garlic?'

'You are too good, dear colleague. And you have no doubt taken notice of the impassive faces of the captured men? It is always so, I believe?'

'Invariably. Zeno, followed by all his school.'

'And does it not seem to you that this suppression, this denial of the outward signs, and as I believe reinforcers if not actually ingredients of the distress – does it not seem to you that this stoical appearance of indifference in fact diminishes the pain?'

'It may well be so: yes.'

'I believe it is so. There were men aboard whom I knew intimately well, and I am morally certain that without this what one might call *ceremony of diminution*, it would have broken their . . .'

'Monsieur, monsieur, monsieur,' cried Dr Ramis' servant. 'The English are filling the bay!'

On the poop they found Captain Pallière and his officers watching the manoeuvres of the *Pompée*, the *Venerable*, the *Audacious* and, farther off, the *Caesar*, the *Hannibal* and the *Spencer* as they worked in on the light, uncertain westerly airs, through the strong, shifting currents running between the Atlantic and the Mediterranean: they were all of them seventy-fours except for Sir James' flagship, the *Caesar*, and she carried eighty guns. Jack stood at some distance, with a detached look on his face; and at the farther rail there were the other quarter-deck Sophies, all making a similar attempt at decency.

'Do you think they will attack?' asked Captain Pallière, turning to Jack. 'Or do you think they will anchor off Gibraltar?'

'To tell you the truth, sir,' said Jack, looking over the sea at the towering Rock, 'I am quite sure they will attack. And you will forgive me for saying, that when you reckon up the forces in presence, it seems clear that we shall all be in Gibraltar tonight. I confess I am heartily glad of it, for it will allow me to repay a little of the great kindness I have met with here.'

There had been kindness, great kindness, from the moment they exchanged formal salutes on the quarter-deck of the *Desaix* and Jack stepped forward to give up his sword: Captain Pallière had refused to take it, and with the most obliging expressions about the *Sophie*'s resistance, had insisted upon his wearing it still.

'Well,' said Captain Pallière, 'let it not spoil our breakfast, at all events.'

'Signal from the Admiral, sir,' said a lieutenant. '*Warp in as close as possible to the batteries.*'

'Acknowledged and make it so, Dumanoir,' said the captain. 'Come, sir: gather we rose-pods while we may.'

It was a gallant effort, and they both of them talked away with a fine perseverance, their voices rising as the batteries on Green Island and the mainland began to roar and the thundering broadsides filled the bay; but Jack found that presently he was spreading marmalade upon his turbot and answering somewhat at random. With a high-pitched shattering crash the stern-windows of the *Desaix* fell in ruin; the padded locker beneath, Captain Pallière's best wine-bin, shot half across the cabin, projecting a flood of champagne, Madeira and broken glass before it; and in the midst of the wreckage trundled a spent ball from HMS *Pompée*.

'Perhaps we had better go on deck,' said Captain Pallière.

It was a curious position. The wind had almost entirely dropped. The *Pompée* had glided on past the *Desaix* to anchor very close to the *Formidable*'s starboard bow, and she was pounding her furiously as the French flagship warped farther in through the treacherous shoals by means of cables on shore. The *Venerable*, for want of wind, had anchored about half a mile from the *Formidable* and the *Desaix* and was plying them briskly with her larboard broadside, while the *Auda-cious*, as far as he could see through clouds of smoke, was abreast of the *Indomptable*, some three or four hundred yards out. The *Caesar* and the *Hannibal* and the *Spencer* were doing their utmost to come up through the calms and the patchy gusts of west-north-west breeze: the French ships were firing steadily; and all the time the Spanish batteries, from the Torre del Almirante in the north right down to Green Island in the south, thundered in the background, while the big Spanish gunboats, invaluable in this calm, with their mobility and their expert knowledge of the reefs and the strong turning currents, swept out to rake the anchored enemy.

The rolling smoke drifted off the land, wafting now this way and now that, often hiding the Rock at the far end of the bay and the three ships out to sea; but at last a steadier breeze sprang up and the *Caesar*'s royals and topgallants appeared above the obscurity. She was wearing Admiral Saumarez' flag and she was flying the signal *anchor for mutual support*. Jack saw her pass the *Audacious* and swing broadside on to the *Desaix* within hailing distance: the cloud around her closed, hiding everything: there was a great stab as of light-ning within the murk, a ball at head-height reaped a file of marines on the *Desaix*'s poop and the whole frame of the powerful ship shuddered with the force of the impact – at least half the broadside striking home.

'This is no place for a prisoner,' reflected Jack, and with a parting look of particular consideration at Captain Pallière, he hurried down on to the quarter-deck. He saw Babbington and young Ricketts standing doubtfully at the hances and called out, 'Get below, you two. This is no time to come it the old Roman – proper flats you would look, cut in half with our own chain-shot' – for chain was coming in now, shrieking and howling over the sea. He shepherded them down into the cable-tier and then made his way to the wardroom quarter-gallery – the officers' privy: it was not the safest place in the world, but there was little room for a spectator between the decks of a man-of-war in action, and he desperately wanted to see the course of the battle.

The *Hannibal* had anchored a little ahead of the *Caesar*, having run up the line of the French ships as they lay pointing north, and she was playing on the *Formidable* and the Santiago battery: the *Formidable* had almost ceased firing, which was as well, since for some reason the *Pompée* had swung round in the current – her spring shot away, perhaps – and she was head-on to the *Formidable*'s broadside, so that she could now only engage the shore-batteries and the gunboats with her starboard guns. The *Spencer* was still far out in the bay: but even so there were five ships of the line attacking three – everything was going very well, in spite of the Spanish artillery. And now through a gap in the smoke torn by the west-north-west breeze, Jack saw the *Hannibal* cut her cable, make sail towards Gibraltar and tack as soon as she had way enough, coming down close inshore to run between the French admiral and the land, and to cross his hawse and rake him. 'Just like the Nile,' thought Jack, and at that moment the *Hannibal* ran aground, very hard aground, and brought up all standing right opposite the heavy guns of the Torre del Almirante. The cloud closed again; and when at last it lifted boats were plying to and fro from the other English ships, and an anchor was carrying out; the *Hannibal* was roaring furiously at three shore-batteries, at the gunboats and, with her forward larboard guns and bow-chasers, at the *Formidable*. Jack found that he was clasping his hands so hard that it needed strong determination to unknot them. The situation was not desperate – was not bad at all. The westerly air had fallen quite away, and now a right breeze was parting the heavy powder-fog, coming from the north-east. The *Caesar* cut her cable, and coming down round the *Venerable* and the *Audacious* she battered the *Indomptable*, astern of the *Desaix*, with the heaviest fire that had yet been heard. Jack could not make out what signal it was she had abroad, but he was cer-

tain it was *cut and wear*, together with engage the enemy
more closely: there was a signal aboard the French admiral
too – *cut and run aground* – for now, with a wind that would
allow the English to come right in, it was better to risk wrecking than total disaster: furthermore, his was a signal easier to
carry out than Sir James', for not only did the breeze stay with
the French after it had left the English becalmed, but the
French already had their warps out and boats by the dozen
from the shore.

Jack heard the orders overhead, the pounding of feet, and
the bay with its smoke and floating wreckage turned slowly
before his eyes as the *Desaix* wore and ran straight for the
land. She grounded with a thumping lurch that threw him off
his balance, on a reef just in front of the town: the *Indomptable*, with her foretopmast gone, was already ashore on Green
Island, or precious near. He could not see the French flagship
at all from where he was, but she would certainly have
grounded herself too.

And yet suddenly the battle went sour. The English ships
did not come in, sweep the stranded Frenchmen clean and
burn or destroy them far less tow them out; for not only did
the breeze drop completely, leaving the *Caesar*, *Audacious*
and *Venerable* with no steerage-way, but almost all the surviving boats of the squadron were busy towing the shattered
Pompée towards Gibraltar. The Spanish batteries had been
throwing red-hot shot for some time, and now the grounded
French ships were sending their excellent gun-crews ashore
by the hundred. Within a few minutes the fire of the shore
guns increased enormously in volume and in accuracy. Even
the poor *Spencer*, that had never managed to get up, suffered
cruelly as she lay out there in the bay; the *Venerable* had lost
her mizzen topmast; and it looked as though the *Caesar* were
on fire amidships. Jack could bear it no longer: he hurried up
on deck in time to see a breeze spring up off the land and the
squadron make sail on the starboard tack, standing eastwards
for Gibraltar and leaving the dismasted, helpless *Hannibal* to

her fate under the guns of the Torre del Almirante. She was firing still, but it could not last; her remaining mast fell, and presently her ensign came wavering down.

'A busy morning, Captain Aubrey,' said Captain Pallière, catching sight of him.

'Yes, sir,' said Jack. 'I hope we have not lost too many of our friends.' The *Desaix*'s quarter-deck was very ugly in patches, and there was a deep gutter of blood running along to the scupper under the wreckage of the poop-ladder. The hammock-netting had been torn to pieces; there were four dismounted guns abaft the mainmast, and the splinter-netting over the quarter-deck bowed and sagged under the weight of fallen rigging. She was canted three or four strakes on her rock, and the least hint of a sea would pound her to pieces.

'Many, many more than I could have wished,' said Captain Pallière. 'But the *Formidable* and the *Indomptable* have suffered worse – both their captains killed, too. What are they doing aboard the captured ship?'

The *Hannibal*'s colours were rising again. It was her own ensign, not the French flag: but it was the ensign reversed, flying with the union downwards. 'I suppose they forgot to take a tricolour when they went to board her and take possession,' observed Captain Pallière, turning to give orders for the heaving of his ship off the reef. Some time later he came back to the shattered rail, and staring out at the little fleet of boats that were pulling with all their might from Gibraltar and from the sloop Calpe towards the *Hannibal*, he said to Jack, 'You do not suppose they mean to retake the ship, do you? What *are* they about?'

Jack knew very well what they were about. In the Royal Navy the reversed ensign was an emphatic signal of distress: the *Calpe* and the people in Gibraltar, seeing it, had supposed the *Hannibal* meant she was afloat again and was begging to be towed off. They had filled every available boat with every available man – with unattached seamen and, above all, with the highly-skilled shipwrights and artificers of the dock-

yard. 'Yes,' he said, with all the open sincerity of one bluff seaman talking to another. 'I do. That is what they are about, for
sure. But certainly if you put a shot across the bow of the
leading cutter they will turn round – they imagine everything
is over.'

'Ah, that's it,' said Captain Pallière. An eighteen-pounder
creaked round and settled squarely on the nearest boat. 'But
come,' said Captain Pallière, putting his hand on the lock and
smiling at Jack, 'perhaps it would be better not to fire.' He
countermanded the gun, and one by one the boats reached
the *Hannibal*, where the waiting Frenchmen quietly led their
crews below. 'Never mind,' said Captain Pallière, patting him
on the shoulder. 'The Admiral is signalling: come ashore with
me, and we will try to find decent quarters for you and your
people, until we can heave off and refit.'

THE QUARTERS ALLOTTED to the *Sophie*'s officers, a house
up at the back of Algeciras, had an immense terrace overlooking the bay, with Gibraltar to the left, Cabrita Point to the
right and the dim land of Africa looming ahead. The first person Jack saw upon it, standing there with his hands behind
his back and looking down on his own dismasted ship, was
Captain Ferris of the *Hannibal*. Jack had been shipmates
with him during two commissions and had dined with him
only last year, but the post-captain was hardly recognizable as
the same man – had aged terribly, and shrunk; and although
they now fought the battle over again, pointing out the various manoeuvres, misfortunes and baffled intentions, he
spoke slowly, with an odd uncertain hesitation, as though
what had happened were not quite real, or had not happened
to him.

'So you were aboard the *Desaix*, Aubrey,' he said, after a
while. 'Was she much cut up?'

'Not so badly as to be disabled, sir, as far as I could collect.
She was not much holed below the waterline, and none of
her lower masts was badly wounded: if she don't bilge they

will put her to rights presently – she has an uncommon sea-manlike set of officers and men.'

'How many did she lose, do you suppose?'

'A good many, I am sure – but here is my surgeon, who certainly knows more about it than I do. May I name Dr Maturin? Captain Ferris. My God, Stephen!' he cried, starting back. He was tolerably used to carnage, but he had never seen anything quite like this. Stephen might have come straight out of a busy slaughterhouse. His sleeves, the whole of the front of his coat up to his stock and the stock itself were deeply soaked, soaked through and through and stiff with drying blood. So were his breeches: and wherever his linen showed it, too, was dark red-brown.

'I beg pardon,' he said, 'I should have shifted my clothes, but it seems that my chest was shattered – destroyed entirely.'

'I can let you have a shirt and some breeches,' said Captain Ferris. 'We are much of a size.' Stephen bowed.

'You have been lending the French surgeons a hand?' said Jack.

'Just so.'

'Was there a great deal to do?' asked Captain Ferris.

'About a hundred killed and a hundred wounded,' said Stephen.

'We had seventy-five and fifty-two,' said Captain Ferris.

'You belong to the *Hannibal*, sir?' asked Stephen.

'I did, sir,' said Captain Ferris. 'I struck my colours,' he said in a wondering tone and at once began to sob, staring open-eyed at them – at one and then at the other.

'Captain Ferris,' said Stephen, 'pray tell me, how many mates has your surgeon? And have they all their instruments? I am going down to the convent to see your wounded as soon as I have had a bite, and I dispose of two or three sets.'

'Two mates, sir,' said Captain Ferris. 'As for their instruments I fear I cannot say. It is good in you, sir – most Christian – let me fetch you this shirt and breeches – you must be damned uncomfortable.' He came back with a bundle of clean clothes wrapped in a dressing-gown, suggested that Dr Maturin might operate in the gown, as he had seen done after the First of June, when there was a similar shortage of clean linen. And during their odd, scrappy meal, brought to them by staring, pitiful maidservants, with red and yellow sentries guarding the door, he said, 'After you have looked to my poor fellows, Dr Maturin – if you have any benevolence left after you have looked to them, I say, it would be a charitable act to prescribe me something in the poppy or mandragora line. I was strangely upset today, I must confess, and I need what is it? The knitting up of ravelled care? And what is more, since we are likely to be exchanged in a few days, I shall have a court-martial on top of it all.'

'Oh, as for that, sir,' cried Jack, throwing himself back in his chair, 'you cannot possibly have any misgivings – never was a clearer case of – '

'Don't you be so sure, young man,' said Captain Ferris. 'Any court-martial is a perilous thing, whether you are in the right or the wrong – justice has nothing much to do with it. Remember poor Vincent of the *Weymouth*: remember Byng – shot for an error of judgment and for being unpopular with the mob. And think of the state of feeling in Gibraltar and at home just now – six ships of the line beaten off by three French, and one taken – a defeat, and the *Hannibal* taken.'

This degree of apprehension in Captain Ferris seemed to Jack a kind of wound, the result of lying hard aground under the fire of three shore-batteries, a ship of the line and a dozen heavy gun-boats, and of being terribly hammered for hours, dismasted and helpless. The same thought, in a slightly different shape, occurred to Stephen. 'What is this trial of which he speaks?' he asked later. 'Is it factual, or imaginary?'

'Oh, it is factual enough,' said Jack.

'But he has done nothing amiss, surely? No one can pretend he ran away or did not fight as hard as ever he could.'

'But he lost his ship. Every captain of a King's ship that is lost must stand his trial at court-martial.'

'I see. A mere formality in his case, no doubt.'

'In *his* case, yes,' said Jack. '*His* anxiety is unfounded – a sort of waking nightmare, I take it.'

But the next day, when he went down with Mr Dalziel to see the *Sophie*'s crew in their disaffected church and to tell them of the flag of truce from the Rock, it seemed to him a little more reasonable – less of a sick fantasy. He told the Sophies that both they and the Hannibals were to be exchanged – that they should be in Gibraltar for dinner – dried peas and salt horse for dinner, no more of these foreign messes – and although he smiled and waved his hat at the roaring cheers that greeted his news, there was a black shadow in the back of his mind.

The shadow deepened as he crossed the bay in the *Caesar*'s barge; it deepened as he waited in the antechamber to report himself to the Admiral. Sometimes he sat and sometimes he walked up and down the room, talking to other officers as people with urgent business were admitted by the secretary. He was surprised to receive so many congratulations on the *Cacafuego* action – it seemed so long ago now as almost to belong to another life. But the congratulations (though both generous and kind) were a little on the cursory side, for the atmosphere in Gibraltar was one of severe and general con-demnation, dark depression, strict attention to arduous work, and a sterile wrangling about what ought to have been done.

When at last he was received he found Sir James almost as old and changed as Captain Ferris; the Admiral's strange, heavy-lidded eyes looked at him virtually without expression as he made his report; there was not a word of interruption, not a hint of praise or blame, and this made Jack so uneasy that if it had not been for a list of heads he had written on a card that he kept in the palm of his hand, like a schoolboy, he would have deviated into rambling explanations and excuses. The Admiral was obviously very tired, but his quick mind extracted the necessary facts and he noted them down on a slip of paper. 'What do you make of the state of the French ships, Captain Aubrey?' he asked.

'The *Desaix* is now afloat, sir, and pretty sound; so is the *Indomptable*. I do not know about the *Formidable* and *Hannibal*, but there is no question of their being bilged; and in Algeciras the rumour is that Admiral Linois sent three officers to Cadiz yesterday and another early this morning to beg the Spaniards and Frenchmen there to come round and fetch him out.'

Admiral Saumarez put his hand to his forehead. He had honestly believed they would never float again, and he had said as much in his report. 'Well, thank you, Captain Aubrey,' he said, after a moment, and Jack stood up. 'I see you are wearing your sword,' observed the Admiral.

'Yes, sir. The French captain was good enough to give it back to me.'

'Very handsome in him, though I am sure the compliment was quite deserved; and I have little doubt the court-martial will do the same. But, you know, it is not quite etiquette to ship it until then: we will arrange your business as soon as possible – poor Ferris will have to go home, of course, but we can see to you here. You are only on parole, I believe?'

'Yes, sir: waiting for an exchange.'

'What a sad bore. I could have done with your help – the squadron is in such a state . . . Well, good day to you, Captain Aubrey,' he said, with a hint of a smile, or at least a lightening in his expression. 'As you know, of course, you are under nominal arrest, so pray be discreet.'

He had known it perfectly well, of course, in theory; but the actual words were a blow to his heart, and he walked through the crowded, busy streets of Gibraltar in a state of quite remarkable unhappiness. When he reached the house where he was staying, he unbuckled his sword, made an ungainly parcel of it and sent it down to the Admiral's secretary with a note. Then he went for a walk, feeling strangely naked and unwilling to be seen.

The officers of the *Hannibal* and the *Sophie* were on parole: that is to say, until they were exchanged for French prisoners of equal rank they were bound in honour to do nothing against France or Spain – they were merely prisoners in more agreeable surroundings.

The days that followed were singularly miserable and lonely – lonely, although he sometimes walked with Captain Ferris, sometimes with his own midshipmen and sometimes with Mr Dalziel and his dog. It was strange and unnatural to be cut off from the life of the port and the squadron at such a moment as this, when every able-bodied man and a good many who should never have got out of their beds at all, were working furiously to repair their ships – an active hive, an ant-hill down below, and up here on these heights, on the thin grass and the bare rock between the Moorish wall and the tower above Monkey's Cove, solitary self-communing, doubt, reproach and anxiety. He had looked through all the Gazettes, of course, and there was nothing about either the *Sophie*'s triumph or her disaster: one or two garbled accounts in the newspapers and a paragraph in the Gentleman's Magazine that made it seem like a surprise attack, that was all. As many as a dozen promotions in the Gazettes, but none for him or Pullings and it was a fair bet that the news of the *Sophie*'s capture had reached London at about the same time as that of the *Cacafuego*. If not before: for the good news (supposing it to have been lost – supposing it to have been in the bag he himself sank in ninety fathoms off Cape Roig) could only have come in a dispatch from Lord Keith, far up the Mediterranean, among the Turks. So there could not be any promotion now until after the court-martial – no such thing as the promotion of prisoners, ever. And what if the trial went wrong? His conscience was very far from being per-fectly easy. If Harte had meant this, he had been devilish successful; and he, Jack, had been a famous green-horn, an egregious flat. Was such malignity possible? Such cleverness in a mere horned scrub? He would have liked to put this to Stephen, for Stephen had a headpiece; and Jack, almost for the first time in his life, was by no means sure of his perfect comprehension, natural intelligence and penetration. The Admiral had not congratulated him: could that conceivably mean that the official view was . . .? But Stephen had no notion of any parole that would keep him out of the naval hospital: the squadron had had more than two hundred men wounded, and he spent almost all his time there. 'You go a-walking,' he said. 'Do for all love go walking up very steep heights – traverse the Rock from end to end – traverse it again and again on an empty stomach. You are an obese subject; your hams quiver as you go. You must weight sixteen or even seventeen stone.'

'And to be sure I do sweat like a mare in foal,' he reflected, sitting under the shade of a boulder, loosening his waist-band and mopping himself. In an attempt at diverting his mind he privately sang a ballad about the Battle of the Nile:

> *We anchored alongside of them like lions bold and free.*
> *When their masts and shrouds came tumbling down,*
> *   what a glorious sight to see!*
> *Then came the bold Leander, that noble fifty-four,*
> *And on the bows of the Franklin she caused her guns to*
> *   roar;*
> *Gave her a dreadful drubbing, boys, and did severely*
> *   maul;*
> *Which caused them loud for quarter cry and down*
> *   French colours haul.*

The tune was charming, but the inaccuracy vexed him: the poor old *Leander* had fifty-two guns, as he knew very well, having directed the fire of eight of them. He turned to another favourite naval song:

There happened of late a terrible fray,
Begun upon our St James's day,
With a thump, thump, thump, thump, thump,
Thump, thump a thump, thump.

An ape on a rock no great way off threw a turd at him, quite unprovoked; and when he half rose in protest it shook its wizened fist and gibbered so furiously that he sank down again, so low were his spirits.

'Sir, sir!' cried Babbington, tearing up the slope, scarlet with hailing and climbing. 'Look at the brig! Sir, look over the point!'

The brig was the *Pasley*: they knew her at once. The hired brig *Pasley*, a fine sailer, and she was crowding sail on the brisk north-west breeze fit to carry everything away.

'Have a look, sir,' said Babbington, collapsing on the grass in a singularly undisciplined manner and handing up a little brass spyglass. The tube only magnified weakly, but at once the signal flying from the *Pasley*'s masthead leapt out clear and plain – *enemy in sight.*

'And there they are, sir,' said Babbington, pointing to a glimmer of topsails over the dark curve of the land beyond the end of the Gut.

'Come on,' cried Jack, and began labouring up the hill, gasping and moaning, running as fast as he could for the tower, the highest point on the Rock. There were some masons up there, working on the building, an officer of the garrison artillery with a splendid great telescope, and some other soldiers. The gunner very civilly offered Jack his glass: Jack leant it on Babbington's shoulder, focused carefully, gazed, and said, 'There's the *Superb*. And the *Thames*. Then two Spanish three-deckers – one's the *Real Carlos*, I am almost sure: vice-admiral's flagship, in any event. Two seventy-fours. No, a seventy-four and probably an eighty-gun ship.'

'*Argonauta*,' said one of the masons.

'Another three-decker. And three frigates, two French.'

They sat there silently watching the steady, calm procession, the *Superb* and the *Thames* keeping their stations just a mile ahead of the combined squadron as they came up the Gut, and the huge, beautiful Spanish first-rates moving along with the inevitability of the sun. The masons went off to their dinner: the wind backed westerly. The shadow of the tower swept through twenty-five degrees.

When they had rounded Cabrita Point the *Superb* and the frigate carried straight on for Gibraltar, while the Spaniards hauled their wind for Algeciras; and now Jack could see that their flagship was indeed the *Real Carlos*, of a hundred and twelve guns, one of the most powerful ships afloat; that one of the other three-deckers was of the same force; and the third of ninety-six. It was a most formidable squadron – four hundred and seventy-four great guns, without counting the hundred odd of the frigates – and the ships were surprisingly well handled. They anchored over there under the guns of the Spanish batteries as trimly as though they were to be reviewed by the King.

'Hallo, sir,' said Mowett. 'I thought you would be up here. I have brought you a cake.'

'Why, thankee, thankee,' cried Jack. 'I am devilish hungry, I find.' He at once cut a slice and ate it up. How extraordinarily the Navy had changed, he thought, cutting another: when he was a midshipman it would never in a thousand years have occurred to him to speak to his captain, far less bring him cakes; and if it had occurred to him he would never have done so, for fear of his life.

'May I share your rock, sir?' asked Mowett, sitting down. 'They have come to fetch the Frenchmen out, I do suppose. Do you think we shall go for 'em, sir?'

'*Pompée* will never be fit for sea these three weeks,' said Jack dubiously. '*Caesar* is cruelly knocked about and must get all her new masts in: but even if they can get her ready before the enemy sail, that only gives us five of the line against ten, or nine if you leave the *Hannibal* out – three hundred and seventy-six guns to their seven hundred odd, both their squadrons combined. We are short-handed, too.'

'*You* would go for them, would not you, sir?' said Babbington; and both the midshipmen laughed very cheerfully.

Jack gave a meditative jerk of his head, and Mowett said, '*As when enclosing harpooners assail, In hyperborean seas the slumbering whale*. What huge things these Spaniards are. The Caesars have petitioned to be allowed to work all day and night, sir. Captain Brenton says they may work all day, but only watch and watch at night. They are piling up juniper-wood fires on the mole to have light.'

It was by the light of these juniper fires that Jack ran into Captain Keats of the *Superb*, with two of his lieutenants and a civilian. After the first surprise, greetings, introductions, Captain Keats asked him to take supper aboard – they were going back now – only a scrap-meal, of course, but some genuine Hampshire cabbage brought straight from Captain Keats' own garden by the *Astraea*.

'It is very kind of you indeed, sir; most grateful, but I believe I must beg to be excused. I had the misfortune to lose the *Sophie*, and I dare say you will be sitting on me presently, together with most of the other post-captains.'

'Oh,' said Captain Keats, suddenly embarrassed.

'Captain Aubrey is quite right,' said the civilian in a sententious voice; and at that moment an urgent messenger called Captain Keats to the Admiral.

'Who was that ill-looking son of a bitch in the black coat?' asked Jack, as another friend, Heneage Dundas of the *Calpe*, came down the steps.

'Coke? Why, he's the new judge-advocate,' said Dundas, with a queer look. Or was it a queer look? The trick of the flames could give anyone a queer look. The words of the tenth Article of War came quite unbidden into his mind: *If any person in the fleet shall cowardly yield or cry for quarter,*

*being convicted thereof by the sentence of a court-martial, shall
suffer death.*

'Come and split a bottle of port with me at the Blue Posts,
Heneage,' said Jack, drawing his hand across his face.

'Jack,' said Dundas, 'there is nothing I should like better,
upon my oath; but I have promised Brenton to give him a
hand. I am on my way this minute – there is the rest of my
party staying for me.' He hurried off into the brighter light
along the mole, and Jack drifted away: dark steep alleys, low
brothels, smells, squalid drinking-shops.

The next day, under the lee of the Charles V wall, with his
telescope resting on a stone, and with a certain sense of spy-
ing or eavesdropping, he watched the *Caesar* (no longer the
flagship) being eased alongside the sheer-hulk to receive her
new lower mainmast, a hundred feet long and more than a
yard across. She got it in so quickly that the top was over
before noon, and neither it nor the deck could be seen for the
number of men working on the rigging.

The day after that, still from his melancholy height, full of
guilt at his idleness and the intense, ordered busyness below,
particularly about the *Caesar*, he saw the *San Antonio*, a
French seventy-four that had been delayed, come in from
Cadiz and anchor among her friends at Algeciras.

The next day there was great activity on the far side of the
bay – boats plying to and fro among the twelve ships of the
combined fleet, new sails bending, supplies coming aboard,
hoist after hoist of signals aboard the flagships; and all this
activity was reproduced in Gibraltar, with even greater zeal.
There was no hope for the *Pompée*, but the *Audacious* was
almost entirely ready, while the *Venerable*, the Spencer and,
of course, the *Superb*, were in fighting trim, and the *Caesar*
was so near the final stages of her refitting that it was just
possible she might be fit for sea in twenty-four hours.

During the night a hint of a Levanter began to breathe from
the east: this was the wind the Spaniards were praying for,
the wind that would carry them straight out of the Gut, once

they had weathered Cabrita Point, and waft them up to
Cadiz. At noon the first of their three-deckers loosed her
foretopsail and began to move out of the crowded road; then
the others followed her. They were weighing and coming out
at intervals of ten minutes or a quarter of an hour to their rendezvous off Cabrita Point. The *Caesar* was still tied up alongside the mole, taking in her powder and shot, with officers,
men, civilians and garrison soldiers working with silent concentrated earnestness.

At length the whole of the combined fleet was under way:
even their jury-rigged capture, the *Hannibal*, towed by the
French frigate *Indienne*, was creeping out to the point. And
now the shrill squealing fife and fiddle broke out aboard the
Caesar as her people manned the capstan bars and began to
warp her out of the mole, taut, trim and ready for war. A
thundering cheer ran all along the crowded shore, from the
batteries, walls and hillside black with spectators; and when
it died away there was the garrison band playing *Come cheer
up my lads, 'tis to glory we steer* as loud as ever they could go,
while the *Caesar*'s marines answered with *Britons strike home*.
Through the cacophony the fife could still be heard: it was
most poignantly moving.

As the *Caesar* passed under the stern of the *Audacious* she
hoisted Sir James's flag once more and immediately afterwards heaved out the signal *weigh and prepare for battle*. The
execution of this was perhaps the most beautiful naval
manoeuvre Jack had ever seen: they had all been waiting for
the signal, they were all waiting and ready with their cables
up and down; and in an unbelievably short space of time the
anchors were catted and the masts and yards broke out in tall
white pyramids of sail as the squadron, five ships of the line,
two frigates, a sloop and a brig, moved out of the lee of the
Rock and formed in line ahead on the larboard tack.

Jack pushed his way out of the tight-packed crowd on the
mile-head, and he was half-way to the hospital, meaning to
persuade Stephen to mount the Rock with him, when he saw

his friend running swiftly through the deserted streets.

'Has she got out of the mole?' cried Stephen, at a considerable distance. 'Has the battle begun?' Reassured, he said, 'I would not have missed it for a hundred pounds: that damned fellow in Ward B and his untimely fancies – a fine time to cut one's throat, good lack a-day.'

'There's no hurry – no one will touch a gun for hours,' said Jack. 'But I am sorry you did not see the *Caesar* warping out: it was a glorious sight. Come up the hill with me, and you will have a perfect view of both squadrons. Do come. I will call in at the house and pick up a couple of telescopes; and a cloak – it grows cold at night.'

'Very well,' said Stephen, after a moment's thought. 'I can leave a note. And we will fill our pockets with ham: then we shall have none of your wry looks and short answers.'

'There they lay,' said Jack, pausing for breath again. 'Still on the larboard tack.'

'I see them perfectly well,' said Stephen, a hundred yards ahead and climbing fast. 'Pray do not stop so often. Come on.'

'Oh Lord, oh Lord,' said Jack at last, sinking under his familiar rock. 'How quick you go. Well, there they are.'

'Aye, aye, there they are: a noble spectacle, indeed. But why are they standing over towards Africa? And why only courses and topsails, with this light breeze? That one is even backing her maintopsail.'

'She's the *Superb*; she does so to keep her station and not over-run the Admiral, for she is a *superb* sailer, you know, the best in the fleet. Did you hear that?'

'Yes.'

'It was rather clever, I thought – witty.'

'Why do they not make sail and bear up?'

'Oh, there is no question of a head-on encounter – probably no action at all by daylight. It would be downright madness to attack their line of battle at this time. The Admiral wants the enemy to get out of the bay and into the Gut, so there will be no doubling back and so that he will have sea-room to make a dash at them: once they get well into the off-ing I dare say he will try to cut off their rear if this wind holds; and it looks like a true three-day Levanter. Look, there the *Hannibal* cannot weather the point. Do you see? She will be on shore directly. The frigate is making sad work of it. They are towing her head round. Handsomely does it – there we are – she fills – set the jib, man – just so. She is going back.'

They sat watching in silence, and all around them they could hear other groups, scattered all over the surface of the Rock – remarks about the strengthening of the wind, the probable strategy to be observed, the exact broadside weight of metal on either side, the high standard of French gunnery, the currents to be met with off Cape Trafalgar.

With a good deal of backing and filling, the combined fleet, now nine ships of the line and three frigates, had formed their line of battle, with the two great Spanish first-rates in the rear, and now they bore away due west-wards before the freshening breeze.

A little before this the British squadron had worn together by signal, and now they were on the starboard tack, under easy sail. Jack's telescope was firmly on the flagship, and as soon as he saw the hoist running up he murmured, 'Here we go.'

The signal appeared: at once the press of canvas almost doubled, and within a few minutes the squadron was racing away after the French and the Spaniards, dwindling in his view – growing smaller every moment as he watched.

'Oh God, how I wish I were with them,' said Jack, with a groan of something like despair. And some ten minutes later, 'Look, there's *Superb* going ahead – the Admiral must have hailed her.' The *Superb*'s topgallant studdingsails appeared as though by magic, port and starboard. 'How she flies,' said Jack, lowering his glass and wiping it: but the dimness was neither his tears nor any dirt on the glass – it was the fading of the day. Down below it had already gone; a tawny late evening filled the town, and lights were breaking out all over it. Presently lanterns could be seen creeping up the Rock to the high points from which perhaps the battle might be seen; and over the water Algeciras began to twinkle, a low-lying curve of lights.

'What do you say to some of that ham?' said Jack.

Stephen said he thought ham might prove a valuable preservative against the falling damps; and when they had been eating for some time in the darkness, with their pocket-handkerchiefs spread upon their knees, he suddenly observed, 'They tell me I am to be tried for the loss of the *Sophie*.'

Jack had not thought of the court-martial since early that morning, when it became certain that the combined fleet was coming out: now it came back to him with an extraordinarily unpleasant shock, quite closing his stomach. However, he only replied, 'Who told you that? The physical gentlemen at the hospital, I suppose?'

'Yes.'

'Theoretically they are right, of course. The thing is officially called the trial of the captain, officers and ship's company; and they formally ask the officers if they have any complaints to make against the captain, and the captain whether he has any to make against the officers; but obviously in this it is only my conduct that is in question. You have nothing to worry about, I do assure you, upon my word and honour. Nothing at all.'

'Oh, I shall plead guilty at once,' said Stephen. 'And I shall add that I was sitting in the powder-magazine with a naked light at the time, imagining the death of the King, wasting my medical stores, smoking tobacco and making a fraudulent return of the portable soup. What solemn nonsense it is' – laughing heartily – 'I am surprised so sensible a man as you should attribute any importance to the matter.'

'Oh, I do not mind it,' cried Jack. 'How you lie,' said Stephen affectionately, but within his own bosom. After a longish pause Jack said, 'You do not rate post-captains and admirals very high among intelligent beings, I believe? I have heard you say some tolerably severe things about admirals, and great men in general.'

'Why, to be sure, something sad seems to happen to your great men and your admirals, with age, pretty often: even to your post-captains. A kind of atrophy, a withering-away of the head and the heart. I conceive it may arise from . . .'

'Well,' said Jack, laying his hand upon his friend's dimly-seen shoulder in the starlight, 'how would you like to place your life, your profession and your good name between the hands of a parcel of senior officers?'

'Oh,' cried Stephen. But what he had to say was never heard, for away on the horizon towards Tangiers there was a flash flash-flash, not unlike the repeated dart of lightning. They leapt to their feet and cupped their ears to the wind to catch the distant roar; but the wind was too strong and presently they sat down again, fixing the western sea with their telescopes. They could distinctly make out two sources, between twenty and twenty-five miles away, scarcely any distance apart – not above a degree: then three: then a fourth and fifth, and then a growing redness that did not move.

'There is a ship on fire,' said Jack in horror, his heart pumping so hard that he could scarcely keep the steady deep-red glow in his object-glass. 'I hope to God it is not one of ours. I hope to God they drown the magazines.'

An enormous flash lit the sky, dazzled them, put out the stars; and nearly two minutes later the vast solemn long rumbling boom of explosion reached them, prolonged by its own echo off the African shore.

'What was it?' asked Stephen at last.

'The ship blew up,' said Jack: his mind was filled with the Battle of the Nile and the long moment when *L'Orient* exploded, all brought back to him with extraordinary vividness – a hundred details he thought forgotten, some very hideous. And he was still among those memories when a second explosion shattered the darkness, perhaps even greater than the first.

After this, nothing. Not the remotest light, not a gun-flash. The wind increased steadily, and the rising moon put out the smaller stars. After a while some of the lanterns began to go down; others remained, and some even climbed higher still; Jack and Stephen stayed where they were. Dawn found them under their rock, with Jack steadily sweeping the Gut – calm now, and deserted – and Stephen Maturin fast asleep, smiling.

Not a word, not a sign: a silent sea, a silent sky and the wind grown treacherous again – all round the compass. At half-past seven Jack saw Stephen back to the hospital, revived himself with coffee and climbed again.

In his journeys up and down he came to know every wind in the path, and the rock against which he leaned was as familiar as an old coat. It was when he was going up after tea on Thursday, with his supper in a sailcloth bag, that he saw Dalziel, Boughton of the *Hannibal* and Marshall bounding down the steep slope so fast that they could not stop: they called out '*Calpe*'s coming in, sir,' and blundered on, with the little dog running round and round them, very nearly bringing them down, and barking with delight.

Heneage Dundas of the fast-sailing sloop *Calpe* was an amiable young man, much caressed by those who knew him for his shining parts and particularly for his skill in the mathematics; but never before had he been the best-loved man in Gibraltar. Jack broke through the crowd surrounding him with brutal force and an unscrupulous use of his weight and his elbows: five minutes later he broke out again and ran like a boy through the streets of the town.

'Stephen,' he cried, bursting open the door, his shining face far larger and higher than usual. 'Victory! Come out at once and drink to a victory! Give you joy of a famous victory, old cock,' he cried, shaking him terribly by the hand. 'Such a magnificent fight.'

'Why, what happened?' asked Stephen, slowly wiping his scalpel and covering up his Moorish hyena.

'Come on, and I will tell you as we drink,' said Jack, leading him into the street full of people, all talking eagerly, laughing, shaking hands and beating one another on the back: down by the New Mole there was the sound of cheering. 'Come on. I have a thirst like Achilles, no, Andromache. It is Keats has the glory of the day – Keats has borne the bell away. Ha, ha, ha! That was a famous line, was it not? In here. Pedro! Bear a hand there! Pedro, champagne. Here's to the victory! Here's to Keats and the Superb! Here's to Admiral Saumarez! Pedro, another bottle. Here's to the victory again! Three times three! Huzza!'

'You would oblige me extremely by just giving the news,' said Stephen. 'With all the details.'

'I don't know all the details,' said Jack, 'but this is the gist of it. That noble fellow Keats – you remember how we saw him shoot ahead? – came up with their rear, the two Spanish first-rates, just before midnight. He chose his moment, clapped his helm a lee and dashed between 'em firing both broadsides – a seventy-four taking on two first-rates! He shot straight on, leaving his smoke-cloud between 'em as thick as peasoup; and each, firing into it, hit the other; and so the *Real Carlos* and the *Hermenegildo* went for each other like fury in the dark. Someone, the *Superb* or the *Hermenegildo*, had knocked away the *Real Carlos'* foretopmast, and it was her topsail that fell over the guns and took fire. And after a while the *Real Carlos* fell on board the *Hermenegildo* and fired her too. Those were the two explosions we saw, of course. But while they were burning Keats had pushed on to engage the *San Antonio*, who hauled her wind and fought back like a rare plucked 'un; but she had to strike in half an hour for, do you see, *Superb* was firing three broadsides to her two, and point-ing 'em straight. So Keats took possession of her; and the rest of the squadron chased as hard as ever they could to the north-north-west in a gale of wind. They very nearly took the

Formidable, but she just got into Cadiz; and we very nearly lost the *Venerable*, dismasted and aground; but they got her off and she is on her way back now, jury-rigged, with a stuns'l boom for a mizzenmast, ha, ha, ha! – There's Dalziel and Marshall going by. Ahoy! Dalziel ahoy! Marshall! Ahoy there! Come and drink a glass to the victory!'

THE FLAG BROKE out aboard the *Pompée*; the gun boomed; the captains assembled for the court-martial.

It was a very grave occasion, and in spite of the brilliance of the day, the abounding cheerfulness on shore and the deep chuckling contentment aboard, each post-captain put away his gaiety and came up the side as solemn as a judge, to be greeted with all due ceremony and led into the great cabin by the first lieutenant.

Jack was already aboard, of course; but his was not the first case to be dealt with. Waiting there in the screened-off larboard part of the dining-cabin there was a chaplain, a hunted-looking man who paced up and down, sometimes making private ejaculations and dashing his hands together. It was pitiful to see how carefully he was dressed, and how he had shaved until the blood came; for if half the general report of his conduct was true there was no hope for him at all.

The moment the next gun sounded the master-at-arms took the chaplain away, and there was a pause, one of those great lapses of time that presently come to have no flow at all, but grow stagnant or even circular in motion. The other officers talked in low voices – they, too, were dressed with particular attention, in the exact uniform regularity that plenty of prize-money and the best Gibraltar outfitters could provide. Was it respect for the court? For the occasion? A residual sense of guilt, a placating of fate? They spoke quietly, equably, glancing at Jack from time to time.

They had each received an official notification the day before, and for some reason each had brought it with him, folded or rolled. After a while Babbington and Ricketts took

to changing all the words they could into obscenities, secretly
in a corner, while Mowett wrote and scratched out on the
back of his, counting syllables on his fingers and silently
mouthing. Lucock stared straight ahead of him into vacancy.
Stephen intently watched the busy unsatisfied questing of a
shining dark-red rat-flea on the chequered sailcloth floor.

The door opened. Jack returned abruptly to this world,
picked up his laced hat and walked into the great cabin,
ducking his head as he came in, with his officers filing in
behind him. He came to a halt in the middle of the room,
tucked his hat under his arm and made his bow to the court,
first to the president, then to the captains to the right of him,
then to the captains to the left of him. The president gave a
slight inclination of his head and desired Captain Aubrey and
his officers to sit down. A marine placed a chair for Jack a few
paces in front of the rest, and there he sat, his hand going to
hitch forward his non-existent sword, while the judge advocate read the document authorizing the court to assemble.

This took a considerable time, and Stephen looked steadily
about him, examining the cabin from side to side: it was like a
larger version of the *Desaix*'s stateroom (how glad he was the
Desaix was safe) and it, too, was singularly beautiful and full
of light – the same range of curved stern-windows, the same
inward-leaning side-walls (the ship's tumblehome, in fact)
and the same close, massive white-painted beams overhead
in extraordinarily long pure curves right across from one side
to another: a room in which common domestic geometry had
no say. At the far end from the door, parallel with the windows, ran a long table; and between the table and the light
sat the members of the court, the president in the middle,
the black-coated judge-advocate at a desk in front and three
post-captains on either side. There was a clerk at a small
table on the left, and to the left again a roped-off space for
bystanders.

The atmosphere was austere: all the heads above the blue
and gold uniforms on the far side of the shining table were

grave. The last trial and the sentence had been quite shockingly painful.

It was these heads, these faces, that had all Jack's attention. With the light behind them it was difficult to make them out exactly; but they were mostly overcast, and all were withdrawn. Keats, Hood, Brenton, Grenville he knew: was Grenville winking at him with his one eye, or was it an involuntary blink? Of course it was a blink: any signal would be grossly indecent. The president looked twenty years younger since the victory, but still his face was impassive and there was no distinguishing the expression of his eyes, behind those drooping lids. The other captains he knew only by name. One, a left-handed man, was drawing – scribbling. Jack's eyes grew dark with anger.

The judge-advocate's voice droned on. 'His Majesty's late Sloop *Sophie* having been ordered to proceed . . . and whereas it is represented that in or about 40′ W 37° 40′ N, Cape Roig bearing . . .' he said, amidst universal indifference.

'That man loves his trade,' thought Stephen. 'But what a wretched voice. It is almost impossible to be understood. Gabble, a professional deformation in lawyers.' And he was reflecting on industrial disease, on the corrosive effects of righteousness in judges, when he noticed that Jack had relaxed from his first rigid posture: and as the formalities went on and on this relaxation became more evident. He was looking sullen, oddly still and dangerous; the slight lowering of his head and the dogged way in which he stuck out his feet made a singular contrast with the perfection of his uniform, and Stephen had a strong premonition that disaster might be very close at hand.

The judge advocate had now reached '. . . to enquire into the conduct of John Aubrey, commander of His Majesty's late sloop the *Sophie* and her officers and company for the loss of the said sloop by being captured on the third instant by a French squadron under the command of Admiral Linois', and Jack's head was lower still. 'How far is one entitled to manipulate one's friends?' asked Stephen, writing *Nothing would give H greater pleasure than an outburst of indignation on your part at this moment* on a corner of his paper: he passed it to the master, pointing to Jack. Marshall passed it on, by way of Dalziel. Jack read it, turned a lowering, grim face without much apparent understanding in it towards Stephen and gave a jerk of his head.

Almost immediately afterwards Charles Stirling, the senior captain and president of the court-martial, cleared his throat and said, 'Captain Aubrey, pray relate the circumstances of the loss of His Majesty's late sloop the *Sophie*.'

Jack rose to his feet, looked sharply along the line of his judges, drew his breath, and speaking in a much stronger voice than usual, the words coming fast, with odd intervals and an unnatural intonation – a harsh, God-damn-you voice, as though he were addressing a most inimical body of men – he said, 'About six o'clock in the morning of the third, to the eastward and in sight of Cape Roig, we saw three large ships apparently French, and a frigate, who soon after gave chase to the *Sophie*: the *Sophie* was between the shore and the ships that chased her, and to windward of the French vessels: we endeavoured by making all sail and were pulling with sweeps – as the wind was very light – to keep to windward of the enemy; but having found notwithstanding all our endeavours to keep to the wind, that the French ships gained very fast, and having separated on different tacks one or the other gained upon each shift of wind, and finding it impracticable to escape by the wind, about nine o'clock the guns and other things on deck were thrown overboard; and having watched an opportunity, when the nearest French ship was on our quarter, we bore up and set the studdingsails; but again found the French ships outsailed us though their studdingsails were not set: when the nearest ship had approached within musket-shot, I ordered the colours to be hauled down about eleven o'clock a.m., the wind being to the eastward and having received several broadsides from the enemy which carried away the maintopgallantmast and foretopsail yard and cut several of the ropes.'

Then, though he was conscious of the singular ineptitude of this speech, he shut his mouth tight and stood looking straight ahead of him, while the clerk's pen squeaked nimbly after his words, writing *and cut several of the ropes*'. Here there was a slight pause, in which the president glanced left and right and coughed again before speaking. The clerk drew a quick flourish after *ropes* and hurried on:

> *Question by the court   Captain Aubrey, have you any reason to find fault with any of your officers or ship's company?*
>
> *Answer   No. The utmost endeavour was used by every person on board.*
>
> *Question by the court   Officers and ship's company of the* Sophie, *have any of you reason to find fault with the conduct of your captain?*
>
> *Answer   No.*

'Let all the evidence withdraw except Lieutenant Alexander Dalziel,' said the judge-advocate, and presently the midshipmen, the master and Stephen found themselves in the dining-cabin again, sitting perfectly mute in odd corners, while from the one side the distant shrieking of the parson echoed up from the cockpit (he had made a determined attempt at suicide) and from the other the drone of the trial went on. They were all deeply affected by Jack's concern, anxiety and rage: they had seen him unmoved so often and in such circumstances that his present emotion shook them profoundly, and disturbed their judgment. They could hear his voice now, formal, savage and much louder than the rest of the voices in the court, saying, 'Did the enemy fire several broadsides at us and at what distance were we when they fired the last?' Mr Dalziel's reply was a murmur, indistinguishable through the bulkhead.

'This is an entirely irrational fear,' said Stephen Maturin, looking at his wet and clammy palm. 'It is but one more instance of the . . . for surely to God, surely for all love, if they had wished to sink him they would have asked "How came you to be there?" But then I know very little of nautical affairs.' He looked for comfort at the master's face, but he found none there.

'Dr Maturin,' said the marine, opening the door.

Stephen walked in slowly and took the oath with particular deliberation, trying to sense the atmosphere of the court: he thus gave the clerk time to catch up with Dalziel's evidence, and the shrill pen wrote:

Question   Did she gain on the Sophie *without her studdingsails set?*

Answer   Yes.

Question by the court   Did they seem to sail much faster than you?

Answer   Yes, both by and large.

Dr Maturin, surgeon of the Sophie, *called and sworn.*

Question by the court   Is the statement you heard made by your captain respecting the loss of the Sophie, *correct as far as your observation went?*

Answer   I think it is.

Question by the court   Are you a sufficient judge of nautical affairs to know whether every effort was used to escape from the force that was pursuing the Sophie?

Answer   I know very little of nautical affairs, but it appeared to me that every exertion was used by every person on board: I saw the captain at the helm, and the officers and ship's company at the sweeps.

Question by the court   Was you on deck at the time the colours were struck and what distance were the enemy from you at the time of her surrender?

Answer   I was on deck, and the Desaix *was within musket-shot of the* Sophie *and was firing at us at the time.*

Ten minutes later the court was cleared. The dining-cabin again, and no hesitation about precedence in the doorway this time, for Jack and Mr Dalziel were there: they were all there, and not one of them spoke a word. Could that be laughter in the next room, or did the sound come from the wardroom of the *Caesar*?

A long pause. A long, long pause: and the marine at the door.

'If you please, gentlemen.'

They filed in, and in spite of all his years at sea Jack forgot to duck: he struck the lintel of the door with a force that left a patch of yellow hair and scalp on the wood and he walked on, almost blinded, to stand rigidly by his chair.

The clerk looked up from writing the word *Sentence*, startled by the crash, and then looked down again, to commit the judge-advocate's words to writing. 'At a court-martial assembled and held on board His Majesty's Ship *Pompée* in Rosia Bay . . . the court (being first duly sworn) proceeded in pursuance of an order from Sir James Saumarez Bart. Rear-Admiral of the Blue and . . . and having examined witnesses on the occasion, and maturely and deliberately considered every circumstance . . .'

The droning, expressionless voice went on, and its tone was so closely allied to the ringing in Jack's head that he heard virtually none of it, any more than he could see the man's face through the watering of his eyes.

'. . . the court is of the opinion that Captain Aubrey, his officers and ship's company used every possible exertion to prevent the King's sloop from falling into the hands of the enemy: and do therefore honourably acquit them. And they are hereby acquitted accordingly,' said the judge-advocate, and Jack heard none of it.

The inaudible voice stopped and Jack's blurred vision saw the black form sit down. He shook his singing head, tightened his jaw and compelled his faculties to return; for here was the president of the court getting to his feet. Jack's clear-

ing eyes caught Keats' smile, saw Captain Stirling pick up
that familiar, rather shabby sword, holding it with its hilt
towards him, while with his left hand he smoothed a piece of
paper by the inkwell. The president cleared his throat again
in the dead silence, and speaking in a clear, seamanlike voice
that combined gravity, formality and cheerfulness, he said,
'Captain Aubrey: it is no small pleasure to me to receive the
commands of the court I have the honour to preside at, that
in delivering to you your sword, I should congratulate you
upon its being restored by both friend and foe alike; hoping
ere long you will be called upon to draw it once more in the
honourable defence of your country.'

Post Captain

1

AT FIRST DAWN the swathes of rain drifting eastwards across the Channel parted long enough to show that the chase had altered course. The *Charwell* had been in her wake most of the night, running seven knots in spite of her foul bottom, and now they were not much above a mile and a half apart. The ship ahead was turning, turning, coming up into the wind; and the silence along the frigate's decks took on a new quality as every man aboard saw her two rows of gun-ports come into view. This was the first clear sight they had had of her since the look-out hailed the deck in the growing darkness to report a ship hull-down on the horizon, one point on the larboard bow. She was then steering north-north-east, and it was the general opinion aboard the *Charwell* that she was either one of a scattered French convoy or an American blockade-runner hoping to reach Brest under cover of the moonless night.

Two minutes after that first hail the *Charwell* set her fore and main topgallants – no great spread of canvas, but then the frigate had had a long, wearing voyage from the West Indies: nine weeks out of sight of land, the equinoctial gales to strain her tired rigging to the breaking-point, three days of lying-to in the Bay of Biscay at its worst, and it was understandable that Captain Griffiths should wish to husband her a little. No cloud of sail, but even so she fetched the stranger's wake within a couple of hours, and at four bells in the morning watch the *Charwell* cleared for action. The drum beat to quarters, the hammocks came racing up, piling into the nettings to form bulwarks, the guns were run out; and the warm, pink, sleepy watch below had been standing to them in the cold rain ever since – an hour and more to chill them to the bone.

Now in the silence of this discovery one of the crew of a gun in the waist could be heard explaining to a weak-eyed staring little man beside him, 'She's a French two-decker, mate. A seventy-four or an eighty: we've caught a tartar, mate.'

'Silence there, God damn you,' cried Captain Griffiths. 'Mr Quarles, take that man's name.'

Then the grey rain closed in. But at present everyone on the crowded quarterdeck knew what lay behind that drifting, formless veil: a French ship of the line, with both her rows of gun-ports open. And there was not one who had missed the slight movement of the yard that meant she was about to lay her foresail to the mast, heave to and wait for them.

The *Charwell* was a 32-gun 12-pounder frigate, and if she got close enough to use the squat carronades on her quarter-deck and forecastle as well as her long guns she could throw a broadside weight of metal of 238 pounds. A French line-of-battle ship could not throw less than 960. No question of a match, therefore, and no discredit in bearing up and running for it, but for the fact that somewhere in the dim sea behind them there was their consort, the powerful 38-gun 18-pounder *Dee*. She had lost a topmast in the last blow, which slowed her down, but she had been well in sight at nightfall, and she had responded to Captain Griffiths's signal to chase: for Captain Griffiths was the senior captain. The two frigates would still be heavily outgunned by the ship of the line, but there was no doubt that they could take her on: she would certainly try to keep her broadside to one of the frigates and maul her terribly, but the other could lie on her bow or her stem and rake her — a murderous fire right along the length of her decks to which she could make almost no reply. It could be done: it had been done. In '97, for example, the *Indefatiga-ble* and the *Amazon* had destroyed a French seventy-four. But then the *Indefatigable* and the *Amazon* carried eighty long guns between them, and the *Droits de l'Homme* had not been able to open her lower-deck ports – the sea was running too high. There was no more than a moderate swell now; and to engage the stranger the *Charwell* would have to cut her off from Brest and fight her for – for how long?

'Mr – Mr Howell,' said the captain. 'Take a glass to the masthead and see what you can make of the *Dee*.'

The long-legged midshipman was half-way to the mizzen-top before the captain had finished speaking, and his 'Aye-aye, sir' came down through the sloping rain. A black squall swept across the ship, pelting down so thick that for a while the men on the quarterdeck could scarcely see the forecastle, and the water ran spouting from the lee-scuppers. Then it was gone, and in the pale gleam of day that followed there came the hail. 'On deck, sir. She's hull-up on the leeward beam. She's fished her . . .'

'Report,' said the captain, in a loud, toneless voice. 'Pass the word for Mr Barr.'

The third lieutenant came hurrying aft from his station. The wind took his rain-soaked cloak as he stepped on to the quarterdeck, and he made a convulsive gesture, one hand going towards the flapping cloth and the other towards his hat.

'Take it off, sir,' cried Captain Griffiths, flushing dark red. 'Take it right off your head. You know Lord St Vincent's order – you have all of you read it – you know how to salute . . .' He snapped his mouth shut; and after a moment he said, 'When does the tide turn?'

'I beg your pardon, sir,' said Barr. 'At ten minutes after eight o'clock, sir. It is almost the end of slack-water now, sir, if you please.'

The captain grunted, and said, 'Mr Howell?'

'She has fished her main topmast, sir,' said the midshipman, standing bareheaded, tall above his captain. 'And has just hauled to the wind.'

The captain levelled his glass at the *Dee*, whose top-gallant-sails were now clear above the jagged edge of the sea: her top-sails too, when the swell raised both the frigates high. He wiped the streaming objective-glass, stared again, swung round to look at the Frenchman, snapped the telescope shut and gazed back at the distant frigate. He was alone there, leaning on the rail, alone there on the holy starboard side of the quarterdeck; and from time to time, when they were not looking at the Frenchman or the *Dee*, the officers glanced thoughtfully at his back.

The situation was still fluid; it was more a potentiality than a situation. But any decision now would crystallize it, and the moment it began to take shape all the succeeding events would follow of themselves, moving at first with slow inevitability and then faster and faster, never to be undone. And a decision must be made, made quickly – at the *Charwell*'s present rate of sailing they would be within range of the two-decker in less than ten minutes. Yet there were so many factors . . . The *Dee* was no great sailer close-hauled on a wind; and the turning tide would hold her back – it was right across her course; she might have to make another tack. In half an hour the French 36-pounders could rip the guts out of the *Charwell*, dismast her and carry her into Brest – the wind stood fair for Brest. Why had they seen not a single ship of the blockading squadron? They could not have been blown off, not with this wind. It was damned odd. Everything was damned odd, from this Frenchman's conduct onwards. The sound of gunfire would bring the squadron up . . . Delaying tactics . . .

The feeling of those eyes on his back filled Captain Griffiths with rage. An unusual number of eyes, for the *Charwell* had several officers and a couple of civilians as passengers, one set from Gibraltar and another from Port of Spain. The fire-eating General Paget was one of them, an influential man; and another was Captain Aubrey, Lucky Jack Aubrey, who had set about a Spanish 36-gun xebec-frigate not long ago with the *Sophie*, a 14-gun brig, and had taken her. The *Cacafuego*. It had been the talk of the fleet some months back; and it made the decision no less difficult.

Captain Aubrey was standing by the aftermost larboard carronade, with a completely abstracted, non-committal look upon his face. From that place, being tall, he could see the whole situation, the rapidly, smoothly changing triangle of three ships; and close beside him stood two shorter figures, the one Dr Maturin, formerly his surgeon in the *Sophie*, and the other a man in black – black clothes, black hat and a streaming black cloak – who might have had *intelligence agent* written on his narrow forehead. Or just the word *spy*, there being so little room. They were talking in a language thought by some to be Latin. They were talking eagerly, and Jack Aubrey, intercepting a furious glance across the deck, leant down to whisper in his friend's ear, 'Stephen, will you not go below? They will be wanting you in the cockpit any moment now.'

Captain Griffiths turned from the rail, and with laboured calmness he said, 'Mr Berry, make this signal. *I am about to . . .*'

At this moment the ship of the line fired a gun, followed by three blue lights that soared and burst with a ghostly effulgence in the dawn: before the last dropping trail of sparks had drifted away downwind she sent up a succession of rockets, a pale, isolated Guy Fawkes' night far out in the sea.

'What the devil can she mean by that?' thought Jack Aubrey, narrowing his eyes, and the wondering murmur along the frigate's decks echoed his amazement.

'On deck,' roared the look-out in the foretop, 'there's a cutter pulling from under her lee.'

Captain Griffiths's telescope swivelled round. 'Duck up,' he called, and as the clewlines plucked at the main and foresails to give him a clear view he saw the cutter, an English cutter, sway up its yard, fill, gather speed, and come racing over the grey sea, towards the frigate.

'Close the cutter,' he said. 'Mr Bowes, give her a gun.'

At last, after all these hours of frozen waiting, there came the quick orders, the careful laying of the gun, the crash of the twelve-pounder, the swirl of acrid smoke eddying briefly on the wind, and the cheer of the crew as the ball skipped across the cutter's bows. An answering cheer from the cutter, a waving of hats, and the two vessels neared one another at a combined speed of fifteen miles an hour.

The cutter, fast and beautifully handled – certainly a smuggling craft – came to under the *Charwell*'s lee, lost her way, and lay there as trim as a gull, rising and falling on the swell. A row of brown, knowing faces grinned up at the frigate's guns.

'I'd press half a dozen prime seamen out of her in the next two minutes,' reflected Jack, while Captain Griffiths hailed her master over the lane of sea.

'Come aboard,' said Captain Griffiths suspiciously, and after a few moments of backing and filling, of fending-off and cries of 'Handsomely now, God damn your soul,' the master came up the stern ladder with a bundle under his arm. He swung easily over the taffrail, held out his hand and said, 'Wish you joy of the peace, Captain.'

'Peace?' cried Captain Griffiths.

'Yes, sir. I thought I should surprise you. They signed not three days since. There's not a foreign-going ship has heard yet. I've got the cutter filled with the newspapers, London, Paris and country towns – all the articles, gentlemen, all the latest details,' he said, looking round the quarterdeck. 'Half a crown a go.'

There was no disbelieving him. The quarterdeck looked utterly blank. But the whispered word had flown along the deck from the radiant carronade-crews, and now cheering broke out on the forecastle. In spite of the captain's automatic 'Take that man's name, Mr Quarles,' it flowed back to the mainmast and spread throughout the ship, a full-throated howl of joy – liberty, wives and sweethearts, safety, the delights of land.

And in any case there was little real ferocity in Captain Griffiths's voice: anyone looking into his close-set eyes would have seen ecstasy in their depths. His occupation was gone, vanished in a puff of smoke; but now no one on God's earth could ever know what signal he had been about to make, and in spite of the severe control that he imposed upon his face there was an unusual urbanity in his tone as he invited his

passengers, his first lieutenant, the officer and the midshipman of the watch to dine with him that afternoon.

'IT IS CHARMING to see how sensible the men are – how
sensible of the blessings of peace,' said Stephen Maturin to
the Reverend Mr Hake, by way of civility.

'Aye. The blessings of peace. Oh, certainly,' said the chaplain, who had no living to retire to, no private means, and who
knew that the *Charwell* would be paid off as soon as she
reached Portsmouth. He walked deliberately out of the wardroom, to pace the quarterdeck in a thoughtful silence, leaving
Captain Aubrey and Dr Maturin alone.

'I thought he would have shown more pleasure,' observed
Stephen Maturin.

'It's an odd thing about you, Stephen,' said Jack Aubrey,
looking at him with affection. 'You have been at sea quite
some time now, and no one could call you a fool, but you
have no more notion of a sailor's life than a babe unborn.
Surely you must have noticed how glum Quarles and Rodgers
and all the rest were at dinner? And how blue everyone has
always looked this war, when there was any danger of peace?'

'I put it down to the anxieties of the night – the long strain,
the watchfulness, the lack of sleep: I must not say the apprehension of danger. Captain Griffiths was in a fine flow of
spirits, however.'

'Oh,' said Jack, closing one eye. 'That was reyther different;
and in any case he is a post-captain, of course. He has his ten
shillings a day, and whatever happens he goes up the captains' list as the old ones die off or get their flag. He's quite
old – forty, I dare say, or even more – but with any luck he'll
die an admiral. No. It's the others I'm sorry for, the lieutenants with their half-pay and very little chance of a ship –
none at all of promotion; the poor wretched midshipmen who
have not been made and who never will be made now – no
hope of a commission. And of course, no half-pay at all. It's
the merchant service for them, or blacking shoes outside St

James's Park. Haven't you heard the old song? I'll tip you a stave.' He hummed the tune, and in a discreet rumble he sang.

> 'Says Jack, "There is very good news, there is peace both
>   by land and by sea;
> Great guns no more shall be used, for we all disbanded
>   be,"
> Says the Admiral, "That's very bad news;" says the cap-
>   tain, "My heart will break;"
> The lieutenant cries, 'What shall I do? For I know not
>   what course for to take."
> Says the doctor, "I'm a gentleman too, I'm a gentleman of
>   the first rank;
> I will go to some country fair, and there I'll set up mounte-
>   bank."

Ha, ha, that's for you, Stephen – ha, ha, ha –

> Says the midshipman, "I have no trade; I have got my
>   trade for to choose,
> I will go to St James's Park gate, and there I'll set black of
>   shoes;
> And there I will set all day, at everybody's call,
> And everyone that comes by, 'Do you want my nice shin-
>   ing balls?' "'

Mr Quarles looked in at the door, recognized the tune and drew in a sharp breath; but Jack was a guest, a superior offi- cer – a master and commander, no less, with an epaulette on his shoulder – and he was broad as well as tall. Mr Quarles let his breath out in a sigh and closed the door.

'I should have sung softer,' said Jack, and drawing his chair closer to the table he went on in a low voice, 'No, those are the chaps I am sorry for. I'm sorry for myself too, naturally – no great likelihood of a ship, and of course no enemy to cruise against if I do get one. But it's nothing in comparison of them. We've had luck with prize-money, and if only it were not for this infernal delay over making me post I should be perfectly happy to have a six months' run ashore. Hunting. Hearing some decent music. The opera – we might even go to Vienna! Eh? What do you say, Stephen? Though I must confess this slowness irks my heart and soul. However, it's nothing in comparison of them, and I make no doubt it will be settled directly.' He picked up *The Times* and ran through the *London Gazette*, in case he should have missed his own name in the first three readings. 'Toss me the one on the locker, will you?' he said, throwing it down. 'The *Sussex Courier*.'

'This is more like it, Stephen,' he said, five minutes later. '*Mr Savile's hounds will meet at ten o'clock on Wednesday, the sixth of November 1802, at Champflower Cross.* I had such a run with them when I was a boy: my father's regiment was in camp at Rainsford. A seven-mile point – prodigious fine country if you have a horse that can really go. Or listen to this: *a neat gentleman's residence, standing upon gravel, is to be let by the year, at moderate terms.* Stabling for ten, it says.'

'Are there any rooms?'

'Why, of course there are. It couldn't be called a *neat* gentleman's residence, without there were rooms. What a fellow you are, Stephen. Ten bedrooms. By God, there's a lot to be said for a house, not too far from the sea, in that sort of country.'

'Had you not thought of going to Woolhampton – of going to your father's house?'

'Yes . . . yes. I mean to give him a visit, of course. But there's my new mother-in-law, you know. And to tell you the truth, I don't think it would exactly answer.' He paused, trying to remember the name of the person, the classical person, who had had such a trying time with his father's second wife; for General Aubrey had recently married his dairy-maid, a fine black-eyed young woman with a moist palm whom Jack knew very well. Actaeon, Ajax, Aristides? He felt that their cases were much alike and that by naming him he would give a subtle hint of the position: but the name would not come, and after a while he reverted to the advertisements. 'There's a great deal to be said for somewhere in the neigbbourhood of Rainsford – three or four packs within reach, London only a day's ride away, and neat gentlemen's residences by the dozen, all standing upon gravel. You'll go snacks with me, Stephen? We'll take Bonden, Killick, Lewis and perhaps one or two other old Sophies, and ask some of the youngsters to come and stay. We'll lay in beer and skittles – it will be Fiddler's Green!'

'I should like it of all things,' said Stephen. 'Whatever the advertisements may say, it is a chalk soil, and there are some very curious plants and beetles on the downs. I am with child to see a dew-pond.'

POLCARY DOWN and the cold sky over it; a searching air from the north breathing over the water-meadows, up across the plough, up and up to this great sweep of open turf, the down, with the covert called Rumbold's Gorse sprawling on the lower edge of it. A score of red-coated figures dotted round the Gorse, and far away below them on the middle slope a ploughman standing at the end of his furrow, motionless behind his team of Sussex oxen, gazing up as Mr Savile's hounds worked their way through the furze and the brown remnants of the bracken.

Slow work; uncertain, patchy scent; and the foxhunters had plenty of time to drink from their flasks, blow on their hands, and look out over the landscape below them – the river winding through its patchwork of fields, the towers or steeples of Hither, Middle, Nether and Savile Champflower, the six or seven big houses scattered along the valley, the whale-backed downs one behind the other, and far away the lead-coloured sea.

It was a small field, and almost everyone there knew everyone else: half a dozen farmers, some private gentlemen from

the Champflowers and the outlying parishes, two militia officers from the dwindling camp at Rainsford, Mr Burton, who
had come out in spite of his streaming cold in the hope of
catching a glimpse of Mrs St John, and Dr Vining, with his
hat pinned to his wig and both tied under his chin with a
handkerchief. He had been led astray early in his rounds – he
could not resist the sound of the horn – and his conscience
had been troubling him ever since the scent had faded and
died. From time to time he looked over the miles of frigid air
between the covert and Mapes Court, where Mrs Williams
was waiting for him. 'There is nothing wrong with her,' he
observed. 'My physic will do no good; but in Christian
decency I should call. And indeed I shall, unless they find
again before I can tell a hundred.' He put his finger upon his
pulse and began to count. At ninety he paused, looking about
for some reprieve, and on the far side of the covert he saw a
figure he did not know. 'That is the medical man they have
been telling me about, no doubt,' he said. 'It would be the
civil thing to go over and say a word to him. A rum-looking
cove. Dear me, a very rum-looking cove.'

The rum-looking cove was sprawling upon a mule, an
unusual sight in an English hunting-field; and quite apart
from the mule there was a strange air about him – his slate-
coloured small-clothes, his pale face, his pale eyes and even
paler close-cropped skull (*his* hat and wig were tied to his
saddle), and the way he bit into a hunk of bread rubbed with
garlic. He was calling out in a loud tone to his companion, in
whom Dr Vining recognized the new tenant of Melbury
Lodge. 'I tell you what it is, Jack,' he was saying, 'I tell you
what it is . . .'

'You sir – you on the mule,' cried old Mr Savile's furious
voice. 'Will you let the God-damned dogs get on with their
work? Hey? Hey? Is this a God-damned coffee-house? I
appeal to you, is this an infernal debating society?'

Captain Aubrey pursed his lips demurely and pushed his
horse over the twenty yards that separated them. 'Tell me

later, Stephen,' he said in a low voice, leading his friend round the covert out of the master's sight. 'Tell me later, when they have found their fox.'

The demure look did not sit naturally upon Jack Aubrey's face, which in this weather was as red as his coat, and as soon as they were round the corner, under the lee of a wind-blown thorn, his usual expectant cheerfulness returned, and he looked eagerly up into the furze, where an occasional heave and rustle showed the pack in motion.

'Looking for a *fox*, are they?' said Stephen Maturin, as though hippogriffs were the more usual quarry in England, and he relapsed into a brown study, munching slowly upon his bread.

The wind breathed up the long hillside; remote clouds passed evenly across the sky. Now and then Jack's big hunter brought his ears to bear; this was a recent purchase, a strongly-built bay, quite up to Jack's sixteen stone. But it did not much care for hunting, and then like so many geldings it spent much of its time mourning for its lost stones: a discontented horse. If the moods that succeeded one another in its head had taken the form of words they would have run, 'Too heavy – sits too far forward when we go over a fence – have carried him far enough for one day – shall have him off presently, see if I don't. I smell a mare! A mare! Oh!' Its flaring nostrils quivered, and it stamped.

Looking round Jack saw that there were newcomers in the field. A young woman and a groom came hurrying up the side of the plough, the groom mounted on a cob and the young woman on a pretty little high-bred chestnut mare. When they reached the post and rail dividing the field from the down the groom cantered on to open a gate, but the girl set her horse at the rail and skipped neatly over it, just as a whimpering and then a bellowing roar inside the covert gave promise of great things.

The noise died away: a young hound came out and stared into the open. Stephen Maturin moved from behind the close-woven thorn to follow the flight of a falcon overhead, and at the sight of the mule the chestnut mare began to caper, flashing her white stockings and tossing her head.

'Get over, you – ,' said the girl, in her pure clear young voice. Jack had never heard a girl say – before, and he turned to look at her with a particular interest. She was busy coping with the mare's excitement, but after a moment she caught his eye and frowned. He looked away, smiling, for she was the prettiest thing – indeed, beautiful, with her heightened colour and her fine straight back, sitting her horse with the unconscious grace of a midshipman at the tiller in a lively sea. She had black hair and blue eyes; a certain ram-you-damn-you air that was slightly comic and more than a little touching in so slim a creature. She was wearing a shabby blue habit with white cuffs and lapels, like a naval lieutenant's coat, and on top of it all a dashing tricorne with a tight curl of ostrich-feather. In some ingenious way, probably by the use of combs, she had drawn up her hair under this hat so as to leave one ear exposed; and this perfect ear, as Jack observed when the mare came crabwise towards him, was as pink as . . .

'There is that fox of theirs,' remarked Stephen, in a conversational tone. 'There is that fox we hear so much about. Though indeed, it is a vixen, sure.'

Slipping quickly along a fold in the ground the leaf-coloured fox went slanting down across them towards the plough. The horses' ears and the mule's followed it, cocked like so many semaphores. When the fox was well clear Jack rose in his stirrups, held up his hat and holla'd it away in a high-seas roar that brought the huntsman tearing round, his horn going twang-twang-twang, and hounds racing from the furze at all points. They hit the scent in the sheltered hollow and they were away with a splendid cry. They poured through the fence; they were half-way across the unploughed stubble, a close-packed body – such music – and the huntsman was right up there with them. The field came thundering round the covert: someone had the gate open and in a moment there was an eager crowd jostling to get through, for it was a devilish unpleasant downhill leap just here. Jack held hard, not choosing to thrust his first time out in a strange country, but his heart was beating to quarters, double-time, and he had already worked out the line he would follow once the press had thinned.

Jack was the keenest of fox-hunters: he loved everything about the chase, from the first sound of the horn to the rancid smell of the torn fox, but in spite of a few unwelcome spells without a ship, he had spent two thirds of his life at sea – his skill was not all he thought it was.

The gate was still jammed – there would be no chance of getting through it before the pack was in the next field. Jack wheeled his horse, called out, 'Come on, Stephen,' and put it at the rail. Out of the corner of his eye he saw the chestnut flash between his friend and the crowd in the gate. As his horse rose Jack screwed round to see how the girl would get over, and the gelding instantly felt this change of balance. It took the rail flying high and fast, landed with its head low, and with a cunning twist of its shoulder and an upward thrust from behind it unseated its rider.

He did not fall at once. It was a slow, ignominious glide down that slippery near shoulder, with a fistful of mane in his right hand; but the horse was the master of the situation now, and in twenty yards the saddle was empty.

The horse's satisfaction did not last, however. Jack's boot was wedged in his near stirrup; it would not come free, and here was his heavy person jerking and thumping along at the gelding's side, roaring and swearing horribly. The horse began to grow alarmed – to lose its head – to snort – to stare wildly – and to run faster and faster across those dark, flint-strewn, unforgiving furrows.

The ploughman left his oxen and came lumbering up the hill, waving his goad; a tall young man in a green coat, a foot-follower, called out 'Whoa there, whoa there,' and ran towards the horse with his arms spread wide; the mule, the last of the vanishing field, turned and raced back to cut the gelding off, swarming along in its inhuman way, very close to the ground. It outran the men, crossed the gelding's path, stood firm and took the shock: like a hero Stephen flung himself off, seized the reins and clung there until Green Coat and the ploughman came pounding up.

The oxen, left staring half-way along their furrow, were so moved by all this excitement that they came very nearly to the point of cutting a caper on their own. But before they had made up their minds it was over. The ploughman was leading the shamefaced horse to the side of the field, while the other two propped raw bones and bloody head between them, listening gravely to his explanations. The mule walked behind.

MAPES COURT was an entirely feminine household – not a man in it, apart from the butler and the groom. Mrs Williams was a woman, in the natural course of things; but she was a woman so emphatically, so totally a woman, that she was almost devoid of any private character. A vulgar woman, too, although her family, which was of some importance in the neighbourhood, had been settled there since Dutch William's time.

It was difficult to see any connexion, any family likeness, between her and her daughters and her niece, who made up the rest of the family. Indeed, it was not much of a house for family likeness: the dim portraits might have been bought at various auctions, and although the three daughters had been brought up together, with the same people around them, in the same atmosphere of genteel money-worship, position-worship and suffused indignation – an indignation that did not require any object for its existence, but that could always find one in a short space of time; a housemaid wearing silver buckles on Sunday would bring on a full week's flow – they were as different in their minds as they were in their looks.

Sophia, the eldest, was a tall girl with wide-set grey eyes, a broad, smooth forehead, and a wonderful sweetness of expression – soft fair hair, inclining to gold: an exquisite skin.

She was a reserved creature, living much in an inward dream whose nature she did not communicate to anyone. Perhaps it was her mother's unprincipled rectitude that had given her this early disgust for adult life; but whether or no, she seemed very young for her twenty-seven years. There was nothing in the least degree affected or kittenish about this: rather a kind of ethereal quality – the quality of a sacrificial object. Iphigeneia before the letter. Her looks were very much admired; she was always elegant, and when she was in looks she was quite lovely. She spoke little, in company or out, but she was capable of a sudden dart of sharpness, of a remark that showed much more intelligence and reflection than would have been expected from her rudimentary education and her very quiet provincial life. These remarks had a much greater force, coming from an amiable, pliant, and as it were sleepy reserve, and before now they had startled men who did not know her well – men who had been prating away happily with the conscious superiority of their sex. They dimly grasped an underlying strength, and they connected it with her occasional expression of secret amusement, the relish of something that she did not choose to share.

Cecilia was more nearly her mother's daughter: a little goose with a round face and china-blue eyes, devoted to ornament and to crimping her yellow hair, shallow and foolish almost to simplicity, but happy, full of cheerful noise, and not yet at all ill-natured. She dearly loved the company of men, men of any size or shape. Her younger sister Frances did not: she was indifferent to their admiration – a long-legged nymph, still given to whistling and shying stones at the squirrels in the walnut-tree. Here was all the pitilessness of youth intact; and she was perfectly entrancing, as a spectacle. She had her cousin Diana's black hair and great dark blue misty pools of eyes, but she was as unlike her sisters as though they belonged to another sex. All they had in common was youthful grace, a good deal of gaiety, splendid health, and ten thousand pounds apiece.

With these attractions it was strange that none of them should have married, particularly as the marriage-bed was never far from Mrs Williams's mind. But the paucity of men, of eligible bachelors, in the neighbourhood, the disrupting effects of ten years of war, and Sophia's reluctance (she had had several offers) explained a great deal; the rest could be accounted for by Mrs Williams's avidity for a good marriage settlement, and by an unwillingness on the part of the local gentlemen to have her as a mother-in-law.

Whether Mrs Williams liked her daughters at all was doubtful: she loved them, of course, and had 'sacrificed everything for them', but there was not much room in her composition for liking – it was too much taken up with being right (*Hast thou considered my servant Mrs Williams, that there is none like her in the earth, a perfect and an upright woman?*), with being tired, and with being ill-used. Dr Vining, who had known her all her life and who had seen her children into the world, said that she did not; but even he, who cordially disliked her, admitted that she truly, whole-heartedly loved their interest. She might damp all their enthusiasms, drizzle grey disapproval from one year's end to another, and spoil even birthdays with bravely-supported headaches, but she would fight parents, trustees and lawyers like a tigress for 'an adequate provision'. Yet still she had three unmarried daughters, and it was something of a comfort to her to be able to attribute this to their being overshadowed by her niece. Indeed, this niece, Diana Villiers, was as good-looking in her way as Sophia. But how unlike these two ways were: Diana with her straight back and high-held head seemed quite tall, but when she stood next to her cousin, she came no higher than her ear, they both had natural grace in an eminent degree, but whereas Sophia's was a willowy, almost languorous flowing perfection of movement, Diana's had a quick, flashing rhythm – on those rare occasions when there was a ball within twenty miles of Mapes she danced superbly; and by candlelight her complexion was almost as good as Sophia's.

Mrs Villiers was a widow: she had been born in the same year as Sophia, but what a different life she had led; at fifteen, after her mother's death, she had gone out to India to keep house for her expensive, raffish father, and she had lived there in splendid style even after her marriage to a penniless young man, her father's aide-de-camp, for he had moved into their rambling great palace, where the addition of a husband and an extra score of servants passed unnoticed. It had been a foolish marriage on the emotional plane – both too passionate, strong, self-willed, and opposed in every way to do anything but tear one another to pieces – but from the worldly point of view there was a great deal to be said for it. It did bring her a handsome husband, and it might have brought her a deer-park and ten thousand a year as well, for not only was Charles Villiers well-connected (one sickly life between him and a great estate) but he was intelligent, cultivated, unscrupulous and active – particularly gifted on the political side: the very man to make a brilliant career in India. A second Clive, maybe, and wealthy by the age of thirty-odd. But they were both killed in the same engagement against Tippoo Sahib, her father owing three lakhs of rupees and her husband nearly half that sum.

The Company allowed Diana her passage home and fifty pounds a year until she should remarry. She came back to England with a wardrobe of tropical clothes, a certain knowledge of the world, and almost nothing else. She came back, in effect, to the schoolroom, or something very like it. For she at once realized that her aunt meant to clamp down on her, to allow her no chance of queering her daughters' pitch; and as she had no money and nowhere else to go she determined to fit into this small slow world of the English countryside, with its fixed notions and its strange morality.

She was willing, she was obliged, to accept a protectorate, and from the beginning she resolved to be meek, cautious and retiring; she knew that other women would regard her as a menace, and she meant to give them no provocation. But her theory and her practice were sometimes at odds, and in any case Mrs Williams's idea of a protectorate was much more like a total annexation. She was afraid of Diana, and dared not push her too far, but she never gave up trying to gain a moral superiority, and it was striking to see how this essentially stupid woman, unhampered by any principle or by any sense of honour, managed to plant her needle where it hurt most.

This had been going on for years, and Diana's clandestine or at least unavowed excursions with Mr Savile's hounds had a purpose beyond satisfying her delight in riding. Returning now she met her cousin Cecilia in the hall, hurrying to look at her new bonnet in the pier-glass between the breakfast-room windows.

'Thou looks't like Antichrist in that lewd hat,' she said in a sombre voice, for the hounds had lost their fox and the only tolerable-looking man had vanished.

'Oh! Oh!' cried Cecilia, 'what a shocking thing to say! It's blasphemy, I'm sure. I declare I've never had such a shocking thing said to me since Jemmy Blagrove called me that rude word. I shall tell Mama.'

'Don't be a fool, Cissy. It's a quotation – literature – the Bible.'

'Oh. Well, I think it's very shocking. You are covered with mud, Di. Oh, you took my tricorne. Oh, what an ill-natured thing you are – I am sure you spoilt the feather. I shall tell Mama.' She snatched the hat, but finding it unhurt she softened and went on, 'Well: and so you had a dirty ride. You went along Gallipot Lane, I suppose. Did you see anything of the hunt? They were over there on Polcary all the morning with their horrid howling and yowling.'

'I saw them in the distance,' said Diana. 'You frightened me so with that dreadful thing you said about Jesus,' said Cecilia, blowing on the ostrich-feather, 'that I almost forgot the news. The Admiral is back!'

'Back already?'

'Yes. And he will be over this very afternoon. He sent Ned with his compliments and might he come with Mama's Berlin wool after dinner. Such fun! He will tell us all about these beautiful young men! Men, Diana!'

The family had scarcely gathered about their tea before Admiral Haddock walked in. He was only a yellow admiral, retired without hoisting his flag, and he had not been afloat since 1794, but he was their one authority on naval matters and he had been sadly missed ever since the unexpected arrival of a Captain Aubrey of the Navy – a captain who had taken Melbury Lodge and who was therefore within their sphere of influence, but about whom they knew nothing and upon whom (he being a bachelor) they, as ladies, could not call.

'Pray, Admiral,' said Mrs Williams, as soon as the Berlin wool had been faintly praised, peered at with narrowed eyes and pursed lips, and privately condemned as useless – nothing like a match, in quality, colour or price. 'Pray, Admiral, tell us about this Captain Aubrey, who they say has taken Melbury Lodge.'

'Aubrey? Oh, yes,' said the Admiral, running his dry tongue over his dry lips, like a parrot, 'I know all about him. I have not met him, but I talked about him to people at the club and in the Admiralty, and when I came home I looked him up in the Navy List. He is a young fellow, only a master and commander, you know – '

'Do you mean he is *pretending* to be a captain?' cried Mrs Williams, perfectly willing to believe it.

'No, no,' said Admiral Haddock impatiently. 'We always call commanders Captain So-and-So in the Navy. Real captains, full captains, we call *post*-captains – we say a man is made post when he is appointed to a sixth-rate or better, an eight-and-twenty, say, or a thirty-two-gun frigate. A *post*-ship, my dear Madam.'

'Oh, indeed,' said Mrs Williams, nodding her head and looking wise.

'Only a commander: but he did most uncommon well in the Mediterranean. Lord Keith gave him cruise after cruise in that little old quarter-decked brig we took from the Spaniards in ninety-five, and he played Old Harry with the shipping up and down the coast. There were times when he well-nigh filled the Lazaretto Reach in Mahon with his prizes – Lucky Jack Aubrey, they called him. He must have cleared a pretty penny – a most elegant penny indeed. And he it was who took the *Cacafuego*! The very man,' said the Admiral with some triumph, gazing round the circle of blank faces. After a moment's pause of unbroken stupidity on their part he shook his head, saying, 'You never even heard of the engagement, I collect?'

No, they had not. They were sorry to say that they had not heard of the *Cacafuego* – was it the same as the Battle of St Vincent? Perhaps it had happened when they were so busy with the strawberries. They had put up two hundred pots.

'Well, the *Cacafuego* was a Spanish xebec-frigate of two and thirty guns, and he went for her in this little fourteen-gun sloop, fought her to a standstill, and carried her into Minorca. Such an action! The service rang with it. And if it had not been for some legal quirk about her papers, she being lent to the Barcelona merchants and not commanded by her regular captain, which meant that technically she was not for the moment a king's ship but a privateer, he would have been made post and given command of her. Perhaps knighted too. But as it was – there being wheels within wheels, as I will explain at another time, for it is not really suitable for young ladies – she was not bought into the service; and so far he has not been given his step. What is more, I do not think he ever will be. He is a vile ranting dog of a Tory, to be sure – or at least his father is – but even so, it was shameful. He may not be quite the thing, but I intend to take particular notice of him – shall call tomorrow – to mark my sense of the action: and of the injustice.'

'So he is not quite the thing, sir?' asked Cecilia.

'Why no, my dear, he is not. Not at all the thing, they tell me. Dashing he may be! indeed, he is; but disciplined – pah! That is the trouble with so many of your young fellows, and it will never do in the service – will never do for St Vincent. Many complaints about his lack of discipline – independence – disobeying orders. No future in the service for that kind of officer, above all with St Vincent at the Admiralty. And then I fear he may not attend to the fifth commandment quite as he should.' The girls' faces took on an inward look as they privately ran over the Decalogue: in order of intelligence a little frown appeared on each as its owner reached the part about Sunday travelling, and then cleared as they carried on to the commandment the Admiral had certainly intended. 'There was a great deal of talk about Mrs – about a superior officer's wife, and they say that was at the bottom of the matter. A sad rake, I fear; and undisciplined, which is far worse. You may say what you please about old Jarvie, but he will not brook undisciplined conduct. And he does not love a Tory, either.'

'Is Old Jarvie a naval word for the Evil One, sir?' asked Cecilia.

The admiral rubbed his hands. 'He is Earl St Vincent, my dear, the First Lord of the Admiralty.'

At the mention of authority Mrs Williams looked grave and respectful; and after a reverent pause she said, 'I believe you mentioned Captain Aubrey's father, Admiral?'

'Yes. He is that General Aubrey who made such a din by flogging the Whig candidate at Hinton.'

'How very disgraceful. But surely, to flog a member of parliament he must be a man of considerable estate?'

'Only moderate, ma'am. A moderate little place the other side of Woolhampton; and much encumbered, they tell me. My cousin Hanmer knows him well.'

'And is Captain Aubrey the only son?'

'Yes, ma'am. Though by the bye he has a new mother-in-law: the general married a girl from the village some months ago. She is said to be a fine sprightly young woman.

'Good heavens, how wicked!' said Mrs Williams. 'But I presume there is no danger? I presume the general is of a certain age?'

'Not at all, ma'am,' said the admiral. 'He cannot be much more than sixty-five. Were I in Captain Aubrey's shoes, I should be most uneasy.'

Mrs Williams brightened. 'Poor young man,' she said placidly. 'I quite feel for him, I protest.'

The butler carried away the tea-tray, mended the fire and began to light the candles. 'How the evenings are drawing in,' said Mrs Williams. 'Never mind the sconces by the door. Pull the curtains by the cord, John. Touching the cloth wears it so, and it is bad for the rings. And now, Admiral, what have you to tell us of the other gentleman at Melbury Lodge, Captain Aubrey's particular friend?'

'Oh, him,' said Admiral Haddock. 'I do not know much about him. He was Captain Aubrey's surgeon in this sloop. And I believe I heard he was someone's natural son. His name is Maturin.'

'If you please, sir,' said Frances, 'what is a natural son?'

'Why . . .' said the admiral, looking from side to side.

'Are sons more natural than daughters, pray?'

'Hush, my dear,' said Mrs Williams.

'Mr Lever called at Melbury,' said Cecilia. 'Captain Aubrey had gone to London – he is always going to London, it appears – but he saw Dr Maturin, and says that he is quite strange, quite like a foreign gentleman. He was cutting up a horse in the winter drawing-room.'

'How very undesirable,' said Mrs Williams. 'They will have to use cold water for the blood. Cold water is the only thing for the marks of blood. Do not you think, Admiral, that they should be told they must use cold water for the marks of blood?'

'I dare say they are tolerably used to getting rid of stains of that kind, ma'am,' said the admiral. 'But now I come to think of it,' he went on, gazing round the room 'what a capital thing it is for you girls, to have a couple of sailors with their pockets full of guineas, turned ashore and pitched down on your very doorstep. Anyone in want of a husband has but to whistle, and they will come running, ha, ha, ha!'

The admiral's sally had a wretched reception; not one of the young ladies joined in his mirth. Sophia and Diana looked grave, Cecilia tossed her head, Frances scowled, and Mrs Williams pursed up her mouth, looked down her nose and meditated a sharp retort.

'However,' he continued, wondering at the sudden chill in the room 'it is no go, no go at all, now that I recollect. He told Trimble, who suggested a match with his sister- in-law, that he had quite given up women. It seems that he was so unfortunate in his last attachment, that he has quite given up women. And indeed he is an unlucky wight, whatever they may call him: there is not only this wretched business of his promotion and his father's cursed untimely marriage, but he also has a couple of neutral prizes in the Admiralty court, on appeal. I dare say that is why he is perpetually fagging up and down to London. He is an unlucky man, no doubt; and no doubt he has come to understand it. So he has very rightly given up all thoughts of marriage, in which luck is everything – has quite given up women.'

'It is perfectly true,' cried Cecilia. 'There is not a single woman in the house! Mrs Burdett, who *just happened to be passing by*, and our Molly, whose father's cottage is directly behind and can see everything, say there is not a woman in the house! There they live together, with a parcel of sailors to look after them. La, how strange! And yet Mrs Burdett, who had a good look, you may be sure, says the window-panes were shining like diamonds, and all the frames and doors had been new-painted white.'

'How can they hope to manage?' asked Mrs Williams. 'Surely, it is very wrong-headed and unnatural. Dear me, I should not fancy sitting down in that house. I should wipe my chair with my handkerchief, I can tell you.'

'Why, ma'am,' cried the admiral, 'we manage tolerably well at sea, you know.'

'Oh, at sea . . .' said Mrs Williams with a smile. 'What can they do for mending, poor things?' asked Sophia. 'I suppose they buy new.'

'I can just see them with their stockings out at heel,' cried Frances, with a coarse whoop, 'pegging away with their needles – "Doctor, may I trouble you for the blue worsted? After you with the thimble, if you please." Ha, ha, ha, ha!'

'I dare say they can cook,' said Diana. 'Men can broil a steak; and there are always eggs and bread-and-butter.'

'But how wonderfully strange,' cried Cecilia. 'How romantic! As good as a ruin. Oh, how I long to see 'em.'

2

THE ACQUAINTANCE WAS not slow in coming. With naval promptness Admiral Haddock invited the ladies of Mapes to dine with the newcomers, and presently Captain Aubrey and Dr Maturin were asked to dinner at Mapes; they were pronounced excellent young men, most agreeable company, perfectly well-bred, and a great addition to the neighbourhood. It was clear to Sophia, however, that poor Dr Maturin needed feeding properly: 'he was quite pale and silent,' she said. But even the tenderest heart, the most given to pity, could not have said the same for Jack. He was in great form from even the beginning of the party, when his laugh was to be heard coming up the drive, until the last repeated farewells under the freezing portico. His fine open battle-scarred countenance had worn either a smile or a look of lively pleasure from the first to the last, and although his blue eye had dwelt a little wistfully upon the stationary decanter and the disappearing remains of the pudding, his cheerful flow of small but perfectly amiable talk had never faltered.

He had eaten everything set before him with grateful voracity, and even Mrs Williams felt something like an affectionate leaning towards him.

'Well,' she said, as their hoof-beats died away in the night, 'I believe that was as successful a dinner-party as I have ever given. Captain Aubrey managed a second partridge – but then they were so very tender. And the floating island looked particularly well in the silver bowl: there will be enough for tomorrow. And the rest of the pork will be delicious, hashed. How well they ate, to be sure: I do not suppose they often have a dinner like that. I wonder at the admiral, saying that Captain Aubrey was not quite the thing. I think he is *very much* the thing. Sophie, my love, pray tell John to put the port the gentlemen left into a small bottle at once, before he locks up: it is bad for the decanter to leave port-wine in it.'

'Yes, Mama.'

'Now, my dears,' whispered Mrs Williams, having left a significant pause after the closing of the door, 'I dare say you all noticed Captain Aubrey's great interest in Sophia – he was quite particular. I have little doubt that – I think it would be very nice if we were all to leave them alone together as much as possible. Are you attending, Diana?'

'Oh, yes, ma'am. I understand you perfectly well,' said Diana, turning back from the window. Far over in the moonlit night the pale road wound between Polcary and Beacon Down, and the horsemen were walking briskly up it.

'I wonder, I wonder,' said Jack, 'whether there is any goose left at home, or whether those infernal brutes have eaten it up. At all events, we can have an omelet and a bottle of claret. Claret. Have you ever known a woman that had any notion of wine?'

'I have not.'

'And damned near with the pudding, too. But what charming girls they are! Did you notice the eldest one, Miss Williams, holding up her wine-glass and looking at the candle

through it? Such grace . . . The taper of her wrist and hand –
long, long fingers.' Stephen Maturin was scratching himself
with a dogged perseverance; he was not attending. But Jack
went on, 'And that Mrs Villiers, how beautifully she held her
head: lovely colouring. Perhaps not such a perfect complexion as her cousin – she has been in India, I believe – but
what deep blue eyes! How old would she be, Stephen?'

'Not thirty.'

'I remember how well she sat her horse . . . By God, a year
or two back I should have – . How a man changes. But even
so, I do love being surrounded by girls – so very different
from men. She said several handsome things about the service – spoke very sensibly – thoroughly understood the
importance of the weather-gage. She must have naval connections. I do hope we see her again. I hope we see them all
again.'

They saw her again, and sooner than they had expected.
Mrs Williams too just happened to be passing by Melbury,
and she directed Thomas to turn up the well-known drive. A
deep and powerful voice the other side of the door was
singing

> You ladies of lubricity
> That dwell in the bordello
> Ha-ha ha-ha, ha-ha ha-hee
> For I am that kind of fellow,

but the ladies walked into the hall quite unmoved, since not
one of them except Diana understood the words, and she was
not easily upset. With great satisfaction they noticed that the
servant who let them in had a pigtail half-way down his back,
but the parlour into which he showed them was disappoint-
ingly trim – it might have been spring-cleaned that morning,
reflected Mrs Williams, drawing her finger along the top of
the wainscot. The only thing that distinguished it from an
ordinary Christian parlour was the rigid formation of the

chairs, squared to one another like the yards of a ship, and the bell-pull, which was three fathoms of cable, wormed and served, and ending in a brass-bound top-block.

The powerful voice stopped, and it occurred to Diana that someone's face must be going red; it was indeed highly coloured when Captain Aubrey came hurrying in, but he did not falter as he cried, 'Why, this is most neighbourly – truly kind – a very good afternoon to you, ma'am. Mrs Villiers, Miss Williams, your servant – Miss Cecilia, Miss Frances, how happy I am to see you. Pray step into the . . .'

'We just happened to be passing by,' said Mrs Williams, 'and I thought we might just stop for a moment, to ask how the jasmin is thriving.'

'Jasmin?' cried Jack.

'Yes,' said Mrs Williams, avoiding her daughters' eyes. 'Ah, the jasmin. Pray step into the drawing-room. Dr Maturin and I have a fire in there: and he is the fellow to tell you all about jasmin.'

The winter drawing-room at Melbury Lodge was a handsome five-sided room with two walls opening on to the garden, and at the far end there stood a light-coloured pianoforte, surrounded by sheets of music and covered by many more. Stephen Maturin rose from behind the piano, bowed, and stood silently watching the visitors. He was wearing a black coat so old that it was green in places, and he had not shaved for three days: from time to time he passed his hand over his rasping jaw.

'Why, you are musicians, I declare!' cried Mrs Williams. 'Violins – a 'cello! How I love music. Symphonies, cantatas! Do you touch the instrument, sir?' she asked Stephen. She did not usually notice him, for Dr Vining had explained that naval surgeons were often poorly qualified and always badly paid; but she was feeling well-disposed today.

'I have just been picking out this piece, ma'am,' said Stephen. 'But the piano is sadly out of tune.'

'I think not, sir,' said Mrs Williams. 'It was the most expen-

sive instrument to be had – a Clementi. I remember its coming by the waggon as though it were yesterday.'

'Pianos do go out of tune, Mama,' murmured Sophia.

'Not Clementi's pianos, my dear,' said Mrs Williams with a
smile. 'They are the most expensive in London. Clementi
supplies the Court,' she added, looking reproachful, as
though they had been wanting in loyalty. 'Besides, sir,' she
said, turning to Jack, 'it was my eldest daughter who painted
the case! The pictures are in the Chinese taste.'

'That clinches it, ma'am,' cried Jack. 'It would be an
ungrateful instrument that fell off, having been decorated by
Miss Williams. We were admiring the landscape with the
pagoda this morning, were we not, Stephen?'

'Yes,' said Stephen, lifting the adagio of Hummel's D major
sonata off the lid. 'This was the bridge and tree and pagoda
that we liked so much.' It was a charming thing, the size of a
tea-tray – pure, sweet lines, muted, gentle colours that might
have been lit by an innocent moon.

Embarrassed, as she so often was, by her mother's strident
voice, and confused by all this attention, Sophia hung her
head: with a self-possession that she neither felt nor seemed
to feel she said, 'Was this the piece you was playing, sir? Mr
Tindall has made me practise it over and over again.'

She moved away from the piano, carrying the sheets, and at
this point the drawing-room was filled with activity. Mrs
Williams protested that she would neither sit down nor take any
refreshment whatsoever; Preserved Killick and John Witsoever,
able seamen, brought in tables, trays, urns, more coal; Frances
whispered 'What ho, for ship's biscuit and a swig of rum,' to
make Cecilia giggle; and Jack slowly began shepherding Mrs
Williams and Stephen out of the room through the french windows in the direction of what he took to be the jasmin.

The true jasmin, however, proved to be on the library wall;
and so it was from outside the library windows that Jack and
Stephen heard the familiar notes of the adagio, as silvery and
remote as a musical-box. It was absurd how the playing

resembled the painting: light, ethereal, tenuous. Stephen Maturin winced at the flat A and the shrill C; and at the beginning of the first variation he glanced uneasily at Jack to see whether he too was jarred by the mistaken phrasing. But Jack seemed wholly taken up with Mrs Williams's account of the planting of the shrub, a minute and circumstantial history.

Now there was another hand on the keyboard. The adagio came out over the sparse wintery lawn with a fine ringing tone, inaccurate, but strong and free; there was harshness in the tragic first variation – a real understanding of what it meant.

'How well dear Sophia plays,' said Mrs Williams, leaning her head to one side. 'Such a sweetly pretty tune, too.'

'Surely that is not Miss Williams, ma'am?' cried Stephen.

'Indeed it is, sir,' cried Mrs Williams. 'Neither of her sisters can go beyond the scales, and I know for a fact that Mrs Villiers cannot read a note. She would not apply herself to the drudgery.' And as they walked back to the house through the mud Mrs Williams told them what they should know about drudgery, taste, and application.

Mrs Villiers started up from the piano, but not so quickly as to escape Mrs Williams's indignant eye – an eye so indignant that it did not lose its expression for the rest of the visit. It even outlasted Jack's announcement of a ball in commemoration of the Battle of Saint Vincent, and the gratification of being the first guests to be bespoke.

'You recall Sir John Jervis's action, ma'am, off Cape Saint Vincent? The fourteenth of February, ninety-seven. Saint Valentine's day.'

'Certainly I do, sir: but' – with an affected simper – 'of course my girls are too young to remember anything about it. Pray, did we win?'

'Of course we did, Mama,' hissed the girls.

'Of course we did,' said Mrs Williams. 'Pray sir, was you there – was you present?'

'Yes, ma'am,' said Jack. 'I was third of the Orion. And so I always like to celebrate the anniversary of the battle with all the friends and shipmates I can bring together. And seeing there is a ballroom here – '

'YOU MAY DEPEND upon it, my dears,' said Mrs Williams, on the way home, 'that this ball is being given in compliment to us – to me and my daughters – and I have no doubt that Sophie will open it with Captain Aubrey. Saint Valentine's day, la! Frankie, you have dribbled chocolate all down your front; and if you eat so many rich pastries you will come out in spots, and then where will you be? No man will look at you. There must have been a dozen eggs and half a pound of butter in that smaller cake: I have never been so surprised in my life.'

Diana Villiers had been taken, after some hesitation, partly because it would have been indecent to leave her behind and partly because Mrs Williams thought there was no possible comparison between a woman with ten thousand pounds and one without ten thousand pounds; but further consideration, the pondering of certain intercepted looks, led Mrs Williams to think that the gentlemen of the Navy might not be so reliable as the local squires and their hard-faced offspring.

Diana was aware of most of the motions of her aunt's mind, and after breakfast the next day she was quite prepared to follow her into her room for 'a little chat, my dear'. But she was quite unprepared for the bright smile and the repeated mention of the word 'horse'. Hitherto it had always meant Sophia's little chestnut mare. 'How good-natured of Sophie to lend you her horse again. I hope it is not too tired this time, poor thing.' But now the suggestion, the downright offer, wrapped in many words, was of a horse for herself. It was a clear bribe to leave the field clear: it was also meant to overcome Sophia's reluctance to deprive her cousin of the mare, and thus to go riding with Captain Aubrey or Dr Maturin herself. Diana accepted the bait, spat out the hook with con-

tempt, and hurried away to the stables to consult with
Thomas, for the great horse-fair at Marston was just at hand.

On the way she saw Sophia coming along the path that led
through the park to Grope, Admiral Haddock's house. Sophia
was walking fast, swinging her arms and muttering 'Larboard,
starboard,' as she came.

'Yo ho, shipmate,' called Diana over the hedge, and she was
surprised to see her cousin blush cherry-pink. The chance
shot had gone straight home, for Sophia had been browsing
in the admiral's library, looking at Navy Lists, naval memoirs,
Falconer's *Dictionary of the Marine*, and the *Naval Chronicle*;
and the admiral, coming up behind her in his list slippers had
said, 'Oh, the *Naval Chronicle*, is it? Ha, ha! This is the one
you want,' – pulling out the volume for 1801. 'Though Miss
Di has been before you – forestalled you long ago – made me
explain the weather-gage and the difference between a xebec
and a brig. There is a little cut of the action, but the fellow
did not know what he was about, so he put in a great quantity
of smoke to hide the rigging, which is most particular in a
xebec. Come, let me find it for you.'

'Oh no, no, no,' said Sophia in great distress. 'I only wanted
to know a little about – ' Her voice died away.

THE ACQUAINTANCE RIPENED; but it did not mature, it
did not progress as fast as Mrs Williams would have liked.
Captain Aubrey could not have been more friendly – perhaps
too friendly; there was none of that languishing she longed to
see, no pallor, nor even any marked particularity. He seemed
to be as happy with Frances as he was with Sophia, and
sometimes Mrs Williams wondered whether he really were
quite the thing – whether those strange tales about sea-officers might possibly be true in his case. Was it not very odd
that he should live with Dr Maturin? Another thing that troubled her was Diana's horse, for from what she heard and from
what little she could understand, it seemed that Diana rode
better than Sophia. Mrs Williams could hardly credit this,

but even so she was heartily sorry that she had ever made the present. She was in a state of anxious doubt: she was certain that Sophia was moved, but she was equally certain that Sophia would never speak to her of her feelings, just as she was certain that Sophia would never follow her advice about making herself attractive to the gentlemen – putting herself forward a little, doing herself justice, reddening her lips before she came into the room.

Had she seen them out one day with young Mr Edward Savile's pack she would have been more anxious still. Sophia did not really care for hunting: she liked the gallops, but she found the waiting about dull and she minded terribly about the poor fox. Her mare had spirit but no great stamina, whereas Diana's powerful, short-coupled bay gelding had a barrel like a vault of a church and an unconquerable heart; he could carry Diana's eight stone from morning till night, and he loved to be in at the kill.

They had been hunting since half past ten, and now the sun was low. They had killed two foxes, and the third, a barren vixen, had led them a rare old dance, right away into the heavy country beyond Plimpton with its wet plough, double oxers, and wide ditches. She was now only one field ahead, failing fast and heading for a drain she knew. At the last check Jack had a lucky inspiration to bear away right-handed, a short-cut that brought him and Sophia closer to hounds than anyone in the field; but now there was a bank, a towering fence, mud in front of it and the gleam of broad water beyond. Sophia looked at the jump with dismay, put her tired horse at it without any real wish to reach the other side, and felt thankful when the mare refused it. She and her mount were quite done up; Sophia had never felt so tired in her life; she dreaded the sight of the fox being torn to pieces, and the pack had just hit off the line again. There was a deadly implacable triumph in the voice of the old bitch that led them. 'The gate, the gate,' called Jack, wheeling his horse and cantering to the corner of the field. He had it half open – an awkward, sagging, left-handed gate – when Stephen arrived. Jack heard Sophia say 'should like to go home – pray, pray go on – know the way perfectly.' The piteous face wiped away his look of frustration; he lost his fixed 'boarders away' expression, and smiling very kindly he said, 'I think I will turn back too: we have had enough for today.'

'I will see Miss Williams home,' said Stephen.

'No, no, please go on,' begged Sophia, with tears brimming in her eyes. 'Please, please – I am perfectly – '

A quick drumming of hooves and Diana came into the field. Her whole being was concentrated on the fence and what lay beyond it, and she saw them only a vague group muddling in a gate. She was sitting as straight and supple as if she had been riding for no more than half an hour: she was part of her horse, completely unaware of herself. She went straight at the fence, gathered her horse just so, and with a crash and a spray of mud they were over. Her form, her high-held head, her contained joy, competent, fierce gravity, were as beautiful as anything Jack or Stephen had ever seen. She had not the slightest notion of it, but she had never looked so well in her life. The men's faces as she flew over, high and true, would have made Mrs Williams more uneasy by far.

Mrs Williams longed for the day of the ball; she made almost as many preparations as Jack, and Mapes Court was filled with gauze, muslins and taffeta. Her mind was filled with stratagems, one of which was to get Diana out of the way for the intervening days. Mrs Williams had no defined suspicions, but she smelt danger, and by means of half a dozen intermediaries and as many letters she managed to have a mad cousin left unattended by his family. She could not do away with the invitation, publicly given and accepted, however, and Diana was to be brought back to Champflower by one of Captain Aubrey's guests on the morning of February the fourteenth.

'Dr Maturin is waiting for you, Di,' said Cecilia. 'He is walking his horse up and down in a fine new bottle-green coat with a black collar. And he has a new tie-wig. I suppose that is why he went up to London. You have made another conquest, Di: he used to be quite horrid, and all unshaved.'

'Stop peering from behind that curtain like a housemaid, Cissy. And lend me your hat, will you?'

'Why, he is quite splendid now,' said Cecilia, peering still and puckering the gauze. 'He has a spotted waistcoat too. Do you remember when he came to dinner in carpet slippers? He really would be almost handsome if he held himself up.'

'A fine conquest,' said Mrs Williams, peering too. 'A penniless naval surgeon, somebody's natural son, and a Papist. Fie upon you, Cissy, to say such things.'

'Good morning, Maturin,' said Diana, coming down the steps. 'I hope I have not kept you waiting. What a neat cob you have there, upon my word! You never found him in this part of the world.'

'Good morning, Villiers. You are late. You are very late.'

'It is the one advantage there is in being a woman. You do know I am a woman, Maturin?'

'I am obliged to suppose it, since you affect to have no notion of time – cannot tell what o'clock it is. Though why the trifling accident of sex should induce a sentient being, let alone such an intelligent being as you, to waste half this beautiful clear morning, I cannot conceive. Come, let me help you to mount. Sex – sex . . .'

'Hush, Maturin. You must not use words like that here. It was bad enough yesterday.'

'Yesterday? Oh, yes. But I am not the first man to say that wit is the unexpected copulation of ideas. Far from it. It is a commonplace.'

'As far as my aunt is concerned you are certainly the first man who ever used such an expression in public.'

They rode up Heberden Down: a still, brilliant morning with a little frost; the creak of leather, the smell of horse, steaming breath. 'I am not in the least degree interested in women as such,' said Stephen. 'Only in persons. There is

Polcary,' he added, nodding over the valley. 'That is where I
first saw you, on your cousin's chestnut. Let us ride over
there tomorrow. I can show you a remarkable family of parti-
coloured stoats, a congregation of stoats.'

'I must cry off for tomorrow,' said Diana. 'I am so sorry, I
have to go to Dover to look after an old gentleman who is not
quite right in the head, a sort of cousin.'

'But you will be back for the ball, sure?' cried Stephen.

'Oh, yes. It is all arranged. A Mr Babbington is to take me
up on his way. Did not Captain Aubrey tell you?'

'I was back very late last night, and we hardly spoke this
morning. But I must go to Dover myself next week. May I
come and beg for a cup of tea?'

'Indeed you may. Mr Lowndes imagines he is a teapot; he
crooks one arm like this for the handle, holds out the other
for the spout, and says, "May I have the pleasure of pouring
you a cup of tea?" You could not come to a better address. But
you also have to go to town again, do you not?'

'I do. From Monday till Thursday.' She reined in her horse
to a walk, and with a hesitation and a shyness that changed
her face entirely, giving it a resemblance to Sophia's, she said,
'Maturin, may I beg you to do me a kindness?'

'Certainly,' said Stephen, looking straight into her eyes and
then quickly away at the sight of the painful emotion in them.

'You know something of my position here, I believe . . .
Would you sell this bit of jewellery for me? I must have something to wear at the ball.'

'What must I ask for it?'

'Would they not make an offer, do you think? If I could get
ten pounds, I should be happy. And if they should give so
much, then would you be even kinder and tell Harrison in
the Royal Exchange to send me this list immediately? Here is
a pattern of the stuff. It could come by the mail-coach as far
as Lewes, and the carrier could pick it up. I must have something to wear.'

Something to wear. Unpicked, taken in, let out, and folded

in tissue-paper, it lay in the trunk that stood waiting in Mr Lowndes's hall on the morning of the fourteenth.

'Mr Babbington to see you, ma'am,' said the servant.

Diana hurried into the parlour – her smile faded – she looked again, and lower than she would have thought possible she saw a figure in a three-caped coat that piped, 'Mrs Villiers, ma'am? Babbington reporting, if you please, ma'am.'

'Oh, Mr Babbington, good morning. How do you do? Captain Aubrey tells me you will be so very kind as to take me with you to Melbury Lodge. When do you please to start? We must not let your horse take cold. I have only a little trunk – it is ready by the front door. You will take a glass of wine before we leave, sir? Or I believe you sea-officers like rum?'

'A tot of rum to keep out the cold would be prime. You will join me, ma'am? It's uncommon parky, out.'

'A very little glass of rum, and put a great deal of water in it,' whispered Diana to the servant. But the girl was too flustered by the presence of a strange dogcart in the courtyard to understand the word 'water', and she brought a dark-brown brimming tumbler that Mr Babbington drank off with great composure. Diana's alarm increased at the sight of the tall, dashing dogcart and the nervous horse, all white of eye and laid-back ears. 'Where is your groom, sir?' she asked. 'Is he in the kitchen?'

'There ain't a groom in this crew, ma'am,' said Babbington, now looking at her with open admiration. 'I navigate myself. May I give you a leg up? Your foot on this little step and heave away. Now this rug – we make it fast aft, with these beckets. All a-tanto? Let go by the head,' he called to the gardener, and they dashed out of the forecourt, giving the white-painted post a shrewd knock as they passed.

Mr Babbington's handling of the whip and the reins raised Diana's dismay to a new pitch; she had been brought up among horse-soldiers, and she had never seen anything like this in her life. She wondered how he could possibly have come all the way from Arundel without a spill. She thought of her trunk behind and when they left the main road, winding along the lanes, sometimes mounting the bank and sometimes shaving the ditch's edge, she said, 'It will never do. This young man will have to be taken down.'

The lane ran straight up hill, rising higher and higher, with God knows what breakneck descent the other side. The horse slowed to a walk – the bean-fed horse, as it proved by a thunderous, long, long fart.

'I beg your pardon,' said the midshipman in the silence.

'Oh, that's all right,' said Diana coldly. 'I thought it was the horse.' A sideways glance showed that this had settled Babbington's hash for the moment. 'Let me show you how we do it in India,' she said, gathering the reins and taking his whip away from him. But once she had established contact with the horse and had him going steadily along the path he should follow, Diana turned her mind to winning back Mr Babbington's kindness and good will. Would he explain the blue, the red, and the white squadrons to her? The weathergage? Tell her about life at sea in general? Surely it must be a very dangerous, demanding service, though of course so highly and so rightly honoured – the country's safeguard. Could it be true that he had taken part in the famous action with the *Cacafuego*? Diana could not remember a more striking disparity of forces. Captain Aubrey must be very like Lord Nelson.

'Oh yes, ma'am!' cried Babbington. 'Though I doubt even Nelson could have brought it off so handsome. He is a prodigious man. Though by land, you know, he is quite different. You would take him for an ordinary person – not the least coldness or distance. He came down to our place to help my uncle in the election, and he was as jolly as a grig – knocked down a couple of Whigs with his stick. They went down like ninepins – both of them poachers and Methodies, of course. Oh, it was such fun, and at Melbury he let me and old Pullings choose our horses and ride a race with him. Three times round the paddock and the horse to be ridden upstairs into the library for a guinea a side and a bottle of wine. Oh, we all love him, ma'am, although he's so taut at sea.'

'Who won?'

'Oh, well,' said Babbington, 'we all fell off, more or less, at different times. Though I dare say he did it on purpose, not to take our money.'

They stopped to bait at an inn, and with a meal and a pint of ale inside him Babbington said, 'I think you are the prettiest girl I have ever seen. You are to change in my room, which I am very glad of, now; and if I had known it was you, I should have bought a pincushion and a large bottle of scent.'

'You are a very fine figure of a man, too, sir,' said Diana. 'I am so happy to be travelling under your protection.'

Babbington's spirits mounted to an alarming degree; he had been brought up in a service where enterprise counted for everything, and presently it became necessary to occupy his attention with the horse. She had meant to allow him only the dash up the drive, but in the event he held the reins all the way from Newton Priors to the door of Melbury Lodge, where he handed her down in state, to the admiration of two dozen naval eyes.

There was something about Diana, a certain piratical dash and openness, that was very attractive to sea-officers; but they were also much attracted by the two Miss Simmonses' doll-like prettiness, by Frances dancing down the middle with the tip of her tongue showing as she kept the measure, by Cecilia's commonplace, healthy good looks, and by all the other charms that were displayed under the blaze of candles in the long handsome ballroom. And they were moon-struck by Sophia's grace as she and Captain Aubrey opened the ball: Sophia had on a pink dress with a gold sash, and Diana said to Stephen Maturin, 'She is lovely. There is not another woman in the room to touch her. That is the most dangerous colour in the world, but with her complexion it is perfect. I would give my eye-teeth for such a skin.'

'The gold and the pearls help,' said Stephen. 'The one

echoes her hair and the other her teeth. I will tell you a thing about women. They are superior to men in this, that they have an unfeigned, objective, candid admiration for good looks in other women – a real pleasure in their beauty. Yours, too, is a most elegant dress: other women admire it. I have remarked this. Not only from their glances, but most positively, by standing behind them and listening to their conversation.'

It was a good dress, a light, flimsy version of the naval blue, with white about it – no black, no concessions to Mrs Williams, for it was understood that at a ball any woman was allowed to make the best of herself; but where taste, figure and carriage are equal, a woman who can spend fifty guineas on her dress will look better than one who can only spend ten pounds.

'We must take our places,' said Diana a little louder as the second violins struck in and the ballroom filled with sound. It was a fine sight, hung with bunting in the naval way – the signal *engage the enemy more closely*, among other messages understood by the sailors alone – shining with bees-wax and candlelight, crowded to the doors, and the lane of dancing figures: pretty dresses, fine coats, white gloves, all reflected in the french windows and in the tall looking-glass behind the band. The whole neighbourhood was there, together with a score of new faces from Portsmouth, Chatham, London, or wherever the peace had cast them on shore; they were all in their best clothes; they were all determined to enjoy themselves; and so far they were succeeding to admiration. Everyone was pleased, not only by the rarity of a ball (not above three in in those parts, apart from the Assembly), but by the handsome, unusual way in which it was done, by the seamen in their blue jackets and pigtails, so very unlike the greasy hired waiters generally to be seen, and by the fact that for once there were more men than women – men in large numbers, all of them eager to dance.

Mrs Williams was sitting with the other parents and chaperons by the double doors into the supper-room, where she could rake the whole line of dancers, and her red face was nodding and smiling – significant smiles, emphatic nods – as she told her cousin Simmons that she had encouraged the whole thing from the beginning. Crossing over in the dance, Diana saw her triumphant face: and the next face she saw, immediately in front of her, was Jack's as he advanced to hand her about. 'Such a lovely ball, Aubrey,' she said, with a flashing smile. He was in gold-laced scarlet, a big, commanding figure: his forehead was sweating and his eyes shone with excitement and pleasure. He took her in with benevolent approval, said something meaningless but kind, and whirled her about.

'Come in and sit down,' said Stephen, at the end of the second dance. 'You are looking pale.'

'Am I?' she cried, looking intently into a mirror. 'Do I look horrible?'

'You do not. But you must not get over-tired. Come and sit down in a fresher air. Come into the orangery.'

'I have promised to stand up with Admiral James. I will come after supper.'

Deserting the supper-table, three sailors, including Admiral James, pursued Diana into the orangery; but they withdrew when they saw Stephen waiting for her there with her shawl.

'I did not think the doctor had it in him,' said Mowett. 'In the *Sophie* we always looked on him as a sort of monk.'

'Damn him,' said Pullings. 'I thought I was getting on so well.'

'You are not cold?' asked Stephen, tucking the shawl round her shoulders; and as though the physical contact between his hand and her bare flesh established a contact, sending a message that had no need of words, he felt the change of current. But in spite of the intuition he said, 'Diana . . .'

'Tell me,' she said in a hard voice, cutting right across him, 'is that Admiral James married?'

'He is.'

'I thought so. You can smell the enemy a great way off.'

'Enemy?'

'Of course. Don't be a fool, Maturin. You must know that married men are the worst enemies women can have. Get me something to drink, will you? I am quite faint with all that fug.'

'This is Sillery; this iced punch.'

'Thank you. They offer what they call friendship or some stuff of that kind – the name don't matter – and all they want in return for this great favour is your heart, your life, your future, your – I will not be coarse, but you know very well what I mean. There is no friendship in men: I know what I am talking about, believe me. There is not one round here, from old Admiral Haddock to that young puppy of a curate, who has not tried it: to say nothing of India. Who the devil do they think I am?' she exclaimed, drumming on the arm of her chair. 'The only honest one was Southampton, who sent an old woman from Madras to say he would be happy to take me into keeping; and upon my honour, if I had known what my life in England, in this muddy hole with nothing but beer-swilling rustics, was going to be, I should have been tempted to accept. What do you think my life is like, without a sou and under the thumb of a vulgar, pretentious, ignorant woman who detests me? What do you think it is like, looking into this sort of a future, with my looks going, the only thing I have? Listen, Maturin, I speak openly to you, because I like you; I like you very much, and I believe you have a kindness for me – you are almost the only man I have met in England I can treat as a friend – trust as a friend.'

'You have my friendship, sure,' said Stephen heavily. After a long pause he said with a fair attempt at lightness, 'You are not altogether just. You look as desirable as you can – that dress, particularly the bosom of that dress, would inflame Saint Anthony, as you know very well. It is unjust to provoke a man and then to complain he is a satyr if the provocation succeeds. You are not a miss upon her promotion, moved by unconscious instinctive . . .'

'Do you tell me I am provocative?' cried Diana.

'Certainly I do. That is exactly what I am saying. But I do not suppose you know how much you make men suffer. In any case, you are arguing from the particular to the general: you have met some men who wish to take advantage of you and you go too far. Not all French waiters have red hair.'

'They all have red hair somewhere about them, and it shows sooner or later. But I do believe you are an exception, Maturin, and that is why I confide in you: I cannot tell you what a comfort it is. I was brought up among intelligent men – they were a loose lot on the Madras side and worse in Bombay, but they were intelligent, and oh how I miss them. And what a relief it is to be able to speak freely, after all this swimming in namby-pamby.'

'Your cousin Sophia is intelligent.'

'Do you really think so? Well, there is a sort of quickness, if you like; but she is a girl – we do not speak the same language. I grant you she is beautiful. She is really beautiful, but she knows nothing – how could she? – and I cannot forgive her her fortune. It is so unjust. Life is so unjust.' Stephen made no reply, but fetched her an ice. 'The only thing a man can offer a woman is marriage,' she went on. 'An equal marriage. I have about four or five years, and if I cannot find a husband by then, I shall . . . And where can one be found in this howling wilderness? Do I disgust you very much? I mean to put you off, you know.'

'Yes, I am aware of your motions, Villiers. You do not disgust me at all – you speak as a friend. You hunt; and your chase has a beast in view.'

'Well done, Maturin.'

'You insist upon an equal marriage?'

'At the very least. I shall despise a woman so poor-spirited, so wanting in courage, as to make a mésalliance. There was a smart little whippersnapper of an attorney in Dover that had the infernal confidence to make me an offer. I have never been so mortified in my life. I had rather go to the stake, or look after the Teapot for the rest of my days.'

'Define your beast.'

'I am not difficult. He must have some money, of course – love in a cottage be damned. He must have some sense; he must not be actually deformed, not too ancient. Admiral Haddock, for example, is beyond my limit, I do not insist upon it, but I should like him to be able to sit a horse and not fall off too often; and I should like him to be able to hold his wine. You do not get drunk, Maturin; that is one of the things I like about you. Captain Aubrey and half the other men here will have to be carried to bed.'

'No, I love wine, but I do not find it often affects my judgment: not often. I drank a good deal this evening, however. As far as Jack Aubrey is concerned, do you not think you may be a little late in the field? I have the impression that tonight may be decisive.'

'Has he told you anything? Has he confided in you?'

'You do not speak as you have just spoken to a tattle-tale of a man, I believe. As far as your knowledge of me goes, it is accurate.'

'In any case, you are wrong. I know Sophie. He may make a declaration, but she will need a longer time than this. She need never fear being left on the shelf – it never occurs to her at all, I dare say – and she is afraid of marriage. How she cried when I told her men had hair on their chests! And she hates being managed – that is not the word I want. What is it, Maturin?'

'Manipulated.'

'Exactly. She is a dutiful girl – a great sense of duty: I think it rather stupid, but there it is – but still she finds the way her mother has been arranging and pushing and managing and angling in all this perfectly odious. You two must have had hogsheads of that grocer's claret forced down your throats. Perfectly odious: and she is obstinate – strong, if you like – under that bread-and-butter way of hers. It will take a great deal to move her; much more than the excitement of a ball.'

'She is not attached?'

'Attached to Aubrey? I do not know; I do not suppose she knows herself. She likes him; she is flattered by his attentions; and to be sure he is a husband any woman would be glad to have – well-off, good-looking, distinguished in his profession and with a future before him, unexceptionable family, cheerful, good-natured. But she is entirely unsuited to him – I am persuaded she is, with her secretive, closed, stubborn nature. He needs someone much more awake, much more alive: they would never be happy.'

'She may have a passionate side, a side you know nothing about, or do not choose to see.'

'Stuff, Maturin. In any case, he needs a different woman and she needs a different man: in a way you might be much more suited to her, if you could stand her ignorance.'

'So Jack Aubrey might answer?'

'Yes, I like him well enough. I should prefer a man more – what shall I say? More grown up, less of a boy – less of a huge boy.'

'He is highly considered in his profession, as you said yourself, just now.'

'That is neither here nor there. A man may be brilliant in his calling and a mere child outside it. I remember a mathematician – they say he was one of the best in the world – who came out to India, to do something about Venus; and when his telescope was taken away from him, he was unfit for civilized life. A blundering schoolboy! He clung to my hand all through one tedious, tedious evening, sweating and stammering. No: give me the politicoes – they know how to live; and they are all reading men, more or less. I wish Aubrey were something of a reading man. More like you – I mean what I say. You are very good company: I like being with you. But he is a handsome fellow. Look,' she said, turning to the window, 'there he is, figuring away. He dances quite well, does he not? It is a pity he wants decision.'

'You would not say that if you saw him taking his ship into action.'

'I mean in his relations with women. He is sentimental. But still, he would do. Shall I tell you something that will really shock you, although you are a medical man? I was married, you know – I am not a girl – and intrigues were as common in India as they are in Paris. There are times when I am tempted to play the fool, terribly tempted. I dare say I should, too, if I lived in London and not in this dreary hole.'

'Tell me, have you reason to suppose that Jack is to your way of thinking?'

'About our suitability? Yes. There are signs that mean a lot to a woman. I wonder he ever looked seriously at Sophie. He is not interested, I suppose? Her fortune would not mean a great deal to him? Have you known him long? But I suppose all you naval people have known one another, or of one another, for ever.'

'Oh, I am no seaman, at all. I first met him in Minorca, in the year one, in the spring of the year one. I had taken a patient there, for the Mediterranean climate – he died – and I met Jack at a concert. We took a liking to one another, and he asked me to sail with him as his surgeon. I agreed, being quite penniless at the time, and we have been together ever since. I know him well enough to say that as for being inter-ested, concerned for a woman's fortune, there never was a man more unworldly than Jack Aubrey. Maybe I will tell you a thing about him.'

'Go on, Stephen.'

'Some time ago he had an unhappy affair with another offi-cer's wife. She had the dash, the style and the courage he loves, but she was a hard, false woman, and she wounded him very deeply. So virginal modesty, rectitude, principle, you know? have a greater charm for him than they might other-wise have had.'

'Ah? Yes, I *see*. I see now. And you have a béguin for her too? It is no use, I warn you. She would never do a thing without her mother's consent, and that is nothing to do with her mother's being in control of her fortune: it is all duty. And you would never bring my aunt Williams round in a thousand years. Still, you may feel on Sophie's side.'

'I have the greatest liking and admiration for her.'

'But no tendre?'

'Not as you would define it. But I am averse to giving pain, Villiers, which you are not.'

She stood up, as straight as a wand. 'We must go in. I have to dance this next bout with Captain Aubrey,' she said, kissing him. 'I am truly sorry if I hurt you, Maturin.'

3

FOR MANY YEARS Stephen Maturin had kept a diary in a crabbed and characteristically secret shorthand of his own. It was scattered with anatomical drawings, descriptions of plants, birds, moving creatures, and if it had been deciphered the scientific part would have been found to be in Latin; but the personal observations were all in Catalan, the language he had spoken most of his youth. The most recent entries were in that tongue.

'February 15 . . . then when she suddenly kissed me, the strength left my knees, quite ludicrously, and I could scarcely follow her into the ball-room with any countenance. I had sworn to allow no such thing again, no strong dolorous emotion ever again: my whole conduct of late proves how I lie. I have done everything in my power to get my heart under the harrow.

'February 21. I reflect upon Jack Aubrey. How helpless a man is, against direct attack by a woman. As soon as she leaves the schoolroom a girl learns to fend off, ward off wild love; it becomes second nature; it offends no code; it is commended not only by the world but even by those very men who are thus repulsed. How different for a man! He has no such accumulated depth of armour; and the more delicate, the more gallant, the more "honourable" he is the less he is able to withstand even a remote advance. He must not wound: and in this case there is little inclination to wound.

'When a face you have never seen without pleasure, that has never looked at you without a spontaneous smile, remains cold, unmoving, even inimical, at your approach, you are strangely cast down: you see another being and you are another being yourself. Yet life with Mrs W can be no party of pleasure; and magnanimity calls for understanding. For the moment it calls in vain. There are depths of barbarity, possibilities I did not suspect. Plain common sense calls for a disengagement.

'JA is uneasy, discontented with himself, discontented with Sophia's *reluctance* – coyness is no word to use for that dear sweet pure affectionate young woman's hesitation. Speaks of wincing fillies and their nonsense: he has never been able to bear frustration. This in part is what Diana Villiers means by his immaturity. If he did but know it the evident mutual liking between him and DV is in fact good for his suit. Sophia is perhaps the most respectable girl I have known, but she is after all a woman. JA is not percipient in these matters. Yet on the other hand he is beginning to look at me with some doubt. This is the first time there has been any reserve in our friendship; it is painful to me and I believe to him. I cannot bring myself to look upon him with anything but affection; but when I think of the possibilities, the physical possibilities I say, why then –

'DV insists upon my inviting her to Melbury to play billiards: she plays well, of course – can give either of us twenty in a hundred. Her insistence is accompanied by an ignoble bullying and an ignoble pretty pretty cajolery, to which I yield, both of us knowing exactly what we are about. This talk of friendship deceives neither of us; and yet it does exist, even on her side, I believe. My position would be the most humiliating in the world but for the fact that she is not so clever as she thinks: her theory is excellent, but she has not the control of her pride or her other passions to carry it into effect. She is cynical, but not nearly cynical enough, whatever she may say. If she were, I should not be obsessed. Quo me rapis? Quo indeed. My whole conduct, meekness, mansuetude, voluntary abasement, astonishes me.

'Quaere: is the passionate intensity of my feeling for Catalan independence the cause of my virile resurrection or its effect? There is a direct relationship, I am sure. Bartolomeu's report should reach England in three days if the wind holds.'

'STEPHEN, STEPHEN, STEPHEN!' Jack's voice came along the corridor, growing louder and ending in a roar as he thrust his head into the room. 'Oh, there you are. I was afraid you had gone off to your stoats again. The carrier has brought you an ape.'

'What sort of an ape?' asked Stephen.

'A damned ill-conditioned sort of an ape. It had a can of ale at every pot-house on the road, and it is reeling drunk. It has been offering itself to Babbington.'

'Then it is Dr Lloyd's lewd mangabey. He believes it to be suffering from the furor uterinus, and we are to open it together when I return.'

Jack looked at his watch. 'What do you say to a hand of cards before we go?'

'With all my heart.'

Piquet was their game. The cards flew fast, shuffled, cut, and dealt again: they had played together so long that each knew the other's style through and through. Jack's was a cunning alternation of risking everything for the triumphant point of eight, and of a steady, orthodox defence, fighting for every last trick. Stephen's was based upon Hoyle, Laplace, the theory of probabilities, and his knowledge of Jack's character.

'A point of five,' said Jack.

'Not good.'

'A quart.'

'To what?'

'The knave.'

'Not good.'

'Three queens.'

'Not good.'

They played. 'The rest are mine,' said Stephen, as the singleton king fell to his ace. 'Ten for cards, and capot. We must stop. Five guineas, if you please; you shall have your revenge in London.'

'If I had not thrown away my hearts,' said Jack, 'I should have had you on toast. What amazing cards you have held these last few weeks, Stephen.'

'Skill enters into this game.'

'It is luck, all luck! You have the most amazing luck with cards. I should be sorry, was you in love with anyone.'

The pause lasted no more than a second before the door opened and the horses were reported alongside, but its effect hung about them for miles as they trotted through the cold drizzle along the London road.

However, the rain stopped while they were eating their dinner at the Bleeding Heart, their half-way point, a cheerful sun came out, and they saw the first swallow of the year, a blue curve skimming over the horse-pond at Edenbridge. Long before they walked into Thacker's, the naval coffee-house, they were far back in their old easy ways, talking without the least constraint about the sea, the service, the possibility of migrant birds navigating by the stars at night, of an Italian violin that Jack was tempted to buy, and of the renewal of teeth in elephants.

'Aubrey, so it is!' cried Captain Fowler, rising from his shadowy box in the far end of the room. 'We were just talking about you. Andrews was here until five minutes ago, telling us about your ball in the country – in Sussex. He said it was the finest thing – girls by the dozen, fine women, such a ball! He told us all about it. Pray,' he said, looking arch, 'are we to congratulate you?'

'Not – not exactly, sir, thank you very much however. Perhaps a little later, if all goes well.'

'Clap on, clap on! Else you will regret it when you are old – damnably mouldy a hundred years hence. Am not I right, Doctor? How do you do? Am I not right? If only he will clap on, we may see him a grandfather yet. My grandson has six teeth! Six teeth in his head already!'

'I SHALL NOT spend long with Jackson, I just want a little ready money – you have stripped me with your infernal run of luck – and the latest news from the prize-court,' said Jack, referring to his prize-agent and man of business. 'And then I shall go to Bond Street. It is a prodigious sum to pay for a fiddle, and I do not think I could square it with my conscience. I am not really a good enough player. But I should just like to handle it again, and tuck it under my chin.'

'A good fiddle would bring you into bloom, and you earned an Amati by every minute you spent on the deck of the *Cacafuego*. Certainly you must have your fiddle. Any innocent pleasure is a real good: there are not so many of them.'

'Must I? I have a great respect for your judgment, Stephen. If you are not long at the Admiralty, perhaps you would step round and give me your opinion of its tone.'

Stephen walked into the Admiralty, gave his name to the porter, and was shown straight past the notorious waiting-room, where an anxious, disconsolate and often shabby crowd of shipless officers were waiting for an interview, an almost certainly hopeless interview.

He was received by an elderly man in a black coat – received with marked consideration and begged to take a seat. Sir Joseph would be with them as soon as the Board rose; they had been sitting an hour longer than had been expected; and in the mean time Black Coat would be happy to deal with certain main heads. They had received Bartolomeu's report.

'Before we begin, sir,' said Stephen, 'may I suggest that I

should use another entrance or that our meetings should take place in another house? There was a fellow lounging about by the hazard on the other side of Whitehall whom I have seen in the company of Spaniards from the embassy. I may be mistaken; it may be mere chance; but – '

Sir Joseph hurried in. 'Dr Maturin, I do apologize for keeping you. Nothing but the Board would have prevented me from . . . How do you do, sir? It is most exceedingly good of you to come up at such short notice. We have received Bartolomeu's report, and we urgently wish to consult you upon several points that arise. May we go through it, head by head? His lordship particularly desired me to let him have the results of our conversation by tonight.'

The British government was well aware that Catalonia, the Spanish province or rather collection of provinces that contained most of the wealth and the industry of the kingdom, was animated by a desire to regain its independence; the government knew that the peace might not last – Bonaparte was building ships as fast as he could – and that a divided Spain would greatly weaken any coalition he might bring into an eventual war. The various groups of Catalan autonomists who had approached the government had made this plain, though it was obvious before: this was not the first time England had been concerned with Catalonia nor with dividing her potential enemies. The Admiralty, of course, was interested in the Catalan ports, shipyards, docks, naval supplies and industries; Barcelona itself would be of incalculable value, and there were many other harbours, including Port Mahon in Minorca, the British possession, so strangely given up by the politicians when they negotiated the recent peace-treaty. The Admiralty, following the English tradition of independent intelligence agencies with little or no communication between them, had their own people dealing with this question. But few of them could speak the language, few knew much about the history of the nation, and none could evaluate the claims of the different bodies that put themselves forward as the true representatives of the country's resistance. There were some Barcelona merchants, and a few from Valencia; but they were limited men, and the long war had kept them out of touch with their friends; Dr Maturin was the Admiralty's most esteemed adviser. He was known to have had revolutionary contacts in his younger days, but his integrity, his complete disinterestedness were never called into question. The Admiralty also had a touching respect for scientific eminence, and no less a person than the Physician of the Fleet vouched for Stephen Maturin's. 'Dr Maturin's *Tar-Water Reconsidered* and his remarks on suprapubic cystotomy should be in every naval surgeon's chest: such acuity of practical observation . . .' Whitehall had a higher opinion of him than Champflower: Whitehall knew that he was a physician, no mere surgeon; that he was a man of some estate in Lérida; and that his Irish father had been connected with the first families of that kingdom. Black Coat and his colleagues also knew that in his character as a physician, a learned man of standing perfectly at home in both Catalan and Spanish, he could move about the country as freely as any native – an incomparable agent, sure, discreet, deeply covered: a man of their own kind. And from their point of view his remaining tinge of Catholicism was but one advantage more. They would have wrung and squeezed their secret funds to retain him, and he would take nothing: the most delicate sounding produced no hint of an echo, no gleam in his purse's eye.

He left the Admiralty by a side door, walked through the park and up across Piccadilly to Bond Street, where he found Jack still undecided. 'I tell you what it is, Stephen,' he said. 'I do not know that I really like its tone. Listen – '

'If the day were a little warmer, sir,' said the shopman, 'it would bring out its fruitiness. You should have heard Mr Galignani playing it when we still had the fire going, last week.'

'Well, I don't know,' said Jack. 'I think I shall leave it for today. Just put up these strings in a paper for me, will you, together with the rosin. Keep the fiddle, and I will let you know one way or the other by the end of the week. Stephen,' he said, taking his friend's arm and guiding him across the busy street, 'I must have been playing that fiddle a good hour and more, and I still don't know my own mind. Jackson was not in the way, nor his partner, so I came straight here. It was odd, damned vexing and odd, for we had appointed to meet. But he was not at home: just this fool of a clerk, who said he was out of town – they expected him, but could not tell when. I shall pay my respects to Old Jarvie, just to keep myself in mind, and then we can go home. I shall not wait for Jackson.'

They rode back, and where they had left the rain there they found it again, rain, and a fierce wind from the east. Jack's horse lost a shoe, and they wasted the best part of the afternoon finding a smith, a surly, awkward brute who sent his nails in too deep. It was dark when they reached Ashdown Forest; by this time Jack's horse was lame, and they still had a long ride before them.

'Let me look to your pistols,' said Jack, as the trees came closer to the road. 'You have no notion of hammering your flints.'

'They are very well,' said Stephen, unwilling to open his holsters (a teratoma in one, a bottled Arabian dormouse in the other). 'Do you apprehend any danger?'

'This is an ugly stretch of road, with all these disbanded soldiers turned loose. They made an attempt upon the mail not far from Aker's Cross. Come, let me have your pistols. I thought as much: what is this?'

'A teratoma,' said Stephen sulkily.

'What is a teratoma?' asked Jack, holding the object in his hand. 'A kind of grenado?'

'It is an inward wen, a tumour: we find them, occasionally, in the abdominal cavity. Sometimes they contain long black hair, sometimes a set of teeth: this has both hair and teeth. It belonged to a Mr Elkins of the City, an eminent cheesemonger. I prize it much.'

'By God,' cried Jack, thrusting it back into the holster and wiping his hand vehemently upon the horse, 'I do wish you would leave people's bellies alone. So you have no pistols at all, I collect?'

'If you wish to be so absolute, no, I have not.'

'You will never make old bones, brother,' said Jack, dismounting and feeling the horse's leg. 'There is an inn, not a bad inn, half a mile off the side-road: what do you say to lying there tonight?'

'Your mind is much disturbed by the thought of these robbers, highwaymen, footpads?'

'I tremble so that I can hardly sit on my horse. It would be stupid to get knocked on the head, to be sure, but I am thinking more of my horse's legs. And then again,' he said, after a pause, 'I have a damned odd feeling: I do not much care to be home tonight. Strange, because I had looked forward to it – lively as a libertyman this morning – and now I do not care for it so much. Sometimes at sea you have that feeling of a lee-shore. Dirty weather, close-reefed top-sails, not a sight of the sun, not an observation for days, no idea of where you are to within a hundred miles or so, and at night you feel the loom of the shore under your lee: you can see nothing, but you can almost hear the rocks grinding out your bottom.'

Stephen made no reply, but wound his cloak higher against the biting wind.

MRS WILLIAMS never came down to breakfast; and quite apart from this the breakfast-room at Mapes was the most cheerful in the house; it looked south-east, and the gauze curtains waved gently in the sun, letting in the smell of spring. It could not have been a more feminine room – pretty white furniture, a green sprigged carpet, delicate china, little rolls and honey, a quantity of freshly-washed young women drinking tea.

One of these, Sophie Bentinck, was giving an account of a

dinner at the White Hart which Mr George Simpson, to whom she was engaged to be married, had attended. 'So then the toasts went round, and when George gave "Sophia" up starts your Captain Aubrey. "Oh," cries he, "I will drink that with three times three. Sophie is a name very dear to my heart." And it could not have been me, you know, for we have never met.' She gazed about her with the benevolence of a good-natured girl who has a ring on her finger and who wishes everybody to be as happy as herself.

'And did he drink it with three times three?' asked Sophia, looking amused, pleased and conscious.

'It was the name of his ship, you know, his first command,' said Diana quickly.

'Of course I know it,' said Sophia with an unusual flush. 'We all know it.'

'The post!' shrieked Frances, rushing out of the room. An expectant pause, a temporary truce. 'Two for my mother, one for Sophie Bentinck with a sweet blue seal of a cupid – no, it's a goat with wings – and one for Di, franked. I can't make out the frank. Who's it from, Di?'

'Frankie, you must try to behave more like a Christian, sweetheart,' said her eldest sister. 'You must not take notice of people's letters: you must pretend to know nothing about 'em.'

'Mama always opens ours, whenever we get any, which isn't often.'

'I had one from Jemmy Blagrove's sister after the ball,' said Cecilia, 'and she said he said she was to say I danced like a swan. Mama was in a horrid wax – correspondence most improper, and anyhow swans did not dance, because of their webbed feet: they sang. But I knew what he meant. So your Mama allows you to correspond?' she said, turning to Sophie Bentinck.

'Oh, yes. But we are engaged, you know, which is quite different,' said Sophie, looking complacently at her hand.

'Tom Postman does not pretend to know nothing about

people's letters,' said Frances. 'He said he could not make out Di's frank either. But the letters he is taking to Melbury are from London, Ireland and Spain. A double letter from Spain, with a vast sum to be paid!'

The breakfast-room at Melbury was cheerful too, but in a different way. Sombre mahogany, Turkey carpet, ponderous chairs, the smell of coffee, bacon and tobacco and wet men: they had been fishing since dawn and now they were half-way through the breakfast to which they were entitled, a breakfast that reached all over the broad white table-cloth: chafing dishes, coffee-pots, toast-racks, a Westphalian ham, a raised pie as yet untouched, the trout they had caught that morning.

'This was the one from under the bridge,' said Jack.

'Post, sir, if you please,' said his servant, Preserved Killick.

'From Jackson,' said Jack. 'And the other from the proctor. Forgive me, Stephen. I will just see what they have to say — what excuse . . . '

'My God,' he cried, a moment later. 'It can *not* be true.' Stephen looked up sharply. Jack passed him the letter. Mr Jackson, his prize-agent, one of the most respectable men in the profession, had failed. He had bolted, run off to Boulogne with what remained of the firm's cash, and his partner had filed his petition in bankruptcy, with no hope of paying six-pence in the pound.

'What makes it so very bad,' said Jack in a low, troubled voice, 'is that I told him to put all *Sophie's* prize-money into the funds as it came in. Some ships take years to be finally condemned, if the owners appeal. He did not do it. He gave me sums he said were interest from funds, but it was not true. He took it all as it came in, kept it in his own hands. It is gone, every last farthing.' He stared out of the window for some time, poising the other letter in his hand.

'This one is from the proctor. It will be about the two neu-trals that were on appeal,' he said, breaking the seal at last. 'I am almost afraid to open it. Yes: just so. Here is my lee-shore.

The verdict is reversed: I am to pay back eleven thousand pounds. I do not possess eleven thousand pence. A lee-shore . . . how can I claw off? There is only one thing for it: I will give up my claim to be made post and beg for a sloop as a commander. A ship I must have. Stephen, lend me twenty pounds, will you? I have no ready money. I shall go up to the Admiralty today. There is not a moment to lose. Oh, I have promised to ride with Sophia: but I can still do it in the day.'

'Take a post-chaise. You must not arrive fagged out.'

'That is what I shall do – you are quite right, Stephen. Thank you. Killick!'

'Sir?'

'Cut along to the Goat and tell them to have a chaise here at eleven. Pack my valise for a couple of nights: no, a week.'

'Jack,' said Stephen urgently, when the servant had left the room, 'do not speak of this to anyone yet, I beg you.'

'YOU ARE LOOKING terribly pale, Captain Aubrey,' said Sophia. 'I do hope you have not had another fall? Come in; please come in and sit down on a chair. Oh dear, I am sure you ought to sit down.'

'No, no, I promise you I have not fallen off my horse this last week,' said Jack, laughing. 'Let us make the most of this burst of sun; we shall get a ducking if we wait. Look at the clouds in the south-west. What a fine habit you are wearing.'

'Do you like it? It is the first time I have put it on. But,' she said, still looking anxiously into his face, which was now an unhealthy red, 'are you sure you would not like a cup of tea? It could be made in a moment.'

'Yes, yes, do step in and have a cup of tea,' cried Mrs Williams from the window, clutching a yellow garment to her throat. 'It will be ready directly, and there is a fire in the small sitting-room. You can drink it together – so cosy. I am sure Sophie is dying for a cup of tea. She would love a cup of tea with you, Captain Aubrey, would you not, Sophie?'

Jack smiled and bowed and kissed her hand, but his iron

determination not to stay prevailed, and in time they rode off along the Foxdene road to the edge of the downs.

'Are you quite sure you did not have a fall?' asked Sophie again, not so much from the idea that he had not noticed it and might recall it with application, as from a desire to express her real concern.

'No,' said Jack, looking at that lovely, usually remote face now gazing at him with such tenderness, such a worried and as it were proprietorial tenderness. 'But I did have a knock-down blow just now. A damned unlooked-for blow. Sophie – I may call you Sophie, mayn't I? I always think of you so – when I was in my *Sophie*, my sloop, I took a couple of neu-trals sailing into Marseilles. Their papers said they were from Sicily for Copenhagen, laden with brimstone. But they were in the very act of running into Marseilles: I was within reach of that battery on the height. And the brimstone was meant for France.'

For Sophia brimstone was something to be mixed with trea-cle and given to children on Fridays: she could still feel the odious lumps between her teeth. This showed in her face, and Jack added, 'They have to have it to make gunpowder. So I sent both these ships into Port Mahon, where they were condemned as lawful prize out of hand, a glaring breach of neutrality; but now at length the owners have appealed, and the court has decided they were not lawful prize at all, that their masters' tale of merely taking shelter from the weather was true. Weather! There was no weather. Scarcely a riffle on the sea, and we stood in under our royals, stuns'ls either side, and the thirty-six-pounders up on the hill making rings in the still water a quarter of a mile wide.'

'Oh, how unjust!' cried Sophie in extreme indignation. 'What wicked men, to tell such lies! You must have risked your life to bring those ships out from under the battery. Of course the brimstone was meant for France. I am sure they will be punished. What can be done? Oh, what can be done?'

'As for the verdict, nothing at all. It is final, I am afraid. But

I must go up and see what other measures – what I can wring out of the Admiralty. I must go today, and I may be away for some time. That is why I bore you with my affairs, to make it plain that I do not go away from Sussex of my own free will, nor with a light heart.'

'Oh, you do not bore – you could not bore me – everything to do with the Navy is – but did you say today? Surely you cannot go today. You must lie down and rest.'

'Today it must be, alas.'

'Then you must not ride. You must take a chaise and post up.'

'Yes. That is just what Stephen said. I will do it: I have ordered one from the Goat.'

'What a dear good man he is: he must be such a comfort to you. Such a good friend. But we must turn back at once, this minute. You must have all the rest you can before your journey.'

When they parted she gave him her hand and said, with an insistent pressure, 'I do pray you have the best of fortune, everything you deserve. I suppose there is nothing an igno-rant girl in the country can do, but – '

'Why there you are, you two,' cried Mrs Williams. 'Chatting away like a couple of inseparables. Whatever can you be talk-ing about all this time? But hush, I am indiscreet. La! And have you brought her back safe and sound, quite intact?'

TWO SECRETARIES, one sure if another failed, wrote as fast as their pens would drive.

> 'To the Marquis Cornwallis
> My Lord,
>   With every disposition to pay the most prompt attention to your Lordship's wishes in favour of Captain Bull, I have greatly to lament that it is not at present in my powers to comply with them. I have the honour to be, etc.

are you there, Bates?'

'Yes, my lord.'

'To Mrs Paulett
Madam,

Although I cannot admit the force of your argument in favour of Captain Mainwaring, there is something so amiable and laudable in a sister contending for the promotion of her brother, that no apology was needed for your letter of the twenty-fourth, which I lose no time in acknowledging.

I am, Madam, etc.

'To Sir Charles Grey, KB.
My dear Sir Charles,

Lieutenant Beresford has been playing a game to get to Ireland, which has lowered him much in my opinion. He is grave and enterprising, but, like the rest of the aristocracy, he thinks he has, from that circumstance, a right to promotion, in prejudice of men of better service and superior merit; which I will never submit to.

Having refused the Prince of Wales, Duke of Clarence, Duke of Kent, and Duke of Cumberland, you will not be surprised that I repeat the impossibility of departing from my principle, which would let in such an inundation upon me as would tend to complete the ruin of the Navy.

Yours very sincerely

'To the Duchess of Kingston,
Madam,

Your Grace is largely correct in the character of Captain Hallows of the Frolic; he has zeal and conduct, and were it not for a certain independence and want of willing submission to his superiors that may be cured

by the passage of time, as well as certain blemishes of a
family nature, I should, exclusive of the interest your
Grace has taken in his fortunes, be very glad to do justice to his merit, were I not precluded from doing so by
the incredible number of meritorious commanders
senior to him, upon half pay, who have prior claims to
any of the very few ships that offer.

I beg leave to assure your Grace that I shall be
happy in an occasion to mark the respect with which I
have the honour to be, Madam,

Your most obedient, humble servant

So much for the letters. Who is upon the list?'

'Captains Saul, Cunningham, Aubrey and Small. Lieutenants Roche, Hampole . . .'

'I shall have time for the first three.'

'Yes, my Lord.'

Jack heard the stentorian laughter as the First Lord and his
old shipmate Cunningham parted with a gun-room joke, and
he hoped he might find St Vincent in a good mood.

Lord St Vincent, deep in his attempts to reform the dockyards, hamstrung by politics, politicians, and his party's uncertain majority in the House, was not much given to good
moods however, and he looked up with an unwelcoming, cold
and piercing eye. 'Captain Aubrey, I saw you here last week. I
have very little time. General Aubrey has written forty letters
to me and other members of the Board and he has been told
that it is not in contemplation to promote you for the action
with the *Cacafuego*.'

'I have come here for another purpose, my Lord. To drop
my claim to post rank in the hope of another sloop. My prize-
agent has failed; two neutral owners have won their appeal
against me; and I must have a ship.'

Lord St Vincent's hearing was not good, and in this innermost shrine of the Navy Jack had lowered his voice; the old
gentleman did not quite catch his meaning. 'Must! What is

this *must?*' he cried. 'Do commanders walk into the Admiralty nowadays and state that they *must* be given a ship? If you *must* be given a ship, sir, what the devil do you mean by parading Arundel with a cockade the size of a cabbage in your hat, at the head of Mr Babbington's supporters, knocking honest freeholders about with a bludgeon? If I had been there, sir, I should have committed you for a brawl, disorderly conduct, and we should have none of this talk of *must*. God damn your impudence, sir.'

'My Lord, I have expressed myself badly. With respect, my Lord, by that unhappy word I meant, that Jackson's failure puts me in the obligation of soliciting your Lordship for a command, sinking my other claim. He has ruined me.'

'Jackson? Yes. However,' said St Vincent coldly, 'if your own imprudence has lost you the fortune your command allowed you to win, you must not expect the Admiralty to feel responsible for finding you another. A fool and his money are soon parted, and in the end it is just as well. As for the neutrals, you know perfectly well, or you ought to know perfectly well, that it is a professional risk: you touch 'em at your peril, and you must make proper provision against an appeal. But what do you do in the event? You fling your money about – ducks and drakes – you talk about marriage, although you know, or ought to know, that it is death to a sea-officer's career, at least until he is made post – you lead drunken parties at a Tory by-election – you come here and say you *must* have a ship. And meanwhile your friends pepper us with letters to say that you *must* be made post. That was the very word the Duke of Kent thought fit to use, put up to it by Lady Keith. It was not an action that entitled you to post rank. What is all this talk about "giving up your claim"? There is no claim.'

'The *Cacafuego* was a thirty-two gun xebec-frigate, my Lord.'

'She was a privateer, sir.'

'Only by a damned lawyer's quibble,' said Jack, his voice rising.

'What the fucking hell is this language to me, sir? Do you know who you are talking to, sir? Do you know where you are?'

'I beg your pardon, my Lord.'

'You took a privateer commanded by God knows who, with a well-manned King's sloop at the loss of three men, and you come here prating about your *claim* to post rank.'

'And eight wounded. If an action is to be rated according to the casualty-list, my Lord, I beg leave to remind you that your flagship at the Battle of St Vincent had one killed and five wounded.'

'Do you presume to stand there and compare a great fleet action with a – '

'With a what, sir?' cried Jack, a red veil appearing in his eye.

The angry voices stopped abruptly. A door opened and closed, and the people in the corridor saw Captain Aubrey stride past, hurry down the stairs and vanish into the courtyard.

'*May* 3. I did beg him not to speak of all this: yet it is known throughout the countryside. He knows nothing about women except as objects of desire (oh quite honourable desire at times): no sisters, a mother who died when he was very young, and has no conception of the power and diabolical energy of a Mrs W. She certainly wrung her information out of Sophia with her customary lack of scruple, and has spread it abroad with malignant excitement and busyness – the same indecent busyness that she displayed in whirling the girls off to Bath. This transparent blackmail of her health: playing on Sophia's tender heart and sense of duty – what easier? All arrangements made in two days. None of her usual slow complaining muddle and whining vacillation for a month, nor yet a week, but two days' strong activity: packed and gone. If this had happened even a week later, with an understanding between them, it would not have mattered. Sophie would have held to her engagement "come Hell or high water". As it is, the circumstances could not be worse. Separation, inconstancy (JA's strong animal spirits, any young man's strong animal spirits), absence, the feeling of neglect.

'What a barbarous animal that Williams is. I should have known nothing of their unseemly departure but for Diana's notes and that sweet child's troubled, furtive visit. I call her child, although she is no younger than DV, whom I look upon in quite another light: though indeed she too must have been exquisite as a child – not unlike Frances, I believe: the same ruthless, innocent cruelty. Gone. What a silence. How am I to tell JA of all this? I am tormented by the thought of striking him in the face.'

Yet the telling was simple enough. He said, 'The girls have gone. Mrs Williams took them away to Bath last Tuesday senight. Sophia came to see me and said she regretted it extremely.'

'Did she leave a message for me?' asked Jack, his sad face brightening.

'She did not. In direct terms, she did not. At times it was difficult to follow her in her agitation. Miss Anna Coluthon, overcome by her position – an unattended girl calling upon a single gentleman. Champflower has not seen such a thing. But I do not mistake when I state that in substance she told me you were to know that she did not leave Sussex of her own free will, nor with a light heart.'

'Do you think I might write to her, under cover to Diana Villiers?' asked Jack.

'Diana Villiers is still here. She does not go to Bath: she stays at Mapes Court,' said Stephen coldly.

The news spread. The decision on the prizes was public knowledge, having been reported in the London papers; and there were enough naval officers in the neighbourhood, some of whom were affected by the agent's defection, to make the extent of the disaster clear. The announcement 'at Wool-hampton, on the 19th instant, to the lady of General Aubrey, a son' merely rounded out the anecdote.

Bath was filled with Mrs Williams's triumph. 'It is certainly a divine retribution, my dears. We were told he was a sad rake, and you will remember I never liked him from the first: I said there was something wrong about his mouth. My instinct is never mistaken. I did not like his eye, neither.'

'Oh, Mama,' cried Frances, 'you said he was the most gentleman-like man you had ever seen, and so handsome.'

'Handsome is as handsome does,' cried Mrs Williams. 'And you may leave the room, Miss Pert. You shall have no pudding, for want of respect.'

It was soon found that other people had never liked Jack either: – his mouth, chin, eyes, lavish entertainment, horses, plans for a pack of hounds, all came in for adverse comment. Jack had seen this process before; he had an outsider's knowledge of it; but although his condemnation was neither gross nor universal, he found it more painful than he had expected – the first cautious reserve of the tradesmen, a certain easiness and assumption in the country gentlemen, an indefinible want of consideration.

He had taken Melbury for a year, the rent was paid, the house could not be sublet; there was no point in removing. He retrenched, sold his hunters, told his men that although it grieved him they must part as soon as they could find places, and stopped giving dinners. His horses were fine animals and he sold one for as much as he had given for it; this satisfied the immediate local duns, but it did not re-establish his credit, for although Champflower was willing to believe in any amount of cloudy wealth (and Jack's fortune had been reckoned very high), it had poverty weighed up to within a pound or two.

Invitations fell off, for not only was he much taken up with his affairs, but he had become prickly, over-sensitive to the least unintentional slight; and presently Mapes was the only place where he dined. Mrs Villiers, supported by the parson, his wife and sister, could perfectly well invite Melbury Lodge.

It was after one of these dinners that they rode back, stabled the cob and the mule and said good night to one another.

'You would not care for a hand of cards, I suppose?' said Jack, pausing on the stairs and looking down into the hall.

'I would not,' said Stephen. 'My mind is turned elsewhere.'

His person, too. He walked fast through the night over Polcary Down, carefully skirted a group of poachers in Gole's Hanger, giving them a wide berth, and paused under a clump of elms that stood, swaying and creaking in the wind, over against Mapes Court. The house was of some antiquity, irregular in spite of its modern alterations, and the oldest wing ended in a blunt square tower: one window lit. He passed quickly through the kitchen-garden, his heart beating, beating, so that when he stood at the little door deep in the base of the tower he could hear it, a sound like the hoarse panting of a dog. His face set in a steady, unmoved acceptance of defeat as he reached for the handle. 'I take my happiness in my hands every time I come to this door,' he said, not trying it for a moment. He felt the lock's silent response: turned it slowly.

He walked up the spiral staircase to the first floor, where Diana lived: a little sitting-room with her bedroom opening out of it, the whole communicating with the rest of the house by a long corridor that opened into the main staircase. There was no one in the sitting-room. He sat down on the sofa and looked attentively at the gold-thread embroidery of a sari that was being turned into a European dress. Under the golden light of the lamp gold tigers tore a Company's officer lying on the spotted ground with a brandy-bottle in his hand: sometimes in his right hand, sometimes in his left, for the pattern had many variations.

'How late you are, Maturin,' said Diana, coming in from her bedroom; she was wearing two shawls over her peignoir and her face was tired – no welcome. 'I was going to bed. However, sit down for five minutes. Eugh, your shoes are covered with filth.'

Stephen took them off and set them by the door. 'There was a gang with lurchers over by the warren. I stepped off the road. You have a singular gift for putting me at a disadvantage, Villiers.'

'So you walked again? Are you not allowed out at night? Anyone would think you were married to that man. How are his affairs, by the way? He seemed cheerful enough this evening, laughing away with that goose Annie Strode.'

'There is no improvement, I am afraid. The shipowners' man of business is an avid brute, with no intelligence, sense, or bowels. Ignorant voracity – a wingless vulture – can soar only into the depths of ignominy.'

'But Lady Keith – ' She stopped. Lady Keith's letter had reached Melbury that morning, and it had not been mentioned at dinner. Stephen passed the sari through his hands, observing that sometimes the Company's officer looked gay, even ecstatic, sometimes agonized. 'If you suppose you have the right to ask me for explanations,' said Diana, 'you are mistaken. We happened to meet, riding. If you think that just because I have let you kiss me once or twice – if you think that just because you have come here when I have been ready to fling myself down the well or play the fool to get away from this odious daily round – nothing but a couple of toothless servants in the house – you are my lover and I am your mistress, you are wrong. I never have been your mistress.'

'I know,' said Stephen. 'I desire no explanation; I assume no rights. Compulsion is the death of friendship, joy.' A pause. 'Will you give me something to drink, Villiers my dear?'

'Oh, I *beg* your pardon,' she cried, with a ludicrous automatic return of civility. 'What may I offer you? Port? Brandy?'

'Brandy, if you please. Listen,' he said, 'did you ever see a tiger?'

'Oh yes,' said Diana vaguely, looking for the tray and the decanter. 'I shot a couple. There are no proper glasses here. Only from the safety of a howdah, of course. You often see them on the road from Maharinghee to Bania, or when you are crossing the mouths of the Ganges. Will this tumbler do? They swim about from island to island. Once I saw one take to the water as deliberately as a horse. They swim low, with their heads up and their tails long out behind. How cold it is in this damned tower. I have not been really warm right through since I came back to England. I am going to bed; it is the only warm place in the house. You may come and sit by me, when you have finished your brandy.'

THE DAYS DROPPED BY, golden days, the smell of hay, a perfect early summer – wasted, as far as Jack was concerned. Or nine parts wasted; for although his naval and legal business grew steadily darker and more complex, he did go twice to Bath to see his old friend Lady Keith, calling up on Mrs Williams in the bosom of her family the first time and meeting Sophia – just happening to meet Sophia – in the Pump Room the second. He came back both elated and tormented, but still far more human, far more like the cheerful resilient creature Stephen had always known.

'I am resolved to break,' wrote Stephen. 'I give no happiness; I receive none. This obsession is not happiness. I see a hardness that chills my heart, and not my heart alone. Hardness and a great deal else; a strong desire to rule, jealousy, pride, vanity; everything except a want of courage. Poor judgment, ignorance of course, bad faith, inconstancy; and I would add heartlessness if I could forget our farewells on Sunday night, unspeakably pathetic in so wild a creature. And then surely style and grace beyond a certain point take the place of virtue – *are* virtue, indeed? But it will not do. No, no, you get no more of me. If this wantonness with Jack continues I shall go away. And if he goes on he may find he has laboured to give himself a wound; so may she – he is not a man to be played with. Her levity grieves me more than I can express. It is contrary to what she terms her principles; even, I believe, to her real nature. She cannot want him as a husband now. Hatred of Sophia, of Mrs W? Some undefined revenge? Delight in playing with fire in a powder-magazine?'

The clock struck ten; in half an hour he was to meet Jack at

Plimpton cockpit. He left the brown library for the brilliant courtyard, where his mule stood gleaming lead-coloured, waiting for him. It was gazing with a fixed, cunning expression down the alley beyond the stables, and following its eyes Stephen saw the postman stealing a pear from the kitchen-garden espalier.

'A double letter for you, sir,' said the postman, very stiff and official, with hurried pear-juice dribbling from the corner of his mouth. 'Two and eightpence, if you please. And two for the Captain, one franked, t'other Admiralty.' Had he been seen? The distance was very great, almost safe.

'Thankee, postman,' said Stephen, paying him. 'You have had a hot round.'

'Why, yes, sir,' said the postman, smiling with relief. 'Parsonage, Croker's, then Dr Vining's – one from his brother in Godmersham, so I'd suppose he'll be over this Sunday – and then right up to young Mr Savile's – his young lady. Never was there such a young lady in the writing line; I shall be glad when they are married, and say it by word of mouth.'

'You are hot, thirsty: you must try a pear – it will keep the humours in motion.'

The main had started when Stephen walked in: a tight-packed ring of farmers, tradesmen, gipsies, horsecopers, country gentlemen, all too excited, the only tolerable thing the courage of the birds there in the pit.

'Evens on the speckled pie! Evens on the speckled pie!' cried a tall gipsy with a red scarf round his neck.

'Done with you,' said Jack. 'Five guineas at even odds on the speckled pie.'

'Done and done,' said the gipsy looking round. His eyes narrowed, and in a jocular, wheedling voice he went on, 'Five guineas, gentleman? Oh, such a purse for a poor travelling man and a half-pay captain! I lays my money down, eh?' He placed the five bright coins on the rim of the pit. Jack thrust out his jaw and matched the guineas one by one. The owners of the birds set them to the ring, clasping them just so and whispering close to their proud close-cropped heads. The cocks stalked out on their toes, darting glances sideways, circling before they closed. Both flew up at the same moment, the steel spurs flashing as they struck; up and up again, a whirlwind in the middle of the pit and a savage roaring all round it.

The speckled pie, staggering, one eye gone and the other streaming blood, stood his ground, peering through the mist for his enemy: saw his shadow and lurched in to get his death-wound. Still he would not die; he stood with the spurs labouring his back until the mere weight of his exhausted opponent bore him down – an opponent too cruelly lacerated to rise and crow.

'Let us go and sit outside,' said Stephen. 'Pot-boy, there, bring us a pint of sherry-wine on the bench outside. Do you mind me, now?'

'Sherry, for all love!' he said. 'The pretentious young whore is wicked enough to call this sherry-wine. Here are letters for you, Jack.'

'The speckled pie did not really want to fight,' said Jack.

'He did not. Though he was a game bird, to be sure. Why did you bet on him?'

'I liked him; he had a rolling walk like a sailor. He was not what you would call a wicked bloody cock, but once he was in the ring, once he was challenged, he would fight. He was a rare plucked 'un, and he went on even when there was no hope at all. I am not sorry I backed him: should do it again. Did you say there were letters?'

'Two letters. Use no ceremony, I beg.'

'Thank you, Stephen. The Admiralty acknowledges Mr Aubrey's communication of the seventh ultimo. This is from Bath: I will just see what Queenie has to say . . . Oh my God.'

'What's amiss?'

'My God,' said Jack again, beating his clenched fist on his knee. 'Come, let's get out of this place. Sophie's to be married.'

They rode for a mile, Jack muttering broken sentences, ejaculations to himself, and then he said, 'Queenie writes from Bath. A fellow by the name of Adams – big estate in Dorset – has made Sophia an offer. Pretty brisk work, upon my soul. I should never have believed it of her.'

'Is this gossip Lady Keith has picked up?'

'No, no, no! She called on Mother Williams for my sake – my idea was she could not refuse to see me when I went down. Queenie knows everybody.'

'Certainly. Mrs Williams would be flattered by the acquaintance.'

'Yes. So she went, and Mrs Williams, tittering with joy, told her the whole thing, every last detail of the estate. Would you have believed it of Sophia, Stephen?'

'No. And I doubt the truth of the report, in so far as it assumes that the offer has been made directly and not through the mother, as a mere proposition.'

'By God, I wish I were in Bath,' said Jack in a low voice, his face dark with anger. 'Who would have believed it of her? That pure face – I should have sworn . . . Those sweet, kindest words so short a while ago; and now already things have gone as far as an offer of marriage! Think of the hand-holding, paddling . . . By God, and such a pure, pure face.'

Stephen said that this was no evidence, that Mrs Williams was capable of any invention; he was intelligent, comforting and wise, and he knew that he might as well have been talking to his mule. Jack's face had closed in a particular hard, determined set; he said he had thought for once he had found a perfectly straightforward girl – nothing hole-in-the-corner, nothing uneasy and complicated – but he would say no more about it; and when they came to the Newton Priors crossroads he said, 'Stephen, I know you mean very, very kindly, but I think I shall ride over the Downs to Wivenhoe. I'm not fit company for man or beast. You will not be wanting the cob? And don't wait supper – I shall get a bite somewhere on the road.'

'KILLICK,' SAID STEPHEN, 'put the ham and a pot of beer in the Captain's room. He may come home late. I am going out.'

He walked slowly at first, his heart and breathing quite undisturbed, but when the familiar miles had passed under him and he started to climb Polcary, the stronger rhythm had returned, increasing as all his resolution fell away, and by the time he reached the top of the hill his heart was keeping time with his brisk busy watch. 'Thump, thump, thump, you fool,' he said smiling as he timed it. 'It is true, of course, that I have never climbed the hill so fast – my legs are in training, ha, ha, ha. A pretty sight I should look. Kind night that covers me.'

More slowly now, his senses keen for the least movement in the wood, in Gole's Hanger or the lane beyond: far on his right hand the barking of a roe-buck in search of a doe, and on his left the distant screaming of a rabbit with a stoat at work upon it. An owl. Dim, fast asleep among its trees, the vague shape of the house, and at its far end the one square eye in the tower, shining out.

Down to the elms, silent and thick-leaved now: the house full-view. And under the elms his own cob tethered to a hazel-bush. He recognized the animal before it whinnied, and he stood stock-still. Creeping forward at its second neigh he stroked its velvet muzzle and its neck, patted it for a while, still staring over its withers at the light, and then turned. After perhaps a hundred yards, with the tower sunk in the trees behind him, he stopped dead and put his hand to his heart. Walked on: a heavy, lumpish pace, stumbling in the ruts, driving himself forward by brute force.

'Jack,' he said at breakfast next morning, 'I think I must leave you: I shall see whether I can find a place on the mail.'

'Leave me!' cried Jack, perfectly aghast. 'Oh, surely not?'

'I am not entirely well, and conceive that my native air might set me up.'

'You do look miserably hipped,' said Jack, gazing at him now with attention and deep concern. 'I have been so wrapped up in my own damned unhappy business – and now this – that I have not been watching you. I am so sorry, Stephen. You must be damned uncomfortable here, with only Killick, and no company. How I hope you are not really ill. Now I recollect, you have been low, out of spirits, these last weeks – no heart for a jig. Should you like to advise with Dr Vining? He might see your case from the outside, if you understand me. I am sure he is not so clever as you, but he might see it from the outside. Pray let me call him in. I shall step over at once, before he starts on his rounds.'

It took Stephen the interval between breakfast and the coming of the post to quiet his friend – 'he knew his disease perfectly – had suffered from it before – it was nothing a man could die of – he knew the cure – the malady was called solis deprivatio.'

'The taking away of the sun?' cried Jack. 'Are you making game of me, Stephen? You cannot be thinking of going to Ireland for the sun.'

'It was a kind of dismal little joke,' said Stephen. 'But I had meant Spain rather than Ireland. You know I have a house in the mountains behind Figueras: part of its roof has fallen in, the part where the sheep live – I must attend to it. Bats there are, free-tailed bats, that I have watched for generations. Here is the post,' he said, going to the window and reaching out. 'You have one letter. I have none.'

'A bill,' said Jack, putting it aside. 'Oh yes you have, though. I quite forgot. Here in my pocket. I happened to see Diana Villiers yesterday and she gave me this note to deliver – said such handsome things about you, Stephen. We said what a capital shipmate you were, and what a hand with a 'cello and a knife. She thinks the world of you . . .'

Perhaps: the note was kind, in its way.

> My dear Stephen,
>
> How shabbily you treat your friends – all these days without a sign of life. It is true I was horribly dis-

agreeable when last you did me the pleasure of calling.
Please forgive me. It was the east wind, or original sin,
or the full moon, or something of that kind. But I have
found some curious Indian butterflies – just their wings
– in a book that belonged to my father. If you are not
too tired, or bespoke, perhaps you might like to come
and see them this evening. D. V.

. . . not that there is any virtue in that. I asked her over to play
with us on Thursday; she knows our trio well, although she
only plays by ear. However since you must go, I will send Killick to make our excuses.'

'Perhaps I may not leave so soon. Let us see what next
week brings; the sheep are covered with wool, after all; and
there is always the chapel for the bats.'

The road, pale in the darkness, Stephen riding deliberately
along it, reciting an imagined dialogue. He rode up to the
door, then tethered his mule to a ring, and he was about to
knock when Diana opened to him.

'Good night, Villiers, he said. 'I thank you for your note.'

'I love the way you say good night, Stephen,' she said, smiling. She was obviously in spirits, certainly in high good looks.
'Are you not amazed to see me here?'

'Moderately so.'

'All the servants are out. How formal you are, coming to the
front door! I am so happy to see you. Come into my lair. I
have spread out my butterflies for you.'

Stephen took off his shoes, sat deliberately on a small chair
and said, 'I have come to pay my adieux. I leave the country
very soon – next week, I believe.'

'Oh, Stephen. . . and will you abandon your friends? What
will poor Aubrey do? Surely you cannot leave him now? He
seems so very low. And what shall I do? I shall have no one to
talk to, no one to misuse.'

'Will you not?'

'Have I made you very unhappy, Stephen?'

'You have treated me like a dog at times, Villiers.'

'Oh, my dear. I am so very sorry. I shall never be unkind again. And so you really mean to go? Oh, dear. But friends kiss when they say good-bye. Come and just pretend to look at my butterflies – I put them out so prettily – and give me a kiss, and then you shall go.'

'I am pitifully weak with you, Diana, as you know very well,' he said. 'I came slowly over Polcary, rehearsing the words in which I should tell you I had come to break, and that I was happy to do so in kindness and friendship, with no bitter words to remember. I cannot do so, I find.'

'Break? Oh dear *me*, that is a word we must never use.'

'Never.'

Yet the word appeared five days later in his diary. 'I am required to deceive JA, and although I am not unaccustomed to deception, this is painful to me. He endeavours to delude me too, of course, but out of a consideration for what he conceives to be my view of right conduct of his relationship with Sophia. He has a singularly open and truthful nature and his efforts are ineffectual, though persistent. She is right: I cannot go away with him in his present difficulties. Why does she increase them? Mere vice? In another age I should have said diabolic possession, and it is a persuasive answer even now – one day herself and none so charming, the next cold, cruel, full of hurt. Yet by force of repetition words that wounded me bitterly not long ago have lost their full effect; the closed door is no longer death; my determination to break grows stronger: it is becoming more than an intellectual determination. I have neither remarked this myself nor found it in any author, but a small temptation, almost an un-temptation, can be more dominant than a great one. I am not strongly tempted to go to Mapes; I am not strongly tempted to drink up the laudanum whose drops I count so superstitiously each night. Four hundred drops at present, my bottled tranquillity. Yet I do so. Killick,' he said, with the veiled dangerous look of a man interrupted at secret work, 'what have you to say to me? You are confused, disturbed in your mind. You have been drinking.'

Killick stepped closer, and leaning on Stephen's chair he whispered. 'There's some ugly articles below, sir, asking for the Captain. A blackbeetle in a scrub wig and a couple of milling coves, prize-fighters. Awkward buggers in little round hats, and I see one of 'em shove a staff under his coat. Bums. Sheriff's officers.'

Stephen nodded. 'I will deal with them in the kitchen. No, the breakfast-room: it looks on to the lawn. Pack the Captain's sea-chest and my small valise. Give me those letters of his. Put the mule to the little cart and drive to the end of Foxdene lane with our dunnage.'

'Aye aye, sir. Pack, mule and cart, and Foxdene it is.'

Leaving the bums grim and wooden in the breakfast-room, Stephen smiled with pleasure: here at last was a concrete situation. He knew where he should find them within a mile or two; but he did not know what it would cost him when, having toiled up the chalky slope in the sun, he met their expressions of cold anger, resentment, and hostility.

'Good morning, now,' he said, taking off his hat. Diana gave him a distant nod and a look that pierced him cruelly. 'You seem to have had a hot walk, Dr Maturin. How eager you must be to see – '

'You will forgive me if I say a word to Captain Aubrey, ma'am,' he said, with a look as cold as her own, and he led the cob aside. 'Jack, they have come to arrest you for debt. We must cross to France tonight and so to Spain. Your chest and the little cart will be at the end of Foxdene lane by now. You shall stay with me at my house: it falls out very well. We may catch the Folkestone packet if we drive hard.' He turned, bowed to Diana, and set off down the hill.

The drum of hooves, Diana's voice calling, 'Ride on, Aubrey. Ride on, I say. I must speak to Maturin,' and she reined in beside him. 'I must speak to you, Maturin. Stephen, would you leave and not say goodbye to me?'

'Will you not let me go, Diana?' he said, looking up, his eyes filling with tears.

'No, no, no,' she cried. 'You must not leave me – go, yes go to France – but write to me, write to me, and come back.' She gripped him hard with her small hand, and she was away, the turf flying behind her horse.

'NOT FOLKESTONE,' said Jack, guiding the mule through the grassy lanes. 'Dover. Seymour has the *Amethyst*; he carries the imperial ambassador across tonight. He will give us a passage – he and I were shipmates in the *Marlborough*. Once aboard a King's ship and we can tell the tipstaff to go to hell.'

Five miles later he said, 'Stephen, do you know what that letter was you brought me? The small one, wafered?'

'I do not.'

'It was from Sophie. A direct letter, sent straight to me, do you hear? She says there have been reports of this Adams fellow and his pretensions, that might have given her friends uneasiness. That there was nothing to it – all God-damned flummery – had scarcely seen him above a dozen times, though he was always closeted with Mama. She speaks of you. Sends you her very kind regards and would be so happy to see you in Bath; the weather there is charming. Christ, Stephen, I have never been so down. Fortune gone, career too maybe, and now this.'

'I CANNOT TELL YOU what a relief it is,' he said, bending to see whether the *Amethyst*'s forestaysail were drawing, 'to be at sea. It is so clear and simple. I do not mean just escaping from the bums; I mean all the complications of life on shore. I do not think I am well suited to the land.'

They were standing on the quarterdeck amidst a crowd of wondering, staring attachés, secretaries, members of the suite, who staggered and lurched, clinging to ropes and to one another as the frigate began to feel the roll and the brisk cross-sea and Dover cliffs vanished in a swathe of summer rain. 'Yes,' said Stephen, 'I too have been walking a tightrope with no particular skill. I have the same sense of enlargement. A little while ago I should have welcomed it without reservation.'

4

TOULON. THE MISTRAL had died away at last, and there was scarcely a fleck of white left on the sea; but the brilliant clarity of the air was still undimmed, so that a telescope from the hills behind the town could pick out even the names of the seven line-of-battle ships in the Petite Rade: the *Formidable* and *Indomptable*, both of eighty guns, and the *Atlas*, *Scipion*, *Intrepide*, *Mont-Blanc* and *Berwick* of seventy-four apiece. English pride might have been hurt at the sight of the last, for she belonged to the Royal Navy until some years before: and had English pride been able to look into the jealously guarded Arsenal it would have been mortified again by seeing two more British seventy-fours, the *Hannibal*, captured during Sir James Saumarez's action in the Gut of Gibraltar in 1801, and the *Swiftsure*, taken in the Mediterranean a few weeks earlier, both of them under active repair.

Indeed activity, extreme activity, was the word for Toulon. The silent, still-green hills, the great headlands, the enormous sweep of the Mediterranean beyond them and the islands, blue and motionless beyond expression, the flood of hot, oppressive light, and then in the middle this noisy little stirring concentrated town, filled with tiny figures – white shirts, blue trousers, the gleam of red sashes – all of them intensely busy. Even under this noonday sun they were toiling like ants – boats pulling from the Arsenal to the Petite Rade, from the Petite Rade to the Grande Rade, from the ships to the quays and back again, men swarming over the fine great ships on the stocks, plying their adzes, caulking-hammers, augers, beetles, harring-poles; gangs of convicts unloading oak from Ragusa, Stockholm tar, Hamburg tow, Riga spars and cordage, all in the din and the innumerable smells of a great port, the reek of open drains, old stagnant water, hot stone, frying garlic, grilling fish that wafted above the whole.

'Dinner,' said Captain Christy-Pallière, closing the file of Death Sentences, F-L. 'I shall start with a glass of Banyuls and some anchovies, a handful of olives, *black* olives; then I believe I may look at Hébert's fish soup, and follow it with a simple langouste in court-bouillon. Possibly his gigot en croûte: the lamb is exquisite now that the thyme is in flower. Then no more than cheese, strawberries, and some trifle with our coffee – a saucer of my English jam, for example. None of your architectural meals, Penhoët; my liver will not stand it in this heat, and we have a great deal of work to do if the *Annibale* is to be ready for sea by next week. There are all Dumanoir's dossiers to deal with – how I wish he would come back. I should have interrogated the Maltese this morning. If we have a good dinner they risk to escape unshot . . .'

'Let us drink Tavel with the lamb,' said Captain Penhoët, who knew that for his part he risked philosophical remarks about digestion – guilt – Pontius Pilate – the odious side of interrogating suspected spies, quite unfit for officers – if he did not interrupt. 'It is – '

'Two roast-beefs to see you, sir,' said an orderly.

'Oh no!' cried Captain Christy-Pallière, 'not at this hour, holy name. Tell them I am not here, Jeannot. I may be back at five. Who are they?'

'The first is Aubrey, Jacques. He claims to be a captain in their navy,' said the orderly, narrowing his eyes and scanning the official slip in his hand. 'Born 1 April 1066, at Bedlam, London. Father's profession, monk: mother's, nun. Mother's maiden name, Borgia, Lucrèce. The other pilgrim is Maturin, Etienne – '

'Quick, quick,' cried Captain Christy-Pallière. 'My breeches, Jeannot, my cravat – ' for ease and commodity he had been sitting in his drawers. 'Son of a whore, my shirt. Penhoët, we must have a real dinner today – find a clothes-brush, Jeannot – this is the English prisoner I was telling you about. Excellent seaman, charming company. You will not mind speaking English, of course. How do I look?'

'So pimping as possible,' said Captain Penhoët in that language. 'Camber the torso, and you will impose yourself of their attention.'

'Show them in, Jeannot,' said Christy-Pallière. 'My dear Aubrey,' he cried, folding Jack in his arms and kissing him on both cheeks, 'how very happy I am to see you! Dear Dr Maturin, be the very welcome. Allow me to present Captain of frigate Penhoët – Captain of frigate Aubrey, and Dr Maturin, at one time my guests aboard the *Desaix*.'

'Your servant, sir,' said Captain Penhoët.

'Domestique, monsieur,' said Jack, still blushing as far as his shirt. 'Penhoët? Je préserve – je ai – le plus vivid rémembrance de vos combatte à Ushant, à bord le *Pong*, en vingt-quatre neuf.' A second of attentive, polite but total blankness followed this, and turning to Christy-Pallière he said, 'How do you say I have the liveliest recollection of Captain Penhoët's gallant action off Ushant in '99?'

Captain Christy-Pallière said this in another kind of French – renewed, far warmer smiles, another British shake-hand – and observed, 'But we may all speak English. My colleague is one of our best translators. Come, let us go and have dinner in a trice – you are tired, dusty, quite fagged up – how far have you come today? How do you stand the heat? Extraordinary for the month of May. Have you seen my cousins in Bath? May we hope for your company for some time? How happy I am to see you!'

'We had hoped you would dine with us,' cried Jack. 'We have livré une table – booked it.'

'You are in my country,' said Christy-Pallière in a tone that allowed of no reply. 'After you, dear friends, I beg. A simple meal – a little inn just outside the town. But it has a muscat

trellis – fresh air – and the man does the cooking himself.'
Turning to Stephen as he shepherded them along the corridor he said, 'Dr Ramis is with us again! He came back from
leave on Tuesday. I will ask him to come and sit with us
after dinner – he could not bear to see us eat – and he will
tell you all the news of our cholera outburst and the new
Egyptian pox.'

'CAPTAIN AUBREY led us such a chase,' he said to Captain
Penhoët, setting pieces of bread to represent the ships of
Admiral Linois's squadron. 'He commanded that little quarter-decked brig the *Sophie* – '
  'I remember myself of him.'
  'And at first he had the weather-gage of us. But he was
embayed – here is the headland, and the wind was so, a
caprice wind.' He fought the battle over again, stage by stage.
'And then he put up his helm in a flash, set his studding-sails
like a conjuring trick and ran through our line, close to the
Admiral. The fox, he knew I dared not risk hitting the flagship! And he knew the *Desaix*'s broadside would come rather
slow! He ran through, and with a little luck – '
  'What is luck?'
  'Chance. He might have escaped. But the Admiral made
my signal to chase, and the *Desaix* was only a week out of
dock quite clean, and she loves a light breeze on the quarter:
and in short . . . I should have blown you out of the sea with
my last broadside, dear friend, if you had not jugged like an
hare.'
  'How well I remember it,' said Jack. 'My heart was in my
boots as I saw you beginning to luff up. But it had gone down
there much earlier, when I saw that you sailed two miles to
my one, without troubling to set your stuns'ls.'
  'It was an exploit of thunder, to run through the line,' said
Captain Penhoët. 'I could almost to wish you had succeeded
the blow. I should have struck as soon as the admiral had fore-
reached my ship. But in principle you English carry too much

guns, is it not? Too many for sail fast in a such breeze – too many to escape oneself.'

'I tossed mine all overboard,' said Jack. 'Though in principle you are right. Yet might we not say that in principle you carry far too many men, particularly soldiers? Remember the *Phoebe* and *Africaine* . . .'

The simple meal wound to its even simpler end – a bottle of brandy and two glasses. Captain Penhoët, exhausted by his efforts, had returned to his office; Stephen had been carried off to Dr Ramis's healthier table, to drink gaseous water from a sulphurous spring; and Cape Sicié had turned purple against the now violet sea. Crickets filled the air with a warm continuous omnipresent churr.

Both Jack and Christy-Pallière had drunk a great deal; they were now telling one another about their professional difficulties, and each was astonished that the other had reason to complain. Christy-Pallière too was caught on the promotion-ladder, for although he was a capitaine de vaisseau, very like a post-captain, there was 'no proper sense of seniority in the French navy – dirty, underhand intrigue everywhere – political adventurers succeeding – real seamen thrust to the wall.' He did not express himself directly, but Jack knew from their conversations a year ago and from the indiscretions of his English Christy cousins, that his friend was but a lukewarm republican, detested the upstart Bonaparte's vulgarity and total ignorance of the sea-service, would have liked a constitutional, liberal monarchy, and was uneasy in his skin – a man devoted to his navy and of course to France, but unhappy in his rulers. Long ago he had spoken in a remarkably informed and perceptive way, about the case of Irish officers in the Royal Navy and the moral dilemma of conflicting loyalties; but at this moment, although four sorts of wine and two of brandy had brought him handsomely into the area of indiscretion, he was solely concerned with his own immediate problems. 'For you it is perfectly simple,' he said. 'You will assemble your interest, your friends and the lords and sirs of your acquaintance; and eventually, with your parliamentary elections, there will be a change of ministry and your evident merits will be recognized. But what is the case with us? Republican interest, royalist influence, Catholic interest, Freemason interest, consular or what they tell me will soon be *imperial* interest, all cutting across one another – a foul hawse. We might as well finish this bottle. You know,' he said, after a pause, 'I am so tired of sitting on my arse in an office. The only hope, the only solution, is a – ' His voice died away.

'I suppose it would be wicked to pray for war,' said Jack, whose mind had followed exactly the same course. 'But oh to be afloat.'

'Oh, very wicked, no doubt.'

'Particularly as the only worth-while war would have to be against the nation we like best. For the Dutch and Spaniards are no match for us now. It makes me stare, every time I think of it, how well the Spaniards build – beautiful, beautiful great ships – and how strangely they handle them. At the Battle of St Vincent – '

'It is all the fault of their admiralty,' cried Christy-Pallière. 'All admiralties are the same. I swear, on the head of my mother, that our admiralty – ' A messenger brought him up short on the brink of high treason; he excused himself, stepped aside and read the note. He read it twice, clearing the fumes of brandy from his head, sobering fast. He was a massive, bear-like man, not as tall as Jack, but stouter, and he could stand his drink: broad, somewhat round-shouldered, with very kind brown eyes – kind, but not foolish; and when he came back to the table, carrying a pot of coffee, they were hard and piercing. He hesitated for some time, sipping the coffee, before he spoke. 'All navies have these problems,' he said slowly. 'My colleague who looks after them here is on leave: I take his place. Here I have a description of a man in a black coat with a telescope on Mount Faron this morning, looking at our installations; medium height, slim, pale eyes, bob wig, grey breeches, speaks French with a southern accent. He has also been talking to a Barcelona merchant, a curious fellow with two feluccas in the darse.'

'Why,' cried Jack, 'that must certainly be Stephen Maturin. I have no doubt of it – he has a telescope. One of Dolland's very best glasses. I am sure he was up there on Faron this morning before I was out of bed, gazing about for his precious birds. He mentioned some monstrous rare pippit or titmouse that lives here. I wonder,' – laughing heartily – 'he did not go up to the fort and beg for the use of their big artillery instruments. Oh no, he is the simplest fellow in the world. I give you my word of honour – unspeakably learned, knows every bug and beetle in the universe, and will have your leg off in an instant – but he should not be allowed out alone. And as for naval installations, he really cannot tell port from starboard, a bonnet from a drabbler, though I have explained a thousand times, and he does try to apply himself, poor fellow. I am sure it must be he, from what you tell me about his speaking to the Barcelona merchant. And in that language, I dare say? He lived in those parts for years, and speaks their lingo like a – like a – why, like a native. We are on our way down there now, to a property he has; and as soon as he has been across to Porquerolles to see some curious shrub that grows on the island and nowhere else, we shall move on. Ha, ha, ha,' he laughed, his big voice full of intense amusement, 'to think of poor good old Stephen being laid by the heels for a spy! Oh, ha, ha, ha!'

There was no possibility of resisting his transparent good faith. Christy-Pallière's eyes softened; he smiled with relief and said, 'So you will vouch for him, then, upon your honour?'

'My hand upon my heart,' said Jack, placing it there. 'My dear sir, surely your men must be a very simple crew, to go round suspecting Stephen Maturin?'

'That is the trouble,' said Christy-Pallière. 'Many of them *are* stupid. But that is not the worst of it: there are other services, the gendarmerie, Fouché's men and all those land people, as you know, and some of them are no wiser. So pray tell your friend to be more discreet. And listen, my dear Aubrey,' he said in a low, significant voice, 'it might be as well if you did not cross to Porquerolles, but pressed on to Spain.'

'Because of the heat?' asked Jack.

Christy-Pallière shrugged. 'If you like,' he said. 'I say no more.' He took a turn up and down the terrace, ordered a fresh bottle, and returned to Jack.

'And so you saw my cousins in Bath?' he said, in quite another, conversational tone.

'Yes, yes! I did myself the honour of calling at Laura Place the first time I was there, and they very kindly asked me to drink tea with them. They were all at home – Mrs Christy, Miss Christy, Miss Susan, Madame des Aguillières and Tom. Charming people, so friendly and welcoming. We talked about you a great deal, and they hoped you might come over soon – sent everything proper, of course, kindest regards – kisses, I believe, from the girls. The second time they invited me to a ramble and a picnic, but unhappily I was bespoke. I was in Bath twice.'

'What did you think of Polly?'

'Oh, a dear girl – full of fun, and so kind to your old – aunt, I believe? And how she rattled away in French! I said several things myself, which she understood straight away, and relayed to the old lady, repeating my signals, as it were.'

'She *is* a dear child,' said her cousin. 'And believe me,' he said very seriously, 'that girl can *cook*. Her coq au vin – ! Her sole normande – ! And she has a deep comprehension of the English pudding. That strawberries jam was hers. A wonderful housekeeper. She has a modest little fortune, too,' he added, looking abstractedly at a tartan working into the port.

'Ah, dear Lord,' cried Jack, with a vehemence that made Christy-Pallière look round with alarm. 'Dear Lord, for the moment I had almost forgot. Shall I tell you why I was in Bath?'

'Do, I beg.'

'It is between ourselves?' Christy-Pallière nodded. 'By God,

I am so wretched about it: it was only that splendid dinner of yours that put it out of my mind these last two hours. Otherwise it has been with me ever since I left England. There was a girl, do you see, that I had met in Sussex – neighbours – and when I had a bad time in the Admiralty court with my neutrals, her mother took her down there, no longer approving of the connection. There was very nearly an understanding between us before then, but somehow I never quite clinched it. Christ, what a fool I was! So I saw her in Bath, but could never come to close quarters: I believe she did not quite like some little attentions I had paid her cousin.'

'Innocent attentions?'

'Well, yes, really; though I dare say they might have been misinterpreted. An astonishingly lovely girl, or rather woman – had been married once, husband knocked on the head in India – with a splendid dash and courage. And then, while I was eating my heart out between the Admiralty and the money-lenders in the City, I learnt that some fellow had made her an offer of marriage – it was spoken of everywhere as a settled thing. I cannot tell you how it hurt me. And this other girl, the one who stayed in Sussex, was so kind and sympathetic, and so very beautiful too, that I – well, you understand me. But, however, as soon as I thought things were going along capitally with her, and that we were very close friends, she pulled me up as though I had run into a boom, and asked me who the devil I thought I was? I had lost all my money by then, as you know; so upon my word, I could scarcely tell what to answer, particularly as I had begun to make out that maybe she was attached to my best friend, and perhaps the other way too, you follow me. I was not quite sure, but it looked damnably like it, above all when they parted. But I was so infernally hooked – could not sleep, could not eat – and sometimes she was charming to me again. So I committed myself pretty far, partly out of pique, do you see? Oh, God damn it all, if only – And then on top of it all there comes a letter from the first girl – '

'A letter to you?' cried Christy-Pallière. 'But this was not an intrigue, as I understand you?'

'As innocent as the day. Not so much as – well, hardly so much as a kiss. It was a surprising thing, was it not? But it was in England, you know, not in France, and things are rather different there: even so, it was astonishing. But such a sweet, modest letter, just to say that the whole thing about the marriage was so much God-damned stuff. It reached me the very day I left the country.'

'Why, then everything is perfect, surely? It is, in a serious young woman, an avowal – what more could you ask?'

'Why,' said Jack, with so wretched a look that Christy-Pallière, who had hitherto thought him a muff to mind having two young women at once, felt a wound in his heart. He patted Jack's arm to comfort him. 'Why, there is this other one, don't you see?' said Jack. 'In honour, I am pretty well committed to her, although it is not the same sort of feeling at all. To say nothing of my friend.'

STEPHEN AND DR RAMIS were closeted in a book-lined study. The great herbal that had been one of the subjects of their correspondence for the past year and more lay open on the table, with a high-detailed map of the new Spanish defences of Port Mahon folded into it. Dr Ramis had just come back from Minorca, his native island, and he had brought several documents for Stephen, for he was his most important contact with the Catalan autonomists. These papers, read and committed to memory, were now crushed black ashes in the fireplace, and the two men had moved on to the subject of humanity at large – man's general unfitness for life as it is lived.

'This is particularly the case with sailors,' said Stephen. 'I have watched them attentively, and find that they are more unsuited for life as it is ordinarily understood than men of any other calling whatsoever. I propose the following reason for this: the sailor, at sea (his proper element), lives in the present. There is nothing he can do about the past at all; and, having regard to the uncertainty of the omnipotent ocean and the weather, very little about the future. This, I may say in passing, accounts for the common tar's improvidence. The officers spend their lives fighting against this attitude on the part of the men – persuading them to tighten ropes, to belay and so on, against a vast series of contingencies; but the officers, being as sea-borne as the rest, do their task with a half conviction: from this arises uneasiness of mind, and hence the vagaries of those in authority. Sailors will provide against a storm tomorrow, or even in a fortnight's time; but for them the remoter possibilities are academic, unreal. They live in the present, I say; and basing itself upon this my mind offers a partially- formed conjecture – I should value your reflections upon it.'

'My lights are yours, for what they may be worth,' said Dr Ramis, leaning back and watching him with a dry, sharp, intelligent black eye. 'Though as you know, I am an enemy to speculation.'

'Let us take the whole range of disorders that have their origin in the mind, the disordered or the merely idle mind – false pregnancies, many hysterias, palpitations, dyspepsias, eczematous affections, some forms of impotence and many more that will occur to you at once. Now as far as my limited experience goes, these we do not find aboard ship. You agree, my dear colleague?'

Dr Ramis pursed his lips, and said, 'With reservations, I believe I may venture to say that I am tempted to do so. I do not commit myself, however.'

'Now let us turn our honest tar ashore, where he is compelled to live not in the present but in the future, with reference to futurity – all joys, benefits, prosperities to be hoped for, looked forward to, the subject of anxious thought directed towards next month, next year, nay, the next generation; no slops provided by the purser, no food perpetually served out at stated intervals. And what do we find?'

'Pox, drunkenness, a bestial dissolution of all moral principle, gross over-eating: the liver ruined in ten days' time.'

'Certainly, certainly; but more than that, we find, not indeed false pregnancies, but everything short of them. Anxiety, hypochondria, displacency, melancholia, costive, delicate stomachs – the ills of the city merchant increased tenfold. I have a particularly interesting subject who was in the most robust health at sea – Hygeia's darling – in spite of every kind of excess and of the most untoward circumstances: a short while on land, with household cares, matrimonial fancies – always in the future, observe – and we have a loss of eleven pounds' weight; a retention of the urine; black, compact, meagre stools; an obstinate eczema.'

'And for you all this is the effect of solid earth beneath the subject's feet? No more?'

Stephen held up his hands. 'It is the foetus of a thought; but I cherish it.'

'You speak of loss of weight. But I find that you yourself are thin. Nay, cadaverous, if I may speak as one physician to another. You have a very ill breath; your hair, already meagre two years ago, is now extremely sparse; you belch frequently; your eyes are hollow and dim. This is not merely your ill-considered use of tobacco – a noxious substance that should be prohibited by government – and of laudanum. I should very much like to see your excrement.'

'You shall, my dear sir, you shall. But I must leave you now. You will not forget my tincture? I shall abandon it entirely once I am in Lérida, but until then it is necessary to me.'

'You shall have it. And,' said Dr Ramis, with a veiled look, 'it is possible that I may send you a note of the first importance at the same time: I shall not know for some hours yet. If I do, it will be in system three. But pray let me feel your pulse before you go. Reedy, intermittent, my friend, just as I thought.'

'What did he mean by that?' said Stephen, referring not to the pulse but to the hypothetical note, and thinking again with some regret of the simplicity of his dealings with plain mercenary agents. Their motives were so clear; their loyalties were to their persons and their purse. The complexities of the entirely honest men, their sudden reticences, the interplay of conflicting loyalties, the personal sense of humour, made him feel old and tired.

'WHY, STEPHEN, here you are at last,' cried Jack, starting straight out of his sleep. 'I sat talking with Christy-Pallière; I hope you did not wait for me.' The subject of their conversation flooded his mind and put out its gaiety; but having gazed at the floor for a moment he looked up with at least an expression of cheerfulness and said, 'You were very nearly taken up for a spy this morning.'

Stephen stopped in his movement towards the desk and stood motionless, unnaturally poised.

'How I laughed when Christy-Pallière read me out your description, looking uncomfortable and prodigious grave; but I assured him on my sacred honour that you were looking for your double-headed eagles, and he was quite satisfied. He made an odd remark, by the way: said, was he in our shoes he should push on for Spain and not go to Porquerolles.'

'Aye, aye? Did he, so?' said Stephen mildly. 'Go back to sleep now, my dear. I conceive he would not choose to traverse the street to see euphorbia praestans, let alone cross an arm of the sea. I have a few notes to write, but I shall not disturb you. Go to sleep: we have a long day head of us.'

Some hours later, in the first grey light, Jack awoke to a faint scratching on the door. His waking mind stated that this was a rat in the bread-room, but his body instantly contradicted it – sleeping or awake his body knew whether it was afloat or not; at no time was it ever unaware of the continual shift and heave of the sea, or of the unnatural stability of the land. He opened his eyes and saw Stephen rise from his guttering candle, open the door, receive a bottle and a folded note. He went back to his table, opened the note, slowly deciphered it, burnt both scraps of paper in the candle flame; without turning round he said, 'Jack, you are awake, I believe?'

'Yes. These last five minutes. A good morning to you, Stephen. Is it going to be hot?'

'It is. And a good morning to you, my dear. Listen,' he said, sinking his voice to no more than a whisper, 'and do not call out or agitate yourself. Do you hear me now?'

'Yes.'

'War will be declared tomorrow. Bonaparte is seizing all British subjects.'

IN THE NARROW BAND of shade under the northern wall of Carcassonne a compassionate gendarme halted his convoy of English prisoners – seamen from detained and captured ships for the most part, a few officers who had been caught by the declaration of war, but some civilians too, travelling gentlemen, servants, grooms and tradesmen, since for the first time in civilized warfare Bonaparte had ordered the arrest of every British subject. They were hot, disconsolate and weary; their bundles had been soaked in a thunderstorm, and at first they had not even the spirit to spread them out in the sun, let alone to take notice of the dilapidated splendour of walls and turrets behind, the view of the new town and the river before them, or even the bear and its leader in the shadow of the next tower but one. But presently the word of the arrival of the convoy spread, and the crowd that had hurried out of the old town to stare was joined by market-women from over the bridge, bringing fruit, wine, bread, honey, sausages, pâté and goat cheeses wrapped in fresh green leaves. Most of the prisoners still had some money (this was only the beginning of their march to the far north-east) and when they had cooled a little, eaten and drunk, they put their clothes to dry and began to look about them.

'What o, the bear,' cried a sailor, quite happy now, with a quart of wine under his brass-buckled belt. 'Can he dance, mate?'

The bear-leader, an ill-looking brute with a patch over one eye and a fortnight's beard, took no notice. But the sailor was not to be put off by the sullenness of foreigners, and he was soon joined by an insistent group of friends, for he was the most popular and influential member of the crew of the pink *Chastity*, a merchantman that had had the unlucky idea of putting into Cette for water the day war was declared. One or two of them began shying stones at the great hairy mass to wake it up, or at least to have the pleasure of seeing it move. 'Avast the stone-throwing,' cried the sailor, his cheerful face clouding. 'You don't want to go a-teasing of bears, cully. Remember Elisha. There's nothing so unlucky as teasing of a bear.'

'You been a-bear-baiting, George, you know you have,' said a shipmate, tossing his stone up and down, not to have the air of abandoning it. 'We been to Hockley together.'

'Bear-baiting is different,' said George. 'The bears at Hockley is willing. This bear ain't. I dare say it's hot. Bears is Greenland creatures.'

The bear certainly looked hot. It was stretched out on what little grass it could find, strangely prostrate. But the clamour had spread; crews of other ships wanted to see it dance, and after some time the bear-leader came up and gave them to understand that the animal was indisposed – could only perform at night – 'im ave airy coat, mister; im ate up whole goat for im dinner; im bellyache.'

'Why, shipmates, there you are. Just as I said,' cried George. 'How would you like dancing in a – great fur pelisse, in this – sun?'

Events had escaped from George's control, however; an English sea-officer, wishing to impress the lady with whom he was travelling, had spoken to the sergeant of gendarmerie, and now the sergeant whistled to the master of the bear.

'Papers,' he said. 'A Spanish passport, eh? A very greasy passport too, my friend; do you sleep with your bear? Joan Margall, born in – what's this place?'

'Lérida, monsieur le sergent,' said the man, with the cringing humility of the poor.

'Lérida. Profession, bear-leader. Eh, bien: a led bear knows how to dance – that is logic. I have to have proof; it is my duty to see the bear perform.'

'Certainly, monsieur le sergent, at once. But the gentlemen will not expect too much from Flora; she is a female bear, and – ' He whispered in the gendarme's ear. 'Ah, ah? Just so,' said the gendarme. 'Well, just a pace or two, to satisfy my sense of duty.'

Dragged up by its chain and beaten by its leader till the dust flew from its shaggy side the bear shuffled forward. The man took a little pipe from his bosom, and playing it with one hand while he held the chain with the other, he hoisted the bear on to its hind legs, where it stood, swaying, amidst a murmur of disapprobation from the sailors. 'Crool buggers, these foringers,' said George. 'Look at his poor nose, with that – great ring.'

'English gents,' said the man, with an ingratiating leer. 'Ornpip.'

He played a recognizable hornpipe, and the bear staggered through a few of the steps, crossing its arms, before sitting down again. Trumpets sounded from the citadel behind the walls, the guard on the Narbonne gate changed, and the sergeant began to bawl 'En route, en route, les prisonniers.'

With avid and shamelessly persistent busyness, the bear-leader hurried up and down the line. 'Remember the bear, gents. Remember the bear. N'oubliez pas l'ours, messieurs-dames.'

SILENCE. THE CONVOY'S dust settled on the empty road. The inhabitants of Carcassonne all went to sleep; even the small boys who had been dropping mortar and clods of earth from the battlements on to the bear disappeared. Silence at last, and the chink of coins.

'Two livres four sous,' said the bear-leader. 'One maravedi, two Levantine coins of whose exact provenance I am uncertain, a Scotch groat.'

'When one sea-officer is to be roasted, there is always another at hand to turn the spit,' said the bear. 'It is an old service proverb. I hope to God I have that fornicating young sod under my command one day. I'll make him dance a hornpipe – oh, such a hornpipe. Stephen, prop my jaws open a little more, will you? I think I shall die in five minutes if you don't. Could we not creep into a field and take it off?'

'No,' said Stephen. 'But I shall lead you to an inn as soon as the market has cleared, and lodge you in a cool damp cellar for the afternoon. I will also get you a collar, to enable you to breathe. We must reach Couiza by dawn.'

THE WHITE ROAD winding, winding, up and up the French side of the Pyrenees, the afternoon sun – the June sun now – beating straight down on the dusty slope: the bear and its leader plodding on. Scorned by carts, feared by horses, they had already walked three hundred and fifty miles, taking a zigzag route to avoid most large towns and the dangerous zone of the coast, and to stay two nights in houses belonging to sure friends. Stephen was leading the bear by the paw, for Jack could not see below his muzzle when his head was on, and in his other hand he had the broad spiked collar that covered the hole through which Jack breathed. He was obliged to put it on for the best part of the day, however, for although this was a remote valley there were houses every few hundred yards, hamlets not three or four miles apart, and fools that kept accompanying them on their way. 'Was it a wise bear? How much did it eat a week? Was it ever wicked? Could he buckle the two ends of his mouth by exhibiting it?' And the nearer they came to the mountains, the more anecdotes of the bears that had been heard of, actually seen, and even killed. Bears, wolves, smugglers and mountain bandits, the Trabucayres and the Migueletes. Communicative fools, cheerful villagers, all eager for a treat, and dogs. Every hamlet, every farmhouse had its swarm of dogs that came out, amazed, howling, yapping and barking, haunting the bear's heels sometimes as far as the next vile swarm; for the dogs, if not the men, knew that there was something unnatural in the bear.

'It will not be long now,' said Stephen. 'At the far end, beyond the trees, I can see the turning of the main Le Perthus road. You can lie in the wood while I walk to the village to find out what is afoot. Should you like to sit down for a moment on this milestone? There is water in the ditch, and you could soak your feet.'

'Oh, I do not mind it,' said Jack, staggering as Stephen altered the rhythm of his walk to peer into the ditch. 'And I dare not soak them again, in any case.' The massive, hairy shape writhed a little – a mechanical attempt at seeing its tattered buttocks, legs and lower paws, dog-lacerated. 'The wood is not very far off, I dare say?'

'Oh, not above an hour or so. It is a beech-wood with an old marle-pit; and you may – I do not assert it, but I say you *may* – see the purple helleborine growing there!'

Lying in the deep cool fern with his collar off Jack felt the sweat still coursing down his chest, and the movement of ants, ticks, unidentified insects invading him; he smelt his own unwashed reek and the moist stench of the skin, imperfectly preserved in turpentine; but he minded none of it. He was too far gone to do anything but lie in the complete relaxation of utter weariness. It had of course been impossible to disguise him: a six-foot, yellow-haired Englishman would have stood out like a steeple in the south of France – a France alive with people tracking fugitives of one kind or another, foreign and domestic; but the price for this attempt was beyond anything he had believed possible. The torment of the ill-fitting, chafing hide, the incessantly-repeated small rasping wounds, the ooze of blood, the flayed soles of his feet, attached to the fur by court-plaster, the heat, the suffocation, the vile uncleanliness, had reached what he had thought the unendurable point ten days, two hundred miles, ago, in the torrid waste of the Causse du Palan.

Was this attempt going to succeed? At the bottom of his heart he had never doubted it to begin with – so long as he did his part (barring some act of God or unaccountable misfortune) neither he nor Stephen Maturin would pass the rest of the war as prisoners, cut off from all possibility of service, promotion, a lucky cruise, cut off from Sophia; cut off, indeed, from Diana. A long war, he made no doubt, for Bonaparte was strong – Jack had been astonished by the state of forwardness of everything he had seen in Toulon: three ships of the line almost ready for launching, a huge quantity of stores, unexampled zeal. Any man bred to the sea, any born sailor, could tell within an hour of being aboard whether a ship was an efficient, happy co-ordinated whole; it was the same with a naval port, and in Toulon his quick, professional eye had seen a great machine running very fast, very smoothly. France was strong; France owned the fine Dutch navy, controlled huge areas of western Europe; England was weak and alone – no allies left at all, as far as he could tell from the fragmentary, partial news they had picked up. Certainly the Royal Navy was weak; he had no doubt of that at all. St Vincent had tried to reform the dockyards rather than build ships, and now there were fewer that could stand in the line of battle than there had been in '93, in spite of all the building and all the captures during the ten years of war: and that again was a reason – quite apart from the obligations of the treaty – why Spain should come in on the side of France – another reason why they should find the frontier closed and Stephen's refuge lost to them, the attempt a failure after all. Had Spain declared? For the last two or three days they had been in the Roussillon, in French Catalonia, and he had not been able to understand anything that Stephen and the peasants said to one another. Stephen was strangely reticent these days. Jack had supposed he knew him through and through in the old uncomplicated times, and he loved all he knew; but now there were new depths, an underlying hard ruthlessness, an unexpected Maturin; and Jack was quite out of his depth.

Stephen had gone on, leaving him. Stephen had a passport into Spain – could move about there, war or no . . . Jack's mind darkened still further and thoughts he dared not formulate came welling up, an ugly swarm.

'Dear God,' he said at last, twisting his head from side to side, 'could I have sweated all my courage out?' Courage gone, and generosity with it? He had seen courage go – men run down hatchways in battle, officers cower behind the capstan. He and Stephen had talked about it: was courage a fixed, permanent quality? An expendable substance, each man having just so much, with a possible end in sight? Stephen had put forward views on courage – varying and relative – dependent upon diet, circumstances, the functioning of the bowels – the costive frequently timid – upon use, upon physical and spiritual freshness or exhaustion – the aged proverbially cautious – courage not an entity, but to be regarded as belonging to different, though related, systems, moral, physical, sexual – courage in brutes, in the castrated – complete integrity, unqualified courage or puerile fiction-jealousy, its effect upon courage – Stoics – the *satietas vitae* and the supreme courage of indifference – indifference, indifference . . .

The tune that Stephen always played on his bear-leader's pipe began to run through his head, mingling with Stephen's voice and half-remembered instances of courage from Plutarch, Nicholas of Pisa and Boethius, a curious little air with archaic intervals, limited to what four fingers and overblowing could do, but subtle, complicated . . .

The roaring of a little girl in a white pinafore woke him; she and some unseen friend were looking for the summer mushrooms that were found in this wood, and she had come upon a fungoid growth.

'Ramón,' she bellowed, and the hollow echoed with the sound, 'Ramón, Ramón, Ramón. Come and see what I have found. Come and see what I have found. Come and see . . .'

On and on and on. She was turned three-quarters from him; but presently, since her companion did not answer, she pivoted, directing her strong voice to the different quarters of the wood.

Jack had already shrunk as far as he could, and now as the child's face veered towards him he closed his eyes, in case she should sense their savage glare. His mind was now all alive; no trace of indifference now, but a passionate desire to succeed in this immediate step, to carry the whole undertaking through, come Hell or high water. 'Frighten the little beast and you will have a band of armed peasants round the wood in five minutes – slip away and you lose Stephen – out of touch, and all our papers sewed inside the skin.' The possibilities came racing one after another; and no solution.

'Come, come, child,' said Stephen. 'You will spoil your voice if you call out so. What have you there? It is a satanic boletus; you must not eat the satanic boletus, my dear. See how it turns blue when I break it with a twig. That is the devil blushing. But here we have a parasol. You may certainly eat the parasol. Have you seen my bear? I left him in the wood when I went to see En Jaume; he was sadly fatigued. Bears cannot stand the sun.'

'En Jaume is my godfather's uncle,' said the child. 'My godfather is En Pere. What is the name of your bear?'

'Flora,' said Stephen; and called, 'Flora!'

'You said *him* just now,' said the child with a frown, and began to roar 'Flora, Flora, Flora, Flora! Oh, Mother of God, what a huge great bear.' She put her hand in Stephen's and murmured, 'Aie, my – in the face of God what a bear.' But her courage returned, and she set to bellowing 'Ramón, Ramón, Ramón! Come and see my bear.'

'Good-bye, poppets,' said Stephen, in time. 'May God go with you.' And waving still to the little figures he said, 'I have firm news at last; mixed news. Spain has not declared war: but the Mediterranean ports are closed to English ships. We must go down to Gibraltar.'

'What about the frontier?'

Stephen pursed his lips. 'The village is filled with police and soldiers: two intelligence men are in charge, searching everything. They have arrested one English agent.'

'How do you know?'

'The priest who confessed him told me. But sure I have never thought of the road itself. I know, I *did* know, another way. Stand over – stand over more this way. The pink roof, and behind it a peak? And to the right of that, beyond the forest, a bare mountain? That is the frontier, joy, and in the dip there is a pass, a path down to Recasens and Cantallops. We will slip across the road after dusk and be there at dawn.'

'May I take off the skin?'

'You may not. I regret it extremely, Jack; but I do not know the path well – there are patrols out, not only for the smugglers but for the fugitives, and we may blunder into one or even two. It is a smugglers' path, a dangerous path indeed, for while the French may shoot you for walking upon it as a man, the smugglers may do the same for looking like a bear. But the second is the proper choice; your smuggler is open to reason, and your patrol is not.'

Half an hour in the bushes by the road, waiting for the long slow train of a battery to pass by – guns, waggons, camp-followers – several coaches, one pulled by eight mules in crimson harness, some isolated horsemen; for now that they could see the frontier-line their caution grew to superstitious lengths.

Half an hour, and then across to the cart-track up to Saint-Jean de l'Albère. Up and up, the moon clearing the forest ahead of them after the first hour; and with the coming of the moon the first breaths of a sirocco from the Spanish plains, a waft from an opened oven-door.

Up and still up. After the last barn the track dwindled to a ribbon and they had to walk in single file; Jack saw Stephen's monstrous bundle – a dark shape, no more – moving steadily a pace or two in front of them, and something like hatred glowed around his stomach. He reasoned: 'The pack is heavy; it weighs fifty or sixty pounds – all our possessions; he too has been going on all these days, never a murmur; the straps wring his back and shoulders, a bloody welt on either side.' But the unwavering determination of that dim form, moving steadily on and on, effortlessly, it seemed, always too fast and never pausing – the impossibility of keeping up, of forcing himself another hundred yards, and the equal impossibility of calling for a rest, drowned his reason, leaving only the dull fire of resentment.

The path meandered, branching and sometimes disappearing among huge ancient widespread beeches, their trunks silver in the moon, and at last Stephen stopped. Jack blundered into him, stood still, and felt a hand gripping him hard through the skin: Stephen guided him into the black velvet shadow of a fallen tree. Over the soughing of the wind he heard a repeated metallic sound, and as he recognized the regular beat – a patrol making too much noise – all notion of the unbreathable air and the intolerable state of his body left him. Low voices now and then, a cough, still the clink-clink-clink of someone's musket against a buckle, and presently the soldiers passed within twenty yards of them, moving down the mountain-side.

The same strong hand pulling him, and they were on the path again. Always this eternal climb, sometimes across the leaf-filled bed of a stream, sometimes up an open slope so steep that it was hands and knees: and the sirocco. 'Can this be real?' he wondered. 'Must it go on for ever?'

The beech-trees gave way to pines: pine-needles under foot, oh the pain. Endless pines on an endless mountain, their roaring tops bowing northwards in the wind.

The shape in front had stopped, muttering 'It should be about here – the second fork – there was a charcoal burner's lay – an uprooted larch, bees in the hollow trunk.'

Jack closed his eyes for a great swimming pause, a respite, and when he opened them again he saw that the sky ahead was lightening. Behind them the moon had sunk into a haze, far down in the deep veiled complicated valleys.

The pines. Then suddenly no more pines – a few stunted bushes, heather, and the open turf. They were on the upper edge of the forest, a forest ruled off sharp, as though by a line; and they stood, silently looking out. After two or three minutes, right up there in the eye of the wind, Jack saw a movement. Leaning to Stephen he said 'Dog?' Soldiers who had had the sense to bring a dog? Loss, dead failure after all this?

Stephen took his head, and whispering right into the hairy ear he said 'Wolf. A young – a young *female* wolf.'

Still Stephen waited, searching the bushes, the bare rocks, from the far left to the far right, before he walked out, paced over the short grass to a stone set on the very top of the slope, a squared stone with a red-painted cross cut into it.

'Jack,' said he, leading him beyond the boundary mark, 'I bid you welcome to my land. We are in Spain. That is my house below – we are at home. Come, let me get your head off. Now you can breathe, my poor friend. There are two springs under the brow of the hill, by those chestnuts, where you can wash and take off the skin. How I rejoice at the sight of that wolf. Look, here is her dung, quite fresh. No doubt this is a wolf's pissing-post: like all the dogs, they have their regular . . .'

Jack sat heavily on the stone, gasping inwards, filling his starved lungs. Some reality other than general suffering returned. 'Wolf's pissing-post: oh, yes.' In front of him the ground fell suddenly – almost a precipice – two thousand feet below there was Spanish Catalonia spread out in the morning light. A high-towered castle just below them on a jutting rock – a lobbed stone would reach it; the Pyrenees folded away and away in long fingers to the plain; square distant fields, vineyards green; a shining river winding left-handed towards the great sweep of the sea; the Bay of Rosas with Cap Creus at the far northern end – home water, and now the hot wind smelt of salt.

'I am happy you were pleased with your wolf,' he said at last in a sleep-walker's voice. 'There are – they are uncommon rare, I dare say.'

'Not at all, my dear. We have them by the score – can never leave the sheep by night. No. Her presence means we are alone. That is why I rejoice. I rejoice. Even so, I think we should go down to the spring: it is under the chestnuts, those chestnuts not two minutes down. That wolfess may be a fool – see her now, moving among the junipers – and I should not wish to fail, just when we have succeeded. Some chance cross-patrol, douaniers rather than soldiers, some zealous sergeant with a carabine . . . Can you get up? God help me, I hardly can.'

The spring, Jack wallowing in it, cold water and grit sweeping off the crass, the stream running filthy, but coming fresh and fresh straight from the rock. Jack luxuriating, drying in the wind, plunging again and again. His body was dead white where it was not cruelly galled, bitten, rasped; his colourless face puffy, sweat-swollen, corpse-like, a tangled yellow beard covering his mouth; his eyes were red and pustulent. But there was life in them, brilliant delight blazing through the physical distress.

'You have lost between three and four stone – ' observed Stephen, appraising his loins and belly.

'I am sure you are right,' said Jack. 'And nine parts of it is in this vile skin, a good three stone of human grease.' He kicked the limp bear with his bleeding foot, damned it once or twice for a son of a bitch, and observed he must take the papers out before setting it alight. 'How it will stink – how it *does* stink, by God. Just hand me along the scissors, Stephen, pray.'

'The bear may serve again,' said Stephen. 'Let us roll it up and thrust it under the bush. I will send for it from the house.'

'Is the house a great way off?'

'Why no,' said Stephen, pointing to the castle. 'It is just there below us, a thousand feet or so – to the right of the white scar, the marble quarry. Though I am afraid it will take us an hour to get there – an hour to breakfast.'

'Is that castle yours, Stephen?'

'It is. And this is my sheepwalk. What is more,' he said, looking sharply at the cowpats, 'I believe those French dogs from La Vaill have been sending their cattle over to eat my grass.'

5

THREE DAYS AFTER crossing the tropic the *Lord Nelson* East-Indiaman, Captain Spottiswood, homeward-bound from Bombay, broached to in a westerly gale; the ship survived, but she lost her maintopmast and its topgallant, carried away her mizzen just above the cap, sprang her fore and main masts, and damaged her rigging to an extraordinary extent. She also lost her boats upon the booms and most of the booms themselves; so, the wind being foul for Madeira, the passengers in a state of panic and the crew near mutiny after a very long and uniformly disagreeable voyage, Mr Spottiswood bore away for Gibraltar, right under his lee, although like all homeward-bound captains he was very unwilling to put into a naval port. As he had expected, he lost many of his English-born sailormen to the press, all prime hands; but he did repair his ship, and as some meagre consolation he did embark a few passengers.

The first to come aboard were Jack Aubrey and Stephen Maturin; they were received by the captain at the head of his officers in some style, for the Company possessed, or at least arrogated to itself, a particular status, and its ships adopted many of the ways of the Royal Navy. There were sensible reasons for some of these – the chequered gunports, for instance, and the general appearance of regularity had persuaded many an enemy cruiser that he had to do with a man-of-war and that he had better look elsewhere – but there were many little pretensions that vexed the real Navy, and King's officers aboard a Company ship were apt to look about them with a carping eye, In this case a critic could have found fault straight away: in spite of the black side-boys in their white gloves, the reception was incorrect – that vague huddle of figures would never have done aboard the *Superb*, for example, in which Jack had dined, and whose hospitality was still ringing in his head, although he could walk straight. Furthermore, he was conscious of a huge grin from the midst of that same huddle, a kind of half-determined nodding and becking, a bashfulness accompanied by familiarity that brought a hint of stiffness into his expression. He spoke with particular civility to Captain Spottiswood, who privately damned him for his condescension, and then turning he recognized the stare.

'Why, Pullings!' he cried, all his ill-humour – a very slight ill-humour in any case – vanishing at once and the hard lines of his face dissolving into a delighted smile. 'How happy I am to see you! How do you do? How are you coming along, eh? Eh?'

'And this is our supercargo, Mr Jennings,' said Captain Spottiswood, not best pleased at having his regular sequence changed. 'Mr Bates. Mr Wand. Mr Pullings you already know, I see.'

'We were shipmates,' said Jack, shaking Pullings's hand with a force in direct proportion to his affection for the young man, a former master's mate and acting-lieutenant in the *Sophie*, who was now beaming over his shoulder at Dr Maturin.

The *Lord Nelson* had never been a happy or a fortunate ship, but within an hour of taking her passengers on board a brisk Levanter sprang up to carry her right out through the strong current of the Gut and into the full Atlantic; and poor

Captain Spottiswood, in the innocence of his heart, reckoned this a great stroke of luck – a good omen at last, perhaps. She was not a very comely ship, either, nor much of a sailer: comfortable for the passengers, roomy for her cargo, certainly; but crank, slow in stays, and near the end of her useful life. This was, in fact, to be her last voyage, and even for her trip in 1801 the underwriters had insisted upon an extra thirty shillings per cent.

It also happened that she was the first Indiaman Jack had ever sailed in, and as he walked about with Pullings during his watch below he gazed with astonishment at the general lumber of the deck and at the casks and water-butts lashed between the guns. Twenty eighteen-pounders and six twelves: an imposing show of force for a merchantman. 'And how many people have you aboard?' he asked.

'Just above a hundred now, sir. A hundred and two, to be exact.'

'Well, well, well,' said Jack. In the Navy they did not think nine men and a powder-boy too much for an eighteen-pounder, seven and a boy for the twelves: a hundred and twenty-four men to fight the guns one side – a hundred and twenty-four beef- and pork-fed Englishmen, and another hundred to trim the sails, work the ship, repel boarders, ply the small arms, and fight the other side on occasion. He glanced at the Lascars squatting around their heap of junk, working under the orders of their turbanned serang; they might be tolerably good seamen in their way, perhaps, but they were very slight, and he could not see five or six of them running out a two-ton gun against the Atlantic roll. This impression of smallness was increased by the fact that most of them were cold; the few European members of the crew were in their shirts, but several of the Lascars had pea-jackets on as well, and all had a blueish tinge in their dark complexions.

'Well, well, well,' said Jack again. He did not like to say more, for his opinion of the *Lord Nelson* was crystallizing fast, and any expression of it could not but give pain – Pullings must feel himself part of the ship. The young man certainly knew that Captain Spottiswood lacked all authority, and that the *Lord Nelson* moved like a log, and that she had twice missed stays off Cape Trafalgar, having to wear round at last: but there was certainly no point in putting this into words. He looked round for something that he could praise with at least an appearance of candour. The gleam of the brass larboard bow-gun caught his eye, and he commended it. 'Really quite like gold,' he said.

'Yes,' said Pullings. 'They do it voluntary – *poojah, poojah*, they say. For days off the island and again when we touched at the Cape, they had a wreath of marigolds around the muzzle. They say their prayers to it, poor fellows, because they think it is like – well, sir, I hardly like to name what they think it is like. But she *is* medium dry, sir, and she *is* roomy – oh, as roomy as a first-rate. I have a vast great spacious cabin to myself. Would you do me the honour of stepping below, sir, and drinking a glass of arrack?'

'I should like it of all things,' said Jack. And stretching himself cautiously on the locker in the vast great spacious cabin, he said, 'How do you come to be here, Pullings, in all your glory?'

'Why, sir, I could not get a ship and they would not confirm me in my rank. "No white lapels for you, Pullings, old cock," they said. "We got too many coves like you, by half." '

'What a damned shame,' cried Jack, who had seen Pullings in action and who knew that the Navy did not and indeed could not possibly have too many coves like him.

'So I tried for a midshipman again, but none of my old captains had a ship themselves; or if they had – and the Honourable Berkely had – no vacancy. I took your letter to Captain Seymour – *Amethyst*, refitting in Hamoaze. Old Cozzens gave me a lift down as far as the Vizes. Captain Seymour received me very polite when I said I was from you, most obliging: nothing starchy or touch-me-not about him,

sir. But he scratched his head and damned his wig when he
opened the letter and read it. He said he would have blessed
the day he could have obliged you, particularly with such
advantage to himself, which was the civillest thing I ever
heard – turned so neat – but that it was not in his power. He
led me to the gun-room and the mids' berth himself to prove
he could not take another young gentleman on to his quarterdeck. He was so earnest to be believed, though in course I
credited him the moment he opened his mouth, that he
desired me to count their chests. Then he gave me a thundering good dinner in his own cabin just him and me – I needed
it, sir, for I'd walked the last twenty miles – and after the pudding we went over your action in the *Sophie*: he knew everything, except quite how the wind had veered, and he made
me tell just where I had been from the first gun to the last.
Then "damn my eyes," says he, "I cannot let one of Captain
Aubrey's officers rot on shore without trying to stretch the little interest I have," and he wrote me one letter for Mr Adams
at the Admiralty and another for Mr Bowles, a great man at
East India House.'

'Mr Bowles married his sister,' observed Jack.

'Yes, sir,' said Pullings. 'But I paid little heed to it just then,
because, do you see, Captain Seymour promised that Mr
Adams would get me an interview with Old Jarvie himself,
and I was in great hopes, for I had always heard, in the service, that he had a kindness for chaps that came in over the
bows. So I got back to town again somehow, and there I was,
double-shaved and all of a tremble in that old waiting-room
for an hour or two. Mr Adams called me in, warns me to speak
up loud and clear to his Lordship, and he is going on to say
about not mentioning the good word you was so kind as to
put in for me, when there's a bloody great din outside, like a
boarding-party. Out he goes to see what's o'clock, and comes
back with his face as blank as an egg. "The old devil," he said,
"he's pressed Lieutenant Salt. Pressed him in the Admiralty
itself, and has sent him off to the tender with a file of

marines. Eight years' seniority, and he has sent him off with a file of Marines." Did you ever hear of it, sir?'

'Never a word.'

'Well, there was this Mr Salt right desperate for a ship, and he bombarded the First Lord with a letter a day for months and turned up every Wednesday and Friday to ask for an interview. And on the last Friday of all, the day I was there, Old Jarvie winked his eye, said "You want to go to sea? Then to sea you shall go, sir," and had him pressed on the spot.'

'An officer? Pressed for a common sailor?' cried Jack. 'I've never heard of such a thing in my life.'

'Nor nobody else: particularly poor Mr Salt,' said Pullings. 'But that's the way it was, sir. And when I heard that, and when people came in and whispered about it, I felt so timid-like and abashed, that when Mr Adams said perhaps I should try another day, I hurried out into Whitehall and asked the quickest way to East India House of the porter. I fell lucky – Mr Bowles was very kind – and so here I am. It's a good berth: twice the pay, and you are allowed a little venture of your own – I have a chest of China embroidery in the after-hold. But Lord, sir, to be in a man-of-war again!'

'It may not be so long now,' said Jack. 'Pitt's back and Old Jarvie's gone – refused the Channel Fleet – if he weren't a first-rate seaman I'd say the devil go with him – and Dundas is at the Admiralty. Lord Melville. I'm pretty well with him, and if only we can spread a little more canvas and get in before all the plums are snapped up, it will go hard if we don't make a cruise together again.'

Spreading more canvas: that was the difficulty. Ever since his disagreeable experience in latitude 33° N. Captain Spottiswood had been unwilling to set even his topgallantsails, and the days passed slowly, slowly by. Jack spent much of his time leaning over the taffrail, staring into the *Lord Nelson*'s gentle wake as it stretched away to the south and west, for he did not care to watch the unhurried working of the ship, and the sight of the topgallantmasts struck down on deck filled him with impatience. His most usual companions were the Misses Lamb, good-natured jolly short-legged squat swarthy girls who had gone out to India with the fishing-fleet – they called it that themselves, cheerfully enough – and who were now returning, maidens still, under the protection of their uncle, Major Hill of the Bengal Artillery.

They sat in a line, with Jack between the two girls and a chair for Stephen on the left; and although the *Lord Nelson* was now in the Bay of Biscay, with a fresh breeze in the south-west and the temperature down in the fifties, they kept the deck bravely, cocooned in rugs and shawls, their pink noses peeping out.

'They say the Spanish ladies are amazingly beautiful,' said Miss Lamb. 'Much more so than the French, though not so elegant. Pray, Captain Aubrey, is it so?'

'Why, upon my word,' said Jack, 'I can hardly tell you. I never saw any of 'em.'

'But was you not several months in Spain?' cried Miss Susan.

'Indeed I was, but nearly all the time I was laid up at Dr Maturin's place near Lérida – all arches, painted blue, as they have in those parts; a courtyard inside, and grilles, and orange-trees; but no ladies of Spain that I recall. There was a dear old biddy that fed me pap – would not be denied – and on Sundays she wore a high comb and a mantilla; but she was not what you would call a beauty.'

'Was you very ill, sir?' asked Miss Lamb respectfully.

'I believe I must have been,' said Jack, 'for they shaved my head, clapped on their leeches twice a day, and made me drink warm goat's milk whenever I came to my senses; and by the time it was over I was so weak that I could scarcely sit my horse – we rode no more than fifteen or twenty miles a day for the first week.'

'How fortunate you were travelling with dear Dr Maturin,' said Miss Susan. 'I truly dote upon that man.'

'I have no doubt he pulled me through – quite lost, but for

him,' said Jack. 'Always there, ready to bleed or dose me, night and day. Lord, such doses! I dare say I swallowed a moderate-sized apothecary's shop – Stephen, I was just telling Miss Susan how you tried to poison me with your experimental brews.'

'Do not believe him, Dr Maturin. He has been telling us how you certainly saved his life. We are so grateful; he has taught us to knot laniards and to splice our wool.'

'Aye?' said Stephen. 'I am looking for the captain.' He peered inquisitively under the empty chair. 'I have news that will interest him; it is of interest to us all. The Lascars are suffering not from the buldoo-panee of their own miasmatic plains, whatever Mr Parley may maintain, but from the Spanish influenza! It is whimsical enough to reflect that we, in our haste, should be the cause of our own delay, is it not? For with so few hands we shall no doubt see our topsails handed presently.'

'I am in no hurry. I wish this voyage would go on for ever,' said Miss Lamb, arousing an echo in her sister alone.

'Is it catching?' asked Jack.

'Oh, eminently so, my dear,' said Stephen. 'I dare say it will sweep the ship in the next few days. But I shall dose them; oh, I shall dose them! Young ladies, I desire you will take physic tonight: I have made up a comfortable little prophylactic bottle for you both, and another, of greater strength, for Major Hill. A whale! A whale!'

'Where away?' cried Mr Johnstone, the first officer. He had been in the Greenland fishery when he was young, and his whole being responded to the cry. He had no answer, for Dr Maturin was squatting like a baboon, resting a telescope on the rail and training it with concentrated diligence upon the heaving sea between the ship and the horizon; but directing his gaze along the tube and staring under his two hands cupped Mr Johnstone presently saw the distant spout, followed by the hint of an immense slow roll, gleaming black against the grey.

'Och, she's no good to you at all,' he said, 'A finwhale.'

'Could you really see its fins that great way off?' cried Miss Susan. 'How wonderful sailors are! But why is it no good, Mr Johnstone? Not quite wholesome, perhaps, like oysters without an R?'

'There she blows!' cried Mr Johnstone, but in a detached, academic voice, from mere habit. 'Another one. See the spout, Miss Susan. Just a single fountain-jet: that means a finner – your right-whale shows two. Aye, aye, there she goes again. There must be a fair-sized pod. No good to man or beast. It vexes my heart to think of all that prime oil swimming there, no good to man or beast.'

'But *why* is the whale no good?' asked Miss Lamb. 'Why, because she is a finwhale, to be sure.'

'My sister means, what is wrong with being a finwhale? Do you not, Lucy?'

'The finner is too hugeous, ma'am. If you are so rash as to make an attempt upon her – if you creep up in the whaleboat and strike your harpoon home, she will bash the boat like a bowl of neeps as she sounds, maybe, and in any case she will run out your two-hundred-fathom whale-line in less than a minute – you bend on another as quick as you can – she runs it out – another, and still she runs. She tows you under, or she carries all away: you lose your line or your life or both. Which is as who should say, be humble, flee ambition. Canst thou draw up Leviathan with a hook? Confine thyself to the right-whale, thy lawful prey.'

'Oh, I will, Mr Johnstone,' cried Miss Lamb. 'I promise you I shall never attack a finwhale all my life.'

Jack liked to see a whale – amiable creatures – but he could tear himself away from them more easily than either Stephen or the person at the mast-head who was supposed to be looking-out, and for some time now he had been watching the white fleck of sails against the darkening westward sky. A ship, he decided at last: a ship under easy sail on the opposite tack.

A ship she was, the *Bellone*, a Bordeaux privateer, one of the most beautiful to sail from that port, high and light as a swan, yet stiff; a thirty-four-gun ship-rigged privateer with a clean bottom, a new set of sails and two hundred and sixty men aboard. A fair proportion of those sharp-eyed mariners were at present in the tops or at the crowded mast-heads, and although they could not exactly make the *Lord Nelson* out, they could see enough to make Captain Dumanoir edge cautiously down for a closer look in the failing light.

What he saw was a twenty-six-gun ship, that was certain; probably a man-of-war, but if so then a partially disabled man-of-war, or her topgallantmasts would never have been down on deck in such a breeze. And as Dumanoir and his second captain gazed and pondered in the main crosstrees all notion of the *Lord Nelson*'s being a man-of-war gradually left them. They were old-experienced sailors; they had seen much of the Royal Navy in the last ten years; and there was something about the *Lord Nelson*'s progress that did not square with their experience.

'She's an Indiaman,' said Captain Dumanoir, and although he was only three parts convinced his heart began to thump and his arm to tremble; he hooked it round the topgallant shrouds and repeated, 'An Indiaman.' Short of a Spanish galleon or treasure-ship, a British Indiaman was the richest prize the sea could offer.

A hundred little details confirmed his judgment; yet he might be wrong; he might be leading his precious *Bellone* into an action with one of those stubby English sixth-rates that carried twenty-four-pounder carronades, the genuine smashers, served by a numerous, well-trained, bloody-minded crew; and although Captain Dumanoir had no sort of objection to a dust-up with any vessel roughly his own size, King's ship or not, he was primarily a commerce-destroyer; his function was to provide his owners with a profit, not to cover himself with glory.

He regained his quarterdeck, took one or two turns, glancing up at the western sky. 'Dowse the lights one by one,' he said. 'And in fifteen minutes' time put her about. Courses and foretopsail alone. Matthieu, Jean-Paul, Petit-André, up you go: let them be relieved every glass, Monsieur Vincent.' The *Bellone* was one of the few French ships of the time in which these orders, together with others concerning the preparation of the guns and small-arms, were received without comment and exactly obeyed.

So exactly that even before the lightening of the day the look-out on the *Lord Nelson*'s forecastle felt the loom of a ship to the windward, a ship sailing on a parallel course and not much above a mile away. What he could not see was that the ship was cleared for action – guns run out, shot-racks charged, cartridge filled and waiting, small-arms served out, splinter-netting rigged, yards puddened, boats towing astern – but he did not like her proximity, nor the lack of lights, and when he had stared awhile, wiping his streaming eyes, he hailed the quarterdeck: between his sneezes he gave Mr Pullings to understand that there was a vessel on the larboard beam.

Pullings' mind, lulled by the long even send of the sea, the regular hum of the rigging, the warmth of his pilot-jacket and blackguardly wool hat, exploded into sharp awareness. He was out of his corner by the binnacle, half-way up the weather shrouds, before the sneezing had stopped: three seconds for a long hard stare, and he turned up the watch with the roar he had learnt aboard HMS *Sophie*. The boarding-netting was already rigging out on the long iron cranes by the time he had shaken Captain Spottiswood into full wakefulness – orders confirmed, beat to action, clear the decks, run out the guns, women down into the hold.

He found Jack on deck in his nightshirt. 'She means business,' he said, over the high beating of the eastern drum. The privateer had put up her helm. Her yards were braced round and she was entering a long smooth curve that would cut the *Lord Nelson*'s present course in perhaps a quarter of an hour;

her main and fore sails were clewed up, and it was clear that she meant to bear down under topsails alone – could do so with ease, a greyhound after a badger. 'But I have time to put my breeches on.'

Breeches, a pair of pistols. Stephen methodically laying out his instruments by the light of a farthing dip.

'What do you make of her, Jack?' he asked.

'Corvette or a damned big privateer: she means business.'

Up on deck. Much more daylight already, and a scene of less disorder than he had feared, a far better state of things. Captain Spottiswood had put the Indiaman before the wind to gain a few minutes' preparation, the French ship was still half a mile away, still under her topsails, still a little dubious, choosing to probe the *Lord Nelson*'s strength rather than make a dash for it.

Captain Spottiswood might lack decision, but his officers did not, nor the most part of his crew: they were used to the pirates of the South China Sea, to the wicked Malays of the Straits, to the Arabs of the Persian Gulf, and they had the boarding-netting rigged out taut and trim, the arms chest open, and at least half the guns run out.

On the crowded quarterdeck Jack snapped in between two sets of orders, said, 'I am at your disposition, sir.' The drawn, hesitant, elderly face turned towards him. 'Shall I take command of the for'ard division?'

'Do, sir. Do.'

'Come with me,' he said to Major Hill, hovering there at the fringe of the group. They ran along the gangway to the forward eighteen-pounders, two under the forecastle, two bare to the thin rain. Pullings had the waist division; the first officer the twelve-pounders on the quarterdeck; Mr Wand the maindeck eighteen-pounders aft, all encumbered in the stateroom and the cabins; and overhead a tall thin midshipman, looking desperately ill, stood shouting weakly at the bow-gun's crew.

The forward division on the larboard side, guns one, three,

five and seven, were fine modern flintlock pieces; two were already run out – primed, cocked and waiting. Number one's port-lid was jammed, its crew prising with their crows and handspikes in the confined space, thumping it with shot, hauling on the port-tackle, all smelling of brown men in violent emotion. Jack bent low under the beams, straddled the gun: with his hands hard on the carriage he lashed out backwards with all his might. Splinters and flakes of paint dropped from the port: it did not budge – seemed built into the ship. Three times. He slipped off, hobbled round to check the breeching, cried 'Bowse her up' and as the gun's muzzle came hard against the port, 'Stand by, stand by.' He pulled the laniard. A spark, a great sullen crash (damp powder, by God), and the gun leapt back under him. The acrid smoke tore out of the shattered port, and as it thinned Jack saw the sponger already at work, his swab right down the barrel of the gun, while the rest of the crew clapped on to the train-tackle. 'They know their business' he thought with pleasure, leaning out and tearing the wreckage from its hooks. 'Crucify that God-damned gunner!' But this was no time for reflection. Number three was still inboard. Jack and Major Hill tailed on to the side-tackles, and with 'One – two – three' they ran it up, the carriage crashing against the port-sill and the muzzle as far out as it could go. Number five had no more than four Lascars and a midshipman to serve it, an empty shot-rack and only three wads: it must have run itself out on the roll when they cast loose. 'Where are your men?' he asked the boy, taking his dirk and cutting the seizing within the clinch.

'Sick, sir, all sick. Kalim is nearly dead – can't speak.'

'Tell the gunner we must have shot and a cheese of wads. Cut along. Now, sir?' to another midshipman.

'Captain asks what did you fire for, sir,' panted the young man.

'To open the port,' said Jack, smiling into his round-eyed, anxious face. 'Tell him, with my compliments, there is nothing like enough eighteen-pound shot on deck. Cut along now.' The boy shut his mouth on the rest of his message and vanished.

Number seven was in good shape: seven men to its crew, powder-boy standing over to starboard with a cartridge in his hands, gun levelled, tackle-falls neatly faked down; all ship-shape. Its captain, a grizzled European, only replied: with a nervous chuckle, keeping his head bent away, feigning to look along the sights. A rum seaman, no doubt, a man who had served with him in some commission, who had deserted, and who was afraid of being recognized. Once a quarter-gunner, to judge from the trimness of the gear. 'I hope he can point his piece as well as he . . .'

Jack straightened from his inspection of the flint and pan and glanced right and left. The hammocks were coming up in relays, piling into the netting. Half a dozen very sick men flogged on deck by the serang's mates, were creeping about with shot, and he was standing behind them, obviously in full control; there was still some confusion on the quarterdeck, but the air of frantic haste had gone. This was a breathing-space, and lucky they were to have it. Fore and aft the India-man looked like a fighting-ship: thinly manned, decks still encumbered, but a fighting-ship. He looked out over the sea: light enough to see the red of the tricolour five hundred yards away – a severe cold light now the rain had stopped, and a grey, grey sea. Wind steady in the west; high cloud except on the horizon; a long even swell. The *Bellone* still had her lar-board tacks aboard: she was hanging off to see what weight of metal the *Lord Nelson* carried. And the *Lord Nelson* was still before the wind, moving heavily – this was one of her many bad points of sailing. If Captain Spottiswood continued to run it was likely that the Frenchman would bear up, and moving two miles for the *Lord Nelson*'s one, cross under her stern and rake her. That was his business: for the moment Jack's world was confined to his guns: there was a comfort in subordination, in small responsibility, no decisions . . . Seven, five and three were well enough: number one was still too cluttered for a full team to work it fast, and a full team it must have. A last sharp look at the privateer – how beautifully she breasted the swell – and he dived under the forecastle.

Hard, fast, dogged, mechanical work, shifting heavy lumps, bales, casks: he found that what he was whistling under his breath was the adagio from Hummel's piece – Sophia's inept playing of it – Diana's rough splendid dash – a jet of intense feeling for Sophia – loving, protective – a clear image of her on the steps of that house. Some fool, Stephen of all people, had said you could not be both busy and unhappy, sad.

The *Bellone*'s opening gun cut short these reflections. Her starboard bow eight-pounder sent a ball skipping along the *Lord Nelson*'s larboard side; and as though he had needed this to set him going, Captain Spottiswood called out his orders. The yards braced round, the seascape turned, and the privateer came into view through the number one gun-port, framed there, bright against the darkness of the low crowded forecastle. The *Lord Nelson* fell off a little, steadied on her new course with the *Bellone* on her larboard quarter, so that now Jack saw no more than her head-sails, four hundred yards away, long musket-shot. And as the Indiaman steadied, so her after guns went off, a six-fold crash, a thin high-pitched cheering, and the word came forward. 'Fire as they bear.'

'This is more like it,' said Jack, plunging out of the forecastle. The long pause before action was always hard to bear, but now in a few seconds everything would vanish but for the living instant – no sadness, no time for fear. Number seven was in good hands, trained right round aft as far as the port would allow, and its captain glaring along the barrel, poised for the roll. The waist guns went off together, and in their eddying smoke – it filled his lungs, a choking exaltation – Jack and Major Hill flung themselves upon the long crows to heave number five, that dull inanimate weight, while the Lascars tailed on to the forward train-tackle to help traverse it to point it at the *Bellone*'s stern, just in view over the dispart-sight. Number seven went off with a poor slow explosion and a great deal of smoke. 'If the powder is all like that,' thought Jack, crouching over number five, his handspike ready to elevate the gun, 'we might as well try boarding right away. But,' he added, 'it is more likely the mumping villain has never drawn it this last week and more.' He waited for the smoke to clear, for the roll of the ship to bring the gun to bear, slowly up and up, and just as he heaved on the laniard he saw the *Bellone* vanish in the white cloud of her own broadside. The gun sprang from under his arched body. He could not see the fall of the shot for the smoke, but from the fine round crash it must have been well pitched up. The privateer's broadside sang and howled overhead – holes in the foretopsail, a bowline hanging loose. The bow-gun overhead went off, and he darted into the forecastle, leaping over the train-tackle as number five was sponged and reloaded. He laid three and one, fired them, and ran back along the line to help run out number five again.

The firing was general now: the *Lord Nelson*'s thirteen larboard guns spoke in ones or twos every half minute or so; the *Bellone*'s seventeen, having fired three steady broadsides in five minutes – a splendid rate even for a man-of-war – had now become irregular, an uninterrupted roll of fire. Her leeward side was veiled in a cloud of smoke that drifted across the intervening sea to join the smoke shot out against the wind by the Indiaman's guns, and through it all there was the stab-stab of orange flame. Only twice could Jack be sure of the flight of his division's shot, once when a flaw in the wind, tearing the curtain aside, showed number seven strike her amidships, just above the main-chains, and again when he saw his own hull her in the bows: her sails were not as pretty as they had been, either, but she had nevertheless closed the distance and she was now on the *Lord Nelson*'s beam, hammering her hard. Would she forge ahead and cross?

There was little time for thought as Jack raced from gun to

gun, bearing a hand, running out, swabbing and loading, but it was clear that the *Bellone* had no heavier guns than eight-pounders, that she meant to tear the Indiaman's sails, rigging and spars to pieces rather than to damage her valuable hull and cargo. There was little doubt that she did not relish the eighteen-pound shot that hit her – three or four between wind and water would be very serious, and a single ball might carry away a straining topmast. If they did not hit her hard soon, she would close – abandon her elegant tactics and close. She was an awkward customer, with her formidable gunnery and her repeated attempts at crossing the *Lord Nelson*'s bows; she would be more awkward still at close quarters. 'Deal with that when we come to it,' he thought, tallying on to a rope.

An enormous ringing crash inside his head and filling the outside world. He was down. Blindly struggling away from number five's recoil, he tried to make out whether he was badly wounded or not – impossible to tell at once. He was not. Number seven had exploded, killing three of its servers, blowing its captain's head to pieces – it was his jaw that had gouged the wound across Jack's forearm – and scattering bits of iron in all directions, wounding men as far away as the mainmast – a splinter of iron had grazed his head, knocking him down. The face he was staring at so stupidly was Pullings's, repeating the words, 'You must go below, sir. Below. Let me give you a hand below.'

He came fully to life and cried, 'Secure that gun,' in a voice that he could hear as if from another throat. By the grace of God what was left of the barrel and the carriage had not burst free from the ring-bolts; they made it fast, slid the bodies overboard, and hurried what was left of its gear over to number five.

Three more rounds, three more of those hammer-blow explosions right by his ear, and the bursting gun, the dead men, his own wound, all merged into the one din and the furious activity of battle.

The smoke was thicker, the *Bellone*'s flashes closer, far closer. She was edging down fast. Faster and faster they worked their guns: with the rest of number seven's crew and two men sent up from a dismounted six-pounder on the quarterdeck they plied them without a second's pause. The metal was hot, so hot the guns kicked clear of the deck, flying back with a terrible note on the breeching. Then the *Bellone*'s guns fired a round of grape, followed by a furious discharge of musketry. The smoke swept away and there she was, right upon them, backing her main topsail to check her way and come alongside. Small-arms cracking in her tops to clear the *Lord Nelson*'s decks, men on her yard-arms to lash her spars to theirs, grappling-irons ready in the waist and bows, a dense swarm on her forecastle and in her foreshrouds.

'All hands to repel boarders,' from the quarterdeck, the grinding crash as they touched, the Frenchmen's cheer and here they were cutlasses slashing the boarding-netting, pole-axes, the flash of swords. He snapped one pistol at a determined face coming through the wrecked number seven port, snatched up the great heavy crow, and with an extraordinary feeling of strength and invulnerability – complete certainty – he flung himself at the men in the netting who were trying to come over the bows – the main attack was in the bows. He stood there with one foot on the broken rail, holding the massive crow in the middle, banging, thrusting, beating them down. All around him the shrieking Lascars fought with their pikes, axes, pistols. A rush of Company's men from the waist and the quarterdeck cleared the gangway, where a dozen privateers had come aboard, and carried on to the forecastle, charging with pikes.

The Indiaman's deck was higher by a good spring than the *Bellone*'s; she had a pronounced tumblehome – her sides sloped inwards – which left an awkward space. But the Frenchmen clung there obstinately, hitting back, striving most desperately, crowding to come aboard. Flung back, yet coming again and again, fresh men by the score and score,

until a heave of the sea separated the ships, and a whole
group clinging to the forechains fell between them, blasted
by Mr Johnstone's blunderbuss fired straight into the mass.
The serang ran out on to the yard-arm and cut the lashing,
the grappling-irons scraped harmlessly over the rail, and the
quarterdeck guns fired three rounds of grape, wounding the
French captain, unshipping the *Bellone*'s wheel, and cutting
her spanker halliards. She shot up into the wind, and if only
the *Lord Nelson* had had enough men both to repel boarders
and fight her guns, she could now have raked the *Bellone* at
ten yards' range; but not a round could she fire – her head
dropped off, and the two ships drifted silently apart.

Jack carried a boy down to the cockpit – both arms slashed
to the bone as he flung them up to guard his face – and
Stephen said, 'Keep your thumb pressed here till I can come
to him. How do we stand?'

'We beat 'em off. Her boats are picking up her men. Two or
three hundred she has. We'll be at it again directly. Hurry,
Stephen, I cannot wait. We must knot and splice. How many
have you here?'

'Thirty or forty,' said Stephen, fastening the tourniquet.
'Boy, you will do very well: lie quiet. Jack, show me your arm,
your head.'

'Another time. A couple of lucky shots and we disabled
him.'

A LUCKY SHOT. How he prayed for it – every time he laid
his gun he prayed for it. 'The name of the Father, the Son,
and the Holy Ghost.' But in the failing wind the smoke lay
thick and heavy all round the *Bellone* – he could see nothing,
and he had only two guns firing now. Number one's breeching had gone at the first discharge, wounding two Lascars and
a midshipman, and the gun was lying on its side, precariously
wedged behind a cask. His crews had thinned – the whole
deck had thinned – and the *Lord Nelson*'s fire had slackened
to a gun a minute, while the *Bellone* kept up a steady thunder

fifty yards to windward. The deck, when he had time to look aft, showed no more than a sparse line of men – no crowded knots at every gun. Some had been wounded, others had run below – the hatches had not been laid – and those that were left were drawn, ashy, weak, their forces drained: they fought without conviction. For a long moment Hill had vanished, but he was back now, laying number three. Jack rammed down the wad, felt behind him for the shot. No shot. That damned powder-boy had run. 'Shot! Shot!' he cried, and there was the boy, waddling from the mainhatch with two heavy balls clasped in his arms – a new boy, absurdly dressed in shore-going rig, new trousers, blue jacket, pigtail in a ribbon. A fat boy. 'Take them from for'ard, you poxed son of a whore,' said Jack into his mute, appalled face, snatching one and thrusting it down the barrel. 'From for'ard, from number one. There's a dozen there. At the double, at the double!' The second wad, rammed hard into the scorching gun. 'Run her up! Run her up!'

Painfully, straining, they forced the great weight up against the roll: one little blue Lascar was vomiting as he heaved. The *Bellone*'s broadside bawled out, all in one; grape and chain, from the shrill scream overhead as they lay to the tackles. He fired, saw Hill snatch the boy from the recoil, and instantly ran forward through the smoke to number three. That damned boy was underfoot. He picked him up, said kindly, 'Stand clear of the guns. You're a good boy – a plucked 'un. Just bring one at a time,' pointing to the forecastle, 'but look alive. Then cartridge. Bear a hand. We must have cartridge.'

The cartridge never came. Jack fired number five, caught a glimpse of topsails towering overhead, saw the *Bellone*'s fore-yards glide into the *Lord Nelson*'s shrouds, and heard an enormous cheering, roaring of boarders behind him, *behind* him. The privateer's boats had slipped round unseen in the smoke and there were a hundred Frenchmen coming up the unprotected starboard side.

They filled the *Lord Nelson*'s waist, cutting the quarter-deck off from the forecastle, and the press of men coming in over the bows through the chain-torn netting was so great they could not fight. Faces, chests, arms, so close to him he could not get his long bar free, a little devilish man clinging round his waist. Down, trampled upon, a passing kick. Up and facing them, hitting short-arm blows – a stab. The crowding force, the weight of men. Back, back, step by step, tripping on bodies, back, back. And then a falling void, an impact faintly, faintly heard, as though from another age.

THE SWINGING LANTERN. He watched it: perhaps for hours. And gradually the world began to fall into place, memory coming back layer by layer, to reach the present. Or nearly so. He could not recall the sequence after the busting of poor Haynes's gun. Haynes, of course: that was his name. A forecastle-man, larboard watch, in the *Resolution*, rated quarter-gunner when they were off the Cape. The rest was darkness: this often happened with a wound. Was he wounded? He was certainly in the cockpit, and that was Stephen moving about among the low, crowded, moaning bodies. 'Stephen,' he said, after a while.

'How then, my dear?' said Stephen. 'How do you find your-self? How are your intellectuals?'

'Pretty well, I thank you. I seem all of a piece.'

'I dare say you are. Limbs and trunk are sound. Coma was all I feared these last few days. You fell down the forehatch. You may take an Almoravian draught, however. The dogs, they did not find half my Almoravian draught.'

'We were taken?'

'Aye, aye, we were taken. We lost thirty-six killed and wounded; and they took us. They plundered us cruelly – stripped to the bone – and for the first few days they kept us under hatches. Here is your draught. However, I extracted a ball from Captain Dumanoir's shoulder and looked after their wounded, and now we are indulged with taking the air on deck. Their second captain, Azéma, is an amiable man, a former King's officer, and he has prevented any gross excess, apart from the plundering.'

'Privateers,' said Jack, trying to shrug. 'But what about those girls? What about the Miss Lambs?'

'They are dressed as men – as boys. I am not sure that they are altogether pleased with the success of their deception.'

'A fair-sized prize-crew?' asked Jack, whose mind had flown to the possibility of retaking the Indiaman.

'Huge,' said Stephen. 'Forty-one. The Company's officers have given their parole; some of the Lascars have taken service for double wages; and the rest are down with this Spanish influenza. They are carrying us into Corunna.'

'Don't they wish they may get us there,' said Jack. 'The chops of the Channel and to westward are alive, with cruisers.'

He spoke confidently; he knew that there was truth in what he said; but limping about the quarterdeck on Tuesday, when Stephen allowed him up, he surveyed the ocean with a feeling of despair. A vast great emptiness, with nothing but the trim *Bellone* a little to windward: not a sail, not the smallest lugger on the world's far rim, nor, after hours of unbroken watching, the least reason why any should appear. Emptiness; and somewhere under the leeward horizon, the Spanish port. He remembered coming from the West Indies in the *Alert*, sailing along the busiest sea-route in the whole Atlantic, and they had not seen a living soul until they were in soundings off the Lizard.

In the afternoon Pullings came on deck, pale Pullings, supported by a Miss Lamb on either side. Jack had already seen Pullings (grape-shot in the thigh, a sword-cut on the shoulder and two ribs stove in), just as he had seen Major Hill (down with the influenza) and all the other men under Stephen's hands, but this was the first time he had seen the girls. 'My dear Miss Lamb,' he cried, taking her free hand, 'I hope I see you well. Quite well?' he said earnestly, meaning 'not too much raped?'

'Thank you, sir,' said Miss Lamb, looking conscious and strange – quite another girl, 'my sister and I are perfectly well.'

'Miss Lambs, your most devoted,' said Captain Azéma, coming from the starboard side and bowing. He was a big dark loose-built man, tough, capable, a sailor – a man after Jack's own heart. 'Misses are under my particular protection, sir,' he said. 'I have persuaded them to carry robes, to resume the form divine,' – kissing his fingers. 'They do not risk the least impertinence. Some of my men are villain buggers indeed, impetuous like one says; but quite apart from my protection, not one, *not one*, would want of respect for such heroines.'

'Eh?' said Jack.

'That's right, sir,' cried Pullings, squeezing them. 'Copper-bottomed heroines, trundling shot, running about like mad, powder, match when my flint flew off, wads!! Joan of Arcs.'

'Did they carry powder?' cried Jack. 'Dr Maturin said trousers, or something of that kind, but I – '

'Oh, you horrid two-faced thing!' cried Miss Susan. 'You *saw* her! You shouted out the most dreadful things to Lucy, the most dreadful things I ever heard in my life. You swore at my sister, sir; you know you did. Oh, Captain Aubrey, fie!'

'*Captain* Aubrey?' observed Azéma, adding the head-money for an English officer to his share of the prize – a very handsome sum.

'She's blown the gaff – I'm brought by the lee,' thought Jack. 'They carried powder – What an amazing spirited thing to do.' 'Dear Miss Lambs,' he said most humbly, 'I beg you to forgive me. The last half-hour of the action – a damned warm action too – is a perfect blank to me. I fell on my head; and it is a perfect blank. But to carry powder was the most amazing spirited thing to do: I honour you, my dears. Please forgive me. The smoke – the trousers – what did I say, so that I may unsay it at once?'

'You said,' began Miss Susan, and paused. 'Well, I forget; but it was monstrous . . .'

The sound of a gun made the whole group jerk, an absurd, simultaneous, galvanic leap: they had all been speaking very loud, being still half deafened from the roar of battle, but a gun touched their innermost ears and they all pivoted at once, mechanical toys pointing directly at the *Bellone*.

She had been under double-reefed topsails all this time, to allow the *Lord Nelson* to keep company, but now men were already laying out on the yard to shake out the reefs, and Captain Dumanoir hailed loud and clear, telling his second to make straight for Corunna, 'all sails outside'. He added a good deal that neither Jack nor Pullings could understand, but the general upshot was plain: his look-out had seen a sail to windward; he was not going to take the slightest risk with so valuable a prize; and he meant to beat up to reconnoitre, and as the case fell out, to salute a friend or neutral, to fight an enemy, or, trusting to the *Bellone*'s magnificent sailing qualities, to lead the strange sail astray.

The *Lord Nelson*, trailing a curtain of dark-brown weed, leaking steadily (her pumps had never stopped since the action), and still short of sails, spars and rigging, could only make four knots, even with her topgallantsails set; but the *Bellone*, now a triple pyramid of white, was at her best close-hauled, and in ten minutes they were two miles away from one another. Jack asked permission to go into the top; Captain Azéma not only entreated him to go anywhere he chose, but lent him Stephen's telescope as well.

'Good day,' said the privateersman in the top. Jack had given him a terrible blow with his bar, but he bore no grudge. 'That is one of thy frigates down there.'

'Oh wee?' said Jack, settling his back against the mast. The distant ship sprang close in his objective-glass. Thirty-six guns; no, thirty-eight. Red pennant. *Naiad*? *Minerve*? She had been going large under easy sail when first she sighted the *Bellone*; then studdingsails had appeared – the last were being sheeted home when first Jack had her steadily under view – as she altered course to close the privateer; then she

saw the Indiaman and altered course again to know more
about her. Upon this the *Bellone* tacked, tacked clumsily, taking an age over what Jack had seen her do in five minutes
from 'helm's a-lee' to 'let go and haul'; he heard them laughing, clowning down there on deck. She stood on this tack
until she was within a mile of the frigate, steadily beating up
against the swell, white water sweeping across her forecastle.
A white puff showed at the frigate's bows, and shifting his
gaze he saw the red ensign break out at her mizzen-peak: he
frowned: he would at least have tried the tricolour or, with
the big American frigates in those waters, the Stars and
Stripes; it might not have worked, but it was worth the
attempt. For her part, the *Bellone* was perfectly capable of
showing French colours without any distinction, to pass for a
national ship and lead the frigate away.

She had done so. She had done just that thing; and the seaman, who had borrowed the glass, licking it with his garlic
tongue, chuckled to himself. Jack knew what was passing
through the frigate-captain's head; far to leeward a ship, probably a merchantship, possibly a prize, but what sort of prize
he could not tell: crossing his bows three-quarters of a mile
away there was a French corvette, not very well handled, not
very fast, peppering him at random-shot. A simple mind
would find no great difficulty about this decision and soon
Jack saw the frigate haul her wind. Her studdingsails disappeared, and she turned to pursue the *Bellone*, setting a press
of staysails. She would deal with the Frenchman and then
come back to see about this hypothetical prize.

'Surely to God you must see she's spilling her wind,' cried
Jack within himself. 'Surely to God you've seen that old trick
before?' They slipped away and away across the distant sea,
the frigate with a fine bold bow-wave at her stern and the
Bellone keeping just beyond the reach of her chasers; and
when they were no more than flecks of white, hull down to
the north-north-east, Jack climbed heavily out of the top. The
seaman gave him a compassionate yet philosophic nod; this

had happened to him before; it was happening to Jack now; it was one of the little miseries of life.

After dark Captain Azéma altered course according to his instructions, and the Indiaman headed into a lonely sea, drawing her slow furrow a hundred miles in the four and twenty hours, never to be seen by the frigate again.

At the far end of that furrow lay Corunna; he had no doubt of Captain Azéma's making his landfall to within a mile or so, for not only was Azéma a thorough-going seaman, but this clear weather continued day after day – perfect weather for observation, for fixing his position. Corunna: Spain. But now that Jack was known for an officer they would never let him ashore. Unless he gave his parole, Azéma would put him in irons, there to lie until the *Bellone* or some chasse-marée carried him to France – his was a valuable carcass.

The next day was a total void: the unbroken round of the sea, the dome of the sky, thin cloud lightening to blue above. And the next was the same, distinguished only by what Jack thought to be the beginnings of the influenza, and a certain skittishness observed in the Misses Lamb, pursued by Azéma's lieutenant and a sixteen-year-old volunteer with flashing eyes.

But Friday's sea was all alive with sails – the ocean was speckled with the sober drab of a fleet of bankers, coming home with codfish from Newfoundland; they could be smelt a mile downwind. And among the bankers a bean-cod, a double-lateen with a host of odd, haphazard-looking sails, a strange vessel with an archaic prow; and a disagreeable reminder that the coast was near – your bean-cod was no ocean crosser. But though the bean-cod was of absorbing interest to a sailor, the plain cutter far down to leeward wiped it entirely from their attention.

'You see the cutter, sir?' said Pullings.

Jack nodded. The cutter was a rig more favoured by the English than the French; it was used by the Navy and by privateers, by smugglers and by those who pursued smugglers, being fast, nimble and weatherly, lying very close to the wind; it was of no great use to merchants. And this particular little vessel was no merchantman: what merchantman would steer that erratic course among the bankers? She did not belong to the Navy, either, for as soon as she sighted the *Lord Nelson* a gaff-topsail appeared above her mainsail, a modern sail not countenanced in the service. She was a privateer.

This was Captain Azéma's opinion too. He had the guns drawn, reloaded and run out on both sides; he was in no particular hurry, because the cutter had to work straight up into the eye of the wind. Furthermore, as she came nearer, tacking and tacking again, it was clear that she had had a rough time of it not long ago – her mainsail was double-reefed, presumably from some recent damage; there were strangely-patched holes all over it and more in her foresail and ragged jib; her upper works had a chewed appearance; and one of her seven little gun-ports on the starboard side had been hastily repaired. There was not much danger to be feared from her, but still he was going to take no risks: he had new boarding-netting rigged out, a great deal of cartridge filled, and shot brought up; and his acting-bosun, helped by all the Lascars who were capable of work, secured the yards.

The *Lord Nelson* was ready long before the cutter fired a gun and hoisted English colours; but she did not reply at once. Azéma looked at Jack and Pullings. 'I will not ask you to go downstairs,' he said, 'but if you will to hail or to signal, I shall be compelled to shoot you.' He smiled, but he had two pistols in his belt and he meant what he said.

Jack said, 'Just so,' and bowed. Pullings smiled diffidently.

The cutter was lying on the Indiaman's bow, her mainsail shivering; Azéma nodded to the man at the wheel. The *Lord Nelson* turned gently, and Azéma said, 'Fire.' The broadside, the eighteen-pounders alone, parted on the downward roll; beautifully grouped, the shots struck the sea just short of the cutter's larboard bow and beam, ricocheting over her, adding new holes to her sails and knocking away the outer third of her bowsprit. Startled by this reception, the cutter tried to fill and come about, but with so little way on her and with her jib flying in the breeze she would not stay. She fell off, giving the *Lord Nelson* her seven six-pounders as she did so, and wore round on the other tack.

The cutter knew she had come up against a tough 'un, a difficult article – half a broadside like this would send her to the bottom; but gathering way she crossed the *Lord Nelson*'s stern, fired again, gybed like a dancer and crossed back to lie upon her starboard bow. At two hundred yards, her six-pounders did the Indiaman's thick sides no harm, but they did cut up her rigging, and it was clearly in the cutter's mind to carry on with this manoeuvre.

Azéma was having none of it. The cutter had gone to and fro in spite of his yawing to fire, and now he brought the wind right abeam, swinging the ship through 90°. He ran down the line of guns, speaking to each crew, and sent a deliberate broadside to the space of sea the cutter had filled two seconds earlier – as though by magic, intuition, telepathy, the cutter's master put his helm a-lee the instant of the call to fire; coming about in a flash and heading for the *Lord Nelson*. He did so again two minutes later, less by magic than by a calculation of the time it would take these gunners to have him in their sights again. He was going to board, and he had only one more short tack to bring him up against the *Lord Nelson*'s bows. Jack could see the men there, cutlasses and boarding-axes ready, twenty-five or thirty of them, the master at the tiller, a long sword in his other hand: in a moment now they would start their cheer.

'Fire,' said Azéma again, and as the smoke cleared there was the cutter with her topsail gone, hanging drunkenly over her side, no captain at the tiller, a heap of men struggling or motionless upon her deck. Her way carried her on past the *Lord Nelson*'s bows, out of reach of the next discharge; and now she was racing away, fleeing to gain a hundred yards or so before the *Lord Nelson*'s ponderous turn should bring her starboard broadside to bear.

She survived it, though it was difficult to see how she did so, with so much white water kicked up all round her; and Azéma, who did not feel passionately about either taking Or sinking her, sent only a few more shots after her before returning to his course. Ten minutes later she had sent up a new jib and foresail and she was dwindling, smaller and smaller among the distant bankers. Jack felt for his watch; he liked to note the beginning and the end of all engagements – it was gone, of course.

'I think it was temerarious, immoral,' said Azéma. 'Suppose he had killed some of my people! He should be broken on the wheel. I should have sunk him. I am too magnanimous. That is not courage, but hardfooliness.'

'I would agree,' said Jack, 'if it had been the other way around. A sloop that does not strike to a ship of the line is a fool.'

'We see things differently,' said Azéma, still cross over the time lost and the damage to his rigging. 'We have different proportions. But at least' – his good humour returning – 'I hope your countrymen will give us a day of rest tomorrow.'

He had his day of rest, and another morning too; but shortly after he had taken his noon observation – 45° 23' N., 10° 30' W. – and had promised his prisoners Spanish bread and real coffee for breakfast, there was the cry of a sail to windward.

Gradually the white blur resolved itself into a brig; and the brig was clearly giving chase. The hours passed: Captain Azéma was thoughtful and preoccupied during dinner – pecked at his food, and from time to time going up on deck. The *Lord Nelson* was under topgallants, with upper and lower studdingsails, which urged her towards Corunna at five or even six knots as the breeze freshened. He set his royals a little after four, anxiously watching to see how the wounded masts would stand the strain; and for a while it seemed that the brig was falling behind.

'Sir,' said Pullings secretly, coming from those airy heights after a long examination of the brig, 'I am almost sure she is the *Seagull*. My uncle was master of her in ninety-nine, and many's the time I have been aboard.'

'*Seagull*?' said Jack, frowning. 'Did she not change to carronades?'

'That's right, sir. Sixteen twenty-four-pounders, very tight in the bridle-ports: and two long sixes. She can hit hard, if only she gets near enough, but she is amazing slow.'

'Slower than this?'

'Much of a muchness, sir. She's just set her skysails. It may make a difference.'

THE DIFFERENCE WAS small, very small – perhaps a table-cloth or two – but in five hours of steady unchanging weather it was enough to bring the *Seagull* within reach of the *Lord Nelson*'s aftermost starboard eighteen-pounder and of a long eight that Captain Azéma had shifted to fire through the stateroom gallery.

For ten sea miles the brig – and now they were sure she was the *Seagull* – could reply only with her bow six-pounder, which did nothing but make a smoke and encourage her crew; but slowly the *Lord Nelson* neared and then crossed a dark band in the sea, where the wind, backed up by the Spanish Cordillera, combined with the ebbing tide to produce a distinct frontier, a sullen, choppy zone haunted by gulls and other inshore birds.

Within five minutes the *Lord Nelson*'s way fell off perceptibly; the song of her rigging dropped tone by tone; and the Seagull ranged up to her starboard quarter. Before the brig crossed the dark water in her turn, she fired the first full broadside of her close-range carronades: it fell short, and so did the next, but a ricocheting twenty-four-pound ball tore through the hammocks and dropped weakly against the mainmast. Captain Azéma looked thoughtfully from the heavy shot to the brig: she still had a quarter of a mile to run before she would lose the full fair breeze. A gain of fifty yards would bring these twenty-four-pounders rattling about his ears, piercing the Indiaman's costly sides and endangering her already damaged masts. His chief feeling was irritation rather than any dread for the outcome: the *Seagull*'s rate of fire and accuracy left much to be desired, whereas he had eight master-gunners aboard; the brig's power of manoeuvring was no greater than his, and he only had to knock away a spar or two to leave her behind and gain the coast. Nevertheless, he was going to need all his concentration.

'She is scarcely commodious, your brig,' he said to Jack. 'We may have serious difficulty with her. I must ask you to go below. Messiers les prisonniers into the hold, if you please – I invite the prisoners to go into the hold.'

There was no denying his authoritative tone. They went below with many a reluctant glance at the evening sea, down hatchway after hatchway to the final grating, which closed over them with a thump and the rattle of a chain. And it was in the crammed bowels of the Indiaman, shut firmly down in the smell of tea, cinnamon and bilgewater that Jack, Pullings, the Company's Europeans and all the passengers witnessed the action. Aural witnesses, of course, no more, since they were below the water-line, with nothing but a swinging lantern and the vague shape of bales to see, but what they heard they heard well. The *Lord Nelson* resonated like a sounding-box to the crash of her eighteen-pounders, transposing the roar an octave lower; and the sea transmitted the *Seagull*'s broadsides – a curious dead thump, like a padded hammer a great way off, a sound devoid of overtones and so distinct that it was sometimes possible to distinguish each of the eight carronades, whose fire would have seemed simultaneous in the open air.

They listened, tried to calculate the direction, worked out the weight of metal – four hundred and thirty-two pounds for the *Lord Nelson*, three hundred and ninety-two for the brig – and the possibility of bringing it into play. 'Azéma is using his big guns alone,' observed Jack. 'Concentrating on her masts, I make no doubt.' Sometimes the *Seagull* hit them, and they cheered, full of speculation as to the place of the strike; once a sudden rush in the well and a renewed activity of the pump made it clear that the *Lord Nelson* had been holed between wind and water, probably in the forepeak; and once a great metallic clang made them think that a gun had been struck; perhaps dismounted.

Towards three o'clock in the morning the candle went out, and they lay in darkness, listening, listening, sometimes regretting their coats, rugs, and pillows and food, and sometimes dozing. The firing went on and on: the *Seagull* had given up her broadsides and was firing gun by gun; the *Lord Nelson* had never done anything else throughout the engagement – a steady, deliberate rhythm hour after hour.

Miss Lamb woke with a scream: 'It was a rat! A monstrous great wet rat! O *how* I regret my trousers!'

Extreme attention slackened as the long night wore on. Once or twice Jack spoke to Major Hill and to Pullings and had no reply. He found that his counting of the shots was mingling with a calculation of the number of sick and wounded under Stephen's hands – with observations made to Sophia – with thoughts of food, of coffee, and the playing of the D minor trio – Diana's rough glissando and the deep sustaining note of the 'cello, as they played three-handed.

A flood of light, the grinding of the chain and grating, and he was conscious that he had been three parts asleep. Not wholly, since he knew that the firing had stopped this last hour and more, but enough to feel shifty and ashamed.

On deck it was raining, a thin drizzle from a high sky – very little wind, and that a land-breeze; Captain Azéma and his people looked deathly pale, tired, but undisturbed – too worn for outward pleasure, but undisturbed. Under her fore and main topsails the *Lord Nelson* was slipping along through the water close-hauled, away from the motionless *Seagull*, far away on her starboard quarter: even at this distance Jack could see that she had suffered badly. Her foreyard was gone, her maintopmast seemed to be tottering, there was a great deal of wreckage on her deck and dangling over her side: four gun-ports beat in: strangely low in the water: pumps hard at work. She had hauled off to refit, to stop her leaks, and the likelihood of her renewing the action – of being able to renew the action – was . . .

Captain Azéma had been bent over a gun, laying it with the very greatest care: he gaged the roll, fired, sending a ball plumb amidships into the repairing party. He waited for the flight of the shot, said 'Carry on, Partre,' and stepped back to his mug of coffee, steaming on the binnacle.

It was perfectly allowable; Jack might have done the same; but there was something so cold-blooded about it that Jack refused a draught from the mug and turned to look at the *Lord Nelson*'s damage and at the coast, barring the whole eastern horizon now. The damage was heavy but not crippling; Azéma had not made quite the landfall he had expected – that was Cape Prior right ahead – but he would be in Corunna road by noon. Jack ignored the second gun: he tried to make out why it should wound him so, for he had no particular friend aboard the *Seagull*. He could not clarify his mind, but he knew he felt the most furious enmity for Azéma, and it was with more than the ordinary leap of delight, of hope revived when all seemed lost, that he saw the first ship round that Spanish headland, heading north. A homeward-bound line-of-battle ship, HMS *Colossus*, followed by the *Tonnant*, eighty.

The mast-head hailed 'Two ships of the line'. But two more followed: a very powerful squadron, all sails abroad, and holding the weather-gage. There was not the slightest chance of escape. Mute, weary consternation; and in the silence Jack stepped to the pointed eighteen-pounder, laid his hand on the lock and said coldly, 'You must not fire that gun, sir. You must strike your colours to the brig.'

6

AT FIVE MINUTES to eight Jack Aubrey walked quickly through the dreary rain over the cobbles of the Admiralty courtyard, pursued by the voice of the hackney coachman. 'Fourpence! Call yourself a gent? The poor bleeding Navy's half-pay shame, that's what I call you.'

He shrugged, and ducking under the overflow from the gutter he hurried into the hall, past the main waiting-room and on to the little office called the Bosun's Chair, for he had a First Lord's appointment, no less. The fire was beginning to draw, sending up a strong writhe of yellow smoke to join the yellow fog outside, and through the yellow shot darts of red, with a pleasant roar and crackle; he stood with his back to the chimneypiece, looking into the rain and mopping his best uniform with a handkerchief. Several figures passed dimly through the Whitehall arch, civilians under umbrellas, officers exposed to the elements: he thought he recognized two or three – certainly that was Brand of the *Implacable* – but the mud deep in the buckles of his shoes occupied him too much for close attention.

He was in a high state of nervous excitement – any sailor waiting to see the First Lord must be in a high state of nervous excitement – yet the surface of his mind was taken up less with his coming interview than with getting the utmost possible service from a single handkerchief and with vague darting reflections upon poverty – an old acquaintance, almost a friend – a more natural state for sea-officers than wealth – wealth very charming – should love to be rich again; but there was the loss of all those little satisfactions of contriving – the triumph of a guinea found in an old waistcoat pocket – the breathless tension over the turn of a card. The hackney-coach had been necessary, however, with the mud ankle-deep, and this damned south-wester: best uniforms did not grow on trees, nor yet silk stockings.

'Captain Aubrey, sir,' said the clerk. 'His lordship will see you now.'

'Captain Aubrey, I am happy to see you,' said Lord Melville. 'How is your father?'

'Thank you, sir, he is very well – delighted with the election, as we all are. But I beg your pardon, my lord. I am out of order. May I offer you my very best congratulations on your peerage?'

'You are very good – very good,' said Lord Melville, and having answered Jack's civil inquiries for Lady Melville and Robert, he went on, 'So you had a lively time of it, coming home?'

'We did indeed, my lord,' cried Jack. 'But I am astonished you should know.'

'Why, it is in the paper – a passenger's letter to her family, describing the Indiaman's capture and recapture. She mentioned you by name – says the handsomest things. Sibbald pointed it out to me.'

That infernal girl, that Lamb, must have sent her letter by the revenue cutter: and there he had been, hurrying up from Plymouth on borrowed money to reach a London filled with bums forewarned, all waiting to arrest him for debt, charmed with the idea of tossing him into the Fleet or the Marshalsea to rot until the war was over and all chance gone. He had known many officers with their careers ruined by a tipstaff – old Baines, Serocold . . . and there he had been, prancing about the town, dressed like the King's birthday for every sneaking attorney to behold. The thought made him feel cold and sick: he said something about 'quite amazed – had posted up from Plymouth with not more than a couple of hours at his father's place – thought he had certainly outrun the news.' Yet it must have made tolerable sense, for Lord Melville only observed in that Scotch voice of his, 'I am sure you used your best endeavours. But I wish you could have come more betimes – weeks, nay, months earlier, before all the plums were gone. I should have liked to do something for you: at the beginning of the war there were commands aplenty. I shall look into this question of promotion that has been urged upon me, but I can hold out no hope of a ship. However, there may be some slight possibility in the Sea-Fencibles or the Impress Service: we are extending both, and they call for active, enterprising men.'

They also called for solvent men, seeing that they were landborne posts: comfort-loving men, devoid of ambition or tired of the sea, willing to look after a kind of fisherman's militia or to attend to the odious work of the press-gang. Clearly it was now or never, all or nothing. Once that hard-faced man the other side of the desk had made a firm offer of a shore appointment there would be no shifting him. 'My lord,' said Jack with all the force and energy he could respect-fully express, 'I like a plum, a post-ship, as much as any man alive; but if I might have four pieces of wood that swim, I should be happy, more than happy, to sail them on any ser-vice, on any station in the world as a commander or anything else. I have been afloat since I was fourteen, sir, and I have never refused any employment their lordships were good enough to offer me. I believe I may promise you would not regret your decision, sir. All I want is to be at sea again.'

'Heu, heu,' said Lord Melville, in his meditating way, pin-ning Jack with a grey stare. 'So you make no stipulation of any kind? There was a great deal of clack about your friends wish-ing you to be made post for the *Cacafuego* affair.'

'None whatsoever, my lord,' said Jack, and shut his mouth. He thought of trying to explain the unfortunate word 'claim' that he had been inspired to use the last time he was in this room: thought better of it, and kept his mouth shut, wearing a look of deferential attention and maintaining it better than he could have done a year ago, although he had a far greater respect for St Vincent than he ever could have for a civilian.

'Weel,' said the First Lord, after a pause, 'I can promise nothing. You can have no conception of the applications, of the interests to be managed, balanced . . . but there might be some remote possibility . . . come and see me next week. In the meantime I will look into this question of promotion, though the post-captain's list is grievously overcharged; and I will turn over the possibilities. Come and see me on Wednesday. Mind me, now, if I do find anything, it will be no plum: that is the one thing I can promise you. But I bind myself in no way at all.'

Jack stood up and made his acknowledgments of his lordship's goodness in seeing him. Lord Melville observed, in an unofficial voice, 'I dare say we shall meet this evening at Lady Keith's: if I can find time, I shall look in.'

'I shall look forward to it extremely, my lord,' said Jack.

'Good day to you,' said Lord Melville, ringing a bell and looking eagerly at his inner door.

'You seem wery cheerful, sir,' said the porter, scanning Jack's face with ancient, red-rimmed eyes. Wery cheerful was an exaggeration; contained satisfaction was more the mark; but at all events it was nothing remotely like the expression of an officer with a flat refusal weighing on his heart.

'Why, Tom, so I am,' said Jack. 'I walked in from Hampstead this morning, as far as Seven Dials. There is nothing like a morning walk to set a man up.'

'Something copper-bottomed, sir?' asked Tom: no tales of morning walks would wash with him. He was old, knowing and familiar; he had known Jack before his first shave, just as he knew almost every other officer on the Navy List below the rank of admiral, and he had a right to a tip if something copper-bottomed turned up while he was on duty.

'Not – not exactly, Tom,' said Jack, looking keenly out through the hall and court to the sodden crowds passing up and down Whitehall – the chops of the Channel, full of shipping; and what cruisers, privateers, chasse-marée, lurking there among them? What unseen rocks? What bums? 'No. But I tell you what it is, Tom: I came out without a cloak and without any money. Just call me a coach and lend me half a guinea, will you?'

Tom had no opinion of sea-officers' powers of discrimination or management on shore; he was not surprised that Jack should have come out lacking the common necessities of life, and from his reading of Jack's expression he was of the opinion that something was on its way – the Fencibles alone would provide a dozen fresh appointments, even if he were not made post. He produced the little coin with a secret, conniving look, and summoned a coach.

Jack plunged into the coach with his hat pulled over his nose and sat huddled low in the corner, peering furtively through the muddy glasses – a curiously deformed, conspicuous figure that excited comment whenever the horse moved at less than a trot. 'An ill-looking parcel of bastards,' he reflected, seeing a bailiff in every full-grown man. 'But my God, what a life. Doing this every day, cooped up with a ledger – what a life.' The cheerless faces went by, hurrying to their dismal work, an endless wet, anxious, cold, grey-yellow stream of people, jostling, pushing past one another like an ugly dream, with here and there a pretty shop-girl or servant to make it more heart-rendingly pathetic.

A convoy of hay-wains came down the Hampstead Road, led by countrymen with long whips. The whips, the drivers' smocks, the horses' tails and manes were trimmed with ribbons, and the men's broad faces shone red, effulgent through the gloom. From Jack's remote and ineffectual schooldays sprang a tag: *O fortunatos nimium, sua si bona norint, agricolas*. 'Come, that is pretty good. How I wish Stephen had been by, to hear it. However, I shall flash it out at him presently.' There would be plenty of opportunity, since they were to travel down the same road that evening to Queenie's rout, and with any luck they would see some agricolas among that pitiable throng.

'Will you tell me about your interview, now?' said Stephen, pushing his report aside and looking into Jack's face with as much attention as the aged porter.

'It was not so bad. Now I have had time to turn it over in

my mind, it was not so bad at all. I think they may promote me or give me a ship: one or the other. If they make me post, there is always the possibility of a post-ship in time, and of acting commands; and if they give me a sloop, why, there I am.'

'What are acting commands?'

'When a post-captain is sick, or wants to go ashore for a while – it often happens when they are peers or members of parliament – another post-captain on half-pay is appointed to his ship for the time being. Shall I tell you about it from the beginning?'

'If you please.'

'It started charmingly. The First Lord said he was happy to see me. No First Lord had ever been happy to see me before, or at least he had always managed to contain it – is there any coffee left in that pot, Stephen?'

'There is not. But you may have some beer presently; it is nearly two o'clock.'

'Well, it began charmingly, but then it took the ugliest vile turn imaginable; he made a sad mouth and said it was a pity I had come so late – *he would have liked to do something for me*. Then he made my heart die within me by prating about the Fencibles and the Impress Service and I knew that somehow I must head him off before he made a direct offer.'

'Why?'

'Oh, it would never do to refuse. If you turn down a ship because she don't suit – because she's on the West Indies station, say, and you don't care for the yellow Jack – it is a black mark against you: you may never be employed again. They don't like you to pick and choose. The good of the service must come first, they say: and they are perfectly in the right of it. Then again, I could not tell him I hated both the Fencibles and the press and that in any event I could accept neither without being laid by the heels.'

'So you evaded the proposal?'

'Yes. Dropping my claim to be made post, I told him anything that would float would do for me. I did not drop it in so many words, but he took the point at once, and after some humming and hawing he spoke of *some remote possibility* next week. And he would consider the matter of promotion. I am not to think him in any way committed, but am to call again next week. From a man like Lord Melville I regard that as pretty strong.'

'So do I, my dear,' said Stephen, with as much conviction as he could put into his voice – a good deal of conviction, for he had had dealings with the gentleman in question, who had been in command of the secret funds these many years past. 'So do I. Let us eat, drink and be merry. There are sausages in the scrutoire; there is beer in the green jug. I shall regale myself on toasted cheese.'

The French privateers had taken away his Breguet watch, as well as most of his clothes, instruments and books, but his stomach was as exact as any timepiece, and as they sat themselves at the little table by the fire, so the church clock told the hour. The crew of the swift-sailing *Bellone* had also taken away the money he had brought from Spain – that had been their first, most anxious care – and since landing at Plymouth he and Jack had been living on the proceeds of one small bill, laboriously negotiated by General Aubrey while their horses waited, and on the hopes of discounting another, drawn on a Barcelona merchant named Mendoza, little known on the London 'change.

At present they were lodging in an idyllic cottage near the Heath with green shutters and a honeysuckle over the door – idyllic in summer, that is to say. They were looking after themselves, living with rigid economy; and there was no greater proof of their friendship than the way their harmony withstood their very grave differences in domestic behaviour. In Jack's opinion Stephen was little better than a slut: his papers, odd bits of dry, garlic'd bread, his razors and small-clothes lay on and about his private table in a miserable squalor; and from the appearance of the grizzled wig that was now acting as a tea-cosy for his milk-saucepan, it was clear that he had breakfasted on marmalade.

Jack took off his coat, covered his waistcoat and breeches with an apron, and carried the dishes into the scullery. 'My plate and saucer will serve again,' said Stephen. 'I have blown upon them. I do wish, Jack,' he cried, 'that you would leave that milk-saucepan alone. It is perfectly clean. What more sanitary, what more wholesome, than scalded milk? Will I dry up?' he called through the open door.

'No, no,' cried Jack, who had seen him do so. 'There is no room – it is nearly done. Just attend to the fire, will you?'

'We might have some music,' said Stephen. 'Your friend's piano is in tolerable tune, and I have found a German flute. What are you doing now?'

'Swabbing out the galley. Give me five minutes, and I am your man.'

'It sounds more like Noah's flood. This peevish attention to cleanliness, Jack, this busy preoccupation with dirt,' said Stephen, shaking his head at the fire, 'has something of the Brahminical superstition about it. It is not very far removed from nastiness, Jack – from cacothymia.'

'I am concerned to hear it,' said Jack. 'Pray, is it catching?' he added, with a private but sweet-natured leer. 'Now, sir,' – appearing in the doorway with the apron rolled under his arm – 'where is your flute? What shall we play?' He sat at the little square piano and ran his fingers up and down, singing,

> *Those Spanish dogs would gladly own*
> *Both Gibraltar and Port Mahon*

and don't they wish they may have it? Gibraltar, I mean.' He went on from one tune to another in an abstracted strumming while Stephen slowly screwed the flute together; and eventually from this strumming there emerged the adagio of the Hummel sonata.

'Is it modesty that makes him play like this?' wondered

Stephen, worrying at a crossed thread. 'I could swear he knows what music is – prizes high music beyond almost anything. But here he is, playing this as sweetly as milk, like an anecdote: Jesus, Mary and Joseph. And the inversion will be worse . . . It is worse – a sentimental indulgence. He takes pains; he is full of good-will and industry; and yet he cannot make even his fiddle utter anything but platitudes, except by mistake. On the piano it is worse, the notes being true. You would say it was a girl playing, a sixteen-stone girl. His face is not set in an expression of sentimentality, however, but of suffering. He is suffering extremely, I am afraid. This playing is very like Sophia's. Is he aware of it? Is he consciously imitating her? I do not know: their styles are much the same in any case – their absence of style. Perhaps it is diffidence, a feeling that *they* may not go beyond certain modest limits. They are much alike. And since Jack, knowing what real music is, can play like a simpleton, may not Sophia, playing like a ninny-hammer . . .? Perhaps I misjudge her. Perhaps it is a case of the man filled with true poetic feeling who can only come out with ye flowery meads again – the channels blocked. Dear me, he is sadly moved. How I hope those tears will not fall. He is the best of creatures – I love him dearly – but he is an Englishman, no more – emotional, lachrymose. Jack, Jack!' he called out. 'You have mistook the second variation.'

'What? What?' cried passionately. 'Why do you break in upon me, Stephen?'

'Listen. This is how it goes,' said Stephen, leaning over him and playing.

'No it ain't,' cried Jack. 'I had it right.' He took a turn up and down the room, filling it with his massive form, far larger now with emotion. He looked strangely at Stephen, but after another turn or two he smiled and said, 'Come, let's improvise, as we used to do off Crete. What tune shall we start with?'

'Do you know St Patrick's Day?'

'How does it go?' Stephen played. 'Oh, that? Of course I know it: we call it Bacon and Greens.'

'I must decline to improve on Bacon and Greens. Let us start with Hosier's Ghost, and see where we get to.'

The music wove in and out, one ballad and its variations leading to another, the piano handing it to the flute and back again; and sometimes they sang as well, the forecastle songs they had heard so often at sea.

> *Come all you brave seamen that ploughs on the main*
> *Give ear to my story I'm true to maintain,*
> *Concerning the* Litchfield *that was cast away*
> *On the Barbary shore by the dawn of the day.*

'The light is failing,' observed Stephen, taking his lips from the flute.

'On the Barbary shore by the dawn of the day,' sang Jack again. 'Oh, such a dying fall. So it is but the rain has let up, thank God,' he said, bending to the window. 'The wind has veered into the east – a little north to east. We shall have a dry walk.'

'Where are we going?'

'To Queenie's rout, of course. To Lady Keith's.' Stephen looked doubtfully at his sleeve. 'Your coat will do very well by candlelight,' said Jack. 'And even better when the middle button is sewn on. Just slip it off, will you, and hand along that hussif? I will make all fast while you put on a neckcloth and a pair of stockings – silk stockings, mind. Queenie gave me this hussif when I first went to sea,' he observed, whipping the thread round the shank of the button and biting it off close to the stuff. 'Now let us set your wig to rights – a trifle of flour from the bread-bag as a bow to fashion – now let me brush your coat – splendid – fit for a levee, upon my word and honour.'

'Why are you putting on that blackguardly cloak?'

'By God,' cried Jack, laying his hand on Stephen's bosom. 'I

never told you. One of the Miss Lambs wrote to her family –
her letter is in the paper – I am mentioned by name – and
that fornicating brute of an attorney will have his men out
after me. I shall muffle myself up and slouch my hat, and
perhaps we may stand ourselves a coach once we get well
into the town.'

'Do you have to go? Is it worth running the risk of a sponging-house and the King's Bench for an evening's diversion?'

'Yes. Lord Melville will be there; and I must see Queenie.
Even if I did not love her so, I have to keep all my naval interest in play – there will be the admiral and half a dozen other
great men. Come. I can explain as we walk. The rout-cake
there is famous, too – '

'I hear the squeaking of a pipistrelle! Hark! Stand still.
There, there again! So late in the year; it is a prodigy.'

'Does it mean good luck?' asked Jack, cocking his ear for
the sound. 'A capital omen, I dare say. But shall we go on
now? Gather just a little headway, perhaps?'

They reached Upper Brook Street at the height of the flood
– flambeaux, links, a tide of carriages waiting to set down at
number three and a counter-current trying to reach number
eight, where Mrs Damer was receiving her friends, a dense
crowd on the pavements to see the guests and pass remarks
upon their clothes, officious unnecessary barefoot boys opening doors or springing up behind, darting and hooting among
the horses in a spirit of fun, wonderfully tedious to the anxious or despondent. Jack had meant to fly straight from the
coach up the steps, but slow groups of fools, either coming
on foot or abandoning their carriages at the corner of
Grosvenor Square, clustered like summer bees in the
entrance and blocked the way.

He sat there on the edge of his seat, watching for a gap.
Arrest for debt was very common – he had always been aware
of it – had had several friends carried off to sponging-houses,
from which they wrote the most piteous appeals – but it had
never happened to him personally and his knowledge of the

process and of the law was vague. Sundays were safe, he was sure, and perhaps the King's birthday; he knew that peers could not be seized, that some places such as the Savoy and Whitefriars were sanctuaries, and he hoped that Lord Keith's house might therefore share these qualities: his longing eyes were fixed upon the open door, the lights within.

'Come on, governor,' cried the driver.

'Mind the step, your honour,' said a boy, holding the door.

'Come on, slow-arse,' shouted the coachman behind. 'You ain't going to plant a tree, are you?'

There was no help for it. Jack stepped out on to the pavement and stood by Stephen in the scarcely-moving throng, hitching his cloak even higher round his face.

'It's the Emperor of Morocco,' said a light brightly-painted whore.

'It's the Polish giant from Astley's.' 'Show us your face, sweetheart.'

'Hold your head up, cock.'

Some thought he was a foreigner, French dog of a Turk, others Old Moore, or Mother Shipton in disguise. He shuffled wretchedly towards the lighted doors, and when a hand clapped down on his shoulder he turned with a ferocity that pleased the crowd more than anything they had seen hitherto, except for Miss Rankin treading on her petticoat and coming down full length. 'Aubrey! Jack Aubrey!' cried Dundas, his old shipmate Heneage Dundas. 'I recognized your back at once – should have recognized you anywhere. How do you do? You have a touch of fever, I dare say? Dr Maturin, how do you do? Are you going in here? So am I, ha, ha, ha. How do you get along?' Dundas had recently been made post into the *Franchise*, 36; he loved the world in general, and his cheerful, affectionate flow of talk carried them across the pavement, up the steps and into the hall.

The gathering had a strong naval flavour, but Lady Keith was also a political hostess and the friend of a great many interesting people: Jack left Stephen in conversation with a gentleman who had discovered the adamantine boron and moved through the great drawing-room, through the less crowded gallery and to a little domed room with a buffet in it: Constantia wine, little pies, rout-cakes, more Constantia. Here Lady Keith found him; she was leading a big man in a sky-blue coat with silver buttons and she said, 'Jack, dear, may I introduce Mr Canning? Captain Aubrey, of the Navy.'

Jack liked the look of this man at once, and during the first meaningless civilities this feeling grew: Canning was a broad-shouldered fellow, and although he was not quite so tall as Jack, his way of holding his small round head up and tilted back, with his chin in the air, made him look bigger, more commanding. He wore his own hair – what there was left of it: short tight curls round a shining calvity, though he was in his thirties, no more – and he looked like one of the fatter, more jovial Roman emperors; a humorous, good-natured face, but one that conveyed an impression of great latent strength. 'An ugly customer to have against you,' thought Jack, earnestly recommending 'one of these voluptuous little pies' and a glass of Constantia.

Mr Canning was a Bristol merchant. The news quite astonished Jack. He had never met a merchant before, out of the way of business. A few bankers and money-men, yes; and a poor thin bloodless set of creatures they seemed – a lower order; but it was impossible to feel superior to Mr Canning. 'I am so particularly happy to be introduced to you, Captain Aubrey,' he said, quickly eating two more little pies, 'because I have known you by reputation for years and because I was reading about you in the paper only yesterday. I wrote you a letter to express my sense of your action with the *Cacafuego* back in '01, and I very nearly posted it: indeed I should have done so, with the least excuse of a nodding acquaintance or a common friend. But it would have been too great a liberty in a complete stranger, alas; and after all, what does my praise amount to? The mere noise of uninformed admiration.'

Jack made the noises of acknowledgment. 'Too kind – an

excellent crew – the Spaniard was unlucky in his dispositions.'

'And yet not so wholly uninformed, neither,' went on Canning. 'I fitted out some privateers in the last war, and I took a cruise in one as far as Goree and in another to Bermuda, so I have at least some notion of the sea. No conceivable comparison, of course; but some slight notion of what such an action means.'

'Was you ever in the Service, sir?' asked Jack.

'I? Why, no. I am a Jew,' said Canning, with a look of deep amusement.

'Oh,' said Jack. 'Ah?' He turned, going through the motions of blowing his nose, saw Lord Melville looking at him from the doorway, bowed and called out 'Good evening.'

'And this war I have fitted out seven, with the eighth on the stocks. Now, sir, this brings me to the *Bellone*, of Bordeaux. She snapped up two of my merchantmen the moment war broke out again, and she took the *Nereid*, my heaviest privateer – eighteen twelve-pounders – the cruise before she took you and your Indiaman. She is a splendid sailer, sir, is she not?'

'Prodigious, sir, prodigious. Close-hauled, with light airs, she ran away from the *Blanche* as easy as kiss my hand: and spilling her wind by way of a ruse, she still made six knots for *Blanche*'s four, though close-hauled is *Blanche*'s best point of sailing. Very well handled, too: her captain was a former King's officer.'

'Yes. Dumanoir – Dumanoir de Plessy. I have her draught,' said Canning, leaning over the buffet, fairly ablaze with overflowing life and enthusiasm, 'and I am building my eighth on her lines exactly.'

'Are you, by God!' cried Jack. Frigate-sized privateers were not uncommon in France, but they were unknown this side of the Channel.

'But with twenty-four-pounder carronades in place of her long guns, and eighteen-pounder chasers. Do you think she will bear 'em?'

'I should have to look at her draught,' said Jack, considering deeply. 'I believe she would, and to spare: but I should have to look at her draught.'

'But that is a detail,' said Canning, waving his hand. 'The real crux is the command. Everything depends on her commander, of course; and here I should value your advice and guidance beyond anything. I should do a great deal to come by the services of a bold, enterprising captain – a thorough-going seaman, of course. A letter-of-marque is not a King's ship, I admit; but I try to run mine in a way no King's officer would dislike – taut discipline, regularity, cleanliness. But no black lists, no hazing, and very little cat. You are no great believer in the cat, sir, I believe?'

'Not I,' said Jack. 'I find it don't answer the purpose, with fighting-men.'

'Fighting-men: just so. That is another thing I can offer – prime fighting-men, prime seamen. They are mostly smugglers' crews, west-countrymen, born to the sea and up to anything: I have more volunteers than I can find room for; I can pick and choose; and those I choose will follow the right man anywhere, put up with all reasonable discipline and behave like lambs. A right privateer's man is no blackguard when he is led by the right captain. I believe I am right there, sir?'

'I dare say you are, sir,' said Jack slowly.

'And to get the right commander I offer a post-captain's pay and allowances for a seventy-four and I guarantee a thousand a year in prize-money. Not one of my captains has made less, and this new ship will certainly do very much better; she will be more than twice the burden of the others and she will have between two and three hundred men aboard. For when you consider, sir, that a private ship of war spends no time blockading, running messages or carrying troops, but only destroying the enemy's commerce, and when you consider that this frigate can cruise for six months at a time, why, the potentialities are enormous . . . enormous.' Jack nodded: they were, indeed. 'But where can I find my commander?' asked Canning.

'Where did you find your others?'

'They were local men. Excellent, in their way, but they govern smallish crews, relatives, acquaintances, men they have sailed with. This is another problem entirely; it calls for a bigger man, a man on another scale. Might I beg for your advice, Captain Aubrey? Can you think of any man, any former shipmate of yours, perhaps, or . . .? I should give him a free hand, and I should back him to the hilt.'

'I should have to consider of it,' said Jack.

'Pray do, pray do,' said Canning. No less than a dozen people came up to the buffet at once, and private conversation was at an end. Canning gave Jack his card, pencilling an address upon it, and said in a low tone, 'I shall be here all the week. A word from you, at any time, and I shall be most grateful for a meeting.'

They parted — indeed they were driven apart — and Jack backed until he was brought up by the window. The offer had been as direct as it could be in decency, to a serving officer: he liked Canning, had rarely taken to any man with such immediate sympathy at first sight. He must be most uncommon rich to fit out a six or seven hundred ton letter-of-marque: a huge investment for a private man. Yet Jack's reflection was one of wonder alone, not of doubt — there was not the least question of Canning's honesty in his mind.

'Come, Jack, come, come,' said Lady Keith, tugging his arm. 'Where are your manners? You are behaving like a bear.'

'Dear Queenie,' said he, with a great slow smile, 'forgive me. I am bemused. Your friend Canning wants to make my fortune. He is your friend?'

'Yes. His father taught me Hebrew — good evening, Miss Sibyl — such a very wealthy young man, so enterprising. He has a vast admiration for you.'

'That shows a proper candour. Does he speak Hebrew, Queenie?'

'Oh, just enough for his bar mitzvah, you know. He is about as much of a scholar as you are, Jack. He has many friends in the Prince of Wales's set, but don't let that put you off – he is not a flash cove. Come into the gallery.'

'Bar mitzvah,' said Jack, in a grave voice, following her into the crowded gallery; and there, momentarily framed by four men in black coats, he saw the familiar red face of Mrs Williams. She was sitting by the fireplace, looking hot and overdressed, and Cecilia sat next to her: for a moment he could not place them in this context; they belonged to another world and time, another reality. There was no empty place beside them, no vacant chair. As Lady Keith led him up to them she murmured something about Sophia; but her discretion swallowed up her meaning.

'Have you come back to England, Captain Aubrey?' said Mrs Williams, as he made his leg. 'Well, well, upon my word.'

'Where are your other girls?' asked Lady Keith, glancing about.

'I was obliged to leave them at home, your ladyship. Frankie has such a feverish cold, and Sophie has stayed to take care of her.'

'She did not know you would be here,' whispered Cecilia.

'Jack,' said Lady Keith, 'I believe Lord Melville is throwing out a signal. He wants to speak with you.'

'The First Lord?' cried Mrs Williams, half rising in her seat and craning. 'Where? Where? Which is he?'

'The gentleman with the star,' said Lady Keith.

'Just a word, Aubrey,' said Lord Melville, 'and then I must be off. Can you come to see me tomorrow instead of next week? It does not throw you out? Good night to you, then – I am obliged to you, Lady Keith,' he called, kissing his hand and waving it, 'your most humble, devoted . . .'

Jack's face and eyes, as he turned back to the ladies, had a fine glow, a hint of the rising sun. By the law of social metaphysics some of the great man's star had rubbed off on him, as well as a little of young Canning's easy opulence. He felt that he was in command of the situation, of any situation, in spite of the wolves outside the door: his calmness surprised him. What were his feelings beneath this strong bubbling cheerfulness? He could not make it out. So much had happened these last few days – his old cloak still smelt of powder – and indeed was still happening, that he could not make them out. Sometimes you receive a knock in action: it may be your death-wound or just a scratch, a graze – you cannot tell at once. He gave up the attempt and turned his full attention to Mrs Williams, inwardly remarking that the Mrs Williams of Sussex and even of Bath was a different animal from the Mrs Williams in a great London drawing-room; she looked provincial and dowdy; and so, it must be admitted, did Cecilia, with her fussy ornaments and frizzled hair – though indeed she was a good-natured child. Mrs Williams was obscurely aware of this; she looked stupid, uncertain, and almost respectful, though he felt that resentment might not be far away. Having observed how affable Lord Melville was very much the gentleman, she told Jack that they had read about his escape in the paper: she hoped his return meant that everything was well with him: but how came he to be in India? She had understood he had withdrawn to the Continent in consequence of some . . . to the *Continent*.

'So I did, ma'am. Maturin and I went to France, where that scoundrel Bonaparte very nearly laid us by the heels.'

'But you came home in an Indiaman. I saw it in the papers – in *The Times*.'

'Yes. She touched at Gibraltar.'

'Ah. I see. So now the mystery is cleared up: I thought I should get to the bottom of it at last.'

'How is dear Dr Maturin?' asked Cecilia. 'I hope to see him.'

'Yes, how is the worthy Dr Maturin?' said her mother. 'He is very well, I thank you. He was in the far room some moments ago, talking to the Physician of the Fleet. What a splendid fellow he is: he nursed me through a most devilish fever I caught in the mountains, and dosed me twice a day until we reached Gibraltar. Nothing else would have brought me home.'

'Mountains – Spain,' said Mrs Williams with strong disapproval. 'You will never get *me* there, I can tell you.'

'So you travelled right down through Spain,' said Cecilia. 'I
dare say it was prodigiously romantic, with ruins, and monks?'

'There were some ruins and monks, to be sure,' said Jack,
smiling at her. 'And hermits too. But the most romantic thing
I saw was the Rock, rearing up there at the end of our road
like a lion. That, and the orange-tree in Stephen's castle.'

'A castle in Spain!' cried Cecilia, clasping her hands.

'Castle!' cried Mrs Williams. 'Nonsense. Captain Aubrey
means some cottage with a whimsical name, my love.'

'No, ma'am. A castle, with towers, battlements, and all that
is proper. A marble roof, too. The only whimsical thing about
it was the bath, which stood just off a spiral staircase, as bald
as an egg: it was marble too, carved out of a single block –
amazing. But this orange-tree was in a court with arches all
round, a kind of cloister, and it bore oranges, lemons, and
tangerines all at the same time! Green fruit, ripe fruit, and
flowers, all at the same time and such a scent. There's
romance for you! Not many oranges when I was there, but
lemons fresh every day. I must have eaten – '

'Am I to understand that Dr Maturin is a man of property?'
cried Mrs Williams.

'Certainly you are, ma'am. A thumping great estate up
where we crossed the mountains – merino sheep – '

'Merino sheep,' said Mrs Williams, nodding, for she knew
the beasts existed – what else could yield merino wool?

' – but his main place is down towards Lérida. By the way, I
have not inquired for Mrs Villiers: how rude of me. I hope
she is well?'

'Yes, yes – she is here,' – dismissing Diana – 'But I thought
he was only a naval surgeon.'

'Did you indeed, ma'am? However, he is a man of considerable estate: a physician, too – they think the world of him in – '

'Then how did he come to be your surgeon?' she asked, in a
sudden last burst of suspicion.

'What easier way of seeing the world? Airy, commodious, and *paid for by the King.*' This was utterly conclusive. Mrs Williams relapsed into silence for some moments. She had heard of castles in Spain, but she could not remember whether they were good or bad: they were certainly one or the other. Probably good, seeing that Lord Melville was so affable. Oh yes, very good – certainly very good.

'I hope he will call – I hope you will both call,' she said at last. 'We are staying with my sister Pratt in George Street. Number eleven.'

Jack was most grateful; unhappily official business – he could not call his time his own – but he was sure Dr Maturin would be delighted; and he begged he might be particularly remembered to Miss Williams and Miss Frances.

'You may have heard, of course, that my Sophie is – ' began Mrs Williams, launched upon the precautionary lie, then regretting it and not knowing how to come off handsomely, ' – that Sophie is, how shall I say – though there is nothing official.'

'There's Di,' whispered Cecilia, poking Jack with her elbow.

She was walking slowly into the gallery between two men, both tall: a dark blue dress, a black velvet band around her throat, splendid white bosom. He had forgotten that her hair was black, *black*, her neck a column and her eyes mere dark smudges in the distance. His feelings needed no analysis: his heart, which had stopped while he searched for the empty place by Mrs Williams, now beat to quarters: a constellation, a galaxy of erotic notions raced through his mind, together with an unmixed pleasure in looking at her. How well-bred she looked! She did not seem pleased, however; she turned her head from the man on her right with a lift of her chin that he knew only too well.

'The gentleman she is walking with is Colonel Colpoys, Admiral Haddock's brother-in-law, from India. Diana is staying with Mrs Colonel Colpoys in Bruton Street. A pokey, inconvenient little house.'

'How beautiful he is,' murmured Cecilia.

'Colonel Colpoys?' cried Mrs Williams.

'No, Mama, the gentleman in the blue coat.'

'Oh, no, my love,' – lowering her voice, speaking behind her hand and staring hard at Canning – 'that gentleman is a jay ee double-u.'

'So he is not beautiful, Mama?'

'Of course not, my dear' – as to an idiot – 'I have just told you he is a' – lowering her voice again – 'jay ee double-u,' pursing her lips and nodding her head with great satisfaction.

'Oh,' said Cecilia, disappointed. 'Well, all I can say,' she muttered to herself, 'is, I wish I had beaux like that following me around. He has been by her all the evening, almost. Men are always following Di around. There is another one.'

The other one, an army officer, was hurrying through the press with a tall thin glass of champagne, bearing it towards her with both hands as though it were a holy object; but before he could urge a fat, staring woman out of his way, Stephen Maturin appeared. Diana's face changed at once – a look of straightforward, almost boyish delight – and as he came up she gave him both hands, crying, 'Oh, Maturin, how very glad I am to see you! Welcome home.'

The soldier, Canning and Jack were watching intently; they saw nothing to give them uneasiness; the delicate pink flush in Diana's face, reaching her ears, was that of spontaneous open uncomplicated pleasure; Maturin's unaltered pallor, his somewhat absent expression, matched her directness. Furthermore, he was looking uncommonly plain – rusty, neglected, undarned.

Jack relaxed in his chair: he had got it wrong, he thought, with a warm and lively pleasure in his mistake: he often got things wrong. He had set up for penetration, and he had got it wrong. 'You are not attending,' said Cecilia. 'You are so busy quizzing the gentleman in blue, that you are not attending. Mama says they mean to go and look at the Magdalene. That is what Dr Maturin is pointing at.'

'Yes? Oh, yes. Certainly. A Guido, I believe?'

'No, sir,' said Mrs Williams, who understood these things better than other people. 'It is an oil painting, a very valuable oil painting, though not quite in the modern taste.'

'Mama, may I run after Dr Maturin and go with them?' asked Cecilia.

'Do, my love, and tell Dr Maturin to come and see me. No, Captain Aubrey, do not get up: you shall tell me about your Spanish journey. There is nothing that interests me more than travel, I declare; and if I had had my health I should have been a great traveller, a second – a second – '

'St Paul?'

'No, no. A second Lady Mary Wortley Montagu. Now tell me about Dr Maturin's establishment.'

Jack could not tell her very much; he had been unwell, delirious at times, and he did not attend to the kind of leases they had in those parts, or the return on capital – Mrs Williams sighed – had not seen the rent-roll, but supposed the estate was 'pretty big' – it took in a good deal of Aragon, as well as Catalonia; it had its drawbacks, however, being sadly infested by porcupines; they were hunted by a pack of pure-bred porcupine-hounds, often by moonlight, the field carrying Cordova-leather umbrellas against the darting of their quills.

'You gentlemen are always so taken up with your sporting, when a little attention to rack-rents and fines and enclosures – I am enclosing Mapes Common – ah, here comes the dear Doctor.'

Stephen's face rarely betrayed much emotion, but her effusive welcome made him stretch his eyes: her first question set him right, however, 'So I hear that you have a marble bath, Dr Maturin? That must be a great comfort to you, in such a climate.'

'Certainly, ma'am. I conceive it to be Visigothic.'

'Not marble?'

'Visigothic marble, my dear madam, from a baptistery destroyed by the Moors.'

'And you have a castle?'

'Oh, it is only a small place. I keep one wing in order, to go up there from time to time.'

'For the porcupine-hunting, no doubt?'

Stephen bowed. 'And for my rents, ma'am. In some ways Spain is a more direct country than England, and when we say rack-rent in those parts, rack-rent is what we mean – why, we make them pay for the use of the instrument.'

Jack found Diana at the buffet where he had had his conversation with Canning: Canning was no longer with her, but his place had been taken by two more soldiers. She did not give Jack both hands, because one was holding a glass and the other a piece of cake, but her greeting was as gay, cheerful and undisguised as it had been for Stephen: even warmer, perhaps, for she moved away from the group to talk with him – a hundred quick, attentive inquiries – and she said 'How we have missed you at Mapes, Aubrey; how I have missed you! A pack of women mewed up together, bottling gooseberries, God help us. There is that odious Mr Dawkins bearing down. We will go and look at Lady Keith's new picture. Here it is. What do you think of her?'

It was clear that the Magdalene had not yet repented: she was standing on a quay with blue ruins in the background – a blue that swept with varying intensities through her robe to the sea – with gold plates, ewers and basins heaped up on a crimson cloth, and an expression of mild complacency on her face. Her blue dress had blown off – a fresh double-reef topsail breeze – and so had a filmy white garment, exposing handsome limbs and a firm, though opulent bosom. Jack had been a long time at sea, and this drew his attention; however, he shifted his gaze after a moment, surveyed the rest of the picture and sought for something appropriate, perhaps even witty, to say. He longed to produce a subtle and ingenious remark, but he longed in vain – perhaps the day had been too full – and he was obliged to fall back on 'Very fine – such a blue.' Then a small vessel in the lower left-hand corner caught his eye, something in the nature of a pink; she was beating up for the harbour, but it was obvious from the direction of the lady's clothes that the pink would be taken aback the moment she rounded the headland. 'As soon as she catches the land-breeze she will be in trouble,' he said. 'She will never stay, not with those unhandy lateens, and there is no room to wear; so there she is on a lee-shore. Poor fellows. I am afraid there is no hope for them.'

'That is exactly what Maturin told me you would say,' cried Diana, squeezing his arm. 'How well he knows you, Aubrey.'

'Well, a man don't have to be a Nostradamus to tell what a sailor will say, when he sees an infernal tub like that laid by the lee. But Stephen is a very deep old file, to be sure,' he added, his good humour returning. 'And a great cognoscento, I make no doubt. For my part I know nothing about painting at all.'

'Nor do I,' said Diana, staring up at the picture. 'She seems to be making a very good thing of it,' – with a chuckle – 'No lack of admirers. Come, let us see if we can find an ice: I am dying of heat and general distress.'

'Look at the outré way Diana has dragged up her hair,' said Mrs Williams as they passed by towards the great drawing-room. 'It is bound to attract attention. It would do Sophie good, to see her walking about like that, as bold as brass, with poor Captain Aubrey. She has positively taken his arm, I protest.'

'Tell me,' said Diana, 'What are your plans? Are you back for good? Shall we see something of you in Sussex?'

'I am not sure,' said Jack. 'Do you see that man saying good-bye to Lady Keith? But you know him – he was talking to you just now. Canning.'

'Yes?' 'He has offered me the command of a – of a letter-of-marque, a private man of war, a thirty-two gun frigate.'

'Oh, Aubrey, how splendid! A privateer is just the thing for you – Have I said something wrong?'

'No. No, not at all – good evening, sir: that was Admiral

Bridges – No, it was just the word privateer. But as Stephen is always telling me, one must not be the prisoner of words.'

'Of course not. Besides, what does it signify? It is just like taking service with the native princes in India: nobody thinks any the less of you and everybody envies the fortune you make. Oh, how well it would suit you – your own master, no fagging up and down to Whitehall, no admirals to make you do tiresome things and snatch great lumps of your prize-money. A perfect idea for a man like you – for a man of spirit. An independent command! A thirty-two gun frigate!'

'It is a magnificent offer: I am in a maze.'

'And in partnership with Canning! I am sure you would get on famously. My cousin Jersey knows him. The Cannings are absurdly rich, and he is very like a native prince; only he is straightforward and brave, which they are not, on the whole.' Her eager face changed, and looking round Jack saw an elderly man standing by him. 'My dear,' said the elderly man, 'Charlotte sends me to tell you she is thinking of going home presently; we have to drop Charles at the Tower before twelve.'

'I shall come at once,' said Diana.

'No, no, you have plenty of time to finish your ice.'

'Have I, truly? May I introduce Captain Aubrey, of the Navy, Admiral Haddock's neighbour? Colonel Colpoys, who is so sweetly kind as to have me to stay.'

Very small talk for a moment, and the colonel went away to see to his horses.

'When shall I see you again? Will you call at Bruton Street tomorrow morning? I shall be alone. You may take me into the park, and to look at the shops.'

'Diana,' said Jack in a low voice, 'there is a writ out against me. I dare not walk about London.'

'You dare not? You are afraid of being arrested?' Jack nodded. 'Afraid? Upon my word, I never expected to hear that from you. What do you think I introduced you for? It was so you might call.'

'Besides, I am under orders for the Admiralty tomorrow.'

'How unfortunate,' said Diana.

'May I come on Sunday?'

'No, sir, you may not. I do not ask men to come to see me so often . . . No, you must certainly consult your safety: of course you must consult your safety. In any case, I shall no longer be in town.'

'Mr Wells's carriage; Sir John Bridges's carriage; Colonel Colpoys's carriage,' cried a footman.

'Major Lennox,' said Diana, as one of her soldiers went by, 'please be very kind and find me my cloak, will you? I must say good-bye to Lady Keith and my aunt,' she observed to herself, gathering her fan and gloves.

Jack followed the procession of Colonel and Mrs Colpoys, Diana Villiers, the unknown Charles, Lennox and Stephen Maturin, and stood bare-headed, exposed on that brightly-lit pavement while the carriages made their slow way down from the mews: no word, however – not so much as a look. At last the women were handed in and stowed away, the carriage moved off, and Jack walked slowly back into the house with Stephen Maturin.

They went up the broad stairs, making their way against the increasing current of guests who had taken their leave; their conversation was fragmentary and unimportant – a few general remarks – but by the time they had reached the top each knew that their harmony was no longer what it had been these last few months.

'I shall make my farewells,' said Stephen, 'and then I believe I shall walk down to the Physical Society. You will stay a little longer with your friends, I imagine? I do beg you to take a coach from the very door itself and to ride all the way home. Here is the common purse. If you are to see the First Lord in the morning, your mind must be in a condition of easy complaisance, in a placid, rested state. There is milk in the little crock – warmed milk will relax the fibres.'

Jack warmed it, added a dash of rum from his case-bottle,

and drank it up; but in spite of his faith in the draught, the fibres remained tense, the placidity of mind a great way off.

Writing a note to tell Stephen that he would be back presently and leaving the candle burning, he walked out on to the Heath. Enough moonlight filtered through the murk to show him his path, pale among the scattered trees; he went fast, and soon he had walked himself into his second wind and a steady rhythm. Into a muck-sweat, too: the cloak became unbearably hot. Steadily on, with the cloak rolled tight under his arm, up hill, down to some ponds, and up again. He almost trod on a courting couple – hard pressed, to lie in such a dismal plash and at such a time – and turned away right-handed, leaving the remote glow of London behind him.

This was the first time in his life he had ever refused a direct challenge. He could hear the whining reasonability of his 'there is a writ out against me' and he blushed in the darkness – pitiful. But how could she have asked him to do such a thing? How could she ask so much? He thought of her with cold hostility. No friend would have done so. She was no fool, no inexperienced girl: she knew what he was risking.

Contempt was very hard to bear. In his place she would have come, bailiffs or no bailiffs; he was sure of that. The Admiralty had sounded a snivelling excuse.

What if he chanced it and appeared at Bruton Street in the morning? If he were to accept the privateer, the appointment in Whitehall would be meaningless. He had been shabbily treated there, more shabbily than any man he could remember, and there was no likelihood, no possibility that tomorrow's meeting would put things right. At the best some unacceptable shore-based post that would salve the First Lord's conscience, that would allow him to say 'We offered him employment, but he did not see fit to accept it.' Conceivably some hulk or storeship; but at all events Lord Melville was not going to make him post and offer him a frigate, the only thing that would do away with the injustice, the only

thing that could find him by a sense of proper usage. The recollection of the way he had been treated rose hotter and hotter in his mind: a wretched mean-spirited disingenuous
shuffling, and men without a tenth part of his claim being
promoted over his head by the dozen. His recommendations
ignored, his midshipmen left on the beach.

With Canning as his First Lord, secretary and Board of
Admiralty all in one, how different it would be! A well-found
ship, a full crew of prime seamen, a free hand, and all the
oceans of the world before him – the West Indies for quick
returns, the cherished cruising-grounds of the Channel fleet,
and if Spain were to come in (which was almost certain), the
Mediterranean sea-lanes he knew so well. But even more, far
beyond the common range of cruisers and private ships of
war, the Mozambique Channel, the approaches to the Isle of
France, the Indian Ocean; and eastwards still, the Spice
Islands and the Spanish Philippines. South of the Line, right
down to the Cape and beyond, there were still French and
Dutch Indiamen coming home. And if he were to stretch
away on the monsoon, there was Manila under his lee, and
the Spanish treasure ships. Even without flying so high, one
moderate prize in those latitudes would clear his debts; a second would set him on his feet again; and it would be strange
if he could not make two prizes in an almost virgin sea.

The name of Sophia moved insistently up into that part of
his mind where words took form. He had repressed it as far
as he was able ever since he ran for France. He was not a
marriageable man: Sophie was as far out of his reach as an
admiral's flag.

She would never have done this to him. In a fit of self-
indulgence he imagined that same evening with Sophie – her
extraordinary grace of movement, quite different from
Diana's quickness, the sweet gentleness with which she
would have looked at him – that infinitely touching desire to
protect. How would he have stood it in fact, if he had seen

Sophie there next to her mother? Would he have turned tail and skulked in the far room until he could make his escape? How would she have behaved?

'Christ,' he said aloud, the new thought striking him with horror, 'what if I had seen them both together?' He dwelt on this possibility for a while, and to get rid of the very unpleasant image of himself, with Sophie's gentle, questioning eyes looking straight at him and wondering, 'Can this scrub be Jack Aubrey?' he turned left and left again, walking fast over the bare Heath until he struck into his first path, where a scattering of birches showed ghastly white in the drizzle. It occurred to him that he should put some order into his thoughts about these two. Yet there was something so very odious, so very grossly indecent, in making any sort of comparison, in weighing up, setting side by side, evaluating. Stephen blamed him for being muddle-headed, wantonly muddle-headed, refusing to follow his ideas to their logical conclusion. 'You have all the English vices, my dear, including muddle-headed sentiment and hypocrisy.' Yet it was nonsense to drag in logic where logic did not apply. To think clearly in such a case was inexpressibly repugnant: logic could apply only to a deliberate seduction or to a marriage of interest.

Taking his bearings, however, was something else again: he had never attempted to do so yet, nor to find out the deep nature of his present feelings. He had a profound distrust for this sort of exercise, but now it was important – it was of the first importance.

'Your money or your life,' said a voice very close at hand.

'What? What? What did you say?'

The man stepped from behind the trees, the rain glinting on his weapon. 'I said, "Your money or your life,"' he said, and coughed.

Instantly the cloak in his face. Jack had him by the shirt, worrying him, shaking him with terrible vehemence, jerking him high off the ground. The shirt gave way: he stood stagger-

ing, his arms out. Jack hit him a great left-handed blow on
the ear and kicked his legs from under him as he fell.

He snatched up the cudgel and stood over him, breathing
hard and waving his left hand – knuckles split: a damned
unhandy blow – it had been like hitting a tree. He was filled
with indignation. 'Dog, dog, dog,' he said, watching for a
movement. But there was no movement, and after a while
Jack's teeth unclenched: he stirred the body with his foot.
'Come, sir. Up you get. Rise and shine.' After a few more
orders of this sort, delivered pretty loud, he sat the fellow up
and shook him. Head dangling, utterly limp; wet and cold; no
breath, no heartbeat, very like a corpse. 'God damn his eyes,'
said Jack, 'he's died on me.'

The increasing rain brought his cloak to mind; he found it,
put it on, and stood over the body again. Poor wretched little
brute – could not be more than seven or eight stone – and as
incompetent a footpad as could be imagined – had been
within a toucher of adding 'if you please' to his demand – no
notion of attack. Was he dead? He was not: one hand scrabbled in vague, disordered motion.

Jack shivered: the heat of walking and of the brief struggle
had worn off in this waiting pause, and he wrapped his cloak
tighter; it was a raw night, with frost a certainty before dawn.
More vain, irritated shaking, rough attempts at revival. 'Jesus,
what a bore,' he said. At sea there would have been no problem, but here on land it was different – he had a different
sense of tidiness ashore – and after a disgusted pause he
wrapped the object in his cloak (not from any notion of
humanity, but to keep the mud, blood and perhaps worse off
his clothes), picked it up and walked off.

Seven stone odd was nothing much for the first hundred
yards, nor the second; but the smell of his warmed burden
grew unpleasant, and he was pleased to see that he was near
the place he had entered the Heath, within sight of his own
lit window.

'Stephen will soon set him right,' he thought: it was known

that Stephen could raise the dead so long as the tide had not changed – had been seen to do it.

But there was no answer to his hail. The candle was low in its socket, with an unsnuffed mushroom of a wick; the fire was almost out; his note still stood propped against the milk jug. Jack put his footpad down, took the candle and looked at him. A grey, emaciated face: eyes almost closed, showing little crescents of white: stubble: blood over one half of it. A puny little narrow-chested cove, no good to man or beast. 'I had better leave him alone till Stephen comes,' he thought. 'I wonder whether there are any sausages left?'

Hours; the ticking of the clock; the quarter-chimes from the church; steady mending of the fire, staring at the flame; the fibres quite relaxed – a kind of placid happiness at last.

The first light brought Stephen. He paused in the doorway, looking attentively at the sleeping Jack and at the wild eyes of the footpad, lashed into a windsor chair.

'Good morning to you, sir,' he said, with a reserved nod. 'Good morning, sir. Oh sir, if you please – '

'Why, Stephen, there you are,' cried Jack. 'I was quite anxious for you.'

'Aye?' said Stephen, setting a cabbage-leaf parcel on the table and taking an egg from his pocket and a loaf from his bosom. 'I have brought a beef-steak to recruit you for your interview, and what passes for bread in these parts. I strongly urge you to take off your clothes, to sponge yourself all over – the copper will answer admirably – and to lie between sheets for an hour. Rested, shaved, coffee'd, steaked, you will be a different man. I urge the more strongly, because there is a louse crawling up your collar – pediculus vestimenti seeking promotion to p. capitis – and where we *see* one, we may reasonably assume the hidden presence of a score.'

'Pah!' said Jack, flinging off his coat. 'This is what comes of carrying that lousy villain. Damn you, sir.'

'I am most deeply sorry, sir: most heartily ashamed,' said the footpad, hanging his head.

'You might take a look at him, Stephen,' said Jack. 'I gave him a thump on the head. I shall go and light the copper and then turn in. You will give me a call, Stephen?'

'A shrewd thump,' said Stephen, mopping and probing. 'A very shrewd thump, upon my word. Does this hurt?'

'No more than the rest, sir. It is benevolent in you to trouble with me . . . but, oh sir, if I might have the liberty of my hands? I itch unbearably.'

'I dare say you do,' said Stephen, taking the bread-knife to the knot. 'You are strangely infested. What are these marks? They are certainly older than last night.'

'Oh, no more than extravasated blood, sir, under your correction. I tried to take a purse over towards Highgate last week. A person with a wench, which seemed to give me a certain . . . however, he beat me cruelly, and threw me into a pond.'

'It may be that your talents do not altogether fit you for purse-taking: certainly your diet does not.'

'Yet it was my diet, or rather my want of diet, that drove me to the Heath. I have not eaten these five days.'

'Pray, have you had any success?' asked Stephen. He broke the egg into the milk, beat it up with sugar and the remaining drops of rum, and began to feed the footpad with a spoon.

'None, sir. Oh how I thank you: ambrosia. None, sir. A black-pudding snatched from a boy in Flask Lane was my greatest feat. Nectar. None, sir. Yet I am sure if a man threatened me with a cudgel in the dark and desired me to give him my purse, I should do so at once. But not my victims, sir; they either beat me, or they declare they have no purse, or they pay no attention and walk on while I cry "Stand and deliver" beside them, or they take to abusing me – why do I not work? Am I not ashamed? Perhaps I lack the presence, the resolution; perhaps if I could have afforded a pistol . . . Might I take the liberty of begging for a little bread, sir? A very little piece of bread? There is a tiger in my bowels, if not in my appearance.'

'You must masticate deliberately. What do you reply to their suggestions?'

'About work, sir? Why, that I should be very glad to have it, that I should do any work I could find: I am an industrious creature, sir. Might I beg for just another slice? I could have added, that it was work that had been my undoing.'

'Truly?'

'Would it be proper to give an account of myself, sir?'

'A brief account of your undoing would be quite proper.'

'I used to live in Holywell Street, sir; I was a literary man. There were a great many of us, brought up to no trade or calling, but with a smattering of education and money enough to buy pens and a quire of paper, who commenced author and set up in that part of town. It was surprising how many of us were bastards; my own father was said to have been a judge – indeed, he may well have been: someone sent me to school near Slough for a while. A few had some little originality – I believe I had a real turn for verse to begin with – but it was the lower slopes of Helicon, sir, the sort of author that writes *The Universal Directory for Taking Alive Rats* or *The Unhappy Birth, Wicked Life and Miserable End of that Deceitful Apostle, Judas Iscariot* and pamphlets, of course – *Thoughts of the Present Crisis*, by a Nobleman, or *A New Way of Funding the National Debt*. For my part, I took to translating for the booksellers.'

'From what language?'

'Oh, all languages, sir. If it was oriental or classical, there was sure to be a Frenchman there before us; and as for Italian or Spanish, I could generally puzzle it out in the end. High Dutch, too: I was quite a proficient in the High Dutch by the time I had run through Fleischhacker's *Elegant Diversions* and Strumpff's *Nearest Way to Heaven*. I did tolerably well, sir, upon the whole, rarely going hungry or without a lodging, for I was neat, sober, punctual, and as I have said, industrious: I always kept my promised day, the printers could read my hand, and I corrected my proofs as soon as they came. But then a bookseller by the name of – but hush, I must name no names – Mr G sent for me and proposed

Boursicot's *South Seas*. I was very happy to accept, for the market was slow, and I had had to live for a month on *The Case of the Druids impartially considered*, a little piece in the *Ladies' Repository*, and the druids did not run to more than bread and milk. We agreed for half a guinea a sheet; I dared not hold out for more, although it was printed very small, with all the notes set in pearl.'

'What might that mean in terms of weekly income?'

'Why, sir, taking the hard places with the smooth, and working twelve hours a day, it might have amounted to as much as five and twenty shillings! I was a cock-a-hoop, for next to the Abbé Prévost, Boursicot is the longest collection of voyages in French I know of, the longest work I had ever engaged in; and I thought I had my living for a great while ahead. My credit was good, so I moved downstairs to the two-pair front, a handsome room, for the sake of the light; I bought some furniture and several books that I should need – some very expensive dictionaries among them.'

'Did you require a dictionary for French, sir?'

'No, sir: I had one. These were Blanckley's *Naval Expositor* and Du Hamel, Aubin, and Saverien, to understand the hard words in the shipwrecks and manoeuvres, and to know what the travellers were about. I find it quite a help in translation to understand the text, sir; I always prefer it. So I worked away in my handsome room, refusing two or three offers from other booksellers and eating in a chop-house twice a week, until the day Mr G sent me his young man to say he had thought better of *my* project of translating Boursicot – that his associates felt the cost of the plate would be too high – and that in the present state of the trade there was no demand for such an article.'

'Did you have a contract?'

'No, sir. It was what the booksellers call a gentleman's agreement.'

'No hope, then?'

'None whatsoever, sir. I tried, of course, and was turned out of doors for my pains. He was angry with me for being ill-used, and he spread tales in the trade of my having grown saucy – the last thing a bookseller can bear in a hack. He even had a harmless little translation of mine abused in the *Literary Review*. I could get no more work. My goods were seized, and my creditors would have had my person too, if I were not so practised at giving them the slip.'

'You are acquainted with bailiffs, arrest for debt, the process of the law?'

'I know few things better, sir. I was born in a debtors' prison, and I have spent years in the Fleet and the Marshalsea. I wrote my *Elements of Agriculture* and my *Plan for the Education of the Young Nobility and Gentry* in the King's Bench.'

'Be so good as to give me a succinct account of the law as it at present stands.'

'JACK,' SAID STEPHEN, 'your watch is called.'

'Hey? Hey?' Jack had the sailor's knack of going instantly to sleep, snatching an hour's rest, and starting straight out of it; but this time he had been very far down, very far away, aboard a seventy-four off the Cape, swimming in a milk-warm phosphorescent sea, and for once he sat there on the side of his bed, looking stupid and bringing himself slowly into the present. Lord Melville, Queenie, Canning, Diana.

'What are you going to do with your prize?' asked Stephen.

'Eh? Oh, him. We ought to turn him over to the constable, I suppose.'

'They will hang him.'

'Yes, of course. It is the devil – you cannot have a fellow walking about taking purses; and yet you do not like to see him hang. Perhaps he may be transported.'

'I will give you twelve and sixpence for him.'

'Do you mean to dissect him already?' – Stephen often bought corpses warm from the gallows. 'And do you really possess twelve and sixpence at this moment? No, no, I'll not take your money – you shall have him as a present. I resign him to you. I smell coffee, toast!'

He sat there eating steak, his bright blue eyes protruding with the effort, and with thought and concentration. They were in fact trying to pierce the future, but they happened to be fixed on his captive, who sat mute with dread upon his chair, very secretly scratching and from time to time making little gestures of submission. One of these caught Jack's attention, and he frowned. 'You sir!' he cried in a strong sea-going voice that brought the poor man's heart to his mouth and stopped his searching hand. 'You, sir! You had better eat this and look sharp about it,' cutting an unctuous gobbet – 'I have sold you to the Doctor, so you must obey his orders now, or you will find yourself headed up in a cask and tossed overboard. Do you mind me, hey?'

'Yes, sir.'

'I must be away now, Stephen. We meet this afternoon?'

'My movements are uncertain: I may look into Seething Lane, though it is scarcely worth while until next week.'

The plunge into the Admiralty courtyard; the waiting-room, with half a dozen acquaintances – disconnected gossip, his mind and theirs being elsewhere; the staircase to the First Lord's room, and there, half-way up, a fat officer leaning against the rail, silent weeping, his slab, pale cheeks all wet with tears. A silent marine watched him from the landing, two porters from the hall, aghast.

Lord Melville had been disagreeably affected by his latest interview, that was plain. He had to collect himself and bring immediate business to mind, and for some moments he leafed through the papers on his desk. He said, 'I have just been treated to a display of emotion that has lowered the officer extremely in my opinion. I know that *you* prize fortitude, Captain Aubrey; that you are not shaken by disagreeable news.'

'I hope I can bear it, my lord.'

'For I must tell you that I cannot make you post for the *Cacafuego* action. I am bound by my predecessor's decision and I cannot create a precedent. A post-ship is therefore out of the question; and as for sloops, there are only eighty-nine in commission, whereas we have four hundred-odd commanders on the list.' He let this sink in, and although there was nothing new about his information – Jack knew the figures by heart, just as he knew that Lord Melville was not being wholly candid, for there were also thirty-four sloops building as well as a dozen for harbour service and in ordinary – its repetition had a deadening effect. 'However,' he went on, 'the former administration also left us a project for an experimental vessel that I am prepared, in certain circumstances, to rate as a sloop rather than a post-ship, although she carries twenty-four thirty-two-pounder carronades. She was designed to carry a particular weapon, a secret weapon that we abandoned after trial, and we are having her completed for general purposes: we have therefore named her the *Polychrest*. Perhaps you would like to see her draught?'

'Very much indeed, my lord.'

'She is an interesting experiment,' he said, opening the portfolio, 'being intended to sail against wind and tide. The projector, Mr Eldon, was a most ingenious man, and he spent a fortune on his plans and models.'

An interesting experiment indeed: he had heard of her. "She was known as the *Carpenter's Mistake*, and no one in the service had ever imagined she would be launched. How had she survived St Vincent's reforms? What extraordinary combination of interest had managed to get her off the stocks, let alone on to them? She had head and stern alike, two maintopsail-yards, a false bottom, no hold, and sliding keels and rudders. The drawing showed that she was being built in a private yard at Portsmouth – Hickman's, of no savoury reputation.

'It is true that the *Polychrest* was primarily designed as a carrier for this weapon; but she was so far advanced that it would have been an unjustifiable waste to abandon her too;

and with the modifications that you see here in green ink, the Board is of the opinion that she will be eminently serviceable in home waters. Her construction does not allow the carrying of stores for a cruise of any duration, but vessels of this size are always required in the Channel, and I have it in contemplation to attach the *Polychrest* to Admiral Harte's squadron in the Downs. For reasons that I shall not enter into, dispatch is called for. Her captain will be required to proceed to Portsmouth immediately, to hasten on her fitting-out, to commission her, and to take her to sea with the utmost expedition. Do you wish to be considered for the appointment, Captain Aubrey?'

The *Polychrest* was a theorizing landsman's vessel, she had been built by a gang of rogues and jobbers; she was to serve under a man he had cuckolded and who would be happy to see him ruined; Cannings's offer would never come again. Lord Melville was no fool, and he was aware of most of these things; he waited for Jack's reply with his head cocked and a considering eye, tapping his fingers on the desk; this was shabby treatment; the *Polychrest* had already been refused; and in spite of his effort with the rating, he would find it hard to justify himself with Lady Keith – even his own conscience, well seared by years and years of office, gave an uneasy twitch.

'If you please, my lord: I should be most grateful.'

'Very good. Then let us make it so. No – no thanks, I beg,' he said, holding up his hand and looking Jack in the eye. 'This is no plum: I wish it were. But you have a broadside weight of metal greater than many a frigate. Given the opportunity, I am sure you will distinguish yourself, and the Board will be happy to make you post as soon as there is fresh occasion. Now as to officers and followers, I shall be glad to fall in with your wishes as far as possible. Your first lieutenant is already appointed: Mr Parker, recommended by the Duke of Clarence.'

'I should be happy to have my surgeon and Thomas

Pullings, my lord, master's mate in the *Sophie*: he passed for lieutenant in '01.'

'You wish him to be made?'

'If you please, my lord.' It was a good deal to ask, and he might have to sacrifice the rest of his patronage; but as he felt the balance of this interview, he could risk it.

'Very well. What else?'

'If I might have two of the midshipmen, my lord?'

'Two? Yes . . . I think so. You mentioned your surgeon. Who was he?'

'Dr Maturin, my lord.'

'Dr Maturin?' said Lord Melville, looking up.

'Yes, my lord: you may have seen him at Lady Keith's. He is my particular friend.'

'Aye,' said Lord Melville, looking down. 'I mind him. Weel, Sir Evan will send you your orders by the messenger today. Or should you rather wait while they are writing out?'

A FEW HUNDRED yards from the Admiralty, in St James's Park, Dr Maturin and Miss Williams paced the gravel by the ornamental pond. 'It never ceases to amaze me,' said Stephen, 'when I see these ducks. Coots – any man can swallow coots, those deeply vulgar birds, and even the half-domesticated mallard. But the high-bred pintail, the scaup, the goldeneye! I have crept on my belly in the freezing bog to catch a glimpse of them a furlong off, only to see them lift and away before I had them in my glass; and yet here they are in the heart of a roaring modern city, swimming about as cool as you please, eating bread! Not taken, not pinioned, but straight in from the high northern latitudes! I am *amazed*.'

Sophia looked earnestly at the birds and said that she too found it truly astonishing. 'Poor coots,' she added, 'they always seem so cross. So that is the Admiralty?'

'Yes. And I dare say Jack knows his fate by now. He will be behind one of those tall windows on the left.'

'It is a noble building,' said Sophia. 'Perhaps we might see it

a little closer to? To see it in its true proportions. Diana said
he was looking quite thin, and not at all well. *Diminished*,
was what she said.'

'He has aged, maybe,' said Stephen. 'But he still eats for six;
and although I should no longer call him grossly obese, he is
far too fat. I wish I could say the same for you, my dear.'
Sophia had indeed grown thinner; it suited her in that it took
away that last hint of childishness and brought out the hidden strength of her features; but at the same time her
removed, mysterious, sleepy look had disappeared, and now
she was a young woman wide awake – an adult. 'If you had
seen him last night at Lady Keith's, you would not have worried. To be sure, he lost the rest of his ear in the Indiaman –
but that was nothing.'

'His ear!' cried Sophia, turning white and coming to a dead
halt in the middle of the Parade.

'You are standing in a puddle, my dear. Let me lead you to
dry land. Yes, his ear, his right ear, or what there was left of it.
But it was nothing. I sewed it on again; and as I say, if you had
seen him last night, you would have been easy in your mind.'

'What a good friend you are to him, Dr Maturin. His other
friends are so grateful to you.'

'I sew his ears on from time to time, sure.'

'What a providence it is that he has you by: I am afraid he
sometimes hazards himself very thoughtlessly.'

'He does, too.'

'Yet I do not think I could have borne to see him. I was very
unkind to him when last we met.' Her eyes filled with tears.
'It is dreadful to be unkind: one keeps remembering it.'
Stephen looked at her with deep affection: she was a lovely
creature, unhappy, with a line across that broad forehead; but
he said nothing.

Clocks all over Westminster began to tell the hour, and
Sophie cried, 'Oh, we are shockingly late. I promised Mama –
she will be so anxious. Come, let us run.'

He gave her his arm and they hurried across the park,

Stephen guiding her, for her eyes were dim with tears and every three steps she glanced over her shoulder to look at the windows of the Admiralty.

These windows, for the most part, belonged to the official apartments of the Lords Commissioners; those which sheltered Jack were on the far side of the building, so placed that he could see the courtyard. He was, in fact, in the waiting-room, where he had spent many an anxious, weary hour in the course of his career, and where he had now been waiting since his interview long enough to count a hundred and twenty-three men and two women walk in or out of the archway. A good many other officers shared the room with him, the company changing as the day wore on; but none of them were waiting, as he was waiting, with their appointment and their orders crackling in their bosoms – his was as strange a case of waiting as the porters had ever seen, and it excited their curiosity.

His was an absurd position. In one pocket he had this beautiful document requesting and requiring him to repair on board His Majesty's sloop *Polychrest*, and in the other a flaccid purse with a clipped groat in it and no more, all the rest having gone in customary presents. The *Polychrest* meant safety, or so he believed, and the Portsmouth mail left at eleven o'clock that night; but he would have to get from Whitehall to Lombard Street without being taken; he would have to traverse London, a conspicuous uniformed figure. In any case he must communicate with Stephen, who expected him at the cottage. Yet he dared not leave the Admiralty: if he were taken at this stage he would hang himself out of mere fury, and he had already had a most unpleasant fright when he was crossing the hall from the Secretary's office and a porter told him that 'a little cove in black and a scrub wig had been asking for him by name.'

'Send him about his business, will you? Is Tom here?'

'Oh, no, sir. Tom's not on duty till Sunday night. A shifty little cove in black, sir.'

For the last forty minutes he had seen this slight black vaguely legal figure crossing and recrossing the passage into Whitehall, peering into coaches as they stopped and even mounting on the step: once he had seen him talking with two burly great fellows, Irish chairmen or bailiff's men dressed as chairmen – a common disguise for bums.

Jack was not in good odour with the porters that day; he had not produced a shower of gold, not as who should say a shower; but they had a smell of the truth and they naturally took his part against the civil power. When one came in with fresh coals he quietly observed, 'Your little chap with the cauliflower ear is still hanging about outside the arch, sir.'

'Cauliflower ear' – had he heard that before how happy he would have been! He darted to the window, and after some minutes of peering he said, 'Be a good fellow and desire him to step into the hall. I will see him at once.'

Mr Scriven, the literary man, came across the courtyard; he was looking old and tired; his ear was hideously swollen. 'Sir,' he said in a voice that quavered with anxiety, 'Dr Maturin bids me tell you that all was well in Seething Lane, and he hopes you will join him at the Grapes, by the Savoy, if you are not bespoke. I am to fetch a coach into the court. I have been trying to do my errand, sir . . . I hope . . .'

'Excellent. Capital. Make it so, Mr – . Bring it into the yard and I am with you.'

At the mention of the Savoy, that blessed haven, the porter's suspicions were confirmed; a benevolent grin spread across his face and he hurried out with Mr Scriven to find a coach, bring it in through the arch (an irregular proceeding) and manoeuvre it so close to the steps that Jack could step in unseen.

'Perhaps it would be wise to sit on the floor, on this cloak, sir,' said Mr Scriven. 'It has been baked,' he added, sensing a certain reluctance. 'And Dr Maturin was good enough to shave me all over, to parboil me in the copper, and to new-clothe me from head to foot.'

'I am sorry I gave your ear such a knock,' said Jack from the depths of the straw. 'Does it hurt a great deal?'

'You are very good, sir. I do not feel it now. Dr Maturin was so kind as to dress it with an ointment from the oriental apothecary's at the corner of Bruton Street, and it is almost insensible. Now, sir, you can sit up, if you choose: we are in the duchy.'

'What duchy?'

'The duchy of Lancaster, sir. From Cecil Street to the other side of Exeter Change it is part of the duchy, neither London nor Westminster, and the law is different – writs not the same as London writs: why, even the chapel is a royal peculiar.'

'Peculiar, is she?' said Jack with real satisfaction. 'A damned agreeable peculiarity, too. I wish there were more of 'em. What is your name, sir?'

'Scriven, sir, at your service. Adam Scriven.'

'You are an honest fellow, Mr Scriven. Here we are: this is the Grapes. Can you pay the man? Capital.'

'Stephen,' he cried, 'how happy I am to see you. We have a chance yet – we breathe! We hope! I have a ship, and if only I can get to Portsmouth, and if she floats, we shall make our fortunes. Here are my orders: there are yours. Ha, ha, ha. What luck did you have? I hope you did not hear bad news. You look pretty hipped.'

'No, no,' said Stephen, smiling in spite of himself. 'I have negotiated the bill on Mendoza. At only twelve and a half per cent discount, which surprised me; but then the bill was backed. Here are eight-five guineas,' sliding a leather bag across the table.

'Thank you, thank you, Stephen,' cried Jack, shaking him by the hand. 'What a charming sound – they ring out like freedom, ha, ha. I am as hungry as a man can well be, without perishing of mere want – nothing since breakfast.' He began to halloo for the woman of the house, who told him he might have a nice pair of ducks or a nice piece of cold sturgeon with cucumber, fresh that morning in Billingsgate.

'Let us start with the sturgeon, and if you put the ducks down to the fire this very minute, they will be ready by the time we have done. What are you drinking, Stephen?'

'Gin and water, cold.'

'What a God-forsaken melancholy tope. Let us call for champagne: it is not every day we get a ship, and such a ship. I will tell you all about it.' He gave Stephen a detailed account of his interview, drawing the *Polychrest*'s curious shape in watered gin. 'She is a vile job, of course, and how she survived Old Jarvie's reforms I cannot conceive. When I looked at her sheer-plan, and when I thought of Canning's frigate, building under his eye according to the draught of the *Bellone* – why, it made me feel very strange, for a moment. But I have scarcely had time to tell you of the handsome offer he made me. Forgive me for a moment while I write him a note to say I regret extremely that official business makes it impossible, and so on: turn it in the most obliging way I can manage, very civil and friendly, and get it into the penny post tonight; for really, it was the handsomest, most flattering offer. I took to Canning amazingly; I hope to see him again. You would like him, Stephen. Full of life, intelligent, gets the point at once, interested in everything – civil, too, delicate and modest; perfectly gentlemanlike; you would swear he was an Englishman. You must meet.'

'That is a recommendation, to be sure; but I am already acquainted with Mr Canning.'

'You know him?'

'We met at Bruton Street today.' In a flash Jack understood why the sound of Bruton Street had run so unpleasantly just now. 'I called on Diana Villiers after walking with Sophie in the park.'

A look of intense pain came over Jack's face. 'How was Sophie?' he asked, looking down.

'She was not looking well. Thinner, unhappy. But she has grown up: I think her more beautiful now than when we knew her in Sussex.'

Jack leant over the back of his chair, saying nothing. A clatter of plates and dishes, a busy waving of table-cloth and napkins, and the sturgeon and the champagne came in. They ate, with a few generalities about sturgeon – a fish-royal – the first time Jack had eaten it – a rather insipid, disappointing fish – and then he said, 'How was Diana?'

'Her spirits appeared sometimes elated and sometimes oppressed; but she was in splendid looks; and she too was full of life.' He might have added, 'And of wanton unkindness.'

Jack said, 'I had no notion you would call at Bruton Street.' Stephen made no reply other than a bend of his head. 'Were there many other people?'

'Three soldiers, an Indian judge, and Mr Canning.'

'Yes. She told me she knew him. Here come the ducks. They look famous, do they not?' he cried with a show of spirit. 'Pray carve them, Stephen. You do it so cleverly. Shall we send some down to Scriven? What do you make of him, by the bye?'

'He is a man, like another. I feel a certain sympathy for him.'

'Do you mean to keep him?'

'I might, too. Will I help you to some stuffing?'

'As much as ever you like. When shall we eat sage and onions again? When he has eaten his duck, do you think Scriven could cut along and take our places on the mail, while we are packing at Hampstead? He might still get insides.'

'It would be safer for you to go post, Jack. The papers have an account of Lady Keith's reception, and your name is in the *Chronicle*, if not the rest: your creditors must have taken notice of it. Their agents in Portsmouth are perfectly capable of meeting the coach. Mr Scriven is thoroughly acquainted with their ingenious devilish malignity: he tells me they are as watchful and eager as thief-takers. You must drive straight to the yard in a post-chaise and go aboard. I will attend to your dunnage and send it down by the waggon.'

'Ain't you coming, Stephen?' cried Jack, pushing his plate away and staring across the table, perfectly aghast.

'I had not thought of going to sea at present,' said Stephen. 'Lord Keith offered me the flagship as physician, but I begged to be excused. I have many things that call for my attention here; and it is a long while since I was in Ireland – '

'But I had taken it absolutely for granted that we were to sail together, Stephen,' cried Jack. 'And I was so happy to bring you these orders. What shall I . . .' He checked himself, and then in a much lower tone he said, 'But of course, I had not the least right to make such an assumption. I do beg your pardon; and I will explain to the Admiralty at once – entirely my fault. A flagship, after all, by God! It is not more than you deserve. I am afraid I have been very presumptuous.'

'No, no, no, my dear,' cried Stephen. 'It is nothing to do with the flagship. I do not give a fig for a flagship. Put that clear out of your mind. I should far prefer a sloop or a frigate. No. It is that I had not quite made up my mind to a cruise just now. However, let us leave things as they stand for the moment. Indeed, I should not like to have the name of a take-it-and-drop it, shilly-shallying, missish "son of a bitch" at the Navy Board,' he said with a smile. 'Never be so put about, joy: it was only the abruptness that disturbed me – I am more deliberate in my motions than you sanguine, briny creatures. I am engaged until the end of the week, but then, unless I write, I will join you with my sea-chest on Monday. Come, drink up your wine – admirable stuff for a little small shebeen – and we will have another bottle. And before we put you aboard your chaise, I will tell you what I know about the English law of debt.'

7

My dear Sir,
        This is to tell you that I have reached Portsmouth a day earlier than I had proposed; to solicit the indul-

gence of not reporting aboard until this evening; and to beg for the pleasure of your company at dinner,

I am, my dear Sir,

Your affectionate humble servant,

Stephen Maturin

HE FOLDED THE PAPER, wrote 'Captain Aubrey, RN, HM Sloop Polychrest', sealed it and rang the bell. 'Do you know where the *Polychrest* lies?' he asked,

'Oh, yes, sir,' replied the man with a knowing smile. 'She's getting her guns in at the Ordnance; and a rare old time of it she had, last tide.'

'Then be so good as to have this note taken to her directly. And these other letters are to be put into the post.'

He turned back to the table, and opening his diary he wrote, 'I sign myself his affectionate humble servant; and affection it is that brings me here, no doubt. Even a frigid, self-sufficing man needs something of this interchange if he is not to die in his unmechanical part: natural philosophy, music, dead men's conversation, is not enough. I like to think, indeed I do think, that JA has as real an affection for me as is consonant with his unreflecting, jovial nature, and I know mine for him – I know how moved I was by his distress; but how long will this affection withstand the attrition of mute daily conflict? His kindness for me will not prevent him from pursuing Diana. And what he does not wish to see, he will not see: I do not imply a conscious hypocrisy, but the *quod volunt credere* applies with particular force to him. As for her, I am at a loss – this kindness and then the turning away as though from an enemy. It is as though in playing with JA she had become herself entangled. (Yet would she ever part with her ambition? Surely not. And he is even less marriageable than I; less a lawful prize. Can this be a vicious inclination? JA, though no Adonis by my measure, is well-looking, which I am not.) It is as though his ludicrous account of my wealth, passing through Mrs Williams and gathering force by the conviction in that block-head's tone, had turned me from an ally, a friend, even an accomplice, into an opponent. It is as though – oh, a thousand wild possibilities. I am lost, and I am disturbed. Yet I think I may be cured; this is a fever of the blood, and laudanum will cool it, distance will cool it, business and action will do the same. What I dread is the contrary heating effect of jealousy: I had never felt jealousy before this, and although all knowledge of the world, all experience, literature, history, common observation told me of its strength, I had no sense of its true nature at all. *Gnosce teipsum* – my dreams appal me. This morning, when I was walking beside the coach as it laboured up Ports Down Hill and I came to the top, with all Portsmouth harbour suddenly spread below me, and Gosport, Spithead and perhaps half the Channel fleet glittering there – a powerful squadron moving out past Haslar in line ahead, all studding-sails abroad – I felt a longing for the sea. It has a great cleanliness. There are moments when everything on land seems to me tortuous, dark, and squalid; though to be sure, squalor is not lacking aboard a man-of-war.

'I am not sure how far JA practised upon Mrs Williams's avid credulity: pretty far, to judge by her obsequious reception of me. It has had this curious result, that JA's stock has risen with her in almost the same proportion as mine. She would have no objection to him if his estate were clear. Nor, I swear, would Sophie. Yet I do believe that that good child is so firm in the principles she has been taught, that she would wither away an old maid, rather than disobey her mother – marry without her consent. No Gretna Green. She is a dear good child; and she is one of those rare creatures in whom principle does not do away with humour. This is no time for roaring mirth, to be sure, but I remember very well to have noted, again and again at Mapes, that she is quietly and privately *jolly*. A great rarity in women (Diana included, apart from an appreciation of wit and now and then a flash of it), who are often as solemn as owls, though given to noisy laughter. How deeply sorry, how more than sorry I should be if she were to take the habit of unhappiness: it is coming on her fast. The structure of her face is changing.' He stood looking out of the window. It was a clear, frosty morning, and the blackguardly town looked as well as it could. Officers passed in and out of the Port Admiral's house, over against the inn; the pavements were full of uniforms, blue coats and red, church-going officers' wives in pretty mantuas, with here and there a fur pelisse; scrubbed children with Sunday faces.

'A gentleman to see you, sir,' said the waiter. 'A lieutenant.'

'A lieutenant?' said Stephen; and after a pause, 'Desire him to walk up.'

A thundering on the stairs, as though someone had released a bull; the door burst inwards, trembling, and Pullings appeared, lighting up the room with his happiness and his new blue coat. 'I'm made, sir,' he cried, seizing Stephen's hand. 'Made at last! My commission came down with the mail. Oh, wish me joy!'

'Why, so I do,' said Stephen, wincing in that iron grip, 'if more joy you can contain – if more felicity will not make your cup overflow. Have you been drinking, Lieutenant Pullings? Pray sit in a chair like a rational being, and do not spring about the room.'

'Oh say it again, sir,' said the lieutenant, sitting and gazing at Stephen with pure love beaming from his face. 'Not a drop.'

'Then it is with present happiness you are drunk. Well. Long, long may it last.'

'Ha, ha, ha! That is exactly what Parker said. "Long may it last," says he; but envious, like, you know – the grey old toad. Howsomever, I dare say even I might grow a trifle sour, or rancid, like, five and thirty years without a ship of my own, and this cruel fitting-out. And he is a good, righteous man, I am sure; though he was proper pixy-led before the captain came.'

'Lieutenant, will you drink a glass of wine, a glass of sherry-wine?'

'You've said it again, sir,' cried Pullings, with another burst of effulgence. ('You would swear that light actually emanated from that face,' observed Stephen privately.) 'I take it very kind. Just a drop, if you please. I am not going to get drunk until tomorrow night – my feast. Would it be proper for me to propose a sentiment? Then here's to Captain Aubrey – my dear love to him, and may he have all his heart desires. Bottoms up. Without him I should never have got my step. Which reminds me of my errand, sir. Captain Aubrey's compliments to Dr Maturin, congratulates him upon his safe arrival, and will be very happy to dine with him at the George this day at three o'clock; has not yet shipped paper, pens, or ink, and begs to be excused the informality of his reply.'

'It would give me great pleasure if you would keep us company.'

'Thankee, sir, thankee. But in just half an hour I am taking the long-boat out off of the Wight. The *Lord Mornington* Indiaman passed Start Point on Thursday, and I hope to press half a dozen prime seamen out of her about dawn.'

'Will the cruising frigates and the Plymouth tenders have left you anything to take?'

'Love you, sir, I made two voyages in her. There are hidey-holes under her half-deck you would never dream of, without you helped to stow men into 'em. I'll have half a dozen men out of her, or you may say, "black's the white of your eye, Tom Pullings." Lieutenant Tom Pullings,' he added, secretly.

'We are short-handed, so?'

'Why it's pretty bad, of course. We are thirty-two men short of our complement, but 'tis not so short as poor. The receiving-ship sent us eighteen Lord Mayor's men and twenty-odd from the Huntingdonshire and Rutland quotas, chaps taken off the parish and out of the gaols – never seen the sea in their life. It's seamen we're short of. Still, we do have a few prime hands, and two old Sophies among 'em – old Allen, fo'c'sleman, and John Lakey, maintop. Do you remember him? You sewed him up very near, the first time you ever sailed with us and we had a brush with an Algerine. He swears you saved his – his privates, sir, and is most uncommon grateful: would feel proper old fashioned without 'em, he says. Oh, Captain Aubrey will lick 'em into shape, I'm certain sure. And there's Mr Parker seems pretty taut; and Babbington and me will have the hide off of any bastard as don't attend to his duty – the Captain need not fear for that.'

'What of the other officers?'

'Why, sir, I have not rightly had time to come to know 'em, not with all this day-of-judgment hell and shindy of fitting-out – purser in the Victualling Yard, gunner at the Ordnance, master in the hold, or where the hold would be if there was a hold, which there ain't.'

'She is constructed on new principles, I find?'

'Well, sir, I hope she's constructed to swim, that's all. I would not say it to any but a shipmate, sir, but I never seen anything like her, Pearl River, Hugli or Guinea coast. You can't tell whether she's coming or going. Not but what she's a gallows deal more handsome than the common run,' he added, as though taking himself up for disloyalty. 'Mr Parker seen to that – gold-leaf, bright-work galore, special patent blacking for the bends and yards, blocks stropped with red leather. Was you ever at a fitting-out, sir?'

'Not I.'

'It's a right old Bedlam,' said Pullings, shaking his head and laughing. 'Dockyard mateys underfoot, stores all over the deck, new drafts milling about like lost souls, nobody knowing who anyone is or where to go – a right old Bedlam, and the Port Admiral sending down every five minutes to know why you're not ready for sea – is everybody observing the Sabbath aboard the *Polychrest*, ha, ha, ha!' In the gaiety of his heart Tom Pullings sang

> 'We'll give you a bit of our mind, old hound:
> Port Admiral, you be damned.

'I haven't had my clothes off since we commissioned her,' he observed. 'Captain Aubrey turns up at crack of dawn – posted all the way – reads himself in to me and Parker and the Marines and half a dozen loobies which was all we had then, and up goes his pennant. And before his last words are rightly out – fail not as you will answer the contrary at your peril – "Mr Pullings, that topsail-sheet block needs a dog-bitch thimble, if you please," in his own voice exactly. But Lord, you should have heard him carrying on at the riggers when he found they had been giving us twice-laid stuff; they had to call the Master-Attendant to soothe his horrid passion. Then "Lose not a minute," says he, driving us all though fit to drop, merry as a grig and laughing when half the people run to the stern thinking it is the bows, and t'other way about. Why, sir, he'll be glad of his dinner, I'm sure: he's not had above a bit of bread and cold beef in his hand since I been aboard, And now I must take my leave. He would give his eye-teeth for a boat-load of thorough-paced seamen.'

Stephen returned to his window, watched the lithe young form of Thomas Pullings weave through the traffic, cross to the far side and hurry away with that easy, loose-limbed rolling gait of his kind towards the Point and his long night's wait in an open boat far out in the Channel. 'Devotion is a fine thing, a moving thing to see,' he reflected. 'But who is going to pay for that amiable young man's zeal? What blows, oaths, moral violence, brutalities?'

The scene had changed: church-going was over, and the respectable part of the town had vanished behind doors, into an odour of mutton; now groups of sailors straggled up and down, walking wide, like countrymen in London, and among them small greasy tradesmen, routs, hucksters, and the thick local girls and women called brutes. A confused bellowing, something between merriment and a riot turning ugly, and the *Impregnable*'s liberty-men, in shore-going rig and a prize divided in their pockets, came staggering by with a troop of whores, a fiddler walking backwards in front of them and small boys skirmishing on every side, like sheepdogs. Some of the whores were old, some had torn dresses with yellow flesh beneath, all had dyed and frizzled hair, and all looked pinched with cold.

The warmth and happiness of young Pullings' joy receded. 'All ports I have seen are much the same,' he reflected. 'All the places where sailors congregate: I do not believe that this reflects their nature, however, but rather the nature of the land.' He sank into a train of thought – man's nature how defined? Where the constant factors of identity? What allows the statement 'I am from which he was aroused by the sight of Jack, walking along with the fine easy freedom of Sunday – no bowed head, no anxious looks over his shoulder. There were many other people in the street, but two, some fifty yards behind Jack and keeping pace with him, caught Stephen's eye: burly fellows, of no obvious trade or calling, and there was something odd about them, some intentness, some want of casual staring about, that made him look harder, withdrawing from the window and fixing them until they came abreast of the George.

'Jack,' he said, 'there are two men following you. Come over here and look out discreetly. There they are, standing on the Port Admiral's steps.'

'Yes,' said Jack. 'I know the one with the broken nose. He tried to come aboard the other day – no go, however; I smoked him at once. I dare say he is putting the other on to my line, the pragmatical bastard. Oh, be damned to them,' he said, hurrying to the fire. 'Stephen, what do you say to a drink? I spent the whole morning in the foretop, starved with cold.'

'A little brandy will answer the case, I think; a glass of right Nantes. Indeed, you look quite destroyed. Drink this up, and we will go straight to the dining-room. I have ordered a halibut with anchovy sauce, mutton, and a venison pasty – simple island fare.'

The worn lines eased out of Jack Aubrey's face, a rosy glow replaced the unhealthy grey; he seemed to fill his uniform again. 'How much better a man feels when he is mixed with halibut and leg of mutton and roebuck,' he said, toying with a piece of Stilton cheese. 'You are a much better host than I am, Stephen,' he observed. 'All the things I stood most in need of but hardly name. I remember a wretched dinner I invited you to in Mahon, the first we ever ate together, and they got it all wrong, being ignorant of Spanish, my sort of Spanish.'

'It was a very good meal, a very welcome meal,' said Stephen. 'I remember it perfectly. Shall we take our tea upstairs? I wish to hear about the *Polychrest*.' The big room was an almost unbroken spread of blue, with here and there a Royal Marine, and conversation was little more private than signals on the open sea.

'We shall make a go of her, once we get used to her ways, I make no doubt,' said Jack. 'She may be a little odd to look at, to the prejudiced eye; but she floats, and that is the essential, do you see? She floats; and as a floating battery – why, I have rarely seen the like! We only have to get her there, and then we have four and twenty thirty-two pounders to bring into play, Carronades, you may say; but thirty-two pounder carronades! We can take on any French sloop afloat, for these are your genuine smashers – we could tackle a thirty-six-gun frigate, if only we could get close enough.'

'By this same argument of proximation you could also set about a three-decker, a first-rate, at six inches; or two, indeed, if you could wedge yourself between them and fire both sides, But believe me, my dear, it is a fallacious argument, God forbid. How far do these carronades of yours fling their vast prodigious missiles?'

'Why, you must engage within pistol shot if you want to hit what you point them at; but at yard-arm to yard-arm, oh, how they smash through the oak!'

'And what is your enemy doing with his long guns, while you labour to approach him? But I am not to teach you your own trade, however,'

'Approach him . . .' said Jack. 'There's the rub. I must have hands to work the ship, We are thirty-two men short of our complement – no hope of another draft – and I dare say you will reject some of the cripples and Abraham-men the receiving-ship has sent us: sad thievish little creatures. Men I must have, and the glass is running out . . . tell me, did you bring Scriven with you?'

'I did, I thought he might be found some small employment.'

'He is an eminent hand at writing, is he not? Pamphlets and such? I have tried dashing off a poster – even three or four volunteers would be worth their weight in gold – but I have had no time, and anyhow it don't seem to answer. Look.' He brought some papers out of his pocket,

'Well,' said Stephen, reading, 'No: perhaps it don't.' He rang the bell and bade the man ask Mr Scriven to walk up. 'Mr Scriven,' he said, 'be so good as to look at these – you see the problem – and to draft a sheet to the purpose, There is paper and ink on the table over there.'

Scriven withdrew to the window, reading, noting and grunting to himself; and Jack, as he sat there, warm and comfortable by the fire, felt a delicious total relaxation creep over his person; it espoused the leather chair, sinking into its curves, no tension anywhere at all. He lost the thread of Stephen's remarks, answering oh and ah at the pauses, or smiling and moving his head with ambiguous appreciation. Sometimes his legs would give a violent twitch, jerking him out of this state of bliss; but each time he sank back, happier than before.

'I said "You do move with the utmost caution, I am sure?" ' said Stephen, now touching him on the knee.

'Oh, certainly,' said Jack, at once grasping the subject. 'I have never set foot on shore except for Sunday, and every boat that comes alongside is examined. In any case, I am moving out to Spithead on tomorrow's tide, which will prevent surprises. I have refused all Dockyard invitations, even the Commissioner himself. The only one I shall accept is

Pullings' feast, where there is no risk of any kind – a little place in Gosport by the landing-stage, quite out of the way. I cannot disappoint him: he is bringing his people and his sweetheart up from the country.' 'Sir,' said Mr Scriven, 'may I show you my attempt?'

£5,OOO a man! (or more)
WEALTH EASE DISTINCTION
YOUR LAST CHANCE OF A FORTUNE!

HMS *Polychrest* will shortly sail to scour the seas of ALL KING GEORGE'S enemies. She is desined to SAIL AGAINST WIND AND TIDE and she will Take, Sink and Destroy the Tyrant's helpless man-of-war, without Mercy, sweeping the Ocean of his Trade. There is no time to be lost! Once the *Polychrest* has gone by there will be no more PRIZES, no more fat French and cowardly Dutch merchantmen, loaded with Treasure, Jewels, Silks, Satins and Costly Delicacies for the immoral and luxurious Usurper's Court.

This Amazing New Vessel, built on Scientific Principles, is commanded by the renowned

CAPTAIN AUBREY!

whose brig *Sophie*, with a 28lb broadside, captured £100,000's worth of enemy shipping last war. 28lb, and the *Polychrest* fires 384lb from either side! So what will she do, in this proportion? More than TWELVE TIMES as much! The Enemy must soon be Bankrupt – the End is Nigh. Come and join the Fun before it is too late, and then set up your Carriage!

Captain Aubrey has been prevailed upon to accept a few more Hands. Only exceptionally wide-awake, intelligent men will be entertained, capable of lifting a Winchester bushel of Gold; but PERHAPS YOU ARE

THE LUCKY MAN! Hurry, there is no time to be lost.
Hurry to the Rendezvous at the – YOU MAY BE THE
LUCKY MAN WHO IS ACCEPTED!

No troublesome formalities. The best of provisions at 16
oz to the pound, 4lb of tobacco a month. Free beer, wine
and grog! Dancing and fiddling aboard. A health-giving,
wealth-giving cruise. Be healthy and wealthy and wise,
and bless the day you came aboard the Polychrest!

GOD SAVE THE KING

'The figures I have ventured to put are merely for the form,'
he said, looking into their faces as they read.

'It is coming it a trifle high,' said Jack, writing sums that
could be attempted to be believed. 'But I like it. I am obliged
to you, Mr Scriven. Will you take it round to the Courier
office and explain to them how it is to be printed? You understand these things admirably. They may strike off a hundred
posters and two hundred as handbills, to be given out where
the country waggons and coaches come in. Here is a couple
of guineas. Stephen, we must get under way. There will still
be light enough to check the new patent slides, and you have
two drafts to sort out: pray do not reject anything that can
haul a rope.'

'You will like to meet the other officers,' he said, as they
stood waiting for their boat. 'They may look a little rough, just
at first. They have been led a devil of a dance with it, with
this fitting-out, especially Parker. The man who was the first
to be offered *Polychrest* dilly-dallied – could not be found,
could not make up his mind – and Pullings, bless him, did
not come until I was here. So it was all on Parker's shoulders.'

He stepped into the boat and sat there silent, thinking
about his first lieutenant. Mr Parker was a man in his middle
fifties, grey, precise, strict, a great one for spit and polish and
details of uniform – this had earned him Prince William's

good word – and brave, active, conscientious; but he tired easily, he did not seem very intelligent, and he was somewhat deaf. Far worse, he had no sense of the men – his black-list was as long as his arm, but the real seamen took little notice of him – and Jack suspected that he had no sense of the sea either. Jack also suspected, more than suspected, that Parker's was the little discipline, the hazing discipline; that under Parker uncontrolled the *Polychrest* would be a flash ship, all paint outside and no order within, the cat in daily use and the crew sullen, unwilling and brutal – an unhappy ship, and an inefficient fighting-machine.

It would not be easy to deal with him. There must be no discord on the quarterdeck; Parker must be seen to be in charge of the day-to-day running of the *Polychrest*, with no easy-going captain to undermine his authority. Not that Jack was in the least easy-going; he was a taut officer and he liked a taut ship, but he had served in one hell afloat, he had seen others, and he wanted no part of it.

'There she lies,' he observed, nodding towards the *Poly-chrest*, a certain defensive note in his voice.

'That is she?' said Stephen. A three-masted vessel – he hesitated to call her a ship, however – very trim, rather high in the water: shining black sides with a brilliant lemon streak broken by twelve portlids, also black; and above the lemon a line of blue, topped with white; gold scroll-work running into the blue from either extremity. 'She does not look so mighty strange to me, except that she seems to have both ends sharp, and no beak-head, in the sense of that dip, that anfractuosity, to which we are accustomed; but after all, the same remarks apply to the curragh in which Saint Brendan made his voyage. I do not understand what all the coil is about.'

'His curragh stayed well? She sailed against wind and tide?'

'Certainly. Did he not reach the Islands of the Blessed?'

BY FRIDAY Jack's spirits were higher than they had been since he took his first command down the long harbour of

Port Mahon and out to sea. Not only had Pullings brought back seven cross but able seamen from the *Lord Mornington*, but Scriven's poster had induced five youths from Salisbury to come aboard 'to ask for details'. And better was in store: Jack and Stephen were on deck, waiting to go to Pullings' feast, waiting in the grey fog until the unhandy crew, badgered by Mr Parker and harassed by the bosun, should succeed in getting the launch into the water, when a wherry came alongside, suddenly appearing through the murk. There were two men in it, dressed in short blue jackets with brass buttons down one side, white trousers, and tarpaulin hats; this with their long pigtails, gold earrings and black silk neckcloths, made them look more like man-of-war's men than was quite right, and Jack stared down at them hard from the rail. To his astonishment he found himself looking straight into the face of Barret Bonden, his former coxswain, and another old Sophie, a man whose name escaped him.

'They may come aboard,' he said. 'Bonden, come aboard. I am very happy to see you,' he went on, as Bonden stood beaming at him on the quarterdeck. 'How do you come along, eh? Pretty spry, I trust? Have you brought me a message?' This was the only rational explanation for the presence of a seaman, bobbing about on the crowded waters of Spithead as though the hottest press in years were a matter of unconcern: but there was no ship's name to the ribbon flying from the hat in Bonden's hand, and there was something about his delighted bearing that kindled hope.

'No, your honour,' said Bonden. 'Which our Joe,' – jerking his thumb at his companion (Joseph Plaice, Bonden's cousin, of course: sheet-anchor man, starboard watch, elderly, deeply stupid, but reliable when sober, and a wonderful hand at a variant of the Matthew Walker knot, sober or speechless) – 'said you was afloat again, so we come round from Priddy's Hard to enter volunteerly, if so be you can find room, sir.' This was as near an approach to open mirth as decency would allow.

'I shall stretch a point for you, Bonden,' said Jack. 'Plaice, you will have to earn your *place* by learning the boys your Matthew Walker.' This flight was beyond Joseph Plaice, but he looked pleased and touched his knuckle to his forehead. 'Mr Parker, enter these men, if you please, and rate them Plaice fo'c'sleman, Bonden my cox'n.'

Five minutes later he and Stephen were in the launch, Bonden steering, as he had steered for Jack in many a bloody cutting-out expedition on the Spanish coast. How did he come to be at liberty at such a time, and how had he managed to traverse the great man-hungry port without being pressed? It would be useless to ask him; he would only answer with a pack of lies. So as they neared the dim harbour entrance Jack said, 'How is your nephew?' meaning George Lucock, a most promising youth whom he had rated midshipman in the *Sophie*.

'Our George, sir?' said Bonden, in a low voice. 'He was in the *York*.' The *York* had foundered in the North Sea with the loss of all hands. 'He was only a foremast jack: pressed out of a Domingoman.'

'He would have made his way,' said Jack, shaking his head. He could see that young man, bright with joy at his promotion, shining in the Mediterranean sun, and the flash of polished brass as he took the noon altitude with his sextant, that mark of the quarterdeck. And he remembered that the *York* had come from Hickman's yard – that there were tales of her having put to sea with timbers in such a state that no lanterns were needed in the hold, because of the glow of rotten wood. At all events she was in no condition to meet a full gale, a North Sea widow-maker.

These thoughts occupied him as they wove through the shipping, ducking under cables that stretched away to the great shadowy forms of three-deckers, crossing the paths of the countless boats plying to and fro, sometimes with outbursts of rage or wit from the licensed watermen – once the cry of 'What ho, the Carpenter's Mistake' floated from behind a buoy, followed by a burst of maniac laughter; and they brought his spirits low.

Stephen remained perfectly mute in some dark study of his own, and it was not until they were coming in to the landing-stage that the sight of Pullings waiting for him lighted some cheerfulness in Jack's mind. The young man was standing there with his parents and an astonishingly pretty girl, a sweet little pink creature in lace mittens with immense blue eyes and an expression of grave alarm. 'I should like to take her home and keep her as a pet,' thought Jack, looking down at her with great benevolence.

The elder Mr Pullings was a farmer in a small way on the skirts of the New Forest, and he had brought a couple of sucking-pigs, a great deal of the King's game, and a pie that was obliged to be accommodated with a table of its own, while the inn provided the turtle soup, the wine and the fish. The other guests were junior lieutenants and master's mates, and to begin with the feast was stiffer and more funereal than might have been wished; Mr Pullings was too shy to see or hear, and once he had delivered his piece about their sense of Captain Aubrey's kindness to their Tom in a burring under-tone whose drift Jack seized only half-way through, he set himself to his bottle with a dreadful silent perseverance. However, the young men were all sharp-set, for this was well past their dinner-hour, and presently the huge amounts of food they ate engendered talk. After a while there was a steady hum, the sound of laughter, general merriment, and Jack could relax and give his attention to Mrs Pullings's low, confidential account of her anxiety when Tom ran away to sea 'with no change of linen, nothing to shift into – not even so much as his good woollen stockings'.

'Truffles!' cried Stephen, deep in the monumental pie, Mrs Pullings's particular dish, her masterpiece (young hen pheasants, boned, stuffed tight with truffles, in a jelly of their own life's blood, Madeira and calves' foot). 'Truffles! My dear madam, where did you find these princely truffles?' – holding one up on his fork.

'The stuffing; sir? We call 'em yearth-grobbets; and Pullings has a little old spayed sow turns 'em up by the score along the edge of the forest.'

Truffles, morells, blewits, jew's ears (perfectly wholesome if not indulged in to excess; and even then, only a few cases of convulsions, a certain rigidity of the neck over in two or three days – nonsense to complain) occupied Stephen and Mrs Pullings until the cloth disappeared, the ladies retired, and the port began to go round. By now rank had evened out: at least one young man was as grand, royal and spreading as an admiral, and in the vinous, candle-lit haze Jack's nagging anxiety about what the *Polychrest* would do in a capful of wind with all that tophamper, about her ballast, trim, construction, crew and stores dropped away, leaving him the cheerful lieutenant he had been not so very long ago.

They had drunk the King, the First Lord ('O bless him, God bless him,' cried Pullings), Lord Nelson with three times three, wives and sweethearts, Miss Chubb (the pink child) and other young ladies; they had carried the elder Mr Pullings to his bed, and they were singing

> *We'll rant and we'll roar like true British sailors,*
> *We'll range and we'll roam over all the salt seas,*
> *Until we strike soundings in the Channel of old*
>   *England:*
> *From Ushant to Scilly 'tis thirty-five leagues.*
>
> *We hove our ship to when the wind was south-west, boys,*
> *We hove our ship to for to strike soundings clear,*
> *Then we filled our main-topsail and bore right away,*
>   *boys,*
> *And right up the Channel our course we did steer.*
>
> *We'll rant and we'll roar . . .*

The din was so great that Stephen alone noticed the door open just enough for Scriven's questing head: he placed a warning hand on Jack's elbow, but the rest were roaring still when it swung wide and the bailiffs rushed in.

'Pullings, pin that whore with the staff,' cried Stephen, tossing his chair under their legs and clasping Broken-nose round the middle.

Jack darted to the window, flung up the sash, jumped on to the sill and stood there poised while behind him the bailiffs struggled in the confusion, reaching out their staffs with ludicrous earnestness, trying to touch him, taking no notice of the clogging arms round their waists, knees and chests. They were powerful, determined fellows; the reward was high, and the mêlée surged towards the open window – one touch amounted to a lawful arrest.

A leap and he was away: but the head tipstaff was fly – he had posted a gang outside, and they were looking up eagerly, calling out 'jump for it, sir – we'll break your fall – it's only one storey.' Holding on to the window he craned out, looking down the lane towards the shore – he could see the gleam of water – towards the place where by rights the Polychrests should be drinking Pullings' beer, sent to them together with the second sucking-pig; and surely Bonden could be relied upon? He filled his lungs and hailed 'Polychrest' in a tone that echoed back from Portsmouth and stopped the mild gossip in the launch stone dead. 'Polychrest!'

'Sir?' came back Bonden's voice out of the dripping gloom.

'Double up to the inn, d'ye hear me? Up the lane. Bring your stretchers.'

'Aye-aye, sir.'

In a moment the launch was empty. Stretchers, the boat's long wooden footrests, meant a row. The captain was no doubt pressing some hands, and they, pressed men themselves, did not mean to miss a second of the fun.

The pounding of feet at the end of the lane, coming nearer: behind, the sway and crash of chairs, oaths, a doubtful battle.

'Here, here! Right under the window,' cried Jack, and there they were, a little wet mob, gasping, gaping up. 'Make a ring, now. Stand from under!' He jumped, picked himself up and cried, 'Down to the boat. Bear a hand, bear a hand!'

For the first moment the gang in the street hung back, but as the head tipstaff and his men came racing out of the inn shouting 'In the name of the law! Way there, in the name of the law!' they closed, and the narrow lane was filled with the sound of hard dry blows, grunts, the crash of wood upon wood. The sailors, with Jack in the middle, pushed fast in the direction of the sea.

'In the name of the law!' cried the tipstaff again, making a most desperate attempt to break through.

' – the law,' cried the seamen, and Bonden, grappling with the bailiff, wrenched the staff from him. He flung it right down the lane, fairly into the water, and said, 'You've lost your commission now, mate. I can hit you now, mate, so you watch out, I say. You watch out, cully, or you'll come home by Weeping Cross.'

The bailiff uttered a low growl, pulled out his hanger and hurled himself at Jack. 'Artful, eh?' said Bonden, and brought his stretcher down on his head. He fell in the mud, to be trampled upon by Pullings and his friends, pouring out of the inn. At this the gang broke and fled, calling out that they should fetch their friends, the watch, the military, and leaving two of their number stretched upon the ground.

'Mr Pullings, press those men, if you please,' cried Jack from the boat. 'And that fellow in the mud. Two more? Capital. All aboard? Where's the Doctor? Pass the word for the Doctor. Ah, there you are. Shove off. Altogether, now, give way. Give way cheerly. What a prime hand he will make, to be sure,' he added in an aside, 'once he's used to our ways – a proper bulldog of a man.'

AT TWO BELLS that morning watch the *Polychrest* was slipping quietly through the cold grey sea, the cold grey air, for at midnight the wind had come a little east of south, and in order not to lose a minute (a ship could be wind bound for weeks on end in the Channel at this season) Jack had given orders to unmoor, although the tide was making. A gentle breeze it was, not enough to dispel the fog or raise more than a ripple on the long oily swell, and the *Polychrest* could have carried a great spread of canvas; however, she was under little more than her topsails, and she ghosted along, with little more than a whisper of water the length of her side. The tall dark form of her captain, much larger in his foul-weather clothes, stood over on the windward side of the quarterdeck. At the sound of the log being heaved, the cry of 'Turn' and 'stop' and the thump of its coming aboard again, he turned. 'Mr Babbington, what do you have?' he called.

'Two knots and a three fathom, if you please, sir.'

Jack nodded. Somewhere out there in the darkness on the larboard bow there would be Selsey Bill, and presently he might have to tack: for the moment he had plenty of room – the persistent howling under the lee came from the horns of the inshore fishing-boats, and they were a good mile away. To seaward there was the thump of a gun every few minutes – a man-of-war bound for Portsmouth, no doubt, on the opposite tack – and the *Polychrest*'s bow carronade answered regularly with quarter charges.

At least there will be four men who know how to handle one by morning,' he reflected.

In a way it was unfortunate that this first acquaintance with his ship should come at a time when there was no horizon, when sea and air could not be told apart; but he was not sorry for it, upon the whole – it gained him some hours at least, it sent Gosport, its squalors and its possible complications far astern, and in any case he had been on fire to know how she handled in the open sea ever since he had set eyes on the *Polychrest*. She had the strangest motion, a kind of nervous lift and shudder like a horse about to shy, as she rose to the swell, a kind of twist in her roll that he had never known before.

Mr Goodridge, the master, could be seen in the glow of the binnacle, standing by the quartermaster at the con. He was a reserved, elderly man of great experience, once the master of a ship of the line, but broken for fighting with the chaplain and only recently put on the list again; and he was as intent upon the *Polychrest*'s behaviour as his captain.

'What do you make of her, Mr Goodridge?' asked Jack, walking over to the wheel.

'Why, sir, for ardent griping, I have never seen the like.'

Jack took the wheel, and indeed, even at the rate of sailing, there was a steady, powerful thrust against him: the *Polychrest* wanted to get her head right up into the eye of the wind. He let her have her way, and then, just before the sails began to shiver the griping stopped; the helm went dead under his hand, and her odd corkscrew motion changed its rhythm entirely. He could not make it out, but stood there puzzling as he gently eased the *Polychrest* back on to her course. It was as though she had two centres of rotation, two pivots: if not three . . . obviously jib, foresail and a reef in the mizzen topsail would keep her off, but that was not the trouble – that would not account for this sluggish helm, this sudden lack of response.

'Three inches in the well, sir,' said the carpenter's mate, making his routine report.

'Three inches in the well, if you please, sir,' said the master.

'Ay,' said Jack. It was negligible: she had not had anything of a trial yet, no working in a heavy sea; but at least it proved that those strange sliding keels and the nameless peculiarity of her quickwork did not mean that the water poured straight in: a comfortable reflection, for he had misgivings. 'No doubt we shall find what trim suits her best,' he observed to the master and went back to the rail, half consciously trying to recreate his quarterdeck pacing in the little *Sophie*, while his mind, worn fine by Pullings' feast, by the prolonged turmoil of unmooring with a foul hawse and by the anxiety of getting under way in a crowded road, turned to the problem of the forces acting upon the vessel.

The new-lit galley stove sent a whiff of smoke eddying aft, together with the smell of burgoo, and at the same time he heard the head-pumps beginning to work. Up and down, up and down, with his hands behind his back and his chin tucked into his griego against the biting air: up and down. The figure of the *Polychrest* was as clear in his mind as if she had been a model held up to a lamp, and he studied her reaction to the creeping influence of the tide, and the lateral thrust of the wind, the eddies deep under her strangely placed rudders . . .

The after-guard were sprinkling the quarterdeck with their buckets, carefully avoiding his walk, and after them came the sand-men. The bosun was on deck: Malloch, a short, bull-like young fellow; had been bosun's mate in the crack *Ixion*. Jack heard his shout and the thwack of his cane as he started a man on the fo'c'sle. And all the time there was the measured thump of the carronade, the now distant gun of the man-of-war, the horns away to port, the steady chant of the man heaving the lead in the chains – 'by the mark nine . . . ho yo ho yo . . . and a quarter nine.'

The rake of the masts was a great consideration, of course. Jack was an intuitive rather than a scientific sailor, and in his mental image of the *Polychrest* her backstays tautened until the angle of her masts looked right and some inner voice said 'Belay there'. The holystones began their steady grinding: the decks could do with it, after the shambles of a hurried fitting-out. These were such familiar sounds and smells, these innumerable difficulties were so very much part of the world he had known from childhood, that he felt as though he had been returned to his own element. It was not that he did not like the land – capital place; such games, such fun – but the difficulties there, the complications, were so vague and imprecise, reaching one behind another, no end to them: nothing a man could get hold of. Here, although life was complex enough in all conscience, he could at least attempt to cope with anything that turned up. Life at sea had the great advantage that . . . something was amiss. He tried to place it, glancing sharply fore and aft in the greyness of approaching day. The fishing-boats that had been sailing on a parallel course were now astern: their melancholy wailing sounded almost from the *Polychrest*'s wake. The Bill must be no great way ahead. It was time to go about. A damned foolish moment to choose, with the people busy, and he would have preferred to wait until the watch below was on deck; but she might have made even more leeway than he had allowed for, and only a fool would run any risk for the sake of neatness.

'We will put her about, Mr Goodridge,' he said.

The bosun started his call. Brooms, buckets, swabs, squeegees, holystones, prayer-books, brass rags flew into sheltered places as his mates roared down the hatches 'All hands, all hands 'bout ship' and then vanished below to drive the sleepers up – those few so worn with toil, seasickness and desolation, that they were unconscious in spite of the carronade and the echoing thunder of the holystones. The score or so of right seamen had been at their stations ten minutes – Pullings and the bosun on the fo'c'sle, the gunner and his mates at the maintack, the carpenter at the foresheet, the Marines at the mainsheet, the maintopmen and the afterguard on the quarterdeck, at the braces – before the last desperate half-clothed bewildered landsman was hunted up, shoved and beaten and cobbed into his place.

'Bear up,' said Jack to the timoneer, waiting for this Bartholomew Fair performance to come to an end – a bosun's mate was now belabouring the former tipstaff with his persuader, to help him understand the difference between a stay and a bowline. And when he felt a little more way on the sloop, saw something like order on deck, and judged the moment ripe, he called, 'Ready about.'

'Ready about, sir,' came the answer.

'Luff up handsomely, now,' he said quietly to the man at the wheel, and then loud and clear, 'Helm's a-lee. Fore topsheet, fore topbowline, stays'l sheet, let go.' The full-bellied curves

of the headsails sagged and collapsed; the *Polychrest* moved
in a long smooth curve up towards the direction of the wind.

'Off tacks and sheets.'

Everything was ready for the decisive order that would
bring the yards flying round; everything was as calm and
unhurried as the sloop's slow curve through this grey, heaving,
formless world; there was time and to spare. And that was
just as well, he thought, seeing the way they were shifting the
sheets over the stays – something between cat's cradle and
puss-in-the-corner.

Her curve was slower now; and now the swell was coming
more and more on to her starboard bow, heaving against her
course. Slowly up and up: within two points of the wind, a
point and a half, and the words 'Mainsail haul' had been long
formed in his mouth when he realized that the deep steady
sound to port and astern, the sound that was coming so clear
and loud through the intent, waiting silence, was that of the
breakers on Selsey Bill. She had made twice and three times
the leeway he and the master had reckoned for. At the same
moment he felt an essential change in her motion, a dead sullenness: she was going to miss stays. She was not going to
travel up into the eye of the wind and carry on beyond it, so
that the sails, braced round, would fill on the larboard side
and bear her out to sea.

A ship that would not stay must wear – she must fall off
from the wind, right round the way she came and much farther still, pivoting about her stern in a great leeward sweep
until she had the wind aft, turning, turning until she could
bring it astern and then at last on her other side, turning still
until she was heading in the direction she desired – a long,
long turn: and in this case, with this tide, swell and wind, the
Polychrest would need a mile to accomplish it, a mile of leeway before she could brace up sharp and head out into the
Channel.

She was losing her headway; her sails were flapping dismally in the silence; with every thrust of the sea she was

nearer the unseen shore. The alternatives flew through his mind: he could let her fall off, set the driver and try again; he could wear and risk it, coming to an anchor if he had cut it too fine – an ignominious, horribly time-wasting process, or he could box-haul her. But dared he box-haul her with this crew? While these possibilities ran past his inner scrutineer a remote corner of his mind called out shrilly against the injustice of missing stays – unknown in such conditions, monstrous, a malignancy designed to make him late on his station, to allow Harte to call him unofficerlike, no seaman, a dawdling Sybarite, a slow-arse. That was the danger: there was no peril in this sea, nothing but a consciousness of having misjudged things, and the likelihood of an ugly, unanswerable rebuke from a man he despised.

These thoughts had their being between the time he heard the splash of the lead and the cry 'By the deep eight'. As the next cry came, 'A half less eight' he said to himself, 'I shall box-haul her.' And aloud, 'Haul up main and mizzen tops'ls. Foretops'l sheet hard a-weather. Foretops'l sharp aback: clap on to that brace. Look alive on the foc's'le there. Lee bowlines, lee bowlines.'

As if she had run into a gentle cushion, the *Polychrest*'s headway stopped – he felt her underfoot – and she began to move backwards, the headsails and her lee-helm paying her round as she went. 'Square main and mizzen yards. Jump to those braces, now.'

She might not like turning up into the wind, but with her strange sharp stern she was very good at going backwards. He had never known such a sternway.

'And a half eight,' from the chains. Round she went: the squared main and mizzen yards lay parallel with the wind, the topsails shaking. Farther, farther; and now the wind was abaft her beam, and by rights her sternway should have stopped; but it did not; she was still travelling with remarkable speed in the wrong direction. He filled the topsails, gave her weather helm, and still she slid backwards in this insane con-

tradiction of all known principles. For a moment all the certainties of his world quivered – he caught a dumbfounded,
appalled glance from the master – and then with a sigh from
the masts and stays, the strangest straining groan, the *Polychrest's* motion passed through a barely perceptible immobility to headway. She brought the wind right aft, then on to her
larboard quarter; and hauling out the mizzen and trimming all
sharp, he set the course, dismissed the watch below, and
walked into his cabin, relief flooding into him. The bases of
the universe were firm again, the *Polychrest* was heading
straight out into the offing with the wind one point free; the
crew had not done very badly, no time worth mentioning had
been lost; and with any luck his steward would have brewed a
decent pot of coffee. He sat on a locker, wedging himself
against the bulkhead as she rolled: over his head there was
the hurrying of feet as ropes were coiled down and made
trim, and then came the long-interrupted sounds of cleaning
– a bear, a great padded, shot-laden block of stone, started
growling on the deck eighteen inches from his ears: he
blinked once or twice, smiled, and smiling went fast asleep.

He was still asleep when the hands were piped to dinner, sleeping still when the gun-room sat down to its gammon
and spinach, and for the first time Stephen saw all the *Polychrest's* officers together – all except for Pullings, who had the
watch, and who was walking the quarterdeck with his hands
behind his back, pacing in as close an imitation of Captain
Aubrey as his form could manage, and remembering, every
now and then, to look stern, devilish, as like a right tartar as
possible, in spite of his bubbling happiness. At the head of
the table sat Mr Parker, an acquaintance of some days' standing, a tall, spare, disapproving man, rather good-looking, apart
from the expression on his face; then the lieutenant of
Marines in his scarlet coat, a black-haired Scotsman from the
Hebrides whose face was so marked by the smallpox that it
was difficult to make out what habitual expression it might

wear; he had a very well-bred turn, however; and Macdonald was his name. Mr Jones the purser, his neighbour, was also a black man, but there the likeness stopped; the purser was a drooping little flaccid man with pendulous cheeks either side of a fleshy red mouth; his face was the colour of cheese, and this uniform pallor swept up his high forehead to a baldness that reached from ear to ear. His straight hair grew only in a fringe round this pool, hanging some way down his neck, and in whiskers; yet a strong beard showed blue on his waxy cheeks, a very powerful growth. His appearance was that of a small shopkeeper; but there was little time to judge of his conversation, for at the sight of his plate he started from the table with a watery belch, rushed staggering to the quarter-gallery, and was seen no more. Then there was the master, still yawning from his morning watch. He was a slight, elderly, grizzled man with bright blue eyes, and he said little as he set to his table at the beginning of the meal: Stephen was habitually silent; the others were feeling their way with their new messmates, and their knowledge that the surgeon was the captain's particular friend acted as a further check.

However, as Stephen's appetite waned, so his desire for information increased, and laying down his knife and fork he said to the master, 'Pray, sir, what is the function of the curious sloping metal-lined cylindrical place immediately in front of my store-room? What is its name?'

'Why, Doctor,' said Mr Goodridge, 'what to call it I do not rightly know, other than an abomination; but the ship-wrights spoke of it as the combustion-chamber, so I take it it was where the secret weapon was stowed. It used to lead out on deck where the fo'c'sle is now.'

'What kind of a secret weapon?' asked Macdonald. 'Something in the nature of a rocket, I believe.'

'Yes,' said the first lieutenant, 'a kind of enormous rocket without a stick. It was the ship that was to be the stick, and those levered chutes for shot were intended to bring her by the head or by the stern for elevation: the weapon was calculated to destroy a first-rate at the distance of a mile, but it had to be amidships, to counteract the roll, and that was the reason for the system of lateral keels and rudders.'

'If the rocket was the calibre of the chamber, then the recoil must have been prodigious,' said Macdonald.

'Prodigious,' said Mr Parker. 'That was why the sharp stern was imagined, to prevent the sudden thrust destroying her bottom – the whole ship recoiled, whereas a square stern, by resisting, would be crushed. Even so, they had to put a mass of timber where the stern-post should be, to take the first impact.' A very exalted personage had been present at the experimental firing that had cost the inventor his life, and he had told Mr Parker that the ship had darted back her whole length, at the same time being pressed down in the water as far as her wing-transoms. The exalted personage had been against it from the start; Mr Congreve, who went down with the party, had said it would never answer; and it had not answered – these innovations never did. Mr Parker was against any break with tradition; it would never answer in the Navy; he did not care for these flint-locks for the guns, for example; although indeed they took a fine polish, and looked well enough, for an inspection.

'How did the poor gentleman come to be killed?' asked the master.

'It seems that he would light the fuse himself, and as it hung fire, he put his head into the chamber to see what was amiss, when it exploded.'

'Well, I am sorry for him,' said Mr Goodridge. 'But if it had to be, it might have been as well if he had sent the ship to the bottom at the same time. A cranker, more unseaworthy craft I never saw, and I have seen a mort in my time. She made more leeway than a common raft between St Helen's and the Bill, for all the sharp floor and sliding keels, and she gripes like a man-trap. Then she goes and misses stays in a mill-pond. There is no pleasing her. She reminds me of Mrs Goodridge – whatever you do is wrong. If the captain had not box-hauled her in a flash, why, I don't know where we might have come to. A most seamanlike manoeuvre, I must say; though I should not have ventured it myself, not with such a ragamuffin crew. And indeed she had more stern way upon her than I should have thought possible. As you say, sir, she was built to recoil, and I thought she was going to go on recoiling until we were brought up all standing on the coast of France. A crinkum-crankum piece of work, in my opinion, and 'tis the Lord's blessing we have a right seaman in command; but what even he will do, or what the Archangel Gabriel would do, if it comes on to blow, I do not know, I am sure. The Channel is not so broad as all that; and in point of searoom, what this here craft requires, is the great Southern Ocean, at its widest part.'

The master's words were prompted by the *Polychrest*'s increasing roll; it sent the bread-barge careering over the table, and a midshipman into Jack's cabin, with the news that the wind was shifting into the east, a little mouse-like child, stiff in his best uniform, with his dirk at his side – he had slept with it.

'Thank you, Mr – ' said Jack. 'I do not believe I remember your name.'

'Parslow, sir, if you please.'

Of course. The Commissioner's protégé, a naval widow's son. 'What have you been doing to your face, Mr Parslow?' he asked, looking at the red, gaping, lint-flecked wound that ran across that smooth oval cheek from ear to chin.

'I was shaving, sir,' said Mr Parslow with a pride he could not conceal. 'Shaving, sir, and a huge great wave came.'

'Show it to the doctor, and tell him, with my compliments, that I should be glad if he would drink tea with me. Why are you in your number one rig?'

'They said – it was thought I ought to show an example to the men, sir, this being my first day at sea.'

'Very proper. But I should put on some foul-weather clothes now. Tell me, did they send you for the key of the keelson?'

'Yes, sir; and I looked for it everywhere. Bonden told me he thought the gunner's daughter might have it, but when I asked Mr Rolfe, he said he was sorry, he was not a married man.'

'Well, well. You have foul-weather clothes?'

'Why, sir, there are a great many things in my chest, my *sea*-chest, that the shopman told Mama I should be equipped with. And I have my father's sou-wester.'

'Mr Babbington will show you what to put on. Tell him with my compliments, that he will show you what to put on,' he added, remembering that gentleman's inhuman barbarity. 'Do not wipe your nose upon your sleeve, Mr Parslow. It ain't genteel.'

'No, sir. Beg pardon, sir.'

'Cut along then,' said Jack irritably. 'Am I a God-damned wet nurse?' he asked his pea-jacket.

On deck he was greeted by a squall of rain mixed with sleet and spray. The wind had increased to a fine fresh breeze, sweeping the fog away and replacing it by a low sky – bands of weeping cloud against a steely grey, black on the eastern horizon; a nasty short choppy sea was getting up against the tide, and although the *Polychrest* was holding her course well enough, she was shipping a good deal of water, and her very moderate spread of canvas laid her over as though she had topgallants abroad. So she was as crank as he had feared; and a wet ship into the bargain. There were two men at the wheel, and from the way they were cramped on to the spokes it was clear they were having to fight hard to keep her from flying up into the wind.

He studied the log-board, made a rough calculation of the position, adding a triple leeway, and decided to wear in half an hour, when both watches would be on deck. He had plenty of room, and there was no point in harassing the few good men he had aboard, particularly as the sky looked changeable, menacing, damned unpleasant – they might have a dirty night of it. And he would get the topgallantmasts down on deck before long. 'Mr Parker,' he said, 'we will take another reef in the foretopsail, if you please.'

The bosun's call, the rush of hands, the volley of orders through Parker's speaking-trumpet – 'Halliards let fly – clap on to that brace – Mr Malloch, touch up those hands at the brace.' The yards came round, the wind spilled from the sail and the *Polychrest* righted herself, at the same time making such a cruel gripe that the man at the con had to fling himself at the wheel to prevent her being taken aback. 'Layout – look alive, there – you, sir, you on the yardarm, are you asleep? Are you going to pass the – weather earing? Damn your eyes, are you going to stow that bunt? Mr Rossall, take that man's name. Lay in.'

Through the clamour Jack watched the men aloft. The man on the yardarm was young Haines, from the *Lord Mornington*; he knew his trade; might make a good captain of the foretop. He saw his foot slip as he scrambled in towards the mast – those horses wanted mousing.

'Send the last man off the yard aft,' called the first lieutenant, red in the face from shouting. 'Start him, Mr Malloch.'

This same old foolery – the last man off was the first man on, the man who went right out on to the yardarm. It was a hard service – it had to be a hard service – but there was no need to make it harder, discouraging the willing hands. The people were going to have plenty to do: it was a pity for them to waste their strength beating one another. And yet again it was easy to seek a cheap popularity by checking an officer in public – easy, and disastrous in the long run.

'Sail ho!' hailed the look-out.

'Where away?'

'Right astern, sir.'

She came up out of a dark smudge of half-frozen rain, a frigate hull-up already, on the same tack as the *Polychrest* and overhauling her very fast. French or English? He was no great way from Cherbourg. 'Make the private signal,' said Jack. 'Mr Parker, your glass, if you please.'

He fixed the frigate in the grey round of the objective, swaying to counterbalance the sloop's roll, pitch and shudder, and as the *Polychrest*'s windward gun went off behind him he saw the blue-white-blue break out aboard her, curving far out to leeward, and the momentary whiff from her answering gun. 'Make our number,' he said, relaxing. He gave orders for the mousing of the horses, desired Mr Parker to see what he could make of the frigate, sent Haines forward, and settled to watch in peace.

'Three of them, sir,' said Mr Parker. 'And I think the first is *Amethyst*.'

Three there were, in line ahead. '*Amethyst* she is, sir,' said the signal midshipman, huddling his book under the shelter of his bosom. They were directly in his wake, steering the same course. But the *Polychrest*'s leeway was such that in a very short while he saw them not head-on, but from an angle, an angle that increased with alarming speed, so that in five minutes he was watching them over the weather quarter. They had already struck their topgallantmasts, but they were still carrying their topsails atrip – their full, expert crews could reef them in a moment. The first was indeed the *Amethyst*; the second he could not make out – perhaps the *Minerve*; the third was the *Franchise*, with his old friend Heneage Dundas aboard, a post captain, in command of a beautiful French-built thirty-six-gun frigate; Dundas, five years junior to him as a lieutenant, thirteen months as master and commander; Jack had cobbed him repeatedly in the midshipmen's berth of Old Ironsides: and would do so again. There he was, standing up on the slide of a quarter-deck carronade, as pleased as Punch, waving his hat. Jack raised his own, and the wind took his bright yellow hair, tearing it from the ribbon behind, and streamed it away north-westward. As if in reply a hoist ran up to the *Franchise*'s mizzen-peak.

'Alphabetic, sir,' said the midshipman, spelling it out. 'P S – oh yes, Psalms. Psalms cxlvii, 10.'

'Acknowledge,' said Jack who was no Biblical scholar.

Two guns from the *Amethyst*, and the frigates tacked in succession, moving like so many models on a sheet of glass: round they went, each exactly in the same piece of water, keeping their stations as though they were linked together. It was a beautifully executed manoeuvre, above all with such a head-sea and such a wind, the result of years of training – a crew that pulled together, officers that knew their ship.

He shook his head, staring after the frigates as they vanished into the gloom. Eight bells struck. 'Mr Parker,' he said, 'we will get the topgallantmasts down on deck, and then we will wear.' By the time the masts were struck there would be no satirical friends to watch from a distance.

'I beg your pardon, sir?' asked Parker, with an anxious poke of his head.

Jack repeated his order and retired to the taffrail to let his first lieutenant carry on.

Glancing at the *Polychrest*'s wake to judge her leeway he noticed a little dark bird, fluttering weakly just over the water with its legs dangling; it vanished under the larboard quarter, and as he moved across to make sure of it, he tripped over something soft, about knee-height, something very like a limpet – the child Parslow, under his sou-wester.

'Why, Mr Parslow,' he said, picking him up, 'you are properly rigged now, I see. You will be glad of it. Run below to the doctor and tell him, if he chooses to see a stormy petrel, he has but to come on deck.'

It was not a stormy petrel, but a much rarer cousin with yellow feet – so rare that Stephen could not identify him until he pittered across a wave so close that those yellow feet showed clear.

'If rarity and the force of the storm are in direct proportion,' he reflected, watching it attentively, 'then we are in for a most prodigious hurricane. I shall not mention it, however.'

A frightful crash forward: the foretopgallantmast brought itself down on deck more briskly than in the smartest frigate, half stunning Mr Parker and plunging Jack into manoeuvres more suitable for a petrel than a mariner. Throughout the night the wind backed until it was blowing hard from the north; there it stayed, north-east, north, or north-west, never allowing more than close-reefed topsails, if that, for nine days on end, nine days of rain, snow, steep wicked seas, and a perpetual fighting for their lives; nine days in which Jack rarely left the deck and young Parslow never once took off his clothes; nine days of wearing, lying to, scudding under bare poles, and never a sight of the sun – no notion of their position within fifty miles and more. And when at last a strong south-wester allowed them to make up their enormous leeway, their noonday observation showed that they were where they had started from.

Early in the blow a lee-lurch, laying the *Polychrest* on her beam-ends, had shot the dazed first lieutenant down the main hatchway, damaging his shoulder, and he had spent the rest of the time in his cot, with the water washing about it often enough, and in great pain. Jack was sorry for the pain, in an abstract way, though it seemed fair that one so fond of inflicting agony should feel a touch of it, but he was heartily glad of Parker's absence – the man was incompetent, incompetent for such a situation as this. He was conscientious, he did his duty as he understood it; but he was no seaman.

The master, Pullings, Rossall, the senior master's mate, the bosun and the gunner were seamen; so were a dozen of the hands. Babbington and Allen, another oldster, were shaping well; and as for the rest of the people, they at least knew what they were to haul upon at the word of command. This long week's blow, when they were close on foundering twice a day and when everybody knew it, had crammed a deal of training into a short time – short when measured by the calendar rather than by mortal dread. Training in manoeuvres of every kind, but particularly in the use of the pumps: they had not stopped for an hour since the second day of the blow.

Now as they sailed up the Channel, passing Selsey Bill with a light air on the quarter and topgallantsails set, with the galley fires lighted at last and a hot dinner in their bellies, he felt that they might not be disgraced when the *Polychrest* reached her station; and she would reach it now, he was sure, even if she had to tide it all the way – no unlikely event, with this wind dying on him. She would not be disgraced: he was short-handed, of course, and there were seventeen men in the sick-bay – two hernias, five bad falls with broken bones, and the rest the usual wounds from falling spars or blocks or ropes crossing a hand or leg. One landsman, an unemployed glover from Shepton Mallet, had been lost overboard, and a thief from the Winchester assizes had gone raving, staring, barking mad off Ushant: yet on the other hand, sea-sickness had vanished, and even the quota-men from the inland gaols could walk about the deck without much danger to themselves or others. The crew were a poor-looking set, upon the whole, but when he had had time to exercise them at the guns, it was not impossible that he might make a passable man-of-war out of the *Polychrest*. He knew her tolerably well now: he and the master (he had a great esteem for Mr Goodridge) had worked out a sail-plan that made the most of what qualities she possessed, and when he could alter her trim to bring her by the head and rake her masts she might do better; but he could not love her. She was a mean-spirited vessel, radically vicious, cross-grained, laboursome, cruel in her unreliability; and he could not love her. She had disappointed him so often when even a log canoe would have risen to the occasion that his strong natural affection for his command had dwindled quite away. He had sailed in some rough old tubs, ponderous things with no perceptible virtue to the outsider, but he had always been able to find excuses for them – they had always been the finest ships in the history of the Navy for some particular quality – and this had never happened to him before. The feeling was so strange, the disloyalty so uncomfortable, that it was some time before he would acknowledge it; and when he did – he was pacing the quarterdeck after his solitary dinner at the time – it gave him such uneasiness of mind that he turned to the midshipman of the watch, who was clinging motionless to a stanchion, and said, 'Mr Parslow, you will find the Doctor in the sick-bay . . .'

'Find him yourself,' said Parslow.

Was it possible that these words had been uttered? Jack paused in his stride. From the rigid blankness of the quartermaster, the man at the wheel, and the gunner's mates busy with the aftermost port carronade, and from the mute writhing of the midshipmen on the gangway, it was clear that they had.

'I tell you what it is, Goldilocks,' went on Parslow, closing one eye, 'don't you try to come it high over me, for I've a spirit that won't brook it. Find him yourself.'

'Pass the word for the bosun's mate,' said Jack. 'Quartermaster, Mr Parslow's hammock, if you please.' The bosun's mate came running aft, his starter in his hand. 'Seize the young gentleman to the gun in my cabin.'

The young gentleman had released his hold on the stanchion; he was now lying on the deck, protesting that he should not be beaten, that he should dirk any man who presumed to lay a hand upon him – he was an officer. The bosun's mate picked him up by the small of the back: the sentry opened and closed the cabin door. A startled cry and then some treble oaths that made the grinning quarterdeck stretch its eyes, the whole punctuated by the measured thump of a rope's end; and then Mr Parslow, sobbing bitterly, was led out by the hand. 'Lash him into his hammock, Rogers,' said Jack. 'Mr Pullings, Mr Pullings, the grog for the midshipmen's berth is stopped until further orders.'

That evening in his cabin he said to Stephen, 'Do you know what those blackguards in the midshipmen's berth did to young Parslow?'

'Whether or no, you are going to tell me,' observed Stephen, helping himself to rum.

'They made him beastly drunk and then sent him on deck. Almost the first day they might have turned in for their watch below, the first time they are not up to their knees in water, they can think of nothing better to do than to make a youngster drunk. They shall not do it again, however. I have stopped their grog.'

'It would be as well if you were to stop the whole ship's grog. A most pernicious custom, a very gross abuse of animal appetite, a monstrous aberration – half a pint of rum, forsooth! I should not have a quarter of the men under my care, was it not for your vile rum. They are brought down with their limbs, ribs, collar-bones shattered, having fallen from the rigging drunk – diligent, stout, attentive men who would never fall when sober. Come, let us pour it secretly away.'

'And have a mutiny on our hands? Thank you very kindly. No: I should rather have them three sheets in the wind now and again, but willing to do their duty the rest of the time. Mutiny. It makes your blood run cold to think of it. Men you have worked with right through the commission and liked, growing cold and secret; no jokes, no singing out, no good will; the ship falling into two camps, with the undecided men puzzled and wretched in between. And then the shot-rolling by night.'

'Shot-rolling?'

'They roll shot along the deck in the night-watches, to let you know their mind, and maybe to catch an officer's legs.'

'As for mutinies in general,' said Stephen, 'I am all in favour of 'em. You take men from their homes or their chosen occupations, you confine them in insalubrious conditions upon a wholly inadequate diet, you subject them to the tyranny of bosun's mates, you expose them to unimagined perils; what is more, you defraud them of their meagre food, pay and allowances – everything but this sacred rum of yours. Had I been at Spithead, I should certainly have joined the mutineers. Indeed, I am astonished at their moderation.'

'Pray, Stephen, do not speak like this, nattering about the service; it makes me so very low. I know things are not perfect, but I cannot reform the world *and* run a man-of-war. In any case, be candid, and think of the *Sophie* – think of any happy ship.'

'There are such things, sure; but they depend upon the whim, the digestion and the virtue of one or two men, and that is iniquitous. I am opposed to authority, that egg of misery and oppression; I am opposed to it largely for what it does to those who exercise it.'

'Well,' said Jack, 'it has done me no good. This afternoon I was savaged by a midshipman, and now I am harassed by my own surgeon. Come, Stephen, drink up, and let us have some music.' But instead of tuning his fiddle he reached beyond it, saying, 'Here is something that will interest you. Have you ever heard of robber-bolts?'

'I have not.'

'This is one.' He held out a short solid copper cylinder with a great nut on the end of it. 'As you know, bolts are to hold the hull together, going right through her timbers; and the best are copper, against the corrosion. They are expensive – I believe two pounds of copper, a short piece of bolt, will pay a shipwright's wages for a day. But if you are a damned villain, you cut off the middle, drive each end home and pocket the money for the length of copper in between. Nobody is any the wiser until the frame opens; and that may not happen until the ship is on the other side of the world. And even then she may founder, leaving no witnesses.'

'When did you know this?'

'I suspected it from the start. I knew she would be a damned job, coming from Hickman's; and then the fellows at the yard were so fulsome, so free with their hampers. But I was certain only the other day. Now that she has worked a little, it is easier to be certain. I pulled this one out with my fingers.'

'Could you not have made representations in the proper quarters?'

'Yes. I could have asked for a survey and waited for a month or six weeks: and then where should I have been? It is a dockyard matter, and you hear very rum tales of ships being passed whatever their state, and small clerks setting up their carriages. No. I preferred to take her out; and indeed, she has withstood quite a blow. I shall have her hove down if ever I can – if ever I can find the right moment, or if she will not float without it.'

They remained silent for a while, and all the time the steady throb of the pumps sounded through the cabin, and, almost keeping time, the barking of the lunatic.

'I must give that man some more of my laudanum,' said Stephen, half to himself.

Jack's mind was still on bolts, timbers, and the other powers that held his ship together. 'What do you say to Parker's shoulder?' he asked. 'He will not be fit for duty for a great while, I dare say? Should lay up ashore, no doubt, and take the waters?'

'Not at all,' said Stephen. 'He is coming along admirably – Dr Ramis's thin water gruel has answered admirably, and the low diet. Properly slung, he may come on deck tomorrow.'

'Oh,' said Jack. 'No sick ticket? No long leave? You do not feel that the waters might help his deafness, too?' He looked wistfully into Stephen's face, but without much hope: in what he conceived to be his duty as a medical man, Stephen Maturin would not budge for man, God or beast. In such matters he was beyond the reach of reason or even of friendship. They never discussed the officers with whom Stephen messed, but Jack's desire to be shot of his first lieutenant, his opinion of Mr Parker, was clear enough to anyone who knew him well: yet Stephen merely looked dogged, reached for the fiddle and ran up and down the scale. 'Where did you get this?' he asked.

'I picked it up in a pawnshop near the Sally-Port. It cost twelve and six.'

'You were not cheated, my dear. I like its tone extremely – warm, mellow. You are a great judge of a fiddle, to be sure. Come, come, there is not a moment to lose; I make my

rounds at seven bells. One, two, three,' he cried, tapping his
foot, and the cabin was filled with the opening movement of
Boccherini's Corelli sonata, a glorious texture of sound, the
violin sending up brilliant jets through the 'cello's involutions,
and they soared up and away from the grind of pumps, the
tireless barking, the problems of command, up, the one
answering the other, joining, separating, twining, rising into
their native air.

A KEEN, PALE, wintry morning in the Downs: the hands at
breakfast, Jack walking up and down.

'The admiral is making our number, sir,' said the signal midshipman.

'Very well,' said Jack. 'Man the gig.' He had been expecting
this since before dawn, when he reported his presence; the
gig was already alongside and his best coat was lying spread
out on his cot. He reappeared, wearing it, and went over the
side to the twittering of the bosun's pipes.

The sea was as calm as a sea can well be; the tide was at
the full, and the whole grey surface under the frozen sky had
the air of waiting – not a ripple, scarcely a hint of living swell.
Behind him, beyond the dwindling *Polychrest*, lay the town of
Deal, and away beyond it, the North Foreland. Ahead of him,
the massive bulk of the *Cumberland*, 74, with the blue ensign
at the mizzen; then two cables' lengths away, the *Melpomene*,
a lovely frigate, then two sloops and a cutter; and beyond
them again, between the squadron and the Goodwin sands,
the whole of the West Indies, Turkey, Guinea and India
trade, a hundred and forty sail of merchantmen lying there in
the road, a wood of masts, waiting for a wind and a convoy,
every yard and spar distinct in this cold air – almost no
colour, only line, but that line unbelievably sharp and clear.

However, Jack had been gazing at this scene ever since the
pale disc of the sun had made it visible, and during the pull to
the flagship his mind was taken up with other things: his
expression was grave and contained as he went up the side,

saluted the quarterdeck, greeted the *Cumberland*'s captain, and was shown into the great cabin.

Admiral Harte was eating kippers and drinking tea, his secretary and a mass of papers on the other side of the table. He had aged shockingly since Jack had last seen him; his shallow eyes seemed to have moved even closer together and his look of falsity to have grown even more pronounced.

'So here you are at last,' he cried – with a smile, however, and reaching up an unctuous hand. 'You must have come dawdling up the Channel; I expected you three tides ago, upon my honour.' Admiral Harte's honour and Jack's dawdling were much on a par, and Jack only bowed. The remark was not intended to be answered, in any case – a mere automatic unpleasantness – and Harte went on, with an awkward assumption of familiarity and good fellowship. 'Sit down. What have you been doing with yourself? You look ten years older. The girls at the back of Portsmouth Point, I dare say. Do you want a cup of tea?'

Money was Harte's nearest approach to joy, his ruling passion: in the Mediterranean, where they had served together, Jack had been remarkably successful in the article of prizes; he had been given cruise after cruise, and he had put more than ten thousand pounds into his admiral's pocket. Captain Harte, as commandant of Port Mahon, had come in for no share of this, of course, and his dislike for Jack had remained unaffected; but now the case was altered; now he stood to gain by Jack's exertions, and he meant to conciliate his good will.

Jack was rowed back again, still over this silent water, but with something less of gravity in his look. He could not understand Harte's drift; it made him uneasy, and the lukewarm tea was disagreeable in his stomach; but he had met with no open hostility, and his immediate future was clear – the *Polychrest* was not to go with this convoy, but was to spend some time in the Downs, seeing to the manning of the squadron and the harassing of the invasion flotilla over the way.

Aboard the *Polychrest* his officers stood waiting for him; the hammocks were up, as neat as art could make them, the decks were clean, the ropes flemished, the Marines geometrically exact as they presented arms and all the officers saluted; yet something was out of tune. The odd flush on Parker's face, the lowering obstinacy on Stephen's, the concern on Pullings', Goodridge's and Macdonald's, gave him a notion of what was afoot; and this notion was confirmed five minutes later, when the first lieutenant came into his cabin and said, 'I am very much concerned to have to report a serious breach of discipline, sir.'

A little after breakfast, while Jack was aboard the admiral, Stephen had come on deck: the first thing he had seen there was a man running aft with a bosun's mate beating him from behind – not an uncommon sight in a man-of-war. But this man had a heavy iron marline-spike between his teeth, held tight with spunyarn, and as he screamed, blood ran from either side of his mouth. He came to a dead halt at the break of the quarterdeck, and Stephen, taking a lancet from his waistcoat pocket, stepped up to him, cut the spunyarn, took the spike and threw it into the sea.

'I remonstrated with him – I told him that the punishment was inflicted upon my orders – and he attacked me with an extreme ferocity.'

'Physically?'

'No, sir. Verbally. He cast out reflections upon my courage and my fitness to command. I should have taken decided measures, but I knew that you were shortly to return, and I understood he was your friend. I hinted that he should withdraw to his cabin: he did not see fit to comply, but stayed pacing the quarterdeck, on the starboard side, although it was represented to him that with the captain out of the ship, this was *my* prerogative.'

'My friendship for Dr Maturin is neither here nor there, Mr Parker: I am surprised that you should have mentioned it. You must understand that he is an Irish gentleman of great eminence in his profession, that he knows very little, almost nothing, of the service, and that he is extremely impatient of being practised upon – being made game of. He does not always know when we are earnest and when we are not. I dare say there has been some misunderstanding in this case. I remember him to have flown out very savagely at the master of the *Sophie* over what he conceived to be a misplaced joke about a trysailmast.'

'A master is not a lieutenant.'

'Now, sir, do you instruct me upon rank? Do you pretend to tell me something that is clear to a newly-joined midshipman?' Jack did not raise his voice, but he was pale with anger, not only at Parker's stupid impertinence but even more at the whole situation, and at what must come. 'Let me tell you, sir, that your methods of discipline do not please me, I had wished to avoid this: I had supposed that when I observed to you that your punishment of Isaac Barrow was perfectly illegal, that you would have taken the hint, And there were other occasions. Let us understand one another. I am not a preachee-flogee captain: I will have a taut ship, by flogging if need be, but I will have no unnecessary brutality. What is the name of the man you gagged?'

'I am sorry to say I do not recall his name for the moment, sir. A landsman, sir – a waister in the larboard watch.'

'It is usual in the service for an efficient first lieutenant to know the names of the men. You will oblige me by finding it directly.'

'William Edwards, sir,' said Parker, some moments later,

'William Edwards. Just so, A scavenger from Rutland: took the bounty. Had never seen the sea or a ship or an officer in his life – no notion of discipline. He answered, I suppose?'

'Yes, sir. Said, "I came as fast as I could, and who are you, any gait?" on being rebuked for slackness.'

'Why was he being started?'

'He left his post without leave, to go to the head.'

'There must be some discrimination, Mr Parker, When he

has been aboard long enough to know his duty, to know the officers and for the officers to know him – and I repeat that it is an officer's duty to know his men – then he may be gagged for answering. If indeed he should do so, a most unlikely event in a ship even half well run, And the same applies to most of the crew; it is useless and detrimental to the good of the service to beat them until they know what is required of them. You, an experienced officer, clearly misunderstood Edwards: you thought he intended gross disrespect. It is exceedingly possible that Dr Maturin, with no experience whatsoever, misunderstood you. Be so good as to show me your defaulters list. This will not do, Mr Parker. Glave, Brown, Stindall, Burnet, all newly-joined landsmen: and so it runs, a list long enough for a first-rate, an ill-conducted first-rate. We shall deal with this later. Pass the word for Dr Maturin.'

This was a Jack Aubrey he had never seen before, larger than life, hard, cold, and strong with a hundred years of tradition behind him, utterly convinced that he was right. 'Good morning, Dr Maturin,' he said. 'There has been a misunderstanding between you and Mr Parker. You were not aware that gagging is a customary punishment in the Navy. No doubt you looked upon it as a piece of rough horseplay.'

'I looked upon it as a piece of extreme brutality. Edwards's teeth are in a state of advanced decay – he has been under my hands – and this iron bar had crushed two molars. I removed the bar at once, and . . .'

'You removed it on medical grounds. You were not aware that it was a customary punishment, awarded by an officer – you knew nothing of the reason for the punishment?'

'No, sir.'

'You did wrong, sir: you acted inconsiderately. And in your agitation, in the heat of the moment, you spoke hastily to Mr Parker. You must express your sense of regret that this misunderstanding should have arisen.'

'Mr Parker,' said Stephen, 'I regret that there has been this misunderstanding. I regret the remarks that passed between us; and if you wish I will repeat my apology on the quarter-deck, before those who heard them.'

Parker reddened, looked stiff and awkward; his right hand, the usual instrument for acknowledging such declarations, was immobilized in his sling. He bowed and said something about 'being entirely satisfied – more than enough – for his part he too regretted any disobliging expression that might have escaped him.'

There was a pause. 'I will not detain you, gentlemen,' said Jack coldly. 'Mr Parker, let the starboard watch be exercised at the great guns and the larboard at reefing topsails. Mr Pullings will take the small-arms men. What is that infernal row. Hallows,' – to the Marine sentry outside the door – 'what is that din?'

'Beg pardon, your Honour,' said the soldier, 'it's the captain's steward and the gun-room steward fighting over the use of the coffee-pot.'

'God damn their eyes,' cried Jack. 'I'll tan their hides – I'll give them a bloody shirt – I'll stop their capers. Old seamen, too: rot them. Mr Parker, let us establish a little order in this sloop.'

'JACK, JACK,' said Stephen, when the lamp was lit, 'I fear I am a sad embarrassment to you. I think I shall pack my chest and go ashore.'

'No, soul, never say that,' said Jack wearily. 'This explana-tion with Parker had to come: I had hoped to avoid it, but he did not catch my drift; and really I am just as glad to have had it out.'

'Still and all, I think I will go ashore.'

'And desert your patients?'

'Sea-surgeons are ten a penny.'

'And your friends?'

'Why, upon my word, Jack, I think you would be better without me. I am not suited for a sea-life. You know far better than I, that discord among the officers is of no use to your ship; and I do not care to be a witness of this kind of brutality, or any party to it.'

'Ours is a hard service, I admit. But you will find as much brutality by land.'

'I am not a party to it by land.'

'Yet you did not so much mind the flogging in the *Sophie*?'

'No. The world in general, and even more your briny world, accepts flogging. It is this perpetual arbitrary harassing, bullying, hitting, brow-beating, starting – these capricious torments, spreadeagling, gagging – this general atmosphere of oppression. I should have told you earlier. But it is a delicate subject, between you and me.'

'I know. It is the devil . . . At the beginning of a commission a raw, ugly crew (and we have some precious hard bargains, you know) – has to be driven hard, and startled into prompt obedience; but this had gone too far. Parker and the bosun are not bad fellows – I did not give them a strong enough lead at the beginning – I was remiss. It will not be the same in the future.'

'You must forgive me, my dear. Those men are dropsical with authority, permanently deranged. I must go.'

'I say you shall not,' said Jack, with a smile.

'I say I shall.'

'Do you know, my dear Stephen, that you may not come and go as you please?' said Jack, leaning back in his chair and gazing at Stephen with placid triumph. 'Do not you know that you are under martial law? That if you was to stir without my leave, I should be obliged to put an R against your name, have you taken up, brought back in irons and most severely punished? What do you say to a flogging through the feet, ha? You have no notion of the powers of a captain of a man-of-war. *He* is dropsical with authority, if you like.'

'Must I not go ashore?'

'No, of course you must not, and that's the end to it. You must make your bed and lie on it.' He paused, with a feeling that this was not quite the epigram that he had wished. 'Now let me tell you of my interview with that scrub Harte . . .'

'If, then, as I understand you, we are to spend some time in this place, you will have no objection to granting me some days' leave of absence. Apart from all other considerations, I must get my dement and my compound fracture of the femur ashore: the hospital at Dover is at an inconsiderable distance – a most eligible port.'

'Certainly,' cried Jack, 'if you give me your word not to run, so that I have all the trouble of careering over the country after you with a posse – a posse navitatum. Certainly. Any time you like to name.'

'And when I am there,' said Stephen deliberately, 'I shall ride over to Mapes.'

8

'A GENTLEMAN TO SEE Miss Williams,' said the maid.

'Who is it, Peggy?' cried Cecilia.

'I believe it is Dr Maturin, Miss.'

'I will come at once,' said Sophia, throwing her needlework into a corner and casting a distracted glance at the mirror.

'It must be for me,' said Cecilia. 'Dr Maturin is my young man.'

'Oh, Cissy, what stuff,' said Sophia, hurrying downstairs.

'You have one, no *two* already,' whispered Cecilia, catching her in the corridor. 'You can't have three. Oh, it's so unfair,' she hissed, as the door closed and Sophia walked into the morning-room with a great air of composure.

'How happy I am to see you,' they said, both together, looking so pleased that a casual observer would have sworn they were lovers, or at least that there was a particular attachment between them.

'Mama will be so disappointed to have missed you,' said

Sophia. 'She has taken Frankie up to town, to have her teeth filed, poor pet.'

'I hope Mrs Williams is well, and Miss Cecilia? How is Mrs Villiers?'

'Diana is not here, but the others are very well, I thank you. How are you, and how is Captain Aubrey?'

'Blooming, blooming, thank you, my dear. That is to say, I am blooming: poor Jack is a little under the weather, what with his new command, and a crew of left-handed hedge-creepers from half the gaols in the kingdom.'

'Oh,' cried Sophie, clasping her hands, 'I am sure he works too hard. Do beg him not to work too hard, Dr Maturin. He will listen to you – I sometimes think you are the only person he will listen to. But surely the men must love him? I remember how the dear sailors at Melbury ran to do whatever he said, so cheerfully; and he was so good to them – never gruff or commanding, as some people are with their servants.'

'I dare say they will come to love him presently, when I they appreciate his virtues,' said Stephen. 'But for the moment we are all at sixes and sevens. However, we have four old Sophies aboard – his coxswain volunteered – and they are a great comfort.'

'I can quite see they would follow him anywhere in the world,' said Sophia. 'Dear things, with their pigtails and buckled shoes. But tell me, is the *Polychrest* really so very – ? Admiral Haddock says she can never swim, but he loves to make our flesh creep, which is very ill-natured in him. He says she has two main topsail yards, in such a sneering, contemptuous way. I have no patience with him. Not that he means it unkindly, of course; but surely it is very wrong to speak lightly of such important things, and to say she will certainly go to the bottom? It is not true, is it, Dr Maturin? And surely two main topsail yards are better than one?'

'I am no sailor, as you know, my dear, but I should have thought so. She is an odd, pragmatical vessel, however, and she has this way of going backwards when they mean her to go forwards. Other ships find it entertaining, but it does not seem to please our officers or seamen. As for her not floating, you may set your mind at rest. We had a nine days' blow that took us far out into the chops of the Channel, with an ugly, pounding sea that partially submerged us, shaking away spars, booms, ropes; and she survived that. I do not suppose Jack was off the deck more than three hours at a time – I remember seeing him lashed to the bitts, up to his middle in the water, bidding the helmsman ease her as the seas came in; and on catching sight of me said, "She'll live yet." So you may be quite easy.'

'Oh dear, oh dear,' said Sophia in a low voice. 'At least, I do hope he eats well, to keep up his strength.'

'No,' said Stephen, with great satisfaction, 'that he does not. I am glad to say he does not eat at all well. I used to tell him over and over again, when he had Louis Durand as his cook, that he was digging his grave with his teeth: he ate far, far too much three times a day. Now he has no cook; now he makes do with our common fare; and he is much the better for it – has lost two stone at least. He is very poor now, as you know, and cannot afford to poison himself; to ruin his constitution: it is true that he cannot afford to poison any guests either, which grieves him. He no longer keeps a table. But you, my dear, how are you? It seems to me that you are more in need of attention than our honest tar.' He had been watching her all this time, and although that unbelievable complexion was as lovely as ever, it was lovely in a lower tone, once the pinkness of surprise had faded; there was tiredness, sorrow, a want of light in her eyes; and something of the straight spring had gone. 'Let me see your tongue, my dear,' he said taking her wrist. 'I love the smell of this house,' he said, as he counted automatically. 'Orris-root, I believe? There was orris-root everywhere in my childhood home – smelt it as soon as you opened the door. Yes, yes. Just as I thought. You are not eating enough. What do you weigh?'

'Eight stone and five pounds,' said Sophia, hanging her head.

'You are fine-boned, sure; but for an upstanding young woman like you it is not nearly enough. You must take porter with your dinner. I shall tell your mother. A pint of good stout will do all that is required: or almost all.'

'A gentleman to see Miss Williams,' said the maid. 'Mr Bowles,' she added, with a knowing look.

'I am not at home, Peggy,' said Sophie. 'Beg Miss Cecilia to see him in the drawing-room. Now I have told a lie,' she said, catching her lip behind her teeth. 'How dreadful. Dr Maturin, would you mind coming for a walk in the park, and then it will be true?'

'With all the pleasure in life, lamb,' said Stephen.

She took his arm and led him quickly through the shrubbery. When they came to the wicket into the park she said, 'I am so wretchedly unhappy, you know.' Stephen pressed her arm, but said nothing. 'It is that Mr Bowles. They want me to marry him.'

'Is he disagreeable to you?'

'He is perfectly hateful to me. Oh, I don't mean he is rude or unkind or in the least disrespectful – no, no, he is the worthiest, most respectable young man. But he is such a bore, and he has moist hands. He sits and gasps – he thinks he ought to gasp, I believe – he sits with me for hours and hours, and sometimes I feel that if he gasps at me just once more, I shall run my scissors into him.' She was speaking very quick, and now indignation had given her colour again. 'I always try to keep Cissy in the room, but she slips away – Mama calls her – and he tries to get hold of my hand. We edge slowly round and round the table – it is really too ridiculous. Mama – nobody could mean to be kinder than my dear Mama, I am sure – makes me see him – she will be so vexed when she hears I was not at home to him today – and I have to teach Sunday school, with those odious little tracts. I don't mind the children, much – poor little things, with their Sundays spoilt, after all that long church – but visiting the cottagers makes me perfectly wretched and ashamed – teaching women twice my age, with families, who know a hundred times more about life than I do, how to be economical and clean, and not to buy the best cuts of meat for their husbands, because it is *luxurious*, and God meant them to be poor. And they are so polite and I know they must think me so conceited and stupid. I can sew a little, and I can make a chocolate mousse, but I could no more run a cottage with a husband and little children in it on ten shillings a week than I could sail a first rate. Who do they think they are?' she cried. 'Just because they can read and write.'

'I have often wondered,' said Stephen. 'The gentleman is a parson, I take it?'

'Yes. His father is the bishop. And I will not marry him, no, not if I have to lead apes in Hell. There is one man in the world I will ever marry, if he would have me – and I had him and I threw him away.'

The tears that had been brimming now rolled down her cheeks, and silently Stephen passed her a clean pocket-handkerchief.

They walked in silence: dead leaves, frosted, withered grass, gaunt trees; they passed the same palings twice, a third time.

'Might you not let him know?' asked Stephen. 'He cannot move in the matter. You know very well what the world thinks of a man who offers marriage to an heiress when he has no money, no prospects, and a load of debts. You know very well what your mother would say to such a proposal: and he is delicate in the point of honour.'

'I did write to him: I said all I could in modesty; and indeed it was the most forward, dreadful thing. It was not modest at all.'

'It came too late . . .'

'*Too late*. Oh, how often I have said that to myself, and with such grief. If he had come to Bath just once again, I know we should have come to an understanding.'

'A secret engagement?'

'No. I should never have consented to that: but an understanding – not to bind him, you understand, but just to say
that I should always wait. Anyhow, that is what I agreed in
myself; but he never came again. Yet I did say it, and I feel
myself bound in honour, whatever happens, unless he should
marry elsewhere. I should wait and wait, even if it means giving up babies – and I should love to have babies. Oh, I am
not a romantic girl: I am nearly thirty, and I know what I am
talking about.'

'But surely now you could make him understand your
mind?'

'He did not come in London. I cannot pursue him, and perhaps distress and embarrass him. He may have formed other
attachments – I mean no blame: these things are quite different with men, I know.'

'There was that wretched story of an engagement to marry
a Mr Allen.'

'I know.' A long pause. 'That is what makes me so cross and
ill-natured,' said Sophia at last, 'when I think that if I had not
been such an odious ninny, so jealous, I might now be . . . But
they need not think I shall ever marry Mr Bowles, for I shall
not.'

'Would you marry without your mother's consent?'

'Oh, no. Never. That would be terribly wrong. Besides,
quite apart from its being wicked – and I should never do it –
if I were to run away, I should not have a penny; and I should
love to be a help to my husband, not a burden. But marrying
where you are told, because it is *suitable*, and *unexceptionable*, is quite different. Quite different. Quick – this way.
There is Admiral Haddock, behind the laurels. He has not
seen us – we will go round by the lake: no one ever comes
there. Do you know he is going to sea again, by the way?' she
asked in another tone.

'In command?' cried Stephen, astonished.

'No. To do something at Plymouth – the Fencibles or the
Impress Service – I did not attend. But he is going by sea. An

old friend is to give him a lift in the *Généreux*.'

'That is the ship Jack brought into Mahon when Lord Nelson's squadron took her.'

'Yes, I know: he was second of the *Foudroyant* then. And the admiral is so excited, turning over all his old uniform-cases and taking in his laced coats. He has asked Cissy and me for the summer, for he has an official residence down there. Cissy is wild to go. This is where I come to sit when I cannot bear it any longer in the house,' she said, pointing to a little green-mouldy Grecian temple, leprous and scaling. 'And this is where Diana and I had our quarrel.'

'I never heard you had quarrelled.'

'I should have thought we could have been heard all over the county, at least. It was my fault; I was horrid that day. I had had Mr Bowles to endure all the afternoon, and I felt as though I had been flayed: so I went for a ride as far as Gatacre, and then came back here. But she should not have taunted me with London, and how she could see him whenever she liked, and that he had not gone down to Portsmouth the next day at all. It was unkind, even if I had deserved it. So I told her she was an ill-natured woman, and she called me something worse, and suddenly there we were, calling names and shouting at one another like a couple of fishwives – oh, it is so humiliating to remember. Then she said something so cruel about letters and how she could marry him any moment she chose, but she had no notion of a half-pay captain nor any other woman's leavings that I quite lost my temper, and swore I should thrash her with my riding-crop if she spoke to me like that. I should have, too: but then Mama came, and she was terribly frightened and tried to make us kiss and be friends. But I would not; nor the next day, either. And in the end Diana went away, to Mr Lowndes, that cousin in Dover.'

'Sophie,' said Stephen, 'you have confided so much in me, and so trustingly . . .'

'I cannot tell you what a relief it has been, and what a comfort to me.'

'. . . that it would be monstrous not to be equally candid with you. I am very much attached to Diana.'

'Oh,' cried Sophia. 'Oh, how I hope I have not hurt you. I thought it was Jack – oh, what have I said?'

'Never be distressed, honey. I know her faults as well as any man.'

'Of course, she is very beautiful,' said Sophia, glancing at him timidly.

'Yes. Tell me, is Diana wholly in love with Jack?'

'I may be wrong,' she said, after a pause, 'I know very little about these things, or anything else; but I do not believe Diana knows what love is at all.'

'THIS GENTLEMAN ASKS whether Mrs Villiers is at home,' said the Teapot's butler, bringing in a salver with a card upon it.

'Show him into the parlour,' said Diana. She hurried into her bedroom, changed her dress, combed her hair up, looked searchingly into her face in the glass, and went down.

'Good day to you now, Villiers,' said Stephen. 'No man on earth could call you a fast woman. I have read the paper twice through – invasion flotilla, loyal addresses, price of Government stock and list of bankrupts. Here is a bottle of scent.'

'Oh thank you, thank you, Stephen,' she cried, kissing him. 'It is the real Marcillac! Where on earth did you find it?'

'In a Deal smuggler's cottage.'

'What a good, forgiving creature you are, Maturin. Smell – it is like the Moghul's harem. I thought I should never see you again. I am sorry I was so disagreeable in London. How did you find me out? Where are you? What have you been doing? You look very well. I dote upon your blue coat.'

'I come from Mapes. They told me you were here.'

'Did they tell you of my battle with Sophie?'

'I understood there had been a disagreement.'

'She angered me with her mooning about the lake and her tragic airs – if she had wanted him, why did she not have

him when she could? I do loathe and despise want of decision – shilly-shallying. And anyhow, she has a perfectly suitable admirer, an evangelical clergyman full of good works:
good connections too, and plenty of money. I dare say he will
be a bishop. But upon my word, Maturin, I never knew she
had such spirit! She set about me like a tiger, all ablaze; and
I had only quizzed her a little about Jack Aubrey. Such a set-
to! There we were roaring away by the little stone bridge,
with her mare hitched to the post, starting and wincing – oh,
I don't know how long – a good fifteen rounds. How you
would have laughed. We took ourselves so seriously; and
such energy! I was hoarse for a week after. But she was
worse than me – as loud as a hog in a gate; and her words
tumbling over one another, in a most horrid passion. But I
tell you what, Maturin, if you really want to frighten a
woman, offer to slash her across the face with your riding
whip, and look as if you meant it. I was quite glad when my
aunt Williams came up, screeching and hallooing loud
enough to drown the both of us. And for her part she was
just as glad to send me packing, because she was afraid for
the parson; not that I would ever have laid a finger on him,
the greasy oaf. So here I am again, a sort of keeper or upper-
servant to the Teapot. Will you drink some of his honour's
sherry? You are looking quite glum, Maturin. Don't be mumchance, there's a good fellow. I have not said an unkind thing
since you appeared: it is your duty to be gay and amusing.
Though harking back, I was just as pleased to come away
too, with my face intact: it is my fortune, you know. You have
not paid it a single compliment, though I was liberal enough
to you. Reassure me, Maturin – I shall be thirty soon, and I
dare not trust my looking-glass.'

'It is a good face,' said Stephen, looking at it steadily. She
held her head up in the hard cold light of the winter sun and
now for the first time he saw the middle-aged woman: India
had not been kind to her complexion: it was good, but nothing to Sophia's; that faintest of lines by her eyes would reach

out; the hint of drawn strength would grow more pronounced – haggard; in a few years other people would see that Sophie had slashed it deep. He hid his discovery behind all the command and dissimulation that he was master of and went on, 'An astonishing face. A damned good figurehead, as we say in the Navy. And it has launched one ship, at least.'

'A good damned figurehead,' she said bitterly.

'Now for the harrow,' he reflected.

'And after all,' she said, pouring out the wine, 'why do you pursue me like this? I give you no encouragement. I never have. I told you plainly at Bruton Street that I liked you as a friend but had no use for you as a lover. Why do you persecute me? What do you want of me? If you think to gain your point by wearing me out, you have reckoned short; and even if you were to succeed, you would only regret it. You do not know who I am at all; everything proves it.'

'I must go,' he said, getting up.

She was pacing nervously up and down the room. 'Go, then,' she cried, 'and tell your lord and master I never want to see him again, either. He is a coward.'

Mr Lowndes walked into the parlour. He was a tall, stout, cheerful gentleman of about sixty, wearing a flowered silk dressing-gown, breeches unbuckled at the knees, and a tea-cosy in lieu of a wig, or nightcap: he raised the cosy and bowed.

'Dr Maturin – Mr Lowndes,' said Diana, with a quick beseeching look at Stephen – deprecation combined with concern, vexation, and the remains of anger.

'I am very happy to see you, sir, most honoured: I do not believe I have had the pleasure,' said Mr Lowndes, gazing at Stephen with extreme intensity. 'I see from your coat that you are not a mad-doctor, sir. Unless, indeed, this is an innocent deception?'

'Not at all, sir. I am a naval surgeon.'

'Very good – you are *upon* the sea but not *in* it: you are not an advocate for cold baths. The sea, the sea! Where should we be without it? Frizzled to a mere toast, sir; parched, desiccated by the simoom, the dread simoom. Dr Maturin would like a cup of tea, my dear, against the desiccation. I can offer you a superlative cup of tea, sir.'

'Dr Maturin is drinking sherry, Cousin Edward.'

'He would do better to drink a cup of tea,' said Mr Lowndes, with a look of keen disappointment. 'However, I do not presume to dictate to my guests,' he added, hanging down his head.

'I shall be very happy to take a cup of tea, sir, as soon as I have drunk up my wine,' said Stephen.

'Yes, yes!' cried Mr Lowndes, brightening at once. 'And you shall have the pot to take with you on your voyages. Molly, Sue, Diana, pray make it in the little round pot Queen Anne gave my grandmama; it makes the best tea in the house. And while it is making, sir, I will tell you a little poem; you are a literary man, I know,' he said, dancing a few paces and bowing right and left.

The butler brought in the tray, looked sharply from Mr Lowndes to Diana: she shook her head slightly, eased her cousin into a wing-chair, tidied him, tied a napkin round his neck, and, as the spirit-lamp brought the kettle to the boil, measured out the tea and brewed it.

'Now for my poem,' said Mr Lowndes. 'Attend! Attend! *Arma virumque cano*, etc. There, ain't it capital?'

'Admirable, sir. Thank you very much.'

'Ha, ha, ha!' cried Mr Lowndes, cramming his mouth with cake, red with sudden pleasure. 'I knew you were a man of exquisite sensibilities. Take the bun!' He flung a little round cake at Stephen's head, and added, 'I have a turn for verse. Sometimes my fancy runs to Sapphics, sometimes to catalectic Glyconics and Pherecrateans – the Priapic metre, my dear sir. Are you a Grecian? Should you like to hear some of my Priapean odes?'

'In Greek, sir?'

'No, sir, in English.'

'Perhaps at another time, sir, when we are alone – when no ladies are present, it would give me great pleasure.'

'You have noticed that young woman, have you? You are a sharp one. But then you are a young man, sir. I too was a young man. As a physical gentleman, sir, do you really think incest so very undesirable?'

'Cousin Edward, it is time for your bath,' said Diana; but he grew confused and unhappy – he was sure it would not do to let that fellow alone with a valuable teapot, but he was too polite to say so; his oblique references to it as 'the dread simoom' were not understood, and it took her five minutes of coaxing to get him out of the room.

'WHAT NEWS FROM Mapes, shipmate?' asked Jack. 'What? I cannot hear a word with all this screeching and bawling overhead.'

'You are as bad as Parker,' said Jack, and poking his head out of the cabin he called, "Vast heaving the after carronades. Mr Pullings, let these hands reef tops'ls. I said "What news from Mapes?"'

'A miscellaneous bag. I saw Sophie alone: she and Diana have parted brass-rags. Diana is looking after her cousin in Dover. I called on her. She asked us both to dinner on Friday, to eat a dish of Dover soles. I accepted for myself, but said I could not answer for you: you might not find it possible to go ashore.'

'She asked me?' cried Jack. 'Are you sure? What is it, Babbington?'

'I beg your pardon, sir, but the flagship is signalling all captains.'

'Very well. Let me know the moment *Melpomene*'s barge touches the water. Stephen, chuck me my breeches, will you?' He was in working clothes – canvas trousers, a guernsey frock and a frieze jacket – and as he stripped the criss-cross of wounds showed plain: bullets, splinters, cutlasses, a boarding-axe; and the last, a raking thrust from a pike, still showed red about the edges. 'Half an inch to the left – if that pike had gone in half an inch to the left, you would have been a dead man,' observed Stephen.

'My God,' said Jack, 'there are times when I wish – however, I must not whine.' From under his clean white shirt he asked, 'How was Sophie?'

'Low in her spirits. She is subjected to the attentions of a moneyed parson.' No reply. No emergence of the head. He went on, 'I also saw to everything at Melbury: all is well there, though the lawyer's men have been hanging about. Preserved Killick asks may he join the ship? I took it upon myself to say that he should come and ask you himself. You will be happy to have the skilled attendance of Preserved Killick. I reduced my femur at the hospital – the leg may be saved – and wished my dement. on to them, with a slime-draught to make him easy. I also bought your thread, music-paper, and strings: these I found at a shop in Folkstone.'

'Thank you, Stephen. I am very much obliged to you. You must have had a damned long ride of it. Indeed, you look dog-tired, quite done up. Just tie my hair for me, like a good fellow, and then you shall turn in. I must get you an assistant, a surgeon's mate: you work too hard.'

'You have some grey hairs,' said Stephen, tying the yellow queue.

'Do you wonder?' said Jack. He buckled on his sword, sat down on the locker, and said, 'I had almost forgot. I had a pleasant surprise today. Canning came aboard! You remember Canning, that admirable chap I liked so much in town, and who offered me his privateer? He has a couple of merchant-men in the road and he came round from the Nore to see them off. I have asked him to dinner tomorrow; and that reminds me . . .' It reminded him of the fact that he had no money, and that he should like to borrow some. He had drawn three lunar months' pay on joining his ship, but his expenses in Portsmouth – customary presents, vails, a bare minimum of equipment – had swallowed twenty-five guineas and more in a week, quite apart from Stephen's loan. It had not allowed him to lay in stores, and that was another thing that was wrong with the running of the *Polychrest* – he hardly knew his officers except on duty. He had invited Parker and he had dined once with the gun-room during their long calm, tiding up the Channel, but he had barely exchanged half a dozen words with Macdonald or Allen, for example, outside the line of duty; yet they were men upon whom the ship, and his own life and reputation, might depend. Parker and Macdonald had private means and they had entertained him well: he had scarcely entertained them at all. He was not keeping up the dignity of a captain: a captain's dignity depended in some degree upon the state of his store-room – a captain must not look a scrub – and as his silly, talkative, consequential temporary steward kept telling him so officiously, is was empty apart from a hundredweight of orange marmalade, a present from Mrs Babbington. 'Where shall I stow the wine, sir? – What shall I do about the live-stock? – When are the sheep coming? – What does your Honour wish me to do about the hen-coops?' Furthermore, he would soon have to invite the admiral and the other captains of the squadron; and tomorrow there would be Canning. Ordinarily he would have turned at once to Stephen, for although Stephen was an abstemious man, indifferent to money beyond the bare necessities of life, and strangely ill-informed, even unperceptive, about discipline, the finer points of ceremonial, the complexity of the service and the importance of entertaining, he would always give way at once when it was represented to him that tradition called for an outlay. He would produce money from the odd drawers and pots where it lay, disregarded, as though Jack were doing him a particular favour by borrowing it: in other hands he would have been the 'easiest touch' afloat. These reflections darted through Jack's mind as he sat there, stroking the worn lion's head on the pommel of his sword; but something in the atmosphere, some chill or reserve or inward scruple of his own, prevented him from completing his sentence before the *Melpomène*'s barge was reported to be in the water.

This was not a Sunday afternoon, with ship-visiting and liberty boats plying to and fro in the squadron; it was an ordinary working day, with all hands creeping up and down the rigging or exercising at the great guns; nothing but a Dover bumboat and a Deal hoveller came anywhere near the *Polychrest*; and yet long before Jack's return it was known throughout the ship that she was on the wing. Where bound, no one could tell, though many tried (to the westward, to Botany Bay, the Mediterranean to carry presents to the Dey of Algiers and redeem Christian slaves). But the rumour was so strong that Mr Parker cleared her hawse, heaved short, and, with a hideous memory of unmooring at Spithead, sent the crew to their stations for this manoeuvre again and again, until even the dullest could find the capstan and his place on the bar. He received Jack back aboard with a look of discreet but earnest inquiry, and Jack, who had seen his preparations, said, 'No, no, Mr Parker, you may veer away astern; it is not for today. Desire Mr Babbington to come into the cabin, if you please.'

'Mr Babbington,' he said, 'you are in a very repellent state of filth.'

'Yes, sir,' said Babbington, who had spent the first dogwatch in the maintop with two buckets of flush from the galley, showing a framework-knitter, two thatchers (brothers: much given to poaching), and a monoglot Finn how to grease the masts, sheets and running-rigging generally, and who was liberally plastered with condemned butter and skimmings from the coppers in which salt pork had been boiled. 'Beg pardon, sir.'

'Be so good as to scrub yourself from clew to earring, to shave – you may borrow Mr Parslow's razor, I dare say – to put on your best uniform and report back here. My compliments to Mr Parker and you are to take the blue cutter to Dover with Bonden and six reliable men who deserve liberty

until the evening gun. The same to Dr Maturin, and I should
be glad to see him.'

'Aye, aye, sir. Oh thank you, sir.'

He turned to his desk:

> *Polychrest*
> in the Downs
>
> Captain Aubrey presents his best compliments to Mrs
> Villiers and much regrets that duty prevents him from
> accepting her very kind invitation to dine on Friday.
> However, he hopes to have the honour, and the plea-
> sure, of waiting on her when he returns.

'Stephen,' he said, looking up, 'I am writing to decline
Diana's invitation – we are ordered to sea tomorrow night.
Should you wish to add a word or send a message? Babbing-
ton is making our excuses.'

'Let Babbington bear mine by word of mouth, if you please.
I am so glad you are not going ashore. It would have been the
extreme of folly, with the *Polychrest* known to be on the station.'

Babbington came in, shining with cleanliness, in a frilled
shirt and fine white breeches.

'You remember Mrs Villiers?' said Jack.

'Oh *yes*, sir. Besides, I drove her to the ball.'

'She is in Dover, at the house where you called for her –
New Place. Be so good as to give her this note; and I believe
Dr Maturin has a message.'

'Compliments: regrets,' said Stephen.

'Now turn out your pockets,' said Jack.

Babbington's face fell. A little heap of objects appeared,
some partially eaten, and a surprising number of coins – silver, a gold piece. Jack returned fourpence, observing that that
would set him up handsomely in cheesecakes, recommended
him to bring back all his men as he should answer the contrary at his peril, and desired him to 'top his boom'.

'It is the only way of keeping him even passably chaste,' he said to Stephen. 'There are a great many loose women in Dover, I am afraid.'

'I beg your pardon, sir,' said Mr Parker, 'but a man by the name of Killick asks permission to come aboard.'

'Certainly, Mr Parker,' cried Jack. 'He is my steward. There you are, Killick,' he said, coming on deck. 'I am happy to see you. What have you got there?'

'Hampers, sir,' said Killick, pleased to see his captain, but unable to restrain a wondering eye from running up and down the *Polychrest*. 'One from Admiral Haddock. T'other from the ladies up at Mapes, or rather, from Miss Sophie, to speak correct: pig, cheeses, butter, cream, poultry and such, from Mapes; game from next door. Admiral's clearing off his land, sir. There's a prime bold roebuck there, sir, hung this sennight past, and any number of hares and such.'

'Mr Malloch, a whip – no, a double whip to the mainyard. Easy with those hampers, now. What's the third bundle?'

'Another roebuck, sir.'

'Where from?'

'Which it fouled the wheels of the tax-cart I come in and hurt its leg, sir,' said Killick, looking at the flagship in the distance with a kind of mild wonder. 'Just half a mile after the turning to Provender bridge. No, I lie – maybe a furlong closer to Newton Priors. So I put it out of its misery, sir.'

'Ah,' said Jack. 'The Mapes hamper is directed to Dr Maturin, I see.'

'It's all one, sir,' said Killick. 'Miss told me to say the pig weighs twenty-seven and a half pound the quarter, and I am to set the hams to the tub the very minute I come aboard – the souse she put aside in thicky jar, knowing you liked 'un. The white puddings is for the Doctor's breakfast.'

'Very good, Killick, very good indeed,' said Jack. 'Stow 'em away. Handsomely with that buck – don't you bruise him on any account.'

'To think a man's heart could break over a soused hog's

face,' he reflected, feigning to turn over the admiral's game; partridge, pheasant, woodcock, snipe, mallard, wigeon, teal, hares. 'You brought the rest of the wine, Killick?'

'Which the bottles broke, sir: all but half a dozen of the burgundy.'

Jack cocked his eye, sighed, but said nothing. Six bottles would do pretty well, with what was left of his corruption from the yard. 'Mr Parker, Mr Macdonald, I hope you will give me the pleasure of dining in the cabin tomorrow? I am expecting a guest.'

They bowed, smiled, and said they should be very happy; they did indeed feel a real pleasure, for Jack had declined the gunroom's last invitation, and this had created an uneasiness in their minds – an unpleasant beginning to a commission.

Stephen said the same in effect, when he could be brought to understand. 'Yes, yes, certainly, of course – much obliged. I did not grasp your meaning.'

'Yet it was plain enough, in all conscience,' said Jack, 'and adapted to the meanest understanding. I said. "Will you have dinner with me tomorrow? Canning is coming, and I have asked Parker, Macdonald and Pullings." '

'My mind dwells with real concern, and yet with what I might term an *inquisitive*, slightly vulgar concern, upon the state of Mother Williams's heart when she finds her dairy, poultry-yard, pig-house, larder, stripped bare. Will it burst? Will it stop beating altogether? Dry to a total desiccation – no great step? What the effect upon her visceral humours? How will Sophie reply? Will she attempt concealment, prevarication? She lies with as much skill as Preserved Killick – a desperate stare, and her face the most perfect damask rose. My mind, I say, wanders in this region, lost. I have no acquaintance with English family life, with English *female* family life: it is to me a region quite unknown.'

It was not a region in which Jack chose to dwell: with a start of intense pain he jerked his mind away. 'Lord, I love that Sophie so,' he cried within. He took a quick turn on deck, going right forward to pat the gammoning of the bowsprit – a private consolation from his very earliest days at sea. When he came back he said, 'A most damnable unpleasant thought has just struck me. I know I must not give Canning swine's flesh, he being a Jew; but can he eat a buck? Is a buck unclean? And hare would not answer, either, for I dare say they are rated with the coney and her kind.'

'I have no idea. You have no Bible, I suppose?'

'Indeed I have a Bible. I used it to check Heneage's signal – The Lord taketh no pleasure in the strength of an horse, do you remember? What did he mean by that, do you suppose? It was not so very witty, or original; for after all, everyone knows the Lord taketh no pleasure in the strength of an horse. He had crossed his tiller-ropes, I dare say. However, I have also been reading it, these last few days.'

'Ah?'

'Yes. I may preach a sermon to the ship's company next Sunday.'

'You? Preach a sermon?'

'Certainly. Captains often do, when no chaplain is carried. I always made do with the Articles of War in the *Sophie*, but now I think I shall give them a clear, well- reasoned – come, what's the matter? What is so very entertaining about my preaching a sermon? Damn your eyes, Stephen.' Stephen was doubled in his chair, rocking to and fro, uttering harsh spasmodic squeaks: tears ran down his face. 'What a spectacle you are, to be sure. Now I come to think of it, I do not believe I have ever heard you laugh before. It is a damned illiberal row, I can tell you – it don't suit you at all. Squeak, squeak. Very well: you shall laugh your bellyful.' He turned away with something about 'pragmatical apes – simpering, tittering' and affected to look into the Bible without the least concern; but there are not many who can find themselves the object of open, whole-hearted, sincere, prostrating laughter without being put out of countenance, and Jack was not one of these few. However, Stephen's mirth died away in time – a few last

crowing whoops and it was over. He got to his feet, and dab-
bing his face with a handkerchief he took Jack by the hand. 'I
am so sorry,' he said. 'I beg your pardon. I would not have
vexed you for the world. But there is something so essentially
ludicrous, so fundamentally comic . . . that is to say, I had so
droll an association of ideas – pray do not take it personally at
all. Of course you shall preach to the men; I am persuaded it
will have a most striking effect.'

'Well,' said Jack, with a suspicious glance, 'I am glad it
afforded you so much innocent merriment at all events.
Though what you find . . .'

'What is your text, pray?'

'Are you making game of me, Stephen?'

'Never, upon my word: would scorn it.'

'Well, it is the one about I say come and he cometh; for I
am a centurion. I want them to understand it is God's will,
and it must be so – there must be discipline – 'tis in the Book
– and any infernal bastard that disobeys is therefore a blas-
phemer too, and will certainly be damned. That it is no good
kicking against the pricks: which is in the Book too, as I shall
point out.'

'You feel that it will make it easier for them to bear their
station, when they learn that it is providential?'

'Yes, yes, that's it. It is all here, you know' – tapping the
Bible. 'There are an amazing number of useful things in it,'
said Jack, with a candid gaze out of the scuttle. 'I had no idea.
And, by the way, it seems that roebuck is not unclean, which
is a comfort, and a very great one, I can tell you. I was quite
anxious about this dinner.'

The next day brought countless duties – the raking of the
Polychrest's masts, the restowing of what part of her ballast
they could come at, the mending of a chain-pump – but this
anxiety remained, to come into full flower in the last quarter
of an hour before the arrival of his guests. He stood fussing in
his day-cabin, twitching the cloth, teasing the stove until its
colour was cherry-pink, worrying Killick and his attendant

boys, wondering whether after all the table should not have been athwart-ships, and contemplating a last-minute alteration. Could it really seat six in even moderate comfort? The *Polychrest* was a larger vessel than the *Sophie*, his last command, but because of the singularity of her construction the cabin had no stern-gallery, no fine curving sweep of windows to give an impression of light, air and indeed a certain magnificence to even a little room; the actual space was greater and the head-room was such that he could stand with no more than a slight stoop, but this space had no generosity of breadth – it drew out in length, narrowing almost to a point aft, and all that it had in the way of day was a skylight and a couple of small scuttles. Leading forward from this shield-shaped apartment was a short passage, with his sleeping-cabin on one side and his quarter-gallery on the other: it was not a true gallery, a projection, in the *Polychrest* at all, of course, nor was it strictly on her quarter, but it served the purpose of a privy as well as if it had been both. In addition to the necessary pot it contained a thirty-two pounder carronade and a small hanging lantern, in case the bull's eye in the port-lid should not be enough to show the unwary guest the consequences of a false step. Jack looked in to see whether it was burning bright and stepped out into the passage just as the sentry opened the door to admit the midshipman of the watch with the message that 'the gentleman was alongside, if you please, sir.'

As soon as Jack saw Canning come aboard he knew his party would be a success. He was dressed in a plain buff coat, with no attempt at a seafaring appearance, but he came up the side like a good 'un, moving his bulk with a strong, easy agility, judging the roll just so. His cheerful face appeared in the gangway, looking sharply from left to right; then the rest of him, and he stood there, quite filling the space, with his hat off and his bald crown gleaming in the rain.

The first lieutenant received him, led him the three paces to Jack, who shook him very warmly by the hand, performed the necessary introductions, and guided the assembled body into the cabin, for he had little temptation to linger in the icy drizzle and none at all to show the *Polychrest* in her present state, to an eye so keen and knowing as his guest's.

Dinner began quietly enough with a dish of codlings caught over the side that morning and with little in the way of conversation apart from banalities – the weather, of course, inquiries after common acquaintance – 'How was Lady Keith? When last seen? What news of Mrs Villiers? Did Dover suit her? Captain Dundas, was he well, and happy in his new command? Had Mr Canning heard any good music lately? Oh yes! Such a *Figaro* at the Opera, he had gone three times.' Parker, Macdonald and Pullings were mere dead weights, bound by the convention that equated their captain, at his own table, with royalty, and forbade anything but answers to proposals set up by him. However, Stephen had no notion of this convention – he gave them an account of nitrous oxide, the laughing gas, exhilaration in a bottle, philosophic merriment; and it did not apply to Canning at all. Jack worked hard with an easy flow of tiny talk; and presently the dead weight began to move. Canning did not refer to the *Polychrest* (Jack noticed this with a pang, but with gratitude as well) apart from saying that she must be a very interesting ship, with prodigious capabilities, and that he had never seen such paintwork – such elegance and taste – the completest thing – one would have supposed a royal yacht – but he spoke of the service in general with obvious knowledge and deep appreciation. Few sailors can hear sincere, informed praise of the Navy without pleasure, and the reserved atmosphere in the cabin relaxed, warmed, grew positively gay.

The codlings were succeeded by partridges, which Jack carved by the simple process of putting one on each man's plate; the corrupt claret began to go about, the gaiety increased, the conversation became general, and the watch on deck heard the sound of laughter coming from the cabin in a steady flow.

After the partridges came no less than four removes of game, culminating in a saddle of venison borne in by Killick and the gun-room steward on a scrubbed scuttle-hatch with a runnel gouged out for the gravy. 'The burgundy, Killick,' murmured Jack, standing up to carve. They watched him earnestly as he laboured, their talk dying away; and they bent with equal attention to their plates.

'Upon my word, gentlemen,' said Canning, laying down his knife and fork, 'you do yourselves pretty well in the Navy – such a feast! The Mansion House is nothing to it. Captain Aubrey, sir, this is the best venison I have ever tasted in my life: it is a *solemn* dish. And such burgundy! A Musigny, I believe?'

'Chambolles-Musigny, sir, of '85. I am afraid it is a little past its prime: I have just these few bottles left – happily my steward does not care for burgundy. Mr Pullings, a trifle of the brown end?'

It was indeed a most capital buck, tender, juicy, full of savour; Jack set to his own mound with an easy mind at last: more or less everybody was talking – Pullings and Parker explaining Bonaparte's intentions to Canning – the new French gunboats, the ship-rigged prams of the invasion flotilla – and Stephen and Macdonald leaning far over their plates to hear one another, or rather to be heard, in an argument that was still mild enough, but that threatened to grow a little warm.

'Ossian,' said Jack, at a moment when both their mouths were full, 'was he not the gentleman that was quite exploded by Dr Johnson?'

'Not at all, sir,' cried Macdonald, swallowing faster than Stephen. 'Dr Johnson was a respectable man in some ways, no doubt, though in no degree related to the Johnstones of Ballintubber; but for some reason he had conceived a narrow prejudice against Scotland. He had no notion of the sublime, and therefore no appreciation of Ossian.'

'I have never read Ossian myself,' said Jack, 'being no great hand with poetry. But I remember Lady Keith to have said that Dr Johnson raised some mighty cogent objections.'

'Produce your manuscripts,' said Stephen.

'Do you expect a Highland gentleman to produce his manuscripts upon compulsion?' said Macdonald to Stephen, and to Jack, 'Dr Johnson, sir, was capable of very inaccurate statements. He affected to see no trees in his tour of the kingdom: now I have travelled the very same road many times, and I know several trees within a hundred yards of it – ten, or even more. I do not regard him as any authority upon any subject. I appeal to your candour, sir – what do you say to a man who defines the mainsheet as the largest sail in a ship, or to belay as to splice, or a bight as the circumference of a rope? And that in a buke that professes to be a dictionary of the English language? Hoot, toot.'

'Did he indeed say that?' cried Jack. 'I shall never think the same of him again. I have no doubt your Ossian was a very honest fellow.'

'He did, sir, upon my honour,' cried Macdonald, laying his right hand flat upon the table. 'And falsum in uno, falsum in omnibus, I say.'

'Why, yes,' said Jack, who was as well acquainted with old omnibus as any man there present. 'Falsum in omnibus. What do you say to omnibus, Stephen?'

'I concede the victory,' said Stephen smiling. 'Omnibus routs me.'

'A glass of wine with you, Doctor,' said Macdonald.

'Allow me to help you to a little of the underside,' said Jack. 'Killick, the Doctor's plate.'

'More dead men, Joe?' asked the sentry at the door, peering into the basket.

'God love us, how they do stow it away, to be sure,' said Joe, with a chuckle. 'The big cove, the civilian – it's a pleasure to see him eat. And there's figgy-dowdy to come, and woodcocks on toast, and then the punch.'

'You ain't forgotten me, Joe?' said the sentry.

'The bottle with the yellow wax. They'll be singing any minute now.'

The sentry put the bottle to his lips, raised it up and up, wiped his mouth with the back of his hand, and observed, 'Rum stuff they drink in the cabin: like blackstrap, only thinner. How's my gent?'

'You'll carry him to his cot, mate: he's coming along royal, sheets aflowing. Which the same goes for buff waistcoat. A bosun's chair for him.'

'Now, sir,' said Jack to Canning, 'we have a Navy dish that I thought might amuse you. We call it figgy-dowdy. You do not have to eat it, unless you choose – this is Liberty Hall. For my part, I find it settles a meal; but perhaps it is an acquired taste.'

Canning eyed the pale, amorphous, gleaming, slightly translucent mass and asked how it was made; he did not think he had ever seen anything quite like it.

'We take ship's biscuit, put it in a stout canvas bag – ' said Jack.

'Pound it with a marlin-spike for half an hour – ' said Pullings.

'Add bits of pork fat, plums, figs, rum, currants,' said Parker.

'Send it to the galley, and serve it up with bosun's grog,' said Macdonald.

Canning said he would be delighted – a new experience – he had never had the honour of dining aboard a man-of-war – happy to acquire any naval taste. 'And really,' he said, 'it is excellent, quite excellent. And so this is bosun's grog. I believe I must beg for another glass. Capital, capital. I was telling you, sir,' he said, leaning confidentially over towards Jack, 'I was telling you some ten or twenty courses back, that I had heard a wonderful *Figaro* at the Opera. You must run up if you possibly can; there is a new woman, La Colonna, who sings Susanna with a grace and a purity I have never heard in my life – a revelation. She drops true on the middle of her note, and it swells, swells . . . Ottoboni is the Contessa, and their duet would bring tears to your eyes. I forget the words, but you know it, of course.' He hummed, his bass making the glasses tremble.

Jack beat the time with his spoon and struck in with 'Sotto i pini . . .'

They sang it through, then through again; the others gazed at them with a mild, bemused, contemplative satisfaction; at this stage it seemed natural that their captain should personate a Spanish lady's maid, and even, somewhat later, three blind mice.

Before the mice, however, there was an event that confirmed them in their affectionate regard for Mr Canning: the port went round, and, the loyal toast being proposed, Canning leapt to his feet, struck his head against a beam and collapsed into his chair as though pole-axed. They had always known it might happen to some land-soldier or civilian, had never actually seen it, and, since he had done himself no lasting injury, they were enchanted. They comforted him, standing round his chair, dressing the lump with rum, assuring him that it was quite all right – it would soon pass – they often banged their heads – no harm in it – no bones broken. Jack called for the punch, telling the steward in a rapid undertone that a bosun's chair was to be rigged, and administered a tot with a medical air, observing, 'We are privileged to drink the King seated in the Navy, sir; we may do so without the least disrespect. Few people know it however – quite recent – it must seem very strange.'

'Yes. Yes.' said Canning, staring heavily straight at Pullings. 'Yes. I remember now.' Then, as the punch spread new life throughout his vitals he smiled round the table and said, 'What a green hand I must look to all you gentlemen.'

It passed, as they had told him it would, and a little while later he joined them in these mice, the Bay of Biscay-o, Drops of Brandy, the Female Lieutenant, and the catch about the lily-white boys, in which he excelled them all, roaring out.

Three, three the rivals
Two, two the lily-white boys, clothed all in green-o,
But one is one and all alone
And evermore shall be so

ending with a power and a depth that none of them could
reach: Boanerges.

'There is a symbolism there that escapes me,' said Stephen,
his right-hand neighbour, when the confused cheering had
died away.

'Does it not refer to – ' began Canning; but the others had
returned to their mice, all singing in voices calculated to
reach the foretop in an Atlantic gale, all except Parker, that is
to say, who could not tell one tune from another and who
merely opened and closed his mouth with an expression of
polite good-fellowship, in a state of exquisite boredom; and
Canning broke off to join them.

He was still with the mice as he was steered into the
bosun's chair and lowered gently into his boat, still with them
as he was rowed over the sea towards the great dark assembly
of ships under the Goodwin sands; and Jack, leaning over the
rail, heard his voice growing fainter – *see* how they run, *see*
how they run – until at last it turned back to Three, three the
rivals, dying quite away.

'That was as successful a dinner-party as I remember,
afloat,' said Stephen at his side. 'I thank you for my part in it.'

'Do you really think so?' said Jack. 'I was so glad you
enjoyed it. I particularly wished to do Canning well: apart
from anything else, he is a very rich man, and one does not
like the ship to look scrape-farthing. I was sorry to call a halt
so soon, however; but I must have a little light for manoeuvring. Mr Goodridge, Mr Goodridge, how is your tide?'

'She'll be making for another glass, sir.'

'Your fender-men are ready?'

'Ready, all ready, sir.'

The wind was fair, but at slack water they were to unmoor

and pass through the squadron and the convoy: Jack had a mortal dread that the *Polychrest* might foul one of the men-of-war or half the straggling convoy, and he had armed a party with long poles to shove her off.

'Then let us step into your cabin.' When they were below he said, 'You have the charts spread out, I see. I believe you are a Channel pilot, Master?'

'Yes, sir.'

'Just as well: I know the West Indian waters and the Mediterranean better than these. Now I want you to lay the sloop half a mile off Gris Nez at three in the morning, the steeple bearing north fifty-seven east and the tower on the cliff south sixty-three east.'

TOWARDS FOUR BELLS in the middle watch Jack came on deck: the *Polychrest* was lying to under foretopsail and mizzen, bowing the swell with her odd nervous lift and jerk. The night was still sharp and clear, bright moonlight, and eastwards a pale host of stars – Altair rising over the dark mass of Cap Gris Nez under the starboard quarter.

And the wind was still this same nipping breeze out of the north-west. But far over on the larboard bow trouble was brewing: no stars above Castor and Pollux, and the moon was sinking towards a black bar right across the horizon. With a falling glass this might mean a blow from the same quarter – an uncomfortable position, with the shore so close under his lee. 'I wish it were over,' he said, beginning his ritual pace. His orders required him to be off the headland at three in the morning, to fire a blue light, and to receive a passenger from a boat that should answer his hail with the word *Bourbon*: he was then to proceed with all possible dispatch to Dover. If no boat appeared or if he were driven off his station by stress of weather, then he was to repeat the operation on the three succeeding nights, remaining out of sight by day.

This was Pullings' watch, but the master was also on deck, standing over by the break of the quarterdeck, keeping an

eye on his landmarks, while the quiet business of the ship
went on. From time to time Pullings trimmed the sails to
keep them exactly balanced; the carpenter's mate reported
the depth of water in the well – eighteen inches, which was
more than was right; the master-at-arms made his rounds;
the glass turned, the bell rang, the sentinels called 'All's well'
from their various posts, the look-outs and the helm were
relieved. The watch took a turn at the pumps; and all the
while the breeze hummed through the rigging, the sum of
the notes rising and falling through a full tone as the ship
rolled, her masts straining their shrouds and braces now this
side, now that.

'Look out afore, there,' called Pullings.

'Aye-aye, thir,' came the distant voice. Bolton, one of the
men pressed from the Indiaman, a glowering, surly, murderous brute with no front teeth – yellow fangs each side of a
lisping gap; but a good seaman. Jack held his watch to the
moonlight: still a long time to go, and now the dark bar in the
north-west had swallowed up Capella. He was thinking of
sending a couple of men to the mast-head when the look-out
hailed. 'Upon deck, thir. Boat on the thtarboard quarter.'

He reached up into the shrouds and swung himself to the
rail, searching the dark sea. Nothing. 'Where away?' he
called.

'Right on the quarter. Maybe half a point off now. Pulling
like hell, three of a thide.'

He caught sight of her as she crossed the path of the moon.
About a mile away: very long, very low, very narrow, more like
a line on the water: travelling fast towards the land. This was
not his boat – wrong shape, wrong time, wrong direction.

'What do you make of her, Mr Goodridge?' he asked.

'Why, sir, she's one of those Deal shells – death-or-money
boats, they call 'em, or guinea-boats as some say; and by the
look of her, she's got a main heavy cargo aboard. They must
have seen a revenue cutter or a cruiser early on, for now
they've got to pull against the ebb, and it runs cruel hard off

the point. Do you mean to snap her up, sir? It's now or never with the race off the headland. What a bit of luck.'

He had not seen one before, but he knew them by reputation, of course: they were more like racing-craft for a quiet river than anything built to face a sea – every notion of safety sacrificed to speed; but the profit on smuggling gold was so great that the Deal men would take them clean across the Channel. They could run away from anything, pulling into the eye of the wind, and although the men were sometimes drowned, they were very rarely caught. Unless, as it might fall out, they chanced to be right under the lee of a pursuer, hampered by a swift tide, and tired out by their long pull. Or if they ran straight into a waiting man-of-war.

Gold packed very small: there might be five or six hundred pounds for him in that frail shell, as well as seven prime hands, the best seamen on the coast – lawful prize, for their protections would be of no sort of use to them whatsoever now. He had the weather-gage. He had but to fill his foretopsail, pay round, set everything she could carry, and bear down. To run from him she would have to pull dead against the tide, and they would not be able to keep that up for long. Twenty minutes: perhaps half an hour. Yes, but then he would have to beat back again to his station; and he knew the *Polychrest*'s powers in that direction, alas.

'There's the best part of an hour to go before three, sir,' said the master at his side. Jack held up his watch again; the master-at-arms held his lantern to light it; the listening quarterdeck fell unnaturally silent. They were all seamen aft, but by now even the framework-knitter in the waist knew what was afoot.

'I only make it seven minutes past, sir,' said the master.

No. It would not do. 'Mind your helm,' snapped Jack as the *Polychrest* yawed a full point to starboard. 'Mr Pullings, check the blue lights,' he said, and resumed his pacing. For the first five minutes it was hard to bear: every time he reached the taffrail there was that boat, drawing in nearer and nearer to the land, but still in extreme danger. After his twentieth turn she had crossed the invisible line into safety: the sloop could no longer cut her off – he could no longer change his mind.

Five bells: he checked their position, bringing the bearing-compass on to the steeple and the tower. The dirty weather in the north-west was skirting the Great Bear now. Six bells, and the blue light soared up, burst, and drifted away to leeward, lighting all their upturned faces with an unnatural emphasis – open mouths, mindless wonder.

'Mr Pullings, be so good as to send a reliable man into the top with a night-glass,' said Jack. And five minutes later, 'Maintop, there. What do you see? Any boat pulling from under the land?'

A pause. 'Nothing, sir. I got the line of surf in my glass, and nothing ain't pulled off yet.'

Seven bells. Three well-lit ships passed out at sea, running down the Channel – neutrals, of course. Eight bells, and the changing watch found the *Polychrest* still there. 'Take her out into the offing, Mr Parker,' said Jack. 'Sink the land entirely, making as little southing as ever you can. We must be here again tomorrow night.'

But the *Polychrest* spent tomorrow night on the other side of the Channel, lying to under Oungeness, shipping such seas that Jack thought he should have to run for the shelter of the Isle of Wight, and report back to the admiral with his tail between his legs, his mission unaccomplished; but the wind chopped round westwards at dawn, and the sloop, pumping hard, began to creep back under close-reefed topsails across the angry water – a sea so short and steep that she proceeded by sickening and often unpredictable jerks, and in the gun-room no amount of fiddles or ingenuity on the parts of the diners would keep their food on the table.

The purser's place was empty, as it usually was as soon as the first reef was taken in; and Pullings was dozing as he sat.

'You do not suffer from the sea-sickness, sir?' said Stephen to Macdonald.

'Why, no, sir. But then I come from the Western Isles, and we are in boats as soon as we are breeched.'

'The Western Isles . . . The Western Isles. There was a Lord of the Isles — of your family, I presume, sir?' — Macdonald bowed. 'And that always seemed to me the most romantic title that ever was. We, indeed, have our White Knight, and the Knight of the Glen, the O'Connor Don, the McCarthy Mor, O'Sionnach the Fox, and so on; but the Lord of the Isles . . . it gives a feeling of indeterminate magnificence. That reminds me: I had the strangest impression today — an impression of time recovered. Two of your men, both by the name of Macrea, I believe, were speaking privately, furbishing their equipment with one piece of pipeclay between them as I stood near them — nothing of any consequence, you understand, just small disagreement about the pipeclay, the first desiring the second to kiss his arse and the second wishing the soul of the first to the Devil and a good deal more to the same effect. And I understood directly, without the least thought or conscious effort of will!'

'You have the Gaelic, sir?' cried Macdonald.

'No, sir,' said Stephen, 'and that is what is so curious. I no longer speak it; I thought I no longer understood it. And yet there at once, with no volition on my part, there was complete understanding. I had no idea the Erse and the Irish were so close; I had imagined the dialects had moved far apart. Pray, is there a mutual understanding between your Hebrideans and the Highlanders on the one, and let us say the native Ulstermen on the other?'

'Why, yes, sir; there is. They converse tolerably well, on general subjects, on boats, fishing, and bawdy. There are some different words, to be sure, and great differences of intonation, but with perseverance and repetition they can make themselves understood very well — a tolerably free communication. There are some Irishmen among the pressed hands, and I have heard them and my marines speaking together.'

'If I had heard them, they would be on the defaulters' list,' said Parker, who had come below, dripping like a Newfoundland dog.

'Why is this?' asked Stephen.

'Irish is forbidden in the Navy,' said Parker. 'It is prejudicial to discipline; a secret language is calculated to foment mutiny.'

'Another roll like that, and we shall have no masts,' said Pullings, as the remaining crockery, the glasses and the inhabitants of the gun-room all shot over to the lee. 'We'll lose the mizzen first, Doctor,' – picking Stephen tenderly out of the wreckage – 'and so we'll be a brig; then we'll lose the foremast, so we'll be a right little old sloop; then we'll lose the main, and we'll be a raft, which is what we ought to have begun as.' By some miracle of dexterity Macdonald had seized, and preserved, the decanter; holding it up he said, 'If you can find a whole glass, Doctor, I should be happy to drink a wee doodly of wine with you, and to lead your mind back to the subject of Ossian. From the obliging way in which you spoke of my ancestor, it is clear that you have a fine delicate notion of the sublime; and sublimity, sir, is the greatest internal evidence of Ossian's authenticity. Allow me to recite you a short description of the dawn.'

ONCE AGAIN the blue light shone down on the deck of the *Polychrest* and the uplifted faces of the watch; but this time it drifted off to the north-east, for the wind had come right round, bringing a thin rain and the promise of more, and this time it was almost instantly answered by musketry on the shore – red points of flame and a remote pop-pop-pop.

'Boat pulling off, sir,' called the man in the top. And two minutes later, 'On deck, on deck there! Another boat, sir. Firing on the first one.'

'All hands to make sail,' cried Jack, and the *Polychrest* woke to urgent life. 'Fo'c'sle, there; cast loose two and four. Mr Rolfe, fire on the second boat as I run inshore. Fire the moment they bear – full elevation. Mr Parker, tops'ls and courses.' They were half a mile off, well out of range of his carronades, but if only he could get under way he would soon shorten it. Oh, for just one long gun, a chaser . . .

The supplementary orders came thick and fast, a continuous, repetitive, exasperated clamour. 'Lay aloft, jump to it, trice up, lay out, lay out – will you lay out there on the maintops'lyard? Let fall, God damn your – eyes, let fall, mizzen tops'l. Sheet home. Hoist with a will, now, hoist away.'

Christ, it was agony: it might have been an undermanned merchantman, a dung-scow in pandemonium: he clasped his hands behind his back and stepped to the rail to prevent himself running forward to sort out the confused bellowing on the fo'c'sle. The boats were coming straight for him, the second firing two or three muskets and a spatter of pistols.

At last the bosun piped belay and the *Polychrest* began to surge forward, lying over to the wind. Keeping his eye on the advancing boats he said, 'Mr Goodridge, lay her in to give the gunner a clear shot. Mr Macdonald, your marksmen into the top – fire at the second boat.'

Now the sloop was really moving, opening the angle between the two boats: but at the same time the first boat began to turn towards her, shielding its pursuer from his fire. 'The boat ahoy,' he roared. 'Steer clear of my stern – pull a-starboard.'

Whether they heard, whether they understood or no, a gap appeared between the boats. The forward carronades went off – a deep crash and a long tongue of flame. He did not see the fall of the shot, but it had no effect on the following boat, which kept up its excited fire. Again, and this time he caught it, a split-second plume in the grey, well short, but in the right direction. The first musket cracked out overhead, followed by three or four together. A carronade again, and this time the ball was pitched well up to the second boat, for the *Polychrest* had moved two or three hundred yards: it must have ricocheted over their heads, for it damped their ardour. They came on still, but at the next shot the pursuing boat spun round, fired a last wanton musket and pulled fast out of range.

'Heave her to, Mr Goodridge,' said Jack. 'Back the mizzen tops'l. The boat, ahoy! What boat?' There was a gabbling out there on the water, fifty yards away. 'What boat?' he hailed again, leaning far over the rail, the rain driving in on his face.

'Bourbon,' came a faint cry, followed by a strong shout, 'Bourbon' again.

'Pull under my lee,' said Jack. The way was off the *Polychrest*, and she lay there pitching and groaning. The boat touched alongside, hooked to the mainchains, and in the glow of the battle-lanterns he saw a body crumpled in the stern-sheets.

'Le monsieur est touché,' said the man with the boathook.

'Is he badly hurt – mauvaisement blessay?'

'Sais pas, commandant. Il parle plus: je crois bien que c'est un macchabée à présent. Y a du sang partout. Vous voulez pas me faire passer une élingue, commandant?'

'Eh? Parlez – pass the word for the Doctor.'

It was not until they had got his patient into Jack's cabin that Stephen saw his face. Jean Anquetil, a nervous, timid-brave, procrastinating, unlucky young man: and he was bleeding to death. The bullet had nicked his aorta, and there was nothing, nothing he could do: the blood was pumping out in great throbs.

'It will be over in a few minutes,' he said, turning to Jack.

'AND SO, SIR, he died within minutes of being brought aboard,' said Jack.

Admiral Harte grunted. He said, 'That is everything he had on him?'

'Yes, sir. Greatcoat, boots, clothes and papers: they are very bloody, I am afraid.'

'Well, that is a matter for the Admiralty. But what about this death-or-money boat?'

So that was the reason for his ill-humour. 'I sighted the boat when I was on my station, sir; there were fifty-three minutes to go before the rendezvous, and if I had borne down I must necessarily have been late – I could never have beaten back in time. You know what the *Polychrest* is on a bowline, sir.'

'And you know the tag about workmen and their tools, Captain Aubrey. Anyhow, there is such a thing as being too scrupulous by half. The fellow was never at the rendezvous at all: these foreigners never are. And in any case, half an hour or so . . . and it positively could not have been more, even with a crew of old women. Are you aware, sir, that *Amethyst*'s boats picked up that Deal bugger as he was running into Ambleteuse with eleven hundred guineas aboard? It makes me mad to think of it . . . made a cock of the whole thing.' He drummed his fingers on the table. The *Amethyst* was cruising under Admiralty orders, Jack reflected; the flag-officer had no share in her prize-money; Harte had lost about a hundred and fifty pounds; he was not pleased. 'However,' went on the admiral, 'it is no use crying over spilt milk. As soon as the wind gets out of the south, I am taking the convoy down. You will wait here for the Guinea-men to join, and the ships in the list Spalding will give you: you are to escort them as far as the Rock of Lisbon, and I have no doubt on your way back you will make good this little mess. Spalding will give you your orders: you will find no cast-iron rigid rendezvous.'

By morning the wind had shifted into the west-north-west, and the blue peter broke out at a hundred foretopmastheads: boats by the score hurried merchant captains, mates, passengers and their relatives from Sandwich, Walmer, Deal and even Dover, and many a cruel extortionate bargain was struck when the flagship's signals, reinforced by insistent guns, made it clear that time was short, that this time was the true departure. Towards eleven o'clock the whole body, apart from those that had fallen foul of one another, was under way in three straggling divisions, or rather heaps. Orderly or disorderly, however, they made a splendid sight, white sails stretching over four or five miles of grey sea, and the high, torn sky sometimes as grey as the one or as white as the other. An impressive illustration of the enormous importance of trade to the island, too; one that might have served the *Polychrest*'s midshipmen as a lesson in political economy and on the powers of the average seaman at evading the press – there were some thousands of them there, sailing unscathed from the very heart of the Impress Service.

But they, in common with the rest of the ship's company, were witnessing punishment. The grating was rigged, the bosun's mates stood by, the master-at-arms brought up his delinquents, a long tally charged with drunkenness – gin had been coming aboard from the bum-boats, as it always did – contempt, neglect of duty, smoking tobacco outside the galley, playing dice, theft. On these occasions Jack always felt gloomy, displeased with everybody aboard, innocent and guilty alike: he looked tall, cold, withdrawn, and, to those under his power, his nearly absolute power, horribly savage, a right hard horse. This was early in the commission and he had to establish an unquestioning discipline; he had to support his officers' authority. At the same time he had to steer fine between self-defeating harshness and (although indeed some of these charges were trivial enough, in spite of his words with Parker) fatal softness; and he had to do so without really knowing three quarters of his men. It was a difficult task, and his face grew more and more lowering. He imposed extra duties, cut grog for three days, a week, a fortnight, awarded four men six lashes apiece, one nine, and the thief a dozen. It was not much, as flogging went; but in the old *Sophie* they had sometimes gone two months and more without bringing the cat out of its red baize bag: it was not much, but even so it made quite a ceremony, with the relevant Articles of War read out, the drum-roll, and the gravity of a hundred men assembled.

The swabbers cleaned up the mess, and Stephen went below to patch or anoint the men who had been flogged –

those, that is to say, who reported to him. The seamen put on their shirts again and went about their business, trusting to dinner and grog to set them right: the landsmen who had not been beaten navy-fashion before were much more affected – quite knocked up; and the thieves' cat had made an ugly mess of thief Carlow's back, the bosun's mate being first cousin to the man he robbed.

He came on deck again shortly before the men were piped to dinner, and seeing the first lieutenant walking up and down looking pleased with himself, he said to him, 'Mr Parker, will you indulge me in the use of a small boat in let us say an hour? I could wish to walk upon the Goodwin sands at low tide. The sea is calm; the day propitious.'

'Certainly, Doctor,' said the first lieutenant, always good-humoured after a flogging. 'You shall have the blue cutter. But will you not miss your dinner?'

'I shall take some bread, and a piece of meat.' So he paced this strange, absolute and silent landscape of firm damp sand with rivulets running to its edges and the lapping sea, eating bread with one hand and cold beef with the other. He was so low to the sea that Deal and its coast were out of sight; he was surrounded by an unbroken disc of quiet grey sea, and even the boat, which lay off an inlet at the far rim of the sand, seemed a great way off, or rather upon another plane. Sand stretched before him, gently undulating, with here and there the black half-buried carcasses of wrecks, some massive, others ribbed skeletons, in a kind of order whose sense escaped him, but which he might seize, he thought, if only his mind would make a certain shift, as simple as starting the alphabet at X – simple, if only he could catch the first clue. A different air, a different light, a sense of overwhelming permanence and therefore a different time; it was not at all unlike a certain laudanum-state. Wave ripples on the sand: the traces of annelids, solens, clams: a distant flight of dunlins, close-packed, flying fast, all wheeling together and changing colour as they wheeled.

His domain grew larger with the ebbing of the tide; fresh sand pits appeared, stretching far, far away to the north under the cold even light; islands joined one another, gleaming water disappeared, and only on the far rim of his world was there the least noise – the lap of small waves, and the remote scream of gulls.

It grew smaller, insensibly diminishing grain by grain; everywhere there was a secret drawing-in, apparent only in the widening channels between the sandbanks, where the water was now running frankly from the sea.

The boat's crew had been contentedly fishing for dabs all this time, and they had filled two moderate baskets with their catch.

'There's the Doctor,' said Nehemiah Lee, 'a-waving of his arms. Is he talking to hisself, or does he mean to hail us?'

'He's a-talking to hisself,' said John Lakes, an old Sophie. 'He often does. He's a very learned cove.'

'He'll get cut off, if he don't mind out,' said Arthur Simmons, an elderly, cross-grained forecastleman. 'He looks fair mazed, to me. Little better than a foreigner.'

'You can stow that, Art Simmons,' said Plaice. 'Or I'll stop your gob.'

'You and who to help you?' asked Simmons, moving his face close to his shipmate's.

'Ain't you got no respect for learning?' said Plaice. 'Four books at once I seen him read. Nay, with these very eyes, here in my head,' – pointing to them – 'I seen him whip a man's skull off, rouse out his brains, set 'em to rights, stow 'em back again, clap on a silver plate, and sew up his scalp, which it was drooling over one ear, obscuring his dial, with a flat-seam needle and a pegging-awl, as neat as the sail-maker of a King's yacht.'

'And when did you bury the poor bugger?' asked Simmons, with an offensive knowingness.

'Which he's walking the deck of a seventy-four at this very moment, you fat slob,' cried Plaice. 'Mr Day, gunner of the

Elephant, by name, better than new, and promoted. So you can stuff that up your arse, Art Simmons. Learning? Why, I seen him sew on a man's arm when it was hanging by a thread, passing remarks in Greek.'

'And my parts,' said Lakey, looking modestly at the gunwale.

'I remember the way he set about old Parker when he gagged that poor bugger in the larboard watch,' said Abraham Bates. 'Those was learned words: even I couldn't understand above the half of 'em.'

'Well,' said Simmons, vexed by their devotion, that deeply irritating quality, 'he's lost his boots now, for all his learning.'

This was true. Stephen retracted his footsteps towards the stump of a mast protruding from the sand where he had left his boots and stockings, and to his concern he found that these prints emerged fresh and clear directly from the sea. No boots: only spreading water, and one stocking afloat in a little scum a hundred yards away. He reflected for a while upon the phenomenon of the tide, gradually bringing his mind to the surface, and then he deliberately took off his wig, his coat, his neckcloth and his waistcoat.

'Oh dear, oh dear,' cried Plaice. 'He's a-taking off his coat. We should never have let him off alone on those — — sands. Mr Babbington said "Do not let him go a-wandering on them – – sands, Plaice, or I'll have the hide off your – back". Ahoy! The Doctor ahoy, sir! Come on, mates, stretch out, now. Ahoy, there!'

Stephen took off his shirt, his drawers, his catskin comforter, and walked straight into the sea, clenching his mouth and looking fixedly at what he took to be the stump of mast under the pellucid surface. They were valuable boots, soled with lead, and he was attached to them. In the back of his mind he heard the roaring desperate hails, but he paid no attention: arrived at a given depth, he seized his nose with one hand, and plunged.

A boathook caught his ankle, an oar struck the nape of his

neck, partly stunning him and driving his face deep into the
sand at the bottom: his foot emerged, and he was seized and
hauled into the boat, still grasping his boots.

They were furious. 'Did he not know he might catch cold?
– Why did he not answer their hail? It was no good his telling
them he had not heard; they knew better; he had not got flannel ears – Why had he not waited for them? – What was a
boat for? – Was this a proper time to go a-swimming? – Did
he think this was midsummer? Or Lammas? – He was to see
how cold he was, blue and trembling like a fucking jelly. –
Would a new-joined ship's boy have done such a wicked
thing? No, sir, he would not. – What would the skipper, what
would Mr Pullings and Mr Babbington say, when they heard
of his capers? – As God loved them, they had never seen anything so foolish: He might strike them blind, else. – Where
had he left his intellectuals? Aboard the sloop?' They dried
him with handkerchiefs, dressed him by force, and rowed
him quickly back to the *Polychrest*. He was to go below
directly, turn in between blankets – no sheets, mind – with a
pint of grog and have a good sweat. He was to go up the side
now, like a Christian, and nobody would notice. Plaice and
Lakey were perhaps the strongest men in the ship, with arms
like gorillas; they thrust him aboard and hurried him to his
cabin without so much as by your leave, and left him there in
the charge of his servant, with recommendations for his present care.

'Is all well, Doctor?' asked Pullings looking in with an anxious face.

'Why, yes, I thank you, Mr Pullings. Why do you ask?'

'Well, sir, seeing your wig was shipped arsy-versy and your
comforter all ends up, I thought may be you had had a misfortune, like.'

'Oh, no: not at all, I am obliged to you. I recovered them
none the worse – I flatter myself there is not such a pair in
the kingdom. The very best Cordova ass's leather. *They* will
not suffer from a thoughtless hour's immersion. Pray, what

was all the ceremony as I came into the ship?'

'It was for the Captain. He was only a little way behind you – came aboard not five minutes ago.'

'Ah? I was not aware he had been out of the ship.'

JACK WAS OBVIOUSLY in high spirits. 'I trust I do not disturb you,' he said. 'I said to Killick, "Do not disturb him on any account, if he is busy." But I thought that with such a damned unpleasant night outside, and the stove drawing so well in, that we might have some music. But first take a sup of this madeira and tell me what you think of it. Canning sent me a whole anker – so good-natured of him. I find it wonderfully grateful to the palate. Eh?'

Stephen had identified the smell that hung about Jack's person and that wafted towards him as he passed the wine. It was the French scent he had bought in Deal. He put down his glass composedly and said, 'You must excuse me this evening, I am not quite well, and I believe I shall turn in.'

'My dear fellow, I am so sorry,' cried Jack, with a look of concern. 'I do hope you have not caught a chill. Was there any truth in that nonsense they were telling me, about your swimming off the sands? You must certainly turn in at once. Should you not take physic? Allow me to mix you a strong . . .'

SHUT FIRMLY in his cabin, Stephen wrote. 'It is unspeakably childish to be upset by a whiff of scent; but I am upset, and I shall certainly exceed my allowance, to the extent of five hundred drops.' He poured himself out a wineglassful of laudanum, closed one eye, and drank it off. 'Smell is of all senses by far the most evocative: perhaps because we have no vocabulary for it – nothing but a few poverty-stricken approximations to describe the whole vast complexity of odour – and therefore the scent, unnamed and unnamable, remains pure of association; it cannot be called upon again and again, and blunted, by the use of a word; and so it strikes afresh every time, bringing with it all the circumstances of its first perception. This is particularly true when a considerable period of time has elapsed. The whiff, the gust, of which I speak brought me the Diana of the St Vincent ball, vividly alive, exactly as I knew her then, with none of the vulgarity or loss of looks I see today. As for that loss, that very trifling loss, I applaud it and wish it may continue. She will always have that quality of being more intensely alive, that spirit, dash and courage, that almost ludicrous, infinitely touching unstudied unconscious grace. But if, as she says, her face is her fortune, then she is no longer Croesus; her wealth is diminishing; it will continue to diminish, by her standard, and even before her fatal thirtieth year it may reach a level at which I am no longer an object of contempt. That, at all events, is my only hope; and hope I must. The vulgarity is new, and it is painful beyond my power of words to express: there was the appearance of it before, even at that very ball, but *then* it was either factious or the outcome of the received notions of her kind – the reflected vulgarity of others; *now* it is not. The result of her hatred for Sophia, perhaps? Or is that too simple? If it grows, will it destroy her grace? Shall I one day find her making postures, moving with artful negligence? That would destroy me. Vulgarity: how far am I answerable for it? In a relationship of this kind each makes the other, to some extent. No man could give her more opportunity for exercising all her worst side than I. But there is far, far more to mutual destruction than that. I am reminded of the purser, though the link is tenuous enough. Before we reached the Downs he came to me in great secrecy and asked me for an antaphrodisiac.

'*Purser Jones*: I am a married man, Doctor.

'*SM*: Yes.

'*Jones*: But Mrs J is a very religious woman, is a very virtuous woman; and she don't like it.

'*SM*: I am concerned to hear it.

'*Jones*: Her mind is not given that way, sir. It is not that she is not fond and loving, and dutiful, and handsome – everything a man could wish. But there you are: I am a very full-blooded man, Doctor. I am only thirty-five, though you might not think it, bald and pot-bellied and cetera and cetera. Sometimes I toss and turn all night, and burn, as the Epistle says; but it is to no purpose, and sometimes I am afraid I will do her a mischief, it is so . . . That is why I went to sea, sir; though I am not suited for a naval life, as you know all too well.

'*SM*: This is very bad, Mr Jones. Do you represent to Mrs Jones that . . .

'*Jones*: Oh, I do, sir. And she cries and vows she will be a better wife to me – hers is not an ungrateful mind, she says – and so, for a day or two, she turns to me. But it is all duty, sir, all duty. And in a little while it is the same again. A man cannot still be asking; and what you ask for is not given free – it is never the same – no more like than chalk and cheese. A man cannot make a whore of his own wife.

'He was pale and sweating, pitiably earnest; said he was always glad to sail away, although he hated the sea; that she was coming round to Deal to meet him; that as there were drugs that promoted venereal desire, so he hoped there might be some that took it away and that I should prescribe it for him, so that they could be sweethearts. He swore "he should rather be cut" than go on like this, and he repeated that "a man could not make a whore of his own wife." '

SOME DAYS LATER the diary continued: 'Since Wednesday JA has been his own master; and I believe he is abusing his position. As I understand it, the convoy was complete yesterday, if not before: the masters came aboard for their instructions, the wind was fair and the tide served; but the sailing was put off. He takes insensate risks, going ashore, and any observation of mine has the appearance of bad faith. This morning the devil suggested to me that I should have him laid by the heels; I could so with no difficulty at all. He presented the suggestion with a wealth of good reasons, mostly of an

altruistic nature, and mentioned both honour and duty; I
wonder he did not add patriotism. To some extent JA is aware
of my feelings, and when he brought her renewed invitation
to dinner he spoke of "happening to run into her again", and
expatiated on the coincidence in a way that made me feel a
surge of affection for him in spite of my animal jealousy. He is
the most inept liar and the most penetrable, with his deep,
involved, long-winded policy, that I have ever met. The dinner was agreeable; I find that given warning I can support
more than I had supposed. We spoke companionably of former times, ate very well, and played – the cousin is one of the
most accomplished flautists I have heard. I know little of DV,
but it appears to me that her sense of hospitality (she is wonderfully generous) overcame all her more turbid feelings; I
also think she has a kind of affection for the both of us;
although in that case, how she can ask so much of JA passes
my understanding. She showed at her best; it was a delightful
evening; but how I long for tomorrow and a fair wind. If it
comes round into the south – if he is windbound for a week
or ten days, he is lost: he must be taken.'

9

THE *POLYCHREST* LEFT her convoy in 380 30' N.,
110 W., with the wind at south-west and the Rock of
Lisbon bearing S87E., 47 leagues. She fired a gun,
exchanged signals with the merchantmen, and wore laboriously round until the wind was on her larboard quarter and
her head was pointing north.

The signals were polite, but brief; they wished one another
a prosperous voyage and so parted company, with none of
those long, often inaccurate hoists that some grateful convoys
would keep flying until they were hidden by the convexity of
the earthly sphere. And although the previous day had been

fine and calm, with an easy swell and warm variable airs from the west and south, the merchant captains had not invited the King's officers to dinner: it was not a grateful convoy, and in fact it had nothing to be grateful for. The *Polychrest* had delayed their departure, so that they had missed their tide and the best part of a favourable breeze, and had held them back in their sailing all the way, not only by her slowness, but by her inveterate sagging to leeward, so that they were all perpetually having to bear up for her, they being a weatherly set of ships. She had fallen aboard the *Trade's Increase* by night, when they were lying-to off the Lizard, and had carried away her bowsprit; and when they met with a strong south-wester in the Bay of Biscay she rolled her mizzenmast out. Her maintopmast had gone with it and they had been obliged to stand by while she set up a jury-rig. Nothing had appeared to threaten their security, not so much as a lugger on the horizon, and the *Polychrest* had had no occasion to protect them or to show what teeth she might possess. They turned from her with loathing, and pursued their voyage at their own far brisker pace, setting topgallants and royals at last.

But the *Polychrest* had little time for attending to the convoy as it disappeared, for this was Thursday, and the people were to be mustered. Scarcely had she steadied on her new course before five bells in the forenoon watch struck and the drum began to beat: the crew came hurrying aft and stood in a cluster abaft the mainmast on the larboard side. They had all been aboard some time now, and they had been mustered again and again; but some were still so stupid that they had to be shoved into place by their mates. However, by this time they were all decently dressed in the purser's blue shirts and white trousers; none showed the ghastly pallor of gaol or/seasickness any more, and indeed the enforced cleanliness, the sea-air and the recent sun had given most the appearance of health. The food might have done something, too, for it was at least as good as that which many of them had been eating, and more plentiful.

The first part of the alphabet happened to contain most of the *Polychrest's* seamen. There were some awkward brutes among them, such as that gap-toothed Bolton, but most were the right strong-faced long-armed bow-legged pigtailed sort; they called out 'Here, sir' to their names, touching their foreheads and walking cheerfully past their captain to the starboard gangway. They gave that part of the ship something of the air of the *Sophie*, an efficient, happy ship, if ever there was one, where even the waisters could hand, reef and steer . . . how fortunate he had been in his lieutenant. But Lord, how few the seamen were! After the letter G there were hardly more than two among all the names that were called. Poor meagre little creatures for the most part little stouter than the boys. And either surly or apprehensive or both: not a smile as they answered their names and crossed over. There had been too much flogging, too much starting: but what else could you do in an emergency? Oldfield, Parsons, Pond, Quayle . . . sad little objects; the last much given to informing; had been turned out of his mess twice already. And they were not the bottom of the barrel.

Eighty-seven men and boys, no more, for he was still thirty-three short of his complement. Perhaps thirty of them knew their duty, and some were learning; indeed, most had learnt a little, and there were no longer the scenes of total incompetence that had made a nightmare of the earliest days. He knew all these faces now; some had improved almost out of recognition; some had deteriorated – too much unfamiliar misery; dull minds unused to learning yet forced to learn a difficult trade in a driving hurry. Three categories: a top quarter of good sound able hands; then the vague middle half that might go up or might go down, according to the atmosphere of the ship and how they were handled; and then the bottom quarter, with some hard cases among them, brutal, or stupid, or even downright wicked. As the last names were called his heart sank farther: Wright, Wilson and Young were the very bottom. Men like them were to be found aboard most men-of-war in a time of hot press, and an established ship's company could wear a certain number without much harm. But the *Polychrest*'s was not an established ship's company; and in any case the proportion was far too high.

The clerk closed the book, the first lieutenant reported the muster complete, and Jack gave them a last look before sending them to their tasks: a thoughtful look, for these were the men he might have to lead on to the deck of a French man-of-war tomorrow. How many would follow him?

'Well, well,' he thought, 'one thing at a time,' and he turned with relief to the problem in hand, to the new-rigging of the *Polychrest*. It would be complicated enough in all conscience, with her strange hull and the calculation of the forces acting upon it, but in comparison with the task of making a crew of man-of-war's men out of the rag, tag, and bobtail from G to Y it was as simple and direct as kiss my hand. And here he was seconded by good officers: Mr Gray, the carpenter, knew his trade thoroughly; the bosun, though still too free with his cane, was active, willing and competent where rigging was concerned; and the master had a fine sense of a ship's nature. In theory, Admiralty regulations forbade Jack to shift so much as his backstays, but Biscay had shifted them for him, and a good deal more besides; he had a free hand, fine calm weather, a long day before him, and he meant to make the most of it.

For form's sake he invited Parker to join their deliberations, but the first lieutenant was more concerned with his paint-work and gold-leaf than with getting the ship to move faster through the water. He did not seem to understand what they were driving at, and presently they forgot his presence, though they listened politely to his plea for a larger crow-foot to extend a double awning – 'In the *Andromeda*, Prince William always used to say that his awning gave the quarter-deck the air of a ballroom.' As he spoke of the dimensions of the heroic euphroe that suspended this awning and the number of cloths that went into the awning itself, Jack looked at

him curiously. Here was a man who had fought at the battle
of the Saintes and in Howe's great action, and yet still he
thought his yard-blacking more important than sailing half a
point closer to the wind. 'I used to tell him it was no use racing one mast against the other in reefing topsails until the
people at least knew how to lay aloft: I was wasting my
breath. Very well, gentlemen,' he said aloud, 'let us make it
so. There is not a moment to lose. We could not ask for better
weather, but who can tell how long it will last?'

The *Polychrest*, fresh from the yard, was reasonably well
supplied with bosun's and carpenter's stores; but in any
event, Jack's intention was rather to cut down than to add.
She had always been crank and overmasted, so that she lay
down in a capful of wind; and her foremast had always been
stepped too far aft, because of her original purpose in life,
which made her gripe even with her mizzen furled – made
her do a great many other unpleasant things too. In spite of
his fervent longing, he could do nothing about the stepping
without official consent and the help of a dockyard, but he
could do something to improve the mast by raking it forward
and by a new system of stays, jibs and staysails; and he could
make her less crank by stubbing her topmasts, striking topgallants, and setting up bentincks, triangular courses that
would not press her down in the water so much and that
would relieve her top-hamper.

This was work he understood and loved; for once he was
not in a tearing hurry, and he paced about the deck, seeing
his plan take form, going from one group to the next as they
prepared the spars, rigging and canvas. The carpenter and his
mates were in the waist, their saws and adzes piling up heaps
of chips and sawdust between the holy guns – guns that lay
still today for the first time since he had hoisted his pennant;
the sailmaker and his two parties spread over the forecastle
and the greater part of the quarterdeck, canvas in every direction; and the bosun piled his coils of rope and his blocks in
due order, checking them on his list, sweating up and down

to his store-room, with no time to knock the hands about or even to curse them, except as a mechanical, unmeaning afterthought.

They worked steadily, and better than he had expected: his three pressed tailors squatted there cross-legged, very much at home, plying needle and palm with the desperate speed they had learnt in the sweat-shop, and an out-of-work nail maker from Birmingham showed an extraordinary skill in turning out iron rings from the armourer's forge: 'Crinkumcankum, round she goes', a twist of his tongs, a knowing triple rap with his hammer, and the glowing ring hissed into a bucket.

Eight bells in the afternoon watch, and the sun pouring down on the busy deck. 'Shall I pipe the hands to supper, sir?' asked Pullings.

'No, Mr Pullings,' said Jack. 'We shall sway up the maintopmast first. Proper flats we should look, was a Frenchman to heave in sight,' he observed, looking up and down the confusion. The foremast was clothed already, with a fine potential spread of canvas but little drawing, for want of stays; the jury-mizzen still wore its little odd lateen, to give steerage-way; but the massive topmast was athwart the gangways, and this, together with the rest of the spars littering the deck, and all the other activities, made it almost impossible to move about – quite impossible to work the ship briskly. There was no room, although the boats were towing astern and everything that could be moved below had disappeared. She was making an easy three knots in the quartering breeze, but any emergency would find her helpless. 'Mr Malloch, there. Is your hawser to the capstan?'

'All along, sir.'

'Hands to the capstan, then. Are you ready at the word, there for'ard?'

'Ready, aye ready, sir.'

'Silence, fore and aft. Heave. Heave handsomely.' The capstan turned, the hawser tightened. It led from the capstan through a block on deck to another block on the mainmast head, thence to the head of the topmast, down to the square fid-hole in its heel, and so back to the topmast head, where it was made fast; bands of spun-yarn held it to the mast at intervals, and as it tightened so it began to raise the head. The topmast, a great iron-hooped column of wood some forty feet long, lay across the waist, its ends protruding far out on either side; as its head rose, so Jack called orders to the party on the other side to ease its heel in over the rail, timing each heave to the roll. 'Pawl, there. Stand to your bars. Heave. Heave and rally. Pawl.' The mast tilted up, nearer and nearer to the vertical. Now it was all inboard, no longer sloping but perfectly upright, swaying with the roll, an enormous, dangerous pendulum in spite of the controlling guys. Its head pointed at the trestle-trees, at the block high on the mainmast: the men in the top guided it through them, and still it rose with the turning of the capstan, to pause with its heel a few feet above the deck while they put on the cap. Up again, and they cut the spun-yarn as it reached the block: another pause, and they set the square over the mainmast head, banging it down with a maul, a thump-thump-thump that echoed through the silent, attentive ship.

'They must be getting the cap over,' said Stephen's patient in the sick-bay, a young topman. 'Oh, sir, I wish I was there. He'll splice the mainbrace for sure – it was nigh on eight bells when you come below.'

'You will be there presently,' said Stephen. 'but none of your mainbrace, none of your nasty grog, my friend, until you learn to avoid the ladies of Portsmouth Point, and the fireships of the Sally-Port. No ardent spirits at all for you. Not a drop, until you are cured. And even then, you would be far better with mild unctuous cocoa, or burgoo.'

'Which she told me she was a virgin,' said the sailor, in a low, resentful tone.

The mast rose up and up, the thrust coming from nearer and nearer to the fid-hole as the spun-yarn bands were cut in succession. They had cast off the hawser in favour of the top-rope; they had got the topmast shrouds over, the stays and the backstays; and now the top-tackle was swaying it up with a smooth, steady motion interrupted only by the roll of the ship. A hitch at this point – the top-rope parting, a block-spindle breaking – might be fatal. The last cautious six inches, and the fid-hole appeared above the trestle-trees. The captain of the top waved his hand: Jack cried 'Pawl, there.' The captain of the top banged home the long iron lid, cried 'Launch ho', and it was done. The topmast could no longer plunge like a gigantic arrow down through the deck, down through the ship's bottom, and send them all to their long account. They eased the top-rope and the mast settled on its lid with a gentle groan, firmly supported below, fore, aft, and on either side.

Jack let out a sigh, and when Pullings reported 'Maintop-mast swayed up, sir,' he smiled. 'Very good, Mr Pullings,' he said. 'Let the laniards be well greased and bowsed taut, and then pipe to supper. The people have worked well, and I believe we may splice the mainbrace.'

'How pleasant it is to see the sun,' he called over the taffrail, later in the afternoon.

'Eh?' said Stephen, looking up from a tube thrust deep into the water.

'I said how pleasant it was to see the sun,' said Jack, smil-ing down at him there in the barge – smiling, too, with gen-eral benevolence. He was warm through and through after months of English drizzle; the mild wind caressed him through his open shirt and old canvas trousers; behind him the work was going steadily along, but now it was a matter for expert hands, the bosun, his mates, the quartermasters and forecastlemen; the mere hauling on ropes was over, and the mass of the crew forward were making cheerful noises – with this day's rational work, with no cleaning and no harass-ing, the feeling aboard had changed. The charming weather and the extra allowance of rum had also helped, no doubt.

'Yes,' said Stephen. 'It is. At a depth of two feet, Fahren-heit's thermometer shows no less than sixty-eight degrees. A southern current, I presume. There is a shark following up, a shark of the blue species, a carcharias. He revels in the warmth.'

'Where is he? Do you see him? Mr Parslow there, fetch me a couple of muskets.'

'He is under the dark belly of the ship. But no doubt he will come out presently. I give him gobbets of decayed flesh from time to time.'

From the sky forward there was a guttural shriek – a man falling from the yard, grabbing at air, almost motionless for a flash of time, head back, strained madly up; then falling, faster, faster, faster. He hit a backstay. It bounced him clear of the side and he splashed into the sea by the mizzen-chains.

'Man overboard!' shouted a dozen hands, flinging things into the water and running about.

'Mr Goodridge, bring her to the wind, if you please,' said Jack, kicking off his shoes and diving from the rail. 'How fresh – perfect!' he thought as the bubbles rushed thundering past his ears and the good taste of clean sea filled his nose. He curved upwards, looking at the rippled silver underside of the surface, rose strongly out of the water, snorting and shak-ing his yellow head, saw the man floundering fifty yards away. Jack was a powerful rather than a graceful swimmer, and he surged through the water with his head and shoulders out, like a questing dog, fixing the point in case the man should sink. He reached him – starting eyes, inhuman face belching water, stretching up, the terror of the deep (like most sailors he could not swim) – circled him, seized him by the root of his pigtail and said, 'Easy, easy, now, Bolton. Hold up.' Bolton writhed and grasped with convulsive strength. Jack kicked him free and bawled right into his ear, 'Clasp your hands, you fool. Clasp your hands, I say. There's a shark just by, and if you splash he'll have you.'

The word *shark* went home even to that terrified, half-drunk, water-logged mind. Bolton clasped his hands as though the force of his grip might keep him safe: he went perfectly rigid: Jack kept him afloat, and there they lay, rising and falling on the swell until the boat picked them up.

Bolton sat confused, obscurely ashamed and stupid in the bottom of the boat, gushing water; to cover his confusion he assumed a lumpish catalepsy, and had to be handed up the side. 'Carry him below,' said Jack. 'You had better have a look at him, Doctor, if you would be so kind.'

'He has a contusion on his chest,' said Stephen, coming back to where Jack stood dripping on the quarterdeck, drying as he leaned on the rail and enjoyed the progress of the work on the running rigging. 'But no ribs are broken. May I congratulate you upon saving him? The boat would never have come up in time. Such promptitude of mind – such decision! I honour it.'

'It was pretty good, was it not?' said Jack. 'This is capital, upon my word,' – nodding to the mainmast – 'and at this rate we shall have the bentincks bent tomorrow. Did you smoke that? I said, the bentincks *bent*. Ha, ha, ha!'

Was he making light of it out of coxcombery, fanfaronade? From embarrassment? No, Stephen decided. It was as genuine as his mirth at his ignoble tiny pun, or adumbration of a pun, the utmost limit of naval wit.

'Was you not afraid,' he asked, 'when you reflected upon the shark – his notorious voracity?'

'Him? Oh, sharks are mostly gammon, you know: all cry and no wool. Unless there's blood about, they prefer galley leavings any day. On the West Indies station I once went in after a jolly and dived plump on to the back of a huge great brute: he never turned a hair.'

'Tell me, is this a matter of frequent occurrence with you? Does it in no way mark an epocha in your life, at all?'

'Epocha? Why, no; I can't say it does. Bolton here must make the twenty-second since I first went to sea: or maybe the twenty-third. The Humane chaps sent me a gold medal once. Very civil in them, too; with a most obliging letter. I pawned it in Gibraltar.'

'You never told me this.'

'You never asked. But there is nothing to it, you know, once you get used to their grappling. You feel good, and worthy – deserve well of the republic, and so on, for a while, which is agreeable, I don't deny; but there is really nothing to it – it don't signify. I should go in for a dog, let alone an able seaman: why, if it were warm, I dare say I should go in for a surgeon, ha, ha, ha! Mr Parker, I think we may rig the sheets tonight and get the stump of the mizzen out first thing tomorrow. Then you will be able to priddy the deck and make all shipshape.'

'It is all ahoo at present, sir, indeed,' said the first lieutenant. 'But I must beg your pardon, sir, for not receiving you aboard in a proper fashion just now. May I offer my congratulations?'

'Why thank you, Mr Parker: an able seaman is a valuable prize. Bolton is one of our best upper-yardsmen.'

'He was drunk, sir. I have him in my list.'

'Perhaps we may overlook it this once, Mr Parker. Now the sheers can go with one foot here and the other by the scuttle, with a guy to the third hoop of the mainmast.'

In the evening, when it was too dark to work but too delightful to go below, Stephen observed, 'If you make it your study to depreciate rescues of this nature, will you not find that they are not valued? That you get no gratitude?'

'Now you come to mention it, I suppose it is so,' said Jack. 'It depends: some take it very kind. Bonden, for example. I pulled him out of the Mediterranean, as I dare say you remember, and no one could be more sensible of it. But most think it no great matter, I find. I can't say I should myself, unless it was a particular friend, who knew it was me, and who went in saying "Why, damn me, I shall pull Jack Aubrey out." No. Upon the whole,' he said, reflecting and looking wise, 'it seems to me, that in the article of pulling people out of the sea, virtue is its own reward.'

They lapsed into silence, their minds following different paths as the wake stretched out behind and the stars rose in procession over Portugal.

'I am determined at last,' cried Stephen, striking his hand upon his knee, 'I am at last determined – determined, I say – that I shall learn to swim.'

'I believe,' said Jack, 'that by the setting of the water tomorrow, we shall have our bentincks drawing.'

'THE BENTINCKS DRAW, the bentincks draw, the bentincks draw fu' weel,' said Mr Macdonald.

'Is the Captain pleased?' asked Stephen.

'He is delighted. There is no great wind to try them, but she seems much improved. Have you not remarked her motion is far more easy? We may have the pleasure of the purser's company once more. I tell you, Doctor, if that man belches of set purpose just once again, or picks his teeth at table, I shall destroy him.'

'That is why you are cleaning your pistols, I presume. But I am glad to hear what you tell me, about these sails. Perhaps now we shall hear less of selvagees and booms – the inner jib, the outer jib – nay, to crown all, the jibs of jibs, God forbid. Your mariner is an honest fellow, none better; but he is sadly given to jargon. Those are elegant, elegant pistols. May I handle them?'

'Pretty, are they not?' said Macdonald, passing the case. 'Joe Manton made them for me. Do these things interest you?'

'It is long since I had a pistol in my hand,' said Stephen. 'Or a small-sword. But when I was younger I delighted in them – I still do. They have a beauty of their own. Then again, they have a real utility. In Ireland, you know, we go out more often than the English do. I believe it is the same with you?'

Macdonald thought it was, though there was a great difference between the Highlands and the rest of the kingdom;

what did Dr Maturin mean by 'often'? Stephen said he meant
twenty or thirty times in a twelvemonth; in his first year at
the university he had known men who exceeded this. 'At that
time I attached a perhaps undue importance to staying alive,
and I became moderately proficient with both the pistol and
the small-sword. I have a childish longing to be at it again.
Ha, ha – carte, tierce, tierce, sagoon, a hit!'

'Should you like to try a pass or two with me on deck?'

'Would that be quite regular? I have a horror of the least
appearance of eccentricity.'

'Oh, yes, yes! It is perfectly usual. In the *Boreas* I used to
give the midshipmen lessons as soon as I had finished exercising the Marines; and one or two of the lieutenants were
quite good. Come, let us take the pistols too.'

On the quarterdeck they foined and lunged, stamping, crying 'Ha!' and the clash and hiss of steel upon steel seduced
the midshipmen of the watch from their duty until they were
banished to the heights, leaving their happier friends to
watch the venomous wicked dart and flash entranced.

'Stop, stop! Hold – belay, avast,' cried Stephen, stepping
back at last. 'I have no breath – I gasp – I melt.'

'Well,' said Macdonald, 'I have been a dead man these ten
minutes past. I have only been fighting speeritually.'

'Sure, we were both corpses from very early in the battle.'

'Bless us all,' said Jack, 'I had no notion you were such a
man of blood, dear Doctor.'

'You must be uncommon deadly when you are in practice,'
said Macdonald. 'A horrid quick murdering lunge. I should
not care to go out with you, sir. You may call me pudding, and
I will bear it meekly. Do you choose to try the pistols?'

Jack, watching from his side of the quarterdeck, was wholly
amazed: he had no idea that Stephen could hold a sword, nor
yet load a pistol, still less knock the pips out of a playing-card
at twenty paces: yet he had known him intimately. He was
pleased that his friend was doing so well; he was pleased at
the respectful silence; but he was a little sad that he could

not join in, that he stood necessarily aloof – the captain could not compete – and he was obscurely uneasy. There was something disagreeable, and somehow reptilian, about the cold, contained way Stephen took up his stance, raised his pistol, looked along the barrel with his pale eyes, and shot the head off the king of hearts. Jack's certainties wavered; he turned to look at his new bentincks, smoothly filled, drawing to perfection. Finisterre would be under their lee by now, some sixty leagues away; and presently, about midnight, he would alter course eastward – eastward, for Ortegal and the Bay.

JUST BEFORE eight bells in the first watch Pullings came on deck, pushing a yawning, bleary-eyed Parslow before him.

'You are a good relief, Mr Pullings,' said the master. 'I shall be right glad to turn in.' He caught the yawn from the midshipman, gaped enormously and went on, 'Well, here you have her. Courses, main and fore tops'ls, forestays'l and jib. Course nor-nor-east, to be altered due east at two bells. Captain to be called if you sight any sail. Oh, my dear cot, how she calls. A good night to you, then. That child could do with a bucket of water over him,' he added, moving towards the hatchway.

Deep in his sleep Jack was aware of the changing watch – sixty men hurrying about in a ship a hundred and thirty feet long can hardly do so in silence – but it did not stir him more than one point from the deepest level of unconsciousness; it did not bring him half so near the surface as the change of course, which followed one hour later. He swam up, between sleeping and waking, knowing that his body was no longer lying in the same relationship to the north. And that the *Polychrest* was going large: the quick nervous rise and fall had given way to a long, easy glide. No roaring or calling out on deck. Pullings had put her before the wind with a few quiet remarks: all wool and no cry: how fortunate he was to have that good young fellow. But there was something not quite right. The sails had been trimmed, yet feet were pattering about at a great rate: through the open skylight he caught quick excited words, and he was fully awake, quite prepared for the opening of his door and the dim form of a midshipman beside his cot.

'Mr Pullings' duty, sir, and he believes there is a sail on the larboard bow.'

'Thank you, Mr Parslow. I shall be with him directly.' He reached the glow of the binnacle as Pullings came sliding down a backstay from the top, thump on to the quarterdeck. 'I think I picked 'un out, sir,' he said, offering his telescope. 'Three points on the larboard bow, maybe a couple of mile away.'

It was a darkish night: an open sky, but hazy at the edges, the great stars little more than golden points and the small ones lost; the new moon had set long ago. When his eyes grew accustomed to the darkness he could make out the horizon well enough, a lighter bar against the black sky, with Saturn just dipping now. The wind had veered a trifle northerly; it had strengthened, and white water flecked the rise of every swell. Several times he thought he had the topsails of a ship in his glass, but every time they dissolved, never to reappear.

'You must have good eyes,' he said. 'She fired a gun, sir, and I caught the flash; but I did not like to call you till I had made certain sure. There she is, sir, just under the sprits'l yard. Tops'ls: maybe mizzen t'garns'l. Close-hauled, I take it.'

'By God, I am getting old,' thought Jack, lowering the glass. Then he saw her, a ghostly flash that did not dissolve – vanished, but reappeared in the same place. A whiteness that the glass showed as a pale bar – topsails braced up sharp so that they overlapped. And a hint of white above: the mizzen topgallant. She was on the starboard tack, close hauled on the fresh north-westerly breeze, probably heading west-south-west or a little south of it. If she had fired a gun, just one gun, it meant that she had consorts – that she was tacking and that they were to do the same. He searched the darkness eastward, and this time he saw one, perhaps two, of those dim but lasting wafts. On this course their paths would intersect. But for how long would the remote unknown hold on to his present tack? No great while, for Cape Ortegal lay under his lee, an iron-bound coast with cruel reefs.

'Let us haul our wind, Mr Pullings,' he said. And to the helmsman, 'Luff up and touch her.'

The *Polychrest* came up and up; the stars turned, sweeping an arc in the sky, and he stood, listening intently for the first flutter of canvas that would mean she was as close to the wind as she would lie. The breeze blew on his left cheekbone now; a dash of spray came over the rail to wet his face, and forward the leech of the foretopsail began to shake.

Jack took the wheel, eased her a trifle. 'Sharp that bowline, there,' he called. 'Mr Pullings, I believe we can come up a trifle more. See to the braces and the bowlines.'

Pullings ran forward over the pale deck: a dark group on the forecastle heaved, 'One, two, three, belay,' and as he came aft so ropes tightened, yards creaked round an extra few inches. Now she was trimmed as sharp as she could be, and gradually Jack heaved on the spokes against the strong living pressure, bringing her head closer, closer to the wind. The pole-star vanished behind the maintopsail. Closer, still closer: and that was her limit. He had not believed she could do so well. She was lying not far from five points off the wind, as opposed to her old six and a half, and even if she made her usual extravagant leeway she could still eat the wind out of the stranger, so long as she had a very careful hand at the wheel and paid great attention to her trim: and he had the feeling she was sagging less, too. 'Thus, very well thus,' he said to the helmsman, looking into his face by the binnacle light. 'Ah, it is Haines, I see. Well, Haines, you will have to oblige me with a double trick at the wheel: this calls for a right seaman. Dyce, do you mind me, now? Not a hair's breadth off.'

'Aye, aye, sir. Dyce it is.'

'Carry on, Mr Pullings. Check all breechings and shot-racks. You may shake out a reef in the maintopsail if the breeze slackens. Call me if you find any change.'

He went below, pulled on his shirt and breeches and lay down on his cot, leafing through Steel's Navy List: but he could not rest, and presently he was on the quarterdeck again, pacing the lee side with his hands behind his back, a glance over the dark sea at every turn.

Two ships, perhaps three, tacking by signal: they might be anything – British frigates, French ships of the line, neutrals. But they might also be enemy merchantmen, slipping out by the dark of the moon: a hint of incautious light as the second rose on the swell made merchantmen more probable; and then again, it was unlikely that. men-of-war should straggle over such an expanse of sea. He would get a better idea as the sky lightened; and in any case, whether they tacked or not, he would have the weather-gage at dawn – he would be up-wind of them.

He watched the side, he watched the wake: leeway she was making, of course; but it was distinctly less. Each heave of the log showed a steady three knots and a half: slow, but he wanted nothing more – at this point he would have reduced sail if she had been moving faster, for fear of finding himself too far away by morning.

Far over the sea on the *Polychrest*'s quarter a flash lit up the sky, and more than a heartbeat later he heard the boom: they were tacking again. Now he and the unknown were sailing on parallel courses, and the *Polychrest* had the weather-gage at its most perfect: she was directly in the eye of the wind from the leading ship of the three – the third was a certainty now, and had been so this last half hour.

Eight bells. It would be light before very long. 'Mr Pullings, keep the watch on deck. In main and mizzen topsails. Mr Parker, good morning to you. Let the galley fires be lit at once, if you please: the hands will go to breakfast as soon as possible – a substantial breakfast, Mr Parker. Rouse up the idlers. And then you may begin to clear the ship for action: we will beat to quarters at two bells. Where are the relief midshipmen? Quartermaster, go cut down their hammocks this instant. Pass the word for the gunner. Now, sir,' – to the appalled Rossall and Babbington – 'what do you mean by this vile conduct? Not appearing on deck in time for your watch? Nightcaps, dirty faces, by God! You are unwashed idle lubbers, both of you. Ah, Mr Rolfe, there you are: how much powder have you filled?'

The preparations went smoothly ahead, and each watch breakfasted in turn. 'Now you'll see summat, mates,' said William Screech, an old Sophie, as he rammed down his meal – cheese and portable soup. 'Now you'll see old Goldilocks cut one of his capers over them forringers.'

'It's time we see summat,' said a landsman. 'Where are all these golden dollars we were promised? It has been more kicks than ha'pence, so far.'

'They are a-lying just to leeward, mate,' said Screech. 'All you got to do, is to mind your duty and serve your gun brisk, and bob's your uncle Dick.'

'I wish I was at home with my old loom,' said a weaver, 'golden dollars or no golden dollars.'

Now the galley fires were dowsed in stench and hissing: the fearnought screens appeared at the hatchways: Jack's cabin vanished, Killick hurrying his belongings to the depths and the carpenters taking away the bulkheads: the gun-room poultry went clucking below in their coops: and all this while Jack stared out over the sea. The eastern sky was showing a hint of light by the time the bosun came to report a difficulty in his puddening – did the Captain wish it to be above the new clench or below? This question took no great consideration, but when Jack had given his answer and could look over the side again, the stranger was there as clear as he could desire: on the dull silver of the sea her hull showed black as it rose, something under a mile away on the starboard quarter. And behind her, far to leeward, the two others. They were no great sailers, that was clear, for although they had a fine spread of canvas abroad they were finding it hard to come up with her: she had hauled up her courses to let them close the distance, and now they were perhaps three parts of a mile from her. One seemed to be jury-rigged. Tucking his glass into his bosom, he climbed to the maintop. At the first glance he took, once he had settled firmly and had brought the leading ship into focus, he pursed his mouth and uttered a silent whistle. A thirty-two, no, a thirty-four gun frigate, no less. At the second he smiled, and without taking his eye from the telescope he called, 'Mr Pullings, pray come into the top. Here, take my glass. What do you make of her?'

'A thirty-two, no, a thirty-four gun frigate, sir. French, by the cut of her jib. No. No! By God, sir, she's the *Bellone*.'

The *Bellone* she was, in her old accustomed cruising-ground. She had undertaken to escort two Bordeaux merchantmen as far as twenty degrees west and forty-five north, and she had brought them successfully across the Bay of Biscay, not without trouble, for they were slow brutes, and one had lost her fore and main topmasts: she had stood by them, but she had no sharper sense of her obligations than any other privateer and now she was keenly interested in this odd triangular thing bobbing about to windward. Her contract had no stipulations against her making prizes during her trip, and for the last quarter of an hour, or ever since she had sighted the *Polychrest*, the *Bellone* had been hauled a point closer to the wind to close her, and the *Bellone*'s captain had been doing exactly what Jack was at now, staring hard through his glass from the top.

The *Bellone*. She could outrun any square-rigged ship afloat, on a wind; but for the next ten or twenty minutes Jack had the initiative. He had the weather-gage, and he could decide whether to bring her to action or not. But this would not last long: he must think fast – make up his mind before she could shoot ahead. She had thirty-four guns to his four and twenty: but they were eight and six pounders – she threw a broadside of a hundred and twenty-six pounds, and with his three hundred and eighty-four he could blow her out of the water, given the right conditions. Only eight-pounders: but they were long brass eight-pounders, beautiful guns and very well served – she could start hitting him at a mile and more, whereas his short, inaccurate carronades, with their scratch crews, needed to be within pistol-shot for any certainty of execution. At fifty yards, or even at a hundred, he could give her such a dose! Near, but not too near. There was no question of boarding her, not with her two or three hundred keen privateersmen, not with this crew. Nor must he be boarded, Lord above.

'Mr Pullins,' he said, 'desire Mr Macdonald to get his men's red jackets off. Fling sailcloth over the guns in the waist. Drabble it about all ahoo, but so that it can be whipped off in a flash. Two or three empty casks on the fo'c'sle. Make her look like a slut.'

How neatly the roles were reversed! This time the *Bellone* had not been preparing herself for a couple of hours; *her* decks would not be clear fore and aft; and she would still be in a state of doubt – it was *she* who would be taken by surprise.

Taken: the word rang like a trumpet. He hurried down to the quarterdeck, his mind made up. 'Mr Parker, what are you about?'

'These mats are to protect my gold-leaf, sir,' said the first lieutenant.

'Do not square them, Mr Parker: they are very well so.' Indeed, they looked charmingly mercantile. 'All hands aft, if you please.'

They stood before him in the grey light, some few delighted, some amazed, many despondent, anxious, apt to stare over the water at that dark shape.

'Shipmates,' he said, loud and clear, smiling at them, 'that fellow down there is only a privateer. I know him well. He has a long row of gun-ports, but there are only six- and eight-pounders behind 'em, and ours are twenty-fours, though he don't know it. Presently I shall edge down on him – he may pepper us a while with his little guns, but it don't signify – and then, when we are so close we cannot miss, why, we shall give him such a broadside! A broadside with every gun low at his mizzen. Not a shot, now, till the drum beats, and then ply 'em like heroes. Thump it into her! Five minutes' brisk and she strikes. Now go to your quarters, and remember, not a shot till the drum beats, and then every ball low at his mizzen. Ply 'em quick, and waste not a shot.' Turning, he saw Stephen watching him from the companion hatchway. 'Good morning, good morning!' he cried, smiling with great affection. 'Here's our old friend the *Bellone* just to leeward.'

'Ay. So Pullings tell me. Do you mean to fight with her?'

'I mean to sink, take, burn or destroy her,' said Jack, a smile flashing across his face.

'I dare say you do. Please to remember the watch they took from me. A Breguet repeater, number 365, with a centre seconds hand. And three pairs of drawers, I should know them anywhere. I must go below.'

The day was dawning fast; the east was golden – a clear sky with white clouds streaked across; the merchantmen were crowding sail to come up with the privateer.

'Mr Parker, lay the hatches, if you please. Mr Macdonald, your best marksmen into the tops at the last minute: they are to sweep the quarterdeck, nothing but the quarterdeck.'

This was his simple plan: he would edge down, never allowing her to forereach him, keeping rigorously to windward, puzzling her as long as he possibly could, and so batter her at close quarters, keeping her there by taking the wind out of her sails. Anything more complex he dared not attempt, not with this ship, not with these men – no quick manoeuvres, no crossing under her stern – just as he dared not hide his men below, these raw hands who had never seen an angry gun.

'Ease her half a point, Mr Goodridge.'

Their courses were converging. How near would the *Bellone* let him come? Every hundred yards meant a minute less of enduring her long-range fire. Nearer, nearer . . .

If he could dismast her, shoot away her wheel – and it was just abaft the mizzen in the *Bellone* . . . Now he could see the white of the faces on her quarterdeck. And yet still they sailed, on and on, drawing together, closer, closer. When would she fire? 'Another quarter, Mr Goodridge. Mr Rossall, you have the Papenburg . . .?'

A puff of smoke from the *Bellone*'s bows, and a shot came skipping along the *Polychrest*'s side. The British colours appeared aboard the Frenchman. 'She's English!' cried a voice in the waist, with such relief, poor fellow. A hail, just audible in a lull of wind: 'Shorten sail and heave to, you infernal buggers.' Jack smiled. 'Slowly, Mr Rossall,' he said. 'Blunder around a little. Half up, down and up again.' The Papenburg flag wavered up to the mizzen peak and appeared at last, streaming out towards the privateer.

'That will puzzle him,' said Jack. The moment's doubt brought the two ships yet closer. Then another shot, one that hit the *Polychrest* square amidships: an ultimatum.

'Up foretopsheet,' cried Jack. He could afford to let the *Bellone* range up a little, and the confusion might gain another half minute.

But now the *Bellone* had had enough: the white ensign came down, the tricolour ran up: the frigate's side vanished in a long cloud and a hundredweight of iron hurtled across the five hundred yards of sea. Three balls struck the *Polychrest*'s hull; the rest screamed overhead. 'Clap on to that sheet there, for'ard,' he cried: and as the sail filled, 'Very well, Mr Goodridge, lay me alongside her at pistol-shot. Our colours, Mr Rossall. Mr Pullings, off canvas, casks over the side.'

An odd gun or two from the *Bellone*, and for a hideous moment Jack thought she was going to tack, cross his stern, and try a luffing-match to gain the wind, hitting him from a distance all the time. 'God send her broadside,' he muttered; and it came, a great rolling crash, but ragged – by no means in the *Bellone*'s finest style. Now the privateer was committed to a quick finish, out of hand. All that remained was to wait while the master took the *Polychrest* down into action, foiling every attempt at forereaching, keeping her just so in relation to the wind and the *Bellone* – to last out those minutes while the gap was narrowed. 'Mr Macdonald, Marines away aloft,' he said. 'Drummer, are you ready?'

Across the water the guns were being run out and aimed again; as the last thrust out its muzzle he roared 'Lie down. Flat down on deck.' This was a mixed broadside, mostly grape: it tore through the lower rigging and across the deck. Blocks rattled down, ropes parted, and there was Macdonald at his side, staggering, a hand clapped to his arm. A wretched little man was running about, trying to get down the fore-hatch: several others on their hands and knees, looking wild, watching to see if he would succeed. The bosun tripped him up, seized him and flung him back to his gun. The smoke cleared, and now Jack could see the dead-eyes in the *Bellone*'s shrouds. 'Stand to your guns,' he cried. 'Stand by. Wait for the drum. All at the mizzen, now.'

The officers and the captains of the guns were traversing the carronades, training them at the *Bellone*, glaring along the barrels. The little drummer's huge eyes were fixed on Jack's face. Closer, even closer . . . He judged the roll, felt the ship reach the long slow peak, and the instant she began to go down he nodded and cried 'Fire!' The drum-roll was drowned by the universal blast of all the starboard guns, stunning the wind, so that the smoke lay thick, impenetrable. He fanned it with his hand, leaning but over the rail. It cleared, sweeping leeward, and he saw the murderous effect – a great gaping hole in the *Bellone*'s side, her mizzenchains destroyed, the mast wounded, three gun-ports beaten in, bodies on her quarterdeck.

A furious, savage cheer from the *Polychrest*. 'Another, another,' he cried. 'Another and she strikes!'

But her colours were flying still, her wheel was unhurt, and on her quarterdeck Captain Dumanoir waved his hat to Jack, shouting orders to his men. To his horror Jack saw that the *Polychrest*'s cursed leeway was carrying her fast aboard the privateer. The Frenchmen, all but the gun-crews, were massing in the bows, some two hundred of them.

'Luff up, Goodridge . . .' and his words were annihilated by the double broadside, the *Bellone*'s and the *Polychrest*'s, almost yardarm to yardarm.

'All hands to repel boarders – pikes, pikes, pikes!' he shouted, drawing his sword and racing to the forecastle, the likely point of impact, vaulting a dismounted gun, a couple of bodies, and reaching it before the smoke cleared away. He stood there with twenty or thirty men around him, waiting for the grinding thump of the two ships coming together. Through the cloud there was an enormous shouting – orders in French – cheering – and now far astern a rending, tearing crash. Clear air, brilliant light, and there was the *Bellone* sheering off, falling off from the wind, turning; and the gap between them was twenty yards already. Her mizzen had gone by the board, and she could not keep to the wind. The fallen mast lay over her starboard quarter, hanging by the shrouds, acting as a huge rudder, swinging her head away.

'To your guns,' he shouted. The *Bellone*'s stern was turning towards them – a raking broadside now would destroy her.

'She's struck, she's struck!' cried a fool. And now the lack of training told – now the disorganized gun-crews ran about – match-tubs upset, shot, cartridge, swabs, rammers everywhere. Some men cheering, others capering like half-wits – guns in, guns out – Bedlam. 'Pullings, Babbington, Parker, get those guns firing – jump to it, God damn you all. Up with the helm, Goodridge – keep her bearing.' He knocked down a lit- tle silly weaver, skipping there for joy, banged two men's heads together, compelled them to their guns, heaved one

carronade in, ran another out, fired it into the *Bellone*'s open
stern, and ran back to the quarterdeck, crying 'Bear up,
Goodridge, bear up, I say.'

And now the vile *Polychrest* would not answer her helm.
Hardly a sheet of her headsails remained after that last broadside, and all her old griping was back. The helm was hard
over, but she would not pay off; and the precious seconds
were flying.

Malloch and his mates were busy with the sheets, knotting
like fury: here and there a carronade spoke out – one twenty-
four-pound ball hit the *Bellone* plumb on the stern-post. But
the privateer had squared her yards; she was right before the
wind, and they were separating at a hundred yards a minute.
Before the headsheets were hauled aft, so that the *Polychrest*
could payoff and pursue the *Bellone*, there was quarter of a
mile of open water between them; and now the *Bellone* was
replying with her stern-chaser.

'Mr Parker, get two guns into the bows,' said Jack. The *Polychrest* was gathering way: the *Bellone*, hampered by her trailing mast, yawed strangely. The distance narrowed. 'Mr
Parslow, fetch me a glass.' His own lay shattered by the fife-
rail.

'A glass? What glass, sir?' The little pale dazed face peered
up, anxious, worried.

'Any glass – a telescope, boy,' he said kindly. 'In the gun-
room. Look sharp.'

He glanced up and down his ship. The bentincks holed like
sieves, two staysails hanging limp, foretopsail in rags, half a
dozen shrouds parted: jibs and mizzen drawing well, however.
Something like order on deck. Two guns dismounted, but one
being crowed up and re-breached. The rest run out, ready,
their crews complete, the men looking eager and determined.
A great heap of hammocks in the waist, blasted out of their
netting by the *Bellone*'s last broadside. The wounded carried
below, skirting the heap.

'The glass, sir.'

'Thank you, Mr Parslow. Tell Mr Rolfe the bow carronades are to fire the moment they can be run out.'

Aboard the *Bellone* they were hacking at the starboard mizzen-shrouds with axes. The last pair parted, the floating mast tore clear, and the frigate surged forward, drawing clear away, going, going from them. But as he watched, her maintopmast lurched, lurched again, and with a heavy pitch of the sea it fell bodily over the side.

A cheer went up from the *Polychrest*. They were gaining on her – they were gaining! The bow carronade went off: the shot fell short, but almost hit the *Bellone* on the ricochet. Another cheer. 'You'll cheer the other side of your faces when she hauls her wind and rakes us,' he thought. The two ships were some five hundred yards apart, both directly before the wind, with the *Polychrest* on the *Bellone*'s larboard quarter: the privateer had but to put her helm a-lee to show them her broadside and rake them from stem to stern. She could not come right up into the wind with no sails aft, but she could bring it on to her beam, and less than that would be enough.

Yet she did not do so. The topmast was cut away, but still the *Bellone* ran before the wind. And focusing his glass upon her stern he saw why – she had no helm to put a-lee. That last lucky shot had unseated her rudder. She could not steer. She could only run before the wind.

They were coming down to the merchantmen now, broad low ships still on the larboard tack. Did they mean to give any trouble? To stand by their friend? They had five gun-ports of a side, and the *Bellone* would pass within a cable's length of them. 'Mr Parker, run out the larboard guns.' No: they did not. They were slowly edging away, heading north: one was a lame duck – juryrigged fore and main topmasts. The *Polychrest*'s bow gun sent a fountain of water over the *Bellone*'s stern. They were gaining. Should he snap up the merchantmen and then go on after the privateer? Content himself with the merchants? At this moment they could not escape: but in five minutes he would be to leeward of them, and slow though they might be, it would be a task to bring them to. In half an hour it would be impossible.

The carronade was firing two shots for the *Bellone*'s one; but that one came from a long eight, a more accurate gun by far. A little before they came abreast of the merchant ships it sent a ball low over the *Polychrest*'s deck, killing a seaman near the wheel, flinging his body on to Parslow as he stood there, waiting for orders. Jack pulled the body off, disentangled the blood-stained child, said 'Are you all right, Parslow?' and in reply to Parker's 'The merchantmen have struck, sir,' he cried, 'Yes, yes. See if it is possible to lace on a bonnet.' A minute gain in speed would allow him to draw up on the *Bellone*, yaw and hammer her with his broadside again. They swept close by the merchantmen, who let fly their sheets in submission. Even in this heat of battle, with the guns answering one another as fast as they could be loaded, powder-smoke swirling between them, bodies on deck, blood running fresh in the scuppers, there were eyes that glanced wistfully at their prizes – fair-sized ships: ten, twenty, even thirty thousand guineas, perhaps. They knew very well that the moment the *Polychrest* had run a mile to leeward, all that money would get under way, spread every possible stitch of canvas, haul to the wind, and fly: kiss my hand to a fortune.

South-east they ran, the merchant ships dwindling fast astern. They ran firing steadily, first the one gaining a little as damaged rigging was repaired, then the other; neither dared risk the pause to bend new sails; neither dared risk sending up a new topmast or topgallants in this steep pitching sea; and as they stood they were exactly matched. The least damage to either would be decisive, the least respite fatal; and so they ran, and the glass turned and the bell rang right through the forenoon watch, hour after hour, in a state of extreme tension – hardly a word on deck, apart from orders – never much more or less than a quarter of a mile away from one another. Both tried setting studdingsails: both had them blown away. Both started their water over the side, lightening themselves by several tons – every trick, device, contrivance known to seamen for an even greater urgency of thrust. At one point Jack thought the *Bellone* was throwing her stores overboard, but it was only her dead. Forty splashes he counted: the slaughter in that close-packed ship must have been appalling. And still they fired.

By noon, when they raised the high land of Spain among the clouds on the southern horizon, the *Polychrest*'s bows were pockmarked with shot-holes, her foremast and foretop-sailyard had been gashed again and again, and she was making water fast. The *Bellone*'s stern was shattered to an extraordinary degree and her great mainsail was a collection of holes; but she was steering again. This she did by a cable veered out of the stern-port, which allowed her to turn a couple of points from the wind – not much, but more than she could do by steering with her sheets. She altered course deliberately on sighting Cape Peñas, and it cost her dear: the drag of the cable lost her a hundred yards – a great distance in that desperate race – and Rolfe, the *Polychrest*'s master-gunner, red-eyed, black with powder, but in his element, sent a ball smashing into her stern-chaser, and from dead silence the *Polychrest* burst into wild cheering. Now the *Bellone* ran mute, apart from musket-fire. But still she ran, and it was Gijon that she was running for. Gijon, a Spanish port and therefore closed to British ships, though open to the French.

Yet there were still some miles to go, and any shot that touched her main yard or her sheets would cripple her. Now her guns were going overboard to win back that hundred yards. Jack shook his head – it would do her little good, with the wind right aft and only headsails left.

'On deck, there,' hailed the look-out. 'A sail on the starboard bow.'

She was a Spanish frigate, rounding Cape Peñas and bearing up for Gijon: she should have been sighted long ago, if every eye had not been fixed upon the flying privateer. 'Damn her,' said Jack, with the fleeting thought that it was strange to see such perfection of canvas, pyramids of white, after all this time staring at tattered rags: and how fast she moved!

An explosion forward – not the right crash of the carronade. Shouts, a high dog-like howling of agony. The overheated gun had burst, killing the gunner stone dead and wounding three more – one man jerking clear of the deck as he screamed, leaping so that twice he escaped from his mates' arms, carrying him below. They slid the gunner over the side, cleared the wreckage, worked furiously to shift the other carronade into its place, but it was a slow job – ringbolts and all had gone; and all the while the *Bellone*'s muskets played on them in the bows.

Now they ran silently, with eager, inveterate malice; the coast drew nearer – the savage cliffs and the white water on the reefs were in view; and without a pause the animal screaming came up from the cockpit far below.

A gun from the Spanish frigate, a hoist of signals. 'Damn her,' said Jack again. The *Bellone* was veering out her cable again to turn to port, to turn for the entrance to Gijon – Dumanoir must haul up a good two points, or he would be on the rocks.

'No you don't, God damn you,' cried Jack. 'Stand to your guns, there. Train 'em sharp for'ard. Three degrees' elevation. Fire as they bear on her main mast. Mr Goodlridge, bring her up.'

The *Polychrest* swerved violently to larboard, bringing her side slanting to the privateer. Her guns went off in succession, three, six and three. Great gaps appeared in the *Bellone*'s mainsail, the yard tilted, held only by the preventerlift; but still she ran.

'The Spaniard is firing, sir,' said Parker. And indeed a shot whipped across the *Polychrest*'s stern. The frigate had altered course to run between them: she was very close.

'Damn him,' said Jack, and taking the wheel he put the ship before the wind, straight for the privateer. He might have time for one more broadside more before the Spaniard crossed his hawse – one chance to cripple the *Bellone* before she cleared the reef and reached the open channel for the port.

'Stand to your guns,' he said in the silence. 'Steady, steady now. Three degrees. For her mainmast. Make sure of every ball.'

He glanced over his shoulder, saw the Spaniard – a magnificent spread of sail – heard her hail loud and clear, clenched his mouth, and spun the wheel. If the Spaniard caught his broadside, that was his affair.

Round, round she came; the helm hard over. The guns went off in one great rolling deliberate thunder. The *Bellone's* mainmast came slowly down, down, right over her side, all her canvas with it. The next moment she was in the surf. He saw the copper of her hull: she drove farther on to the reef in two great heaves and there lay on her side, the waves making a clean breach over her.

'AND SO, SIR, I drove her on to the rock before Gijon. I wished to send in the boats to burn her at low tide, but the Spaniards represented to me that she was in territorial waters, and that they should oppose any such measure. They added, however, that she was hopelessly bilged, her back broken.'

Admiral Harte stared at him with sincere dislike. 'So as I understand it,' he said, 'you left these valuable merchantmen when you could have tossed a biscuit on to their deck, to chase a blackguardly privatee, which you did not take either.'

'I destroyed her, sir.'

'Oh, I dare say. We have all heard of these ships driven on the rocks and bilged and so on and so forth, and then next month they reappear as good as new. It is easy enough to say "I drove her on the rocks". Anyone can say that, but no one has yet got any head-money or gun-money out of it – not a brass farthing. No, no, it is all the fault of this damn-fool sail-plan of yours: if you could have spread your topgallants you would have had plenty of time to pick up the merchants and then have really knocked hell out of the bugger you claim to have destroyed. These bentincks, in anything but a gale wind – I have no notion of them.'

'I could never have worked to windward of the convoy without them, sir; and I do assure you that with the *Polychrest* a greater spread of canvas would only have pressed her down.'

'So we are to understand that the less sail you spread the faster you go?' said Harte, with a look at his secretary, who tittered. 'No, no: an admiral is generally reckoned to know more about these things than a commander -- let us hear no more of this fancy rig. Your sloop is peculiar enough, without making her look like a poxed cocked hat, the laughing-stock of the fleet, creeping about at five knots because you don't choose to set more sail. Anyhow, what have you to say about this Dutch galliot?'

'I must confess she ran clean away from me, sir.'

'And who picked her up the next day, with her gold- dust and elephant's teeth? *Amethyst*, of course. *Amethyst* again, and you were not even in sight. I don't touch a – that is to say, you don't share. Seymour is the lucky man: ten thousand guineas at the lowest mark. I am deeply disappointed in you, Captain Aubrey. I give you what amounts to a cruise in a brand-new sloop, and what do you do with it? You come back empty-handed – you bring her in looking like I don't know what, pumping night and day, half her spars and cordage gone, five men dead and seven wounded, with a tale about driving a little privateer on to some more or less imaginary rocks and clamouring for a refit. Don't tell me about bolts and twice-laid stuff,' he said, holding up his hand. 'I've heard it all before. And I've heard about your carrying on ashore, before I came in. Let me remind you that a captain is not allowed to sleep out of his ship without permission.'

'Indeed, sir?' asked Jack, leaning forward. 'May I beg you to be more particular? Am I reproached with sleeping out of my ship?'

'I never said you *slept* out of it, did I?' said Harte.

'Then may I ask what I am to understand by your remark?'

'Never mind,' said Harte, fiddling with his paper-knife: and then in an unconquerable jet of waspishness, 'but I will tell you this – your topsails are a disgrace to the service. Why can't you furl them in a body?'

The malignance was too obvious to bite. Crack frigates with a full, expert crew might furl their sails in a body rather than in the bunt, but only in harbour or for a Spithead review. 'Well,' said Harte, aware of this, 'I am disappointed in you, as I say. You will go on the Baltic convoys, and the rest of the time I dare say the sloop will be employed up and down the Channel. That's more your mark. The Baltic convoy should be complete in a few days' time. And that reminds me: I have had a very extraordinary communication from the Admiralty. Your surgeon, a fellow by the name of Maturin, is to be given this sealed envelope; he is to have leave of absence, and they have sent down an assistant to take his place while he is away and to help him when he sees fit to return to his duty. I wish he may not give himself airs – a sealed envelope, forsooth.'

10

THE POST-CHAISE drove briskly forward over the Sussex downs, with Stephen Maturin and Diana Villiers sitting in it with the glasses down, very companionably eating bread and butter.

'So now you have seen your dew-pond,' she said comfortably. 'How did you like it?'

'It came up to my highest expectations,' said Stephen. 'And I had looked forward to it extremely.'

'And I look forward to Brighton extremely too: I hope I may be as pleased as you are. Oh, I cannot fail to be delighted, can I, Maturin? A whole week's holiday from the Teapot! And even if it rains all the time, there is the Pavilion – how I long to see the Pavilion.'

'Was not candour the soul of friendship, I should say, "Why

Villiers, I am sure it will delight you," affecting not to know that you were there last week.'

'Who told you?' she asked, her bread and butter poised.

'Babbington was there with his parents.'

'Well, I never said I had not been – it was just a flying visit – I did not see the Pavilion. That is what I meant. Do not be disagreeable, Maturin: we have been so pleasant all the way. Did he mention it in public?'

'He did. Jack was much concerned. He thinks Brighton a very dissolute town, full of male and female rakes – a great deal of temptation. He does not like the Prince of Wales, either. There is an ill-looking smear of butter on your chin.'

'Poor Jack,' said Diana, wiping it off. 'Do you remember – oh how long ago it seems – I told you he was little more than a huge boy? I was pretty severe about it: I preferred something more mature, a fully-grown man. But how I miss all that fun and laughter! What has happened to his gaiety? He is growing quite a bore. Preaching and moralizing. Maturin, could you not tell him to be less prosy? He would listen to you.'

'I could not. Men are perhaps less free with such recommendations than you imagine. In any case I am very sorry to say we are no longer on such terms that I could venture anything of the kind – if indeed we ever were. Certainly not since last Sunday's dinner. We still play a little music together now and then, but it is damnably out of tune.'

'It was not a very successful dinner: though I took such care with the pudding. Did he say anything?'

'In my direction? No. But he made some illiberal flings at Jews in general.'

'That was why he was so glum, then. I *see*.'

'Of course you see. You are not a fool, Villiers. The preference was very marked.'

'Oh no, no, Stephen. It was only common civility. Canning was the stranger, and you two were old friends of the house; he had to sit beside me, and be attended to. Oh, what is that bird?'

'It is a wheatear. We have seen between two and three hundred since we set out, and I have told your their name twice, nay, three times.'

The postillion reined in, twisted about and asked whether the gentleman would like to see another dew-pond? There was one not a furlong off.

'I cannot make it out,' said Stephen, climbing back into the chaise. 'The dew, per se, is inconsiderable; and yet they are full. They are always full, as the frog bears witness. *She* does not spawn in your uncertain, fugitive ponds; *her* tadpoles do not reach maturity in your mere temporary puddle; and yet here they are – ' holding out a perfect frog the size of his little finger nail – 'by the hundred, after three weeks of drought.'

'He is entrancing,' said Diana. 'Pray put him out, on the grass. Do you think I may ask what this delightful smell is, without being abused?'

'Thyme,' said Stephen absently. 'Mother of thyme, crushed by our carriage-wheels.'

'So Aubrey is bound for the Baltic,' said Diana, after a while. 'He will not have this charming weather. I hate the cold.'

'The Baltic and northwards: just so,' said Stephen, recollecting himself. 'Lord, I wish I were going with him. The eider-duck, the phalarope, the narwhal! Ever since I was breeched I have pined to see a narwhal.'

'What will happen to your patients when you are gone?'

'Oh, they have sent me a cheerful brisk noisy good-natured foolish young man with scrofulous ears – a vicious habit of body – to be my assistant. Those who are not dead will survive him.'

'And where are you going now? Lord, Stephen, how prying and inquisitive I am. Just like my aunt Williams. I trust I have not been indiscreet.'

'Oh,' cried Stephen, suddenly filled with a strong temptation to tell her that he was going to be landed on the Spanish coast at the dark of the moon – the classical temptation of the secret agent in his loneliness, but one that he had never felt before. 'Oh, 'tis only a dismal piece of law-business. I shall go to town first, then to Plymouth, and so perhaps to Ireland for a while.'

'To town? But Brighton is quite out of your way – I had imagined you had to go to Portsmouth, when you offered me a lift. Why have you come so far out of your way?'

'The dew-ponds, the wheatears, the pleasure of driving over grass.'

'What a dogged brute you are, Maturin, upon my honour,' said Diana. 'I shall lay out for no more compliments.'

'No, but in all sadness,' said Stephen, 'I like sitting in a chaise with you; above all when you are like this. I could wish this road might go on for ever.'

There was a pause; the chaise was filled with waiting; but he did not go on, and after a moment she said with a forced laugh, 'Well done, Maturin. You are quite a courtier. But I am afraid I can see its end already. There is the sea, and this must be the beginning of the Devil's Punchbowl. And will you really drive me up to the door in style? I thought I should have to arrive in a pair of pattens – I brought them in that little basket with the flap. I am so grateful; and you shall certainly have your narwhal. Pray, where are they to be had? At the poulterer's, I suppose.'

'You are too good, my dear. Would you be prepared to reveal the address at which you are to be set down?'

'Lady Jersey's, in the Parade.'

'Lady Jersey's?' She was the Prince of Wales's mistress: and Canning was a member of that set.

'She is a Villiers cousin by marriage, you know,' said Diana quickly. 'And there is nothing in those vulgar newspaper reports. They like one another: that is all. Why, Mrs Fitzherbert is devoted to her.'

'Ay? Sure, I know nothing of these things. Will I tell you about poor Macdonald's arm, now?'

'Oh, *do*,' cried Diana. 'I have been longing to ask, ever since we left Dover.'

They parted at Lady Jersey's door, having said nothing more, amidst the flurry of servants and baggage: tension, artificial smiles.

'A GENTLEMEN to see Miss Williams,' said Admiral Haddock's butler.

'Who is it, Rowley?' asked Sophia.

'The gentleman did not mention his name, ma'am. A sea-officer, ma'am. He asked for my master, and then for Miss Williams, so I showed him into the library.'

'Is he a tall, very good-looking midshipman?' asked Cecilia. 'Are you sure he did not ask for me?'

'Is he a commander?' asked Sophia, dropping her roses.

'The gentleman is in a cloak, ma'am: I could not see his rank. He might be a commander, though – not a midshipman, oh no, dear me. He come in a four-horse shay.'

From the library window Stephen saw Sophia running across the lawn, holding up her skirt and trailing rose-petals. She took the steps up to the terrace three at a time: 'A deer might have taken them with such sweet grace,' he observed. He saw her stop dead and close her eyes for a second when she understood that the gentleman in the library was Dr Maturin; but she opened the door with hardly a pause and cried, 'What a delightful surprise! How kind to come to see us. Are you in Plymouth? I thought you were ordered for the Baltic.'

'The *Polychrest* is in the Baltic,' he said, kissing her heartily. 'I am on leave of absence.' He turned her to the light and observed, 'You are looking well – very well – quite a remarkable pink.'

'Dear, dear Dr Maturin,' she said, 'you really must not salute young ladies like that. Not in England. Of course I am pink – scarlet, I dare say. You kissed me!'

'Did I, my dear? Well, no great harm. Do you take your porter?'

'Most religiously, in a silver tankard: I almost like it, now.

What may I offer you? The admiral always takes his grog about this time. Are you in Plymouth for long? I do hope you will stay.'

'If you could give me a cup of coffee, you would do me a most essential service. I lay at Exeter, and they gave me the vilest brew . . . No, I am on the wing – I sail with this tide – but I did not like to pass without paying my respects. I have been travelling since Friday, and to sit with my friends for half an hour is a charming respite.

'Since Friday? Then perhaps you have not heard the splendid news?'

'Never a word, at all.'

'The Patriotic Fund have voted Captain Aubrey a sword of a hundred guineas, and the merchants a piece of plate, for destroying the *Bellone*. Is it not splendid news? Though no more than he deserves, I am sure – indeed, not nearly enough. Will he be promoted, do you think?'

'For a letter of marque, a privateer? No. And he does not look for it. Promotion is the very devil these days. There are not enough ships to go round. Old Jarvie did not build them, but he did make men post. So we have herds of unemployed captains; shoals of unpromoted commanders.'

'But none so deserving as Captain Aubrey,' said Sophia, dismissing the rest of the Navy List. 'You have not told me how he is.'

'Nor have you asked after your cousin Diana.'

'How shocking of me; I beg your pardon. I hope she is quite well.'

'Very well. In charming spirits. We drove from Dover to Brighton together some days ago: she is to spend a week with Lady Jersey.'

It was clear that Sophia had never heard of Lady Jersey. She said, 'I am so glad. No one can be better company than Diana when she is in – ' she quickly changed 'a good temper' to a weak 'in charming spirits.'

'As for Jack, I am sorry to say I cannot congratulate *him*

upon charming spirits; nor indeed upon any spirits at all. He is unhappy. His ship is a very miserable vessel; his admiral is a scrub; he has a great many worries ashore and afloat. And I tell you bluntly, my dear, he is jealous of me and I of him. I love him as much as I have loved any man, but often these last months I have wondered whether we can stay in the same ship without fighting. I am no longer what small comfort I was to him, but a present irritation and a constraint – our friendship is constrained. And the tension, cooped up in a little small ship day after day, is very great – covert words, the risk of misunderstanding, watching the things we say or even sing. It is well enough when we are far out in the ocean. But with Channel service, in and out of the Downs – no, it cannot last.'

'Does he know of your feelings for Diana? Surely not. Surely, to his best friend, he would never . . . He loves you dearly.'

'Oh, as to that – yes, I believe he does, in his own way; and I believe if he had never been led into this by a series of unhappy misunderstandings, he would never have "crossed my hawse", as he would put it. As for his knowing the nature of my feelings, I like to think he does not. Certainly not with any sharp clarity, in the forefront of his mind. Jack is not quick in such matters; he is not in any way an analytical thinker, except aboard a ship in action: but light creeps in, from time to time.'

They were interrupted by the appearance of the coffee, and for some time they sat without speaking, each deep in thought.

'You know, my dear,' said Stephen, stirring his cup, 'where women are concerned, a man is very helpless against direct attack. I do not mean in the nature of a challenge, which of course he is bound in honour to take up, but in the nature of a plain statement of affection.'

'I could not, could not possibly write to him again.'

'No. But if for example the *Polychrest* were to put in here, which is very likely in the course of the summer, you could perfectly well ask, or the Admiral could ask him to give you

and your sister a lift to the Downs – nothing more usual-
nothing more conducive to an understanding.'

'Oh, I could never do so. Dear Dr Maturin, do but think
how immodest, how pushing – and the risk of a refusal. I
should die.'

'Had you seen his tears over your kindness, your hampers,
you would not speak of refusal. He was all a-swim.'

'Yes, you told me in your dear letter. But no, really, it is
quite impossible – unthinkable. A man might do so, but for a
woman it is quite impossible.'

'There is much to be said for directness.'

'Oh, yes, yes! There is. Everything would be so much simpler if one only said what one thought, or felt. Tell me,' she
said shyly, after a pause, 'may I say something to you, perhaps
quite improper and wrong?'

'I should take it very friendly in you, my dear.'

'Then if you were perfectly direct with Diana, and proposed
marriage to her, might not we all be perfectly happy? Depend
upon it, that is what she expects.'

'I? Make her an offer? My dearest Sophie, you know what
kind of a match I am. A little ugly small man, with no name
and no fortune. And you know her pride and ambition and
connections.'

'You think too little of yourself, indeed you do. Far, far too
little. You are much too humble. In your own way you are
quite as good looking as Captain Aubrey – everybody says so.
Besides, you have your castle.'

'Honey-love, a castle in Spain is not a castle in Kent. Mine
is mostly ruin – the sheep shelter in the part with a roof. And
the great part of my land is mere mountain; even in peace-
time it hardly brings me in two or three hundred English
pounds a year.'

'But that is *plenty* to live on. If she loves you just a little,
and I cannot see how any woman could not, she would be
delighted with an offer.'

'Your sweet partiality blinds you, my dear. And as for love –

love, that amiable, unmeaning word – however you may define it, I do not believe she knows what it is, as you told me once yourself. Affection, kindness, friendship, good nature sometimes, yes: beyond that, nothing. No. I must wait. It may come, perhaps; and in any case, I am content to be a pis aller. I too know how to wait. I dare not risk a direct refusal – perhaps a contemptuous refusal.'

'What is a pis aller?'

'What one accepts when one can do no better. It is my only hope.'

'You are too humble. Oh, you are. I am sure you are mistaken. Believe me, Stephen: I am a woman, after all.'

'Besides, I am a Catholic, you know. A Papist.'

'What does that matter, above all to her? Anyhow, the Howards are Catholics – Mrs Fitzherbert is a Catholic.'

'Mrs Fitzherbert? How odd you should mention her. My dear, I must go. I thank you for your loving care of me. I may write again? There was no unkindness because of my letters?'

'None. I do not mention them.'

'Not for a month or so, however: and perhaps I may pass by Mapes. How is your Mama, your sisters? May I ask after Mr Bowles?'

'They are very well, thank you. As for him,' she said, with a flash of her eye, the calm grey growing fierce, 'I sent him about his business. He became impertinent – "Can it be that your affections are engaged elsewhere?" says he. "Yes, sir, they are," I replied. "Without your mother's consent?" he cried, and I desired him to leave the room at once. It was the boldest thing done this age.'

'Sophie, your very humble servant,' said Stephen, standing up. 'Pray make my compliments to the Admiral.'

'Too humble, oh far too humble,' said Sophie, offering her cheek.

TIDES, TIDES, the Cove of Cork, the embarkation waiting on the moon, a tall swift-pacing mule in the bare torrid mountains quivering in the sun, palmetto-scrub, Señor don Esteban Maturin y Domanova kisses the feet of the very reverend Lord Abbot of Montserrat and begs the honour of an audience. The endless white road winding, the inhuman landscape of Aragon, cruel sun and weariness, dust, weariness to the heart, and doubt. What was independence but a word? What did any form of government matter? Freedom: to do what? Disgust, so strong that he leant against the saddle, hardly able to bring himself to mount. A shower on the Maladetta, and everywhere the scent of thyme: eagles wheeling under thunder-clouds, rising, rising. 'My mind is too confused for anything but direct action,' he said. 'The flight disguised as an advance.'

The lonely beach, lanterns flashing from the offing, an infinity of sea. Ireland again, with such memories at every turn. 'If I could throw off some of this burden of memory,' said Stephen to his second glass of laudanum, 'I should be more nearly sane. Here's to you, Villiers, my dear.' The Holyhead mail and two hundred and seventy miles of rattling jerking, falling asleep, waking in another country: rain, rain, rain: Welsh voices in the night. London, and his report, trying to disentangle the strands of altruism, silliness, mere enthusiasm, self-seeking, love of violence, personal resentment; trying too to give the impossible plain answer to the question 'Is Spain going to join France against us, and if so, when?' And there he was in Deal once more, sitting alone in the snug of the Rose and Crown, watching the shipping in the Downs and drinking a pot of tea: he had an odd detachment from all this familiar scene – the uniforms that passed outside his bow-window were intimately well known, but it was as though they belonged to another world, a world at one or two removes, and as though their inhabitants, walking, laughing, talking out there on the other side of the pane were mute, devoid both of colour and real substance.

Yet the good tea (an unrivalled cholagogue), the muffin, the comfort of his chair, the ease and relaxation after these weeks and months of jading hurry and incessant motion – tension, danger and suspicion too – insensibly eased him back into this frame, re-attached him to this life of which he had been an integral part. He had been much caressed at the Admiralty; a very civil, acute, intelligent old gentleman called in from the Foreign Office had said the most obliging things; and Lord Melville had repeatedly mentioned their sense of obligation, their desire to acknowledge it by some suitable expression of their esteem – any appointment, any request that Dr Maturin might choose to make would receive the most earnest and sympathetic consideration. He was recalling the scene and sipping his tea with little sounds of inward complacency when he saw Heneage Dundas stop on the pavement outside, shade his eyes, and peer in through the window, evidently looking for a friend. His nose came into contact with the glass, and its tip flattened into a pale disc. 'Not unlike the foot of a gasteropod,' observed Stephen, and when he had considered its loss of superficial circulation for a while he attracted Dundas's attention, beckoning him in and offering him a cup of tea and a piece of muffin.

'I have not seen you these months past,' said Dundas in a very friendly tone. 'I asked for you several times, whenever *Polychrest* was in, and they told me you was on leave. How brown you are! Where have you been?'

'In Ireland – tedious family business.'

'In Ireland? You astonish me. Every time I have been in Ireland it has rained. If you had not told me, I should have sworn you had been in the Med, ha, ha, ha. Well, I asked for you several times: I had something particular to say. Excellent muffin, eh? If there is one thing I like better than another with my tea, it is a well-turned piece of muffin.' After this promising beginning, Dundas fell strangely mute: it was clear that he wanted to say something of importance, but did not know how to get it out handsomely – or, indeed, at all. Did he want to borrow money? Was some disease preying on his mind?

'You have a particular kindness for Jack Aubrey, Dr Maturin, I believe?'

'I have a great liking for him, sure.'

'So have I. So have I. We were shipmates even before we were rated midshipmen – served in half a dozen commissions together. But he don't listen to me, you know; he don't attend. I was junior to him all along, and that counts, of course; besides, there are some things you cannot tell a man. What I wanted to say to you was, do you think you might just hint to him that he is – I will not say ruining his career, but sailing very close to the wind? He does not clear his convoys – there have been complaints – he puts into the Downs when the weather is not so very terrible – and people have a tolerable good notion why, and it won't answer, not in Whitehall.'

'Lingering in port is a practice not unknown to the Navy.'

'I know what you mean. But it is a practice confined to admirals with a couple of fleet actions and a peerage behind them, not to commanders. It won't do, Maturin. I do beg you will tell him so.'

'I will do what I can. God knows what will come of it. I thank you for this mark of confidence, Dundas.'

'The *Polychrest* is trying to weather the South Foreland now; I saw her from the *Goliath*, missing stays and having to wear again. She has been over the way, looking at the French gunboats in Etaples. She should manage it when the sea-breeze sets in; but God help us, what leeway that ship does make. She has no right to be afloat.'

'I shall take a boat and meet her,' said Stephen. 'I am quite impatient to see my shipmates again.'

They received him kindly, very kindly; but they were busy, anxious and overwrought. Both watches were on deck to moor the *Polychrest*, and as he watched them at their work it was clear to Stephen that the feeling in the ship had not improved at all. Oh very far from it. He knew enough about the sea to tell the difference between a willing crew and a dogged, sullen set of men who had to be driven. Jack was in his cabin, writing his report, and Parker had the deck: was the man deranged? An incessant barking flow of orders, threats, insults, diversified with kicks and blows: more vehement than when Stephen had left the ship, and surely now there was a note of hysteria? Not far behind him in vociferation there was Macdonald's replacement, a stout pink and white young man with thick pale lips; his authority extended only to his soldiers, but he made up for this by his activity, bounding about with his cane like a jack-in-a-box.

When he went below this impression was confirmed. His assistant, Mr Thompson, was not perhaps very wise nor very skilful – his attempt at a Cheseldon's lithotomy had an ominous smell of gangrene – but he did not seem at all brutal or even unkind; yet as they went round their patients there was not a smile – proper answers, but no sort of interchange, no friendliness whatsoever, except from one old Sophie, a Pole by the name of Jackruckie, whose hernia was troubling him again. And even his strange jargon (he spoke very little English) was uneasy, conscious, and inhibited. In the next cot lay a man with a bandaged head. Gummata, the sequelae of an old depressed fracture, malingering? In an eager attempt to justify his diagnosis, Thompson darted a pointing finger at the man's head, and instantly the crooked protective arm shot up.

By the time he had finished his rounds and settled in his cabin, the *Polychrest* was moored. Jack had gone off to make his report, and something nearer to peace had come down on the ship. There was only the steady grind of the pumps and the now almost voiceless bark of the first lieutenant getting the courses, the *square* courses, and topsails furled in a body, smooth enough for a royal review.

He walked into the gun-room, which was empty but for the Marine officer. He was reclining upon two chairs with his feet on the table; and craning up his neck he cried, 'Why, you must be the sawbones back again. I'm glad to see you. My name is Smithers. Forgive me if I do not get up; I am quite fagged out with mooring the ship.'

'I noticed that you were very active.'

'Pretty brisk, pretty brisk. I like my men to know who's who and what's what and to move smart – they'll smart else, you catch my meaning, ha, ha. They tell me you are quite a hand with a cello. We must have a bout some night. I play the German flute.'

'I dare say you are a remarkable performer.'

'Pretty brisk, pretty brisk. I don't like to boast, but I fancy I was the best player at Eton in my time. If I chose to do it professionally, I should make twice what they give me for fighting His Majesty's wars for him – not that the pewter matters to *me*, of course. It's precious slow in this ship, don't you find? Nobody to talk to; nothing but ha'penny whist and convoy-duty and looking out for the French prams. What do you say to a hand of cards?'

'Is the captain returned, do you know?'

'No. He won't be back for hours and hours. You have plenty of time. Come let us have a hand of piquet.'

'I play very little.'

'You need not be afraid of him. He'll be pulling down to Dover against the tide – he's got a luscious piece there – won't be back for hours and hours. A luscious piece, by God: I could wear it. I'd have a mind to cut him out, if he weren't my captain: it's a wonder what a red coat will do, believe you me. I dare say I could, too; she invited all the officers last week, and she looked at me . . .'

'You cannot be speaking of Mrs Villiers, sir?'

'A pretty young widow – yes, that's right. Do you know her?'

'Yes, sir: and I should be sorry to hear her spoken of with disrespect.'

'Oh, well, if she's a friend of yours,' cried Smithers, with a knowing leer, 'that's different. I have said nothing. Mum's the word. Now what about our game?'

'Do you play well?'

'I was born with a pack of cards in my hand.'

'I must warn you I never play for small stakes: it bores me.'

'Oh, I'm not afraid of you. I've played at White's – I played at Almack's with my friend Lord Craven till daylight put the candles out! What do you think of that?'

The other officers came down one by one and watched them play; watched them in silence until the end of the sixth partie, when Stephen laid down a point of eight followed by a quart major, and Pullings, who had been sitting behind him, straining his stomach to the groaning-point to make him win, burst out with 'Ha, ha, you picked a wrong 'un when you tackled the Doctor.'

'Do be quiet, can't you, when gentlemen are playing cards. And smoking that vile stinking pipe in the gun-room – it is turning the place into one of your low pot-houses. How can a man concentrate his mind with all this noise? Now you have made me lose my score. What do you make it, Doctor?'

'With repique and capot, that is a hundred and thirty; and since I believe you are two short of your hundred, I must add your score to mine.'

'You will take my note of hand, I suppose?'

'We agreed to play for cash, you remember.'

'Then I shall have to fetch it. It will leave me short. But you will have to give me my revenge.'

'Captain's coming aboard, gentlemen,' said a quartermaster. Then reappearing a moment later, 'Port side, gents.' They relaxed: he was returning with no ceremony.

'I must leave you,' said Stephen. 'Thank you for the game.'

'But you can't go away just when you have won all that money,' cried Smithers.

'On the contrary,' said Stephen. 'It is the very best moment to leave.'

'Well, it ain't very sporting. That's all I say. It ain't very sporting.'

'You think not? Then when you have laid down the gold you may cut double or quits. Sans revanche, eh?'

Smithers came back with two rouleaux of guineas and part of a third. 'It's not the money,' he said. 'It's the principle of the thing.'

'Aces high,' said Stephen, looking impatiently at his watch. 'Please to cut.'

A low heart: knave of diamonds. 'Now you will have to take my note for the rest,' said Smithers.

'Jack,' said Stephen, 'may I come in?'

'Come in, come in, my dear fellow, come in,' cried Jack, springing forward and guiding him to a chair. 'I have scarcely seen you – how very pleasant this is! I cannot tell you how dreary the ship has been without you. How brown you are!'

In spite of an animal revulsion at the catch of the scent that hung about Jack's coat – never was there a more unlucky present – Stephen felt a warmth in his heart. His face displayed no more than a severe questioning, professional look, however, and he said, 'Jack, what have you been doing to yourself? You are thin, grey – costive, no doubt. You have lost another couple of stone: the skin under your eyes is a disagreeable yellow. Has the bullet-wound been giving trouble? Come, take off your shirt. I was never happy that I had extracted all the lead; my probe still seemed to grate on something.'

'No, no. It has quite healed over again. I am very well. It is only that I don't sleep. Toss, turn, can't get off, then ill dreams and I wake up some time in the middle watch – never get off again, and I am stupid all the rest of the day. And damned ill-tempered, Stephen; I sway away on all top-ropes for a nothing, and then I am sorry afterwards. Is it my liver, do you think? Not yesterday, but the day before I had a damned unpleasant surprise: I was shaving, and thinking of something else; and Killick had hung the glass aft the scuttle instead of its usual place. So just for a moment I caught sight of my face as though it was a stranger looking in. When I understood it was me, I said, "Where did I get that damned forbidding ship's corporal's face?" and determined not to look like that again – it reminded me of that unhappy fellow Pigot, of the *Hermione*. And this morning there it was again, glaring back at me out of the glass. That is another reason why I am so glad to see you: you will give me one of your treble-shotted slime-draughts to get me to sleep. It's the devil, you know, not sleeping: no wonder a man looks like a ship's corporal. And these dreams – do you dream, Stephen?'

'No, sir.'

'I thought not. You have a head-piece . . . however, I had one some nights ago, about your narwhal; and Sophie was mixed up with it in some way. It sounds nonsense, but it was so full of unhappiness that I woke blubbering like a child. Here it is, by the way.' He reached behind him and passed the long tapering spiral of ivory.

Stephen's eyes gleamed as he took it and turned it slowly round and round in his hands. 'Oh thank you, thank you, Jack,' he cried. 'It is perfect – the very apotheosis of a tooth.'

'There were some longer ones, well over a fathom, but they had lost their tips, and I thought you would like to *get the point, ha, ha, ha.*' It was a flash of his old idiot self, and he wheezed and chuckled for some time, his blue eyes as clear and delighted as they had been long ago: wild glee over an infinitesimal grain of merriment.

'It is a most prodigious phenomenon,' said Stephen, cherishing it. 'How much do I owe you, Jack?' He put his hand in his pocket and pulled out a handkerchief, which he laid on the table, then a handful of gold, then another, and scrabbled for the odd coins, observing that it was foolish to carry it loose: far better made a bundle of.

'Good God,' cried Jack, staring. 'What on earth have you been at? Have you taken a treasure-ship? I have never seen so much money all at once in my life.'

'I have been stripping a jackeen that annoyed me: the young nagin, the coxcomb in the red coat. The *lobster*, as you would say.'

'Smithers. But this is gaming, Stephen, not mere play.'

'Yes. He seemed concerned at his loss: a lardish sweat. But he has all the appearance of wealth – all its petulant arrogance, certainly.'

'He has private means, I know; but you must have left him very short – this is more than a year's pay.'

'So much the better. I intended he should smart.'

'Stephen, I must ask you not to do it again. He is an underbred puppy, I grant you, and I wonder the jollies ever took him, they being so particular; but the ship is in a bad enough way as it is, without getting a name for gaming. Will you not let him have it back?'

'I will not. But since you wish it, I shall not play with him again. Now how much do I owe you, my dear?'

'Oh, nothing, nothing. Do me the pleasure of accepting it as a present. Pray do. It was very little, and the prize paid for it.'

'You took a prize, so?'

'Yes. Just one. No chance of any more – the *Polychrest* can be recognized the moment she is hull up on the horizon, now that she is known. I am sorry you were not aboard, though it did not amount to much: I sold my share to Parker for seventy-five pounds, being short at the time, and he did not make a great deal out of it. She was a little Dutch shalloop, creeping along the back of the Dogger, laden with deals; and we crept just that trifle less almighty slow. A contemptible prize – we should have let her go in the *Sophie* – but I thought I ought to blood the hands at last. Not that it did much good. The ship is in a bad way; and Harte rides me hard.'

'Pray show me your honorary sword and the merchants' piece of plate. I called upon Sophie, and she told me about them.'

'Sophie?' cried Jack, as though he had been kicked. 'Oh. Oh, yes – yes, of course. You called upon her.' As an attempt at diverting his mind to happier thoughts, this was not a success. After a moment he said, 'I am sorry, they are not here. I ran short again. For the time being, they are in Dover.'

'Dover,' said Stephen, and thought for a while, running the narwhal's horn through his fingers. 'Dover. Listen, Jack, you take insane risks, going ashore so often, particularly in Dover.'

'Why particularly in Dover?'

'Because your often presence there is notorious. If it is notorious to your friends, how much more so to your enemies? It is known in Whitehall; it must be known to your creditors in Mincing Lane. Do not look angerly now, Jack, but let me tell you three things: I must do so, as a friend. First, you will certainly be arrested for debt if you continue to go ashore. Second, it is said in the service that you cling to this station; and what harm that may do you professionally, you know better than I. No, let me finish. Third, have you considered how you expose Diana Villiers by your very open attentions, in circumstances of such known danger?'

'Has Diana Villiers put herself under your protection? Has she commissioned you to say this to me?'

'No, sir.'

'Then I do not see what right you have to speak to me in this way.'

'Sure, Jack, my dear, I have the right of a friend, have I not? I will not say duty, for that smells of cant.'

'A friend who wants a clear field, maybe. I may not be very clever, no God-damned Macchiavelli, but I believe I know a ruse de guerre when I see one. For a long time I did not know what to think about you and Diana Villiers – first one thing and then another – for you are a devilish sly fox, and break back upon your line. But now I see the reason for this standing off and on, this "not at home", and all this damned unkind treatment, and all this cracking-up of clever, amusing Stephen Maturin, who understands people and never preaches, whereas I am a heavy-handed fool that understands nothing. It is time we had a clear explanation about Diana Villiers, so that we may know where we stand.'

'I desire no explanations. They are never of any use, particularly in matters of this kind, where what one might term *sex-*

uality is concerned – reason flies out of the window; all candour with it. In any case, even where this passion is not concerned, language is so imperfect, that . . .'

'Any bastard can cowardly evade the issue by a flood of words.'

'You have said enough, sir,' said Stephen, standing up. 'Too much by far: you must withdraw.'

'I shall not withdraw,' cried Jack, very pale. 'And I will add, that when a man comes back from leave as brown as a Gibraltar Jew, and says he had delicate weather in Ireland, he lies. I will stand by that, and I am perfectly willing to give you any satisfaction you may choose to ask for.'

'It is odd enough,' said Stephen, in a low voice, 'that our acquaintance should have begun with a challenge, and that it should end with one.'

'DUNDAS,' HE SAID, in the small room of the Rose and Crown, 'how good of you to come so soon. I am sorry to say I must ask you to be my second. I tried to follow your excellent suggestion, but I mishandled it – I did not succeed. I should have seen he was in a state of unhappy passion, but I persisted untimely, and he called me a coward and a liar.'

Dundas's face changed to one of horror. 'Oh, that is very bad,' he cried. 'Oh, Lord.' A long, unhappy pause. 'No question of an apology, I suppose?'

'None whatsoever. One word he did withdraw,' – Captain Aubrey presents his compliments to Dr Maturin, and begs to say that an expression escaped him yesterday evening, a common expression to do with birth, that might have been taken to have a personal bearing. None was intended, and Captain Aubrey withdraws that word, at the same time regretting that, in the hurry of the moment, he made use of it. The other remarks he stands by – 'but the gratuitous lie remains. It is not easy of digestion.'

'Of course not. What a sad, sad business. We shall have to

fit it in between voyages. I feel horribly responsible. Maturin, have you been out before? I should never forgive myself if anything were to happen to you. Jack is an old hand.'

'I can look after myself.'

'Well,' said Dundas, looking at him dubiously, 'I shall go and see him at once. Oh, what a damned unlucky thing. It may take some time, unless we can arrange it tonight. That is the wretched thing about the Navy: soldiers can always settle out of hand, but with us I have known an affair hang fire three months and more.'

It could not be arranged that night, for on the evening tide the *Polychrest* was ordered to sea. She bore away to the southwest with a couple of store-ships, carrying with her more than her usual load of unhappiness.

The news of their disagreement spread throughout the ship; the extent and the deadly nature of it were quite unknown, but so close an intimacy could not come to a sudden end without being noticed, and Stephen watched the reactions of his shipmates with a certain interest. He knew that in many ships the captain played the part of a monarch and the officers that of a court – that there was eager competition for Caesar's favour; but he had never thought of himself as the favourite; he had never known how much the respect paid to him was a reflection of the great man's power. Parker, who revered authority far more than he disliked his captain, drew away from Stephen; so did the featureless Jones; and Smithers did not attempt to conceal his animosity. Pullings behaved with marked kindness in the gun-room; but Pullings owed everything to Jack, and on the quarterdeck he seemed a little shy of Stephen's company. Not that he was often put to this trial, however, for convention required that the principals in a duel, like bride and bridegroom, should see nothing of one another before they reached the altar. Most of the old Sophies shared Pullings' distress; they looked at him with anxious constraint, never with unkindness; but it was clear to

Stephen that quite apart from any question of interest, their prime loyalty lay with Jack, and he embarrassed them as little as he could.

He spent the chief of his time with his patients – the lithotomy called for radical measures: a fascinating case and one that called for hours of close surveillance – reading in his cabin, and playing chess with the master, who surprised him by showing particular consideration and friendliness. Mr Goodridge had sailed as a midshipman and master's mate with Cook; he was a good mathematician, an excellent navigator, and he would have reached commissioned rank if it had not been for his unfortunate battle with the chaplain of the *Bellerophon*.

'No, Doctor,' said he, leaning back from the board, 'you may struggle and wruggle as you please, but I have him pinned. It is mate in three.'

'It is muchwhat like,' said Stephen. 'Must I resign?'

'I think you must. Though I like a man that fights, to be sure. Doctor,' he said, 'have you reflected upon the phoenix?'

'Not, perhaps, as often as I should have done. As I remember, she makes her nest in Arabia Felix, using cinnamon for the purpose; and with cinnamon at six and eight-pence, surely this is a thoughtless thing to do?'

'You are pleased to be facetious, Doctor. But the phoenix, now, is worth your serious consideration. Not the bird of the tales, of course, which cannot be attempted to be believed in by a philosophical gentleman like you, but what I might call the bird behind the bird. I should not care to have it known in the ship, but in my opinion, the phoenix is Halley's comet.'

'Halley's comet, Mr Goodridge?' cried Stephen.

'Halley's comet, Doctor; and others,' said the master, pleased with the effect of his words. 'And when I say opinion, I might say fact, for to a candid mind the thing is proved beyond the slightest doubt. A little calculation makes it plain. The best authors give 500, 1416, and 7006 years as the proper intervals between phoenixes; and Tacitus tells us that one appeared under Sesostris, another under Amasis, another in the reign of the third Ptolemy, and another in the twentieth year of Tiberius; and we know of many more. Now let us take the periods of Halley's, Biela's, Lexel's, and Encke's comets and plot them against our phoenixes, just allowing for lunar years and errors of computation in the ancients, and the thing is done! I could show you calculations, with respect to their orbits, that would amaze you; the astronomers are sadly out, because they do not take account of the phoenix in their equations. They do not see that for the ancients the pretended phoenix was a poetical way of saying a blazing heavenly phenomenon – that the phoenix was an emblem; and they are too proud and sullen and dogged and wanting in candour to believe it when told. The chaplain of the *Bellerophon*, who set up for an astronomer, would not be convinced. I stretched him out on deck with a heaving-mallet.'

'I am quite convinced, Mr Goodridge.'

'It ruined my career,' – with a fiery look into the past – 'It ruined my career; but I should do it again, the contumelious dog, the . . . however, I must not swear; and he was a clergyman. Since then I have not told many people, but in time I mean to publish – *The Phoenix Impartially Considered, A Modest Proposal*, by an Officer of Rank in the Royal Navy – and that will flutter some dovecotes I could mention; that will bring them up with a round turn. My phoenixes, Doctor, tell me we may expect a comet in 1805; I will not give the month, because of a doubt in Ussher as to the exact length of the reign of Nabonidus.'

'I shall look forward to it with confident expectation,' said Stephen; and he reflected, 'I wish they could foretell an end to this waiting.'

'How strangely I dread the event,' he said, sitting down by his patient and counting his respirations, 'and yet how hard I find it to wait.'

In the far corner of the sick-bay the low murmur of conversation began again; the men were used to his presence, and to his absences – more than once a messmate had brought in the forbidden grog, walking right past the Doctor without being noticed – and he did not disturb them. At present two Highlanders were talking slowly to an Irishman, slowly and repetitively in Gaelic, as he lay there on his stomach to ease his flayed back.

'I follow them best when I do not attend at all,' observed Stephen. 'When I do not strain, or try to isolate any word. It is the child in long clothes that understands, myself in Cahirciveen. They are of the opinion that we shall anchor in the Downs before eight bells. I hope they are right; I hope I find Dundas.'

They were right, and before the way was off the *Polychrest* he heard the sentry hail a boat and the answering cry of '*Franchise*' that meant her captain was coming aboard. The bosun's pipe, the proper respect shown to a post captain, the stumping of feet overhead, and then 'Captain Dundas's compliments, and might he have a word with Dr Maturin, when at leisure?'

Discretion was of first importance in these matters, and Heneage Dundas, knowing how public a spoken word might be in a crowded sloop, had written his message on a piece of paper. 'Will half past six on Saturday suit? In the dunes. I will come for you.' He handed the paper, with a grave, meaning look. Stephen glanced at it, nodded, and said, 'Perfect. I am obliged to you. Will you give me a lift ashore? I should spend tomorrow in Deal, should I not? Perhaps you would be so very kind as to mention it to Captain Aubrey.'

'I have: we may go now, if you wish.'

'I will be with you in two minutes.' There were some papers that must not be seen, a few manuscripts and letters that he prized; but these were almost ready, and his necessary bag was at hand. In two minutes he followed Dundas up the companion-ladder and they rowed away over the calm sea to Deal. Speaking in such a way as to be clear to Stephen alone, Dundas gave him to understand that Jack's second, a Colonel

Rankin, could not get down until tomorrow night – Friday; that he had seen Rankin earlier in the week, and that they had decided on an excellent spot near the castle often used for this purpose and convenient in every way. 'You are provided, I suppose?' he asked, just before the boat touched.

'I think so,' said Stephen. 'If not, I will call on you.'

'Goodbye, then,' said Dundas, shaking his hand. 'I must go back to my ship. If I do not see you before, then at the time we agreed.'

Stephen settled in at the Rose and Crown, called for a horse, and rode slowly towards Dover, reflecting upon the nature of dunes; upon the extraordinary loneliness surrounding each man; and on the inadequacy of language – a thought that he would have developed to Jack if he had been given time. 'And yet for all its inadequacy, how marvellously well it allows them to deal with material things,' he said, looking at the ships in the roadstead, the unbelievable complexity of named ropes, blocks, sails that would carry the crowd of isolated individuals to the Bosphorus, the West Indies, Sumatra, or the South Sea whaling grounds. And as he looked, his eyes running along the odd cocked-hat form of the *Polychrest* he saw her captain's gig pull away from the side, set its lugsail, and head for Dover.

'Knowing them both, as I do,' he observed, 'I should be surprised if there were much liking between them. It is a perverse relationship. That, indeed, may be the source of its violence.'

Reaching Dover, he went directly to the hospital and examined his patients: his lunatic was motionless, crouched in a ball, sunk even below tears; but Macdonald's stump was healing well. The flaps were as neat as a parcel, and he noted with pleasure that the hair on them continued to grow in its former direction.

'You will soon be quite well,' he said, pointing this out to the Marine. 'I congratulate you upon an excellent healthy constitution. In a few weeks' time you will rival Nelson,

spring one-handed from ship to ship – happier than the
Admiral in that you have your sword-arm still.'

'How you relieve my mind,' said Macdonald. 'I had been
mortally afraid of gangrene. I owe you a great deal, Doctor:
believe me, I am sensible of it.' Stephen protested that any
butcher, any butcher's boy, could have done as much – a simple operation – a real pleasure to cut into such healthy flesh –
and their conversation drifted away to the likelihood of a
French invasion, of a breach with Spain, and to the odd
rumours of St Vincent impeaching Lord Melville for malversation, before it returned to Nelson.

'He is a hero of yours, I believe?' said Macdonald.

'Oh, I hardly know anything of the gentleman,' said
Stephen. 'I have never even seen him. But from what I understand, he seems quite an active, zealous, enterprising officer.
He is much loved in the service, surely? Captain Aubrey
thinks the world of him.'

'Maybe,' said Macdonald. 'But he is no hero of mine.
Caracciolo sticks in my gullet. And then there is his example.'

'Could there be a better example, for a sea-officer?'

'I have been thinking, as I lie here in bed,' said Macdonald.
'I have been thinking of justification.' Stephen's heart sank:
he knew the reputation of the Scots for theological discussion, and he dreaded an outpouring of Calvinistical views,
flavoured, perhaps, with some doctrines peculiar to the Royal
Marines. 'Men, particularly Lowlanders, are never content
with taking their sins upon their own heads, or with making
their own law; a young fellow will play the blackguard, not
because he is satisfied that his other parts will outweigh the
fact, but because Tom Jones was paid for lying with a woman
– and since Tom Jones was a hero, it is quite in order for him
to do the same. It might have been better for the Navy if Nelson had been put to a stable bucket when he was a wee bairn.
If the justification that a fellow in a play or a tale can provide,
is enough to confirm a blackguard, think what a live hero can
do! Whoremongering – lingering in port – hanging officers

who surrender on terms. A pretty example!' Stephen looked at him attentively for signs of fever; they were certainly there, but to no dangerous degree at present. Macdonald stared out of the window, and whatever he may have seen there, apart from the blank wall, prompted him to say, 'I hate women. They are entirely destructive. They drain a man, sap him, take away all his good: and none the better for it themselves.' After a pause, 'Nasty, nasty queans.'

Stephen said, 'I have a service to beg of you, Mr Macdonald.'

'Name it, sir, I beg: nothing could give me greater pleasure.'

'The loan of your pistols, if you please.'

'For any purpose but to shoot a Marine officer, they are yours and welcome. In my canteen there, under the window, if you would be so good.'

'Thank you, I will bring them back, or cause them to be brought, as soon as they have served their purpose.'

The evening, as he rode back, was as sweet as an early autumn evening could be, still, intensely humid, a royal blue sea on the right hand, pure dunes on the left, and a benign warmth rising from the ground. The mild horse, a good-natured creature, had a comfortable walk; it knew its way, but it seemed to be in no hurry to reach its stable – indeed, it paused from time to time to take leaves from a shrub that he could not identify; and Stephen sank into an agreeable languor, almost separated from his body: a pair of eyes, no more, floating above the white road, looking from left to right. 'There are days – good evening to you, sir' – a parson went by, walking with his cat, the smoke from his pipe keeping him company as he walked – 'there are days,' he reflected, 'when one sees as though one had been blind the rest of one's life. Such clarity – perfection in everything, not merely in the extraordinary. One lives in the very present moment; lives intently. There is no urge to be doing: being is the highest good. However,' he said, guiding the horse left-handed into the dunes, 'doing of some kind there must be.' He slid from

the saddle and said to the horse, 'Now how can I be sure of
your company, my dear?' The horse gazed at him with glistening, intelligent eyes, and brought its ears to bear. 'Yes, yes, you
are an honest fellow, no doubt. But you may not like the
bangs; and I may be longer than you choose to wait. Come,
let me hobble you with this small convenient strap. How little
I know about dunes,' he said, pacing out his distance and
placing a folded handkerchief at the proper height on a sandy
slope. 'A most curious study – a flora and a fauna entirely of
its own, no doubt.' He spread his coat to preserve the pistols
from the sand and loaded them carefully. 'What one is *bound*
to do, one usually does with little acknowledged feeling; a
vague desperation, no more,' he said, taking up his stance. Yet
as he did so his face assumed a cold, dangerous aspect and
his body moved with the easy precision of a machine. The
sand spat up from the edge of the handkerchief; the smoke
lay hardly stirring;' the horse was little affected by the noise,
but it watched idly for the first dozen shots or so.

'I have never known such consistently accurate weapons,'
he said aloud. 'I wonder, can I still do Dillon's old trick?' He
took a coin from his pocket, tossed it high, and shot it fair
and square on the top of its rise, between climbing and
falling. 'Charming instruments indeed: I must cover them
from the dew.' The sun had set; the light had so far diminished that the red tongue of flame lit up the misty hollow at
each discharge; the handkerchief was long ago reduced to its
component threads. 'Lord, I shall sleep tonight. Oh, what a
prodigious dew.'

In Dover, sheltered by the western heights, the darkness
fell earlier. Jack Aubrey, having done what little business he
had to do, and having called in vain at New Place – 'Mr
Lowndes was indisposed: Mrs Villiers was not at home' – sat
drinking beer in an ale-house near the Castle. It was a sad,
dirty, squalid little booth – a knocking-shop for the soldiers
upstairs – but it had two ways out, and with Bonden and
Lakey in the front room he felt reasonably safe from surprise.

He was as low as he had ever been in his life, a dull, savage
lowness; and the stupidity that came from the two pots he
had drunk did nothing to raise it. Anger and indignation were
his only refuge, and although they were foreign to his nature,
he was steadily angry and indignant.

An ensign and his flimsy little wench came in, hesitated on
seeing Jack, and settled in the far corner, slapping and pushing each other for want of words. The woman of the house
brought candles and asked whether he should like anything
more; he looked out of the window at the gathering twilight
and said no – what did he owe her, and for the men in the
tap?

'One and ninepence,' said the woman; and while he felt in
his pockets she stared him full in the face with an open, ignorant, suspicious, avid curiosity, her eyes screwed close and
her upper lip drawn back over her three yellow teeth. She did
not like the cloak he wore over his uniform; she did not like
the sobriety of his men, nor the way they kept themselves to
themselves; again, gentlemen as were gentlemen called for
wine, not beer; he had made no response to Betty's advances
nor to her own modest proposal of accommodation; she
wanted no pouffes in her house, and she should rather have
his room than his company.

He looked into the tap, told Bonden to wait for him at the
boat, and walked out by the back way, straight into a company of whores and soldiers. Two of the whores were fighting
there in the alley, tearing one another's hair and clothes, but
the rest were cheerful enough, and two of the women called
to him, coming alongside to whisper their talents, their
prices, and their clean bill of health.

He walked up to New Place. The demure look that accompanied the 'not at home' had convinced him that he should
see Diana's light. A faint glow between the drawn curtains up
there: he checked it twice, walking up and down the road,
and then fetched a long cast round the houses to reach a lane
that led behind New Place. The palings of the wilderness

were no great obstacle, but the walled inner garden needed
his cloak over the broken glass on top and then a most determined run and leap. Down in the garden the noise of the sea
was suddenly cut off – a total, listening silence and the falling
dew as he stood there amongst the crown imperials. Gradually the silence listened less; there were sounds inside the
house – talking from various windows, somebody locking
doors, closing the lower shutters. Then a quick heavy thud-
ding on the path, the deep wuff-wuff of dog Fred, the mastiff,
who was free of the garden and the yard by night, and who
slept in the summerhouse. But dog Fred was a mute creature;
he knew Captain Aubrey – thrust his wet nose into his hand
– and said no more. He was not altogether easy in his mind,
however, and when at last Jack gained the mossy path he followed him to the house, grumbling, pushing the back of his
knees. Jack took off his coat, folded it on the ground, and
then his sword: Fred at once lay on the coat, guarding both it
and the sword.

For months and months past a builder had been replacing
the roof-tiles of New Place; his improvised crane, with its
pulley, projecting from the parapet and its rope hung there
still, hooked to a bucket. Jack quickly made the ends fast,
tried it, took the strain, and swung himself up. Up, hand over
hand, past the library, where Mr Lowndes was writing at his
desk, past a window giving on to the stairs, up to the parapet.
From this point it was only a few steps to Diana's window, but
half-way up, before ever he reached the parapet, he had recognized Canning's great delighted laugh, a crowing noise that
rose from a deep ass, a particular laugh, that could not be
mistaken. For all that he went the whole way, until he was
there, sitting on the parapet with a sharp-angled view of all of
the room lat mattered. For three deep breaths he might have
burst through: it was extraordinarily vivid, the lit room, the
faces, their expressions picked out by the candlelight, their
intense life and their unconsciousness of a third person.
Then shame, unhappiness, extreme weariness put out the

rest, extinguished it utterly. No rage, no fire: all gone, and nothing to take their place. He moved some paces off to hear and see no more, and after a while he reached out to the end of the crane for the rope; automatically he frapped the two strands, took a sailor's grip on it, swung himself out into the darkness, and went down, down and down, pursued by that intensely amused laughter.

STEPHEN SPENT Friday morning writing, coding and decoding; he had rarely worked so fast or so well, and he had the agreeable feeling that he had produced a clear statement of complex situation. From a moral scruple he had refrained from his habitual dose, and he had spent the greater part of the night in a state of lucid consideration. When he had tied up all the ends, sealed his papers in a double cover and addressed the outer to Captain Dundas, he turned to is diary. 'This is perhaps the final detachment; and this perhaps the only way to live – free, surprisingly light and well, no diminution of interest but no commitment: a liberty I have hardly ever known. Life in its purest form – admirable in every way, only for the fact that it is not living, as I have ever understood the word. How changes the nature of time! The minutes and the hours stretch out; there is leisure to see the movement of the present. I shall walk out beyond Walmer Castle, by way of the sand-dunes: there is a wilderness of time in that arenaceous world.'

Jack also took a spell at his writing-table, but in the forenoon he was called away to the flagship.

'I have worn you down a trifle, my spark,' thought Admiral Harte, looking at him with satisfaction. 'Captain Aubrey, I have orders for you. You are to look into Chaulieu. *Thetis* and *Andromeda* chased a corvette into the harbour. She is believed to be the *Fanciulla*. There are also said to be a number of gunboats and prams preparing to move up the coast. You are to take all possible measures, consistent with the safety of your ship, to disable the one and to destroy the others. And the utmost despatch is essential, do you hear me?'

'Yes, sir. But for form's sake, I must represent to you that the *Polychrest* needs to be docked, that I am still twenty-three men short of my complement, that she is making eighteen inches of water an hour in a dead calm, and that her leeway renders inshore navigation extremely hazardous.'

'Stuff, Captain Aubrey: my carpenters say you can perfectly well stay out another month. As for her leeway, we all make leeway: the French make leeway, but they are not shy of running in and out of Chaulieu.' In case the hint should not have been clear enough, he repeated his last remark, dwelling on the word *shy*.

'Oh, certainly, sir,' said Jack with real indifference. 'I spoke, as I say, purely for form's sake.'

'I dare say you want your orders in writing?'

'No, thank you, sir; I believe I shall remember them quite easily.'

Returning to the ship he wondered whether Harte understood the nature of the service he required of the *Polychrest* – how very like a death-warrant these orders might be: he was not much of a seaman. On the other hand, he had vessels at his command more suitable by far for the intricate passage of the Ras du Point and the inner roads – the *Aetna* and the *Tartarus* would do the job admirably. Ignorance and malice in fairly even parts, he decided. Then again, Harte might have relied upon his contesting the order, insisting upon a survey, and so dishing himself; if so, he had chosen the moment well, as far as the *Polychrest* was concerned. 'But what does it signify?' he said, running up the side with a look of cheerful confidence. He gave the necessary orders, and a few minutes later the blue peter broke out at the foretopmasthead, with a gun to call attention to it. Stephen heard the gun, saw the signal, and hurried back to Deal.

There were several other Polychrests ashore – Mr Goodridge, Pullings to see his sweetheart, Babbington with his doting parents, half a dozen liberty-men. He joined them on the shingle, where they were bargaining for a hoveller, and in ten minutes he was back in the pharmaceutical-bilge-water-damp-book smell of his own cabin. He had hardly closed his door before a hundred minute ties began to fasten insensibly on him, drawing him back into the role of a responsible naval surgeon, committed to complex daily life with a hundred other men.

For once the *Polychrest* cast prettily to larboard and bore away on the height of the tide. A gentle breeze abaft the beam carried her shaving round the South Foreland, and by the time the hands were piped to supper they were in sight of Dover. Stephen came on deck by way of the fore-hatch from the sick-bay, and walked into the bows. As he stepped on to the forecastle the talk stopped dead, and he noticed an odd, sullen, shifty glance from old Plaice and Lakey. He had grown used to reserve from Bonden these last few days, for Bonden was the captain's coxswain, and he supposed Plaice had caught it by family affection; but it surprised him from Lakey, a noisy man with an open, cheerful heart. Presently he went below again, and he was busy with Mr Thompson when he heard 'All hands 'bout ship' as the *Polychrest* stood out into the offing. It was generally known that they were bound down-Channel to look into a French port: some said Wimereux, others Boulogne, and some pushed as far as Dieppe; but when the gun-room sat down to supper the news went about that Chaulieu was their goal.

Stephen had never heard of the place. Smithers (who had recovered his spirits) knew it well: 'My friend, the Marquis of Dorset, was always there in his yacht, during the peace; and he was for ever begging me to run across with him – "'Tis absolutely no more than a day and a night in my cutter," he would say. "You should come, George – we can't do without you and your flute."'

Mr Goodridge, who looked thoughtful and withdrawn, added nothing to the conversation. After a discussion of yachts, their astonishing luxury and sailing qualities, it returned to Mr Smithers's triumphs, his yacht-owning friends, and their touching devotion to him; to the fatigues of the London season, and the difficulty of keeping debutantes at a decent distance. Once again Stephen noticed that all this pleased Parker; that although Parker was a man of respectable family and, in his way, a 'hard horse', he encouraged Smithers, listening attentively, and as it were taking something of it to himself. It surprised Stephen, but it did not raise his spirits; and leaning across the table he said privately to the master, 'I should be obliged, Mr Goodridge, if you would tell me something about this port.'

'Come with me, then, Doctor,' said the master. 'I have the charts spread out in my cabin. It will be easier to explain with these shoals laid down before us.'

'These, I take it, are sandbanks,' said Stephen. 'Just so. And the little figures show the depth at high water and at low: the red is where they are above the surface.'

'A perilous maze. I did not know that so much sand could congregate in one place.'

'Why, it is the set of the tides, do you see – they run precious fast round Point Noir and the Prelleys – and these old rivers. In ancient times they must have been much bigger, to have carried down all that silt.'

'Have you a larger map, to give me a general view?'

'Just behind you, sir, under Bishop Ussher.'

This was more like the maps he was used to: it showed the Channel coast of France, running almost north and south below Etaples until a little beyond the mouth of the Risle, where it tended away westwards for three or four miles to form a shallow bay, or rather a rounded corner, ending on the west with the Ile Saint-Jacques, a little pear-shaped island five hundred yards from the shore, which then resumed its southerly direction and ran off the page in the direction of Abbeville. In the inner angle of this rounded corner, the point where the coast began to run westward, there was a rectangle marked Square Tower, then nothing, not even a hamlet, for a mile westward, until a headland thrust out into the sea for two hundred yards: a star on top of it, and the name Fort de la Convention. Its shape was like that of the island, but in this case the pear had not quite succeeded in dropping off the mainland. These two pears, St Jacques and Convention, were something less than two miles apart, and between them, at the mouth of a modest stream called the Divonne, lay Chaulieu. It had been a considerable port in mediaeval times, but it had silted up; and the notorious banks in the bay had still further discouraged its trade. Yet it had its advantages: the island sheltered it from western gales and the banks from the north; the fierce tides kept its inner and outer roads clear, and for the last few years the French government had been cleaning the harbour, carrying an ambitious breakwater out to protect it from the north-east, and deepening the channels. The work had gone on right through the Peace of Amiens, for Chaulieu revived would be a valuable port for Bonaparte's invasion-flotilla as it crept up the coast from every port or even fishing-village capable of building a lugger right down to Biarritz – crept up to its assembly-points, Etaples, Boulogne, Wimereux and the rest. There were already over two thousand of these prams, cannonières and transports, and Chaulieu had built a dozen.

'This is where their slips are,' said Goodridge, pointing to the mouth of the little river. 'And this is where they are doing most of their dredging and stone-work, just inside the harbour jetty. It makes the harbour almost useless for the moment, but they don't care for that. They can lie snug in the inner road, under Convention; or in the outer, for that matter, under St Jacques, unless it comes on to blow from the north-east. And now I come to think of it, I believe I have a print. Yes: here we are.' He held out an odd-shaped volume with long strips of the coast seen from the offing, half a dozen to a page. A dull low coast, with nothing but these curious chalky rises each side of the mean village: both much of a height, and both, as he saw looking closely, crowned by the unmistakable hand of the industrious, ubiquitous Vauban.

'Vauban,' observed Stephen, 'is like aniseed in a cake: a little is excellent; but how soon one sickens – these inevitable pepper-pots, from Alsace to the Roussillon.' He turned back to the chart. Now it was clear to him that the inner road, starting just outside the harbour and running up north-east past the Fort de la Convention on its headland, was protected by two long sandbanks, half a mile off the shore, labelled West Anvil and East Anvil; and that the outer road, parallel to the first, but on the seaward side of the Anvils, was sheltered on the east by the island and on the north by Old Paul Hill's bank. These two good anchorages sloped diagonally across the page, from low left to high right, and they were separated by the Anvils: but whereas the inner road was not much above half a mile wide and two long, the outer was a fine stretch of water, certainly twice that size. 'How curious that these banks should have English names,' he said. 'Pray, is this usual?'

'Oh, yes: anything by sea, we feel we own, just as we call Setubal St Ubes, and Coruña The Groyne, and so on: this one here we call the Galloper, after ours, it being much the same shape. And the Anvils we call anvils because with a north-wester and a making tide, the hollow seas bang away on them rap-rap, first the one and the other, like you was in a smithy. I ran in here once in a cutter, by the Goulet' – pointing to the narrow passage between the island and the main – 'in '88 or '89, with a stiff north-wester, into the inner road, and the spoondrift came in off the bank so thick you could hardly breathe.'

'There is an odd symmetry in the arrangement of these banks, and in these promontories: perhaps there may be a connection. What a maze of channels! How shall you come in? Not by the Goulet, I presume, since it is so close to the fort on the island – I should not have called it a promontory: it is an island, though from the print it looks much the same, being seen head-on.'

'It depends on the wind, of course; but with anything north, I should hope to follow the channel between the Galloper and Morgan's Knock to the outer road, run past St Jacques, and then either go between the Anvils or round the tail of the West Anvil to come to the harbour-mouth; then out again on the ebb, with God's blessing, by the Ras du Point – here, beyond the East Anvil – and so get into the offing before Convention knocks our masts away. They mount forty-two pounders: a mighty heavy gun. We must start to come in on the first half of the flood, do you see, to get off if we touch and to do our business at high water. Then away with the ebb, so as not to be heaved in by the making tide when they have chawed us up a little, and we have not quite the control we could wish. And chaw us up they will, playing their heavy pieces on us, unless we can take them by surprise: capital practice those French gunners make, to be sure. How glad I am I left the *Modest Proposal* with Mrs G., fair-copied and ready for the press.'

'So the tide is all-important,' observed Stephen, after a pause.

'Yes. Wind and tide, and surprise if we can manage it. The tides we can work. I reckon to bring her there, with the island bearing due south and the square tower south-east a half east, with the flood, not of tomorrow night, but of the night after – Sunday, as ever is. And we must pray for a gentle west or north-west breeze to take us in: and out again, maybe.'

11

STEPHEN SAT BY his patient in the gently rocking sickbay. He had almost certainly pulled him through the crisis – the faint thready pulse had strengthened this last hour, temperature had dropped, breathing was almost normal but this triumph occupied only a remote corner of his mind: the rest was filled with dread. As a listener, a half unconscious listener, he had heard too much good of himself – 'The Doctor is all right – the Doctor will not see us abused – the Doctor is for liberty – he has instruction; he has the French – he is an Irish person, too.' The murmur of conversation at the far end had dropped to an expectant silence; the men were looking eagerly towards him, nudging one another; and a tall Irishman, visiting a sick shipmate, stood up, his face turned towards the Doctor. At his first movement Stephen slipped out of the sick-bay: on the quarterdeck he saw Parker, talking with the Marine lieutenant, both gazing at a line-of-battle ship, a three-decker standing south-west with all her canvas abroad, studdingsails port and starboard, tearing down the Channel with a white bow-wave streaming along her side. Two midshipmen, off duty, sat making a complex object out of rope in the gangway. 'Mr Parslow,' said Stephen, 'pray be so good as to ask the Captain if he is at leisure.'

'I'll go when I've finished this,' said Parslow coolly, without getting up.

Babbington dropped his fid, kicked Parslow vehemently down the ladder and said, 'I'll go, sir.' A later moment he came running back. 'Captain has Chips with him just now, sir, but will be very happy in five minutes.'

Very happy was a conventional phrase, and it was obvious that Captain Aubrey had had an unpleasant conversation with his carpenter: there was a lump of rotten wood with a drawn bolt in it on his desk and a shattered, bludgeoned look on his face. He stood up, awkward, doubtful, embarrassed, his head bent under the beam.

'I am sorry to have to ask for this interview, sir,' said Stephen. 'But it is probable there will be a mutiny tomorrow night, when the ship is in with the French coast. The intention is to carry her into Saint-Valery.'

Jack nodded. This confirmed his reading of the situation – the Sophies' downcast, wretched looks, the men's demeanour, the twenty-four-pound shot that had left their racks to trundle about the deck in the middle watch. His ship was falling to pieces under his feet, his crew were falling away from their duty and their allegiance. 'Can you tell me who are the ringleaders?'

'I cannot. No, sir: you may call me many things, but not an informer. I have said enough, more than enough.'

No. Many surgeons, with a foot in each world, were more than half in sympathy with mutineers: there had been that man at the Nore, and the unfortunate Davidson they hanged for it at Bombay. And even Killick, his own servant, even Bonden – and they must have known something of what was brewing – would not inform on their shipmates, although they were very close to him.

'Thank you for having come to see me,' he said stiffly. When the door had closed behind Stephen he sat down with his head in his hands and let himself go to total unhappiness – to something near despair – so many things together, and now this cold evil look: he reproached himself most bitterly for not having seized this chance for an apology. 'If only I could have got it out; but he spoke so quick, and he was so very cold. Though indeed, I should have looked the same if any man had given me the lie; it is not to be borne. What in God's name possessed me? So trivial, so beside the point – as gross as a schoolboy calling names – unmanly. However, he shall make a hole in me whenever he chooses. And then again, what should I have the air of, suddenly growing abject now that I know he is such a deadly old file?' Yet throughout this period of indulgence some other part of his brain was dealing with the immediate problem, and almost without a transition he said, 'By God, I wish I had Macdonald.' This had nothing to do with a desire for comfort or council – he knew that Macdonald disapproved of him – but for efficiency. Macdonald was an officerlike man; this puppy Smithers was not. Still, he might not be wholly inept.

He rang his bell, and said, 'Pass the word for Mr Smithers.'

'Sit down, Mr Smithers. Tell me over the names of your Marines, if you please. Very good: and there is your sergeant, of course. Now listen to what I say. Think of each of these men separately, with great attention, and tell me whether or no each is to be relied upon.' 'Why, of course they are, sir,' cried Smithers. 'No, no. Think, man, think,' said Jack, trying to force some responsibility from that pink smirk. 'Think, and reply when you have really thought. This is of the very first consequence.'

His look was exceedingly penetrating and savage; it had effect. Smithers lost countenance and began to swear. He did evidently put his mind into painful motion; his lips could be seen moving, telling over the muster; and after some time he came up with the answer, 'Perfectly reliable, sir. Except for a man called – well, he has the same name as me; but no sort of connection, of course – a Papist from Ireland.'

'You will answer for that? You are dead certain of what you say? I say dead certain?'

'Yes, sir,' said Smithers, staring, terribly upset.

'Thank you, Mr Smithers. You are to mention this conversation to no one, That is a direct, absolute order. And you are to display no uneasiness. Pray desire Mr Goodridge to come here at once.'

'Mr Goodridge,' he said, standing at his chart-table, 'be so good as to give me our position.'

'Exact, sir, or within a league or two?' asked the master, with his head on one side and his left eye closed.

'Exact.'

'I must bring the log-board, sir.' Jack nodded. The master returned, took up scale and compasses, and pricked the chart. 'There, sir.'

'I see. We are under courses and topsails?'

'Yes, sir. We agreed to run down easy for Sunday's tide, if you remember, so as not to hang about in the offing, we being so recognizable.'

'I believe, I believe,' said Jack, studying the chart and the board, 'I believe that we may catch this evening's tide. What do you say, Master?'

'If the wind holds, sir, so we may, by cracking on regardless. I should not care to answer for the wind, though. The glass is rising.'

'Not mine,' said Jack, looking at his barometer. 'I should like to see Mr Parker, if you please: and in the meantime it would be as well to get the stuns'ls, royals and skylines into the tops.

'Mr Parker, we have a mutiny on our hands. I intend to take the *Polychrest* into action at the earliest possible moment, by way of dealing with the situation. We shall crowd sail to reach Chaulieu tonight. But before making sail I shall speak to the men. Let the gunner load the two aftermost guns with grape. The officers are to assemble on the quarterdeck at six bells – in ten minutes – with their side-arms. The Marines will fall in with their muskets on the fo'c'sle. No hurry or concern will be shown before that time. When all hands are called the guns will be traversed for'ard, with an oldster standing by each one. When I have spoken to the hands and we make sail, no man is to be struck or started until further orders.'

'May I offer an observation, sir?'

'Thank you, Mr Parker, no. Those are my orders.'

'Very good, sir.'

He had no confidence in Parker's judgment. If he had asked the advice of any man aboard it would have been Goodridge. But this was his responsibility as captain of the ship and his alone. In any case, he felt that he knew more about mutinous hands than anyone on the quarterdeck of the *Polychrest*: as a disrated midshipman he had served before the mast in a discontented ship on the Cape station – he knew it from the other side. He had a great affection for the foremast jack, and if he did not know for certain what would go with the lower deck, at least he was quite sure what would not.

He looked at his watch, put on his best coat, and walked on to the quarterdeck. Six bells in the forenoon watch. His officers were gathering round him, silent, very grave.

'All hands aft, if you please, Mr Parker,' he said. The shrill pipes, the roaring down hatchways, the stampede, the red coats trooping forward through the throng. Silence, but for the tapping of the reef-points overhead.

'Men,' said Jack, 'I know damned well what's going on. I know damned well what's going on; and I won't have it. What simple fellows you are, to listen to a parcel of makee-clever sea-lawyers and politicians, glib, quick-talking coves. Some of you have put your necks into the noose. I say your necks into the noose. You see the *Ville de Paris* over there?' Every head turned to the line-of-battle ship on the horizon. 'I have only to signal her, or half a dozen other cruisers, and run you up to the yardarm with the Rogue's March playing. Damned fools, to listen to such talk. But I am not going to signal to the *Ville de Paris* nor to any other king's ship. Why not? Because the *Polychrest* is going into action this very night, that's why. I am not going to have it said in the fleet that any Polychrest is afraid of hard knocks.'

'That's right,' said a voice – Joe Plaice, well out in front, his mouth wide open.

'It's not you, sir,' said another, unseen. 'It's him, old Parker, the hard-horse bugger'.

'I'm going to take the *Polychrest* in tonight,' Jack went on, in a growing roar of conviction, 'and I'm going to hammer the Frenchmen in Chaulieu, in their own port, dy'e hear me? If there's any man here afraid of hard knocks, he'd better stay behind. Is there any man here, afraid of hard knocks?'

A kind of universal growl, not ill-natured: some laughter; further cries of 'that hard-horse bugger'.

'Silence fore and aft. Well, I'm glad there ain't. There are some awkward hands among us still – look at that wicked ugly slab-line – and some men that talk too much, but I never thought there was a faint heart aboard. They may say the *Polychrest* ain't very quick in stays; they may say she don't furl her tops'ls all that pretty; but if they say she's shy, if they say she don't like hard knocks, why, black the white of my eye.

When we thumped it into the *Bellone*, there wasn't a single foremast jack that did not do his duty like a lion. So we'll run into Chaulieu, I say, and we'll hammer Bonaparte. That's the right way to bring the war to an end – that's the right way, not listening to a set of galley-rangers and clever chaps – and the sooner it's over and you can go home, the better I'll be pleased. I know it's not a bed of roses, looking after our country the way we have to. Now I tell you this, and mark what I do say. There is going to be no punishment over this business: it will not even be logged, and there's my word upon it. There is going to be no punishment. But every man and boy must attend to his duty tonight, he must mind it very carefully, because Chaulieu is a tough nut to crack – an awkward set of shoals – an awkward tide – and we must be every hand to his rope, and haul with a will, d'ye hear? Quick's the word and sharp's the action. Now I am going to pick some men for the barge, and then we shall crowd all the sail she can bear.' He walked into the tight crowd of men, into the low buzz of talk, the whispers, and silence went before him. Smiling, confident faces, worried faces or blank, some apprehensive, some brute-terrified and savage. 'Davis,' he said, 'go along into the barge.' The man's eyes were frightened as a wild beast's: he darted looks left and right. 'Come on, now, come along, you heard what I said,' said Jack quietly, and Davis lumbered aft, bowed and unnatural. The silence was general now, the atmosphere quite different. But he was not going to leave these men to have dinner with their messmates and try some desperate foolery. He was in a state of exceedingly acute awareness; he had no shadow of a doubt of the men he chose. 'Wilcocks, into the barge. Anderson.' He was far in among them. He had no weapons. 'Johnson. Look alive.' The tension was heightening very fast; it must go no higher. 'Bonden, into the barge,' he said, looking over his coxswain's head. 'Me, sir?' cried Bonden piteously. 'Cut along,' said Jack. 'Bantock, Lakey, Screech.' The low excited talk had begun again on the periphery. Men who could not be suspected were being sent into the barge: they were going aft, down the stern ladder and into the boat towing behind: this was no punishment, nor no threat of punishment. He flemished down the offending slab-line in a seamanlike manner and walked back to the quarterdeck.

'Now, Polychrests,' he said, 'now we are going to crack on until she groans again. Stuns'ls aloft and alow, royals, and, damn me, royal stuns'ls and skys'ls if she'll bear 'em. The sooner we're there, the sooner we're home. Topmen, upper-yardmen, are you ready?'

'Ready, aye ready, sir.' A comfortable, good body of sound – relief, thankfulness?

'Then at the word, up you go. Lay aloft!'

The *Polychrest* bloomed like a white rose. Her rarely-used studdingsails stretched out brilliant white one after another, her brand-new royals shone high, and above them all, her hitherto unseen skysails twinkled in the sun. The ship groaned and groaned again as they were sheeted home; she plunged her forefoot deep while behind her the barge raced along in her wake, the water almost to its gunwales.

IF THE *POLYCHREST* could be said to have a good point of sailing, it was with the wind three points abaft the beam; and here the wind stayed all day, scarcely varying from west-north-west by north, and blowing with a gentle urgency that kept all eyes aloft for the safety of her royals and skysails. She was cracking on indeed, racing down the Channel as though their lives depended upon it, making so much water that Mr Gray the carpenter, coming up from the well, officially registered his protest. She did carry away a skysail, and at one point a large unidentified object tore from her bottom, but the leagues raced away in her wake, and Jack, perpetually on the quarterdeck, could almost have loved her.

On the forecastle the watch below were at their make and mend; the watch on duty were kept busy, necessarily busy, trimming sail; and everybody seemed to be enjoying the speed, the racing tension to get the last ounce out of her. His orders about starting were being punctually obeyed; and so far no man or boy seemed to move any slower for it. The men in the barge had been brought aboard, lest it should tow under, and they had had their dinner in the galley: he was not afraid of them now – their influence was gone, their ship-mates avoided them. Davis, the really dangerous brute for a sudden reckless explosion, seemed wholly amazed; and Wilcocks, the eloquent attorney's clerk turned pickpocket, could find no one to listen to him. The seamen, for the most part, had turned with their usual calm volatility from one dis-aster to the interval before the next. For the moment he had the situation in hand.

His only anxiety was the wind. As the afternoon wore on it grew fainter and more irregular, giving every sign of falling away altogether with the setting of the sun: as the damp evening settled from the sky, with the dew tightening the rig-ging, it revived a little, still breathing from the longed-for north-west; but there was no trusting to it. By six o'clock they had run off their distance, standing in to raise the unmistak-able tower and headland of Point Noir, with a cross-bearing on Camaret; but now, as they steered east-south-east to make the coast a little north of Chaulieu, the haze thickened, thickened, until at the very entrance to Chaulieu bay itself, they found themselves in a fog, their royals faint blurs high over the deck – a fog that lay a little above the smoothly swelling surface of the sea, and that was torn in long wafts of thick and clear, faintly luminous from the rising moon.

They were no more than a little late for their tide, and they stood in steadily with the master at the con and two leads going without a pause – 'By the deep eight, by the deep eight, by the mark ten, a quarter less ten, by the deep nine, and a half seven, by the mark five, a quarter less five, and a half four.' The bottom was shelving fast. 'We are on the edge of the outer bank, sir,' said the master, looking at the sample of shelly ooze from the lead. 'All well. Tops'ls alone, I believe.'

'She is yours, Mr Goodridge,' said Jack, and he stood back a step, while the ship whispered through the water and the master took her in. She had been cleared for action long before; the hands were silent and attentive; the ship answered her helm promptly as she worked through the channels, sheets and braces tightening at the word. 'That will be the Galloper,' said the master, nodding towards a stretch of pale water on the starboard bow. 'Starboard a point. Two points. Steady – easy, now. As she goes. Port your helm. Hard over.' Silence. Dead silence in the fog.

'Morgan's Knock to larboard, sir,' he said, coming aft. Jack was glad to hear it. Their last sure cross-bearing seemed a terribly long time ago; and this was blindman's buff: it was water he did not know. With Morgan's Knock astern, they would have to bear westward round the tail of Old Paul Hill's bank, and then head a little south of east and so into the outer road, crossing the Ile Saint-Jacques. 'Starboard three points,' said the master, and the ship swung to the west. It was wonderful how these old Channel pilots knew their sea: by the smell and feel of it, no doubt. 'Mind your bowline, for'ard there,' called the master in a low voice. A long, long pause, with the *Polychrest* close-hauled to the now freshening breeze. 'Down with your helm, now. Steady, steady. As she goes. Look, sir, on the larboard bow – that's St Jacques.' A tear in the fog, and there, about a mile away, rose a tall white mass with a fortification on its top and half-way down its side.

'Well done, Mr Goodridge, well done indeed.'

'On deck, there,' hailed the look-out. 'Sail on the larboard beam. Oh, a mort of craft,' he added conversationally. 'Eight, nine – a proper old crowd of 'em.'

'They'll be at the far end of the outer road, sir,' said the master. 'We are in it now.'

The breeze was tearing great windows in the fog, and gazing over to port Jack had a sudden vision of an assembly of fair-sized vessels, ship- and brig-rigged, bright in the moonlight. These were his prey, the transports and cannonières for the invasion.

'You are happy that they are in the outer road, Mr Goodridge?' he asked.

'Oh, yes, sir. We just had St Jacques bearing south-south-east. There's nothing but open water between you and them.'

'Down with your helm,' said Jack. With the wind on her larboard quarter the *Polychrest* ran through the sea, going fast in with the tide, straight for the gun-vessels.

'Out tompions,' he said. 'Stand to your guns.' He meant to run right in among them, firing both sides, to get the very most out of the surprise and the first discharge, for a moment after it all hell would break loose from the batteries, and the men would never be so steady again. The mist had drifted across again, but it was clearing – he could see them dimly, coming closer and closer.

'Not a gun till . . .' he called, and a shock threw him flat on the deck. The *Polychrest* was brought up all standing. She had run full tilt on to the West Anvil.

This was plain as he got to his feet and the clearing of the fog showed one fort right astern and another almost exactly alike on the starboard bow, forts that woke to instant life with a shattering roar, a blast of flame that lit the sky. They had mistaken Convention for St Jacques, the inner road for the outer: they had come in by a different channel, and the vessels were separated from him by an impassable spit of sand. Those ships were in the inner, not the outer road. By some miracle the *Polychrest* had all her masts still standing: she lifted on the swell and ground a little farther on to the bank.

'Up sheets,' he shouted, full voice – no call for silence now. 'Up sheets.' The strain on the masts eased. 'Parker, Pullings, Babbington, Rossall, get the guns aft.' If she were only hanging by her forefoot this might bring her off. On the far side of the bank a great flurry of canvas – ships getting under way in every direction – and amidst this confusion two distinct well-ordered shapes steering to cross his bows. Gun-brigs, which marked their presence by two double jets of fire, meaning to rake him from stern to stern. 'Leave the fo'c'sle guns,' he cried. 'Mr Rossall, Adams, keep up a steady fire on those brigs.'

Now the moon shone out with surprising brilliance, and as the wind blew away the smoke, it showed the batteries as clear as day. It showed the whole inner road, crowded with shipping – a corvette moored right up against Convention, under its guns; certainly the ship *Thetis* and *Andromeda* had chased in, his quarry. 'A damned-fool place to moor her' – one thought among countless others racing through his head. It showed the deck of the *Polychrest*, most of the men well disciplined, over their amazement, working fast at the guns, trundling them aft, not much concerned by the thunder of the forts. St Jacques was firing wide, afraid of hitting its own people ahead of the *Polychrest*. Convention had not yet got the range: the iron hail was still high overhead. The gun-brigs were more dangerous.

He clapped on to a rope, helped run a gun aft, called for coigns to wedge them until they could make fast.

'All the people aft. All hands, all hands aft. We'll jounce her off. All jump together at the word. One, two. One, two.' They jumped, a hundred men together: would their weight and the weight of the guns slide her off into deep water? 'One, two. One, two.' It would not. ''Vast jumping.' He ran forward, looking hard and quick right round the port; glanced at his watch. A quarter past nine – not much left of the flood. 'Get all the boats over the side. Mr Parker,' he said, 'carronade into the barge.'

She had to be got off. A bower anchor carried out, dropped in deep water and heaved upon would bring her off: but even the barge could not bear the weight of such an anchor. A larger vessel must be cut out. A ball passed within a few feet of him, and its wind made him stagger. A cheer from forward, as the starboard carronade hit one of the gun-brigs square on the figurehead. Something had to be cut out. The transports were all crowding sail for the Ras du Point; they could not be caught in time. There were some small luggers in the harbour mouth; the corvette alone under Convention's guns. Absurdly close under Convention's guns, moored fore and aft, fifty yards from the shore, broad-side and headed towards St Jacques. Why not the corvette herself? He dismissed the question as absurd. But why not? The risk would be enormous, but no greater than lying here under the cross-fire, once the batteries had the range. It was very near to wild mad recklessness; but it was not quite there. And with the corvette in his possession there would be no need to carry out an anchor – a time-consuming job.

'Mr Rossall,' he said, 'take the barge. Draw off the fire of those brigs. Plenty of cartridge, a dozen muskets. Make all the noise you can – shout – sing out.' The barge-crew dropped over the side. Drawing a deep breath he shouted above the guns, 'Volunteers, volunteers to come along with me and cut out that corvette. Richards, serve out cutlasses, pistols, axes. Mr Parker, you will stay in the ship,' – The men would not follow Parker: how many would follow *him*? 'Mr Smithers, the red cutter: you and your Marines board over her starboard bow. Mr Pullings, blue cutter to her larboard quarter, and the moment you are aboard cut her cables. Take axes. Then lay aloft and let fall her tops'ls. Attend to nothing else at all. Pick your men: quick. The rest come along with me and look alive, now. There's not a moment to be lost.' Killick handed him his pistols and he dropped into his gig, never looking behind him. The Polychrests poured over the side, thump thump thump down into the boats. The clash of arms, a voice bawling in his ear 'Squeeze up, George. Make room, can't you?' How many men in the boats? Seventy? Eighty? Even more, A magnificent rise in his heart, all the blackness falling clear away,

'Give way,' he said. 'Silence, all boats. Bonden, right over the bank. Go straight for her.' A crash behind him as a salvo from Convention took away the *Polychrest*'s foretopmast.

'No great loss,' he said, settling in the stern-sheets with his sword between his knees, They touched once, a bare scrape, on the top of the sand-bank, then they were beyond it, in the inner road, going straight for the corvette half a mile away. The risk was enormous – she might have two hundred men aboard – but here again there was the chance of surprise. They would scarcely expect to be boarded from a grounded ship, not right under their own guns. Too far under their own guns – what a simple place to moor – for the Convention battery was high-perched up on the headland: its guns could never be depressed so far as to sweep the sea two or three hundred yards in front of the fort. Only five hundred yards to go, The men were pulling like maniacs, grunt, grunt, grunt, but the boat was crammed, heavy and encumbered – no room to stretch to their oars. Bonden wedged next to him, little Parslow – that child should never have come – the purser, deathly pale in the moonlight, the villainous face of Davis; Lakey, Plaice, all the Sophies . . .

Four hundred yards, and at last the corvette had woken to her danger. A hail. An uneven broadside, musketry. And now musketry crackling all along the shore. A deluge of water from Convention's great guns, no longer firing at the *Poly-chrest* but at her boats, and missing only by a very little. And all the time the barge, banging away behind them at the gun-brigs with its little six-pounder carronade, roaring, firing muskets, wonderfully diverting attention from this silent rush across the inner road. Convention again, at extreme depression, but firing over them.

Two hundred yards, one. The other boats drawing ahead, Smithers to the right, Pullings turning left-handed to go round her stern.

'Mizzen chains, Bonden,' he said, loosening his sword in its scabbard.

A shattering burst of fire, a great roaring – the Marines were boarding her over the bows.

'Mizzen chains it is, sir,' said Bonden, heaving on the tiller.

A last broadside overhead, and the boat came kissing against the side.

Up. He leapt on the high roll, his hands catching the dead-eyes. Up. No boarding-netting, by God! Men thrusting, grasping all round him, one holding his hair. Up and over the rail, through the thin fringe of defenders – a few pikes, swabs, a musket banging in his ear – on to the quarterdeck, his sharp sword out, pistol in his left hand. Straight for the group of officers, shouting 'Polychrest! Polychrest!' a swarm of men behind him, a swirling scuffle by the mizzenmast, an open maul, men grappling silently, open extreme brutal violence. Fired his pistol, flinging it straight at the next man's face. Babbington on his left running full into the flash and smoke of a musket – he was down. Jack checked his rush and stood over him; lunging hard he deflected the plunging bayonet into the deck. His heavy sword carried on, and now with all his weight and strength he whipped it up in a wicked backhanded stroke that took the soldier's head half off his body.

A little officer in the clear space in front of him, sword-point darting at his breast. Swerve and parry, and there they were dancing towards the taffrail, their swords flashing in the moonlight. A burning stab in his shoulder, and before the officer could recover his point Jack had closed, crashing the pommel into his chest and kicking his legs from under him. 'Rendez-vous,' he said.

'Jé mé rendre,' said the officer on the deck, dropping his sword. 'Parola.'

Firing, crashing, shouting in the bows, in the waist. And now Pullings was over the side, hacking at the cables. Red coats, dark in the moonlight, clearing tbe starboard gangway, and everywhere, everywhere the shout of Polychrest. Jack raced forward at the tight group by the mainmast, mostly officers; they were backing, firing their pistols, pointing swords and pikes, and behind them, on the landward side, their men were dropping into the boats and into the water by the score.

Haines ran past him, dodging through the fight, and hurled himself aloft, followed by a string of other men.

Here was Smithers, shouting, sweating, a dozen other Marines – they had reached the quarterdeck from the bows. Now Pullings, with a bloody axe in his hand, and the top-sails were letting fall, mizzen, main and fore – men already at the sheets.

'Capitaine,' cried Jack, 'Capitaine, cessez effusion sang. Rendez-vous. Hommes desertés. Rendez-vous.'

'Jamais, monsieur,' said the Frenchman, and came for him with a furious lunge.

'Bonden, trip up his heels,' said Jack, parrying the thrust and cutting high. The French captain's sword flashed up. Bonden ran beneath it, collared him, and it was over.

Goodridge was at the wheel – where had he come from? – calling like thunder for the foretopsail to be sheeted home; already the land was gently receding, gliding, sliding back-wards and away.

'Capitaine, en bas, dessous, s'il vous plait. Toutes officiers dessous.' Officers giving up their swords; Jack taking them, passing them to Bonden. Incomprehensible words – Italian? 'Mr Smithers, put 'em in the cable-tier.'

An isolated scuffle and a single shot on the forecastle, to join the firing from the shore. Bodies on deck: the wounded crawling.

She was heading westward, and the blessed wind was just before her beam. She must go round the tail of the West Anvil before she could tack to reach the *Polychrest*, and all the way she would be sailing straight into the fire of St Jacques: half a mile's creep, always closer to that deadly rak-ing battery .

'Foresail and driver,' cried Jack. The quicker the better, and above all she must not miss stays. She seemed to be handling beautifully, but if she missed stays she would be cut to pieces.

Convention was firing behind them: wildly at present,

though one great ball passed through all three topsails. He hurried forward to help sort out the foresail tack. The deck was swarming with Polychrests – they called out to him: tearing high spirits, some quite beside themselves. 'Wilkins,' he said, putting his hand on the man's shoulder, 'you and Shaddock start getting the corpses over the side.'

She was a trim little vessel. Eighteen, no, twenty guns. Broader than the *Polychrest*. *Fanciulla* was her name – she was indeed the *Fanciulla*. Why did St Jacques not fire? 'Mr Malloch, clear away the small bower and get a cable out of a stern-port.' Why did they not fire? A triple crash abaft the mainmast – Convention hulling the corvette – but nothing from St Jacques. St Jacques had not yet realized that the *Fanciulla* had been carried – they thought she was standing out to attack the grounded *Polychrest*. 'Long may it last,' he said. The tack was hard down, the corvette moving faster through the water – slack water now. He looked at his watch, holding it up to the moon: and a flash from St Jacques showed him just eleven. They had smoked him at last. But the tail of the sandbank was no great way off.

'I killed one, sir,' cried Parslow, running across the deck to tell him. 'I shot him into the body just as he was going for Barker with a half-pike.'

'Very good, Mr Parslow. Now cut along to the cable-tier and give Mr Malloch a hand, will you? Mr Goodridge, I believe we may go about very soon.'

'Another hundred yards, sir,' said the master, his eyes fixed on St Jacques. 'I must just get those two turrets in a line.'

Nearer, nearer. The towers were converging. 'All hands, all hands,' shouted Jack. 'Ready about ship. Mr Pullings, are you ready, there?' The towers blazed out, vanished in their own smoke, the corvette's mizzen topmast went by the board, sheets of spray flew over the quarterdeck. 'Ready oh! Helm's a-lee. Up tacks and sheets. Haul mains'l, haul.' Round she came, paying off all the faster for the loss of her after sails. 'Haul of all, haul with a will.' She was round, had spun like a cutter, and now with the wind three points free she was running for the *Polychrest* – the *Polychrest* with no foremast, no maintopgallant and only the stump of her bowsprit, but still firing her forward carronades and cheering thinly as the *Fanciulla* ran alongside, came up into the wind on the far side of the channel and dropped anchor.

'All well, Mr Parker?' hailed Jack.

'All's well, sir. We are a little knocked about, and the barge sank alongside; but all's well.'

'Rig the capstan, Mr Parker, and make a lane for the cable.' The roar of guns, the din of shot hitting both ships, tearing up the water, and passing overhead, drowned his voice. He repeated the order and went on, 'Mr Pullings, veer the cutter under the stern to take the line.'

'Red cutter was stove by that old topmast, sir, and I'm afraid the Marine's painter came adrift like, somehow. Only your gig left, sir. The Frenchmen went ashore in all theirn.'

'The gig, then. Mr Goodridge, as soon as the cable is to, start heaving ahead. Pullings, come with me.' He dropped into the gig, took the line in his hand – their life-line – and said, 'We shall need at least twenty more men for the capstan. Ply to and from as quick as ever you can, Pullings.'

The *Polychrest* again, and hands reaching eagerly from the stem-port for the line. A mortar-shell burst, brilliant orange, closer to the gun-brigs than to its target.

'Hot work, sir,' said Parker. 'I wish you joy of your prize.' He spoke with an odd hesitation, forcing the words: in the light of the flashes he looked an old, old man, bent and old.

'Thankee, Parker. Pretty warm. Clap on to the line, there. Heave hearty.' The line came in hand over hand, followed briskly by a small hawser, and then far more slowly by a great heavy snake of cable. Pullings' men kept coming aboard, and at last the cable was to the capstan. While the bars were being swifted, Jack looked at his watch again: just past midnight: the tide had been ebbing for half an hour.

'Heave away,' he called to the *Fanciulla*. 'Now, Polychrests, step out. Heave hearty. Heave and rally.' The capstan span, the pawls going click-click-click; the cable began to rise from the sea, to tighten, squirting water.

And now, with the gun-brigs sheering off, frightened by the shell, St Jacques let fly – heavy mortars, all the guns they possessed. A shot killed four men at the bars; the maintop mast toppled over the forecastle; the gig was knocked to pieces alongside just as its last man left it. 'Heave. Heave and rally,' cried Jack, slipping in the blood and kicking a body out of his way as he forced the bar round. 'Heave. Heave.' The cable rose right from the sea, almost straight. The men saved from the gig flung themselves on the bars. 'Heave, heave. She moves!' Clear through the roar of guns they could hear, or rather feel, the grind of the ship's bottom shifting over the sand. A kind of gasping cheer: the pawls clicked once more, twice, and then they were flat on their faces, no resistance in the bars at all, the capstan turning free. A ball had cut the cable.

Jack fell with the rest. He was trampled upon. Clearing himself from the limbs and bodies he leapt to the rail. 'Goodridge! Goodridge ahoy! Can you bring her alongside?'

'I dare not, sir. Not on the ebb. I've only got a couple of fathoms here. No boat?'

'No boat. Heave in quick and bend on another line. D'ye hear me, now?' He could scarcely hear himself. The gun-brigs had worked round and were firing over the bank from near the harbour. He stripped off his coat, laid down his sword and went straight in; and as he dived a jagged piece of iron caught him on the head, sending him deep under. But dazed or not his body swam on, and he found his hands scrabbling at the *Fanciulla*'s side. 'Haul me aboard,' he cried.

He sat, gasping and streaming, on deck. 'Is there anyone here can swim?' Not a word, no answer. 'I'll try on a grating,' said an anxious voice.

'Give me the line,' he said, walking to the stern-ladder.

'Won't you sit down, sir, and take a dram? You're all bloody,

sir,' said Goodridge, with a beseeching look into his face. Jack
shook his head impatiently, and the blood spattered the deck.
Every second counted, on the ebb. Even now there was six
inches less of water round the *Polychrest*. He went down the
ladder, let himself into the water and pushed off, swimming
on his back. The sky was in a state of almost continual corus-
cation: between the flashes the moon shone out, her face
bent like a shield. Abruptly he realized that there were two
moons, floating apart, turning; and Cassiopeia was the wrong
way about. Water filled his throat. 'By God, I'm tiring. Wits
going,' he said, and slid round in the water, straining his head
up and taking his bearings. The *Polychrest* was far over on his
left: not ahead. And hailing; yes, they were hailing. He took a
turn with the line round his shoulder and concentrated his
whole spirit on swimming, fixing the ship, plunging with
every stroke, fixing it again: but such feeble strokes. Of
course, it was against the tide: and how the line dragged.

'Thus, very well thus,' he said, changing his direction to
allow for the current. In the last twenty yards his strength
seemed to revive, but he could only cling there under her
stern – no force in his arms to get aboard. They were fussing
about, trying to haul him in. 'Take the line, God damn you
all,' he cried in a voice that he heard from a distance. 'Carry it
for'ard and heave, heave . . .'

At the foot of the stern-ladder Bonden lifted him out of the
water, guided him up, and he sat on a match-tub while the
capstan turned fast, then slower, slower, slower. And all the
time they heaved the slow steady swell lifted the *Polychrest*'s
stern and set it down with a thump on the hard sand; and all
the French artillery played upon her. The carpenter hurried
past with still another wad to stop a shot-hole; they had
hulled the *Polychrest* perhaps a dozen times since he had
been back aboard, but now he was utterly indifferent to their
fire – a mere background, a nuisance, a hindrance to the one
thing that really mattered. 'Heave and rally, heave and rally,'
he cried. The full strain was on: not a click from the capstan-

pawls. He staggered to an empty place on a bar and threw his weight forward, slipping in blood, finding his feet again. Click: and the whole capstan was groaning. Click. 'She moves,' whispered the man next to him. A slow, hesitant grind, and then as the swell came along from aft she lifted clear. 'She swims! She swims!' Wild cheering, and an answering cheer from over the water.

'Heave, heave,' he said. She must be pulled full clear. Now the capstan turned, now it fairly span, faster than the cable could be passed forward, and the *Polychrest* surged heavily right into the deep channel. "Vast heaving. All hands to make sail. Mr Parker, everything that can be set.'

'What? I beg pardon, sir? I did not – ' It did not matter. The seamen who had heard were aloft: the tattered mainsail dropped, the mainstaysail almost whole, and the *Polychrest* had steering-way. She was alive under him, and the life rose into his heart, quite filling him again. 'Mr Goodridge!' he shouted with new strength, 'cut your cables and lead me out by the Ras du Point. Veer out a towline as soon as you are under way.'

'Aye, aye, sir.' He took the wheel, moving her over to the windward side of the channel, so that her leeway should not run her aground again. Lord, how heavy she was, and how she wallowed on the swell! How low in the water, too. A little more sail appeared – mizzen topmast staysail, a piece of driver, odd scraps; but they gave her two knots, and with the run of the tide, setting straight down the channel, he should carry her out of range in ten minutes. 'Mr Rolfe.'

'Mr Rolfe's dead, sir.'

His mate, then: the guns back into their places.' It was no good asking Parker; the man was only just holding himself upright. 'Mr Pullings, take some lively hands forward and see if you can pick up the towline. What is it, Mr Gray?'

'Six foot of water below, sir, if you please. And the Doctor says may he put the wounded into your cabin? He moved 'em from the cockpit to the gun-room, but now it's all awash.'

'Yes. Certainly. Can you come at any more of the holes? We'll have the pumps going directly.'

'I'll do my best, sir; but I fear it's not the shot-holes. She's opening like a flower.'

A fury of shot drowned his words, some of it glowing red, for now they had the furnaces at work: mostly wide and astern, but three went home, jarring the water-logged ship from stem to stern and cutting the last of her starboard mizzen shrouds. Babbington came staggering aft, one sleeve hanging empty, to report the towline aboard and made fast to the knight-heads.

'Very good, Mr Babbington. Allen, take some hands below and help Dr Maturin move the wounded into the cabin.' He realized that he was shouting with great force, and that there was no need to be shouting. Everywhere, apart from one wicked long gun in the Convention battery, there was silence: silence and dimness, for the moon was dipping low. He felt the towline tighten, plucking at the *Polychrest*; and she gave a little spurt. The corvette just ahead had set her courses as well as main and fore topsails, and they were busy clearing the wreck of her mizzen topmast. What a pretty thing she was, taut and trim: great strength in her pull – she would be a fast one.

They were running along the landward edge of the East Anvil – the bank was above the surface now, with a gentle surf breaking over it – and ahead of them was the opening of the Ras du Point, full of the transports. They too seemed unaware of the *Fanciulla*'s changed character – sitting ducks – the chance of a lifetime.

'Mr Goodridge, there. How are your guns?'

'Prime, sir, prime. Brass twelve-pounders: and four eights. Plenty of cartridge filled.'

'Then lead right through those transports, will you?'

'Aye aye, sir.'

'Jenkins, how is our powder?'

'Drowned, sir. The magazine is drowned. But we got three rounds a gun, and shot a-plenty.'

'Then double-shot 'em, Jenkins, and we'll give them a salute as we pass by.'

It would be no stylish broadside; there were scarcely enough men even to fire both sides, let alone run the guns in and out, loading fast; but it would mark the point. And it was in his orders. He laughed aloud; and he laughed too to find that he was holding himself up by the wheel.

The moonlight faded; the Ras du Point glided very slowly nearer. Pullings had set up some kind of a jury-rig forward, and another sail was drawing. Parslow was fast asleep under the shattered fife-rail.

Now there was movement, agitation, among the transports. He heard a hail, and a muffled response from the *Fanciulla*, followed by low laughter. Sails appeared, and with them confusion.

The *Fanciulla* was a hundred yards ahead. 'Mr Goodridge,' called Jack, 'back your maintops'l a trifle.' The *Polychrest* ploughed heavily on, closing the distance. The transports were moving in several directions: at least three had fallen foul of one another in the narrow channel. The moments passed in dreamlike procession, and then suddenly there it was, the immediate vivid action, vivid even after all this saturation of noise and violence. One transport on the port bow, two hundred yards away; three locked together, aground, to starboard. 'Fire as they bear,' said Jack, putting down the helm two points. At the same moment the *Fanciulla* burst into flame and smoke – a much shriller crash. Now they were in the middle of them, firing both sides. The grounded vessels waved lanterns, shouting something that could not be heard. Another, having missed stays, drifted down the *Polychrest*'s side after the last carronade had shot its final charge. Her yards caught in the *Polychrest*'s remaining shrouds; some bright spirit lashed her main yard fast; and standing there right under the mouth of her empty guns her commander said he had struck.

'Take possession, Mr Pullings,' said Jack. 'Keep close under my lee. You can only have five men. Mr Goodridge, Mr Goodridge! Stand on.'

In half an hour the channel was clear of floating transports. Three had grounded. Two had run themselves ashore. One had sunk – the twenty-four pound smashers at close range – and the rest had doubled into the outer road or back to Chaulieu, where one was set ablaze by red-hot shot from St Jacques. And in half an hour, the time to run the length of the channel and to wreak all this havoc, the *Polychrest* was moving so heavily, keeping such a strain on the towline, that Jack hailed the *Fanciulla* and the transport to come alongside.

He went below, Bonden holding him by the arm, confirmed the carpenter's desperate report, gave orders for the wounded to be moved into the corvette, the prisoners to be secured, his papers brought, and sat there as the three vessels rocked on the gentle swell of slack water, watching the tired men carry their shipmates, their belongings, all the necessaries out of the *Polychrest*.

'It is time to go, sir,' said Parker, with Pullings and Rossall standing by him, ready to lift their captain over.

'Go,' said Jack. 'I shall follow you.' They hesitated, caught the earnestness of his tone and look, crossed and stood hovering on the rail of the corvette. Now the veering breeze blew off the land; the eastern sky was lightening; they were out of the Ras du Point, beyond the shoals; and the water in the offing was a fine deep blue. He stood up, walked as straight as he could to a ruined gun-port, made a feeble spring that just carried him to the *Fanciulla*, staggered, and turned to look at his ship. She did not sink for a good ten minutes, and by then the blood – what little he had left – had made a pool at his feet. She went very gently, with a sigh of air rushing through the hatches, and settled on the bottom, the tips of her broken masts showing a foot above the surface.

'Come, brother,' said Stephen in his ear, very like a dream.
'Come below. You must come below – here is too much blood
altogether. Below, below. Here, Bonden, carry him with me.'

12

Fanciulla
The Downs
20 September 04

My dear Sir,

By desire of your son William, my brave and
respectable midshipman, I write a hasty line to inform
you of our brush with the French last week. The claim
of distinction which has been bestowed on the ship I
commanded, I must entirely, after God, attribute to the
zeal and fidelity of my officers, amongst whom your son
stands conspicuous. He is very well, and I hope will
continue so. He had the misfortune of being wounded
a few minutes after boarding the *Fanciulla*, and his arm
is so badly broken, that I fear it must suffer amputation.
But as it is his left arm, and likely to do well under the
great skill of Dr Maturin, I hope you will think it an
honourable mark instead of a misfortune.

We ran into Chaulieu road on the 14th instant and
had the annoyance of grounding in a fog under the
cross-fire of their batteries, when it became necessary
to cut out a vessel to heave us off. We chose a ship
moored under one of the batteries and proceeded with
all dispatch in the boats. It was in taking her that your
son received his wound: and she proved to be the Ligurian corvetto *Fanciulla* of 20 guns, with some French
officers. We then proceeded to attack the transports,
your son exerting himself all this time with the utmost
gallantry, of which we took one, sank one, and drove

five ashore. At this point the *Polychrest* unfortunately sank, having been hulled by upwards of 200 shot and having beaten five hours on the bank. We therefore proceeded in the prizes to the Downs, where the court-martial, sitting yesterday afternoon in the *Monarch*, most honourably acquitted the *Polychrest's* officers for the loss of their ship, not without some very obliging remarks. You will find a fuller account of this little action in my Gazette letter, which appears in tomorrow's newspaper, and in which I have the pleasure of naming your son; and since I am this moment bound for the Admiralty, I shall have the pleasure of mentioning him to the First Lord.

My best compliments wait on Mrs Babbington, and I am, my dear Sir,

With great truth, sincerely yours,
Jno. Aubrey

PS. Dr Maturin desires his compliments, and wishes me to say, that the arm may very well be saved. But, I may add, he is the best hand in the Fleet with a saw, if it comes to that; which I am sure will be a comfort to you and Mrs Babbington.

'KILLICK,' HE CRIED, folding and sealing it. 'That's for the post. Is the Doctor ready?'

'Ready and waiting these fourteen minutes,' said Stephen in a loud, sour voice. 'What a wretched tedious slow hand you are with a pen, upon my soul. Scratch-scratch, gasp-gasp. You might have written the Iliad in half the time, and a commentary upon it, too.'

'I am truly sorry, my dear fellow – I hate writing letters: it don't seem to come natural, somehow.'

'Non omnia possumus omnes,' said Stephen, 'but at least we can step into a boat at a stated time, can we not? Now here is your physic, and here is your bolus; and remember, a quart of porter with your breakfast, a quart at midday . . .'

They reached the deck, a scene of very great activity: swabs, squeegees, holystones, prayer-books, bears grinding in all directions; her twenty brass guns hot with polishing; the smell of paint; for the Fanciullas, late Polychrests, had heard that their prize was to be bought into the service, and they felt that a pretty ship would fetch a higher price than a slattern – a price that concerned them intimately, since three-eighths of it would be theirs.

'You will bear my recommendations in mind, Mr Parker,' said Jack, preparing to go down the side.

'Oh yes, sir,' cried Parker. 'All this is voluntary.' He looked at Jack with great earnestness; apart from any other reason, the lieutenant's entire future hung on what his captain would say of him at the Admiralty that evening.

Jack nodded, took the side-ropes with a careful grasp and lowered himself slowly into the boat: a ragged, good-natured, but very brief cheer as it pushed off, and the Fanciullas hurried back to their scouring, currying and polishing; the surveyor was due at nine o'clock.

'A little to the left – to the *larboard*,' said Stephen. 'Where was I? A quart of porter with your dinner: no wine, though you may take a glass or two of cold negus before retiring; no beef or mutton – fish, I say, chicken, a pair of rabbits; and, of course, Venerem omitte.'

'Eh? Oh, her. Yes. Certainly. Quite so. Very proper. Rowed of all – run her up.' The boat ground through the shingle. They ploughed across the beach, crossed the road into the dunes. 'Here?' asked Jack.

'Just past the gibbet – a little dell, a place I know, convenient in every way. Here we are.' They turned a dune and there was a dark-green post-chaise and its postillion eating his breakfast out of a cloth bag.

'I wish we could have worked the hearse,' muttered Jack.

'Stuff. Your own father would not recognize you in that bandage and in this dirty-yellow come-kiss-me-death exsanguine state: though indeed you look fitter for a hearse than many a subject I have cut up. Come, come, there is not a moment to lose. Get in. Mind the step. Preserved Killick, take good care of the Captain: his physic, well shaken, twice a day; the bolus thrice. He may offer to forget his bolus, Killick.'

'He'll take his nice bolus, sir, or my name's not Preserved.'

'Clap to the door. Give way, now; give way all together. Step out! Lay aloft! Tally! And belay!'

They stood watching the dust of the post-chaise; and Bonden said, 'Oh, I do wish as we'd worked the hearse-and-coffin lark, sir: if they was to nab him now, it would break my heart.'

'How can you be so simple, Bonden? Do but think of a hearse and four cracking on regardless all the way up the Dover Road. It would be bound to excite comment. And you are to consider, that a recumbent posture is bad for the Captain at present.'

'Well, sir. But, a hearse is sure: no bum ever arrested a corpse, as I know of. Howsoever, it's too late now. Shall you pull back along of us, sir, or shall we come for you again?'

'I am obliged to you, Bonden, but I believe I shall walk into Dover and take a boat back from there.'

THE POST-CHAISE whirled through Kent, saying little. Ever since Chaulieu Jack had been haunted by the dread of tipstaffs. His return to the Downs, with no ship and a couple of prizes, had made a good deal of noise – very favourable noise, but still noise – and he had not set foot on shore until this morning, refusing invitations even from the Lord Warden himself. He was moderately well-to-do; the *Fanciulla* might bring him close on a thousand pounds and the transport a hundred or two; but would the Admiralty pay head-money according to the *Fanciulla*'s muster-roll when so many of her people had escaped on shore? And would his claim for gun-money for the destroyed transports be allowed? His new prize-agent had shaken his head, saying he could promise nothing but delay; he had advanced a fair sum, however, and Jack's bosom had the pleasant crinkle of Bank of England notes. Yet he was nowhere near being solvent, and passing through Canterbury, Rochester and Dartford he cowered deep in his corner. Stephen's assurances had little force with him: he knew he was Jack Aubrey, and it seemed inevitable that others too should see him as Jack Aubrey, debtor to Grobian, Slendrian and Co. for £11,012 6s 8d. With better reason it seemed to him inevitable that those interested should know that he must necessarily be summoned to the Admiralty, and take their steps accordingly. He did not get out when they changed horses; he passed most of the journey keeping out of sight and dozing – he was perpetually tired these days – and he was asleep when Killick roused him with a respectful but firm 'Time for your bolus, sir.'

Jack eyed it: this was perhaps the most nauseating dose that Stephen had ever yet compounded, so vile that health itself was scarcely worth the price of swallowing it. 'I can't get it down without a drink,' he said.

'Hold hard,' cried Killick, putting his head and shoulders out of the window. 'Post-boy, ahoy. Pull in at the next public, d'ye hear me, there? Now, sir,' – as the carriage came to a stop – 'I'll just step in and see if the coast is clear.' Killick had spent little of his life ashore, and most of that little in an amphibious village in the Essex mud; but he was fly; he knew a great deal about landsmen, most of whom were crimps, pickpockets, whores, or officials of the Sick and Hurt Office, and he could tell a gum a mile off. He saw them everywhere. He was the worst possible companion for a weak, reduced, anxious debtor that could well be found, the more so in that his absolute copper-bottomed certainty of being a right deep file, no sort or kind of a flat, carried a certain conviction. By way of a ruse de guerre he had somehow acquired a clergyman's hat, and this, combined with his earrings, his yard of pigtail, his watchet-blue jacket with brass buttons, his white trousers and low silver-buckled shoes, succeeded so well that several customers followed him from the tap-room to gaze while he leaned in and said to Jack, 'It's no go, sir. I seen some slang coves in the tap. You'll have to drink it in the shay. What'll it be, sir? Dog's nose? Flip? Come, sir,' he said, with the authority of the well over the sick in their care, or even out of it, 'What'll it be? For down it must go, or it will miss the tide.' Jack thought he would like a little sherry. 'Oh no, sir. No wine. The Doctor said, *No wine*. Porter is more the mark.' He brought back sherry – had been obliged to call for wine, it being a shay – and a mug of porter; drank the sherry, gave back such change as he saw fit, and watched the bolus go gasping, retching down, helped by the porter. 'That's thundering good physic,' he said. 'Drive on, mate.'

The next time he woke Jack it was from a deeper sleep. 'Eh? What's amiss?' cried Jack. 'We'm alongside, sir. We'm there.'

'Ay. Ay. So we are,' said Jack, gazing at the familiar doorway, the familiar courtyard, and suddenly coming to life. 'Very well. Killick, stand off and on, and when you see my signal, drive smartly in and pick me up again.'

He was sure of a fairly kind reception at the Admiralty: the cutting-out of the *Fanciulla* had been well spoken of in the service and very well spoken of in the press – it had come at a time when there was little to fill the papers and when people were feeling nervous and low in their spirits about the invasion. The *Polychrest* could not have chosen a better moment for sinking; nothing could have earned her more praise. The journalists were delighted with the fact that both ships were nominally sloops and that the *Fanciulla* carried almost twice as many men; they did not point out that eighty of the Fanciullas were peaceable Italian conscripts, and they were good enough to number the little guns borne by the transports in the general argument. One gentleman in the *Post*, particularly dear to Jack's heart, had spoken of 'this gallant, nay, amazing feat, carried out by a raw crew, far below its complement and consisting largely of landsmen and boys. It must show the French Emperor the fate that necessarily awaits his invasion flotilla; for if our lion-hearted tars handle it so roughly when it is skulking behind impenetrable sand-banks under the cross-fire of imposing batteries, what may they not do should it ever put to sea?' There was a good deal more about hearts of oak and honest tars, which had pleased the Fanciullas – the more literate hearts perpetually read it to the rest from the thumbed copies that circulated through the ship – and Jack knew that it would please the Admiralty too: in spite of their lordly station they were as sensitive to loud public praise as common mortals. He knew that this approval would grow after the publication of his official letter, with its grim list of casualties – seventeen dead and twenty-three wounded – for civilians liked to have sailors' blood to deplore, and the more a victory cost the more it was esteemed. If only little Parslow could have contrived to get himself knocked on the head it would have been perfect. He also knew something that the papers did not know, but that the Admiralty did: the *Fanciulla*'s captain had not had the time or the wit to destroy his secret papers, and for the moment the French private signals were private no longer – their codes were broken.

But as he sat there in the waiting-room thoughts of past misdeeds filled his uneasy mind; anything that Admiral Harte's malignance could do would have been done; and in fact he had not behaved irreproachably in the Downs. Stephen's warning had fallen on a raw conscience: and it could only have come through Dundas – Dundas, who was so well placed to know what they thought of his conduct here. If his logs and order-books were sent for, there would be some things he would find hard to explain away. Those strokes of profound cunning, those little stratagems that had seemed individually so impenetrable, now in the mass took on a sadly imbecile appearance. And how did the *Polychrest* come to be on the sand-bank in the first place? Explain that, you infernal lubber. So he was more than usually pleased when Lord Melville rose from behind his desk, shook him warmly by the hand, and cried, 'Captain Aubrey, I am delighted to see you. I said you would be sure to distinguish yourself, do you recall?

I said so in this very room. And now you have done so, sir: the
Board is content, pleased, eminently satisfied with its choice
of you as commander of the *Polychrest*, and with your conduct at Chaulieu. I wish you could have done so with less
cost: I am afraid you suffered terribly both in your ship's company and in your person. Tell me,' he said, looking at Jack's
head, 'what is the nature of your wounds? Do they . . . do they
hurt?'

'Why, no, my lord, I cannot say they do.'

'How were they inflicted?'

'Well, my lord, the one was something that dropped on my
head – a piece of mortar-shell, I imagine; but luckily I was in
the water at the time, so it did little damage, only tearing off a
handsbreadth of scalp. The other was a sword-thrust I did not
notice at the moment, but it seems it nicked some vessel, and
most of my blood ran out before I was aware. Dr Maturin said
he did not suppose there was more than three ounces left,
and that mostly in my toes.'

'You are in good hands, I find.'

'Oh yes, my lord. He clapped a red-hot iron to the place,
brought up the bleeding with a round turn, and set me up
directly.'

'Pray what did he prescribe?' asked Lord Melville, who
was intensely interested in his own body, and so in bodies in
general.

'Soup, my lord. Enormous quantities of soup, and barley-
water, and fish. Physic, of course – a green physic. And porter.'

'Porter? Is porter good for the blood? I shall try some today.
Dr Maturin is a remarkable man.'

'He is indeed, my lord. Our butcher's bill would have been
far, far longer but for his devotion. The men think the world
of him: they have subscribed to present him with a gold-
headed cane.'

'Good. Good. Very good. Now I have your official letter
here, and I see that you mention all your officers with great
approval, particularly Pullings, Babbington and Goodridge,

the master. By the bye, I hope young Babbington's wound is not too grave? His father voted with us in the last two divisions, out of compliment to the service.'

'His arm was broken by a musket-shot as we boarded, my lord, but he tucked it into his jacket and fought on in a most desperate fashion; and afterwards, as soon as it was dressed, he came on deck again and behaved extremely well.'

'So you are truly satisfied with all your officers? With Mr Parker?'

'More than satisfied with them all, my lord.'

Lord Melville felt the hint of evasion, and said, 'Is he fit to command?' looking straight into Jack's eye.

'Yes, my lord.'

Turmoil of conscience: immediate loyalty and fellow-feeling overcoming good sense, responsibility, love of truth, love of the service, all other considerations.

'I am glad to hear it. Prince William has been pressing us for some time on the subject of his old shipmate.' He touched his bell, and a clerk came in with an envelope; at the sight of it Jack's heart began to beat wildly, his thin sparse blood to race about his body; yet his face turned extremely pale. 'This is an interesting occasion, Captain Aubrey: you must allow me the pleasure of being the first to congratulate you on your promotion. I have stretched a point, and you are made post with seniority from May 23rd.'

'Thank you, my lord, thank you very much indeed,' cried Jack, flushing scarlet now. 'It gives me – it gives me very great pleasure to receive it from your hands – even greater pleasure from the handsome way in which it is given. I am very deeply obliged to you, my lord.'

'Weel, weel, there we are,' said Lord Melville, quite touched. 'Sit down, sit down, Captain Aubrey. You are looking far from well. What are your plans? I dare say your health requires you to take some months of sick-leave?'

'Oh no, my lord! Oh, very far from it. It was only a passing weakness – quite gone now – and Dr Maturin assures me that my particular constitution calls for sea air, nothing but sea air, as far from land as possible.'

'Well, you cannot have the *Fanciulla*, of course, since she will not be rated a post-ship – what the gods give with one hand they take away with the other. And seeing that you cannot have her, then in compliment to you, it seems but just that she should be given to your first lieutenant.'

'Thank you, my lord,' said Jack, with a face so dashed and glum that the other looked at him with surprise.

'However,' he said, 'I think we may hold out some hope of a frigate. The *Blackwater*: she is on the stocks, and all being well she may be launched in six months. That will give you time to recover your strength, to see your friends, and to watch over her fitting-out from the very beginning.'

'My lord,' cried Jack, 'I do not know how to thank you for your goodness to me, and indeed I am ashamed to ask for more, having had so much. But to be quite frank with you, my affairs were thrown into such a state of confusion by the breaking of my prize-agent, that something is quite necessary to me. A temporary command, or anything.'

'You were with that villain Jackson?' asked Lord Melville, looking at him from under his bushy eyebrows. 'So was poor Robert. He lost better than two thousand pound, a ca'hoopit sum. Weel, weel. So you would accept an acting-command, however short?'

'Most willingly, my lord. However short or however inconvenient. With both hands.'

'There may be some slight fleeting remote possibility – I do not commit myself, mind. The *Ethalion*'s commander is sick. There is Captain Hamond's *Lively*, and Lord Carlow's *Immortalité*; they both wish to attend parliament, I know. There are other service members too, but I have not the details in my head. I will desire Mr Bainton to look into it when he has a moment. There is no certainty in these matters, you understand. Where are you staying, since you will not be rejoining the *Fanciulla*?'

'At the Grapes, in the Savoy, my lord.'

'In the Savoy?' said Lord Melville, writing it down. 'Och aye. Just so. Now have we any more official business?'

'If I might be permitted an observation, my lord. The *Polychrest*'s people behaved exceedingly well; they could not have done better. But if they were left together in a body, there might be unpleasant consequences. It seems to me they would be far better drafted in small parties to ships of the line.'

'Is this a general impression, Captain Aubrey, or can you bring forward any names, however tentatively?'

'A general impression, my lord.'

'It shall be attended to. So much for business. If you are not bespoke, it would give Lady Melville and me great pleasure if you would dine with us on Sunday. Robert will be there, and Heneage.'

'Thank you, my lord; I shall be very happy indeed to wait upon Lady Melville.'

'Then let me wish you joy once more, and bid you a very good day.'

JOY. AS HE walked heavily, solemnly down the stairs, it mounted in him, a great calm flood-tide of joy. His momentary disappointment about the *Fanciulla* (he had counted on her – such a quick, stiff, sweet-handling, weatherly pet) entirely vanished by the third step – forgotten, overwhelmed – and by the landing he had realized his happiness almost to the full. He had been made post. He was a post-captain; and he would die an admiral at last.

He gazed with quiet benevolence at the hall-porter in his red waistcoat, smiling and bobbing at the foot of the stairs.

'Give you joy, sir,' said Tom. 'But oh dear me, sir, you're improperly dressed.'

'Thankee, Tom,' said Jack, rising a little way out of his beatitude. 'Eh?' He cast a quick glance down his front.

'No, no, sir,' said Tom, guiding him into the shelter of the hooded leather porter's chair and unfastening the epaulette on his left shoulder to transfer it to his right. 'There. You had your swab shipped like a mere commander. There: that's better. Why, bless you, I did that for Lord Viscount Nelson, when he come down them stairs, made post.'

'Did you indeed, Tom?' said Jack, intensely pleased. The thing was materially impossible, but it delighted him and he emitted a stream of gold – a moderate stream, but enough to make Tom very affable, affectionate, and brisk in hailing the chaise and bringing it into the court.

HE WOKE SLOWLY, in a state of wholly relaxed comfort, blinking with ease; he had gone to bed at nine, as soon as he had swallowed his bolus and his tankard of porter, and he had slept the clock round, a sleep full of diffused happiness and a longing to impart it – a longing too oppressed by languor to have any effect. Some exquisite dreams: the Magdalene in Queenie's picture saying, 'Why do not you tune your fiddle to orange-tawny, yellow, green and this blue, instead of those old common notes?' It was so obvious: he and Stephen set to their tuning, the 'cello brown and full crimson, and they dashed away in colour alone – such colour! But he could not seize it again; it was fading into no more than words; it no longer made evident, luminous good sense. His bandaged head, mulling about dreams, how they sometimes made sense and how sometimes they did not, suddenly shot from the pillow, all the pink happiness wiped off it. His coat, which had slipped from the back of the chair, looked exactly like the coat of yesterday. But there, exactly squared and trimmed on the chimney-piece, stood that material sail-cloth envelope, that valuable envelope or wrapper. He sprang out of bed, fetched it, returned, poised it on his chest above the sheets, and went to sleep again.

Killick was moving about the room, making an unnecessary noise, kicking things not altogether by accident, cursing steadily. He was in a vile temper: he could be smelt from the pillow. Jack had given him a guinea to drink to his swab, and he had done so conscientiously, down to the last penny, being brought home on a shutter. 'Now sir,' he said, coughing artificially. 'Time for this ere bolus.' Jack slept on. 'It's no good coming it the Abraham, sir. I seen you twitch. Down it must go. Post-captain or no post-captain,' he added, possibly to himself, 'you'll post it down, my lord, or I'll know the reason why. And your nice porter, too.'

About twelve Jack got up, stared at the back of his head with his shaving-mirror and the looking-glass – it seemed to be healing well, but as Stephen had shaved the whole crown, leaving the long hair at the back, he had an oddly criminal look of alopecia or the common mange – dressed in civilian clothes, and walked out to see the light of day, for none ever reached the Grapes, at any time of the year. Before leaving he asked at the bar for an exact description of the Savoy, the boundaries of the sanctuary; he was particularly interested in these old survivals, he said.

'You may go as far as Falconer's Rents, and then cut through to Essex Street and go along as far as the fourth house from the corner, then right back to the City side of Cecil Street; but don't ever you cross it, nor don't ever you pass the posts in Sweating-house Lane, your honour, or all is up. You pee, up,' said the Grapes, who heard this piece about interesting old survivals a hundred times a year.

He walked up and down the streets of the Duchy, stepped into a coffee-house, and idly picked up the paper. His own Gazette letter leapt straight out of the open page at him, with its absurdly familiar phrasing, and his signature, quite transmogrified by print. On the same page there was a piece about the action: it said that our gallant tars were never happier than when they were fighting against odds of twelve and an eighth to one, which was news to Jack. How had the man arrived at that figure? Presumably by adding up all the guns and mortars in the batteries and all the vessels afloat in the bay and dividing by the *Polychrest*. But apart from this odd notion of happiness, the man obviously had sense, and he obviously knew something about the Navy: Captain Aubrey, said he, was known as an officer who was very careful of his men's lives – 'That's right,' said Jack – and he asked how it came about that the *Polychrest*, with all her notorious defects, was sent on a mission for which she was so entirely unsuited, when there were other vessels – naming them – lying idle in the Downs. A casualty-list of a third of the ship's company called for explanation: the *Sophie*, under the same commander, had taken the *Cacafuego* with a loss of no more than three men killed.

'Parse that, you old – ,' said Jack inwardly, to Admiral Harte.

Wandering out, he came to the back of the chapel: an organ was playing inside, a sweet, light-footed organ hunting a fugue through its charming complexities. He circled the railings to come to the door, but he had scarcely found it, opened it and settled himself in a pew before the whole elaborate structure collapsed in a dying wheeze and a thick boy crept from a hole under the loft and clashed down the aisle, whistling. It was a strong disappointment, the sudden breaking of a delightful tension, like being dismasted under full sail.

'What a disappointment, sir,' he said to the organist, who had emerged into the dim light. 'I had so hoped you would bring it to a close.'

'Alas, I have no wind,' said the organist, an elderly parson. 'That chuff lad has blown his hour, and no power on earth will keep him in. But I am glad you liked the organ – it is a Father Smith. A musician, sir?'

'Oh, the merest dilettante, sir; but I should be happy to blow for you, if you choose to go on. It would be a sad shame to leave Handel up in the air, for want of wind.'

'Should you, indeed? You are very good, sir. Let me show you the handle – you understand these things, I am sure. I must hurry to the loft, or these young people will be here. I have a marriage very soon.'

So Jack pumped and the music wound away and away, the separate strands following one another in baroque flights and twirls until at last they came together and ran to the final magnificence, astonishing the young couple who had come silently in, and who were sitting furtive, embarrassed, nervous and intensely clean in the shadows, with their landlady and a midwife; for they had not paid for music – only the simplest ceremony. They were absurdly young, pretty creatures, with little more than a gasp between them; and they had anticipated the rites by a hairsbreadth under full term. But the parson joined them very gravely, telling them that the purpose of their union was the getting of children, and that it was better to marry than to burn.

When it was over they came to life again, regained their colour, smiled, seemed very pleased with being married, amazed at themselves. Jack kissed the pink bride, shook the other child by the hand, wishing him all possible good fortune, and walked out into the air, smiling with pleasure. 'How happy they will be, poor young things – mutual support – no loneliness – no God-damned solitude – tell happiness and sorrows quite openly – sweet child, not the least trace of the shrew – trusting, confident – marriage a very capital thing, quite different from – by God, I am on the wrong side of Cecil Street.'

He turned to cross back, and as he turned he collided with a sharp youth who had darted after him through the traffic with a paper in his hand. 'Captain Aubrey, sir?' asked the youth. Escape to the other side was impossible. He shot a glance behind him – surely they could not hope to make the arrest with just this younker? 'They told me at the Grapes I should find you walking about the Duchy, your honour.' There was no menace in his voice, only a modest satisfaction. 'I should have hollered out, but for manners. '

'Who are you?' asked Jack, still poised to deal with him.

'Tom's nevvy, your honour, if you please, the duty-porter. Which I was to give you this,' – handing the letter.

'Thankee, boy,' said Jack, unpoising himself. 'You are a sharp lad. Tell your uncle I am obliged to him: and this is for your errand.'

A gap appeared in the traffic and he darted back into Lancaster, back to the Grapes, called for a glass of brandy, and sat down in greater flutter of spirits than he had ever known.

'No brandy, sir,' said Killick, cutting the pot-boy off at the head of the stairs and confiscating the little glass. 'No spirits of wine, the Doctor said. Swab-face, you jump to the bar and draw the Captain a quart of porter: and none of your guardomoves with the froth.'

'Killick,' said Jack, 'God damn your eyes. Cut along to the kitchen and desire Mrs Broad to step up. Mrs Broad, what have you for dinner? I am amazing sharp-set.'

'No beef or mutton, Mr Killick says,' said Mrs Broad, 'but I have a nice loin of weal, and a nice piece of wenison, as plump as you could wish; a tender young doe, sir.'

'The wenison, if you please, Mrs Broad; and perhaps you would send me up some pens and a pot of ink. Ah dear God,' he said to the empty room, 'a tender young doe.'

> The Grapes
> Saturday

My dear Stephen, he wrote

> Oh wish me joy – I am made post! I never thought it would be, though he received me in the kindest way; but then suddenly he popped it out, signed, sealed and delivered, with seniority from May 23rd. It was like a prodigious unexpected vast great broadside from a three-decker, but of happiness: I could not get it all aboard directly, I was so taken aback, but by the time I had smuggled myself back to the Grapes I was swelling like a rose – so happy. How I wish you had been there! I celebrated with a quart of your vile porter and a bolus, and turned in at once, quite fagged out.
>
> This morning I was very much better, however, and

in the Savoy chapel I said the finest thing in my life. The parson was playing a Handel fugue, the organ-boy deserted his post, and I said 'it would be a pity to leave Handel up in the air, *for want of wind*,' and blew for him. It was the wittiest thing! I did not smoke it entirely all at once, however, only after I had been pumping for some time; and then I could hardly keep from laughing aloud. It may be that post-captains are a very witty set of men, and that I am coming to it.

But then you very nearly lost your patient. Like a fool I strayed out of bounds: a little chap heaves in sight, sings out, 'Captain A!' and I say, 'This claps a stopper over all: Jack, you are brought by the lee.' But, however, it was orders to join the *Lively*.

She is only a temporary command, and of course as acting-captain I do not take my friends with me; but I do beg you, my dear Stephen, to sail with me as my guest. The Polychrests will be paid off – Parker is to have the *Fanciulla*, in compliment to me, which is as cruel a kindness as the world has seen since that fellow in the play, but I have looked after the *Polychrest*'s people – so there will be no difficulty of any kind. Pray come. I cannot tell you what pleasure it would give me. And to be even more egotistical in what I am afraid is a sadly egotistical letter, let me say, that having had your care, I should never trust my frame to a common saw-bones again – my health is far from good, Stephen.

She is a crack frigate, with a good reputation, and I believe we shall have orders for the West Indies – think of the bonitoes, the bosun birds, the turtles, the palm-trees!

I am sending Killick with this – heartily glad I am to be shot of him too, such a pragmatical brute he has grown, with his physic-spoon – and he will see our dunnage round to the Nore. I am dining with Lord Melville on Sunday; Robert will run me down in his curricle, and I shall sneak aboard that night, without touching at an inn. Then, I swear to God, I shall not set foot ashore until I can do so without this wretched fear of being taken to a sponging-house and then to a debtor's prison.

Yours most affectionately

'Killick!' he shouted.

'Sir?'

'Are you sober?'

'As a judge, sir.'

'Then pack my shore-going trunk all but my uniform and number one scraper, take it down to the Nore, aboard the *Lively*, and give the first lieutenant this chit: we join her on Sunday night, temporary command. Then proceed to the Downs: give this letter to the Doctor and this to Mr Parker – it has good news for him, so give it into his hands yourself. If the Doctor chooses to join the *Lively*, take his sea-chest and anything else he wants, no matter what – a stuffed whale or a double-headed ape got with child by the bosun. My sea-chest, of course, and what we saved from the *Polychrest*. Repeat your instructions. Good. Here is what you will need for the journey, and here is five shillings for a decent glazed hat: you may skim the other into the Thames. I will not have you go aboard the *Lively* without a Christian covering to your head. And get yourself a new jacket, while you are about it. She is a crack frigate.'

She was a crack frigate, she was indeed; and seeing that a wheel came off Robert's curricle in a remote and midnight ditch Jack was obliged to go aboard her in the glare of the risen sun, passing through the crowded streets of Chatham – a considerable trial to him after an already trying night. But this was nothing to the trial of meeting Dr Maturin on the water; for Stephen had been inspired to put off from the shore at about the same time, though from a different place, and their courses converged some three furlongs from the frigate's side. Stephen's conveyance was one of the *Lively*'s

cutters, which saluted Jack by tossing oars, and which fell
under his wherry's lee, so that they pulled in close company,
Stephen calling out pleasantly all the way. Jack caught a
frightened glance from Killick, noticed the wooden composure of the midshipman and the cutter's crew, saw the grinning face of Matthew Paris, an old Polychrest, Stephen's
servant, once a framework knitter and still no kind of seaman
– no notion of common propriety in his myopic, friendly gaze.
And as Stephen rose to wave and hoot, Jack saw that he was
dressed from head to foot in a single tight dull-brown garment; it clung to him, and his pale, delighted face emerged
from a woollen roll at the top, looking unnaturally large. His
general appearance was something between that of an atten-
uated ape and a meagre heart; and he was carrying his narwhal horn. Captain Aubrey's back and shoulders went
perfectly rigid: he adopted the features of one who is smiling;
he even called out, 'Good morning to you – yes – no – ha, ha.'
And as he recomposed them to a look of immovable gravity
and unconcern, the thought darted through his mind, 'I
believe the wicked old creature is drunk.'

Up and up the side – a long haul after the *Polychrest* – the
wailing of the calls, the stamp and clash of the Marines presenting arms, and he was aboard.

Mathematical precision, rigorous exactitude fore and aft:
he had rarely seen a more splendid array of blue and gold on
the quarterdeck: even the midshipmen were in cocked hats
and snowy breeches. The officers stood motionless, bareheaded. The naval lieutenants, the Marine lieutenants; then
the master, the surgeon, the purser, and a couple of black
coats, chaplain and schoolmaster, no doubt; and then the
flock of young gentlemen, one of whom, three feet tall and
five years of age, had his thumb in his mouth, a comfortably
jarring note in all this perfection of gold lace, ivory deck,
ebony seams.

Jack moved his hat to the quarterdeck, tilting it no more
than an inch or so, because of his bandage. 'We got a rogue,'

whispered the captain of the foretop. 'A proud son of wrath, mate,' replied the yeoman of the sheets. The first lieutenant stepped forward, a grave, severe, tall thin man. 'Welcome aboard, sir,' said he. 'My name is Simmons.'

'Thank you, Mr Simmons. Gentlemen, good morning to you. Mr Simmons, pray be so good as to name the officers.' Bows, civil mutterings. They were youngish men, except for the purser and the chaplain; a pleasant-looking set, but reserved and politely distant. 'Very well,' said Jack to the first lieutenant, 'we will muster the ship's company at six bells, if you please, and I shall read myself in then.' Leaning over the side he called, 'Dr Maturin, will you not come aboard?' Stephen was no more of a mariner now than he had been at the outset of his naval career, and it took him a long moment to clamber snorting up the frigate's side, propped by the agonized Killick, a moment that increased the attentive quarterdeck's sense of expectation. 'Mr Simmons,' said Jack, fixing him with a hard, savage eye, 'this is my friend Dr Maturin, who will be accompanying me. Dr Maturin, Mr Simmons, the first lieutenant of the *Lively*.'

'Your servant, sir,' said Stephen, making a leg: and this, thought Jack, was perhaps the most hideous action that a person in so subhuman a garment could perform. Hitherto the *Lively*'s quarterdeck had taken the apparition nobly, with a vexing, remote perfection; but now, as Mr Simmons bowed stiffly, saying, 'Servant, sir,' and as Stephen, by way of being amiable, said, 'What a splendid vessel, to be sure – vast spacious decks: one might almost imagine oneself aboard an Indiaman,' there was a wild shriek of childish laughter – a quickly smothered shriek, followed by a howl that vanished sobbing down the companion-ladder.

'Perhaps you would like to come into the cabin,' said Jack, taking Stephen's elbow in an iron grip. 'Your things will be brought aboard directly, never trouble yourself' – Stephen cast a look into the boat and seemed about to break away.

'I shall see to it myself at once, sir,' said the first lieutenant.

'Oh, Mr Simmons,' cried Stephen, 'pray bid them be very tender of my bees.'

'Certainly, sir,' said the first lieutenant, with a civil inclination of his head.

Jack got him into the after-cabin at last, a finely-proportioned, bare, spacious cabin with a great gun on either side and little else but the splendid curving breadth of the stern-windows: Hamond was clearly no Sybarite. Here he sat on a locker and gazed at Stephen's garment. It had been horrible at a distance; it was worse near to – far worse. 'Stephen,' he said, 'I say, Stephen . . . Come in!'

It was Paris, with a rectangular sail-cloth parcel. Stephen ran to him, took it from his arms with infinite precaution and set it on the table, pressing his ear to its side. 'Listen, Jack,' he said, smiling. 'Put your ear firmly to the top and listen while I tap.' The parcel gave a sudden momentary hum. 'Did you hear? That shows they are queen-right – that no harm has come to their queen. But we must open it at once; they must have air. There! A glass hive. Is it not ingenious, charming? I have always wanted to keep bees.'

'But how in God's name do you expect to keep bees in a man-of-war?' cried Jack. 'Where in God's name do you expect them to find flowers, at sea? How will they eat?'

'You can see their every motion,' said Stephen, close against the glass, entranced. 'Oh, as for their feeding, never fret your anxious mind; they will feed with us upon a saucer of sugar, at stated intervals. If the ingenious Monsieur Huber can keep bees, and he blind, the poor man, surely we can manage in a great spacious xebec?'

'This is a frigate.'

'Let us never split hairs, for all love. There is the queen! Come, look at the queen!'

'How many of those reptiles might there be?' asked Jack, holding pretty much aloof.

'Oh, sixty thousand or so, I dare say,' said Stephen carelessly. 'And when it comes on to blow, we will ship gimbals for the hive. This will preserve them from undue lateral motion.'

'You think of almost everything,' said Jack. 'Well, I will wear the bees, like Damon and Pythagoras – ho, a mere sixty thousand bees in the cabin don't signify, much. But I tell you what it is, Stephen: you don't always think of quite everything.'

'You refer to the queen's being a virgin?' said Stephen. 'Not really. No. What I really meant was, that this is a crack frigate.'

'I am delighted to hear it. There she goes – she lays an egg! You need not fear for her virginity, Jack.'

'And in this frigate they are very particular. Did not you remark the show of uniforms as you came aboard – an admiral's inspection – a royal review.'

'No, I cannot truthfully say that I did. Tell me, brother, is there some uneasiness on your mind?'

'Stephen, will you for the love of God take off that thing?'

'My wool garment? You have noticed it, have you? I had forgot, or I should have pointed it out, Have you ever seen anything so deeply rational? See, I can withdraw my head entirely: the same applies to the feet and the hands. Warm, yet uncumbering; light; and above all healthy – no constriction anywhere! Paris, who was once a framework knitter, made it to my design; he is working on one for you at present.'

'Stephen, you would favour me deeply by taking it right off. It is unphilosophical of me, I know, but this is only an acting-command, and I cannot afford to be laughed at.'

'But you have often told me that it does not matter what one wears at sea. You yourself appear in nankeen trousers, a thing that I should never, never countenance, And this' – plucking at his bosom with a disappointed air – 'partakes of the nature both of the Guernsey frock and of the free and easy pantaloon.'

THE *LIVELY* HAD remained in commission throughout the peace; her people had been together many years, with few

changes among the officers, and they had their own way of
doing things. All ships were to some degree separate kingdoms, with different customs and a different atmosphere:
this was particularly true of those that were on detached service or much by themselves, far from their admirals and the
rest of the fleet, and the *Lively* had been in the East Indies
for years on end – it was on her return during the first days of
the renewed war that she had had her luck, two French Indiamen in the same day off Finisterre. When she was paid off,
Captain Hamond had no difficulty in manning her again, for
most of his people re-entered, and he even had the luxury of
turning volunteers away. Jack had met him once or twice – a
quiet, thoughtful, unhumorous, unimaginative man in his
forties, prematurely grey, devoted to hydrography and the
physics of sailing, somewhat old for a frigate-captain – and as
he had met him in the company of Lord Cochrane, he had
seemed rather to want colour, in comparison with that ebul-
lient nobleman. His first impression of the *Lively* did not alter
during the ceremonies of mustering and quarters: she was
obviously a most competent ship with a highly efficient crew
of right man-of-war's men; probably a happy ship in her quiet
way, judging from the men's demeanour and those countless
very small signs that a searching, professional eye could see –
happy, yet taut; a great distance between officers and men.
But as he and Stephen were sitting in the dining-cabin, waiting for their supper, he wondered how she had come by her
reputation as a crack frigate. It was certainly not from her
appearance, for although everything aboard was unexception-
ally shipshape and man-of-war fashion, there was no extraordinary show of perfection, indeed nothing extraordinary at all,
apart from her huge yards and her white manilla cordage: her
hull and portlids were painted dull grey, with an ochre streak
for the gun-tier, her thirty-eight guns were chocolate-
coloured, and the only obvious piece of brass was her bell,
which shone like burnished gold. Nor was it from her fighting
qualities, since from no fault of her own she had seen no

action with anything approaching a match for her long eighteen-pounders. Perhaps it was from her remarkable state of readiness. She was permanently cleared for action, or very nearly so: when the drum beat for quarters she might almost have gone straight into battle, apart from a few bulkheads and a minimum of furniture; the two quarterdeck goats walked straight down the ladder by themselves, the hen-coops vanished on an ingenious slide, and the guns in his own cabins were cast loose, something he had never seen before in an exercise. She had a Spartan air: but that in itself was not enough to explain anything, although it did not arise from poverty – the *Lively* was well-to-do; her captain had recently bought himself a seat in Parliament, her officers were men of private means even before their fortunate stroke, and Hamond insisted upon a handsome allowance from the parents of his midshipmen.

'Stephen,' he said, 'how are your bees?'

'They are very well, I thank you; they show great activity, even enthusiasm. But,' he added, with a slight hesitation, 'I seem to detect a certain reluctance to return to their hive.'

'Do you mean to say you let them out?' cried Jack. 'Do you mean that there are sixty thousand bees howling for blood in the cabin?'

'No, no. Oh no. Not above half that number; perhaps even less. And if you do not provoke them, I am persuaded you may go to and fro without the least concern; they are not froward bees. They will have gone home by morning, sure; I shall creep in during the middle watch and close their little wicket. But perhaps it might be as well, were we to sit together in this room tonight, just to let them get used to their surroundings. A certain initial agitation is understandable after all, and should not be discountenanced.'

Jack was not a bee, however, and his initial agitation was something else again. It was clear to him that the *Lively* was a closed, self-sufficing community, an entity to which he was an outsider. He had served under acting-captains himself, and he knew that they could be regarded as intruders – that they could excite resentment if they took too much upon themselves. They had great powers, certainly, but they were wise not to use them. Yet on the other hand, he might have to fight this ship; the ultimate responsibility, the loss of reputation or its gain was his, and although he was here only for the time, and although he was not the real owner, he was not going to play King Log. He must move with care, and at the same time with decision . . . a difficult passage. An awkward first lieutenant could prove the very devil. By the grace of God he had a little money in hand: he would be able to entertain them decently for the present, although he could not keep Hamond's table, with half a dozen to dinner every day. He must hope for another advance from his agent soon, but for the moment he would not look poverty-stricken. There was a Latin tag about poverty and ridicule – elusive: no hand at Latin. He must not be ridiculous; no captain could afford to be ridiculous. 'Stephen, oh my dear fellow,' he said to the tell-tale compass over his cot (for he was in his sleeping-cabin), 'what induced you to put on that vile thing? What a singular genius you have for hiding your talent under a bushel – a bushel that no one could possibly have foreseen.'

In the gun-room, however, another sound of things was heard. 'No, gentlemen,' said Mr Floris, the surgeon. 'I do assure you he is a great man. I have read his book until it is dog-eared – a most luminous exposition, full of pregnant reflections, a mine of nervous expressions. When the Physician of the Fleet came to inspect us, he asked me whether I had read it, and I was happy to show him my copy, interleaved and annotated, and to tell him that I required my assistants to get whole passages by heart. I tell you, I long to be introduced to him. I long for his opinion on poor Wallace.'

The gun-room was impressed; it had a deep respect for learning, and but for that unfortunate remark about East Indiamen it would have been ready to accept the wool garment as a philosopher's vagary, a knitted Diogenes' tub.

'Yet if he has been in the service,' said Mr Simmons, 'what are we to make of his remark about the East Indiaman? It was very like a direct affront, and it was delivered with a strangely knowing leer.'

Mr Floris looked at his plate, but found no justification there. The chaplain coughed, and said that perhaps they should not judge by appearances – perhaps the gentleman had had a momentary absence – perhaps he meant that the Indiaman was the very type of sea-going luxury, which indeed it was; a well-appointed Indiaman was to be preferred, in point of comfort, to a first-rate.

'That makes it worse,' observed the third lieutenant, an ascetic young man so tall and thin that it was difficult to see where he could sleep at length, if not in the cable-tier.

'Well, for my part,' said the senior Marine, the caterer to the mess, 'I shall drink to his health and eternal happiness in a glass of this excellent Margaux, as sound as a nut, whatever the parson may say. Such an example of courage as coming aboard like Badger-Bag, with a narwhal-horn in one hand and a green umbrella in the other, has never come under my observation. Bless him.'

The gun-room blessed him, but without much conviction, except for Mr Floris; and they went on to discuss the health of Cassandra, the last of the *Lively*'s gibbons, the last of that numerous menagerie which she had borne away from Java and the remoter islands of the eastern seas. They did not discuss their acting-captain at all: he had come with the reputation of a seaman and a fighter; of a rake and of a protégé of Lord Melville. Captain Hamond was a supporter of Lord St Vincent; and he had gone to Parliament to vote with St Vincent's friends; and Lord St Vincent, who hated Pitt and his administration, was working to impeach Lord Melville for malversation of the secret funds and to get him out of the Admiralty. The *Lively*'s officers all shared their captain's views – strong Whigs to a man.

BREAKFAST WAS SOMETHING of a disappointment. Captain Hamond had always drunk cocoa, originally to encourage the crew to do the same and then because he liked it, whereas Jack and Stephen were neither of them human until the first pot of coffee was down, hot and strong.

'Killick,' said Jack, 'toss this hog's wash over the side and bring coffee at once.'

'Ax pardon, sir,' said Killick, seriously alarmed. 'I forgot the beans, and the cook's got none.'

'Then jump to the purser's steward, the gun-room cook, the sick-bay, anywhere, and get some, or your name will not be Preserved much longer, I can tell you. Cut along. God-damned lubber, to forget our coffee,' he said to Stephen, with warm indignation.

'A little pause will make it all the more welcome when it comes, sure,' said Stephen, and to divert his friend's mind he took up a bee and said, 'Be so good as to watch my honey-bee.' He put it down on the edge of a saucer in which he had made a syrup of cocoa and sugar; the bee tasted to the syrup, pumped a reasonable quantity, took to the air, hovered before the saucer, and returned to the hive. 'Now, sir,' said Stephen, noting the time on his watch, 'now you will behold a prodigy.'

In twenty-five seconds two bees appeared, questing over the saucer with a particular high shrill buzz. They pitched, pumped syrup, and went home. After the same interval four bees came, then sixteen, then two hundred and fifty-six; but when four minutes had elapsed this simple progression was obscured by earlier bees who knew the way and who no longer had to fix either their hive or the syrup.

'Now,' cried Stephen, from out of the cloud, 'have you any doubt of their power to communicate a locus? How do they do it? What is their signal? Is it a compass-bearing? Jack, do not offer to molest that bee, I beg. For shame. It is only resting.'

'Beg pardon, sir, but there ain't a drop of coffee in the barky. Oh God almighty,' said Killick.

'Stephen, I am going to take a turn,' said Jack, withdrawing from the table in a sly undulatory motion and darting through the door with hunched shoulders.

'Why they call this a crack frigate,' he said, swilling down a glass of water in his sleeping-cabin, 'I cannot for the life of me imagine: not a drop of coffee among two hundred and sixty men.'

The reason became apparent to him some two hours later, when the port-admiral signalled *Lively proceed to sea*. 'Acknowledge,' said Jack, this news being brought to him. 'Mr Simmons, we will unmoor, if you please.'

The unmooring was a pleasure to watch. At the pipe of All hands to unmoor ship the men flowed rather than ran to their stations; there was no stampede along the gangways, no stream of men blundering into one another in their haste to escape the rope's end; as far as he could see there was no starting, and there was certainly very little noise. The capstan-bars were pinned and swifted, the Marines and afterguard manned them, the piercing fife struck up Drops of Brandy, and one cable came in while the other went out. A midshipman from the forecastle reported the best bower catted; the first lieutenant relayed this to Jack, who said, 'Carry on, Mr Simmons.'

Now the *Lively* was at single anchor, and as the capstan turned again so she crept across the sea until she was immediately over it. 'Up and down, sir,' called the bosun.

'Up and down, sir,' said the first lieutenant to Jack.

'Carry on, Mr Simmons,' said Jack. This was the crucial moment: the crew had both to clap on fresh nippers – the bands that attached the great cable to the messenger, the rope that actually turned on the capstan – for a firmer hold, and to loose the topsails so as to sail the anchor out of the ground. In even the best-managed ships there was a good deal of hullabaloo at such a time, and in this case, with the tide running across the wind – an awkward cast in which split-second timing was called for – he expected a rapid volley, a broadside of orders.

Mr Simmons advanced to the break of the quarterdeck, glancing quickly up and down, said, 'Thick and dry for weighing,' and then, before the rush of feet had died away, 'Make sail.' No more. Instantly the shrouds were dark with men racing aloft. Her topsails, her deep, very well cut topsails were let fall in silence, sheeted home, the yards hoisted up, and the *Lively*, surging forward, weighed her anchor without a word. But this was not all: even before the small bower was fished, the jib, forestaysail and foretopgallant had appeared and the frigate was moving faster and faster through the water, heading almost straight for the Nore light. All this without a word, without a cry except for an unearthly hooting of Woe, woe, woe high in the upper rigging. Jack had never seen anything like it. In his astonishment he looked up at the main topgallant yard, and there he saw a small form hanging by one arm; it swung itself forward on the roll of the ship and fell in a sickening curve towards the maintopmaststay. Almost unbelievably it caught this rope, and then, altogether unbelievably, shot up from one piece of rigging to another to the fore-royal and sat there.

'That is Cassandra, sir,' said Mr Simmons, seeing Jack's face of horror. 'A sort of Java ape.'

'God help us,' said Jack, recovering himself. 'I thought it was a ship's boy gone mad. I have never seen anything like it – this manoeuvre, I mean. Do your people usually make sail according to their own notions?'

'Yes, sir,' said the first lieutenant, in civil triumph.

'Well. Very well. The *Lively* has her own way of doing things, I see. I have never seen . . .' The frigate was heeling to the breeze, marvellously alive, and he stepped to the taffrail, where Stephen, dressed in a sad-coloured coat and drab small-clothes, stood conversing with Mr Randall, bending to hear his tiny pipe. Jack looked at the dark water slipping fast by her side, curving deep under the chains; she was making seven knots already, seven and a half. He looked at her wake, fixing an anchored seventy-four and a church tower – hardly a trace of leeway. He leant over the larboard quarter, and there, one point on the larboard bow, was the Nore light. The wind was two points free on the starboard tack, and any ship he had sailed in would be aground in the next five minutes.

'You are happy about your course, Mr Simmons?' he said.

'Quite happy, sir,' said the first lieutenant.

Simmons knew his ship, that was obvious: he most certainly knew her capabilities. Jack repeated this – he was convinced of it; it must be so. But the next five minutes were as unhappy as any he had ever spent – this beautiful, beautiful ship a mere hulk, dismasted, bilged . . . During the moments when the *Lively* was racing through the turbid shoaling water at the edge of the bank and where a trifle of leeway would wreck her hopelessly, he did not breathe at all. Then the bank was astern.

With as much impassivity as he could summon he drew in the good sparkling air and desired Mr Simmons to set course for the Downs, where he was to pick up some supernumeraries and, if Bonden had not vanished, his own coxswain, seeing that Captain Hamond had taken his with him to London. He set to pacing the windward side of the quarterdeck, keenly watching the behaviour of the *Lively* and her crew.

No wonder they called her a crack frigate: her sailing qualities were quite out of the ordinary, and the smooth quiet discipline of her people was beyond anything he had seen: her speed in getting under way and making sail had something unnatural about it, as eerie as the cry of the gibbon in the rigging.

The familiar low, grey, muddy shores glided by; the sea was a hard metallic grey, the horizon in the offing ruled sharply from the mottled sky, and the frigate ran on, the wind now one point free, as though a precise, undeviating rail were guiding her. Merchantmen were coming in for the London river, four sail of Guineamen, and a brig of war for Chatham, apart from the usual hovellers and peterboats: how flabby and loose they looked, by comparison.

The fact of the matter was that Captain Hamond, a gentleman of a scientific turn of mind, had chosen his officers with
great care and he had spent years training his crew; even the
waisters could hand, reef and steer; and for the first years he
had raced them mast against mast in furling and loosing sail,
putting them through every manoeuvre and combination of
manoeuvres until they reached equality at a speed that could
not be improved upon. And today, jealous for the honour of
their ship, they had excelled themselves; they knew it very
well, and as they passed near their acting-captain they
glanced at him with discreet complacency, as who should say,
'We showed you a thing or two, cock; we made you stretch
your eyes.'

What a ship to fight, he reflected: if he met one of the big
French frigates, he could make rings round her, beautifully
built though they were. Yes. But what of the Livelies themselves? They were seamen, to be sure, quite remarkable seamen; but were they not a little elderly, on the whole, oddly
quiet? Even the ship's boys were stout hairy fellows, rather
heavy for lying out on the royal yards; and most of them
talked gruff. Then there were a good many brown and yellow
men aboard. Low Bum, who was now at the wheel, steering
wonderfully small, had had no need to grow a pigtail when he
entered at Macao; nor had John Satisfaction, Horatio Jelly-
Belly or half a dozen of his shipmates. Were they fighting
men? The Livelies had had none of the incessant cutting-out
expeditions that made danger an everyday affair and so dis-
armed it: circumstances had been entirely different – he
should have read her log to see exactly what she had done.
His eye fell on one of the quarterdeck carronades. It was
painted brown, and some of the dull, scrubbed paint overlapped the touch-hole. It had not been fired for a long while.
Certainly he should look at the log to see how the Livelies
spent their day.

On the leeward side Mr Randall told Stephen that his
mother was dead, and that they had a tortoise at home; he

hoped the tortoise did not miss him. Was it really true that
the Chinese never ate bread and butter? Never, at any time
whatsoever? He and old Smith messed with the gunner, and
Mrs Armstrong was very kind to them. Plucking at Stephen's
hand to draw his attention, he said in his clear pipe, 'Do you
think the new captain will flog George Rogers, sir?'

'I cannot tell, my dear. I hope not, I am sure.'

'Oh, I hope he does,' cried the child, with a skip. 'I have never
seen a man flogged. Have you ever seen a man flogged, sir?'

'Yes,' said Stephen.

'Was there a great deal of blood, sir?'

'Indeed there was,' said Stephen. 'Several buckets full.'

Mr Randall skipped again, and asked whether it would be
long to six bells. 'George Rogers was in a horrid passion, sir,'
he added. 'He called Joe Brown a Dutch galliot-built bugger,
and damned his eyes twice: I heard him. Should you like to
hear me recite the points of the compass without a pause,
sir? There is my Papa beckoning. Good-bye, sir.'

'Sir,' said the first lieutenant, stepping across to Jack, 'I
must beg your pardon, but there are two things I forgot to
mention. Captain Hamond indulged the young gentlemen
with the use of his fore-cabin in the mornings, for their
lessons with the schoolmaster. Should you wish to continue
the custom?'

'Certainly, Mr Simmons. A capital notion.' 'Thank you, sir.
And the other thing was that we usually punish on Mondays
in the *Lively*.'

'On Mondays? How curious.'

'Yes, sir. Captain Hamond thought it was well to let defaulters have Sunday for quiet reflection.'

'Well, well. Let it be so, then. I had meant to ask you what
the ship's general policy is, with regard to punishment. I do
not like to make any sudden changes, but I must warn you, I
am no great friend to the cat.'

Simmons smiled. 'Nor is Captain Hamond, sir. Our usual
punishment is pumping: we open a sea-cock, let clean water

in to mix with what is in the bilges, and pump it out again – it keeps the ship sweet. We rarely flog. In the Indian Ocean we were nearly two years without bringing the cat out of its bag; and since then, not above once in two or three months. But I am afraid that today you may think it necessary: an unpleasant case.'

'Not article thirty-nine?'

'No, sir. Theft.'

Theft it was said to be. Authority, speaking hoarse and official through the mouth of the master-at-arms, said it was theft, riotous conduct, and resisting arrest. With the ship's company assembled aft, the Marines drawn up, and all the officers present, he led his victim before the captain and said, 'Did steal one ape's head . . .'

'It's all lies,' cried George Rogers, still clearly in a horrid passion.

'. . . the property of Evan Evans, quarter-gunner . . .'

'It's all lies.'

'And being desired to step aft . . .'

'It's all lies, lies!' cried Rogers.

'Silence, there,' said Jack. 'You shall have your turn, Rogers. Carry on, Brown.'

'And on being told I had information that led me to believe he was in possession of this head, and on being desired, civil, to step aft and verify the statements of Evan Evans, quarter-gunner, larboard watch,' said the master-at-arms, swivelling his eyes alone in the direction of Rogers, 'did call out expressions of contempt: was in liquor; and endeavoured to conceal hisself in the sail-room.'

'All lies.'

'And when roused out, did offer violence to Button, Menhasset and Mutton, able seamen.'

'It's all lies,' cried Rogers, beside himself with indignation. 'All lies.'

'Well, what did happen?' said Jack. 'Tell me in your own words.'

'I will, your honour,' said Rogers, glaring round, pale and trembling with fury. 'In my own Gospel words. Master-at-arms comes for'ard – which I was taking a caulk, my watch below – tips me a shove on the arse, begging your pardon, and says, "Get your skates on, George; you're fucked." And I up and says, "I don't care for you, Joe Brown, nor for that fucking little cunt Evans." No offence, your honour; but that's the Gospel truth, to show your honour the lies he tells, with his "verify the statements". It's all lies.'

There seemed to be a more familiar ring about this version; but it was followed by a rambling account of who pushed whom, in what part of the ship, with contradictory evidence from Button, Menhasset and Mutton, and remarks on character; and it seemed that the main issue might be lost in a discussion of who lent someone two dollars off of Banda, and was never repaid, in grog, tobacco, or any other form.

'What about this ape's head?' said Jack.

'Here, sir,' said the master-at-arms, producing a hairy thing from his bosom.

'You say it is yours, Evans; and you say it is yours, Rogers? Your own property?'

'She's my Andrew Masher, your honour,' said Evans.

'He's my poor old Ajax, sir, been in my ditty-bag ever since he took sick off the Cape.'

'How can you identify it, Evans?'

'Anan, sir?'

'How do you know it is your Andrew Masher?'

'By her loving expressions, sir, your honour. By her expressions. Griffi Jones, stuffed animals, Dover, is giving me a guinea for her tomorning, yis, yis.'

'What have you to say, Rogers?'

'It's all lies, sir!' cried Rogers. 'He's my Ajax. Which I fed him from Kampong – shared my grog, ate biscuit like a Christian.'

'Any distinguishing marks?'

'Why, the cut of his jib, sir: I know him anywheres, though shrivelled.'

Jack studied the ape's face, which was set in an expression of deep, melancholy contempt. Who was telling the truth? Both thought they were, no doubt. There had been two ape's heads in the ship, and now there was only one. Though how anyone could pretend to recognize the features of this wizened red coconut heavy in his hand he could not tell. 'Andrew Masher was a female, I take it, and Ajax a male?' he said.

'That's right, your honour.'

'Beg Dr Maturin to come on deck, if he is not engaged,' said Jack. 'Dr Maturin, is it possible to tell the sex of an ape by its teeth, or that kind of thing?'

'It depends on the ape,' said Stephen, looking eagerly at the object in Jack's hands. 'This, for example,' he said, taking it and turning it about, 'is an excellent specimen of the male simia satyrus, Buffon's wild man of the woods: see the lateral expansion of the cheeks, mentioned by Hunter, and the remains of that particular throat-sac, so characteristic of the male.'

'Well, there you are,' said Jack. 'Ajax it is. Thank you very much, Doctor. The charge of theft is dismissed. But you must not knock people about, Rogers. Has anyone something to say in his favour?'

The second lieutenant stepped forward, said that Rogers was in his division – attentive to his duty, generally sober, a good character, but apt to fly into a passion. Jack told Rogers that he must not fly into a passion; that flying into a passion was a very bad thing – it would certainly lead him to the gallows, if indulged in. He was to command his temper, and do without grog for the next week. The head was confiscated temporarily, for further examination – indeed, it had already vanished into the cabin, leaving Rogers looking somewhat blank. 'I dare say you will get it back in time,' said Jack, with more conviction than he felt. The other defaulters, all guilty of uncomplicated drunkenness, were all dealt with in the same way; the grating was unrigged; the cat, still in its bag, returned to its resting-place; and shortly after the hands were piped to dinner. Jack invited the first lieutenant, the officer and midshipman of the watch, and the chaplain to dine with him, and resumed his pacing.

His thoughts ran on gunnery. There were ships, and plenty of them, that hardly ever exercised the great guns, hardly fired them except in action or for saluting, and if this was the case with the *Lively*, he would change it. Even at close quarters it was as well to hit where it hurt most; and in a typical frigate-action accuracy and speed were everything. Yet this was not the *Sophie*, with her pop-guns: a single broadside from the *Lively* would burn well over a hundredweight of powder – a consideration. Dear *Sophie*, how she blazed away . . .

He identified the music that was running so insistently through his head. It was the piece of Hummel's that he and Stephen had played so often at Melbury Lodge, the adagio. And almost at once he had the clearest visual image of Sophia standing tall and willowy by the piano, looking confused, hanging her head.

He turned short in his stride and brought his mind to bear strongly on the question in hand. But it was no use; the music wove in among his calculations of powder and shot; he grew more agitated and unhappy, and clapping his hands together with a sudden report he said to himself, 'I shall run through the log and see what their practice really is – tell Killick to uncork the claret – he did not forget *that*, at all events.'

He went below, noticed the smell of midshipmen in the fore-cabin, walked through into the after-cabin, and found himself in total darkness.

'Close the door,' cried Stephen, swarming past him and clapping it to.

'What's amiss?' asked Jack, whose mind had moved so deep into naval life that he had forgotten the bees, as he might have forgotten even a vivid nightmare.

'They are remarkably adaptable – perhaps the most adaptable of all social insects,' said Stephen, from another part of the cabin. 'We find them from Norway to the burning wastes of the Sahara; but they have not grown quite used to their surroundings yet.'

'Oh God,' said Jack, scrabbling for the handle. 'Are they all out?'

'Not all,' said Stephen. 'And learning from Killick that you expected guests, I conceived you might prefer them away. There is so much ignorant prejudice against bees in a dining-room.' Something was crawling on Jack's neck; the door had completely vanished; he began to sweat heavily. 'So I thought to create an artificial night, when, in the course of nature, they return to their hive. I also made three fires for the sake of the smoke: these did not have the desired effect, however. It may be that the darkness is too complete. Let us compromise with a twilight – dark, but not too dark.' He raised a corner of sailcloth, and a beam of sun showed an incalculable number of bees on every vertical surface and on most of those that were flat; bees flying in a jerky, meaningless fashion from point to point; fifty or so sitting on his coat and breeches. 'There,' said Stephen, 'that is far, far better is it not? Urge them to mount on your finger, Jack, and carry them back to their hive. Gently, gently, and on no account exhibit, or even feel, the least uneasiness: fear is wholly fatal, as I dare say you know.'

Jack had the door-handle; he opened it a crack and glided swiftly through. 'Killick!' he shouted, beating at his clothes.

'Sir?'

'Go and help the Doctor. Bear a hand, now.'

'I dursn't,' said Killick.

'You don't mean to tell me you are afraid, a man-of-war's man?'

'Yes I am, sir,' said Killick.

'Well, clear the fore-cabin and lay the cloth there. And

uncork a dozen of claret.' He plunged into his sleeping-cabin and tore off his stock – there was something creeping beneath it. 'What is there for dinner?' he called.

'Wenison, sir. I found a prime saddle at Chators', the same as the ladies sent us from Mapes.'

'Gentlemen,' said Jack, as the last stroke of six bells in the afternoon watch was struck and his guests arrived, 'you are very welcome. I am afraid we may have to sit a little close, but for the moment my friend is engaged in a philosophical experiment aft. Killick, tell the Doctor we hope to see him when he is at leisure. Go on,' he muttered, clenching his fist secretly and vibrating his head at the steward. 'Go on, I say: you can call through the door.'

Dinner ran very well. The *Lively* might be Spartan in her appearance and cabin furniture, but Jack had inherited an excellent cook, accustomed to sea-borne appetites, and his guests were well-bred men, easy within the strict limits of naval etiquette – even the midshipman of the watch, though mute, was mute gracefully. But the sense of rank, of deference to the captain, was very strong, and as Stephen's mind was clearly far away, Jack was pleased to find in the chaplain a lively, conversible man, with little notion of the solemnities of dining in the cabin. Mr Lydgate, the Perpetual Curate of Wool, was a cousin of Captain Hamond's, and he was taking this voyage for the sake of his health, leaving his living not for a new career but for a temporary change of air and scenery. The air of Lisbon and Madeira was particularly recommended; that of Bermuda even more so; and this, he understood, was their destination?

'It may well be,' said Jack. 'I hope so, indeed; but with the changing face of the war there is no certainty about these things. I have known captains lay in stores for the Cape, only to find themselves ordered to the Baltic at the last moment. Everything must depend on the good of the service,' he added piously; and then feeling that remarks of this kind might have a damping effect, he cried, 'Mr Dashwood, the wine stands by you: the good of the service requires that it should circulate. Mr Simmons, pray tell me about the ape that so astonished me this morning. The living ape.'

'Cassandra, sir? She is one of half a dozen that came aboard at Tungoo; the surgeon says she is a Tenasserim gibbon. All hands are very fond of her, but we are afraid she is pining. We rigged her out in a flannel jacket when we came into the chops of the Channel, but she will not wear it; and she will not eat English food.'

'Do you hear, Stephen?' said Jack. 'There is a gibbon aboard, that is not well.'

'Yes, yes,' said Stephen, returning to the present. 'I had the pleasure of meeting her this morning, walking hand in hand with the very young gentleman: it was impossible to tell which was supporting which. A fetching, attractive creature, in spite of its deplorable state. I look forward eagerly to dissecting it. Monsieur de Buffon hints that the naked callosities on the buttocks of the hylobates may conceal scent glands, but he does not go so far as to assert it.'

A chill fell on the conversation, and after a slight pause Jack said, 'I think, my dear fellow, that the ship's company would be infinitely more obliged to you, was you to cure it, than for putting Monsieur de Buffon right – for putting Cassandra in order, rather than a Frenchman, eh, eh?'

'Yet it is the ship's company that is killing her. That ape is a confirmed alcoholic; and from what little I know of your foremast jack, no earthly consideration will prevent him from giving rum to anything he loves. Our monk-seal in the Mediterranean, for example: it drowned in a state of besotted inebriation, with a fixed smile upon its face; and when fished up and dissected, its kidneys and liver were found to be ruined, very much like those of Mr Blanckley of the Carcass bomb-ketch, an unpromoted master's mate of sixty-three whom I had the pleasure of opening at Port Mahon, a gentleman who had not been sober for five and thirty years. I met this gibbon a little after the serving out of the grog – it had plunged from an upper pinnacle at the first notes of Nancy Dawson – and the animal was hopelessly fuddled. It was conscious of its state, endeavoured to conceal it, and put its black hand in mine with an embarrassed air. Who is that very young gentleman, by the way?'

He was Josiah Randall, they told him, the son of the second lieutenant, who had come home to find his wife dead, and this child unprovided for – no near family at all. 'So he brought him aboard,' said Mr Dashwood, 'and the Captain rated him bosun's servant.'

'How very, very painful,' said Jack. 'I hope we have some action soon; there is nothing like it for changing the current of a man's mind. A French frigate, or a Spaniard, if they come in; there is nothing like your Spaniard for dogged fighting.'

'I dare say you have seen a great deal of action, sir?' said the parson, nodding towards Jack's bandage.

'Not more than most, sir,' said Jack. 'Many officers have been far more fortunate.'

'Pray what would you consider a reasonable number of actions?' asked the parson. 'I was astonished, on joining the ship, to find that none of the gentlemen could tell me what a pitched battle was like.'

'It is so much a question of luck, or perhaps I should say of Providence,' said Jack, with a bow to the cloth. 'Where one is stationed, and so on. After all,' he said, pausing, for on the verge of his mind there was a witticism, if he could but grasp it. 'After all, it takes two to make a quarrel, and if the French don't come out, why, you cannot very well have a battle all by yourself. Indeed, there is so much routine work, blockading and convoy-duty and carrying troops, you know, that I dare say half the lieutenants of the Navy List have never seen action at all, in the sense of a meeting of ships of equal force, or of fleets. More than half, perhaps.'

'I never have, I am sure,' said Dashwood.

'I *saw* an action when I was in the *Culloden* in ninety-eight,' said Simmons. 'A very great action; but we ran aground, and never could come up. It nearly broke our hearts.'

'It must have been a sad trial,' said Jack. 'I remember how you carried out warps, pulling like heroes.'

'You were at the Nile, sir?'

'Yes, yes. I was in the *Leander*. I remember coming on deck just as the *Mutine* rounded to under your stern, to try to heave you off.'

'So you were in a great battle, Captain Aubrey,' said the chaplain eagerly. 'Pray, can you tell me what it was like? Can you give me some impression of it?'

'Why, sir, I doubt that I could, really, any more than I could give you much impression of let us say a symphony or a splendid dinner. There is a great deal of noise, more noise than you would believe possible; and time does not seem to have the same meaning, if you follow me; and you get very tired. And afterwards you have to clear up the mess.'

'Ah, that is what I wanted to know. And is the din so very great?'

'It is enormous. At the Nile, for example, we had the *Orion* blow up near us, and we all conversed in shouts for ten days after. But St Vincent was noisier. In what we call the slaughter-house, where I was stationed at St Vincent – that is the part of the gun-deck in the middle of the ship, sir – you have sixteen thirty-two pounders in a row, all roaring away as fast as they can load and fire, recoiling and jumping up with a great crash when they are hot, and running out again to fire; and then just overhead you have another row of guns thundering on the deck above. And then the smashing blow as the enemy's shot hits you, and maybe the crash of falling spars above, and the screams of the wounded. And all this in such a smoke you can hardly see or breathe, and the men cheering like mad, and sweating and gulping down water when there is a second's pause. At St Vincent we fought both sides, which doubled the row. No: that is what you remember – the huge noise everywhere, the flashes in the darkness. And,' he added, 'the importance of gunnery – speed and accuracy and discipline. We were firing a broadside every two minutes, and they took three and a half or four – that's what wins the day.'

'So you were at St Vincent too,' said the parson. 'And at what other actions, if I am not too indiscreet – I mean, apart from this last most daring capture, of which we have all read?'

'Only small affairs – skirmishing in the Mediterranean and the West Indies in the last war – that kind of thing,' said Jack.

'There was the *Cacafuego*, sir, I believe,' said Mr Simmons, with a smile.

'It must have been wonderful, when you were young, sir,' said the midshipman, sick with envy. 'Nothing ever happens now.'

'I am sure you will forgive me if I seem personal,' said the chaplain, 'but I should like to form an image of the officer who has seen, as you say, a moderate amount of fighting. In addition to your fleet actions, about how many others have you taken part in?'

'Why, upon my word, I forget,' said Jack, feeling that the others had an unfair advantage of him, and feeling too that parsons were out of place in a man-of-war. He signalled to Killick for fresh decanter and the roast; and as he set to carving the flow of his mind changed as thoroughly as if an eighteen-pound shot had hulled the frigate. He felt a rising oppression in his bosom and choked, standing bowed there, carving the venison. The first lieutenant had long ago seen that Mr Lydgate's persistence was disagreeable to Captain Aubrey, and he turned the conversation back to animals aboard. Dogs in ships he had known: the Newfoundland that so lovingly brought a smoking grenade; the *Culloden*'s pet crocodile; cats . . .'

'Dogs,' said the chaplain, who was not one to leave his corner of the table silent long. 'That reminds me of a question I had meant to put to you gentlemen. This short watch that is about to come, or rather these two short watches – why are they called *dog* watches? Where, heu, heu, is the *canine* connection?'

'Why,' said Stephen, 'it is because they are curtailed, of course.'

A total blank. Stephen gave a faint inward sigh; but he was used to this. 'Mr Butler, the bottle stands by you,' said Jack. 'Mr Lydgate, allow me to help you to a little of the undercut.'

It was the midshipman who first reacted. He whispered to his neighbour Dashwood, 'He said, cur-tailed: the *dog*-watch is *cur*-tailed. Do you twig?'

It was the sort of wretched clench perfectly suited to the company. The spreading merriment, the relish, the thunderous mirth, reached the forecastle, causing amazement and conjecture: Jack leaned back in his chair, wiping the tears from his scarlet face, and cried, 'Oh, it is the best thing – the best thing. Bless you, Stephen – a glass of wine with you. Mr Simmons, if we dine with the admiral, you must ask me, and I will say, "Why, it is because *they have been docked*, of course." No, no. I am out. *Cur-tailed* – cur-tailed. But I doubt I should ever be able to get it out gravely enough.'

They did not dine with the admiral, however; no loving messages answered their salute to the flagship; but the moment they dropped anchor in the crowded Downs Parker came aboard from the *Fanciulla* with his brand-new epaulette, to congratulate and to be congratulated. Jack felt a certain pang when the boat answered the *Lively*'s hail with '*Fanciulla*', meaning that her captain was aboard; but the sight of Parker's face as it came level with the deck and the affection that beamed from it, did away with all repining. Parker looked ten, fifteen years younger; he came up the side like a boy; he was wholly and absolutely delighted. He most bitterly regretted that he was under orders to sail within the hour, but he solemnly engaged Jack and Stephen to dine with him at the very next meeting; he thought *curtailed* by far the best thing he had ever heard in his life – should certainly repeat it – but he had always known that Dr Maturin was a towering intellect – was still taking his pill, morning and evening, and should continue to do so until the end of his life; and on leaving he took Jack's hesitant 'Captain Parker would not be offended if he suggested a relaxation – a *curtailing* of the cat, as he might say' very well indeed. He said he should pay the utmost attention to advice from such a – such an esteemed quarter, such a very, very highly esteemed quarter. On saying good-bye he took both Jack's hands in his and, with tears in his small, close-set eyes, he said, 'You don't know what it means, sir, success at fifty-six – success at last. It changes a man's whole, eh heart. Why I could kiss the ship's boys.'

Jack's eyebrows shot into his bandage but he returned Parker's fervent grip and saw him to the gangway. He, was profoundly touched and he stood there looking after the boat as it pulled over to the beautiful little sloop until the first lieutenant came up to him and said, 'Mr Dashwood has a request to make, sir, if you please. He would like to take his sister down to Portsmouth: she is married to a Marine officer there.'

'Oh, certainly, Mr Simmons. She will be very welcome. She may have the after-cabin. But stay, the after-cabin is filled with . . .'

'No, no, sir. He would not hear of putting you out – it is only his sister. He will sling a hammock in the gun-room, she shall have his cabin. That is how we always did these things when Captain Hamond was aboard. Shall you be going ashore, sir?'

'No. Killick will go to pick up my coxswain and some stores and salve against bee-stings; but I shall stay aboard. Keep a boat for Dr Maturin, however: I believe he will wish to go. Good day to you, ma'am,' he said, moving aside and taking off his hat as Mrs Armstrong, the gunner's wife, shook the gangway with her bulk. 'Take care – hold on to the side-ropes with both hands.'

'Bless you sir,' said Mrs Armstrong with a jolly wheeze, 'I been in and out of ships since I was a little maid.' She took one basket between her teeth, two more under her left arm, and dropped into the boat like a midshipman.

'That is an excellent woman, sir,' said the first lieutenant, looking down into the hoveller. 'She nursed me through a fever in Java when Mr Floris and the Dutch surgeons had given me up.'

'Well,' said Jack, 'there were women in the Ark, so I suppose there must be some good in 'em; but generally speaking I have never known anything but trouble come of shipping them on a voyage – quarrels, discussions, not enough to go round, jealousies. I do not even care for them in port – drunkenness, and a sick-list as long as your arm. Not that this has the least bearing on Mrs Gunner of course, or the other warrant officers' wives – still less to Mr Dashwood's sister. Ah, Stephen, there you are – Simmons withdrew – 'I was just telling the first lieutenant that you would probably be going ashore. You will take the barge, will you not? Two of the supernumeraries are not to report aboard until the morning, so you will have all the time in the world.'

Stephen looked at him with his strange pale unblinking eyes. Had that old constraint returned, that curious misery? Jack was looking conscious – unnaturally, inappropriately gay: a wretched actor. 'Shall you not go, Jack?' he said.

'No, sir,' said Jack. 'I shall stay aboard. Between ourselves,' he added in a much lower tone, 'I do not believe I shall ever willingly set foot on shore again: indeed, I have sworn an oath never to risk arrest. But,' he cried, with that painful, jarring, artificial assumption of levity that Stephen knew so well, 'I must beg you to get some decent coffee when you go. Killick is no judge. He can tell good wine from bad, as you would expect in a smuggler; but he is no judge of coffee.'

Stephen nodded. 'I must also buy some issue-peas,' he said. 'I shall call at New Place, and I shall look into the hospital. Have you any messages?'

'Compliments, of course, best compliments: and my very kindest wishes to Babbington and the other wounded Polychrests – this is for their comforts, if you please. Macdonald, too. Please tell Babbington I am particularly sorry not to be able to visit him – it is quite impossible.'

13

IT WAS DRAWING towards evening when Stephen left the hospital: his patients were doing well – one shocking belly-wound had astonished him by living – and Babbington's arm was safe; his professional mind was easy and content as he walked up through the town towards New Place. His professional mind: but the whole of the rest of his spirit, feeling out with un-logical antennae, sensing the immaterial, was in such a state of preparedness that he was not in any way surprised to see the house boarded and shut up.

It seemed that the mad gentleman had been driven away in a coach and four 'weeks and weeks ago' or 'some time last month, maybe' or 'before we got in the apples', bowing from the window and laughing fit to burst his sides; and that the coachman wore a black cockade. The servants followed in the waggon the next day, a week after, some time later, going to a little place in Sussex, to Brighton, to London town. His informants had not noticed the lady these last weeks. Mr Pope, the butler at New Place, was a proud, touch-me-not gentleman; all the servants were a stiff London lot, and kept themselves to themselves.

Less downright in his approach than Jack, Stephen opened the simple lock of the garden gate with a piece of wire, and the kitchen door with a Morton's retractor. He walked composedly up the stairs, through the green-baize door and into the hall. A tall thirty-day clock was still going, its weight nearly touching the ground; a solemn tock-tock that echoed through the hall and followed him up into the drawing-room. Silence; a perfection of dust-sheets, rolled carpets, ranged furniture; rays of light that came through the shutters, motes turning in them; moths; the first delicate cobwebs in unexpected places, such as the carved mantelpiece in the library, where Mr Lowndes had written some lines of Sappho large on the wall in chalk.

'An elegant hand,' said Stephen, as he stood to consider it. *'The moon has set, and the Pleiades; midnight is gone; the hours wear by, and here I lie alone: alone. Perhaps and here I, Sappho, lie alone*, to give the sex. No. The sex is immaterial. It is the same for both.'

Silence; anonymous perfection; unstirring air – never a waft or a movement; silence. The smell of bare boards. A tall-boy with its face turned to the wall.

In her room the same trim bare sterility; even the looking-glass was shrouded. It was not so much severe, for the grey light was too soft, as meaningless. There was no waiting in this silence, no tension of any kind: the creaking of the boards under his feet contained no threat, no sort of passion: he could have leapt or shrieked without affecting the inhuman vacuum of sense. It was as meaningless as total death, a skull in a dim thicket, the future gone, its past wiped out. He had the strongest feeling of the déjà-vu that he had ever experienced, and yet it was familiar enough to him, that certain knowledge of the turn of a dream, the sequence of words that would be said by a stranger in a coach and of his reply, the disposition of a room he had never seen, even to the pattern of the paper on its walls.

In the waste-paper-basket there were some balled-up sheets, the only imperfection, apart from the living clock, in this desert of negation, and the only exception to the completeness of his déjà-vu. 'What indeed am I looking for?' he said, and the sound of his voice ran through the open rooms. 'An out-of-date announcement of my death?' But they were lists in a servant's hand, quite meaningless, and one paper where a pen had been tried – spluttering lines of ink that might have had a meaning once, but none that could be understood. He tossed them back, stood for a long moment listening to his heart, and walked straight into her dressing-room. Here he found what he had known he should find: the stark bareness, the pretty satinwood furniture huddled against the wall was of no importance, did not signify; but here, coming from no particular shelf or cupboard, there was the ghost of her scent, now a little stronger, now so tenuous that his most extreme attention could hardly catch it.

'At least,' he said, 'this is not the horror of the last.' He closed the door with the greatest caution, walked down into the hall; stopped the clock, setting his mark upon the house, and let himself out into the garden. He turned the lock behind him, walked along the leaf-strewn, already neglected paths, out by the green door and so to the road along the coast. With his hands behind his back and his eyes on this road as it streamed evenly beneath him, watching its flow while there was still any day to see, he followed it until he reached the lights of Deal. Then, remembering that he had left his boat at Dover, he turned and paced the smooth miles back again. 'It is very well,' he said. 'I should have sat in the parlour of an inn, in any case, until I could return and go to bed without any conversation or civilities. This is better by far. I rejoice in this even, sandy road, stretching on and on for ever.'

THE MORNING WAS RICH in such events as the introduction of Mr Floris, the surgeon, his invitation to view the sick-bay, equipped with his personally-invented wind-sail to bring fresh air below, and his flattering eagerness, his flattering *deferential* eagerness for Dr Maturin's opinion on Wallace – as clear a case for instant suprapubic cystotomy as Stephen had ever seen; and the appearance of Mrs Miller and her child, bright and early, for the *Lively* was at single anchor, with the blue peter flying.

She was a pretty young woman with a decided air, and with a hint not of boldness but rather of that freedom which a wedding-ring and the protection of a child provides. Not that any of this was visible when Jack greeted her on the quarter-deck, however; all was demure gratitude and apologies for the intrusion. Little Brydges would be no trouble, she assured him – he was thoroughly accustomed to ships – had been to Gibraltar and back – was never sick, and never cried.

'Why, ma'am,' said Jack, 'we are delighted to have the honour of your company, and wish it were for farther than Portsmouth. If a man cannot give a brother-officer's wife and sister a lift, things are in a sad way. Though I believe we may look forward to the pleasure of having you with us for quite a while; the wind is getting round into that God – that bothersome southerly quarter.'

'Uncle John,' said young Brydges, 'why are you nodding and winking at Mama? She has not talked to the Captain too much, yet; and I dare say she will stop directly. And I have said nothing at all.'

'Stephen,' said Jack, 'may I come in? I hope I have not woken you – was you asleep?'

'No,' said Stephen. 'Not at all.'

'Well, the gun-room is in rather a taking. It seems that a round million of your reptiles got into their cocoa-pot this morning – immolated themselves by the hundred, crawling in at the spout. They say that the wear and anxiety of such another breakfast would make them give up the service.'

'Did they note down the exact time?'

'Oh, I am sure they did. I am sure that in the intervals of avoiding attack, eating their breakfast, and navigating the ship, they hurried off to check the precise moment by the master's twin chronometers. Ha, ha.'

'You speak ironically, no doubt. But this is a striking instance of sagacity in bees. I feed them with a syrup of cocoa and sugar. They connect the scent of cocoa with their nourishment. They discover a new source of cocoa-scent; they busily communicate this discovery to their fellows, together with its location, and there you have the whole situation – as satisfactory a proof as you could wish to see.

Tomorrow I hope the gun-room will note down the time of
their first appearance. I bet you a considerable sum of money
that it will be within ten minutes either side of seven bells,
the moment at which they were first fed.'

'Do you mean that they will rush in again?'

'So long as the gun-room continues to drink heavily-
sugared cocoa, I see no reason why they should ever stop. It
will be interesting to see whether this knowledge is passed on
to all the subsequent generations of bees. I thank you, Jack,
for telling me this: no discovery has given me so much satisfaction for years. Once it has been thoroughly tested – a
sequence of some weeks or months – I shall communicate it
to Monsieur Huber.'

His waxy, tormented face had such a glow of pleasure that
Jack could not find it in his heart to fulfil his promise to the
gun-room. They might caulk their bulkheads, key-holes, sky-
lights, drink tea or coffee, shroud themselves in mosquito
netting for a day or so – what was a little discomfort, on
active service? He said, 'I have a treat for you today, Stephen
– a pretty young woman for dinner! Dashwood's sister came
aboard this morning, a very fine young woman indeed. A pleasure to look at, and very well behaved – went straight below
and has never been seen since.'

'Alas, I must beg to be excused. I am only waiting for my
opiates to have their effect, and then I shall operate. Mr
Floris is waiting for me, and his mates are sharpening the bis-
touries at this very moment. I should have preferred to wait
until we reached Haslar, but with this wind I presume it will
take a couple of days or so; and the patient cannot wait. They
are eager to see the operation; I am equally eager to gratify
them. That is why I am resting my limbs at present; it would
never do to make a blunder in such a demonstration. Besides,
we must consider our patient. Oh, certainly. He must feel
assured of a steady hand, when we are groping in his vitals
with our instrument, for it will be some little while before we
tally and belay.'

The patient, the unhappy Wallace, might feel assured of a
steady hand as he was led, or rather propelled, to the bench,
stupefied with opium, dazed with rum, and buoyed up with
accounts of the eminence of the hand that was going to deal
with him; but he was assured of little else, to judge by his
staring pallor. His messmates led him to his place and made
him fast in a seamanlike manner: one seized his pigtail to a
ring-bolt, another gave him a bullet to bite upon, and a third
told him he was saving at least a hundred guineas by being
there – no physical gent with a gold-headed stick would think
of opening him for less.

'Gentlemen,' said Stephen, turning back his cuffs, 'you will
observe that I take my point of departure from the iliac crest;
I traverse thus, and so find my point of incision.'

So, in the fore-cabin, Jack held the point of his carver over
a dimple in the venison pasty and said, 'Allow me to cut you a
little of this pasty, ma'am. It is one of the few things I can
carve. When we have a joint, I usually call upon my friend Dr
Maturin, whom I hope to introduce to you this afternoon. He
is such a hand at carving.'

'If you please, sir,' said Mrs Miller. 'It looks so very good.
But I cannot quite believe what you say about carving. You
cut out the *Fanciulla* only the other day, and surely that was a
very pretty piece of carving.'

While these delights were going forward, the *Lively* stood
across the Channel, close-hauled to the freshening south-
west breeze with her starboard tacks aboard, under topgallants and a fine spread of staysails.

'Now, Mr Simmons,' said Jack, appearing upon deck, 'this is
very capital, is it not? How she does love to sail upon a bowline.' It was a warm, bright afternoon, with patches of cloud
moving across the sky, and her brilliant canvas, her white rigging, shone splendid against them as she heeled to the wind.
There was nothing of the yacht about her; her paintwork was
strictly utilitarian and even ugly; but this one point of snowy
cordage, the rare manilla she had brought back from the

Philippines, raised her to an uncommon height of beauty –
that, and of course, her lovely, supple command of the sea.
There was a long, even swell from the south and a surface
ripple that came lipping along her weather bow, sometimes
sending a little shower of spray aft across the waist, with
momentary rainbows in it. This would be a perfect afternoon
and evening for gunnery.

'Tell me, Mr Simmons,' he said, 'what has been your practice in exercising the great guns?'

'Well, sir,' said the first lieutenant, 'we used to fire once a
week at the beginning of the commission, but Captain
Hamond was so checked by the Navy Board for expenditure
of powder and ball that he grew discouraged.' Jack nodded:
he too had received those querulous, righteous, indignant
letters that ended so strangely with 'your affectionate
friends'. 'So now we only fire by divisions once a month.
Though of course we run them in and out at least once a
week at quarters.'

Jack paced the windward side of the quarterdeck. Rattling
the guns in and out was very well, but it was not the same
thing as firing them. Nothing like it at all. Yet a broadside
from the *Lively* would cost ten guineas. He considered, turning it over in his mind; stepped into the master's cabin to look
at the charts, and sent for the gunner, who gave him a statement of cartridge filled, powder at hand, and an appreciation
of each gun. The four long nine-pounders were his darlings,
and they did most of the firing in the *Lively*, worked by him,
his mates and the quarter-gunners.

The horizon beyond the larboard bow was broken now by
the irregular line of the French coast, and the *Lively* heaved
about on the other tack. How beautifully she handled! She
came smoothly up into the wind, paid off and filled in a
cable's length, hardly losing any way at all. In spite of her
spread of canvas, with all the staysail sheets to be passed
over, scarcely a quarter of an hour passed between the pipe of
All hands about ship and the moment when the mastmen

began flemishing their ropes and making pretty, while France dropped out of sight astern.

What a ship to handle – no noise, no fuss, no shadow of a doubt as to whether she would stay. And she was making eight knots already: he could eat the wind out of any square-rigged craft afloat. But what was the good of that, if he could not hit his enemy when he came up with him?

'We will make a short board, Mr Norrey,' he said to the master, who now had the watch. 'And then you will be so good as to lay her in half a mile from Balbec, under topsails.'

'Stephen,' he said, some minutes later, 'how did your operation go?'

'Very prettily, I thank you,' said Stephen. 'It was as charming a demonstration of my method as you could wish: a perfect case for immediate intervention, good light, plenty of elbow-room. And the patient survived.'

'Well done, well done! Tell me, Stephen, would you do me a kindness?'

'I might,' said Stephen, looking shrewish.

'It is just to shift your brutes into the quarter-gallery. The guns are to fire in the cabin, and perhaps the bang might be bad for them. Besides, I do not want another mutiny on my hands.'

'Oh, certainly. I shall carry the hive and you shall fix the gimbals. Let us do it at once.'

When Jack returned, still trembling and with the sweat running down the hollow of his spine, it was time for quarters. The drum beat and the Livelies hurried to their stations in the usual way; but they knew very well that this was no ordinary ritual, not only from the gunner's uncommon activity and knowing looks, but also because Mrs Miller had been desired to step down into the hold, with a midshipman bearing an armful of cushions to show her the way: asked if she minded a bang, had replied, 'Oh no, I love it.'

The frigate was gliding along half a mile from the shore under topsails alone, so close in that the members of a flock of sheep could be seen on the green grass, surrounding their shepherd as he stared out to sea; and the Livelies were not surprised, after they had been reported present and sober, sir, to hear the order 'Out tompions.'

Some of the tompions needed a furious heave to get them out, they having sat in the muzzles of their guns for so long, but as the frigate approached the battery guarding the little port of Balbec all the guns were staring at it with their iron eyes wide open. This was a little battery of three twenty-four pounders on an islet outside the creek, and it vanished in its own smoke at extreme range, so that only its immense tricolour could be seen floating over the cloud.

'We will fire the guns in succession, Mr Simmons,' said Jack, 'with a half-minute interval between each. I will give the word. Mr Fanning, note down the fall of each shot with the number of the gun.'

The French gunners were accurate but slow – shorthanded, no doubt. They knocked away the *Lively*'s stern lantern with their third salvo, but they did not do more than make a hole in her maintopsail before the frigate was within the range that Jack had chosen – before he gave the word to fire. The *Lively* was slow and inaccurate – little notion of independent fire, almost none of elevation. Only one shot from her starboard guns hit the battery at all, and her last gun was followed by a derisive cheer from the land.

The frigate was coming abreast of the battery, a little over a quarter of a mile away. 'Are those after guns run out, Mr Simmons?' asked Jack. 'Then we will give them a broadside.' As he waited for the long roll, one twenty-four pounder hulled the *Lively* in the mizzen-chains and another passed over the quarterdeck with a deep howl. He noticed that two of the midshipmen bobbed to the ball and then looked anxiously to see whether he had noticed: they had not been under fire before. 'Fire!' said Jack, and the whole ship erupted in a vast roaring crash, trembling to her keelson. For a moment the smoke blotted out the sun, then raced away to leeward. Jack stretched eagerly over the rail: this was a little better – stones knocked sideways, the flag leaning drunkenly. The Livelies were cheering; but they were not running up their guns with anything like the speed they furled their topsails. The minutes dragged by. The battery sent a ball into the *Lively*'s stern. 'Perhaps that was the quarter-gallery,' he thought, with a spurt of hope through his boiling impatience. 'Shiver the maintops'l. Hard a-starboard. Will you get those guns run up, Mr Simmons?' The range was lengthening, drawing out and out. A ball hit the boats on the booms, scattering planks and splinters. 'Port your helm. Thus, thus. Fire. Ready about, ready oh!'

Only two of her shots had gone home, but one of them had silenced a gun, hitting the embrasure fair and square. The *Lively* came about, fired her larboard guns in succession – the men had their shirts off now – and then a broadside. As she came abreast of the battery for the second time, gliding smoothly up much nearer to and with her carronades ready to join in, the little garrison was seen to be pulling furiously for the shore, all crammed into one small boat, for the other had gone adrift, its painter cut. 'Fire,' said Jack, and the battery leapt in a cloud of dust and chips of stone.

'How are our boats?' he asked a quarterdeck midshipman.

'Your gig has been hit, sir. The others are all right.'

'Cutter away. Mr Dashwood, be so good as to take the cutter, spike up any serviceable guns and carry what is left of the colours to Mrs Miller with the *Lively*'s compliments. And just secure that boat of theirs, will you? Then we shall be all square.'

The frigate lay gently pitching on the swell while the cutter hurried across the sea and back. There was nothing in the little port except fishing craft: nothing to be done there. 'However,' he said, when the boats were hoisted in, 'the good of the service requires us to batter the battery a little more. Up jib. We really must see if we can do better than four and a half minutes between broadsides, Mr Simmons.'

To and fro she went, shattering and pulverizing the heap of rubble, the gun-crews very pleased with themselves and plying their pieces with great zeal if not much accuracy.

By the time she sailed away her practice was a little better, the co-ordination was a trifle nearer what he could wish, and the men were more accustomed to the crash and leap of their deadly charges; but of course it was still pitifully slow.

'Well, Mr Simmons,' he said to the first lieutenant, who was looking at him with a certain uneasiness, 'that was not bad at all. Number four and seven fired very well. But if we can manage three accurate broadsides in five minutes, then there will be nothing that can stand against us. We must salute every French battery we pass like this – so much more fun than firing at a mark – and our affectionate friends cannot handsomely object. I hope we shall have a little more Channel duty before they send us foreign.'

HE WOULD NOT have formed this wish if he had known how surprisingly soon it was to be fulfilled. The *Lively* had not anchored in Spithead before orders came off desiring and directing him to proceed immediately to Plymouth to take charge of a north-bound convoy – Bermuda was off for the next few weeks, perhaps for good. The port admiral's boat also brought a young man from Jack's new agent, bearing a cheque for a hundred and thirty pounds more than Jack had dared hope for, and a letter from General Aubrey announcing his return from St Muryan, the rottenest of all the rotten Cornish boroughs, the property of his friend Mr Polwhele, on the simple platform of Death to the Whigs. 'I have composed my maiden speech,' wrote the General, 'and am to deliver it on Monday. It will dish them completely – such corruption you would not credit, hardly. And I shall deliver another, worse, after the recess, if they do not do something for us. We have bled for our country, and may I be damned if our country shall not bleed for us, moderately.' The *moderately* was scratched out, and the letter concluded by desiring Jack to enter his little brother's name on the ship's books, 'as it might come in useful, some day.' Jack's face took on a very thoughtful cast; it was not that he disliked the sentiment about bleeding – he was all for it; but he knew his father's notions of discretion, alas. They bundled Mrs Miller ashore, as proud as Pontius Pilate with her piece of flag, and carried on their zigzag course down the Channel against the west and south-west winds, pausing only to celebrate Jack's wealth and General Aubrey's election by beating a battery on the headland of Barfleur into the ground and destroying the semaphore-station at Cap Levi. The frigate spent barrel after barrel of powder and scattered some tons of iron over the French landscape; her gunnery improved remarkably. Next to the pleasure of shooting at a fellow man, the Livelies loved destroying his works; no shooting at the mark at sea could possibly have given them such delight or have increased their zeal a tenth part as much as shooting at the windows of the semaphore-station, with their guns at their utmost elevation. And when at last they hit them, when the glass and frames vanished with a crash, they cheered as though they had sunk a ship of the line; and the whole quarterdeck, including the chaplain, laughed and simpered like a holiday.

He would not have formed the wish, if he had known that it would mean depriving Stephen of the tropical delights he had promised, to say nothing of the pleasure of walking about on land himself, unhunted, with never an anxious glance behind, in Madeira, Bermuda or the West Indies, unharassed by any but the French, and perhaps the Spaniards and the yellow fever.

Yet there it was, formed and fulfilled; and here he was, under the lee of Drake's Island, with Plymouth Hoe on his larboard bow, waiting for the 92nd Foot to get into their transports in Hamoaze: and a long business it would be, judging from their present state of total unpreparedness.

'Jack,' said Stephen, 'shall you call on Admiral Haddock?'

'No,' said Jack. 'I shall not. I have sworn not to go ashore, you know.'

'Sophie and Cecilia are still there,' observed Stephen.

'Oh,' cried Jack, and took a turn up and down the cabin. 'Stephen,' he said, 'I shall not go. What in God's name have I to offer her? I have thought about it a great deal. It was wrong and selfish in me to pursue her to Bath – I should never have done it; but I was hurried along by my feelings, you know – I did not reflect. What sort of a match am I? Post, if you like, but up to the ears in debt, and with nothing much in the way of prospects if Melville goes. A chap that goes sneaking and skulking about on land like a pickpocket with the thief takers on his line. No. I am not going to pester her as once I did. And I am not going to tear my heart to pieces again: besides, what can she care for me, after all this?'

14

'BEG PARDON, ma'am, but can you tell me where Miss Williams is?' asked the Admiral's butler. 'There is a gentleman to see her.'

'She will be down presently,' said Cecilia. 'Who is it?'

'Dr Maturin, ma'am. He particularly told me to say, Dr Maturin.'

'Oh, show him in to me, Rowley,' cried Cecilia. 'I'll entertain him. Dear Dr Maturin, how do you do? How come you are here? Oh, I am amazed, I declare! What a splendid thing about Captain Aubrey, the dear man, and the *Fanciulla*: but to think of the poor *Polychrest*, all sunk beneath the wave – but you saved your clothes, however, I dare say? Oh, we were so pleased to read the Gazette! Sophie and I held hands and skipped about like lambs in the pink room, roaring out Huzzay, huzzay! Though we were in such a taking – Lord, Dr Maturin, such a taking! We wept and wept, and I was all swollen and horrid for the port admiral's ball, and Sophie would not even go at all, not that she missed much –

a very stupid ball, with all the young men stuck in the door and only the old codgers dancing – call that dancing! – by order of rank. I only stood up once. Oh, how we wept – handkerchiefs all sopping, I do assure you – and of course it is very sad. But she might have thought of us. We shall never be able to hold up our heads again! I think it was very wrong of her – she might have waited until we were married. I think she is a – but I must not say that to you, because I believe you were quite smitten once, ages and ages ago, were you not?'

'What upset you so?'

'Why, Diana, of course. Didn't you know? Oh, Lord.'

'Pray tell me now.'

'Mama said I was never to mention it. And I never will. But if you promise not to tell, I will whisper it. Di has gone into keeping with that Mr Canning. I thought that would surprise you. Who ever would have guessed it? Mama did not, although she is so amazing wise. She was in a horrid rage – she still is. She says it has quite ruined our chances of a decent marriage, which is such a shame. Not that I mind so much about a *decent* marriage; but I should not like to be an old maid. That is quite my aversion. Hush, I hear her door closing: she is coming down. I will leave you together, and not play gooseberry. I may not be six foot tall, but at least no one can say I am a gooseberry. You won't tell, will you? Remember, you promised.'

'Sophie, my dear,' he said, kissing her, 'how do you do? I will answer your questions at once. Jack is made post. We came in that frigate by the little small island. He has an acting command.'

'Which frigate? Where? Where?'

'Come,' said Stephen, swivelling the admiral's great brass telescope on its stand. 'There you have him, walking on the quarterdeck in his old nankeen trousers.'

There in the bright round paced Jack, from the hances to the aftermost carronade and back again.

'Oh,' she cried, 'he has a bandage on his head. Not – not his poor ears again?' she murmured, focusing the glass.

'No, no, a mere scalp-wound. Not above a dozen stitches.'

'Will he not come ashore?' she asked.

'He will not. What, set foot on land to be arrested for debt? No friend of his but would stop him by force – no woman with any heart of friendship in her would ask it.'

'No, no. Of course. I was forgetting . . .'

Each time he turned he glanced up to Mount Edgcumb, to Admiral Haddock's official residence. Their eyes seemed to meet, and she started back.

'Is it out of focus?' asked Stephen.

'No, no. It is so prying to look like this – indecent. How is he? I am so very glad that – I am quite confused – everything is so sudden – I had no idea. How is he? And how are you? Dear Stephen, how are you?'

'I am very well, I thank you.'

'No, no, you are not. Come, come and sit down at once. Stephen, has Cissy been prattling?'

'Never mind,' said Stephen, looking aside. 'Tell me, is it true?'

She could not reply, but sat by him and took his hand. 'Now listen, honey,' he said, returning the kindness of her clasp.

'Oh, I beg your pardon,' cried Admiral Haddock, putting his head in at the door and instantly withdrawing.'

'Now listen, honey. The *Lively*, the frigate, is ordered up-Channel, to the Nore, with these foolish soldiers. She will sail the minute they are ready. You must go aboard this afternoon and ask him to give you a lift to the Downs.'

'Oh, I could never, never do such a thing. It would be very, very improper. Forward, pushing, bold, improper.'

'Not at all. With your sister, perfectly proper, the most usual thing in the world. Come now, my dear, start packing your things. It is now or never. He may be in the West Indies next month.'

'Never. I know you mean so very kindly – you are a darling, Stephen – but a young woman cannot, *cannot* do such things.'

'Now I have no time at all, none, acushla,' said Stephen, rising. 'So listen now. Do what I say. Pack your bonnet: go aboard. Now is the time. Now, or there will be three thousand miles of salt unhappy sea between you, and a waste of years.'

'I am so confused. But I cannot. No, I never will. I cannot. He might not want me.' The tears overflowed: she wrung her handkerchief desperately, shaking her head and murmuring, 'No, no, never.'

'Good day to you, now, Sophie,' he said. 'How can you be so simple. So missish? Fie Sophie. Where's your courage, girl? Sure, it is the one thing in the world he admires.'

IN HIS DIARY he wrote, 'So much wretchedness, misery and squalor I do not believe I have ever seen collected together in one place, as in this town of Plymouth. All the naval ports I have visited have been cold smelly blackguardly places, but for pox-upon-pox this Plymouth bears the bell. Yet the suburb or parasite they call Dock goes even beyond Plymouth, as Sodom outran Gomorrah: I wandered about its dirty lanes, solicited, importuned by its barbarous inhabitants, male, female and epicene, and I came to the poor-house, where the old are kept until they can be buried with some show of decency. The impression of meaningless absolute unhappiness is with me yet. Medicine has brought me acquainted with misery in many forms; I am not squeamish; but for complications of filth, cruelty, and bestial ignorance, that place, with its infirmary, exceeded any thing I have ever seen or imagined. An old man, his wits quite gone, chained in the dark, squatting in his excrement, naked but for a blanket; the idiot children; the whipping. I knew it all; it is nothing new; but in this concentration it overcame me so that I could no longer feel indignation but only a hopeless nausea. It was the merest chance that I kept my appointment with the chaplain to listen to a concert – my feet, more civil than my mind, led me to the place. Curious music, well played, particularly the trumpet: a German composer, one Molter. The music, I believe, had nothing to say, but it provided a pleasant background of 'cellos and woodwinds and allowed the trumpet to make exquisite sounds – pure colour tearing through this formal elegance. I grope to define a connection that is half clear to me – I once thought that this was music, much as I thought that physical grace and style was virtue; or replaced virtue; or was virtue on another plane. But although the music shifted the current of my thoughts for a while, they are back again today, and I have not the spiritual energy to clarify this or any other position. At home there is a Roman stone I know (I often lay there to listen to my night jars) with *fui non sum non cum* carved on it; and there I have felt such a peace, such a *tranquillitas animi et indolentia corporis*. Home I say, which is singular: yet indeed there is still a glow of hatred for the Spaniards under these indulgent, unmanly ashes – a living attachment to Catalan independence.' He looked out of the cabin window at the water of the Sound, oily, with the nameless filth of Plymouth floating on it, a bloated puppy, and dipped his pen. 'Yet on the other hand, will this glow ever blaze up again, when I think of what they will do with independence? When I let my mind dwell on the vast potentiality for happiness, and our present state? Such potentiality, and so much misery? Hatred the only moving force, a petulant unhappy striving – childhood the only happiness, and that unknowing; then the continual battle that cannot ever possibly be won; a losing fight against ill-health – poverty for nearly all. Life is a long disease with only one termination and its last years are appalling: weak, racked by the stone, rheumatismal pains, senses going, friends, family, occupation gone, a man must pray for imbecility or a heart of stone. All under sentence of death, often ignominious, frequently agonizing: and then the unspeakable levity with which the faint chance of happiness is thrown away for some jealousy, tiff, sullenness, private vanity, mistaken sense of honour, that deadly, weak and silly notion. I am not acute in my perceptions – my whole conduct with Diana proves it – but I would have sworn that Sophie had more bottom; was more straightforward, direct, courageous. Though to be sure, I know the depth of Jack's feeling for her, and perhaps she does not.' He looked up from his page again, straight into her face. It was outside the window, a few feet below him, moving from left to right as the boat pulled round the frigate's stern; she was looking up beyond the cabin window towards the taffrail, with her mouth slightly open and her lip caught behind her upper teeth, with an expression of contained alarm in her immense upturned eyes. Admiral Haddock sat beside her, and Cecilia.

When Stephen reached the quarterdeck the admiral was uttering his thoughts on manilla cordage, and Jack and Sophie were standing some distance apart, looking extraordinary conscious. 'His appearance,' reflected Stephen, 'is not so much that of concern as of consternation. His wits are overset: how very much at random he answers the admiral.'

'And all that, my dears, has to be tarred, in the case we are rigged with common hemp,' said the admiral.

'Tarred, sir?' cried Sophie. 'Oh, indeed. With – with a tar-brush, I dare say?' Her voice died away, and she blushed again.

'So I entrust the girls to you, Aubrey,' said the admiral. 'I shift the responsibility on to your shoulders – two great girls is a very shocking responsibility – and send 'em aboard on Thursday.'

'Upon my word, sir, you are very good – but not fit for a lady. That is to say, very fit for a lady; but cramped. Should be very happy, more than happy, to show Miss Williams any attention in my power.'

'Oh, never mind them. They are only girls, you know – they can rough it – don't put yourself out. Think what you will save them in pin-money. Stow them anywhere. Berth them with the Doctor, ha, ha! There you are, Dr Maturin. I am happy to see you. You would not mind it, eh? Eh? Ha, ha, ha. I saw you, you sly dog. Take care of him, Aubrey; he is a sly one.' The scattered officers on the quarterdeck frowned: the Admiral belonged to an older, coarser Navy; and he had been dining with his carnal colleague, the port admiral. 'So that is settled, Aubrey? Capital, capital. Come, Sophie; come, Cecilia: into the chair – hang on to your petticoats; mind the wind. Oh,' he added in what passed for a whisper, as the girls were lowered away in the ignominy of a bosun's chair, 'a word in your ear, Aubrey. Have you read your father's speech? I thought not. "And now let us turn to the Navy," said he to the House. "Here too we find that the former administration allowed, nay, *encouraged* the grossest laxity and unheard-of corruption. My son, a serving officer, tells me that things were very bad – the wrong officers promoted through mere influence, the ropes and sails not at all the thing; and to crown all, Mr Speaker, sir, women, *women* allowed on board! Scenes of unspeakable debauchery, fitter, oh far fitter, for the French." Now if you will take an old man's advice, you will clap a stopper over all by express. It will do you no good in the service. Let him stick to the army. A word to the wise, eh, eh? You get my meaning?'

With a look of infinite cunning, the Admiral went over the side, attended by the honours due to his splendid rank; and having stood watching respectfully for the proper length of time, Jack turned to a messenger. 'Pass the word for the carpenter,' he said. 'Mr Simmons, be so good as to select our very best hands with holystone and swab and send them aft. And tell me, who of the officers is the most remarkable for taste?'

'For taste, sir?' cried Simmons.

'Yes, yes, artistic taste. You know, a sense of the sublime.'

'Why, sir, I don't know that any of us is much gifted in that line. I do not remember the sublime ever having been men-

tioned in the gun-room. But there is Mallet, sir, carpenter's
crew, who understands these things. He was a receiver of
stolen property, specializing in pretty sublime pieces, as I
understand it – old masters and so on. He is rather old himself, and not strong, so he helps Mr Charnock with the join-
ery and fine-work; but I am sure he understands things in the
sublime way as well as anyone in the ship.'

'We will have a word with him. I need some ornaments for
the cabin. He can be trusted ashore, I suppose?'

'Oh dear me, no, sir. He has run twice, and at Lisbon he
tried to get ashore in a barrel, from the wrong side of the bar.
And once he stole Mrs Armstrong's gown and tried to slip
past the master-at-arms, saying he was a woman.'

'Then he shall go with Bonden and a file of Marines. Mr
Charnock,' he said to the waiting carpenter, 'come along with
me and let us see what we can do to the cabin to make it fit
for a lady. Mr Simmons, while we are settling this, pray let
the sailmaker start making a sailcloth carpet: black and white
squares, exactly like the *Victory*. There is not a moment to be
lost. Stephen, my hero,' he said, in the comparative privacy of
the fore-cabin, putting one arm round him in a bear-like hug,
'ain't you amazed, delighted and amazed? Lord, what luck I
have some money! Come and give me your ideas on improving the cabin.'

'The cabin is very well as it is. Perfectly adequate. All that is
needed is another hanging bed, a simple cot, with the proper
blankets and pillows. A water-carafe, and a tumbler.'

'We can shift the bulkhead a good eighteen inches for'ard,'
said Jack. 'By the bye, you will not object to the bees going
ashore, just for a while?'

'They did not go ashore for Mrs Miller. There were none of
these tyrannical caprices for Mrs Miller, I believe. They are
just growing used to their surroundings – they have started a
queen-cell!'

'Brother, I insist. I should send my bees ashore for you,
upon my sacred honour. Now there is a great favour I must

ask you. I believe I have told you how I dined with Lord
Nelson?'

'Not above two or three hundred times.'

'And I dare say I described those elegant silver plates he
has? They were made here. Please would you go ashore and
order me four, if it can be done with this? If not, two. They
must have a hawser-laid rope-border. You will remember that?
The border, the rim, must be in the form of a hawser-laid
rope. Mallet,' he said, turning to a very elderly young man
with lank sparse curls who stood bowing and undulating
beside the first lieutenant, 'Mr Simmons tell me you are a
man of taste.'

'Oh, sir,' cried Mallet, bridling, 'I protest he is too sweetly
kind. But I had some slight pretensions in former days. I contributed my mite to the Pavilion, sir.'

'Very good. Now I want some ornaments for the cabin, do
you understand? A looking-glass, a vast great looking-glass.
Curtains. Delicate little chairs. Perhaps a – what do you call
the thing? – a pouffe. Everything suitable for a young lady.'

'Yes, sir. I understand perfectly. In what style, sir? Chinois-
erie, classical, directoire?'

'In the *best* style, Mallet. And if you can pick up some pictures, so much the better. Bonden will go with you, to see
there are no purser's tricks, no Raphaelos passed off for Rem-
brandts. He will carry the purse.'

The last days of Stephen's stay in the *Lively* were tedious
and wearing to the spirit. The cabin was scrubbed and
scrubbed again; it reeked of paint, beeswax and turpentine,
sailcloth; its two cots were slung in different positions several
times a day, with stork flowers in match-tubs arranged about
them; the whole was shut up, forbidden ground, except for a
space where he had to lie in disagreeable proximity to Jack,
who tossed and snorted through the night. And whereas the
general atmosphere in the frigate grew more and more like
that of the *Polychrest* on the verge of mutiny, with sullen looks
and murmuring, her captain was in a wearisome flow of spir-

its, laughing, snapping his fingers, skipping heavily about the deck. The married officers looked at him with malignant satisfaction; the rest with disapproval.

Stephen walked up to Admiral Haddock's house, where he sat with Sophie in the summerhouse overlooking the Sound. 'You will find him very much changed,' he observed. 'You might not think so at the present moment, but he has in fact lost much of his gaiety of heart. In comparison of what he was, he is sombre, and less inclined to make friends. I have noticed it particularly in this ship – distinctly more remote from his officers and the crew. Then again, he suffers frustration with more patience than he used; he cares less passionately about many things. Indeed, I should say that the boy has quite vanished now – certainly the piratical youth of my first acquaintance is no longer to be seen. But when a man puts on maturity and invulnerability, it seems that he necessarily becomes indifferent to many things that gave him joy. I do not, of course, refer to the pleasure of your company,' he added, seeing her look of alarm. 'Upon my word, Sophie, you are in prodigious fine looks today,' he said, narrowing his eyes and peering at her. 'Your hair – I dare say you have been brushing it? No: what it comes to is this, that he is a better officer, and a duller man.'

'Dull? Oh, Stephen.'

'But his future worries me, I must confess. From what I understand there may be changes in Whitehall from one day to the next. His influence is small; and good, capable officer though he undoubtedly is, he may never get another ship. There are some hundreds of post-captains unemployed. I passed several of them on that sparse barren dismal grass-plat they call the Hoe, looking hungrily at the shipping in the Sound. This acting-command will soon be over, and then he will be on the shore. At present there are just eighty-three sea-going ships of the line in commission, a hundred and one frigates, and maybe a score of other post-ships. And Jack is 587th in a list of 639. It would have been simpler if he had remained a commander, or even a lieutenant: there are so many more opportunities for employment.'

'But surely, General Aubrey being in Parliament must be a very good thing?'

'Sure, if he could be induced to keep his mouth shut, it might be. But just now he is on his hind legs in the House, busily stamping Jack as a double-dyed Tory. And St Vincent and his friends, you know, are rabid Whigs – the general feeling of the service is whiggish to a degree.'

'Oh dear. Oh dear. Perhaps he will take a splendid prize. He does deserve it so. The Admiral says the *Lively* is one of the best sailers that ever was; he is full of admiration for her.'

'So she is. She runs along with a most surprising smooth velocity, a pleasure to behold, and her hands are most attentive to their duty. But, my dear, the day of splendid prizes is gone. At the beginning of the war there were French and Dutch Indiamen: there is not one left on the seas at present. And he would have to cut out a dozen *Fanciullas* to pay off his debts, so that he could set foot on shore without danger – by the bye, he is coming to see you on Sunday. How happy we shall be to be rid of him for a while – pray keep him as long as ever you can, or the men will break out in open rebellion. Not only are they compelled to scrub the ship below the water-line, but now they are required to comb the lambs.'

'How very happy we shall be to see you both. Pray, are lambs a part of the ship? I have read the Marine Dictionary until the pages have begun to come out, to understand the actions; but I do not remember any lambs.'

'They may well be. There are horses, fishes, cats, dogs and mice in their barbarous jargon; and bears; so I dare say there are lambs, rams, ewes, wethers and tegs. But these particular animals are for your nourishment: they are literally lambs. He has laid in stores that would be excessive for a pair of ogresses – a cask of petits-fours (they will be damnably stale), four Stilton cheeses, a tub of scented soap, forsooth, hand-towels – and now, I say, these lambs are required to be washed and combed twice a day. Keep him to dinner – let him sup with you – and perhaps we may have a little peace.'

'What would he like to eat? A pudding, of course; and perhaps souse. And what would you like, Stephen? Something with mushrooms in it, I know.'

'Alas, I shall be a hundred miles away. I have one commission to perform for Captain Aubrey, and then I hoist myself into this evening's coach. I do not expect to be gone for long. Here is my direction in London: I have written it on a card for you. Pray send me word how you liked your voyage.'

'Shall you not be coming, Stephen?' cried Sophia, clasping his arm. 'What will happen to me?'

'No, my dear. I cast you adrift. Sink or swim, Sophie; sink or swim. Where is my hat? Come, give me a buss, and I must away.'

'Jack,' said he, walking into the cabin, 'what are you at?'

'I am trying to get this God-damned plant to stand upright. Do what I may, they keep wilting. I water them before breakfast and again in the last dog-watch, and still they wilt. Upon my word, it is too bad.'

'What do you water them with?'

'The best water, straight from the scuttle-butt.'

'If you anoint them with the vile decoction we drink and wash in, of course they wilt. You must send ashore for some rain-water; and at that rate of watering, some aquatic plants.'

'What an admirable notion, Stephen. I shall do so at once. Thank you. But apart from these poxed vegetables, don't you think it looks tolerably well? Comfortable? Homelike? The gunner's wife said she had never seen the like: all she could suggest was somewhere to hang their clothes, and a pincushion.'

The cabin resembled a cross between a brothel and an undertaker's parlour, but Stephen only said that he agreed with Mrs Armstrong and suggested that it might be a little less like a state funeral if the tubs were not quite so rigidly arranged about each cot. 'I have your plates,' he said, holding out a green-baize parcel.

'Oh, thank you, thank you, Stephen. What a good fellow you are. Here's elegance, damn my eyes. How they shine! Oh, oh,' his face fell. 'Stephen, I do not like to seem ungrateful, but I did say hawser-laid, you know. The border was to be hawser-laid.'

'Well, and did I not say, "Let there be a hawser about the periphery" and did he not say, the shopman, God's curse upon him, the thief, "Here, sir, is as pretty a hawser as Lord Viscount Nelson himself could desire"?'

'And so it is. A capital hawser. But surely my dear Stephen, you must be aware, after all this time at sea, that a hawser is *cable-laid*, not hawser-laid?'

'I am not. And I absolutely decline to hear more of the matter. A hawser not hawser-laid – what stuff. I badger the silversmith early and late, and we are to be told that hawsers are not hawser-laid. No, no. The wine is drawn, it must be drunk. The frog has neither feathers nor wool, and yet she sings. You will have to sail up to the Downs, eating the bread of affliction off your cable-laid baubles, and wetting it with the tears of misery; and I may tell you, sir, that you will eat it without me. Essential business calls me away. I shall put up at the Grapes, when I am in London: I hope to be there well before Michaelmas. Pray send me a line. Good day to you, now: God bless.'

THE GRAPES WERE home in Catalonia when Dr Maturin left the Abbot of Montserrat. All through the country as he rode his swift-trotting mule westwards, the vineyards had their familiar shattered, raped appearance; in the villages the streets ran purple-red with lees and the hot air was heavy with fermentation – an early year, an auspicious year. Melons everywhere, ten for a realillo, figs drying all round Lérida, oranges bronze on the trees. Then a more decided autumn in Aragon; and throughout the green Basque country rain, solid rain day after day, pursuing him even to the dark lonely beach where he stood waiting for the boat, the drops running off his sodden cloak and vanishing into the shingle underfoot.

The surge and grind of waves withdrawing, then at last the sound of careful oars and a low call through the rain: Abraham and his seed for ever.'

'Wilkes and liberty,' said Stephen. 'Let go the kedge, Tom.' Splashes, a thump; and then, very close to him, 'Are you there? Let me give you a back, sir. Why, you are all wet.'

'It is on account of the rain.'

Rain pouring off the deck of the lugger; rain flattening the waves the whole length of the Channel; rain pelting down in the streets of London, overflowing from the Admiralty's gutter.

'How it rains,' said the young gentleman in a flowered dressing-gown and nightcap who received him. 'May I take your cloak, sir, and spread it by the fire?'

'You are very good, sir, but since Sir Joseph is not in the way, I believe I shall go straight to my inn. I have been travelling hard.'

'I am infinitely concerned, sir, that both the First Lord and Sir Joseph should be at Windsor, but I will send a messenger at once, if you are quite sure that Admiral Knowles will not do.'

'This is essentially a political decision, as I take it. It would be better to wait until tomorrow, though by God the matter presses.'

'They should have started back tonight, I know: and from the orders Sir Joseph left with me, I am sure I should not do wrong to invite you to breakfast with him – to come to his official apartment as early as you think fit.'

The Grapes were fast asleep, shuttered, dark, and so unwilling to reply that they might all have died of the plague. He had a despairing vision of never being fed again, of passing the night in the hackney-coach or a bagnio. 'Perhaps we had better try the Hummums,' he said wearily.

'I'll just give 'em one more knock,' said the coachman, 'the stiff-necked bloody set of dormice.' He rattled his whip against the shutters with righteous venom, and at last life spoke in the dripping void, asking 'who it was?'

'It's a gent as wants to come in out of the rain,' said the coachman. 'He ain't no bleeding mermaid, he says.'

'Why, it's you, Dr Maturin,' cried Mrs Broad, opening the door with many a creak and gasp. 'Come in. There's been a fire in your room since Tuesday. God preserve you, sir, how wet you are. Let me take your cloak – it weighs a ton.'

'Mrs Broad,' said Stephen, yielding it with a sigh, 'pray be so kind as to give me an egg and a glass of wine. I am faint with hunger.'

Enveloped in a flannel garment, the property of the late Mr Broad, he gazed at his skin: it was thick, pale, sodden, lifeless; where it had had his shirt or drawers about it, as upon his belly, it showed a greyish-blue tinge, elsewhere the indigo of his stockings and the snuff-coloured dye of his coat had soaked so deep that his penknife reached blood before the end of it.

'Here's your egg, sir,' said Mrs Broad, 'with a nice piece of gammon. And here are some letters come for you.'

He sat by the fire, devouring his food, with the letters balanced on his knee. Jack's strong hand, remarkably neat. Sophie's round, disconnected script: yet the down-strokes had determination in them.

'This will be all blotted with tears,' ran Sophie's, 'for although I shall try to make them fall to one side of my writing-desk, I am afraid some will drop on the paper, there are so many of them.' They had, indeed; the surface of the letter was mottled and uneven. 'Most of them are tears of pure undiluted happiness, for Captain Aubrey and I have come to an understanding – we are never to marry anyone else, ever! It is *not* a secret engagement, which would be very wrong; but it is so like one, that I fear my conscience must have grown sadly elastic. I am sure you can see the difference, even if no one else can. How happy I am! And how very, very kind you have been to me . . .' 'Yes yes, my dear,' said Stephen, skipping some prettily-detailed expressions of gratitude, some particularly obliging remarks, and a highly-detailed account of the interesting occasion when, becalmed off the Isle of Wight on a Saturday evening 'so warm and balmy, with the dear sailors singing on the forecastle and dancing to the squeaky fiddle, and Cecilia being shown the stars by Mr Dredge of the Marines', they came to their understanding in the cabin, 'yes, yes. Come to the point, I beg. Let us hear about these other tears.'

The point came on the back of page three. Mrs Williams had flown into a horrid passion on their return – had wondered what Admiral Haddock could possibly have been thinking about – was amazed that her daughter could so have exposed herself with a man known to be in difficulties – a fortune-hunter, no doubt – had Sophia no conception of her sacred duty to her mother – to a mother who had made such endless sacrifices? – Had she no idea of religion? Mrs Williams insisted upon an instant cessation of intercourse; and if that man had the impudence to call, he should be shown the door – not that Mrs Williams imagined he dared show his face on land. It was very well to go and capture this little French ship and get his name in the newspapers, but a man's first duty was to his creditors and his bank-account. Mrs Williams's head was not to be turned by these tales: none of *her* family had ever had their names in the newspapers, she thanked God, except for the announcement of their marriage in *The Times*. What kind of a husband would such a man make, always wandering off into foreign parts whenever the whim took him, and attacking people in that rash way? Some folk might cry up her precious Lord Nelson, but did Sophie wish to share poor Lady Nelson's fate? Did she know what a mistress meant? In any case, what did they know of Captain Aubrey? He might very well have liaisons in every port, and a large quantity of natural children. Mrs Williams was very far from well.

The tears had fallen thicker here by far: spelling and syntax had gone astray: two lines were blotted out. 'But I shall wait for ever, if need be,' was legible, and so was 'and I am sure, quite sure, that he will too.' Stephen sniffed, glanced at the lines that said 'she must hurry now, to catch the post,' smiled at the 'yours, *very* affectionately, Sophie,' and picked up Jack's letter. With an overwhelming yawn he opened it, lay down on the bed with the candle near the pillow, and focused his drooping eyes on the paper, '*Lively*, at sea. September 12, '04. My dear Stephen . . .' September 12: the day Mendoza was in EI Ferrol. He forced his eyes wide open. The lines seemed to crackle with life and happiness, but still they swam. 'Wish me joy!' Well, so I do, too. 'You will never guess the news I have to tell you!' Oh yes I shall, brother: pray do not use so many points of admiration. 'I have the best part of a wife!! viz, her heart!!' Stephen sniffed again. An intolerably tedious description of Miss Williams, whom Stephen knew a good deal better than Captain Aubrey – her appearance, virtues. 'So direct – straightforward – nothing hole in the corner, if you understand me – no damned purser's tricks – must not swear, however, – like a 32 lber.' Could he really have likened Sophie to a thirty-two pounder? It was quite possible. How the lines did swim. 'He must not speak disrespectfully of his putative mother-in-law, but . . .' What did Jack imagine putative to mean? 'Would be perfectly happy if only . . . ship . . . join me at Falmouth . . . Portsmouth . . . convoy . . . Madeira, the Cape Verdes! Coconut-trees! . . . must hurry not to miss the post.' Coconut-trees, immeasurably tall palms waving, waving . . . Deus ex machina.

He awoke in daylight from a deep uninterrupted sleep, feeling happy, called for coffee, buns and a dram of whisky, read their letters again, smiling and nodding his head, as he breakfasted, drank to their happiness, and took his papers from their oiled-silk roll. He sat at the table, decoding, drawing up his summary. In his diary he wrote, 'All happiness is a good: but if theirs is to be bought by years of waiting and perhaps disgrace, then even this may come too dear. JA is older than he was by far, perhaps as mature as it is in his nature to be; but he is only a man, and celibacy will never do for him. Ld Nelson said, Once past Gibraltar, every man is a bachelor. What will tropical warmth, unscrupulous young women, a fixed habit of eating too much, and high animal spirits accomplish? What a renewed fire, a renewed challenge from Diana? No, no. If no deus ex machina appears at this interesting juncture, the whole turns into a sad, sad, long-drawn-out, ultimately squalid tragedy. I have seen a long engagement, the dear knows. Yet as I understand it, Ld Melville is nearly down: in this trade there are facts he cannot reveal – he cannot defend himself, nor, consequently, his friends. NB I slept upwards of nine hours this night, *without a single drop*. This morning I saw my bottle on the chimney-piece, untouched: this is unparalleled.'

He closed his book, rang the bell, and said, 'Young gentlewoman, be so good as to call me a hackney-coach.' And to the coachman, 'The Horseguards' Parade.'

Here he paid the man, watched him drive off, and after a turn or two he walked quickly to a small green door that led to the back of the Admiralty.

There was lather still on Sir Joseph's pink jowls as he hurried in and begged Stephen to sit by the fire, to look at the paper, to make himself comfortable – victuals would be up directly – he would not be a moment. 'We have been most anxious for you, Dr Maturin,' he said, coming back, neat and trim. 'Mendoza was taken at Hendaye.'

'He had nothing on him,' said Stephen, 'and the only knowledge he could betray is already useless. Spain is coming into the war.'

'Ah,' said Sir Joseph, putting down his cup and looking at him very hard. 'It is a firm commitment?'

'It is. They are wholly engaged. That is why I ventured to call so late last night.'

'How I wish I had been here! How I cursed Windsor when the messenger met us just this side of Staines. I knew it must

be something of the very first importance: the First Lord said
the same.'

Stephen took his short statement from his pocket and said,
'An armament is fitting out in Ferrol, the ships of the San
Ildefonso treaty: here is a list of the vessels. Those marked
with a cross are ready for sea with six months' stores aboard.
These are the Spanish regiments stationed in and about the
port, with an appreciation of their commanding officers: I do
not place great reliance upon the remarks in the case of those
names that are followed by a mark of interrogation. These are
the French regiments actually upon the march.' He passed
the sheet.

'Perfectly, perfectly,' said Sir Joseph, looking at it greedily –
he loved a tabulated list, numbers, factual intelligence, rather
than the usual vague impressions and hearsay. 'Perfect. This
corresponds very closely to what we have from Admiral
Cochrane.'

'Yes,' said Stephen. 'A little too perfect, maybe. Mendoza
was an intelligent agent, but he was a paid agent, a professional. I do not vouch for it personally, although I think it
highly probable. But what I do vouch for, and what induced
me to reach you at the earliest possible moment, is the programme that has been settled between Paris and Madrid.
Madrid has been under increasing pressure since July, as you
know: now Godoy has yielded, but he refuses to declare until
the treasure-ships reach Cadiz from Monte Video. Without
this vast amount of specie Spain is very nearly bankrupt. The
ships in question are frigates of the Spanish navy: the *Medea*,
of forty guns, and the *Fama*, *Clara*, and *Mercedes*, all of 34.
The *Fama* is said to be an uncommon swift sailer; the others
are well spoken of. The squadron is commanded by Rear-
Admiral don José Bustamente, a capable and determined
Officer. The total value of the specie embarked at Monte
Video was five million, eight hundred and ten thousand
pieces of eight. These ships are expected in Cadiz early October, and once the news that the treasure is landed has

reached Madrid, we are expected a declaration of war, the Sarastro incident being the casus belli. Without this treasure Madrid will be so embarrassed that a rising in Catalonia, supported by the vessels now off Toulon, would have every likelihood of success.'

'Dr Maturin,' cried Sir Joseph, shaking his hand, 'we are infinitely obliged to you. It had to come, sooner or later, as we all knew — but to have the very moment, or something close to it . . . ! There is still time to act. I must tell Lord Melville at once: he will certainly wish to see you. Mr Pitt must know immediately — oh, how I curse that Windsor visit — forgive me a moment.' He ran out of the room. Stephen at once took Sir Joseph's untasted coffee and poured it into his own cup.

He was drinking it still when Sir Joseph came back, discouraged. 'He is at that wretched inquiry: he will not be free for some hours, and every minute counts. However, I have sent a note . . . we must act at once. It is a cabinet decision, of course; but I have no doubt that we must act at once. God send the wind stays fair: the time is very short.'

'You intend a decisive action, I take it?'

'Certainly. I cannot answer for the cabinet, but if my advice is attended to, the bold stroke is only once. Is it the mortality of the thing that you refer to? he asked with a smile.

'The morality of the thing is not my concern,' said Stephen. 'I present the state of fact, with the observation that action would greatly increase the chance of Catalan success. Tell me, how does the inquiry go?'

'Badly, very badly. You and I know that Lord M's hands are tied: he cannot in honour account for the secret funds, and his enemies, some of whom know this as well as we do, are taking full advantage of the situation. I must not say more, because I am an official.' He was indeed an official, a permanent official, one of the most powerful in the Admiralty; and every First Lord except St Vincent had followed his advice. He was also something of an entomologist, and when, after a pause, he said, 'What news from the other world, Dr

Maturin?' Stephen recollected himself, felt in his bosom, and replied, 'Great news, sir. Bless me, I was so hurried I had almost forgot. The ingenious priest of Sant Marti found her, or him, or them, this summer. A little crushed, a little spoilt by the rain, but still recognizable.' Between the pages of his opened pocket-book lay a depressed Clouded Yellow, a genetic freak with both its starboard wings bright green, the others gold.

'A true gynandromorph!' cried Sir Joseph, bending over the creature. 'I have never see one in my life before. Perfectly male the one side, perfectly female the other. I am amazed, sir, amazed. This is almost as astonishing as your news.'

Butterflies, moths, the dubious privilege of having two sexes at once, and an aged clerk came in, whispered in Sir Joseph's ear, and tiptoed out.

'We shall know in half an hour or so. Dr Maturin, let me ring for some more coffee; it has gone down strangely.'

'If you please. Now, Sir Joseph, may I speak to you in an unofficial or at the most a semi-official way, about a naval friend of mine, in whom I am particularly interested?'

'By all means. Pray do.'

'I refer to Captain Aubrey. Captain John Aubrey.'

'Lucky Jack Aubrey? Yes, yes: he cut out the *Fanciulla* – a very creditable little action. But you know that perfectly well, of course – you were there!'

'What I should like to ask is, whether he has good prospects of employment.'

'Well,' said Sir Joseph, leaning back and considering. 'Well. I do not have a great deal to do with patronage or appointments: that is not my department. But I do know that Lord Melville has a regard for him, and that he intended to advance his interests in time; possibly in the command of a vessel now on the stocks. His recent promotion, however, was intended as a full reward for his past services; and perhaps he would be well advised to expect nothing but the occasional acting, temporary command for some considerable period. The pressure on patronage is very great, as you know. Then again, I am afraid it is all too likely that Lord M may have left us before the proposed command can, shall I say, *eventuate*; his successor may have other views; and if this is so, your friend's chances are – well . . .' He waved his hand. 'There are, I believe, a certain number of objections to set against his brilliant services: and he is unfortunate in his choice of a father. Are you acquainted with General Aubrey, my dear sir?'

'I have met the gentleman. He did not strike me as being very wise.'

'Every speech of his is said to be worth five votes to the other side; and he makes a surprising number of them. He has a tendency to address the House on subjects he does not quite understand.'

'It would be difficult for him to do otherwise, unless the Commons were to discuss the strategy of a fox-chase.'

'Exactly so. And naval affairs are his chief delight, alas. If there should be even a partial change of administration, his son is likely to be looked upon with a jaundiced eye.'

'You confirm all that I had supposed, Sir Joseph. I am obliged to you.'

They returned to their butterflies, to beetles – Sir Joseph had not attended to beetles as much as he could have wished – to a discussion of Cimarosa – an excellent performance of *Le Astuzie Feminili* at Covent Garden – Sir Joseph adjured Dr Maturin to hear it – he himself had heard it twice and would be going a third time tonight – charming, charming – but his eye kept wandering to a severe, accurate clock, and his defence of Cimarosa, though earnest, occupied no more than a quarter of his mind.

The aged clerk returned, ten years younger, skipping with excitement, handed a note, and darted out.

'We act!' cried Sir Joseph, ringing a number of bells. 'Now I must find the ships. Mr Akers, files A12 and 27 and the current dockets. Mr Roberts, copying-clerks and messengers to stand by. Dr Maturin, Lord Melville's compliments, his very particular compliments, and he begs the favour of a word with you at twenty minutes past eleven precisely. Now, my dear sir, will you accompany the squadron? A negotiation might prove possible; it would be better by far than the *main forte*.'

'I will. But I must not appear. It would destroy my value as an agent. Give me a gentleman who speaks Spanish, and I will speak through him. And may I say this? To deal with Bustamente you must send a powerful squadron – ships of the line – to allow him to yield with honour. An overwhelming force, or he will fight like a lion. These are frigates in high training, and, for Spain, high discipline: ships to be reckoned with.'

'I will attend to what you say, Dr Maturin. With the disposition of our fleets I promise nothing. Have you any further counsels or observations – one moment, Mr Robinson – or remarks?'

'Yes, sir. I have a request to make – I have a favour to beg. As you are aware, I have accepted nothing, at any time, for what services I may have been able to perform, in spite of the Admiralty's very obliging insistence.'

Sir Joseph looked grave, but said he was sure that any request from Dr Maturin would receive the most sympathetic attention.

'My request is, that Captain Aubrey, in the *Lively*, should form part of the squadron.'

Sir Joseph's face cleared wonderfully. 'Certainly: I think I may promise that on my own responsibility,' he said. 'I believe Lord Melville would wish it: it may be the last thing he can do for his young friend. But is that all, sir? Surely, that cannot be all?'

'That is all, sir. You oblige me most extremely: I am deeply obliged to you, Sir Joseph.'

'Lord, Lord,' cried Sir Joseph, waving away the obligation with a file. 'Let me see: she has a surgeon, of course. I cannot in decency supersede him – besides, that would not answer.

You must have a temporary rank – you shall go in her with a temporary rank, and join early in the morning. The full instructions will take some time to draw up – the Board must sit – but they will be ready by this evening, and you can go down with the Admiralty messenger. You will not object to travelling in the darkness?'

THE RAIN WAS no more than a drizzle by the time Stephen came out into the park, but it was enough to prevent him from wandering among the bookstalls of Wych Street as he had intended, and he returned to the Grapes. There he sat in a high leather chair, staring at the fire, his mind ranging in many, many directions or sometimes merely turning on itself in a comfortable lethargy, until the grey daylight faded into a dim, unemphatic night, foggy and suffused with orange from the lamps outside. The coming of an Admiralty messenger aroused him from his delicious sense of inhabiting a body with indefinite, woollen bounds, and he realised that he had not eaten since his biscuit and madeira with Lord Melville.

He called for tea and crumpets, a large number of crumpets, and with candles lit on the table by his side, he read what the messenger had brought: a friendly note from Sir Joseph, confirming that the *Lively* should be sent and observing 'that in compliment to Dr Maturin he had given orders that the temporary commission should be modelled as closely as possible upon that granted to Sir J. Banks, of the Royal Society', which he hoped might give pleasure; the commission itself, an imposing document, entirely handwritten because of the rarity of its form, with Melville's signature smudged with haste; an official letter requesting and directing him to proceed to the Nore to join his ship forthwith; a later note from Sir Joseph to say that the instructions could not be ready until after midnight, begging his pardon for the delay, and enclosing a ticket for *Le Astuzie Feminili* – it might help Dr Maturin to pass the hours agreeably, and persuade him to do justice to Cimarosa, 'that amiable phoenix'.

Sir Joseph was a wealthy man, a bachelor; he liked to do himself well; and the ticket was for a box, a small box high on the left-hand side of the house. It gave a better view of the audience and the band than the stage, but Stephen settled into it with a certain complacency; he leant his hands, still greasy from the crumpets, upon the padded edge and looked down at the groundlings – his fellows on almost every other occasion – with some degree of spiritual as well as physical loftiness. The house was filling rapidly, for the opera was much talked of, much in fashion, and although the royal box away on his right was empty, nearly all the others had people in them, moving about, arranging chairs, staring at the audience, waving to friends; and immediately opposite him there was a group of naval officers, two of whom he knew. Beneath him, in the pit, he recognized Macdonald with his empty sleeve pinned across his coat, sitting next to a man who must surely be his twin brother, they were so alike. There were other faces he knew: all London that attended to music seemed to be there, and some thousands that did not – an animated scene, a fine buzz of conversation, the sparkle of jewels; and now that most of the audience was thoroughly settled, the waving of fans.

The house darkened and the first notes of the overture quelled the greater part of the talk, muting the rest. Stephen turned his eyes and his attention to the band. Poor thin pompous overblown stuff, he thought; not unpleasant, but quite trivial. What was Sir Joseph thinking of, to compare this man with Mozart? He admired the red-faced 'cellist's bowing, however – agile, determined, brisk. To his right a flash of brightness drew his eye: a party of latecomers walking into their box and letting in the light from the door at the back. Goths: Moorish barbarity. Not, indeed, that the music had much to say: not that his attention had been wrenched painfully from something that required close concentration. Though it would have been all one to those grass-combing Huns, had it been Orpheus in person.

A charming harp came up through the strings, two harps running up and down, an amiable warbling. Signifying nothing, sure; but how pleasant to hear them. Pleasant, oh certainly it was pleasant, just as it had been pleasant to hear Molter's trumpet; so why was his heart oppressed, filled with an anxious foreboding, a dread of something imminent that he could not define? That arch girl posturing upon the stage had a sweet, true little voice; she was as pretty as God and art could make her; and he took no pleasure in it. His hands were sweating.

A foolish German had said that man thought in words. It was totally false; a pernicious doctrine; the thought flashed into being in a hundred simultaneous forms, with a thousand associations, and the speaking mind selected one, forming it grossly into the inadequate symbols of words, inadequate because common to disparate situations – admitted to be inadequate for vast regions of expression, since for them there were the parallel languages of music and painting. Words were not called for in many or indeed most forms of thought: Mozart certainly thought in terms of music. He himself at this moment was thinking in terms of scent.

The orchestra and the people on the stage pumped busily up to the obvious climax: it blared out – the house burst into a roar of applause, and in the latecomers' box he saw Diana Villiers, clapping politely but with no great enthusiasm, not looking at the stage with its smirking bowing actors but at someone deeper in the box behind her. Her head was turned in a curve he would have recognized in an even greater crowd: her long white gloves, pointing upwards, beat steadily together as she talked over the general din, her expression and the movements of her head pushing her meaning through the noise.

There was another woman beside her – Lady Jersey, he thought – and four men behind. Canning; two officers in scarlet and gold; a civilian with the high colour and oyster eye of Hanover and the ribbon of the Garter across his breast – a minor royal. This was the man to whom she was speaking: he looked stupid, uncomprehending; but pleased, almost lively.

Stephen watched with no particular emotion but with extreme accuracy. He had noted the great leap of his heart at the first moment and the disorder in his breathing, and he noted too that this had no effect upon his powers of observation. He must in fact have been aware of her presence from the first: it was her scent that was running in his mind before the curtain fell; it was in connection with her that he had reflected upon these harps.

Now the applause had stopped, but Diana's hands were still raised, and leaning forward he watched with an even greater intensity. She was moving her right hand as she talked to the man behind her and by Christ she was moving it with a *conscious* grace. The door at the back of the box opened. Another broad blue ribbon, and the women stood up, bobbed. He could not see the face for the tall standing men, but he could see, he did see this essential change confirmed – her whole movement, from the carriage of her head to the pretty flirt of her ostrich-fan was subtly altered. Bows, more bobs, laughter, the door closed, the outward-facing group reformed: the figure reappeared in another box. Stephen took no notice of him, did not care if he were the Duke of Hell, but concentrated his utmost attention upon Diana to prove what he knew to be the fact. It was so: everything showed it, and he extracted the last dreg of pain from the knowledge, the spectacle. She was on display. The purity of wild grace was gone, and the thought that from now on he must associate vulgarity with his idea of her was so painful that for a while he could not think clearly. Not that it was in the least obvious to anyone who knew her less well, or who valued that purity less highly, and not that it detracted in any way from the admiration of the men in the audience or of her companions, for it was done with great instinctive art; but the woman in the box over there was not one to whom he would have paid any attention, at any time.

She was uneasy. She felt the intensity of his gaze and from

time to time she looked round the house; and each time she did so he dropped his eyes, as he would have done, stalking a doe: there were plenty of people looking at her from the pit and the other boxes – indeed, she was perhaps the finest woman there, in her low sky-blue dress and the diamonds in her black, high-piled hair. In spite of his precaution their eyes crossed at last: she stopped talking. He meant to rise and bow, but there was no power whatsoever in his legs. He was astonished, and before he could grip the pad in front of him to raise himself the curtain had gone up and the harps were racing through glissando after glissando.

That my body should be affected to this point, he said, is something beyond my experience. I have felt the great nausea before, God knows, but this want of control . . . Did the Diana I last saw at New Place ever exist in fact? A creation of my own? Can you create a unicorn by longing?

Through the music and the caterwauling on the stage the insistent knocking at the locked door of his box disturbed the course of his reflection. He did not reply, and presently it went away. Had he had a hand in her death? He shook his head to deny it.

At last the curtain came sweeping down and the light increased. The box over there was empty, a pair of long white gloves drooped over the plush in front; and the band was playing God save the King. He sat on, and in time the standing slowly-moving crowd below shuffled out, a few people darting back for forgotten hats, and the place was empty, an enormous shell. The people of the house walked about the emptiness with an everyday step, picking up rubbish, putting out the lights.

Two said, 'There's a gent still there, up in the box.'

'Is he drunk?'

'Perhaps he thinks there is another act; but there ain't no more, thank God.'

'Come, sir,' they said, opening the door with their little key, 'it's all over now. This is the end of the piece.'

LONG BEFORE DAWN the *Lively*'s warm, smelly, close-packed gun-deck awoke to violent and unexpected life, the strong-voiced bosun's mates roaring 'All hands! All hands unmoor ship. Rise and shine! Show a leg there! Tumble up, tumble up, tumble up!' The Livelies – the male Livelies, for there were about a hundred women aboard – tore themselves from their pink companions or their more prosaic wives, tumbled up into the wet darkness and unmoored the ship, as they were desired. The capstan turned, the fiddle squeaked, the temporary ladies hurried ashore, and the Nore light faded astern: the frigate stood for the North Foreland with a favourable tide and a quartering wind.

The officer of the watch checked the noise of speculation, but it continued under the cover of the rumbling holystones while the people washed the decks. What was up? Had Boney started his invasion? Something was up, or they would never have been ordered to sea with only half their water filled. Port admiral's barge had come alongside, a civilian and an officer: one gent was with the captain yet. No news so far, but that there Killick or Bonden would know before breakfast-time was over.

In the gun-room the wonder was quite as great, and quite as uninformed; but it had a depth of apprehension and uneasiness that was lacking before the mast. Word had gone about that Dr Maturin was aboard again, and although they liked him well enough, they dreaded what he might bring with him.

'Are you quite sure?' they asked Dashwood, who had had the morning watch.

'I would not positively take my oath,' he said, 'because he was muffled against the rain, and it was dark. But I have never seen anyone else on earth come up the side like a left-handed bear: you would never believe it could be done, without you see it. I should be certain, if the boat had not answered "aye aye".'

'That decides it,' said Mr Simmons. 'The Admiral's coxswain

could never have made such a mistake. It must have been some commissioned officer that the Captain knew well enough to call him his dear fellow; an old shipmate, no doubt. It cannot be Dr Maturin.'

'Certainly not,' said Mr Randall.

'Never in life,' said the master.

The purser, whose cabin had been out of reach of the bees, was more concerned with the political aspects of their sudden move, and with the wretched state of his stores. 'I have not above fifty fathoms of duck aboard,' he said, 'and not a scrap of sennit. What will become of us when we cross the line? What will become of us at Madeira, even: to say nothing of Fernando Poo? And Fernando Poo is our destination, I am very sure, for reasons of high strategy.'

Some time before this, Jack, having given directions to put to sea, came back in his nightshirt and watch-coat to his cabin, where his immediate orders lay, next to the sheaf of detailed instructions and a fat sealed envelope marked Not to be opened until latitude 43° N. He looked somewhat ecclesiastical, but also deeply concerned. 'Dear Stephen,' he said, 'thank you a thousand times for coming down so quick; I hardly hoped to see you before Falmouth. But I find I have lured you aboard on false pretences – Madeira and the West Indies are quite exploded. I am ordered to proceed to sea with the utmost possible dispatch – rendezvous off the Dodman.' He held the paper close to the light. 'Rendezvous with *Indefatigable*, *Medusa* and *Amphion*. Strange. And sealed orders not to be opened until so and so. What can they mean by that, Stephen?'

'I have no idea,' said Stephen.

'God damn and blast the Admiralty and all its lords,' cried Jack. 'Utmost dispatch – muck up all one's plans – I do apologize most humbly, Stephen.' He read on. 'Hey, hey, Stephen? I thought you had no idea: I thought you had just chanced to come down with the messenger. But in case of separation of one or more . . . certain eventualities and all that, I am requested and directed to avail myself of the counsels and advice of S. Maturin, esquire, MD etc., etc., appointed pro hac vice a captain in the Royal Navy . . . his knowledge and discretion.'

'It is possible that you may be required to undertake some negotiations, and that I may be of use in them.'

'Well, I must be discreet myself, I find,' said Jack, sitting down and looking wonderingly at Stephen. 'But you did say . . .'

'Now listen, Jack, will you? I am somewhat given to lying: my occasions require it from time to time. But I do not choose to have any man alive tell me of it.'

'Oh no, no, no,' cried Jack. 'I should never dream of doing such a thing. Not,' he added, recollecting himself and blushing, 'not when I am in my right mind. Quite apart from my love for you, it is far, far too dangerous. Hush: mum's the word. Tace is the Latin for a candle. I quite understand – am amazed I did not smoke it before: what a deep old file you are. But I twig it now.'

'Do you, my dear? Bless you.'

'But what takes my breath away, what flabbergasts me to this high pitch,' said Jack, 'is, that they should have given you a temporary commission. The Navy, you know, is uncommon jealous of rank, very sparing of such compliments. I hardly remember ever to have heard of it, except once. They must think the world of you in Whitehall.'

'I wonder at it too, this insistence upon a commission. It struck me at the time. I am sensible of the compliment, but puzzled. Why should I not have been your guest?'

'I have it,' cried Jack. 'Stephen, may I ask without indiscretion whether this could be a – what shall I say? – a *profitable* expedition?'

'It might be, too.'

'Then they mean to cut you in on the prize-money. Depend upon it, they mean you to share as a captain. These are Admiralty orders, so no flag gets a share: if it comes to anything, your cut should be pretty handsome.'

'What a pretty thought in Sir Joseph; remarkably delicate in him. I do not regret sending him my gynandromorph by the messenger now: the fellow seemed amazed, as well he might – a princely gift. Tell me, what would be a captain's share of – I name a hypothetical sum – a million pounds?'

'Taken by a squadron with four, no, five, captains in it? Let me see, fives into ten is two, and eights into two hundred, five and twenty – seventy-five thousand pounds. But there are no prizes like that afloat these days, my poor Stephen, more's the pity.'

'Seventy-five thousand pounds? How absurd. What could Sir Joseph imagine I should do with such a sum? What could any reasonable man do with such a sum?'

'I can tell you what I should do,' cried Jack, his eyes ablaze. He darted out of the cabin in spite of the cry of 'Stay!' to see whether the inner jibs were drawing, and every bowline harp-string taut. Having harassed the watch for some minutes he returned, leaving tart, unfavourable comments behind him.

'I hope this skipper is not going to turn into a jib and stays'l jack,' said the captain of the foretop.

'I don't like the look of it at all,' said the yeoman of the sheets. 'This giving of himself such airs is something new.'

'Perhaps he has a rendezvous with his Miss,' said Blue Edward, the Malay. 'God damn my eye, I should crack on, if I had such a Miss to see, Sophie by name.'

'No disrespectful words, Blue Edward,' cried George Allen. 'For I won't abide it.'

'A man might, of course, make a circumambulation of Lapland, or emulate Banks in the Great South Sea,' observed Stephen. 'But tell me, Jack, how did your journey go? How did Sophie withstand the motion of the vessel? Did she take her porter with her meals?'

'Oh, admirably, admirably!' It had been the most perfect series of warm, gentle days, scarcely a fleck of white water – Simmons had made a magnificent show with royals and sky-sails, and studdingsails aloft and alow; she had never seen anything more beautiful, she said – the lively had left the *Amethyst* standing: red faces on her quarterdeck – and then there had been some charming dead calms, the whole day long – they had often talked of Stephen – how they had missed him! – and she had been so kind to that youngster Randall, who wept when poor Cassandra died – Randall senior loved her to distraction; so did the whole gun-room – they had dined twice with the officers – Cecilia seemed very well with Dredge, of the Marines – Jack was grateful to him for drawing her off – certainly Sophie had drunk her porter, and a glass of bosun's grog – had eaten splendidly: Jack loved a girl that tucked in hearty – and as for the future, they were full of hope, but . . . could do with very little . . . no horses . . . cottage . . . potatoes. 'Stephen,' he said, 'you are asleep.'

'I am not,' said Stephen. 'You just mentioned the last syllable of recorded time with evident approval. But I am weary, I confess. I travelled all night, and yesterday was something of a trial. I will turn in, if I may. Where must I sleep?'

'There's a question,' said Jack. 'Where should you berth, in fact? Of course you shall sleep in my cot; but officially where should you be? That would puzzle Solomon. What seniority did they give you?'

'I have no idea. I did not read the document, apart from the phrase. *We, reposing especial trust and confidence in S.M.,* which pleased me.'

'Well, I suppose you are junior to me; so you shall have the leeward side of the cabin and I the windward, and every time we go about, we shall change sides, ha, ha, ha. Ain't I a rattle? But seriously, I suppose you should be read in to the ship's company – an amazing situation.'

'If there is any doubt, pray do no such thing. It would be far better for me to remain unobserved. And Jack, in all this that has passed between us, all that you may have guessed, I rely wholly upon your discretion, eh? There are moments when my life might turn upon it.'

He had every reason to rely upon Jack, who could keep

close counsel; but not all captains were so discreet, and when the *Medusa* came tearing out of Plymouth with a dark gentleman aboard, known to speak Spanish – a gentleman who remained closeted with the captains of the *Lively*, the *Amphion* and the *Medusa*, and Dr Maturin while they were lying to off the Dodman, waiting for the *Indefatigable* to join – the general opinion of the ship was that they were bound for Cadiz, that Spain had come in or was just about to come in; and this gave a great deal of simple pleasure, for hitherto Spanish merchantmen had been immune from capture. In a sea swept almost clear of prizes, they ploughed steadily along past cruisers, through blockading squadrons, laughing and kissing their hands, their holds so full of wealth that a foremast jack might make five years' pay in one pleasant Saturday afternoon.

At last the *Indefatigable* hove in sight, a heavy forty-gun frigate, making heavy weather of it too, close-hauled on the westerly gale with green seas keeping her beak-head clean and the signal flying *Form in line astern: make all suitable sail*.

Now, as the four frigates, in a perfect line, each two cables from the next, stretched away to the south-south-west, came a tedious, frustrating time for the Livelies: the topmen were rarely on deck, but it was not to make sail. In order to keep rigidly to her station in the *Amphion*'s wake, the *Lively* was perpetually reefing, clewing up, hauling down jibs, staysails, spanker, starting sheets. And when the sealed orders were opened – when, after the captains' last conference aboard the *Indefatigable*, it became certain knowledge that they were to intercept a Spanish squadron from the River Plate to Cadiz, this impatience grew to such a height that they welcomed the dirty look of Sunday evening. A vast unformed blackness filled the south and western sky, an enormous swell was running, so great that men who had scarcely set foot on shore for years were sick; the wind boxed the compass, blowing now hot, now cold, and the sun went down in an ill-looking bank of livid purple with green lights showing through. Cape Finis-

terre was not far under their lee, and they doubled their
preventer-stays and rolling-tackle, roused up storm-canvas,
secured the boats on the booms, double-breeched their guns,
struck the topgallants down on deck, and made all snug.

At two bells in the middle watch the wind, which had been
blowing fitfully from the south-west, backed suddenly into
the north, hurling itself against the mountainous swell with
tripled force – thunder just overhead, lightning, and such a
deluge of rain that a storm-lantern on the forecastle could not
be seen from the quarterdeck. The maintopmast staysail blew
out of its boltrope, vanishing ghostly to leeward in pale strips
of cloth. Jack sent more hands to the wheel, rigged relieving-
tackles, and came into the cabin, where Stephen lay swinging
in his cot, to tell him that it was coming on to blow.

'How you do exaggerate, brother,' said Stephen. 'And how
you drip! The best part of a quart of water has run off your
person in this short space of time – see how it sweeps to and
fro, defying gravity.'

'I love a good blow,' said Jack, 'and this is one of your genuine charmers; for, do you see, it must hold the Spaniards
back, and the dear knows we are very short of time. Was they
to slip into Cadiz before us, what flats we should look.'

'Jack, do you see that piece of string hanging down? Would
you have the goodness to tie it to the hook over there, to reat-
tach it? It came undone. Thank you. I pull upon it to moderate the motion of the cot, which exacerbates all my
symptoms.'

'Are you unwell? Queasy? Sick?'

'No, no. Not at all. What a foolish suggestion. No. This
may be the onset of a very serious malady. I was bitten by a
tame bat a little while ago, and I have reasons to doubt its
sanity: it was a horseshoe bat, a female. It seems to me that I
detect a likeness between my symptoms and the Ludolphus'
description of his disease.'

'Should you like a glass of grog?' asked Jack. 'Or a ham
sandwich, with luscious white fat?' he added, with a grin.

'No, no, no,' cried Stephen. 'Nothing of the kind. I tell you, this is a serious matter, calling for . . . there it goes again. Oh, this is a vile ship: the *Sophie* never behaved so – wild, unmeaning lurches. Would it be too much to ask you to turn down the lamp and to go away? Surely this is a situation that requires all your vigilance? Surely this is no time to stand idly smirking?'

'Are you sure there is nothing I can fetch you? A basin?'

'No, no, no.' Stephen's face assumed a pinched, mean expression: his beard showed black against the nacreous green. 'Does this sort of tempest last long?'

'Oh, three or four days, no more,' said Jack, staggering with the lee-lurch. 'I will send Killick with a basin.'

'Jesus, Mary, Joseph,' said Stephen. 'There she goes again.' In the trough of the enormous waves the frigate lay becalmed, but as she rose, so the gale took her and laid her down, down and down, in a never-ending roll, while her fore-foot heaved up until her bowsprit pointed at the racing clouds. 'Three days of this,' he thought. 'No human frame can withstand it.'

Happily it was only the tail of the notorious September blow that the *Lively* had to deal with. The sky cleared in the morning watch; the glass rose, and although she could show no more than close-reefed topsails it was plain that she would spread more by noon. Dawn showed a sea white from horizon to horizon, a sea with nothing on it but the waterlogged wreck of a Portuguese bean-cod, and far to windward the *Medusa*, apparently intact. Jack was now senior captain, and he signalled her to make more sail – to make for their next rendezvous off Cape Santa Maria, the landfall for Cadiz.

Towards noon he altered course due south, which brought the wind on the *Lively's* quarter, easing her motion greatly. Stephen appeared on deck, still very grave, but more humane. He and Mr Floris and Mr Floris's assistants had spent the morning dosing one another; they had all suffered more or less from the onset of diseases (orchitis, scurvy, the fell Ludolphus' palsy), but in Dr Maturin's case at least the attack had been averted by a judicious mixture of Lucatellus' balsam and powder of Algaroth.

After dinner the *Lively* exercised the great guns, swell or no, rattling them in and out, but also firing broadside after broadside, so that the frigate was preceded by a cloud of her own making as she ran southwards at eleven knots, some twenty leagues off the coast of Portugal. The recent training had had effect, and although the fire was still painfully slow – three minutes and ten seconds between broadsides was the best they could do – it was more accurate by far, in spite of the roll and pitch. A palm-tree trunk, drifting by on the starboard bow three hundred yards away, was blown clear of the water on the first discharge; and they hit it again, with cheers that reached the *Medusa*, before it went astern. The *Medusa* also put in an hour's strenuous practice; and aboard the *Medusa* too, a good many hands were employed carefully picking over the round-shot, choosing the most spherical and chipping off flakes of rust. But most of the Medusa's time was taken up with trying to overhaul the *Lively*; she set topgallants before the *Lively* had shaken out the last reef in her topsails, and she tried studdingsails and royals as the breeze moderated, only to lose two of her booms, without the gain of half a mile. The *Lively*'s officers and her sailmaker watched with intense satisfaction; but underlying their pleasure there was a haunting anxiety – were they going to be in time to cut the Spanish squadron off from Cadiz? And even if they were, would the *Indefatigable* and *Amphion* reach the rendezvous before the clash? The Spanish reputation for courage, if not for seamanship, stood high; and the odds were very great – a forty-gun frigate and three thirty-fours against a thirty-eight and a thirty-two; for Jack had explained the tactical situation to his officers as soon as he had opened his sealed orders – as soon as there was no danger of communication with the shore. The same anxiety, that they might be too late, was general throughout the ship: there was scarcely a man aboard

who did not know what came from the River Plate, and those
few – a person from Borneo and two Javanese – were told.
'It's gold, mate. That's what they ship from the River Plate:
gold and silver, in chests and leather bags.'

All through the day the wind declined, and all through the
night; and whereas the log had once taken the line straight
off the reel, tearing it away to show twelve and even thirteen
knots, heave after heave, at dawn on the last day of September it had to be helped gently off and veered away, so that the
midshipman of the watch could announce a dismal 'Two and
a fathom, sir, if you please.'

A day of light variable airs, mostly in their teeth – whistling
fore and aft, and prayers that were answered by a fair breeze
on Thursday, October 2. They passed Cape St Vincent later
that day, under royals, with the *Medusa* in company, and they
had been exercising the guns for some time – a very particular salute for that great headland, just visible from the masthead on the larboard beam when the bosun came aft and
spoke to the first lieutenant. Mr Simmons pursed his lips,
looked doubtful, hesitated, and then stepped across to Jack.
'Sir,' he said, 'the bosun represents to me, that the men, with
the utmost respect, would wish you to consider whether it
might be advisable not to fire the bow guns.'

'They do, do they?' cried Jack, who had caught some odd,
reproachful glances before this. 'Do they also think it advisable to double the ration of grog?'

'Oh no, sir,' said the sweating crew of the gun nearest at
hand.

'Silence, there,' cried Mr Simmons. 'No, sir: what they
mean is – that is to say, there is a general belief that firing the
bow guns checks her way; and time being so short . . .'

'Well, there may be something in what they say. The
philosophers don't believe it, but we will not run the risk. Let
the bow guns be run in and out, and fired in dumb show.'

A pleased smile spread along the deck. The men wiped
their faces – it was 80° in the shade of the sails – tightened

the handkerchiefs round their foreheads, spat on their hands, and prepared to whip their iron monsters in and out in under two minutes and a half. After a couple of broadsides – in for a penny, in for a pound – and some independent firing, the tension, strongly present throughout the ship since Finisterre, suddenly rose to the highest pitch. *Medusa* was signalling a sail one point on the larboard quarter.

'Up you go, Mr Harvey,' said Jack to a tall, light midshipman. 'Take the best glass in the ship. Mr Simmons may lend you his.'

Up he went, up and up with the glass slung over his shoulder, up to the royal pole and the tie; poor Cassandra could hardly have outstripped him. Presently his voice came floating down. 'On deck, there, *Amphion*, sir. I believe she has sent up a jury foretopmast.'

The *Amphion* she was, and bringing up the breeze she joined company before the fall of night. Now they were three, and the next morning found them at their last rendezvous, with Cape Santa Maria bearing north-east, thirty miles away, visible from the fighting-tops in the brilliant light.

The three frigates, with Sutton of the *Amphion* now senior captain, stood off and on all day, their mastheads thick with telescopes, perpetually sweeping the western sea, a vast blue rolling sea, with nothing between them and America except, perhaps, the Spanish squadron. In the evening the *Indefatigable* joined, and on the fourth day of October the frigates spread wide to cover as great an area as possible, still remaining within signalling distance: silently they beat up and down – gunnery had been laid aside since Cape St Vincent, for fear of giving the alarm. Aboard the *Lively* almost the only sound was the squeaking of the grindstone on the forecastle as the men sharpened their cutlasses and pikes, and the chip-chip-chip of the gunner's party scaling the shot.

To and fro, to and fro, wearing every half hour at the first stroke of the ship's bell, men at every masthead watching the other frigates for a signal, a dozen glasses scanning the remote horizon.

'Do you remember Anson, Stephen?' said Jack, as they paced the quarterdeck. 'He did this for weeks and weeks off Paita. Did you ever read his book?'

'I did. How that man wasted his opportunities.'

'He went round the world, and worried the Spaniards out of their wits, and took the Manilla galleon – what more could you ask?'

'Some slight attention to the nature of the world round which he sailed so thoughtlessly. Apart from some very superficial remarks about the sea-elephant, there is barely a curious observation in the book. He should certainly have taken a naturalist.'

'If he had had you aboard, he might be godfather to half a dozen birds with curious beaks; but on the other hand, you would now be ninety-six. How he and his people ever stood this standing off and on, I do not know. However, it all ended happy.'

'Not a bird, not a plant, not a smell of geology . . . Shall we have some music after tea? I have written a piece I should like you to hear. It is a lament for the Tir nan Og.'

'What is the Tir nan Og?'

'The only bearable part of my country: it vanished long ago.'

'Let us wait until the darkness falls, may we? Then I am your man: we will lament to your heart's content.'

DARKNESS; A LONG, long night in the stifling gun-deck and the cabins, little sleep, and many a man, and officer too, taking a caulk on deck or in the tops. Before dawn on the fifth the decks were being cleaned – no trouble in getting the hands to tumble up – and the smoke from the galley fire was streaming away on the steady north-east wind, when the forward look-out, the blessed Michael Scanlon, hailed the deck with a voice that might have been heard in Cadiz – the *Medusa*, the last ship in the line of frigates as they stood to the north, was signalling four large sail bearing west by south.

The eastern sky lightened, high wisps of cloud catching the golden light from below the horizon; the milky sea grew brilliant, and there they were, right aft, beating up for Cadiz, four white flecks on the rim of the world.

'Are they Spaniards?' asked Stephen, creeping into the maintop.

'Of course they are,' said Jack. 'Look at their stumpy topmasts. Here, take my glass. On deck, there. All hands stand by to wear ship.'

At the same moment the signal to wear and chase broke out aboard the *Indefatigable*, and Stephen began his laborious descent, propped by Jack, Bonden, and a bosun's mate, clinging to his tail until tears came into the poor man's eyes. He had prepared his lines of argument for Mr Osborne, but he wished to pass them over in his mind before he conferred with him aboard the *Indefatigable*, whose captain was in command of the squadron as commodore. He went below, his heart beating at an unusual pace. The Spaniards were gathering together, signals passing between them: negotiations would be delicate; oh, very delicate indeed.

Breakfast, a scrappy meal. The Commodore signalling for Dr Maturin: Stephen upon deck with a cup of coffee in one hand and a piece of bread and butter in the other as the cutter was lowered away. How very much closer they were, so suddenly! The Spaniards had already formed their battle-line, standing on the starboard tack with the wind one point free, and they were so near that he could see their gun-ports — every one of them open, yawning wide.

The British frigates, obeying the signal to chase, had broken their line, and the *Medusa*, the southernmost ship and therefore the foremost once they had worn, was running straight before the wind for the leading Spanish ship; a few hundred yards behind her there was the *Indefatigable*, steering for the second Spaniard, the *Medea*, with Bustamente's flag at the mizzen; then came the *Amphion*; and bringing up the rear, the *Lively*. She was closing the gap fast, and as soon as Stephen had been bundled into the cutter she spread her foretopgallant, crossed the *Amphion*'s wake, and steered for the *Clara*, the last ship in the Spanish line.

The *Indefatigable* yawed a trifle, backed her topsails, hoisted Stephen aboard, and plunged on. The Commodore, a dark, red-faced, choleric man, very much on edge, hurried him below, paid very little attention to his words as he ran over the heads of the argument that was to persuade the Spanish admiral to yield, but sat there drumming his fingers on the table, breathing fast with angry excitement. Mr Osborne, a quick, intelligent man, nodded, staring into Stephen's eyes: he nodded, taking each point, and nodded again, his mouth tight shut. '. . . and lastly,' said Stephen, 'induce him by all possible means to come across, so that we may concert our answer to unforeseen objections.'

'Come, gentlemen, come,' cried the Commodore, running on deck. Closer, closer: they were well within range, all colours abroad; within musket-shot, the Spanish decks crowded with faces; within pistol-shot.

'Hard over,' said the Commodore. The wheel spun and the big frigate turned with a roar of orders to round to and lie on the admiral's starboard beam, twenty yards to windward. The Commodore took his speaking-trumpet. 'Shorten sail,' he cried, aiming it at the *Medea*'s quarterdeck. The Spanish officers spoke slightly to one another; one of them shrugged his shoulders. There was dead silence all along the line: wind in the rigging, the lapping of the sea.

'Shorten sail,' he repeated, louder still. No reply: no sign. The Spaniard held his course for Cadiz, two hours away. The two squadrons ran in parallel lines, gliding silently along at five knots, so close that the low sun sent the shadow of the Spanish topgallantmasts across the English decks.

'Fire across his bows,' said the Commodore. The shot struck the water a yard before the *Medea*'s forefoot, the spray sweeping aft. And as though the crash had broken the spell of silence and immobility there was a quick swirl of movement aboard the *Medea*, a shout of orders, and her topsails were clewed up.

'Do your best, Mr Osborne,' said the Commodore. 'But by God he shall make up his mind in five minutes.'

'Bring him if you possibly can,' said Stephen. 'And above all, remember Godoy has betrayed the kingdom to the French.'

The boat pulled across and hooked on. Osborne climbed aboard the Spanish frigate, took off his hat and bowed to the crucifix, the admiral and the captain, each in turn. They saw him go below with Bustamente.

And now the time dragged slow. Stephen stood by the mainmast, his hands tight clasped behind his back: he hated Graham, the commodore: he hated what was going to happen. He tried with all his force to follow and to influence the argument that was carrying on half a pistol shot away. If only Osborne could bring Bustamente aboard there might be a fair chance of an arrangement.

Mechanically he glanced up and down the line. Ahead of the *Indefatigable* the *Medusa* lay rocking gently beside the *Fama*; astern of the *Medea* the *Amphion* had now slipped round under the *Mercedes*'s lee, and in the rear lay the *Lively*, close to windward of the *Clara*. Even to Stephen's unprofessional eye, the Spaniards were in a remarkable state of readiness; there was none of that hurried flight of barrels, coops, livestock, tossed into the sea to clear the decks, that he had seen often enough in the Mediterranean. At each gun, its waiting, motionless crew; and the smoke from the slow-match in every tub wafted in a thin blue haze along the long range of cannon.

Graham was pacing up and down with a quick uneven step. 'Is he going to be all night?' he said aloud, looking at the watch in his hand. 'All night? All night?'

A quarter of an endless hour, and all the time the sharp smell of burning match in their nostrils. Another dozen turns and the Commodore could bear it no longer.

'A gun for the boat,' he cried, and again a shot whipped across the *Medea*'s bows.

Osborne appeared on the Spanish deck, clambered down into the boat, came aboard the *Indefatigable*, shaking his head. His face was pale and tense. 'Admiral Bustamente's compliments, sir,' he said to the Commodore, 'but he cannot entertain your proposals. He cannot consent to being detained. He nearly yielded when I spoke of Godoy,' he said to Stephen, aside. 'He hates him.'

'Let me go across, sir,' cried Stephen. 'There is still time.'

'No, sir,' cried the Commodore, a wild, furious glare in his face. 'He has had his time. Mr Carrol, lay me across her bows.'

'Lee braces – ' The cry was drowned by the *Mercedes*'s crashing broadside as she fired straight into the *Amphion*.

'Signal close engagement,' said the Commodore, and the vast bay roared and echoed with a hundred guns. A great pall of smoke formed at once, rising and drifting away south-west, and within the pall the flashes of the guns followed one another in a continuous blaze of lightning. An enormous din, trembling heart and spine: Stephen stood there near the mainmast, with his hands behind his back, looking up and down; there was the cruel taste of powder in his mouth, and in his bosom he felt the rising fierce emotion of a bull-fight – the furious cheering of the gun-crews was invading him. Then the cheering was cut off, drowned, annihilated by a blast so huge that it wiped out thought and almost consciousness: the *Mercedes* blew up in a fountain of brilliant orange light that pierced the sky.

Spars, great shapeless timbers rained down out of the pillar of smoke, a severed head, and now through their fall there was the roar of guns again. The *Amphion* had moved up to the leeward side of the *Medea*, and the Spaniard was between two fires.

Cheer upon cheer, a rolling fire, and the powder-boys ran by in an unbroken stream. Cheers, and then one greater than

the rest, quite different, a great exultant cry 'She's struck! The
admiral has struck!'

The fire was slackening all along the line. Only the *Lively*
was still hammering the *Clara*, while the *Medusa* was sending
a few shots after the distant *Fama*, who, having struck, had
nevertheless borne up: she was flying, uninjured, under a
press of sail to leeward.

A few minutes later the *Clara's* colours came down. The
Lively shot ahead alongside the *Indefatigable* and Jack hailed
the Commodore. 'Give you joy, sir. May I go in chase?'

'Thankee, Aubrey,' called the Commodore. 'Chase for all
you are worth – she has the treasure aboard. Crack on: we are
all chewed up.'

'May I have Dr Maturin, sir? My surgeon is aboard the
prize.'

'Yes, yes. Bear a hand, there. Don't let her get away, Aubrey,
do you hear me?'

'Aye aye, sir. Briskly the cutter, now.' The *Lively* wore clear
of the crippled *Amphion*, just shaving her bowsprit, sheeted
home her topgallants and headed south-west. The *Fama*,
untouched in her masts and rigging, was already three miles
off, stretching away for a band of deeper blue, a stronger
wind that might carry her to the Canaries, or allow her to
double back by night for Algeciras.

'Well, old Stephen,' cried Jack, hauling him inboard by
main force, 'that was a hearty brush, eh? No bones broke, I
trust? All sober and correct? Why, your face is black with
powder-smoke. Go below – the gun-room will lend you a
basin until the cabin is set to rights – wash, and we will go on
with our breakfast as soon as the galley fire is lit again. I will
be with you once we have knotted and spliced the worst of
the danger.'

Stephen looked at him curiously. He was bolt upright,
larger than life, and he seemed fairly to glow with light. 'It
was a necessary stroke,' said Stephen.

'Indeed it was,' said Jack. 'I do not know much about politics, but it was a damned necessary stroke for me. No, I don't mean that,' he cried, seeing Stephen jut out his lower lip and look away. 'I mean she let fly at us, and if we had not replied, why truly, we should have been in a pretty mess. She dismounted two guns with her first broadside. Though to be sure,' he added with a delighted chuckle, 'it was necessary in the other meaning too. Come, go below, and I will join you presently. We shall not be up with her – ' nodding towards the distant *Fama* ' – much before noon, if that.'

Stephen went down into the cockpit. He had been in several actions, but this was the first time he had ever heard laughter coming from the place where men paid for what went on on deck. Mr Floris's two assistants and three patients were sitting on chests round the midshipmen's table, where the fourth patient, a simple fracture of the femur, had just been splinted and bandaged: he was telling them how in his haste he had left the rammer in his gun; it had been fired straight into the *Clara*'s side, and Mr Dashwood, seeing it sticking there, had spoken quite sharp and sarcastic – 'It shall be stopped from your pay, Bolt,' says he, 'you wicked dog.'

'Good morning, gentlemen,' said Stephen. 'Since Mr Floris is not aboard, I have come to see whether I may be of any assistance.'

The surgeon's mates leapt up; they became extremely grave, endeavoured to hide their bottle, assured him of their great obligation, but these men represented the whole of the butcher's bill – two splinter wounds, superficial, one musketball, and this femur.

'Apart from John Andrews and Bill Owen, who lost the number of their mess, in consequence of the figurehead of that old *Mercedes* cutting 'em in two,' observed the femur. 'Which she fired very wild, though willing,' said another seaman. 'And mostly at our rigging. Do you know, sir, we thumbed in seventeen broadsides in eight and twenty minutes, by Mr Dashwood's watch. Seventeen broadsides in just short of a glass!'

The *Lively*, knotting and splicing, fetched the *Fama*'s wake and settled down to a serious, a grave and concentrated stern-chase. They were a little short-handed, for want of the prize-crew and Mr Simmons aboard the *Clara*, and when Stephen walked into the cabin he found it still cleared for action, the guns still warm, the smell of battle, a Spanish eighteen-pound ball rolling among the splinters, under the gaping hole it had made in the *Lively*'s side; the place bare and deserted, a clean sweep fore and aft apart from half the forward bulk-head and a single chair, upon which there sat the Spanish captain, staring at the pommel of his sword.

He rose and made a distant bow. Stephen stepped up and introduced himself, speaking French; he said that he was sure Captain Aubrey would wish don Ignacio to take a little refreshment – what might he offer? Chocolate, coffee, wine?

'Damn it, I had clean forgot him,' said Jack, appearing in the gutted cabin. 'Stephen, this is the captain of the *Clara*. Monsieur, j'ai l'honneur de introduire une amie, le Dr Maturin: Dr Maturin, l'espagnol capitaine, don Garcio. Please explain that I beg he will take a little something – vino, chocolato, aguardiente?'

With immovable gravity the Spaniard bowed and bowed again; he was extremely grateful, but he would take nothing for the moment. A stilted conversation followed, ragging on until Jack had the idea of begging don Ignacio to rest in the first lieutenant's cabin until dinner time.

'I had clean forgot him,' he said again, returning. 'Poor devil: I know what it feels like. Life scarcely worth living, for a while. I made him keep his sword; it takes away a little of the sting, and he fought as well as he could. But dear Lord, it makes you feel low. Killick, how much mutton is there left?'

'Two legs, sir, and the best part of the scrag end. There's a nice piece of sirloin, sir; plenty for three.'

'The mutton, then: and Killick, lay for four – the silver plates.'

'Four, sir? Aye aye, sir: four it is.'

'Let us take our coffee on to the quarterdeck: that poor don Garcio haunts me. By the way, Stephen, you have not congratulated me. The *Clara* struck to us, you know.'

'I wish you joy, my dear. I do indeed. I wish you may not have bought it too high. Come, give me the tray.'

The squadron and the prizes were far astern; the *Medusa* too had been detached to chase the *Fama*, but she was a great way off, hull down. The Spaniard seemed to be about the same distance ahead as when they began, or even a little more, but the Livelies looked quite unconcerned as they hurried about with fresh cordage, blocks, and bales of sailcloth, casting a casual eye at the chase from time to time. The ease and freedom of battle were still about the decks; there was a good deal of talk, particularly from the topmen re-reaving the rigging high above, and laughter. Quite unbidden a carpenter's mate, padding by with a rough-pole on his shoulder, said to Jack, 'It won't be long now, sir.'

'They smashed most of our stuns'l booms,' observed Jack, 'and we never touched one of theirs. Just wait till we rig 'em out.'

'She seems to be running extremely fast,' said Stephen. 'Yes. She is a flyer, certainly: they say she cleaned her bottom at the Grand Canary, and she has the sweetest lines. There! See, she's heaving her guns overboard. You see the splash? And another. She will be starting her water over the side presently. You remember how we pumped and pulled in the *Sophie*? Ha, ha. You heaved on your sweep like a hero, Stephen. *She* cannot sweep, however; no, no, *she* cannot sweep. There goes the last of her starboard guns. See how she draws away now – a charming sailer; one of the best they have.'

'Yet you mean to catch her? The *Medusa* is falling far behind.'

'I do not like to show away, Stephen, but I will bet you a dozen of any claret you choose to name against a can of ale that we lay her aboard before dinner. You may not think it, but her only chance of escape is a ship of the line heaving up ahead, or our carrying a mast away. Though she may wing us, too, if she keeps her chasers.'

'Will you not touch on wood when you say that? I take your wager, mind.'

Jack looked secretly at him. The dear creature's spirits were recovering a little: he must have been sadly shocked by that explosion. 'No,' he said. 'This time I shall defy fate: I did so, in any case, when I desired Killick to lay four places. The fourth is for the captain of the *Fama*. I shall invite him. I shall not give him back his sword, however, it was a shabby thing to do, to strike and then run.'

'All ready, sir,' said Mr Dashwood. 'Capital, capital: that was brisk work. Rig 'em out, Mr Dashwood, if you please.'

On either side of the *Lively*'s topgallants, topsails and courses there appeared her studdingsails, broadening her great spread of canvas with a speed, a perfect efficiency that made the *Fama*'s heart sink and die.

'There goes her water,' said the master, who had her scuppers fixed in his glass.

'I believe you may set water-sails,' said Jack, 'and clew up the mizzen tops'l.'

Now the *Lively* began to lean forward, throwing up the water with her forefoot so that it raced creaming right down her side to join her wake. Now she was really showing her paces; now she was eating the wind out of the *Fama*; and the distance narrowed. Never a sail that was not drawing perfectly, attended every moment by the crew – the now silent crew. A smooth, steady, urgent progression, the very height of sailing.

The *Fama* had almost everything abroad already, but now she tried her driver too, boomed far out. Jack and all the officers on the quarterdeck shook their heads simultaneously: it would never answer – it would not set well with the wind so far aft. She began to steer wild, and simultaneously they all nodded. A yaw that lost her two hundred yards – her wake was no longer a straight line.

'Mr Dashwood,' said Jack, 'the gunner may try the bow gun. I should like to win my bet.' He looked at his watch. 'It is a quarter to one.'

The starboard bow-gun spoke out, ringing faint after the din of battle: a plume of water astern of the *Fama*, white against the blue. The next, a very deliberate shot, was well pitched up, some thirty yards to one side of her. Another, and this must have passed low over her deck, for she yawed again, and now the *Lively* was coming up hand over hand.

The interval before the next gun was reaching its close: their ears were ready for the crash. But while they hung up there waiting for it there was an immense tumultuous cheering forward. It spread aft in a flash: the lieutenant came running through the crowd of men, pushing through them as they shook hands and clapped one another on the back. He took off his hat, and said, 'She has struck, sir, if you please.'

'Very good, Mr Dashwood. Be so kind as to take possession and send her captain back at once. I expect him to dinner.'

The *Lively* raced up, turned into the wind, folded her wings like a bird and lay athwart the *Fama*'s hawse. The boat splashed down, crossed, and returned. The Spanish captain came up the side, saluted, presented his sword with a bow: Jack passed it to Bonden, just behind him, and said, 'Do you speak English, sir?'

'A little, sir,' said the Spaniard.

'Then I should be very happy to have your company at dinner, sir. It is waiting in the cabin.'

They sat at the elegant table in the transformed cabin. The Spaniards behaved extremely well; they ate well, too, having been down to biscuit and chick-peas these last ten days; and as the courses followed one another their perfect dignity relaxed into something far more human. The bottles came and went: the tension wore away and away – talk flowed free in Spanish, English and a sort of French. There was even laughter and interruption, and when at last the noble pudding gave way to comfits, nuts and port, Jack sent the

decanter round, desiring them to fill up to the brim; and raising his glass he said, 'Gentlemen, I give you a toast. I beg you
will drink Sophia.'

'Sophia!' cried the Spanish captains, holding up their
glasses.

'Sophie,' said Stephen. 'God bless her.'

H.M.S.
Surprise

1

'BUT I PUT IT to you, my lord, that prize-money is of essential importance to the Navy. The possibility, however remote, of making a fortune by some brilliant stroke is an unparalleled spur to the diligence, the activity, and the unremitting attention of every man afloat. I am sure that the serving members of the Board will support me in this,' he said, glancing round the table. Several of the uniformed figures looked up, and there was a murmur of agreement: it was not universal, however; some of the civilians had a stuffed and non-committal air, and one or two of the sailors remained staring at the sheets of blotting-paper laid out before them. It was difficult to catch the sense of the meeting, if indeed any distinct current had yet established itself: this was not the usual restricted session of the Lords Commissioners of the Admiralty, but the first omnium gatherum of the new administration, the first since Lord Melville's departure, with several new members, many heads of department and representatives of other boards; they were feeling their way, behaving with politic restraint, holding their fire. It was difficult to sense the atmosphere, but although he knew he did not have the meeting entirely with him, yet he felt no decided opposition – a wavering, rather – and he hoped that by the force of his own conviction he might still carry his point against the tepid unwillingness of the First Lord. 'One or two striking examples of this kind, in the course of a long-protracted war, are enough to stimulate the zeal of the whole fleet throughout years and years of hardship at sea; whereas a denial, on the other hand, must necessarily have a – must necessarily have the contrary effect.' Sir Joseph was a capable, experienced chief of naval intelligence; but he was no orator, particularly before such a large audience; he had not struck upon the golden phrase; the right words had escaped him, and he was conscious of a certain negative, unpersuaded quality in the air.

'I cannot feel that Sir Joseph is quite right in attributing such interested motives to the officers of our service,' remarked Admiral Harte, bending his head obsequiously towards the First Lord. The other service members glanced quickly at him and at one another: Harte was the most eager pursuer of the main chance in the Navy, the most ardent snapper-up of anything that was going, from a Dutch herring-buss to a Breton fishing-boat.

'I am bound by precedent,' said the First Lord, turning a vast glabrous expressionless face from Harte to Sir Joseph. 'There was the case of the *Santa Brigida* . . .'

'The *Thetis*, my lord,' whispered his private secretary. 'The *Thetis*, I mean. And my legal advisers tell me that this is the appropriate decision. We are bound by Admiralty law: if the prize was made before the declaration of war the proceeds escheat to the Crown. They are droits of the Crown.'

'The strict letter of the law is one thing, my lord, and equity is another. The law is something of which sailors know nothing, but there is no body of men more tenacious of custom nor more alive to equity and natural justice. The position, as I see it, and as they will see it, is this: their Lordships, fully aware of the Spaniards' intention of entering the war, of joining Bonaparte, took time by the forelock. To carry on a war with any effect, Spain needed the treasure shipped from the River Plate; their Lordships therefore ordered it to be intercepted. It was essential to act without the loss of a moment, and the disposition of the Channel Fleet was such that – in short, all we were able to send was a squadron consisting of the frigates *Indefatigable*, *Medusa*, *Amphion* and *Lively*; and they had orders to detain the superior Spanish force and to carry it into Plymouth. By remarkable exertions, and, I may say, by the help of a remarkable stroke of intelligence, for which I claim no credit, the squadron reached Cape Santa Maria in time, engaged the Spaniards, sank one and took the others after a determined action, not without grievous loss on our side. They carried out their orders; they deprived the enemy of the sinews of war; and they brought home five million pieces of eight. If now they are to be told that these dollars, these pieces of eight, are, contrary to the custom of the service, to be regarded not as prize-money at all but as droits of the Crown, why then, it will have a most deplorable effect throughout the fleet.'

'But since the action took place before the declaration of war . . .' began a civilian.

'What about *Belle Poule* in '78?' cried Admiral Parr.

'The officers and men of our squadron had nothing to do with any declaration,' said Sir Joseph. 'They were not to meddle with affairs of state, but to execute the orders of the Board. They were fired upon first; then they carried out their duty according to their instructions, at no small cost to themselves and with very great advantage to the country. And if they are to be deprived of their customary reward, if, I say, the Board, under whose orders they acted, is to appropriate this money, then the particular effect upon the officers concerned, who have been led to believe themselves beyond the reach of want, or of anything resembling want, and who have no doubt committed themselves upon this understanding, will be – ' he hesitated for the word.

'Lamentable,' said a rear-admiral of the Blue. 'Lamentable. And the general effect upon the service, which will no longer have this splendid example of what zeal and determination can accomplish, will be far wider, far more to be deplored. This is a discretionary matter, my lord – the precedents point in contrary directions, and none has been tried in a court of law – and I put it to you with great earnestness that it would be far better for the Board to use its discretion in the favour of the officers and men concerned. It can be done at no great expense to the country, and the example will repay that expense a hundredfold.'

'Five million pieces of eight,' said Admiral Erskine, long-ingly, in the midst of a general hesitation. 'Was it indeed as much as that?'

'Who are the officers primarily concerned?' asked the First Lord.

'Captains Sutton, Graham, Collins and Aubrey, my lord,' said the private secretary. 'Here are their files.'

There was a silence while the First Lord ran through the papers, a silence broken only by the squeak of Admiral Erskine's pen converting five million pieces of eight to pounds sterling, dividing the result into its customary prize-shares and coming out with the answer that made him whis-tle. At the sight of these files Sir Joseph knew the game was up: the new First Lord might know nothing of the Navy, but he was an old parliamentary hand, an astute politician, and there were two names there that were anathema to the pre-sent administration. Sutton and Aubrey would throw the damnable weight of party politics into the wavering balance; and the other two captains had no influence of any kind, parliamentary, social or service, to redress it.

'Sutton I know in the House,' said the First Lord, pursing his mouth and scribbling a note. 'And Captain Aubrey . . . the name is familiar.'

'The son of General Aubrey, my lord,' whispered the secretary.

'Yes, yes. The member for Great Clanger, who made such a furious attack upon Mr Addington. He quoted his son in his speech on corruption, I remember. He often quotes his son. Yes, yes.' He closed the personal files and glanced at the gen-eral report. 'Pray, Sir Joseph,' he said after a moment, 'who is this Dr Maturin?'

'He is the gentleman about whom I sent your Lordship a minute last week,' said Sir Joseph. 'A minute in a yellow cover,' added with a very slight emphasis – an emphasis that would have been the equivalent of flinging his ink-well at the First Lord's head in Melville's time.

'Is it usual for medical men to be given temporary post-

captain's commissions?' went on the First Lord, missing the
emphasis and forgetting the significance of the yellow cover.
All the service members looked up quickly, their eyes running
from one to the other.

'It was done for Sir Joseph Banks and for Mr Halley, my
lord, and I believe, for some other scientific gentlemen. It is
an exceptional compliment, but by no means unknown.'

'Oh,' said the First Lord, conscious from something in Sir
Joseph's cold and weary gaze that he had made a gaffe. 'So it
has nothing to do with this particular case?'

'Nothing whatsoever, my lord. And if I may revert for a
moment to Captain Aubrey, I may state without fear of contradiction that the father's views do not represent the son's.
Far from it, indeed.' This he said, not from any hope that he
could right the position, but by way of drowning the gaffe – of
diverting attention from it – and he was not displeased when
Admiral Harte, still hoping to curry favour and at the same
time to gratify a personal malevolence, said, 'Would it be in
order to call upon Sir Joseph to declare a personal interest?'

'No sir, it would not,' cried Admiral Parr, his port-wine face
flushing purple. 'A most improper suggestion, by God.' His
voice trailed away in a series of coughs and grunts, through
which could be heard 'infernal presumption – new member –
mere rear-admiral – little shit.'

'If Admiral Harte means to imply that I am in any way concerned with Captain Aubrey's personal welfare,' said Sir
Joseph with an icy look, 'he is mistaken. I have never met the
gentleman. The good of the service is my only aim.'

Harte was shocked by the reception of what he had
thought rather a clever remark, and he instantly pulled in his
horns – horns that had been planted, among a grove of others, by the Captain Aubrey in question. He confounded himself in apologies – he had not meant, he had not wished to
imply, what he had really intended – not the least aspersion
on the most honourable gentleman . . .

The First Lord, somewhat disgusted, clapped his hand on

the table and said, 'But in any event, I cannot agree that five million dollars is a trifling expense to the country; and as I have already said, our legal advisers assure me that this must be considered as droits of the Crown. Much as I personally should like to fall in with Sir Joseph's in many ways excellent and convincing suggestion, I fear we are bound by precedent. It is a matter of principle. I say it with infinite regret, Sir Joseph, being aware that this expedition, this brilliantly successful expedition, was under your aegis; and no one could wish more wealth and prosperity to the gentlemen of the Navy than myself. But our hands are tied, alas. However, let us console ourselves with the thought that there will be a considerable sum left over to be divided: nothing in the nature of millions, of course, but a considerable sum, oh yes. Yes. And with that comfortable thought, gentlemen, I believe we must now turn our attention . . .'

They turned it to the technical questions of impressment, tenders and guardships, matters outside Sir Joseph's province, and he leant back in his chair, watching the speakers, assessing their abilities. Poor, on the whole; and the new First Lord was a fool, a mere politician. Sir Joseph had served under Chatham, Spencer, St Vincent and Melville, and this man made a pitiful figure beside them: they had had their failings, particularly Chatham, but not one would so have missed the point – the whole expense in this case would have been borne by the Spaniards; it would have been the Spaniards who provided the Royal Navy with the splendid example of four youngish post-captains caught in a great shower, a downpour, of gold – the money would not have left the country. Naval fortunes were not so common; and the fortunes there were had nearly all been amassed by admirals in lucrative commands, taking their flag-share for innumerable captures in which they personally took no part whatsoever. The captains who fought the ships – those were the men to encourage. Perhaps he had not made his point as clearly or as forcibly as he should have done: he was not in form after a

sleepless night with seven reports from Boulogne to digest.
But in any case, no other First Lord except perhaps St Vincent would have made the question turn on party politics.
And quite certainly not a single one of them would have
blurted out the name of a secret agent.

Both Lord Melville (a man who really understood intelligence – a splendid First Lord) and Sir Joseph were much
attached to Dr Maturin, their adviser on Spanish and especially Catalan affairs, a most uncommon, wholly disinterested
agent, brave, painstaking, utterly reliable and ideally qualified, who had never accepted the slightest reward for his services – and such services! It was he who had brought them
the intelligence that had allowed them to deliver this crippling blow. Sir Joseph and Lord Melville had devised the
temporary commission as a means of obliging him to accept a
fortune, supplied by the enemy; and now his name had been
brayed out in public – not even in the comparative privacy of
the Board, but in a far more miscellaneous gathering – with
the question openly directed at the chief of naval intelligence. It was unqualifiable. To rely on the discretion of these
sailors whose only notion of dealing with an enemy as cunning as Bonaparte was to blow him out of the water, was
unqualifiable. To say nothing of the civilians, the talkative
politicians, whose nearest approach to danger was a telescope
on Dover cliffs, where they could look at Bonaparte's invasion
army, two hundred thousand strong, camped on the other
side of the water. He looked at the faces round the long table;
they were growing heated about the relative jurisdictions of
the impress service proper and the gangs from the ships –
admiral called to admiral in voices that could be heard in
Whitehall, and the First Lord seemed to have no control of
the meeting whatsoever. Sir Joseph took comfort from this –
the gaffe might be forgotten. 'But still,' he said to himself,
drawing the metamorphoses of a red admiral, egg, caterpillar,
chrysalis and imago on his pad, 'what shall I say to him when
we meet? What kind of face can I put on it, when I see him?'

IN WHITEHALL a grey drizzle wept down upon the Admiralty, but in Sussex the air was dry – dry and perfectly still. The smoke rose from the chimney of the small drawing-room at Mapes Court in a tall, unwavering plume, a hundred feet before its head drifted away in a blue mist to lie in the hollows of the downs behind the house. The leaves were hanging yet, but only just, and from time to time the bright yellow rounds on the tree outside the window dropped of themselves, twirling in their slow fall to join the golden carpet at its foot, and in the silence the whispering impact of each leaf could be heard – a silence as peaceful as an easy death.

'At the first breath of a wind those trees will all be bare,' observed Dr Maturin. 'Yet autumn is a kind of spring, too; for there is never a one but is pushed off by its own next-coming bud. You see that so clearly farther south. In Catalonia, now, where you and Jack are to come as soon as the war is over, the autumn rains bring up the grass like an army of spears; and even here – my dear, a trifle less butter, if you please. I am already in a high state of grease.'

Stephen Maturin had dined with the ladies of Mapes, Mrs Williams, Sophia, Cecilia and Frances – traces of brown windsor soup, codfish, pigeon pie, and baked custard could be seen on his neck-cloth, his snuff-coloured waistcoat and his drab breeches, for he was an untidy eater and he had lost his napkin before the first remove, in spite of Sophia's efforts at preserving it – and now he was sitting on one side of the fire drinking tea, while Sophia toasted him crumpets on the other, leaning forward over the pink and silver glow with particular attention neither to scorch the crumpet by holding it too close nor to parch it by holding it too far down. In the fading light the glow caught her rounded forearm and her lovely face, exaggerating the breadth of her forehead and the perfect cut of her lips, emphasising the extraordinary bloom of her complexion. Her anxiety for the crumpet did away with the usual reserve of her expression; she had her younger sister's trick of showing the tip of her tongue when she was concentrating, and this, with so high a degree of beauty, gave her an absurdly touching appearance. He looked at her with great complacency, feeling an odd constriction at his heart, a feeling without a name: she was engaged to be married to his particular friend, Captain Aubrey of the Navy; she was his patient; and they were as close as a man and a woman can be where there is no notion of gallantry between them – closer, perhaps, than if they had been lovers. He said, 'This is an elegant crumpet, Sophie, to be sure: but it must be the last, and I do not recommend another for you, my dear, either. You are getting too fat. You were quite haggard and pitiful not six months ago; but the prospect of marriage suits you, I find. You must have put on half a stone, and your complexion . . . Sophie, why do you thread, transpierce another crumpet? Who is that crumpet for? For whom is that crumpet, say?'

'It is for me, my dear. Jack said I was to be firm – Jack loves firmness of character. He said that Lord Nelson . . .'

Far, far over the still and almost freezing air came the sound of a horn on Polcary Down. They both turned to the window. 'Did they kill their fox, I wonder, now?' said Stephen. 'If Jack were home, he would know, the animal.'

'Oh, I am so glad he is not out there on that wicked great bay,' said Sophia. 'It always managed to get him off, and I was always afraid he would break his leg, like young Mr Savile. Stephen, will you help me draw the curtain?'

'How she has grown up,' said Stephen privately. And aloud, as he looked out of the window, holding the cord in one hand, 'What is the name of that tree? The slim exotic, standing on the lawn?'

'We call it the pagoda-tree. It is not a real pagoda-tree, but that is what we call it. My uncle Palmer, the traveller, planted it; and he said it was very like.'

As soon as she had spoken Sophia regretted it – she regretted it even before the sentence was out, for she knew where the word might lead Stephen's mind.

These uneasy intuitions are so often right: to anyone who

had the least connection with India the pagoda-tree must necessarily be associated with those parts. Pagodas were small gold coins resembling its leaves, and shaking the pagoda-tree meant making an Indian fortune, becoming a nabob – a usual expression. Both Sophia and Stephen were concerned with India, because Diana Villiers was said to be there, with her lover and indeed keeper Richard Canning. Diana was Sophia's cousin, once her rival for the affections of Jack Aubrey, and at the same time the object of Stephen's eager, desperate pursuit – a dashing young woman of surprising charms and undaunted firmness of character, who had been very much part of their lives until her elopement with Mr Canning. She was the black sheep of the family, of course, the scabbed ewe, and in principle her name was never mentioned at Mapes; yet it was surprising how much they knew about her movements and how great a place she occupied in their thoughts.

The newspapers had told them a great deal, for Mr Canning was something of a public figure, a wealthy man with interests in shipping and in the East India Company, in politics (he and his relations owned three rotten boroughs, appointing members to sit for them, since they could not sit themselves, being Jews), and in the social world, Mr Canning having friends among the Prince of Wales's set. And rumour, making its way from the next county, where his cousins the Goldsmids lived, had told them more. But even so, they had nothing like the information that Stephen Maturin possessed, for in spite of his unworldly appearance and his unfeigned devotion to natural philosophy, he had wide-reaching contacts and great skill in using them. He knew the name of the East Indiaman in which Mrs Villiers had sailed, the position of her cabin, the names of her two maids, their relations and background (one was French, with a soldier brother taken early in the war and now imprisoned at Norman Cross). He knew the number of bills she had left unpaid, and their amount; he knew a great deal about the storm that had raged so violently in the Canning, Goldsmid and Mocatta families, and that was still raging, for Mrs Canning (a Goldsmid by birth) had no notion of a plurality of wives, and she called upon all her relations to defend her with a furious, untiring zeal – a storm that had induced Canning to leave for India, with an official mission connected with the French establishments on the Malabar coast, a rare place for gathering pagodas.

Sophia was right: these were indeed the thoughts that flooded into Stephen's mind at the name of that unlucky tree – these and a great many more, as he sat silently by the glow of the fire. Not that they had far to travel; they hovered most of the time at no great distance, ready to appear in the morning when he woke, wondering why he was so oppressed with grief; and when they were not immediately present their place was marked by a physical pain in his midriff, in an area that he could cover with the palm of his hand.

In a secret drawer of his desk, making it difficult to open or close, lay docketed reports headed *Villiers, Diana, widow of Charles Villiers, late of Bombay, Esquire*, and *Canning, Richard, of Park Street and Coluber House, co. Bristol*. These two were as carefully documented as any pair of State suspects working for Bonaparte's intelligence services; and although much of this mass of paper had come from benevolent sources, a good deal of it had been acquired in the ordinary way of business, and it had cost a mint of money. Stephen had spared no expense in making himself more unhappy, his own position as a rejected lover even clearer.

'Why do I gather all these wounds?' he wondered. 'With what motive? To be sure, in war any accession of intelligence is an advance: and I may call this a private war. Is it to persuade myself that I am fighting still, although I have been beaten out of the field? Rational enough, but no doubt false – too glib it is.' He uttered these remarks in Catalan, for being something of a polyglot he had a way of suiting his train of thought to the language that matched it best – his mother

was a Catalan, his father an Irish officer, and Catalan, English, French, Castilian came to him as naturally as breathing,
without preference, except for subject.

'How I wish I had held my tongue,' thought Sophie. She
looked anxiously at Stephen as he sat there, bent and staring
into the red cavern under the log. 'Poor dear thing,' she
thought, 'how very much he is in need of darning – how very
much he needs someone to look after him. He really is not fit
to wander about the world alone; it is so hard to unworldly
people. How could she have been so cruel? It was like hitting
a child. A child. How little learning does for a man – he
knows almost nothing: he had but to say "Pray be so good as
to marry me" last summer and she would have cried "Oh yes,
if you please". I *told* him so. Not that she would ever have
made him happy, the . . .' Bitch was the word that struggled to
make itself heard; but it struggled in vain. 'I shall never love
that pagoda-tree again. We were so pleasant together, and
now it is as though the fire had gone out . . . it will go out,
too, unless I put another log on. And it is quite dark.' Her
hand went out towards the bell-pull to ring for candles,
wavered, and returned to her lap. 'It is terrible how people
suffer,' she thought. 'How lucky I am: sometimes it terrifies
me. Dearest Jack . . .' Her inner eye filled with a brilliant
image of Jack Aubrey, tall, straight, cheerful, overflowing with
life and direct open affection, his yellow hair falling over his
post-captain's epaulette and his high-coloured weather-
beaten face stretched in an intensely amused laugh: she
could see the wicked scar that ran from the angle of his jaw
right up into his scalp, every detail of his uniform, his Nile
medal, and the heavy, curved sword the Patriotic Fund had
given him for sinking the *Bellone*. His bright blue eyes almost
vanished when he laughed – all you saw were shining slits,
even bluer in the scarlet flush of mirth. Never was there anyone with whom she had had such fun – no one had ever
laughed like that.

The vision was shattered by the opening of the door and a

flood of light from the hall: the squat thick form of Mrs
Williams stood there, black in the doorway, and her loud
voice cried, 'What, what is this? Sitting alone in the dark?'
Her eyes darted from the one to the other to confirm the suspicions that had been growing in her mind ever since the
silence had fallen between them – a silence of which she was
perfectly aware, as she had been sitting in the library close to
a cupboard in the panelling: when this cupboard door was
open, one could not help hearing what was said in the small
drawing-room. But their immobility, their civil, surprised
faces turned towards her, convinced Mrs Williams of her mistake and she said with a laugh, 'A lady and gentleman sitting
alone in the dark – it would never have done in my time, la!
The gentlemen of the family would have called upon Dr
Maturin for an explanation. Where is Cecilia? She ought to
have been keeping you company. In the dark . . . but I dare
say you were thinking of the candles, Sophie. Good girl. You
would not credit, Doctor,' she said, turning towards her guest
with a polite look; for although Dr Maturin was scarcely to be
compared with his friend Captain Aubrey, he was known to
be the possessor of a marble bath and of a castle in Spain – a
castle in Spain! – and he might very well do for her younger
daughter: had Cecilia been sitting in the dark with Dr
Maturin she would never have burst in. 'You would not credit
how candles have risen. No doubt Cecilia would have had
the same idea. All my daughters have been brought up with a
strict sense of economy, Dr Maturin; there is no waste in this
house. However, if it had been Cecilia in the dark with a
beau, that would never have done; the game would not have
been worth the candle, ahem! No sir, you would never believe
how wax has gone up since the beginning of the war. Sometimes I am tempted to turn to tallow; but poor though we are,
I cannot bring myself to it – at least not in the public rooms.
However, I have two candles burning in the library, and you
shall have one: John need not light the sconces in here. I was
obliged to have two, Dr Maturin, for I have been sitting with

my man of business all this time — nearly all this time. The
writings and the contracts and the settlements are so very
long and complicated, and I am an infant in these matters.'
The infant's estate ran far beyond the parish boundaries, and
tenants' babies as far away as Starveacre, on being told 'Mrs
Williams will come for you', would fall mute with horror. 'But
Mr Wilbraham throws out some pretty severe reflections on
us all for our *dilatoriness*, as he calls it, though I am sure it is
not our fault, with Captain A so far away.'

She bustled away for the candle, pursing her mouth. These
negotiations were drawing out in length, not from any petulance on the part of Mr Wilbraham, but because of Mrs
Williams's iron determination not to part with her daughter's
virginity or her ten thousand pounds until an 'adequate provision', a binding marriage-settlement, had been signed, sealed,
and above all, the hard cash delivered. It was this that was
hanging fire so strangely: Jack had agreed to all the conditions, however rapacious; he had tied up his property, pay,
prospects and future prize-money for the benefit of his
widow and any off-spring of this union for ever, in the most
liberal way, as though he had been a pauper; but still the
actual money did not appear, and not a step would Mrs
Williams move until it was in her hands, not in promises, but
in minted gold or its copper-bottomed, Bank of England guaranteed equivalent.

'There,' she said, coming back and looking sharply at the
log which Sophia had put on the fire. 'One will be enough,
will it not, unless you wish to read? But I dare say you still
have plenty to talk about.'

'Yes,' said Sophia, when they were alone again. 'There is
something I should like to ask you. I have been meaning to
draw you aside ever since you came . . . It is dreadful to be so
ignorant, and I would not have Captain Aubrey know it for
the world; and I cannot ask my mother. But with you it is
quite different.'

'One may say anything at all to a medical man,' said

Stephen, and a look of professional, anonymous gravity came over his face, partly overlaying its look of strong personal affection.

'A medical man?' cried Sophia. 'Oh, yes. Of course: certainly. But what I really meant, dear Stephen, was this war. It has been going on for ever now, apart from that short break. Going on for ever – and oh how I wish it would stop – for years and years, as long as I can remember; but I am afraid I have not always paid as much attention as I should. Of course, I do know it is the French who are so wicked; but there are all these people who keep coming and going – the Austrians, the Spaniards, the Russians. Pray, are the Russians a good thing now? It would be very shocking – treason no doubt – to put the wrong people in my prayers. And there are all those Italians, and the poor dear Pope: and only the very day before he left, Jack mentioned Pappenburg – he had hoisted the flag of Pappenburg, by way of a ruse de guerre; so Pappenburg must be a country. I was despicably false, and only nodded, looking as wise as I could, and said, Ah, Pappenburg." I am so afraid he will think me ignorant: which of course I am, but I cannot bear him to know it. I am sure there are quantities of young women who know where Pappenburg is, and Batavia, and this Ligurian Republic; but we never *did* such places with Miss Blake. And this Kingdom of the Two Sicilies: I can find one on the map, but not the other. Stephen, pray tell me the present state of the world.'

'Is it the state of the world, my dear?' said Stephen, with a grin – no professional look left at all. 'Well now, for the moment, it is plain enough. On our side we have Austria, Russia, Sweden and Naples, which is the same as your Two Sicilies; and on his he has a whole cloud of little states, and Bavaria and Holland and Spain. Not that these alliances are of much consequence one side or the other: The Russians were with us, and then against us until they strangled their Czar, and now with us; and I dare say they will change again, when the whim bites. The Austrians left the war in '97 and

then again in the year one, after Hohenlinden: the same thing
may happen again any day. What matters to us is Holland and
Spain, for they have navies; and if ever this war is to be won,
it must be won at sea. Bonaparte has about forty-five ships of
the line, and we have eighty-odd, which sounds well enough.
But ours are scattered all over the world and his are not.
Then again the Spaniards have twenty-seven, to say nothing
of the Dutch; so it is essential to prevent them from combining, for if Bonaparte can assemble a superior force in the
Channel, even for a little while, then his invasion army can
come across, God forbid. That is why Jack and Lord Nelson
are beating up and down off Toulon, bottling up Monsieur de
Villeneuve with his eleven ships of the line and seven
frigates, preventing them from combining with the Spaniards
in Cartagena and Cadiz and Ferrol; and that is where I am
going to join him as soon as I have been to London to settle
one or two little points of business and to buy a large quantity
of madder. So if you have any messages, now is the time; for,
Sophie, I am upon the wing.' He stood up, scattering crumbs,
and the clock on the black cabinet struck the hour.

'Oh, Stephen, must you go?' cried Sophie. 'Let me brush
you a little. Will you not stay supper? Pray, do stay supper – I
will make you toasted cheese.'

'I will not, my dear, though you are very kind,' said Stephen,
standing like a horse as she brushed at him, turned down his
collar and twitched at his cravat – since his disappointment
he had grown less nice about his linen; he had given up the
practice of brushing his clothes or his boots, and neither his
face nor his hands were particularly clean. 'There is a meeting of the Entomological Society that I might just be able to
attend, if I hurry. There, there, my dear, that will do: Mary
and Joseph, I am not going to Court – the entomologists do
not set up for beaux. Now give me a kiss, like a good creature,
and tell me what I am to say – what messages I am to give to
Jack.'

'How I wish, oh how I wish I were going with you . . . It

would be of no use begging him to be prudent, not to take risks, I suppose?'

'I will mention it, if you choose. But believe me, honey, Jack is not an imprudent man – not at sea. He never takes a risk without he has weighed it very carefully: he loves his ship and his men too much, far too much, to run them into any unconsidered danger – he is not one of your wild, hit-or-miss, fire-eating rapparees.'

'He would not do anything rash?'

'Never in life. It's true, you know; quite true,' he added, seeing that Sophia was not wholly persuaded that Jack at sea and Jack ashore were two different persons.

'Well,' she said, and paused. 'How long it seems; everything seems to take so very long.'

'Nonsense,' said Stephen, with an assumed liveliness. 'Parliament rises in a few weeks' time; Captain Hamond will go back to his ship, and Jack will be thrown on the beach again. You will see as much of him as your heart could desire. Now what shall I say?'

'Give him my dearest love, Stephen, if you please; and pray, pray, take the greatest care of yourself, too.'

DR MATURIN WALKED into the Entomological Society's meeting as the Reverend Mr Lamb began his paper on Certain Non-Descript Beetles found on the Shore at Pringle-juxta-Mare in the Year 1799. He sat down at the back and listened closely for a while; but presently the gentleman strayed from his theme (as everyone had known he would) and began to harangue the gathering on the hibernation of swallows; for he had found a new prop for his theory – not only did they fly in ever – decreasing circles, conglobulate in a mass and plunge to the bottoms of quiet ponds, but they also took refuge in the *shafts of tin-mines*, 'of Cornish tin-mines, gentlemen!' Stephen's attention wandered, and he glanced over the restless entomologists; several he knew – the worthy Dr Musgrave, who had favoured him with a prime

carena quindecimpunctata; Mr Tolston, of stag-beetle fame;
Eusebius Piscator, that learned Swede – and surely the
plump back and powdered queue looked familiar? It was odd
how one's eye must take in and store innumerable measurements and proportions; a back was almost as recognisable as
a face. This applied also to gait, stance, lift of head: what
countless references at every turn! This back was turned from
his with an odd, unnatural twist, and its owner's left hand was
raised, resting on his jaw in such a way as to shield his face:
no doubt it was this twist that had caught his eye; yet in all
their dealings he had never seen Sir Joseph writhe himself
into such an attitude.

'. . . and so, gentlemen, I believe I may confidently state
that the hibernation of swallows, *and of all the other
hirondines*, is conclusively proved,' said Mr Lamb, with a defiant glare at his audience.

'I am sure were are all very grateful to Mr Lamb,' said the
chairman, in an atmosphere of general discontent, with some
cross shuffling of feet and murmuring. 'And although I am
afraid that we are now short of time – perhaps not all the
papers can be read – allow me to call on Sir Joseph Blain to
favour us with his remarks on A True Gynandromorph
recently added to his Cabinet.'

Sir Joseph half rose in his place and begged to be excused –
he had left his notes behind – he was not perfectly well, and
would not try the patience of the meeting by trying to speak
without 'em – he begged pardon, but thought he would retire.
It was only a passing indisposition, he said, to reassure the
company: the company would not have cared if it had been
the great spotted leprosy – three entomologists were already
on their feet, eager for immortality in the society's Proceedings. 'What am I to infer from this?' asked Stephen of himself, as Sir Joseph passed with a distant bow; and during the
following account of luminous beetles, lately received from
Surinam – a fascinating account, which he should certainly
read with great attention later – a cold presentiment formed

in his bosom. He carried this presentiment with him from the meeting; but he had not walked a hundred yards before a discreet messenger accosted him and gave him a card with a cipher and an invitation not to Sir Joseph's official apartments but to a little house behind Shepherd Market.

'How good of you to come,' said Sir Joseph, seating Stephen by the fire in what was clearly his library, study and drawing-room; it was comfortable, even luxurious, in the style of fifty years before; and cases of butterflies alternated with pornographic pictures on the walls – emphatically a private house. 'How truly kind.' He was nervous and ill at ease, and he said 'how truly kind' again: Stephen said nothing. 'I begged you to come here,' Sir Joseph went on, 'because this is my private shall I say *refuge*, and I feel I owe you a private explanation. When I saw you this evening I was not expecting you; my conscience gave me a rude jerk – it put me about strangely, because I have exceedingly disagreeable news for you, news that I should rather have any other man deliver but that necessarily falls to me. I had prepared myself for it at our meeting tomorrow morning; and I should have done it well enough, I dare say. But seeing you suddenly there, in that atmosphere . . . To put it in a word,' he said, putting down the poker with which he had been teasing the fire, 'there has been a grave indiscretion at the Admiralty – your name was mentioned and insisted upon at a general meeting, in direct connexion with the action off Cadiz.' Stephen bowed, but still said nothing. Sir Joseph, looking at him covertly, went on. 'Of course, I drowned the indiscretion at once, and afterwards I let it be understood that you were aboard by chance, that you were bound for some undefined Eastern region in a scientific or quasi-diplomatic capacity in which a commission would be necessary for your status, for your eventual negotiations, citing the precedent of Banks and Halley – that its connexion with this incident was purely fortuitous and coincidental, occasioned only by the need for extreme haste. This I have put about as the true inside story, far more secret than the interception, known only to the initiated and not to be divulged on any account: it should answer with most of the sailors and civilians who were present. The fact remains that in spite of my efforts you are somewhat blown upon; and this necessarily calls our whole programme into question.'

'Who were the gentlemen present?' asked Stephen. Sir Joseph passed him a list. 'A considerable gathering . . . There is a strange levity,' he said coldly, 'a strange weak irresponsibility, in playing with men's lives and a whole system of intelligence in this manner.'

'I entirely agree,' cried Sir Joseph. 'It is monstrous. And I say so with the more pain since it is I who am partly at fault. I had minuted the First Lord on the subject and I wholly relied upon his discretion. But no doubt I had allowed myself to become too much accustomed to a chief upon whom I could rely without question – there never was a closer man than Lord Melville. A parliamentary government is hopeless for intelligence: new men come in, politicians rather than professionals, and we are all to seek. Your dictatorship is the only thing for intelligence: Bonaparte is far, far better served than His Majesty. But I must not evade the second unhappy issue. Although it will be a matter of public notoriety in a few days' time, I feel I must tell you myself that the Board means to treat the Spanish treasure as droits of the Crown – that is to say, it will not be distributed as prize-money. I did everything in my power to avert this decision, but I am afraid it is irrevocable. I tell you this in the faint hope that it might prevent you from committing yourself to any course of action on the contrary assumption; even a few days' warning is perhaps better than none at all. I also tell you, with the utmost regret, because I am aware that you have another interest in this – in this matter. I can only hope, alas without much conviction, that my warning may have some slight . . . you follow me. And as for my personal expressions of extreme regret, intense chagrin and concern, upon my word, I scarcely know how to phrase them with a tenth of the force they require.'

'You are very good,' said Stephen, 'and I am most sensible of this mark of confidence. I will not pretend that the loss of a fortune can be a matter of indifference to any man: I do not feel any emotion other than petty vexation at the moment, though no doubt I shall in time. But the interest to which you so obligingly refer is another matter: allow me to make it clear. I particularly wished to serve my friend Aubrey. His agent absconded with all his prize-money; the court of appeal reversed the condemnation of two neutral vessels, leaving him £11,000 in debt. This happened when he was on the point of becoming engaged to a most amiable young woman. They are deeply attached to one another; but since her mother, a widow with considerable property under her own control, is a deeply stupid, griping, illiberal, avid, tenacious, pinchfist lickpenny, a sordid lickpenny and a shrew, there is no hope of marriage without his estate is cleared and he can make at least some kind of settlement upon her. That was the position I flattered myself I had dealt with; or rather that you, a kind fate and the conjuncture had dealt with for me. That was the understanding of all concerned. What am I now to tell Aubrey when I join him at Minorca? Does anything accrue to him from this action at all?'

'Oh yes, certainly: there will certainly be an ex gratia payment: indeed, it might clear the debts you mention, or very nearly: but it will not be wealth, oh dear me no; far from it. But, my dear sir, you speak of Minorca. Do I collect that you mean to continue with our original plan, in spite of this wretched unnecessary contretemps?'

'I believe so,' said Stephen, studying the list again. 'There is so much to be gained from our recent contacts; so much to be lost by not . . . In this case it seems to me essentially a question of time: as far as common loose talk and confidential rumour are concerned, I must in all probability outrun it, since I sail tomorrow night. Information of this seeping kind is unlikely to move as fast as a determined traveller; and in any event you have dealt with the more obvious prattlers.

This is the only name here I am afraid of' – pointing to the list – 'He is, as you know, a paederast. Not that I have any-thing against paederasty myself – each man must decide for himself where beauty lies and surely the more affection in this world the better – but it is common knowledge that some paederasts are subject to pressures that do not apply to other men. If this gentleman's meetings with Monsieur de La Tapetterie could be discreetly watched, and above all if La Tapetterie could be neutralised for a week, I should have no hesitation in carrying on with our former arrangement. Even without these precautions, I doubt I should put it off; these are the merest conjectures, after all. And it is no use sending Osborne or Schikaneder – Gomez will put his head into no man's hands but mine; and without that contact the new sys-tem falls to pieces.'

'That is true. And of course you understand the local posi-tion far better than any of us. But I do not like to think of you running this added risk.'

'It is very slight, if indeed it exists at the moment – negligi-ble if I have a fair wind and if you caulk this leak, this purely conjectural leak. For this one voyage it does not weigh at all, compared with the common daily hazards of the trade. After-wards, if silly chatter has its usual effect, clearly I shall not be useful for some time – not until you rehabilitate me, ha, ha, with your quasi-diplomatic or scientific mission to the Cham of Tartary. When I come back from it I shall publish such papers on the cryptogams of Kamschatka that no one will ever set the mark of intelligence upon my head again.'

2

TO AND FRO, to and fro, from Cape Sicié to the Giens peninsula, wear ship and back again, all day long, week after week, month after month, whatever the weather; after

the evening gun they stood out into the offing and at dawn
they were back again, the inshore squadron of frigates watching Toulon, the eyes of the Mediterranean fleet, those line-of-
battle ships whose topsails flecked the southern horizon,
Nelson waiting for the French admiral to come out.

The mistral had been blowing for three days now and the
sea showed more white than blue, with the off-shore wind
cutting up little short waves that sent spray flying over the
waist of the ship: the three frigates had reduced sail at noon,
but even so they were making seven knots and heeling until
their larboard chains were smothered in the foam.

The tediously familiar headland of Cape Sicié came closer
and closer; in this sparkling clean air under the pure sky they
could see the little white houses, carts creeping on the road
up to the semaphore station and the batteries. Closer, almost
within range of the high-perched forty-two pounders; and
now the wind was coming in gusts off the high ground.

'On deck, there,' hailed the lookout at the mast-head.
'Naiad's showing a waft, sir.'

'Hands wear ship,' said the lieutenant of the watch, more
from form than anything else, for not only did the Lively have
a crew that had worked together for years, but also she had
carried out this manoeuvre several hundred times in this very
stretch of water and the order was scarcely needed. Routine
had taken the edge off the Livelies' zeal, but nevertheless the
boatswain had to call out 'Handsomely, handsomely, now,
with that bleeding sheet'; for the crew had been brought to
such a pitch of silent efficiency that the frigate ran the risk of
darting her jib-boom over the taffrail of the Melpomene, her
next ahead, whose talents and sailing qualities could not have
recommended her anywhere.

However, round they went in succession, each wearing in
the spot where her leader had turned; they hauled their wind
and re-formed their rigid line, heading for Giens once more,
Naiad, Melpomene, Lively.

'I do hate this wearing in succession,' said one thin midshipman to another thin midshipman, 'It does not give a man a chance: nothing can you see, not a sausage, no not a sausage; nor yet a smell of one,' he added, peering forward through the rigging and sails towards the gap between the peninsula and the island of Porquerolles.

'Sausage,' cried the other. 'Oh, Butler, what an infernal bloody thing to say.' He, too, leaned over the top of the hammocks, staring towards the passage; for at any moment now the *Niobe* might appear from her cruise, watering at Agincourt Sound and working back along the Italian coast, badgering the enemy and picking up what supplies she could find, and it would be the *Lively*'s turn next. 'Sausage,' he cried above the mistral, as he stared, 'hot, crisp, squirting with juice as you bite 'em – bacon – mushrooms!'

'Shut up, fat-arse,' whispered his friend, with a vicious pinch. 'The Lord is with us.'

The officer of the watch had moved away over to leeward at the clash of the Marine sentry's salute; and a moment later Jack Aubrey stepped out of the cabin, muffled in a griego, with a telescope under his arm, and began to pace the quarterdeck, the holy windward side, sacred to the captain. From time to time he glanced up at the sails: a purely automatic glance – nothing called for comment, of course: she was a thoroughly efficient machine, working smoothly. For this kind of duty the *Lively* would function perfectly if he were to stay in his cot all day. No reproach was possible, even if he had felt as liverish as Lucifer after his fall, which was not the case; far from it; he and the men under his command had been in a state of general benignity these many weeks and months, in spite of the tedium of a close blockade, the hardest and most wearisome duty in the service; for although wealth may not bring happiness, the immediate prospect of it provides a wonderfully close imitation and last September they had captured one of the richest ships afloat. His glance, then, was filled with liking and approval; yet still it did not contain that ingenuous love with which he had gazed at his first command, the short, thick, unweatherly *Sophie*. The *Lively* was not really his ship; he was only in temporary command, a jobbing-captain until such time as her true owner, Captain Hamond, should return from his seat at Westminster, where he represented Coldbath Fields in the Whig interest; and although Jack prized and admired the frigate's efficiency and her silent discipline – she could flash out a full suit of canvas with no more than the single quiet order 'Make sail', and do so in three minutes forty-two seconds – he could not get used to it. The *Lively* was a fine example, an admirable example, of the Whiggish state of mind at its best; and Jack was a Tory. He admired her, but it was with a detached admiration, as though he were in charge of a brother—officer's wife, an elegant, chaste, unimaginative woman, running her life on scientific principles.

Cape Cépet lay broad on the beam, and slinging his telescope he hoisted himself into the ratlines – they sagged under his weight – and climbed grunting into the maintop. The topmen were expecting him, and they had arranged a studdingsail for him to sit on. 'Thankee, Rowland,' he said, 'uncommon parky, hey? Hey?' and sank down upon it with a final grunt, resting his glass on the aftermost upper deadeye of the topmast shrouds and training it on Cape Cépet: the signal-station leapt into view, bright and clear, and to its right the eastern half of the Grande Rade with five men-of-war in it, seventy-fours, three of them English. *Hannibal*, *Swiftsure* and *Berwick*: they were exercising their crews at reefing aboard the *Hannibal*, and quantities of people were creeping up the rigging of the *Swiftsure*, landmen under training, perhaps. The French nearly always had these captured ships in the outer Rade; they did it to annoy, and they always succeeded. Twice every day it vexed him to the heart, for every morning and every afternoon he went aloft to peer into the Rade. This he did partly out of professional conscience, although there was not the slightest likelihood of their coming out unless they had thick weather and such a gale of wind that the English fleet would be blown off station; and partly because it was some sort of exercise. He was growing fat again, but in any case he had no intention of getting out of the way of running up and down the rigging, as some heavy captains did: the feel of the shrouds under his hands, the give and spring of live rigging, the heave and swing on the roll as he came over into the top made him deeply happy.

The rest of the anchorage was coming into view, and with a frown Jack swung his glass to inspect the rival frigates: seven of them still, and only one had moved since yesterday. Beautiful ships: though in his opinion they over-raked their masts.

Now the moment was coming. The church tower was almost in line with the blue dome, and he focused with renewed attention. The land hardly seemed to move at all, but gradually the arms of the Petite Rade opened, and there was the inner harbour, a forest of masts, all with their yards across, all in apparent readiness to come out and fight. A vice-admiral's flag, a rear-admiral's, a commodore's broad pennant: no change. The arms were closing; they glided imperceptibly together, and the Petite Rade was closed.

Jack shifted his aim until the Faro hill came into sight, then the hill behind it, and he searched the road for the little inn where he and Stephen and Captain Christy-Pallière had eaten and drunk such a capital dinner not so very long ago, together with another French sea-officer whose name he forgot. Precious hot then: precious cold now. Wonderful food then – Lord, how they had stuffed! – precious short commons now. At the thought of that meal his stomach gave a twinge: the *Lively*, though she considered herself the wealthiest ship on the station and conducted herself with a certain reserve towards the paupers in company, was as short of fresh provisions, tobacco, firewood and water as the rest of the fleet, and because of a murrain among the sheep and measles in the pigsty even her officers' stores were being eked out with the wicked old salt horse of his 'young gentleman' days, while all hands had been eating ship's biscuits for a great

while now. There was a small shoulder of not altogether
healthy mutton for Jack's dinner: 'Shall I invite the officer of
the watch?' he wondered. 'It is some time since I had I anyone to the cabin, apart from breakfast.' It was some time, too,
since he had spoken to anyone on a footing of real equality or
with any free exchange of minds. His officers – or rather
Captain Hamond's officers, for Jack had had no hand in
choosing or forming them – entertained him to dinner once a
week in the gunroom, and he invited them quite often to the
cabin, almost always breakfasting with the officer and midshipman of the morning watch; but these were never very
cheerful occasions . . .' The gentlemanly, but slightly Ben-
thamite, gunroom were strict observers of the naval etiquette
that prevented any subordinate from speaking to his captain
without being spoken to first; and they had grown thoroughly
used to Captain Hamond, to whose mind this was a congenial rigour. And then again they were a proud set of men –
most of them could afford to be – and they had a horror of
the ingratiating manoeuvres, the currying of favour that was
to be seen in some ships, or any hint of it: once they had had
an overpliable third lieutenant wished upon them, and they
had obliged him to exchange into the *Achilles* within a couple
of months. They carried this attitude pretty high, and without
disliking their temporary commander in the very least –
indeed they valued him exceedingly both as a seaman and a
fighting captain – they unconsciously imposed an Olympian
role upon him; and at times the silence in which he lived
made him feel utterly forlorn. At times only, however, for he
was not often idle; there were duties that even the most perfect first lieutenant could not take off his hands, and then
again in the forenoon he supervised the midshipmen's lessons
in his cabin. They were a likeable set of youngsters, and even
the Godlike presence of the captain, the severity of their
schoolmaster, and the scrubbed, staid example of their elders
could not repress their cheerfulness. Even hunger could not
do so, and they had been eating rats this last month and

more, rats caught in the bowels of the ship by the captain of
the hold and laid out, neatly skinned, opened and cleaned,
like tiny sheep, in the orlop, for sale at a price that rose week
by week, to reach its present shocking rate of fivepence a
knob.

Jack was fond of the young, and like many other captains
he took great care of their professional and social education,
of their allowances, and even of their morals; but his con-
stancy at their lessons was not entirely disinterested. He had
been a stupid boy at figures in his time, badly taught aboard,
and although he was a natural-born seaman he had only managed to pass for lieutenant by feverish rote-learning, the
interposition of Providence, and the presence of two friendly
captains on the board. In spite of his dear friend Queenie's
patient explanations of tangents, secants and sines, he had
never had a really firm grasp of the principles of spherical
trigonometry; his navigation had been a plain rule-of-thumb
progress from A to B, plane-sailing at its plainest; but fortunately the Navy had always provided him, as it provided all
other commanders, with a master learned in the art. Yet now,
perhaps affected by the scientific, hydrographic atmosphere
on the *Lively*, he studied the mathematics, and like some
other late-developers he advanced at a great pace. The
school-master was an excellent teacher when he was sober,
and whatever the midshipmen may have made of his lessons,
Jack profited by them: in the evenings, after the watch was
set, he would work lunars or read Grimble on Conic Sections
with real pleasure, in the intervals between writing to Sophie
and playing on his fiddle. 'How amazed Stephen will be,' he
reflected. 'How I shall come it the philosopher over him: and
how I wish the old soul were here.'

But this question of whether he should invite Mr Randall
to dinner was still in suspense, and he was about to decide it
when the captain of the top coughed significantly. 'Beg parding, your honour,' he said, 'but I think *Naiad*'s seen something.' The Cockney voice came strangely from his yellow

face and slanting eyes; but the *Lively* had been in Eastern waters for years and years, and her crew, yellow, brown, black and nominally white, had worked so long together that they all spoke with the accent of Limehouse Reach, Wapping or Deptford Yard.

High Bum was not the only man to have caught the flurry of movement on the deck of the next in line ahead. Mr Randall junior swarmed inwards from his spray-soaked post on the sprit-sail yardarm and ran skipping along the deck towards his messmates: his seven-year-old pipe could be heard in the top as he cried, 'She's rounding the point! She's rounding the point!'

The *Niobe* appeared as though by magic from the midst of the overlapping Hyères islands, tearing along under courses and topsails and throwing a fine white bow-wave. She might be bringing something in the way of food, something in the way of prizes (all the frigates had agreed to share), and in any case she meant a break from this extreme monotony; she was heartily welcome. 'And here's the *Weasel*,' piped the infant child.

The *Weasel* was a big cutter, the messenger that plied all too rarely from the fleet to the inshore frigates. She too would almost certainly be bringing stores, news of the outside world – what a happy combination!

The cutter was under a perfect cloud of sail, heeling over at forty-five degrees; and the squadron, hove-to off Giens, cheered as they saw her fetch the *Niobe*'s wake and then cross to windward, with the obvious intention of making a race of it. Topgallants and an outer jib broke out aboard the frigate, but the fore-topgallant split as it was sheeted home, and before the agitated Niobes could blunt up the Weasel was on her starboard beam, wronging her cruelly, taking the wind right out of her sails. The *Niobe*'s bow-wave diminished and the cutter shot past, cheering madly, to the delight of one and all. She had the *Lively*'s number flying – orders aboard for *Lively* – and she came down the line, rounding to under

the frigate's lee, her enormous mainsail flapping, cracking
like a shooting-gallery. But she made no motion towards
launching a boat: lay there with her captain bawling through
the wind for a line.

'No stores?' thought Jack in the top, frowning. 'Damn this.'
He put a leg over the side, feeling for the futtock-shrouds:
but someone had seen a familiar purple bag handing up
through the cutter's main-hatch, and there was a cry of 'Post'.
At this word Jack leant out for the backstay and shot down on
deck like a midshipman, forgetting his dignity and laddering
his fine white stockings. He stood within a yard of the quartermasters and the mate of the watch as the two bags came
jerking across the water. 'Bear a hand, bear a hand there,' he
called out; and when at last the bags were inboard he had to
make a strong effort to control his impatience while the midshipman passed them solemnly to Mr Randall, and while Mr
Randall brought them across the quarterdeck, took off his
hat, and said, '*Weasel* from the flag, sir, you please.'

'Thank you, Mr Randall,' said Jack, carrying them with a
fair show of deliberation into his cabin. Here he raped the
seals of the post-bag with furious haste, whipped off the cord
and riffled through the letters: three covers directed to Captain Aubrey, H.M.S. *Lively*, in Sophie's round but decided
hand, fat letters, triple at the very least. He thrust them into
his pocket, and smiling he turned to the little official bag, or
satchel, opened the tarred canvas, the oiled-silk inner envelope and then the small cover containing his orders, read
them, pursed his lips and read them again. 'Hallows,' he
called. 'Pass the word for Mr Randall and the master. Here,
letters to the purser for distribution. Ah, Mr Randall, signal
Naiad, if you please – permission to part company. Mr Norrey, be so good as to lay me a course for Calvette.'

FOR ONCE there was no violent hurry; for once that 'jading
impression of haste, of *losing not a minute*, forsooth' of which
Stephen had complained so often, was absent. This was the

season of almost uninterrupted northerly winds in the western Mediterranean, of the mistral, the gargoulenc and the tramontane, all standing fair for Minorca and the *Lively*'s
rendezvous; but it was important not to arrive off the island
too soon, not to stand off and on arousing suspicion; and as
Jack's orders, with their general instructions 'to disturb the
enemy's shipping, installations and communications' allowed
him a great deal of latitude, the frigate was now stretching
away across the Gulf of Lyons for the coast of Languedoc,
with as much sail as she could bear and her lee rail vanishing
from time to time under the racing white water. The morning's gunnery practice – broadside after broadside into the
unopposing sea – and now this glorious rushing speed in the
brilliant sun had done away with the cross looks and murmurs of discontent of the day before – no stores and no
cruise; these damned orders had cheated them of their little
cruise at the very moment they had earned it, and they
cursed the wretched *Weasel* for her ill-timed antics, her silly
cracking-on, her passion for showing away, so typical of those
unrated buggers. 'Was she had come along like a Christian
not a Turk, we should have been gone halfway to Elba,' said
Java Dick. But this was yesterday, and now brisk exercise,
quick forgetfulness, the possibility of something charming
over every fresh mile of the opening horizon, and above all
the comfortable pervading sense of wealth tomorrow, had
restored the *Lively*'s complacency. Her captain felt it as he
took a last turn on deck before going into his cabin to receive
his guests, and he felt it with a certain twinge of emotion, difficult to define: it was not envy, since he was wealthier than
any group of them put together, wealthier in *posse*, he added,
with a habitual crossing of his fingers. Yet it was envy, too:
they had a ship, they were part of a tightly-knit community.
They had a ship and he had not. Yet not exactly envy, not as
who should say envy . . . fine definitions fled down the wind,
as the glass turned, the Marine went forward to strike four
bells, and the midshipman of the watch heaved the log. He

hurried into the great cabin, glanced at the long table laid
athwartships, his silver plates blazing in the sun and sending
up more suns to join the reflected ripple of the sea on the
deck head (how long would the solid metal withstand that
degree of polishing?), glasses, plates, bowls, all fast and trim
in their fiddles, the steward and his mates standing there by
the decanters, looking wooden. 'All a-tanto, Killick?' he said.

'Stock and fluke, sir,' said his steward, looking beyond him
and signalling with an elegant jerk of his chin.

'You are very welcome, gentlemen,' said Jack, turning in the
direction of the chin. 'Mr Simmons, please to take the end of
the table; Mr Carew, if you will sit – easy, easy.' The chaplain,
caught off his balance by a lee-lurch, shot into his seat with
such force as almost to drive it through the deck. 'Lord Garron here; Mr Fielding and Mr Dashwood, pray be so good,' –
waving to their places. 'Now even before we begin,' he went
on, as the soup made its perilous way across the cabin, 'I
apologise for this dinner. With the best will in the world –
allow me, sir,' – extracting the parson's wig from the tureen
and helping him to a ladle – 'Killick, a nightcap for Mr Carew,
swab this, and pass the word for the midshipman of the
watch. Oh, Mr Butler, my compliments to Mr Norrey, and I
believe we may brail up the spanker during dinner. With the
best will in the world, I say, it can be but a Barmecide feast.'
That was pretty good, and he looked modestly down but it
occurred to him that the Barmecides were not remarkable for
serving fresh meat to their guests, and there, swimming in
the chaplain's bowl, was the unmistakable form of a bargeman, the larger of the reptiles that crawled from old biscuit,
the smooth one with the black head and the oddly cold taste
– the soup, of course, had been thickened with biscuit-
crumbs to counteract the roll. The chaplain had not been
long at sea; he might not know that there was no harm in the
bargeman, nothing of the common weevil's bitterness; and it
might put him off his food. 'Killick, another plate for Mr
Carew: there is a hair in his soup. Barmecide . . . But I partic-

ularly wished to invite you, since this is probably the last time I shall have the honour. We are bound for Gibraltar, by way of Minorca; and at Gibraltar Captain Hamond will return to the ship.' Exclamations of surprise, pleasure, civilly mixed with regret. 'And since my orders require me to harry the enemy installations along the coast, as well as his shipping, of course, I do not suppose we shall have much leisure for dining once we have raised Cape Gooseberry. How I hope we shall find something worthy of the *Lively*! I should be sorry to hand her over without at least a small sprig of laurel on her bows, or whatever is the proper place for laurels.'

'Does laurel grow along this coast, sir?' asked the chaplain. 'Wild laurel? I had always imagined it to be Greek. I do not know the Mediterranean, however, apart from books; and as far as I recall the ancients do not notice the coast of Languedoc.'

'Why, it has been gathered there, sir, I believe,' said Jack. 'And it is said to go uncommon well with fish. A leaf or two gives a haut relievo, but more is deadly poison, I am told.'

General considerations upon fish, a wholesome meat, though disliked by fishermen; Dover soles commended; porpoises, frogs, puffins rated as fish for religious purposes by Papists; swans, whales and sturgeon, fish royal; an anecdote of a bad oyster eaten by Mr Simmons at the Lord Mayor's banquet.

'Now this fish,' said Jack, as a tunny replaced the souptureen, 'is the only dish I can heartily recommend: he was caught over the side by that Chinaman in your division, Mr Fielding. The short one. Not Low Bum, nor High Bum, nor Jelly-belly.'

'John Satisfaction, sir?'

'That's the man. A most ingenious, cheerful fellow, and handy; he spun a long yarn with hairs from his messmates' pigtails and baited the hook with a scrap of pork-rind shaped like a fish, and so caught him. What is more, we have a decent bottle of wine to go with him. Not that I claim any credit for the wine, mark you; it was Dr Maturin that had the choosing of it – he understands these things – grows wine himself. By the bye, we shall touch at Minorca to pick him up.'

They should be delighted to see him again – hoped he was very well – looked forward much to the meeting. 'Minorca, sir?' cried the chaplain, however, having mulled over it. 'But did we not give Minorca back to the Spaniards? Is it not Spanish now?'

'Why, yes, so it is,' said Jack. 'I dare say he has a pass to travel: he has estates in those parts.' 'The Spaniards are far more civilised than the French in this war, as far as travel is concerned,' observed Lord Garron. 'A friend of mine, a Catholic, had leave to go from Santander to St James of Compostella because of a vow – no trouble at all – travelled as a private gentleman, no escort, nothing. And even the French are not so bad when it comes to men of learning. I saw in *The Times* the *Weasel* brought that a scientific cove from Birmingham had gone over to Paris to receive a prize from their Institute. It is your scientific chaps who are the ones for travelling, war or no war; and I believe, sir, that Dr Maturin is a genuine smasher in the scientific line?'

'Oh indeed he is,' cried Jack. 'A sort of Admiral Crichton – whip your leg off in a moment, tell you the Latin name of anything that moves,' – his eye caught a brisk yellow weevil hurrying across the table-cloth – 'speaks languages like a walking Tower of Babel, all except ours. Dear Lord,' he said, laughing heartily, 'to this day I don't believe he knows the odds between port and starboard. Suppose we drink his health?'

'With all my heart, sir,' cried the first lieutenant, with a conscious look at his shipmates, all of whom shared it more or less, as Jack had noticed at their first appearance in the cabin. 'But if you will allow me – *The Times*, sir, that Garron refers to, had a far, far more interesting announcement – a piece of news that filled the gunroom, which has the liveliest recollection of Miss Williams, with unbounded enthusiasm.

Sir, may I offer you our heartiest congratulations and wish you joy from all of us, and suggest that there is one toast that should take precedence even over Dr Maturin?'

Lively,
at sea
Friday, 18th

Sweetheart,

We drank your health with three times three on Monday; for the fleet tender brought us orders while we were polishing Cape Sicie, together with the post and your three dear letters, which quite made up for our being *diddled* out of our cruise. And unknown to me it also brought a copy of *The Times* with our announcement in it; which I had not yet seen, even.

I had invited most of the gunroom to dinner, and that good fellow Simmons brought it out, desiring to drink your health and happiness and saying the handsomest things about you – they had the liveliest recollection of Miss Williams in the Channel, all too short, were your most devoted, etc., very well put. I went as red as a new-painted tompion and hung my head like a maiden, and upon my honour I was near-hand blubbering like one, I so longed for you to be by me in this cabin again – it brought it back so clear. And he went on to say he was authorised by the gunroom to ask, should you prefer a tea-pot or a coffee-pot, with a suitable inscription? Drinking your health recovered me, and I said I thought a coffee-pot, begging the inscription might say that the *Lively* preserved the *liveliest* memory. That was pretty well received, and even the parson (a dull dog) laughed hearty in time, when the bonne mot was explained to him.

Then that night, standing in with a fine top-gallant-sail breeze, we raised Cape Gooseberry and bore away for the signal-station: we landed a couple of miles from

it and proceeded across the dunes to take it from
behind, for just as I suspected its two twelve-pounders
were so placed that they could only fire out to sea or at
the most sweep 75° of the shore, if traversed. It was a
long grind, with the loose sand flying in the wind they
always have in these parts filling our eyes and noses and
getting into the locks of our pistols. The parson says
that the Ancients did not notice this coast; and the
Ancients knew what they were about, deep old files –
one infernal dust-storm after another. But, however, we
got there at last, steering by compass, without their
smoking us, gave a cheer and carried the place directly.
The Frenchmen left as we came in, all except a little
ensign, who fought like a hero until Bonden collared
him from behind, when he burst into tears and flung
down his sword. We spiked the guns, destroyed the
semaphore, blew up the magazine and hurried back to
the boats, which had pulled along, carrying their signal-
books with us. It was a neat piece of work, though slow:
if we had had to reckon with tides, which there are
none of here, you know, we should have been sadly out.
The Livelies are not used to this sort of caper, but some
of them shape well, and they all have willing minds.

The little officer was still in a great passion when
we got him aboard. We should never have dared to
show our faces, says he, had the *Diomède* still been on
the coast; his brother was aboard her, and she would
have blown us out of the water; someone must have
told us – there were traitors about and he had been
betrayed. He said something to the effect that she had
gone down to Port-Vendres three days or three hours
before, but he spoke so quick we could not be certain –
no English, of course. Then, something of a cross-sea
getting up as we made our offing, he spoke no more,
poor lad: piped down altogether, sick as a dog.

The *Diomède* is one of their heavy forty-gun eighteen-pounder frigates, just such a meeting as I have been longing for and do long for ever more now, because – don't think badly of me sweetheart – I must give up the command of this ship in a few days' time, and this is my last chance to distinguish myself and earn another; and as anyone will tell you, a ship is as necessary to a sailor as a wife, in war-time. Not at once, of course, but well before everything is over. So we bore away for Port-Vendres (you will find it on the map, down in the bottom right-hand corner of France, where the mountains run down to the sea, just before Spain) picking up a couple of fishing-boats on the way and raising Cape Bear a little after sunset, with the light still on the mountains behind the town. We bought the barca-longas' fish and promised them their boats again, but they were very glum, and we could not get anything out of them – 'Was the *Diomède* in Port-Vendres? – Yes: perhaps. – Was she gone for Barcelona? – Well, maybe. – Were they a pack of Tom Fools, that did not understand French or Spanish? – Yes, Monsieur' – spreading their hands to show they were only Jack-Puddings, and sorry for it. And the young ensign, on being applied to, turns haughty – amazed that a British officer should so far forget himself as to expect him to help in the interrogation of prisoners; and a piece about Honneur and Patier, which would have been uncommon edifying, I dare say, if we could have understood it all.

So I sent Randall in one of the barca-longas to look into the port. It is a long harbour with a dog-leg in it and a precious narrow mouth protected by a broad mole and two batteries, one on each side, and another of 24-pounders high up on Béar: a tricky piece of navigation, to take a ship in or out with their infernal tramontane blowing right across the narrow mouth, but an excellent sheltered harbour inside with deep water up to the quays. He came back; had seen a fair amount of shipping inside, with a big square-rigged vessel at the far end; could not be sure it was the *Diomède* – two boats rowing guard and the dark of the moon – but it was likely.

Not to bore you with the details, dear, dear Sophie, we laid out five hawsers an-end with our best bower firm in gritty ooze to warp the frigate out in case the high battery should knock any spars away, stood in before dawn with a moderate NNE breeze and began hammering the batteries guarding the entrance. Then when there was plenty of light, and a brilliant day it was too, we sent all the ships' boys and such away in the boats, wearing the Marines' red coats, pulling up the coast to a village round the next headland; and as I expected, all the horse-soldiers, a couple of troops of 'em, went pounding along the winding coast road (the only one) to stop them landing. But before daylight we had sent off the barca-longas, crammed with men under hatches, to the other side of Béar, right inshore; and at the signal they dashed for the land close-hauled (these lateens lie up amazingly), landed at a little beach this side of the cape, jumped round to the back of the southern battery, took it, turned its guns on the other over the water and knocked it out, or what the frigate had left of it. By now our boats had come flying back and we jumped in; and while the frigate kept up a continual fire on the coast road to keep the soldiers from coming back, we pulled as fast as we could for the harbour. I had great hopes of cutting her out, but alas she was not the *Diomède* at all – only a hulking great storeship called the *Dromadaire*. She gave no real trouble, and a party took her down the harbour under topsails; but then an unlucky gust coming off the mountains and being an unweatherly awkward griping beast, very much by the head, she stuck fast in the harbour-mouth and bilged directly, on the mole. So we burnt her to the

water-line, set fire to everything else except the fishing-
boats, blew up the military works on either side with
their own powder, and collected all our people: Killick
had spent part of his time shopping, and he brought
soft tack, fresh milk, butter, coffee, and as many eggs as
he could get into his hat. The Livelies behaved well –
no breaking into wine-shops – and it was pretty to see
the Marines formed on the quay, as trimly squared as at
divisions, although indeed they looked pitiful and lost
in checkered shirts and seamen's frocks. We returned
to the boats, all sober and correct, and proceeded to the
frigate.

But now the fort up on Cape Béar was playing on
the frigate, so she had warped out; and a couple of gunboats came down the coast to get between us and her.
They were peppering us with grape from their 18-
pounders, and there was nothing for it but to close
them; which we did, and I have never been so surprised
in my life as when I saw my launch's crew just as we
were about to board the nearest. As you know, they are
mostly Chinamen or Malays – a quiet civil well-
behaved set of men. One half of 'em dived straight into
the sea and the rest crouched low against the gunwale.
Only Bonden and Killick and young Butler and I gave
something of a cheer as we came alongside, and I said
to myself, 'Jack, you're laid by the lee; you have gone
along with a set of fellows that won't follow you.' However, there was nothing for it, so we gave our sickly
cheer and jumped aboard.

He paused, the ink drying on his pen: the impression was still
immensely strong – the Chinese swarming over the side at
the last second to avoid the musketry, silently tackling their
men in pairs, one tripping him up, ignoring blows, the other
cutting his throat to the bone, instantly leaving him for the
next – systematic, efficient, working from aft forward, with

nothing but a few falsetto cries of direction: no fury, no hot
rage. And immediately after the first assault, the Javamen
shooting up the other side, having dived under the keel, their
wet brown hands gripping the rail all along the gunboat's
length: Frenchmen shrieking, running up and down the slippery deck, the great lateen flapping to and fro; and still that
silent close-work, knife alone, and cords – a terrible quiet
eagerness. His own opponent in the bows, a thickset determined seaman in a woollen cap, going over the side at last,
the water clouding red over him. Himself shouting 'Belay that
sheet, there. Down with her helm. Prisoners to the fore-
hatch,' and Bonden's shocked reply. 'There ain't no prisoners,
sir.' And then the deck, bright, bright red in the sun: the Chinamen squatting in pairs, methodically, quickly stripping the
dead, the Malays piling the heads in neat heaps like round-
shot, and one routing in the belly of a corpse. Two men at the
wheel already, their spoil next to them in a bundle: the sheet
properly belayed. He had seen some ugly sights – the slaughter-house of a seventy-four during a hard-fought fleet engagement, boardings by the dozen, the bay of Aboukir after the
Orion blew up – but he felt his stomach close and heave: the
taking was professional, as professional as anything could be,
and it sickened him with his trade. A strong impression: but
how to convey it when you are no great hand with a pen? In
the lamplight he stared at the gash in his forearm, fresh blood
still oozing through the bandage, and reflected; all at once it
occurred to him that of course he had not the slightest wish
to convey it; nor anything like it. As far as dear Sophie was
concerned life at sea was to be – why, not exactly an eternal
picnic, but something not altogether unlike; occasional hard-
ships, to be sure (shortage of coffee, fresh milk, vegetables),
and guns going off now and then, and a clash of swords, but
without any real people getting hurt: those that happened to
die did so instantly, from wounds that could not be seen; they
were only figures in the casualty list. He dipped his pen and
went on.

But I was mistaken; they boarded over both sides, behaved remarkably, and the work was over in a few minutes. The other gunboat sheered off as soon as the *Lively*, shooting very neat with her bow guns, sent a couple of balls over her. So we took the boats in tow, joined the frigate, made sail in double-quick time, recovered our hawsers, and stood out to sea, steering ESE½E; for I am afraid we cannot drop down to Barcelona after the *Diomède*, as that would get us far to the leeward of Minorca and I might be late for my rendezvous, which would never do. As it is, we have time and to spare, and expect to raise Fornells at dawn.

Dearest Sophie, you will forgive these blots, I trust; the ship is skipping about on a short cross-sea as we lie hove-to, and most of the day I have spent trying to be in three places at once if not more. You will say I ought not to have gone ashore at Port-Vendres, and that it was selfish and unfeeling to Simmons; and indeed generally speaking a captain should leave these things to his first lieutenant – it is his great chance for distinguishing himself. But I could not quite tell how they would behave, do you see? Not that I doubted their conduct, but it seemed to me they were perhaps the kind of men who would fight best in a defensive battle or a regular fleet action – that perhaps they lacked the speed and dash for this sort of thing, for want of practice – they have done no cutting-out. That is why I carried it out in broad day-light, it being easier to see what goes wrong; and glad I am I did, too, for it was nip and tuck at moments. Upon the whole they all behaved well – the Marines did wonders, as they always do – but once or twice things might have taken an awkward turn. The ship was hulled in a few places, her foremast wounded in the hounds, her cross-jack yardarm carried away, and her rigging cut up a little; but she could fight an action tomorrow, and our losses were very slight, as you will see from the public letter. Her captain suffered from nothing but extreme apprehension for his personal safety and the total loss of his breakfast-cup, shattered in being struck down into the hold on clearing for action.

But I promise not to do so again; and this is a promise I dare say Fate will help me keep, for if this wind holds, I should be in Gibraltar in a few days, with no ship to do it from.

Do it from, he wrote again; and leaning his head on his arms he went fast asleep.

'FORNELLS ONE POINT to the starboard bow, sir,' said the first lieutenant.

'Very good,' said Jack in a low voice. His head was aching as though it might split and he was filled with gloom which so often came after an action. 'Keep her standing off and on. Is the gunboat cleaned up yet?'

'No, sir. I am afraid she is not,' said Simmons.

Jack said nothing. Simmons had had a hard day yesterday, barking his shins cruelly as he ran up the stone steps of Port-Vendres quay, and naturally he was less active; but even so Jack was a little surprised. He walked over to the side and looked down into their prize: no, she most certainly had not been cleaned. The severed hand that he had last seen bright red was now blackish brown and shrunken – you would have said a huge dead spider. He turned away, looked aloft at the boatswain and his party in the rigging, over the other side at the carpenter and his mates at work on a shot-hole, and with what he meant to be a smile he said, 'Well, first things first. Perhaps we shall be able to send her away for Gibraltar this evening. I should like to have a thorough look at her first, however.' This was the first time he had ever had to reproach Simmons even by implication, and the poor man took it very hard; he hobbled along, just keeping pace with his captain,

his face so concerned that Jack was about to utter some soft-
ening remark when Killick appeared again.

'Coffee's up, sir,' he said crossly; and as Jack hurried into
his cabin he heard the words 'stone cold now – on the table
since six bells – told 'im again and again – enough trouble to
get it, and now it's left to go cold.' They seemed to be
addressed to the Marine sentry, whose look of shocked horror, of refusal to hear or participate in any way, was in exact
proportion to the respect, even to the awe, in which Jack was
held in the ship.

In point of fact the coffee was still so hot that it almost
burnt his mouth. 'Prime coffee, Killick,' he said, after the first
pot. A surly grunt, and without turning round Killick said, 'I
suppose you'll be wanting another 'ole pot, sir.'

Hot and strong, how well it went down! A pleasurable
activity began to creep into his dull, torpid mind. He
hummed a piece of *Figaro*, breaking off to butter a fresh piece
of toast. Killick was a cross-grained bastard, who supposed
that if he sprinkled his discourse with a good many sirs, the
words in between did not signify: but still he had procured
this coffee, these eggs, this butter, this soft tack, on shore and
had put them on the table the morning after a hot engagement – ship still cleared for action and the galley knocked
sideways by the fire from Cape Béar. Jack had known Killick
ever since his first command, and as he had risen in rank so
Killick's sullen independence had increased; he was angrier
than usual now because Jack had wrecked his number three
uniform and lost one of his gloves: 'Coat torn in five places –
cutlash slash in the forearm which how can I ever darn *that*?
Bullet 'ole all singed, never get the powder-marks out.
Breeches all a-hoo, and all this nasty blood everywhere, like
you'd been a-wallowing in a lay-stall, sir. What Miss would
say, I don't know, sir. God strike me blind. Epaulette 'acked,
fair 'acked to pieces. (Jesus, what a life.)'

Outside he could hear pumps, the hose carrying across,
and the cry of 'Wring and pass, wring and pass,' that meant

swabs were going aboard the gunboats; and presently, after Killick had displayed his yesterday's uniform again, with a detailed reminder of its cost, Mr Simmons sent to ask whether he had a moment.

'Dear me,' thought Jack, 'was I so very unpleasant and forbidding? Ask him to step in. Come in, come in, Mr Simmons; sit down and have a cup of coffee.'

'Thank you, Sir,' said Simmons, casting a reconnoitring look at him. 'Wonderful odour, grateful to the mind. I ventured to disturb you, sir, because Garron, going through the cabin of the gunboat, found this in a drawer. I have not your command of French, sir, but glancing through I thought you ought to see it at once.' He passed a broad flat book, its covers made of sheet-lead.

'Hey, hey!' cried Jack, with a bright and lively eye. 'Here's a palm in Gilead, by God – private signals – code by numbers – lights – recognition in fog – Spanish and other allied signals. What does bannière de partance mean, do you think? Pavillon de beaupré, that's a jack. Misaine's the foremast, though you might not think it. Hunes de perroquet? Well, damn the hunes de perroquet, the pictures are clear enough. Charming, ain't they?' He turned back to the front. 'Valid until the twenty-fifth. They change with the moon, I suppose. I hope we may profit by it – a little treasure while it lasts. How do you come along with the gunboat?'

'We are pretty forward, sir. She will be ready for you as soon as her decks are dry.' There was a superstition in the Navy that damp was mortal to superior officers and that its malignant effects increased with rank; few first lieutenants turned out before the dawn washing of the decks was almost finished, and no commander or post-captain until they had been swabbed, squeegeed and flogged dry. The gun-boat was being flogged at this moment.

'I had thought of sending her down to Gibraltar with young Butler, a responsible petty-officer or two, and the crew of the launch. He did very well – pistolled her captain – and so did they, in their heathen fashion. The command would do him good. Have you any observations to offer, Mr Simmons?' he asked, seeing the lieutenant's face.

'Well, sir, since you are so good as to ask me, might I suggest another crew? I say nothing whatsoever against these men – quiet, attentive, sober, give no trouble, never brought to the gangway – but we took the Chinamen out of an armed junk with no cargo, almost certainly a pirate, and the Malays out of a proa of the same persuasion, and I feel that if they were sent away, they might be tempted to fall to their old ways. If we had found a scrap of evidence, we should have strung 'em up. We had the yardarm rigged, but Captain Hamond, being a magistrate at home, had scruples about evidence. There was some rumour of their having ate it.'

'Pirates? I see, I see. That explains a great deal. Yes, yes; of course. Are you sure?'

'I have no doubt of it myself, both from the circumstances and from remarks that they have let fall since. Every second vessel is a pirate in those seas, or will be if occasion offers, right round from the Persian Gulf to Borneo. But they look upon things differently there, and to tell you the truth, I should be loath to see High Bum or John Satisfaction swinging in a noose now; they have improved wonderfully since they came among us; they have given up praying to images and spitting on deck, and they listen to the tracts Mr Carew reads them with proper respect.'

'Oh, *now*, there's no question,' cried Jack. 'If the Judge Advocate of the Fleet were to tell me to hang an able seaman, let alone the captain of the maintop, I should tell him to – I should decline. But, as you say, we must not lead them into temptation. It was only a passing thought; she might just as well stay in company. Indeed, it would be better. Mr Butler shall have her, though; pray be so good as to pick a suitable crew.'

The gunboat stayed in company, and at dusk the *Lively's* launch pulled round under her stern on its way inshore,

towards the dark loom of the island. Mr Butler, packing his
own quarterdeck, ordered the salute in a voice that started
deep and shot up into a strangled, blushing squeak, his first
experience of the anguish of command.

Jack, wrapped in a boat-cloak, with a dark-lantern between
his knees, sat in the stern-sheets, filled with pleasurable
anticipation. He had not seen Stephen Maturin for a vast
stretch of time, made even longer by the grinding monotony
of the blockade: how lonely he had been for the want of that
harsh, unpleasant voice! Two hundred and fifty-nine men living in promiscuity, extreme promiscuity for the lower-deck,
and the two hundred and sixtieth a hermit: of course it was
the common lot of captains, it was the naval condition, and
like all other lieutenants he had strained every nerve to reach
this stark isolation; but admitting the fact made precious little odds to what it felt like. No consolation in philosophy.
Stephen would have seen Sophie only a few weeks ago, perhaps even less; he would certainly have messages from her,
possibly a letter. He put his hand secretly to the crinkle in his
bosom, and lapsed into a reverie. A moderate following sea
heaved the launch in towards the land; with the rhythm of
the waves and the long even pull and creak of the oars he
dozed, smiling in his almost sleep.

He knew the creek well, as indeed he knew most of the
island, having been stationed there when it was a British possession; it was called Cala Blau, and he and Stephen had
often come over from Port Mahon to watch a pair of red-
legged falcons that had their nest on the cliff above.

He recognised it at once when Bonden, his coxswain, looked
up from the glowing compass and gave a low order, changing
course a trifle. There was the curious peaked rock, the ruined
chapel on the skyline, the even blacker place low on the cliff-
face that was in fact a cave where monk-seals bred. 'Lay on
your oars,' he said softly, and flashed the dark-lantern towards
the shore, staring through the darkness. No answering light.
But that did not worry him. Give way,' he said, and as the oars

dipped he held his watch to the light. They had timed it well: ten minutes to go. Not that Stephen had, or by his nature ever could have, a naval sense of time; and in any event this was only the first of the four days of rendezvous.

Looking eastwards he saw the first stars of the Pleiades on the clear horizon; once before he had fetched Stephen from a lonely beach when the stars were just so. The launch lay gently pitching, kept just stern-on by a touch of the oars. Now the Pleiades had heaved clear, the whole tight constellation. He signalled again. 'Nothing more likely than he cannot strike a light,' he thought, still without any apprehension. 'In any case, I should like to walk there again; and I shall leave him a private sign. Run her in, Bonden,' he said. 'Handsomely, handsomely. No noise at all.'

The boat slipped over the black, starlit water, pausing twice again to listen: once they heard the snort of a seal breaking surface, then nothing until the sand grated under her bows.

Up and down the water-line of the half-moon beach, with his hands behind his back, turning over various private marks that might make Stephen smile if he missed this first rendezvous: some degree of tension, to be sure, but none of the devouring anxiety of that first night long ago, south of Palamós, when he had had no idea of his friend's capabilities.

Saturn came up behind the Pleiades; up and up, nearly ten degrees from the edge of the sea. He heard stones rattle on the cliff-path above. With a lift of his heart he looked up, picked out the form moving there, and whistled low *Deh vieni, non tardar*.

No reply for a moment, then a voice from half-way up, 'Captain Melbury?'

Jack stood behind a rock, took a pistol from his belt and cocked it. 'Come down,' he said pleasantly; and directing his voice into the cave, 'Bonden, pull out.'

'Where are you?' whispered the voice at the foot of the cliff.

When Jack was certain that there was no movement on the path above he stepped from the rock, walked over the sand,

and shone his light on a man in a brown cloak, an olive-faced man with a fixed, wary expression, exaggerated in this sudden light against the darkness. He came forward, showing his open hands, and said again, 'Captain Melbury?'

'Who are you, sir?' asked Jack.

'Joan Maragall, sir,' he whispered in the clipped English of the Minorcans, very like that of Gibraltar. 'I come from Esteban Domanova. He says, Sophia, Mapes, Guarnerius.'

Melbury Lodge was the house they had shared; Stephen's full name was Maturin y Domanova; no one else on earth knew that Jack had once nearly bought a Guarnerius. He uncocked the pistol and thrust it back.

'Where is he?'

'Taken.'

'Taken?'

'Taken. He gave me this for you.'

In the beam of the lantern the paper showed a straggle of disconnected lines: *Dear J* – some words, lines of figures – the signature S, tailing away off the corner, a wavering curve.

'This is not his writing,' whispering still in the darkness, caution rising still over this certainty of complete disaster. 'This is not his hand.'

'He has been tortured.'

3

UNDER THE SWINGING lamp in the cabin, he looked intently into Maragall's face. It was a tough, youngish, lined face, pock-marked and with bad teeth; an ill-looking cast in one eye, but the other large and as it were gentle. What to make of him? The fluent Minorcan English, perfectly comprehensible but *foreign*, was difficult to judge for integrity: the open sheet of paper under the lamp had been written with a piece of charcoal; almost the whole message had crumbled away or smudged. *Do not* – perhaps wait; then several words underlined with only the line remaining – *send this* – a name: St Joseph? – *not to trust.* Then the traces of figures, five painful rows of them, and the trailing S.

The whole thing might be an elaborate trap: it might also be intended to incriminate Stephen. He listened to the run of words, examined the paper, weighed the possibilities, with his mind working fast. There were times when there was something very young and slightly ridiculous about Jack; it was a side of him that Sophie loved beyond measure; but no one looking at him now, or in action, would have believed in its existence.

He led Maragall through his narrative again – the first trouble following a denunciation to the Spanish authorities, quickly settled by the production of an American passport and the intervention of the vicar-general: Señor Domanova was an American of Spanish origin. Then the interference of the French, their removal of the suspect to their own headquarters in spite of violent protests. The jealousy between the French and Spanish allies at all levels, administration, army, navy, civilian population – the French way of behaving as though they were in conquered territory, which was bringing even Catalans and Castilians together. Particular hatred for this alleged French purchasing commission, which was in fact an intelligence unit, small but very active, recently joined by a Colonel Auger (a fool) and Captain Dutourd (brilliant) straight from Paris, busily recruiting informers, as bad as the Inquisition. Growing detestation of the French, almost universal apart from some opportunists and the leaders of the Fraternitat, an organisation that hoped to use them rather than the English against the Castilians – to win Catalan independence from Napoleon rather than George III.

'And you belong to a different organisation, sir?' said Jack.

'Yes, sir. I am the head of the Confederacio on the island; that is why I know Esteban so well. That is why I have been able to get messages in and out of his cell. We are the only

organisation that has wide support, the only one that really
does anything apart from to make speeches and denuncia-
tions. We have two men in their place in the day-time, and
my brother, which is a priest, has been in several times:
myself was able to take him the laudanum he asked for and
speak him a few minutes through the bars, when he told me
the words I was to say.'

'How is he?'

'Weak. They are quite pitiless.'

'Where is he? Where is their headquarters?'

'Do you know Port Mahon?'

'Yes. Very well.'

'Do you know where the English commandant used to
live?'

'Martinez's place?'

'Is right. They have taken it over. The little house at the
back of the garden they use for questioning – farther from the
street. But you can hear the shrieks from St Anna's. Sometimes, at three or four in the morning, they carry bodies down
and throw them into the harbour behind the tanneries.'

'How many are there?'

'Five officers now, and a guard quartered in the Alfonso
barracks. A dozen men on duty at a time – the guard changes
at seven. No sentries outside, no show, all very quiet and
retired. Then there are a few civilians, interpreters, servants,
cleaners; two of them belong to us, as I have say – said.'

Eight bells struck; the watch changed overhead. Jack
glanced at the barometer – sinking, sinking.

'Listen, Mr Maragall,' he said. 'I shall tell you my general
course of action: be so good as to make any observations that
occur to you. I have a French gunboat here, captured yesterday: I shall run her into Port Mahon, land a party say at Johnson's Steps or Boca Chica, march up in detached groups
behind St Anna's to the garden wall, take the house as silently
as possible and either return to the gunboat or behind the
town to Cala Garau. The weak points are, entrance into the

port, guides, alternative lines of retreat. In the first place, can you tell me whether there is any French ship in? How are French vessels received, what are the formalities, visits, moorings?'

'This is far from my line. I am a lawyer, an advocate,' he said, after a long pause. 'No, there is no French ship in at present. When they come, they exchange signals off Cape Mola – but what signals? Then there is the pratique boat, for plague and health; if they have a clean bill of health it leads them to their moorings, otherwise to the quarantine reach. I believe the French moor above the customs house. The captain waits on the port-admiral – but when? I could tell you this, all this, if I had time. My cousin is the doctor.'

'There is no time.'

'Yes, sir, there is time,' said Maragall slowly. 'But can you indeed enter the port? You rely on their not firing on French colours, on confusing signals?'

'I shall get in.'

'Very well. Then if now you put me ashore before light, I shall meet you in the pratique boat or tell my cousin what he must do – meet you in any case, deal with what formalities there may be and tell you what we have managed to arrange. You have said guides—certainly: other lines of retreat, yes. I must consult.'

'You take this to be a feasible plan, I collect?'

'Yes. To get in, yes. To get out – well, you know the harbour as well as I do. Guns, batteries all the way for four miles. It is the only plan, however, with so little time. It would be terrible to run in, and then to arouse suspicion by some little nonsense that my friends could tell you in a moment. You are unwilling to put me ashore, are you not?'

'No sir. I am no great politician or judge of character, but my friend is: I am happy to stake my head on his choice.' Sending for the officer of the watch he said, 'Mr Fielding, we shall run in. To Cala Blau?' – looking at Maragall, who nodded. 'To Cala Blau. All sail she will bear; blue cutter to be ready at a moment's notice.' Fielding repeated the order and hurried out, calling 'Watch, watch, about ship,' before he was past the sentry. Jack listened to the running feet for a moment, and said, 'While we stand in, let us go over the details. May I offer you some wine – a sandwich?'

'FOUR BELLS, sir,' said Killick, waking him. 'Mr Simmons is in the cabin.'

'Mr Simmons,' said Jack in a harsh, formal voice. 'I am taking the gunboat into Port Mahon at sunset. This is an expedition in which I shall ask none of the officers to come with me; I believe none is intimately acquainted with the town. I should like those of the launch's crew who choose to volunteer, but it must be represented to them, that this is an expedition in which – it is an expedition of some danger. The pinnace is to remain at the cave at Cala Blau from the coming midnight until the following sunset, when, unless it receives orders, it is to rejoin the ship at the rendezvous I have marked here. The launch at Rowley's Creek, with the same orders. They are to be victualled for a week. The frigate will stand off and on to windward of Cape Mola, having sent them in, and close with the land at dawn under French colours, remaining out of gunshot, however; I hope to join her at that time or during the course of the day. If I do not appear by six o'clock she is to proceed to the first rendezvous without loss of time; and after cruising twenty-four hours there, to Gibraltar. Here are your orders; you will see that I have written clearly what I now repeat – there is to be no attempt whatsoever at any rescue, These orders are to be followed to the letter.' The idea of these good, brave, but essentially unenterprising and unimaginative men plunging about an unknown countryside, with the frigate a prey to the Spanish gunboats or the great batteries of St Philip's or Cape Mola made him repeat these words. Then, after a slight pause and in a diffident tone, he said, 'My dear Simmons, here are some personal papers and letters that I will trouble you with, if I may, to be sent home from Gibraltar in the event of things going amiss.'

The first lieutenant looked down, and then up again into Jack's face; he was profoundly troubled, and he was obviously seeking for his words. Jack did not wish to hear them: this was his own affair – he was the only man aboard, apart from his followers, who knew Port Mahon backwards, above all the only one who had been in Molly Harte's garden and her music-room; and at this pitch of cold tension he wanted no gestures of any kind, either. He had no emotion to spare for anyone else. 'Be so good, Mr Simmons, as to speak to the launch's crew,' he said with a trace of impatience. 'Those who wish to come will be taken off duty; they must rest. And I should like a word with my coxswain. The gunboat is to come alongside; I shall go into her when I am ready. That will be all, Mr Simmons.'

'Yes, sir,' said Simmons. He turned in the door and paused, but Jack was already busy with his preparations.

'Killick,' he said, 'my sword is dull from yesterday. Take it to the armourer; I want it shaving-sharp. And bid him look at my pistols: new flints. Bonden, there you are. You remember Mahon?'

'Like the palm of my hand, sir.'

'Good. We are taking the gunboat in this evening. The Doctor is in prison there, and they are torturing him. You see that book? It has their signals in it: check the gunboat's flags and lanterns and see everything is there. If not, get it. Take your money and warm clothes: we may end up in Verdun.'

'Aye aye, sir. Here's Mr Simmons, sir.'

The first lieutenant reported that the entire launch's crew had volunteered: he had taken them off duty. 'And, sir,' he added, 'the officers and men will take it very unkind indeed if some of them may not come along – if you will not pick from them. I do beg you will not disappoint me and the whole gun-room, sir.'

'I know what you mean, Simmons – honour their feelings –

should feel the same myself. But this is a very particular, hey, expedition. My orders must stand. Is the gunboat alongside?'

'Just ranging up on the quarter now, sir.'

'Let Mr West and his mates check her rigging before I go aboard, in half an hour. And the launch's crew are to be provided with red woollen hats, Mediterranean style,' he said, looking at his watch.

'Yes, sir,' said Simmons in a flat, dead, wretched tone. Half an hour later Jack came on deck in a shabby uniform and Hessian boots, a cloak and a plain cocked hat. Glancing at the sky he said, 'I shall not return to the ship until after Port Mahon, Mr Simmons. At eight bells in the afternoon watch, pray send the launch across. Good-bye.'

'Good-bye, sir.'

They shook hands. Jack nodded to the other officers, touched his hat, and they piped him down the side.

As soon as he was aboard the gunboat he took the tiller and sent her racing away down to leeward with the fresh breeze on her larboard quarter. The island rose in the south, headland after headland stretching away, and he brought her up in a long sweet curve. She was not one of the regulation Toulon gunboats, or the heavy Spanish creatures that swept out from Algeciras every time there was a calm, creeping over the still water; she was not one of those port-bound floating carriages for a single heavy gun, or he would never have brought her away, but a half-decked barca-longa with a long slide that allowed her gun to be run in and stowed against her short thick forward-raking mast – a vessel perfectly capable of running down the Mediterranean, and of sweeping in and out of any port.

She was no fairy, though. As he brought her up and up into the wind the tiller was hard under his hand, and he felt the weight of that gun forward. Yet once she was close up, right up, pointing even closer than five, she held her course, never offering to fall to or gripe, but shouldering the short seas bravely; and the spray came whistling aft.

This was the sort of thing he understood. The immense lateen on its curving yard was not so familiar as a square rig nor a cutter, but the essence was the same, and he was like a good horseman riding a well-spirited horse from another stable. He put the gunboat through all her paces – unspectacular, but dogged, firm and sure – tracing great curves round the frigate, weaving to and fro until the sun sloped far westwards.

He brought her under the *Lively*'s lee, signalled for the launch, and went below. While the red-hatted crew came aboard he sat in the late captain's cabin, a low triangular cupboard aft, studying the charts and the signal-book: not that he had much need of either – the Minorcan waters were home to him, and the rows of flags and lights were sharp in his mind – but any contact with the ship at this point meant a waste of that particular strength he should need in a few hours' time. In a few hours, if only the dropping glass and the ugly look of the sky did not mean a full gale of wind.

Bonden reported all hands present and sober, and he went on deck. He was completely withdrawn: he shook his head impatiently at the ragged, spontaneous cheer, put his helm astarboard and bore away for the eastern cape. He saw Killick lurking there against his orders, looking sullen, with a basket of food and some bottles, but he looked beyond him for the quartermaster, handing over the tiller and giving him the course to steer; and then he began his steady pace to and fro, gauging the progress of the wind, the speed of the gunboat, the changing lie of the land.

The shore went by a mile to starboard, well-known headlands, beaches, creeks turning slowly; very like a dream; and the men were quiet. He had a momentary feeling that his pace and turn, pace and turn in this silence was taking him from reality, spoiling his concentration, and he went below, crouching into the cabin.

'You are up to your God-damn-ye capers again, I see,' he said coldly.

Killick dared not speak, but put cold mutton, bread and

butter, and claret in front of him. 'I must eat,' he said to himself, and deliberately set to his meal: but his stomach was
closed – even the wine seemed hard in his gullet. This had
not happened to him before, in no action, emergency or crisis. 'It don't signify,' he said, pushing the things aside.

When he came on deck again the sun was only a span from
the high land to the west, and broad on the starboard bow lay
Cape Mola. The wind had freshened, blowing gusty, and the
men were baling: it would be touch and go to round the cape,
and they might have to sweep in. But so far the timing was
right. He wanted to pass the outer batteries in the light, with
his French colours clearly seen, and to move up the long harbour as darkness fell. He glanced up at the tricolour at the
peak, at the hoists that Bonden had ready laid out at the sig-
nal-halliards, and he took the helm.

Now there was no time for reflection: now the whole of his
person was engaged in governing immediate material problems. The headland and the white surf were racing towards
them; he must round the point just so, and even with the
nicest judgment a back-eddy off the cliff might lay him right
down or sweep him away to leeward.

'Right, Bonden,' he said, as the signal-station came into
view. The stoppered flags shot up, broke out and showed
clear. His eye darted from the sea and the straining sail to the
height, where the Spanish ensign flew still in the breeze. If
his was the right signal, it would dip. Motionless up there,
motionless, and flat as a board in the distance. Motionless
and then at last it jerked down and up again.

'Acknowledge,' he said. 'Start the sheet. Stand by the halliards, there.' The seamen were in their places, silent, glancing from the sky to the rigid sail. Bracing himself and
tightening his mouth he brought up the helm: the gunboat
answered instantly, her lee-rail vanishing deeper and deeper
under the foam: the wind was abeam, she lay over, over, and
here was St Philips on his larboard bow. A broad line of white
scum, marking the edge of the full wind, a quarter of a mile

ahead: she was through it, shooting into the calm water under the lee of the cape, gliding on an even keel.

'Satisfaction, take the helm,' he said. 'Bonden, con the ship.'

The two sides, the approach to the harbour, were running together, and where they almost joined lay the narrow mouth with its heavy batteries on either side. Some of the casemates were lit, but there was still light enough over the water for a watcher to take notice of an officer at the helm – an unnatural sight. Nearer, nearer: and the gunboat moved silently through the mouth, close enough to toss a biscuit on to the muzzles of the forty-two-pounders at the water's edge. A voice in the twilight called out, 'Parlez-vous français?' and cackled: another shouted 'Hijos de puta.'

Ahead lay the broad stretch with the hospital island in it, the Lazaretto, a good mile away on the starboard bow; the last reflection of the day had left the hilltops, and the long harbour was filled with a deep purple, shading to blackness. Fitful gusts from the tramontane outside ruffled its surface, ugly gusts sometimes; and there beyond the lights – they were increasing every moment – was the gap in the hills where just such a gust had laid the Agamemnon on her beam ends in '98.

'Brail up,' he said. 'Out sweeps.' He fixed the Lazaretto Island, staring till his eyes watered; and at last a boat put off. 'Silence fore and aft,' he called. 'No hailing, no speaking: d'ye hear me there?'

'Boat on the starboard bow, sir,' murmured Bonden in his ear.

He nodded. 'When I wave my hand so,' he said, 'in sweeps. When I wave again, give way.'

Slowly they drew together, and although his mind was as cool and lucid as he could wish, he found he had stopped breathing: he heaved in a deep draught with a sigh, and the boat hailed, 'Ohé, de la barca.'

'Ohé,' he repeated, and waved his hand.

The boat ran alongside, hooked on, and a man made a

blundering leap for the rail; Jack caught his arms and lifted him clear over, looking into his face – Maragall. The boat shoved off; Jack nodded significantly to Bonden, waved his hand, and led Maragall into the cabin.

'How is he?' he whispered.

'Alive – still there – they talk of moving him. I have sent no message, received none.' His face was strained and deadly pale, but he moved it into the shape of a smile, and said, 'So you are in. No trouble. You are to lie off the old victualling wharf; they have given you the dirty filth-place, because you are French. Listen, I have four guides, and the church will be open. At half after two o'clock I put fire to Martinez's warehouse close to the arsenal – Martinez it was denounced him. This will allow a friend, an officer, to move the troops; by three there will be no soldiers or police within a quarter of a mile of the house. Our two men who work there will be at the church to show the way inside the house. Right?'

'Yes. How many men inside tonight?'

'Boat hailing, sir,' said Bonden, thrusting in his head.

They leapt from their seats, and Maragall stared out over the water. The lights of Mahon were showing round the point, silhouetting a black felucca a hundred yards away. The felucca hailed again. 'He asks what it is like outside,' whispered Maragall.

'Blowing hard – close-reefed topsails.'

Maragall called out in Catalan, and the felucca dropped astern, out of the lights. Back in the cabin he wiped his face, muttering, 'Oh, if only we had had more time, more time. How many men? Eight and a corporal: probably all five officers and one interpreter, but the colonel may not have come back. He is playing cards at the citadel. What is your plan?'

'Land in small parties between two and three o'clock, reach St Anna's by the back streets, take the rear wall and the garden house. If he is there, away at once, the way we came. If not, cross the patio, seal the doors and work through the house. Silently if possible, and fall back on the gunboat. If there is a row, then out across country: I have boats at Cala Blau and Rowley's Creek. You can manage horses? Do you need money?'

Maragall shook his head impatiently. 'It is not only Esteban,' he said. 'Unless the other prisoners are released, he is pointed at − identified, and God knows how many others with him. Besides, some of them are our men.'

'I see,' said Jack.

'He would tell you that himself,' whispered Maragall urgently. 'It must look like a rising of all the prisoners.'

Jack nodded, peering out of the stern window. 'We are almost in. Come on deck for the mooring.'

The old victualling-wharf was coming closer, and with it the stench of stagnant filth. They slid past the customs house, all lit up, and into the darkness beyond. The pratique boat hailed, backing water and turning back down the harbour. Maragall replied. A few moments later Bonden murmured 'In sweeps' and steered the gunboat gently up along the black and greasy side. They made fast to a couple of bollards and lay there in silence, with the lap of water on the starboard side and the diffused noise of the town on the other. Beyond the stone quay there was a vague plain of rubbish, a disused factory on the far side, a rope-walk, and a shipbuilder's yard with broken palings. Two unseen cats were howling in the middle of the rubbish.

'You understand me?' insisted Maragall. 'He would say exactly the same.'

'It makes sense,' said Jack sharply.

'He would say so,' repeated Maragall. 'You know where you are?'

'There's the Capuchins' church. And that is St Anna's,' he said, jerking his head towards a tower. It stood high over them, for at this point, the far end of the harbour, a cliff rose sheer from the low ground, a long cliff beginning in the middle of the town, so that this part of Mahon rode high above the water.

'I must go,' said Maragall. 'I shall be here at one with the guides. Think, I beg of you, think what I have said: it must be all.'

It was eight o'clock. They carried out a kedge, moored the gunboat stern-on with the sweeps ready at hand and lay there in squalid loneliness: Jack had a meal served out to the men in messes of six, crowded into the little cabin, while the rest sheltered under the half-deck – only one light, little movement or sound, no appearance of activity.

How well they bore the waiting! A low murmur of talk, the faint click of dice; the fat Chinese snoring like a hog. They could believe in an omniscient leader, who had everything in hand – meticulous preparations, wisdom, local knowledge, sure allies: Jack could not. Every quarter the church bells chimed all over Port Mahon; and one, with a cracked treble, was St Anna's, which he had often heard from that very garden house with Molly Harte. A quarter past; the half-hour; nine. Ten.

He found himself staring up at Killick, who said, 'Three bells, sir. Gentleman back presently. Here's coffee, sir, and a rasher. Do get summat in your gaff, sir, God love us.'

Like every other sailor Jack had slept and woken in all latitudes at all hours of the night and day; he too had the trick of springing out of a deep sleep ready to go on deck, highly developed by years and years of war; but this time it was different – he was not only bright awake and ready to go on deck – he was another man; the cold desperate tension was gone and he was another man. Now the smell of their foul anchorage was the smell of coming action – it took the place of the keen whiff of powder. He ate his breakfast with eager voracity and then went forward in the quarter moonlight to talk to his crew, squatting under the half-deck. They were astonished at his contained high spirits, so different from the savage remoteness of the run down the coast; astonished, too, that they should outlast the stroke of one, of half past, the waiting and no Maragall.

It was nearly two o'clock before they heard steps running on the quay. 'I am sorry,' he said, panting. 'To make people to move in this country . . . Here they are, guides. All's well. St Anna's at three, yes? I shall be there.'

Jack smiled and said, 'Three it is. Good-bye.' And turning to the shadowy guides, 'Cuatro groupos, cinco minutos each, eh? Satisfaction, then Java Dick: Bonden, bring up the rear.' He stepped ashore at last, the stiff, unyielding ground after months at sea.

He had thought he knew Port Mahon, but in five minutes of climbing up through these dark sleeping alleys, with no more than a cat flitting in the doorways and once the sound of a baby being hushed, he was lost; and when they came crouching through a low stinking tunnel he was astonished to find himself in the familiar little square of St Anna's. The church door was ajar: they pushed silently in. One candle in a side-chapel, and by the candle two men holding white hand-kerchiefs. They whispered to the guide, a priest or a man dressed as a priest, and came forward to speak to him. He could not make out what they said, but caught the word loch several times repeated, and when the door opened again he saw a red glow in the sky. The back of the church was filling as the guides led in his other groups: close-packed silent men, smelling of tar. The glow again, and he went to look out – a fire down by the harbour, with smoke drifting fast away to the south, lit red from below – and as he looked he heard a shriek: high bubbling agony cut off short. It came from a house no great way off.

Here was Bonden with the last party, doubling across the square. 'Did you hear that, sir? Them buggers are at it.'

'Silence, you God-damn fool,' he said, very low.

The clock whirred and struck: three. Maragall appeared from the shadows. 'Come on,' said Jack, ran from the square to the alley in the corner, up the alley, along the high blank wall to where a fig-tree leaned over the top. 'Bonden, make me a back.' He was up. 'Grapnels.' He hooked them around the trunk, whispered 'Land soft, land soft, there,' and dropped into the court.

Here was the garden house, its windows full of light: and inside the long room three men standing over a common rack; one civilian at a desk, writing; a soldier leaning against the door. The officer who was shouting as he leant over the rack moved sideways to strike again and Jack saw that it was not Stephen spreadeagled there on the ground.

Behind him there was the soft plump of men dropping from the wall. 'Satisfaction,' he whispered, 'your men round the other side, to the door. Java Dick – that archway with the light. Bonden, with me.'

The bubbling shriek rose again, huge, beyond human measure, intolerable. Inside the room the strikingly handsome youth had turned and now he was looking up with a triumphant smile at the other officers. His coat and his collar were open, and he had something in his hand.

Jack drew his sword, opened the long window: their faces turned, indignant, then shocked, amazed. Three long strides, and balancing, with a furious grip on his hilt, he cut forehand at the boy and backhand at the man next to him. Instantly the room was filled – bellowing noise, rushing movement, blows, the thud of bodies, a shout from the last officer, chair and table crashing down, the black civilian with two seamen on top of him, a smothered scream. The soldier shooting out of the door – an animal cry beyond it; and silence. The demented, inhuman face of the man on the rack, running with sweat.

'Cast him off,' said Jack, and the man groaned, shutting his eyes as the strain relaxed.

They waited, listening: but although they could easily hear the voices of three or four soldiers arguing on the ground floor and someone whistling sweet and true upstairs, there was no reaction. Loud voices, didactic, hortatory, going on and on, unchanged.

'Now for the house,' said Jack. 'Maragall, which is the guard-room?'

'The first on the left under the archway.'

'Do you know any of their names?'

Maragall spoke to the men with the handkerchiefs. 'Only Potier, the corporal, and Normand.'

Jack nodded. 'Bonden, you remember the door into the front patio? Guard that with six men. Satisfaction, your party stays in this court. Java, yours each side of the door. Lee's men come along with me. Silence, silence, eh?'

He walked across the court, his boots loud on the stones and soft feet padding by him: a moment's pause for a last check and he called out 'Potier.' In the same instant, like an echo from up the stairs came the shout 'Potier', and the whistling, which had stopped, started again, stopped, and 'Potier!' again, louder. The argument in the guardroom slackened, listening; and again, 'Potier!'

'J'arrive, mon capitaine,' cried the corporal; he came out of the room, still talking into it before he closed the door. A sob, an astonished gasp, and silence. Jack called 'Normand,' and the door opened again; but it was a surly, questioning, almost suspicious face that craned out, slammed the door to at what it saw.

'Right,' said Jack, and flung his sixteen stone against it. The door burst inwards, shuddering as it swung; but there was only one man left this side of the crowded open window: they hunted him down in one quick turn. Shrieks in the courtyard.

'Potier,' from above, and the whistling moved down the stairs, 'qu'est-ce que ce remue-ménage?'

By the light of the big lantern under the arch Jack saw an officer, a cheerful, high-coloured officer, bluff good humour and a well-fitting uniform, so much the officer that he felt a momentary pause. Dutourd, no doubt.

Dutourd's face, about to whistle again, turned to incredulity: his hand reached to a sword that was not there.

'Hold him,' said Jack to the dark seamen closing in. 'Maragall, ask him where Stephen is.'

'Vous êtes un officier anglais, monsieur?' asked Dutourd, ignoring Maragall.

'Answer, God rot your bloody soul,' cried Jack with a flush of such fury that he trembled.

'Chez le colonel,' said the officer. 'Maragall, how many are there left?' 'This person is the only man left in the house: he says Esteban is in the colonel's room. The colonel is not back yet.'

'Come.'

Stephen saw them walk into his timeless dream: they had been there before, but never together. And never in these dull colours. He smiled to see Jack, although poor Jack's face was so shockingly concerned, white, distraught. But when Jack's hands grappled with the straps his smile changed to an almost frightened rigour: the furious jet of pain brought the two remote realities together.

'Jack, handsomely, my dear,' he whispered as they eased him tenderly into a padded chair. 'Will you give me something to drink, now, for the love of God? En Maragall, valga'm Deu,' he said, smiling over Jack's shoulder.

'Clear the room, Satisfaction,' said Jack, breaking off – several prisoners had come up, some crawling, and now two of them made a determined rush at Dutourd, standing ghastly, pressed into the corner.

'That man must have a priest,' said Stephen.

'Must we kill him?' said Jack.

Stephen nodded. 'But first he must write to the colonel – bring him here – say, vital information – the American has talked – it will not wait. Must not: vital.'

'Tell him, sir,' said Jack to Maragall, looking back over his shoulder, with the look of profound affection still on his face. 'Tell him he must write this note. If the colonel is not here in ten minutes I shall kill him on that machine.'

Maragall led Dutourd to the desk, put a pen in his hand.

'He says he cannot,' he reported. 'Says his honour as an officer – '

'His what?' cried Jack, looking at the thing from which he
had unstrapped Stephen.

Shouting, scuffling, a fall on the way up.

'Sir,' said Bonden, 'this chap comes in at the front door.'
Two of his mates propped a man into the room. 'I'm afraid the
prisoners nobbled him on the way up.'

They stared at the dying, the dead colonel, and in the pause
Dutourd whipped round, dashed out the lamp, and leapt
from the window.

'While trying to escape,' said Stephen, when Java Dick
came up to report. 'Oh, altogether too – too – Jack, what
now? I cannot scarcely crawl, alas.'

'We carry you down to the gunboat,' said Jack.

Maragall said, 'There is the shutter they carry their dead
suspects on, behind the door.'

'Joan,' said Stephen to him, 'all the papers that matter are in
the press to the right of the table.'

Gently, gently down through the open streets, Stephen
staring up at the stars and the clean air reaching deep into his
lungs. Dead streets, with one single figure that glanced at this
familiar cortège and looked quickly away: right down to the
quays and along. The gunboat: Satisfaction's party there
before them, ready at the sweeps. Bonden reporting 'All present and sober, sir, if you please.' Farewell, farewell, Maragall:
God go with you and may no new thing arise. The black water
slipping by faster, faster, lipping along her side. The strangled
chime of a clock among the neat bundles of loot under the
half-deck. Silence behind them: Mahon still fast asleep.

Lazaretto Island left astern; the signal lanterns swaying up,
answered from the battery with the regulation hoist and a last
derisive cry of 'Cochons'. And the blessed realisation that the
dawn was bringing its usual slackening of the tramontane –
and that the sail down to leeward was the Lively.

'God knows I should do the same again,' said Jack, leaning

on the helm to close her, the keen spray stinging his tired, reddened eyes. 'But I feel I need the whole sea to clean me.'

4

'WILL THE INVALID gentleman take a little posset before he goes?' asked the landlady of the Crown. 'It is a nasty raw day – Portsmouth is not Gibraltar – and he looks but palely.' She was on the point of appropriating the chambermaid's 'more fit for a hearse than a shay' when it occurred to her that this might cast a reflection upon the Crown's best post-chaise, now standing at the door.

'Certainly, Mrs Moss; a capital idea. I will carry it up. You put a warming-pan in the chaise, I am sure?'

'Two, sir, fresh and fresh this last half-hour. But if it was two hundred, I would not have him travel on an empty stomach. Could you not persuade him to stay dinner, sir? He should have a goose-pie; and there is nothing more fortifying than goose-pie, as the world in general knows.'

'I will try, Mrs Moss; but he is as obstinate as a bee in a bull's foot.'

'Invalids, sir,' said Mrs Moss, shaking her head, 'is all the same. When I nursed Moss on his death-bed, he was that cross and fractious! No goose-pie, no mandragore, no posset, not if it was ever so.'

'Stephen,' he cried, with a meretricious affectation of gaiety, 'just toss this off, will you, and we will get under way. Is your great-coat warming?'

'I will not,' said Stephen. 'It is another of your damned possets. Am I in childbed, for all love, that I should be plagued, smothered, destroyed with caudle?'

'Just a sip,' said Jack. 'It will set you up for the journey. Mrs Moss does not quite like your travelling; and I must say I

agree with her. However, I have bought you a bottle of Dr
Mead's Instant Invigorator; it contains iron. Now just a drop,
mixed with the posset.'

'Mrs Moss – Mrs Moss – Dr Mead – iron, forsooth,' cried
Stephen. 'There is a very vicious inclination in the present
age, to – '

'Great-coat, sir,' said Killick. 'Warm as toast. Now step into
it before it gets cold.'

They buttoned him up, tweaked him into shape, and carried him downstairs, one at each elbow, so that his feet
skimmed the steps, to where Bonden was waiting by the
chaise. They packed him into the stifling warmth with understanding smiles over his head as he cried out that they were
stifling him with their God-damned rugs and sheepskins –
did they mean to bury him alive? Enough damned straw
underfoot for a regiment of horse. Killick and Bonden were
cramming in the few last wisps and Jack was at the other
door, about to get in, when he felt a touch upon his shoulder.
Turning he saw a man with a battered face and a crowned
staff in his hand – a quick glance showed two others at the
horses' heads and a reinforcement of burly sheriff's officers
with clubs. 'Captain Aubrey, sir?' said the man. 'In the name
of the law, I must ask you to come along with me – little matter of Parkin and Clapp – judgment summons. No trouble,
sir? We will walk along quietly, no scandal? I'll come behind,
if you prefer it, and Joe will lead the way.'

'Very well,' said Jack, and leaning in at the window he said,
'Stephen, I am nabbed – Parkin and Clapp – a caption.
Please see Fanshaw. I'll write to you at the Grapes, maybe
join you there. Killick, get my valise out. Bonden, you go
along with the Doctor: look after him, eh?'

'Which sponging-house?' asked Stephen.

'Bolter's. Vulture Lane,' said the tipstaff. 'Every luxury, every
consideration, all conweniencies.'

'Drive on,' said Jack.

'MATURIN, MATURIN, my dear Maturin,' cried Sir Joseph, 'how extremely shocked I am, how concerned, how deeply moved.'

'Ay, ay,' said Stephen testily, 'it is showy enough to look at, no doubt, but these are only the superficial sequelae. There is no essential lesion. I shall do very well. But for the moment I was obliged to beg you to visit me here; I could not manage the stairs. It was benevolent of you to come; I wish I could receive you better.'

'No, no, no,' cried Sir Joseph. 'I like your quarters excessively – another age – most picturesque – Rembrandt. What a splendid fire! I trust they make you comfortable?'

'Yes, I thank you. They are used to my ways here. Perfect, if only the woman of the house did not take it upon herself to play the physician, merely because I keep my bed some hours every day. "No, ma'am," I say to her, "I will not drink Godfrey's Cordial, nor try Ward's drop. I do not tell you how to dress this salmagundy, for you are a cook; pray do not tell me how to order my regimen, for as you know, I am a medical man." "No sir," says she, "but our Sarah, which she was in just the same case as you, having been overset at the bear-baiting when six months gone, took great adwantage from Godfrey; so pray, sir, do try this spoonful." Jack Aubrey was just the same. "I do not pretend to teach you to sail your sloop or poop or whatever you call the damned machine; do not therefore pretend – " But it is all one. Nostrums from the fairground quack, old wives' remedies – bah! If rage could reunite my sinews, I should be as compact as a lithosperm.'

Sir Joseph had intended to suggest the waters of Bath, but now he said, 'I hope your friend is well? I am infinitely obliged to him; it was a most heroic stroke. The more I reflect upon it, the more I honour him.'

'Yes. Yes, it was. It appears to me that these coups can be brought off only by enormous pains, forethought, preparation, or by taking them on the volley; and for that a very particular quality is required, a virtue I hardly know how to name. *Baraka*, say the Moors. He possesses it in a high degree; and what would be criminal temerity in another man is right conduct in him. Yet I left him in a sponging-house at Portsmouth.'

Amazement; concern. 'Yes. His virtue seems to apply only at sea; or in his maritime character. He was arrested for debt at the instance of a coven of attorneys. Fanshaw, his agent, tells me it was for a sum of seven hundred pounds. Captain Aubrey was aware that the Spanish treasure was not to be regarded as prize, but he had no notion that the news had spread in England; nor, I must confess, had I, since there has been no official announcement. However, I must not importune you with private discontents.'

'My dear sir, my dear Maturin – I beg you will always speak to me as a personal friend, a friend who has a great esteem for you, quite apart from all official considerations.'

'That is kind, Sir Joseph; it is very kind. Then I will tell you, that I fear his other creditors may get wind of his renewed difficulties and so load him with processes that he will be hopelessly involved. My means do not allow me to extricate him; and although the ex gratia payment you were good enough to mention may eventually extinguish the greater part of his debt, it will leave a considerable sum. And a man may rot in prison as thoroughly for a few hundred as for ten thousand pounds.'

'Has it not been paid?'

'No, sir. And I detect a certain reluctance in Fanshaw to make an advance upon it – these things are so unusual, says he, the event dubious, the delay unknown, and his capital was so very much engaged.'

'It is not my province, of course: the sluggish Transport Board and the still more sluggish Ticket Office have to pass the vouchers. But I think I can promise something like despatch. In the meantime Mr Carling will speak a private word to Fanshaw, and I am sure you will be able to draw on him for the sum you mention. Mention.'

'Should you like a window open, Sir Joseph?'

'If it would not incommode you. Do you not find it a trifle warm yourself?'

'I do not. The tropic sun is what I require, and a bushel of sea-coals is its nearest equivalent. But it would scarcely answer for a normally-constituted frame, I agree. Pray take off your coat – loosen your neckcloth. I do not stand on ceremony, as you see, with my nightcap and catskin comforter.' He began to heave on a system of cords and purchases connected with the window, but sank back, muttering, 'Jesus, Mary and Joseph. No grip, no grip at all. Bonden!'

'Sir?' said Bonden, instantly appearing at the door.

'Just clap on to that slab-line, and tally and belay right aft, will you now?' said Stephen, glancing at Sir Joseph with covert pride. Bonden gaped, caught the Doctor's intention, and moved forward. But with his hand on the rope he paused and said, 'But I don't hardly know, sir, that draught would be the thing. We ain't so spry this morning.'

'You see how it is, Sir Joseph. Discipline all to pieces; never an order carried out without endless wrangling. Damn you, sir.'

Bonden sulkily opened the window an inch or two, poked the fire and left the room, shaking his head.

'I believe I *shall* take off my coat,' said Sir Joseph. 'So a warm climate would suit, you tell me?'

'The hotter the better. As soon as I can, I mean to go down to Bath, to wallow in the warm and sulphurous—'

'Just what I was about to observe!' cried Sir Joseph. 'I am delighted to hear it. It was the very thing I should have recommended if' – if you had not looked so very savage, explosive, obstinate and cantankerous, he thought; but said 'if it had been my place to advise you. The very thing to brace the fibres; my sister Clarges knew of a case, not perhaps quite identical . . .' He felt he was on dangerous ground, coughed, and without a transition said, 'But to return to your friend: will not his marriage set him up? I saw the announcement in

The Times, and surely I understand the young lady to be a very considerable heiress? Lady Keith told me the estate is very handsome; some of the best farm-land in the county.'

'That is so, sure. But it is in her mother's hands entirely; and this mother is the most unromantic beast that ever urged its squat thick bulk across the face of the protesting earth; whereas Jack is not. He has the strangest notions of what constitutes a scrub, and the greatest contempt for a fortune-hunter. A romantic creature. And the most pitiful liar you can imagine: when I had to tell him the Spanish treasure was not prize, but that he was a pauper again, he feigned to have known it a great while – laughed, comforted me as tender as a woman, said he had been quite resigned to it these months past, desired me not to fret – he did not mind it. But I know all that night he wrote to Sophia, and I am morally certain he released her from her engagement. Not that that will have the slightest effect upon *her*, the honey bun,' he added, leaning back on his pillows with a smile.

Bonden walked in, staggering under the weight of two butts of coal, and made up the fire.

'Sir Joseph, you will take some coffee? Perhaps a glass of Madeira? They have an excellent sercial here, that I can conscientiously recommend.'

'Thank you, thank you – perhaps I might have a glass of water? A glass of cold water would be most acceptable.'

'A glass of water, Bonden, if you please, and a decanter of Madeira. And if I find another raw egg beaten up in rum on the tray, Bonden, I shall fling it at your head. That,' he said, sipping his wine, 'was the most painful aspect of my journey, the breaking of my news. Even more painful than the fact that my let us call it *interrogation* was carried out by the French, the nation I love best.'

'What civilised man does not? Their rulers, politicians, revolutions set apart, and this horrible engouement for Bonaparte.'

'Just so. But these were not new men. Dutourd was an engineer, ancien régime, and Auger a dragoon – regular, traditional officers. That was the horrible part. I had thought I knew the nation through and through – lived there, studied in Paris. However, Jack Aubrey had a short way with them. Yes. As I was saying, he is a romantic creature: after this affair he tossed his sword into the sea, though I know the value he had for it. Then again, he loves to make war – no man more eager in the article of battle; but afterwards it is as though he did not feel that war consisted of killing your opponents. There is a contradiction here.'

'I am so glad you are going to the Bath,' said Sir Joseph, whom the conflicts within the heart of a frigate-captain he had never seen interested less than the restoration of his friend's health; for although in ordinary relationships the chief of naval intelligence more nearly resembled an iceberg than a human being, he had a real affection, a real warmth of affection for Maturin. 'I am delighted, because you will meet my *successor* there, and I shall be down from time to time. I shall look forward extremely to enjoying your company, and to bringing you better acquainted with him.' He felt the strength of Stephen's gaze at the word successor, relished it for a moment, and went on. 'Yes. I shall be retiring presently, to my Sabine beetles; I have a little place in the Fens, a Paradise for coleoptera. How I look forward to it! Not without a certain regret, of course; yet this is lessened by the fact that I leave my concerns – our concerns – in good hands. You are acquainted with the gentleman.'

'Indeed?'

'Yes. When you desired me to send a confidential person to take down your report because of the state of your hands – oh, it was barbarous, barbarous, to have used you so – I begged Mr Waring to come. You sat with him for two hours!' he said, savouring the triumph.

'You astonish me. I am amazed,' said Stephen crossly. But then a smile spread across his face: that subfusc, entirely unremarkable man, that Mr Waring, would answer charmingly. He had done his work with no fuss of any kind, efficiently; and his only questions had been immediately to the point; he had given nothing away – no special knowledge, no particular interest; and he might have been some dull, respectable civil servant in the middle reaches of the hierarchy.

'He has the greatest admiration for your work, and a thorough grasp of the situation. Admiral Sievewright will appear for him – a much better system – but you will deal directly with him when I am gone. You will agree very well, I am sure: he is a *professional*. It was he who dealt with the late Monsieur de La Tapetterie. I believe, by the bye, that you gave him to understand that you had some other papers or observations that lay somewhat outside the limits of your report.'

'Yes. If you will be so good as to pass me that leather-covered object – thank you. The Confederacio burnt the house – how those fellows love a blaze – but before we left I desired their chief to remove the important papers, from which I offer you this, as a personal present for your retirement. It comes to you by right, since your name appears in it – les agissements néfastes de Sir Blaine on page three, and le perfide Sir Blaine on page seven. It is a report drawn up nominally by Colonel Auger but in fact by the far more brilliant Dutourd for your homologue in Paris, showing the present state of their military intelligence network in the eastern part of the Peninsula, *including Gibraltar*, with appreciation of the agents, details of payment, and so on. It is not finished, because the gentleman was cut short in mid-paragraph, but it is tolerably complete, and authentic even to the very blood stains. You will find a certain number of surprises, particular Mr Judas Griffiths; but on the whole I hope it will gratify you. Oh, that we had such a document for England! In my yesterday's state of knowledge it seemed to me a document that should pass from my hands directly to yours,' he said, handing it over.

Sir Joseph plucked it from him with a glittering eye, hurried over to the light and sat there hunched sideways, devouring the neat pages, accounts and lists. 'The dog,' he exclaimed in an undertone. 'The cunning dog – Edward Griffiths, Edward Griffiths, say your prayers, my man – in the very embassy itself? – so Osborne was right – the hound – God bless my soul.'

'Well,' he said aloud, 'I shall have to share this with my colleagues at the Horse Guards and the Foreign Office, of course; but the document itself I shall keep – Ie perfide Sir Blaine – to gloat upon in my leisured ease: such a document! I am so grateful, Maturin.' He made as though to shake hands, but recollected himself at the sight of Stephen's, touched it gently, and said, 'If it comes to exchanging surprises, I own myself beat out of the ring.'

THE POSTMAN was a rare visitor to Mapes. Mrs Williams's bailiff lived in the village, and her man of business called on her once a week; she had few relations with whom she was on letter-writing terms, and those few wrote seldom. Yet to the eldest daughter of the house the postman's step, his way of opening the iron gate, was perfectly distinct, and as soon as she heard it she flew from the still-room, along three corridors and down the stairs into the hall. She was too late, however. The butler had already placed *The Ladies' Fashionable Intelligencer* and a single letter on his salver and he was walking towards the breakfast-room.

'Is there anything for me, John?' she cried.

'Just the magazine and a threepenny one, Miss Sophia,' said the butler. 'I am taking them to my mistress.'

Sophia instantly detected the evasion and said, 'Give me that letter at once, John.'

'My mistress says I am to take everything to her, to prevent mistakes.'

'You must give it to me directly. You could be taken up and hanged for keeping people's letters; it is against the law.'

'Oh, Miss Sophie, it would be as much as my place is worth.'

At this point Mrs Williams came out of the breakfast-room,

took the post, and disappeared, her black eyebrows joining on her forehead. Sophie followed her, heard the rip of the cover, and said, 'Mama, give me my letter.'

Mrs Williams turned her angry dark-red face to her daughter and cried, 'Do you give orders in this house, miss? For shame. I forbade you to correspond with that felon.'

'He is not a felon.'

'Then what is he in prison for?'

'You know perfectly well, Mama. It is for debt.'

'In my opinion that is worse: defrauding people of their money is far worse than knocking them on the head. It is aggravated felony. Anyhow, I have forbidden you to correspond.'

'We are engaged to be married: we have every right to correspond. I am not a child.'

'Stuff. I never gave more than a conditional consent, and now it is all over. I am quite ill and weary with telling you so. All these fine words of his – so much pretence. We had a narrow escape; many unprotected women have been taken in by fine words, and high-flown specious promises with not a scrap of solid Government stock to support them when it comes to the point. You say you are not a child; but you *are* a child in these matters, and you need protecting. That is why I mean to read your letters; if you have nothing to be ashamed of, why should you object? Innocence is its own shield, I have always found – how cross and wicked you look, oh fie upon you, Sophia. But I am not going to let you be made a victim of by the first man that takes a fancy to your fortune, Miss, I can tell you. I shall have no hugger-mugger correspondence in my house; there has been enough of that, with your cousin going into keeping, or coming upon the town, or whatever you like to call it in your modern flash way of speaking; there was nothing of that kind when I was a girl. But then in my day no girl would ever have been so bold as to speak to her mother like that, nor so wickedly undutiful; even the most brazen chit would have died of shame first, I am very sure.' Mrs

Williams's spate flowed slower during the last sentences, for she was greedily reading as she spoke. 'Anyhow,' she said, 'all this headstrong violence of yours is quite unnecessary – you have brought on my migraine for nothing – the letter is from Dr Maturin, and you need not blush to have it read:

' "My dear Miss Williams,

I must beg your pardon for dictating this letter; a misfortune to my hand makes it difficult for me to write. I at once executed the commission you were kind enough to honour me with, and I was so fortunate as to obtain all the books on your list through my bookseller, the respectable Mr Bentley, who allows me a discount of thirty percent." ' Something like pinched approval showed in the lower parts of Mrs Williams's face. ' "What is more, I have a messenger, in the shape of the Reverend Mr Hinksey, the new rector of Swiving Monachorum, who will be passing through Champflower on his way to be read in, or inducted, as I believe I should say." Quite right; we say inducted for a clergyman. La, Sophie, we shall be the first to see him!' Mrs Williams's moods were violent, but changeable. ' "He has a vast carriage, and being as yet unprovided with a family, undertakes to place Clerk of Eldin, Duhamel, Falconer and the rest on the seat; which will save you not only the waiting, but also the sum of half a crown, which is not to be despised." No, indeed: eight of 'em make a pound; not that some fine gentlemen seem to think so. "I rejoice to hear that you will be at Bath, since this will afford me the pleasure of paying my respects to your Mama —I shall be there from the twentieth. But I trust this visit may not mean a decline in her health, or any uneasiness about her former complaint." He is always so considerate about my sufferings. He really might do for Cissy: if she could get him, that would mean a physician in the family, always at hand. And what does a little Popery signify? We are all Christians, I believe. "Pray tell her that if I can be of any service, I am at her command: my direction will be, at Lady Keith's, in Landsdowne Crescent. I shall be alone, as Captain Aubrey is detained in Portsmouth." He is quite of my way of thinking, I see; has cut off all connections, like a well-judging man. "And so, my dear Miss Williams, with my best compliments to your Mama, to Miss Cecilia and to Miss Frances . . ."

. . . and so on and so forth. A very pretty, respectful letter, quite properly expressed; though he might have found a frank, among all his acquaintances. A man's hand, I see, not a woman's. He must certainly have dictated this letter to a gentleman. You may have it, Sophie. I shall not at all object to seeing Dr Maturin in Bath; he is a sensible man – *he* is no spendthrift. He might do very well for Cecilia. Never was a gentleman that needed a wife more; and certainly your sister is in need of a husband. With all these militia officers about, and the example she has had, there will be no holding her – the sooner she is safely married the better. I desire you will leave them together as much as possible in Bath.'

BATH, WITH ITS terraces rising one above another in the sun; the abbey and the waters; the rays of the sun slanting through the steam, and Sir Joseph Blaine and Mr Waring walking up and down the gallery of the King's bath, in which Stephen sat boiling himself to total relaxation, dressed in a canvas shift and lodged in a stone niche, looking Gothic. Other male images sat in a range either side of him, some scrofulous, rheumatic, gouty or phthisical, others merely too fat, gazing without much interest at female images, many of them in the same case, on the other side; while a dozen pilgrims stumbled about in the water, supported by attendants. The powerful form of Bonden, in canvas drawers, surged through the stream to Stephen's niche, handed him out, and walked him up and down, calling 'By your leave, ma'am – make a lane there mate' with complete self-possession, this being his element, whatever the temperature.

'He is doing better today,' said Sir Joseph.

'Far better,' said Mr Waring. 'He walked the best part of a mile on Thursday, and to Carlow's yesterday. I should never have believed it possible – you saw his body?'

'Only his hands,' said Sir Joseph, closing his eyes. 'He must have uncommon strength of will – uncommon strength of constitution.'

'He has, he has,' said Sir Joseph, and they walked up and down again for a while. 'He is going back to his seat. See, he climbs in quite nimbly; the waters have done him the world of good – I recommended them. He will be going up to Landsdowne Crescent in a few minutes. Perhaps we might walk slowly up through the town – I am childishly eager to speak to him.

'Strong, yes, certainly he is strong,' he said, threading through the crowd. 'Let us cross into the sun. What a magnificent day; I could almost do without my great-coat.' He bowed towards the other side, kissing his hand. 'Your servant, ma'am. That was an acquaintance of Lady Keith's large properties in Kent and Sussex.'

'Indeed? I should have taken her for a cook.'

'Yes. A very fine estate, however. As I was saying, strong; but not without his weaknesses. He was blaming his particular friend for romantic notions the other day – the friend who is to marry the daughter of that woman we saw just now – and if I had not been so shocked by his condition, I should have been tempted to laugh. He is himself a perfect Quixote: an enthusiastic supporter of the Revolution until '93; a United Irishman until the rising, Lord Edward's adviser – his cousin, by the way – '

'Is he a Fitzgerald?'

'The wrong side of the blanket. And now Catalan independence. Or perhaps I should say, Catalan independence from the beginning, simultaneously with the others. But always heart and soul, blood and purse in some cause from which he can derive no conceivable personal benefit.'

'Is he romantic in the common sense?'

'No. So chaste indeed that at one time we were uneasy: Old Subtlety was particularly disturbed. There was one liaison, however, and that set our minds at rest. A young woman of very good family: it ended unhappy, of course.'

In Pulteney Street they were stopped by two groups of acquaintances, and by one gentleman so highly-placed that there was no cutting him short; it was therefore some time before they reached Landsdowne Crescent, and when they asked for Dr Maturin they learnt that he had company. However, after a moment they were asked to walk up, and they found him in bed, with a young lady sitting beside him. She rose and curtseyed – an unmarried young lady. Their lips tightened; their chins retreated into the starched white neckcloths: this young person was far, far too beautiful to be described as company, alone in a gentleman's bedroom.

'My dear, allow me to name Sir Joseph Blaine and Mr Waring: Miss Williams,' said Stephen.

They bowed again, filled with a new respect for Dr Maturin, and of a different kind; for as she turned and faced the light they saw that she was a perfectly lovely girl, dewy, fresh, a nonpareil. Sophie did not sit down; she said she must leave them – indeed she must, alas; she was to attend her mother to the Pump Room and the clock had already struck – but if they would forgive her she must first . . . She rummaged in her covered basket, brought out a bottle, a silver tablespoon wrapped in tissue paper, and a box of gilded pills. She filled the spoon, guided it with fixed attention towards Stephen's mouth, poured the glaucous liquid in, fed him two pills and with a firm benevolence watched them until they had gone down.

'Well, sir,' said Sir Joseph, when the door had closed, 'I congratulate you upon your physician. A more beautiful young lady I do not remember to have seen, and I am old enough to have seen the Duchess of Hamilton and Lady Coventry before they were married. I should consent to have my old cramps redoubled, to be dosed by such a hand; and I, too, should swallow it like a lamb.' He smirked. Mr Waring also smirked.

'Be so good as to state your pleasure, gentlemen,' said Stephen sharply.

'But seriously, upon my honour,' said Sir Joseph, 'and with the greatest possible respect for Miss – I do not believe I have ever had so much pleasure in the sight of a young lady – such grace, such freshness, such colour!'

'Ha,' cried Stephen, 'you should see her when she is in looks – you should see her when Jack Aubrey is by.'

'Ah, so *that* is the young lady in question? *That* is the gallant captain's betrothed? Yes. How foolish of me. I should have caught the name.' This explains everything. A pause. 'Tell me, my dear Doctor, is it true that you are somewhat recovered?'

'Very much so, I thank you. I walked a mile without fatigue yesterday; I dined with an old shipmate; and this afternoon I intend dissecting an aged male pauper with Dr Trotter. In a week I shall be back in town.'

'And a hot climate, you feel, would recover you entirely? You can stand great heat?'

'I am a salamander.'

They gazed at the salamander, pitifully small and distorted in that great bed; he still looked more fit for a hearse than a chaise, let alone a sea-voyage; but they bowed to superior knowledge, and Sir Joseph said, 'Then in that case, I shall have no scruple in taking my revenge; and I believe I shall surprise you as much as you surprised me in London. There's many a true word spoken in jest.'

A variety of other wise saws sprang to Stephen's indignant mind – words and feathers are carried off by the wind; as is the wedding, so is the cake; do not speak Arabic in the house of the Moor; pleasures pass but sorrows stay; love, grief and money cannot be concealed – but he uttered no more than a sniff, and Sir Joseph continued in his prosy voice, 'There is a custom in the department, that when the chief retires, he has certain traditional privileges; just as an admiral, on hauling down his flag, may make certain promotions. Now there is a frigate fitting out at Plymouth to take our envoy, Mr Stanhope, to Kampong. The command has been half-promised to three different gentlemen and there is the usual – in short, I may have the disposal of it. It appears to me that if you were to go, with Captain Aubrey, this would rehabilitate you in your purely scientific character; do not you agree, Waring?'

'Yes,' said Waring.

'It will, I trust and pray, restore your health; and it will remove your friend from the dangers you have mentioned. There is everything to be said for it. But there is this grave disadvantage: as you are aware, everything, *everything* decided by our colleagues in the other departments of the Admiralty or the Navy Office is either carried out with end-less deliberation if indeed it ever reaches maturity, or in a furious hurry. Mr Stanhope went aboard at Deptford a great while ago, with his suite, and waited there a fortnight, giving farewell dinners; then they dropped down to the Nore, where he gave two more; then their Lordships noticed that the *Surprise* lacked a bottom, or masts, or sails, put him ashore in a tempest, and sent her round to Plymouth to be refitted. In the interval he lost his oriental secretary, his cook and a valet, and the prize bull he was to take to the Sultan of Kampong pined away; while the frigate lost most of her active officers by transfer and a large proportion of her men by the port-admiral's drafts. But now all is changed! Stores are hurrying aboard night and day, Mr Stanhope is posting down from Scotland, and she must sail within the week. Should you be fit to join her, do you think? And is Captain Aubrey at large?'

'Perfectly fit, my dear,' cried Stephen, flushing with new life. 'And Aubrey left his sponging-house the moment Fanshaw's clerk released him, one tide ahead of a flood of writs. He instantly repaired aboard the press-tender, went up to the Pool of London, and so to ground at the Grapes.'

'Let us turn to the details.'

'BONDEN,' CRIED STEPHEN, 'take pen and ink, and write — '

'Write, sir?' cried Bonden.

'Yes. Sit square to your paper, and write: Landsdowne Crescent – Barret Bonden, are you brought by the lee?'

'Why, yes, sir; that I am – fair broached-to. Though I can read pretty quick, if in broad print; I can make out a watch-bill.'

'Never mind. I shall show you the way of it when we are at sea, however: it is no great matter – look at the fools who write all day long – but it is useful, by land. You can ride a horse, sure?'

'Which I *have* rid a horse, sir; and three or four times, too, when ashore.'

'Well. Be so good as to step – to *jump* – round to the Paragon and let Miss Williams know that if her afternoon walk should chance to lead her by Landsdowne Crescent, she would oblige me infinitely; then to the Saracen's Head – my compliments to Mr Pullings, and I should be very glad to see him as soon as he has a moment.'

'Paragon it is, sir, and Saracen's Head: to proceed to Lands-downe Crescent at once.'

'You may run, Bonden, if you choose. There is not a moment to be lost.'

The front door banged; feet tearing away left-handed down the crescent, and a long, long pause. A blackbird singing for the faint approach of spring in the gardens the other side of the road; the dismal voice of a corn-cutter chanting 'Work if I had it – Work if I had it' coming closer, dying away. Reflections upon the aetiology of corns; upon Mrs Williams's bile-duct. The front door again, echoing in the empty house – the Keiths and all their servants but a single crone were away – footsteps on the stairs, continual gay prattle. He frowned. The door opened and Sophia and Cecilia walked in, with Bonden winking and jerking his thumb behind their heads.

'Lord, Dr Maturin,' cried Cecilia, 'you are abed! I declare. Why, I am in a gentleman's bedroom at last – that is to say, I don't mean at last at all, but how are you? I suppose you have just come from the bath, and are sweating. Well, and how are you? We met Bonden just as we were going out, and I said at once, I must ask how he does: we have not seen you since Tuesday! Mama was quite –'

A thundering double knock below; Bonden vanished. Powerful sea-going voices on the stairs – a booming remark about the 'oakum-topped piece' which could only refer to Cecilia and her much-teazed yellow hair – and Mr Pullings made his appearance, a tall, kind-looking, loose-limbed young man, a follower of Jack Aubrey's, as far as so unfortunate a captain could be said to have followers.

'You know Mr Pullings of the Navy, I believe?' said Stephen.

Of course they knew him – he had been twice to Melbury Lodge – Cecilia had danced with him. 'Such fun!' she cried, looking at him with great complacency. 'How I love balls.'

'Your Mama tells me you also have a fine taste in art,' said Stephen. 'Mr Pullings, pray show Miss Cecilia Lord Keith's new Titian: it is in the gallery, *together with a great many other pictures*. And Pullings, explain the battle scene, the Glorious First of June. Explain it in particular detail, if you please,' he called after them. 'Sophie, my dear, briskly now: take pen and paper. Write:

"Dear Jack,

We have a ship, *Surprise*, for the East Indies, and must join at Plymouth instantly. . . ."

ha, ha, what will he say to that?'

'*Surprise!*' was what he said, in a voice that made the windows of the Grapes' one-pair front tremble. In the bar Mrs Broad dropped a glass. 'The Captain's had a surprise,' she said, gazing placidly at the pieces. 'I hope it is a pleasant one,' said Nancy, picking them up. 'Such a pretty gentleman.' The travel-worn Pullings, discreetly turned to the window as Jack read his letter, spun about at the cry. '*Surprise!* God love my heart, Pullings: do you know what the Doctor has done? He has found us a ship – *Surprise* for the East Indies – join at once. Killick, Killick! Sea-chest, portmanteau, small valise; and jump round to the office: insides on the Plymouth mail.'

'You won't go down by no mail-coach, sir,' said Killick, 'nor no po'shay neither, not with all them bums lining the shore. I'll lay on a hearse, a genteel four-'orse-'earse.'

'*Surprise!*' cried Jack again. 'I have not set foot in her since I was a midshipman.' He saw her plain, lying there a cable's length from him in the brilliant sunshine of English Harbour, a trim, beautiful little eight-and-twenty, French-built with a bluff bow and lovely lines, weatherly, stiff, a fine sea-boat, fast when she was well-handled, roomy, dry . . . He had sailed in her under a taut captain and an even tauter first lieutenant – had spent hours and hours banished to the masthead – had done most of his reading there – had carved his initials on the cap: were they still to be seen? She was old, to be sure, and called for nursing; but what a ship to command . . . He dismissed the ungrateful thought that there was never a prize to be looked for in the Indian Ocean – swept clear long ago – and said, 'We could give *Agamemnon* mainsail and topgallants, sailing on a bowline . . . I shall have the choice of one or two officers, for sure. Shall you come, Pullings?'

'Why, in course, sir,' – surprised.

'Mrs Pullings no objection? No:— eh?'

'Mrs Pullings will pipe her eye, I dare say; but then presently she will brighten up. And I dare say she will be main pleased to see me back again at the end of the commission; more pleased than now is, maybe. I get sadly underfoot, among the brooms and pans. It ain't like aboard ship, sir, the marriage-state.'

'Ain't it, Pullings?' said Jack looking at him wistfully.

> Stephen went on with his dictation: '*Surprise*, to carry H.M. envoy to the Sultan of Kampong. Mr Taylor at the Admiralty is *au courant*: has the necessary papers all ready. I calculate that if you take the Bath road and fork off at Dayrolle's you should pass Wolmer Cross at about four in the morning of the third, thus going aboard during the debtors' truce of Sunday. I shall wait for you at the Cross for a while in a chaise, and if I am not so fortunate as to see you, I shall proceed with Bonden and expect you at the Blue Posts. She is a frigate, it appears, of the smaller kind; she is short of officers, men, and – unless Sir Joseph spoke in jocular hyperbole – of a bottom.
>
> In haste –

Mend your pace, Sophie. Come come. You would never grow fat as a scrivener. Cannot you spell hyperbole? Is it done at last, for all love? Show.'

'Never,' cried Sophie, folding it up. 'I believe you have put in more than ever I said,' said Stephen, narrowing his eyes. 'You blush extremely. Have you at least the rendezvous just so?'

'Wolmer Cross at four in the morning of the third. Stephen, I shall be there. I shall get out of my window and over the garden wall: you must take me up at the corner.'

'Very well. But why will you not walk out at the front door like a Christian? And how are you going to get back? You will be hopelessly compromised if you are seen stalking about Bath at dawn.'

'So much the better,' said Sophie. 'Then I shall have no reputation left whatsoever, and shall have to be married as soon as possible – why did I not think of that before? Oh Stephen, you have beautiful ideas.'

'Well. At the corner, then, at half past three. Put on a warm cloak, two pair of stockings, and thick woollen drawers. It will be cold; we may have to wait a great while; and even then as like as not we shall not see him, which will chill you even more – for you are to consider, that a disappointment on top of the falling damps – hush: give me the letter.'

Half past three in the morning; a strong north-easter howling among the chimney-pots of Bath; the sky clear, and a lop-sided moon peering down into the Paragon. The door of number seven opened just enough to let Sophie out and then slammed with a most horrid crash, drawing the attention of a group of drunken soldiers, who instantly gave tongue. Sophie walked with a great air of resolution and purpose towards the corner, seeing with despair no sign of a coach – nothing but a row of doorways stretching on for ever under the moon, quite unearthly, strange, inhuman, deserted, and inimical. Steps behind her, overtaking – faster and faster; a low cry, 'It's me, miss, Bonden,' and in a moment they were round the corner, climbing into the old leather smell of the first of two post-chaises drawn up at a discreet distance from the house. The postboys' red jackets looked black in the moon.

Her heart was going so fast that she could hardly speak for five minutes. 'How strange it is at night,' she said when they were climbing out of the town. 'As though everyone were dead. Look at the river – it is perfectly black. I have never been out at this time before.'

'No, my dear, I do not suppose you have,' said Stephen.

'Is it like this every night?'

'It is sweeter sometimes – this cursed wind blows warm in other latitudes – but always at night the old world comes into its own. Hark there, now. Do you hear her? She must be in the woods above the church.' The hellish shrieking of a vixen it was, enough to chill the blood of an apostle; but Sophie was busy peering at Stephen in the faint moonlight, plucking his garments. 'Why,' she cried, 'you have come out without even so much as your dreadful torn old great-coat. Oh,

Stephen, how can you be so abandoned? Let me wrap you in
my cloak; it is lined with fur.'

Stephen eagerly resisted the cloak, explaining that once the
skin had a certain degree of protection, once it was protected
from dissipating its natural heat by a given depth of integu-
ment, then all other covering was not only superfluous but
harmful.

'The case is not the same with a horseman, however,' he
said. 'I strongly recommended Thomas Pullings to place a
sheet of oiled silk between his waistcoat and his shirt before
setting out; the mere motion of the horse, independently of
the velocity of the wind, would carry away the emanent cushion of warmth, could it pierce so far. In a reasonably-constructed coach, on the other hand, we need fear nothing of
the kind. Shelter from the wind is everything; the contented
Eskimo, sheltered in his house of snow, laughs at the tempest, and passes his long winter's night in hospitable glee. A
reasonably-constructed carriage, I say: I should never advise
you to career over the steppes of Tartary in a tarantass with
your bosom bare to the winds, or covered only with a cotton
shift. Nor yet a jaunting-car.'

Sophia promised that she should never do so; and wrapped
in this capacious cloak they once again calculated the distance from London to Bath, Pullings's speed in going up,
Jack's in coming down. 'You must make up your mind not to
be disappointed, my dear,' said Stephen. 'The likelihood of his
keeping – not the appointment, but rather the suggestion that
I threw out, is very slight. Think of the accidents in a hundred miles of road, the possibility, nay the likelihood, of his
falling off – the horse flinging him down and breaking its
knees, the dangers of travel, such as footpads, highwaymen
. . . but hush, I must not alarm you.'

The post-chaises had slowed to little more than a walk. 'We
must be near the Cross,' said Stephen, looking out of the window. Here the road mounted between trees – the white ribbon was lost in long patches of total darkness. Into the trees,

whistling and sighing in the north-easter; and there, in one of the pools of light among them, stood a horseman. The post-boy caught sight of him at the same moment, reined in, and called back to the chaise behind, 'It's Butcher Jeffrey, Tom. Shall ee turn around?'

'There's two more of un behind us, terrible great murdering devils. Do ee bide still, Amos, and be meek. Mind master's horses, and tip 'em the civil.'

The quick determined clip of hooves, and Sophia whispered, 'Don't shoot, Stephen.'

Glancing back from the open window, Stephen said, 'My dear, I have no intention of shooting. I have – ' But now here was the horse pulled up at the window, its hot breath steaming in, and a great dark form leaning low over its withers, shutting out the moonlight and filling the chaise with the civilest murmur in the world, 'I beg your pardon, sir, for troubling you – '

'Spare me,' cried Stephen. 'Take all I have – take this young woman – but spare me, spare me!'

'I knew it was you, Jack,' said Sophia, clasping his hand.

'I knew directly. Oh, I am so glad to see you, my dear!'

'I will give you half an hour,' said Stephen. 'Not a moment more: this young woman must be back in her warm bed before cock-crow.'

He walked back to the other chaise, where Killick, with infinite satisfaction, was telling Bonden of their departure from London – a hearse as far as Putney, with Mr Pullings in a mourning-coach behind, bums by the score on either side of the road, pulling their hats off and bowing respectful. 'I wouldn't a missed it, I wouldn't a missed it, no, not for a bosun's warrant.'

Stephen paced up and down; he sat in the chaise; he paced up and down – conversed with Pullings on the young man's Indian voyages, listened greedily to his account of the prostrating heat of the Hooghly anchorages, the stifling country behind, the unforgivable sun, the heat beating even from the moon by night. 'If I do not reach a warm climate soon,' he observed, 'you may bury me, and say, "He, of mere misery, perished away."' He pressed the button of his repeater, and in a lull of the wind the little silvery bell struck four and then three for the quarters. Not a sound from the chaise ahead; but as he stood, irresolute, the door opened, Jack handed Sophia out and cried, 'Bonden, back to the Paragon in t'other coach with Miss Williams. Come down by the mail. Sophie, my dear, jump in. God bless you.'

'God bless and keep you, Jack. Make Stephen wrap himself in the cloak. And remember, for ever and ever – whatever they say, for ever and ever and ever.'

5

THE SUN BEAT down from its noon-day height upon Bombay, imposing a silence upon that teeming city, so that even in the deepest bazaars the steady beat of the surf could be heard – the panting of the Indian Ocean, dull ochre under a sky too hot to be blue, a sky waiting for the south-west monsoon; and at the same moment far, far to the west-ward, far over Africa and beyond, it heaved up to the horizon and sent a fiery dart to strike the limp royals and topgallants of the *Surprise* as she lay becalmed on the oily swell a little north of the line and some thirty degrees west of Greenwich.

The blaze of light moved down to the topsails, to the courses, shone upon the snowy deck, and it was day. Suddenly the whole of the east was day: the sun lit the sky to the zenith and for a moment the night could be seen over the starboard bow, fleeting away towards America. Mars, setting a handsbreadth above the western rim, went out abruptly; the entire bowl of the sky grew brilliant and the dark sea returned to its daily blue, deep blue.

'By your leave, sir,' cried the captain of the afterguard,

bending over Dr Maturin and shouting into the bag that covered his head. 'If you please, now.'

'What is it?' asked Stephen at last, with a bestial snarl.

'Nigh on four bells, sir.'

'Well, what of it? Sunday morning, surely to God, and you would be at your holystoning?' The bag, worn against the moon-pall, stifled his words but not the whining tone of a man jerked from total relaxation and an erotic dream. The frigate was stifling between-decks; she was more than ordinarily overcrowded with Mr Stanhope and his suite; and he had slept on deck, walked upon by each changing watch.

'These old pitch-spots,' said the captain of the afterguard in a wheedling, reasoning voice. 'What would the quarterdeck look like with all these old pitch-spots when we come to rig church?' Then, as Dr Maturin showed signs of going to sleep again, he returned to 'By your leave, sir. By your leave, if you please.'

In the heat the tar on the rigging melted and fell on the deck; the pitch used in caulking the seams melted too; and Stephen, plucking off his bag, saw that they had scrubbed, sanded and holystoned all round him – that he was in a spotted island, surrounded by impatient seamen, eager to be done with their work so that they could shave and put on their Sunday clothes. Sleep was hopelessly gone: he stood up, took his head right out of the bag, muttering. 'No peace in this infernal hulk, or tub – persecution – Judaic superstitious ritual cleanliness – archaic fools,' and walked stiffly to the side. But as he stood the sun shot a grateful living warmth right into his bones: a cock in the nearby coop crowed, standing on tiptoe, and instantly a hen cried that she had laid an egg, an egg! He stretched, gazed about him, met the stony, disapproving faces of the afterguard and realised that the gumminess of his feet was caused by tar, pitch and resin on his shoes: a trail of dirty footsteps led across the clean deck from the place where he had slept to the rail where he now stood. 'Oh, I beg your pardon, Franklin,' he cried, 'I have dirtied the floor, I find. Come, give me a scraper – sand – a broom.'

The harsh looks vanished. 'No, no,' they cried – it was only a little pitch, not dirt – they would have it off in a moment. But Stephen had caught up a small holystone and he was earnestly spreading the pitch far, deep and wide, surrounded by a ring of anxious, flustered seamen when four bells struck, and to the infinite distress of the afterguard a huge shadow fell across the deck – the captain, stark naked and carrying a towel.

'Good morning, Doctor,' he said. 'What are you about?'

'Good morning, my dear,' said Stephen. 'It is this damned spot. But I shall have him out. I shall extirpate this spot.'

'What do you say to a swim?'

'With all my heart. In less than a moment. I have a theory – a trifle of sand, there, if you please. A small knife. No. No, my hypothesis was unsound. Perhaps aqua-regia, spirits of salt . . .'

'Franklin, show the Doctor how we do it in the Navy. My dear fellow, if I might suggest taking off your shoes? Then they might not have to scrub right through the deck and leave His Excellency without a roof to his head.'

'An excellent suggestion,' said Stephen. He tiptoed barefoot to a carronade and sat looking at his upturned soles. 'Martial tells us that in his day the ladies of the town had *sequi me* engraved upon their sandals; from which it is reasonable to conclude, that Rome was uncommon muddy, for sand would scarcely hold the print. I shall swim the whole length of the ship today.'

Jack stepped on to the western rail and looked down into the water. It was so clear that he could see the light passing under the frigate's keel: her hull projected a purple underwater shadow westwards, sharp head and stern but vague beneath because of her trailing skirts of weeds – a heavy growth in spite of her new copper, for they had been a great while south of the tropic. No ominous lurking shape, however; only a school of shining little fishes and a few swimming crabs. 'Come on, then,' he said, diving in.

The sea was warmer than the air, but there was refreshment in the rush of bubbles along his skin, the water tearing through his hair, the clean salt taste in his mouth. Looking up he saw the silvery undersurface, the *Surprise*'s hull hanging down through it and the clean copper near her water-line reflecting an extraordinary violet into the sea: then a white explosion as Stephen shattered the mirror, plunging bottom foremost from the gangway, twenty feet above. His impetus bore him down and down, and Jack noticed that he was holding his nose: he was holding it still when he came to the surface, but then relinquished it to strike out in his usual way – short, cataleptic jerks, with his eyes tightly shut and his mouth clenched in savage determination. Some inherent leading quality about his person kept him very low in the water, his nose straining just clear of the surface; but he had made great progress since the day Jack had first dipped him over the side in a running bowline three days out from Madeira, two thousand miles and many weeks sailing to the north: or rather many weeks of trimming sail, hoping to catch a hint of a breeze in their royals and flying kites, and whistling for a wind; for although they had picked up the north-east trades off the Canaries and had run down twenty-five degrees of latitude, day after day of sweet sailing, hardly touching a sheet or a brace and often logging two hundred miles between noon and noon, the sun growing higher with every latitude they took, they had run into the Variables far north of the line, and hitherto they had not had a hint of the south-east trades, in spite of the fact that at this time of the year they were to be expected well above the equator. Three hundred miles now of calm or of capricious often baffling breezes – weeks of towing the ship's head round to take advantage of them, heaving round the yards, getting the fire-engine into the tops to wet the sails, buckets of water whipped up to the royals to help them draw – only to find the breeze die away or desert them to ruffle the sea ten miles away. But mostly dead calm and the *Surprise* drifting imperceptibly westwards on the equatorial current, very slowly turning upon herself. A lifeless sea, the swell invisible but for the sickening heave of the horizon as she rolled with no sail to steady her; almost no birds, very few fishes – the single turtle and yesterday's booby a nine days' wonder; never a sail under the pure dome of the sky; the sun beating down twelve hours a day. And they were running short of water . . . how long would the short allowance last? He dismissed the calculations for the moment and swam towards the boat towing behind, where Stephen was clinging to the gunwale and calling out something about the Hellespont, incomprehensible for the gasping.

'Did you see me?' he cried as Jack came nearer. 'I swam the entire length: four hundred and twenty strokes without a pause!'

'Well done,' said Jack, swinging himself into the boat with an easy roll. 'Well done indeed.' Each stroke must have propelled Stephen a little less than three inches, for the *Surprise* was only a twenty-eight gun ship, a sixth-rate of 579 tons – the kind so harshly called a jackass frigate by those not belonging to her. 'Should you like to come aboard? Let me give you a hand.'

'No, no,' cried Stephen, drawing away. 'I shall manage perfectly well. For the moment I am taking my ease. I thank you, however.' He hated to be helped. Even at the beginning of the voyage, when his poor twisted limbs would hardly carry him along the deck he had detested it, and yet daily he had made a stated number of turns from the taffrail to the break of the head and back again; daily, after they had reached the height of Lisbon, he had crawled into the mizzen-top, allowing no man but Bonden to attend him, while Jack watched in agony from below and two hands darted about on deck with a fender to break his fall. And every evening he forced his mutilated hand to skip up and down the muted strings of his 'cello, while his set face turned a paler grey. But Lord, what progress he had made! This last frantic swim would have

been infinitely beyond his strength only a month ago, to say
nothing of their time in Portsmouth.

'What were you saying about the Hellespont?' he asked.
'How wide is it?'

'Why, not above a mile or so – point-blank range from
either side.'

'The next time we go up the Mediterranean,' said Stephen,
'I shall swim it.'

'I am sure you will. If one hero could, I am sure another
can.'

'Look, look! Surely that is a tern, just above the horizon,'
cried Stephen.

'Where away?'

'There, there,' said Stephen, releasing his hold to point. He
sank at once, bubbling; but his pointing hand remained above
the surface. Jack seized it, heaved him inboard and said,
'Come, let us dart up the stern-ladder. I can smell our coffee,
and we have a busy morning ahead of us.' He took the
painter, pulled the boat up to the frigate's stern, and guided
the ladder into Stephen's grasp.

The bell struck; and at the pipe of the bosun's call the hammocks came flying up, close on two hundred of them, to be
stowed with lightning rapidity into the nettings, with their
numbers all turned the same way; and in the rushing current
of seamen Jack stood tall and magnificent in a flowered silk
dressing-gown, looking sharply up and down the deck. The
smell of coffee and bacon was almost more than he could
bear, but he meant to see this operation through: it was by no
means as brisk as he could wish, and some of those hammocks were flabby, dropsical objects. Hervey would have to
start using a hoop again. Pullings, who had the morning
watch, was forward, causing a hammock to be relashed in an
un-Sunday tone of voice – he was obviously of the same opinion. It was Jack's usual custom to invite the officer of the
morning watch and one of the youngsters to breakfast with
him, but this was to be a particularly social day later on, and

Callow, the squeaker in question, had burst out into an eruption of adolescent spots, enough to put a man off his appetite. Dear Pullings would certainly forgive him.

An eddy in the tide brought a civilian staggering over the quarterdeck. This was Mr Atkins, the envoy's secretary, an odd little man who had already given them a deal of trouble – strange notions of his own importance, of the accommodation possible in a small frigate, and of sea-going customs; sometimes high and offended, sometimes over-familiar.

'Good morning, sir,' said Jack.

'Good morning, Captain,' cried Atkins, falling into step as Jack started his habitual pacing – no idea of the sacro-sanctity of a captain, and in spite of his before-breakfast shrewishness Jack could hardly tell him of it himself. 'I have good news for you. His Excellency is far better today – far better than we have seen him since the beginning of the trip. I dare say he will take the air presently. And I think I may venture to hint,' he whispered, taking Jack's reluctant arm and breathing into his face, 'that an invitation to dinner might prove acceptable.'

'I am delighted to hear that he is better,' said Jack, disengaging himself. 'And I trust that we may soon have the pleasure of his company.'

'Oh, you need not be anxious – you need not make any great preparations. H.E. is quite simple – no distance or pride. A plain dinner will do very well. Shall we say today?'

'I think not,' said Jack, looking curiously at the little man by his side. 'I dine with the gunroom on Sunday. It is the custom.'

'But surely, Captain, surely no previous engagement can stand in the way – His Majesty's direct representative!'

'Naval custom is holy at sea, Mr Atkins,' said Jack, turning away and raising his voice. 'Foretop, there. Mind what you are about with that euphroe. Mr Callow, when Mr Pullings comes aft, be so good as to give him my compliments, and I should be glad if he would breakfast with me. I hope you will join us, Mr Callow.'

Breakfast at last, and the tide of Jack's native good humour rose. They were cramped, the four of them, in the coach – the great cabin had been given over to Mr Stanhope – but confinement was part of naval life, and easing himself round in his chair he stretched his legs, lit his cigar and said, 'Tuck in, youngster. Don't mind me. Look, there is a whole pile of bacon under that cover; it would be a sad shame to send it away.'

In the agreeable pause that followed, broken only by the steady champ of the midshipman's jaws as he engulfed twenty-seven rashers, they heard the cry pass through the ship. 'D'ye hear there, fore and aft? Clean for muster at five bells. Duck frocks and white trousers. D'ye hear there, clean shirt and a shave at five bells.' They also heard, clear through the thin cabin bulkhead, the metallic voice of Mr Atkins, apparently haranguing his chief, and Mr Stanhope's quiet replies. The envoy was a remote, gentle, grey man, very well-bred, and it was a wonder that he should ever have attached such a bustling fellow to his service; Mr Stanhope had been ill when he came aboard, had suffered abominably from sea-sickness as far as Gibraltar, then again right down to the Canaries; and he relapsed in the heavy swell of the doldrums, when the *Surprise*, log-like on the heaving sea, often seemed to be about to roll her masts out. This relapse had been accompanied by a fit of the gout which, flying to his stomach, had kept him in his cabin. They had seen very little of the poor gentleman.

'Tell me, Mr Callow,' said Jack, partly out of a wish not to hear too much and partly to make his guest welcome, 'how is the midshipman's mess coming along? I have not seen your ram this week or more.' The ancient creature palmed off upon the unsuspecting caterer as a hogget had been a familiar sight, stumping slowly about upon the deck.

'Pretty low, sir,' said Callow, withdrawing his hand from the bread-barge. 'We ate him in seventy north, and now we are down to the hen. But we give her all our bargemen, sir, and she may lay an egg.'

'You ain't down to millers, then?' said Pullings.

'Oh yes we are, sir,' cried the midshipman. 'Threepence, they have reached, which is a God-damned – a crying shame.'

'What are millers?' asked Stephen.

'Rats, saving your presence,' said Jack. 'Only we call 'em millers to make 'em eat better; and perhaps because they are dusty, too, from getting into the flour and peas.'

'My rats will not touch anything but the best biscuit, slightly moistened with melted butter. They are obese; their proud bellies drag the ground.'

'Rats, Doctor?' cried Pullings. 'Why do you keep rats?'

'I wish to see how they come along – to watch their motions,' said Stephen. He was in fact conducting an experiment, feeding them with madder to see how long it took to penetrate their bones, but he did not mention this. His was a secretive mind; the area of reticence had grown and grown and now it covered the globular, kitten-sized creatures that dozed through the hot nights and blazing days in his storeroom.

'Millers,' said Jack, his mind roaming back to his famished youth. 'In the aftermost carline-culver of the larboard berth there is a hole where we used to put a piece of cheese and catch them in a noose as they poked their heads out on their way along the channel to the bread-room. Three or four a night in the middle watch we used to catch, on the Leeward Islands station. Heneage Dundas' – nodding to Stephen – 'used to eat the cheese afterwards.'

'Was you a midshipman in the *Surprise*, sir?' cried young Callow, amazed, *amazed*. If he had thought about it at all, he would have supposed that post-captains sprang fully armed from the forehead of the Admiralty.

'Indeed I was,' said Jack.

'Good heavens, sir, she must be very, very old. The oldest ship in the fleet, I dare say.'

'Well,' said Jack, 'she is pretty old, too. We took her early in the last war – she was the French *Unité* – and she was no chicken then. Could you manage another egg?'

Callow leapt, jerked almost out of his chair by Pullings's under-table hint, changed his *Yes, sir, if you please* to *No, sir, thank you very much*, and stood up.

'In that case,' said Jack, 'perhaps you will be so good as to desire your messmates to come into the cabin, with their logs.'

The rest of the morning, until five bells in the forenoon watch, he spent with the midshipmen, then with the bosun, gunner, carpenter and purser, going over their accounts: stores were well enough: plenty of beef, pork, peas and bis- cuit for six months, but all the cheese and butter had to be condemned – hardened as he was, Jack recoiled from the samples Mr Bowes showed him – and worse, far worse, the water was dangerously short. Some vile jobbery in the cooper- age had provided the *Surprise* with a ground-tier of casks that drank almost as much as the ship's company, and the new- fangled iron tank had silently leaked its heart out. He was still deep in paper when Killick came in, carrying his best uniform coat, and jerked his chin at him.

'Mr Bowes, we must finish this later,' said Jack. And as he dressed – the good broadcloth seemed three inches thick in this shattering heat – he thought about the water, about his position, so far westward after these weeks of drifting that when they did pick up the south-east trades he might find it difficult to weather Cape St Roque in Brazil. He could see the *Surprise* exactly on the chart; his repeated lunars agreed closely with the chronometers and with the master's and Mr Hervey's reckonings; and on the chart he could see the coast of Brazil, not much above five hundred miles away. Further- more, near the line the trades often came from due south. While he was worrying with these problems and his buttons, neckcloth and sword-belt, he felt the ship heel to the wind, heel again, and very gently she began to speak – the sound of live water running along her side. He glanced at the compass overhead. WSW½W. Would it die at once?

When he came on to the crowded, even hotter deck it was

still blowing. She just had steerage-way, as close-hauled as she could be – yards braced up twanging-taut, sails like boards. His plump, myopic first lieutenant, Mr Hervey, sweating in his uniform, smiled nervously at him, though with more confidence than usual. Surely this was right?

'Very good, Mr Hervey,' he said. 'This is what we have been whistling for, eh? Long may it last. Perhaps we might keep her a little off – fore and main-sheets – give her a fathom.' Hervey, thank God, was not one of your touchy first lieutenants, needing perpetual management. He had no great opinion of his own seamanship – nor had anyone else – and so long as he was treated kindly he never took offence. Hervey relayed the orders; the *Surprise* began to slip through the water as though she meant to cut the line diagonally before nightfall; and Jack said, 'I believe we may beat to divisions.'

The first lieutenant turned to Nicolls, the officer of the watch, and said, 'Beat to divisions.' Nicolls said to the mate of the watch, 'Mr Babbington, beat to divisions,' and Babbington opened his mouth to address the drummer. But before any sound emerged, the Marine, with a set and hieratic expression, woke the thunder in his drum, tan-tarara-tan, and all the officers hurried off to their places.

As a warning or advertisement the drumbeat was a failure, there being nothing unexpected about it whatsoever. The ship's company had been lining the quarterdeck, the gangways and the forecastle for some time, standing along the appointed seams in the deck while the midshipmen fussed about them, trying to make them stand upright, keep in order and toe the line, tweaking neckerchiefs, lanyards, hat-ribbons. But the muster was understood by all hands to be a formal ceremony, as formal as a dance, a slow, solemn dance with the captain opening the ball.

This he did as soon as all the officers had reported to Hervey and Hervey had informed him of the fact. He turned first to the Marines. From their position on the after part of the quarterdeck they had no benefit from the awning, but stood

there in rigid pipeclay and scarlet perfection, their muskets
and faces blazing in the sun. He returned their officer's salute
and walked slowly along the line. His opinion on the set of a
leather stock, the amount of powder in their hair, the number
and brilliance of their buttons, was of no value; in any case
Etherege, their lieutenant, was a competent officer and it
would certainly be impossible to fault him. But Jack's role in
all this was to be the eye of God, and he carried out his
inspection with impersonal gravity. As a man he felt for the
Marines broiling there; as a captain he left them to their
motionless suffering – the tar was already dripping on the
awnings as the sun gathered even greater strength – and with
the words 'Very creditable, Mr Etherege,' he turned to the
first division of the seamen, the forecastlemen, headed by Mr
Nicolls, the second lieutenant. They were the best seamen in
the ship, all rated able; most of them middle-aged, some
quite elderly; but none, in all those years at sea, had yet
learnt to stand to attention. Their straw hats flew off at his
approach and their toes remained fairly near the line, but this
was the height of their formality. They smoothed down their
hair, hitched up their loose white home-made trousers,
looked round, smiled, coughed, gaped about, staring: very
unlike the soldiers. A comforting set of forecastlemen, he
reflected, as he passed slowly along the silent deck with Mr
Hervey, seamen salted to the bone: several bald pates
strangely white in the suffused glare under the awning – a
striking contrast with their dark brown faces – but all with
their remaining hair gathered in a long tail behind, sometimes
helped out with tow. Such a mass of sea-going knowledge
there: but as he returned Nicolls's parting salute he noticed
with a sudden shock that the lieutenant's face was ill-shaved
and that the man himself, his linen and his uniform, were
dirty. He had scarcely ever seen such a thing before in an officer: nor had he often seen such a look of veiled indifference
and weariness.

On to the foretopmen under Pullings, who greeted him as

though they had never met before with a 'Present, properly dressed and clean, sir,' and fell in behind the captain and the first lieutenant. Here was worldliness, here was sinful vanity: all hands were in their best clothes, of course, snowy trousers and frocks with blue open collars; but the younger foretopmen had ribbons sewn into their seams, gorgeous handkerchiefs shawlwise round their necks, curling side locks falling low and gold earrings gleaming among them.

'What is the matter with Kelynach, Mr Pullings?' he asked, stopping.

'He fell off the topgallant yardarm on Friday, sir.'

Yes. Jack remembered the fall. A spectacular but a lucky one, a direct plunge on the roll that sent him clear of spars and ropes into the sea, from which he was fished with no trouble of any kind. It could hardly account for this glum look, dull eye, lifelessness. Questions yielded nothing: he was 'quite well, sir: prime.' But Jack had seen that puffed face and sunken eye before; he had seen it too often; and when he came to Babbington's waisters and saw it again in Garland, an 'innocent' whose lifetime at sea had not taught him to wield more than a swab and that badly, a gigantic simpleton who always laughed and simpered whenever he was mustered, he said to Hervey, 'What do you make of this man?'

The first lieutenant thrust his head forward to focus Garland's face and replied, 'That is Garland, sir: a good fellow, attentive to his duty, but not very bright.'

No blushing merriment, no sidling, followed this remark; the innocent stood like an ox.

Jack passed on to the gunners, honest slow bellies for the most part, whom he had found in the usual state of neglect, but whose lives he would make a misery until they learnt to serve their pieces as they ought to serve their God. Young Conroy was the last in the division: a blue-eyed youth as tall as Jack but much slimmer, with an absurdly beautiful mild smooth girl's face; his beauty left Jack totally unmoved (this could not be said for all his shipmates) but the bone ring that

fastened his handkerchief did not. On the outward face of
the bone, a shark's vertebra, Conroy had worked so perfect a
likeness of the *Sophie*, Jack's first command, that he recognised her at once. Conroy was probably related to someone
who had belonged to her: yes, there had been a quartermaster
of the same name, a married man who always remitted his
pay and prize-money home. Was he sailing with an old shipmate's son? Age, age; dear me. This was no time to speak, and
in any case, Conroy, though not dumb, had such a shocking
stutter as to make him nearly so. But he would look into the
muster-book when he had a moment.

Now the forecastle, where he was received by the bosun,
the carpenter and the gunner, suffering and motionless in
their rarely-worn uniforms; and at once the oppressive feeling
of great age fell away, for these were the frigate's standing
officers, and one of them, Rattray, had been with her from
the beginning. He had been bosun of the *Surprise* when Jack
was a master's mate in her, and Jack felt painfully young
under his keen, grey, respectful but somewhat cynical eye.
He felt that this eye pierced straight through his post-captain's epaulette and did not think much of what it saw below,
was not deceived by the pomp. Inwardly Jack agreed, but
withdrawing into his role he stiffened as they exchanged the
formal courtesies, and passed on with some relief to the master-at-arms and the ship's boys, taking a mean revenge in
reflecting once more that Rattray had never been much of a
bosun from the point of view of discipline and that now he
was past his prime in the article of rigging too. The boys
seemed spry enough, though here again there were more
spots than was usual or pleasant; and one had a monstrous
black mark on the shoulder of his frock. Tar.

'Master-at-arms, said Jack, 'what is the meaning of this?'

'It dropped on him from the rigging, sir, this last minute:
which I see it fall.' The boy, a stunted little adenoidal creature
with a permanently open mouth, looked perfectly terrified.

'Well,' said Jack, 'I suppose we may call it an act of God. Do not let it happen again, Peters.' Then seeing at the edge of his official gaze that three of the boys in the back row had worked one another into a hopeless pitch of strangled mirth, mutely writhing, he passed quickly on to the larboard waisters and the after-guard. Here the quality fell off dismally: a stupid, unhandy set of lubbers on the whole, though some of the recent landsmen might improve. Most of them looked cheerful, good-natured fellows; only three or four right hard bargains from the gaols; but here again he saw more gloomy, lack-lustre faces.

The ship's company was done: not a bad company at all, and for once he was not undermanned. But poor ailing Simmons, his predecessor, had let discipline grow slack before he died; the months in Portsmouth had done no good; and Hervey was not the man to build up an efficient crew. He was an amiable, conscientious fellow, very good company when he could overcome his diffidence, and a profound mathematician; but he could not see from one end of the ship to the other, and even if he had had the eyes of a lynx, he was no seaman. Still worse, he had no authority. His kindliness and ignorance had played Old Harry with the *Surprise*; and anyhow it would have called for an exceptional officer to cope with the loss of half the frigate's people, drafted off by the port-admiral, and their replacement by the crew of the *Racoon*, turned over to the *Surprise* in a body on returning from a four years' commission on the North American station without being allowed to set foot on shore. The Racoons and the Surprises and the small draft of landsmen still had not mixed; there were still unpleasant jealousies, and the ratings were often absurdly wrong. The captain of the foretop did not know his business, for example; and as for their gunnery . . . But this was not what he was worrying about as he walked into the galley. He had an enchanting ship, frail and elderly though she might be, some good officers, and good material. No: what haunted him was the thought of scurvy. But he might be mistaken; these dull looks might have a hundred other causes; and surely it was too early in the voyage for scurvy to break out?

The heat in the galley brought him up all standing. It had been gasping hot on deck, even with the blessed breeze: here it was like walking straight into a baker's oven. But the three-legged cook – three-legged because both his own had been shot away on the Glorious First of June, and he had supplemented the two provided by the hospital with a third, ingeniously seized to his bottom, to prevent him from plunging into his cauldrons or his range in a heavy sea. The range was now cherry-pink in the gloom, and the cook's face shone with sweat.

'Very trim, Johnson. Capital,' said Jack, backing a step.

'Ain't you going to inspect the coppers, sir?' cried the cook, his brilliant smile vanishing, so that in the comparative darkness his whole face seemed to disappear.

'Certainly I am,' said Jack, drawing on the ceremonial white glove. With this he ran his hand round the gleaming coppers, gazed at his fingers as though he really expected to find them deeply crusted with old filth and grease. A drop of sweat trembled on the end of his nose and more coursed down inside his coat, but he gazed at the pease-soup, the ovens and the two hundredweight of plum-duff, Sunday duff, before making his way to the sick-bay where Dr Maturin and his raw-boned Scotch assistant were waiting for him. Having made the round of the cots (one broken arm, one hernia with pox, four plain poxes) with what he intended to be encouraging remarks – looking better – soon be fit and well – back with their messmates for crossing the line – he stood under the opening of the air-sail, profiting by the relative coolness of 105°, and said privately to Stephen, 'Pray go along the divisions with Mr M'Alister while I am below. Some of the men seem to me to have an ugly look of the scurvy. I hope I am wrong – it is far too early – but it looks damnably like it.'

Now the berth-deck, with an ill-looking cat that sat defying them with studied insolence, its arms folded, and its particu-

lar friend, an equally mangy green parrot, lying on its side,
prostrated with the heat, that said 'Erin go bragh' in a low
tone once or twice as Jack and Hervey paced along with
bowed heads past the spotless mess-tables, kids, benches,
chests, the whole clean-swept deck checkered with brilliant
light from the gratings and the hatchways. Nothing much
wrong here; nor in the midshipmen's berth, nor of course in
the gunroom. But in the sail-room, where the bosun joined
them again, a very shocking sight – mould on the first staysail he turned over, and worse as the others were brought out.

This was lubber's work, slovenly and extremely dangerous.
Poor Hervey wrung his hands, and the bosun, though made
of sterner stuff, was quickly reduced to much the same condition. Jack's unfeigned anger, his utter contempt for the
excuses offered – 'it happens so quick near the line – no fresh
water to get the salt out – the salt draws the damp – hard to
fold them just so with all these awnings' – made a shattering
impression on Rattray.

His remarks upon the efficiency required in a man-of-war
were delivered in little more than a conversational tone, but
they were not inaudible, and when he emerged after having
looked at the holds, cable-tiers and fore-peak, the frigate's
people had an air of mixed delight and apprehension. They
were charmed that the bosun had copped it – all of them,
that is to say, who would not be spending their holy Sunday
afternoon in 'rousing them all out, sir, every last storm-stays'l,
every drabbler, every bonnet: do you hear me, now?' – but
apprehensive lest their own sins be discovered, lest they cop
it next; for this skipper was a bleeding tartar, mate, a right
hard horse.

However, he returned to the quarterdeck without biting or
savaging anyone in his path, peered up between the awnings
at the pyramid of canvas, still just drawing, and said to Mr
Hervey, 'We will rig church, if you please.'

Chairs and benches appeared on the quarterdeck; the cut-
lass-rack, decently covered with signal flags, became a read-

ing-desk; the ship's bell began to toll. The seamen flocked aft; the officers and the civilians of the envoy's suite stood at their places, waiting for Mr Stanhope, who walked slowly to his chair on the captain's right, propped on the one side by his chaplain and on the other by his secretary. He looked grey and wan among all these mahogany-red faces, almost ghost-like: he had never wanted to go to Kampong; he had not even known where Kampong was until they gave him this mission; and he hated the sea. But now that the *Surprise* was sailing on the gentle breeze her roll was far less distressing – hardly perceptible so long as he kept his eyes from the rail and the horizon beyond – and the familiar Church of England service was a comfort to him among all these strange intricacies of rope, wood and canvas and in this intolerably heated unbreathable air. He followed its course with an attention as profound as that of the seamen; he joined in the well-known psalms in a faint tenor, drowned by the deep thunder of the captain on his left and yet sweetly prolonged in the remote, celestial voice of the Welsh lookout high on the fore-royal jacks. But when the parson announced the text of his ser-mon, Mr Stanhope's mind wandered far away to the coolness of his parish church at home, the dim light of sapphires in the east window, the tranquillity of the family tombs, and he closed his eyes.

He wandered alone. The moment the Reverend Mr White said, 'The sixth verse of Psalm 75: *promotion cometh neither from the east, nor from the west, nor from the south,*' the flag-ging devotion of the midshipmen to leeward and of the lieu-tenants to windward revived, sprang to vivid life. They sat forward in attitudes of tense expectancy; and Jack, who might be called upon to preach himself, if he were to command a ship without a chaplain, reflected, 'A flaming good text, upon my word.'

Yet when at length it appeared that promotion cameth not from the north either, as the sharper midshipmen had sup-posed, but rather from a course of conduct that Mr White proposed to describe under ten main heads, they slowly sank back; and when even this promotion was found to be not of the present world, they abandoned him altogether in favour of reflections upon their dinner, their Sunday dinner, the plum-duff that was simmering under the equatorial sun with no more than a glowing cinder to keep it on the boil. They glanced up at the sails, flapping now as the breeze died away: they pondered on the likelihood of a studdingsail being put over the side, to swim in. 'If I can square old Babbington,' thought Callow, who had also been invited to dine in the gun-room at two o'clock, 'I shall get two dinners. I can dart below the moment we have shot the sun, and – '

'On deck there,' came from the sky. 'On deck there. Sail ho!'

'Where away?' called Jack, as the chaplain broke off.

'Two points on the starboard bow, sir.'

'Keep her away, Davidge,' said Jack to the man at the wheel, who, though in the midst of the congregation, was not of it, and who had never opened his mouth for hymn, psalm, response or prayer. 'Carry on, Mr White, if you please: I beg your pardon.'

Looks darted to and fro across the quarterdeck – wild sur-mise, intense excitement. Jack felt extreme moral pressure building up all round him, but, apart from a quick glance at his watch, he remained immovable, listening to the chaplain with his head slightly on one side, grave, attentive.

'Tenthly and lastly,' said Mr White, speaking faster.

Below, in the airy shadowed empty berth-deck, Stephen walked up and down, reading the chapter on scurvy in Blane's *Diseases of Seamen*: he heard the hail, paused, paused again, and said to the cat, 'How is this? The cry of a sail and no tur-moil, no instant activity? What is afoot?' The cat pursed its lips. Stephen reopened his book and read in it until he heard the two-hundredfold 'Amen' above his head.

On deck the church was disappearing in the midst of a uni-versal excited buzz – glances at the captain, glances over the hammock-cloths towards the horizon, where a flash of white could be seen on the rise. The chairs and benches were hurried below, the hassocks turned back to wads for the great guns, the cutlasses resumed their plain Old Testament character, but since the first nine heads of Mr White's discourse had taken a long, long time, almost till noon itself, sextants and quadrants already came tumbling up before the prayer-books had vanished. The sun was close to the zenith, and this was nearly the moment to take his altitude. The quarterdeck awning was rolled back, the pitiless naked light beat down; and as the master, his mates, the midshipmen, the first lieutenant and the captain took their accustomed stations for this high moment, the beginning of the naval day, they had no more shadow than a little pool of darkness at their feet. It was a solemn five minutes, particularly for the midshipmen – their captain insisted upon accurate observation – and yet no one seemed to care greatly about the sun: no one, until Stephen Maturin, walking up to Jack, said, 'What is this I hear about a strange sail?'

'Just a moment,' said Jack, stepping to the quarterdeck bulwark, raising his sextant, bringing the sun down to the horizon and noting his reading on the little ivory tablet. 'Sail? Oh, that is only St Paul's Rocks, you know. They will not run away. If this breeze don't die on us, you will see 'em quite close after dinner – prodigiously curious – gulls, boobies, and so on.'

The news instantly ran through the ship – rocks, not ships; any God-damned lubber as had travelled farther than Margate knew St Paul's Rocks – and all hands returned to their keen expectation of dinner, which followed immediately after the altitude. The cooks of all the messes stood with their wooden kids near the galley; the mate of the hold began the mixing of the grog, watched with intensity by the quartermasters and the purser's steward; the smell of rum mingled with that of cooking and eddied about the deck; saliva poured into a hundred and ninety-seven mouths; the bosun stood with

his call poised on the break of the forecastle. On the gangway
the master lowered his sextant, walked aft to Mr Hervey and
said, 'Twelve o'clock, sir: fifty-eight minutes north.'

The first lieutenant turned to Jack, took off his hat, and
said, 'Twelve o'clock, sir, if you please, and fifty-eight minutes
north.'

Jack turned to the officer of the watch and said, 'Mr
Nicolls, make it twelve.'

The officer of the watch called out to the mate of the
watch, 'Make it twelve.'

The mate of the watch said to the quartermaster, 'Strike
eight bells'; the quartermaster roared at the Marine sentry,
'Turn the glass and strike the bell!' And at the first stroke
Nicolls called along the length of the ship to the bosun, 'Pipe
to dinner.'

The bosun piped, no doubt, but little did the quarterdeck
hear of it, for the clash of mess-kids, the roaring of the cooks,
the tramp of feet and the confused din of the various messes
banging their plates. In this weather the men dined on deck,
among their guns, each mess fixing itself as accurately as possible above its own table below, and so Jack led Stephen into
his cabin.

'What did you think of the people?' he asked. 'You were
quite right,' said Stephen. 'It is scurvy. All my authorities
agree – weakness, diffused muscular pain, petechia, tender
gums, ill breath – and M'Alister has no doubt of it. He is an
intelligent fellow; has seen many cases. I have gone into the
matter, and I find that nearly all the men affected come from
the *Racoon*. They were months at sea before being turned
over to us.'

'So that is where the mischief lies,' cried Jack. 'Of course.
But you will be able to put them right. Oh yes, you will set
them up directly.'

'I wish I could share your confidence; I wish I could feel
persuaded that our lime-juice were not sophisticated. Tell
me, is there anything green grows upon those rocks of yours?'

'Never a blade, never a single blade,' said Jack. 'And no water, either.'

'Well,' said Stephen, drawing up his shoulders. 'I shall do my best with what we have.'

'I am sure you will, my dear Stephen,' cried Jack, flinging off his coat and with it part of his care. He had an unlimited faith in Stephen's powers; and although he had seen a ship's company badly hit by the disease, with hardly enough hands to win the anchor or make sail, let alone fight the ship, he thought of the forties, of the great western gales far south of the line, with an easier mind. 'It is a great comfort to me to have you aboard: it is like sailing with a piece of the True Cross.'

'Stuff, stuff,' said Stephen peevishly. 'I do wish you would get that weak notion out of your mind. Medicine can do very little; surgery less. I can purge you, bleed you, worm you at a pinch, set your leg or take it off, and that is very nearly all. What could Hippocrates, Galen, Rhazes, what can Blane, what can Trotter do for a carcinoma, a lupus, a sarcoma?' He had often tried to eradicate Jack's simple faith; but Jack had seen him trepan the gunner of the *Sophie*, saw a hole in his skull and expose the brain; and Stephen, looking at Jack's knowing smile, his air of civil reserve, knew that he had not succeeded this time, either. The Sophies, to a man, had *known* that if he chose Dr Maturin could save anyone, so long as the tide had not turned; and Jack was so thoroughly a seaman that he shared nearly all their beliefs, though in a somewhat more polished form. He said, 'What do you say to a glass of Madeira before we go to the gunroom? I believe they have killed their younger pig for us, and Madeira is a capital foundation for pork.'

Madeira did very well as a foundation, burgundy as an accompaniment, and port as a settler; though all would have been better if they had been a little under blood-heat. 'How long the human frame can withstand this abuse,' thought Stephen, looking round the table, 'remains to be seen.' He

was eating biscuit rubbed with garlic himself, and he had
drunk thin cold black coffee, on grounds both of theory and
personal practice; but as he looked round the table he was
obliged to admit that so far the frames were supporting it tolerably well. Jack, with a deep stratum of duff upon a couple
of pounds of swine's flesh and root-vegetables, was perhaps a
little nearer apoplexy than usual, but the bright blue eyes in
his scarlet face were not suffused – there was no immediate
danger. The same could be said for the fat Mr Hervey, who
had eaten and drunk himself out of his habitual constraint:
his round face was like the rising sun, supposing the sun to
wrinkle with merriment. All the faces there, except for
Nicolls's, were a fine red, but Hervey's outshone the rest.
There was an attaching simplicity about the first lieutenant;
no striving contention, no pretence, no sort of aggression.
How would such a man behave in hand-to-hand action?
Would his politeness (and Hervey was very much the gentleman) put him at a fatal disadvantage? In any event, he was
quite out of place here, poor fellow; far more suitable for a
parsonage or a fellowship. He was the victim of innumerable
naval connections, an influential family full of admirals
whose summum bonum was a flag and who by means of
book-time and every other form of decent corruption meant
to impel him into command at the earliest possible age. He
had passed for lieutenant before a board of his grandfather's
protégés, who gravely wrote that they had examined 'Mr Hervey . . . who appears to be twenty years of age. He produceth
Certificates . . . of his Diligence and Sobriety; he can splice,
knot, reef a sail, work a Ship in sailing, shift his Tides, keep a
Reckoning of a Ship's Way by Plane Sailing and Mercator;
observe by Sun or Star, and find the Variation of the Compass, and is qualified to do the Duty of an able Seaman and
Midshipman' – all lies, but for the mathematical part, since
he had almost no real sea-going experience. He would be
made commander as soon as they reached his uncle, the
admiral on the East India station; and a few months later he

would be an anxious, ineffectual, diffident post-captain. He
and the purser would have been happier if they had changed
places; Bowes, the purser, had been unable to go to sea as a
boy, but being enamoured of the naval life (his brother was a
captain) he had bought a purser's place, and in spite of his
club-foot he had distinguished himself in several desperate
cutting-out expeditions. He was always on deck, understood
the manoeuvres perfectly, and prided himself on sailing a
boat; he knew a great deal about the sea, and although he was
not a particularly good purser he was an honest one: an
uncommon bird. Pullings was much as he had always been, a
thin, amiable, loose-limbed youth, delighted to be a lieutenant (his highest ambition), delighted to be in the same
ship as Captain Aubrey: how did he manage to remain so
tubular, eating with the thoughtless avidity of a wolf? Harrowby, the master: a broad, spade-shaped face set in a smile –
he was smiling now, with his wide mouth open at the corners,
the middle closed. It gave an impression of falsity; perhaps
unfairly, for although the master was an ignorant, confident
man there might be no conscious duplicity there. No teeth.
Fair receding hair worn cropped; a vast domed forehead, ordinarily pale, now red and beaded with sweat. An indifferent
navigator, it seemed. He owed his advance to Gambier, that
evangelical admiral, and when ashore he was a lay-preacher,
belonging to some west-country sect. Stephen often saw him
in the sick-bay, coming to visit the invalids. 'There is good in
them all,' he said. 'We must try to bring them up to our level.'

Maturin: 'How do you propose to effect this?'

Harrowby: 'I rely upon unction and personal magnetism.'

Yet he did in fact bring them wine and chicken; he wrote
letters for them and gave or lent small sums of money. He
was ready and eager to give; perhaps readier than others to
receive. Active: zealous; healthy; extremely clean; somewhat
excited. He caught Stephen's eye and smiled wider, nodding
kindly.

Etherege, the Marine lieutenant, was as red as his coat; at

the moment he was surreptitiously undoing his belt, looking round with a general benevolence. A small round-headed man who rarely spoke; yet he gave no impression of taciturnity – his lively expression and his frequent laugh took the place of conversation. He had indeed very little to say, but he was welcome wherever he went.

Nicolls: he was something else again. The only comparatively pale face in the cheerful ring: a black-haired man, self-contained, not one to be pushed about. He would have been the skeleton at this orderly, somewhat formal feast if he had not been making an obvious effort at conviviality; but his face was set in unhappiness, and his present application to the port did not seem to be doing him much good. Stephen had seen much of him in Gibraltar, years before, and they had dined together with the 42nd Foot at Chatham, when Nicolls had had to be carried back to his ship, singing like a canary-bird; but that was immediately before his marriage and no doubt he was in a state of nervous tension. In those days Stephen had thought him a typical sea-officer, somewhat reserved but good company, one of those who naturally combined good breeding with the necessary roughness of their profession, with a bulkhead between the two. Typical sea-officer: the phrase was not without meaning, but how to define it? In every gathering of sailors you would see a few from whom the rest seemed variants; but how few to colour a whole profession! To colour it – to set its tone. Off-hand he could not think of more than a dozen out of the hundreds he had met: Dundas, Riou, Seymour, Jack, perhaps Cochrane; but no, Cochrane ashore was too flamboyant to be typical, too full of himself, too conscious of his own value, too much affected by that Scotch love of a grievance; and there was that unfortunate title hanging about his neck, a beloved millstone. There was something of Cochrane in Jack, a restless impatience of authority, a strong persuasion of being in the right; but not enough to disqualify him, not nearly enough; and in any case it had been diminishing fast these last years.

What were the constants? A cheerful resilience; a competent readiness; an open conversability; a certain candour. How much of this was the sea, the common stimuli? How much was the profession the choice of those who shared a particular cast of mind?

'The captain is under way,' whispered his neighbour, touching his shoulder and bending to speak in his ear.

'Why, so he is,' said Stephen, getting to his feet. *'He has catted his fish.'*

They slowly climbed the companion-ladder. The heat on deck was even greater than below now that the breeze had died away entirely. On the larboard side a sail had been lowered into the water, buoyed at its extremities and weighted in the middle to form a swimming-bath, and half the ship's company were splashing about in it. To starboard, perhaps two miles away, lay the rocks, no longer anything like ships at all, but still dazzling white from the edge of the deep blue sea to their tops, some fifty feet above the surface in the case of the biggest – so white that the slow surf showed creamy in comparison. A cloud of gannets sailed overhead, with a mingling of dark, smaller terns: every now and then a gannet dived straight down into the sea with a splash like a four-pounder ball.

'Mr Babbington, pray lend me your spy-glass,' cried Stephen; and when he had gazed for a while, 'Oh how I wish I were there. Jack – that is to say, Captain Aubrey – may I have a boat?'

'My dear Doctor,' said Jack, 'I am sure you would not have asked, if you had remembered it was Sunday afternoon.' Sunday afternoon was holy. It was the men's only holiday, wind, weather and the malice of the enemy permitting, and they prepared for it with enormous labour on Saturday and on Sunday morning. 'Now I must go below and see to that infernal sail-room,' he said, turning quickly away from his friend's disappointment. 'You will not forget that we are to call upon Mr Stanhope before quarters?'

'I will pull you across, if you choose,' said Nicolls, a moment later. 'I am sure Hervey will let us have the jolly-boat.'

'How very good-natured of you,' cried Stephen, looking into Nicolls' face – somewhat vinous, but perfectly in command of himself. 'I should be infinitely obliged. Give me leave to fetch a hammer, some small boxes, a hat, and I am with you.'

They crawled along the barge, the launch and one of the cutters to the jolly-boat – they were all towing behind, to prevent them opening in the heat – and rowed away. The cheerful noise faded behind them; their wake lengthened across the glassy sea. Stephen took off his clothes and sat naked in his sennit hat; he revelled in the heat, and this had been his daily practice since the latitude of Madeira. At present he was a disagreeable mottled dun colour from head to foot, the initial brown having darkened to a suffused grey; he was not much given to washing – fresh water was not to be had, in any event – and the salt from his swimming lay upon him like dust.

'I was contemplating upon sea-officers just now,' he observed, 'and trying to name the qualities that make one cry, "That man is a sailor, in the meliorative sense". From that I went on to reflect that the typical sea-officer is as rare as your anatomically typical corpse; that is to say, he is surrounded by what for want of a better word I may call unsatisfactory specimens, or sub-species. And I was carried on to the reflection that whereas there are many good or at least amiable midshipmen, there are fewer good lieutenants, still fewer good captains, and almost no good admirals. A possible explanation may be this: in addition to professional competence, cheerful resignation, an excellent liver, natural authority and a hundred other virtues, there must be the far rarer quality of resisting the effects, the dehumanising effects, of the exercise of authority. Authority is a solvent of humanity: look at any husband, any father of a family, and note the absorption of the person by the persona, the individual by the role. Then multiply the family, and the authority, by some hundreds and see the effect upon a sea-captain, to say nothing of an absolute monarch. Surely man in general is born to be oppressed or solitary, if he is to be fully human; unless it so happens that he is immune to the poison. In the nature of the service this immunity cannot be detected until late: but it certainly exists. How otherwise are we to account for the rare, but fully human and therefore efficient admirals we see, such as Duncan, Nelson . . .'

He saw that Nicolls's attention had wandered and he let his voice die away to a murmur with no apparent end, took a book from his coat pocket and, since the nearer sky was empty of birds, fell to reading in it. The oars squeaked against the tholes, the blades dipped with a steady beat, and the sun beat down: the boat crept across the sea.

From time to time Stephen looked up, repeating his Urdu phrases and considering Nicolls's face. The man was in a bad way, and had been for some time. Bad at Gibraltar, bad at Madeira, worse since St Jago. Scurvy was out of the question in this case: syphilis, worms?

'I beg your pardon,' said Nicolls with an artificial smile. 'I am afraid I lost the thread. What were you saying?'

'I was repeating phrases from this little book. It is all I could get, apart from the Fort William grammar, which is in my cabin. It is a phrase-book, and I believe it must have been compiled by a disappointed man: *My horse has been eaten by a tiger, leopard, bear; I wish to hire a palanquin; there are no palanquins in this town, sir – all my money has been stolen; I wish to speak to the Collector: the Collector is dead, sir —I have been beaten by evil men.* Yet salacious too, poor burning soul: *Woman, wilt thou lie with me?*'

With an effort at civil interest Nicolls said, 'Is that the language you speak with Achmet?'

'Yes, indeed. All our Lascars speak it, although they come from widely different parts of India: it is their lingua franca. I chose Achmet because it is his mother-tongue; and he is an obliging, patient fellow. But he cannot read or write, and that is why I ply my grammar, in the hope of fixing the colloquial: do you not find that a spoken language wafts in and out of your mind, leaving little trace unless you anchor it with print?'

'I can't say I do: I am no hand at talking foreign – never was. It quite astonishes me to hear you rattling away with those black men. Even in English, when it comes to anything more delicate than making sail, I find it . . .' He paused, looked over his shoulder and said there was no landing this side; it was too steep-to; but they might do better on the other. The number of birds had been increasing as they neared the rock, and now as they pulled round to its southern side the terns and boobies were thick overhead, flying in and out from their fishing-grounds in a bewildering intricacy of crossing paths, the birds all strangely mute. Stephen gazed up into them, equally silent, lost in admiration, until the boat grounded on weed-muffled rock and tilted as Nicolls ran it up into a sheltered inlet, heaved it clear of the swell, and handed Stephen out.

'Thank you, thank you,' said Stephen, scrambling up the dark sea-washed band to the shining white surface beyond: and there he stopped dead. Immediately in front of his nose, almost touching it, there was a sitting booby. Two, four, six boobies, as white as the bare rock they sat on – a carpet of boobies, young and old; and among them quantities of terns. The nearest booby looked at him without much interest; a slight degree of irritation was all he could detect in that long reptilian face and bright round eye. He advanced his finger and touched the bird, which shrugged its person; and as he did so a great rush of wings filled the air – another booby landing with a full crop for its huge gaping child on the naked rock a few feet away. 'Jesus, Mary and Joseph,' he murmured, straightening to survey the island, a smooth mound like a vast worn molar tooth, with birds thick in all the hollows. The hot air was full of their sound, coming and going; full of the

ammoniac smell of their droppings and the reek of fish; and
all over the hard white surface it shimmered in the heat and
the intolerable glare so that birds fifty yards up the slope
could hardly be focused and the ridge of the mound wavered
like a taut rope that had been plucked. Waterless, totally arid.
Not a blade of grass, not a weed, not a lichen: stench, blazing
rock and unmoving air. 'This is a paradise,' cried Stephen.

'I am glad you like it,' said Nicolls, sitting wearily down on
the only clean spot he could find. 'You don't find it rather
strong for paradise, and hell-fire hot? The rock is burning
through my shoes.'

'There is an odour, sure,' said Stephen. 'But by paradise I
mean the tameness of the fowl; and I do not believe it is they
that smell.' He ducked as a tern shot past his head, banking
and braking hard to land. 'The tameness of the birds before
the Fall. I believe this bird will suffer me to smell it; I believe
that much, if not all the odour is that of excrement, dead fish,
and weed.' He moved a little closer to the booby, one of the
few still sitting on an egg, knelt by it, gently took its wicked
beak and put his nose to its back. 'They contribute a good
deal, however,' he said. The booby looked indignant, ruffled,
impenetrably stupid; it uttered a low hiss, but it did not move
away – merely shuffled the egg beneath it and stared at a crab
that was laboriously stealing a flying-fish, left by a tern at the
edge of a nest two feet away.

FROM THE TOP of the island he could see the frigate, lying
motionless two miles off, her sails slack and dispirited: he
had left Nicolls under a shelter made from their clothes
spread on the oars, the only patch of shade on this whole
marvellous rock. He had collected two boobies and two terns:
he had had to overcome an extreme reluctance to knock
them on the head, but one of the boobies, the red-legged
booby, was almost certainly of an undescribed species; he had
chosen birds that were not breeding, and by his estimate of
this rock alone there were some thirty-five thousand left. He

had filled his boxes with several specimens of a feather-eating moth, a beetle of an unknown genus, two woodlice apparently identical with those from an Irish turf stack, the agile thievish crab, and a large number of ticks and wingless flies that he would classify in time. Such a haul! Now he was beating the rock with his hammer, not for geological specimens, for they were already piled in the boat, but to widen a crevice in which an unidentified arachnid had taken refuge. The rock was hard; the crevice deep; the arachnid stubborn. From time to time he paused to breathe the somewhat purer air up here and to look out towards the ship: eastwards there were far fewer birds, though here and there a gannet cruised or dived with closed wings, plummeting into the sea. When he dissected these specimens he should pay particular attention to their nostrils; there might well be a process that prevented the inrush of water.

Nicolls. The flow, the burst of confidence, hingeing upon what chance word? Something tolerably remote, since he could not remember it, had led to the abrupt statement, 'I was ashore from the time *Euryalus* paid off until I was appointed to the *Surprise*; and I had a disagreement with my wife.' Protestants often confessed to medical men and Stephen had heard this history before, always with the ritual plea for advice – the bitterly wounded wife, the wretched husband trying to atone, the civil imitation of a married life, the guarded words, politeness, restraint, resentment, the blank misery of nights and waking, the progressive decay of all friendship and communication – but he had never heard it expressed with such piercing desolate unhappiness. 'I had thought it might be better when I was afloat,' said Nicolls, 'but it was not. Then no letter at Gibraltar, although *Leopard* was there before us, and *Swiftsure*: every time I had the middle watch I used to walk up and down composing the answer I should send to the letters that would be waiting for me at Madeira. There were no letters. The packet had come and gone a fortnight before, while we were still in Gibraltar; and there were no letters. I had really thought there must be a remaining . . . but, however, not so much as a note. I could not believe it, all the way down the trades; but now I do, and I tell you, Maturin, I cannot bear it, not this long, slow death.'

'There is certain to be a whole bundle of them at Rio,' said Stephen. 'I, too, received none at Madeira – virtually none. They are sure to be sent to Rio, rely upon it; or even to Bombay.'

'No,' said Nicolls, with a toneless certainty. 'There will be no letters any more. I have bored you too long with my affairs: forgive me. If I were to rig a shelter with the oars and my shirt, would you like to sit down under it? Surely this heat will give you a sun-stroke?'

'No, I thank you. Time is all too short. I must quickly explore this stationary ark – the Dear knows when I shall see it again.'

Stephen hoped Nicolls would not resent it later. Regular confession was far more formal, far less detailed and spreading, far less satisfactory in its unsacramental aspect; but at least a confessor was a priest his whole life through, whereas a doctor was an ordinary being much of the time – difficult to face over the dinner-table after such privities.

He returned to his task, thump, thump, thump. Pause: thump, thump, thump. And as the crevice slowly widened he noticed great drops falling on the rock, drying as they fell. 'I should not have thought I had any sweat left,' he reflected, thumping on. Then he realised that drops were also falling on his back, huge drops of warm rain, quite unlike the dung the countless birds had gratified him with.

He stood up, looked round, and there barring the western sky was a darkness, and on the sea beneath it a white line, approaching with inconceivable rapidity. No birds in the air, even on the crowded western side. And the middle distance was blurred by flying rain. The whole of the darkness was lit from within by red lightning, plain even in this glare. A moment later the sun was swallowed up and in the hot gloom water hurtled down upon him. Not drops, but jets, as warm as the air and driving flatways with enormous force; and between the close-packed jets a spray of shattered water, infinitely divided, so thick he could hardly draw in the air. He sheltered his mouth with his hands, breathed easier, let water gush through his fingers and drank it up, pint after pint. Although he was on the dome of the rock the deluge covered his ankles, and there were his boxes blowing, floating away. Staggering and crouching in the wind he recovered two and squatted over them; and all the time the rain raced through the air, filling his ears with a roar that almost drowned the prodigious thunder. Now the squall was right overhead; the turning wind knocked him down, and what he had thought the ultimate degree of cataclysm increased tenfold. He wedged the boxes between his knees and crouched on all fours.

Time took on another aspect; it was marked only by the successive lightning-strokes that hissed through the air, darting from the cloud above, striking the rock and leaping back into the darkness. A few weak, stunned thoughts moved through his mind – 'What of the ship? Can any bird survive this? Is Nicolls safe?'

It was over. The rain stopped instantly and the wind swept the air clear; a few minutes later the cloud had passed from the lowering sun and it rode there, blazing from a perfect, even bluer sky. To westward the world was unchanged, just as it always had been apart from white caps on the sea; to the east the squall still covered the place he had last seen the ship; and in the widening sunlit stretch between the rock and the darkness a current bore a stream of fledgling birds, hundreds of them. And all along the stream he saw sharks, some large, some small, rising to the bodies.

The whole rock was still streaming – the sound of running water everywhere. He splashed down the slope calling 'Nicolls, Nicolls!' Some of the birds – he had to avoid them as he stepped – were still crouching flat over their eggs or nestlings; some were preening themselves. In three places there were jagged rows of dead terns and gannets, charred though damp, and smelling of the fire. He reached the spot where the shelter had been: no shelter, no fallen oars: and where they had hauled up the boat there was no boat.

He made his way clean round the rock, leaning on the wind and calling in the emptiness. And when for the second time he came to the eastern side and looked out to sea the squall had vanished. There was no ship to be seen. Climbing to the top he caught sight of her, hull down and scudding before the wind under her foretopsail, her mizzen and main-topmast gone. He watched until even the flicker of white disappeared. The sun had dipped below the horizon when he turned and walked down. The boobies had already set to their fishing again, and the higher birds were still in the sun, flashing pink as they dived through the fiery light.

6

IT WAS THE barge that took him off at last, the barge under Babbington, with a powerful crew pulling double-banked right into the eye of the wind.

'Are you all right, sir?. he shouted, as soon as they saw him sitting there. Stephen made no reply, but pointed for the boat to come round the other side.

'Are you all right, sir?' cried Babbington again, leaping ashore. 'Where is Mr Nicolls?'

Stephen nodded, and in a low croak he said, 'I am perfectly well, I thank you. But poor Mr Nicolls . . . Do you have any water in that boat?'

'Light along the keg, there. Bear a hand, bear a hand.' Water. It flowed into him, irrigating his blackened mouth and cracking throat, filling his wizened body until his skin broke out into a sweat at last; and they stood over him, wondering, solicitous, respectful, shadowing him with a piece of sail-cloth. They had not expected to find him alive: the disappearance of Nicolls was in the natural course of events. 'Is there enough for all?' he asked in a more human tone, pausing.

'Plenty, sir, plenty; another couple of breakers,' said Bonden. 'But sir, do you think it right? You won't burst on us?'

He drank, closing his eyes to savour the delight. 'A sharper pleasure than love, more immediate, intense.' In time he opened them again and called out in a strong voice, 'Stop that at once. You, sir, put that booby down. Stop it, I say, you murderous damned raparees, for shame. And leave those stones alone.'

'O'Connor, Boguslavsky, Brown, the rest of you, get back into the boat,' cried Babbington. 'Now, sir, could you take a little something? Soup? A ham sandwich? A piece of cake?'

'I believe not, thank you. If you will be so good as to have those birds, stones, eggs, handed into the boat, and to carry the two small boxes yourself, perhaps we may *shove off*. How is the ship? Where is it?'

'Four or five leagues south by east, sir: perhaps you saw our topgallants yesterday evening?'

'Not I. Is she damaged – people hurt?'

'Pretty well battered, sir. All aboard, Bonden? Easy, sir, easy now: Plumb, bundle up that shirt for a pillow. Bonden, what are you at?'

'I'm coming it the umbrella, sir. I thought as maybe you wouldn't mind taking the tiller.'

'Shove off,' cried Babbington. 'Give way.' The barge shot from the rock, swung round, hoisted jib and mainsail and sped away to the south-east. 'Well, sir,' he said, settling to the tiller with the compass before him, 'I'm afraid she was rather knocked about, and we lost some people: old Tiddiman was swept out of the heads and three of the boys went adrift before we could get them inboard. We were so busy looking at the sky in the west that we never had a hint of the white squall.'

'White? Sure it was as black as an open grave.'

'That was the second. The first was a white squall from due south, a few minutes before yours: it often happens near the line, they say, but not so God-damn hard. Anyhow, it hit us without a word of warning – the Captain was below at the time, in the sail-room – hit us tops'l high – almost nothing on the surface and laid us on our beam-ends. Every sail blown clean out of its bolt-rope before we could touch the sheets or halliards; not a scrap of canvas left.'

'Even the pendant went,' said Bonden. 'Yes, even the pendant went: amazing. And main and mizzen topmasts and fore-topgallant, all over to leeward, and there we were on our beam-ends, all ports open and three guns breaking loose. Then there was the Captain on deck with an axe in his hand, singing out and clearing all away, and she righted. But we had hardly got her head round before the black squall hit us – Lord'

'We got a scrap of canvas on to the foretopmast,' said Bonden, 'and scudded, there being these guns adrift on deck and the Captain wishful they should not burst through the side.'

'I was at the weather-earing,' said Plumb, stern-oar, 'and it took me half a glass to pass it; and it blew so hard it whipped my pig-tail close to the boom-iron, took a double turn in it, and Dick Turnbull had to cut me loose. That was a cruel hard moment, sir..' He turned his head to show the loss – fifteen years of careful plaiting, combing, encouraging with best Macassar oil, reduced to a bristly stump three inches long.

'But at least,' said Babbington, 'we did fill our water-casks. Then we rigged a jury mizzen and maintopmast; and we've been beating up ever since.'

An infinity of details – Babbington's low anxious inquiries after Nicolls – the surprisingly ready, philosophical acceptance of his death – more details of yards sprung, bowsprit struck by lightning, great exertions day and night – and Stephen slept, the piece of cake in his hand.

'There she lays,' said Bonden's voice through his dispersing dream. 'They've sent up a foretopgallant. Captain will be

main glad to see you, sir. Said you could never last on that –
rock; on deck all day and night – hands 'bout ship every glass.
God love us,' he said with a chuckle, remembering the ferocious compulsion, the pitiless driving of men three parts dead
with fatigue, 'he was quite upset.'

He had indeed been quite upset, but the news from the
mast-head that the returning barge carried an animate surgeon reassured the greater part of his mind: he was still in
strong anxiety for Nicolls, however, and the two emotions
showed on his face as he leant over the rail – gravity, and yet a
flush of pleasure and a smile that would be spreading.
Stephen came nimbly up the side, almost like a seaman. 'No,
no, I am perfectly well,' he said, 'but I am deeply concerned
to tell you, that Mr Nicolls and the boat vanished entirely. I
searched the rocks that evening, the next day and the next:
no trace at all – '

'I am most heartily sorry for it,' said Jack, shaking his head
and looking down. 'He was a very good officer.' After a
moment he said, 'Come, you must go below and to bed.
M'Alister shall physic you. Mr M'Alister, pray take Dr
Maturin below - '

'Let me carry you, sir,' said Pullings. 'I will give you a hand,'
said Hervey. The whole quarterdeck and the greater part of
the ship's company were gazing at the resuscitated Doctor,
his older shipmates with plain delight, the others with heavy
wonder: Pullings went so far as to push between the captain
and the surgeon and to seize him by the arm. 'I have not the
least wish to go below,' said Stephen sharply, twitching himself away. 'A pot of coffee is all that I require.' He moved a little way aft, caught sight of Mr Stanhope, and cried, 'Your
Excellency, I must beg your pardon for not having kept my
engagement with you on Sunday.'

'Allow me to congratulate you upon your preservation,' said
Mr Stanhope, advancing and shaking hands; he spoke with
more than his ordinary formality, for Stephen was mother-
naked; and although Mr Stanhope had seen naked men

before, he had never seen one with eyes so reddened by the salt and the intolerable sun that they shone like cherries, nor one so wizened, so wrinkled in his loose blackened skin, so encrusted and cadaverous.

'I wish you joy of your rescue, Doctor,' said Mr Atkins, the only man aboard who was not pleased to see the barge return: Stephen was attached to the mission in an artfully vague capacity, and the envoy's instructions required him to seek Dr Maturin's advice; Mr Atkins's advice or indeed presence was nowhere mentioned and he was consumed with jealousy. 'May I fetch you a towel or some other garment?'— with a look at Stephen's scrofulous shrunken belly.

'You are very officious, sir; but this is the garment in which I shall appear before God; I find it answers pretty well. It may be termed my birthday suit.'

'That has choked the bugger off,' said Pullings to Babbington, just above his breath, out of a motionless face. 'That is one in his bleeding eye.'

IN THE MORNING he appeared, eager and sharp-set at the breakfast-table, on the first stroke of the bell. 'Are you sure you should not stay abed?' cried Jack.

'Never in life, soul,' said Stephen, reaching for the coffee-pot, 'am I not telling you for ever that I am well? A slice of that ham, if you please. No, in all sobriety, if it had not been for poor unhappy Nicolls, I should have been glad to be marooned. It was uncomfortable – I was roasted, to be sure – but it has done extraordinary things to my sinews, more than the waters of Bath in a hundred years. No pain, no awkwardness! I could dance a jig, and an elegant jig. And quite apart from that, what else would have allowed me day after day of detailed observation? The arthropods alone . . . Before I went to bed last night, before I *turned in*, I threw down a mass of undigested notes, and merely for the arthropods there were seventeen pages! You shall see them. You shall have the maidenhead of my observations.'

'I shall be very happy; thank you, Stephen.' 'Then I sponged myself repeatedly, from head to foot, with *fresh* water, your blessed fresh water; and I slept – I slept! It was like falling slowly into a bottomless void, so deep that this morning I had difficulty in recalling the events of yesterday – a vague recollection of the sick-bay that I had to piece together from fragments that came swimming up. I fear I shall have a sad report for you when I have made my rounds this morning.'

'Certainly you look less like a burnt-offering than you did yesterday,' said Jack, peering affectionately into his face. 'Your eyes are almost human. But,' he said, feeling that this was not perfectly civil, 'they will behold a charming sight on deck – we have picked up the south-east trade at last! It is coming more southerly than I could wish, but I believe we shall weather Cape St Roque. At all events we shall cross the line before noon – we have been making seven and eight knots since the beginning of the middle watch. Another cup? Tell me, Stephen, what did you drink on that infernal rock?'

'Boiled shit.' Stephen was chaste in his speech, rarely an oath, never an obscene word, never any bawdy: his reply astonished Jack, who looked quickly at the tablecloth. Perhaps it was a learned term he had misunderstood. 'Boiled shit,' he said again. Jack smiled in a worldly fashion, but he felt the blush rising. 'Yes. There was one single pool of rainwater left in a hollow. The birds defecated in it, copiously. Not with set intent – the whole rock is normally deep in their droppings – but enough to foul it to the pitch of nausea. The next day was hotter, if possible, and with the reverberation the liquid rose to an extraordinary temperature. I drank it, however, until it ceased to be a liquid at all; then I turned to blood. Poor unsuspecting boobies' blood, tempered with a little sea-water and the expressed juice of kelp. Blood . . . Jack, this Cape St Roque, of which you speak so anxiously, is in Brazil, is it not, the home of the vampire?'

'I beg your pardon, sir, for interrupting you,' said Hervey, appearing at the door, 'but you desired me to let you know when the maintopgallant was ready to be swayed up.'

Left alone Stephen looked at his nail-less hand, flexed it with great complacency – remarkable intension: precise, unwavering – carried out a delicate operation on the ham with his pocket-lancet, and walked forward to the sick-bay, observing, 'I could not have done that before I was broiled alive, desiccated, mummified: bless the sun in his power.'

They crossed the line that day, but with muted ceremonies. It was not only the loss of their shipmates and of Mr Nicolls – a loss emphasised by the sale of their clothes at the capstan head – but there was not much spirit of fun in the ship. Badger-Bag came aboard with his trident, shaved the boys and the younger hands in a perfunctory manner, mulcted Stephen, Mr Stanhope and his people of six and eightpence a head, splashed a fair amount of water about the forecastle and the waist of the ship, and withdrew.

'That was our Saturnalia,' said Jack. 'I hope you did not dislike it?'

'Not at all. I am wholly in favour of innocent mirth; but I wonder you suffered it, with so much work on hand – all these spars, ropes and sails lying about half destroyed, and time, as you tell me, so precious.'

'Oh, you must not interfere with custom. They will work double-tides tomorrow – they will be in much better heart. Custom –'

'You are hag-ridden by custom, in the Navy,' said Stephen. 'Bells; an esoteric language – I will not say jargon; unmeaning ceremonies. The selling of poor Nicolls's clothes, for example, seemed to me gross impiety. And to Mr Stanhope, too. He is a far more interesting man than you might suppose; reads; plays a delicate flute. But I am not come here to be prating of the envoy. I have something far graver to tell you. The incessant labours of the last week have exhausted the men; many who showed no signs of scurvy at the last examination are now affected: here is my list. Virtually all the Racoons, many Surprises, and four landsmen. What is worse, the squall, in wrecking my store-room, has made the strangest magma of my drugs, to say nothing of the remaining and more than doubtful lime juice. I tell you officially, my dear, and will put it in writing if you choose, that I cannot be answerable for the consequences unless green vegetables, fresh meat and above all citrus fruits are provided within a few days. If I understand you, you mean to skirt the extremity of eastern Brazil; and eastern Brazil,' he cried, looking greedily through the open port westwards, 'is notoriously supplied with all these commodities.'

'So it is,' said Jack. 'And with vampires.'

'Oh, do not imagine I have not examined my conscience,' cried Stephen, laying his hand on Jack's bosom. 'Do not suppose I am unaware of my eagerness to set foot upon the New World at the earliest possible moment. But come and look at my suppurating five-year-old amputation, my re-opening once-healthy wounds, my purulent gums, imposthumes, low fevers, livid extravasations.'

'I was hardly serious,' said Jack. 'But. the fact is, there are many things I have to take into account.' There were indeed. This was a very long voyage, and already he had lost a great deal of time. With the Cape in the hands of the Dutch again he must get right down to the forties, to the great unfailing westerlies that would carry him into the Indian Ocean at two hundred miles a day, to catch the tail of the south-west monsoon somewhere about the height of Madagascar. His orders required him to touch at Rio, which was not much above a thousand miles away, no great distance if the hardwon trades held true; whereas if he stood in with the land he might lose them. He would certainly be entangled with the Portuguese officials if he called at Recife, for example: interminable delay at the best, and at the worst some ugly incident, detention, even violence, they being so very jealous of a foreign man-of-war anywhere but Rio. Delay, perhaps a row, and even then no certainty of supplies. And although Stephen was speaking in good faith, the dear creature was so passion-

ate a philosopher, with his bugs, vampires . . . 'Let me consider of it, Stephen,' he said. 'I will come to the sickbay.'

'Very well. And as we go, pray consider of this, too: my rats
have vanished. The squall did not take them. Their cage was
undamaged, but its door was open. I turn my back for five
minutes to take the air on St Paul's Rock, and my valuable
rats disappear! If this is one of your naval customs, I could
wish you all crucified at your own royal-yards; and flayed alive
before you are nailed up. This is not the first time I have suffered so. An asp off Fuengirola: three mice in the Gulf of
Lyons. Rats I had brought up by hand, cosseted since Berry
Head, crammed with best double-refined madder in spite of
their growing reluctance – and now all is lost, the entire
experiment rendered nugatory, utterly destroyed!'

'Why did you feed them with madder?'

'Because Duhamel tells us that the red is fixed and concentrated in their bones. I wished to find the rate of penetration,
and to know whether it reached the marrow. I shall know in
time, however: M'Alister and I will dissect all suitable subjects, for the effect will be passed to those that ate them, of
course; and I tell you soberly, Jack, that if you persist in this
dogged, self-defeating hurry, hurry, hurry, clap on more sails,
not a moment to be lost, then most of the people will pass
through our hands, including, no doubt, that black thief
whose very bones will blush for shame.' He uttered these
words in a high shriek at the entrance to the sick-bay, to make
himself heard above the armourer's forge, where they were
fashioning a new iron-horse, to replace that carried away in
the squall.

Jack looked at the crowded berth; he breathed the fetid air
that no wind-sail would carry away; he stood by while
Stephen and M'Alister undid bandages and showed him the
effects of scurvy upon old wounds; he did not give an inch
even when they led him to their chief witness, the five-year-
old amputated stump. But when they showed him a box of
teeth and sent for their walking cases to see how easily even

molars came out and to make him palpate their rotting gums he said he was satisfied and hurried aft.

'Killick,' he said, 'I shall not be having any dinner today. Pass the word for Mr Babbington.' Here at least was something pleasant to take the charnel-house smell away. 'Ah, Mr Babbington, there you are: sit down. I dare say you know why I have sent for you?'

'No, sir,' said Babbington instantly. It was worth denying everything as long as he could.

'How is your servitude coming along, eh? You must be close on your time.'

'Five years, nine months and three days, sir.' After six years on ships' books a midshipman might pass for lieutenant, might change from a reefer, a nonentity discharged or disrated at pleasure, to a godlike commissioned officer; and Babbington knew the date to the very hour.

'Yes. Well, I am going to give you an order as acting-lieutenant in poor Nicolls's place. By the time we reach the Admiral you will have your time and you can sit your board; and I dare say the Admiralty will confirm the appointment. They will never fail you on seamanship, I am very sure, but it might be wise to beg Mr Hervey to give you a hand with your double altitudes.'

'Oh thank you, thank you, sir,' cried Babbington, suffused with joy. It was not wholly unexpected (he had bought one of Nicolls's coats on the off-chance), but it had been far from certain. Braithwaite, the other senior midshipman (who had bought two coats, two waistcoats, two pair of breeches) had as good a claim to the step; and some sharp words had passed between Babbington and his captain at Madeira ('This ship is not a floating brothel, sir'), sharper still about relieving the watch in time. It was an exquisite moment, and the kind words with which Jack finished – 'shaping well – responsible, officerlike – should feel as easy with Babbington keeping a watch as any officer on the ship' – brought tears to Babbington's eyes. Yet in the midst of his joy his heart smote him, and pausing at the door after the usual acknowledgements he turned and said, in a faltering voice, 'You are so very kind to me, sir – always have been – that it seems a blackguardly thing. You might not have done it, if . . . but I did not exactly lie, however.'

'Eh?' cried Jack, astonished. In time it appeared that Babbington had eaten of the Doctor's rats; and that he was sorry now. 'Why, no, Babbington,' said Jack. 'No. That was an infernal shabby thing to do; mean and very like a scrub. The Doctor has been a good friend to you – none better. Who patched up your arm, when they all swore it must come off? Who put you into his cot and sat by you all night, holding the wound? Who – ' Babbington could not bear it; he burst into tears. Though an acting-lieutenant he wiped his eyes on his sleeve, and through his sobs he gave Jack to understand that unknown hands had wafted these prime millers into the larboard midshipmen's berth; that although he had had no hand in their cutting-out – indeed, would have prevented it, having the greatest love for the Doctor, so much so that he had fought Braithwaite over a chest for calling the Doctor 'a Dutch-built quizz' – yet, the rats being already dead, and dressed with onion-sauce, and he so hungry after rattling down the shrouds, he had thought it a pity to let the others scoff the lot. Had lived with a troubled conscience ever since: had in fact expected a summons to the cabin.

'You would have been living with a troubled stomach if you had known what was in 'em; the Doctor had – '

'I tell you what it is, Jack,' said Stephen, walking quickly in. 'Oh, I beg your pardon.'

'No, stay, Doctor. Stay, if you please,' cried Jack.

Babbington looked wretchedly from one to the other, licked his lips and said, 'I ate your rat, sir. I am very sorry, and I ask your pardon.'

'Did you so?' said Stephen mildly. 'Well, I hope you enjoyed it. Listen, Jack, will you look at my list, now?'

'He only ate it when it was dead,' said Jack.

'It would have been a strangely hasty, agitated meal, had he ate it before,' said Stephen, looking attentively at his list. 'Tell me, sir, did you happen to keep any of the bones?'

'No, sir. I am very sorry, but we usually crunch 'em up, like larks. Some of the chaps said they looked uncommon dark, however.'

'Poor fellows, poor fellows,' said Stephen in a low, inward voice.

'Do you wish me to take notice of this theft, Dr Maturin?' asked Jack.

'No, my dear, none at all. Nature will take care of that, I am afraid.'

He wandered back to the sick-bay, and there, when he had carried out some dressings, he asked M'Alister how many lived in the larboard midshipmen's berth. On being told six he wrote out a prescription and desired M'Alister to make it up into six boluses.

On deck Stephen was conscious of being closely, furtively watched; and after dinner, at a time when he was judged to be in a benevolent frame of mind, he was not surprised to receive a deputation from the young gentlemen, all washed and wearing coats in spite of the heat. They, too, were very sorry they had eaten his rats; they, too, begged his pardon; and they should never do so again.

'Young gentlemen,' he said, 'I have been expecting you. Mr Callow, be so good as to take this note, with my best compliments to the Captain.' He wrote 'Can the services of the young gentlemen and the clerk be dispensed with for a day?', folded it and handed it over. In the interval he gazed at Meadows and Scott, first-class volunteers aged twelve and fourteen; the captain's clerk, a hairy sixteen with his wrists far beyond the sleeves of his last year's jacket; Joliffe and Church, fifteen-year old midshipmen: all thinner, hungrier than their mothers could have wished. And they gazed covertly back at him, their habitual thoughtless merriment quenched, turned to a pasty solemnity.

'The Captain's compliments, sir,' said Callow, 'and he says with the greatest possible ease. A week, if you choose.'

'Thank you, Mr Callow. You will oblige me by swallowing this bolus. Mr Joliffe, Mr Church . . .'

THE *SURPRISE* LAY hove-to, the precious trade-wind singing through her rigging, fleeting away unused. Broad on her starboard beam Cape St Roque advanced into the sea, a bold headland, so thickly covered with tropical forest that not a patch of bare earth, not a rock could be seen except at the edge of the sea, where the surf broke upon a shining beach, indented here and there with creeks that ran into the trees.

One of these inlets had a stream – its turbid waters could be seen mingling with the blue, spreading on either side of the little bar – and by following its course one could make out the roofs of a village some way inland. Just these roofs, nothing more: the whole of the rest of the New World was ancient luxuriating forest, a solid mass of different shades of green – not a wisp of smoke, not a hut, not a track.

Jack's telescope, poised on the hammock-cloth, brought the forest so close that he could see half-fallen trunks, held in a tangle of gigantic creepers, new trees pushing through, even the flashing scarlet of a bird, the very colour of a blaze of flowers a little to the right; but most of the time he kept it fixed upon the roofs, the stream, hoping hour after hour to surprise a movement there.

His idea had seemed brilliant in the morning light, with Brazil looming in the west: they would not go to Recife nor any other port, but coast along and send the launch ashore at the nearest fishing village; no trouble with any authorities, almost no loss of time. Stephen was convinced that any cultivated stretch of this shore would provide what he needed. 'All we require is greenstuff,' he said, looking at Cape St Roque. 'And what, outside the Vale of Limerick, could be greener than that?' Then they saw these canoes running up the creek, and the roofs beyond. As Stephen was the only officer aboard who spoke Portuguese and who could be sure of the sick-bay's needs, it was sensible that he should go; but he had had to be persuaded, and on leaving, with a partially-concealed wild secret grin on his face, he had sworn upon his honour that he was uninfluenced by vampires – that he should not bring a single vampire aboard.

Behind Jack the work of the ship was going on; they were taking advantage of this pause to new-reeve most of the rigging on the mainmast and to re-stow the booms; but it was going forward slowly, with the bosun and his mates driving the sparse, dispirited crew with more noise and less effect than usual. The sound of distant wrangling came from the carpenters in the forward cockpit; and Mr Hervey was in an unusual passion, too. 'Where have you been, Mr Callow?' he cried. 'It is ten minutes since I told you to bring me the azimuth compass.'

'Only at the head, sir,' said Callow, glancing nervously at the Captain's back.

'The head, the head! Every single midshipman gives me that lame old excuse today. Joliffe is at the head, Meadows is at the head, Church is at the head. What is the matter with you all? Have you eaten something, or is it a wicked false-hood? I will not have this skulking. Do not trifle with your duty, sir, or you will find yourself at the masthead pretty soon, I can tell you.'

Six bells struck, and Jack turned to keep his appointment to drink tea with Mr Stanhope. He liked the envoy more the better he knew him, though Mr Stanhope was one of the most ineffectual men he had met; there was something touching about his anxiety to give no trouble, his gratitude for all they did for him in the way of accommodation, his hope-lessly misdirected consideration for the hands, and his forti-tude – never a word of complaint after the squall and all its wreckage. Once he had established that Jack and Hervey were connected with families he knew, he treated them as human beings; all the others as dogs – but as good, quite

intelligent dogs in a dog-loving community. He was ceremoni-
ous, naturally kind, and he had a great and oppressive sense
of duty. He greeted Jack with renewed apologies for doing so
in the Captain's own cabin. 'You must be sadly cramped, I am
afraid,' he said. 'Quite miserably confined; a great trial,' and
poured him a cup of tea in a way that reminded Jack irresistibly of his great-aunt Lettice: the same priestly gestures,
the same droop of the wrist, the same grave concentration.
They talked about His Excellency's flute, a quarter-tone too
high in this extraordinary heat; about Rio and the refreshments to be expected there; about the naval custom of having
thirteen months in the year; and Mr Stanhope said, 'I have
often meant to ask you, sir, why my naval friends and
acquaintance so often refer to the *Surprise* as the *Nemesis*.
Was her name changed – was she taken from the French?'

'Why, sir, it is more a kind of nickname that we have in the
service, much as we call *Britannia* Old Ironsides. You may
remember the *Hermione*, sir, in '97?'

'A ship of that name? No, I believe not.'

'She was a thirty-two-gun frigate, on the West Indies station;
and I am sorry to say her people mutinied, killed their officers,
and carried her into La Guayra, on the Spanish Main.'

'Oh, oh, how deeply shocking. I am distressed to hear it.'

'It was an ugly business; and the Spaniards would not give
her up, either. So, to put it in a word, Edward Hamilton, who
had the *Surprise* then, went and cut her out. She was moored
head and stern in Puerto Cabello, one of the closest harbours
in the world, under their batteries, which had some two hundred guns in 'em; and the Spaniards were rowing guard, too,
since the *Surprise* had stood in with the land, and they were
aware of her motions. Still, that night he went in with the
boats, boarded her and brought her away. He killed a hundred and nineteen of her crew, wounded ninety-seven, with
very little loss, though he was shockingly knocked about himself – oh, it was a most brilliant piece of service! I would have
given my right hand to be there. So the Admiralty changed

Hermione's name to *Retribution*, and in the service people called the *Surprise* the *Nemesis*, seeing that . . .' Through the open skylight he heard the masthead hail the deck: the launch had put off from the shore, followed by two canoes. Mr Stanhope went on for some time, gently prosing away about nemesis, retribution, just deserts, the inevitability of eventual punishment for all transgressions – crime bore within it the fatal seeds of the criminal's undoing – and lamenting the depravity of the mutineers. 'But no doubt they were led on, incited by some wretched Jacobin or Radical, and plied with spirits. To attack properly-constituted authority in such a barbarous fashion —! I trust they were severely dealt with?'

'We have a short way with mutineers, sir. We hanged all we could lay our hands on; ran 'em up the yardarm directly, with the "Rogue's March" playing. An ugly business, however,' he added; he had known the infamous Captain Pigot, the cause of the mutiny, and he had known several of the decent men who had been goaded into it. An odious memory. 'Now, sir, if you will forgive me, I believe I must go on deck, to see what Dr Maturin has brought us.'

'Dr Maturin is returning? I rejoice to hear it. I will come with you, if I may. I have a great esteem for Dr Maturin: a most valuable, ingenious gentleman; I have no objection to a little originality – my friends often quiz me for it myself. May I beg you to give me your arm?'

Valuable and ingenious he might be, thought Jack, fixing him with his glass, but false he was too, and perjured. He had voluntarily sworn to have no truck with vampires, and there, attached to his bosom, spread over it and enfolded by one arm, was a greenish hairy thing, like a mat – a loathsome great vampire of the most poisonous kind, no doubt. 'I should never have believed it of him: his sacred oath in the morning watch and now he stuffs the ship with vampires; and God knows what is in that bag. No doubt he was tempted, but surely he might blush for his fall?'

No blush; nothing but a look of idiot delight as he came slowly up the side, hampered by his burden and comforting it in Portuguese as he came.

'I am happy to see that you were so successful, Dr Maturin,' he said, looking down into the launch and the canoes, loaded with glowing heaps of oranges and shaddocks, red meat, iguanas, bananas, greenstuff. 'But I am afraid no vampires can be allowed on board.'

'This is a sloth,' said Stephen, smiling at him. 'A three-toed sloth, the most affectionate, discriminating sloth you can imagine!' The sloth turned its round head, fixed its eyes on Jack, uttered a despairing wail and buried its face again in Stephen's shoulder, tightening its grip to the strangling-point.

'Come, Jack, disengage his right arm, if you please: you need not be afraid. Excellency, pray be so good – the left arm, gently disengaging the claws. There, there, my fine fellow. Now let us carry him below. Handsomely, handsomely; do not alarm the sloth, I beg.'

THE SLOTH WAS not easily alarmed; as soon as it was provided with a piece of hawser stretched taut in the cabin it went fast to sleep, hanging by its claws and swaying with the roll as it might have done in the wind-rocked branches of its native forest. Indeed, apart from its candid distress at the sight of Jack's face it was perfectly adapted for a life at sea; it was uncomplaining; it required no fresh air, no light; it throve in a damp, confined atmosphere; it could sleep in any circumstances; it was tenacious of life; it put up with any hardship. It accepted biscuit gratefully, and pap; and in the evenings it would hobble on deck, walking on its claws, and creep into the rigging, hanging there upside down and advancing two or three yards at a time, with pauses for sleep. The hands loved it from the first, and would often carry it into the tops or higher; they declared it brought the ship good luck, though it was difficult to see why, since the wind rarely blew east of south, and that but feebly, day after day.

Yet the fresh provisions had their astonishingly rapid effect; in a week's time the sick-bay was almost empty, and the *Surprise*, fully manned and cheerful, had recovered her old form, her high-masted, trim appearance. She returned to her exercising of the great guns, laid aside for the more urgent repairs, and every day the trade-wind carried away great wafts of her powder-smoke: at first this perturbed the sloth; it scuttled, almost ran, below, its claws going clack-clack-clack in the silence between one broadside and the next; but by the time they had passed directly under the sun and the wind came strong and true at last, it slept through the whole exercise, hanging in its usual place in the mizzen catharpins, above" the quarterdeck carronades, just as it slept through the Marines' musketry and Stephen's pistol-practice.

All through this tedious, tedious passage, even in the northeast trades, the frigate had not shown of her best, but now with the steady urgent rush of air, this strong ocean of wind, she behaved like the old *Surprise* of Jack Aubrey's youth. He was not satisfied with her trim, nor with the present rake of her masts, nor with the masts themselves, far less with the state of her bottom; yet still, with the wind just far enough abaft the beam for the studding-sails to set pretty, she ran with the old magical life and thrust, a particular living, supple command of the sea that he would have recognised at once, if he had been set down upon her deck blindfolded.

The sun had gone down in a brief crimson blaze; the night was sweeping up from the east over a moonless sky, a deeper blue with every minute; and every wave-top began to glow with inner fire. The acting third lieutenant paused in his strut on the windward side of the sloping quarterdeck and called over to leeward, 'Mr Braithwaite, are you ready with the log, there?' Babbington did not dare come it very high with his former messmates yet, but he cut many a charming caper over the midshipmen of the starboard berth – balm to his soul – and this unnecessary question was intended only to compel Braithwaite to reply, 'All ready and along, sir.'

The bell struck. Braithwaite heaved the log clear of the stronger phosphorescence racing down the frigate's side: the line tore off the reel. At the quartermaster's cry he checked the run, jerked the pin, hauled the log aboard and shouted, 'We've done it! We've done it! Eleven on the nose!'

'It's not true!' cried Babbington, his dignity all sunk in delight. 'Let's have another go.'

They heaved the log again, watched it dwindle in the shining turmoil of the wake, more brilliant now with the darkening of the sky, and with his fingers on the running line Babbington nipped on the eleventh knot itself, shrieking 'Eleven!'

'What are you at?' asked Jack, behind the excited huddle of midshipmen.

'I am just checking Mr Braithwaite's accuracy, sir,' said the third lieutenant. 'Oh sir, we are doing eleven knots! Eleven knots, sir; ain't it prime?'

Jack smiled, felt the iron-taut backstay, and walked forward to where Stephen and Mr White, the envoy's chaplain, were crouching on the forecastle, braced against the lean of the ship and clinging haphazard to anything, kevils, beckets, even the burning metal of the horse. 'Is it settled yet?' he asked.

'We are waiting for the agreed moment, sir,' said the chaplain. 'Perhaps you would be so good as to keep time and see all's fair: a whole bottle of pale ale depends upon this. The moment Venus sets, Dr Maturin is to read from the first page he opens, by the phosphorescence alone.'

'Not footnotes,' said Stephen.

Jack glanced up, and there against the Southern Cross, high on the humming topgallant forestay, was the sloth, rocking easy with the rhythm of the ship. 'I doubt you have too much starlight,' he said. At this speed the frigate's bow-wave rose high, washing the lee head-rails with an unearthly blue-green light and sending phosphorescent drops over them, even more brilliant than the wake that tore out straight behind them, a ruled line three miles long gleaming like a flow of metal. For a moment Jack fixed the glowing spray as it was whirled inboard and then across the face of the foresail by the currents from the jibs and staysail, and then he turned his eyes westwards, where the planet was as low on the horizon as she could be. The round glow touched the sea, reappeared on the rise, vanished entirely; and the starlight distinctly lost in power. 'She dips,' he cried.

Stephen opened the book, and holding it with the page to the bow-wave he read,

> 'Speed the soft intercourse from soul to soul
> And waft a sigh from Indus to the Pole.

Mr White, I exult, I triumph. I claim my bottle; and Lord, Lord, how I shall enjoy it – such a thirst! Captain Aubrey, I beg you will share our bottle. Come, Lethargy,' he called directing his voice into the velvet sky.

'Oh, oh!' cried the chaplain, staggering into the booms. 'A fish – a fish has hit me! A flying-fish hit me in the face.'

'There is another,' said Stephen, picking it up. 'You notice that your high fishes fly paradoxically with the wind. I conceive there must be an upward draught. How they gleam – a whole flight, see, see! Here is a third. I shall offer it, lightly fried, to my sloth.'

'I cannot imagine,' said Jack, recovering the chaplain and guiding him along the gangway, 'what that sloth has against me. I have always been civil to it, more than civil; but nothing answers. I cannot think why you speak of its discrimination.'

Jack was of a sanguine temperament; he liked most people and he was surprised when they did not like him. This readiness to be pleased had been damaged of recent years, but it remained intact as far as horses, dogs and sloths were concerned; it wounded him to see tears come into the creature's eyes when he walked into the cabin, and he laid himself out to be agreeable. As they ran down to Rio he sat with it at odd moments, addressing it in Portuguese, more or less, and feed-

ing it with offerings that it sometimes ate, sometimes allowed
to drool slowly from its mouth; but it was not until they were
approaching Capricorn, with Rio no great distance on the
starboard bow, that he found it respond.

The weather had freshened almost to coldness, for the
wind was coming more easterly, from the chilly currents
between Tristan and the Cape; the sloth was amazed by the
change; it shunned the deck and spent its time below. Jack
was in his cabin, pricking the chart with less satisfaction than
he could have wished: progress, slow, serious trouble with the
mainmast – unaccountable headwinds by night – and sipping
a glass of grog; Stephen was in the mizzentop, teaching Bonden to write and scanning the sea for his first albatross. The
sloth sneezed, and looking up, Jack caught its gaze fixed upon
him; its inverted face had an expression of anxiety and concern. 'Try a piece of this, old cock,' he said, dipping his cake
in the grog and proffering the sop. 'It might put a little heart
into you.' The sloth sighed, closed its eyes, but gently
absorbed the piece, and sighed again.

Some minutes later he felt a touch on his knee: the sloth
had silently climbed down and it was standing there, its
beady eyes looking up into his face, bright with expectation.
More cake, more grog: growing confidence and esteem. After
this, as soon as the drum had beat the retreat, the sloth
would meet him, hurrying towards the door on its uneven
legs: it was given its own bowl, and it would grip it with its
claws, lowering its round face into it and pursing its lips to
drink (its tongue was too short to lap). Sometimes it went to
sleep in this position, bowed over the emptiness.

'IN THIS BUCKET,' said Stephen, walking into the cabin, 'in
this small half-bucket, now, I have the population of Dublin,
London and Paris combined: these animalculae – what is the
matter with the sloth?' It was curled on Jack's knee, breathing
heavily: its bowl and Jack's glass stood empty on the table.
Stephen picked it up, peered into its affable, bleary face,

shook it, and hung it upon its rope. It seized hold with one fore and one hind foot, letting the others dangle limp, and went to sleep.

Stephen looked sharply round, saw the decanter, smelt to the sloth, and cried, 'Jack, you have debauched my sloth.'

On the other side of the cabin-bulkheads Mr Atkins said to Mr Stanhope, 'High words between the Captain and the Doctor, sir. Hoo, hoo! Pretty strong – he pitches it pretty strong: I wonder a man of spirit can stomach it. I should give him a thrashing directly.'

Mr Stanhope had no notion of listening behind bulk-heads, and he did not reply; but he could not prevent himself from catching isolated sentiments, such as '. . . tes moeurs crapuleuses . . . tu cherches à corrompre mon paresseux . . . va donc, eh, salope . . . espèce de fripouille', for the dialogue had switched to French on the entrance of the wooden-faced Killick. 'I hope they will not be late for our whist,' he murmured. Now that the air had grown breathable Mr Stanhope's strength had revived, and he looked forward keenly to these evenings of cards, the only break in the unspeakable tedium of ocean travel.

They were not late. They appeared at the stroke of the hour; but their faces were red, and Stephen was seen to cheat in order to have the envoy as his partner. Jack played abominably; Stephen with a malignant concentration, darting out his trumps like a serpent's tooth; he excelled himself in post-mortems, showing clearly how his opponents might have drawn the singleton king, saved the rubber, trumped the ace, and the evening broke up with no slackening of the tension; they looked at him nervously as they settled the monstrous score, and with a factitious air of cheerfulness Jack said, 'Well, gentlemen, if the master's reckoning is as deadly accurate as Dr Maturin's leads, and if the wind holds, I believe you will wake up tomorrow in Rio de Janeiro: I feel the loom of the land – I feel it in my bones.'

In the dead hour of the middle watch he appeared on deck

in his night-shirt, looked attentively at the log-board by the binnacle-light, and desired Pullings to shorten sail at eight bells. He appeared again, like a restless ghost, at five bells, and backed his topsails for a while. His calculations were remarkably exact, and he brought the frigate into Rio just as the sun rose behind her and bathed the whole fantastic spectacle in golden light. Yet even this did not answer: even this did not close the breach: Stephen, on being routed out of bed to behold it, observed 'that it was curious how vulgar Nature could be at times – meretricious, ad captandum vulgus effects – very much the kind of thing attempted to be accomplished at Astley's or Ranelagh, and fortunately missed of'. He might have thought of other observations, for the sloth had been very slowly sick all night in his cabin, but at this moment the *Surprise* erupted in flames and smoke, saluting the Portuguese admiral as he lay there in a crimson seventy-four under Rat Island.

Jack went ashore with Mr Stanhope after breakfast, his bargemen shaved and trim in sennit hats and snowy duck and himself in his best uniform; and when he came back there was not the least trace of reserve, propitiation or hauteur in his expression. Bonden was carrying a bag, and from far off the cry of Post went round the waiting ship.

'Captain's compliments and should be happy if you could spare him a moment,' said Church, the rattivore. Then grasping Stephen's sleeve he added in an urgent whisper, 'And sir, please, please would you put in a good word for Scott and me to go ashore? We have deserved it.'

Wondering just how Mr Church thought he had deserved anything short of impalement, Stephen walked into the cabin. It was filled with a rosy smile, with contentment and the smell of porter; Jack sat there at his table behind a number of opened letters from Sophia, two glasses and a jug. 'There you are, my dear Stephen,' he cried. 'Come and drink a glass of porter, with the Irish Franciscans' compliments. I have had five letters from Sophie, and there are some for you

– from Sussex too, I believe.' They were lying on a heap of others addressed to Dr Maturin, and the hand was undoubtedly Sophia's. 'What a splendid hand she writes, don't you find?' said Jack. 'You can make out every word. And, really, such a style! Such a style! I wonder how she could have got such a style: they must be some of the best letters that were ever wrote. There is a piece here about the garden at Melbury and the pears, that I will read to you presently, as good as anything in all literature. But do not mind me, I beg, if you choose to look at yours now – do not stand on ceremony.'

'I will not,' said Stephen absently, putting them into his pocket and shuffling through the rest – Sir Joseph, Ramis, Waring, four unknowns. 'Tell me, were there any letters for Mr Nicolls?'

'Nicolls? No, none. Plenty for the rest of the gunroom, however. Killick!'

'What now, sir?' said Killick angrily, with a spoon in his hand.

'Gunroom steward: post. And bring another jug. Stephen, just look at this, will you?' He handed a letter: Mr Fanshaw presented his compliments to Captain Aubrey, and had the honour to state that he had this day received the sum of £9,755 13s 4d from the Admiralty, representing an ex gratia payment to Captain A in respect of the detention of His Most Catholic Majesty's ships *Clara*, *Fama*, *Medea* and *Mercedes*; that their Lordships did not have it in contemplation to make any payment of head-money or gun-money, nor for the hulls; and that the above-mentioned sum, less sundry advances as per margin and the usual commission, had been paid into Captain A's account with Messrs Hoare's banking house.

'It is not what you would call handsome,' said Jack laughing, 'but a bird in the hand is worth any amount of beating about the bush, don't you agree? And it pretty well clears me of debt: now all I need is a couple of moderate prizes, and then upon my word I cannot see what Mother Williams can possibly object to. To be sure, there is not a smell of a merchantman left this side of Batavia; not lawful prize, I mean, and God preserve me from sending in another neutral; but still, they have some privateers cruising from the Isle of France, and a brush with one or two of them . . .' The old eager piratical gleam was in his eye; he looked five years younger. 'But Stephen, I have been thinking about you. I must heave the ship down, re-stow her – Mr Stanhope's dunnage and presents are all ahoo in the after-hold – get her more by the head, shift all manner of things; and it occurred to me, now you are so amazing agile, should not you like to take a week's leave and ride into the interior? Jaguars, ostriches, unicorns – '

'Oh Jack, how truly good of you! I had to put violence upon myself to come away from Cape St Roque, to abandon that vegetable magnificence. The Brazilian forest is the haunt of the tapir, the boa, the peccary! You may find it hard to credit, Jack, but never yet have I beheld a boa.'

BOAS HE HAD BEHELD, and handled too; hummingbirds; fire-flies; the toucan in his glory, peering from his nest; the anteater and her child, tinted purple by the sunrise over a desolate swamp; armadillos, three kinds of New World monkey; a true tapir he had seen, before he came back to the ship at Rio, having worn three horses and Mr White, his companion, to a shadow. Here, riding at single anchor, he found a strangely altered *Surprise*, with a thirty-six gun frigate's mainmast, her fore and mizzen raked strongly aft, and her sides repainted black and white – the Nelson checker. 'It is a plan of my own,' said Jack, welcoming him aboard, 'something between the *Lively* and the old *Surprise* I knew as a boy. It will move her in light airs, with her narrow entrance, do you see, and above all give her an extra knot under a press of canvas. You are going to object to her top-hamper, I know' – Stephen was gaping up at an immature parrot – 'but I have tossed out all my shingle-ballast and replaced it with pig-iron – I cannot tell you how kind the Admiral has been – and we have stowed it low. She is as stiff as – why, as stiff as you can imagine; and if we cannot get an extra knot I shall be amazed. We may need it, for *Lyra* was in, and she tells us Linois has passed into the Indian Ocean with a ship of the line, two frigates and a corvette. You remember Linois, Stephen?'

'Monsieur de Linois, who captured us in the *Sophie*? Yes, yes. I remember him perfectly. A cheerful, polite gentleman, in a red waistcoat.'

'And a prodigious good seaman, too; but if I can help it, he shall not catch us again, not in his seventy-four. The frigates are another matter: the *Belle-Poule* is a heavy great brute, forty guns to our twenty-eight, and twenty-four-pounders; but the *Semillante* is smaller, and we should stand a chance with her, if only I can get our people to move brisk and fire straight. That would be something like a prize, eh? Ha, ha!'

'Do you apprehend any immediate danger? Have these vessels been seen at the Cape?'

'No, no, they are ten thousand miles away. They have come into the Indian Ocean by the Sunda Strait.'

'Then is it not perhaps a little premature to . . .'

'Not a bit, not a bit. Even from the service point of view, there is not a moment to be lost. The crew is not half worked up – nothing like the Livelies, not a patch on the Sophies; and then again, you know, I do so long to be married! The idea of being married drives a man, by God: you can have no idea. Married to Sophie, I mean: I beg pardon if I have spoke awkward again.'

'Why, my dear, I am no great friend to marriage, as you know; and sometimes I wonder whether you may not set too great a store on a contract compelling you to be happy – whether any arrival can amount to the sum of voyages – whether, in fact, it would not be better to travel indefinitely.' His own letters from Sophia told a wretched tale of persecution; Mrs Williams's health was really breaking up – the President of the College of Physicians and Sir John Butler were not men to be deceived by vapours or hypochondria, and there were some ugly, ugly symptoms – but her strong restless mind seemed to have gathered fresh energy. Sometimes touchingly pale and racked with pain (she bore real pain with great fortitude), sometimes her red, angry self, she was battering her daughter with Mr Hincksey, the new parson. In an exhausted voice from what she called her death-bed she would beg her daughter to give up this Captain Aubrey, who would never make her happy, who was going to India everyone knew why – who was going to India after that woman – and to let her mother die in peace, knowing her safely married and settled in Swiving rectory, so near at hand, among all their connections, so comfortable, not in seaside lodgings the other end of England or in Peru; married and settled with a man all her friends approved, a man with handsome private means and brilliant prospects, a man who could make a proper provision for her and who would look after her sisters when their mother was gone – poor motherless girls! A man to whom Sophie was not indifferent, whatever she might say. Captain Aubrey would soon get over it, if indeed he was not over it already, in the arms of some trollop: as his precious Lord Nelson said, every man was a bachelor once he was beyond Gibraltar; and India was a great way beyond Gibraltar, if the atlas was to be believed. In any case, Admiral Haddock and every gentleman of the Navy she had ever known, all said 'Sea-water and distance wash love away'; they were all of the same opinion. She only spoke for Sophie's good; and she implored her not to refuse this one, this last request, for the sake of her sisters, even if her mother's happiness meant nothing to her.

Stephen knew Hincksey, the new rector, a tall, well-looking, gentlemanlike man; a sound scholar; nothing of the evangelical; amusing, witty, kind. Stephen loved and esteemed Sophie more than any woman he knew, but he expected heroic virtue in no one: not heroic virtue of long duration, with few allies and they ten thousand miles away. Ten thousand miles, and how many weeks, months, even years? Time meant one thing in an active, ever-changing life; quite another in a remote provincial house, cooped up with a strong woman devoid of scruple, convinced of her divine rectitude.

In any case, Mrs Williams's fear and detestation of debt was wholly genuine, and this gave her argument a strength and truth far beyond her ordinary reach; in her quiet, settled part of the country imprisonment – imprisonment! – for debt did not happen, and the shocking tales she heard from outlying regions or from the dissolute, giddy metropolis concerned only raffish adventurers or worse; though her whole childhood had been tinged by whispered apocalyptic accounts of people so abandoned by God as to have lost their capital in the South Sea Bubble. By her own efforts Mrs Williams, like all the people she knew, might have earned fivepence a day at weeding or plain sewing, though some of the gentlemen might have done a little better at haysel and harvest; the accumulation of a hundred pounds was utterly beyond their powers, that of ten thousand beyond their imagination; and they worshipped capital with an unshakeable, uncomprehending, steady devotion, not devoid of superstitious practices.

Stephen had reflected upon this at the time of reading Sophie's letters; he had reflected upon it as he walked in the Brazilian forest, gazing at vast cataracts of orchids and butterflies the size of soup-plates; he reflected upon it now. The infinitesimal time of thought! The interval was barely long enough for Jack's expression to change from embarrassment to a hint of puzzled anxiety, sensing the motive behind Stephen's words, before a message with the news of the launch putting off with Mr Stanhope aboard turned it to pleasure and relief. 'I was so afraid we should miss the tide,' he said, running up the ladder into the swarming anthill on deck. Swarming but orderly: whatever he might say about their being only half worked up, the Surprises moved about their preparations to get under way with diligent purpose; the

Racoon was now forgotten, the land men had left the plough and the loom far far behind; and in their battles ashore with the crew of the *Lyra* the frigate's libertymen had fought as a body – there was not a man whose straw hat did not fly a ribbon with *Surprise* embroidered on it.

The ceremony of reception – Mr Stanhope never came aboard incognito – the clash of the Marines presenting arms, the long-expected order 'Up anchor', the bosun's pipe, and the crunch of the soldiers' boots as they ran to their places at the capstan bars.

The spell on land, prolonged to the last possible minute, had restored Mr Stanhope's spirits; but, thought Stephen, looking into his face, it had not done a great deal for his health: it had also taken away his sea-legs. He and Stephen were discussing the official letters that had reached him from England and from India when the tide turned against the wind, and the *Surprise*, heading out to sea, began to caper like a rocking-horse.

'You will forgive me, Dr Maturin,' he said. 'I think I will lie down. I have little hope of its doing any good, I know that in an hour's time this cold salivation will reach its paroxysm and that I shall become an inhuman being, unfit for decent company for how long, oh Lord, how long?' Stephen stayed with him as long as human comfort was supportable, then left him to his valet and a bucket, observing, 'You will be better soon, very soon; you will grow accustomed to the motion far sooner than you did in the Channel, off Gibraltar, off Madeira; your sufferings will soon be at an end.'

Little did he believe it, however: he had read books of voyages, he had conversed with Pullings, who, sailing with the China-bound East Indiamen, had made this trip several times; and he knew the reputation of the high southern latitudes. For this was not an ordinary passage to India; the Cape of Good Hope had been handed back to the Dutch with bows and smiles in the year two – clearly it would have to be taken from them again, but in the mean-time the *Surprise* must run

down far to the south of Africa, to the roaring forties, make
her easting, and so northwards to the waters where the summer monsoon blew,

The frigate ran down the trades as though she were determined to make up for lost time; the difference in her sailing
was apparent to everyone aboard – easier, faster, more stylish
by far. Jack was charmed; he explained to Stephen that she
was very like a thoroughbred mare – needed a light careful
hand – had to be steered small – had beautiful rnanners *on* a
wind and stayed like a cutter – but a captious fellow might
fault her going large: a very slight tendency to steer wild, that
called for great attention at the helm, to prevent her being
pooped. 'I should be sorry indeed to see her pooped,' he said,
shaking his head. 'Was she to broach to, I should not like to
answer for that damned foremast yard; nor yet for the mast
itself, the only thing I could not replace. You remember the
partners, for example?' Stephen had a vague recollection of
Jack striking a marlinspike into wood, and soft splinters flying; he, too, shook his head, looking grave; and in decency he
paused a moment before asking 'when he might reasonably
hope to see an albatross?'

'Poor dear,' said Jack, his mind still with his ship, 'I am
afraid she is growing old: all the spirit in the world, but anno
domini can't be beat. Albatross? Why, I dare say we may sight
one before we reach the height of the Cape. I will put it in
orders that you are to be told the moment an albatross is
seen.'

Day after day the figure of the noon altitude rose: 26°16′,
29°47′, 30°58′; every day the air grew colder – guernsey
frocks and fur hats were seen, pitiably reduced by their passage through the tropics, and the officers' uniforms were no
longer a torment to them; and every day, several times every
day, Stephen was called on deck to see mollyhawks, Cape
pigeons, petrels, for now they were in the rich waters of the
south Atlantic, waters that could and did support Leviathan,
who might often be seen sporting in the distance – once

indeed a bump in the night, a momentary check in the frigate's way, showed that they had come into immediate contact with him.

South and south for ever, beyond the zone where the trades were born, boring steadily through uncertain variable airs – cold, cold airs – towards the roaring forties, where the west wind, sweeping without a pause round the whole watery globe, would carry them eastwards beyond the tip of Africa. Week after week of determined sailing, with the sun lower at every noon, lower and as it were smaller: brilliant, but with no warmth in it: while at the same time the moon seemed to grow.

It was strange to see how quickly this progress took on the nature of ordinary existence: the *Surprise* had not run off a thousand miles before the unvarying routine of the ship's day, from the piping up of the hammocks to the drumbeat of 'Heart of Oak' for the gunroom dinner, thence to quarters and the incessantly-repeated exercising of the guns, and so to the setting of the watch, obliterated both the beginning of the voyage and its end, it obliterated even time, so that it seemed normal to all hands that they should travel endlessly over this infinite and wholly empty sea, watching the sun diminish and the moon increase.

Both were in the pale sky on a memorable Thursday when Stephen and Bonden resumed their customary places in the mizzentop, dismissing its ordinary inhabitants and settling down upon the folded studdingsails. Bonden had graduated from pot-hooks and hangers far north of the line; he had skimmed his ignoble slate overboard in 3°S; now he was yardarm to yardarm with pen and ink, and as the southern latitude mounted, so his neat hand grew smaller and smaller and smaller.

'Verse,' said Stephen. It was an inexpressible satisfaction to Bonden to write in metre: with a huge childish grin he opened his inkhorn and poised his attentive pen – a booby's quill.

'Verse,' said Stephen again, gazing at the illimitable blue-grey sea and the lop-sided moon above it. 'Verse:

> *Then we upon our globe's last verge shall go.*
> *And view the ocean leaning on the sky;*
> *From thence our rolling neighbors we shall know,*
> *And on the lunar world securely pry* by God I believe I
> see the albatross.'

' . . . believe I see the albatross,' said Bonden's lips silently. 'It don't rhyme. Another line, sir, maybe?' But receiving no answer from his rigid teacher he looked up, followed his gaze, and said, 'Why so you do, sir. I dare say he will fetch our wake directly, and overhaul us. Wonderful great birds they are, though something fishy, without you skin 'em. There are some old-fashioned coves that has a spite against them, which they say they bring ill winds.'

The albatross came nearer and nearer, following the ship's wake in a sinuous path, never moving its wings but coming up at such a pace that what was a remote fleck when Stephen first saw it was an enormous presence by the time Bonden had finished his receipt for albatross pie. An enormous white presence with black wing-tips, thirteen feet across, poised just astern: then it banked, shot along the side, vanished behind the cloud of sails, and reappeared fifty yards behind the ship.

Messenger after messenger ran into the mizzentop. 'Sir, there's your albatross, two points on the larboard quarter.' Achmet reported it in Urdu, and immediately afterwards his dull blue face was thrust aside by a ship's boy from the quarterdeck with 'Captain's compliments, sir, and he believes he has seen the bird you was asking after.'

'Maturin, I say, Maturin, here's your albatross!' This was Bowes, the purser, clambering up by the power of his hands, trailing his game leg.

At last Bonden said, 'My watch is called, sir. I must be

going, asking your pardon, or Mr Rattray will give me the rub. May I send up a pea-jacket, sir? 'Tis mortal cold.'

'Ay, ay. Do, do,' murmured Stephen, unhearing, rapt in admiration.

The bell struck, the watch changed. One bell, two bells, three; the drum for quarters, the beating of retreat – no guns for once, thank God; and still he gazed and still in the fading light the albatross wheeled, dropped astern, occasionally alighting for some object thrown overboard, ran up in a long series of curves, the perfection of smooth gliding ease.

The days that followed were among the most trying that Stephen had spent at sea. Some of the forecastlemen, old South Sea whalers, were passionate albatross-fishers: after his first vehement outburst they would not offer to do it when he was on deck, but as soon as he went below a line would be privily veered out and the great bird would come flapping in, to be converted into tobacco-pouches, pipe-stems, hot dinners, down comforters to be worn next the skin, and charms against drowning – no albatross ever drowned: as many as half a dozen were following the ship now, and not one of them was ever seen to drown, blow rough, blow smooth. He knew that morally his case was weak, for he had bought and skinned the first specimens: he was most unwilling to invoke authority, but he was much occupied in the sick-bay – the opening of case 113 (three-year old pork that had seen its time in the West Indies station) had produced something surprising in the dysentery way: two pneumonias as well – and in the end, worn out by darting up and down, he appealed to Jack.

'Well, old Stephen,' said he, 'I will give the order, if you wish: but they won't like it, you know. It's against custom: people have fished for albatrosses and mutton-birds ever since ships came into these seas. They won't like it. You will get wry looks and short answers, and half the older hands will start prophesying woe – we shall run into a widow-maker, or hit a mountain of ice.'

'From all I read, and from all Pullings tells me, it would be safe enough to foretell a gale of wind, in forty degrees south.'

'Come,' said Jack, reaching for his fiddle. 'Let us play the Boccherini through before we turn in. We may not have another chance this side of the Cape, with your upsetting the natural order of things.'

The wry looks, the reproachful tones, began the next morning; so did the prophecies. Many a grizzled head was shaken on the forecastle, with the ominous words, profoundly true and not altogether outside Stephen's hearing. 'We shall see what we shall see.'

South and south she ran, flanking across the west wind, utterly alone under the grey sky, heading into the immensity of ocean. From one day to the next the sea grew icy cold, and the cold seeped into the holds, the berth-deck and the cabins, a humid, penetrating cold. Stephen came on deck reflecting with satisfaction upon his sloth, now a parlour-boarder with the Irish Franciscans at Rio, and a secret drinker of the altar-wine. He found the frigate was racing along under a press of canvas, lying over so that her deck sloped like a roof and her lee chains were buried in the foam; twelve and a half knots with the wind on her quarter – royals, upper and lower studdingsails, almost everything she had; her starboard tacks aboard, for Jack still wanted a little more southing. He was there, right aft by the taffrail, looking now at the western sky, now up at the rigging. 'What do you think of this for a swell?' he cried.

Blinking in the strong cold wind Stephen considered it: vast smooth waves, dark, mottled with white, running from the west diagonally across the frigate's course, two hundred yards from crest to crest: they came with perfect regularity, running under her quarter, lifting her high, high, so that the horizon spread out another twenty miles, then passing ahead, so that she sank into the trough, and her courses, her lower sails, sagged in the calm down there. In one of these valleys that he saw was an albatross flying without effort or concern,

a huge bird, but now so diminished by the vast scale of the
sea that it might have been one of the smaller gulls. 'It is
grandiose,' he said.

'Ain't it?' said Jack. 'I do love a blow.' There was keen pleasure in his eye, but a watchful pleasure too; and as the ship
rose slowly up he glanced again at the topsail-studdingsail. As
she rose the full force of the wind laid her over, and the studdingsail-boom strained forward, bending far out of the true.
All the masts and yards showing this curving strain: they all
groaned and spoke; but none like the twisting studdingsail-
booms. A sheet of spray flew over the waist, passing through
the rigging and vanishing over the larboard bow, soaking Mr
Hailes the gunner as it passed. He was going from gun to gun
with his mates, putting preventer-breechings to the guns, to
hold them tighter against the side. Rattray was among the
booms, making all fast and securing the boats: all the responsible men were moving about, with no orders given; and as
they worked they glanced at the Captain, while he, just as
often, put out his hand to test the strain on the rigging, and
turned his head to look at the sky, the sea, the upper sails.

'This is cracking on,' said Joliffe.

'It will be cracking off, presently,' said Church, 'if he don't
take in.'

For a glass and more the watch on deck had been waiting
for the order to lay aloft and reduce sail before the Lord
reduced it Himself: yet still the order did not come. Jack
wanted every last mile out of this splendid day's run; and in
any case the frigate's tearing pace, the shrill song of her rigging, her noble running lift and plunge filled him with
delight, a vivid ecstasy that he imagined to be private but that
shone upon his face, although his behaviour was composed,
reserved and indeed somewhat severe – his orders cracked
out sharp and quick as he sailed her hard, completely identified with the ship. He was on the quarterdeck, yet at the
same time he was in the straining studdingsail-boom, gauging
the breaking-point exactly.

'Yes,' he said, as though a long period of time had not passed. 'And it will be more grandiose by half before the end of the watch. The glass is dropping fast, and it will start to blow, presently. Just you wait until this sea gets up and starts to tumble about. Mr Harrowby, Mr Harrowby, another man to the wheel, if you please. And we will get the flying jib and stuns'ls off her.'

The bosun's pipe, the rush of feet, and her tearing speed sensibly diminished. Mr Stanhope, clinging to the companion-ladder, cruelly in the way, said, 'It is a wonder they do not fall off, poor fellows. This is exhilarating, is it not? Like champagne.'

So it was, with the whole ship vibrating and a deep bass hum coming from the hold, and the clean keen air searching deep into their lungs: but well before nightfall the clean keen air blew so strong as to whip the breath away as they tried to draw it in, and the *Surprise* was under close-reefed topsails and courses, topgallant-masts struck down on deck, running faster still, and still holding her course south-east.

During the night Stephen heard a number of bumps and cries through his sleep, and he was aware of a change of course, for his cot no longer swung in the same direction. But he was not prepared for what he saw when he came on deck. Under the low grey tearing sky, half driving rain, half driving spray, the whole sea was white – a vast creaming spread as far as eye could see. He had seen the Bay of Biscay at its worst, and the great south-west gales on the Irish coast: they were nothing to this. For a moment the whole might have been a wild landscape, mountainous yet strangely regular; but then he saw that the whole was in motion, a vast majestic motion whose size concealed its terrifying dreamlike speed. Now the crests and troughs were enormously greater; now they were very much farther apart; and now the crests were curling over and breaking as they came, an avalanche of white pouring down the steep face. The *Surprise* was running almost straight before them, east by south; she had managed to

strike her mizzentopmast at first light – anything to diminish
the wind-pressure aft and thus the risk of broaching-to – and
man-ropes were rigged along her streaming deck. As his eyes
reached the level of the quarterdeck he saw a wave, a green-
grey wall towering above the taffrail, racing towards them –
swift inevitability. He strained his head back to see its top,
curving beyond the vertical as it came yet still balancing with
the speed of its approach, a beard of wind-torn spray flying
out before it. He heard Jack call an order to the man at the
wheel: the frigate moved a trifle from her course, rose, tilting
her stern skywards so that Stephen clung backwards to the
ladder, rose and rose; and the mortal wave swept under her
counter, dividing and passing on to smother her waist in foam
and solid water, on to bar the horizon just ahead, while the
ship sank in the trough and the shriek of the rigging sank an
octave as the strain slackened.

'Seize hold, Doctor,' shouted Jack. 'Take both hands to it.'

Stephen crept along the life-line, catching a reproachful
look from the four men at the wheel, as who should say 'Look
what you done with your albatrosses, mate', and reached
the stanchion to which Jack was lashed. 'Good morning, sir,'
he said.

'A very good morning to you. It is coming on to blow.'

'What?'

'It is coming on to blow,' said Jack, with greater force.
Stephen frowned, and looked astern through the haze of
spray; and there, whiter than the foam, were two albatrosses,
racing across the wind. One wheeled towards the ship, rose
to the height of the taffrail and poised there in the eddy not
ten feet away. He saw its mild round eye looking back at him,
the perpetual minute change of its wing-feathers, its tail;
then it banked, rose on the wind, darted down, and its wings
raised high it paddled on the face of an advancing cliff of
water, picked something up and shot away along the valley of
the wave before it broke.

Killick appeared with a sour, mean look on his face, all

screwed up against the wind; he passed the coffee-pot from the bosom of his jacket; Jack put the spout into his mouth and drank. 'You had better go below,' he shouted; to Stephen. 'Go below and have some breakfast: you may not get another hot meal, if it turns nasty.'

The gunroom was of the same opinion. They had their table spread with boiled ham, beef-steaks, and a sea-pie, all held down as tight as double-rove fiddles would hold them, but all mingling their gravy in reckless confusion.

'Sea-pie, Doctor?' said Etherege, beaming at him. 'I have kept you a piece.'

'If you please.' Stephen held out his plate, received the piece on the top of the rise; and as the frigate shot down the face of the wave so the pie rose in the air. Etherege instantly pinned it with his practised fork, held it until she reached the trough and gravity went to work again.

Pullings gave him a selected biscuit, and told him with a smile 'that the glass was falling yet; it had to be worse before it got better', and begged him 'to blow out his luff while he might'.

The purser was telling them of an infallible method of cal-culating the height of waves by simple triangulation when Hervey plunged into the gunroom, spouting water like an inverted fountain. 'Oh dear, oh dear,' he said, throwing his tarpaulins into his cabin and putting on his spectacles. 'Give me a cup of tea, Babbington, there's a good fellow. My fingers are too numb to turn the tap.'

'The tea has gone by the board, sir. Would coffee do?'

'Anything, anything, so long as it is warm and wet. Is there any sea-pie left?' They showed him the empty dish. 'Why, here's a pretty thing,' he cried. 'All night on deck, and no sea-pie.' When ham had mollified him, Stephen said, 'Why did you spend all night on deck, pray?'

'The skipper would not go below, though I begged him to turn in; and I could not very well do so with him on deck. I have a noble nature,' said Hervey, smiling now through the ham.

'Are we in extreme peril then?' asked Stephen. Oh yes, they assured him, with grave, anxious faces; they were in horrid danger of foundering, broaching-to, running violently into Australia; but there was a hope, just a very slight hope, of their meeting with a mountain of ice and clambering on to it – as many as half a dozen men might be saved. When they had exercised their wit for some considerable time, Hervey said, 'The skipper is worried about the foretopmast. We went aloft to look at it, and – would you credit it? – the force of the wind upon us as we went aloft threw the ship a point off her course. The coaking just above the cap is not what any of our friends could wish; and if a cross-sea sets in, and we start to roll, I shall start saying my prayers.'

'Mr Stanhope begs Dr Maturin to spare him a minute, when conwenient,' said Killick in his ear.

He found them sitting in the cold dark cabin by the light of a purser's dip: Mr White, Atkins, a young attaché called Berkeley, on chairs with their feet in the water that swilled fore and aft with a dismal sound, all wearing greatcoats with the collars turned up; Mr Stanhope half lying on the couch; servants lurking in the shadows. Apparently they had not been fed; and their spirit-stoves would not work. They were all quite silent.

Mr Stanhope was extremely obliged to Dr Maturin for coming so quick; he did not wish to give the least trouble, but should be grateful if he might be told whether this was the end? Water was coming in through the sides; and a seaman had given his valet to understand that this was the gravest sign of all. One of the young gentlemen had confirmed this to Mr Atkins, adding, that being pooped was more likely than actual foundering, or breaking in two; though neither possibility was to be overlooked. What did being *pooped* imply? Could they be of any use?

Stephen said that as far as his understanding went, the real danger lay in a following wave striking the back of the ship such a buffet as to twirl it sideways to the wind, when it would lie down, receive the next wave broadside-on, and so be overwhelmed; hence the necessity for speed, for flying before the wind with all sail that could be set, and for steering with due attention, to outrun and to avoid these blows. Yet they were to consider, that as the ship was exposed to the full force of the blast when it was on the top of the monstrous wave, so it was sheltered in the hollow some fifty feet below, where nevertheless the forward speed must be maintained, to enable the ship to be guided in the desired direction and to diminish the relative velocity of the ensuing wave; and that this necessarily called for a nice adjustment of the various sails and ropes in all their complexity. But as far as he could tell, all these things were being done with conscientious diligence; and for his part, under such a commander, with such a crew and such a vessel, he felt no rational apprehension whatsoever. 'Captain Aubrey has repeatedly stated in my hearing, that the *Surprise* is the very finest frigate of her tonnage in the Royal Navy.' The water coming in was inconvenient and even disconcerting, but it was a usual phenomenon in such circumstances, particularly in aged vessels; it was what the mariners termed 'the working of the ship'. And he cautioned them against too literal a belief in the words of the sailors: 'They take an obscure delight in practising upon us landlubbers.'

Once he was relieved of the sensation of imminent death, Mr Stanhope relapsed into the appalling dry sea-sickness that had struck him in the night. As Stephen and the chaplain helped him into his cot he said, with an attempt at a smile, 'So grateful – not quite suited for sea-travel – never undertake sea-voyage again – if there is no way home by land, shall stay in Kampong for ever.'

But the others grew indignant, shrill and vocal. Mr. White thought it scandalous that government should have sent them in so small a boat, and one that leaked. Did Dr Maturin realise that it was very *cold* at sea? Far colder than on land. Mr Atkins said that the officers he had questioned replied in an off-hand manner or not at all; and that surely the Captain should have waited upon His Excellency with an explanation before this. Last night's supper had been disgracefully under-done: he should like to see the Captain.

'You will find him on the quarterdeck,' said Stephen. 'I am sure he will be happy to listen to your complaints.'

In the silence that followed this Mr Berkeley said in a lugubrious tone, 'and all our chamber-pots are broken.'

Stephen made his way forward to the sick-bay, through the soaking, smelly berth-deck where the watch below were sleeping, fully-clothed, sleeping in spite of the tremendous pitch and the roar, for all hands had been called three times that night. He found the usual accidents, the bangs and bruises of a furious storm; one man had been flung against the fluke of an anchor, another had pitched head-first down the fore-hatch as it was being battened down, another had contrived to impale himself on his own marlinspike; but nothing that went beyond the surgeons' powers. What wor-ried them was their worst pneumonia, an elderly seaman named Woods; it had been touch and go with him before the storm, and now the prodigious shaking, the absence of rest, had turned the scale. Stephen listened to his breathing, felt his pulse, exchanged a few low words with M'Alister, and fin-ished his round in silence.

On deck he found the scene changed once more. The wind had increased and it had backed three points; the nature of the sea had changed. Now, instead of the regular procession of vast rollers, there was a confusion of waves running across, bursting seas that filled the valleys with leaping spray: the underlying pattern was still the same, but now the crests were a quarter of a mile apart and even higher than before, though at times this was less evident because of the turmoil between. There were no albatrosses anywhere in sight. Yet still the frigate ran on at this racing speed under the precious scrap of canvas forward, rising nobly to the gigantic waves, shouldering the cross-seas aside: the launch had been carried

away in spite of the bosun's treble gripes, but there seemed to
be no other damage. She was beginning to roll now, as well as
pitch; and on each plunge her head and the lee side of her
forecastle vanished under white water.

All the officers were on deck, wedged into odd corners. Mr
Bowes, unrecognisable in tarpaulins, caught Stephen as a
weather-lurch knocked him off his balance and guided him
along the life-line to the Captain, still standing there by his
stanchion. He waited while Jack told Callow to go below and
read the barometer, and then said, 'Woods, of the afterguard,
is sinking fast; if you wish to see him before he dies, you must
come soon.'

Jack reflected, automatically calling out his orders to the
men at the wheel. Dared he leave the deck at this stage? Callow came crawling aft. 'Rising, sir,' he shouted.

'It's risen two lines and a half. And Mr Hervey desires me to
say, the relieving tackles are hooked on.'

Jack nodded. 'That means a stronger blow,' he said, glancing at the foretopsail, mould-eaten in the tropics: but they
had done all they could to strengthen it, and so far the storm-
canvas held. 'I'll come now, while I can.' He cast himself off,
called the master and Pullings to take his place, and blundered heavily below. In the cabin he drank off a glass of wine
and flexed his arms. 'I am sorry to hear what you tell me
about poor old Woods,' he said, still in the same hoarse roar;
then, moderating his voice, 'Is there no hope?' Stephen shook
his head. 'I say, Stephen, I hope Mr Stanhope and his people
are not too tumbled about – not too upset.'

'No. I told them the *Surprise* was a capital ship, and that all
was well.'

'So it is, too, as long as the foretopsail holds. She is the
bravest ship that ever swam. And if the glass is right, this will
blow out in a couple of days. Come, let us go along?'

'Do not be too distressed: it is horrible to see and hear, but
he feels nothing. It is a very easy death.' Horrible it was.
Woods was a leaden blue, and the animal sound of his

laboured breath sounded louder, close to, than the all-pervading din. He might have recognised Jack; he might not. His open mouth and half-closed eyes showed little change. Jack did his duty, said the words expected of a captain – it touched him to the quick – spent a few moments with the other men, and hurried back to his stanchion.

A quarter of an hour, yet what a change! When he went below the frigate had no more than a ten-degree roll: now her larboard cathead touched green water. And still they came sweeping up from the black westwards, the gigantic streaming seas, taller than ever – impossibly tall— and their foam filled her waist five feet deep, while the whole of her forecastle vanished as she plunged. Still she rose, pouring water, spouting from her scuppers: every time she rose. More heavily now?

In the cabin one of Mr Stanhope's servants, half drunk, had managed to blow himself up with a spirit-stove: miserably burnt, and shattered by falling against a gun, he was being patched up by the surgeons. Mr White, Mr Atkins and Mr Berkeley, all of whom had struggled earnestly in London to reach this position, sat wedged together on the couch, with their feet tucked up out of the water, staring in front of them. Hour after hour.

On deck the day was fading, if that grey shrieking murk could be called day. Yet still Jack could see the rollers sweeping towards her stern from half a mile away, their white tops clear: their whole length traversed the sky as the frigate rolled; and two monstrous waves, too close to one another, exploded in ruin just astern, to be swept up into a still greater whole that thundered as it came, vast and overwhelming. And above the thunder as it passed his waiting ear caught a sharp gun-like crack, a crash forward, and the foremast went by the board. The foretopsail, ripped from its yard, vanished far ahead, a flickering whiteness in the gloom.

'All hands, all hands,' he roared. Already the ship was steering wild, yawing off her course. He glanced back. They were running down into the trough: unless they could get her before the wind – could get some headsail on her – the next wave would poop her. She would broach to and take the next sea on her beam.

'All hands – ' his voice tearing blood from his throat – 'Pullings, men into the foreshrouds. It's gone above the cap. Forestays'l, forestays'l! Come along with me. Axes! Axes!'

In the momentary lull of the deepest trough he raced along the gangway, followed by twenty men: a cross-sea broke over the side waist-deep: they ploughed through and they were on the forecastle before the ship, slewed half across the wind, began to rise – before the next wave was more than half-way to them. Men were swarming up the weather ratlines, forcing themselves up against the strength of the gale; their backs made sail enough to bring her head a little round before the sea struck them with an all-engulfing crash and spout of foam – far enough round for the wave to take her abaft the beam, and still she swam. The axes cleared the wreckage. Bonden was out on the bowsprit, hacking at the foretopmaststay that still held fast to the floating mast, slewing the ship around; holding his breath Jack swarmed out after him, his head under the foam, feeling for the gaskets of the forestaysail, snugged down tight under the stay. He had it – his hands, many hands were tearing at the lashings, so tight they would not, would not come.

'Hold on!' roared in his ear, and there was a strong hand pressing on his neck: then an unimaginable force of water, a weight and a strength past anything – the third wave that broached the frigate squarely to.

The pressure slackened. His head was above water, and now there were more men in the shrouds. Again the thrust of the gale on them brought her head round, helped by a savage cross-sea; but they could not hold there for ever – a few more minutes of this and the shrouds would be swept clear. Down again as she plunged, and running his hand along the sail he found the trouble – the down-hauler had fouled the clew:

stray lines from the wreckage in the hanks. 'Knife!' he roared as his head came clear. It was in his reaching hand: a lightning slash, and all sprang free.

'Hold on! Hold on!' and again the thunder of a falling sea, a mountainous wave: the intolerable pressure on his chest: the total certainty that he must not let go of the sail clutched under him: his legs curled round the bowsprit to hold on: hold on . . . strength going. But here was breath again in his bursting lungs and he reared up out of the water bawling, 'Man the halliards. D'ye hear me aft? Man the halliards there!'

In slow jerks the sail rose up the stay, filled: they sheeted home. But now she was broadside on, wallowing. Oh would it be in time? Slowly, heavily she turned as the forestaysail took the strain, the great wave racing up – turned, turned just enough and took it on her quarter: rose to the height, and the full blast in the head-sail set her right before the wind. Faster and faster she moved, steering nimbly now; for though the last blow had flung the men from the wheel the relieving-tackles held; and the next wave passed harmlessly under her stern.

He swarmed in, clinging to the knightheads for a moment as she plunged again, and then he was on the forecastle: it was clear of wreckage: the sail set well. He called the men down from the shrouds and moved along the gangway. 'Any hands lost, Hervey?' was asked, with his arms round the stanchion.

'No, sir. Some hurt, but they have all come aft. Are you all right, sir?'

Jack nodded. 'She steers better,' he said. 'Dismiss the watch below. Grog for all hands: serve it out in the half-deck. Pass the word for the bosun.'

All night. The officers stayed on deck that endless night or spent a few brief spells in the gunroom, sitting between dreaming and waking, listening gravely, concentrated upon that one triangle of rigid canvas forward. After an hour Jack

found the trembling that had affected his entire body die
away, and with it even the consciousness of his body. The
wheel was relieved. Relieved again: again. Continually his
croaking voice called out orders, and twice he sent picked
parties forward, strengthening, frapping, making all as fast as
ever they could in a night that cut to the bone. A little before
dawn the wind veered a point, two points, blowing with sudden flaws, vacuums that hurt his ears; it reached a screaming
note more savage than anything he had heard and his heart
hurt him for the staysail, for the ship – an edge of sentiment
and self-pity, with Sophia's name hovering on the edge of
utterance aloud. Then slowly, slowly, the shriek dropped half
a tone, another, and another: a low buffeting roar at last,
when the faint straggling light showed a sea white from rim to
rim, with the steady procession of great rollers in their due
solemn ordered ranks once again – vast indeed, but no longer
maniac. No cross-sea; very little roll; and the *Surprise* scudding over the desolation, passing every sea under her counter,
her waist with no more than a foot of water swirling about it.
An albatross broad on the starboard beam. He cast off his
lashings and moved stiffly forward. 'We will ship the pumps,
Mr Hervey, if you please. And I believe we may get a scrap of
maintopsail on her.'

PEACE, PEACE. Madagascar lay astern and the Cormorins;
the shattered hulk that had crept north of the fortieth parallel, trailing ends of rope and pumping day and night, was now
as trim as art and a limited supply of paint could make her.
An expert eye would have seen a great deal of twice-laid stuff
in the rigging and an odd scarcity of boats on the booms; it
would have stared with amazement at the attachments of the
rudder; and it would have noted that in spite of fair and moderate breeze the frigate carried nothing above her topsails.
She dared not; although with her new foretopmast and her
fresh paintwork she looked 'as pretty as a picture', her inward
parts had suffered. Jack spoke so often of her butt-ends and

her hanging knees that Stephen said, 'Captain Aubrey, your butt-ends and your hanging knees cannot be attempted to be rectified, as I understand you, until you have her *docked*, three thousand miles away; so may I beg you to clap a stopper over all and to accept the inevitable with a decent appearance of unconcern? If we fall apart, why, we fall apart, and there is the end to it. For my part, I have every confidence of reaching Bombay.'

'What I know, and what you don't know,' cried Jack, 'is that I have not so much as a single ten-inch spike left aboard.'

'God set a flower upon you, my dear, with your ten-inch spike,' said Stephen. 'Of course I know it: you have mentioned them daily these last two hundred leagues, together with your hanging-ends and double-sister-blocks; and nightly too, prattling in your sleep. Bow, bow to predestination or at least confine yourself to silent prayer.'

'Not so much as a ten-inch spike, not a mast or boom but what is fished,' said Jack, shaking his head. And it was true: yet with an irritating complacency Mr Stanhope, his suite, and now even Dr Maturin cried out that this was delightful now – that was the only way of travelling – a post-chaise on the turnpike road was nothing in comparison of this – they should recommend it to all their friends.

Certainly it was delightful for the passengers, the smooth sea, the invigorating breeze carrying them steadily into warmer airs; but in the latitude of the Isle of France Jack, his carpenter and boatswain, and all his seamanlike officers, looked out eagerly for a French privateer – a spare topmast or so, a few spars, a hundred fathoms of one-and-a-half-inch rope would have made them so happy! They stared with all their might, and the Indian Ocean remained as empty as the South Atlantic; and here there were not even whales.

On and on she sailed, in warmer seas but void, as though they alone had survived Deucalion's flood; as though all land had vanished from the earth; and once again the ship's routine dislocated time and temporal reality so that this progress was an endless dream, even a circular dream, contained within an unbroken horizon and punctuated only by the sound of guns thundering daily in preparation for an enemy whose real existence it was impossible to conceive.

STEPHEN LAID DOWN his pistols, wiped the barrels with his handkerchief and shut the case. They were warm from his practice, but still the bottle hanging from the foreyardarm swung there intact. It was not the fault of the pistols, either; they were the best Joe Manton could produce, and the purser had hit the mark three times. It was true that Stephen had been firing left-handed, the right having suffered worse at Port Mahon; but a year ago he would certainly have knocked the bottle down, left hand or not. Pressing? Trying too hard? He sighed; and pondering over the nature of muscular and nervous co-ordination he groped his way up into the mizzentop: Mr Atkins gazed after him, more nearly convinced that it would be safe to quarrel with him once they reached Bombay.

Reaching the futtock-shrouds, Stephen took a sudden determination: if his body would not obey him in one way it should in another. He seized the ropes that ran outwards to the rim of the platform, and instead of making his way into the top by writhing through them he forced his person grunting upwards, a diagonal reversed climb with his back towards the sea and himself hanging at an angle of forty-five degrees, and so reached his goal by the path a seaman would have taken – a sailor, but no landsman bound by the ordinary law of gravity. Bonden was still peering down the lubber's hole, the way Stephen had always come before, the safe, direct, logical, but ignominious road; and his unsuccessful attempt at disguising his astonishment when he turned was a consolation to Stephen's mind: its element of vanity glowed cherry-pink. Mastering a laboured gasp that would have ruined the effect, he said, 'Let us go straight to verse.' This was all that one inspiration could accomplish and he paused, as if in thought, until his heart was beating normally. 'Verse,' he said again. 'Are you ready, Barret Bonden? Then dash away.

> *Thus to the Eastern wealth through storms we go,*
> *But now, the Cape once doubled, fear no more:*
> *A constant trade-wind will securely blow,*
> *And gently lay us on the spicy shore.'*

'An elegant sentiment, sir,' said Bonden. 'As good as Dibdin any day. If you wanted to crab it, which far from me be it, you might say the gent was a trifle out in his trade-wind, this rightly being the monsoon, as we call it by sea. And as for wealth, why, that's poetic licence; or, as you might say, all my eye. Spice maybe; I'm not saying anything against spice, nor yet spicy shores, though most of them is shit begging your pardon, in Indian ports. But wealth, I make so bold as to laugh, ha, ha; why, sir, bating a few privateers out of the Isle of France and Reunion there's not a prize for us in this whole Indian mortal Ocean, not from here to Java Head, not since Admiral Rainier cleaned up Trincomalee. Unless maybe we take on Admiral Linois on his seventy-four, that chased us so cruel hard in the poor old *Sophie*. God love us, he was a merry old gentleman; you remember him, sir?' Certainly Stephen remembered him; and that bitter chase in the Mediterranean – the loss of their ship – their capture. Bonden's face changed from smiling reminiscence to stony reserve: he slid his book into his bosom as Mr Callow's hideous face appeared above the rail with the Captain's compliments and did Dr Maturin intend shifting his coat?

'Why in God's name would I shift my coat?' cried Stephen. 'What is more, I have no coat on, at all.'

'Perhaps he thought you might like to put one on for Mr Stanhope's dinner, sir: a genteel way of alluding to it. It is within minutes of three bells, sir: the sand is almost out. And he particularly begs you, sir, to come down through the – to come down the usual way.'

'Mr Stanhope's dinner,' said Stephen in an undertone. He stood up and stared down at the quarterdeck, where, except for her captain, all the frigate's officers were gathered in their full-dress uniforms. Just so. He had forgotten the invitation. How remote it seemed, that quarterdeck, crowded with blue coats, red coats and half a dozen black, with the busy check-shirted seamen moving among them: no great distance vertically – fifty feet or so – but still how remote. He knew all the men there, liked several of them, loved young Babbington and Pullings; and yet he had the impression of living in a vacuum. It came to him strongly now, though some of the upturned faces were winking and nodding at him: he slid his legs through the lubber's hole with a grave expression on his face and began his laborious descent.

'So full a ship, so close-packed a world, moving urgently along, surrounded by its own vacuum; each man bombinating in his own, no doubt. My journal, re-read but yesterday, gives me this same impression: an egocentric man living amidst pale shades. It reflects none of the complex, vivid life of this crowded vessel. In its pages, my host (whom I esteem) and his people hardly exist, nor yet the gunroom, he reflected during intervals of conversation as he sat at the envoy's left, stuffed rapidly into his best coat by Jack's powerful hand, breeched and brushed in one minute twenty seconds flat while the Marine sentry, under penalty of death, held the half-hour glass concealed in his hand to prevent the striking of the bell – as he sat there eating up the last long-preserved delicacies from Mr Stanhope's store and drinking milk-warm claret in honour of the Duke of Cumberland's birthday. But he was not without a social conscience, and aware that he had caused great uneasiness, that his very, very dirty face and hands reflected discredit upon the ship, he exerted himself to talk, to be agreeable; and even, after the port had gone round and round, to sing.

Mr Bowes, the purser, had obliged the company with an endless ballad on the battle of the First of June, in which he had served a gun: it was set to the tune of 'I was, d'ye see, a Waterman,' but he produced its slow length in an unvarying tone, neither shout nor cry but nearly allied to both, pitched in the neighbourhood of lower A, with his eyes fixed bravely on a knot in the deckhead above Mr Stanhope. The envoy smiled bravely, and in the thundering chorus of 'To make 'em strike or die' his neighbours made out his piping treble.

The frigate could boast no high standard of musical accomplishment: Etherege had never really known the tune of his comic song; and now, bemused by Mr Stanhope's port, he forgot the words too; but when at last he abandoned it, after three heavy falls, he assured them that well sung, by Kitty Pake for example, it was irresistibly droll – how they had laughed! But he was no hand at a song, he was sorry to say, though he loved music passionately; it was far more in the Doctor's line – the Doctor could imitate cats on the 'cello to perfection – would deceive any dog you cared to bring forward.

Mr Stanhope turned his worn, polite face towards Stephen, blinking in a shaft of sunlight that darted through a scuttle on the roll; and Stephen noticed, for the first time, that the faded blue eyes were showing the first signs of that whitish ring, the arcus senilis. But from the far end of the table Mr Atkins called out, 'No, no, your Excellency; we must not trouble Dr Maturin; his mind is far above these simple joys.'

Stephen emptied his glass, set his eyes upon the appropriate knot, tapped the table and began,

> *'The seas their wonders might reveal*
> *But Chloe's eyes have more:*
> *Nor all the treasure they conceal,*
> *Can equal mine on shore.'*

His harsh, creaking voice, indicating rather than striking the note, did nothing to improve the ship's reputation; but now Jack was accompanying him with a deep booming hum

that made the glasses vibrate, and he went on with at least
greater volume,

> *'From native Ireland's temp'rate coast*
> *Remove me farther yet,*
> *To shiver in eternal frost,*
> *Or melt with India's heat.'*

At this point he saw that Mr Stanhope would not be able to
outlast another verse: the heat, the want of air (the *Surprise*
had the breeze directly aft and almost none came below), the
tight-packed cabin, the necessary toasts, the noise, had done
their work; and the rapidly-whitening face, the miserable
fixed smile, meant a syncope within the next few bars.

'Come, sir,' he said, slipping from his place. 'Come. A
moment, if you please.' He led him to his sleeping-cabin, laid
him down, loosened his neckcloth and waistband, and when
some faint colour began to return, he left him in peace.
Meanwhile the party had broken up, had tiptoed away; and
unwilling to answer inquiries on the quarterdeck, Stephen
made his way forward through the berth-deck and the sick-
bay to the head of the ship, where he remained throughout
the frigate's evening activities, leaning on the bowsprit and
watching the cutwater sheer through mile after mile of
ocean, parting it with a sound like tearing silk, so that it
streamed away in even curves along the *Surprise*'s side to join
her wake, now eight thousand miles in length. The unfin-
ished song ran in his head, and again and again he sang
beneath his breath,

> *Her image shall my days beguile*
> *And still my dream shall be . . .*

Dream: that was the point. Little contact with reality, perhaps – a child of hope – a potentiality – infinitely better left
unrealised. He had been most passionately attached to Diana

Villiers, and he had felt a great affection for her, too, a strong affection as from one human being to another in something of the same case; and that, he thought, she had returned to some degree – all she was capable of returning. To what degree? She had treated him very badly both as a friend and a lover and he had welcomed what he called his liberation from her: a liberation that had not lasted, however. No great while after his last sight of her 'prostituting herself in a box at the Opera' – a warm expression by which he meant consciously using her charms to please other men – the unreasoning part of his mind evoked living images of these same charms, of that incredible grace of movement when it was truly sponta- neous; and very soon his reasoning mind began to argue that this fault, too, was to be assimilated to the long catalogue of defects that he knew and accepted, defects that he felt to be outweighed if not cancelled by her qualities of wit and des- perate courage: she was never dull, she was never cowardly. But moral considerations were irrelevant to Diana: in her, physical grace and dash took the place of virtue. The whole context was so different that an unchastity odious in another woman had what he could only call a purity in her: another purity: pagan, obviously – a purity from another code alto- gether. That grace had been somewhat blown upon to be sure, but there was enough and to spare; she had destroyed only the periphery; it was beyond her power to touch the essence of the thing, and that essence set her apart from any woman, any person, he had ever known.

This, at least, was his tentative conclusion and he had trav- elled these eight thousand miles with a continually mounting desire to see her again; and with an increasing dread of the event – desire exceeding dread, of course.

But Lord, the infinite possibilities of self-deception – the difficulty of disentangling the countless strands of emotion and calling each by its proper name – of separating business from pleasure. At times, whatever he might say, he was surely lost in a cloud of unknowing; but at least it was a peaceful cloud at present and sailing through a milky sea towards a possible though unlikely ecstasy at an indefinite remove was, if not the fulness of life, then something like its shadow.

PEACE, STILL DEEPER peace. The languid peace of the Arabian Sea in the south-west monsoon; a wind as steady as the trades but gentler, so gentle that the battered *Surprise* had her topgallants abroad and even her lower studdingsails, for she was in an even greater hurry than usual. Her stores were so low now that for weeks past the gunroom had been living on ship's provisions, salt beef, salt pork, biscuit and dried peas, and the midshipmen's berth reported no single rat left alive: what was worse, Stephen and M'Alister had cases of scurvy on their hands once more.

But the lean years were thought to be almost over. At one time Harrowby had wished to steer for the Nine Degree Channel and the Laccadives; but Harrowby was an indifferent, timid navigator and Jack, overruling him, had laid her head for Bombay itself; and now they had been running north-east by east so long that by dead reckoning the *Surprise* should have been a hundred miles east of the Western Ghauts, another Ark stranded in the hills of Poona. But consulting with Pullings, working his lunars again and again, dragging his brighter midshipmen repeatedly through the calculations in search of an error, worshipping his chronometers, and making the necessary corrections, Jack was almost certain of his position. Sea-birds, native craft far off, a single merchantman that fled, crowding sail on the horizon without waiting to learn if they were French or English – the first sail they had seen in four months – and above all, soundings in eleven fathoms, a bottom of shelly white sand like Direction Bank, strengthened him in his persuasion that he was in 18°34′N, 72°29′E, and that he should make his landfall the next day. He stood on the quarterdeck, glancing now over the side, now up at the masthead, where the sharpest eyes and the best glasses in the ship were trained steadily eastwards.

Stephen's confidence in Captain Aubrey's seamanship was as entire, as blind, as Jack's in the medical omniscience of Dr Maturin; and untroubled by the cares that now oppressed his friend he sat in the mainchains, as naked as Adam and much the same colour, trailing a purse-net in the sea.

The chains, broad planks jutting horizontally from the outside of the ship to spread the shrouds wider than her extreme breadth, provided the most comfortable seat imaginable; he had all the advantage of the sun, of solitude (for the chains were well below the rail), and of the sea, which ran curving past under his feet, sometimes touching them with a warm caress, sometimes sending an agreeable shower of spray over his person; and as he sat he sang 'Asperges me, Domine, hyssopo – but those qualities

    were of course

      most apparent when she was poor

        lonely and oppressed

          what shall I find now?

            what, what development?

              if indeed I call? hyssopo

                et super nivem dealbabor.

Asperges me . . .'

A passing sea-snake broke his song, one of the many he had seen and failed to catch: he veered out his line, willing the creature to enter the purse. But an empty purse had no charm for the serpent; it swam on with scarcely a hesitation in its beautiful proud easy glide.

Above and behind him he could hear Mr Hervey's usually conciliating voice raised in passion, wanting to know whether those sweepers were ever coming aft – whether this bloody shambles was ever going to look like the deck of a man-of-war. Another voice, low, inward and confidential, was that of Babbington, who had borrowed Stephen's Hindustani phrasebook: over and over again he was repeating 'Woman, wilt thou lie with me?' in that language, staring impatiently north-eastwards. Like many sailors he could sense the loom of the land, a land with thousands of women upon it, every one of whom might perhaps lie with him.

'No great guns this evening, Doctor,' said Pullings, leaning over the rail. 'We are priddying for tomorrow. I reckon we shall raise Malabar Hill before it's dark, and the Admiral lays there in Bombay. We must be shipshape for the Admiral.'

Bombay: fresh fruit for his invalids, iced sherbets for all hands, enormous meals; the marvels of the East; marble palaces no doubt; the Parsees' silent towers; the offices of the Commissioners for the former French settlements, counters and factories on the Malabar coast: the residence of Mr Commissioner Canning.

'How happy you make me, Mr Pullings,' said Stephen. 'This will be the first evening since thirty south that we shall be spared that inhuman – hush, hush! Do not stir. I have it! Ha, ha, my friend: at last!' He hauled in his line, and there in the net lay a sea-snake, a slender animal, shining black and brilliant yellow, quite amazing.

'Don't ee touch her, Doctor,' cried Pullings. 'She's a sea-serpent.'

'Of course she is a sea-serpent. That has been the whole purpose of my fishing ever since we reached these waters. Oh what a lovely creature.'

'Don't ee touch her,' cried Pullings again. 'She's deadly poison. I seen a man die in twenty minutes – '

'Land ho,' hailed the lookout. 'Land broad on the starboard beam.'

'Jump up to the masthead, Mr Pullings, if you please,' said Jack, 'and let me know what you see.'

A thunder of feet as the whole ship's company rushed to stare at the horizon, and the *Surprise* took on a list to starboard. Stephen held his close-meshed net at a prudent distance; the serpent writhed furiously, coiled and struck like a powerful spring released.

'On deck there,' roared Pullings. 'It's Malabar Hill itself, sir; and I see the island plain.'

The serpent, blind out of its own element, bit itself repeat-edly, and presently it died. Before Stephen could bring it inboard, to its waiting jar of spirit, its colours were already fading: but as he climbed in over the rail, so a waft of air took the frigate's sails aback, a breath of heavy air off the land, with a thousand unknown scents, the green smell of damp vegetation, palms, close-packed humanity, another world.

7

FRESH FRUIT for the invalids, to be sure, and enormous meals for those who had time to eat them; but apart from the omnipresent smell and a little arrack that came aboard by stealth, the wonders of the East, the marble palaces, remained distant, half-guessed objects for the *Surprise*. She was taken straight into the naval yard, and there they stripped her to the bone; they took out her guns and cleared her holds to come to her bottom, and what they found there made the master-attendant clear the dry-dock as fast. as ever he could, to bring her in before she sank at her moorings.

The Admiral visited her in state; he was a jolly, rose-pink admiral and he said the kindest things about the *Surprise*; but he instantly deprived Jack of his first lieutenant, appointing Mr Hervey to an eighteen-gun sloop as master and comman-der, thereby throwing all the labour of refitting on to the cap-tain's shoulders.

The Admiral had a conscience, however; and he knew that Mr Stanhope was of some importance. He spoke the good word to the master-attendant, and all the resources of a well-equipped yard lay open to the *Surprise*. The daughter of the horse-leech was moderation made flesh compared to Captain Aubrey let loose in a Tom Tiddler's ground strewn with pitch, hemp, tow, cordage, sailcloth by the acre, copper in gleaming sheets, spars, blocks, boats and *natural-grown* knees; and although he, too, was afire to wander on the coral strand beneath the coconut-palms, he said, 'While this lasts, not a man shall leave the ship. Gather ye rose-pods while ye may, as dear Christy-Pallière used to say.'

'May you not find the men grow wilful and discontented? May they not, with a united mind, rush violently from the ship?'

'They will not be pleased. But they know we must catch the monsoon with a well-found ship; and they know they are in the Navy – they have chosen their cake, and must lie on it.'

'You mean, they cannot have their bed and eat it.'

'No, no, it is not quite that, neither. I mean – I wish you would not confuse my mind, Stephen. I mean it is only a week or so, to snap up everything that can be moved before *Ethalion* or *Revenge* come in, screeching for spars and cables; then I dare say we can take it easier, with native caulkers from the yard, and some liberty for our people. But there is a vast deal of work to be done – you saw her spirketing? – weeks and weeks of work; and we must hurry.'

From his earliest acquaintance with the Navy, Stephen had been oppressed by this sense of hurry – hurry to look over the next horizon, hurry to reach a certain port, hurry to get away from it in case something should be happening in a distant strait: and hurry now, not only to gather rose-pods, but to catch the monsoon. If they did not set the envoy down in Kampong by a given date, Jack would be obliged to beat all the way back against head-winds, losing months of valuable time, time that might be spent in active warfare. 'Why,' cried he, 'the war might be over before we round the Cape, if we miss the north-east monsoon: a pretty state of affairs.'

And in the immediate future there was this matchless opportunity for making the dear *Surprise* what she had been, and what she ought to be again. Stephen cared for none of these things; the fire that vainly urged Jack to go ashore burnt with a devouring, an irresistible force in him.

He left Jack caressing a massive baulk of timber, the finest teak in the island. He said, 'My patients are in the hospital; Mr Stanhope is recovering with the Governor; there is no place for me here. I must devote a certain amount of time to the shore – a variety of reasons require my presence on the shore.'

'I dare say you must,' said Jack absently. 'Mr Babbington, Mr Babbington! Where is that infernal slowbelly of a carpenter? I dare say you must: but however busy you are, do not miss the getting out of our lower masts. We go alongside the sheer-hulk, and they lift 'em out like kiss my hand – it is the prettiest thing in the world. I shall send word the day before – you would be very sorry to miss the sheer-hulk.'

Stephen came aboard from time to time, once with a mathematical Parsee who wished to see the frigate's navigation tables; once with a child of unknown race who had found him lost among the blue buffaloes of the Aungier maidan, in danger of being trampled, and who had led him back by the hand, talking all the way in an Urdu adapted to the meanest understanding; and once with a Chinese master-mariner, a Christian from Macao, a spoilt priest, with whom he conversed in Latin, showing him the working of the patent chain-pump. And now and then he appeared at Jack's lodgings, where in theory he, too, had his bed and board. Jack was too discreet to ask him where he slept when they did not meet, and too well-bred to comment on the fact that sometimes he walked about in a towel, sometimes in European dress, and sometimes in a loose shirt, hanging over white pantaloons, but always with an expression of tireless secret delight.

As for sleeping, he lay where he chose, under trees, on verandas, in a caravanserai, on temple steps, in the dust among rows of other dust-sleepers wrapped as it were in shrouds – wherever extreme bodily fatigue laid his down. Nowhere in the crowded city, accustomed to a hundred races and innumerable tongues, did he excite the least comment as he wandered through the bazaars, the Arab horse-lines, among the toddy-groves, in and out of temples, pagodas, churches, mosques, along the strand, among the Hindu funeral pyres, through and through the city, gazing at the Mahrattas, Bengalis, Rajputs, Persians, Sikhs, Malays, Siamese, Javans, Philippinoes, Khirgiz, Ethiopians, Parsees, Baghdad Jews, Sinhalese, Tibetans; they gazed back at him, when they were not otherwise employed, but with no particular curiosity, no undue attention, certainly with no kind of animosity. Sometimes his startling pale eyes, even more colourless now against his dusky skin, called for a second wondering glance; and sometimes he was taken for a holy man. Oil was poured on him more than once, and tepid cakes of a sweet vegetable substance were pressed into his hand with smiles; fruit, a bowl of yellow rice; and he was offered buttered tea, fresh toddy, the juice of sugar-cane. Before the partners of the mainmast were renewed he came home with a wreath of marigolds round his bare dusty shoulders, an offering from a company of whores: he hung the wreath on the right-hand knob of his blackwood chair and sat down to his journal.

'I had expected wonders from Bombay; but my heated expectations, founded upon the Arabian Nights, a glimpse of the Moorish towns in Africa, and books of travel, were poor thin insubstantial things compared with the reality. There is here a striving, avid and worldly civilisation, of course; these huge and eager markets, this incessant buying and selling, make that self-evident; but I had no conception of the ubiquitous sense of the holy, no notion of how another world can permeate the secular. Filth, stench, disease, "gross superstition" as our people say, extreme poverty, promiscuous universal defecation, do not affect it: nor do they affect my sense of the humanity with which I am surrounded. What an agreeable city it is, where a man may walk naked in the heat if it pleases him! I was speaking today with an unclothed Hindu religious, a parama-hamsa, on the steps of a Portuguese church, a true gymnosophist; and I remarked that in such a climate wisdom and clothing might bear an inverse propor-

tion to one another. But measuring my garment with his hand
he observed that there was not one single wisdom.

'Never have I so blessed this facility for coming by a superficial knowledge of a language. My Fort William grammar, my
trifle of Arabic, and above all my intercourse with Achmet
and Butoo, bear such fruit! Had I been dumb, I might almost
as well have been blind also: what is the sight of a violin, and
the violin lying mute? This dear child Dil teaches me a great
deal, talking indefatigably, a steady flow of comment and narrative, with incessant repetition where I do not understand –
she insists on being understood, and no evasion deceives her.
Though I do not believe Urdu is her mother-tongue. She and
the crone with whom she lives converse in quite a different
language: not a familiar word. The ancient gentlewoman,
offering me the child for twelve rupees, assured me she was a
virgin and wished to show me the fibula that guaranteed her
state. It would have been quite superfluous: what could be
more virginal than this tubular fearless creature that looks me
directly in the face as though I were a not very intelligent
tame animal, and that communicates her thoughts, views,
the moment they are born as though I, too, were a child? She
can throw a stone, leap, climb like a boy; and yet she is no
garçon manqué neither, for in addition to this overflowing
communicative affection she also has a kind of motherliness
and wishes to rule my movements and my diet for my own
good – disapproves my smoking bhang, eating opium, wearing trousers of more than a given length. Choleric, however:
on Friday she beat a doe-eyed boy who wished to join himself
to us in the palm-grove, threatening his companions with a
brickbat and with oaths that made them stare. She eats vora-
ciously: but how often in the week? She owns one piece of
cotton cloth that she wears sometimes as a kilt, sometimes as
a shawl; an oiled black stone that she worships perfunctorily;
and her fibula. When fed she is, I believe, perfectly happy;
longing only, but with no real hope, for a silver bangle. Almost
all the children here are encumbered with them, and clank as

they go. How old is she? Nine? Ten? The menarche is not far off – a hint of a bosom, poor child. I am tempted to purchase her: above all I should wish to preserve her in this present state, not sexless, but unaware of her sex, free of her person and of all the gutters and bazaars of Bombay, wholly and immediately human: wise, too. But only Joshua could halt the sun. In a years time or less she will be in a brothel. Would a European house be better? A servant, washed and confined? Could I keep her as a pet? For how long? Endow her? It is hard to think of her lively young spirit sinking, vanishing in the common lot. I shall advise with Diana: I have a groping notion of some unidentified common quality.

'This city has immense piety, but old Adam walks about; bodies I have seen, some starved to death, some clubbed, stabbed, or strangled; and in any mercantile city one man's evil is another's good. Yet a materialism that would excite no comment in Dublin or Barcelona shocks the stranger in Bombay. I was sitting under the towers of silence on Malabar hill, watching the vultures – such a view! I had taken Jack's glass, but I did not need it, they were so very tame, even the *yellow-billed* Pharaoh's hen, which, Mr Norton tells me, is most uncommon west of Hyderabad – and collecting some anomalous bones when Khowasjee Undertaker spoke to me, a Parsee in a plum-coloured hat. Having come from Mr Stanhope, I was in European clothes, and he addressed me in English – did not I know it was forbidden to take up bones? I replied that I was ignorant of the customs of his country, but that I understood the bodies of the dead were exposed upon these towers to be devoured, or taken away piecemeal, by vultures – that the bodies thus became bonus nullius – that if property in the flesh could be conceived, then it was vested in the vulture; and that the vulture, relinquishing its title, surely in natural justice gave me a right to this femur, this curiously distorted hyoid? But that I was unwilling to offend any man's opinions, and that I should content myself with contemplating the remains rather than taking them away: my

interest was not that of a ghoul, still less that of a glue-
merchant; but of a natural philosopher.

'He, too, was a philosopher, he said: the philosophy of
number. Should I like to hear him extract a cube root? I
might name any figure I pleased. A surprising performance:
the answers came as quick as my piece of rib could write
them in the dust. He was enchanted, and he would have
gone on for ever, if I had not mentioned Napier's bones,
Gunter's scales – the applied mathematics of navigation –
lunars – the necessary tables. Here I ventured out of my
depth; was unable to satisfy him as to their nature, and therefore proposed carrying him to the ship. His curiosity overcame his evident alarm: he was gratified by the attention,
pleased with the instrument; and on returning to land he
invited me to drink tea at his counting-house – he is a considerable merchant. Here, at my request, he gave me a succinct
account of his life; and I was disappointed but not surprised
to find him a complacent pragmatical worldly fellow. Little do
I know of the mathematics or the law; but the few mathe-
maticians and lawyers I have met seem to me to partake of
this sterility in direct proportion to their eminence: it may be
that they are satisfied with an insufficient or in the case of
lawyers almost wholly factitious order. However that may be,
this man appears to have turned his benevolent ancient creed
into an arid system of mechanical observances: so many
hours devoted to stated ceremonies, so much of acknowledged income set aside for alms (no question of charity here,
I believe), and a rancorous hatred for the Khadmees, who disagree with his sect, the Shenshahees, not on any point of
doctrine, but over the dating of their era. I might have been
in Seething Lane. I do not imagine he is a typical Parsee,
however, in anything but his alert, painstaking attention to
business. Among other things, he is an insurer, a maritime
insurer, and he spoke of the rise in premiums, plotting them
against the movements, or the rumoured movements, of
Linois's squadron, an armament that fills not only the Com-

pany with alarm, but also all the country ships: premiums are now higher than they were in Suffren's time. His family has innumerable commercial interests: Tibetan borax, Bencoolen nutmeg, Tuticorin pearls my memory retains. A cousin's banking-house is closely connected with the office of the Commissioners for the former French Settlements. He could have told me a great deal about them, if it had not been for his sense of caution; even so, he spoke with some freedom of Richard Canning, for whom he expressed respect and esteem. He told me little I did not already know, but he did confirm that their return is set for the seventeenth.

'He could tell me nothing about the Hindu ceremony on the shores of the bay this coming moon: neither cared nor knew. For this I must turn once again to Dil; though indeed her notions of religion are so eclectic as to lead her into confusion. God will not be merciful to him who through vanity wears long trousers, she tells me (a Muslim teaching); and at the same time she takes it for an acknowledged truth that I am a were-bear, a decayed were-bear out of a place, an inept rustic demon that has strayed into the city; and that I can certainly fly if I choose, but with a blundering flight, neither efficient nor in the right direction – a belief she must have taken from the Tibetans. She is right in supposing that I need guidance, however.

'The seventeenth. If Jack is accurate in his calculations (and in these matters I have never known him fail) I should have three weeks before the ship is ready. I am impatient for their arrival now, although when we came in I more than half dreaded it. What a wonderful interlude this has been, a piece of my life lifted quite out – '

'Why, there you are, Stephen,' cried Jack. 'You are come home, I find.'

'That is true,' said Stephen with an affectionate look: he prized statements of this kind in Jack. 'So are you, joy; and earlier than usual. You look perturbed. Do you find the heat affects you? Take off some of these splendid garments.'

'Why, no; not more than common,' said Jack, unbuckling his sword. 'Though it is hellfire hot and close and damp. No. I looked in on the off-chance . . . I had to dine with the Admiral, as you know, and there I heard something that made my blood run cold; and I thought I ought to tell you. Diana Villiers is here, and that man Canning. By God, I wish the ship were ready for sea. I could not stand the meeting. Ain't you amazed – shocked?'

'No. No, truly I am not. And for my part I must tell you, Jack, I look forward to the meeting extremely. They are not in fact in Bombay, but they are expected on the seventeenth.'

'You knew she was here?' cried Jack, Stephen nodded. 'You are a close one, Stephen,' said Jack, looking at him sideways.

Stephen shrugged: he said, 'Yes, I suppose I am. I have to be, you know. That is why I am alive. And one's mind takes the bent . . . but I beg your pardon if I have not been as free and open with you as I should have been. This is delicate ground, however.'

There was a time when they were rivals, when Jack felt so strongly about Diana that this was very dangerous ground indeed. Jack had nearly wrecked his career because of her, and his chance of marrying Sophia. In retrospect he resented it bitterly, just as he resented her unfaithfulness, although she owed him no fidelity. He hated her, in a way; he thought her dangerous, if not evil; and he dreaded an encounter – dreaded it for Stephen more than for himself.

'No, no, my dear fellow, not at all,' he said, shaking Stephen by the hand. 'No. I am sure you are right. In keeping your counsel, I mean.'

After a pause Stephen said, 'And yet I am surprised you should not have heard of their presence, if not in England, then here: I have been regaled with accounts of their cohabitation at every dinner I have attended, every tea-drinking, almost every casual encounter with a European.'

He had indeed. The coming of Richard Canning and Diana Villiers had been a godsend to Bombay, bored as it was with the Gujerat famine and the endless talk of a Mahratta war. Canning had an important official position, he had great influence with the Company, and he lived in splendour; he was an active, stirring man, ready and eager to take up any challenge, and he made it clear that he expected their ménage to be accepted. Several of the highly-placed officials had known her father, and those with Indian concubines made no difficulty; nor did the bachelors; but the European wives were harder to persuade. Few had much room to cast stones, but hypocrisy has never failed the English middle class in any latitude, and they flung them in plenty with delighted, shocked abandon – rocks, boulders, limited in size only by fear for their husband's advancement. Conciliating discretion had never been among Mrs Villiers's qualities, and if subjects for malignant gossip had been wanting she would have provided them by the elephant-load. Canning spent much of his time in the French possessions and in Goa, and during his absence the good ladies kept telescopes trained on Diana's house. With extravagant lamentation they mourned the death of Mr James, of the 87th Foot, killed by Captain Macfarlane, the wounding of a member of Council, and less important hostilities: these affairs were spoken of with religious horror, while the many other quarrels in that liverish, over-fed, parboiled community, much given to murder by consent, were passed over as amiable weaknesses, the natural consequence of the heat. Mr Canning was of a jealous disposition, and unsigned letters kept him informed of Diana's visitors, imaginary and real.

'Sir, sir,' cried Babbington, on the veranda.

In his strong voice Jack called out, 'Hallo.'

The staircase trembled, the door burst open, and Babbington's smile appeared in the gloom. It faded at the sight of his captain's harsh expression. 'What are you doing ashore, Babbington?' asked Jack. 'Two pairs of shrouds cut in the eyes, and you are ashore?'

'Why, sir, the Governor's kolipar brought the mail, and I thought you might choose to see it right away.'

'Well,' said Jack, the gloom lightening. 'There is something in what you say.' He grasped the bag and hurried into the next room, coming out a few moments later with a packet for Stephen and disappearing again.

'Well, sir,' said Babbington. 'I must not keep you.'

'You must not keep your strumpet either,' said Stephen, glancing out of the window.

'Oh, sir,' cried Babbington. 'She is not a strumpet, She is a clergyman's daughter.'

'Then why do you perpetually borrow important sums of money from the only person in the ship weak enough to lend them to you? Two pagodas last week. Four rupees six pice the week before.'

'Oh, but she only lets her friends – her friend – help her with the rent – it is somewhat in arrears. I put up there, you know, when I can get ashore; which is precious rare. But it is true, you have been very good to me, sir.'

'You do? You do? Well, let me tell you this, Mr Babbington: such things can lead very far; and clergymen are not all they seem. You will remember what I told you about gummata and the third generation? Many an example may you see in the bazaars. How should you like to see your grandson bald, stunted, and gibbering, toothless and decrepit before the age of twelve? I beg of you to take care. Any woman is a source of great potential danger to a sailorman.'

'Oh, I will, sir. I will,' cried Babbington, who had been peering secretly through the slatted blind, 'But do you know, sir, it is the most ridiculous thing – I seem to have left the ship without any money in my pocket.'

Stephen listened to him hurtling down the stairs, sighed, and turned to his letters.

Sir Joseph was concerned almost entirely with beetles of one kind or another; he would be infinitely grateful if his dear Maturin, happening to stumble upon any of the Bupestrids, would remember him. But an enigmatic postscript gave him the key to Mr Waring's letter, which seemed to be about a stupid, quarrelsome, litigious set of common acquaintances, but which in fact gave him a view of the political situation: in Catalonia British military intelligence was backing the wrong horse, as usual; in Lisbon the embassy was having conversations with still another dubious representative of the resistance; there was danger of a schism in the movement, and they longed for his return.

News from his private agent: Mrs Canning was making preparations for a voyage to India, to confront her husband. The Mocattas had found out that he was obliged to be in Calcutta before the next rains, and she was to travel in the *Warren Hastings*, bound for that uncomfortable port.

Sophie had omitted to date three of her letters with anything more definite than the day of the week, and he opened them in the wrong order. His first impression was that of time entirely dislocated – Cecilia placidly expecting a baby (how I look forward to being an aunt!) without any apparent sacrifice of her maidenhead or adverse comment from her friends; Frances removed to the desolate shores of Lough Erne, and there shivering in the company of somebody called Lady F and longing for the return of one Sir O. A second reading made the situation clearer: both Sophie's younger sisters had married, Cecilia to a young Militia officer, and Frances, emulating her sister's triumph (how she must have changed, said Stephen) to this soldier's much older cousin, an Ulster landowner who represented County Antrim at Westminster while Frances lived with his aged mother at Floodesville, drinking confusion to the Pope twice a day in elderberry wine. There was joy, even exultation, at her sisters' happiness (Cecilia at least adored the marriage state; it was even more fun than she had expected, although they were only in lodgings at Gosport, and would have to stay there until Sir Oliver could be induced to *do something* for his cousin) and a detailed description of their weddings, conducted with great propriety and in splendid weather, by Mr Hincksey, their own dear vicar being from home; but they were not really happy letters; they were not the letters he would have liked to read.

A third reading convinced him that Cecilia's marriage had been tolerably hasty; that Mrs Williams had been obliged to yield on all fronts, the brisk young soldier having undermined her citadel; but that she had had her way with Sir Oliver Floode, a wealthy man, and a dreary. And this third reading confirmed his impression of despondency. Mrs Williams's spirits had revived with the excitement of the marriages and her victory over Sir Oliver's attorney; but now her health was on the wane again, and she complained much of her loneliness. Now that she and Sophia were alone she had reduced the number of her servants, had shut up the tower wing, and had given up entertaining; almost their only visitor was Mr Hincksey, who dropped in every other day or so, and who dined with them whenever he took Mr Fellows's duty.

Now that there was nothing else to occupy her mind she renewed her persecution of Sophia, volubly when she was well, in pale gasps when she was confined to her bed. 'And the strange thing is, that although I hear his name so very often, Mr Hincksey is a real comfort to me; he is a truly friendly man, and a good man, as I was sure he would be from your recommendation of him – he thinks so highly of "dear unworldly Dr Maturin", and you would blush, I am sure, to hear us speaking about you, as we so often do. He never obtrudes his feelings or distresses me; and he is as kind as can be to my Mama, even when she is not quite discreet. He preaches exceedingly well – no enthusiasm or hard words and no what I suppose you would call eloquence either – and it is a pleasure to hear him, even when he speaks of *duty*, which he does pretty often. And I must say he practises what he preaches: he is the most dutiful son. It makes me feel wretched and ashamed. His mother . . .' Stephen did not care about old Mrs Hincksey: she was a beautiful old lady, so kind and gentle, but perfectly deaf . . . 'Humbug: the woman can hear quick enough if she chooses,' said Stephen. 'All these unscrupulous advantages, and white hair too.' He skipped to the part that worried him most. Sophia found it very strange that Jack had not written. 'Why, you fat-headed girl, cannot you see that a man-of-war must outfly the swiftest post?' She was sure that Jack would never, never do anything unkind on purpose; but the best of men were thoughtless and forgetful at times, particularly when they had a great deal to do, like the captain of a man-of-war; and there was the old saying about distance and salt water doing away with other feelings. Nothing was more natural than a man should grow tired of an ignorant country girl like Sophia – that even quite ardent feelings should wear out in a man who had so many other things to think of, and such high responsibilities. Above all she did not wish to be a clog on Jack, either in his career (Lord St Vincent was dead set against marriage) or in anything else; he might have friends in India, and she would be perfectly miserable if, because of her, he felt himself bound or in any way entangled.

'The catalyst in all this is the General,' observed Stephen, comparing the letter with earlier examples of Sophie's hand. 'It is wrote hasty, and in some agitation of spirit. The spelling is even poorer than usual.' Sophie passed it off as a trifling incident, but her amusement was forced and unconvincing. General Aubrey, together with Jack's new stepmother, a jolly, vulgar young woman, until recently a dairy-maid, and their little boy, had descended upon Mapes, fortunately at a time when Mrs Williams was in Canterbury with Mrs Hincksey. Sophie gave them the best dinner she could, with several bottles of wine, alas. General Aubrey belonged to another civilisation, a civilisation untouched by the age of enlightenment or the spread of the bourgeoisie, one that had passed away in the counties nearer London long before Sophie was born and one to which her essentially urban, respectable, middle-class family had never belonged at any time. She had been brought up in a quiet, staid, manless house and she did not know what to make of his gallantries, his praise of Jack's taste (Cecilia would have been more at home with him); nor of his observation that Jack was a sad dog – always had been – but she was not to mind it – Jack's mother never had. Sophia would not mind half a dozen love-children, he was sure.

General Aubrey was not a disreputable man; he was kind and well-bred in his camp and country way; but he was chuckle-headed and impulsive; and when he was nervous (Sophia had no idea that a man of nearly seventy could be shy) and in wine, he felt he had to be talking: his outré facetiousness, his broad, earthy pleasantries shocked her extremely, and he seemed to her a coarse, licentious, rakish, unprincipled caricature of his son. Her only consolation was that the General and her mother had not come into contact; and that her mother had not seen the second Mrs Aubrey.

She remembered the General's loud, candid voice, so reminiscent of his son's, calling out from the end of the long table that Jack 'had not a groat to bless himself with – never would have – all the Aubreys were unlucky with money – they had to be lucky in marriage'. She remembered the endless pause after dinner, with the little boy poking holes in the fire-screen: the concentrated urgency with which she willed the General to have done with his bottle, to come in, drink his tea and go away before her mother's return, now long overdue. She remembered how she and the laughing Mrs Aubrey had supported him into the carriage – the interminable farewells – the General recalling some endless anecdote about a fox-chase and losing himself in it while the child played havoc with the flowerbeds, shrieking like a barn-owl. Then ten minutes later, while she was still shattered, her mother's return, the scene, the cries, tears, swooning, bed, extreme pallor, reproaches.

'Stephen: I say, Stephen, I ain't interrupting you, am I?' said Jack, coming out of his room with a letter in his hand. 'Here's a damned thing. Here's Sophie writing me the damnedest rigmarole. I can't show it you – some very private things in it, you understand me – but the drift of it is, that if I choose to feel myself free, nothing would make her happier. Free to do what, in God's name? God damn and blast my eyes, we are engaged to be married, ain't we? If it were any other woman on earth, I should think there was some other man hanging about. What the devil can she mean by it? Can you make head or tail of it?'

'It may be that someone has fabricated – it may be that someone has told her that you have come to India to see Diana Villiers,' said Stephen, hiding his face with shame as he spoke. This was a direct attempt at keeping them apart, for his own purposes – partly for his own purposes. It was wholly uncandid, of course, and he had never been uncandid with Jack before. It filled him with anger; but still he went on, 'or that you may see her here.'

'Did she know Diana was in Bombay?' cried Jack.

'Sure it was common knowledge in England.'

'So Mother Williams knew?' Stephen nodded.

'Ah, that is Sophie, from clue to earing,' cried Jack, with such a radiant smile. 'Can you imagine a sweeter thing to say? And such modesty, do you see? As if anyone could look at Diana after – however,' he said, recollecting himself and looking deprecatingly at Stephen, 'I don't mean to say anything wrong, or uncivil. But not a reproach, not an unkind word in the whole letter – Lord, Stephen, how I love that girl.' His bright blue eyes clouded, ran over, and he wiped them with his sleeve. 'Never a hint of being ill-used, though I know damned well what kind of life that woman leads her: to say nothing of filling her mind with ugly tales. A shocking life – you know Cecilia and Frankie are gone off, married? – that makes it even worse. Lord, how I shall press on with the refitting! Even faster now. I long to get back into the Atlantic or the Med: these are not waters where a man can look for any distinction now, far less any wealth. If only we had picked up a single decent prize off the Isle of France, I should write to her to come out to Madeira, and be damned to . . . A few hundred would buy us a neat cottage. How I should love a neat cottage, Stephen – potatoes, cabbages, and things.'

'Upon my word, I cannot tell why you do not write, prize or no prize. You have your pay, for all love.'

'Oh, that would not be right, you know. I am nearly clear of debt, but there is still a couple of thousand to find. It would scarcely be honourable to pay it off with her fortune, and then only have seven shillings a day to offer her.'

'Do you pretend to teach me the difference between honourable and dishonourable conduct?'

'No, no, of course not – pray don't fly out at me, Stephen. I have spoke awkward again. No, what I mean is, it would not be right for *me*, do you understand? I could not bear it, to have Mrs Williams call me a fortune-hunter. It is different in Ireland, I know – oh damn it, I am laid by the lee again – I do not mean you are a fortune-hunter, but you see it differently in your country. *Autre pays, autre merde*. But in any case, she has sworn never to marry without her mother's consent: so that claps a stopper over all.'

'Never in life, my dear. If Sophie comes to Madeira Mrs Williams will be bound either to give her consent or to face a delighted neighbourhood. She was obliged to the same course in the case of Cecilia, I believe.'

'Would not that be rather Jesuitical, Stephen?' said Jack, looking into his face.

'Not at all. Consent unreasonably withheld may justifiably be compelled. I am concerned with Sophie's happiness and yours, rather than with pandering to Mrs Williams's sordid whims. You must write that letter, Jack; for you are to consider, Sophie is the beauty of the world; whereas although you are tolerably well-looking in your honest tarpaulin way, you are rather old and likely to grow older; too fat, and likely to grow even fatter – nay, obese.' Jack looked at his belly and shook his head. 'Horribly knocked about, earless, scarred: brother, you are no Adonis. Do not be wounded,' he said, laying his hand on Aubrey's knee, 'when I say you are no Adonis.'

'I never thought I was,' said Jack.

'Nor when I add that you are no Fox either: no flashing wit

to counterbalance want of looks, wealth, grace and youth.'

'Sure I never set up for a wit,' said Jack. 'Though I can bring out a good thing on occasion, given time.'

'And Sophie, I say again, has real beauty: and there are Adonises, witty, moneyed Adonises, in England. Again, she is led a devil of a life. Two younger sisters have married: you are aware of the importance of marriage to a young woman – the status, the escape, the certified guarantee of *not having failed*, the virtual certainty of a genteel subsistence. You are a great way off, ten thousand miles and more: you may be knocked on the head from one moment to the next, and at no time is there more than a two-inch plank between you and the grave. You are half the world away from her and yet within half a mile of Diana. She knows little or nothing of the world, little or nothing of men apart from what her mother tells her – small good, you may be sure. Lastly, there is her high sense of duty. Now although Sophie carries humanity to a high pitch of perfection, no young woman more, still she is human and she is affected by human considerations. I do not say for a moment that she coldly weighs them up; but considerations, the pressures, are there, and they are very strong. You must certainly write your letter, Jack. Take pen and ink.'

Jack gazed at him for a while with a heavy, troubled countenance, then stood up, sighed, pulled in his belly, and said, 'I must go down to the yard: we are shipping the new capstan this evening. Thank you for what you have told me, Stephen.'

It was Stephen who took pen and ink and sat down to his diary. 'I must go down to the yard, said he: we are stepping the new capstan this evening. Had there been powder-smoke in the room, a tangible enemy at hand, there would have been none of this hesitation, no long stare: he would have known his mind and he would have acted at once, with intelligent deliberation. But now he is at a stand. With that odious freedom I prattled on: in doing so I overcame my shame; but it was bitter cruel and sharp while it lasted. In the instant between his asking, could I make head or tail of it? and my reply, the Devil said to me, "If Aubrey is really vexed with Miss Williams, he will turn to Diana Villiers again. You already have your work cut out with Mr Canning." I fell at once. Yet already I have almost persuaded myself that my subsequent words were the same as those an honest man would have used: myself, if this *attachment* had not existed. Liaison I cannot say, since liaison implies a mutual attraction and I have no sort of evidence for this other than my oh so fallible intuition. I long for the seventeenth. Already I am beginning to murder time, like an ardent boy: such an ugly crime. The sea-festival will perhaps knock six innocent hours on the head.'

The ceremony took place all along the shore of Back Bay, from Malabar Point to the Fort; and the broad parklike stretch of grass before the Fort was one of the best places for viewing the preparations. Like all Hindu ceremonies he had seen, this appeared to be going forward with great excitement, great good humour, and a total lack of organisation. There were some groups already on the strand, with their leaders standing waist-deep, wafting flowers into the sea; but most of the inhabitants of Bombay seemed to have gathered here on the green to mill about in their best clothes, laughing, singing, beating drums, eating sweetmeats and saucers of cooked food from tiny stalls, breaking off now and then to form a vague procession, chanting a shrill and powerful hymn. Great warmth, an infinite variety of smells and colours, the bray of conchs, deep hooting trumpets, countless people; and winding in and out among the people elephants with crowded castles on their backs, bullock-carts, hundreds and hundreds of palanquins, horsemen, holy cows, European carriages.

A warm hand slipped into his, and looking down Stephen saw Dil smiling up at him. 'Art very strangely clothed, Stephen,' she said. 'I almost took thee for a topi-wallah. I have a whole leaf of pondoo: come and eat it before it spills. Mind thy good bazaar shirt in the dung – it is far too long, thy shirt.' She led him across the trampled grass to the rising glacis of the fort, and there, finding an empty place, they sat down. 'Lean thy head forward,' she said, unfolding the leaf and setting the turgid mess between them. 'Nay, nay, *forward, more forward.* Dost not see thy shirt all slobbered, oh for shame. Where wast thou brought up? What mother bore thee? *Forward.*' Despairing of making him eat like a human being, she stood up, licked his shirt clean, and then, folding her brown jointless legs under her she squatted close in front of him. 'Open thy mouth.' With an expert hand she moulded the pondoo into little balls and fed him. 'Close thy mouth, Stephen. Swallow. Open. There, maharaj. Another. There, my garden of nightingales. Open. Close.' The sweet, gritty unctuous mass flowed into him, and all the time Dil's voice rose and fell. 'Thou canst not eat much better than a bear. Swallow. Pause now and belch. Dost not know how to belch? Thus. I can belch whenever I choose. Belch twice. Look, look; the Mahratta chiefs.' A splendid group of horsemen in crimson with gold-embroidered turbans and saddle-cloths. 'That is the Peshwa in the middle: and there the Bhonsli rajah – har, har, mahadeo! Another ball and all is gone. Open. Thou hast fifteen teeth above and one less below. There is a European carriage, filled with Franks. Pah, I can smell them from here, stronger than camels. They eat cow and pig – it is perfectly notorious. Thou hast no more skill in eating with thy fingers than a bear or a Frank, poor Stephen: art thou a Frank at times?' Her eyes were fixed upon him with alert penetrating curiosity, but before he could reply they had darted off to an approaching line of elephants, so covered with housings, paint, howdahs and tinsel that below nothing could be seen but their feet shuffling in the dust and before nothing but their gilt, silver-banded tusks and questing trunks.

'I shall sing thee the Marwari hymn to Krishna,' said Dil, and began in a nasal whine, slicing the air with her right hand as she sang. Another elephant crossed in front of them, a trim pole set up on the howdah, bearing a streamer that read

Revenge as it floated on the breeze: most of the ship's star-board maintop men were there, clinging to one another in a tight mass, while their larboard colleagues ran behind, calling out that they had had their spell, mates, and fair was fair. A competing elephant from the *Goliah*, almost hidden by a mass of delighted seamen in shore-going rig, white sennit hats and ribbons. Mr Smith, a sea-officer of the small, trim, brisk, round-headed, port-wine kind, once shipmates with Stephen in the *Lively* and now second in the *Goliah*, rode by on a camel, with his legs folded negligently over the creature's neck to the manner born: he cut nimbly between the ele-phant and the bank, with his face at Stephen's level, some fif-teen feet away: the Goliahs roared out to Mr Smith, waving bottles and cheering, and Smith waved back to them. His mouth could be seen opening and closing, but no sound pierced through the din. Dil sang on, hypnotised by her unvarying chant and the flow of words.

More and more Europeans appeared, now that the day was growing cooler. Carriages of every kind. A disreputable drove of midshipmen from the *Revenge* and the *Goliah*, mounted on little Arab horses, asses and an astonished bullock.

More and more Europeans; and incomparably more Hin-dus, for now the climax was coming near. The strand was almost covered with white-robed brown figures and the sound of horns drowned the low thunder of the sea; yet even so the crowds on the green grew thicker still, and now the carriages advanced at a walk, when they advanced at all. Ris-ing dust, heat, merriment: and above all this immense activity the kites and vultures wheeled in the untroubled sky – effort-less rings, higher and higher, the highest losing themselves at last, black specks that vanished in the blue. Dil sang on and on.

Bringing his eyes down from the vultures and the glare, Stephen found himself looking directly into Diana's face. She was sitting in a barouche under the shade of two apricot-coloured umbrellas with three officers, leaning forward with lively interest to see what had stopped them. Immediately in front of the carriage two bullock-carts had locked their wheels together: the drivers stood there shouting at one another, while the bullocks leaned inwards together against the yoke, closing their eyes, and from behind the shutters the purdah-ladies shrieked abuse, advice and orders. With a dense procession filing by for ever on the right-hand side and the steep slope of the glacis on the left, it was clear that the barouche would have to wait until the bullocks were disentangled: she twisted round with a movement Stephen had forgotten but that was as familiar as the beat of his heart. The servants perched behind with the umbrellas ducked and swerved to give her a better view, but there was no retreat through the crowd and she sat back in her seat, saying something to the man opposite her that made him laugh; and the apricot shadow swept over them again.

She was, if anything, better looking than when he had seen her last: she was a little too far from him to be sure, but it seemed that the climate, her almost native climate, which turned so many Englishmen yellow, had been kind to her, bringing to her a glow that he had not seen in England. At all events that remembered perfection of movement was there: nothing studied about that sinuous turn, nothing that loosened all his judgment so.

'What is amiss with thee?' asked Dil, breaking off and looking up at him.

'Nothing,' said Stephen, staring still. 'Art sick?' she cried, standing up and spreading her hands upon his heart.

'No,' said Stephen. He smiled at her and shook his head: he was quite composed.

She squatted, still staring up; and Diana, looking quickly from side to side, made some mechanical smiling reply to her neighbour's remark. Her eyes swept along the glacis, passed over Stephen, suddenly returned and paused, with a growing look of doubt and then the most extreme astonishment, and all at once her face changed to frank delight: it flushed, turned pale; she opened the door and sprang to the ground, leaving astonishment behind her.

She ran up the slope, and Stephen, rising, stepped over Dil and took her by her outstretched hands. 'Stephen, upon my soul and honour!' she cried. 'Stephen, how glad I am to see you!'

'I am glad to see you too, my dear,' he said, grinning like a boy.

'But in God's name how come you to be here?'

By sea, by ship – the usual way – brief explanations cut again and again by amazement – ten thousand miles – health, looks, mutual civilities – unabashed staring, smiles – how very, very brown you are! 'Your skin is fairer than I saw it last,' he said.

'Stephen,' muttered Dil again.

'Who is your sweet companion?' asked Diana.

'Allow me to name Dil, my particular friend and guide.'

'Stephen, tell the woman to take her foot from off my khatta,' said Dil, with a stony look.

'Oh daughter, I beg thou wilt forgive me,' cried Diana, bending and brushing the dust off Dil's rag. 'Oh how sorry I am. If it is spoilt, thou shalt have a sari made of Gholkand silk, with two gold threads.'

Dil looked at the trodden place. She said, 'It will pass,' and added, 'Thou dost not smell like a Frank.'

Diana smiled and wafted her handkershief at the child, spreading the scent of attar from Oudh. 'Pray take it, Dil-Gudaz,' she said. 'Take it, melter of hearts, and dream of Sivaji.'

Dil writhed her head away, the conflict between pleasure and displeasure plain on her averted face; but pleasure won and she took the handkerchief with a supple, pretty bow, thanked the Begum Lala and smelt it voluptuously. Behind them there was the sound of bullock-carts tearing free: the syce stood hovering to say the way was clear, the press extremely great and the horses in a muck-sweat.

less about the earth. Dil is alive. This boy is living.' For some time the boy, a creature with huge eyes, had been smiling at him between bracelets; they were well acquainted before Stephen said, 'Boy wilt thou tell me the cost of those bracelets?'

'Pandit,' said the boy, his teeth flashing, 'the truth is my mother and my father; I will not lie to thee. There are bracelets for every degree of wealth.'

WHEN HE FOUND Dil she was playing a game so like the hop-scotch of his youth that he felt the stirring of that ancient anxiety as the flat stone shuffled across the lines towards Paradise. One of her companions hopped exulting to the goal itself, her anklets clashing as she went. But it was false, cried Dil, she had not hopped fair – a blind hyaena could have seen her stagger and touch the ground: glaring about with clenched fists to call heaven and earth to witness she caught sight of Stephen and abandoned the match, calling out as she left them, that they were daughters of whores – they would be barren all their lives.

'Shall we go now?' she asked. 'Art so very eager, Stephen?' She found the notion of Stephen as a bridegroom irresistibly comic.

'No,' he said. 'Oh no. I know the way; have been there many times. I have another service to beg of thee – to take this letter to the ship.'

Her face clouded: she pushed out her lower lip: her whole body expressed displeasure and negation. 'Thou art not afraid to take it in the dark?' he asked, glancing at the sun, no more than its own breadth above the sea.

'Bah,' she cried, kicking the ground. 'I want to go with thee. Besides, if I do not go with thee, where are my three wishes? There is no justice in the world.'

It had never been difficult to make out the nature of Dil's wishes, whatever their number: from the first day of their friendship she had spoken of bracelets, silver bracelets; she

had told him, objectively and at length, the size, weight and
quality of every kind in the Presidency as well as those current in the neighbouring province and kingdoms; and he had
seen her kick more than one well-furnished clanking child
from mere envy. They walked to a grove of coconut-palms
overlooking Elephanta Island. 'I have never yet seen the
caves,' he observed, and took a cloth parcel from his bosom.
As though she, too, had been warned in a dream, Dil stopped
breathing and watched with motionless intensity. 'Here is the
first wish,' he said, taking out one bangle. 'Here is the second,' taking out two. 'And here is the third,' taking out three
more.

She reached forward a hesitant hand and touched them
lightly; her fearless and cheerful expression was now timid,
very grave. She held one for a moment; put it solemnly down;
looked at Stephen gazing at the island in the bay. Put it
silently on and squatted there amazed, staring at her arm and
the gleaming band of silver: put on another and another; and
the rapture of possession seized her. She burst into wild
laughter, slipped them all on, all off, all on in a different
order, patting them, talking to them, giving them each a
name. She leapt up and spun, jerking her thin arms to make
the bracelets clink. Then suddenly she dropped in front of
Stephen and worshipped him for a while, patting his feet –
earnest, loving thanks broken by exclamations – how had he
known? – preternatural wisdom nothing to him, of course –
did he think them better this way round or that? – such a
blaze of light! – might she have the cloth they were wrapped
in? She took them off, comforting them, put them on again –
how smoothly they slipped! – and sat there pressed against
his knee, gazing at the silver on her arms.

'Child,' he said, 'the sun has set. It is the dark of the moon
and we must go.'

'Instantly,' she cried. 'Give me the chit and I fly to the ship;
straight to the ship, ha, ha, ha!'

She ran skipping down the hill: he watched her until she

vanished in the twilight, her gleaming arms held out like wings and the letter grasped in her mouth.

HE HAD SEEN the house often enough from the outside – was familiar with its walls, windows, entrances – a retired house deep behind its courts and inner walled gardens; but he was surprised to find how large it was inside. A small palace, in fact: not so large as the commissioner's residence; but very much finer, being made of white marble, cool and intricately fretted in the room where he stood, an octagonal room, domed, with a fountain in the middle of it.

Under the dome, a gallery, screened with this same marble lace: a staircase curving down from the gallery to the place where Stephen stood; and on the fifth step above him, three small pots, a brass pan for gathering filth; on the sixth a short brush made of finely-divided toddy-palm frond, and a longer brush – virtually a broom. A scorpion had hidden under the pan, but it did not judge the shelter adequate and he was watching its uneasy movements among the pots. Moving between them it balanced its claws and tail, rising on its legs with a certain grace.

At the sound of voices he looked up: shapes could be seen flitting through the pierced gallery, and Diana, followed by another woman, appeared at the top of the stairs. Most women show at a disadvantage, viewed from below: not Diana. She was dressed in light blue muslin trousers, tight at the ankle, and a sleeveless jacket above a deep, deep blue sash: remarkably tall and slim: the foreshortening effect quite overcome. She cried 'Maturin,' and ran down the stairs. She caught her right foot on the pan and her left on the handle of the larger brush: the impetus of her run carried her clear of the remaining implements, the remaining stairs, and Stephen caught her at the bottom. He held her lithe body in his arms, kissed her on both cheeks, and set her on her feet.

'Pray take notice of the scorpion, ma'am,' he called to the elderly woman on the stairs. 'He is beneath the little broom.'

'Maturin,' cried Diana again, 'I am still amazed to see you, utterly *amazed*. It is impossible you should be standing here – much more astonishing than sitting there in the crowd by the Fort, like a dream. Lady Forbes, may I introduce Dr Maturin? Dr Maturin, Lady Forbes, who is so kind as to live with me.'

She was a dumpy woman, dressed in a haphazard way with ornaments here and there; but she had taken great care over her large face, which was painted out of resemblance to humanity, and with her wig, whose curls stood in order low on her forehead. She recovered from her deep curtsey, saying, 'He is an odd-looking bugger; a streak of the tar-brush, I dare say. God damn this leg. I shall never get up. How do you do, sir? So happy. Was you born in India, sir? I remember some Maturins on the Coromandel coast.'

Diana clapped her hands: servants flowed into the room – exclamations of deep and even tragic concern at her danger and at the mess; soft, deprecating murmurs; bows; anxiety; gentle, immovable obstinacy. At last an aged person was brought in and he carried the pan away; the scorpion was removed in wooden tweezers; two different servants gathered up what was left. 'Forgive me, Maturin,' she said. 'You cannot imagine what it is, keeping house with so many different castes – one cannot touch this, another cannot touch that; and half of them are only copy-cats – such stuff: of course a radha-vallabhi can touch a pot. However, let us try whether they can give us anything to wet our whistles with. Have you eaten yet, Maturin?'

'I have not,' he said. She clapped her hands again. A fresh company appeared, a score of different people; and while Diana was issuing her orders – there was more wrangling, exhortation and laughter than he would have expected out-side Ireland – he turned to Lady Forbes and said, 'It is remarkably cool here, ma'am.'

'*Wrangle, wrangle, wrangle,*' said Lady Forbes. '*She has no idea of managing her servants: never had when she was a girl.* Yes, sir; it is sunk for the purpose; quite underground, you know. *God's my life, I hope she calls for the champagne: I am fair parched. Will she think this young fellow worth it? Ay, there's the point. Canning is very near with his wine.* But there is the inconvenience that it floods; I remember two foot of mud on the floor, in Raghunath Rao's time; for it belonged to him then, you know. However, there was really no rain this monsoon; no rain at all, hardly. Presently there will be another famine in Gujerat, and the tedious creatures will be dying off in droves, and making one's morning ride so disagreeable.' The parts of her conversation that were intended for herself were uttered in a deeper tone; but there was no variation in the volume of sound.

'Villiers,' he said, 'pray what language were you speaking to them?'

'That was Banga-Bhasa; they speak it in Bengal. I brought some of my father's people back when I was in Calcutta. But come, tell me all about your voyage — a good passage? — what did you come in?'

'A frigate: the *Surprise*.'

'Such a good name! You could have — do not beat me if I say knocked me down with a feather — when I saw you in that wicked old shirt on the glacis. Exactly what I should have expected you to wear in this climate — so much more sensible than broadcloth. Do you admire my trousers?'

'Extremely.'

'*Surprise*. Well, you astonish me. Admiral Hervey did speak of a frigate with a nephew of his on board; but he said the *Nemesis*. Is Aubrey in command? Of course he must be, or you would not be here. Is he married yet? I saw the announcement in *The Times*, but no marriage yet.'

'I believe it is to be any minute now.'

'All my Williams cousins will be married,' she observed, with a slight check in her bubbling gaiety. 'Here is the champagne at last. Lord, I could do with a glass. I hope you are as thirsty as I am, Maturin. Let us drink to his health and happiness.'

'With all my heart.'

'Tell me,' said Diana, 'has he grown up at all?'

'I do not think that you would see a greater maturity,' said Stephen. As I grow older, so I coarsen, he thought, emptying his glass.

A greybeard with a silver mace advanced towards Diana, bowed, and thumped three times: immediately low tables came hurrying in, and great silver trays with innumerable dishes, most of them very small. 'You will forgive me my dear,' said Lady Forbes, rising. 'You know I never sup.'

'Of course,' said Diana, 'and as you pass by, would you be very kind and see that everything is ready? Dr Maturin will be staying in the lapis lazuli room.'

They sat on a divan, with the tables grouped in front of them. She explained the dishes with great volubility and a fair amount of open greed. 'You will not mind eating in the Indian way? I love it.' She was in tearing high spirits, laughing and talking away at a splendid rate, as though she had been long deprived of company. 'How it becomes her to laugh,' he reflected. 'Dulce loquentem, dulce ridentem – most women are solemn owls. But then few have such brilliant teeth.' He said, 'How many teeth have you in your head, now, Villiers?'

'Lord, I don't know. How many should I have? They are all there, in any event. Ha, he has given us bidpai chhatta; how I loved it as a child – still do. Let me help you. Do you think Aubrey would like to dine here, with his officers? I could ask the Admiral. He is a vicious man, but he can be vastly pleas-ant when he chooses – fool of a wife, but then so many naval wives are impossible. And some of the dockyard people: just men.'

'I cannot answer for him, of course; but I do know he is much taken up with his ship. She is being heaved up and heaved down; vital pieces are being sawed out of her bowels; she was much shattered south of the Cape. He has refused all invitations apart from the Admiral's dinner; and that was a holiday of obligation.'

'Oh well: damn Aubrey. But I cannot tell you how glad I am to see you, Stephen. I have been so lonely, and you were in my mind, as clear as a bell, just before I saw you. You are no great shakes at eating in the Indian way, I see . . . Oh my God, what have you done with your poor hands?'

'It is of no consequence,' said Stephen, darting them out of sight. 'They were injured – caught in a machine. It is of no consequence; it will soon pass.'

'I will feed you.' She sat cross-legged on a cushion in front of him, dipping into a dozen bowls, dishes, plates, and feeding him with balls that exploded in a pink glow inside his stomach, others that cooled and dulcified his palate. He looked attentively at her firm round legs under the blue muslin, and the play of her loins as she leant from side to side or towards him.

'What was that thin child I saw you with?' she asked. 'A Dhaktari? Too pale for a Gond. She spoke poor Urdu.'

'I never asked her; nor did she question me. Tell me, Villiers, what must I do? I wish to ensure that she will eat to her hunger every day. At present she begs or steals most of her food. I may buy her for twelve rupees; so the thing should be simple. But it is not. I do not wish to put her into a way of earning an honest living – plying her needle, for example. She has no needle, nor does she feel the need for one. Nor do I wish to entrust her to the good Portuguese sisters, to be clothed and converted. Yet surely there must be some solution?'

'I am sure there is,' said Diana. 'But I should have to know much more about her before I could say anything of the least real use – her caste, and so on. You never believe the difficulties that can cause, when you are thinking of a place for a child. She may be an untouchable: probably is. Send her whenever you have any message for me, and then I can find out. In the meantime she must certainly come here if ever she is hungry. We shall find a way, I am sure. But you will be a great simpleton if you pay twelve rupees, Stephen; three is more the mark. Another piece?'

'If you please; and do not let us neglect the pale ale at your elbow.'

Ales; sherbet; mangosteens: the sky itself turned pale while they talked of Indian pastrycooks; the frigate's voyage, her purpose and intent; Mr Stanhope, sloths, the great men of Bombay. Her only references to Canning were oblique: 'On her good days, Lady Forbes can be an entertaining companion; and at all events she keeps me in countenance – I need it, you know'; and 'I rode sixty miles the day before yesterday, and sixty the day before that, right over the Ghauts. That was why I was here so much earlier than I had expected. There was some tedious business to be discussed with the Nizam and suddenly I could not bear it any longer and came on alone, leaving the elephants and camels to follow. They should be here on the seventeenth.'

'Many elephants and camels?'

'No. Thirty elephants and maybe a hundred of camels. Bullock-carts too, naturally. But even a small train takes an endless time to get moving: you run mad and start to scream.

'And do you indeed travel with thirty elephants?'

'This was only a small journey: to Hyderabad, no more. When we go right across we take a hundred, and all the rest in proportion. It is like an army. Oh, Stephen, I wish you could have seen half the things I saw this last time! Leopards by the dozen, all kinds of birds and monkeys, a python that had eaten a deer, and a well-grown young tiger – not up to our Bengal standards, but a tolerable fine beast. Tell me, Stephen, what can I show you? This is my country, after all, and I should love to lead you about. I am my own mistress for the next few days.'

'God bless you, my dear: I should like to see the caves of Elephanta, if you please, a bamboo forest, and a tiger.'

'Elephanta I can promise – we will make up a party at the end of the week and ask Mr Stanhope; he is a charming man – prodigious gallant to me in London – and your parson friend. The bamboo forest, too. The tiger I will not swear to. I am sure the Peshwa will try to drive one for us in the Poona hills; but they have had rain there and with the jungle so thick . . . however, if we do miss of a tiger there, I can promise you half a dozen in Bengal. For when you have set the old gentleman down in Kampong, you must come back to Calcutta, I collect?'

PERHAPS IT WAS a mistake to invite Mr Stanhope; the day was intolerably hot and humid; all he wanted to do was to lie on his bed with a punkah sighing over him, at least moving the unbreathable air. But he thought it his duty to wait on Mrs Villiers, and he particularly wished to see Dr Maturin, who had unaccountably vanished these last days; so overcoming his nausea and putting a little carmine on his yellow cheeks, he embarked on the heavy, oily swell, and there being no hint of a breeze they rowed him the six evil miles across the bay.

Mr Atkins sat by him and in a rapid, excited whisper he told His Excellency of the discoveries he had made. Mr Atkins was never long in any community before he mastered all the gossip: he had found out, he said, that this Mrs V was not a respectable person, that she was in fact the mistress of a Jew merchant – 'a Jew, for God's sake!' – and that her impudent presence in Bombay aroused indignation; that Dr Maturin was aware of the couple's criminal conversation; and that he had therefore betrayed Mr Stanhope into a false position – His Majesty's representative giving countenance to a connection of this sort!

Mr Stanhope said little in reply, but when he landed he was stiffer and more reserved than usual: in spite of his elaborate courtesy to Diana, his praise for the magnificent array of tents, umbrellas, carpets, cooling drinks (which reminded him of Ascot); for the lumpish statue of the elephant and the astonishing, *astonishing* wealth of sculpture in the caves, his want of cordial enjoyment affected the whole company.

He called Stephen aside as they were walking to the caves

and said, 'I am very much disturbed in my mind, Dr Maturin;
I have word from Captain Aubrey that we are to embark on
the seventeenth! I had counted upon at least another three
weeks. Dr Clowes's course of bleeding and slime-baths lasts
another three weeks.'

'This must be some extravagant wild flight of naval hyperbole. How often do we not read of passengers urged to appear
on board at let us say Greenwich or the Downs on a given date,
only to find that the mariners have not the least intention of
sailing, either for want of inclination or even for the want of the
very sails themselves? You may set your mind at rest, sir: to my
certain knowledge the *Surprise* was without her masts only a
very short time ago. It is materially impossible she should sail
on the seventeenth. I wonder at his precipitancy.'

'Have you seen Captain Aubrey recently?'

'I have not. Nor, to my shame, have I called upon Dr
Clowes since Friday. Have you found benefit from his slime?'

'Dr Clowes and his colleagues are excellent physicians, I
am sure; and they are most attentive; but they do not seem to
have prevailed with the liver complaint. They are afraid it
may fly to the stomach, and fix itself there. However . . . my
main purpose in begging for these few moments was to tell
you that we have received overland despatches on which I
should value your advice: and may I at the same time hint
that perhaps you have not been quite as assiduous in attending at the office as ideal perfection might require? We have
been unable to find you these last days, in spite of repeated
applications to the ship and to your lodgings in the town. No
doubt your birds have drawn you away – have seduced you
from your usual exact punctuality. '

'I beg pardon, Your Excellency; I shall attend this afternoon, and at the same time we can discuss your liver with Dr
Clowes.'

'I should be most infinitely obliged, Dr Maturin. But we are
neglecting our duty in the most disgraceful manner. Dear
Mrs Villiers,' he cried, casting a haggard eye upon the feast

spread in front of the caves, 'this is princely, princely – Lucullus dines with Lucullus, upon my word.'

Mr White, the chaplain, to whom Atkins had at once communicated his discoveries, was as reserved as his patron; he was also deeply shocked by some of the female and hermaphrodite sculptures; and an unidentified creature had bitten him on the left buttock when he sat upon it. He remained heavy and stolid throughout the entertainment.

Mr Atkins and the young men of the envoy's suite were less affected by the atmosphere, however, and they made enough noise to give the impression of a party that was enjoying itself: Atkins more than any; he was easy and familiar; he talked loudly, without restraint, and during the picnic he called out to Stephen 'not to let the bottle stand by him – it was not every day they could swill champagne.' After it he led Diana to a particularly striking group at the back of the second cave, and holding up a lamp he desired her to take notice of the flowing curves, the delicious harmony, the balance, worthy of the well-known Greek sculptor Phidias. She was astonished at his assurance, the way in which he held her elbow and breathed on her; but supposing that he was in wine she did not formalise upon it – only detached herself, regretted that she had been so simple as to follow him, and rejoiced at the sight of Stephen hurrying towards them.

Mr Atkins continued in high spirits, however, and when the party broke up on the Bombay shore he thrust his head into her palanquin and said, 'I shall come up and see you one of these evenings,' adding with an arch look that left her speechless, 'I know where you live.'

Later that day Stephen returned to the house on Malabar Hill and said to Diana, 'Mr Stanhope desires his best compliments to Mrs Villiers, and his heartfelt thanks for an unforgettably delightful afternoon. Lady Forbes, your servant. Do not you find it uncommon hot, ma'am?'

Lady Forbes gave him a vague, frightened smile, and presently she left the room.

'Maturin, did you ever know such a wretched miserable damned picnic in your life?' said Diana. She was wearing an ugly, hard blue dress, tediously embroidered with pearls, and a rope of very much larger pearls in a loop to her middle. 'But it was kind of him to send his compliments, his best compliments, to a fallen woman.'

'What stuff you talk, Villiers,' he said.

'I have fallen pretty low for an odious little reptile like that Perkins to take such liberties. Christ, Maturin, this is a vile life. I never go out without the danger of an affront: and I am alone, cooped up in this foul place all the time. There are only half a dozen women who receive me willingly; and four of them are demireps and the others charitable fools – such company I keep! And the other women I meet, particularly those I knew in India before – oh, how they know how to place their darts! Nothing obvious, because I can hit back and Canning could break their husbands, but sharp enough, and poisonous, my God! You have no notion what bitches women are. It makes me so furious I cannot sleep – I get ill – I am bilious with rage and I look forty. In six months I shall not be fit to be seen.'

'Sure, my dear, you deceive yourself. The first moment I saw you, I remarked that your complexion was even finer than it was in England. This impression was confirmed when I came here, and examined it at leisure.'

'I wonder that you should be so easily taken in. It is only so much trompe-couillon, as Amélie calls it: she is the best woman-painter since what's-her-name.'

'Vigée Lebrun?'

'No. Jezebel. Look here,' she cried, drawing a finger down her cheek and showing a faint smear of pink.

Stephen looked at it closely. He shook his head. 'No. That is not the essence, at all. Though in passing I must warn you against the use of ceruse: it may desiccate and wrinkle the deeper layers. Hog's lard is more to the point. No, the essence is your spirit, courage, intelligence, and gaiety; they are unaffected; and it is they that form your face – you are responsible for your face.'

'But how long do you think any woman's spirit can last, in this kind of life? They dare not use me so badly when Canning is here, but he is so often away, going to Mahé and so on; and then when he is here, there are these perpetual scenes. Often to the point of a break. And if we break, can you imagine my future? Penniless in Bombay? It is unthinkable. And to feel bound by cowardice is unthinkable, too. Oh, he is a kind keeper, I do not say he is not; but he is so hellish jealous – Get out,' she shouted at a servant in the doorway. 'Get out!' again, as he lingered, making deprecatory gestures; and she shied a decanter at his head.

'It is so humiliating to be suspected,' she said, 'I know half the servants are set to watch. If I did not stand up for myself there would be a troop of black eunuchs, great flabby things, in no time at all. That is why I have my own people . . . Oh, I get so tired of these scenes. Travelling is the only thing that is even half bearable – going somewhere else. It is an impossible situation for a woman with any spirit. Do you remember what I told you, oh a great while ago, about married men being the enemy? Here I am, delivered up to the enemy, bound hand and foot. Of course it is my own fault; you do not have to tell me of it. But that does not make the life any less wretched. Living large is very well, and certainly I love a rope of pearls as much as any woman; but give me even a grisly damp cold English cottage.'

'I am sorry,' said he in a harsh formal voice, 'that you should not be happy. But at least it does give me some slightly greater confidence, a perceptibly greater justification, in making my proposal.'

'Are you going to take me into keeping too, Stephen?' she asked, with a smile.

'No,' he said, endeavouring to imitate her. He privately crossed his bosom, and then, speaking somewhat at random in his agitation, he went on, 'I have never made a woman an offer of marriage – am ignorant of the accepted forms. I am sorry for my ignorance. But I beg you will have the goodness, the very great goodness, to marry me.' As she did not reply, he added, 'It would oblige me extremely, Diana.'

'Why, Stephen,' she said at last, still gazing at him with candid wonder. 'Upon my word and honour, you astonish me. I can hardly speak. It was the kindest thing you could possibly have said to me. But your friendship, your affection, is leading you away; it is your dear good heart full of pity for a friend that . . .'

'No, no, no,' he cried passionately. 'This is a deliberate, long-meditated statement, conceived a great while since, and matured over twelve thousand miles and more. I am painfully aware,' he said, clasping and unclasping his hands behind his back, 'that my appearance does not serve me; that there are objections to my person, my birth, and my religion; and that my fortune is nothing in comparison with that of a wealthy man. But I am not the penniless nonentity I was when we first met; I can offer an honourable if not a brilliant marriage; and at the very lowest I can provide my wife – my widow, my relict – with a *decent competence*, an assured future.'

'Stephen darling, you honour me beyond what I can express; you are the dearest man I know – by so very far my best friend. But you know I often speak like a fool when I am angry – fly out farther than I mean – I am an ill-tempered woman, I am afraid. I am deeply engaged to Canning; he has been extremely good to me . . . And what kind of a wife could I make for you? You should have married Sophie: she would have been content with very little, and you would never have been ashamed of her. Ashamed – think what I have been – think what I am now: and London is not far from Bombay; the gossip is the same in both. And having had this kind of life again, could I ever . . . Stephen, are you unwell?'

'I was going to say, there is Barcelona, Paris, even Dublin.'

'You are certainly unwell; you look ghastly. Take off your coat. Sit in your shirt and breeches.'

'Sure I have never felt the heat so much.' He threw off his coat and neckcloth.

'Drink some iced water, and put your head down. Dear Stephen, I wish I could make you happy. Pray do not look so wretched. Perhaps, you know, if it were to come to a break . . .'

'And then again,' he said, as though ten silent minutes had not passed, 'it is not a question of very little, by European standards. I have about ten thousand pounds, I believe; an estate worth as much again, and capable of improvement. There is also my pay,' he added. 'Two or three hundred a year.'

'And a castle in Spain,' said Diana, smiling. 'Lie still, and tell me about your castle in Spain. I know it has a marble bath.'

'Aye, and a marble roof, where it has a roof at all. But I must not practise on you, Villiers; it is not what you have here. Six, no five habitable rooms; and most of them are inhabited by merino sheep. It is a romantic ruin, surrounded by romantic mountains; but romance does not keep the rain away.'

He had made his attempt, delivered his charge, and it had failed: now his heart beat quietly again. He was speaking in a companionable, detached voice about merino sheep, the peculiarities of a Spanish rent-roll, the inconveniences of war, a sailor's chances of prize-money, and he was reaching for his neckcloth when she interrupted him and said, 'Stephen, what you said to me turned my head about so much I hardly know what I answered. I must think. Let us talk about it again in Calcutta. I must have months and months to think. Lord, how pale you have gone again. Come, put on a light gown and we will sit in the court for the fresh air: these lamps are intolerable indoors.'

'No, no. Do not move.'

'Why? Because it is Canning's gown? Because he is my lover? Because he is a Jew?'

'Stuff. I have the greatest esteem for Jews, so far as anyone can speak of a heterogenous great body of men in such a meaningless, illiberal way.'

Canning walked into the room, a big man who moved lightly on his feet. 'How long has he been outside?' thought Stephen; and Diana said, 'Canning, Dr Maturin finds the heat a little much. I am trying to persuade him to put on a gown and to sit by the fountain in the peacock court. You remember Dr Maturin?'

'Perfectly, and I am very happy to see him. But my dear sir, I am concerned that you should not be entirely well. It is indeed a most oppressive day. Pray give me your arm, and we will take the air. I could do with it myself. Diana, will you call for a gown, or perhaps a shawl?'

'How much does he know about me?' wondered Stephen as they sat there in the relative coolness, Canning and Diana talking quietly of his journey, the Nizam, and a Mr Norton. It seemed that Mr Norton's best friend had run away into the Nizam's dominions with Mrs Norton.

'He gives nothing away,' Stephen reflected. 'But that in itself is significant: and he has not asked after Jack, which is more so. His bluff, manly air cannot be assumed, however; it is very like Jack's and it certainly represents a great deal of the man; but I also perceive a gleam of hidden intelligence. How I wish he had Lady Forbes's gift of displaying his secret mind. Mr Norton, the ornithologist?' he asked aloud.

'No,' said Diana, 'he is interested in birds.'

'So interested,' said Canning, 'that he went off as far as Bikanir for a kind of sand-grouse, and when he came back Mrs Norton had flown. I do not think it a pretty thing, to seduce a friend's wife.'

'I am sure you are right,' said Stephen. 'But is it indeed a possible offence? A booby girl may be led away by a wicked fellow, to be sure, but a woman, a married woman? For my part I do not believe that any marriage was ever yet broken by an outside force. Let us suppose that Mrs Norton is confronted with a choice between claret and port; she decides that she does not care for claret but that she does care for port. From that moment she is wedded to her muddy brew~

and it is impertinent to assure her that claret is her true delight. Nor does it seem to me that any great blame attaches to the bottle she prefers.'

'If only there were a breath of air from the sea,' said Canning, with his deep belly-laugh, 'I should tear your analogy limb from limb: besides, you would never have ventured upon it – a foul bottom, if ever there was one. But my point is that Norton was Morton's particular friend: Norton took him into his house, and he made his way into Norton's bed.'

'That was not pretty, I must confess: it savours of impiety.'

'I have not asked after our friend Aubrey,' cried Canning. 'Have you news of him? I believe we are to drink to his happiness – perhaps we should even do so now.'

'He is here, in Bombay: his frigate, the *Surprise*, is refitting in Bombay.'

'You astonish me,' said Canning.

'I doubt that very much, my friend,' said Stephen inwardly: he listened to Canning's exclamations upon the service, its ubiquity, its wide commitments – Jack's excellence as a sailor – sincere and reiterated hopes for his happiness – and then he stood up, saying he believed he must beg permission to withdraw; it was some time since he had been to his lodgings and work was waiting for him there; his lodgings were near the yard; he looked forward to the walk.

'You cannot walk all the way to the dockyard,' said Canning. 'I shall send for a palanquin.'

'You are very good, but I prefer to walk.'

'But my dear sir, it is madness to stroll about Bombay at this time of night. You would certainly be knocked on the head. Believe me, it is a very dangerous city.'

Stephen was not easily overcome, but Canning obliged him to accept an escort, and it was at the head of a train of bearded, sabre-bearing Sikhs that he paced through the deserted outer streets, not altogether pleased with himself ('Yet I like the man, and do not entirely grudge him the satisfaction of knowing that I am off the scene, and that I do in fact live at such and such an address'), down the hill, with the funeral pyres glowing on the shore, the scent of burning flesh and sandal-wood; through quiet avenues tenanted by sleeping holy cows; pariah dogs and one gaunt leafless tree covered with roosting kites, vultures, crows, through the bazaars, filled now by shrouded figures lying on the ground; through the brothel quarter by the port – life here, several competing musics, bands of wandering sailors: but not a *Surprise* among them. Then the long quiet stretch outside the wall of the yard, and as they turned a corner they fell upon a band of Moplahs, gathered in a ring. The Moplahs straightened, hesitated, gauging their strength, and then fled, leaving a body on the ground. Stephen bent over it, holding the Sikhs' lantern; there was nothing he could do, and he walked on.

From a distance he was surprised to see a light burning in their house; and he was more surprised, on walking in, to find Bonden there fast asleep: he was leaning over the table with his head on his bandaged arms; and both arms and head were covered with an ashy snow – the innumerable flying creatures that had been drawn to the lamp. A troop of geckoes stood on the table to eat the dazzled moths.

'Here you are at last, sir,' he cried, starting up, scattering the geckoes and his load of dead. 'I'm right glad to see you.'

'It is kind in you to say so, Bonden,' said Stephen. 'What is up?'

'All hell is up, sir, pardon the expression. The Captain is in a terrible taking over you, sir – reefers and ship's boys relaying one another here, messengers sent up every hour – was you there yet? and afeared to go back and say no you wasn't and no word either. Poor Mr Babbington in irons and young Mr Church and Callow flogged in the cabin with his own hands and didn't he half lay it on, my eye – they howled as piteous as cats.'

'Why, what's afoot?'

'What's afoot? Only blue murder, that's all. No liberty, all shore-leave stopped, barky warped out into the basin, no bumboats allowed alongside for a drop of refreshment, and all hands at it, working double tides, officers too. No liberty at all, though promised weeks ago. You remember how the old *Caesar* got her new masts in by firelight in Gib before our brush with the Spaniards? Well, it was like that, only day after day after bleeding day – every hand that could hale on a rope, sick or not, gangs of lascars, which he hired 'em personal, drafts from the flagship, riggers from the yard – it was like a fucking ant-heap, begging your pardon, and all in the flaming sun. No duff on Sunday! Not a soul allowed on shore, bar shrimps that was no use aboard and these here messengers at the double. Which I should not be here myself, but for my arm.'

'What was it?'

'Boiling tar, sir. Hot and hot off of the foretop, but nothing to what the Captain's been ladling out. We reckon he must have word of Linois; but any rate it has been drive, drive, drive. Not a dead-eye turned in on Tuesday, and yet we rattled down the shrouds today and we sail on tomorrow's tide! Admiral did not believe it possible; I did not believe it possible, nor yet the oldest fo'c'sleman; and like I said or meant to say Mr Rattray took to his bed the Monday, wore out and sick: which half the rest of the people would a done the same if they dared. And all the time it was "Where's the Doctor – God damn you, sir, can't you find the Doctor, you perishing swab?" Right vexed he was. Excellency's baggage aboard in double quick time – guns for the boats every five minutes – ball over their heads to encourage 'em to stretch out. God love us all. Here's a chit he gave me for you, sir.'

> *Surprise*
> Bombay

Sir

  You are hereby required and directed to report aboard H M Ship under my command immediately upon receipt of this order

> I am, etc.
> Jno. Aubrey

'It is dated three days ago,' observed Stephen.

'Yes, sir. We been handing it from one to the next, by turns. Ned Hyde spilt some toddy on the corner.'

'Well, I shall read it tomorrow: I can hardly see tonight, and we must get a couple of hours' sleep before sunrise. And does he indeed mean to sail upon the tide?'

'Lord, yes, sir. We'm at single anchor in the channel. Excellency's aboard, powder-hoy alongside and the last barrels stowing when I left her.'

'Dear me. Well, cut along to the ship now, Bonden: my compliments to the Captain and I shall be with him before the full. Why do you stand there, Barret Bonden, like a stock, or image?'

'Sir, he'll call me a lubber and a fool and I don't know what all if I come back without you; and I tell you straight it will be a file of Marines to carry you back to the ship the moment he knows you're here. I've followed him these many years, sir, and I've never known him so outrageous: lions ain't in it.'

'Well, I shall be there before she sails. You need not hurry to the ship, you know,' he said, pushing the unwilling, anxious, despondent Bonden out of the door and locking it behind him.

Tomorrow would be the seventeenth. There might be other factors, but he was certain that one reason for this furious drive was Jack's desire to get him out of Bombay before Canning and Diana should return. No doubt he meant it kindly; no doubt he was afraid of an encounter between the two men. It was an ingenious piece of manipulation; but although Stephen was under naval law he was not to be moved about quite so easily. He had never cared for laws at any time.

He threw off his clothes, poured water over himself, and sat down to write a note to Diana. It would not do: he had hit the wrong tone. Another version, and the sweat running down his fingers blurred the words. Canning was a formidable enemy; sharp, silent, quick. If indeed he was an enemy at all: the danger of over-reaching oneself— Byzantine convolutions, too cunning by half. The nausea of perpetual suspicion and intrigue: a hopeless nostalgia for a plain direct relationship – for cleanliness. He reached for another sheet: it appeared that the enemy was at sea – he begged pardon for not taking leave – looked forward to a meeting in Calcutta – reminded her of the promised tiger, sent his compliments to Mr Canning, and was sure he might confide his little protégée to her kindness – he was just about to purchase the child for –

'That puts me in mind of my purse,' he said. He found it, a small cloth bag, hung it round his neck, and put on a kind of shirt. Out into the cooler, cleaner air. Through the streets again, more peopled now with the gardeners bringing in their fruit and vegetables – barrows, asses, bullocks and camel carts making their way carefully through the grey darkness, pariah dogs flitting behind them. In the bazaars there were small lamps everywhere, and the glow of braziers – a general stirring: people picking up their beds and carrying them indoors or turning them into stalls. On through the Gharwal caravanserai, past the Franciscan church, past the Jain temple to the alley where Dil lived.

The alley was unusually crowded; already there were people filling in from side to side, and it was only by urging a Brahmin bull in front of him that he was able to reach the triangular booth made of planks and wedged against a buttress. The old woman was sitting in front of it, with a wavering lamp on her right side, a white-robed man on the other, Dil's body in front of her, partly covered with a piece of cloth. On the ground, a bowl with some marigolds in it and four brass coins. The people pressed in a half circle facing her, listening gravely to her harsh, angry voice.

He sat down in the second rank – went down with a grunt, as though his legs had been cut from under him – and he felt an intolerable pain rising in his heart. He had seen so much death that he could not be mistaken: but after some time the hard acceptance he had learnt cleared his mind at least. The

old woman was calling upon the crowd for money: breaking
off to tell the Brahmin that a very little wood would do –
wrangling with him, insisting. The people were kind: many
words of comfort, sympathy and praise, small offerings added
to the bowl; but it was a desperately poor neighbourhood and
the coins did not amount to half a dozen logs.

'Here is no one of her caste,' said the man next to Stephen;
and other people murmured that that was the cruel pity of
the thing – her own people would have seen to the fire. But
with a famine coming, no man dared look beyond the caste
he belonged to. 'I am of her caste,' said Stephen to the man in
front of him, touching his shoulder. 'Tell the woman I will
buy the child. Friend, tell the woman I will buy the child and
take it down. I will attend to the fire.'

The man looked round at him. Stephen's eyes were remote;
his cheeks hollow, lined and dirty; his hair straggled over his
face: he might well have been mad, or in another state –
removed. The man glanced at his grave neighbours, felt their
qualified approval, and called out, 'Grandmother, here is a
holy man of thy caste who from piety will buy the child and
take it down: he will also provide the wood.'

More conversation – cries – and a dead silence. Stephen
felt the man thrust the purse back into his bosom, patting
and arranging his shirt round the string.

After a moment he stood up. Dil's face was infinitely calm;
the wavering flame made it seem to smile mysteriously at
times, but the steady light showed a face as far from emotion
as the sea: contained and utterly detached. Her arms showed
the marks where the bracelets had been torn off, but the
marks were slight: there had been no struggle, no desperate
resistance.

He picked her up, and followed by the old woman, a few
friends and the Brahmin, he carried her to the strand, her head
lolling against his shoulder. The dawn broke as they went down
through the bazaar: three parties were already there before
them, at the edge of the calm sea beyond the wood-sellers.

Prayers, lustration; chanting, lustration: he laid her on the pyre. Pale flames in the sunlight, the fierce rush of blazing sandalwood, and the column of smoke rising, rising, inclining gently away as the breeze from the sea set in.

'. . . nunc et in hora mortis nostrae,' he repeated yet again, and felt the lap of water on his foot. He looked up. The people had gone; the pyre was no more than a dark patch with the sea hissing in its embers; and he was alone. The tide was rising fast.

8

THE *SURPRISE* LAY at single anchor, well out in the channel: the wind was fair, the tide near the height of flood, and her captain stood at the rail, staring at the distant land with a grim look on his face. His hands were clasped behind his back: they clenched a little from time to time. Young Church came bounding up from the midshipmen's berth into the expectant silence, filled with some unreasoning delight of his own, and he met the warning eye of his messmate Callow, who murmured, 'Watch out for squalls.'

Jack had already seen the boat pulling away from the flagship, but this was not the boat he was waiting for; it was a man-of-war's cutter, with an officer and his sea-chest in the stern sheets – his new first lieutenant sent by the facetious admiral the moment he returned from a shooting-expedition up country. The boat that Jack was looking for would be a native craft, probably filthy, and he was still looking for it when the cutter hooked on to the chains and the officer ran up the side.

'Stourton, sir,' he said, taking off his hat. 'Come aboard to join, sir, if you please.'

'I am happy to see you at last, Mr Stourton,' said Jack with a constrained smile on his lowering face. 'Let us go into the coach.' He cast another glance shoreward before leading the way, but nothing did he see.

They sat in silence while Jack read the Admiral's letter, and Stourton looked covertly at his new captain. His last had been a gloomy, withdrawn, hard-drinking man, at war with his officers, perpetually finding fault, and flogging six days a week. Stourton, and every other officer aboard who did not wish to be broke, had been forced into tyranny: between them they had made the *Narcissus* the prettiest ship, to look at, east of Greenwich, and they could cross upper yards in twenty-two seconds – a true spit-and-polish frigate, with the highest rate of punishment and desertion in the fleet.

Stourton's reputation was that of the hard-horse first lieutenant of the *Narcissus*. He did not look like a slave-driver, but like a decent, pink, very close-shaved, conscientious, brisk young man: however, Jack knew what the habit of power could do, and putting the Admiral's letter away he said, 'Different ships have different ways, sir, as you are aware. I do not mean to criticise any other commander, but I desire to have things done my way in *Surprise*. Some people like their deck to look like a ball-room: so do I, but it must be a fighting ball-room. Gunnery and seamanship come first, and there never was a ship that fought well without she was a happy ship. If every crew can ply their gun brisk and hit the mark, and if we can make sail promptly, I do not give a damn for an occasional heap of shakings pushed under a carronade. I tell you this privately, for I should not wish to have it publicly known; but I do not think a man deserves flogging for a handful of tow. Indeed, in *Surprise* we do not much care for rigging the grating, either. Once the men understand their duty and have been brought to a proper state of discipline, officers who cannot keep them to it without perpetually starting them or flogging them do not know their business. I hate dirt and slovenliness, but I hate a flash ship, all spit and polish and no fighting spirit, even worse. You will say a slovenly ship cannot fight either, which is very true: so you will please to ensure the pure ideal, Mr Stourton. Another thing that I should like to say, so that we may understand one another from the beginning, is that I hate unpunctuality.' Stourton's face fell still further: through no fault of his own he had been abominably late reporting aboard. 'I do not say this for you, but the young gentlemen are blackguards in the middle and morning watches; they are late in relieving the deck. Indeed, there is little sense of time in this ship; and at this very moment, at top of flood, I am kept waiting . . .'

There was the sound of a boat coming alongside, then a thin, high wrangling about the fare. Jack cocked his ear and shot upon deck with a face of thunder.

Surprise, at sea

Sweetheart,

We have picked up the moonsoon, after baffling winds and light airs among the Laccadives, and at last I can turn to my letter again with an easy mind: we are sailing through the Eight Degree channel with flowing sheets, Minicoy bearing NNW four leagues. The people are recovering from our refit in Bombay, when I must confess I pushed them pretty hard, and the dear ship is stretching away south-east under all plain sail like a thoroughbred on Epsom Downs. I was not able to do all I could have wished in the yard, as I was determined to sail on the seventeenth; but although we are not altogether pleased with her shifting backstays nor her trim, we did *make hay while the sun shone*, as they say, and with the wind two points free she handles as sweet as a cutter – a vastly different *Surprise* from the pitiful thing we brought in, frapped like St Paul's barky and pumping day and night. We logged 172 miles yesterday, and next week, at this rate, we should go south about Ceylon and bear away for Kampong; and it will be strange if in two thousand miles of ocean we do not overcome her very slight tendency to gripe (it is no more). And even with her present trim, I am confident we can eat the wind out of any man-of-war in these seas. She can bear a great press of sail, and with our clean bottom, I believe we could give even lively skysails and perhaps an outer jib.

Indeed it is a great pleasure to feel her answer to a light air and stand up stiff to a strong breeze; and if only we were heading west rather than east, I should be perfectly happy. Was she homeward bound, she should be under topgallants and studdingsails too, for all it is Sunday afternoon.

Our people behaved uncommon well in Bombay, and I feel truly obliged to them. What a capital fellow Tom Pullings is! He worked like a black, driving the hands day and night; and then when the Admiral sent this Mr Stourton to be first lieutenant over poor Pullings's head (all the labour of refitting being over), not a word of complaint, nor a hint of being ill-used. It was heavy work, as heavy as I can remember, and the boatswain being sick, even more fell to his share: I do not believe he went out of the ship above once, saying in his cheerful way 'that he knew Bombay – had often been there before – it was no more than Gosport to him'. Fortunately there was a rumour that Linois's squadron was off Cape Comorin, and that kept the men to their task with a will: I did not contradict it, you may be sure, though I cannot conceive he should have beat so far westwards, yet.

Lord, how we toiled in the broiling sun! Mr Bowes, the purser, was a great support – are you not amazed? But he is the most seamanlike officer; and he and Bonden (until he boiled himself with tar) supplied the boatswain's place to admiration. William Babbington, too, is an excellent young man; though he was harpooned by a lamentable trollopy wench the moment he set foot ashore, and eventually was obliged to be placed

under restraint. However, when we really set to, in consequence of a damned odd contretemps I shall tell you
about, he behaved nobly. And young Callow, the very
hideous boy, is shaping well: it was very good for the
midshipmen to see a thorough refit carried through at
the double, with some operations that are rarely done
when a ship is in commission; and I kept them by me
all the time: I hardly went ashore either, apart from
duty-calls and a dinner with the Admiral.

Now here, dearest Sophie, I enter into shoaling
water, without a chart; and I am afraid I may run myself
aground; being, as you know, no great hand with a pen.
However, I shall carry on as best I can, trusting in your
candour to read me aright. Scarcely an hour before I
received your last packet, I was amazed to learn Diana
Villiers was in Bombay; and that you knew, and
Stephen knew, she was there. Two things came into my
mind directly. In the first place I conceived it might
cause you uneasiness was I to go ashore, she being
there; and in the second, I was much concerned for
Stephen. I break no confidence (for he has never spoke
to me about such matters; not plain, I mean) when I
tell you he has been and I fear still is much attached to
Diana. He is a deep old file, and I do not pretend to any
great penetration; but I love him more than anyone but
you, and strong affection supplies what intellect don't –
he lit up like a boy when we reached soundings (I wondered at it at the time) and he lit up again when I mentioned her name, though he tried to hide it. He had
known she was in Bombay from the beginning. When
he landed he found out she was away, up country, but
that she should be back on the seventeenth. He had
the strongest intention of seeing her; and there is no
shaking him, of course. I turned it over in my mind and
it was certain to me, that either she would use him barbarously, or he would fight Canning: or both. He is bet-

ter than he was; far, far better; but he is in no fit state to fight or to be treated rough.

So I decided to get away to sea by that date; all the more so, that it would bring me home earlier. And by going very hard at our refitting, I flattered myself I had brought it off. But I must say I had my doubts. He vanished for days and days; and I was very dissatisfied with him for cutting a muster and for not being aboard to see to his stores and the sick-bay – there was no finding him, no word from him; and when Mr Stanhope came aboard he mentioned having been with him and Mrs Villiers to Elephanta Island. I had made up my mind to put him under arrest if I could lay my hands on him; but I could not. I was angry, as well as being very concerned; and I determined, when he came aboard, to give him an official rebuke, as well as a piece of my private mind, as a friend.

We were at single anchor in the channel, blue peter at the fore since daybreak, when his boat appeared at last; and what with the heat, the anxiety, the jaded feeling of having been up all night, and some foolish words with the envoy's secretary, who would be making a nuisance of himself, I was ready to give him a trebly-shotted broadside. But when I saw him, my heart failed me: you would not credit how unhappy and ill he looked. He is as dark as a native, with the sun; but yet he somehow looked pale – grey is more the mark.

I am afraid she must have been most bitterly unkind, for although we have been at sea some days now, and although we are back in our regular course, sailing with a fair wind for escort on a warm sea, which is the best way I know of setting the ugly side of shore-life far astern, his spirits don't recover. I could almost wish for some benign plague to break out in the ship, to rouse him; but so far only Babbington is on the sick-list – the rest of the ship's company are amazingly well, apart from Mr Rattray and a couple of men with the sun-stroke. I have never seen him so low, and now I am very glad I did not reprove him: apart from anything else, it would have been precious awkward, living together mewed up so close together as we are, block by block, with Mr Stanhope and his people taking up all the room. However, at least I think we may hope it is all over, and salt water and absence will waste it away. He is sitting over against me now, on the starboard locker, studying in a Malay dictionary, and you would say he was quite old. How I wish we could find one of Mons. de Linois's frigates and lay her aboard, yardarm to yardarm: we ply our guns pretty brisk now, and I make no doubt we should thump it into her with some effect. There is nothing like it for suddenly raising your spirits.

And even a man-of-war, which don't fetch much in the way of prize-money, being in general handled rough before you can get possession of her, would set us up in a neat cottage. I have been thinking so of this neat cottage, Sophie! Pullings understands everything in the earthy line, his people having a farm; and I have been talking to him about gardening, and it is clear to me that with proper attention two people (not much given to luxury) could feed admirably well off a rood of moderate land. I should never grow tired of fresh green stuff, nor potatoes for that matter, after so many years of hard tack. In this drawing you will see I have attended to the due rotation of crops: plot A is root vegetables for the first year. Heaven knows when you will see the plan: but with any luck we may fall in with the Company's China fleet, and if we do, I shall send this and the rest of my packet by one of them – many of the homeward-bound China ships don't touch at Calcutta or Madras – and then you may have it before Christmas. However, the fleet's motions depend upon

Linois's; if he is anywhere near the Straits they won't
sail; so perhaps I shall be my own postman after all.'

He drifted into a reverie, seeing trim rows of cabbages, cauli-
flowers, leeks; stout and well-grown, untouched by caterpillars, wireworms, leatherjackets or the dread onion-fly; a
trout-stream at the bottom of the garden with good pasture
along its banks, and on the good pasture a mild pair of cows,
Jersey cows. Following the stream down he saw the Channel
at no great distance, with ships upon it; and through the temperate haze upon this sea he was conscious of Stephen smiling at him.

'Will you tell me what you were musing upon, now?' said
Stephen. 'It must have been rarely pleasant.'

'I was thinking about marriage,' said Jack, 'and the garden
that goes with it.'

'Must you have a garden when you are married?' cried
Stephen. 'I was not aware.'

'Certainly,' said Jack. 'I had provided myself with a prize,
and my cabbages were already springing up in rank and file. I
don't know how I shall bear to cut the first. Stephen,' he
cried, suddenly breaking off, 'should you like to see a relic of
my youth? I had hoped to show it to you when we were alongside the sheer-hulk, but you did not turn up; however, I have
preserved it. The sight will raise your heart.'

'I should be happy to see a relic of your youth,' said
Stephen, and they walked on to the calm deck, calm with the
peace of Sunday afternoon, calm and placidly crowded. The
awning rigged for church was rigged still; and beneath its
shade the gunroom officers, Mr Stanhope's people, and most
of the midshipmen took their ease, or as much of it as they
could; for now that church was over, the cabin's, the coach's,
the gunroom's and the berth's hencoops and smaller live-
stock, including Mr Stanhope's nanny-goat had reappeared,
and since there was little air to temper the fiery sun – the
Surprise was running before the wind – they were all crowded

into the shade. Yet at the same time the officer of the watch
took his ritual turns fore and aft with a telescope under his
arm, while the mate and the midshipman of the watch paced
all the quarterdeck that was available on the other side, the
timoneer stood at the wheel, the quartermaster conned the
ship, two boys, the duty-messengers, stood meek as mice,
though often trodden upon, in their due places, and an eager
young Bombay mongoose threaded busily among them all,
frightening the hens. Jack paused to compliment Mr White
on his sermon (a strongly-worded confutation of Arminian-
ism) and to inquire for Mr Stanhope, who had managed to
take a little dry toast and broth, and who hoped to recover his
sea-legs in a day or two.

   Followed by Stephen, he moved forward along the gangway,
filled with seamen in their Sunday rig – many a splendid
Indian handkerchief – some gazing over the hammock-cloths
at the empty sea or conversing with their mates in the chains,
some walking up and down, revelling in idleness; and so to
the forecastle, which was deeply packed with men: for not
only was it too hot to stay below, but a game was in progress,
the ancient country game of grinning through a horse-collar,
with a prize for who should be the most hideous. The collar
was the hoop through which hammocks had to be passed,
and the probable winner, to judge from the infinite mirth,
was the loblolly boy, the surgeons' lay assistant. A weak head
for figures had undone him as a butcher in the Bahamas, but
he was a firm hand at the operating-table, and no mean dis-
sector. Ordinarily he remained at a certain distance from the
unlearned, but now, with Sunday's grog and the stirring of his
youth, he was grinning like a Goth, amaranthine-purple with
the strain. Grinning, that is to say, until his suffused eyes met
Stephen's, when its face resolved itself into a reasonable
shape, assumed a sickly look between greeting and confusion, simpered unhappily, but lacked the quickness to remove
itself from the hoop.

   Silently as a ghost, and unseeing, Jack climbed slowly up

the foremast shrouds, thrust his head through the lubber's hole, heard the click of dice – the deadly, illegal, fifty-strokes-at-the-gangway dice – and the horrified cry 'It's the skipper.' He looked down to guide Stephen's hands, and when at last he heaved himself into the top the men were standing in a huddle, mute by the larboard dead-eyes: they were used to an unnaturally active captain, but the foretop – and of a Sunday! – and through the lubber's hole! – it passed human belief. Faster Doudle, the only one whose wits could stand the strain, had swept the dice into his mouth: he stood now fixing the horizon with an absent gaze, a strikingly criminal expression on his face. Jack gave them a remote passing look and a smile, said 'Carry on, carry on,' and sat down on a studding-sail to haul Stephen through, in spite of his peevish cries of 'perfectly capable of coming up – have repeatedly mounted by the futtock-shrouds – scores of times – pray do not encumber me with your needless solicitude.'

Once up, he, too, sat upon the studdingsail, and gasped for a while: he put enormous effort into climbing, and now the sweat was running down his meagre cheeks. 'So this – this is the foretop,' he observed. 'I have been into the mizzentop, and the maintop, but never here. It is very like the others; very like indeed. The same ingenious arrangements of caps, double masts, and those round things – have you noticed, my dear sir, that it is virtually identical with the rest?'

'An odd coincidence, ain't it?' said Jack. 'I do not believe I have ever heard it remarked upon before.'

'And is your relic here?'

'Why, no; not exactly. It is a little higher up. You do not mind going a little higher up?'

'Not I,' said Stephen, glancing aloft to where the topmast soared, up and up through the brilliant diffused light, the only straight object in a billowy whiteness criss-crossed with curving ropes. 'You mean to the next story, or stage? Certainly. Then in that case I shall take off my coat, breeches, stockings. Lambswool stockings at three and nine the pair, are not to be hazarded lightly.' As he sat unfastening his knee-buckles he stared heavily at the men by the rail. 'Faster Doudle,' he said, 'has my rhubarb answered? How are your bowels, my good friend? Show me your tongue.'

'Oh, not on Sunday, Doctor,' said Jack. Faster Doudle was a valuable upper-yard man; he had no wish to see him at the gangway. 'You are forgetting that today is Sunday. Mellish, take great care of the Doctor's wig. Put the watch and the money into it, and the handkerchief on top. Come now: clap on to the shrouds, Doctor, not the ratlines, and always look up, not down. Take it easy; and I will follow you and place your feet.'

Up and up they went, passing the lookout perched on the yardarm, who assumed an attitude of intense vigilance. Still higher; and Jack swarmed round the mast, up into the cross-trees, and heaved Stephen's now submissive body into place, passed a line round it, and called upon him to open his eyes.

'Why, this is superb,' he cried, convulsively hugging the mast. They were poised high above the surface of the sea; and all that was visible of the distant, narrow deck through the topsails and courses seemed peopled with dolls, fore-shortened dolls that moved with disproportionate strides, their feet reaching too far in front and too far behind. 'Superb,' he said again. 'How vast the sea has become! How luminous!'

Jack laughed to see his evident pleasure, his bright and attentive wondering eye, and said, 'Look for'ard.'

The frigate had no headsails set, the wind being aft, and the taut lines of the forestays plunged slanting down in a clean, satisfying geometry; below them the ship's head with its curving rails, and then the long questing bowsprit, reach-ing far out into the infinity of ocean: with a steady, measured, living rhythm her bows plunged into the dark blue water, splitting it, shouldering it aside in dazzling foam.

He sat for a long while, gazing down. With the long, slow pitch – no roll – they were swept fifty feet forward through the air each time the frigate put her head down; then slowly up to the vertical, a pause, and the forward rush again. 'How much airier it is, at this great height,' he observed at last.

'Yes,' said Jack. 'It is always so. In the light air, for example, your royals will give you as much thrust as the courses. Even more.' He looked up at the royal pole, rising bare into the unclouded sky, and he was weighing the dynamic advantages of a fidded mast with one part of his mind when another part told him he was being uncivil – that Stephen had asked him a question, and was waiting for an answer. He reconstructed the words as well as he could – 'had he ever considered the ship thus seen as a figure of the present – the untouched sea before it as the future – the bow-wave as the moment of perception, of immediate existence?' and replied, 'I cannot truly say I have. But it is a damned good figure; and all the more to my liking, as the sea is as bright and toward today as ever your heart could wish. I hope it pleases you, old Stephen?'

'It does indeed. I have rarely been more moved – delighted; and am most sensible of your kindness in carrying me up. I dare say you, for your part, have been here pretty often?'

'Lord, when I was a mid in this very ship, old Fidge used to masthead me for a nothing – a fine seaman, but testy: died of the yellow jack in ninety-seven – and I spent hours beyond number here. This is where I did nearly all my reading.'

'A venerable spot.'

'Ah,' cried Jack, 'if I had a guinea for every hour I have spent up here, I should not be worrying about prizes; nor discounting bills on my next quarter's pay. I should have been married long ago.'

'This question of money preoccupies your mind. Mine, too, at times: how pleasant it would be, to be able to offer one's friend a rope of pearls! And then again, such deeply stupid men are able to come by wealth, often by no exertion, by no handling or even possession of merchandise, but merely by writing figures in a book. My Parsee, for example, assured me that if only he had the hard word about Linois's whereabouts, he and his associates would make lakh upon lakh of rupees.'

'How would he do that?'

'By a variety of speculations, particularly upon rice. Bombay cannot feed itself, and with Linois off Mahé, for instance, no rice ships would sail. Clearly the price would rise enormously, and the thousands of tons in the Parsee's nominal possession would sell for a very much greater sum. Then there are the funds, or their Indian equivalent, which lie far beyond my understanding. Even an untrue word, intelligently spread and based upon the statement of an honest man, would answer, I collect: it is called rigging the market.'

'Aye? Well, damn them for a pack of greasy hounds. Let me show you my relic. I preserved it south of Madagascar, and I preserved it in Bombay. You will have to stand up. Steady, now – clap on to the cheek-bolt. There!' He pointed to the cap, a dark, worn, rope-scored, massive block of wood that embraced the two masts. 'We cut it out of greenheart in a creek on the Spanish main: it is good for another twenty years. And here, do you see, is my relic.' On the broad rim of the square hole that sat on the topmast head there were the initials JA cut deep and clear, supported on either side by blowsy forms that might have been manatees, though mermaids were more likely – beer-drinking mermaids.

'Does not that raise your heart?' he asked.

'Why,' said Stephen, 'I am obliged to you for the sight of it, sure.'

'But it does raise your heart, you know, whatever you may say,' said Jack. 'It raises it *a hundred feet above the deck*. Ha, ha – I can get out a good thing now and then, given time – oh ha, ha, ha! You never smoked it – you was not aware of my motions.'

When Jack was as amused as this, so intensely amused throughout his whole massive being, belly and all, with his scarlet face glorious and shining and his blue eyes darting mirth from their narrowed slits, it was impossible to resist.

Stephen felt his mouth widen involuntarily, his diaphragm contract, and his breath beginning to come in short thick pants.

'But I am truly grateful to you, my dear,' he said, 'for having brought me to this proud perilous eminency, this quasi-apex, this apogee; you have indeed lifted my heart, in the spirit and in the flesh; and I am now resolved to mount up daily. I now despise the mizzentop, once my ultima Thule; and I even aspire to that knob up there,' – nodding to the truck of the royal. 'What an ape, or even I may say an obese post-captain can accomplish, that also I can do.'

These words, and the conviction with which they were uttered, wiped the laugh off Jack's face. 'Each man to his own trade,' he began earnestly. 'Apes and I are born. . .' The look-out's hail 'On deck there,' directed nevertheless straight up at the captain, 'sail ho!' cut him short.

'Where away?' he cried.

'Two points on the larboard bow, sir.'

'Mr Pullings. Mr Pullings, there. Be so good as to send my glass into the fore crosstrees.'

A moment later Mr Callow appeared, having run from the cabin to the crosstrees without a pause; and the white fleck in the south-east leapt nearer – a ship, close-hauled on the starboard tack: topsails and courses, taking it easy. Already there was a hint of her dark hull on the rise. She would be about four leagues away. At the moment the *Surprise* was running seven or eight knots with no great spread of canvas; and she had the weather-gauge. There was plenty of time.

'Lose not a minute' was engraved on his heart, however, and saying 'Shin up to the jacks, Mr Callow: do not watch the chase, but the sea beyond her. Doctor, pray do not stir for the moment,' he hailed the deck for his coxswain and swung him-self into the shrouds with a speed just short of hurry. He met the ascending Bonden, said, 'Bring the Doctor down hand-somely, Bonden. He is to be dressed, full rig, in the top,' and so reached the quarterdeck.

'What have they seen, Captain?' cried Atkins, running towards him. 'Is it the enemy? Is it Linois?'

'Mr Pullings, all hands to make sail. Maintopgallants'l, stuns'ls and royal; and scandalise the foretops'l yard.'

'Maintopgallants'l, stuns'ls and royal, and scandalise foretops'l yard it is, sir.'

The boatswain's call piped with a fine urgency; the ship was filled with the unaccustomed click of Sunday shoes; and Jack heard Atkins's shrill voice cut off suddenly as the afterguard bowled him over; in a few moments the wild melee had resolved itself into ordered groups of men aloft and alow, each at his appointed rope. The orders came in the dead silence: in quick succession the sails were sheeted home, and as each filled on the steady breeze so a stronger impulse sent the ship faster through the water – her whole voice changed, and the rhythm of her pitch; all far more living, brilliantly awake. At the last cry of 'Belay' Jack looked at his watch. It was pretty well; they were not Livelies yet, not by a minute and forty seconds; but it was pretty well. He caught a look of whistling astonishment on his new first lieutenant's face, and he smiled privately.

'South-south-west a half south,' he said to the helmsman. 'Mr Pullings, I believe you may dismiss the watch below.'

The watch below did in fact vanish into the berth-deck, but only to take off its best shirts, embroidered at the seams with ribbons, its spotless white trousers, and little low-cut shoes with bows; it reappeared a few minutes later in working clothes and gathered on the forecastle, in the head and the foretop, staring fixedly at the sail on the horizon.

By this time Jack had begun his ritual pace from the break of the quarterdeck to the taffrail: at each turn he glanced up at the rigging and across the sea to the distant chase – for chase she had become in the frigate's predatory eyes, although in fact she was not in flight: far from it – her course lay rather towards the *Surprise* than from her. At this moment she was a whiteness just clear of the larboard lower studding-

sail, and if she held her luff she would soon disappear behind
it. Now that the whole of the fresh impulse had been transmitted to the frigate's hull, now that her upper masts had
ceased their momentary complaint and that the backstays
were less iron-taut, she was racing through the water: she had
nothing on her mizzenmast; on her main, topsail, topgallant
with studdingsails on either side, and royal, her mainsail
being hauled up to let the wind into her foresail; and on her
foremast, the course with both lower studdingsails spread
like wings, no topsail – the maintopsail would have becalmed
it – but the topsail yard on the masthead and its studdingsails
set. She was running very smoothly, rippling over the swell
with an eager forward thrust, not a hint of steering wild: their
courses should converge in about an hour at this rate. Rather
less: he might have to reduce sail. And if the chase wore and
fled, he still had his spritsail and the kites in hand, as well as
an advantage of some two or three knots, in all likelihood.

The civilians had been reduced to silence or shepherded
below; Mr Stourton was hurrying quietly about, making ready
for the possible order to clear for action; and in the silence of
voices, but almost silence of the following wind, all that was
to be heard was the steady run of water along her side, an
urgent bubbling rush that mingled with the higher excited
tumult of her wake.

Six bells. Braithwaite, the mate of the watch, came to the
rail with the log. 'Is the glass clear?' he cried. 'All clear, sir,'
said the quartermaster.

Braithwaite heaved the log. It shot astern. 'Turn,' he said, as
the mark tore through his fingers, the reel screeching aloud.

'Stop!' shouted the quartermaster, twenty-eight seconds
later.

'Eleven knots and six fathoms, sir, if you please,' reported
Braithwaite to Pullings, official gravity fighting a losing battle
with delight. All hands were listening nakedly, a murmur of
intense satisfaction ran through the ship.

'Give it her,' said Pullings, and stepped closer to Jack's path.

'How do we come along, Mr Pullings?' said he.

'Eleven knots and six fathoms, sir, if you please,' said Pullings with a grin.

'Hey, hey,' cried Jack. 'I scarcely believed it could be so much.' He looked lovingly along her deck and up to where her pendant flew out in a curving flame fifty foot long, almost straight ahead. She was indeed a noble ship: she always had been, but she had never run eleven knots six fathoms off the reel when he was a boy. By now the chase had vanished from his view, and if she held her course he would not see her again until she was within gunshot, unless he went forward. Stephen was sitting on the capstan, eating a mangosteen and staring at the mongoose as it played with his handkerchief, tossing it up, catching it, worrying it to death.

'We are running eleven knots six,' said Jack.

'Oh,' said Stephen, 'I am sorry to hear it – most concerned. Is there no remedy?'

'I fear not,' said Jack, shaking his head. 'Do you choose to walk forward?'

From the forecastle she was even nearer than he had expected: hull up – same sails, same course.

'I speak under correction, and with great diffidence,' said Stephen as Jack fixed her in his glass, 'but I should have supposed our progress satisfactory, seeing that the vessel is notoriously weak and old, even decrepit. See how she dashes the foam aside – see how the water is as it was *excavated* in a deep trough on either bow. I can see a yard of her copper at least: I never remember to have seen so deeply down her side. From the flying spray alone – and my good coat is soaked – I should have judged our pace adequate; unless indeed we are to indulge in this modern frenzy for speed.'

'It is not our speed that is unsatisfactory,' said Jack. He lowered the telescope, wiped the object-glass, and peered again. 'It is that ugly Dutch-built interloping tub.' And to be sure the tension on the forecastle had been slackening fast as the probable nature of the chase became more and more apparent. In all likelihood she was one of the Company's country ships, bound for Bombay. What else would have held an untroubled course, with a man-of-war bearing down on her under a press of sail? Her chequered sides, her ten gunports, her martial air, might deceive foreigners; but the Navy had smoked her at once for a vile merchantman, no enemy nor no prize.

'Well, I am glad we did not clear away even the bow-chasers,' said Jack, walking aft. 'Proper flats we should have looked, if we had run alongside, stripped and bristling with guns. Mr Pullings, you may take in the royal and the topgal-lant-studdingsails.'

Half an hour later the two ships lay hove-to with backed topsails, wallowing in the swell, and the master of the *Seringapatam* came across Navy-fashion in an elegant barge with a uniformed crew. He came grunting up the side, fol-lowed by a Lascar with a parcel, saluted the quarterdeck and limped towards Jack with a smile on his face and his hand held out. 'You do not recognise me, sir,' he said. 'Theobald, of the *Orion*.'

'Theobald, God love you,' cried Jack, all his reserve vanish-ing at once. 'How happy I am to see you. Killick, Killick — where is that mumping villain?'

'What now?' said Killick angrily, two feet behind him. 'Sir.'

'Iced punch in the coach, and bear a hand.'

'How d'ye do, Killick?' said Theobald.

'Tolerable, sir, I thank you: up to my duty, sir, though hardu-ous. We was wholly grieved to hear of your mishap, sir.'

'Thankee, Killick. Yet it is a saving in neat's leather, you know. We made out the *Surprise* the moment you was top-sails up,' he said to Jack. 'I never thought to see that taut old mainmast again.'

'You had no notion of our being Linois?'

'God bless you, no! He will be in the Isle of France by now, if not at the Cape. Quite out of these waters.'

They walked into the forecabin; and when at last they walked out again, Theobald was a fine deep crimson and Jack not much lighter; and their strong nautical voices could be heard from one end of the ship to the other. Theobald gripped the side-ropes, and by the strength of his arms alone he let himself down, his face disappearing like a setting sun. When he had seen his friend bob over the water and swarm aboard the *Seringapatam*, and when the ships had parted with the usual civilities, Jack turned to Stephen and said, 'Well, that was a sad disappointment for you, I am afraid: not so much as a gun. Come and help me finish the punch: it is the last of the snow, and God knows when you will have a cool drink again, this side of Java.'

In the cabin he said, 'I must beg your pardon for not naming Theobald to you. But there is nothing so tedious as sitting by when two old shipmates are calling out, "Do you remember the three days' blow in the Mona Passage? – Do you remember Wilkins and his timenoguy? – What has happened to old Blodge?" He is a fine fellow, however, capital seaman; but having no interest he could not get a command – eighteen years a lieutenant. Indeed, having contrived to blow off his leg, he could not get a ship, either; so he turned to the Company, and here he is commanding a tea-wagon. Poor chap: how lucky I am, in comparison of him.'

'Certainly. I feel much for the gentleman. But he seems to be of a sanguine humour, and Pullings tells me the captains of Indiamen become exceedingly rich – they shake the pagoda-tree like true British tars.'

'Rich? Oh, yes, they wallow in gold. But he will never hoist his flag! No, no, poor fellow, *he* will never hoist his flag. However, old shipmate or not, he had wretched news for us: first, that Linois had taken his squadron off to the Isle of France to refit – they must be infernally short of stores, with no port this side of the ocean – so they cannot be back in these waters this monsoon, if at all: not within three thousand miles of us. And second, that the Company's China fleet has sailed – he had had news of them in the Sunda Strait – so we shall not meet 'em.'

'What of it?'

'I had so looked forward to getting my packet off to England. And I am sure you would have liked to do the same. However, salt water washes away disappointment as well as other things. I have often been amazed at how you forget, after a few days at sea. You might be sailing in Lethe, once you have sunk the land. I said, you might be sailing in Lethe, once you have sunk the land.'

'Yes. I heard you. I do not agree. What is the object behind you, on the locker?'

'It is a case of pistols.'

'No, no. The ill-wrapped parcel, from which feathers protrude.'

'Oh, that. I had meant to show it you earlier. Theobald brought it me. It is for Sophie – a paradise-bird. Was it not handsome in him? But he was always as open-handed as the day. He picked it up some time ago, in the Spice Islands; and he very candidly told me he had meant it for his sweetheart, to put in her hat. But it seems she turned sour and threw him over for a cove in the law line, I believe: the Secondary of the Poultry Compter. He did not mind it much, he said – what could a fellow with a wooden leg expect? – and he wished them happiness in this very bowl. But he hoped it would bring me better luck. Do you feel it might be a trifle ostentatious in a hat? Perhaps more suitable for a chimney-piece, or a fire-screen?'

'What emerald splendour! What a demi-ruff – I hardly know what to call it. What a tail! Never have I beheld such extreme delicate magnificence. A cock bird, of course.' He sat handling the brilliant feathers, the improbable streaming tail; and Jack pondered mildly over a joke, or pun, connecting this fowl with the Poultry Compter; but abandoned it as heartless to Theobald.

Stephen said, 'Have you ever contemplated upon sex, my dear?'

'Never,' said Jack. 'Sex has never entered my mind, at any time.'

'The burden of sex, I mean. This bird, for example, is very heavily burdened; almost weighed down. He can scarcely fly or pursue his common daily round with any pleasure to himself, encumbered by a yard of tail and all this *top-hamper*. All these extravagant plumes have but one function – to induce the hen to yield to his importunities. How the poor cock must glow and burn, if these are, as they must be, an index of his ardour.'

'That is a solemn thought.'

'Were he a capon, now, his life would be easier by far. These spurs, these fighting spurs, would vanish; his conduct would become peaceable, social, complaisant and mild. Indeed, were I to castrate all the Surprises, Jack, they would grow fat, placid and unaggressive; this ship would no longer be a man-of-war, darting angrily, hastily from place to place; and we should circumnavigate the terraqueous globe with never a harsh word. There would be none of this disappointment in missing Linois.'

'Never mind the disappointment. Salt water will wash it away. You will be amazed how unimportant it will seem in a week's time – how everything will fall into place.'

It was the true word: once the *Surprise* had turned south about Ceylon to head for the Java Sea, the daily order seized upon them all. The grind of holystones, the sound of swabs and water on the decks at first light; hammocks piped up, breakfast and its pleasant smells; the unvarying succession of the watches; noon and the altitude of the sun, dinner, grog; Roast Beef of Old England on the drum for the officers; moderate feast; quarters, the beating of the retreat, the evening roar of guns, topsails reefed, the setting of the watch; and then the long warm starlight, moonlit evenings, often spent on the quarterdeck, with Jack leading his two bright midshipmen through the intricate delights of astral navigation. This life, with its rigid pattern punctuated by the sharp imperative sound of bells, seemed to take on something of the nature of eternity as they slanted down towards the line, crossing it in ninety-one degrees of latitude east of Greenwich. The higher ceremonies of divisions, of mustering by the open list, church, the Articles of War, marked the due order of time rather than its passage; and before they had been repeated twice most of the frigate's people felt both past and future blur, dwindling almost into insignificance: an impression all the stronger since the *Surprise* was once more in a lonely sea, two thousand miles of dark blue water with never an island to break its perfect round: not the faintest smell of land even on the strongest breeze – the ship was a world self-contained, swimming between two perpetually-renewed horizons. Stronger still, because in these waters there was no eager impatience to see over the eastward rim: they sailed with no relation to an enemy, nor to any potential prize. The Dutch were bottled up; the French had disappeared; the Portuguese were friends.

They were not idle. Mr Stourton had a high notion of a first lieutenant's duties, a religious horror of anything approaching dirt or shakings; his speaking-trumpet was rarely out of his hand, and the cry of 'Sweepers, sweepers!' resounded through the ship as often as the voice of the cuckoo in May, and with something of the same intonation.

He had at once fallen in with his captain's views on discipline, and with great relief; but the force of habit was strong, and the *Surprise* might have been inspected by an admiral any day without having to blush for it. Stourton was much more efficient than Hervey; it was clear that he could see to the daily running of the ship – in a thoroughly-worked-up frigate with a captain who knew what he was about, any fairly competent officer could have done so, but Stourton did it excellently. It is true that the midshipmen's berth often wished him in hell in the early morning, but his natural cheerfulness was a real addition to the domestic comfort of the gunroom.

The frigate's sailing qualities were Jack's concern, however. His master, Harrowby, was no phoenix, either in navigation or seamanship. In the hurry of their departure Harrowby had allowed an imperfect stowing of the hold, and the ship, as soft-mouthed as a filly with her fine narrow entry, would neither lie as close to the wind as Jack could have wished nor stay with the smooth and certain rapidity that was in her power. She was splendid, sailing large – had never been better; but by the wind she left much to be desired; there was a slowness, a tendency to gripe, and want of ease that no fresh combination of sails would overcome; and it was not until they reached the line that pumping their water from one tier to another and shifting several thousand shot brought her by the stern enough to give him some ease of mind: it was only a half-measure, to be sure, and the true solution must wait until they could land a mass of stores, come at the ballast and the ground-tier, and restow the hold; but even this alteration in her trim made her a pleasure to steer.

He had a great deal to do; so had the frigate's people; but there were many evenings when the hands danced and sang on the forecastle, and when Jack and Stephen played, sometimes in their narrow coach, sometimes on the quarterdeck, and sometimes in the great cabin – trios with Mr Stanhope, who blew a tremulous, small-voiced flute, and who had a great deal of sheet-music by him.

The envoy's delicate health had taken great benefit from Bombay, and after his week of sea-sickness his strength and spirits recovered remarkably. He and Stephen often sat together, hearing one another their Malay verbs or rehearsing his address to the Sultan of Kampong. It was to be delivered in French, a language that Mr Stanhope did not possess in great perfection: nor, it was to be presumed, did the sultan, but there was a French resident at Kampong, and Mr Stanhope felt that for his master's credit he must be word-perfect, and they went through it again and again, breaking down every time at 'roi des trente-six parapluies, et très illustre seigneur de mille éléphants', Mr Stanhope transposing the seigneur and the elephants out of mere nervousness. The address was to be translated phrase by phrase into Malay by his new oriental secretary, a gentleman of mixed parentage from Bencoolen, found for the envoy by the Governor of Bombay. Mr Atkins looked upon the new arrival with hatred and suspicion; he tried to make Mr Ahmed Smyth's life miserable, but outwardly at least he was unsuccessful, for in the oriental secretary the Malay predominated, and his large, black, somewhat oblique eyes shone with merriment.

Mr Stanhope tried to keep the peace between them, but often and often Atkins's harsh, nasal voice would be heard issuing from the cabin – little or no privacy in a vessel thirty yards long with two hundred men crammed into it – complaining of some infringement of his prerogatives, some slight; and then the envoy's gentle, conciliating murmur, assuring him Smyth was a very good, well-behaved, civil, attentive fellow – that he meant no harm, had no idea of encroaching. Ahmed Smyth was popular in the ship although, being a Mahommedan and suffering from his liver, he drank no wine; and when the rearrangement of the frigate's bowels set free a space long enough to swing a hammock in, Mr Stourton had it screened off as a cabin for *the foreign gentleman*. This so vexed Atkins, who was obliged to share with poor Mr Berkeley, with whom he was no longer on speaking terms, that he came to Stephen and begged him to use his influence with the captain, to put an end to a gross injustice, a monstrous abuse of authority.

'I cannot interfere with the running of the ship,' said Stephen.

'Then H.E. will have to have a word with Aubrey himself,' said Atkins. 'It is intolerable. Every day this nigger finds some new way of provoking me. If he don't take care, I shall provoke him, I can tell you.'

'Do you mean you will fight him?' asked Stephen. 'That is a course no one with your welfare at heart could advise.'

'Thank you, thank you, Dr Maturin,' cried Atkins, grasping his hand. He was extremely sensitive to even the most fallacious appearance of affection, poor man. 'But that is not what I meant. Oh no. A man of my family does not fight with a half-caste nigger clerk, not even a Christian. After all, un gentilhomme est toujours gentilhomme.'

'Compose yourself, Mr Atkins,' said Stephen, for the enthusiasm with which Atkins spoke these last words brought the blood to his nose and ears. 'In these latitudes, indulgence in passion may bring on a calenture. I do not like your mottled face; you eat too much, drink too much; and are a likely victim.'

Yet it was Mr Stanhope that suffered from the calenture. One afternoon when Ahmed Smyth dined with the gunroom, Atkins could be heard ranting away in the cabin. Some feet above the open skylight the carpenter rested his mallet and said privately to his mate, 'If I was His Excellency, I should put that bugger into the jolly-boat with a pound of cheese, and bid him look out for another place.'

'How he does badger and worry the poor old gent, to be sure. You would think they was married. I feel for him: poor old gent – always a civil word.'

A little later Mr Stanhope's valet brought his master's compliments – he begged to be excused from their party at whist, and would be most grateful for a word with Dr Maturin at his leisure. Stephen found him looking tired and old and discouraged: it was this wretched bile again, he thought, and should be infinitely obliged for half of a blue pill, or whatever Dr Maturin judged proper. A thready, uneven pulse, a high temperature; dry skin, an anxious face, a brilliant eye: Stephen prescribed bark, his favourite slime-draught, and a blue-coloured placebo.

They had some effect, and Mr Stanhope was more comfortable in the morning. Yet his strength did not return, nor his appetite; Stephen was not pleased with his patient, whose temperature rose and fell, with an alternation of febrile

excitement and languor that he had never seen before. Mr
Stanhope found the heat very hard to bear, yet every day they
drew nearer to the equator, and every day the wind died to
the smallest breeze between ten and two. They set up a wind-
sail for him, to direct the air into the cabin, where he lay, dry,
thin, yellow, suffering from continual nausea, but always
polite, always grateful for any attention, apologetic.

Stephen and M'Alister had a fair library of books on tropical medicine; they read them through and through, and
admitted to one another, but in Latin, that they were at sea.
'There is at least one thing we can do,' observed Stephen. 'We
can get rid of one external source of irritation.'

Mr Atkins was forbidden the cabin on doctor's orders, and
Stephen spent most of his nights there, generally accompanied by the valet or Mr White. He was fond of the envoy; he
wished him very well; but above all he was professionally
committed. This was a case in which close Hippocratic attention must take the place of drugs; the patient was too weak,
the disease too little understood, for any radical measures;
and he sat by Mr Stanhope's bedside watch after watch while
the ship moved quietly through the phosphorescent sea.
This, he reflected, was his true occupation; this, not the self-
destructive pursuit of a woman far beyond his reach. Medicine, as he saw it, was largely impersonal, and although its
effect might be humane, Atkins would have received much
the same care. What were his motives, beyond a desire for
knowledge, an itch for cataloguing, measuring, naming,
recording?

His mind wandered away, losing itself in intricate paths;
and when he found that his half-waking consciousness was
suffused with a rosy pleasure, and that there was a smile
upon his face, he brought up his vague ideas with a jerk, to
find that in fact between two bells and the three that had just
struck he had been musing upon Diana Villiers, or rather
upon her laughter, particularly bubbling and gay, unaffectedly

musical, and the way the hair curled at the nape of her neck.

'Did you do the Heautontimoroumenos at school?' whispered Mr Stanhope.

'I did, too,' said Stephen. 'But at sea it is different. I was dreaming of Dr Bulkeley at school and his terrible black face; I really thought I saw him there in the cabin. How he frightened me when I was a little chap. But, however, we are at sea – it is different. Tell me, is it nearly daylight yet? I thought I heard three bells.'

'Very soon now. Just raise your head, will you now, till I turn your pillow.' Fresh sheets, sponging, a spoonful of animal soup, sordes removed from his cracked lips, black in the candlelight. At four bells Mr Stanhope fell into a rambling account of the etiquette at the Sultan's court – Mr Smyth told him the Malay rulers were very particular about precedence; His Majesty's representative must not give way to any improper claim; he hoped he should do right . . .

Sponging, a change of position, the small personal ignominies – Mr Stanhope was as shamefaced as a girl. Day after day Stephen felt the balance shift and vary; but after a fortnight of unremitting care he walked into the sick-bay, his eyes sunk and dark-rimmed with fatigue, and said 'Mr M'Alister, a good morning to you. I believe we may cry Io triumphe, at least as far as the anorexia is concerned. We had a pretty crisis at four with a laudable exudation, and a little after six the patient took eleven ounces of animal soup! It is the animal soup that bears the bell away – the animal soup for ever! The vicious anomaly of the pulse remains, and the palpable liver; but I think we may look forward to a gain in weight and strength.'

By day they slung his cot on the weather-side of the quarterdeck, and the Surprises were happy to see him again. He and his people and his baggage, presents and livestock had been a great nuisance to them these fifteen thousand miles now; but, as they said, the Excellency was a civil gentleman – always had a civil word, not like some touch-me-not sodomites – and they were used to him. They liked what they were used to, and they rejoiced to see him getting better as the frigate slipped away south and eastwards through stronger, cooler winds.

Much fresher winds, and more uncertain: sometimes they would fairly box the compass, and now it was no unusual thing for the *Surprise* to strike her topgallantmasts down on deck, hand her courses, and proceed under close-reefed topsails alone.

It was on such a day as this, a Sunday with Jack dining in the gunroom, where the conversation was running on the wild beasts to be met with in Java, whose western tip, the opening of the Sunda Strait, they hoped to raise on Monday, that Mr Stanhope's valet rushed in, his face horrified, staring and distraught. Stephen left his plate; a few minutes later he sent for Mr M'Alister. Already rumours were flying round the ship – the envoy had been struck down by the strong fives, or apoplexy; he had choked over his wine and blood, thick blood, was gushing black from his mouth; he was to be opened by the surgeon within the hour and the instruments were sharpening this minute; he was dead.

When he came back to the damped, silent, apprehensive feast, Stephen sat to his meal, and eating it up with no apparent emotion he said to Jack, 'We have taken the first measures, and he is relatively comfortable; but his state is very grave and it is essential that he should be set down on land, the nearest firm land. And until we can reach it the motion of the ship should be reduced as far as possible. Another four and twenty hours of this bucketing must have a fatal issue. May I trouble you for the wine?'

'Mr Harrowby, Mr Pullings, pray come with me,' said Jack, throwing down his napkin. 'Mr Stourton, you will excuse us.'

In a few moments all the sea-officers had gone, leaving only Etherege and the purser: they pushed the cheese towards Stephen, the pudding and the wine, watching silently and uneasily as he made his hearty meal.

Jack stood at the charts, with Pullings and the master beside him. The ship's course had been altered to bring the wind on her quarter and she was lasking along with an easy motion under little more than her foretopsail: the latest log-board readings had been fetched and her position was clearly and certainly set down: 5°13´S, 103°37´E, Java Head beating WSW 70 leagues. 'We could fetch Bencoolen on this tack,' he said, 'but not in four and twenty hours. Or bear up for Telanjang . . . no: not with this cross-sea. Does he need a civilised town, a hospital, or will any land answer? That is the point.'

'I will find out, sir,' said Pullings: and coming back he said, 'Any land at all, he says.'

'Thank you, Pullings. You know these waters – you must have run through the straits a dozen times: have you anything to suggest?'

'Pulo Batak, sir,' said Pullings at once, touching the coast of Sumatra with the dividers. 'Inside Pulo Batak. We watered there twice in the *Lord Clive*, both coming and going. It is a right bold shore, forty fathom water not a cable's length from the land, and a clean bottom. At the head of the bay there is a stream comes out of the rock – sweet water you can fill directly into the boats. It ain't civilised – nothing but some lit-tle naked black men that beats drums in the woods – but it's purely calm, and the island shelters it from anything but a nor-wester.'

'Very well,' said Jack, hanging over the chart. 'Very well. Mr Harrowby, lay off the course for Pulo Batak, if you please.' He went on deck to see what sail she could bear and still remain on a fairly even keel: at midnight he was still there, and at dawn; and as the wind failed, so the *Surprise* silently blos-somed, sail by sail, into a pyramid of whiteness. They needed every ounce of thrust to reach Pulo Batak in twenty-four hours.

Their noon altitude showed a fair day's run, and a little after dinner-time – no pipes, no drum – they made their landfall. Pullings, at the fore royal jacks, was certain of it: a rounded head with two peaks bearing north-east. The ship ghosted along on the unruffled sea, her lofty skysails giving her four knots.

There was also the strange attraction of the land heaving her in, and presently the whole of the eastern sky was barred with dark mountains, growing greener as she stood on and on. The island guarding the little bay was clear from the deck, with a hint of gentle surf on its westward face, and it looked very much as though the *Surprise* would drop her anchor within the time laid down: there was still an hour to go.

The best bower was already at the cat-head and all was cleared away when the land-breeze set untimely in, coming off strong and gusty, and bringing with it the strong scent of rotting vegetation. The sails slackened, flapped, and her way began to fall off. Jack sent for the deep-sea line. It splashed into the sea far forward, and running aft down the side came the familiar cry, strangely muted. 'Watch, watch, bear away, veer away,' and at last the answer he had expected: 'No ground, sir, no ground with two hundred fathom.'

'ALL BOATS AWAY, Mr Stourton,' he said. 'We must tow her in. Let us hope we reach soundings before the tide sets too strong against us. Mr Rattray, bend another shot of cable to the small bower, if you please; and rouse out the new eight-inch hawser.'

Pullings took her in, conning the ship from the foreyard-arm; and when the ebb began to run so hard against them that the boats could no longer give her any headway at all they dropped the small bower in a prodigious depth – something over ninety fathoms to hold their ground. This was deeper water than Jack had ever anchored in, and in his anxiety he twice asked Thomas Pullings if he knew what he was at. 'Mr Pullings, are you happy about our berth?'

They were standing immediately above the hawse-hole, with a group of extremely grave forecastlemen, old experienced seamen, behind them. 'Yes, sir,' said Pullings. 'We rode here three days in the *Clive*: I am sure of the bearings, and the bottom is as clean as Gurnard Point. If we veer out to the bitter-end, I will answer for it.'

'Below, there,' cried Jack down the hatch. 'Double the stoppers, clap on two dogs, and veer out to the bitter-end.'

The *Surprise* was going fast astern: the cable straightened, rising in a drooping curve and dragging the anchor over the sea-bed far below. A fluke dug into the bottom, dragged a little further, and held firm: the cable rose again, much higher, much straighter; and as it took the full strain it stretched taut, squirting water, and then brought her up, riding steady.

Throughout the tide Pullings stood there, the responsibility heavy on him, watching the cable and the shore, keeping three tall trees in a line to make sure she did not move, drift helplessly out to sea, out to the strong current that set north-west up the coast, so that they might have to beat up for days before they reached the bay again. The ebb ran faster, even faster, gurgling round her stem.

'I never heard of an anchor holding, well-nigh apeak, not in a hundred fathom water,' observed an elderly hand. 'It stands to reason, on account of the compression of wolume.'

'You pipe down, Wilks,' cried Pullings, turning sharp upon him. 'You and your God-damned wolumes.'

'Which I only passed the remark,' said Wilks, but very quietly.

How cruel fast it ebbed! But it was slackening, surely it was slackening? Babbington joined him on the forecastle. 'What's o'clock?' asked Pullings.

'It wants five minutes of half-tide,' said Babbington. Together they stared at the cable. 'But it is slackening faster already,' he said, and Pullings felt his heart warm to him. After a moment Babbington went on, 'We are to buoy the cable and slip, as soon as we can tow again. They are making a kind of litter to pass him over the side in.'

The ebb ran its course at last; the barge pulled out with the tow-line, buoying the cable in its way; and Pullings went aft, feeling young once more.

'Are you ready there below, Mr Stourton?' called Jack. 'All ready, sir,' came the muffled reply.

'Then slip the cable. Mr Pullings, take the jolly-boat and lead in. Boats away, and stretch out there, d'ye hear me?'

They stretched out; they pulled with a will, and the frigate towed sweetly. But even so it was late evening before she glided past the island, down the sheltered inlet with its tall, jungle-covered sides, green cliffs or bare rock rising sheer from the water, down to the far end, where there was a little white crescent of beach and an astonishing waterfall plunging down the black rocks to one side of it, almost the only sound in that strangely oppressive air. The land, which had seemed so green and welcoming from a distance, took on altogether another appearance as they drew in; and two hundred yards from the shore a swarm of black flies settled heavily on the ships and the boats, crawling about the rigging, the sails, the deck, and the people.

Thirty hours, not twenty-four, had gone by before they lifted Mr Stanhope's litter out of the barge and set it gently down on the sand.

The little beach seemed even smaller to Jack as he walked about it. The jungle pressed in on all sides: huge improbable fronds overhung the sea-wrack, and the still air – no land-breeze here in this lost inlet – was filled with the smell of decay and the hum of mosquitoes. He had heard the sound of a drum in the forest as they came in, and now that his ears were accustomed to the roar of the waterfall he heard it again, some way inland, and to the north; but there was no telling how far off.

A troop of fruit-bats, each five feet across, flew low over the open space and into a vast, creeper-covered tree; following their sinister flight he thought he saw a dark, man-sized form moving through the mass of green below and he stepped eagerly towards it. But the jungle-wall was impenetrable, the only paths being tunnels two or three feet high. He turned and looked out over the strand and to sea. They had rigged two tents, and a fire was burning, bright already in the twilight; a top-lantern had been set up, and Etherege was posting his Marines. Beyond the tents lay the ship, no more than a cable's length away but still in twenty fathom water; she was moored fore and aft to trees on the outward-curving shores, and they had laid out the best bower to seaward: she looked huge and tall in this confined space, and lights were moving about on the main-deck, behind her open ports. Beyond her rose the island, blocking out the sea. She would lie safe there, even if it came on to blow; and her guns commanded every approach. But he had an uneasy feeling of being watched, and presently he moved down towards the tents.

'Mr Smyth,' he said, meeting the oriental secretary, 'have you been here before?'

'No, sir,' said Smyth. 'This is not a part of the country the Malays frequent. Oh no. It belongs to the Orang Bakut, a little black naked people. There – you can hear their drums. They communicate with drums.'

'Aye. I dare say . . . is the Doctor with his patient?'

'No, sir. He is in the other tent, preparing his instruments.'

'Stephen, may I come in?' he said, ducking under the doorway. 'What is your news?'

Stephen tested the edge of his catlin, shaving the hair from his forearm, and said, 'We shall operate as soon as there is light enough, if his strength recovers a little in the night. I have represented to him the alternatives – the delicacy of such an intervention in a body worn by disease: the inevitably fatal outcome of delay. He has made his mind up to the operation as a matter of duty: Mr White is with him now. I wish his resolution may not falter. I shall require two more chests and some leather-bound rope.'

It was not Mr Stanhope's resolution that faltered, but his vital spirit. All night the noises of the jungle kept him from sleep; the drums on either side of the bay disturbed his mind; the motionless heat was more than he could bear; and towards three in the morning he died, talking quietly about the ceremonies at the Sultan's court and the importance of yielding to no improper claim; the drums and his official reception having as it were run into one another. He had little real notion of dying. Through the remaining hours of darkness Stephen and the chaplain sat with him, listening to the noises outside the tent: the croaking and chuckling of innumerable reptiles; unidentified and countless shrieks, hoots, grunts, against a deep background of steady sound; the roar of a tiger, frequently repeated from different places; the continually shifting drums, now close, now far.

They buried him in the morning at the head of the bay, with the Marines firing volleys over his grave and the ship thundering out an envoy's salute, raising clouds of birds and flying-foxes all round the reverberating cove: all the officers attended in full dress, their swords reversed, and most of the ship's company.

JACK TOOK ADVANTAGE of their sheltered anchorage to correct the frigate's trim; and while this was going forward the carpenter made a wooden cross: they painted it white, and before the paint was dry the *Surprise* stood out to sea, her cables recovered and stowed in the tier, smelling of the mephitic ooze.

Jack looked out of the stern window at the distant, receding land, dull purple now, with a rainstorm beating down on it. He said, 'We came on a fool's errand.'

Stephen said, as though in reply,

> 'All all of a piece throughout
> Thy chase had a beast in view
> Thy wars brought nothing about
> Thy lovers were all untrue.'

'But still,' said Jack, after a long pause, 'but still, we are homeward bound. Homeward bound at last! I am afraid I am required to touch at Calcutta; but it will be touch and go – Calcutta fare thee well, and home as fast as she will fly. Indeed,' he added, having reflected for a while, for a whistling pause, 'if we start to fly this very moment, we may yet overhaul the China fleet, and send our packets off. They are slow, close-reef topsails-every-night old tubs, for all their man-of-war airs and graces. You should not have said that about lovers, Stephen.'

9

IT WAS IN latitude eighty-nine east that the frigate caught them. A string of lights had been seen towards the end of the middle watch, and as the sun came up most of the *Surprise*'s people were on deck to contemplate the cloud of sails that stretched along the horizon: thirty-nine ships and a brig in two separate bodies.

They had scattered somewhat in the night, and now they were closing up in response to their commodore's signals, the laggards crowding sail on the moderate north-east breeze. The leeward division, if such a wandering heap could be called a division, was made up of country ships bound for Calcutta, Madras or Bombay, and some foreigners who had joined them for safety from pirates and to profit by their exact nagivation; it straggled for three miles along the distant sea. But those to windward, all sixteen of them the larger kind of Indiamen that made the uninterrupted voyage from Canton to London, were already in a formation that would not have done much discredit to the Navy.

'And are you indeed fully persuaded that they are not men-of-war?' asked Mr White. 'They look wonderfully like, with their rows of guns; wonderfully like, to a landsman's eye.'

'They do, do they not?' said Stephen. 'It is their study so to appear; but I believe that if you look closer you will see water-butts placed, *stowed*, between the guns, and a variety of bales on deck, which would never be countenanced in the service. And the various flags and streams that fly in the appropriate places are quite different: I am not prepared to say just in what the difference lies, but to the seaman it is instantly apparent – they are not the *royal* insignia. Then again, you will have noticed that the Captain has given orders to close them; which I conceive he would scarcely have done, had they been an enemy fleet of such magnitude.'

'He said, "Keep your luff," and followed it with an oath,' said the chaplain, narrowing his eyes.

'It is all one,' said Stephen. 'They speak in tropes, at sea.'

From his perch in the main crosstrees Pullings summoned William Church aloft, a very small midshipman in his first voyage, who seemed rather to have shrunk than to have grown in the course of it. 'Now, younker,' he said, 'you are always nattering about the wealth of the Orient and the way you never seen none of it in Bombay nor parts east but only mud and flies and a mortal lot of sea: well, now, just take a look through this spyglass at the ship wearing the pendant. She's the *Lushington*: I made two voyages in her. Then. next astern there's the *Warley*: a very sweet sailer – works herself, almost – and fast, for an Indiaman: trim lines – you could take her for a heavy frigate, if you had not been aboard. You see they carry forestaysails, just as we do: they are the only merchantmen you will ever see with a forestaysail. Some call it impertinence. And then the one with her topsail atrip, that they are making such a cock of trimming – Judas Priest, what a Hornchurch fair! They have forgot to pass the staysail sheet – you see the mate in a passion, a-running along the gang-way? I can hear him from here. It is always the same with these Lascars: they are tolerable good seamen, sometimes, but they forget their ABC, and they can't be got to do their duty brisk, no not if it is ever so. Then on her quarter, with the patched inner jib, that's the *Hope*: or maybe she's the *Ocean* – they're much of a muchness, out of the same yard and off of the same draught. But any gait, all of 'em you see in this weather line, is what we call twelve-hundred-tonners; though to be sure some gauges thirteen and even fifteen hundred ton, Thames measurement. *Wexford*, there, with her brass fo'c'sle eight-pounder winking in the sun, she does: but we call her a twelve hundred ton ship.'

'Sir, might it not be simpler to call her a fifteen hundred ton ship?'

'Simpler, maybe: but it would never do. You don't want to be upsetting the old ways. Oh dear me, no. God's my life, if the Captain was to hear you carrying on in that reckless Jacobin, democratical line, why, I dare say he would turn you adrift on a three-inch plank, with both your ears nailed down to it, to learn you bashfulness, the way he served three young gentlemen in the Med. No, no: you don't want to go arsing around with the old ways: the French did so, and look at the scrape it has gotten them into. But what I called you up here for, was to show you this here wealth of the Orient. Just you look ahead of the commodore to the leading ship, *Ganges*, if I don't mistake, and now cast your eye to old slowbelly in the rear, setting his topgallants and sagging to leeward something cruel. Look hard, now, because you will not likely see such a sight again; for there you have a clear six millions of money, not counting the officers' private ventures. Six million of money: God love us, what a prize!'

The officers who were wafting this enormous treasure across the ocean in their leisurely East-India fashion were well rewarded for doing so; this pleased them, because, among other things, it allowed them to be magnificently hospitable; and they were the most hospitable souls afloat. No sooner had Captain Muffit, the commodore, made out the frigate's tall mainmast in the light of dawn, than he sent for his chief steward, his head Chinese and his head Indian cook; and signals broke out aboard the *Lushington*: the one to the *Surprise, Request honour of captain's and officers' company to dinner*, the other to the convoy, *All ships: pretty young female passengers required dine frigate's officers. Repeat young. Repeat pretty.*

The *Surprise* ran within a cable's length of the *Lushington*. Boats plied to and fro along the fleet, bringing young women in silk dresses and eager officers in blue and gold. The India-man's splendid stateroom was filled with people, filled with cheerful noise – news of Europe, of India and the farther East; news of the war, of common acquaintances, gossip; inane but cheerful conversation; riddles! toasts to the Royal Navy, to the Honourable East-India Company, to trade's increase – and the frigate's officers filled themselves with splendid food, with charming wine. Mr Church's neighbour, a lovely rounded creature with golden hair, treated him with the attentive respect due to his uniform, urging him to try a little more of this lacquered duck, a trifle of pork, a few more slices of pineapple, calling for Canton buns, exchanging her third plate of pudding with him – no one would notice: but even her overflowing goodwill sought to restrain his hand at last. It sought in vain: Church had secured to himself a cake in the form of the Kwan-Yin pagoda; there were eight stories still to go, and his beloved captain's motto was Lose not a minute. He lost none in small-talk, at all events, but silently ate on and on. She looked anxiously round – gazed at the frigate's surgeon, sitting in moody silence opposite her – but found no help. When the ladies withdrew, instantly followed by Babbington, who muttered something about 'his handker-chief being left in the boat', she paused by the *Lushington*'s chief officer and said, 'Pray, sir, take care of the blue child; I am sure he will do himself a mischief.'

She watched him apprehensively as he went down the side; but her eye could not follow, nor her heart conceive, his rapid progress from the frigate's deck to the midshipmen's berth, where those who had been obliged to stay aboard were sitting down to a feast sent across by the Indiaman.

For his part Jack could not manage a second dinner when he reached the *Surprise* again, nor indeed anything of a solid nature; but throwing off his coat, neckcloth, waistcoat and breeches, he called for nankeen trousers and coffee. 'You will join me in another pot, Stephen?' he said. 'Lord, how delightful it is to have room to move.' The envoy's suite, apart from Mr White, who was too poor to pay his passage, had removed into an Indiaman, and the great cabin was itself again. 'And how glad I am to be shot of that wicked little scrub Atkins.'

'He was a nuisance, but he was not a wicked man. Weak he was, and silly.'

'When you say weak you say all the rest. You are much too inclined to find excuses for scrubs, Stephen: you preserved that ill-conditioned brute Scriven from the gallows, nourished him in your bosom, gave him your countenance, and who paid for it? J. Aubrey paid for it. Here is the coffee – after such a dinner your soul calls out for coffee . . . A most capital dinner, upon my word. The duck was the best I have ever tasted.'

'I was sorry to see you help yourself to him a fourth time: duck is a melancholy meat. In any case the rich sauce in which it bathed was not at all the thing for a subject of your corpulence. Apoplexy lurks in dishes of that kind. I signalled to you, but you did not attend.'

'Is that why you were looking so mumchance?'

'I was displeased with my neighbours, too.'

'The nymphs in green? Delightful girls.'

'It is clear you have been a great while at sea, to call those sandy-haired coarse-featured pimply short-necked thick-fingered vulgar-minded lubricious blockheads by such a name. Nymphs, forsooth. If they were nymphs, they must have had their being in a tolerably rank and stagnant pool: the wench on my left had an ill breath, and turning for relief I found her sister had a worse; and the upper garment of neither was free from reproach. Worse lay below, I make no doubt. "La, sister," cries the one to the other, breathing across me – vile teeth; and "La, sister," cries the other. I have no notion of two sisters wearing the same clothes, the same flaunting meretricious gawds, the same tortured Gorgon curls low over their brutish criminal foreheads; it bespeaks a superfetation of vulgarity, both innate and studiously acquired. And when I think that their teeming loins will people the East . . . Pray pour me out another cup of coffee. Confident brutes.' He might have added that these young ladies had instantly started to talk to him about a Mrs Villiers of Bombay who had just reached Calcutta – the Doctor must have heard of her in Bombay? – she was nothing but an adventuress, how dreadful – they had seen her at the Governor's, dressed very outrée; not at all good-looking; they wondered at the reports – people were obliged to receive her and pretend not to know, because her *gentleman-friend* – say 'protector', sister – was vastly impor-tant, lived in the highest style, quite princely – it was said she was ruining him. He was a vastly genteel creature – tall – such an air and address, you would almost think he was one of us – he had looked at Aggie in such a particular way! They both tittered into their balled-up grubby handkerchiefs, slap-ping one another behind his bowed back.

He was turning it over in his mind whether to say, 'These women spoke malignantly about Diana Villiers, which angered me: I asked her to marry me in Bombay, and I am to have her reply in Calcutta. I have meant to tell you this for some time: candour required such a statement earlier. I trust you will forgive my apparent lack of candour,' when Jack said, 'Well, and so you did not altogether like them, I collect? I am sorry for it. My neighbour and I agreed wonderfully well – Muffit, I mean. The girl my other side was a ninnyhammer: no bosom. I thought these girls with no bosoms were exploded long ago. I took to him amazingly; a thorough-going seaman, not at all the usual Company's commander – not that I mean to imply they are not seamen; but they are rather pianissimo, if you know what I mean.'

'I know what pianissimo means.'

'He has exactly my idea about stepping the royal-mast *abaft* the topgallant with its heel on the top-cap; he actually has it rigged so, as I dare say you noticed, and swears it gives him an extra knot in moderate airs. I am determined to try it. He is an excellent fellow: he promised to put our packet aboard a pilot-boat the moment he was in soundings.'

'I wish you may have desired Sophie to come to Madeira,' muttered Stephen.

'And he has some notions of gunnery, too, which is rare enough even in the Navy. He does his best to exercise his people, but he is most pitifully equipped, poor fellow.'

'There seemed to me a formidable array of guns. More than we possess, if I do not mistake.'

'They were not guns, my poor Stephen. They were cannonades.'

'What are cannonades?'

'Why, they are cannonades – medium eighteens. How can I explain. You know a *carronade*, I am sure?'

'Certainly I do. The short thing on slides, ignoble in its proportions, that throws an immense ball. I have noticed several about the ship.'

'What a lynx you are, upon my honour: nothing escapes you. And clearly you know a cannon, a great gun? Well now, conceive of an unlucky bastard cross between the two, something that weighs a mere twenty-eight hundredweight and jumps in the air and breaks its breeching every time you offer to fire it, and that will not strike true at five hundred yards, no not at fifty, and there you have your cannonade. But even if the Company had some notion of its own interests and gave him real guns, who is to fire them off? He would need three hundred and fifty men, and what has he got? A hundred and forty, most of them cooks and stewards: and Lascar cooks and stewards at that. Dear Lord above, what a way to trundle six millions about the world! Yet he has sound views on stepping a royal; I am determined to try it, if only on the foremast.'

Two days later the *Surprise*, alone on a misty heaving sea, was trying it. The carpenter and his crew had wrought all morning, and now, dinner having been cut short, the long mast was swaying up through the intricate tracery of the rigging. This was a delicate task in a heavy swell, and Jack had not only heaved to but he had stopped the midday grog: he wanted no fuddled enthusiasm heaving on the top-rope, and he knew very well that the delay would stimulate zeal – that no one would put up with a moment's dawdling – that no man would presume to pause to gasp in the oppressive, thundery heat for fear of what his mates would do.

Up and up it went, and peering with half-closed eyes into the glare of the covered sun, he guided it inch by inch, coordinating the successive heaves with the pitching of the ship. The last half foot, and the whole ship's company held its breath, eyes fixed on the heel of the mast. It crept a little higher, the new top-rope creaking in the block and sending down a cloud of shakings: then with a jerk and a shudder along its whole length the heel lifted over the top-cap.

'Handsomely, handsomely!' cried Jack. A trifle more: at the masthead the bosun flung up his hand. 'Lower away.' The top-rope slackened; the heel of the mast settled down inside the step; and it was done.

The Surprises let out a universal sigh. The maintopsail and forecourse dropped like the curtain at the end of a harrowing drama; they were sheeted home, and the bosun piped belay. The frigate answered at once, and as he felt the way on her Jack gazed up at the new royal-mast, rigidly parallel with the topgallant and rising high above with a splendid promise of elastic strength: he felt a dart of pure joy, not merely because of the mast, nor because of the sweet motion of the ship – his own dear ship – nor yet because he was afloat and in command. It was a plenitude of being —

'On deck, there,' called the lookout in a hesitant, deprecating howl. 'Sail on the larboard bow. Two maybe.' Hesitant, because reporting the China fleet for a third time was absurd;

deprecating, because he should have done so long ago, instead of staring at the perilous drama of the mast.

His hail excited little interest, or none: grog was to be served out the moment the mast was secured and the yard across. Willing hands, well ahead of orders, were busy with the two pair of shrouds, the stoppings on the yard; impatient men were waiting in the crosstrees ready to clap on the braces. However, Jack and his first lieutenant looked attentively at the hazy ships, looming unnaturally large some four miles ahead and growing rapidly clearer as the frigate sailed towards them – she was making five knots already on the steady north-east wind.

'Who is that old-fashioned fellow who carries his mizzentopmast staysail *under* the maintop?' said Stourton. 'I believe I can make out two more behind them. I am astonished they should have come up with us so soon; after all . . .'

'Stourton – Stourton,' cried Jack, 'it is Linois. Haul your wind! Hard a-port, hard over. Let fall the maincourse, there. Strike the pendant. Forestaysail: maintopgallant. Marines, Marines, there: clap on to the mainbrace. Bear a hand, bear a hand. Mr Etherege, stir up your men.'

Babbington came running aft to report the foreroyalyard across, and the frigate's sudden turn, coinciding with a heavy roll, threw him off his balance: he fell sprawling at his captain's feet. 'Butcher!' cried Jack, 'Mr Babbington, this is carrying a proper deference too far.'

'Yard across, sir, if you please,' said Babbington: and seeing the wild glee on Jack's face, the mad brilliance of his eye, he presumed on their old acquaintance to say, 'Sir, what's afoot?'

'Linois is afoot,' said Jack, with a grin. 'Mr Stourton, backstays to that mast at once, and preventers. Do not let them set up the shrouds too taut; we must not have it wrung. All stuns'ls and kites into the tops. Give her what sail she can carry. And then I believe you may prepare to clear for action.'

Slinging his glass, he ran up the masthead like a boy. The *Surprise* had spun round on her heel; she was now steadying

on her course, close-hauled and heading north, leaning far
over to larboard as the sail increased upon her and her bow-
wave began to fling the water wide. The Frenchmen were
fading a little in the haze, but he could see the nearest signalling. Both had been sailing on a course designed to intercept the *Surprise* – they had seen him first – and now they
were following his turn in chase. They would never fetch his
wake unless they tacked, however; they had been too far
ahead for that. Beyond them he could make out a larger ship:
another farther to the south-west, and something indistinct
on the blurred horizon – perhaps a brig. These three were still
sailing large, and clearly the whole squadron had been in line
abreast, strung out to sweep twenty miles of sea; and they
were standing directly for the path the slow China fleet
would traverse next day.

Thunder had been grumbling and crashing since the morning, and now in the midst of a distant peal there was the
sound of a gun. The Admiral, no doubt, calling in his leeward
ships.

'Mr Stourton, he called, 'Dutch ensign and two or three
hoists of the first signal-flags that come to hand, with a gun to
windward – two guns.'

The French frigates were cracking on: topgallant staysails
appeared, outer jib, jib of jibs. They were throwing up a fine
bow-wave, and the first was making perhaps eight knots, the
second nine; but the distance was drawing out, and that
would never do – his very first concern was to find out what
he had to deal with.

Below him the deck was like an ant-hill disturbed; and he
could hear the crash of the carpenters' mallets below as the
cabin bulkheads came down. It would be some minutes
before the apparent confusion resolved itself into a trim,
severe pattern, a clean sweep fore and aft, the guns cast
loose, their crews standing by them, every man at his station,
sentries at the hatchways, damp fearnought screens rigged
over the magazines, wet sand strewn over the decks. The men

had been through these motions hundreds of times, but never in earnest: how would they behave in action? Pretty well, no doubt: most men did, in this kind of action, if they were properly led: and the Surprises were a decent set of men; a little over-eager with their shot at first, perhaps, but that could be dealt with . . . how much powder was there filled? Twenty rounds apiece was yesterday's report, and plenty of wads: Hales was a good conscientious gunner. He would be as busy as a bee at this moment, down there in the powder-room.

This drawing away would never do. He would give them another two minutes and then take his measures. The second frigate had passed the first. She was almost certainly the thirty-six gun *Sémillante*, with twelve-pounders on her main-deck: the *Surprise* could take her on. He moved out on to the yardarm for a better view, for they lay on his quarter and it was difficult to count the gun-ports. Yes, she was the *Sémillante*; and the heavy frigate behind her was the *Belle Poule*, forty, with eighteen-pounders – a very tough nut to crack, if she was well handled. He watched them dispassionately. Yes, they were well-handled: both somewhat crank, probably from want of stores; and both slow, of course; they must be trailing a great curtain of weed, after so many months in this milk-warm water, and they were making heavy weather of it. Beautiful ships, however, and their people obviously knew their duty – *Sémillante* sheeted home her foretopmast staysail in a flash. In his opinion *Belle Poule* would do better with less canvas abroad; her foretopgallant seemed to be pressing her down; but no doubt her captain knew her trim best.

Braithwaite appeared, snorting. 'Mr Stourton's duty, sir, and the ship is cleared for action. Do you choose he should beat to quarters, sir?'

'No, Mr Braithwaite,' said Jack, considering: there was no question of action yet awhile, and it would be a pity to keep the men standing about. 'No. But pray tell him I should like sail to be discreetly reduced. Come up the bowlines a trifle and give the sheets half a fathom or so – nothing obvious, you understand me. And the old number three foretopsail is to be bent to a hawser and veered out of the lee sternport.'

'Aye, aye, sir,' said Braithwaite, and vanished. A few moments later the frigate's speed began to slacken; and as the strain came on to the drag-sail, opening like a parachute beneath the surface, it dropped further still.

Stephen and the chaplain stood at the taffrail, staring over the larboard quarter. 'I am afraid they are coming closer,' said Mr White. 'I can distinctly see the men on the front of the nearer one: and even on the ship behind. See, they fire a gun! And a flag appears! Your glass, if you please. Why, it is the English flag! I congratulate you, Dr Maturin; I congratulate you on our deliverance: I confess I had apprehended a very real danger, a most unpleasant situation. Ha, ha, ha! They are our friends!'

'Haud crede colori,' said Stephen. 'Cast your eyes aloft, my dear sir.'

Mr White looked up at the mizzen-peak, where a tricolour streamed out bravely. 'It is the French flag,' he cried. 'No. The Dutch. We are sailing under false colours! Can such things be?'

'So are they,' said Stephen. 'They seek to amuse us; we seek to amuse them. The iniquity is evenly divided. It is an accepted convention, I find, like bidding the servant – ' A shot from the *Sémillante's* bow-chaser threw up a plume of water a little way from the frigate's stern, and the parson started back. ' – say you are not at home, when in fact you are eating muffin by your fire and do not choose to be disturbed.'

'I often did so,' said Mr White, whose face had grown strangely mottled. 'God forgive me. And now here I am in the midst of battle. I never thought such a thing could happen – I am a man of peace. However, I must not give a bad example.'

A ball, striking the top of a wave, ricocheted on to the quarter-deck by way of the neatly piled hammocks. It fell with a harmless dump and two midshipmen darted for it, struggled briefly until the stronger wrested it away and wrapped it lovingly in his jacket. 'Good heavens,' cried Mr White. 'To fire great iron balls at people you have never even spoken to – barbarity is come again.'

'Will you take a turn, sir?' asked Stephen.

'Willingly, sir, if you do not think I should stand here, to show I do not care for those ruffians. But I bow to your superior knowledge of warfare. Will the Captain stay up there on the mast, in that exposed position?'

'I dare say he will,' said Stephen. 'I dare say he is turning over the situation in his mind.'

Certainly he was. It was clear that his first duty, having reconnoitred the enemy, was to reach the China fleet and do everything possible to preserve it: nor had he the least doubt that he could outsail the Frenchmen, with their foul bottoms – indeed, even if they had been clean he could no doubt have given them a good deal of canvas, fine ships though they were: for it was they who had built the *Surprise* and he who was sailing her – it stood to reason that an Englishman could handle a ship better than a Frenchman. Yet Linois was not to be underestimated, the fox. He had chased Jack in the Mediterranean through a long summer's day, and he had caught him.

The two-decker, now so near that her identity was certain – the *Marengo*, 74, wearing a rear-admiral's flag —had worn, and now she was close-hauled on the larboard tack, followed by the fourth ship and the distant brig. The fourth ship must be the *Berceau*, a 22-gun corvette: the brig he knew nothing about. Linois had *worn*: he had not tacked. That meant he was favouring his ship. Those three, the *Marengo*, *Berceau* and the brig, standing on the opposite tack, meant to cut him off, if the frigates managed to head him: that was obvious – greyhounds either side of a hare, turning her.

The last shot came a little too close – excellent practice, at this extreme range. It would be a pity to have any ropes cut away. 'Mr Stourton,' he called, 'shake out a reef in the fore-topsail, and haul the bowlines.'

The *Surprise* leapt forward, in spite of her drag-sail. The *Sémillante* was leaving the *Belle Poule* far behind, and to leeward; he knew that he could draw her on and on, then bear up suddenly and bring her to close action – hammer her hard with his thirty-two-pounder carronades and perhaps sink or take her before her friends could come up. The temptation made his breath come short. Glory, and the only prize in the Indian Ocean . . . the pleasing image of billowing smoke, the flash of guns, masts falling, faded almost at once, and his heart returned to its dutiful calculating pace. He must not endanger a single spar; his frigate must join the China fleet at all costs, and intact.

His present course was taking Linois straight towards the Indiamen, half a day's sail away to the east, strung out over miles of sea, quite unsuspecting. Clearly he must lead the Frenchmen away by some lame-duck ruse, even if it meant losing his comfortable weather-gauge – lead them away until nightfall and then beat up, trusting to the darkness and the *Surprise*'s superior sailing to shake them off and reach the convoy in time.

He could go about and head south-east until about ten o'clock: by then he should have fore-reached upon Linois so far that he could bear up cross ahead of him in the darkness and so double back. Yet if he did so, or offered to do so, Linois, that deep old file, might order the pursuing frigates to hold on to their northerly course, stretching to windward of the *Surprise* and gaining the weather-gauge. That would be awkward in the morning; for fast though she was, she could not outrun *Sémillante* and *Belle Poule* if they were sailing large and she was beating up, as she would have to beat up, tack after tack, to warn the China fleet.

But then again, if Linois did that, if he ordered his frigates northwards, a gap would appear in his dispositions after a quarter of an hour's sailing, a gap through which the *Surprise* could dart, bearing up suddenly and running before the wind with all the sail she could spread and passing between the

Belle Poule and the *Marengo,* out of range of either; for Linois's dispositions were based upon the chase moving at nine or ten knots – no European ship in these waters could do better, and hitherto *Surprise* had not done as well. *Berceau*, the corvette, farther to leeward, might close the gap; but although she might knock away some of his spars, it was unlikely that she could hold him long enough for the *Marengo* to come up. If she had a commander so determined that he would let his ship be riddled, perhaps sunk – a man who would run him aboard – why then, that would be a different matter.

He looked hard over the sea at the distant corvette: she vanished in a drift of rain, and he shifted his gaze to the two-decker. What was in Linois's mind? He was running east-south-east under easy sail: topsails, forecourse clewed up. One thing Jack was certain of was, that Linois was infinitely more concerned with catching the China fleet than with destroying a frigate.

The moves, the answers to those moves on either side, the varying degrees of danger, and above all Linois's appreciation of the position . . . He came down on deck, and Stephen, looking attentively at him, saw that he had what might be called his battle-face: it was not the glowing blaze of immediate action, of boarding or cutting out, but a remoter expression altogether – cheerful, confident, but withdrawn – filled with natural authority. He did not speak, apart from giving an order to hitch the runners to the mastheads and to double the preventer-backstays, but paced the quarterdeck with his hands behind his back, his eyes running from the frigates to the line-of-battle ship. Stephen saw the first lieutenant approach, hesitate, and step back. 'On these occasions,' he reflected, 'my valuable friend appears to swell, actually to increase in his physical as well as his spiritual dimensions: is it an optical illusion? How I should like to measure him. The penetrating intelligence in the eye, however, is not capable of measurement. He becomes a stranger: I, too, should hesitate to address him.'

'Mr Stourton,' said Jack. 'We will go about.'

'Yes, sir. Shall I cast off the drag-sail, sir?'

'No: and we will not go about too fast, neither: space out the orders, if you please.'

As the pipes screeched 'All hands about ship' he stood on the hammocks, fixing the *Marengo* with his glass, pivoting as the frigate turned up into the wind. Just after the cry of 'Mainsail haul' and the sharp cutting pipe of belay, he saw a signal run up aboard the flagship and the puff of a gun on her poop. The *Sémillante* and the *Belle Poule* had begun their turn in pursuit, but now the *Sémillante* paid off again and stood on. The *Belle Poule* was already past the eye of the wind when a second gun emphasised the order, the order to stand on northwards and gain the weather-gauge, and she had to wear right round to come up on to her former tack. 'Damn that,' murmured Jack: the blunder would narrow his precious gap by quarter of a mile. He glanced at the sun and at his watch. 'Mr Church,' he said, 'be so good as to fetch me a mango.'

The minutes passed: the juice ran down his chin. The French frigates stood on to the north-north-west, growing smaller. First the *Sémillante* and then the *Belle Poule* crossed the wake of the *Surprise*, gaining the weather-gage: there was no changing his mind now. The *Marengo*, her two tiers of guns clearly to be seen, lay on the starboard beam, sailing a parallel course. There was no sound but the high steady note of the wind in the rigging and the beat of the sea on the frigate's larboard bow. The far-spaced ships scarcely seemed to move in relation to one another from one minute to the next – there seemed to be all the peaceful room in the world.

The *Marengo* dropped her foresail: the angle widened half a degree. Jack checked all the positions yet again, looked at his watch, looked at the dog-vane, and said, 'Mr Stourton, the stuns'ls are in the tops, I believe?'

'Yes, sir.'

'Very well. In ten minutes we must cast off the drag-sail,

bear up, set royals, stuns'ls aloft and alow if she will bear them, and bring the wind two points on the quarter. We must make sail as quick as ever sail was made, brailing up the driver and hauling down the staysails at the same time, of course. Send Clerk and Bonden to the wheel. Lower the starboard port-lids. Make all ready, and stand by to let go the drag-sail when I give the signal.'

Still the minutes dropped by; the critical point was coming, but slowly, slowly. Jack, motionless upon that busy deck, began to whistle softly as he watched the far-off Linois: but then he checked himself – he wanted no more than a brisk top-gallant breeze. Anything more, or anything like a hollow sea, would favour the two-decker, the tall, far heavier ship; and he knew, to his cost, how fast these big French seventy-fours could move.

A last glance to windward: the forces were exactly balanced: the moment had come. He drew a deep breath, tossed the hairy mango stone over the side, and shouted, 'Let go there.' An instant splash. 'Hard a-port.' The Surprise turned on her heel, her yards coming round to admiration, sails flashing out as others vanished, and there close on her starboard quarter was her foaming wake, showing a sweet tight curve. She leapt forward with a tremendous new impulse, her masts groaning, and settled on her new course, not deviating by a quarter of a point. She was heading exactly where he had wanted her to head, straight for the potential gap, and she was moving even faster than he had hoped. The higher spars were bending like coach-whips, just this side of carrying away. 'Mr Stourton, that was prettily executed: I am very pleased.'

The Surprise was tearing through the water, moving faster and faster until she reached a steady eleven knots and the masts ceased their complaint. The backstays grew a shade less rigid, and leaning on one, gauging its tension as he stared at the Marengo, he said, 'Main and fore royalstuns'ls.'

The Marengo was brisk in her motions – well-manned – but

the move had caught her unawares. She did not begin her turn until the *Surprise* had set her royal studdingsails and her masts were complaining again as they drove her five hundred tons even faster through the sea: her deck leaning sharply, her lee head rails buried in the foam, the sea roaring along her side, and the hands standing mute – never a sound fore and aft.

Yet when the *Marengo* did turn she bore up hard to bring the wind on her starboard quarter, settling on a course that would give her beautiful deep-cut sails all possible thrust to intercept the *Surprise* at some point in the south-west – to cut her off, that is to say, if she could not find another knot or so. At the same time the flagship sent up hoist after hoist of signals, some directed, no doubt, at the still invisible corvette to leeward and others to bring the *Sémillante* and the *Belle Poule* pelting down after the *Surprise*.

'They will never do it, my friend,' said Jack. 'They did not send up double preventer-stays half an hour ago. They cannot carry royals in this breeze.' But he touched a belaying pin as he said this: royals or no, the situation was tolerably delicate. The *Marengo* was moving faster than he had expected, and the *Belle Poule*, whose earlier mistake had set her well to leeward, was nearer than he could wish. The two-decker and the heavy frigate were the danger; he had no chance at all against the *Marengo*, very little against the *Belle Poule*, and both these ships were fast converging upon his course. Each came on surrounded by an invisible ring two miles and more in diameter – the range of their powerful guns. The *Surprise* had to keep well out of these rings, above all out of the area where they would soon overlap; and the lane was closing fast.

He considered her trim with the most intense concentration: it was possible that he was pressing her down a trifle aft – that there was a little too much canvas abroad, driving her by force rather than by love. 'Haul up the weather-skirt of the maincourse,' he said. Just so: that was distinctly sweeter; a more airy motion altogether. The dear *Surprise* had always loved her headsails, 'Mr Babbington, jump forward and tell me whether the spritsail will stand.'

'I doubt it, sir,' said Babbington, coming aft. 'She throws such an almighty bow-wave.'

Jack nodded: he had thought as much. 'Spritsail-topsail, then,' he said, and thanked God for his new strong royal-mast, that would take the strain. How beautifully she answered! You could ask anything of her. Yet still the lane was narrow enough, in all conscience: the *Marengo* was crowding sail, and now the *Surprise* was racing into the zone of high danger. 'Mr Callow,' he said to the signal-midshipman, 'strike the Dutch colours. Hoist our own ensign and the pendant.' The ensign broke out at the mizzen-peak; a moment later the pendant, the mark of a man-of-war and no other, streamed from the main. The *Surprise* was particular about her pendant – had renewed it four times this commission, adding a yard or two each time – and now its slim tapering flame stretched out sixty feet, curving away beyond her starboard bow. At the sight there was a general hum of satisfaction along the deck, where the men stood tense, strongly moved by the tearing speed.

Now he was almost within random-shot of the *Marengo*'s bow guns. If he edged away the *Belle Poule* and the *Sémillante* would gain on him. Could he afford to hold on to this present course? 'Mr Braithwaite,' he said to the master's mate, 'be so good as to heave the log.'

Braithwaite stepped forward, paused for a moment at the sloping lee-quarter to see where he could toss it into a calm patch outside the mill-race rushing along her side, flung the log wide through the flying spray, and shouted 'Turn!' The boy posted on the hammock-netting with the reel held it high; the line tore off, and a moment later there was a shriek. The quartermaster had the boy by one foot, dragging him inboard; and the reel, torn from his hand, raced away astern.

'Fetch another log, Mr Braithwaite,' said Jack with intense satisfaction, 'and use a fourteen-second glass.' He had seen the whole line run off the reel only once in his life, when he was a midshipman homeward-bound in the packet from Nova Scotia: and the *Flying Childers* boasted of having done it too – the *Childers* also claimed to have lost their boy. But this was no time to be regretting the preservation of young puddinghead, Bent Larsen – for although it was clear that at this speed they would do it, that they would cross the *Marengo* and start to increase the distance within a few minutes, yet nevertheless they were running towards the nearest point of convergence, and it was always possible to mistake by a few hundred yards. And some French long brass eights threw a ball very far and true.

Would Linois fire? Yes: there was the flash and the puff of smoke. The ball fell short. The line was exact, but having skipped five times the ball sank three hundred yards away. So did the next two; and the fourth was even farther off. They were through, and now every minute sailed carried them farther out of range.

'Yet I must not discourage him,' said Jack, altering course to bring the *Surprise* a little closer. 'Mr Stourton, ease off the foresail sheet and hand the spritsail-topsail. Mr Callow, signal *enemy in sight: ship of the line, corvette and brig bearing east, two frigates bearing north-north-west. Request orders*, with a gun to windward. Keep it flying and repeat the gun every thirty seconds.'

'Yes, sir. Sir, may I say the corvette is bearing south-east now?'

She was indeed. The lifting rainstorm showed her on the *Surprise*'s larboard bow, well ahead of the *Marengo*, and to leeward. The turning wind in the squall had set her half a mile to the west. Grave: grave.

It was in the corvette's power to bring him to action, unless he edged away into the extreme range of the frigates – the *Sémillante* had overhauled the *Belle Poule* once again. But to bring him to close action the corvette would have to stand his raking fire, and it would need a most determined commander to take his ship right in against such odds. He would probably bear up at long gunshot and exchange a distant broadside or two. Jack had no sort of objection to that – on the contrary: ever since he had set the *Surprise* for the gap, showing what she could really do in the way of speed, giving away her qualities, he had been trying to think of some means of leading Linois on in a hopeful chase that would take him far to the southward before nightfall. The signal was well enough in its way, but its effect would not last. The drag-sail would scarcely take again – they must have smoked it; but a yard coming down with a run as though it had been shot away, why, that would answer. And he could give any of them the mizzen or even the maintopsail.

'Mr Babbington, the corvette will engage us presently. When I give the word, let the maintopsail come down with a run, as though her fire had had effect. But neither the yard nor the sail must be hurt. Some puddening on the cap – but I leave it to you. It must look like Bedlam, all ahoo, and yet still be ready to set.'

It was just the kind of caper Babbington would delight in; Jack had no doubt of his producing an elegant chaos. But he would have to go briskly to work. The *Berceau* was coming down under a cloud of canvas, as fast as ever she could run; and as Jack watched he saw her set her fore-royal flying. She was steering to cross ahead of the *Surprise* – she lay on her beam at this moment – and although she was now within range she held her fire.

'Mr Babbington,' cried Jack, without taking his eyes from the *Berceau*, 'should you like your hammock sent up?'

Babbington slid down a backstay, scarlet with toil and haste. 'I am sorry to have been so slow, sir,' he said. 'All is stretched along now, and I have left Harris and Old Reliable in the top, with orders to keep out of sight and let go handsomely when hailed.'

'Very good, Mr Babbington. Mr Stourton, let us beat to quarters.'

At the thunder of the drum Stephen took the startled chaplain by the arm and led him below. 'This is your place in action, my dear sir,' he said in the dimness. 'These are the chests upon which Mr M'Allister and I operate; and these' – waving the lantern towards them – 'are the pledgets and tow and bandages with which you and Choles will second our endeavours. Does the sight of blood disturb you?'

'I have never seen it shed, in any quantity.'

'Then here is a bucket, in case of need.'

Jack, Stourton and Etherege were on the quarterdeck; Harrowby stood a little behind them, conning the ship; the other officers were at the guns, each to his own division. Every man silently watched the *Berceau* as she ran down, a beautiful, trim little ship, with scarlet topsides. She was head-on now, coming straight for the frigate's broadside; and Jack, watching closely through his glass, could see no sign of her meaning to bear up. The half-minute signal-gun beside him spoke out again and again and again, and yet still the *Berceau* came on into the certainty of a murderous raking fire. This was more determination than ever he had reckoned on. He had done the same himself, in the Mediterranean: but that was against a Spanish frigate.

Another two hundred yards and his heavy carronades would reach the *Berceau* point-blank. The signal-gun again; and again. 'Belay there,' he said; and much louder, 'Mr Pullings, Mr Pullings – a steady, deliberate fire, now. Let the smoke clear between each shot. Point low on her foremast.'

A pause, and on the upward roll the purser's gun crashed out, the smoke sweeping ahead. A hole appeared in the corvette's spritsail and a cheer went up, drowned by the second gun. 'Steady, steady,' roared Jack, and Pullings ran down the line to point the third. The ball splashed close to the corvette's bow, and as it splashed she answered with a shot from her chaser that struck the mainmast a glancing blow. The firing came down the line, a rippling broadside: two shots went home in the corvette's bows, another hit her chains, and there were holes in her foresail. Now it began forward again, and as the range narrowed so they hit her hard with almost every shot or swept her deck from stem to stern – there were two guns dismounted aboard her, and several men lying on the deck. Broadside after deliberate broadside, the whole ship quivering in the thunder – the jets of flame, the thick powder-smoke racing ahead. Still the *Berceau* held on, though her way was checked, and now her bow-guns answered with chain-shot that shrieked high through the rigging, cutting ropes and sails as it went. 'A little more of this, and I shall not need my caper,' thought Jack. 'Can he mean to lay me aboard? Mr Pullings, Mr Babbington, briskly now, and grape the next round. Mr Etherege, the Marines may – ' His words were cut off by a furious cheer. The *Berceau's* foretopmast was going: it gave a great forward lurch, the stays and shrouds parted and it fell in a ruin of canvas, masking the corvette's forward guns. 'Hold hard,' he cried. 'Maintop, there. Let go.'

The *Surprise's* topsail billowed out, came down, collapsed; and across the water they heard a thin answering cheer from the shattered corvette.

A forward gun sent a hail of grape along the *Berceau's* deck, knocking down a dozen men and cutting away her colours. 'Cease fire there, God rot you all in hell,' cried Jack. 'Secure those guns. Mr Stourton, hands to knot and splice.'

'She struck,' said a voice in the waist, as the *Surprise* swept on. The *Berceau*, hulled again and again, low in the water and by the head, swung heavily round, and they saw a figure running up the mizzen-shrouds with fresh colours. Jack took his hat off to her captain, standing there on his bloody quarterdeck seventy yards away; the Frenchman returned the salute, but still, as his remaining larboard guns came to bear he fired a ragged broadside after the frigate, and then, as she reached the limit of his range, another, in a last attempt at preventing her escape. A vain attempt: not a shot came home, and the *Surprise* was still far ahead of the

Marengo on her larboard quarter and the two frigates away
to starboard.

Jack glanced at the sun: no more than an hour to go, alas.
He could not hope to lead them very far this moonless night,
if indeed he could lead them at all for what was left of the
day. 'Mr Babbington, take your party into the top and give the
appearance of trying to get things shipshape – you may cock-
bill the yard. Mr Callow – where is that midshipman?'

'He was carried below, sir,' said Stourton. 'Hit on the head.'

'Mr Lee, then. Signal *partial engagement, heavy damage;
request assistance. Enemy bearing north-north-east and north-
north-west*, and carry on with the half-minute gun. Mr Stourton, a fire in the waist would do no harm: plenty of smoke.
One of the coppers filled with slush and tow might answer.
Let there be some turmoil.'

He walked to the taffrail and surveyed the broad sea astern.
The brig had gone to the assistance of the *Berceau*: the
Marengo maintained her position on the larboard quarter,
coming along at a fine pace and perhaps gaining a little. As he
expected, she was signalling to the *Sémillante* and the *Belle
Poule* – a talkative nation, though gallant – and she was no
doubt telling them to make more sail, for the *Belle Poule* set
her main-royal, which instantly carried away. For the moment
everything was well in hand.

He went below. 'Dr Maturin,' he said, 'what is your casualty-list?'

'Three splinter-wounds, sir, none serious, I am happy to
report, and one moderate concussion.'

'How is Mr Callow?'

'There he is, on the floor – on the *deck* – just behind you. A
block fell upon his head.'

'Shall you open his skull?' asked Jack, with a vivid recollection of Stephen trepanning the gunner on the quarterdeck of
the *Sophie*, exposing his brains, to the admiration of all.

'No. Oh, no. I am afraid his condition would not justify the
step. He will do very well as he is. Now Jenkins here had a

truly narrow escape, with his splinter. When M'Alister and I cut it out —'

'Which it came off of the hounds of the mainmast, sir,' said Jenkins, holding up a wickedly sharp piece of wood, two feet long.

' – we found his innominate artery pulsing against its tip. The twentieth part of an inch more, or a trifling want of attention, and William Jenkins would have become an involuntary hero.'

'Well done, Jenkins,' said Jack. 'Well done indeed,' and he went on to inquire after the other two – a forearm laid open, and an ugly scalp-wound. 'Is this Mr White?' catching sight of another body.

'Yes. He was a little overcome when we raised John Saddler's scalp and desired him to hold it while we sewed it on: yet there was virtually no blood. A passing syncope: he will be quite recovered by a little fresh air. May he go on deck, presently?'

'Oh, this minute, if he chooses. We had a slight brush with the corvette – such a gallant fellow: he came on most amazingly until Mr Bowes brought his foremast by the board – but now we are running before the wind, far out of range. Let him come on deck by all means.'

On deck the black smoke was belching from the frigate's waist, streaming away ahead of her, the ship's boys were hurrying about with swabs, buckets and the fire engine, Babbington was roaring cursing in the top, waving his arms, all hands looked pleased with themselves and sly; and the pursuers had gained a quarter of a mile.

Far on the starboard beam the sun was sinking behind a blood-red haze; sinking, sinking, and it was gone. Already the night was sweeping up from the east, a starless night with no moon, and pale phosphorescent fire had begun to gleam in the frigate's wake.

After sunset, when the French sails were no more than the faintest hint of whiteness far astern, to be fixed only by the recurrent flash of the admiral's top-lantern, the *Surprise* sent up a number of blue lights, set her undamaged main-topsail, and ran fast and faster south-westwards.

At eight bells in the first watch she hauled to the wind in the pitchy darkness; and having given his orders for the night, Jack said to Stephen, 'We must turn in and get what sleep we can: I expect a busy day tomorrow.'

'Do you feel that M. de Linois is not wholly deceived?'

'I hope he is, I am sure: he ought to be, and he has certainly come after us as if he were. But he is a deep old file, a through-going seaman, and I shall be glad to see nothing to the east of us, when we join the China fleet in the morning.'

'Do you mean he might dart about and fling himself between us, guided by mere intuition? Surely that would argue a prescience in the Admiral exceeding the limits of our common humanity. A thorough-going seaman is not necessarily a seer. Attention to the nice adjustment of the sails is one thing; vaticination another. Honest Jack, if you snore in that deep, pragmatical fashion, Sophie is going to spend many an uneasy night. It occurs to me,' he said, looking at his friend, who, according to his long-established habit, had plunged straight into the dark comfortable pit of sleep from which nothing would rouse him but the cry of a sail or a change in the wind, 'it occurs to me, that our race must have a natural propensity to ugliness. You are not an ill-looking fellow, and were almost handsome before you were so pierced, blown up and banged by the enemy and so exposed to the elements; and you are to marry a truly beautiful young woman; yet I make no doubt you will between you produce little common babies, that mewl, pewl and roar all in that same tedious, deeply vulgar, self-centred monotone, drool, cut their teeth, and grow up into plain blockheads. Generation after generation, and no increase in beauty; none in intelligence. On the analogy of dogs, or even of horses, the rich should stand nine foot high and the poor run about under the table. This does not occur: yet the absence of improvement never stops men desiring the company of beautiful women. Not indeed that when I think of Diana I have the least notion of children. I should never voluntarily add to the unhappiness of the world by bringing even more people into it in any case; but even if that were in my mind, the idea of Diana as a mother is absurd. There is nothing maternal about her whatsoever: her virtues are of another kind.' He turned the wick down to a small line of blue flame and crept on to the steeply-sloping deck, where he wedged himself between a coil of rope and the side and watched the dim tearing sea, the clearing sky with stars blazing in the gaps of cloud, reflecting upon Diana's virtues, defining them, and listening to the successive bells, the responding cry of 'All's well' right round the ship, until the first lightening of the eastern sky.

'I've brought you a mug of coffee, Doctor,' said Pullings, looming at his side. And when you have drunk it up, I am going to call the skipper. He will be most uncommon pleased.' He still spoke in his quiet night-watch voice, although the idlers had been called already, and the ship was filling with activity.

'What will please him so, Thomas Pullings? You are a good creature, to be sure, to bring me this roborative, stimulating drink: I am obliged to you. What will please him so?'

'Why, the Indiamen's toplights have been in sight this last glass and more, and when dawn comes up I dare say we shall see them a-shaking out the reef in their topsails just exactly where he reckoned to find 'em: such artful navigation you would scarcely credit. He has come it the Tom Cox's traverse over Linois.'

Jack appeared, and the spreading light showed forty sail of merchantmen stretched wide along the western sea; he smiled, and opened his mouth to speak when the spreading light also betrayed the *Surprise* to a distant vessel in the east, which instantly burst into a perfect frenzy of gunfire, like a small and solitary battle.

'Jump up the masthead, Braithwaite,' he said, 'and tell me what you make of her.'

The expected answer came floating down. 'That French brig, sir. Signalling like fury. And I believe I make out a sail bearing something north of her.'

It was just as he had feared: Linois had sent the brig northwards early in the night, and now she was reporting the presence of the *Surprise*, if not of the China fleet, to her friends over the horizon.

The long-drawn-out ruse had failed. He had meant to draw Linois so far to the south and west during the night that the *Surprise*, doubling back towards the China fleet in the darkness, would be far out of sight by morning. With the frigate's great speed (and how they had cracked on!) he should have done it: yet he had not. Either one of the French squadron had caught the gleam of her sails as she ran northwards through the pursuing line, or Linois had had an intuition that something was amiss – that he was being attempted to be made a fool of – and had called off the chase, sending the brig back to his old cruising-ground and then following her with the rest of his ships after an hour or so, crowding sail for the track of the China fleet. Yet his ruse had not failed entirely: it had gained essential time. How much time? Jack set course for the Indiamen and made his way into the crosstrees: the accursed brig lay some four leagues off, still carrying on like a Guy Fawkes' night, and the farther sail perhaps as much again – he would scarcely have seen her but for the purity of the horizon at this hour, which magnified the nick of her topgallants in the line of brilliant sky. He had no doubt that she was one of the frigates, and that the whole of Linois's squadron, less the corvette, was strung out on the likely passage of the Indiamen. They could outsail the convoy; and with this unvarying monsoon there was no avoiding them. But they could not outsail the convoy by a great deal: and it would take Linois the greater part of the day to concentrate his force and come up with the China fleet.

THE SENIOR CAPTAINS came hurrying aboard the *Surprise*, headed by Mr Muffit, their commodore. The signal flying from the frigate's maintruck and the commodore's energetic gathering of the stragglers had given them a general idea of the situation; they were anxious, disturbed, grave; but some, alas, were also garrulous, given to exclamation, to blaming the authorities for not protecting them, and to theories about where Linois had really been all this time. The Company's service was a capable, disciplined body, but its regulations required the commodore to listen to the views of his captains in council before any decisive action; and like all councils of war this was wordy, indefinite, inclined to pessimism. Jack had never so regretted the superior rigour of the Royal Navy as he did during the vague discourse of a Mr Craig, who was concerned to show what might have been the case, had they not waited for the Botany Bay ship and the two Portuguese.

'Gentlemen,' cried Jack at last, addressing himself to the three or four other determined men at the table, 'this is no time for talking. There are only two things for it: we must either run or fight. If you run, Linois will snap up your fleet piecemeal, for I can stop only one of his frigates, while the *Marengo* can sail five leagues to your three and blow any two of you out of the water. If we fight, if we concentrate our force, we can answer him gun for gun.'

'Who is to fight the guns?' asked a voice.

'I will come to that, sir. What is more, Linois is a year out of a dockyard and he is three thousand miles from the Isle of France: he is short of stores, and single spar or fifty fathom of two-inch rope is of a hundred times more consequence to him than it is to us – I doubt there is a spare topmast in his whole squadron. In duty he must not risk grave damage: he must not press home his attack against a determined resistance.'

'How do you know he has not refitted in Batavia?' 'We will leave that for the moment, if you please,' said Jack. 'We have no time to lose. Here is my plan. You have three more ships than Linois reckoned for: the three best-armed ships will wear men-of-war pendants and the blue ensign – '

'We are not allowed to wear Royal Navy colours.'

'Will you give me leave to proceed, sir? That is entirely my responsibility, and I will take it upon myself to give the necessary permission. The larger Indiamen will form in line of battle, taking all available men out of the rest of the convoy to work the guns and sending the smaller ships away to leeward. I shall send an officer aboard each ship supposed to be a man-of-war, and all the quarter-gunners I can spare. With a close, well-formed line, our numbers are such that we can double upon his van or rear and overwhelm him with numbers: with one or two of your fine ships on one side of him and *Surprise* on the other, I will answer for it if we can beat the seventy-four, let alone the frigates.'

'Hear him, hear him,' cried Mr Muffit, taking Jack by the hand. 'That's the spirit, God's my life!'

In the confusion of voices it became clear that although there was eager and indeed enthusiastic support, one captain even beating the table and roaring, 'We'll thump 'em again and again,' there were others who were not of the same opinion. Who had ever heard of merchant ships with encumbered decks and few hands holding out for five minutes against powerful men-of-war? – most of them had only miserable eighteen-pounder cannonades – a far, far better plan was to separate: some would surely escape – the *Dorsetshire* was certain she could outrun the French – could the gentleman give any example of a ship with a 270 lb broadside resisting an enemy that could throw 950 lb?

'Whisht, Mr Craig,' said Muffit before Jack could reply. 'Do you not know Captain Aubrey is the gentleman who commanded the *Sophie* brig when she took the *Cacafuego*, a 32-gun frigate? And I believe, sir, *Sophie* threw no great broadside?'

'Twenty-eight pounds,' said Jack, reddening.

'Why,' cried Craig. 'I spoke only out of my duty to the Company. I honour the gentleman, I am sure, and I am sorry I did not just recollect his name. He will not find me shy, I believe. I spoke only for the Company and my cargo; not for myself.'

'I believe, gentlemen,' said Muffit, 'that the sense of the council is in favour of Captain Aubrey's plan, as I am myself. I hear no dissentient voice. Gentlemen, I desire you will repair aboard your ships, fill powder, clear away your guns, and attend to Captain Aubrey's signals.'

ABOARD THE *SURPRISE* Jack called his officers to the cabin and said, 'Mr Pullings, you will proceed to the *Lushington* Indiaman with Collins, Haverhill and Pollyblank. Mr Babbington to *Royal George* with the brothers Moss. Mr Braithwaite, to the brig to repeat signals: take the spare set with you. Mr Bowes, can I persuade you to look to the *Earl Camden*'s guns? I know you can point them better than any of us.'

The purser flushed bright with pleasure, and chuckled: if the Captain wished, he would certainly abandon his cheese and candles, though he did not know how he should like it; and he begged for Evans and Strawberry Joe.

'That is settled, then,' said Jack. 'Now, gentlemen, this is a delicate business: we must not offend the Company's officers, and some of them are very touchy – the least sense of ill-feeling would be disastrous. The men must be made to understand that thoroughly: no pride, no distance, no reference to tea-waggons, or how we do things in the Navy. Our one aim must be to keep their guns firing briskly, to engage Linois closely, and to wound his spars and rigging as much as ever we can. Hulling him or killing his people is beside the point: he would give his bosun for a stuns'l boom, and with the best will in the world we shall never sink a seventy-four. We must fire like Frenchmen for once. Mr Stourton, you and I will work out a list of the gunners we can spare, and while I am sharing them among the Indiamen you will take the ship to the eastward and watch Linois's motions.'

Within an hour the line had formed, fifteen handsome

Indiamen under easy sail a cable's length apart and a fast-sailing brig to repeat signals; boats plied to and from the smaller ships bringing volunteers for the guns; and all that forenoon Jack hurried up and down the line in his barge, dispensing officers, gunners, discreet advice and encouragement, and stores of affability. This affability was rarely forced, for most of the captains were right seamen, and given their fiery commodore's strong lead they set to with a determination that made Jack love them. Decks were clearing fast; the three ships chosen for pendants, the *Lushington*, the *Royal George* and the *Earl Camden*, began to look even more like men-of-war, with whitewashers over their sides disguising them fast, and royal yards crossed; and the guns ran in and out without a pause. Yet there were some awkward captains, lukewarm, despondent and reserved, two of them timid old fools; and the passengers were the cruellest trial – Atkins and the other members of Mr Stanhope's suite could be dealt with, but the women and the important civilians called for personal interviews and for explanations; one lady, darting from an unlikely hatch, told him she should countenance no violence whatsoever – Linois should be reasoned with – his passions would certainly yield to reason – and Jack was kept very busy. It was only from time to time, as he sat in the barge next to Church, his solemn aide-de-camp, that he had leisure to ponder the remark 'How do you know he has not refitted in Batavia?'

He did not know it: yet his whole strategy must be based upon that assumption. He did not *know* it, but still he was willing to risk everything upon his intuition's being sound: for it was a matter of intuition – Linois's cautious handling of his ship, a thousand details that Jack could hardly name but that contrasted strongly with the carefree Linois of the Mediterranean with Toulon and its naval stores a few days' sail away. Yet moral certainty could fade: he was not infallible, and Linois was old in war, a resourceful, dangerous opponent.

Dinner aboard the *Lushington* with Captain Muffit was a relief. Not only was Jack desperately sharp-set, having missed his breakfast, but Muffit was a man after his own heart: they saw eye to eye on the formation of the line, the way to conduct the action – aggressive tactics rather than defence – and on the right dinner to restore a worn and badgered spirit.

Church appeared while they were drinking coffee. '*Surprise* signalling, sir, if you please,' he said. '*Sémillante, Marengo* and *Belle Poule* bearing east by south about four leagues: *Marengo* has backed topsails.'

'He is waiting for *Berceau* to come up,' said Jack. 'We shall not see him for an hour or two. What do you say, sir, to a turn on deck?'

Left alone, the midshipman silently devoured the remains of the pudding, pocketed two French rolls, and darted after his captain, who was standing with the commodore on the poop, watching the last boats pull away from the line, filled with passengers bound for the hypothetical safety of the lee-ward division.

'I cannot tell you, sir,' said Muffit in a low voice, 'what a feeling of peace it gives me to see them go: deep, abiding peace. You gentlemen have your admirals and commissioners, no doubt, and indeed the enemy to bring your spirits low; but passengers . . . "Captain, there are mice in this ship! They have ate my bonnet and two pairs of gloves. I shall complain to the directors: my cousin is a director, sir." "Captain, why cannot I get a soft-boiled egg in this ship? I told the young man at India House my child could not possibly be expected to digest a hard yolk." "Captain, there are no cupboards, no drawers in my cabin, nowhere to hang anything, no room, no room, no room, d'ye hear me, sir?" There will be all the room you merit where you are going to – ten brimstone shrews packing into one cabin in a country ship, ha ha. How I love to see 'em go; the distance cannot be too great for me.'

'Let us increase it, then. Give them leave to part company, throw out the signal to tack in succession again, and there you have two birds in one bush. It is a poor heart that never rejoices.'

The flags ran up, the ships to leeward acknowledged and made sail, and the line prepared to go about. First the *Alfred*, then the *Coutts*, then the *Wexford*, and now the *Lushington*: as she approached the troubled wake where the *Wexford* had begun her turn, Mr Muffit took over from his chief mate and put her about himself, smooth, steady, and exact. The *Lushington* swung through ninety degrees and the *Surprise* came into view on her port bow. The sight of her low checkered hull and her towering masts lifted Jack's heart, and his grave face broke into a loving smile; but after this second's indulgence his eyes searched beyond her, and there, clear on the horizon, were the topgallantsails of Linois's squadron.

The *Lushington* steadied on her course. Mr Muffit stepped back from the rail, mopping his face, for the turn had brought the sun full on to the poop, where the awning had long since been replaced by splinter-netting, which gave no protection from the fiery beams: he hurried to the side and stood watching the centre and the rear. The line was reformed, heading south-east with the larboard tacks aboard, a line of ships a mile and a half long, lying between the enemy and the rest of the convoy, a line of concentrated fire, nowhere strong, but moderately formidable from its quantity and from the mutual support of the close order. A trim line, too: the *Ganges* and the *Bombay Castle* were sagging away a little to leeward, but their intervals were correct. The East India captains could handle their ships, of that there was no doubt. They had performed this manoeuvre three times already and never had there been a blunder nor even a hesitation. Slow, of course, compared with the Navy; but uncommon sure. They could handle their ships: could they fight them too? That was the question.

'I admire the regularity of your line, sir,' said Jack. 'The Channel fleet could not keep station better.'

'I am happy to hear you say so,' said Muffit. 'We may not have your heavy crews, but we do try to do things seaman-like. Though between you and me and the binnacle,' he added in a personal aside, 'I dare say the presence of your people may have something to do with it. There is not one of us would not sooner lose an eye-tooth than miss stays with a King's officer looking on.'

'That reminds me,' said Jack, 'should you dislike wearing the King's coat for the occasion, you and the gentlemen who are to have pendants? Linois is devilish sly, and if his spyglass picks up the Company's uniform in ships that are supposed to be men-of-war, he will smoke what we are about: it might encourage him to make a bolder stroke than we should care for.'

It was a wounding suggestion; it was not happily expressed; Muffit felt it keenly. He weighed the possible advantage, the extreme gravity of the situation, and after a moment he said he should be honoured – most happy.

'Then let us recall the frigate, and I will send across all the coats we possess.'

The *Surprise* came running down the wind, rounded-to outside the line and lay there with her foretopsail to the mast, looking as easy and elegant as a thoroughbred.

'Good-bye, Captain Muffit,' said Jack, shaking his hand. 'I do not suppose we shall see one another again before the old gentleman is with us: but we are of one mind, I am sure. And you must allow me to add, that I am very happy to have such a colleague.'

'Sir,' said Captain Muffit, with an iron grasp, 'you do me altogether too much honour.'

The lively pleasure of being aboard his own ship again – her quick life and response after the heavy deliberation of the Indiaman – her uncluttered decks, a clean sweep fore and aft – the perfect familiarity of everything about her, including the remote sound of Stephen's 'cello somewhere below, improvising on a theme Jack knew well but could not name.

The frigate moved up to the head of the line, and on his strangely thin quarterdeck – only the more vapid youngsters left and the master, apart from Etherege and Stourton – he listened to his first lieutenant's report of Linois's motions. The report confirmed his own impressions: the Admiral had gathered his force, and his apparent delay was in fact an attempt at gaining the weather-gauge and at making sure of what he was about before committing himself.

'I dare say he will put about as soon as ever he fetches our wake,' he observed, 'and then he will move faster. But even so, I doubt he will be up with us much before sunset.' He gave directions for making free with all the officer's coats aboard and walked over to the taffrail, where Mr White was standing alone, disconsolate and wan.

'I believe, sir, this is your first taste of warfare,' he said. 'I am afraid you must find it pretty wearisome, with no cabin and no proper meals.'

'Oh, I do not mind that in the least, sir,' cried the chaplain. 'But I must confess that in my ignorance I had expected something more shall I say exciting? These slow, remote manoeuvres, this prolonged anxious anticipation, formed no part of my image of a battle. Drums and trumpets, banners, stirring exhortations, martial cries, a plunging into the thick of the fray, the shouting of captains – this, rather than interminable waiting in discomfort, in suspended animation, had been my uninformed idea. You will not misunderstand me if I say, I wonder you can stand the boredom.'

'It is use, no doubt. War is nine parts boredom, and we grow used to it in the service. But the last hour makes up for all, believe me. I think you may be assured of some excitement tomorrow, or perhaps even this evening. No trumpets, I am afraid, nor exhortations, but I shall do my best in the shouting line, and I dare say you will find the guns dispel the tedium. You will like that, I am sure: it raises a man's spirits amazingly.'

'Your remark is no doubt very just; and it reminds me of my duty. Would not a spiritual, as well as a physical preparation be proper?'

'Why,' said Jack, considering, 'we should all be most grateful, I am sure, for a Te Deum when the business is done. But at this moment, I fear it is not possible to rig church.' He had served under blue-light captains and he had gone into bloody action with psalms drifting in the wake, and he disliked it extremely. 'But if it were possible,' he went on, 'and if I may say so without levity, I should pray for a swell, a really heavy swell. Mr Church, signal *tack in succession*. All hands about ship.' He mounted the hammock-netting to watch the brig that lay outside the line, where all the long file could see her: a great deal would depend on Braithwaite's promptness in repeating signals. The hoist ran up, the signal-gun fired to windward. 'I shall give them a moment to brood over it,' he said inwardly, paused until he saw the scurrying stop on the forecastle of the *Alfred*, just astern, and then cried 'Ready oh! Helm's a-lee.'

This movement brought the Indiamen to the point where the *Surprise* had turned, while the *Surprise*, on the opposite tack, passed each in succession, the whole line describing a sharp follow-my-leader curve; and as they passed he stared at each with the most concentrated attention. The *Alfred*, the *Coutts*, each with one of his quartermasters aboard: in her zeal the *Coutts* ran her bowsprit over the *Alfred*'s taffrail, but they fell apart with no more damage than hard words and a shrill piping in the Lascar tongue. The *Wexford*, a handsome ship in capital order; she could give the rest her maintopsail and still keep her station; a fine eager captain who had fought his way out of a cloud of Borneo pirates last year. Now the *Lushington*, with Pullings standing next to Mr Muffit on the quarterdeck – he could see his grin from here. And there were several other Royal Navy coats aboard her. *Ganges*, *Exeter* and *Abergavenny*: she still had water-butts on her deck: what was her captain thinking of? Gloag, a weak man, and old. 'God,' he thought, 'never let me outlive my wits.' Now a gap in the centre for the. *Surprise*. *Addington*, a flash, nasty ship: *Bombay Castle*, somewhat to leeward – her bosun and *Old Reliable* were still at work on the breechings of her guns. *Camden*, and there was Bowes limping aft as fast as he could go to move his hat as the *Surprise* went by. He had never made a man so happy as when he entrusted *Camden's* guns to the purser: yet Bowes was not a bloody-minded man at all. *Cumberland*, a heavy unweatherly lump, crowding sail to keep station. *Hope*, with another dismal old brute in command – lukewarm, punctilious. *Royal George*, and she was a beauty; you would have sworn she was a postship. His second-best coat stood there on the quarterdeck, its epaulette shining in the sun: rather large for her captain, but he would do it no discredit – the best of them all after Muffit. He and Babbington were laughing, side by side abaft the davits. *Dorset*, with more European seamen than usual, but only a miserable tier of popguns. *Ocean*, a doubtful quantity.

'Sir,' said Stourton, 'Linois is putting about, if you please.'

'So he is,' said Jack, glancing aft. 'He has fetched our wake at last. It is time to take our station. Mr Church, signal *reduce sail*. Mr Harrowby, be so good as to place the ship between *Addington* and *Abergavenny*.' Up until the present Linois had been continually manoeuvring to gain the wind, and to gather his forces, making short tacks, standing now towards the Indiamen, now from them. But he had formed his line at last, and this movement was one of direct pursuit.

While the *Surprise* lay to he turned his glass to the French Squadron: not that there was any need for a telescope to see their positions, for they were all hull-up – it was the detail of their trim that would tell him what was going on in Linois's mind. What he saw gave him no comfort. The French ships were crowding sail as though they had not a care in the world. In the van the *Sémillante* was already throwing a fine bow-wave; close behind *Marengo* was setting her royals; and although the *Belle Poule* lay quarter of a mile astern she was drawing up. Then there was the *Berceau*: how she managed to spread so much canvas after the drubbing she had received he could not conceive – an astonishing feat: very fine seamen aboard the *Berceau*.

In the present position, with the Indiamen under easy sail on the starboard tack with the wind two points free, and Linois five miles away, coming after them from the eastwards on the same tack, Jack could delay the action by hauling his wind – delay it until the morning, unless Linois chose to risk a night-action. There was a good deal to be said for delay – rest, food, greater preparation; and their sailing-order was not what he could have wished. But, on the other hand, a bold front was the very essence of the thing. Linois must be made to believe that the China fleet had an escort, not a powerful escort perhaps, but strong enough to inflict serious damage, with the help of the armed Indiamen, if he pushed home his attack. As for the sailing-order, there would be too much risk of confusion if he changed it now; they were not used to these manoeuvres; and in any case, once the melee began, once the smoke, din and confusion of close action did away with the rigid discipline of the line and with communication, those captains who really meant to lay their ships alongside an enemy would do so: the others would not.

The tactics that he had agreed upon with Muffit and that had been explained to the captains were those of close, enveloping action: the line of battle to be maintained until the last moment and then to double upon the French ships, to take them between two or even three broadsides, overwhelming them with numbers, however weak the fire of each Company ship. If a regular doubling was not possible, then each captain was to use his judgment to bring about the same position – a cluster of ships round every Frenchman, cutting up his sails and rigging at the closest range.

Now, after hours of reflection, he still thought this idea the best: close range was essential to make the indifferent guns bite hard; and if he were Linois, he should very much dislike being surrounded, hampered, and battered by a determined swarm, above all if some men-of-war were mingled with the Indiamen. His greatest dread, after the doubtful fighting qualities of the merchantmen, was that of a distant cannonade, with the heavy, well-pointed French guns hitting his ships from a thousand yards.

Linois vanished behind the foresail of the *Addington* as the *Surprise* glided into her place in the centre of the line. Jack looked up at the masthead, and felt a sudden overwhelming weariness: his mind was running clear and sharp, and the continual variation of the opposed forces presented itself as a hard, distinct point on a graph; but his arms and legs were drained of strength. 'By God,' he thought, 'I am growing old: yesterday's brush and talking to all these people has knocked me up. But at least Linois is still older. If he comes on, maybe he will make a blunder. God send he makes a blunder. Bonden,' he cried, 'run up to the masthead and tell me how they bear.'

They bore three points on the quarter: two and a half points on the quarter: *Belle Poule* had set her forestaysail and she had closed with the two-decker: they were coming up hand over fist. The hails followed one another at steady intervals, and all the time the sun sank in the west. When at last Bonden reported the *Sémillante* at extreme random-shot of the rear of the line, Jack said to the signal-midshipman, 'Mr Lee, *edge away one point*; and get the next hoists ready: *prepare to wear all together at the gun: course south-east by east: van engage to windward on coming up, centre and rear to leeward.*'

This was the aggressive manoeuvre of a commander eager to bring on a decisive action. Wearing would reverse the order of sailing and send the whole line fast and straight for the French squadron close-hauled on the opposite tack – a line that would divide on coming up and threaten to take them between two fires. It would throw away the advantage of the wind, but he dared not tack all together – too dangerous an evolution by far in close order – and even this simultaneous wearing was dangerous enough, although a few minutes of edging away would make it safer. Indeed, Linois might well take it as a mark of confidence.

Now they had edged away from the wind; the line was slanting farther south, with the wind just before the beam. 'Carry on, Mr Lee,' he said, and turned to watch the repeating-brig. The signals ran up aboard her, brisk and clear. 'I must give the Indiamen time to make them out,' he said, deliberately pacing to and fro. The slow-match for the signal-gun sent its acrid smoke across the deck, and he found his breath coming short: everything, *everything*, depended on this manoeuvre being carried out correctly. If they turned in a disordered heap, if there was irresolution, Linois would smoke his game and in five minutes he would be among them, firing both sides with his thirty-six and twenty-four-pounders. Another turn: another. 'Fire,' he said. 'All hands wear ship.'

Up and down the line of orders echoed, the bosuns' pipes shrilled out. The ships began their turn, bringing the wind aft, right astern, on the larboard quarter, on to the beam and beyond, the yards coming round, round, and harder round until the whole line, with scarcely an irregularity, was close-hauled on the larboard tack, each having turned in its place, so that now the *Ocean* led and the *Alfred* brought up the rear.

A beautifully-executed evolution, almost faultless. 'Mr Lee: *make more sail hoist colours.*' Blue, because Admiral Hervey in Bombay was a vice-admiral of the blue. The *Surprise*, being under Admiralty orders, wore the white. Handsome colours, and imposing: but the speed of the line did not increase: 'Signal: *Ocean make more sail: repeat Ocean make more sail,*' cried Jack. 'And give him two guns.'

Ahead of them now, and broad on the larboard bow, there was the French squadron in a rigid line, colours flying: the Admirals' flag at the mizzen. The two lines were drawing together at a combined speed of fourteen knots: in less than five minutes they would be within range.

Jack ran forward, and as he reached the forecastle Linois fired a gun. But a blank gun, a signal-gun, and its smoke had hardly cleared before the French ships hauled their wind, heading north-north-west and declining the engagement.

Back on his quarterdeck Jack signalled *Tack in succession*, and the line came about, stretching towards the setting sun. In the depths the 'cello was still singing away, deep and meditative; and all at once the elusive name came to him – it was the Boccherini suite in D minor. He smiled, a great smile filled with many kinds of happiness. 'Well, gentlemen,' he said, 'that was pretty creditable in the Indiamen, hey, hey?'

'I should scarcely have believed it, sir,' said Stourton. 'Not a single ship fell foul of another. It was giving them time to edge away that did it, no doubt.'

'Linois did not care for it,' said Etherege. 'But until the very last moment I did not think he would sheer off, night-action or no night-action.'

Harrowby said, 'The Company officers are a well-behaved set of men. Many of them are serious.'

Jack laughed aloud. Out of piety or superstition he would not even formulate the thought, 'He mistook the situation: he has made his blunder', far less put it into words: he touched a belaying-pin and said, 'He will spend the night plying to windward, while we lie to. His people will be worn out for the morning action. Ours must get all the rest we can manage: and food. Mr Stourton, since we have lost our purser, I must ask you to see to the serving-out of the provisions. Let the men make a good hearty supper – there are some hams in my store-room. Where is my steward? Pass the word for – '.

'Here I am sir, and have been a-standing by the bitts this half-glass and more,' said Killick in his disagreeable injured whine, 'a-holding of this sanglewich and this here mug of wine.'

The burgundy went down more gratefully than any wine he had ever drunk, strengthening his heart, dispelling weariness.

'So there is to be no battle after all?' said the chaplain, moving from the shadows and addressing either Etherege or the master. 'They appear to be slanting off at a great pace. Can it be timidity? I have often heard that the French are great cowards.'

'No, no, don't you believe it, Mr White,' said Jack. 'They

have tanned my hide many a time, I can tell you. No, no: Linois is only reculing pour mew sauter, as he would say. You shall not be disappointed; I believe we may promise you a brisk cannonade in the morning. So perhaps you might be well advised to turn in directly and get all the sleep you can. I shall do the same, once I have seen the captains.'

All that night they lay to, with stern-lanterns and top-lights right along the line, each watch in turn at quarters and fifty night-glasses trained on Admiral Linois's lights as he worked up to windward. In the middle watch Jack woke for a few minutes to find the ship pitching heavily: his prayer had been answered, and a heavy swell was setting in from the south. He need not dread the Frenchmen's distant fire. Accuracy, long range and a calm sea were birds tarred with the same feather.

Dawn broke calm, sweet and clear over the troubled sea, and it showed the French and British lines three miles apart. Linois had, of course, spent all the night in beating up, so that now he had the weather-gauge without any sort of a doubt – now he could bring on the action whenever he chose. He had the power, but did not seem inclined to use it. His squadron backed and filled, rolling and pitching on the swell. After some time the *Sémillante* left her station, came down to reconnoitre within gunshot, and returned: still the French hung aloof, lying there on the beam of the English line, with their heads north-west; and the heat of the day increased.

The swell from some distant southern tempest ran across the unvarying north-east monsoon, and every few minutes the sharp choppy seas sent an agreeable spray flying over the *Surprise*'s quarterdeck. 'If we engage her from the leeward,' observed Jack, with his eyes fixed on the *Marengo*, 'she will find it damned uncomfortable to open her lower ports.' She carried her lower guns high, like most French line of battle ships, but even so, with her side pressed down by this fine breeze and with such a sea running, her lower deck would be flooded – all the more so in that she was somewhat crank, somewhat inclined to lie over, no doubt from want of stores deep in her hold. If Linois could not use his lower tier, his heaviest guns, the match would be more nearly even: was that the reason why he was lying there backing and filling, when he was master of the situation, with a convoy worth six millions under his lee? What was in his mind? Plain hesitation? Had he been painfully impressed by the sight of the British line lying to all night, a long string of lights, inviting action in the morning instead of silently dispersing in the darkness, which they would surely have done if yesterday's bold advance had been a ruse?

'Pipe the hands to breakfast' he said. 'And Mr Church, be so good as to let Killick know that if my coffee is not on deck in fifteen seconds he will be crucified at noon. Doctor, a very good morning to you. Ain't it a pure day? Here is the coffee at last – will you take a cup? Did you sleep? Ha, ha, what a capital thing it is to sleep.' He had had five hours in his wool-lined well, and now new vigorous life flowed through him. He knew he was committed to an extremely dangerous undertaking, but he also knew that he should either succeed or that he should fail creditably. It would be a near-run thing in either event, but he had not launched himself, his ship, and fifteen hundred other men into a foolhardy enterprise: the anxiety was gone. One of the reasons for this was the new feeling right along the line of battle: the captains had handled their ships well and they knew it; the success of their manoeuvre and Linois's retreat had done wonders for the fighting spirit of those who had been somewhat backward, and now there was a unanimity, a readiness to fall in with the plan of attack, that delighted him.

However, he knew how early-morning sprightliness could anger his friend, and he contented himself with walking up and down, balancing his coffee-cup against the heavy motion of a ship hove-to, and champing a ship's biscuit dipped in ghee.

Breakfast was over, and still the French squadron made no move. 'We must help him to make up his mind,' said Jack.

The signals ran up: the British line filled on the starboard tack and stood away to the westward under topsails and courses alone. At once the frigate's motion became easier, a smooth, even glide; and at once the French ships in the distance wore round on the opposite tack, slanting down southwards for the Indiamen.

'At last,' said Jack. 'Now just what will he do?' When he had watched them long enough to be sure that this was not an idle move but the certain beginning from which all things must follow he said, 'Stephen, it is time for you to go below. Mr Stourton, beat to quarters.'

The drum, more stirring even than a trumpet, volleyed and thundered. But there was nothing to be done: the *Surprise* had long been stripped for battle, her yards puddened and slung with chains, splinter-netting rigged, powder filled and waiting, shot of all kinds at hand, match smoking in little tubs along the deck; the men ran to their stations and stood or knelt there, gazing out over their guns at the enemy. The French were coming down under easy sail, the *Marengo* leading: it was not clear what they meant to do, but the general opinion among the older seamen was that they would presently wear round on to the same tack as the Indiamen, steer a parallel course and engage the centre and van in the usual way, using their greater speed to pass along it; whereas others thought Linois might cross their wake and haul up to engage from leeward so that he could use his lower guns, now shut up tight behind their port-lids, with green water dashing against them. At all events they and all the frigate's company were convinced that the time of slow manoeuvring was over – that in a quarter of an hour the dust would begin to fly: and there was silence throughout the ship, a grave silence, not without anxiety, and an urgent longing for it to start.

Jack was too much taken up with watching his line and with interpreting Linois's movements to feel much of this brooding impatience; but he, too, was eager for the moment of grappling and of certainty, for he knew very well that he was faced with a formidable opponent, capable of daring, unusual tactics. Linois's next move took him by surprise, however: the Admiral, judging that the head of the long British line was sufficiently advanced for his purposes, and knowing that the Indiamen could neither tack nor sail at any great speed, suddenly crowded sail. It was a well-concerted manoeuvre: every French ship and even the brig blossomed out in a great spread of white canvas: royals appeared, stud-dingsails stretched out like wings, doubling the breadth of the ships and giving them a great and menacing beauty as they ran down upon the merchantmen. For a moment he could understand neither their course nor their evolution, but then it came to him with instant conviction. 'By God, he said, 'he means to break the line. Lee: *tack in succession: make all practicable sail.*'

As the signal broke out, it became even more certain that this was so. Linois was setting his heavy ship straight at the gap between the *Hope* and the *Cumberland*, two of the weakest ships. He meant to pass through the line, cut off the rear, leave a ship or two to deal with what his fire had left, luff up and range along the lee of the line, firing his full broadside.

Jack snatched Stourton's speaking-trumpet, sprang to the taffrail and hailed his next astern with all his force: '*Addington*, back your topsail. I am tacking out of the line.' Turning he cried, 'All hands about ship. Hard over. Harrowby, lay me athwart the *Marengo's* hawse.'

Now the long hard training told: the frigate turned in a tight smooth curve with never a check, moving faster and faster as they packed on sail after sail. She tore through the water with her lee-chains deep in white foam, heading close-hauled for the point where her course would cut the *Marengo's*, somewhere short of the British line if this speed could be maintained. He must take her down and hold the *Marengo* until the van ships could follow him, could reach him and give the *Surprise* their support. With her speed it was possible, so long as he lost no important spars; to be sure, it meant running straight into *Marengo*'s broadside, yet it might be done, particularly in such a sea. But if he did it, if he was not dismasted, how long could he hold her? How long would it take for the van to reach him? He dared not disrupt the line: the merchantmen's safety depended entirely on its strength and unity and the mutual support of its combined fire in close order.

Poised at the break of the quarterdeck he checked the position once more: the *Surprise* had already passed three ships, the *Addington*, *Bombay Castle* and *Camden*, moving up in the opposite direction towards their turning-point; and they were making sail – the gap had closed. On the port bow, a long mile away to the north-east, the *Marengo* with white water breaking against her bows. On the port quarter, still a mile away, the *Alfred* and the *Coutts* had made their turn and they were setting topgallantsails: the *Wexford* was in stays, and it looked as though the eager *Lushington* might fall foul of her. He nodded: it could be done – indeed, there was no choice.

He jumped down the ladder and hurried along the gun-crews; and he spoke to them with a particular friendliness, a kind of intimacy: they were old shipmates now; he knew each man, and he liked the greater part of them. They were to be sure not to waste a shot – to fire high for this spell, on the upward roll – ball and then chain as soon as it would fetch – the ship might get a bit of a drubbing as they ran down, but they were not to mind it: the Frenchman could not open his lower ports, and they should serve him out once they got snug athwart his bows – he knew they would fire steady – let them watch Old Reliable: he had never wasted a shot all this commission – and they were to mind their priming. Old Reliable winked his only eye and gave a chuckle.

The first ranging shot from the *Marengo* plunged into the sea a hundred yards out on the larboard beam, sending up a tall white plume, torn away by the wind. Another, closer and to starboard. A pause, and now the *Marengo*'s side disappeared behind a white cloud of smoke, spreading from her bows to her quarter: four shots of the thundering broadside struck home, three hitting the frigate's bows and one her cathead.

He looked at his watch, told his clerk to note down the time, and kept it in his hand as he paced up and down with Stourton at his side until the next great rippling crash. Far more accurate: white water leapt all round her, topmast high, so many twenty-four-pound shot struck home that her hull rang again: way was momentarily checked: she staggered; holes appeared in her fore and mainsails, and a clutter of blocks fell on to the splinter-netting over the waist. 'Just under two minutes,' he observed. 'Indifferent brisk.' The *Surprise* took no more than one minute twenty seconds between broadsides. 'But thank God her lower ports are shut.' Before *Marengo* fired the next the frigate would be quarter of a mile nearer.

The *Sémillante*, *Marengo*'s next astern, opened fire with her forward guns. He saw one ball travelling from him, racing astern, as he reached the taffrail in his ritual to and fro, a distinct ball with a kind of slight halo about it.

'Mr Stourton, the bow gun may fire.' It would do no harm; it might do good, even at this range; and the din would relieve the silent men. The two minutes were gone: some seconds past: and the *Marengo*'s careful, deliberate broadside came, hitting the *Surprise* like a hammer, barely a shot astray. And immediately after that six guns from the *Sémillante*, all high and wide.

Stourton reported, 'Spritsail yard gone in the slings, sir. The carpenter finds three foot in the well: he is plugging a couple of holes under the water-line, not very low.' As he spoke the bow gun roared out and the encouraging, heady smell of powder-smoke came aft.

'Warm work, Mr Stourton,' said Jack, smiling. 'But at least *Sémillante* cannot reach us again. The angle is too narrow. When *Marengo* starts firing grape, let the men lie down at their guns.'

Fine on the port bow he could see the last of the *Marengo*'s
guns running out. They were waiting for the roll. He glanced
round his sparse quarterdeck before he turned in his walk.
Bonden and Carlow at the wheel, Harrowby behind them,
conning the ship; Stourton calling out an order at the hances
– sail-trimmers to the foretopsail bowline – over to leeward
the signal midshipman, then Callow with his bandaged head
to run messages, and young Nevin, the clerk, with his slate in
his hand; Etherege watching the Indiamen through his little
pocket-glass. All the Marines, apart from the sentry at the
hatchway, were scattered among the gun-crews.

The crash of the broadside, and of the bow-gun, and of the
twenty shot hitting her, came in one breath – an extreme violence of noise. He saw the wheel disintegrate, Harrowby
jerked backwards to the taffrail, cut in two; and forward there
was a screaming. Instantly he bent to the speaking-tube that
led below, to the men posted at the relieving-tackles that
could take over from the wheel. 'Below there. Does she
steer?'

'Yes, sir.'

'Thus, very well thus. Keep her dyce, d'ye hear me?'

Three guns had been dismounted, and splinters, bits of
carriage, bits of rail, booms, shattered boats littered the decks
as far aft as the mainmast, together with scores of hammocks
torn from their netting: the jibboom lurched from side to
side, its cap shot through: cannon-balls, scattered from their
racks and garlands, rumbled about the heaving deck: but far
more dangerous were the loose guns running free – concentrated, lethal weight, gone mad. He plunged into the disorder
forward – few officers, little co-ordination – catching up a
bloody hammock as he ran. Two tons of metal, once the cherished larboard chaser, poised motionless on the top of the
roll, ready to rush back across the deck and smash its way
through the starboard side: he clapped the hammock under it
and whipped a line round the swell of its muzzle, calling for
men to make it fast to a stanchion; and as he called a loose 36

lb shot ran crack against his ankle, bringing him down. Stourton was at the next, a carronade still in its carriage, trying to
hold it with a handspike as it threatened to plunge down the
fore hatchway and thence through the frigate's bottom: the
coamings round the hole yielded like cardboard: then the forward pitch took off the strain – the gun rolled towards the
bows, and as it gathered speed they tripped it, throwing it
over on to its side. But the same pitch, the same shift of
slope, working upon the loose gun amidships, under the
gangway, sent it faster and faster through the confused group
of men, each with his own notion of how to stop it, so that it
ran full tilt against the side abaft the fore-chains, smashed
through and plunged into the sea. Oh for his officers! – high
discipline did away with the men's initiative – but those he
had left were hard at their duty: Rattray out on the perilous
bowsprit already with two of his mates, gammoning the jib-
boom before it carried away; Etherege with half a dozen
Marines tossing the balls over the side or securing them; Callow and his boat's crew heaving the wreckage of the launch
free of the guns.

He darted a look at the *Marengo*. All but two of her guns
were run out again: 'Lie flat,' he roared, and for the space of
the rising wave there was silence all along the deck, broken
only by the wind, the racing water, and an odd ball grumbling
down the gangway. The full broadside and the howl of grape
tearing over the deck; but too high, a little hurried. Rattray
and his mates were still there, working with concentrated
fury and bawling for ten fathom of two-inch rope and more
handspikes. The *Surprise* was still on her headlong course,
her way only slightly checked by the loss of her outer jib and
the riddling of her sails: and now the rear Indiaman opened
fire from half a mile. There were holes in the *Marengo*'s fore-
topsails. And he doubted she would get in another broadside
before the *Surprise* was so close on her bow that the broadside guns would no longer bear – could not be trained far
enough forward to reach her. If the *Marengo* yawed off her

course to bring the *Surprise* into her fire, then Linois's plan was defeated: at this speed a yaw would carry the two-decker east of the unbroken line.

He limped back to the quarterdeck, where young Nevin was on his hands and knees, being sick. 'All's well, Bonden?' he asked, kneeling to the tube. 'Below there. Ease her half a point. Another half. Belay.' She was steering heavy now.

'Prime, sir,' said Bonden. 'Just my left arm sprung. Carlow copped it.'

'Give me a hand with t'other, then,' said Jack, and they slid Harrowby over the taffrail. Away astern, beyond the splash of the body, six of the Indiamen were already round: they were coming down under a fine press of sail, but they were still a long way off. Wide on the port bow the *Marengo* was almost within his reach at last. 'Stand to your guns,' he cried. 'Hard for'ard. Do not waste a shot. Wait for it. Wait for it.'

'Five foot water in the well, sir,' said Stourton.

Jack nodded. 'Half a point,' he called down the pipe again, and again the ghostly voice answered 'Half a point it is, sir.' Heavy she might be, heavy she was; but unless she foundered in the next minute he would hit the *Marengo*, hit her very, very hard. For as the *Surprise* came closer to crossing the *Marengo*'s bows, so her silent broadside would come into play at last, and at close range.

Musketry crackling on the *Marengo*'s forecastle: her Marines packed into her bows and foretop. Another hundred yards, and unless *Marengo* yawed he would rake her: and if she did yaw then there they would lie, broadside to broadside and fight it out.

'Mr Stourton, some hands to clew up and to back the fore-topsail. Callow, Lee, Church, jump along for'ard.' Closer, closer: the *Marengo* was still coming along with a splendid bow-wave; the *Surprise* was moving slower. She would cross the *Marengo* at something under two hundred yards, and already she was so near the two-decker that the Indiamen had stopped firing from fear of hitting her. Still closer, for the full force of the blow: the crews crouched tense over their pointed guns, shifting them a trifle for the aim with a total concentration, indifferent to the musket-balls.

'Fire,' he said, as the upward roll began. The guns went off in a long roar: the smoke cleared, and there was the *Marengo*'s head and forecastle swept clean – ropes dangling, a staysail flying wild.

'Too low,' he cried. 'Pitch 'em up; pitch 'em up. Callow, Church – pitch 'em up.' There was no point in merely killing Frenchmen: it was rigging, spars, masts that counted, not the blood that now ran from the *Marengo*'s bow scuppers, crimson against her streak of white. The grunting, furious work of running in, swabbing, loading, ramming, running out; and number three, the fastest gun, fired first.

'Clew up,' he shouted above the thunder. 'Back foretop- sail.' The *Surprise* slowed, lost her way, and lay shrouded in her own smoke right athwart the *Marengo*'s bows, hammering her as fast as ever the guns could fire. The third broadside merged into the fourth: the firing was continuous now, and Stourton and the midshipmen ran up and down the line, pointing, heaving, translating their captain's hoarse barks into directed fire – a tempest of chain. After their drubbing the men were a little out of hand, and now they could serve the Frenchmen out their fire was somewhat wild and often too low: but at this range not a shot flew wide. The powder-boys ran, the cartridges came up in a racing stream, the gun-crews cheered like maniacs, stripped to the waist, pouring with sweat, taking their sweet revenge; thumping it into her, cramming their guns to the muzzle. But it was too good to last. Through the smoke it was clear that Linois meant to run the *Surprise* aboard – run the small frigate bodily down or board her.

'Drop the forecourse. Fill foretopsail,' he cried with the full force of his lungs: and down the tube, 'Two points off.' He must at all costs keep on the *Marengo*'s bows and keep hitting her – she was a slaughter-house forward, but nothing vital had yet carried away. The *Surprise* forged on in a sluggish, heavy turn, and the two-decker's side came into view. They were opening their lower ports, running out the great thirty-six-pounders in spite of the sea. One shift of her helm to bring them to bear and the *Surprise* would have the whole shattering broadside within pistol-shot. Then they could clap the lower ports to, for she would be sunk.

Etherege, with four muskets and his servant to load them, was firing steadily at the *Marengo*'s foretop, picking off any man who showed. Half a mile astern, the British van opened fire on the *Sémillante* and *Belle Poule*, who had been reaching them this last five minutes: smoke everywhere, and the thunder of the broadsides deadened the breeze.

'Port, port, hard a-port,' he called down the tube; and straightening, 'Maincourse, there.' Where was her speed, poor dear *Surprise*? She could just keep ahead of the *Marengo*, but only by falling away from the wind so far that her guns could not bear and her stern was pointing at the *Marengo*'s bows. Fire slackened, died away, and the men stared aft at the *Marengo*: two spokes of her wheel would bring the Frenchman's broadside round – already they could see the double line of muzzles projecting from their ports. Why did she not yaw? Why was she signalling?

A great bellowing of guns to starboard told them why. The *Royal George*, followed by the two ships astern of her, had left the line, the holy line, and they were coming up fast to engage the *Marengo* on the other side while the van was closing in from the west, threatening to envelop him – the one manoeuvre that Linois dreaded.

The *Marengo* hauled her wind, and her swing brought the frigate's guns into play again. They blazed out, and the two-decker instantly replied with a ragged burst from her upper starboard guns so close that her shot went high over the frigate's deck and the burning wads came aboard – so close that they could see the faces glaring from the ports, a biscuit-toss away. For a moment the two ships lay broadside to broad-side. Through a gap torn in the *Marengo*'s quarterdeck bul-wark Jack saw the Admiral sitting on a chair; there was a grave expression on his face, and he was pointing at some-thing aloft. Jack had often sat at his table and he instantly recognised the characteristic sideways lift of his head. Now the *Marengo*'s turn carried her farther still. Another burst from her poop carronades and she was round, close-hauled, presenting her stern to a raking fire from the frigate's remain-ing guns – two more were dismounted and one had burst – a fire that smashed in her stern gallery. Another broadside as she moved away, gathering speed, and a prodigious cheer as her cross-jack yard came down, followed by her mizzen and topgallantmast. Then she was out of range, and the *Surprise*, though desperately willing, could not come round nor move fast enough through the sea to bring her into reach again.

The whole French line had worn together: they hauled close to the wind, passed between the converging lines of Indiamen, and stood on.

'Mr Lee,' said Jack. '*General chase.*'

IT WOULD NOT do. The Indiamen chased, cracking on until their skysails carried away, but still the French squadron had the heels of them; and when Linois tacked to the eastward, Jack recalled them.

The *Lushington* was the first to reach him, and Captain Muffit came aboard. His red face, glorious with triumph, came up the side like a rising sun; but as he stepped on to the bloody quarterdeck his look changed to shocked astonish-ment. 'Oh my God,' he cried, looking at the wreckage fore and aft – seven guns dismantled, four ports beat into one, the boats on the booms utterly destroyed, shattered spars every-where, water pouring from her lee-scuppers as the pumps brought it gushing up from below, tangled rope, splinters knee-deep in the waist, gaping holes in the bulwarks, fore and mainmast cut almost through in several places, 24 lb balls lodged deep. 'My God, you have suffered terribly. I give you the joy of victory,' he said, taking Jack's hand in both of his, 'but you have suffered most terribly. Your losses must be shocking, I am afraid.'

Jack was worn now, and very tired: his foot hurt him abominably, swollen inside his boot. 'Thank you, Captain,' he said. 'He handled us roughly, and but for the *George* coming up so nobly, I believe he must have sunk us. But we lost very few men. Mr Harrowby, alas, and two others, with a long score of wounded: but a light bill for such warm work. And we paid him back. Yes, yes: we paid him back, by God.'

'Eight foot three inches of water in the well, if you please, sir,' said the carpenter. 'And it gains on us.'

'Can I be of any use, sir?' cried Muffit. 'Our carpenters, bosuns, hands to pump?'

'I should take it kindly if I might have my officers and men back, and any help you can spare. She will not swim another hour.'

'Instantly, sir, instantly,' cried Muffit, starting to the side, now very near the water. 'Lord, what a battering,' he said, pausing for a last look.

'Ay,' said Jack. 'And where I shall replace all my gear this side of Bombay I do not know – not a spar in the ship. My comfort is, that Linois is even worse.'

'Oh, as for masts, spars, boats, cordage, stores, the Company will be delighted – oh, they will think the world of you, sir, in Calcutta – nothing too much, I do assure you. Your splendid action has certainly preserved the fleet, as I shall tell 'em. Yardarm to yardarm with a seventy-four! May I give you a tow?'

Jack's foot gave him a monstrous twinge. 'No, sir,' he said sharply. 'I will escort you to Calcutta, if you choose, since I presume you will not remain at sea with Linois abroad; but I will not be towed, not while I have a mast standing.'

10

THE COMPANY did think the world of him, indeed. Fireworks; prodigious banquets, treasures of naval stores poured out; such kind attentions to the crew while the *Surprise* was repairing that scarcely a man was sober or single from the day they dropped anchor to the day they weighed it, a sullen, brutal, debauched and dissipated band.

This was gratitude expressed in food, in entertainment on the most lavish scale in oriental splendour, and in many, many speeches, all couched in terms of unmixed praise; and it brought Jack into immediate contact with Richard Canning. At the very first official dinner he found Canning at his right – a Canning filled with *affectionate* admiration, who eagerly claimed acquaintance. Jack was astonished: he had scarcely thought twice about Canning since Bombay, and since the engagement with Linois not at all. He had been perpetually busy, nursing the poor shattered fainting *Surprise* across the sea, even with a favourable wind and the devoted help of every Indiaman whose people could find footing aboard her; and Stephen, with a sick-bay full, and some delicate operations, including poor Bowes's head, had barely exchanged a dozen unofficial words with him that might have brought Diana or Canning to his mind.

But here was the man at his side, friendly, unreserved and apparently unconscious of any call for reserve on either part, present to do him honour and indeed to propose his health in a well-turned, knowledgeable and really gratifying speech, a speech in which Sophia hovered, decently veiled, together with Captain Aubrey's imminent, lasting, and glorious happiness. After the first stiffness and embarrassment Jack found it impossible to dislike him, and he made little effort to do so, particularly as Stephen and he seemed so well together. Besides, any distance, any coldness on a public occasion would have been so marked, so graceless and so churlish that he could not have brought himself to it, even if the offence had been even greater and far more recent. It occurred to him that in all probability Canning had not the least notion of having cut him out long ago – oh so long ago: in another world.

Banquets, receptions, a ball that he had to decline, because that was the day they buried Bowes; and it was a week before he ever saw Canning in private. He was sitting at his desk in his cabin with his injured foot in a bucket of warm oil of sesame, writing to Sophie 'the sword of honour they have presented me with is a very handsome thing, in the Indian taste, I believe, with a most flattering inscription; indeed, if kind words were ha'pence, I should be a nabob, and oh sweetheart a married nabob. The Company, the Parsee merchants and the insurers have made up a splendid purse for the men, that I am to distribute; but in their delicacy – ' when Canning was announced.

'Beg him to step below,' he said, placing a whale's tooth upon his letter, against the fetid Hooghly breeze. 'Mr Canning, a good morning to you, sir: pray sit down. Forgive me for receiving you in this informal way, but Maturin will flay me if I rise up from my oil without leave.'

Civil inquiries for the foot – vastly better, I thank you – and Canning said, 'I have just pulled round the ship, and upon my word I do not know how you ever brought her in. I absolutely counted forty-seven great shot between what was left of your cutwater and the stump of the larboard cat head and even more on the starboard bow. Just how did the *Marengo* lay?'

Few landsmen would have had more than the briefest general account, but Canning had been to sea; he owned privateers and he had fought one of them in a spirited little action. Jack told him just how the *Marengo* lay; and led on by Canning's close, intelligent participation in every move, every shift of wind, he also told him how the *Sémillante* and *Belle Poule* had lain, and how the gallant *Berceau* had tried to lay, drawing diagrams in oil of sesame on the table-top.

'WELL,' SAID CANNING with a sigh, 'I honour you, I am sure: it was the completest thing. I would have given my right hand to be there . . . but then I have never been a lucky man, except perhaps in trade. Lord, lord, how I wish I were a sailor, and a great way from land.' He looked down-spirited and old; but reviving he said, 'It was the completest thing – the Nelson touch.'

'Ah no, sir, no,' cried Jack. 'There you mistake it. Nelson would have had *Marengo*. There was a moment when I almost thought we might. If that noble fellow McKay in *Royal George* could only have brought up the rear a little faster, or if Linois had lingered but a minute to thump us again, the van would have been up, and we had him between two fires. But it was not to be. It was only a little brush, after all – another indecisive action; and I dare say he is refitting in Batavia at this moment.'

Canning shook his head, smiling. 'It was not altogether unsuccessful, however,' he said. 'A fleet worth six million of money has been saved; and the country, to say nothing of the Company, would have been in a strange position if it had been lost. And that brings me to the purpose of my visit. I am come at the desire of my associates to find out, with the utmost tact and delicacy, how they may express their sense of your achievement in something more – shall I say *tangible*? – than addresses, mountains of pilau, and indifferent burgundy. Something perhaps more negotiable, as we say in the City. I trust I do not offend you, sir.'

'Not in the least, sir,' said Jack.

'Well now, seeing that anything resembling a direct gratification is out of the question with a gentleman of your kind – '

'Where, *where* do you get these wild romantic notions?' thought Jack, looking wistfully into his face.

'— some members suggested a service of plate, or Sur-ajud-Dowlah's gold-mounted palanquin. But I put it to them, that a service of plate on the scale they suggested would take a year or so to reach your table, that to my personal knowl-

edge you were already magnificently supplied with silver
[Jack possessed six plates, at present in pawn], and that a
palanquin, however magnificent, was of little use to a sea-
officer; and it occurred to me that freight was the answer to
our problem. Am I too gross, speaking with this freedom?'

'Oh no, no,' cried Jack. 'Use no ceremony, I beg.' But he
was puzzled: freight-money, that charming unlooked-for,
unlaborious, almost unearned shower of gold, fell only on
those fortunate captains of men-of-war who carried treasure
for Government or for the owners of bullion or specie who
did not choose to trust their concentrated wealth to any conveyance less sure; it amounted to two or three per cent of the
value carried, and very welcome it was. Although it was far
rarer than prize-money (the sea-officer's only other road to a
decent competence) it was surer; it had no possible legal difficulties attached, and no man had to risk his ship, his life or
his career in getting it. Like every other sailor, Jack knew all
about freight-money, but none had ever come his way: he felt
a glowing benevolence towards Canning. Yet still he was in a
state of doubt: bullion travelled *out* to India, not back to England; the Company's wealth sailed home in the form of tea
and muslin, Cashmere shawls . . . He had never heard of bullion homeward-bound.

'You may be aware that the *Lushington* was carrying Borneo
rubies, one of our shipments of gems,' said Canning. 'And we
have a consignment of Tinnevelly pearls as well as two
parcels of sapphires. The whole amounts to no great value, I
fear, not even quarter of a million; but it takes no room, either
– you would not be incommoded. May I hope to persuade
you to convey it, sir?'

'I believe you may, sir,' said Jack, 'and I am exceedingly
obliged to you for the, hey, delicate, gentlemanlike way this
offer has been made.'

'You must not thank me, my dear Aubrey: there is not the
least personal obligation. I am only the mouthpiece of the
Company. How I wish I could be of some direct service. If

there is any way in which I can be of use, I should be most happy – would it, for example, be of any interest to you to send a message to England? If you were to put a few thousand into Bohea and mohair futures, you might well clear thirty percent before you were home. Some cousins and I keep up an overland mail, and the courier is on the wing. He goes by way of Suez.'

'Mohair futures,' said Jack, in a wondering voice. 'I should be tolerably at sea, there, I am afraid. But I tell you what it is, Canning, I should be infinitely obliged if your man would take me a private letter. You shall have it in ten minutes – how kind, how very kind.'

He turned Canning over to Pullings for a thorough tour of the ship, with a particular recommendation that he should view the stringers abaft the manger, and the state of the bitts, and resumed his letter.

> Sophie dear, here is the prettiest thing in the world – John Company is stuffing the ship with treasure— you and I are to get freight, as we say – shall explain it to you later: very like prize, but the men don't share, nor the Admiral neither, this time, since I am under Admiralty orders, is not that charming? No vast great thumping sum, but it will clear me of debt and set us up in a neat cottage with an acre or two. So you are hereby required and directed to proceed to Madeira forthwith and here is a note for Heneage Dundas who will be delighted to give you a passage in *Ethalion* if he is still on the packet-run or to find one of our friends bound there if he is not. Lose not a moment: you may knit your wedding-dress aboard. In great haste, and with far greater love, Jack. PS Stephen is very well. We had a brush with Linois.

> Old Heneage,
>   As you love me, give Sophie a passage to Madeira.

Or if you cannot, stir up Clowes, Seymour, Rieu – any of our reliable, sober friends. And if you can ship a respectable woman as, say boatswain's servant, you would infinitely oblige

Yours ever,

Jack Aubrey

PS *Surprise* had a mauling from *Marengo*, 74, but paid her back with interest, and the moment her bow-knees are something like, I put to sea. This comes overland, and I dare say it will outrun me by a couple of months.

'Here you are, sir,' he cried, seeing Canning's hulk darken the cabin-door. 'Signed, sealed and delivered. I am most uncommon grateful.'

'Not at all. I shall give it to Atkins directly, and he will take it to the courier before he leaves.'

'Atkins? Mr Stanhope's Atkins?'

'Yes. Dr Maturin gave him a chit for me: it seems that with the envoy dying in that unhappy way, he was out of a place. Are you acquainted with him?'

'He came out in *Surprise*, of course: but really I hardly saw anything of the gentleman.'

'Ah? Indeed? That reminds me, I have not had the pleasure of seeing Maturin for some days now.'

'Nor have I. We meet at these splendid dinners, but otherwise he is busy at the hospital or running about the country looking for bugs and tigers.'

'BE SO GOOD as to call me an elephant,' said Stephen.

'Sahib, at once. Does the sahib prefer a male elephant, or a female elephant?'

'A male elephant. I should be more at home with a male elephant.'

'Would the sahib wish me to bring him to a house of boys? Cleaned, polite boys like gazelles, that sing and play the flute?'

'No, Mahomet: just the elephant, if you please.'

The enormous grey creature knelt down, and Stephen looked closely into its wise little old eye, gleaming among the paint and embroidery.

'The sahib places his foot here, upon the brute.'

'I beg your pardon,' murmured Stephen at the vast archaic ear, and mounted. They rode down the crowded Chowringhee, Mahomet pointing out objects of interest. 'There lives Mirza Shah, decrepit, blind: kings trembled at his name. There Kumar the rich, an unbeliever; he has a thousand concubines. The sahib is disgusted. Like me, the sahib looks upon women as tattling, guileful, tale-bearing, noisy, contemptible, mean, wretched, unsteady, harsh, inhospitable; I will bring him a young gentleman that smells of honey. This is the Maidan. The Sahib sees two peepul-trees near the bridge, God give him sight for ever. That is where the European gentlemen come to fight one another with swords and pistols. The building beyond the bridge is a heathen temple, full of idols. We cross the bridge. Now the sahib is in Alipur.'

In Alipur: vast walled gardens, isolated houses; here a Gothic ruin with a true pagoda in its grounds, there a homesick Irishman's round tower. The elephant padded up a gravel drive to a portico, very like the portico of an English country house apart from the deep recesses on either side for the tigers, and the smell of wild beasts that hung beneath its roof. They paced out and looked not at but towards him with implacable eyes: their chains still dragged upon the ground, yet their faces were so close together that their whiskers mingled, and it was impossible to say from which cavernous chest came the growl that filled the echoing porch with this low, continuous sound. The porter's infant child, woken by the organ-note, applied himself to a winch, and the tigers were heaved apart.

'Infant child,' said Stephen, 'state the names and ages of thy beasts.'

'Father of the poor, their names are Right and Wrong. They are of immemorial antiquity, having been in this portico even before I was born.'

'Yet the territory of the one overlaps the territory of the other?'

'Maharaj, my understanding does not reach the word *overlap*; but no doubt it is so.'

'Child, accept this coin.'

Stephen was announced, '*Here is that physical chap again,*' said Lady Forbes, peering at him under her shading hand. '*You must admit he has a certain air – has seen good company – but I never trust these half-castes.* Good afternoon, sir: *I trust I see you well, my Sawbones Romeo: they have been at it hammer and tongs and thrown in the bloody coal-scuttle, too: she would have reduced me to tears, if I had any left to shed.* You find me at my tea, sir. May I offer you a cup? I lace it with gin, sir; the only thing against this hot relaxing damp. Kumar – *where is that black sodomite?* Another cup. So you have buried poor Stanhope, I hear? Well, well, we must all come to it: that's my comfort. Lord, the young men I have seen buried here! Mrs Villiers will be down presently. Perhaps I will pour you another cup and then help her with her gown. *She will be lying there stark naked, sweating under the punkah: I dare say you would like to go and help her yourself, young fellow, for all your compassé airs. Don't tell me you have no – la, I am a coarse old woman; and to think I was once a girl, alas, alas.*'

'Stephen, my conquering hero,' cried Diana, coming in alone, 'how glad I am to see your phiz at last! Where have you been all these days? Did you not have my note? Sit down, do, and take off your coat. How can you bear this wicked heat? We are beside ourselves with stickiness and vexation, and you look as cool as – how I envy you. Is that your elephant outside? I will have him led into the shade at once – you must never leave an elephant in the sun.' She called a servant, a stupid man who did not understand her directions at once, and her voice rose to a tone that Stephen knew well.

'When I saw an elephant coming up the drive,' she said, smiling again, 'I thought it was that bore Johnstone; he is always calling. Not that he is really a bore – an interesting man, in fact; an American: you would like him – have you ever met an American? – nor had I before this: perfectly civilised, you know; all that about their spitting on the floor is so much stuff – and immensely rich, too – but it is embarrassing, and a source of these perpetual God-damned scenes. How I hate a man that makes scenes, particularly in this weather, when the least exertion brings you out in a mucksweat. Everybody is furious in this weather. But what made you come on an elephant, Stephen, dressed in a bloom-coloured coat?'

It was clear to a man with far less knowledge of morphology than Stephen possessed that there was nothing under Diana's gown, and he looked out of the window with a light frown: he wished his mind to be perfectly clear.

He said, 'The elephant stands for splendour and confidence. These last weeks, ever since the ship turned back from the Sumatra coast, I have noticed a look of settled and increasing anxiety upon my face. I see it when I shave: I also feel the set of my features, head, neck, shoulders – the expressive parts. From time to time I look and again I verify that it is indeed this expression of an indwelling, undefined, and general apprehension or even dread. I dispel it; I look cheerful and alert, perhaps confident; and in a few moments it is there again. The elephant is to deal with this. You will remember the last time we met I begged you would do me the honour of marrying me.'

'I do, Stephen,' cried Diana, blushing: he had never seen her blush, and it moved him. 'Indeed I do. But oh why did you not say so long ago – at Dover, say? It might have been different then, before all this.' She took a fan from the table and stood up, flicking it nervously. 'God, how hot it is today,' she said, and her expression changed. 'Why wait till now? Anyone would say I had brought myself so low that you could do something quixotic. Indeed, if I were not so fond of you – and I am fond of you, Maturin: you are a friend I love – I might call it a great impertinence. An affront. No woman of any spirit will put up with an affront. I have *not* degraded myself.' Her chin began to pucker; she mastered it and said, 'I have not come down to . . .' But in spite of her pride the tears came running fast: she bowed her head on his shoulder, and they ran down his bloom-coloured coat. 'In any case,' she said between her sobs, 'you do not really wish to marry me. You told me yourself, long ago, the hunter does not want the fox.'

'What the devil are you about, sir?' cried Canning from the open door.

'What is that to you, sir?' said Stephen, turning sharp upon him.

'Mrs Villiers is under my protection,' said Canning. He was pale with fury.

'I give no explanations to any man for kissing a woman, unless it is his wife.'

'Do you not?'

'I do not, sir. And what does your protection amount to? You know very well Mrs Canning will be here in the *Hastings* on the sixteenth. Where is your protection then? What kind of consideration is this?'

'Is that true, Canning?' cried Diana.

Canning flushed deeply. 'You have been tampering with my papers, Maturin. Your man Atkins has been tampering with my papers.' He stepped forward and in his passion he gave Stephen a furious open-handed blow.

Instantly Diana thrust a table between them and pushed Canning back, crying out, 'Pay no attention, Stephen. He does not mean it – it is the heat – he is drunk – he will apologise. Leave the house at once, Canning. What do you mean by this low vulgar brawling? Are you a groom, a pot-boy? You are ridiculous.'

Stephen stood with his hands behind his back: he, too, was very pale, apart from the red print of Canning's hand.

Canning, at the door, snatched up a chair and beat it on the ground: he wrenched the back apart, flung it down, and ran out.

'Stephen,' said Diana, 'do not notice it. Do not, *do not* fight him. He will apologise – he will certainly apologise. Oh, do not fight him – promise me. He will apologise.'

'Perhaps he will, my dear,' said Stephen. 'He is in a sad way entirely, poor fellow.' He opened the window. 'I believe I will go out this way, if I may: I do not altogether trust your tigers.'

'CAPTAIN ETHEREGE, SIR,' he said, 'will you do me a service, now?'

'With all the pleasure in life,' said Etherege, turning his round benevolent face from the scuttle, where he held it in the hope of air.

'Something happened today that caused me uneasiness. I must beg you to call upon Mr Canning and desire him to give me satisfaction for a blow.'

'A blow?' cried Etherege, his face instantly changing to a look of profound concern. 'Oh dear me. No apology in that case, I presume? But did you say Canning? Ain't he a Jew? You don't have to fight a Jew, Doctor. You must not put your life at risk for a Jew. Let a file of Marines tan his unbelieving hide and ram a piece of bacon down his throat, and leave it at that.'

'We see things differently,' said Stephen. 'I have a particular devotion to Our Lady, who was a Jewess, and I cannot feel my race superior to hers; besides, I feel for the man; I will fight him with the best will in the world.'

'You do him too much honour,' said Etherege, dissatisfied and upset. 'But you know your own business best, of course. You cannot be expected to stomach a blow. And yet again, having to fight a commercial fellow is like being forced into an unequal match, or having to marry a maid-servant because you have got her with child. Should you not like to fight someone else? Well, I shall have to put on my regimentals. I should not do it for anyone but you, Maturin, not in this damned heat. I hope he can find a second that understands these things, a Christian, that's all.' He went to his cabin, worried and displeased; reappeared in his red coat, already damp with sweat, and putting his head through the door he made a last appeal. 'Are you sure you would not like to fight somebody else? A bystander, say, who saw the blow?'

'It might not have quite the same effect,' said Stephen, shaking his head. 'And Etherege, I may rely upon your discretion, of course?'

'Oh, I know what o'clock it is,' said Etherege crossly. 'As early as possible, I suppose? Will dawn suit?' and Stephen heard him muttering 'Obstinate – don't listen to reason – pig-headed,' as he went down the gangway.

'What is the matter with our lobster?' asked Pullings, coming into the gunroom. 'I have never seen him so hellfire grum. Has he caught the prickly heat?'

'He will be cooler, and more collected, in the evening.'

On his return Etherege was much cooler, and almost satisfied. 'Well, at least he has some respectable friends,' he said. 'I spoke to Colonel Burke, of the Company's service, a very gentlemanlike man, quite the thing, and we agreed on pistols, at twenty paces. I hope that suits?'

'Certainly. I am obliged to you, Etherege.'

'The only thing I have left to do, is to view the ground: we agreed to meet after the Chief Justice's party, when it will be cooler.'

'Oh, never trouble your kind heart, Etherege; I shall be content with any usual ground.'

Etherege frowned, and said, 'No, no. I do hate any irregularity in affairs of this kind. It is strange enough already, without the seconds not viewing the ground.'

'You are too good. I have prepared you a bowl of Iced punch: pray drink off a glass or so.'

'You have been preparing your pistols, too,' said Etherege, nodding at the open case. 'I do recommend corning the powder uncommon fine – but I am not to tell *you* anything about powder and shot. This is capital punch: I could drink it for ever.'

Stephen walked into the great cabin. 'Jack,' he said, 'it is weeks since we played a note. What do you say to a bout this evening, if you are not too taken up with your bollards and capstan-bars?'

'Have you come aboard, my plum?' cried Jack, looking up from the bosun's accounts with a beaming face. 'I have such news for you. We are to carry treasure, and the freight will see me clear.'

'What is freight?'

'It means I am clear of debt.'

'That is news indeed. Ha, ha, I give you joy, with all my heart. I am delighted – amazed.'

'I will explain it to you, with figures, the moment my accounts are done. But damn paper-work for today. Had you any particular music in mind?'

'The Boccherini C major, perhaps?'

'Why, that is the strangest thing – the adagio has been running through my head this last hour and more, yet I ain't in the least melancholy. Far from it, ha. ha.' He rosined his bow, and said, 'Stephen, I took your advice. I have written to Sophie, asking her to come out to Madeira. Canning sends it overland.'

Stephen nodded and smiled, hummed the true note and found it on his 'cello. They tuned, nodded, tapped three times, each with his eye fixed on the other's bow, and dashed away into the brilliant, heart-lifting first movement.

On and on, lost in the music, intertwined, a lovely complexity of sound; on through the near-desperation of the adagio, on and on with such fire and attack to the very height and the majestic, triumphant close.

'Lord, Stephen,' said Jack, leaning back and laying his fiddle carefully down, 'we have never played so well.'

'It is a noble piece. I revere that man. Listen, Jack: here are

some papers I must confide to you – the usual things. I fight
Canning in the morning, alas.'

A dense curtain fell instantly, cutting off all but formal
communication between them. After a pause Jack said, 'Who
is your second?'

'Etherege.'

'I will come with you. That was why there was all that firing
on the quarterdeck, of course. You would not mind it, if I
were to have a word with him?'

'Not at all. But he is gone to the Chief Justice's: he is to
view the ground with a Colonel Burke after the party. Never
vex your heart for me, Jack: I am used to these things – more
used to them than you, I dare say.'

'Oh, Stephen,' said Jack, 'this is a damned black ending to
the sweetest day.'

'THIS IS WHERE we usually settle our affairs, in Calcutta,'
said Colonel Burke, leading them across the moonlit Maidan.
'There is the road over the Alipur bridge, do you see, conveniently near at hand; and yet behind these trees it is as discreet and secluded as you could wish.'

'Colonel Burke,' said Jack, 'as I understand it, the offence
was not given in public. I believe any expression of regret
would meet the case. I have a great esteem for your principal,
and I say this out of consideration for him; pray do all you can
– my man is deadly.'

Burke gave him a broad stare. 'So is mine,' he said in an
offended tone. 'He dropped Harlow like a bird, in Hyde Park.
But even if he were not, it would not signify. He don't want
pluck, as I know very well; I should not be here, else. Of
course, if your man chooses to put with a blow, and turn the
other cheek, I have nothing more to say. Blessed are the
peacemakers.'

Jack commanded himself; there was little hope of piercing
through Burke's deep stupidity, but he went on. 'Canning
must certainly have been in wine. The least admission of this

– a general expression – will answer. It will be satisfactory, and if need be I shall use my authority to make it so.'

'Confine your man to his quarters, you mean? Well, you have your own ways in the Navy, I see. It would scarcely answer with us. I will carry your message, of course, but I cannot answer for its coming to anything. I have never had a principal more determined to give satisfaction in a regular way. He is a rare plucked 'un.'

IN HIS JOURNAL Stephen wrote, 'At most times the diarist may believe he is addressing his future self: but the real height of diary-writing is the gratuitous entry, as this may prove to be. Why should tomorrow's meeting affect me in this way? I have been out many, many times. It is true my hands are not what they were; and in growing older I have lost the deeply illogical but deeply anchored conviction of immortality; but the truth of the matter is that now I have so much to lose. I am to fight Canning: made as we are, it was inevitable, I suppose; but how deeply I regret it. I cannot feel ill-will towards him, and although in his present state of confused passion and shame and disappointment I have no doubt he will try to kill me, I do not believe he feels any towards me, except as the catalyst of his unhappiness. For my part I shall, sub Deo, nick his arm, no more. Good Mr White would call my sub Deo gross blasphemy and I am tempted to throw down some observations on the matter; but peccavi nimis cogitatione, verbo, et opere – I must find my priest and go quickly to sleep: sleep is the thing, sleep with a quietened mind.'

From this sleep – but a sleep troubled by hurrying, disjointed dreams – Jack woke him at two bells in the morning watch; and as they dressed they heard young Babbington on deck singing *Lovely Peggy* in a sweet undertone, as cheerful as the rising day.

They came out of the cabin, into the deathly reek lying over the Hooghly and the interminable mud-flats, and at the gangway they found Etherege, M'Alister and Bonden.

Under the peepul-trees on the deserted Maidan a silent group was waiting for them: Canning, two friends, a surgeon, and some men to keep the ground: two closed carriages at a distance. Burke came forward. 'Good morning, Gentlemen,' he said. 'There is no accommodating the affair. Etherege, if you are happy that there is light enough, I think we should place our men; unless, of course, your principal chooses to withdraw.'

Canning was wearing a black coat, and he buttoned it high over his neckcloth. There was light enough now – a fine clear grey – to see him perfectly: perfectly composed, grave and withdrawn; but his face was lined and old, colourless.

Stephen took off his coat and then his shirt, folding it carefully. 'What are you doing?' whispered Jack.

'I always fight in my breeches: cloth carried into a wound makes sad work, my dear.'

The seconds paced out the ground, examined the pistols, and placed their men. A third closed carriage drew up.

With the familiar butt and the balanced weight in his hand, Stephen's expression changed to one of extreme coldness: his pale eyes fixed with impersonal lethal intensity upon Canning, who had taken up his stance, right foot forward, his whole body in profile. All the men there stood motionless, silent, concentrated as though upon an execution of a sacrament.

'Gentlemen,' said Burke, 'you may fire upon the signal.' Canning's arm came up, and along the glint of his own barrel Stephen saw the flash and instantly loosened his finger from the trigger. The enormous impact on his side and across his breast came at the same moment as the report. He staggered, shifted his unfired pistol to his left hand and changed his stance: the smoke drifted away on the heavy air and he saw Canning plain, his head high, thrown back with that Roman emperor air. The barrel came true, wavered a trifle, and then steadied: his mouth tightened, and he fired. Canning went straight down, rose to his hands and knees calling for his second pistol, and fell again. His friends ran to him, and Stephen turned away. 'Are you all right, Stephen?' He nodded, still as hard and cold as ever, and said to M'Alister, 'Give me that lint.' He mopped the wound, and while M'Alister probed it, murmuring, 'Struck the third rib; cracked it – deviated across the sternum – the ball is awkwardly lodged – meant to kill you, the dog – I'll clap a cingulum about it,' he watched the far group. And his heart sank; the wicked, reptilian look faded, giving way to one of hopeless sadness. That dark flow of blood under the feet of the men gathered round Canning could mean only one thing: he had missed his aim.

M'Alister, holding the end of the bandage in his mouth, followed his glance and nodded, 'Subclavian, or aorta itself,' he muttered through the cloth. 'I will just pin this end and step over for a word with our colleague.'

He came back, and nodded gravely. 'Dead?' said Etherege, and looked hesitantly at Stephen, wondering whether to congratulate him: the look of utter dejection kept him silent. While Bonden drew the charge from the second pistol and ranged them both in their cases, Etherege walked over to Burke: they exchanged a few words, saluted formally, and parted.

People were already moving about the Maidan; the eastern sky showed red; Jack said, 'We must get him aboard at once. Bonden, hail the carriage.'

11

THE TIGERS had gone, and servants were openly carrying things away.

'Good morning, ma'am,' said Jack, springing up. Diana curtseyed. 'I have brought you a letter from Stephen Maturin.'

'Oh how is he?' she cried.

'Very low: a great deal of fever, the ball is badly lodged; and in this climate, a wound – but you know all about wounds in this climate.'

Her eyes filled with tears. She had expected hardness, but not this cold anger. He was taller than she had remembered him, altogether bigger and more formidable. His face had changed, the boy quite gone, vanished beyond recall: a hard, commanding eye: the only thing she recognised, apart from his uniform, was his yellow hair, tied in a queue. And even his uniform had changed: he was a post-captain now.

'You will excuse me, Aubrey,' she said, and opened the note. Three straggling uneven lines. 'Diana: you must come back to Europe. The *Lushington* sails on the fourteenth. Allow me to deal with any material difficulties: rely upon me at all times. I say at all times. Stephen.'

She read it slowly, and again, peering through the mist of tears. Jack stood, his back turned, looking out of the window with his hands behind his back.

Beneath the anger and the distaste for being there, his mind was filled with questions, doubts, a hurry of feelings that he could not easily identify. Righteousness, except where faulty seamanship was concerned, or an offence against Naval discipline, was unfamiliar to him. Was he a contemptible scrub, to harbour this enmity against a woman he had pursued? The severity that filled him from head to toe – was it an odious hypocrisy, fit to damn him in a decent mind? He had gone near to wrecking his career in his pursuit of her: she had preferred Canning. Was this holier-than-thou indignation mere pitiful resentment? No, it was not: she had hurt Stephen terribly; and Canning, that fine man, was dead. She was no good, no good at all. Yet that meeting under the trees could have taken place over the most virtuous of women, the world being what it was. Virtue: he turned it over, vaguely watching a horseman winding through the trees. He had attacked her 'virtue' as hard as ever he could; so where did he stand? The common cant *it is different for men* was no comfort. The horseman came in sight again, and his horse into

full view: perhaps the most beautiful animal he had ever
seen, a chestnut mare, perfectly proportioned, light, powerful. She shied at a snake on the drive and reared, a lovely
movement, and her rider sat easy, kindly patting her neck.
Virtue: the one he esteemed above all was courage; and
surely it included all the rest? He looked at her ghostlike
image in the window-pane: she possessed it – never a doubt
of that. She was standing there perfectly straight, so slim and
frail he could break her with one hand: a tenderness and
admiration he had thought quite dead moved in him.

'Mr Johnstone,' said a servant.

'I am not at home.'

The horseman rode away.

'Aubrey, will you give me a passage home in your ship?'

'No ma'am. The regulations do not admit of it; in any case
she is unfit for a lady, and I have another month and more of
refitting.'

'Stephen has asked me to marry him. I could act as a nurse.'

'I regret extremely my orders will not allow it. But the *Lushington* sails within the week; and if I can be of any assistance,
I should be most happy.'

'I always knew you were a weak man, Aubrey,' she said, with
a look of contempt. 'But I did not know you were a scrub. You
are much the same as every man I have ever known, except for
Maturin – false, weak, and a coward in the end.'

He made his bow and walked out of the room with an
appearance of composure. In the drive he passed a cook
pushing a hand-cart loaded with brass pots and saucepans.
'Am I indeed a scrub?' he asked, and the question tormented
him all the way to Howrah, where the frigate lay. The
moment he saw her tall mainmast high above the mass of
shipping he walked even faster, ran up the gangway, passed
through the waiting officers and shipwrights, and went below.
'Killick,' he said, 'find out if Mr M'Alister is busy with the
Doctor: if he is not, I wish to see him.'

Stephen was in the great cabin, the airiest, lightest place in the ship: there seemed to be a good deal of activity in there. M'Alister came out, with a drawing in his hand, followed by the bosun, the carpenter, and several of their mates. He looked anxious and upset. 'How is he?' asked Jack.

'The fever is far too high, sir,' said M'Alister, 'but I hope it will come down when we have extracted the ball. We are almost ready now. But it is very badly placed.'

'Should he not be taken to the hospital? Their surgeons could give you a hand. We can have a litter ready in a moment.'

'I did suggest it, of course, as soon as we found the bullet right under the pericardium – flattened and deflected, you understand. But he has no opinion of the military surgeons, nor of the hospital. They sent to offer their assistance not half an hour since, and I confess I should welcome it – the pericardium, hoot, toot – but he insists on performing the operation himself, and I dare not cross him. You will excuse me now, sir: the armourer is waiting to make this extractor he has designed.'

'May I see him?'

'Yes. But pray do not disturb him, or agitate his mind.'

Stephen was lying on a series of chests, propped up with his back against a thrum-mat, the whole covered with sailcloth: over against him, showing his naked chest in the fullest light, a large mirror, slung by a system of blocks and lines: beside him, within reach, a table covered with lint, tow, and surgical instruments – crowbills, retractors, a toothed demilune.

He looked at Jack and said, 'Did you see her?'

'Yes.'

'I am deeply obliged to you for going. How was she?'

'Bearing up: she has all the spirit in the world. Stephen, how do you feel?'

'What was she wearing?'

'Wearing? Oh, a sort of dress of some sort, I suppose. I did not attend.'

'Not black?'

'No. I should have noticed that. Stephen, you look damnably feverish. Shall I have the skylight unshipped, for air?'

Stephen shook his head. 'There is some little fever, of course, but not enough to cloud my mind to any degree. That may come later. I wish Bates would hurry with my davier.'

'Will you let me bring the Fort William man, just to stand by? He could be here in five minutes.'

'No, sir. I do this with my own hand.' He looked at it critically, and said, more or less to himself, 'If it could undertake the one task, it must undertake the other: that is but justice.'

M'Alister came back, holding a long-nosed instrument with little jaws, straight from the armourer's forge. Stephen took it, compared its curve with his drawing, snapped its levered beak, and said, 'Cleverly made – neat – charming. M'Alister, let us begin. Pray call for Choles, if he is sober.'

'Is there anything I can do?' asked Jack. 'I should very much like to help. May I hold a basin, or pass the tow?'

'You may take Choles's place, if you wish, and hold my belly, pressing firmly, thus, when I give the word. But have you a head and a stomach for this kind of thing? Does blood upset you? Choles was a butcher, you know.'

'Bless you, Stephen, I have seen blood and wounds since I was a little boy.'

Blood he had seen, to be sure; but not blood, not this cold, deliberate ooze in the slow track of the searching knife and probe. Nor had he heard anything like the grind of the demilune on living bone, a few inches from his ear as he leant over the wound, his head bent low not to obscure Stephen's view in the mirror.

'You will have to raise the rib, M'Alister,' said Stephen. 'Take a good grip with the square retractor. Up: harder, harder. Snip the cartilage.' The metallic clash of instruments: directions: perpetual quick swabbing: an impression of brutal force, beyond anything he had conceived. It went on and on and on. 'Now, Jack, a steady downward pressure. Good. Keep it so. Give me the davier. Swab, M'Alister. Press, Jack, press.'

Deep in the throbbing cavity Jack caught a glimpse of a leaden gleam; it clouded; and there, half-focused, was the long-nosed instrument searching, deeper and deeper. He closed his eyes.

Stephen drew his breath and held it, arching his back: in the silence Jack could hear the ticking of M'Alister's watch close to his ear. There was a grunt, and Stephen said, 'Here she is. Much flattened. M'Alister, is the bullet whole?'

'Whole, sir, by God, quite whole. Not a morsel left. Oh, brawly feckit!'

'Easy away, Jack. Handsomely with the retractor, M'Alister: a couple of pledgets, and you may begin to sew. Stay: look to the Captain, while I swab. Hartshorn – put his head down.'

M'Alister heaved him bodily into a chair: Jack felt his head pressed down between his knees and the pungent Hartshorn searching his brain. He looked up and saw Stephen: his face was now perfectly grey, glistening with sweat; it was barely human, but somewhere about it there was a look of surly triumph. Jack's eye moved down to Stephen's chest, ploughed open from side to side, deep, deep; and white bone bare . . . Then M'Alister's back hid the wound as he set to work – a competent back, expressing ease and a share in the triumph. Competent activity, short technical remarks; and there was Stephen, – his chest swatched in a white bandage, sponged, relaxed, leaning back with his eyes half-closed. 'You took the time, M'Alister?' he asked.

'Twenty-three minutes just.'

'Slow . . .' His voice trailed away, reviving after a moment to say, 'Jack, you will be late for your dinner.'

Jack began to protest that he should stay, but M'Alister put his finger to his lips and led him on tiptoe to the door. More of the ship's company than was right were hanging about outside it. Discipline seemed to have been forgotten. 'The ball is out,' he said. 'Pullings, let there be no noise abaft the mainmast, no noise at all,' and walked into his sleeping-cabin.

'You look wholly pale yourself, sir,' said Bonden. 'Will you take a dram?'

'You will have to change your coat, your honour,' said Killick. 'And your breeches, too.'

'Christ, Bonden,' said Jack, 'he opened himself slowly, with his own hands, right to the heart. I saw it beating there.'

'Ah, sir, there's surgery for you,' said Bonden, passing the glass. 'It would not surprise any old Sophie, however; such a learned article. You remember the gunner, sir? Never let it put you off your dinner. He will be as right as a trivet, never you fret, sir.'

The dinner was a splendid affair, eaten off a blaze of gold; and without reflecting he swallowed a pound or two of some animal aswim in a fiery sauce. His neighbours were affable, but after they had exhausted the common topics they gave him up as a heavy fellow, and he made his way mutely through the succeeding courses, each with its own wine. In the comparative silence he heard the conversation of the two civilians opposite, the one a deaf and aged judge with green spectacles and a braying voice, the other a portly member of council: towards the end of dinner they were both flushed, and far from steady. Their subject was Canning, his unpopularity, his bold and independent activity. 'From all I hear,' said the judge, 'you gentlemen will be inclined to present the survivor with a pair of gold-inlaid pistols, if not a service of plate,'

'I do not speak for myself,' said the member of council, 'since Madras is the scene of my labours, but I believe there are some here who will shed no tears in their mourning-coaches.'

'And what about the woman? Is it true they mean to expel her as an undesirable person? I should prefer to see a good old-fashioned flogging at the cart's tail; it is many years since I have had that pleasure, sir. Should you not itch to hold the whip? For *undesirable person* is only to be construed in the administrative sense, in this case.'

'Buller's wife called to see how she was supporting her misfortune; she was not admitted, however.'

'Prostrated, of course; quite prostrated, I am sure. But tell me about the fire-eating Irish sawbones. Was the woman his . . .'

An aide-de-camp came up behind them and whispered between their heads. The judge cried, 'What? Eh? Oh I was not aware.' He brought his spectacles some way down his nose and peered at Jack, who said, 'You are speaking of my friend Dr Maturin, sir. I trust the woman to whom you have referred is in no way connected with the lady who honours Maturin and me with her acquaintance.'

No, no, they assured him – they meant not the least offence to the gentleman – would be happy to withdraw any facetious expression – would never dream of speaking of a lady known to Captain Aubrey with disrespect – they hoped he would drink a glass of wine with them. By all means, said he; and presently the judge was led away.

The next day, on the padded quarterdeck of the *Surprise*, Jack received Diana with less rigour than she had expected. He told her that Maturin was sleeping at the moment, but if she chose to sit below with Mr M'Alister she would learn all that could be learnt about his state, and if Stephen woke, M'Alister might let her in. He sent down all that the *Surprise* could offer in the way of refreshments, and when she went away at last, after a long vain wait, he said, 'I hope you will have better luck another time; but indeed this sleep is the greatest blessing: it is the first he has had.'

'Tomorrow I cannot get away; there is so much to be done. On Thursday, if I may?'

'Certainly; and if any of my officers can be of use, we should be most happy. Pullings and Babbington you know. Or Bonden for an escort? These docks are hardly the place for a lady.'

'How kind. I should be glad of Mr Babbington's protection.'

'LORD, BRAITHWAITE,' said Friday's Babbington, double-shaved, shining in his gold-laced hat, 'how I love that Mrs Villiers.'

Braithwaite sighed and shook his head. 'She makes the rest look like brutes from Portsmouth Point.'

'I shall never look at another woman again, I am sure. Here she comes! I see her carriage beyond the dhow.'

He ran to hand her up the gangway and to the quarter-deck. 'Good day to you, ma'am,' said Jack. 'He is considerably better, and I am happy to say he has ate an egg. But there is still a great deal of fever, and I beg you will not upset or cross him in any way. M'Alister says it is most important not to cross him in any way.'

'Dear Maturin,' she said, 'how glad I am to see you sitting up. Here are some mangosteens; they are the very thing for a fever. But are you sure you are well enough to see visitors? They frighten me so, Aubrey, Pullings, Mr M'Alister, and now even Bonden, telling me not to tire you or vex you, that I think I should go almost at once.'

'I am as strong as an ox, my dear,' said he, 'and infinitely recovered by the sight of you.'

'At all events, I shall try not to upset you or cross you in any way. First let me thank you for your dear note. It was a great comfort, and I am following your directions.'

He smiled, and said in a low voice. 'How happy you make me. But Diana, there is the sordid aspect – common requirements – bread and butter. In this envelope – '

'Stephen, dear, you are the best of creatures. But I have bread and butter, and jam too, for the moment. I sold a thumping great emerald the Nizam gave me, and I have booked the only decent cabin in the *Lushington*. I shall leave everything else behind – just abandon it where it lies. The underbred frumps of Calcutta may call me names, but they shall not say I am interested.'

'No. No indeed,' said Stephen. 'The *Lushington*: roomy, comfortable, twice our size, the best sherry I have ever drunk.

Yet I wish – you know, I wish you could have come home in the *Surprise*. It would have meant waiting another month or so, but . . . You did not think to ask Jack?'

'No, my dear,' she said tenderly. 'I did not: how stupid of me. But then there are the maids, you know; and I should hate you to see me seasick, green, squalid and selfish. It will make little odds in the long run, however. I dare say you will catch us up – we shall see one another at Madeira; or at all events in London. It will not be long. How parched you look. Let me give you something to drink. Is this barley-water?'

They talked quietly – barley-water, mangosteens, eggs, the tigers of the Sunderbands – or rather she talked and he lay there looking grave, transparent, but deeply happy, uttering a word or two. She said, 'Aubrey will certainly take great care of you. Will he make as good a husband as he does a friend, I wonder? I doubt it; he knows nothing whatsoever about women. Stephen, you are growing very tired. I shall go now. The *Lushington* sails at some impossible hour of the morning – at high tide. Thank you for my ring. Good-bye, my dear.' She kissed him, and her tears dropped on his face.

THE FETID OOZE of the Hooghly gave way to the clearer sea of the Bay of Bengal, to the right dark blue of the Indian Ocean; the *Surprise*, homeward-bound at last, spread her wings to the monsoon and raced away south-westwards in the track of the *Lushington*, now two thousand miles ahead.

She carried a sodden, disgruntled, flabby crew, a steel box filled with rubies, sapphires, and pearls in chamois bags, a raving surgeon, and an anxious commander.

He sat the night-watches through by Stephen's cot ever since the fever had reached its present shocking height: M'Alister would have spelled him, or anyone of the gunroom, but delirium had unlocked Stephen's secret mind and although much of what he said was in French or Catalan, or meaningless except in the context of his private nightmare, much was direct, clear and specific. A less secret man might not have been so communicative: it poured out of Stephen's unconscious mouth in a torrent.

Quite apart from official secrets, there were things Jack did not want any other man to hear. He was ashamed to hear them himself – for a man as proud as Stephen (and Lucifer could not hold a candle to him) it would be death to know that even the closest friend had heard his naked statements of desire and all his weaknesses laid as bare as Judgment Day. Discourses on adultery and fornication; imagined conversations with Richard Canning on the nature of the marriage-bond; sudden apostrophes – 'Jack Aubrey, you, too, will pierce yourself with your own weapon, I fear. A bottle of wine inside you, and you will go to bed to the next wench that shows a gleam, quit with regretting it all your days. You do not know chastity.' Embarrassing words: *Jew* is an unearned distinction; *bastard* is another. They should be brothers: both at least are difficult friends, if not impossible, since both are sensitive to pricks unknown to the general.'

So there Jack sat, sponging him from time to time, and the watches changed and the ship ran on and on, and he thanked God he had officers he could trust to see to her routine. He sat sponging him, fanning him, and listening against his will, distressed, anxious, wounded at times, bored.

He was no great hand at sitting mute and still hour after hour, and the stress of hearing painful words was wearing – the stimulus lost its point in time – and a jaded weariness supervened: a longing for Stephen to be quiet. But Stephen, so taciturn in life, was loquacious in delirium, and his subject was the human state as a whole. He also had an inexhaustible memory: Jack heard whole chapters of Molina, and the greater part of the Nicomachean Ethics.

Embarrassment and shame at his unfair advantage were bad enough, but even worse was the confusion of all his views: he had looked upon Stephen as the type of philosopher, strong, hardly touched by common feelings, sure of himself and rightly so; he had respected no landsman more.

This Stephen, so passionate, so wholly subjugated by Diana, and so filled with doubt of every kind, left him aghast; he would not have been more at a loss if he had found the *Surprise* deprived of her anchors, ballast and compass.

'Arma virumque cano,' began the harsh voice in the darkness, as some recollection of Diana's mad cousin set Stephen's memory in motion.

'Well, thank God we are in Latin again,' said Jack. 'Long may it last.'

Long indeed; it lasted until the Equatorial Channel itself, when the morning watch heard the ominus words.

' . . . ast illi solvuntur frigore membra

vitaque cum gemitu fugit indignata sub umbras',
followed by an indignant cry for tea – for 'green tea, there. Is there no one in this vile ship that knows how to look after a calenture? I have been calling and calling.'

Green tea, or a change in the wind (it was now a little west or north), on the intercession of St Stephen, lowered the fever from one hour to the next, and M'Alister kept it down with bark; but it was succeeded by a period of querulous peevishness that Jack found as trying as the Aeneid; and even he, with his experience of the seaman's long-suffering kindliness to a shipmate, wondered to see how they bore it: the surly, spoilt, consequential Killick called 'that infamous double-poxed baboon' and yet running with all his might to bring a spoon; Bonden submitting patiently to assault with a kidney-dish; elderly, ferocious forecastlemen soothing him as they gently carried his chair to favoured points on deck, only to be cursed for every breeze, and every choice.

Stephen was a wretched patient; sometimes he looked to M'Alister as an omniscient being who would certainly produce the one true physic; sometimes the ship resounded to the cry of 'Charlatan', and drugs would be seen hurtling through the scuttle. The chaplain suffered more than the rest: most of the officers haunted other parts of the ship when the convalescent Maturin was on the quarterdeck, but

Mr White could not climb and in any case his duty required him to visit the sick – even to play chess with them. Once, goaded by a fling about Erastianism, he concentrated all his powers and won: he had to bear not only the reproachful looks of the helmsman, the quartermaster at the con, and the whole gunroom, but a semi-official rebuke from his captain, who thought it 'a poor shabby thing to set back an invalid's recovery for the satisfaction of the moment', and the strokes of his own conscience. Mr White was in a hopeless position, for if he lost, Dr Maturin was quite as likely to cry out that he did not attend; and fly into a passion.

Stephen's iron constitution prevailed, however, and a week later, when the frigate layoff a remote uninhabited island in the Indian Ocean whose longitude was set down differently in every chart he went ashore; and there, on a day to be marked with a white stone, a white boulder indeed, he made the most important discovery of his life.

The boat pulled through a gap in the coral reef to a strand with mangroves on the left and a palm-capped headland to the right; a strand upon which Jack had set up his instruments and where he and his officers were gazing at the pale moon, with Venus clear above her, like a band of noon-day necromancers.

Choles and M'Alister lifted him out and set him on the dry sand; he staggered a little, and they led him up the beach to the shade of an immense unnamed ancient tree whose roots formed a comfortable ferny seat and whose branches offered fourteen different kinds of orchids to the view. There they left him with a book and a paper of cigars while the surveying of the anchorage and the astronomical observations went forward, a work of some hours.

The instruments stood on a carefully levelled patch of sand, and as the great moment approached the tension could be felt even from the tree. A deadly hush fell over the group, broken only by Jack's voice reading off figures to his clerk.

'Two seven four,' he said, straightening his back at last. 'Mr Stourton, what do you find?'

'Two seven four, sir, exactly.'

'The most satisfactory observation I have ever made,' said Jack. He clapped the eyepiece to and cast an affectionate glance at Venus, sailing away up there, distinct in the perfect blue once one knew where to look. 'Now we can stow all this gear and go aboard.'

He strolled up the beach. 'Such a charming observation, Stephen,' he called out as he came near the tree. 'I am sorry to have kept you so long, but it was worth it. All our calculations tally, and the chronometers were out by twenty-seven mile. We have laid down the island as exactly – my God, what is that monstrous thing?'

'It is a tortoise, my dear. The great land-tortoise of the world: a new genus. He is unknown to science, and in comparison of him, your giants of Rodriguez and Aldabra are inconsiderable reptiles. He must weight a ton. I do not know that I have ever been so happy. I am in such spirits, Jack! How you will ever get him aboard, I cannot tell; but nothing is impossible to the Navy.'

'Must we get him aboard?'

'Oh, no question about it. He is to immortalise your name. This is Testudo aubreii for all eternity; when the Hero of the Nile is forgotten, Captain Aubrey will live on in his tortoise. There's glory for you.'

'Why, I am much obliged, Stephen, I am sure. I suppose we might parbuckle him down the beach. How did you come by him?'

'I wandered a little way inland, looking for specimens – that box is filled with 'em: such wealth! Enough for half a dozen monographs – and there he was in an open space, eating Ficus religiosa. I plucked some high shoots he was straining for, and he followed me down here, eating them. He is the most confiding creature, wholly without distrust. God help him and his kind when other men find out this island. See his gleaming eye! He would like another leaf. It does me good to see him. This tortoise has quite recovered me,' he cried, putting his arm round the enormous carapace.

THE TORTOISE TURNED the scale, as M'Alister said, his wit heated by the tropical sun; its presence had a more tonic effect than all the bark, steel and bezoar in the frigate's medicine-chest. Stephen sat with Testudo aubreii by the hen-coops day after day as the *Surprise* ran down her southing; he increased in weight; his temper grew mild, equable, benevolent.

On her outward voyage the *Surprise* had done well enough, when she was neither crippled nor headed by foul winds; and it might have been thought that zeal had done all it could. But now she was homeward-bound. The words were magic to her people, many of whom had wives or sweethearts; even more so to her captain, who was (he hoped) to be married, and who was heading not only for a bride but also for the real theatre of war, for the possibility of distinction, of a Gazette to himself, and indeed of prizes, too. Then again the Company had done her proud – no royal dockyard's niggling over a halfpennyworth of tar – and her sumptuous refit, her new sails, new copper, beautiful Manilla cordage, had brought back much of her youth: it had not dealt with certain deep-seated structural defects, the result of age and the *Marengo*'s handling of her, but for the moment all was well, and she raced southwards as though she had a galleon in chase.

The ship's company was in the highest training now: their action had had its great cementing effect, but long before that the hands had settled down to a solid understanding, and an order was hardly given before it was carried out. The wind stood fair until they were far below Capricorn; day after day she logged her two hundred miles; pure, urgent sailing, all hands getting the last ounce out of her – the beautiful way of naval life that half-pay officers in their dim lodgings remember as their natural existence.

Outward-bound they had not seen a sail from the height of the Cape to the Laccadives; this time they sighted five and spoke three, an English bark-rigged privateer, an American bound for the China seas, and a storeship for Ceylon; each gave them news of the *Lushington*, whose lead, according to the storeship, was now little more than seven hundred miles.

The warm sea grew cooler, almost cold; waistcoats appeared in the night-watches, and the northern constellations were no longer to be seen. Then, in fifty fathom water not far from the Otter shoal, they were startled by the barking of penguins in the mist, and the next day they reached the perpetual westerlies and the true change of climate.

Now it was pea-jackets and fur caps as the *Surprise* beat up, tack upon tack, boring into the wind under storm-canvas, or flanked away southwards in search of a kinder gale, or lay a-try, fighting for every mile of westing against the barrier of violent air. The petrels and the albatrosses joined company: the midshipmen's berth, then the gunroom, and then the cabin itself was down to salt beef and ship's bread again – the lower deck had never left it – and still the wind held in the west, with such thick weather that there was no observation for days on end.

The tortoise had been struck down into the hold long since; he slept on a padded sack through the long, long rounding of the Cape; his master did much the same, eating, gaining strength, and sorting his respectable Bombay collections, and his scraps – alas, too hurried – from other lands. He had little to do: the inevitable sailors' diseases the men had brought with them from Calcutta had been dealt with by M'Alister before he was recovered, and since then the ship, awash with the pure juice of limes, had been remarkably healthy: hope, eagerness and merriment had their usual effect – and the *Surprise* was not only a happy ship but a merry one. He had dealt with the coleoptera and he was deep in the vascular cryptograms before the frigate turned her head north at last.

Five days of variable winds and light airs, warmer by far, in which the *Surprise* sent up her topgallant masts for the first time in weeks, and then on a temperate, moonlit night, when Stephen was sitting by the taffrail with Mr White, watching him draw the fascinating pattern of the rigging —black shadows on the ghostly deck, pools of darkness – a waft heeled the ship, upsetting the Indian ink, and the phosphorescent water streamed along her larboard side. The heel increased: the hissing bubbles rose to a continual song.

'If this is not the blessed trade,' said Pullings, 'I am a Dutchman.'

No Dutchman he. It was the true south-east trade, gentle but sure, hardly varying a point. The *Surprise* set a noble spread of canvas and glided on for the tropic line: the days grew warmer and warmer; the hands recovered from their battle with the Cape, and now there was singing on the forecastle, and the sound of the hornpipe called The Surprise's Delight. But there was no heaving to for any thought of a swim this bout, even when they were so far beyond Capricorn once more that Jack said, 'We shall raise St Helena in the morning.'

'Shall we touch?' asked Stephen.

'Oh no,' said he.

'Not even for a dozen bullocks? Are not you tired of junk?'

'Not I. And if you think there is any device, any ruse, that can take you ashore to collect bugs, pray think again.'

And there in the brilliant dawn a black point broke the horizon, a black point with a cloud floating over it. Presently it showed clearer still, and Pullings pointed out the principal charms of the island: Holdfast Tom, Stone Top, and Old Joan Point – he had landed several times, and he did wish he could show the Doctor the bird that haunted Diana's Peak, a cross between an owl and a poll-parrot, with a curious bill.

The frigate made her number to the tall signal-station and asked, 'Are there orders for *Surprise*? Is there any mail?'

'No orders for *Surprise*,' said the signal-station, and paused for a quarter of an hour. 'No mail,' it said at last. 'Repeat: no orders, no letters for *Surprise*.'

'Pray ask if the *Lushington* has passed by,' said Stephen.

'*Lushington* called: left for Madeira seventh instant: all well aboard,' said the station.

'Bear up,' said Jack, and the frigate filled and stood on. 'Muffit must have been lucky round the Cape. He will beat us to the Lizard, and make his voyage in under six months. Did he risk the Mozambique Channel, the dog?'

ANOTHER DAWN, OF the exquisite purity that is frightening – the perfection must break and fade. This time it was the cry of a sail that brought all hands tumbling up faster than a bosun's pipe. She was standing southwards on the opposite tack: a man-of-war, in all probability. Half an hour later it was certain that she was a frigate, and that she was edging down. All hands stood by to clear for action, and the *Surprise* made the private signal. She replied, together with her number: *Lachesis*. The tension died away, to be replaced by a pleasant expectancy. 'We shall have some news at last,' said Jack; but as he spoke another hoist broke out, 'Charged with despatches,' and she hauled her wind. She might not heave to, not even for an admiral.

'Ask her if she has any mail,' said Jack; and with his glass to his eye he read the answer before the signal-midshipman: 'No mail for *Surprise*.'

'Well, be damned to you for a slab-sided tub,' he said as they drew rapidly apart: and at dinner he said, 'You know what it is, Stephen, I wish we did not have that parson aboard. White is a very good fellow; nothing against him personally; I like him, and should be happy to serve with him in any way, ashore. But at sea it is always reckoned bad luck to carry parsons. I am not in the least superstitious myself, as you know, but makes the hands uneasy. I would not have a chaplain in any ship of mine if I could help it. Besides, they are out of place in a man-of-war: it is their duty to tell us to turn the other cheek, and it don't answer, not in action. I did not care for that ill-looking bird that crossed our bows, either.'

'It was only a common booby – from Ascension, no doubt. This grog is the vilest brew, even with my cochineal and ginger in it: how I long for wine again . . . a good full-bodied red. Will I tell you something? The more I know of the Navy, the more I am astonished that men of a liberal education should be so weak as to believe in bugaboos. In spite of your eagerness to be home, you declined sailing on a Friday, with your very pitiful excuse about the capstan. You will advance the plea that it is for the sake of the men; and to that I will reply, ha, ha.'

'You may say what you please, but these things work: I could tell you tales that would raise the wig off your head.'

'All your sea-omens are omens of disaster; and of course, with man in his present unhappy state, huddled together in numbers far too great and spending all his surplus time and treasure in beating out his brother's brains, any gloomy foreboding is likely to be fulfilled; but your corpse, your parson, your St Elmo's fire is not the cause of the tragedy.'

Jack shook his head, unconvinced; and after chewing on his wooden beef for some time he said, 'As for your liberal education, I, too, can say ha, ha. We sailors are hardly educated at all. The only way to make a sea-officer is to send him to sea, and to send him young. I have been afloat, more or less, since I was twelve; and most of my friends never went much beyond the dame's school. All we know is our profession, if indeed we know that – I should have tried the Mozambique channel. No: we are not the sort of men that educated, intelligent, well-brought-up young women cross a thousand miles of sea for. They like us well enough ashore, and are kind, and say Good old Tarpaulin when there is a victory. But they don't marry us, not unless they do it right away – not unless we board them in our own smoke. Given time to reflect, as often as not they marry parsons, or clever chaps at the bar.'

'Why, as to that, Jack, you undervalue Sophie: to love her is a liberal education in itself. Of course you are an educated man, in that sense. Besides, lawyers make notoriously bad husbands, from their habit of incessant prating; whereas your sailor has been schooled to mute obedience,' said Stephen; and to divert the sad current of Jack's mind he added, 'Giraldus Cambrensis asserts, that the inhabitants of Ossory can change into wolves at their pleasure.'

Back with his cryptogams his conscience troubled him: he had been so steadily fixed upon his own pursuit —the hope of Madeira, the certainty of London – that he had paid little attention to Jack's anxiety, an anxiety that, like his own, had been growing as the vague charming future became more sharply defined, more nearly the decisive present. He, too, was oppressed by a feeling that this great happiness of travelling month after month towards a splendid end was soon to be broken: a sense not indeed of impending disaster but rather of some uneasiness that he could not well define.

'That was the unluckiest stroke,' he said, thinking of Jack's *they marry parsons*. 'Absit, o absit omen,' for the deepest of his private superstitions, or ancestral pieties, was *naming calls*.

He found the chaplain alone in the gunroom, setting up a problem on the chess-board, 'Pray, Mr White,' he said, 'among the gentlemen of your cloth, have you ever met a Mr Hincksey?'

'Mr *Charles* Hincksey?' asked the chaplain, with a civil inclination of his head.

'Just so. Mr Charles Hincksey.'

'Yes. I know Charles Hincksey well. We were at Magdalen together: we used to play fives, and walk great distances. A delightful companion – no striving, no competition – and he was very well liked in the university: I was proud to know him. An excellent Grecian, too, and well-connected; so well-connected that he has two livings now, both of them in Kent, the one as fat as any in the county and the other capable of improvement. And yet, you know, I do not believe any of us grudged or envied him, even the men without benefices. He is a good, sound preacher, in the plain, unenthusiastic way: I dare say he will be a bishop soon; and so much the better for our church.'

'Has the gentleman no faults?'

'I dare say he has,' said Mr White, 'though upon my honour I cannot call any to mind. But even if he were another Chartres I am sure people would still like him. He is one of your tall, handsome fellows, not at all witty or alarming, but always good company. How he has escaped marriage until now I cannot tell: the number of caps set in his direction would furnish a warehouse. He is not at all averse to the state, I know; but I dare say he is hard to please.'

NOW THE DAYS flew by: each was long in itself, but how quickly they formed a week, a fortnight! The baffling winds and calms of the outward voyage restored the average by sweeping the ship northwards across the line and up into the trades with hardly a pause, and presently the peak of Tenerife lay there on the starboard beam, a gleaming triangle under its private cloud, nearly a hundred miles away.

The first consuming eagerness to reach Madeira was in no way diminished; never for a moment did Jack cease driving the fragile ship with a spread of sail just this side of recklessness; but in both Aubrey and Maturin there was this increasing tension, dread of the event combining with the delight.

The island loomed up in the north against a menacing sky; before sunset it vanished in rain, a steady downpour from low cloud that washed runnels in the new paint on the frigate's sides; and in the morning there was Funchal road, filled with shipping, and the white town brilliant behind it in the sparkling air. A frigate, the *Amphion*; the *Badger* sloop of war; several Portuguese; an American; innumerable tenders, fishermen and small craft; and at the far end, three Indiamen with their super yards on deck. The *Lushington* was not among them.

'Carry on, Mr Hales,' said Jack; the guns saluted the castle, and the castle thundered back, the smoke rolling wide over the bay.

'For'ard there. Let go.' The anchor splashed into the sea and the cable raced after it; but before the anchor could bite and swing the ship, there was the boom of guns again. Jack looked for a newcomer, staring seawards, before he realised that the Indiamen were saluting the *Surprise*. The *Lushington* must have told them of the brush with Linois, and they were pleased.

'Give them seven, Mr Hales,' he said. 'Lower down the barge.'

Stephen was to go down the side first. He hesitated in the gangway, and Bonden, taking it for a physical uncertainty, whispered, 'Easy does it, sir. Give me your foot.'

Jack followed him to the sound of bosun's pipes, and they rowed ashore, sitting side by side in their best uniforms, facing the bargemen, all shaved, all in white frocks, wearing broad white hats with long ribbons bearing the name *Surprise*. The only words Jack spoke were 'Stretch out.'

They went straight to their agent's correspondent, a Madeira Englishman. 'Welcome, sir,' cried he. 'As soon as I heard the Indiamen I know it must be you. Mr Muffit was in last week, and he told us about your noble action. Allow me to wish you joy, sir, and to shake you by the hand.'

'Thank you, Mr Henderson. Tell me, is there any young lady in the island for me, brought either by a King's ship or an Indiaman?'

'Young lady, sir? No, not that I know of. Certainly not in any King's ship. But the Indiamen only got in on Monday, cruelly mauled in the Bay, she might still be in one of them. Here are their passenger-lists.'

Jack's eyes raced down the names, and instantly they fixed on *Mrs Villiers*. Two lines farther down *Mr Johnstone*. 'But this is the *Lushington*'s,' he cried.

'So it is,' said the agent. 'The others are overleaf – *Mornington*, *Bombay Castle* and *Clive*.'

Twice Jack ran through them, and a third time slowly: there was no Miss Williams.

'Is there any mail?' he asked in a flat voice.

'Oh no, sir. Nobody would have looked for *Surprise* at the Island these many months yet. They would not even know you had sailed, at home. I dare say your mail is aboard *Bellerophon*, with the last convoy down. But now I come to think on it, there was a message left in the office for a Dr Maturin, belonging to the *Surprise*; left by a lady from the *Lushington*. Here it is.'

'My name is Maturin,' said Stephen. He recognised the hand, of course, and through the envelope he felt the ring. He said, 'Jack, I shall take a turn. Good day to you, sir.'

He walked steadily uphill wherever the path mounted, and in time he climbed through the small fields of sugar-cane, through the orchards, through the terraced vineyards, and to the chestnut forest. Up through the trees until they died away to scrub and the scrub to a parched meagre vegetation; and so, beyond all paths now, to the naked volcanic scree lying in falls beneath the central ridge of the island. There was a little sleety snow lying in the shadows up here, and he scooped handfuls of it to eat; he had wept and sweated all the water out of his body; his mouth and throat were as dry and cracked as the barren rock he sat on.

He had walked himself into a dull apathy of mind, and although his cheeks were still wet – the wind blew cold upon them – he was beyond the immediate pain. Below there stretched a tormented landscape, sterile for a great way, then wooded; minute fields beyond, a few villages, and then the whole south sea-line of the island, with Funchal under his right hand; the shipping like white flecks; and beyond, the ocean rising to meet the sky. He looked at it all with a certain residual interest. Behind the great headland westwards lay the Camara de Lobos: seals were said to breed there.

The sun was no more than a handsbreadth above the horizon, and in the innumerable ravines the shadow reached from rim to rim, almost as dark as night. 'To get down – that will be a problem,' he said aloud. 'Any man can go up – oh, almost indefinitely – but to go down and down sure-footed, that is another thing entirely.' It was his duty to read the letter, of course, and in the last gleam of day he took it from his pocket: the tearing of the paper – a cruel sound. He read it with a hard, cruel severity; yet he could not prevent a kind of desperate tenderness creeping over his face at the end. But it would not do – weakness would never do – and with the same appearance of indifference he looked about for a hollow in the rocks where he could lie.

Toward the setting of the moon his twitching exhausted body relaxed and sank into the darkness at last: some hours of dead sleep – a total absence. The circling sun, having lit Calcutta and then Bombay, came up on the other side of the world and blazed full on his upturned face, bringing him back into himself by force. He was still dazed with sleep when he sat up and although he was conscious of an extreme pain he could not immediately name it. The dislocated elements of memory fell back into place: he nodded, buried the ancient small iron ring that he had still clasped in his hand – the letter had blown away – and found a last patch of snow to rub his face.

He was at the foot of the mountain by the afternoon, and as he was walking through Funchal he met Jack in the cathedral square.

'I hope I have not kept you?' he said.

'No. Not at all,' said Jack, taking him by the elbow. 'We are watering. Come and drink a glass of wine.'

They sat down, too heavy and stupid to be embarrassed. Stephen said, 'I must tell you this: Diana has gone to America with a Mr Johnstone, of Virginia: they are to be married. She was under no engagement to me – it was only her kindness to me in Calcutta that let my mind run too far: my wits were astray. I am in no way aggrieved; I drink to her.'

They finished their bottle, and another; but it had no effect of any kind, and they rowed back to the ship as silently as they had come.

Her water completed and fresh provision brought aboard, the *Surprise* weighed and stood out to sea, going east about the island and heading into a dirty night. The gaiety forward contrasted strangely with the silence farther aft: as Bonden remarked, the ship 'seemed by the stern'. The men knew that something was amiss with the skipper, they had not sailed so long with him without being able to interpret the look on his face, the captain of a man-of-war being an absolute monarch at sea, dispensing sunshine or rain. And they were concerned for the Doctor, too, who looked but palely; yet the general opinion was that they had both eaten some foreign mess ashore – that they would be better in a day or two, with a thundering dose of rhubarb – and seeing that no rough words came from the quarterdeck they sang and laughed as they won the anchor and made sail, in tearing high spirits; for this was the last leg and they had a fair wind for the Lizard. Wives and sweethearts and paying off – Fiddler's Green in sight at last!

The heaviness in the cabin was not a gloom, but rather a weary turning back to common life, to a commonplace life without much meaning in it – certainly no brilliant colour. Stephen checked the sick-bay and had a long session with M'Alister over their books; in a week or so the ship would be paid off, and they would have to pass their accounts, justifying upon oath the expenditure of every drachm and scruple of their drugs and comforts for the last eighteen months, and M'Alister had a morbidly tender conscience. Left to himself, Stephen looked at his private stock of laudanum, his bottled fortitude: at one time he had made great use of it, up to four thousand drops a day, but now he did not even draw the cork. There was no longer any need for fortitude: he felt nothing at present and there was no point in artificial ataraxy. He went to sleep sitting in his chair, slept through the exercising of the guns and far into the middle watch. Waking abruptly he found light coming under his door from the great cabin, and there he found Jack, still up, reading over his remarks for the Admiralty hydrographer: innumerable soundings, draughts of the coastline, cross-bearings; valuable, conscientious observations. He had become a scientific sailor.

'Jack,' he said abruptly, 'I have been thinking about Sophie. I thought about her on the mountain. And it occurs to me – the simplest thing: why did we not think of it before? – that there is no certainty whatsoever about the courier. So many, many miles overland, through wild countries and desert; and in any case the news of Canning's death must have travelled fast. It may have overtaken the courier; it must certainly have affected Canning's associates and their designs; there is every reason to believe that your message never reached her.'

'It is kind of you to say that, Stephen,' said Jack, looking at him affectionately, 'and it is capital reasoning. But I know the news reached India House six weeks ago. Brenton told me. No. They used to call me Lucky Jack Aubrey, you remember; and so I was, in my time. But I am not as lucky as all that. Lord Keith told me luck has its end, and mine is out. I set my sights too high, that's all. What do you say to a tune?'

'With all my heart.'

With the rain coming down outside and the hanging lamp swinging wide as the sea got up, they soared away through their Corelli, through their Hummel, and Jack had his bow poised for Boccherini when he brought it screeching down on the strings and said, 'That was a gun.'

They sat motionless, their heads up, and a dripping midshipman knocked and burst in. 'Mr Pullings's compliments, sir,' he said, 'and he believes there is a sail to leeward.'

'Thank you, Mr Lee. I shall be on deck directly.' He snatched up his cloak and said, 'God send it is a Frenchman. I had rather meet a Frenchman now than – ' He vanished, and Stephen put the instruments away.

On deck the cold rain and the freshening south-wester took his breath away after the air of the cabin, where the tropical heat, stored up under the line, still seeped from the hold. He came up behind Pullings, who was crouched at the rail with his glass. 'Where away, Tom?' he said.

'Right on the quarter, sir, I reckon, in that patch of half moonlight. I caught the flash, and just for a moment I thought I saw her putting about. Will you take a look, sir?'

Pullings could see her tolerably well, a ship under topsails three miles off, standing from them on the starboard tack – a ship that had signalled to some unseen consort or convoy that she was going about; but he was attached to his captain, he was distressed by his unhappiness, and he wished to offer him this small triumph.

'By God, Pullings, you are right. A ship. On the starboard tack, close-hauled. Wear, clew up topsails, fetch her wake, and see how near she will let us come. There is no hurry now,' he muttered. Then raising his voice, 'All hands wear ship.'

The pipes and the roaring bosun's mate roused the sleeping watch below, and some minutes later the *Surprise* was running down to cross the stranger's wake under courses alone, almost certainly invisible in this darkness. She had the wind two points free and she gained steadily, creeping up on the stranger, guns run out, shielded battle-lanterns faintly glowing along the main-deck, bell silenced, orders given in an undertone. Jack and Pullings stood on the forecastle, staring through the rain: there was no need for a glass now, none at all; and a break in the cloud had shown them she was a frigate.

If she was what he hoped she was, he would give her such a broadside in the first moment, and before the surprise was over he would cross under her stern and rake her twice, perhaps three times, and then lie upon her quarter. Closer, closer: he heard her bell; seven bells in the graveyard watch, and still no hail. Closer, and the sky was lightening in the east.

'Stand by the clew-lines,' he called softly. 'Bellow, mind your priming.' Still closer: his heart was pounding like a mallet. 'Let fall,' he cried. The topsails flashed out, they were sheeted home in an instant and the *Surprise* surged forward, racing up on the stranger's quarter.

Shouts and bellowing ahead. 'What ship is that?' he roared into the confusion. 'What ship is that?' And over his shoulder, 'Back foretops'l. Man clew-garnets.'

The *Surprise* was within pistol-shot, all her guns bearing, and he heard the returning hail '*Euryalus*. What ship is that?'

'*Surprise*. Heave to or I sink you,' he replied; but the true fire had gone. Under his breath he said, 'God damn you all to hell, for a set of lubbers.' Yet hope said it might still be a ruse, and as the ships came up into the wind he stood there still, twice his natural size and all aglow.

But *Euryalus* she was, and there was Miller in his night-shirt on the quarterdeck: Miller, far senior to him. He pitied the officer of the watch, the lookouts; there would be the devil to pay – many a bloody back in the morning. 'Aubrey,' hailed Miller, 'where the devil do you come from?'

'East Indies, sir. Last from the Island.'

'Why the devil did you not make the night-signal like a Christian? If this is a joke, sir, a God-damned pleasantry, I am not amused. Where the hell is my cloak? I am getting wet. Mr Lemmon, Mr Lemmon, I will have a word with you presently, Mr Lemmon. Aubrey, instead of arsing about like a jack-in-the-box, just you run down to *Ethalion* and tell him to mend his pace. Good day to you.' He disappeared with a savage growl; and from the bow port under Jack's feet a voice said '*Euryalus*?'

'What?' said an answering voice from *Euryalus*'s aftermost port.

'Ballocks to you.'

The *Surprise* bore up, ran leisurely down to the straggling *Ethalion* in the growing light – a shamefully great way off – made the private signal and repeated Captain Miller's order.

The *Ethalion* acknowledged, and Jack was laying the course for Finisterre when Church, the signal midshipman

this watch, and an inexpert one, too, said, 'She is signalling
again, sir.' He stared through his telescope, struggled with the
leaves of his book, and with the help of the yeoman he slowly
read it off. '*Captain Surprise I have two wool*— no, *women for
you.* Next hoist. *One young. Please come to breakfast.*'

Jack took the wheel, bawling out, 'Make sail, bear a hand,
bear a hand, bear a hand, look alive.'

The *Surprise* shot across the *Ethalion*'s bows and rounded
to under her lee. He gazed across with a look of extreme
apprehension, trying to believe and to disbelieve; and
Heneage Dundas called out from her quarterdeck, 'Good
morning, Jack; I have Miss Williams here. Will you come
across?'

The boat splashed down, half-filling in the choppy sea; it
pulled across; Jack leapt for the side, raced up, touched his
hat to the quarterdeck, crushed Dundas in his arms, and was
led to the cabin, unshaved, unwashed, wet, ablaze with joy.

Sophie curtseyed, Jack bowed; they both blushed
extremely, and Dundas left them, saying he would see to
breakfast.

Endearments, a hearty kiss. Endless explanations, perpetually interrupted and re-begun – dear Captain Dundas, so infinitely considerate, had exchanged into this ship – had been
away on a cruise – and they had been obliged to chase a privateer almost to the Bahamas, and had very nearly caught
him. Several shots had been fired!

'I tell you what it is, Sophie,' cried Jack, 'I have a parson
aboard! I have been cursing him up hill and down dale for a
Jonah, but now how glad I am: he shall marry us this morning.'

'No, my dear,' said Sophia. 'Properly, and at home, and with
Mama's consent, yes – whenever you like. She will never
refuse now; but I did promise it. The minute we get home,
you shall marry me in Champflower church, if you really wish
it. But if you don't, I will sail round and round the world with
you, my dear. How is Stephen?'

'Stephen? Lord, sweetheart, what a selfish brute I am – a

most shocking damned thing has happened. He thought he was to marry her, he longed to marry her – it was quite understood, I believe. She was coming home in an Indiaman, and at Madeira she left her and bolted with an American, a very rich American, they say. It was the best thing that could possibly have happened for him, but I would give my right hand to have her back, he looks so low. Sophie, it would break your heart to see him. But you will be kind, I know.'

Her eyes filled with tears, but before she could reply her maid came in, bobbed severely to Jack, and said breakfast was ready. The maid disapproved of the whole proceeding; and from the frightened, deprecating look of the steward behind her, it was clear that she disapproved of sailors, too.

Breakfast, with Dundas giving Jack a circumstantial account of his exchange and of the privateer and insisting on a rehearsal of the action with Linois, was a long, rambling meal, with dishes pushed aside and pieces of toast representing ships, which Jack manoeuvred with his left hand, holding Sophia's under the table with his right, and showing the disposition of his line at different stages of the battle, while she listened with eager intelligence and a firm grasp of the weather-gauge. A rambling, exquisite meal, that was brought to a close by the fury of Captain Miller's repeated guns.

They came on deck; Jack called for a bosun's chair to be rigged, and while it was preparing Stephen and Sophie waved to one another without a pause, smiling and crying out, 'How are you, Stephen?' 'How are you, my dear?' Jack said, 'Heneage, I am so very much obliged to you, so deeply obliged. Now I have but to run Sophie and my treasure home, and the future is pure Paradise.'

The Mauritius
Command

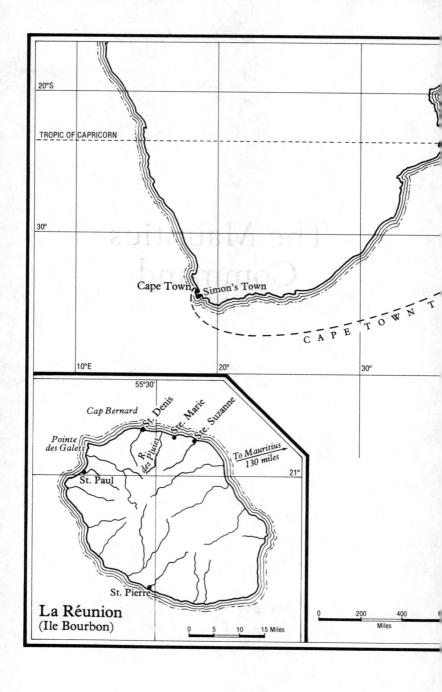

20°S

TROPIC OF CAPRICORN

30°

Cape Town · Simon's Town

C A P E   T O W N   T

10°E   20°   30°

55°30′

Cap Bernard

Pointe
des Galets

St. Denis

Ste. Marie

Ste. Suzanne

R. des Pluies

To Mauritius
130 miles

21°

St. Paul

St. Pierre

La Réunion
(Ile Bourbon)

0   5   10   15 Miles

0   200   400

Miles

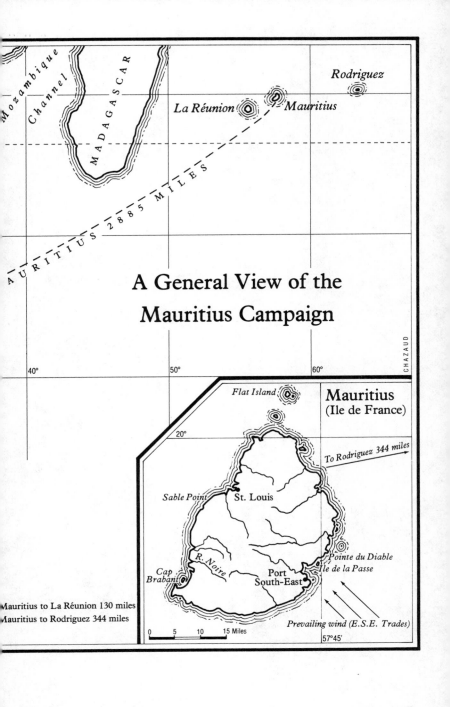

Mozambique Channel

MADAGASCAR

Rodriguez

La Réunion ◎ ⟲ Mauritius

─ ─ MAURITIUS 2885 MILES

A General View of the
Mauritius Campaign

CHAZAUD

40° 50° 60°

Flat Island ◎

Mauritius
(Ile de France)

20°

To Rodriguez 344 miles →

Sable Point   St. Louis

R. Noire

Cap
Brabant

Port
South-East

Pointe du Diable
Ile de la Passe

Mauritius to La Réunion 130 miles
Mauritius to Rodriguez 344 miles

Prevailing wind (E.S.E. Trades)

0   5   10   15 Miles

57°45'

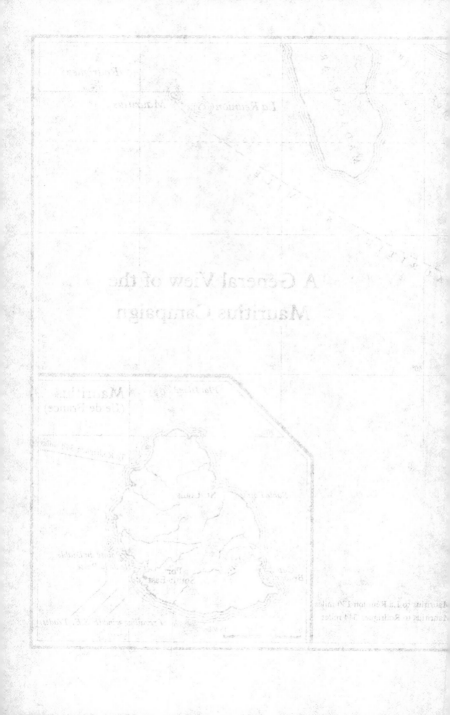

A General View of the

Mauritius Campaign

Author's Note

Sometimes the reader of a novel, particularly a novel set in another age, likes to know whether the events have any existence outside the author's mind, or whether, like the characters, they are quite imaginary.

There is no doubt a great deal to be said for complete freedom within a context of historical accuracy, but in this case the groundwork of the tale, a little-known campaign in the Indian Ocean, is factual; and as far as the geography, the manoeuvres, the ships taken, burnt, sunk or destroyed, the battles, triumphs and disasters are concerned, the writer has kept close to contemporary accounts, to the log-books and despatches of the officers who fought the actions, and to the Admiralty records. Apart from the necessary fictions at the beginning and the very end, he has not done anything to neaten history except for the omission of a few confusing, unimportant ships whose fleeting presence was neither here nor there; nor has he thought fit to gild the lily by adding in any way to the Royal Navy's pugnacious resourcefulness in time of adversity.

P.O'B

1

CAPTAIN AUBREY of the Royal Navy lived in a part of
Hampshire well supplied with sea-officers, some of
whom had reached flag-rank in Rodney's day while others
were still waiting for their first command. The more fortunate
had large, comfortable houses overlooking Portsmouth, Spithead, St Helens, the Isle of Wight, and the constant procession of men-of-war; and Captain Aubrey might have been
among them, since as a commander and as a young post-captain he had done so well in prize-money that he was known in
the service as Lucky Jack Aubrey. But want of a ship, the failure of his agent, his ignorance of business, and the sharp
practice of an attorney had reduced him to half-pay and no
more; and in fact his cottage lay on the northern slope of the
Downs, not far from Chilton Admiral, and the rising hill shut
out all the sea, together with most of the sun.

This cottage, though picturesque among its ash trees and
even romantic, ideally suited for two in the early days of his
marriage, was neither large nor comfortable; it had always
been low-ceilinged, pokey and inconvenient, but now that it
also contained two babies, a niece, a ruined mother-in-law,
some large pieces of furniture from Mapes Court, Mrs
Williams's former home, and a couple of servants, it was
something like the Black Hole of Calcutta, except that
whereas the Hole was hot, dry and airless, Ashgrove Cottage
let in draughts from all sides, while the damp rising from the
floor joined the leaks in the roof to form pools in many of the
rooms. These people Captain Aubrey maintained on nine
shillings a day, paid half-yearly and often long after the anx-
iously-awaited date; and although in his mother-in-law he
had a remarkable economist to help him, the effort of doing
so had imprinted an expression of abiding worry on a face
that nature had meant to look cheerful – an expression that
sometimes had a touch of frustration in it as well, for Captain

Aubrey, a scientific as well as a natural-born sailor, devoted to hydrography and navigation, was deeply concerned with a plan for finding the longitude at sea by the moons of Jupiter, and although he ground the mirrors and lenses for his telescope himself he would dearly have loved to be able to spend a guinea or two on brass-work from time to time.

At some distance below Ashgrove Cottage a deep lane led up through the fungus-smelling woods. The heavy autumnal rains had turned the clayey bottom into a quagmire, and through this quagmire, sitting sideways upon his horse with his feet so withdrawn from the mud that he appeared to be crouching on its back, like an ape, rode Dr Maturin, Captain Aubrey's closest friend, the surgeon in many of the ships he had commanded, a small, indefinably odd and even ill-looking man with pale eyes and a paler face, topped by the full-bottomed wig that marked him as a physician, if a somewhat old-fashioned one. He was, for him, unusually well dressed in a snuff-coloured coat with silver buttons and buckskin breeches; but the effect was spoilt by the long black sash that he wore wound three times round his waist, which gave him an outlandish air in the English countryside. On his saddle-bow lay a net, filled with a variety of mushrooms – bolets of all kinds, blewits, chanterelles, Jew's ears – and now, seeing a fine flush of St Bruno's collops, he sprang from his horse, seized a bush, and scrambled up the bank. As he did so an uncommonly large black and white bird lifted from among the trees, its vast wings labouring in the calm. Maturin's hand darted into the folds of his sash, whipped out a little spy-glass and presented it well before the bird, now harried by a pair of crows, crossed the valley and vanished over the hill that divided Ashgrove Cottage from the sea. With great satisfaction he stared after it for a while and then lowered his glass to the cottage itself. To his surprise he noticed that the little home-made observatory had been moved a considerable distance to the right, a good furlong, indeed, to a point where the ridge dropped fifty feet. And there, standing by its characteristic dome and overtopping it as Captain Gulliver might have overtopped a temple in Lilliput, stood Captain Aubrey, resting an ordinary naval glass upon the dome and peering steadfastly at some object far remote. The light was full on him; his face was sharp and clear in Maturin's telescope, and with a shock the Doctor saw not only that look of anxiety but also the marks of age and unhappiness. Stephen Maturin had thought of Aubrey as powerful resilient cheerful youth itself for so long that this change and the slow, weary motion as the distant figure closed the instrument and stood up, his hand pressed to an old wound in his back, were unusually distressing. Maturin closed his glass, picked the mushrooms and whistled his horse, a little Arab that came like a dog, looking affectionately into his face as he made his awkward journey down the bank with his hatful of collops.

Ten minutes later he stood at the door of the observatory. Captain Aubrey's bottom now protruded from it, entirely filling the gap. 'He must have his telescope as nearly horizontal as it will go, and he bending double over it,' reflected Dr Maturin. 'There is no weight lost in these posteriors, however: would still tip the beam at fifteen stone.' Aloud he said, 'Hola, Jack.'

'Stephen!' cried Jack, shooting out backwards with surprising nimbleness in so large a man and seizing his friend by both hands. His pink face was scarlet with pleasure, and a slight answering flush appeared in Maturin's. 'How very happy I am to see you, old Stephen! How are you? Where have you been? Where have you been all this time?' But recollecting that Dr Maturin, as well as being a medical man, was also an intelligence agent – that his movements were necessarily obscure – that his appearance might well be connected with the recent Spanish declaration of war upon France – he hurried on, 'Looking after your affairs, no doubt. Splendid, splendid. You are staying with us, of course. Have you seen Sophie?'

'I have not. I paused at the kitchen door, asked the young

woman was the Captain at home, and hearing domestic sounds within – the massacre of the innocents came to my mind – I merely left my offering and my horse and came along. You have moved the observatory.'

'Yes. It was no great task, however: the whole contraption don't weigh three hundredweight. Killick and I just unshipped the dome – it is copper from the old *Diomed* that the Dockyard let me have – and then we clapped on a couple of purchases and rolled it up in a forenoon.'

'How is Killick?' asked Stephen. Killick had been Jack's servant these many years; the three had been shipmates in several commissions, and Stephen valued him.

'Very well, I believe. I had news of him from Collard of *Ajax*; he sent a shark's backbone walking-stick for the twins. I had to turn him away, you know.'

Stephen nodded and said, 'Did the observatory not answer by the house, so?'

'Yes, it did,' said Jack hesitantly. 'But I tell you what it is, Stephen: from here you can see the Wight and the Solent, the tip of Gosport and Spithead. Quick, come and have a look – she will not have moved yet.'

Stephen lowered his face to the eyepiece, shading it with his hands; and there, inverted on a pale luminous background, hung a misty three-decker, almost filling the disc. As he shifted the focus she sprang sharp and clear into view. Brilliantly clear: her sails, topgallants down to courses, limp in the flat calm: the cable out of her hawsehole as her boats ahead carried out the warps to bring her to her mooring. Whilst he gazed he heard Jack's explanations – this was his new six-inch speculum – three months' grinding and buffing – finished off with the finest Pomeranian sludge – Miss Herschel's help invaluable – he had taken off a shade too much on the rim and had very nearly given up heart when she put him in the way of recovering it – admirable woman.

'Why, it is not the *Victory*,' cried Stephen as the ship began to move. 'It is the *Caledonia*. I can see the Scotch arms. Jack,

I can positively see the Scotch arms! At this distance! You are the speculum-maker of the world, so you are.'

Jack laughed with pleasure. 'Well do you see, it is the purest day for viewing,' he said modestly. 'Never a shimmer even by the water's edge. How I hope it will hold out until tonight. I will show you such a double star in Andromeda, less than a second of arc apart. Think of that, Stephen. Less than a second apart! With my three-inch glass I could never resolve anything much better than two. Should you not like to see a double less than a second apart?'

'Sure, it must be prodigious. But for my part I should as soon watch the shipping. Such life, such activity, and we Olympian above it all. Do you not spent hours and hours up here?'

'I do, Stephen, I do indeed. But I beg you will not mention it at the house. Sophie don't mind my stargazing, however late – and we shall have to sit up until three this morning before I can show you Jupiter – but staring at the Solent ain't astronomy. She don't say anything, but it makes her low in her spirits to think I am pining for the sea.'

'Do you pine much, Jack?' asked Stephen, but before Captain Aubrey could answer their attention was distracted by a clamour from the cottage, by Mrs Williams's hoarse martial voice, the shrill, defiant replies of the servant she was rebuking. Sometimes the motionless air carried the words up the hill with perfect clarity, and they heard the cry 'a foreign gentleman left them in my kitchen' several times repeated, but generally the passionate voices overlaid one another, and they were further confused by the echo from the hanging wood on the other side of the valley, by the wail of children, and by the repeated slamming of a door.

Jack shrugged his shoulders: yet after a pause he looked benevolently down at his friend, surveying him. 'You have not really told me how you are, Stephen,' he said. 'How do you do in fact?'

'Amazingly well, I thank you, Jack. I took the waters at

Caldas de Bohi not long ago, and derived great benefit from them.' Jack nodded: he knew the place, a village in the Pyrenees not far from Dr Maturin's high sheepwalk; for Stephen, though an Irishman, had property in those parts, coming down to him from his Catalan grandmother. 'And as well as growing as supple as a fawn,' continued Dr Maturin, 'I was able to make a number of valuable observations on the cretins of Bohi. Bohi is largely inhabited by idiots, my dear.'

'Bohi is not the only place, not by a long chalk. Look at the Admiralty, and what do you see? A general as First Lord, that is what you see. Would you believe it, Stephen? And the first thing this infernal redcoat does, is to take away one of the captain's eighths – he reduces our prize-money by a third, which is stark, raving lunacy. And then, quite apart from the idiots in Whitehall, this village has half a dozen; they squeak and gibber in the market-place. And in sober earnest, Stephen, I am sometimes cruelly worried by the twins. They do not look over bright to me, and I should take it very kind, was you to survey them privately. But I dare say you would like to look at the garden first?'

'I should like it of all things. And the bees.'

'Why, as to the bees, they seem to have piped down these last few weeks. That is to say, I have not been very close since I tried to take their honey, but I have not noticed them about. It must be more than a month since I was stung. But if you would like to see them, let us take the upper path.'

The hives stood in a trim row on white painted stools, but never a bee was to be seen. Stephen peered into the entrances, saw the telltale cobweb, shook his head and observed, 'It is the fell wax-moth.' He prised a skep from its stool and held it out, inverted, showing the dirty wreck of combs, with the vile grubs spinning their cocoons.

'The wax-moth!' cried Jack. 'Is there something I should have done?'

'No,' said Stephen. 'Not that I know of.'

'I would not have had it happen for the world. I am so concerned. Sophie and I valued them extremely, as your present.'

'Never mind,' said Stephen. 'I shall bring you some more, of a bolder stock. Pray let us view the garden.'

In the Indian Ocean Captain Aubrey had dreamed of a cottage, with a little land to it: rows of turnips, carrots, onions, cabbages and beans; now his dream was realized. But it had taken no account of the blackfly, the wireworm, the turnip-beetle, the leather-jacket, the green-fly and the black, the cabbage white. The rows were there, half an acre of them, dug as straight as a ruler in the poor, shallow, spewy, earth, and in them stood some dwarfish plants. 'Of course,' said Jack, 'there is nothing to be seen at this time of the year; but I mean to get three to four loads of dung on to the land this winter, and that will make a marvellous difference. I have already put some to my Brunswick cabbages, beyond Sophie's rose-garden. This way.' As they skirted the meagre potatoes he pointed over the hedge and said, 'That is the cow.'

'I thought it must be a cow: for milk, I make no doubt?'

'Just so. Vast great quantities of milk, butter, cream, veal: that is to say, we look forward to them presently. At the moment she happens to be dry.'

'Yet she does not look gravid. Rather the reverse, indeed: lean, Pharaonic, cadaverous.'

'Well, the fact of the matter, Stephen,' said Jack, staring at the cow, 'the fact of the matter is that she refuses the bull. He is game enough, oh Lord, yes; but she will have nothing to say to him. Then he flies into a hellfire passion, bellowing and tearing up the ground; and we go without milk.'

'From a philosophical point of view, her behaviour is logical enough. Reflect upon the continual, wearisome pregnancies, the price of a momentary and I may say aleatory pleasure. Reflect upon the physical discomfort of a full udder, to say nothing of the necessary parturition, with its attendant perils. I do not mention the uneasiness of seeing one's offspring turned into a blanquette de veau; for this is peculiar to the cow. Were I a female of any kind, I should beg to decline these general cares; and were I, in this particular case, a heifer, I should certainly choose to remain dry. Yet it must be confessed that from a domestical point of view celibacy in a cow takes on a different aspect entirely: here the general good calls out for teeming loins.'

'Yes,' said Jack. 'It does. Now here is Sophie's garden. It will be full of roses, come next June. Do you think they look a trifle spindly, Stephen? Do you think I should cut them back very hard, this winter?'

'Nothing do I know about gardening,' said Maturin. 'Nothing at all. But perhaps they may be a little, shall I say, rachitic?'

'I don't know how it is,' said Jack, 'I don't seem to have much luck with ornamental plants: that was supposed to be a lavender hedge, do you see? The roots came from Mapes. However, come and look at my cabbages. I am quite proud of them.' They passed through a wicket-gate and came to a plot at the back of the cottage: a sea of greenery, with a noble steaming dunghill beyond it. 'There,' cried Jack, 'have you ever seen the like?'

'I have not,' said Stephen.

'You may think them rather close, but I reasoned this way: for slinging hammocks we allow fourteen inches a man; now a man will eat a cabbage, and the part cannot be greater than the whole; so I set them by that reckoning, and it has answered amazingly.' He laughed with satisfaction. 'Do you remember the old Roman that could not bear to cut 'em?'

'Diocletian, I believe.'

'Just so. How I understand him. And yet, you know, whenever I do bring myself to spoil a rank, precious little encouragement do I get. Always this silly cry of caterpillars. Lord, if they had ate a tenth part of what we have ate in the way of weevils and bargemen in our biscuit, month in month out, on blockade, they would thank Heaven fasting for an honest green caterpillar.'

They stood a while, contemplating the cabbage-patch, and

in the stillness Stephen could actually hear the innumerable jaws at work. His eyes wandered from the mass of green to the dunghill: on top of it he noticed the bolets, chanterelles, blewits and collops that he had picked a little while before. The crash of a slamming door above interrupted their meditations; this was followed by the sound of heavy steps within, and the back-door opened, to display a square, red-faced woman, the spit of Mrs Williams but for a cast in her left eye and, when she spoke, a shrill Welsh voice. She had her box on her shoulder.

'Why, Bessie,' cried Jack. 'Where are you going? What are you about?'

Passion so choked the woman that for a moment her lips moved with never a sound; then all at once the words came darting out, accompanied by so venomous a look that Stephen crossed himself. 'A character, a character, that's all I want. Near with the sugar, nearer with the tea. A character I want, is all.' With this she vanished round the corner of the cottage.

Jack looked after her, and observed in a low voice, 'That makes the fourth this year. It is the damnedest thing, Stephen: I managed a ship's company of three hundred odd as easy as kiss your hand, but I cannot get the least notion of discipline into this establishment.' He paused, brooding, and added, 'You know very well I was no friend to the cat at sea; but rot me, I can see it has its uses.' Another reflective pause in which his face took on the stem, implacable expression of one who orders a dozen lashes to be laid on; then this look was replaced by one of concern and he cried, 'Oh Stephen, what a wretched host I am. You must be clemmed. Come in, come in, and we'll have a glass of grog. This way: you will not mind walking through the scullery – no ceremony, eh? Sophie must be somewhere in front.'

As he spoke a minute window opened above their heads and Sophie's head emerged. Her distracted look instantly changed to open delight, the sweetest smile. 'Oh Stephen,' she cried, 'how very happy I am to see you. Come in. I shall be down directly.' Stephen plucked off his hat, bowed and kissed his hand, though indeed he could perfectly well have reached hers from where he stood.

'Step in,' said Jack, 'and mind your head on the beam.'

The only thing in the scullery apart from a vast copper and its smell of boiling baby-clothes was a young woman on a chair with her apron over her head, rocking mutely to and fro. Three paces carried them through it however, into a narrow passage and so to the parlour, a pleasant little room with a bow window, made more spacious by a number of sea-going devices such as lockers under the windows and compact brassbound ship's furniture, yet somewhat marred by incongruous great objects never designed for a cottage, such as a high-backed caned seat for five or six people and a long-case clock whose hood would not fit under the ceiling and which therefore stood bareheaded in a corner, shedding desolation. Jack had scarcely time to ask Dr Maturin whether the bow did not remind him of the stem-window of the brig in which they had first sailed together when there was the sound of steps on the stairs and Sophie ran in. She kissed Stephen with sisterly affection and holding him by both hands scrutinized him for his health, his happiness and his general welfare with a tenderness that went straight to his heart, talking all the time with extreme rapidity – 'she was amazed, delighted – where had he been? – had he been quite well? – he could not imagine how pleased she was – had he been here long? – why had not Jack called her? – she had missed a quarter of an hour of him – she was sure the twins would remember him – they would be so excited – and little Cecilia too of course – he was hungry, was he not? – he would take a piece of seed-cake – how was he?'

'I am very well, I thank you. And you too, my dear, you are blooming, blooming.' She was indeed. She had caught up most of the wisps of hair he had seen streaming from the window, but one had escaped and its disorder enchanted him; yet for all the complacency with which he gazed upon her he could not conceal from his private mind that the tendency to plumpness he had once warned her of was quite gone, that were the present flush of pleasure not on her face she might look worn and even haggard, and that her hands, once so elegant, were now coarse and reddened.

Mrs Williams walked in. Stephen rose to bow, to ask after her health and that of her other daughters, and to answer her questions. He was about to sit down again after a tolerably detailed account of Mrs Williams' providential recovery when she cried, 'Not on the settle, Doctor Maturin, if you please. It is bad for the cane. You will be more comfortable in Captain Aubrey's chair.'

A thump and a dismal howling above-stairs called Sophie from the room, and presently Jack went after her. Mrs Williams, feeling that she had been a little abrupt in the matter of his sitting, gave Stephen a history of the settle since its manufacture in Dutch William's time: she had brought it with her from dear Mapes, where no doubt he remembered it in the summer drawing-room; she liked Captain A's cottage to have something of the air of a gentleman's house, and in any case she could not bear leaving so valuable, so historical a piece to her tenant, a worthy sort of man no doubt, but something in the commercial line, and people in that walk of life would not scruple to sit on it. The clock also came from Mapes, the most accurate clock in the county.

'A handsome clock it is too,' said Stephen. 'A regulator, I believe. Could it not be set a-going?'

'Oh, no, sir,' said Mrs Williams with a pitying look. 'Was it to be set a-going, the works would instantly start to wear.' From this she carried on to wear in general and the prohibitive cost of repairs, with an aside about Captain A's being handy in the house.

Captain Aubrey's voice, though well calculated to carry from one end of a ship to another in a gale, was less suited to the confidential domestic whisper, and at intervals in Mrs

Williams's stream of words his deep rumble could be heard, not perhaps quite as good-humoured as once it was, expostulating about a fair-sized piece of ham that could be dressed, a sea-pie that could be knocked up in a moment. Stephen turned his attention to Mrs Williams, and shading his eyes with his hand he studied her carefully. It appeared to him that her misfortune had had remarkably little effect on her: her restless, aggressive urge to dominate seemed if anything to have increased; she looked well, and as happy as it was in her nature to be. Her frequent references to her former grandeur might have been references to a myth in which she did not herself believe, a dream from which she had wakened to her present reality. Perhaps she had been born to play the part of a contriving manager with two hundred a year, so that at last she was fulfilling her real purpose. Was it a remarkable display of courage, or was it stark insensibility? For some time now she had been on the subject of servants, producing the usual threadbare observations with great conviction and volubility. In her young days they had been perfect; now they were difficult to find, impossible to keep, idle, false, dishonest, and often downright evil. 'Only this morning, only this very morning,' she said, 'I caught the cook fingering a heap of toadstools. Can you imagine such wickedness, Dr Maturin? To finger toadstools and then to touch my grandchildren's food with her nasty hands! There's a Welshwoman for you!'

'Did you attend to her explanation, ma'am?'

'Of course not, Lies, all lies, you know, in the kitchen. I flung them out of the door and gave her a piece of my mind. Character, forsooth! Don't she wish she may get it.'

After a short pause Stephen said, 'I saw an osprey this morning in that noble hanger over the way.'

'Did you, sir, indeed? Well, I declare. In that little wood we see from the window? It is quite well, for Hampshire. But when you know the neighbourhood as well as I know it, you will find that it is nothing in comparison of the woods at Mapes. They stretched into the next county, sir, and they were full of ospreys. Mr Williams used to shoot any number of 'em. I dare say this osprey of yours was a stray from Mapes.'

For some time Stephen had been aware of a snuffling behind the door. Now it opened and a little girl with yellow hair and a heavy cold came bursting in. She stared at him with an arch look, then buried her head in her grandmother's lap; to Stephen's relief all Mrs Williams's entreaties that she should stand up, that she should shake the gentleman's hand and give him a kiss, were in vain, and there she reclined, while her grandmother gently stroked her hair.

Mrs Williams had never, to Stephen's knowledge, shown the least kindness to her daughters; her face, voice and manner were unfitted for the expression of kindness; yet here it was, glowing in her whole squat person as she explained that this was little Cecilia, the child of her middle daughter, who was following her husband's regiment and who therefore could not look after her, poor thing.

'I should have known her anywhere,' said Stephen. 'A fine child.'

Sophie returned and the child at once began to shout, 'Aunt, Aunt, Cook tried to poison me with toadstools.' She kept up this unvaried cry for some time, and over it Stephen said to Sophie, 'I am strangely remiss: you must forgive me. I am come to beg you all to dine with me, and I have not yet delivered my invitation.'

'You are very good,' said Mrs Williams at once, 'but I am afraid that would be quite impossible, because – ' she looked about for some reason why it should be quite impossible, but was obliged to take refuge in hushing the child. Stephen went on, 'I am staying at the Crown in Petersfield, and have bespoke a variety of dishes:'

Sophie asked how he could be so monstrous; he was staying at the cottage, and dining there too. Again the door opened, and both women eagerly turned to Jack. 'How they do talk,' reflected Stephen: this was the first time he had ever seen the slightest possible evidence of a relationship between Sophie and her improbable mother.

'Uncle Aubrey,' cried Cecilia, 'Cook tried to poison me and the twins with toadstools.'

'What stuff,' said Jack. 'Stephen, you dine and sleep with us. The galley is all ahoo today, but there will be a capital sea-pie.'

'Jack,' said Stephen, 'I have bespoke dinner at the Crown. These dishes will be on the table at the appointed hour, and if we are not there, they will go to waste entirely. '

This remark, he noticed, had a striking effect upon the women. Although they still protested that he should not go, the conviction and the volume of their arguments declined. Stephen said nothing: at times he looked out of the window, at others he watched Sophie and her mother, and their kinship became more apparent. Where did it lie? Certainly not in tone of voice, nor in any particular feature or physical movement. Conceivably it arose from a certain not childish but rather un-adult expression common to both, an expression that a French colleague of his, a physiognomist and a follower of Lavater, had called 'the English look', attributing it to frigidity, a well-known characteristic of Englishwomen, and thus to an ignorance of the warming, ripening delights of physical love. 'If Dupuytren was right, and if this is indeed the case,' he reflected, 'then Jack, with his ardent temperament, must be strangely put about.' The flood of talk continued. 'How well he bears it,' thought Stephen, remembering Jack's short way with cackle on the quarterdeck. 'I honour his forebearance.' Compromises made their appearance: some should go, some should stay. Eventually, after a very long typical family discussion that often began again where it had started, it was agreed that Jack should go, that Stephen should return the next morning for breakfast, and that Mrs Williams, for some reason, should content herself with a little bread and cheese.

'Nonsense, ma'am,' cried Jack, goaded beyond civility at

last, 'there is a perfectly good piece of ham in the larder, and the makings of a monstrous fine great sea-pie.'

'But at least, Stephen, you will have time to see the twins before you leave,' said Sophie quickly. 'For the moment they are quite presentable. Pray show them, my dear. I will be with you in a moment.'

Jack led him up the stairs into a little sloping room, upon whose floor sat two bald babies, dressed in fresh frocks. They had pale, globular faces, and in the middle of each face a surprisingly long and pointed nose called the turnip to an impartial observer's mind. They looked at Stephen steadily: they had not yet reached the age of any social contact whatsoever and there was not the least doubt that they found him uninteresting, dull, even repellent; their eyes wandered elsewhere, dismissing him, both pairs at exactly the same moment. They might have been infinitely old, or members of another genus.

'Very fine children,' said Stephen. 'I should have known them anywhere.'

'I cannot tell one from t'other,' said Jack. 'You would not credit the din they can kick up if things are not quite to their liking. The one on the right is probably Charlotte.' He stared at them; they stared at him, unwinking. 'What do you think of them, Stephen?' he asked, tapping his forehead significantly.

Stephen resumed his professional role. He had delivered some scores of babies at the Rotunda in his student days, but since then his practice had lain among adults, particularly among seafaring adults, and few men of his professional standing could have been worse qualified for this task; however, he picked them up, listened to their hearts and lungs, opened their mouths and peered within, bent their limbs, and made motions before their eyes.

'How old are they?' he asked.

'Why, they must be quite old by now,' said Jack. 'They seem to have been here forever. Sophie will know exactly.'

Sophie came in, and to his pleasure Stephen saw both the

little creatures lose their eternal, ancient look; they smiled, wriggled and jerked themselves convulsively with joy, mere human larvae.

'You need not be afraid for them,' he said, as he and Jack walked over the fields towards their dinner. 'They will do very well; they may even turn out a pair of phoenixes, in time. But I do beg you will not countenance that thoughtless way people have of flinging them up into the air. It is liable to do great harm, to confuse their intellects; and a girl, when grown into a woman, has greater need of her intellect than a man. It is a grievous error to fling them to the ceiling.'

'God's my life!' cried Jack, pausing in his stride. 'You don't tell me so? I thought they liked being tossed up —they laugh and crow and so on, almost human. But I shall never do it again, although they are only girls, poor little swabs.'

'It is curious, the way you dwell upon their sex. They are your own children, for all love, your very flesh; and yet I could almost suppose, and not only from your referring to them as *swabs*, a disobliging term, that you were disappointed in them, merely for being girls. It is, to be sure, a misfortune for *them* – the orthodox Jew daily thanks his Maker for not having been born a woman, and we might well echo his gratitude – but I cannot for the life of me see how it affects *you*, your aim being, as I take it, posterity, a vicarious immortality: and for that a girl is if anything a better assurance than a boy.'

'Perhaps it is a foolish prejudice,' said Jack, 'but to tell you the truth, Stephen, I had longed for a boy. And to have not one girl but two – well, I would not have Sophie know it for the world, but it is a disappointment, reason how I may. My heart was set on a boy: I had it all worked out in my mind. I should have taken him to sea at seven or eight, with a good schoolmaster aboard to give him a thorough grounding in mathematics and even perhaps a parson for the frills, Latin and morality and so on. He should have spoken French and Spanish as well as you do, Stephen; and I could have taught him a deal of seamanship. Even if I could get no ship for years and years, I knew just what admirals and captains to place him with; he would not have lacked for friends in the service; and if he had not been knocked on the head first, I should have seen him made post by twenty-one or -two. Maybe I should have seen him hoist his flag at last. I could help a boy along, at sea; and the sea is the only thing I know. What use can I possibly be to a parcel of girls? I cannot even give them portions.'

'By the law of averages the next is very likely to be a boy,' said Stephen, 'and then you will carry out your benevolent scheme.'

'There is no likelihood of another. None at all,' said Jack. 'You have not been married, Stephen – but I cannot explain – should never have mentioned it. This is the stile to the turn-pike: you can see the Crown from here.'

They said nothing as they walked along the road. Stephen reflected upon Sophie's confinement: he had not been present, but he understood from his colleagues that it had been unusually difficult and prolonged – a bad presentation – yet there had been no essential lesion. He also reflected upon Jack's life at Ashgrove Cottage; and standing before the fire in the Crown, a fine great, posting-inn on the main Portsmouth road, he said, 'Were we to speak generally, we might say that upon the whole sailors, after many years of their unnatural, cloistered life, tend to regard the land as Fiddler's Green, a perpetual holiday; and that their expectations cannot be attempted to be fulfilled. What the ordinary landsman accepts as the common lot, the daily round of domestic ills, children, responsibilities, the ordinary seaman is apt to look upon as a disappointment of his hopes, an altogether exceptional trial, and an invasion of his liberty.'

'I catch your drift, old Stephen,' said Jack with a smile, 'and there is a great deal in what you say. But not every ordinary seaman has Mrs Williams to live with him. I am not complaining, mark you. She is not a bad sort of a woman at all; she does her best according to her own lights, and she is truly devoted to the children. The trouble is that I had somehow got the wrong notion of marriage. I had thought there was more friendship and confidence and unreserve in it than the case allows. I am not criticizing Sophie in the least degree, you understand – '

'Certainly not.'

' – but in the nature of things . . . The fault is entirely on my side, I am sure. When you are in command, you get so sick of the loneliness, of playing the great man and so on, that you long to break out of it; but in the nature of things it don't seem possible.' He relapsed into silence.

After a while Stephen said, 'So if you were ordered to sea, brother, I collect you would not rage and curse, as being snatched away from domestic felicity – the felicity, I mean, of a parent guiding his daughters' first interesting steps?'

'I should kiss the messenger,' said Jack.

'This I had supposed for some time now,' murmured Stephen.

'For one thing, I should be on full pay,' continued Jack, 'and for another, there would be a chance of prize-money, and I might be able to give them portions.' At the word prize-money the old piratical look gleamed in his bright blue eye and he straightened to his full height. 'And indeed I have some hopes of a ship. I pepper the Admiralty with letters, of course, and some days ago I wrote to Bromley: there is a frigate fitting out in the Dockyard, the old *Diane*, doubled and braced with Snodgrass's diagonals. I even pester Old Jarvie from time to time, though he don't love me. Oh, I have half a dozen irons in the fire – I suppose you have not been up to anything, Stephen? Not another *Surprise*, with an envoy for the East Indies?'

'How come you to ask such a simple question, Jack? Hush: do not gape, but look privily towards the stair. There is a most strikingly handsome woman.'

Jack glanced round, and there in fact was a most strikingly handsome woman, young, spry, a lady very much alive, wearing a green riding-habit; she was aware of being looked at, and she moved with even more grace than nature had provided.

He turned heavily back to the fire. 'I have no use for your women,' he said. 'Handsome or otherwise.'

'I never expected you to utter so weak a remark,' said Stephen. 'To lump all women together in one undiscriminated heap is as unphilosophical as to say . . .'

'Gentlemen,' said the host of the Crown, 'your dinner is on the table, if you please to walk in.'

It was a good dinner, but even the soused hog's face did not restore Captain Aubrey's philosophy, nor give his expression the old degree of cheerfulness that Stephen had known outlast privation, defeat, imprisonment and even the loss of his ship.

After the first remove, which had been entirely taken up with memories of earlier commissions and former shipmates, they spoke of Mrs Williams's affairs. That lady, having lost her man of business by death, had been unfortunate in her choice of a new one, a gentleman with a scheme of investment that must infallibly yield seventeen and a half per cent. Her capital had been engulfed and with it her estate, though up until the present she still retained the house whose rent paid the interest on the mortgage. 'I cannot blame her,' said Jack. 'I dare say I should have done the same myself: even ten per cent would have been wonderfully tempting. But I wish she had not lost Sophie's dowry too. She did not choose to transfer it until the Michaelmas dividends were due, and in decency we could hardly press her, so it all went, being in her name. I mind the money, of course, but even more than that I mind its making Sophie unhappy. She feels she is a burden, which is the greatest nonsense. But what can I say? I might as well talk to the cathead.'

'Allow me to pour you another glass of this port,' said Stephen. 'It is an innocent wine, neither sophisticated nor muddy, which is rare in these parts. Tell me, who is the Miss

Herschel of whom you spoke with such warm approbation?'

'Ah, now, that is another case altogether: there is a woman who bears out all you say about heaps,' cried Jack. 'There is a woman you can talk to as one rational being to another. Ask her the measure of an arc whose cosine is nought, and instantly she replies pi upon two: it is all there, in her head. She is sister to the great Mr Herschel.'

'The astronomer?'

'Just so. He honoured me with some most judicious remarks on refraction when I addressed the Royal Society, and that is how I came to know her. She had already read my paper on the Jovian moons, was more than civil about it, and suggested a quicker way of working my heliocentric longitudes. I go to see her every time she comes down to Newman's observatory, which is pretty often, and we sit there either sweeping for comets all night or talking about instruments. She and her brother must have made some hundreds in their time. She understands telescopes from clew to earring, and it was she who showed me how to figure a speculum, and where to get my superfine Pomeranian sludge. And it is not mere theory: I have seen her walking round and round a post in Newman's stableyard for a good three hours without a break, putting the last touches to a six-inch mirror – it will never do to take your hand from the surface at that stage, you know – taking snuff from a saucer every hundred paces. An admirable woman; you would love her, Stephen. And she sings, too – hits the note plumb in the middle, as pure as the Carlotta.'

'If she is Mr Herschel's sister, I presume she is a lady of a certain age?'

'Oh, yes, she must be sixty or so: she could never have come by such a knowledge of double stars in less. Sixty at least. Yet it is all one. Whenever I come home from a night with Miss Herschel there are wry looks, a tolerably frigid welcome.'

'Since it has physical effects, the sorrow and woe that is in marriage no doubt belongs to the province of the physician,' said Stephen. 'But I am as little acquainted with it as I am with gardening, or domestic economy.'

He was brought nearer acquainted the next morning, when he walked up to breakfast at the cottage. He was far too early, and the first sight that met his eye was the twins flinging their pap about and shrieking as they did so, while their grandmother, protected by a coarse canvas bib and apron, endeavoured to feed them with a spoon and little Cecilia wallowed in the bowl itself; he recoiled into the arms of the servant-girl carrying a basket of malodorous cloths, and worse might have happened if Sophie, suddenly appearing from above, had not whipped him away into the garden.

After a little general conversation from which it appeared that Jack had enjoyed his dinner, had come home singing, and was now grinding the coffee himself, she said, 'Oh, Stephen, how I wish you could help him to a ship. He is so unhappy here. He spends hours up on the hill, looking at the sea through his telescope, and it breaks my heart. Even if it were only for a short cruise – the winter is coming on, and the damp is so bad for his wound – any sort of ship at all, even if it were only a transport, like dear Mr Pullings.'

'How I wish I could, my dear; but what is the voice of a ship's surgeon in the councils of the great?' said Stephen, with a veiled though piercing glance to see whether any of her husband's knowledge of his double character had been sacrificed to marital confidence. Her next words and her totally unconscious air reassured him: she said, 'We saw in the paper that you were called in when the Duke of Clarence was ill, and I thought that perhaps a word from you . . .'

He said, 'Honey, the duke knows Jack very well, by reputation – we spoke of his action with the *Cacafuego* – but he also knows that recommending Jack for a command would be the worst service he could do him. His Highness is in bad odour with the Admiralty.'

'But surely they could not refuse the King's own son?'

'They are terrible men at the Admiralty, my dear.'

Before she could reply the church clock of Chilton Admiral told the hour, and on the third stroke Jack's hail of 'Coffee's up' followed by his manly form and some remarks about the wind having backed two points in the night – heavy rain for sure – broke up their conference.

Breakfast was spread in the parlour, and they walked into a fine smell of coffee, toast and wood-smoke: the ham stood on the table, flanked by Jack's own radishes, each the size of a moderate pippin, and a solitary egg. 'There is the great advantage of living in the country,' he said. 'You get your vegetables really fresh. And that is our own egg, Stephen! Do help yourself. Sophie's crab-apple jelly is by your side. Damn that chimney; it will not draw when the air is anything south of west. Stephen, let me pass you an egg.'

Mrs Williams brought Cecilia in, so starched that she held her arms from her sides, like an imperfectly-articulated doll. She came and stood by Stephen's chair, and while the others were busily wondering why there was no news from the rectory, where the birth of a child had been hourly expected these many days past, she told him loud and clear that they never had coffee except on birthdays and when there had been a victory, and that her uncle Aubrey usually drank small beer, whereas her aunt and grandmama drank milk: if he liked, she would butter his toast for him. She had buttered a good deal of his coat too before Mrs Williams, with a delighted shriek, plucked her away, remarking that there never was such a forward child for her years; Cecilia, her mother, could never have buttered a piece of toast so prettily at that age.

Jack's attention was elsewhere; his ear was cocked; his cup was poised; several times he looked at his watch. 'The post!' exclaimed Mrs Williams at the thundering double knock on the door, and Jack made a visible effort to sit still in his chair until the servant appeared, saying 'A letter and a book, sir, if you please, and a shilling to pay.'

Jack felt in his pocket, frowned, and called across the table, 'Have you a shilling in change, Stephen? Here's nothing small.'

Stephen too plunged his hand into his breeches and came up with a mixed bag of currency, English, French and Spanish. 'The gentleman has three gold pieces,' said Cecilia, 'and a large quantity of silver.' But Stephen was deaf: he picked out twelve pence and handed them over, saying 'Never mind me, I beg.'

'Well, if you will all forgive me . . .' said Jack, breaking the seal. Mrs Williams craned her neck to make out all she could from her indifferent point of vantage, but before she could move to a better, her curiosity was satisfied. 'Oh,' said Jack, throwing the letter down, 'it is only that fellow Bromley. I always knew he was a rake; now I know he is a scrub into the bargain. However, here is the *Naval Chronicle*. That is always worth reading. My dear, Stephen's cup is empty.' He turned first to the appointments and promotions. 'Goate is made post at last; I am heartily glad of it.' Considerations upon the merits and demerits of Captain Goate and other acquaintances, also made post. Then, after a calculating pause, Jack said, 'You know, Stephen, our losses last year were not as heavy as I made out last night. Listen: *Jupiter*, 50, wrecked in Vigo Bay; *Leda*, 38, wrecked off Milford Haven; *Crescent*, 36, wrecked off Jutland; *Flora*, 32, wrecked off Holland; *Meleager*, 36, wrecked on Barebush Cay; *Astraea*, 32, wrecked off Anagado. Only five frigates, you see. And as for the post-ships, only *Banterer*, 22, wrecked in the St Lawrence; *Laurel*, 22, taken by the *Canonnière*, 50 – you remember the *Canonnière*, Stephen? I pointed her out to you once, when we were looking into Brest. An ancient old ship, built somewhere about 1710, but an amazing fine sailer; she can still give most of our heavy frigates topgallants on a bowline. Stephen, what's amiss?'

Stephen was gazing through the acrid smoke at Cecilia, who, bored with the conversation, had opened the clock's door with her greasy hands to get at the pendulum, a heavy jar of quicksilver.

'Oh, let the poor little treasure be,' said Mrs Williams, looking at her granddaughter with the fondest admiration.

'Madam,' said Stephen, his heart in pain for the exquisite mechanism, 'she will do herself a mischief. That quicksilver is most delicately poised; furthermore it is poison.'

'Cecilia,' said Jack, 'cut along now. Run away and play.'

Contention, tears, Mrs Williams's nimble protective tongue, and Sophie led her niece from the room. Mrs Williams was not at all pleased, but in the silence the sound of the passing-bell came clear from the church; it instantly diverted her mind, and she cried, 'That must be for poor Mrs Thwaites. She was due last week, and they sent for the man-midwife last night. There, Captain Aubrey.' These last words were delivered with an inimical jerk of her head, a retaliation, as it were, for his list of male wreckage and death, an assertion of women's sacrifice.

Sophie returned with the news that a horseman was approaching the cottage. 'It is news of poor Mrs Thwaites, no doubt,' said Mrs Williams, looking hard at Jack again. But she was mistaken. It was a boy from the Crown, with a letter for Jack: he was to wait for an answer.

' "Lady Clonfert presents her compliments to Captain and Mrs Aubrey, and would be most grateful for a passage to the Cape. She promises to take up no room and to give no trouble whatsoever; and flatters herself that Mrs Aubrey will, as a fellow-sailor's wife, understand and support this sadly informal and hurried application. She also proposes, if perfectly convenient to Mrs Aubrey, to do herself the honour of waiting upon her in the forenoon," ' read Captain Aubrey aloud, with a very high degree of astonishment, adding, 'Certainly she may have a lift to the Cape, whenever I happen to be going there, ha, ha.'

'Jack,' said Stephen, 'a word with you, if you please.'

They walked out into the garden, pursued by Mrs

Williams's angry voice – 'A most improper application – no compliments to me – and disgracefully ill-wrote; she has spelt promises with one m – I have no patience with these attempts at thrusting oneself into a strange house.'

At the end of the wan row of carrots Stephen said, 'I must beg your pardon for having evaded your question last night. I have in fact been *up to something*, as you put it. But first I must speak very briefly of the position in the Indian Ocean. Some months ago four new French frigates slipped out of the Channel ports, ostensibly for Martinique – that was the general rumour on shore, and that was the destination stated in the orders delivered to their respective captains: but no doubt these captains also carried sealed orders, to be opened somewhere south of Finisterre. At all events the frigates never reached the Antilles. Nothing was heard of them until they reached Mauritius, where they upset the balance of power in those waters entirely. The news of their presence reached England a very short while ago. They have already taken two Indiamen, and clearly they threaten to take many more. Government is extremely concerned.'

'I am sure of it,' cried Jack. Mauritius and La Réunion lay right in the path of the eastern trade, and although the Company's ships were usually well enough armed to deal with the privateers and pirates that swarmed in those seas, while the Royal Navy, by stretching its resources to the utmost, could just contain the French men-of-war, the sudden arrival of four frigates would be catastrophic: furthermore, the Frenchmen had excellent deepwater harbours in Port-Louis and Port South-East and St Paul's, sheltered from the frequent hurricanes and full of marine stores, whereas the Navy's nearest base was the Cape, more than two thousand miles to the south.

Stephen was silent for a moment. 'Do you know the *Boadicea*?' he asked abruptly.

'*Boadicea*, thirty-eight? Yes, of course. A weatherly ship, though slow: fitting foreign for the Leeward Islands station. Charles Loveless has her.'

'Well, listen now: this vessel, this frigate, is to be diverted to the Cape. And Captain Loveless, as you say, was to take her there to form part of a squadron made up of what the Admiral could spare: a force intended not only to counteract the French frigates but to take their bases away from them. In short, to capture La Réunion and Mauritius, to install a governor, and to possess them as colonies, valuable not only in themselves but as posts along this most interesting route.'

'A capital notion,' said Jack. 'It has always seemed absurd to me, that islands should not be English – unnatural.' He spoke a little at haphazard, because he had noted – oh, with what keen attention – Stephen's 'Captain Loveless *was* to take her.' Might this possibly be an acting command?

Stephen frowned. 'I was to accompany this force, together with the proposed governor,' he went on. 'And I was in a position to offer a certain amount of advice; that is to say, I was consulted on various points. It did not appear to me that Captain Loveless was fitted for the political side of the task, either mentally or physically; but he has great interest at the Admiralty. However, his malady increased upon him, and in spite of my colleague's efforts and of my own he is now on shore with an obstinate tenesmus that will keep him there. In London I caused it to be suggested that Captain Aubrey would be admirably suited for the vacant command – ' Jack gripped his elbow with a force that made him catch his breath, but he continued ' – that it was probable he would accept it in spite of his domestic situation and of the very short notice, and that I should be seeing him myself directly. Alternative names were advanced; some very frivolous objections to do with seniority and the flying of some kind of flag, some trumpery mark of distinction, were raised, for it seemed desirable that the person, or the ship, in question should be so ornamented . . .' With a prodigious effort Jack swallowed the words 'A broad pendant, a commodore's broad pendant for God's sake!' and Stephen continued, 'and most unhappily several people had to be consulted.' He bent to pick a stalk of grass and put it into his mouth; for some time he shook his head, and the farther end of the grass magnified its motion, showing anger, disapprobation, or a most decided negative. Jack's heart, raised by the mere mention of a broad pendant, the sailor's sweetest dream short of the admiral's flag itself, sank into the dark, everyday world of half-pay. 'Most unhappily, I say,' went on Stephen, 'for although I carried my point, it is evident that at least one of those consulted has been talking. The rumour has already spread about the town. Lady Clonfert's appearance is clear proof of that; her husband is on the Cape station, captain of the *Otter*. Oh, oh, it is always the same thing – gabble, gabble, gabble, blab, blab, blab, like a parcel of geese on a common, or a pack of old women . . .' his voice soared shrill in indignation, and Jack was aware that he was giving instances of loose talk, of intelligence conveyed to the enemy by spreading gossip; but Jack's glowing mind was filled with a picture of the *Boadicea*, her simpering figure-head with its vast bosom spreading over the frigate's fine sea-worthy bows – a trifle slow, perhaps, and he had seen her miss stays; but a careful stowing of her hold to bring her by the stern might make a world of difference, and cross-cat-harpins; Charles Loveless had no notion of cross-cat-harpins, still less of Bentinck shrouds. He found Stephen's eye fixed angrily upon him, bent his head with an expression of the gravest attention, and heard the words, 'As though the French were deaf, dumb, blind, incompetent! That is why I am most unwillingly obliged to give you this short summary. In any other event I should infinitely have preferred the news to reach you through the proper channels, without the least explanation – your provisional orders are at the port-admiral's office this minute – for not only does this require speaking openly of what should not be mentioned at all, but I am extremely averse to appearing in the role of fairy godmother, a purely fortuitous fairy godmother in this case. It can inflict an apparent, though fallacious, burden of obligation, and cause great damage to a relationship.'

'Not to ours, brother,' said Jack, 'not to ours. And I will not thank you, since you don't like it; but Lord, Stephen, I am a different man.' He was indeed. Taller, younger, pinker, his eyes blazing with life. His stoop had gone, and a great boyish grin kept ruining his attempted gravity.

'You will not mention this to Sophie, nor to any other person,' said Stephen, with a cold, penetrating glare.

'Must I not even start looking to my sea-chest?'

'What a fellow you are, Jack!' cried Stephen, in great disgust. 'Of course you must not, not until the port-admiral's messenger is come. Cannot you see the obvious cause and effect? I should have thought it plain even to the meanest intelligence.'

'A ship!' cried Jack, springing heavily into the air. There were tears in his eyes, and Stephen saw that he might wish to shake hands at any minute. He disliked all effusion, privately thinking the English far too much given to weeping and the flow of soul; he pursed his lips with a sour expression, and put his hands behind his back. He said, 'Plain to the meanest intelligence: I appear – you have a ship. What must Sophie conclude? Where is my character?'

'How long do you think the port-admiral's messenger will be, Stephen?' asked Jack, with nothing but a loving smile at these harsh words.

'Let us hope he outpaces Lady Clonfert by a few minutes at least, if only to prove that casual gossip does not necessarily have to run faster than official orders every single time. How we shall ever win this war I cannot tell. In Whitehall they know perfectly well that success in the Mauritius enterprise is of capital importance, and yet some fool must be prating. I cannot express my abhorrence of their levity. We reinforce the Cape, and tell them so: they instantly reinforce the Ile de France, that is to say, Mauritius. And so it runs, all, all of a piece throughout: Mr Congreve invents a military rocket with vast potentialities – we instantly inform the world, like a hen that has laid an egg, thus throwing away all the effect of surprise. The worthy Mr Snodgrass finds out a way of rendering old ships serviceable in a short time and at little expense: without a moment's pause we publish his method in all the papers, together with drawings, lest some particular should escape our enemy's comprehension.'

Jack looked as solemn as he could, and shook his head; but very soon he turned a beaming face to Stephen and asked, 'Do you imagine this will be one of your standoff-and-on capers? Ordered to sea at a moment's notice, recalled, turned on shore for a month, all your hands drafted elsewhere, and then sent to the Baltic at last in your hot-weather clothes?'

'I do not. Quite apart from the absolute importance of the operation, there are many members of the Board and of the ministry that have their money in East India stock: ruin the Company and you ruin them. No, no: there is likely to be a wonderful degree of celerity in this case, I believe.'

Jack laughed aloud with pleasure, and then observed that they must be getting back to the house – the boy from the Crown was waiting for an answer. 'I shall have to give that wretched woman a lift,' he added. 'You cannot refuse a brother-officer's wife, the wife of a man you know; but Lord, how I wish I could get out of it. Come, let us walk in.'

'I cannot advise it,' said Stephen. 'Sophie would detect you instantly. You are as transparent as a bride. Stay here till I desire Sophie to make your joint reply to Lady Clonfert: you cannot be seen until you have your orders.'

'I shall go to the observatory,' said Jack. It was here that Stephen found him some minutes later, with his telescope trained on the Portsmouth road. 'Sophie has answered,' said Stephen, 'and every woman in the house is now scrubbing the parlour and changing the lace window-curtains; they turned me out with very little ceremony, I can tell you.'

The promised rain began to fall, drumming briskly on the copper dome: there was just room for them both, and there they crouched in silence for a while. Beneath the bubbling current of his pure joy, Jack longed to ask whether Stephen had in some way arranged Captain Loveless's tenesmus; but although he had known Stephen intimately these many, many years, there was something about him that forbade questioning.

Presently, his mind sobering, he reflected on the Indian Ocean, on the fine blue-water sailing with the south-east trade-wind, the perilous inshore navigation among the coral reefs surrounding La Réunion and Mauritius; on the typical Admiralty decision to send one frigate to counterbalance four; on the immense difficulty of maintaining even a blockade, above all in the hurricane months, let alone that of landing upon those islands, with their few harbours (and those fortified), their broad reefs, the perpetual heavy surf on their inhospitable shores; on the question of water, and on the nature of the force likely to oppose him. To oppose him, that is to say, if ever he reached the station. Furtively stretching out to touch a piece of wood, he said, 'This hypothetical squadron, Stephen, have you any idea of its strength, and what it might have to deal with?'

'I wish I had, my dear,' said Stephen. 'The *Néréide* and the *Sirius* were mentioned, to be sure, together with the *Otter* and the possibility of another sloop; but beyond that everything is nebulous. Vessels that Admiral Bertie had at the time of his latest despatches, dated more than three months ago, may very well be off Java by the time the squadron is actually formed. Nor can I speak to what Decaen may have had in Mauritius before this reinforcement, apart from the *Canonnière* and possibly the *Sémillante* – they range so wide. On the other hand I can tell you the names of their new frigates. They are the *Vénus, Manche, Bellone* and *Caroline*.'

'*Vénus, Manche, Bellone, Caroline*,' said Jack, frowning. 'I have never heard of a single one of 'em.'

'No. As I said, they are new, quite new: they carry forty guns apiece. Twenty-four pounders, at least in the case of the *Bellone* and the *Manche*: perhaps in the others too.'

'Oh, indeed?' said Jack, his eye still to his telescope. The rosy glow in his mind had strange lurid edges to it now. Those were in fact the French navy's most recent, very heavy frigates, the envy of the British dockyards. Buonaparte had all the forests of Europe at his command, splendid Dalmatian oak, tall northern spars, best Riga hemp; and although the man himself was the merest soldier, his ship-builders turned out the finest vessels afloat and he had some very capable officers to command them. Forty guns apiece. The *Néréide* had thirty-six, but only twelve-pounders: *Boadicea* and *Sirius*, with their eighteen-pounders, might be a match for the Frenchmen, particularly if the French crews were as new as their ships; but even so, that was a hundred and sixty guns to a hundred and ten to say nothing of the broadside weight of metal. Everything would depend on how those guns were handled. The other forces at the Cape hardly entered into the line of count. The flagship, the ancient *Raisonable*, 64, could no more be considered a fighting unit than the antique French *Canonnière*: he could not offhand recall the smaller vessels on the station, apart from the *Otter*, a pretty eighteen-gun ship-sloop: but in any case, if it came to a general action, the frigates alone must bear the brunt. The *Néréide* he knew of, the crack frigate of the West Indies station, and in Corbett she had a fighting captain; Pym he knew by reputation; but Clonfert of the *Otter* was the only captain he had ever sailed with . . . Across the round of his objective-glass travelled a purposeful Marine, mounted on a horse. 'O blessed form,' murmured Jack, following him behind a haystack with his telescope, 'he will be here in twenty minutes. I shall give him a guinea.' All at once the Indian Ocean, the Mauritius command, took on a new, infinitely more concrete reality: the characters of Admiral Bertie, Captain Pym, Captain Corbett and even Lord Clonfert assumed a great practical importance: so did the immediate problems of a new command. Although his intimacy with Stephen Maturin did not allow him to ask questions that might be judged impertinent, it was of such a rare kind that he could ask for money without the least hesitation. 'Have you any money, Stephen?' he said, the

Marine having vanished in the trees. 'How I hope you have. I shall have to borrow the Marine's guinea from you, and a great deal more besides, if his message is what I dearly trust. My half-pay is not due until the month after next, and we are living on credit.'

'Money, is it?' said Stephen, who had been thinking about lemurs. There were lemurs in Madagascar: might there not be lemurs on Réunion? Lemurs concealed among the forests and the mountains of the interior? 'Money? Oh, yes, I have money galore.' He felt in his pockets. 'The question is, where is it?' He felt again, patted his bosom, and brought out a couple of greasy two-pound notes on a country bank. 'That is not it,' he muttered, going through his pockets again. 'Yet I was sure – was it in my other coat? – did I perhaps leave it in London? – you are growing old, Maturin – ah, you dog, there you are!' he cried triumphantly, returning to the first pocket and drawing forth a neat roll, tied with tape. 'There. I had confused it with my lancet-case. It was Mrs Broad of the Grapes that did it up, finding it in a Bank of England wrapper that I had – that I had neglected. A most ingenious way of carrying money, calculated to deceive the pick-pocket. I hope it will suffice.'

'How much is it?' asked Jack.

'Sixty or seventy pound, I dare say.'

'But, Stephen, the top note is a fifty, and so is the next. I do not believe you ever counted them.'

'Well, never mind, never mind,' said Stephen testily. 'I meant a hundred and sixty. Indeed, I said as much, only you did not attend.'

They both straightened, cocking their ears. Through the beating of the rain came Sophie's voice calling 'Jack! Jack!' and rising to a squeak as she darted into the observatory, breathless and wet. 'There is a Marine from the port-admiral,' she said between her gasps, 'and he will not give his message except into your own hands. Oh, Jack, might it be a ship?'

A ship it was. Captain Aubrey was required and directed to

repair aboard HMS *Boadicea* and to take upon himself the command of the said vessel, for which the enclosed order was to be the warrant: he was to touch at Plymouth, there to receive on board R.T. Farquhar, Esquire, at the Commissioner's office, and any further orders that might be transmitted to him at that place. These stately, somewhat inimical documents (as usual, Captain Aubrey was to fail not, at his peril), were accompanied by a friendly note from the Admiral, asking Jack to dine with him the next day, before going aboard.

Now that direct action was legitimate, it burst forth with such force that Ashgrove Cottage was turned upside-down in a moment. At first Mrs Williams clung tenaciously to her scheme for changing the parlour curtains, clamouring that it must be done – what would Lady Clonfert think? – and protesting that she should not be overborne; but her strength was as nothing compared with that of a newly-appointed frigate-captain burning to join his ship before the evening gun, and in a few minutes she joined her daughter and the distracted maid in brushing uniforms, madly darning stockings and ironing neck-cloths, while Jack trundled his sea-chest in the attic and roared down to know where was his neat's-foot oil, and who had been at his pistols? adjuring them 'to bear a hand', 'to look alive', 'to lose not a minute below there', 'to light along the sextant-case'.

Lady Clonfert's arrival, so much in the forefront of Mrs Williams's mind not an hour before, passed almost unnoticed in the turmoil, a turmoil increased by the howling of neglected children, which reached its paroxysm as her coachman thundered on the door. A full two minutes of strenuous battering passed by before the door was opened and she was able to walk into the naked parlour, whose old curtains lay on one end of the settle and the new on the other.

Poor lady, she had but a sad time of it. She had dressed with particular care in garments designed not to offend Mrs Aubrey by being too fashionable or becoming yet at the same

time to beguile Captain Aubrey, and she had prepared an artless speech about sailors' wives, Clonfert's respect and affection for his old shipmate, and her perfect familiarity with life
aboard a man-of-war, together with some slight hints as to her
acquaintance with General Mulgrave, the First Lord, and
with Mrs Bertie, the wife of the Admiral at the Cape. This
she delivered to Stephen, wedged into a dim corner by the
clock under a drip, with some charming asides to Sophie; and
she was obliged to repeat it when Jack appeared, trailing cobwebs from the attic and bearing his chest. It is difficult to
sound artless twice in quick succession, but she did her best,
for she was sincerely devoted to the prospect of escaping an
English winter, and the idea of seeing her husband again
filled her with a pleasurable excitement. Her confusion
caused her bosom to rise and fall, a blush to overspread her
pretty face, and from his corner Stephen observed that she
was doing quite well against heavy odds – that Jack, at least,
was not unmoved by her distress. Yet he also noticed, with
regret, a certain stiffening in Sophie's attitude, a constraint in
her civil smile, and something near acerbity in her reply to
Lady Clonfert's suggestion that she too might darn the Captain's stockings and make herself useful during the voyage.
Mrs Williams's stony reserve, her repeated sniff, her ostentatious busyness, he took for granted; but although he had long
known that jealousy formed part of Sophie's character – perhaps the only part that he could have wished otherwise – he
was grieved to see it thus displayed. Jack had caught the signals as quickly as his friend – Stephen saw his anxious glance
– and his cordiality towards Lady Clonfert, never very great,
sensibly diminished; although he did repeat what he had said
at the beginning – that he should be happy to carry her ladyship to the Cape. What had preceded that glance, to make it
so anxious? Dr Maturin lapsed into a meditation upon the
marriage state: monogamy, an aberration? How widely spread
in time and place? How strictly observed? From this train of
thought he was aroused by Jack's strong voice stating that her

ladyship was certainly aware of the tediousness of tiding down the Channel, that he strongly recommended her posting to Plymouth, that he begged stores and baggage might be kept to a minimum, and that once again he must urge the most exact punctuality however short the notice: 'for his part he should gladly lose a tide to be of use, but on the King's service he must not lose a minute.'

Now everybody was standing up: soon Jack had led Lady Clonfert, under an umbrella, to her carriage, had firmly closed the door upon her, and was back in the house, his face radiating universal goodwill, as though she were utterly dismissed.

Mrs Williams was abusing Lady Clonfert's tippet, complexion and morals with a volubility that Stephen could not but admire, yet Jack's statement that a couple of hours would see his dunnage corded up, that Stephen would oblige him infinitely by riding straight to Gosport in order to bring back John Parley in Newman's dogcart to pack the telescope, and that he was determined to go aboard before the evening gun and to get the *Boadicea* to sea on the ebb, struck her dumb. It had no such effect on her daughter, however, who instantly produced a number of reasons why Jack could certainly not join tonight: the state of his linen would bring discredit on the service; it would be shockingly rude to dear, kind Admiral Wells not to dine with him, most impolitic if not direct insubordination; and Jack had always been such a friend to discipline. Besides, it was raining. It was clear to Stephen that she was not only horrified at losing Jack so soon but that she was also sorry for her recent – shrewishness was far too strong a word – for she now ran straight on into praise of their visitor. Lady Clonfert was a most elegant, well-bred woman, with remarkably fine eyes; her wish to join her husband was in every way meritorious and understandable; her presence aboard would certainly please the gunroom, indeed the whole ship's company.

Sophie then returned to arguments against Jack's leaving

quite so soon: tomorrow morning would be far, far better in every way; they could not possibly have his clothes ready before then. In spite of her nimble wit, logical arguments soon began to run short, and Stephen, feeling that at any moment she might resort to others, even to tears, or appeal to him for support, slipped quietly out of the room. He communed with his horse in its outhouse for a while, and when he came back he found Jack at the door, staring up at the scudding clouds, with Sophie, looking exceptionally beautiful in her anxiety and emotion, beside him. 'The glass is rising,' said Jack thoughtfully, 'but the wind is still due south . . . and when you consider where she lays, right up the harbour, there is not a hope of getting her out on this tide. No, my dear; perhaps you are right. Perhaps I should not go aboard until tomorrow. But tomorrow, sweetheart,' he said, looking fondly down, 'tomorrow at the crack of dawn you lose your husband to his natural element.'

2

UPON THAT DAMP element, always unstable, often treacherous, but for the moment both warm and kind, Captain Aubrey dictated an official letter to his happy clerk:

> *Boadicea*, at sea

Sir,

I have the honour to acquaint you, that at dawn on the seventeenth instant, the Dry Salvages bearing SSE two leagues, His Majesty's ship under my command had the good fortune to fall in with a French national ship of war with a prize in company. On the *Boadicea*'s approach she bore up, abandoning her prize, a snow, whose topmasts were struck down on deck. Every exertion was made in this ship to come up with the enemy, who endeavoured to lead us among the shoals of the Dry Salvages; but missing stays in consequence of the loss of her mizzen topmast, she struck upon a reef. Shortly afterwards, the wind having fallen to a flat calm, and the rocks sheltering her from the *Boadicea*'s guns, she was boarded and carried by the boats, when she proved to be the *Hébé*, formerly His Majesty's twenty-eight-gun frigate *Hyaena* but now mounting twenty-two twenty-four-pounders, carronades, and two long nines, with a complement of 214 men, commanded by Mons. Bretonnière, lieutenant de vaisseau, her captain having been killed in the action with the prize. She was thirty-eight days out of Bordeaux, on a cruise, and had taken the English vessels named in the margin.

My first lieutenant, Mr Lemuel Akers, an old and deserving officer, commanded the *Boadicea*'s boats and led the attack in the most gallant manner; while Lieutenant Seymour and Mr Johnson, master's mate, displayed great activity. Indeed I am happy to say, that the conduct of the *Boadicea*'s people gave me great satisfaction, and I have no greater loss to deplore than two men slightly wounded.

The snow was secured without delay: she is the *Intrepid Fox* of Bristol, A. Snape master, from the Guinea Coast, laden with elephants' teeth, gold-dust, grains of Paradise, hides, and skins. In view of the value of her cargo, I have thought proper to send her into Gibraltar, escorted by the *Hyaena* under the command of Lieutenant Akers.

I have the honour to be, etc.

Captain Aubrey watched his clerk's flying pen with great benevolence. The letter was true in essence, but like most official letters it contained a certain number of lies. Jack did not think Lemuel Akers a deserving officer, and the lieutenant's gallantry had in fact been confined to roaring at the *Hébé* from the stern-sheets of the launch, to which his wooden leg confined him, while the conduct of several of the *Boadicea*'s people had filled their new captain with impatience, and the snow had not been secured without delay.

'Do not forget the wounded at the bottom of the page, Mr Hill,' he said. 'James Arklow, ordinary, and William Bates, Marine. Now be so good as to let Mr Akers know that I shall have a couple of private letters for him to take to Gibraltar.'

Left alone in the great cabin he glanced out of the stern-window at the calm, crowded, sunlit sea, with his prizes lying upon it and boats plying to and fro, the *Hébé*'s or rather the *Hyaena*'s rigging full of men putting the last touches to her repairs, the shrouds of her new mizzen rattled down already: he had a first-rate bosun in John Fellowes. Then he reached out for a sheet of paper and began: 'Sweetheart – a hasty line to bring you my dear love and tell you all is well. We had an amazing prosperous voyage down as far as 35°30′, with a fine double-reefed topsail quartering breeze – *Boadicea*'s best point of sailing in her present trim – all the way from the moment we sank Rame Head right across the Bay and almost to Madeira. We put into Plymouth at the height of flood on Monday night – black, with squalls of sleet and blowing hard – and since we had made our number to Stoke Point, Mr Farquhar was ready waiting, bag and baggage, at the Commissioner's office. I sent to Lady Clonfert's inn, desiring her to be at the quay by twenty minutes past the hour; but through some mistake she did not appear, and I was obliged to proceed to sea without her.

'However, to cut things short, this pretty wind carried us across the Bay, where the *Boadicea* proved she was a dry, wholesome ship, and at one time I thought we should raise the Island in just over a week. But then it backed into the south-east and I was obliged to stretch away for Tenerife, cursing my luck: and at four bells in the morning watch I happened to be on deck to make sure the master, an ignorant old man, did not run us on the Dry Salvages as he had nearly run us on Penlee Point, when there, right under our lee at the dawn of day, was a Frenchman, lying to with her prize. She had scarcely a chance, for the prize, a well-armed Guinea-man, had mauled her briskly before she was taken; her rig-ging was all ahoo, she was bending a new foretopsail, and many of her people were in the Guineaman, setting her to rights: and of course she was not half our size. And since we had the weather-gage we could afford to yaw and let fly with our bow guns: not that it did her much harm, apart from flus-tering her people. However, she did her best, peppering us with her stern-chaser and trying to lead us into the four-fathom water of the Dog-Leg Passage. But I sounded that channel when I was a midshipman in the *Circe*, and since we draw twenty-three foot, I did not choose to follow her, although there was no swell worth speaking of. Had she got through, we might have lost her, *Boadicea* being a trifle slug-gish (though you will not repeat that anywhere, my dear); but we knocked away her mizzen topmast – she missed stays in the turn of the passage – ran on to the reef, and there being no wind could not beat across. So we lowered the boats and took her without much trouble, though I am sorry to say her commanding officer was wounded – Stephen is patching him up at this moment, poor fellow.

'There was no glory in it, sweetheart, not the least hint of danger; but the charming thing is, that she can just be called a frigate. She was our old *Hyaena*, a jackass twenty-eight as ancient as the Ark, that the French took when I was a boy: she was overgunned, of course, and they reduced her to what they rate a corvette, with twenty-four pounder carronades and a couple of long nines – I scarcely recognized her at first, she was so changed. But she is still a frigate for us, and of course she will be bought into the service (she is a fine sailer too, particularly on the wind, and we hauled her clear with no damage at all, bar a fathom or two of her copper being scraped off). And then there is head-money, and above all this

Guineaman. She is no prize to us, being English, but she is salvage, and she does represent a certain amount of cash, which, the kitchen copper being in the state it is, will not be unwelcome. Unfortunately the Admiral shares. Although mine were Admiralty orders, the cunning old dog added some nonsense of his own, to make sure of one of my eights if I took anything; and this he did in the most barefaced way, after dinner, laughing cheerfully, ha, ha. All admirals are tarred with the same brush, I fear, and I dare say we shall find the same thing at the Cape.' He had scarcely written the last word before Stephen's grave warnings about close counsel came to his mind: he carefully changed it to 'our destination', and then returned to the Guineaman. 'Ordinarily she would have been crammed with blacks for the West Indies, which would have added much to her value; but perhaps it was just as well that there were none. Stephen grows so outrageous the minute slavery is mentioned, that I dare say I should have been obliged to set them ashore to prevent his being hanged for mutiny. Only the last time I dined in the gunroom, Akers, the first lieutenant, got on to the subject, and Stephen handled him so severely, I was obliged to intervene. Mr Farquhar is of the same opinion with Stephen, and I am sure they are right – it is a very ugly thing to see, indeed – yet sometimes I cannot help feeling that a couple of biddable, able-bodied young blacks that attended to their duty and could give no month's warning might come in uncommon handy at Ashgrove Cottage. And now I am on the cottage, I have written to Ommaney to send you all he will advance on the *Hyaena* directly, with which I beg you will instantly buy yourself a pelisse and tippet against its infernal draughts, and . . .' There followed a list of domestic improvements to be made: the copper, of course; the parlour chimney to be rebuilt; Goadby to be set to work on the roof; a newly-calved Jersey cow to be bought with Mr Hick's advice. 'My dear, time is flying,' he went on. 'They are hoisting in *Hyaena*'s boats, and the snow has won her anchor. We may touch at St Helena, but otherwise I must take my leave until we reach our port. God bless and keep you, sweetheart, and the children.' He sighed; smiled, and was about to seal when Stephen walked in, looking mean and pinched. 'Stephen,' he said, 'I have just written to Sophie. Have you any message?'

'Love, of course. And compliments to Mrs Williams.'

'Lord,' cried Jack, writing fast, 'thank you for reminding me. I have explained about Lady Clonfert,' he observed, as he closed the letter up.

'Then I trust you kept your explanation short,' said Stephen. 'Circumstantial details destroy a tale entirely. The longer, the less credible.'

'I merely stated that she did not appear at the rendezvous, and passed on.'

'Nothing about three o'clock in the morning, the hocus-pocus at the inn, signals disregarded, the boat being made to row as though we were escaping from the Day of Judgment, and the lady ditched?' asked Stephen, with the unpleasant creaking noise that was his nearest approach to a laugh.

'What a rattle you are, to be sure,' said Jack. 'Come now, Stephen, how is your patient?'

'Why, he has lost a great deal of blood, it cannot be denied; but then on the other hand I have rarely seen a man with so much blood to lose. He should do very well, with the blessing. He has the late captain's cook with him, a famous artist, and desires he may be kept aboard, if agreeable to the gallant victor.'

'Capital, capital. A famous artist in the galley will set the crown on a very pretty morning's work. Was it not a very pretty morning's work, Stephen?'

'Well,' said Stephen, 'I wish you joy of your capture with all my heart; but if by "pretty" we are to understand an elegant economy of means, I cannot congratulate you. All this banging of great guns for so pitiful a result as the mizzen topmast of a little small slip of a thing, and it embarrassed among the rocks, the creature – Armageddon come before its time. And the infamous backing and filling before the Guineaman is even approached, in spite of her captain's ardent pleas; and all this interminable while no one is allowed to set foot upon these rocks, on the grounds that not a minute is to be lost. Not a minute, forsooth: and forty-seven are wantonly thrown away – forty-seven minutes of invaluable observation that will never be made up.'

'What I know, Stephen, and what you don't know,' began Jack, but a messenger interrupted him: with the Captain's leave, Mr Akers was ready to go aboard. On deck Jack found the south-west breeze setting in steadily, just as if it had been ordered, a perfect breeze to waft the *Hyaena* and her charge to Gibraltar. He gave his letters to the first lieutenant, again recommended the utmost vigilance, and urged him towards the side. Mr Akers displayed a tendency to linger, to express his extreme gratitude for his command (and indeed the recovered *Hyaena* meant his promotion) and to assure Captain Aubrey that if a single prisoner showed his nose above the hatchway it should instantly be blown off with his own grapeshot, but presently he was gone; and leaning over the rail Jack watched the *Boadicea*'s boats carrying him and his companions away. Some went to the man-of-war, to work the ship and guard the prisoners; some to the *Intrepid Fox*, to strengthen her sickly and diminished crew: a surprising number of men in both cases.

Few captains, far from a press-gang, a receiving-ship or any other source of hands, could have smiled at the sight of so many of them pulling awkwardly away to other vessels, never, in all probability, to be seen again, but Jack beamed like the rising sun. Captain Loveless had had excellent connections, and the *Boadicea* a plethoric crew: a good average crew, upon the whole, with no more than a fair share of landsmen and with a gratifying proportion of hands who deserved their rating of able seaman; yet with a number of hard cases too, not worth the food they ate nor the space they occupied, while the last draft had been made up entirely of quota-men from

Bedfordshire, odd misfits, petty criminals and vagrants, not one of whom had ever used the sea. The *Hébé*'s English prisoners, right sailormen taken out of British ships for the most part, together with a couple of prime hands pressed from the *Intrepid Fox*, far more than compensated for their loss; and now, with real satisfaction, Jack watched eight sodomites, three notorious thieves, four men whose wits were quite astray, and a parcel of inveterate skulkers and sea-lawyers go off for good. He was also happy to be rid of a great lout of a midshipman who made the youngsters' lives a burden to them: but above all he was delighted to be seeing the last of his first lieutenant. Mr Akers was a harsh, greying, saturnine man with one leg; the pain from his wound often made him savagely ill-tempered; and he did not see eye to eye with Jack on a number of matters, including flogging. Yet far more important, honourable wound or not, Akers was no seaman: when Jack had first stepped aboard the frigate he found her lying with two round turns and an elbow in her cables, a very disgusting sight; they had lost an hour and twenty minutes clearing their hawse, with *Boadicea*'s signal to proceed to sea flying all the time, reinforced by guns at frequent intervals: and this impression of busy, angry inefficiency had grown stronger day by day.

So there it was: he had made two charming captures; at the same time he had freed himself of men whose presence would have gone far towards preventing the frigate's becoming a fully efficient instrument for distressing the enemy, let alone a happy ship, and he had done so in a way that would confer the utmost benefit on Mr Akers. That was where the prettiness lay. He was now in command of a crew whose collective seamanship was already tolerably good in spite of the remaining fifty or sixty raw hands, and whose gunnery, though of the lowest standard, as it so often was under officers whose one idea of action was a yardarm-to-yardarm engagement where no shot could miss, was certainly capable of improvement. 'Vast capabilities, ma'am, vast capabilities,' he murmured; and then his smile changed to an inward chuckle as he recollected that for once his low cunning had over-reached Stephen Maturin: for what Jack knew, and what Stephen did not, was that those forty-seven minutes had made all the difference between salvage and no salvage, between the *Boadicea's* right to an eighth of the Guineaman's value and a mere letter of thanks from her owners. The *Intrepid Fox* had been taken at forty-six minutes past ten on Tuesday, and if he had accepted the surrender of the French prize-master one moment before twenty-four hours had passed, by sea-law the Guineaman would not have been salvage at all. And as for Stephen's passing three quarters of an hour on the Dry Salvages, searching for problematical bugs, Jack had set him down on remote oceanic rocks before now, and had been obliged to have him removed by armed force, long, long after the appointed time: but, however, he would make it up to him – there were coral reefs in plenty on the far side of the Cape.

'Frigate signalling, sir, if you please,' said the signal-midshipman. '*Permission to part company.*'

'Say *carry on,*' replied Jack. 'And add *happy return.*' The *Hyaena* dropped her topsails neatly, sheeted them home and gathered way, followed by the Guineaman a cable's length to leeward; and having watched them for a while, true on their course for Gibraltar, Jack gave orders that would carry the *Boadicea* slanting away towards the tropic line, close-hauled on the freshening breeze, and walked into his great cabin. The bulkheads, knocked down when the frigate cleared for action, were already back in place, and the two massive eighteen-pounders were housed again, fore and aft; but the starboard gun was still warm, and the smell of powder and slow-match hung about the air, the most exhilarating scent by land or sea. The beautiful room was all his own, with its noble space and its gleaming curve of stern-windows, in spite of his distinguished passenger; for although Mr Farquhar was to be a governor, his status was still highly theoretical, since it depended on the defeat of a powerful French squadron and on the conquest of the islands he was to govern; and for the moment he had to be content with what would otherwise have been the captain's dining-cabin. Jack threw one last loving glance at his captures, dwindling northwards over the sparkling light-blue sea, and called out, 'Pass the word for Mr Seymour, Mr Trollope and Mr Johnson.'

Seymour, the second lieutenant, and Trollope, the third, followed by Johnson, a master's mate, hurried in, looking pleased but somewhat apprehensive: they knew very well that the *Boadicea*, though successful, had not distinguished herself, particularly in the operation of hauling the *Hyaena* off her innocuous ledge of rock and towing her clear of the channel and they were by no means sure what their new captain would have to say. Seymour and Johnson might almost have been brothers, short, pink, chubby men with round heads and fresh open faces upon which their expression of respectful sobriety seemed less natural than cheerfulness: they were the kind of men Jack had seen a hundred times in his career, and he was happy to have them aboard. He had seen other Trollopes too; Trollope was a big man, black-haired, with a dark, unhumorous, determined face and a strong jaw; he might be a right hard-horse lieutenant under the wrong kind of commander, or a devil of a captain himself, if ever he reached post rank. But for the moment he was young; he was not yet set. They were all young, though Johnson might be nearing thirty – old for his station.

Jack knew very well what was in their minds; as a lieutenant he had often been summoned to bear the blame for others' shortcomings. But what he did not know was that the deferential expression on the faces of these capable, enterprising, seasoned young men was the outcome not merely of respect for his rank but of something resembling awe of his reputation in the service: in his fourteen-gun brig the *Sophie* he had taken the thirty-two-gun Spanish *Cacafuego*; he was one of the few frigate-captains who had ever attacked a

French ship of the line, a seventy- four; as acting-captain of
the *Lively* he had compelled the *Clara* and the *Fama*,
Spaniards of equal force, to strike to him in the memorable
frigate-action off Cadiz; and in cutting-out operations and in
generally harassing the enemy he had few equals among
those of his standing in the Navy list. Jack neither knew it nor
suspected it, partly because he still felt very much their contemporary, and partly because he sincerely regarded his more
outstanding actions as the effect of luck: he had happened to
be on the spot, and in his place any other sea-officer would
have done the same. This was not false modesty: he had
known officers by the score, good officers, excellent seamen,
their courage beyond question, who had served throughout
the wars without any chance of distinguishing themselves;
men on convoy-duty, in transports, or even in the ships of the
line perpetually blockading Brest and Toulon, who very often
encountered danger, but from the violence of the sea rather
than that of the enemy, and who therefore remained obscure,
often unpromoted and always poor: had they been in the right
place at the right time, they would have done as well or better: it was a question of luck.

'Well, gentlemen,' he said, 'this is quite a pleasant beginning to a voyage. But we have lost Mr Akers. Mr Seymour,
you will be so good as to take his place.'

'Thank you, sir,' said Seymour.

'And Mr Johnson, you have passed for lieutenant, I
believe?'

'Oh, yes, sir. On the first Wednesday in August, 1802,' said
Johnson, blushing and then turning remarkably pale. He had
passed, but as it happened for so many other midshipmen
with no influence, the longed-for commission had never
come. All these years he had been a master's mate, a senior
midshipman, no more, the likelihood of promotion fading
with every birthday; it had almost vanished now, and he
seemed fated to end his career as a master at the best, a mere
warrant-officer until he was thrown on the beach, with never

a command of his own. And in the *Boadicea* there were midshipmen with claims far higher than his own: Captain Loveless had shipped the godson of one admiral, the nephew of another, and the heir of the member for Old Sarum; whereas Johnson's father was only a retired lieutenant.

'Then,' said Jack, 'I shall give you an order as acting-lieutenant, and let us hope the Admiral at the Cape will confirm it.'

Johnson, flushed scarlet now, brought out his acknowledgments, and Jack hurried on, 'For I will not disguise from you, gentlemen, that the Cape is our destination. And what you may not know, is that there are four French forty-gun frigates waiting for us round the other side of it. Now today's little brush was very well in its way. It pleased the raw hands – entered 'em, as you might say – and it clapped a stopper over the *Hébé*'s capers; she had been playing Old Harry with our trade these past few weeks. So I believe we may drink a glass of wine to it. Probyn!' he called, Probyn being his steward. 'Rouse out a bottle of Madeira and then jump forward and see that the French captain's cook is comfortably stowed: use him civil. Here's to the *Hyaena*, ex-*Hébé*, then; and a safe landfall to her.' They drank gravely, certain that this was by no means all the Captain had to say. 'Very well in its way,' he continued, 'but I scarcely suppose that anyone of you would have called it pretty.'

'Not quite in your Minorca style, sir,' said Trollope. Jack looked hard at the lieutenant. Had they ever been shipmates? He could not recall his face.

'I was a midshipman in *Amelia*, sir, when you brought the *Cacafuego* into Mahon. Lord, how we cheered the *Sophie*!'

'Was you, though?' said Jack, somewhat embarrassed. 'Well, I am glad it was not the *Cacafuego* we came upon today, let alone one of those Frenchmen round the Cape; because although the Boadiceas seem a willing, decent set upon the whole – no sign of shyness that I could see – their gunnery is pitiful beyond all description. And as for pulling, never, never have I seen so many creatures in human shape incapable of handling an oar: in the red cutter there was not one single man apart from old Adams and a Marine that knew how to pull. But it is the gunnery that is my chief concern: pitiful, pitiful . . . Broadside after broadside at five hundred yards and even less; and where did they go? Not aboard the Frenchman, gentlemen. The only shot that told was the one fired from the bow-chaser, and that was pointed by Jack of the breadroom, who had no business to be on deck at all. Now do but imagine that we had run into a well worked-up French frigate, hulling us with her twenty-four-pounders at the best part of a mile: for their practice is devilish accurate, as I dare say you know.' In the solemn pause that followed he refilled their glasses and went on, 'But thank God this happened early: it could not have fallen better. The raw hands are over their sea-sickness; they are all pleased with themselves, poor honest lubbers; and every foremast Jack is richer by a year's pay, all won in a sunny morning. They must be made to understand that by teaching them their duty we are putting them in the way of getting more. They will attend now, with a good heart; no need for rattans and the rope's end. By the time we reach the Cape, gentlemen, I trust that every man and boy on the ship's books will at least be able to pull an oar, hand and reef a sail, load, point and fire a musket and a gun: and if they can learn no more than that, and to be obedient to command, why, we shall be in a fair way to meet any French frigate on the far side of it.'

With the lieutenants gone, Jack considered for a while. He had no doubt that they were entirely with him; they were the sort of men he knew and liked; but there was still a great deal to be done. With their help he might make the *Boadicea* into a most lethal floating battery of tremendous power; but still she had to be brought to the scene of action, brought as rapidly as the elements would allow. He sent for the master and the bosun, and to them he stated that he was not satisfied with the frigate's sailing, either in the article of speed or in that of lying close to the wind.

There followed a highly technical conference in which he encountered steady resistance from Buchan, the master, an elderly man set in his ways, who would not admit that any restowing of the hold, any attempt to bring her by the head, would have the least favourable effect. Slow she had always been and slow she always would be: he had always stowed the hold in exactly the same way, ever since he had been in her. The bosun, on the other hand, a young man for his important office, a seaman through and through, brought up in the North Sea colliers, was as eager as his captain to get the best out of the *Boadicea*, even if it meant trying something new. He spoke feelingly on the good effect of cat-harpins, well-sniftered in; he entirely agreed with the plan for raking the foremast; Jack's heart warmed to him.

At least a part of Mr Buchan's sullenness arose from hunger. The gunroom dined at one o'clock, an hour now long past; and although today dinner would have been indifferent in any case, its absence rendered the master positively morose. The bosun had dined at noon together with the carpenter and the gunner, and Buchan, smelling both food and grog upon him, hated his cheerful face; even more his steady flow of talk.

Jack too was somewhat given to worshipping his belly, and when he had dismissed them he walked into the coach: here he found Stephen and Mr Farquhar, eating cake. 'Do I interrupt you?' he asked: not at all, they said, clearing a space for him among the books, documents, maps, proclamations and broadsheets that they were trying to reassemble after the abrupt disappearance and reappearance of their quarters. 'I hope I see you well, sir?' he said to Mr Farquhar, who had suffered more than most in the Bay of Biscay and who had spent much of the time since rising from his cot in conference with Dr Maturin, the two of them deep in papers, talking foreign to the intense vexation of their servants, two ship's boys told off to look after them, who liked to indulge their natural curiosity – a curiosity much stimulated by their ship-

mates before the mast, eager to know what was afoot. Farquhar had lost a stone, and his lean, intelligent, hook-nosed
face still had a greenish tinge, but he replied that he had
never felt better in his life, that the tremendous din of battle,
the more than Jovian thunder of the guns, had completed the
work – with a civil bow to Stephen – of Dr Maturin's preternatural physic, so that he felt like a boy again; he had a boy's
appetite, a restless eagerness to be at table. 'But,' he went on,
'you must first allow me to congratulate you most heartily
upon your splendid victory. Such instant decision, such a
determined onslaught, and such a happy issue!'

'You are too kind, sir, too kind by half. But as for the happy
issue that you are so obliging as to mention, it has one aspect
that cannot but rejoice us all. We have the French captain's
cook aboard, and I am come' – turning towards Stephen – 'to
ask whether you think he might be persuaded . . . ?'

'I have already attended to him,' said Stephen. 'A sucking
pig, one of a large surviving farrow, was one of the few casualties aboard the *Hébé*, and I understand that it is to provide a
first example of his powers. I have also seen to it that Monsieur Bretonnière's wine and comforts have been transferred:
to these I thought fit to add his late captain's stores; foie gras
in jars, truffles in goose-grease, pieces of goose in goose-
grease, a large variety of dried sausages, Bayonne hams, pot-
ted anchovies; and among the rest of the wine, twenty-one
dozens of Margaux of '88, with the long cork, together with
an almost equal quantity of Château Lafite. Sure, I cannot
tell how we shall ever get through them all; yet it would be
the world's shame to let such noble wine go back, and in
these conditions another year must see it the mere ghost of
itself.'

The claret never saw another year, however, nor did that
splendid vintage go to waste: with steady application and
with some help from Bretonnière and other guests from the
gunroom Jack and Stephen drank almost every drop as the
days went by. And there were days enough in all conscience,

since the kind winds of their departure deserted them well north of the line, and sometimes they would lie on the oily, heaving sea, drifting slowly towards America on the equatorial current, with the *Boadicea's* figurehead simpering all round the compass and the frigate nearly rolling her masts by the board. Ten days on end when she wallowed with flaccid sails on the stagnant water, clean in herself but so surrounded by the filth of three hundred men – by Admiral Brown as the old hands called it – and by her own empty beef-casks, peelings and general rubbish that Jack was obliged to take the jolly-boat a quarter of a mile away for his morning's swim, while at the same time he caused the crew to tow their ship, thus rendering the view more agreeable and training them in the art of managing an oar, so beating two birds with one bush, as he put it, or even three, since after they had pulled her for an hour or two it was the *Boadicea's* custom to lower a sail into the pure, tepid water, buoying its outer corners and thereby making a shallow pool in which those who could not swim – the great majority – might splash about and enjoy themselves, perhaps learning how to stay afloat in the process.

But they crossed the line itself in style, with studdingsails aloft and alow, and with more than the usual merriment, for when they reduced sail to let Neptune come aboard, accompanied by an outrageously lewd Amphitrite and Badger-Bag, he found no less than a hundred and twenty-three souls who had to be made free of the equator by being lathered with rancid grease – tar was forbidden, being in short supply – and shaved with a piece of barrel-hoop before being ducked.

Southward still, with Canopus and Achernar high overhead, and Jack showed his attentive midshipmen the new constellations, Musca, Pavo, Chamaeleon and many more, all glowing in the warm, pellucid air.

Strange, unpredictable weather, for even when the *Boadicea* found the trades in 4° south they proved apathetic and fitful. It was clear that this was not to be a rapid passage,

but although Jack often whistled for a breeze, a stronger
breeze, he was not deeply worried by the length of their voyage: his ship was well-found, several storms of rain had filled
her water, and her men were remarkably healthy; and as the
weeks turned into months it came to him that this was a
happy period, a time set apart, lying between the anxieties of
home on the one hand and those that would surely be waiting
for him in the Indian Ocean, where his real work would
begin. And then although he longed for the 'real thing' to
start, he knew that no power on earth could bring him to it
any earlier: he and Fellowes had done all they could to
increase the frigate's rate of sailing, and they had accomplished much; but they could not command the wind. So
with a tranquil conscience and that fatalism which sailors
must acquire if they are not to perish of frustration, he
rejoiced in this opportunity for making the *Boadicea* into
something like his notion of a crack frigate, a fighting-
machine manned entirely by able seamen, man-of-war's men,
everyone of them an expert gun-layer and a devil with the
boarding-axe and cutlass.

Insensibly the lubberly part of the *Boadicea*'s crew began to
resemble sailormen as the unchanging naval routine came to
be their only real way of life, a life in which it was natural and
inevitable that all hands should be piped just before eight
bells in the middle watch and that the sleepers should start
from their hammocks to the muster and then to the scrubbing of the decks in the first light of dawn; that all hands
should be piped to dinner at eight bells in the forenoon
watch, that this dinner should consist of cheese and duff on
Monday, two pounds of salt beef on Tuesday, dried peas and
duff on Wednesday, one pound of salt pork on Thursday,
dried peas and cheese on Friday, two more pounds of salt
beef on Saturday, a pound of salt pork and some such treat as
figgy-dowdy on Sunday, always accompanied by a daily pound
of biscuit; that at one bell dinner should be followed by a pint
of grog, that after supper (with another pint of grog) all hands

should repair to their action-stations at the beat of the drum, and that eventually hammocks should be piped down so that the watch below might have four hours of sleep before being roused again at midnight for another spell on deck. This and the perpetual living movement of the deck underfoot, and the sight of nothing but the Atlantic Ocean clear round the horizon, nothing but endless sea and sky, cut them off from the land so completely that it seemed another world, with no immediacy at all, and they adopted the values of the sea.

They also came to resemble sailormen in appearance, since one hour and forty minutes after the *Boadicea* had passed under the tropic of Cancer the carpenter's mate banged two brass nails into the deck, exactly twelve yards apart: twelve yards of duck, needles and thread were served out to each man, together with sennet, and they were desired to make themselves hot-weather frocks, trousers and broad-brimmed hats. This they did, helped by their handier colleagues, to such effect that at next Sunday's divisions the landsmen dressed in a mixture of rag-fair clothes and purser's slops, old leather breeches, greasy waistcoats and battered hats, had vanished, and their captain paced along lines of men as clean and white in their way as the Marines, drawn up on the quarterdeck, were clean and red in theirs.

There were still some fools belonging to the afterguard who were only good for heaving on a given rope; there were a dozen or so in either watch whose heads could not stand the swingeing ration of grog and who were continually punished for drunkenness; and there were some remaining hard cases; but on the whole he was pleased with them: a very decent set of men. He was pleased with his officers too, apart from Buchan and the purser, a very tall yellow-faced man with knock-knees and huge splay feet, upon whose books Jack kept a very sharp eye indeed: all three lieutenants seconded him with admirable zeal, and the older midshipmen were of real value.

Not the least part of that wonderfully lucky stroke off the

Dry Salvages was the *Boadicea*'s acquisition of a large quantity of ammunition. Regulations confined Jack to a hundred
round-shot for each of his long eighteen-pounders, and he
had to hoard them with jealous care, for there was no certainty of any more at the Cape – a wretched situation in
which he knew that if he did not train his gun-crews by firing
live they would not know how to do it when the moment
came, and that if he did then at the same critical juncture
they might have nothing left to fire – but from that blessed
day onwards the *Boadicea*'s daily exercise with the great guns
had not been the usual dumb-show. Certainly the crews rattled their eighteen-pounders in and out, going through all the
motions of firing them, from casting loose to housing; but
since the *Hébé*'s twenty-four-pound balls fitted the *Boadicea*'s
carronades and her nine-pound the two chase-guns, every
evening heard their savage roar: every man was accustomed
to the deadly leap of the recoiling gun, to the flash and the
din and to seizing his tackle, rammer or wad with automatic
speed in the dense swirling powder-smoke. And on high days,
as when they saluted the tropic of Capricorn with a double
broadside, it was a pleasure to see their spirit: they demolished a raft of empty beef-barrels at something over five hundred yards and ran their guns up again, cheering madly, to
blast the scattered remains in a trifle less than two minutes.
It was nothing like the mortal rate of fire that Jack so valued;
it was not even the three broadsides in five minutes that was
coming to be thought normal by those captains who cared for
gunnery, far less the three in two minutes that Jack had
achieved in other commissions; but it was accurate, and a
good deal faster than some ships he knew.

   This 'time out', this happy interval with a straightforward
and agreeable task in hand, sailing through warm seas with
winds that, though often languid, were rarely downright contrary, sailing southwards in a comfortable ship with an excellent cook, ample stores and good company, had its less
delightful sides, however.

His telescope was a disappointment. It was not that he could not see Jupiter: the planet gleamed in his eyepiece like a banded gold pea. But because of the ship's motion he could not keep it there long enough or steadily enough to fix the local time of its moons' eclipses and thus find his longitude. Neither the theory (which was by no means new) nor the telescope was at fault: it was the cleverly weighted cradle slung from the maintopgallantmast stay that he had designed to compensate for the pitch and roll that did not answer, in spite of all his alterations; and night after night he swung there cursing and swearing, surrounded by midshipmen armed with clean swabs, whose duty it was to enhance the compensation by thrusting him gently at the word of command.

The young gentlemen: he led them a hard life, insisting upon a very high degree of promptitude and activity; but apart from these sessions with the telescope, which they loathed entirely, and from their navigation classes, they thoroughly approved of their captain and of the splendid breakfasts and dinners to which he often invited them, although on due occasion he beat them with frightful strength on the bare breech in his cabin, usually for such crimes as stealing the gunroom's food or repeatedly walking about with their hands in their pockets. For his part he found them an engaging set of young fellows, though given to lying long in their hammocks, to consulting their ease, and to greed; and in one of them, Mr Richardson, generally known as Spotted Dick, because of his pimples, he detected a mathematician of uncommon promise. Jack taught them navigation himself, the *Boadicea*'s schoolmaster being incapable of maintaining discipline, and it soon became apparent to him that he should have to keep his wits as sharp as his razor not to be outstripped by his pupil in the finer points of spherical trigonometry, to say nothing of the stars.

Then there was Mr Farquhar. Jack esteemed him as an intelligent, capable, gentlemanlike man with remarkable powers of conversation, excellent company for the space of a dinner, although he drank no wine, or even for a week; but Mr Farquhar had been bred to the law, and perhaps because of this a little too much of his conversation took the form of questioning, so that Jack sometimes felt that he was being examined at his own table. Furthermore, Mr Farquhar often used Latin expressions that made Jack uneasy, and referred to authors Jack had never read: Stephen had always done the same (indeed, it would have been difficult to refer to any author with whom Jack was acquainted apart from those who wrote on fox-hunting, naval tactics, or astronomy), but with Stephen it was entirely different. Jack loved him, and had not the least objection to granting him all the erudition in the world, while remaining inwardly convinced that in all practical matters other than physic and surgery Stephen should never be allowed out alone. Mr Farquhar, however, seemed to assume that a deep knowledge of the law and of the public business embraced the whole field of useful human endeavour.

Yet Mr Farquhar's vastly superior knowledge of politics and even his far more galling superiority at chess would have been as nothing if he had had some ear for music: he had none. It was their love of music that had brought Jack and Stephen together in the first place: the one played the fiddle and the other the 'cello, neither brilliantly, yet both well enough to take deep pleasure in their evening concerts after retreat; they had played throughout every voyage they had made together, never interrupted by anything but the requirements of the service, the utmost extremity of foul weather, or by the enemy. But now Mr Farquhar was sharing the great cabin, and he was as indifferent to Haydn as he was to Mozart; as he observed, he would not give a farthing candle for either of them, or for Handel. The rustling of his book as they played, the way he tapped his snuffbox and blew his nose, took away from their pleasure; and in any case, Jack, brought up in the tradition of naval hospitality, felt bound to do all he could to make his guest comfortable, even to the extent of giving up his fiddle in favour of whist, which he did not care for, and of calling in the senior Marine lieutenant as the fourth, a man he did not much care for either.

Their guest was not always with them, however, for during the frequent calms Jack often took the jolly-boat and rowed away to swim, to inspect the frigate's trim from a distance, and to talk with Stephen in private. 'You cannot possibly dislike him,' he said, skimming over the swell towards a patch of drifting weed where Stephen thought it possible they might find a southern variety of sea-horse or a pelagic crab related to those he had discovered under the line, 'but I shall not be altogether sorry to set him down on shore,'

'I can and do dislike him intensely when he pins my king and a rook with his lurking knight,' said Stephen, 'At most other times I find him a valuable companion, an eager, searching, perspicacious intelligence. To be sure, he has no ear at all, but he is not without a tincture of poetry: he has an interesting theory on the mystic role of kings, founded upon his study of tenures in petty serjeanty,'

Jack's concern with petty serjeanty was so slight that he carried straight on, 'I dare say I have been in command too long. When I was a lieutenant, messing with the rest, I used to put up with people far, far more trying than Farquhar, There was a surgeon in the *Agamemnon* that used to play 'Greensleeves' on his flute every evening, and every evening he broke down at exactly the same place. Harry Turnbull, our premier – he was killed at the Nile —used to turn pale as he came nearer and nearer to it. That was in the West Indies, and tempers were uncommon short but no one said anything except Clonfert. It don't sound much, 'Greensleeves', but it was a pretty good example of that give and take there has to be, when you are all crammed up together for a long commission: for if you start falling out, why, there's an end to all comfort, as you know very well, Stephen. I wish I may not have lost the way of it, what with age and the luxury of being post – the luxury of solitude.'

'So you are acquainted with Lord Clonfert, I find? What kind of a man is he, tell?'

'Ours was a very slight acquaintance,' said Jack evasively. 'He only came into the ship just before we were ordered home, and then he exchanged into the *Mars*.'

'An able, dashing man, I believe?'

'Oh,' said Jack, gazing beyond Stephen's head at the *Boadicea*, a lovely sight on the lonely sea, 'the *Agamemnon*'s wardroom was crowded, she wearing a flag; so I hardly knew him. But he has made quite a reputation for himself since those days.'

Stephen sniffed. He was perfectly aware of Jack's dislike for saying anything unpleasant about a former shipmate, and although he honoured the principle in theory, in practice he found it somewhat irritating.

Jack's acquaintance with Lord Clonfert had in fact been brief, but it had left its mark. They had been ordered away with the boats to take, burn or destroy a privateer lying far up a broad, shallow creek, out of range of the *Agamemnon*'s guns, an estuary lined with mangroves, whose unbuoyed channels through the mudbanks presented many interesting problems of navigation, particularly as the boats had to advance against the fire of the privateer and of some guns planted on the shore.

Clonfert's boats took the north channel, Jack's the southern; and by the time for the final dash across the open water where the privateer was moored Clonfert's were grouped behind a spit of land somewhat nearer to the ship than Jack's. Jack emerged from the narrow channel, waved his hat, gave a cheer, urged his men 'to stretch out now, like good 'uns' and steered straight for the enemy's starboard mainchains through the heavy smoke, convinced that Clonfert's party would board on the other side. He heard the answering cheer, but it was the cheer of spectators rather than of participants: Clonfert's boats did not intend to stir. Jack realized this in the last fifty yards, but he was committed and it was too late to do anything but race on. The privateersmen fought hard: they killed several Agamemnons, among them a midshipman to whom Jack was much attached, and wounded many more. For some minutes it was doubtful who should drive whom over the side – a cruel, bitter little action, vicious hand-to-hand murder in the fading light – and then the French Captain, flinging his empty pistols at Jack's head, leapt the rail and swam for it, followed by most of his remaining men. It was not the safety of the shore that he was seeking, however, but the second battery of guns that he had mounted there; and these he turned straight on to the ship, to sweep her deck with grape at point-blank range. Although Jack had received a shrewd rap on the head, his wits were about him still, and before the first discharge he had cut the cables and let fall the foretopsail to the nascent land-breeze, so that there was already way upon her when the fire began. With the luck that never deserted him in those days he steered her through the one channel in which she would not ground, and the light air took her out; though not before the grapeshot had wounded another man, cut away the crossjack halliards, and scored him across the ribs with a wound like a blow from a red-hot poker, knocking him flat into a pool of blood. They picked up the other boats and returned to the *Agamemnon*, Clonfert taking over.

Jack was scarcely conscious of going up the side. He grieved extremely for the boy who had been killed; his mind was dulled by pain and by the fever that followed so quickly in that climate; and Clonfert's eager explanation – 'he was right up against a mudbank – he was pinned down by the shore-battery – it would have been suicide to move – he was in the very act of landing to take it from behind when Aubrey made his gallant dash' – seemed to him uninteresting and unimportant. Later, when he was fit for duty again, it did seem to him a little strange that the official letter should have omitted his name and have given Clonfert quite so much credit; though indeed Clonfert was senior to him at that time;

and then again half a dozen privateersmen, unable to swim, had taken refuge below, where they had had to be overcome after Clonfert's taking over. But by that time Clonfert had exchanged into the *Mars*; and Jack, homeward-bound in the *Agamemnon*, soon forgot the incident, retaining only an inward conviction that Clonfert was either singularly muddle-headed and unenterprising or that he was somewhat shy. None of the other officers in the wardroom offered an opinion – their silence was significant – and in the turmoil of the succeeding years Jack would scarcely have remembered Clonfert but for the noise he made sometimes in the newspapers, as when he was cast in damages for criminal conversation with Mrs Jennings, or on the occasion of his court-martial for striking another officer on the quarterdeck of HMS *Ramillies*, and sometimes more creditably in the Gazette. His court-martial had led to his being dismissed the service, and although after some time he had been reinstated by order-in-council he necessarily lost seniority: on the other hand, during the interval he took service with the Turks, and the experience proved uncommonly useful when, as a king's officer once more, he attached himself to Sir Sydney Smith. He was with that somewhat flamboyant gentleman at Acre when Smith forced Buonaparte to retire, and in other creditable actions, mostly on shore; and Smith praised him highly in his public letters: indeed Clonfert and the Admiral agreed well together – they were both seen walking about London wearing Oriental robes – and it was due to him that Clonfert was made a commander, his present rank. Jack was well aware that Gazettes might suppress truth and suggest falsehood, but he knew that they could not possibly invent victories such as the destruction of a Turkish squadron or the spiking of the guns of Abydos; and on these occasions it occurred to him that he might have been mistaken about Clonfert's want of courage. The reflection did not linger, however: quite apart from the fact that Clonfert was not a man whom Jack had taken to, he was a follower of Smith; and

Smith, though dashing, was a vain, showy man who had given Nelson much uneasiness in the Mediterranean. Jack's admiration and respect for Nelson was such that his opponents could find no friend in Captain Aubrey. His mind ran on to admirals, their rivalries, the ill effect of these rivalries, the problems of high and necessarily remote command.

'Why, brother, what a study you are in,' said Stephen. 'We shall certainly row clean through my weed, if you go on at this unconsidered pace. Pray, what is in your mind? Dread of the French, no doubt?'

'Certainly,' said Jack, shipping his oars, 'they make my heart die within me. But what concerns me most, as we get nearer to the Cape, is the possibility of a pendant, and what comes with it.'

'I do not understand you – a little to the left, if you please; I believe I see a cephalopod among the wrack. He is gone, the thief. Row gently, joy, and I shall trail my little net. I do not understand you: the ship has a perfectly good pendant at this moment; surely you must have noticed it.' He nodded towards the *Boadicea*, from whose masthead dropped the long streamer that showed she was in commission.

'What I mean is the broad pendant.' Stephen looked stupid. 'The *broad* pendant, Stephen, that shows you are a commodore: and what comes with it is high command. For the first time you are as who should say a flag, an admiral; and you have an admiral's responsibilities of command.'

'What of it, my dear? To my certain knowledge you have always exercised command efficiently: I doubt I could have done much better myself. You say belay, and he belayeth. What more can you desire, for all love?' Stephen spoke with only a small part of his attention: all the rest was concentrated upon the cephalopod, though indeed he did murmur something about commodores – he remembered them perfectly – the chief Indiaman of the fleet that had succoured them so providentially after their affray with Monsieur de Linois had been called the commodore.

'Why, don't you see,' cried Jack, his mind fixed upon this question of command, 'it has always been the command of a single ship. You are bred up to it – it comes natural. But high command is something you come to suddenly, with no experience. There are captains under you; and handling the captains of a squadron, each one of them God the Father of his own quarterdeck, is a very different matter from handling a ship's company under your own eye. You can rarely choose them and you can rarely get rid of them; and if you do not handle them right, then the squadron is inefficient, and there's the devil to pay with tar. A good understanding is more important than I can tell you. Nelson could do it as easy as kiss my hand . . . the band of brothers, you know . . .' His voice trailed away, and as he watched Stephen grubbing among the weed he thought of cases where admirals or commodores had lacked the Nelson touch: a melancholy list – bitter ill-feeling, indecisive actions, golden opportunities thrown away for lack of support, strict obedience to the letter of the Fighting Instructions, courts-martial, and above all the enemy roaming about the sea unchecked. 'Corbett's reputation is sound enough, so is Pym's,' he said almost to himself, and then louder, 'But now I come to think of it, Stephen, you should know all about Clonfert. He is a countryman of yours, an eminent chap, I dare say, in Ireland.'

'Sure, it is an Irish title,' said Stephen, 'but Clonfert is as much an Englishman as you are yourself. The family name is Scroggs. They have some acres of bog and what they call a castle near Jenkinsville in the bleak north – I know it well; anthea foetidissima grows there – and a demesne south of the Curragh of Kildare, forfeited Desmond land; but I doubt he has ever set foot on it. A Scotch agent looks after what rents he can rack out of the tenants.'

'But he is a peer, is he not? A man of some real consequence?'

'Bless your innocence, Jack: an Irish peer is not necessarily a man of any consequence at all. I do not wish to make any uncivil reflection on your country – many of my best friends are Englishmen – but you must know that this last hundred years and more it has been the practice of the English ministry to reward their less presentable followers with Irish titles; and your second-rate jobbing backstairs politician, given a coronet of sorts and transplanted into a country where he is a stranger, is a pitiful spectacle, so he is; a flash Brummagem imitation of the real thing. I should be sorry if the Irish peers, for the most part of them, were Irishmen. Apart from certain naval lords, that the ministry dare not have in the English House, they are a shabby crew, upon the whole, out of place in Ireland and ill at ease in England. I do not speak of your Fitzgeralds or Butlers, you understand, still less of the few native families that have survived, but of what is commonly called an Irish peer. Clonfert's grandfather, now, was a mere – Jack, what are you about?'

'I am taking off my shirt.'

'To swim so soon after dinner, and such a dinner? I cannot advise it. You are very corpulent; full of gross, viscous humours after these weeks and months of Poirier's cooking. And now we are come to the point, my dear, it is my clear duty to warn you against gule, against ungoverned appetite . . . a brutish vice, inductive mainly to the sin of Eve . . . bulimy, bulimy . . . dinners have killed more men than ever Avicenna healed . . .' he prosed away while Jack took off his trousers. 'So you are determined on your bathe?' he said, looking at his naked companion. 'Will you let me see your back, now?' He ran his fingers over the dull-blue scar and asked, 'Do you feel it, these days?'

'Just a trifle, this morning,' said Jack. 'But otherwise, from the time we cleared the Channel until yesterday, never a twinge. A swim,' he said, slipping over the side and plunging deep into the pure blue water with his long yellow hair streaming out behind him, 'is the very thing for it,' he continued, rising to the surface and blowing hard. 'God, it is so refreshing, even though it is as warm as milk. Come on,

Stephen, bathe while you may. For tomorrow we reach the cold current setting north, the green water and the westerlies, I trust; you will have your mollymawks and your pintadoes and maybe your albatrosses, but there will be no more swimming till the Cape.'

3

EVER SINCE the *Boadicea* had made her landfall all hands had been in a state of feverish activity, putting the last touches to her beauty: now it was almost over, and she stood into False Bay with a fair breeze rounding her studdingsails and wafting the reek of fresh paint along with her. The only stage still to obscure her spotless black and white Nelson checker was that occupied by the carpenters' mates, applying carmine with anxious care to the lips, cheeks and bosom of the opulent though insipid British queen.

Jack, already fine in his best uniform, stood by the starboard rail of the quarterdeck with Mr Farquhar beside him. A little farther forward the gunner blew on his slow-match by the brass nine-pounder: all the other guns were housed, ranged with the perfection of the Guards on parade, their breeching pipeclayed. Seymour was a conscientious first lieutenant, and the deck was a pleasure to behold – the gleaming pallor of the wood, the ebony of the seams new-paid with pitch, the falls precisely flemished, a series of exact helices that no man dared disturb, the few pieces of brass the captain would permit blazing in the sun, no speck of dust to be seen from stem to stern, the hen-coops, the surviving swine struck down into the hold together with the goat, which, in the general silence, could be heard bleating angrily for its long-overdue tobacco. The general silence, for all hands were on deck in their Sunday frocks, and they gazed earnestly, mutely at the shore, upon which people could now be seen walking about – walking about on dry land, among trees! – most of them perceptibly black: the only sounds to be heard, apart from the goat, were the bark of the master conning the ship from the forecastle, the ritual answers of the timoneer, the chant of the leadsman in the chains: 'By the mark, fifteen: by the mark, fifteen: and a half, fifteen: by the deep, sixteen: and a half, fifteen', and the conversational voice of the Captain as he pointed out various objects to his guest.

'That flat rock is what we call Noah's Ark, and far over there is Seal Island – the Doctor will like that. And beyond the Ark where you see the white water is the Roman Rock: we shall pass between the two. Indeed, we shall open Simon's Bay at any minute now. Mr Richardson, pray see if the Doctor has finished – whether he can come on deck – he would be sorry to miss all this. Yes, there we are,' he went on, with his telescope to his eye as the inner harbour came into full view. '*Raisonable*, do you see? The two-decker. Then *Sirius*: *Néréide* laying inside her, a very pretty berth: then a brig I cannot make out at all. Mr Seymour, what do you make of the brig with her topmasts on deck?' At this point Stephen appeared, blinking in the strong light, wiping his bloody hands on a woollen nightcap and looking squalid. 'Ah, there you are, Doctor,' cried Jack. 'Have you finished sawing up poor young Francis? How is he coming along? Prime, I dare say?' Francis, until today the most popular topman in the ship, endeavouring to gild the *Boadicea*'s maintopgallant truck, had lost his hold, making a most spectacular fall from that giddy eminence, missing the deck (and certain death) by the grace of the frigate's roll, but grazing her number twelve portlid with such force as to play havoc with his thoracic cage and above all to smear the bleeding paintwork, the grass-combing bugger.

'He may do,' said Stephen. 'These young fellows are made of steel and a particularly resilient leather. So that is Africa.' He looked greedily at the shore, the known haunt of the aard-vark, the pangolin, the camelopard; of birds without number, roaming at large amidst a flora of extraordinary wealth, headed by the ostrich. 'And that,' pointing towards a remote headland, 'is the all-dreaded Cape of Storms itself, I make no doubt?'

'Not exactly,' said Jack. 'The Cape is far astern: I am sorry you did not see it. We came round precious close while you was busy. But before that you did see the Table Mountain, did you not? I sent a messenger.'

'Yes, yes. I felt most obliged to you, in spite of the unchristian hour. It might also be compared with Ben Bulben.'

'Curious, ain't it? And now here on the larboard bow – no, the larboard – you have Simon's Bay, a sweet anchorage. And there's *Raisonable*, wearing the flag.'

'Would that be a line-of-battle ship?' asked Farquhar. 'A most imposing vessel.'

'I doubt any sixty-four would ever lie in the line nowadays,' said Jack. 'In any case, the *Raisonable* was built fifty years ago, and if she fired a full broadside she might fall to pieces; but I am glad she looks imposing. Then comes *Sirius*, a much more powerful ship in fact, although she has but one tier of guns; thirty-six eighteen-pounders, much the same broadside weight of metal as ours. Then another frigate, do you see? *Néréide*, thirty-six; but only twelve-pounders. Then that odd little brig-of-war.'

'Pray, sir, why are they not at sea?' asked Farquhar. 'As I understand it, those and a smaller vessel called the *Otter* are almost all we have to guard the Indian trade. I ask out of mere curiosity.'

'Oh,' said Jack, 'this is the tail-end of the hurricane season up there. They could hardly be blockading the Mauritius in the hurricane season. They are probably in to refit and to take in stores – nothing for them up there, two thousand miles to the north . . . Mr Johnson, I believe you may begin to reduce sail.'

His eyes were fixed to his glass: the *Boadicea* had made her number and he was watching for the master-attendant's boat

to put off. There it was, just leaving the pier. Although the
frigate was now under fore and main topsails alone, still she
glided in, heaved on by the moderate south-east swell and the
making tide, and the shore came fast towards him. The
moment he had the Admiralty House square on he would
begin his salute; and while he waited for that moment to
come he had the strangest feeling that at the first gun England and his whole voyage south would vanish into the past.

'Carry on, Mr Webber,' he said, and as he spoke the nine-
pounder bawled out its respects with a tongue of fire in a
cloud of smoke.

'Fire one,' said the gunner; and the echoes came hurrying
back from the mountains. 'Fire two. Fire three . . .' By the
seventeenth gun the great bay was alive with crossing rever-
berations, and before they had died away a puff of smoke
appeared on the *Raisonable*'s side, followed a second later by
the deep report. Nine guns she fired, the reply due to a captain, and after the ninth the *Boadicea*'s signal-midshipman,
young Weatherall, piped, 'Flag signalling, sir.' Then his voice
broke to a harsh bass as he went on, *'Captain repair aboard
flag.'*

'Acknowledge,' said Jack. 'Lower away the gig. Where's my
coxswain? Pass the word for my coxswain.'

'I am sorry, sir,' said Johnson, blushing. 'Moon is drunk. '

'Damn him,' said Jack. 'Crompton, jump into the gig. Mr
Hill, are these all my papers? Every last one?' Clasping the
packet of sealed, canvas-covered documents to his bosom he
ran down the side, caught the heaving gig on the height of its
rise, and said, 'Shove off.'

It was many, many years since he had last been here, a midshipman, an oldster, in the *Resolution*, yet how exactly he
remembered it all; there were a few more civilian houses in
the village at the bottom of the bay, but everything else was
just the same – the steady beat of the surf, the mountains,
the men-of-war's boats crossing to and fro, the hospital, the
barracks, the arsenal: he might himself have been a lanky boy,

returning to the *Resolution* after catching Roman-fish off the rocks. He was filled with a pleasurable excitement, with countless memories, yet at the same time with an apprehension that he could not define.

'Boat ahoy?' asked the *Raisonable*.

'*Boadicea*,' replied the acting coxswain in a voice of brass; and then more quietly he said, 'Rowed of all.' The gig kissed against the tall flank of the flagship, the sideboys ran down with their scarlet man-ropes, the bosun started his call, and Jack was piped aboard. As he took off his cocked hat he realized with a shock that the tall bowed white-haired figure who answered his salute was the Admiral Bertie he had last seen in Port of Spain as the lithe, lively, wenching captain of the *Renown*; and some part of his busy mind said to him, beneath all the rest, 'Perhaps you are not so very young yourself, either, Jack Aubrey.'

'Here you are at last, Aubrey,' said the Admiral, shaking his hand. 'I am very happy to see you. You know Captain Eliot?'

'Yes, sir; we were shipmates in the *Leander* in ninety-eight. How do you do, sir?'

Before Eliot could reply with anything more than an extension of the friendly smile that he had worn ever since Jack's face appeared, the Admiral went on, 'I dare say those papers are for me? Come along; let's have a look at them in the cabin.' Splendour; opulence; carpets; a portrait of Mrs Bertie, looking plump and comfortable. 'Well,' he said, wrestling with the outer covers, 'so you had a tedious passage of it: but did you have any luck on your way down? They used to call you Lucky Jack Aubrey in the Mediterranean, I remember. God damn these seals.'

'We saw barely a sail, sir; but we did have a little brush off the Dry Salvages, and retook the old *Hyaena*.'

'Did you? Did you, indeed? Well, I am heartily glad of it . . .' The papers were free now, and as he glanced through them he said, 'Yes. I have been expecting these. We must take them along to the Governor at once. But you have a politico aboard, I see? A Mr Farquhar? He must come too: I shall send my barge, by way of compliment; you cannot be too careful with these political gents. You had better order some cool clothes, too; it is a twenty-mile ride to Cape Town. The Governor will not object to nankeen trousers and a round jacket.' He gave his orders and called for a bottle of wine. 'This is the right Diamant of the year one, Aubrey,' he said, sitting down again. 'Too good for you young fellows but you did retake the old *Hyaena* . . . I was a midshipman in her. Yes.' His washed-out blue eyes looked back over forty-five years, and he observed, 'That was in the days before carronades.' Returning to the present he drank his wine, saying, 'I trust your luck will hold, Aubrey: you need it, on this station. Well, and so we shall have to fag over that damned mountain, a wearying ride in this infernal dust – dust everywhere, rain or shine; a whole nation of swabbers would never come to an end of it. I wish we did not have to go. If it were not for the political side, I should get you to sea the minute you had your water aboard. The situation is far worse than ever it was before you left England – far worse than when these orders were written. The French have snapped up two more India-men, this side of the Ten Degree channel, the *Europe* and the *Streatham*: homeward-bound Indiamen, worth a mint of money.'

'Lord, sir, that is very bad,' cried Jack.

'Yes, it is,' said the Admiral, 'and it is going to get even worse unless we bring it up with a round turn, and smartly at that. That is what we must do: it is feasible, and it must be done. Oh, yes, it is feasible, with a certain amount of initia-tive . . . and maybe I should add good fortune too, though luck don't bear talking about.' He touched wood, considered for a while, and then said, 'Listen, Aubrey, before your Mr Farquhar comes aboard – before we start getting entangled in political considerations – I shall lay the position before you as clearly as I can. There are four French frigates based on Mauritius and Réunion, in addition to the force they had there last year: they can use Port Louis or Port South-East in Mauritius and Saint-Paul in Réunion, and separately or in pairs they can range out as far as the Nicobars and beyond – the whole Indian Ocean. You can't catch them out there; we can't convoy all the Eastern trade – we do not possess the ships; and you can't blockade them forever. So you must either destroy them in detail in their home waters or eventually you must take their bases away from them. Now with this in mind, we have seized and garrisoned Rodriguez with part of the Fifty-Sixth and some Bombay sepoys, for your water in the first place, and in the second as a base for the reinforcements that are supposed to come from India in time. There are only about four hundred men on the island at present, but we hope for more next year – it is a question of transports. You know Rodriguez?'

'Yes, sir. I have not touched there, however.' Rodriguez: a remote and tolerably barren speck of land alone in the ocean, three hundred and fifty miles eastward of Mauritius: he had viewed it from the masthead of his dear *Surprise*.

'So at least you have your water. As for ships, you have *Boadicea*, of course; *Sirius*, with a good steady captain in Pym, as regular as a clock; *Néréide* – she is only a twelve-pounder, and getting on in years, but Corbett keeps her in very good order though he is rather undermanned; *Otter*, a fast, useful eighteen-gun sloop, in very good order too. Lord Clonfert has her: she should be in any moment now. And I can let you have *Raisonable* except in the hurricane months, for she cannot bear a hard blow. She is not all she was when I was a boy, but we careened her a few weeks ago, and she is quite fast. At least she is a match for the *Canonnière*, who is older still; and she makes a show. I might conceivably be able to add the *Magicienne* from Sumatra, in time, and the *Victor*, another sloop. But even without them, I conceive that, *Raisonable* cancelling out *Canonnière*, three well worked-up frigates and a powerful sloop would not be reckoned out of the way for dealing with four Frenchmen.'

'Certainly not, sir,' said Jack. The Admiral was speaking as though Jack's pendant were a certainty.

'No one will pretend it is an easy task, however. The Frenchmen are *Vénus*, *Manche*, *Caroline* – it was she who took the last two Indiamen – and *Bellone*, all new forty-gun frigates. As for the rest, they have the *Canonnière*, as I have said, still mounting her fifty guns, our brig the *Grappler*, several avisos and a few smaller things. And I warn you, Aubrey, if you hoist your pendant, I cannot let you have a captain under you. If you shift into the *Raisonable* for the time being, Eliot can replace you in *Boadicea*; but I cannot let you have a captain under you.' Jack bowed. He had scarcely relied upon it: on the remoter stations there were few post-captains to spare; and then again if a commodore did have a captain under him, that commodore was entitled to a third of the Admiral's share of prize-money.

'May I ask whether we have any intelligence of their land-forces, sir?' he said.

'Yes, but I wish it were more exact. On Mauritius General Decaen has the best part of two regiments of the line, and his militia may amount to ten thousand or so. Our information from Réunion is more scanty, but is seems that General Desbrusleys has much the same. Oh, it is a tough nut to crack, I grant you; but cracked it must be, and at the earliest possible moment. You have to strike hard and fast with your forces concentrated while theirs are dispersed: in a word, you have to go in and win. Government will be in a rare old taking when the news of the *Europe* and the *Streatham* reaches England, and this is the kind of situation where you must produce results at once. I do not mention the country's interests, of course; but I do say that from a purely personal point of view there is probably a knighthood or even a baronetcy if you succeed; and if you don't, why it is the beach and half-pay for the rest of your life.'

A midshipman darted in. 'The captain's duty, sir,' said he, 'and should you wish a compliment to the gentleman in the barge?'

'Certainly,' said the Admiral. 'As to a flag.' In the pause that followed he gazed abstractedly at his wife's portrait. 'Should you not like a baronetcy, Aubrey? I am sure I would. Mrs Bertie fairly longs to wipe her sister's eye.'

THE UNOFFICIAL PART of Simon's Town, though little more than a hamlet, had drinking-booths, wine-shops and places of entertainment enough for a town of moderate size; and into one of those, at dusk, walked Stephen Maturin, bearing a bunch of orchids. He was tired, thirsty, and covered from head to foot with African dust; but he was happy, having spent his first half-day ashore walking up a mountain clothed with a vegetation largely unknown to him and inhabited by remarkable birds, some of which he recognized from their published descriptions: he had also seen three quarters of a female spotted hyaena, and he found the remaining piece, including its wistful face, removed to some distance, in the act of being devoured by his old friend the bearded vulture – a pleasant combination of the present and the past, of two far-distant worlds.

He called for wine and water, mingled them in proportion to his thirst, placed his orchids in the water-jug, and drank until at last he began to sweat again. Apart from the landlord and three pretty Malay girls at the bar, there were only two other people in the twilit room, a very large officer in a uniform he could not make out, a vast gloomy man with a great deal of dark whisker, not unlike a melancholy bear, and his smaller, inconspicuous companion, who sat at his ease in shirtsleeves, with his breeches unbuttoned at the knee. The sad officer spoke a fluent though curious English devoid of articles: the smaller man's harsh and grating accent was clearly that of Ulster. They were discussing the Real Presence, but he had not made out the thread of their discourse before they both burst out 'No Pope, no Pope, no Pope,' the sad officer in the deepest bass that Stephen had ever heard. At the bar the Malay girls politely echoed 'No Pope' and as though it were a signal they brought candles and set them about the room. The light fell on Stephen's orchids and upon the contents of his handkerchief, fourteen curious beetles, collected for his friend Sir Joseph Blaine, formerly the chief of naval intelligence; he was considering one, a bupestrid, when he became aware of a darkness by his side, the melancholy bear, gently swaying. 'Golovnin, fleet lieutenant, captain of Imperial Majesty's sloop *Diana*,' said he, clicking his heels.

Stephen rose, bowed, and said, 'Maturin, surgeon of Britannic Majesty's ship *Boadicea*. Please to take chair.'

'You have soul,' observed Golovnin, nodding at the orchids. 'I too have soul. Where did you find them, flowers?'

'In mountain,' said Stephen. Golovnin sighed; and taking a small cucumber from his pocket he began to eat it. He made no reply to Stephen's proffer of wine, but after a while he said, 'What is their name, flowers?'

'Disa grandiflora,' said Stephen, and a long silence fell. It was broken by the Ulsterman, who, tired of drinking alone, brought his bottle over and set it on Stephen's table without the least ceremony. 'I am McAdam, of the *Otter*,' he remarked, sitting down. 'I saw you at the hospital this morning.' Now, by the light of the candle, Stephen recognized him, not from that morning but from many years ago: William McAdam, a mad-doctor with a considerable reputation in Belfast, who had left Ireland after the failure of his private asylum. Stephen had heard him lecture, and had read his book on hysteria with great applause. 'He will not last long,' observed McAdam, referring to Golovnin, now weeping on to the orchids.

'Nor will you, colleague,' thought Stephen, looking at McAdam's pallid face and bloodshot eye.

'Will you take a wee drink?'

'Thank you, sir,' said Stephen, 'I believe I shall stay with my negus. What is it that you have in your bottle, pray?'

"Och, it's a brandy they distill hereabouts. Raw, rot-gut

stuff; I drink it experimentally, not from indulgence. He' – pointing an unsteady finger at Golovnin – 'drinks it from nostalgia, as the nearest to his native vodka; I encourage him.'

'You alluded to an experiment?' said Stephen. 'Yes. Strobenius and others allege that a man dead drunk on grain-spirits falls backwards: on brandy he falls forwards. And if that is true, it tells us something about the motor centres, if you understand the expression. This gentleman here is my corpus vile. Yet it is wonderful how he holds out. This is our third bottle, and he has drunk glass for glass with me.'

'I honour your devotion to science, sir.'

'I do not give a fart in hell for science,' said McAdam. 'Art is all. Medicine is an art or it is nothing. Medicine of the mind, I mean; for what is your physical medicine, apart from purges and mercury and bark, what your murderous chirurgical tricks? They may, with luck, suppress symptoms: no more. On the other hand, where is the true *fons et origo* of nine tenths of your vicious constitutions of body? The mind, that's where it is,' he said, tapping his forehead. 'And what heals the mind? Art: nothing else. Art is all. That is my realm.'

It occurred to Stephen that McAdam was perhaps a somewhat seedy practitioner of this or any other art; a man furthermore whose inward torments were clearly printed on his face. But as they talked of the interaction of mind and body, of interesting cases they had seen – false pregnancies – inexplicable remissions – their experience afloat – the inverse relationship of constipation and courage – the proved efficacity of placebos – his opinion of McAdam rose: indeed, a mutual esteem came into being, and McAdam's arrogant, didactic tone grew even civil. He was telling Stephen about his patients aboard the *Otter* – most of the Otters were, *sensu stricto*, mentally deranged, and there was one case that McAdam would describe and name, were it not for professional secrecy, a fascinating and particularly subtle chain of symptoms – when without any warning Golovnin fell off his chair, grasping the orchids. He lay motionless, still in the attitude of sitting; but he fell sideways, a wholly inconclusive result. At the sound of the crash the landlord paced to the door and whistled. Two enormous sailors walked in, and murmuring, 'Come, Vasily Mikhailovitch; come, little father,' they carried their captain out into the darkness.

'He has not hurt my flowers, however,' said Stephen, smoothing their petals. 'They are, in their essentials, quite intact. You have no doubt remarked the curious spiral convolution of the ovary, so typical of the whole order. Though perhaps your realm does not extend to botany, at all?'

'It does not,' said McAdam. 'Though twisted ovaries are well within it; and twisted testicles too – I speak in figure, you understand: I am jocose. No. The proper study of mankind is man. And I may observe, Dr Maturin, that this eager prying into the sexual organs of vegetables on your part seems to me . . .'

What it seemed to Dr McAdam did not appear, for his tide too had now reached the full. He rose; his eyes closed, and he pitched straight into Stephen's arms, falling, as Stephen noted, forwards.

The landlord brought one of the wheelbarrows that he kept under the porch, and with the help of a black, Stephen wheeled McAdam towards the pier, passing several bodies of cheerful liberty-men as he went. He hailed each party in turn, asking for any Otters; but no man chose to leave the sheltering darkness and sacrifice a moment of his shore-leave, and Stephen heard nothing but facetious replies – '*Otter*'s bound for the Rio Grande' – '*Otter*'s paid off at the Nore' – '*Otter* was broke up for firewood last Wednesday week' – until he met a group of Néréides. A familiar voice cried, 'It's the Doctor,' and there was the powerful form of Bonden at his side, Jack Aubrey's coxswain from his earliest command.

'Bonden, sir. Do you remember me?'

'Of course I remember you, Bonden,' said Stephen, shaking his hand. 'And am delighted to see you again. How do you do?'

'Pretty spry, thank you, sir; and I hope I see you the same? Now just you shove off, Darkie' – to the black – 'I'll take care of this here barrow.'

'The question is, Bonden,' said Stephen, giving the black two stuivers and a penny, 'the question is, how shall I find the means of conveying my charge to his ship, always supposing that his ship is here at all, which seems to be a matter of some doubt? He is the surgeon of the *Otter*, Bonden, a learned man, though somewhat original; and at the moment disguised in drink.'

'*Otter*, sir? She come in on the turn of the tide, not ten minutes ago. Never you fret, I'll square our boat-keeper directly and take him out.' He hurried away: a little later the *Néréide*'s jolly-boat appeared at the step, and Bonden carried the body into it. In spite of the dimness Stephen noticed that Bonden moved stiffly; and this stiffness became more apparent as he pulled out across the harbour towards the distant sloop.

'You are stiff, Barret Bonden,' said Stephen. 'In another man I should say he had certainly been flogged; but that can scarcely be the case with you. I trust this is not a wound, or a rheumatism from the falling damps?'

Bonden laughed, but without much mirth, and said, 'Oh, it was four dozen at the gangway, all right, sir, and two more for luck: brass on the lock of the number seven gun not bright enough.'

'I am amazed, Bonden: amazed,' said Stephen, and indeed he was. Bonden had never been flogged to his knowledge; and even in a flogging ship fifty lashes was a savage punishment for anything but a most serious crime. 'And grieved. Let us row over to the *Boadicea*, and I shall give you some salve.'

'It's all right now, sir, thanking you kindly. I was aboard you this afternoon, but it was not for no salve: you will find the letter we wrote, a-laying there in your cabin.'

'What is it all about, tell?'

'Well, sir,' said Bonden, resting on his oars: but by this time they were close to the larboard side of the *Otter*, and in reply to her hail Bonden called, 'Your doctor coming aboard: request a line.' The *Otter* was perfectly used to this: a whip with a bowline appeared over the side; Bonden slipped it under McAdam's arms; and the surgeon vanished upwards.

'Well, sir,' said Bonden again, pulling slowly towards the *Boadicea*, 'this is the way of it. When me and Killick, on the Leeward Islands station, heard the Captain was afloat again, we went to join him, in course: and there was plenty more in other ships did likewise – old Sophies, old Surprises, even an old Polychrest, Bolton, that slab-sided cove the Captain pulled out of the sea. Oh, was he to new-commission a ship, he'd have no trouble finding a ship's company: not like some – ' He swallowed the coarse expression with a cough and went on, 'Howsoever, we put in our request, and Captain Dundas, a very affable gent and a friend of the Captain's as you know full well, sir, discharged us into *Néréide*, Captain Corbett, for the Cape: which he was so kind as to say he was sorry to lose us, and give Killick a pot of guava-jelly for the Captain. But *Néréide*'s short-handed: because why? because the men run whenever they can. There was Joe Lucas, of our mess, as swam three mile, with bladders, off St Kitts, sharks and all: was brought back, flogged, and swum it again, with his back like a raw steak. And today, with only twelve liberty-men out of the whole crew, two of 'em are off for the mountain, in spite of all them wild beasts, I know for certain fact, leaving thirty-eight months' pay and their prize-money. So, do you see, we are afraid, Killick and me and the rest, that Captain Corbett will not discharge us into the *Boadicea*; and so we wrote this letter to you, sir. Because not liking to put ourselves in the Captain's way, being that he's to hoist his pendant any minute as they say, and therefore too busy, we hoped you might put in a good word, just casual, at the right moment.'

'Of course I shall. But you could very well have addressed Captain Aubrey himself; he has the kindest recollection of you – often speaks of his real coxswain, and much regrets your absence.'

'Does he, though?' said Bonden, with a chuckle of satisfaction. 'But even so, we'd take it very kind in you to say a word: it would come more proper, like, from you. And we are main anxious to be out of *Néréide*.'

'She is not altogether a happy ship, I collect?'

'No, sir, she ain't.' He rested on his oars again, and looking a little sideways at Stephen he added, 'She's a shot-rolling ship: that's what she is.'

Stephen knew nothing about the sailing of ships, theoretical or practical; but he did know that when a crew started trundling cannon-balls about the deck under the cover of darkness, then something was very much amiss; for the next stage was mutiny. He also knew that in any normal ship it would be unthinkable for an unusually steady, sober man like Bonden to be flogged.

'I'm not complaining, mark you,' said Bonden. 'Nor I'm not setting up in judgment: there are some right bastards in the *Néréide*, before the mast and elsewheres; and when things reach a certain pitch, in such a ship the cat falls on the just and the unjust alike. I can take fifty lashes as well as the next man, I hope; though I may say as how it was the first time the cat and me came acquainted – oh, I was beat like a drum when I was a little chap in the *Thunderer*, but that was only the master-at-arms' admonition, as we say. His cane, sir. No. What I mean is, that in the first place me and Killick and the rest want to get back to our own captain: and in the second, we want to get out before things turn nasty. And at the gait they are going now – well, I shouldn't give much for Captain Corbett's life, nor some of his officers, come an action, or even maybe a dirty night with no moon; and we want no part in it.'

'Ugly, Bonden, very ugly,' said Stephen, and no more until they were alongside the *Boadicea*, when he said, 'Good night, now; and thank you for rowing me home.'

He turned in with Leguat's Voyage, with its fascinating account of the solitaire, and Sparmann; and late in the middle watch he heard Jack come aboard. But it was not until quite late in the morning that they met, Stephen having been called to the sick-bay to deal with an alcoholic coma that had suddenly started to gush blood at the ears; and when they did meet it was clear to him that both his crapulous night and his crapulous morning (the sick-bay had smelt like a distillery) were to be prolonged. Captain Aubrey had the yellow, puffy look of one who has drunk far too much – so much indeed that his twenty-mile ride back had not worked it off. 'Twenty miles, *more* than twenty miles, on a damned screw that flung me down three times, and spoilt my best nankeen trousers,' he said. His steward had broken the coffee-pot: his French cook had gone ashore with Bretonnière to join the other prisoners of war, and never more would there be brioche for breakfast. But infinitely more than even the missing coffee was the fact that the Admiral had promised Jack his orders and had not produced them. An interminable, inconclusive conference with the Governor, Mr Farquhar and two general officers of a stupidity remarkable even for the army: then an equally long supper with the soldiers, determined to make their guest drunk. And all this while no orders. By the time Jack set off on his glandered mare the Admiral had long since gone to bed; the flag-lieutenant knew nothing about any orders, written or even contemplated. So here he was, as he told Stephen in the cabin, not knowing *where* he was: there had been no word about his pendant at any time. So here he was, left hanging up in the air: perhaps the expedition would not take place at all: and if it did, after months of delay, perhaps he was not intended to command at all – there had been a furtive, evasive look in the eye of the Admiral's secretary, an ill-looking, untrustworthy swab, for all he was a parson. There had been no mention of higher command in his original sailing orders, and although the Admiral had certainly spoken as though the matter were settled, the appointment no doubt lay at his discretion: the Admiral might have changed his mind: he might have been influenced by the opinion of the council. And then earlier there had been that ominous '*if* you hoist your pendant'.

'Let us take a turn on deck,' he said. 'My head seems to be made of hot sand. And Stephen, might I beg you, implore you, not to smoke those vile things in the cabin? It is your pot-house all over again, like that soldiers' mess last night.'

They reached the quarterdeck in time to see an odd figure come up the side, a young man dressed in a gaudy coat and a little gaudy hat. He had come up the starboard side, the offi-cers' side, and as he advanced towards Mr Seymour he saluted. The first lieutenant hesitated: not so Jack. 'Turn that fellow off the ship,' he roared. Then, in a lower voice, holding his hand to his aching forehead, 'What the devil does he mean by it, prancing about the deck of a King's ship improp-erly dressed, like a jack-pudding?' The young man got into a boat, and was rowed away by a crew of merry-andrews, all in much the same kind of rig.

Jack's steward cautiously sidled near, muttering something about 'the gunroom's pot', and Stephen said, 'I believe he means that coffee's up.'

It was: and as they drank it benignity returned, helped by fresh cream, bacon, eggs, pig's fry, the last of the true French short bastards, toasted, and Sophie's orange marmalade.

'I am sorry I was so cursed snappish just now, about your cigar,' said Jack, pushing back his chair at last and undoing his waistcoat. 'Pray smoke, Stephen. You know I like the smell.'

'Ay,' said Stephen. He broke a cigar in three, crumbled one piece, moistened it with a few drops of coffee, rolled it in paper, and lit it with a voluptuous indraught. 'Listen, now, will you?' he said. 'Bonden, Killick and some others are aboard the *Néréide*, and wish to return to you. All tastes are to be found in nature, we are told; and it is to be presumed that they like the brutal, arbitrary, tyrannical exercise of power.'

'Oh,' cried Jack, 'how very, very pleased I am! It will be like old times. I have rarely regretted anything so much as having to part with them. But will Corbett ever let them go? He's devilish short-handed; and it's only a courtesy, you know, except to a flag. Why, a man like Bonden is worth his weight in gold.'

'Corbett does not seem to be aware of his value, however: he gave him fifty lashes.'

'Flogged Bonden?' cried Jack, going very red. 'Flogged my cox'n? By God, I . . .'

A nervous young gentleman brought the news that the Commander-in-chief's flag-lieutenant had been seen putting off from the shore and the captain of the *Otter* from his sloop, and that Mr Seymour thought Captain Aubrey might like to know.

'Thank you, Mr Lee,' said Jack, and he went on deck: Lord and Lady Clonfert had been far, far from his mind, but they came back with a rush as he saw the *Otter*'s gig, pulled by the same merry-andrews of just before breakfast, approaching the *Boadicea*. It was at about the same distance as the *Raison-able*'s barge, but the flag-lieutenant paused by the flagship to exchange a bellowed and apparently very amusing conversation with a friend on her poop, and before it was over the gig was alongside.

Clonfert was piped aboard, a slight, strikingly handsome, youthful-looking man in full uniform with a star on the bosom of his coat and a singular expression of expectation and uneasiness on his face. He flushed as Jack shook his hand, saying, 'I am happy to see you again, Clonfert; but I heartily wish I had better news for you. Come into my cabin.' Once there he went on, 'I am very much concerned to tell you, that because of an unfortunate misunderstanding about the time, I was obliged to leave Plymouth without Lady Clonfert.'

'Oh,' said Clonfert, with a look of bitter contrariety on his mobile face. 'I was afraid that might be so. I sent early to enquire, but it seems that the message I sent by one of my officers could not be received.'

'An officer?' cried Jack. 'I had no notion – an officer, in that rig?'

'I am sorry it did not meet with your approval, sir,' said Clonfert stiffly. 'But it is my custom to dress my gig's crew in my own colours – it is usual enough in the service, I believe – and the gentlemen under my command fall in with my humour. I confess it is irregular, however.'

'Well, it can lead to misunderstanding. Still, it is cleared up now, and I have delivered my damned unwelcome news – I regret it extremely, but I am sure that Lady Clonfert will have taken the next Indiaman. She will have travelled in much greater comfort, and she should be here within the next week or so, for we made but a slow passage of it. You will dine with me? We have a sucking-pig, and I recall you was fond of sucking-pig in the *Agamemnon*.'

Clonfert flushed again at the name of the ship: he darted an intensely suspicious glance at Jack, and then with an artificial air he said he must beg to be excused – with infinite reluctance he must plead a previous engagement – but that in taking his leave he must be allowed to express his sense of Captain Aubrey's great politeness in having intended to bring Lady Clonfert to the Cape; he was pénétré, pénétré.

He brought it off well enough to make Jack, whose conscience was far from easy on that score, feel something of a scrub; and if he had not tripped on his way out of the cabin the performance would have been well-nigh perfect. The flag-lieutenant was already on deck, talking and laughing with Seymour, when Jack saw his visitor to the side; and Jack's searching eye saw that the jolly young man was the bearer not of the unimportant inconclusive temporizing verbal order that he had so dreaded – that he had so reasonably dreaded, from the tone of last night's conference – but of an important folder bound up with tape, red official tape.

In the cabin once more he received the folder; but first he

had to listen to the flag-lieutenant's message. 'The Admiral desires me to say, sir, that he was taken unwell just after the meeting; that he was unable to give you your orders as he had intended; but that he dictated them from his bed at the earliest possible moment. In fact, sir, he dictated them to me, the secretary not being in the way.'

'So you know what is in them, I dare say?'

'Yes sir; and may I be the first to wish you joy of your pendant, sir?'

'Thank you, Mr Forster,' said Jack, with the full sun lighting up his heart and bowels, his whole being. 'Thank you very much indeed. I trust the Admiral's indisposition causes him no pain or distress? I could wish him restored to the most amazing health and happiness immediately.' The flag-lieutenant thought that perhaps the Admiral had eaten something; for his part he had recommended a dose of rhubarb; and Jack listened to him with an appearance of steady solicitous attention. Jack looked decently solemn, but his mind was swimming in happiness, a happiness made all the more wholly concrete, real and tangible when the flag-lieutenant's recollections of an occasion upon which he too had eaten something came to an end and Jack could cut the tape and see that his orders were addressed to Commodore Aubrey. Yet underlying this pure felicity there was another level of consciousness, a hard, sober determination to come straight into direct contact with the 'real thing', to see exactly what it amounted to, to gauge the limits of his possible initiative, to weigh up the forces in presence, and to start dealing with the situation at once.

The orders were clear, concise, and urgent: the Admiral had obviously had his way. Commodore Aubrey was directed and required to repair aboard the *Raisonable*; to hoist his pendant; to take the ships and vessels named in the margin under his command; to proceed to sea with the utmost dispatch; to seek out and destroy the French cruisers operating south of 10°S and west of 70°E, and, with the cooperation of

the officer commanding the land forces on Rodriguez (which
were to be reinforced at the appropriate juncture), to undertake the reduction of the French possessions of the Ile Bourbon, otherwise Ile de la Réunion, otherwise Ile Buonaparte,
and of the Mauritius, otherwise Ile de France, together with
that of the French ships and vessels in the seas thereto adja-
cent: he was to attend to the general directions in the
attached schedules A and B; and in all political matters or
those having a bearing on contact with the civil population he
was to seek the advice of William Farquhar, Esquire, H.M.
Governor-Designate, and in the absence of Mr Farquhar then
that of Dr Stephen Maturin.

The schedules, together with various appreciations, charts,
hydrographical notes, and estimates of the French strength,
mostly derived from the American merchantmen that passed
to and fro, were in separate packets; and among them was a
paper bearing the superscription Lieutenant Johnson, R.N.,
Boadicea. 'What is this?' asked Jack.

'The Admiral has confirmed your acting-order for Mr Johnson,' said the flag-lieutenant. 'It is his commission.' Jack nodded, a fresh jet of pleasure overcoming the underlying gravity
for a moment, and the flag-lieutenant went on, 'I am also to
say, sir, that the Admiral desires you will use your own discretion entirely as far as *Raisonable* is concerned, and shift your
pendant just as you see fit: he knows her condition only too
well. He asks for this list of followers and servants to be sent
to him in Cape Town, and he hopes you will see proper to
maintain the following appointments. He much regrets that
time and his present indisposition do not allow him to communicate the confidential remarks upon your captains personally, in the usual manner, and begs you will forgive this
hasty scribble.' He passed a half sheet of paper, folded and
sealed, and said, 'I believe that is all, sir, apart from Mr Shepherd's message: he says that since you will need a commodore's secretary he begs to recommend his cousin, Mr
Peter. Mr Peter has been several months on this station and is

thoroughly *au courant*, He is in Simon's Town at the moment
– rode over with me – if you choose to see him.'

'I should be happy to see Mr Peter,' said Jack, strongly
aware of the importance of these civilities, of the importance
of good relations throughout the squadron.

Decency required Jack to refresh the flag-lieutenant;
decency required the flag-lieutenant to see his share of the
bottle out within ten minutes, in order to leave the new commodore free for the innumerable tasks awaiting him; but
although the young man did his best, no period of Jack's life
had ever passed so slowly.

When Mr Forster had gone at last, Jack summoned Johnson and said, 'I wish you joy of your commission, Mr Johnson.
Here it is. The Admiral has confirmed your acting-order, and
I am very sure you deserve it.' He handed over the precious
document, even more precious perhaps to Johnson than his
pendant was to Jack – certainly less loaded with responsibility – and both to cut short the flood of thanks and to gain a
few minutes he said, 'Pray be so good as to send the bosun as
soon as possible,' while to the bosun he said, 'Mr Fellowes, I
do not suppose we have a broad pendant in the colour-chest?
If not, I should be obliged if you would have one run up
directly. '

'Aye aye, sir,' said the bosun, trying to suppress a grin,
'broad pendant it is.' Out of piety, a dread of offending fate by
presumption, Jack had never ordered one to be made: he had
felt the temptation very strongly – he had longed to cherish it
in private – but he had waited until it should be certain. On
the other hand the Boadiceas had turned the matter over in
their heads well north of the line, ferreting about and fitting
odd scraps together; they had become convinced of the need
for such an object, and it had been lying by these last four
thousand miles.

The bosun hurried off forward: Jack broke the Admiral's
seal and read: 'Captain Pym of the *Sirius* is a thoroughly reliable, conscientious officer, but wanting in initiative; Captain

Corbett of the *Néréide*, though he keeps an excellent discipline and is of outstanding value as a fighting commander, has a tendency to irascibility that is to be regretted; he is on bad terms with Captain Lord Clonfert of the *Otter*, and the two should not be sent together on detached service if it can be avoided. Lord Clonfert has distinguished himself recently in several minor actions of a most dashing nature; and he, like Captain Corbett, has a considerable acquaintance with the waters off Réunion and Mauritius.' The confidential remarks told Jack perhaps rather more about the Admiral than the captains; but he had scarcely formulated this reflection before Fellowes came hurrying back, bearing the beautiful pendant in his arms. Jack looked at it with an affectation of detachment that could scarcely have deceived his daughters, far less the bosun. 'Thank, you, Mr Fellowes,' he said. 'Pray put it on the locker, and then ask the Doctor, with my compliments, whether he can spare a moment.'

He was drawing on the breeches of his best full-dress uniform when Stephen walked in. 'I thought you might like to see something new,' he said, adding, not without pride, '*Ex Africa surgit semper aliquid novo, – novi*, eh?'

'To what do you refer?' asked Stephen, gazing about the cabin.

'Cannot you see anything that strikes you dumb with awe, the mark of a living commodore, very nearly the most exalted being on the face of the earth?'

'The ornamental cloth? Oh, that: I had understood you to say something new. That cloth I saw daily in the bosun's cabin when his bowels were disturbed, long ago: I took it for a sign of his office, or perhaps the banner of some bosuns' guild.' Then, feeling obscurely that he had not quite fulfilled his friend's expectations, he added, 'But it is an amazingly handsome flag, upon my honour; and so neatly sewn. I dare say you will hang it up, presently; and sure it will do us all great credit, the pretty thing.'

If there had been little secrecy aboard the frigate, there was even less in the squadron. No one had failed to remark the flag-lieutenant's arrival, nor his prolonged stay in the *Boadicea*, nor the subsequent desertion of the flagship by a troop of the Admiral's servants and followers, nor yet Captain Aubrey's passage across the harbour: when the swallow-tailed pendant broke out at the *Raisonable*'s masthead, therefore, not a ship or vessel present let a second go by before starting the thirteen-gun salute due to the man it symbolized. The salutes merged with one another and with their echoes, filling the bay with a sullen roar, a cloud of smoke that drifted over Jack as he stood there on the poop, not directly looking at his pendant, but feeling its presence with oh such intensity: the moment his thunderous reply was done, he returned to the signal lieutenant and said, 'All captains, Mr Swiney.'

He received them in the Admiral's great cabin: the *Raisonable* was not the *Hibernia* nor yet the *Victory*, but still this was a noble room, full of dappled reflected light, and as they filed in their blue and white and gold made it look nobler still. Pym of the *Sirius* came first, a big man, as tall as Jack and fatter; his congratulations were as frank and unreserved as his fine friendly open face, and Jack's heart warmed to him. Corbett followed, a small dark round-headed man whose set expression of determined, angry authority was now softened into a look of the deference and the pleasure proper to this occasion. He had fought several most creditable actions in the West Indies, and in spite of Bonden Jack looked at him with respect: with hopeful anticipation, too. Corbett's good wishes were almost as cordial as Pym's, although there might have been the slightest hint of resentment, of merit and local knowledge passed over: but in any event they were far more hearty than Clonfert's formal 'Allow me to offer my felicitations, sir.'

'Now, gentlemen,' said Commodore Aubrey, when this stage was over, 'I am happy to tell you that the squadron is to proceed to sea with the utmost dispatch. I should therefore be obliged for a statement of each ship's readiness, her condition: not a detailed statement, you understand – that can come later – but a general notion. Lord Clonfert?'

'The sloop I have the honour to command is always ready to put to sea,' said Clonfert. That was mere rodomontade: no ship was always ready to put to sea unless she never used up any water, stores, powder or shot; and the *Otter* had just come in from a cruise. They all knew it, Clonfert as well as any once the words were out of his mouth. Without allowing the awkward pause to last more than a moment, however, Jack went straight on, receiving a more rational account from Pym and Corbett, from which it appeared that the *Sirius*, though well-found in general, badly needed careening, and that she was having great trouble with her water-tanks, new-fangled iron affairs that had been wished on her in Plymouth and that leaked amazingly. 'If there is one thing that I detest more than anything,' said Captain Pym, staring round the table, 'it is innovations.' The *Sirius* had rummaged her hold to come at the tanks, so even with the best will in the world, and working double-tides, she could scarcely be ready for sea before Sunday. The *Néréide*, though apparently fit to sail the moment she had filled her water, was really in a much sadder way: she was old, as the Commodore knew, and according to Captain Corbett's carpenter her navel-futtocks could be removed with a shovel; while she was certainly iron-sick fore and aft, if not amidships too; but far worse than that, she was shockingly undermanned. Captain Corbett was sixty-three hands short of his complement: a shocking figure.

Jack agreed that it was a very shocking figure, to be sure. 'But let us hope that the next homeward-bound Indiaman to put in will solve the difficulty with sixty-three prime hands and a few supernumaries.'

'You are forgetting, sir, that ever since their disagreement with Government about the running of the colony the Company's ships no longer touch at the Cape.'

'Very true,' said Jack, with a covert glance at Clonfert. He covered his lapse by saying that he should visit their ships in the course of the afternoon, when he would hope to see their detailed statements of condition, and suggested that they should now discuss some claret that he had taken from a Frenchman on his way down. The last of the Lafite appeared, together with something in the farinaceous line from the *Boadicea*'s galley. 'Capital wine,' said Pym. 'As sound as a nut,' said Corbett. 'So you found a Frenchman, sir?'

'Yes,' said Jack, and he told them about the *Hébé*: it was not much of an action, but the mere talk of banging guns, the *Hyaena* restored to the list, the prize neatly salvaged, caused the formal atmosphere to relax. Reminiscence flowed with the claret: comparable actions and old shipmates were called to mind: laughter broke out. Jack had never served with either Pym or Corbett, but they had many acquaintances in common throughout the service: when they had spoken of half a dozen, Jack said, 'You knew Heneage Dundas in the West Indies, of course, Captain Corbett?' thinking that this might jog his mind.

'Oh, yes, sir,' said Corbett: but no more. 'That will not wash, however,' said Jack within: and aloud, 'Lord Clonfert, the bottle stands by you.'

All this time Clonfert had been sitting silent. A shaft of light, falling on his star, sent a constellation of little prismatic dots flashing high: now, as he leant forwards to the bottle, they all swept down. He filled his glass, passed the bottle on, and moved perhaps by some notion of repairing his unpleasant relationship with Corbett and possibly at the same time of winning an ally in this meeting where he could not but feel at a disadvantage, he said, 'Captain Corbett, a glass of wine with you.'

'I never drink a glass of wine with any man, my lord,' replied Corbett.

'Captain Corbett,' said Jack quickly, 'I was astonished to learn about the Russian brig lying inside the *Néréide*, and even more astonished when the Admiral told me that her captain had served under you.'

'Yes, sir, he was in the *Seahorse* when I had her, serving as a volunteer to learn our ways: and he picked them up pretty well, I must confess. His people are scarcely what we should rate ordinary, but I dare say he will knock some seamanship into them in time. They have a fine sense of discipline in those parts: a thousand lashes are not uncommon, I believe.'

The talk ran on about the unfortunate *Diana* – her sailing from the Baltic on a voyage of discovery at a time of peace between England and Russia – her arrival, all unsuspecting, in Simon's Town to learn that war had been declared – her curious status – her curious build – her people's curious ways ashore.

Eight bells struck: they all stood up. Jack detained Corbett for a moment and said, 'Before I forget it, Captain Corbett, my coxswain and some other men are aboard the *Néréide*. Here, I have jotted down their names. You will oblige me by having 'em sent over.'

'Certainly, sir,' said Corbett. 'Of course . . . But I beg you will not think I intend the least disrespect if I venture to repeat that I am cruelly short-handed.'

'So I understand,' said Jack. 'But I do not mean to rob you: far from it. You shall have an equal number from the *Boadicea*, and I believe I may even be able to let you have a few more. We pressed some good men among the *Hébé*'s prisoners.'

'I should be most uncommon grateful, sir,' said Corbett, brightening at once. 'And I shall send your men back the moment I reach the ship.'

It was with his own coxswain at his side, therefore, that the Commodore put off for his tour of the squadron. 'This is like old times, Bonden,' he said, as they approached the *Sirius*. 'Yes, sir; only better,' murmured Bonden: and then, in answer to the frigate's hail, he roared 'Pendant,' in a voice to wake the dead.

It did not startle the *Sirius*, however: from the moment of Captain Pym's return all hands had turned to – dinner cut

short, grog gulped down – in order to give her an entirely artificial and fallacious appearance, designed to make her appear
what she was not. They had done so with a will, being proud
of their ship, and although there had been no time for any
lavish repainting, the *Sirius* that the Commodore beheld was
as unlike her workaday self as the concentrated effort of two
hundred and eighty-seven men and several women (some
regular, others less so) could make her. Seeing that she was
virtually disembowelled because of her tanks, they had not
been able to turn her into a larger version of a royal yacht, as
they could have wished; but apart from the pyramids of
nameless objects on deck, decently shrouded with awnings
and tarpaulins, she was very presentable, and Jack was
pleased with what he saw. He did not believe it, of course;
nor was he expected to believe it: the whole thing, from the
whitewashed coal in the galley to the blackened balls in the
shot-garlands, was a ritual disguise. Yet it had a relationship
to the facts, and he gained the impression of a fine steady
ship in moderately good order with competent officers and a
decent crew largely composed of man-of-war's men – she had
been in commission these three years and more. Captain
Pym had set up a splendid array of bottles and cakes in his
cabin, and as Jack lowered a Bath bun whose specific gravity
somewhat exceeded that of platinum he reflected that its
consistency was in all likelihood a fair symbol of the ship –
steady, regular, rather old-fashioned, reliable; though perhaps
not apt to set the Indian Ocean in a blaze.

Next the *Néréide*. She had had no real need to turn to in
order to achieve the full effect that the *Sirius* had aimed at,
yet from the mute, weary sullenness of her crew and the anxious, jaded, harassed look of her officers, every man jack
aboard had been hard at it, gilding the lily for this occasion.
Jack liked a taut ship, and of course a clean ship, but the total
perfection of the *Néréide*'s vast expanse of brass alone
oppressed him: he went through with his inspection, that
being due to those who had toiled so hard and to so little pur-

pose, but he made his tour of the silent, rigid frigate with no
pleasure at all. His real business lay below, however, among
the navel-futtocks; and there in the depths with the captain,
his nervous first lieutenant and his nervous carpenter, he
found that Corbett had not exaggerated greatly. Her timbers
were indeed in a bad way: yet, he reflected as he prodded
about with a spike, the Simon's Town surveyor might be right
in saying that they would last another two or three seasons,
whereas unless Jack was out in his reckoning the rot on the
upper deck would spread more rapidly than that. As a young
fellow, a midshipman in those very waters, he had been disrated for misconduct, for venery, and turned before the mast:
infinitely against his will he had been a foremast jack for six
months. That ship's standard of spit and polish had been
nothing remotely like the *Néréide*'s, but she had had a tartar
of a captain and a driving first lieutenant, and he knew to his
cost just what it took in labour to produce even half this
result. And those months, so wretched at first and indeed
most of the time, had also given him something that few officers possessed: an intimate understanding of life at sea from
the men's point of view, a comprehension from within. He
knew their language, spoken and silent; and his interpreta-
tion of the looks he had seen before coming below, the constraint, the veiled sideways glances, the scarcely perceptible
nods and signs, the total lack of anything resembling cheerfulness, depressed him extremely.

Corbett was a brisk man with figures, however: he produced his detailed statement of the *Néréide*'s condition,
neatly ruled in black and red, at the same time as his Madeira
and sweet biscuits. 'You are very well found in powder and
shot, I see,' Jack remarked, glancing over the columns.

'Yes, sir,' said Corbett. 'I don't believe in flinging it into the
ocean: besides, your genuine recoil does so plough up the
deck.'

'It does; and the *Néréide*'s deck is a most remarkable sight, I
must confess. But do you not find it answers, to have your

men handy with the guns – accurate at a distance?'

'Why, sir, as far as my experience goes, it don't make much odds. I have always engaged yardarm to yardarm, when they could not miss if they tried. But I don't have to tell *you* anything about close engagement, sir, not after your action with the *Cacafuego*, ha, ha.'

'Still, there is something to be said for the other school of thought – something to be said for knocking away the enemy's sticks from a mile off and then lying athwart his hawse,' observed Jack mildly.

'I am sure you are right, sir,' said Corbett, without the least conviction.

If the *Néréide* had been as like a royal yacht as a man-of-war could very well be, the *Otter*, at first glance, was the yacht itself. Jack had never, in all his life, seen such a display of gold leaf; and rarely had he seen all shrouds and stays wormed with vermilion yarn and the strops of the blocks covered with red leather. At second glance it seemed perhaps a little much, touching on the showy, just as the perfection of tailoring on Clonfert's quarterdeck – even the midshipmen had laced cocked hats, breeches, and Hessian boots with gold tassels – had a hint of costume rather than of uniform about it: and as he stood there Jack noticed to his surprise that Clonfert's officers appeared rather a vulgar set. They could not help their undistinguished faces, of course, but their stance, now too rigid, like tailor's dummies, now too lounging and, easy by far, was something else again; so was their underbred open staring, their direct listening to what their captain had to say to him. On the other hand, no great perspicacity was required to see that the atmosphere aboard the *Otter* was as unlike that in the *Néréide* as possible: the lower-deck Otters were a cheerful, smiling crew, and it was clear that they liked their captain; while the standing officers, the bosun, the gunner and the carpenter (those essential pillars), seemed steady, valuable, experienced men. The *Otter's* decks, rigging and gingerbread-work had surprised him; her cabin surprised him even more. Its not inconsiderable size was much increased by looking-glasses in gilt frames; these reflected a remarkable number of cushions piled up on a Turkish sofa, and the Arabian Nights were even more strongly called to mind by scimitars hanging on the bulkhead against a Persian carpet, a gilt mosque-lamp swinging from the beam, and a hubblebubble. Among all this the two twelve-pounders looked homely, brutish, drab, and ill-at-ease.

The ritual offerings appeared, brought in by a black boy in a turban, and Jack and Clonfert were left alone: a certain awkwardness became manifest at once. With advancing years Jack had learnt the value of silence in a situation where he did not know what to say. Clonfert, though slightly older in spite of his youthful appearance, had not, and he talked – these baubles were from his Syrian campaign with Sir Sydney – the lamp a present from Dgezzar Pasha – the scimitar on the right from the Maronite Patriarch – he had grown so used to Eastern ways that he could not do without his sofa. Would not the Commodore sit down? The Commodore had no notion of lowering himself to within inches of the deck – what could he do with his legs? – and replied that he should as soon keep an eye on the *Boadicea*'s boats as they pulled briskly between the arsenal and the frigate, filling her magazines and shot-lockers with what he hoped would prove a most persuasive argument. Then the Commodore would surely taste a little of this Constantia and toy with an Aleppo fig: Clonfert conceived that they made an interesting combination. Or perhaps a trifle of this botargo?

'I am infinitely obliged to you, Clonfert,' said Jack, 'and I am sure your wine is prodigious good; but the fact of the matter is, that *Sirius* gave me a great deal of capital port and *Néréide* a great deal of capital Madeira; so what I should really prize beyond anything at this moment is a cup of coffee, if that is possible.'

It was not possible. Clonfert was mortified, chagrined, desolated, but he drank no coffee; nor did his officers. He really was mortified, chagrined and desolated, too. He had already been obliged to apologize for not having his statement of condition ready, and this fresh blow, this *social* blow, cast him down extremely. Jack wanted no more unpleasantness in the squadron than already existed; and even on the grounds of common humanity he did not wish to leave Clonfert under what he evidently considered a great moral disadvantage; so pacing over to a fine narwhal tusk leaning in a corner he said, in an obliging manner, 'This is an uncommonly fine tusk.'

'A handsome object, is it not? But with submission, sir, I believe horn is the proper term. It comes from a unicorn. Sir Sydney gave it to me. He shot the beast himself, having singled it out from a troop of antelopes; it led him a tremendous chase, though he was mounted on Hassan Bey's own stallion – five and twenty miles through the trackless desert. The Turks and Arabs were perfectly amazed. He told me they said they had never seen anything like his horsemanship, nor the way he shot the unicorn at full gallop. They were astounded.'

'I am sure they were,' said Jack. He turned it in his hands, and said, with a smile, 'So I can boast of having held a true unicorn's horn.'

'You may take your oath on it, sir. I cut it out of the creature's head myself.'

'How the poor fellow does expose himself,' thought Jack, on his way back to the *Raisonable*: he had had a narwhal tusk in his cabin for months, bringing it back from the north for Stephen Maturin, and he was perfectly acquainted with the solid heft of its ivory, so very far removed from horn. Yet Clonfert had probably thought that the first part was true. Admiral Smith was a remarkably vain and boastful man, quite capable of that foolish tale: yet at the same time Admiral Smith was a most capable and enterprising officer. Apart from other brilliant actions, he had defeated Buonaparte at Acre: not many men had such grounds for boasting. Perhaps Clonfert was of that same strange build? Jack hoped so with all his heart – Clonfert might show away with all the unicorns in the world as far as Jack was concerned, and lions too, so long as he also produced something like the same results.

His meagre belongings had already come across from the *Boadicea*; they had already been arranged by his own steward as he liked them to be arranged, and with a contented sigh Jack sat easy in an old Windsor chair with arms, flinging his heavy full-dress coat on to a locker. Killick did not like seeing clothes thrown about: Killick would have to lump it.

But Killick, who had dashed boiling water on to freshly-ground coffee the moment the *Raisonable*'s barge shoved off from the *Otter*, was a new man. Once cross-grained, shrewish, complaining, a master of dumb and sometimes vocal insolence, he was now almost complaisant. He brought in the coffee, watched Jack drink it hissing hot with something like approval, hung up the coat, uttering no unfavourable comment, no rhetorical 'Where's the money going to come from to buy new epaulettes when all the bullion's wore off, in consequence of being flung down regardless?' but carried on with the conversation that Jack's departure had interrupted. 'You did say, sir, as how they had no teeth?'

'Not a sign of them, Killick. Not a sign, before I sailed.'

'Well, I'm right glad on it' – producing a handkerchief with two massive pieces of coral in its folds – 'because this will help to cut 'em, as they say.'

'Thank you, Killick. Thank you kindly. Splendid pieces, upon my word: they shall go home in the first ship.'

'Ah, sir,' said Killick, sighing through the stern-window, 'do you remember that wicked little old copper in the back-kitchen, and how we roused out its flue, turning as black as chimney-sweeps?'

'That wicked little old copper will be a thing of the past, when next we see the cottage,' said Jack. 'The *Hébé* looked after that. And there will be a decent draught in the parlour, too, if Goadby knows his business.'

'And them cabbages, sir,' went on Killick, in an ecstasy of

nostalgia. 'When I last see 'em, they had but four leaves apiece.'

'Jack, Jack,' cried Stephen, running in. 'I have been sadly remiss. You are promoted, I find. You are a great man – you are virtually an admiral! Give you joy, my dear, with all my heart. The young man in black clothes tells me you are the greatest man on the station, after the Commander-in-chief.'

'Why, I am commodore, as most people have the candour to admit,' said Jack. 'But I did mention it before, if you recollect. I spoke of my pendant.'

'So you did, joy; but perhaps I did not fully apprehend its true significance. I had a cloudy notion that the word commodore and indeed that curious little flag were connected with a ship rather than with a man – I am almost sure that we called the most important ship in the East India fleet, the ship commanded by the excellent Mr Muffit, the commodore. Pray explain this new and splendid rank of yours.'

'Stephen, if I tell you, will you attend?'

'Yes, sir.'

'I have told you a great deal about the Navy before this, and you have not attended. Only yesterday I heard you give Farquhar a very whimsical account of the difference between the halfdeck and the quarterdeck, and to this day I do not believe you know the odds between . . .' At this point he was interrupted by the black-coated Mr Peter with a sheaf of papers, by a messenger from the general at Cape Town, and by Seymour, with whom he worked out a careful list of those men who could be discharged into the *Néréide*, either in the light of their own crimes or in that of the frigate's more urgent needs, and lastly by the Commander-in-chief's secretary, who wished to know whether his cousin Peter suited, to say that Admiral Bertie, now much recovered, sent his compliments: without wishing to hurry the Commodore in any way, the Admiral would be overjoyed to hear that he had put to sea.

'Well, now, Stephen,' said Jack at last, 'this commodore lark: in the first place I am not promoted- at all – it is not a rank but a post, and J. Aubrey does not shift from his place on the captains' list by so much as the hundredth part of an inch. I hold this post just for the time being, and when the time being is over, if you follow me, I go back to being a captain again. But while it lasts I am as who should say an acting temporary unpaid rear-admiral; and I command the squadron.'

'That must warm your heart,' said Stephen. 'I have often known you chafe, in a subordinate position.'

'It does: the word is like a trumpet. Yet at the same time . . . I should not say this to anyone but you, Stephen, but it is only when you have an enterprise of this kind on your hands, an enterprise where you have to depend on others, that you understand what command amounts to.'

'By others you mean the other commanders, I take it? Sure, they are an essential factor that must be thoroughly understood. Pray open your mind upon them, without reserve.' Jack and Stephen had sailed together in many ships, but they had never discussed the officers: Stephen Maturin, as surgeon, had messed with them, and although he was the captain's friend he belonged to the gunroom: the subject was never, never raised. Now the case altered: now Stephen was Jack's political colleague and adviser; nor was he bound in any way to the other commanding officers. 'Let us begin with the Admiral; and Jack, since we are to work openly together, we must speak openly: I know your scruples and I honour them, yet believe me, brother, this is no time for scruples. Tell, do you look for full, unreserved support from Mr Bertie?'

'He is a jolly old boy,' said Jack, 'and he has been as kind and obliging to me as I could wish: he confirmed my acting-order for Johnson at once – a most handsome compliment. As long as all goes well, I make no doubt he will back us to the hilt; apart from anything else, it is entirely in his interest. But his reputation in the service – well, in Jamaica they called him Sir Giles Overreach, from the fellow in the play, you know; and he certainly overreached poor James. A good officer, mark you, though he don't see much farther through a brick wall than another man.' He considered for a while before saying, 'But if I made a mistake, I should not be surprised to be superseded: nor if I stood between him and a plum. Though as things stand, I cannot see how that could come about.'

'You have no very high opinion of his head, nor of his heart.'

'I should not go as far as that. We have different ideas of what is good order in a ship, of course . . . no, I shall tell you one thing that makes me uneasy about his sense of what is right. This Russian brig. She is an embarrassment to everybody. The Admiral wishes her away, but he will not take the responsibility of letting her go. He will not accept the responsibility of making her people prisoners, either – among other things they would have to be fed, with everything charged against him if Government disapproved. So what he has done is to make the captain give his word not to escape and has left him lying there, ready for sea: he is trying to starve Golovnin out by allowing no rations for his men. Golovnin has no money and the merchants will not accept bills drawn on Petersburg. The idea is that he will break his word and disappear some dirty night when the wind is in the north-west. His word means nothing to a foreigner, said the Admiral, laughing; he wondered Golovnin had not gone off six months ago – he longed to be rid of him. He took it so much as a matter of course – did not hesitate to tell it – thought it such a clever way of covering himself – that it made my heart sink.'

Stephen said, 'I have noticed that some old men lose their sense of honour, and will cheerfully avow the strangest acts. What else affects your spirits, now? Corbett, I dare say? In that case the beadle within has quite eaten up the man.'

'Yes: he is a slave-driver. I do not say a word against his courage, mark you; he has proved that again and again. But by my book his ship is in very bad order indeed. She is old too, and only a twelve-pounder. Yet with the odds as they are, I cannot possibly do without her.'

'What do you say to the captain of the *Sirius*?'

'Pym?' Jack's face brightened. 'Oh, how I wish I had three more Pyms in three more *Siriuses*! He may be no phoenix, but he is the kind of man I like – three Pyms, and there would be your band of brothers for you. I should have to do myself no violence, keeping on terms with three Pyms. Or three Eliots for that matter: though he will not be with us long, more's the pity. He means to invalid as soon as ever he can. As it is, I shall have to humour Corbett to some degree, and Clonfert; for without there is a good understanding in a squadron, it might as well stay in port. How I shall manage it with Clonfert I can hardly tell: I must not get athwart his hawse if I can avoid it, but with that damned business of his wife I am half way there already. He resented it extremely – refused my invitation, which is almost unheard-of in the service, previous engagement or not: and there was no previous engagement. This is an odd case, Stephen. When we talked about him some time ago, I did not like to say I had my doubts about his conduct – an ugly thing to say about any man. But I had, and I was not the only one. Yet maybe I was not as wise as I supposed, for although he still looks like a flash cove in a flash ship, he did distinguish himself up the Mediterranean with Admiral Smith.'

'That, I presume, was where he came by his star? It is an order I have never seen.'

'Yes, the Turks handed out quite a number, but they were thought rather absurd, and not many officers asked permission to wear them: only Smith and Clonfert, I believe. And he has also carried out some creditable raids and cutting-out expeditions in these waters. He knows them well, and he has a native pilot; the *Otter* draws little water, even less than the *Néréide*, so he can stand in among the reefs; and according to Admiral Bertie he might almost be setting up as a rival to Cochrane in the matter of distressing the enemy.'

'Yes: I have heard of his enterprise, and of his ship's ability to go close to the shore. I shall no doubt have to be with him from time to time, to be landed and taken off. But just now you spoke of the odds. How do you see them at present?'

'Simply in terms of ships and guns, and only from the point of view of fighting at sea, they are rather against us. Then if you allow for the fact that we shall be more than two thousand miles from our base while they are in their home waters, with supplies at hand, why, you might say that they are in the nature of three to five. In the Channel or the Mediterranean I should put it nearer evens, since we are at sea all the time in those parts, and they are not: but their heavy frigates have been out the best part of a year now, plenty of time to work up their crews, given competent officers; and upon the whole the French officers are a competent set of men. But all this is very much up in the air – there are so many unknowns in the equation. For one thing, I know nothing of their captains, and everything depends on them. Once I catch sight of them at sea I shall be able to reckon the odds more accurately.'

'Once you have had a brush with them, you mean?'

'No. Once I have seen them, even hull down on the horizon.'

'Could you indeed judge of their abilities at so remote a view?'

'Of course,' said Jack a little impatiently. 'What a fellow you are, Stephen. Any sailor can tell a great deal from the way another sailor sets his jib, or goes about, or flashes out his stuns'ls, just as you could tell a great deal about a doctor from the way he whipped off a leg.'

'Always this whipping off of a leg. It is my belief that for you people the whole noble art of medicine is summed up in the whipping off of a leg. I met a man yesterday – and he was so polite as to call on me today, quite sober – who would soon put you into a better way of thinking. He is the *Otter*'s surgeon, I should probably have to cultivate his acquaintance in any event, for our own purposes, since the *Otter* is, as you would say, an inshore prig: but I do not regret it now that I have met him, He is, or was, a man of shining parts, But to return to our odds: you would set them at five to three in favour of the French?'

'Something of that kind. If you add up guns and crews and tonnage it is a great deal worse; but of course I cannot really speak to the probability until I see them, Yet although I have sent a hundred Boadiceas to lend a hand aboard the *Sirius*, and although I know Pym is doing his utmost to get her ready for sea, our own ship has to take in six months' stores, and I should love to careen her too, the last chance of a clean bottom for God knows how long – I cannot see how we can sail before Saturday's tide. I shall keep the people hard at it, and harry the arsenal until they wish me damned, but apart from that there is nothing I can do: there is nothing that the Archangel Gabriel could do. So what do you say to some music, Stephen? We might work out some variations on "Begone Dull Care".'

4

THE SQUADRON, standing north-east with the urgent tradewind on the beam, made a noble sight; their perfect line covered half a mile of sea – and such a sea: the Indian Ocean at its finest, a sapphire not too deep, a blue that turned their worn sails a dazzling white. *Sirius*, *Néréide*, *Raisonable*, *Boadicea*, *Otter*, and away to leeward the East India Company's fast-sailing armed schooner *Wasp*, while beyond the *Wasp*, so exactly placed that it outlined her triangular courses, floated the only bank of cloud in the sky, the flat-bottomed clouds hanging over the mountains of La Réunion, themselves beneath the horizon.

The Cape and its uneasy storms lay two thousand miles astern, south and westward, eighteen days' sweet sailing; and by now the crews had long since recovered from the extreme exertion of getting their ships ready for sea three tides before it seemed humanly possible. But once at sea new exertions awaited them: for one thing, the perfection of this line, with each ship keeping station on the pendant at exactly a cable's length, could be achieved only by incessant care and watchfulness. The *Sirius*, with her foul bottom, kept setting and taking in her topgallants; the *Néréide* had perpetually to struggle against her tendency to sag to leeward; and Jack, standing on the poop of the *Raisonable*, saw that his dear but somewhat sluggish *Boadicea* was having an anxious time of it – Eliot was fiddling with his royals – while only the pendant-ship, fast in spite of her antiquity, and the *Otter* were at ease. And for another, all the ships except the *Boadicea* were disturbed, upset and harassed by the Commodore's passion for gunnery.

He had begun as soon as they sank Cape Agulhas, and although they were by no means reconciled to the exercise they were used to his ways; they were quite sure what the Commodore would be at at this point in the afternoon watch when they saw the *Raisonable* signal to the *Wasp* and then bid the squadron wear together. Up and down the line the bosuns' calls shrilled high and clear, the hands stood poised upon their toes (for the competition between the ships was very keen, the horror of public disgrace very great), and the moment the *Raisonable* deviated from her line the others began their turn: round they came, as trim as could be, forming the line with their larboard tacks aboard, the wind one point free, a reversed line, with the *Otter* leading. They had no great press of sail and this was a simple manoeuvre; even so, it was well executed; there was not much amiss with their seamanship, reflected Jack, looking over the taffrail at the *Néréide*'s masts, all in one line, eclipsing those of the *Sirius*, her next astern. Meanwhile the schooner had cast off the targets, and she was making sail with remarkable diligence, being eager to run out of range as soon as possible.

It was an understandable eagerness, for as usual the *Otter* opened a fine brisk fire a little before her guns could really be said to bear, and her wilder shot whipped up the sea between the schooner and the target. Her second broadside was nearer the mark, and might have hit it if the Otters had waited for the top of the roll: her third resembled the first, except that one ball did skip over the target: and she did not manage a fourth. Jack, watch in hand, was calling the figures to the mathematical midshipman he had brought with him when the *Boadicea* spoke out, pitching her shot a trifle high but sweeping the hypothetical deck; her second broadside struck the enemy square amidships, and with rapturous cries her third and fourth demolished the floating wreckage. 'One minute fifty-five seconds,' wrote Spotted Dick upon his slate, following it with two points of admiration. 'As they bear, Mr Whittington,' called Jack. The *Raisonable* was understood to play no competitive role in all this: because of her age she could not blaze away with the single, timber-shattering roar of a younger ship, but every third gun of her lower deck, half charged, and several of her lighter pieces produced a slow rolling fire that would have done a certain amount of damage. Far more damage than the full but almost comically inept broadsides of the *Néréide*: two broadsides only, and those fired so high that no more than a single shot went home – a shot almost certainly fired by one of the quarter-gunners that Jack had most reluctantly sent into her. Then came *Sirius*, with two deliberate broadsides and then her five aftermost guns as the battered target went astern: slow but quite accurate at this moderate range.

Jack had neither the time nor the powder for any more. As soon as the guns were housed he signalled *Tack in succession* and called the schooner under his lee. From the moment they weighed from Simon's Town he had watched the sailing of the ships under his command with a very close attention, but never had he kept his glass so fixedly upon anyone of them as now he kept it upon the *Wasp* as she came racing up close-hauled, throwing white water right down her lee-rail. She was a beautiful craft, beautifully handled, and she sailed closer to the wind than he would have thought possible; yet his anxious, worn expression did not lighten when she rounded to and lay there under the *Raisonable*'s quarter, her captain looking up at her lofty poop with an inquiring face.

Jack nodded absently to the schooner, told the signal-lieutenant to summon the captain of the *Sirius*, stepped aft with a speaking-trumpet and hailed the *Boadicea*, desiring her acting-captain to come aboard. The Commodore received them rather formally in the fore-cabin, where Mr Peter handed Eliot written orders to proceed to the Mauritius in company with the *Sirius*, there to lie off Port-Louis, the capital and the chief port, in the north-west of the island, and to rendezvous with the rest of the squadron on that station: in the intervening time they were to watch the motions of the enemy and to gain all the information they could. To these orders Jack added a clear direction not to engage in any action unless the odds were heavily in their favour, together with some advice about arriving off Sable Point after dark and sending in boats to look into the harbour at crack of dawn, so that they could pullout against the sea-breeze. Then, in his care for the *Boadicea*, he was going on to beg Eliot not to carry too great a press of sail, not to set his royals – a spar carried away in these latitudes was a terrible loss – she must be humoured, not drove – when he realized that he sounded more like a mother-hen than was quite right. He stifled his recommendation about the *Boadicea*'s starboard cathead, saw them over the side, watched their ships steer north, and went below again, going right aft to the great cabin, where Stephen sat at a table, encoding letters on paper of surprising thinness.

'The great advantage of these ark-like vessels,' observed Stephen, 'is that one can at least speak in privacy. The Admiral, with his luxury of dining-room, bedroom, ante-chamber, fore-cabin, and then this magnificence with the balcony behind, could riot at his ease; the Commodore can freely speak his mind. A mind that is, I fear, oppressed by melancholy thoughts?'

'Yes: commodious, ain't it?' said Jack, stepping out on to the stern-gallery, from which he could see the *Wasp*, rising and falling ten feet on the long smooth swell and shivering her foretopsail from time to time to keep her pace down to that of the two-decker. Coming back he said, 'Stephen, I do so hate this vile scheme of yours.'

'I know you do, my dear,' said Stephen, 'You have frequently mentioned it. And each time I have replied, that in the first place the contacts and the information I seek are of essential importance; and in the second, that the risk is negligible. I walk two hundred paces along a strand clearly defined by palm-trees; I call at the second house I see – a house of which I have an accurate drawing – I make a contact of inestimable value, receive my information, deliver these documents, whose extreme tenuity, you see' – holding them out – 'renders them edible, as tradition doth require – I walk back to the boat and so to your swift-sailing machine, to join you, with the blessing, for breakfast. I promise not to linger, Jack, though La Réunion is another Ophir, to the philosophic mind.'

Jack paced up and down: all that Stephen said was perfectly reasonable. Yet not so many years ago Jack had fetched him out of Port Mahon more dead than alive, Port Mahon in Minorca, where he had been caught on a secret mission, interrogated with all the barbarity of the Inquisition, and very nearly destroyed.

'Minorca was entirely different,' said Stephen. 'In that case I had been undermined at home. Here the possibility does not exist.'

'It is not only that,' said Jack, coming to a halt in front of a chart of the coast of La Réunion. 'Just look at these God-damned reefs. Think of the surf. I have told you again and again, Stephen, these inshore waters are hellish dangerous – reefs everywhere, half of 'em uncharted, the most tremendous surf. I know what I am talking about. I was here as a boy. There is scarcely a beach where you can land in safety, even when the swell is more moderate by half. To get into your Petite Anse you must run through a gap in the reef not a cable's length across even at high tide, by moonlight. And what if this Company's chap don't find it? He is no pilot for these waters: admits it candidly.'

'The alternative is to go in the *Otter*. Clonfert does know these shores; and he has a native pilot. And since I shall have to spend some time in the *Otter* sooner or later, I am eager to know her captain. Much will depend upon our understanding.'

'Certainly he knows this coast,' said Jack, 'but then the coast knows him. He has been in and out a score of times on this east side alone. The *Otter* is very recognizable, and if any fishing-boat or aviso or watchman on the cliffs sees her standing in, then every soldier and militiaman on the island will be running about, shooting the first thing that stirs. No: if it has to be, then the schooner is the right choice. Her captain is a steady young fellow and a good seaman; nothing flash or gimcrack about him or his *Wasp*. Besides, there is the time.'

'Sure, I should prefer the schooner. She leaves us at Rodriguez for Bombay, as I understand it, and that will preserve my character a little longer.'

'Well,' said Jack in the most unwilling voice. 'But I tell you, Stephen, I shall give him absolute orders to return immediately if he cannot make out his leading marks at once, or at the least sign of movement ashore. And Stephen, I must tell you this, too: if the scheme goes wrong, I cannot land a party to bring you off.'

'It would be madness to attempt any such thing,' said Stephen placidly; and after a slight pause, 'Honest Jack, would it be uncivil to remind you, that time waits for no man? This also applies, they tell me, to the tide.'

'Then at least,' cried Jack, 'I can send Bonden with you, and have a carronade mounted in the boat.'

'That would be kind; and might I suggest that black men

for the boat's crew would be a diabolically cunning stroke, by way of amusing the enemy? For we must assume that he sees in the dark, the creature.'

'I shall attend to it this minute,' said Jack, and he left Stephen to his encoding.

A LITTLE BEFORE FOUR bells in the afternoon watch Dr Maturin was lowered like a parcel on to the heaving deck of the *Wasp*, where Bonden seized him, cast off the five fathoms of stout line that had held him motionless (no one had the least opinion of his powers of self-preservation, at sea) and led him aft, whispering, 'Don't forget to pull off your hat, sir.'

It was a round hat of French manufacture, and Stephen took it off to the schooner's quarterdeck and to her captain with something of an air; then turning about with the intention of waving it to Jack he found that he was gazing over a broad lane of sea at the *Raisonable*'s stolid figurehead. The schooner had already crossed the two-decker's bows, and she was now flying goose-winged towards the clouds that hung over La Réunion.

'If you will step this way, sir,' said the captain of the *Wasp*, 'I believe we shall find our dinner ready.'

At the same moment Killick mounted to the poop of the *Raisonable*, where Jack was staring after the schooner, and stated, with something of his old acerbity, that 'the gentlemen were treading on one another's toes in the halfdeck this ten minutes past: and his honour still in his trousers.' Abruptly Jack realized that he had forgotten his invitation to the wardroom, that he was improperly dressed – north of Capricorn once more he had reverted to the free and easy ducks – and that he was in danger of committing unpunctuality. He darted below, huddled on his uniform, and shot into the great cabin just as five bells struck. Here he received his guests, the sailors in their best blue coats, the soldiers in their scarlet, and all of them red-faced in the heat, for they had had their finery on for the last half hour at least: presently he led them to the dining-table, where the skylight admitted the rays of the ardent sun, and they grew redder still. At the beginning of a cruise, and often right through it, these feasts, theoretically the gathering of equals for social intercourse but in fact the almost obligatory attendance of men belonging to different steps of a rigid and never-forgotten hierarchy, tended to be ponderous affairs. Jack was perfectly aware of it, and he exerted himself to give some semblance of spontaneity to his entertainment. He tried very hard, and at one point, feeling for the sufferings of the Marine captain whose stock was bringing him nearer and nearer to a cerebral congestion, he even though of bidding them take off their heavy coats: but that would never do – a disproportioned thought indeed – for although he naturally liked his guests to enjoy themselves, he must not conciliate their goodwill by the least improper concession; they must enjoy themselves within the limits of naval convention, and these limits certainly did not extend to turning the cabin into a bawdy-house. He confined himself to ordering the awning, removed for Stephen's aerial voyage, to be rigged again, and water to be dashed upon the deck.

Although his heart was not in it, he laboured on: yet artificial conviviality is rarely infectious, and still they sat, hot, prim, polite. Convention required that no man but Jack Aubrey should initiate any conversation, and since they had not yet taken the measure of their new Commodore they obeyed it religiously. Presently he began to run short of topics, and he was reduced to urging them to eat and drink. For his own part he could only go through the motions of eating – his stomach was quite closed – but as a grateful coolness began to come down from the shaded skylight, wafted by the unvarying south-east trade, the bottle went about more briskly. Even before the port came to the table each man had a shining, glazed appearance, a tendency to stare and hold himself very straight, and each man behaved with even greater care as the decanter went its rounds – tolerably dismal rounds, as Jack could not but inwardly confess.

Dinner in the *Wasp*'s low triangular cabin was a very different matter. Since this coming night's activity called for a mind as clear as it could be Stephen had begged for thin cold coffee: Mr Fortescue drank no wine at any time, so the bottle he had provided for his guest stood untouched between the lime-juice and the tall brass pot while the two of them devoured a great mound of curry so Vesuvian that it paled the tropic sun. Each had early discovered the other's passionate concern with birds; and now, after a modest though fully-detailed account of petrels he had known, Mr Fortescue observed that there was nothing like a sailor's life for bringing a man acquainted with the world.

'Sir, sir,' cried Stephen, waving a Bombay duck, 'how can you speak so? Every ship I have sailed upon might have been called the Tantalus. They have carried me to remote countries, within reach of the paradise-bird, the ostrich, the sacred ibis; they have set me down in a variety of smelly and essentially identical havens; and then, almost without exception, they have hurried me away. The wealth of the Indies is within my grasp, and I am hurried away to another stinking port a thousand miles away, where exactly the same thing occurs. In candour I must not deny that the intervening ocean may reveal wonders that more than compensate the tedium of one's confinement, the Judaic ritual of life aboard – I have beheld the albatross! – but these are fleeting glimpses: we know nothing of the birds' economy, the interesting period of their loves, their solicitude for their young, their domestic tasks and cares. Yet all this is just at hand, attained by enormous expense of spirit and of the public treasure: and it is thrown away. No: I can conceive of no more deeply frustrating life for a naturalist than that of a sailor, whose lot it is to traverse the world without ever seeing it. But perhaps, sir, you have been more fortunate?'

Mr Fortescue, though freely admitting the justice of Dr Maturin's observations in general, had indeed been more fortunate, particularly in respect of the great albatross,

Diomedea exulans, to which the Doctor had so feelingly referred: he had been cast away on Tristan da Cunha, where he had lived with and upon albatrosses, thousands and thousands of albatrosses, to say nothing of the penguins, terns, skuas, prions, the indigenous gallinule and a hitherto nondescript finch. He had sat with albatrosses right through their incubation; he had weighed, measured, and eaten their eggs; he had attended to their nuptial ceremonies; and, having been cast away with a piece of pencil and the Complete Practical Navigator, whose blank pages served for notes and measurements, he had, to the best of his poor abilities, drawn them.

'And were you indeed able to make illustrated notes?' cried Stephen, his eyes gleaming. 'How I wish, oh how I wish, that you might be persuaded to communicate them, at some not too distant time!'

As it happened, said Mr Fortescue, reaching for the book, they were just at hand, entirely at Dr Maturin's service; and he rather thought that there might be some specimens – eggs, skins, and bones – in the locker upon which he sat.

They were still with their albatrosses at nightfall, when the chaotic mountains of La Réunion stood black against the afterglow, and when Jack, with the taste of brass in his mouth and an aching head, began his pacing of the poop, glancing westward at each turn, although there could not be the slightest chance of seeing the *Wasp* much before dawn. It was a pacing that continued as the stars swept widdershins round the southern sky and watch succeeded watch: nervous and uneasy at first, it settled into a mechanical to and fro of his body, leaving his mind to run clear. By this stage he was fairly peaceful, and between watching the stars he ran over his calculations, always coming up with the same comforting result: La Réunion lay at the apex of a triangle whose base was the squadron's course during the afternoon and then the night, its southern arm the *Wasp*'s path taking Stephen in, an arm some fifty miles long. He had kept the squadron under topsails alone, and having checked the rate of sailing each time the log was heaved he was confident that they would have run off eighty miles at about four bells in the morning watch, reaching the point at which the northern arm of the triangle, that of the schooner bringing Stephen back, should meet the base, making a neat isosceles of the whole. In these seas, with their perfectly steady wind, such calculations could be made with remarkable accuracy; and here the only important variable was the time Stephen spent ashore, which Jack provisionally set at three hours.

The middle watch wore on: once a flying squid struck against the great stern-lantern: otherwise the quiet night-routine of the ship moved along its invariable course. The wind sang an even note in the rigging, the water slipped along the side, the phosphorescent wake stretched out, a straight line broken by the bow-wave of the *Otter*, two cables' lengths astern; and at each stroke of the bell the sentinels called out from their stations, 'All's well', 'All's well', right round the ship and up and down the squadron.

'I hope to God they are right,' said Jack. He stepped down to the quarterdeck and looked at the log-board again. He was strongly tempted to go up into the top or even to the masthead; but that would singularize the whole thing too much – draw too much attention to it – and he returned to his lonely poop, only desiring the officer of the watch to send a good man aloft with a night-glass and bid him keep a sharp look-out.

He was still on the poop when the eastern stars began to pale: the morning watch had been called long since and men were moving about the dim deck, sprinkling sand. Jack's certainties had vanished an hour ago: his neat isosceles triangle had fled down the wind, routed by a thousand fresh unknown quantities. He stood still now, leaning on the rail and searching the horizon from the west to south-west. The blazing rim of the sun thrust up; light shot into the eastern sky; and the lookout hailed 'Sail ho.'

'Where away?' cried Jack.

'On the starboard beam, sir. *Wasp*. A-lying to.'

And there indeed she was, hull-down, well to the east, her triangular sails just nicking the rising sun. Jack called down to the quarterdeck, 'Make sail to close her,' and resumed his pacing. The steady grind of holystones, the slap of swabs: full day-time life returned to the *Raisonable* as she set her topgallants and ran fast along the line that should cut the schooner's path. When his powerful glass had shown him Stephen walking about far over there, Jack went below, said, 'Breakfast in the after-cabin, Killick,' and stretched himself out on his cot for a while. Presently he heard the officer of the watch call for a bosun's chair, agitated cries of 'Handsomely, handsomely, there. Boom him off the backstay,' and a little later Stephen's familiar step.

'Good morning, Stephen,' he said. 'You look as pleased as Punch – the trip was to your liking, I hope and trust?'

'The most delightful trip, I thank you, Jack; and a very good morning to you too. Most delightful . . . look!' He held out his two hands, opened them cautiously and disclosed an enormous egg.

'Well, it is a prodigious fine egg, to be sure,' said Jack: then, raising his voice, 'Killick, light along the breakfast, will you? Bear a hand, there.'

'Other things have I brought with me,' said Stephen, drawing a green-baize parcel from his pocket and a large cloth bag. 'But nothing in comparison with the truly regal gift of that most deserving young man Fortescue. For what you see there, Jack, is nothing less than the concrete evidence of the albatross's gigantic love. Whereas this' – pointing to the gently heaving parcel – 'is no more than a poll-parrot of the common green, or West African, species, too loquacious for its own good.' He undid the baize, snipped the band confining the parrot's wings, and set the bird upon its feet. The parrot instantly cried. 'A bas Buonaparte. Salaud, salaud, salaud,' in a metallic, indignant voice, climbed on to the back of his chair, and began to preen its ruffled feathers. 'The cloth bag, on the other hand, contains some of the finest coffee I have ever tasted; it grows to great advantage upon the island.'

Breakfast appeared, and when they were alone again Jack said, 'So you did not spend all your time ashore bird's nesting, I collect. Would it be proper to tell me anything about the rest of your journey?'

'Oh, that,' said Stephen, setting his egg sideways upon a butter-dish to see it at a better angle. 'Yes, yes: it was a straightforward piece of routine, perfectly simple, as I told you. Fruitful, however. I shall not tell you about my interlocutor – far better to know nothing in these cases – apart from saying that I take him to be a wholly reliable source, exceptionable only in his prolonged retention of this indiscreet fowl, a fault of which he was himself most sensible. Nor shall I trouble you with the political aspect: but I have a clear notion of the military side. I believe it to be a true statement of the position, and am not without hope that it will give you pleasure. In the first place, our accession of strength is as yet unknown: in the second, the two most recently captured Indiamen, the *Europe* and the *Streatham*, are in St Paul's road, on the other side of the island, together with their captor, the frigate *Caroline*, whose inward parts are alleged to require some attention that will keep her there for perhaps a fortnight. In fact her captain, a most amiable young man called Feretier, is attached to the wife of the Governor, General Desbrusleys, a passionate gentleman who is at odds with Captain Saint-Michiel, the commandant of St Paul's, and with most of the other officers on La Réunion. At present he is at Saint-Denis: his forces amount to something over three thousand men, including the militia; but they are stationed at various points, twenty and even thirty miles apart over difficult mountain country; and although St Paul's is strongly defended by batteries and fortifications mounting, let us see, nine and eight is seventeen – I write seven and I retain one; five and five is ten, and with the one that I retained, eleven – mounting a hundred and seventeen guns, you may consider it practicable, in spite of the difficulty of landing on these shores, to which you have so frequently adverted. This rude sketch shows the approximate location of the batteries. This the disposition of the troops. You will forgive me for labouring the obvious when I say, that if you do decide to act, then celerity is everything. "Lose not a minute", as you would put it.'

'Lord, Stephen, how happy you make me,' said Jack, taking the paper and comparing it with his chart of St Paul's roadstead and the shore. 'Yes, yes: I see. A crossing fire, of course. Forty-two-pounders, I dare say; and well served, no doubt. There is no possibility of cutting the Indiamen or the frigate out, none at all, without we take the batteries. And that we cannot do with our Marines and seamen: but three or four hundred soldiers from Rodriguez would just tip the scale, I do believe. We could not hold the place, of course, but we might take the ships – there is a fair chance that we take the ships.' He stared at the paper and at his chart. 'Yes: a tough nut, to be sure; but if only I can persuade the soldiers on Rodriguez to move at once, and if only we can get our men ashore, I believe we can crack it. St Paul's is on the leeward side, where the surf is not so wicked unless the wind lies in the west . . . but I quite take your point about losing no time, Stephen . . .' He ran out of the cabin, and a few moments later Stephen, turning the egg over in his hands, heard the *Raisonable* begin to speak as she bore up for Rodriguez, spreading sail after sail: the masts complained, the taut rigging sang with a greater urgency, the sound of the water racing along her side mounted to a diffused roar; the complex orchestra of cordage, wood under stress, moving sea and wind, all-pervading sound, exalting to the sea-borne ear – a sound that never slackened day or night while the squadron made good its five hundred miles with the strong, steady south-east wind just abaft the beam.

RODRIGUEZ: THE LOW dome of the island lay clear on the starboard bow at dawn on Thursday, a greenish dome, its sky-

line stuck with palm-trees, in a green lagoon; all round the
immense surrounding reef the white of breakers, and beyond
it the intense blue of the open sea, uninterrupted for five
thousand miles to windward. A man-of-war bird passed a few
feet overhead, its long forked tail opening and closing as it
glided through the swirling currents about the forestaysail
and the jibs, but neither Jack nor Stephen moved their steady
gaze from the land. On a flat tongue of land with a large
house upon it and some huts, neat rows of tents could
already be seen: no great number of them, but enough to
shelter the three or four hundred soldiers that might make
the descent on La Réunion a possibility, if only their commanding officer could be induced to stir. Jack had seen combined operations by the score, few of them a pleasant
memory; and the likelihood of miserable jealousies between
army and navy, the divided command, to say nothing of
divided councils, were clear in his mind. He was superior to
Lieutenant-Colonel Keating in rank, but that gave him a
mere precedence, no right to issue orders: it would have to be
a true, willing cooperation or nothing. He must rely upon his
powers of exposition: and as though an unremitting glare
might carry conviction, he kept the glass trained on the
house, moving it only occasionally to glance at the gap in the
surf that showed the narrow passage into the lagoon.

Stephen's mind was largely taken up with the same considerations; yet part of it was also aware, vividly aware, that the
island gliding towards him was the home of an enormous
land tortoise, not perhaps quite so vast as *Testudo aubreii*, discovered and named by himself on a comparable island in this
same ocean, but even so one of the wonders of the world;
and, more important still, that until recently it had been the
home, the only home, of the solitaire, a bird in some ways
resembling the dodo, equally extinct alas, but still less known
to science, even in fragmentary remains. He turned over a
number of approaches to this subject, none wholly satisfactory, given Jack's gross insensibility to all science without an

immediate application: for Captain Aubrey, as for the rest of brute creation, there were only two kinds of birds, the edible and the inedible. Even after prolonged meditation, during which the squadron reduced sail for the first time in fifty-two hours, he could produce no more than a timid 'Were we compelled to stay a short while . . .' that passed unnoticed, for as he spoke Jack raised his speaking-trumpet and hailed the *Néréide*, saying 'Lead in, if you please, Captain Corbett. And preserve us from evil.'

'Amen,' said a forecastleman automatically, glancing at the Commodore with horror as soon as the word was out of his mouth.

'. . . perhaps I might be allowed a party,' continued Stephen, 'a very small party, consisting only of ambulant cases . . .' He would have added 'to look for bones', if the Commodore's eager determined expression had not convinced him that he might as well have pleaded with the ship's figurehead.

The barge splashed down into the calm waters of the lagoon, its crew stretched out as they were bid, and this same eager determined expression advanced with long strides up the coral beach to meet Colonel Keating. They exchanged salutes, shook hands, and the soldier said, 'You will not remember me, sir, but I was at a dinner given in your honour at Calcutta after your magnificent defence of the China fleet.'

'Certainly I remember you, sir,' said Jack, who had indeed some recollection of this tall, lean figure – a long-nosed, capable face that raised his hopes, 'and am very happy to see you again.'

The Colonel looked pleased, and as he led Jack through a double hedge of his men, Englishmen of the 56th Foot on the one side, turbaned sepoys of the 2nd regiment of Bombay Infantry on the other, he observed, 'How delighted we were to see you coming in. We have been so cruelly bored on this dismal rock, these last few months – reduced to tortoise-races – nothing to look forward to except the arrival of the

main body next year – nothing to shoot except guinea-fowl.'
Jack instantly seized upon the opening and said, 'If we are of
the same mind, Colonel, I believe I can do away with your
boredom. I can offer you something better than guinea-fowl
to shoot at.'

'Can you, by God?' cried the soldier, with a look as keen as
Jack's. 'I rather hoped something might be afoot, when I saw
you come ashore so quick.'

In the tents, drinking tepid sherbet, Jack stated the case:
he felt almost certain that the Colonel, though mute, was
with him, but even so his heart thumped strangely as he
spoke the words that must bring the answer, positive, negative, or temporizing: 'And so, sir, I should value your appreciation of the position.'

'Sure, I am of your mind entirely,' said Keating straight away.
'There are only two things that make me hesitate – hesitate as
the officer commanding the troops on Rodriguez, I mean, not
as Harry Keating. The first is that I have barely four hundred
men here, a mere advance-party to build the fort and prepare
the lines. It was never imagined that I should move until the
arrival of the main body with the next monsoon, and I might
be broke for stirring, for leaving my command. Yet as against
that, I know the Company loves you like a son, so I might
equally well be broke for not falling in with your plan of campaign. As far as that goes, then, I should choose to follow my
own inclination, which is the same as yours, sir. The second is
this question of landing through the surf – the choice of our
disembarkation. As you pointed out so candidly, there lies the
crux. For with no more than your Marines and what seamen
you can spare – say six hundred men with my few companies
– it must necessarily be nip and tuck. My men, and particularly the sepoys, are not clever in boats: if we do not land
cleanly and carry their works out of hand, a neat *coup de main*,
there will be the Devil to pay, once their columns start coming
in from Saint-Denis and the other places. If I could be satisfied on that point, I should cry done directly.'

'I cannot pretend to be well acquainted with the western side of the island myself,' said Jack, 'but I have two captains here with a vast deal of local knowledge. Let us hear what they have to say.'

Colonel Keating's conscience longed to be satisfied, and it would have taken far less to do so than Corbett's vehement assertion that landing on the west side, north of St Paul's, so long as the wind stayed in the south-east, which it did three hundred days in the year, was as easy as kiss my hand, particularly when this was reinforced by Clonfert's still more positive statement that even with a westerly wind he would undertake to set a thousand men ashore in a sheltered cove accessible through gaps in the reef known to his black pilot. But the Colonel was less pleased when the two captains disagreed violently upon the best place for the landing, Clonfert maintaining that the St Giles inlet was the obvious choice, Corbett that no one but a blockhead would attempt anything but the Pointe des Galets, adding, in reply to Clonfert's objection that it was seven miles from St Paul's, that he conceived the opinion of a post-captain with a *real* knowledge of these waters, acquired over many years of service on the station during this war and the last, was likely to carry more weight than that of a very young commander. The Colonel retired into a grave, formal absence while the captains wrangled, the veiled personalities growing more naked until the Commodore called both to order, not without asperity. And somewhat later Keating's delight in the company of the sailors was damped again when Lord Clonfert abruptly excused himself before the end of dinner and left the tent as pale as he had been red at the beginning of the meal – a redness attributable to the Commodore's words, delivered in what was meant to be the privacy of the nascent fort: 'Lord Clonfert, I am exceedingly concerned that this display of ill-feeling should have taken place, above all that it should have taken place in the presence of Colonel Keating. You forget the respect due to senior officers, sir. This must not occur again.'

'LORD, STEPHEN,' cried Jack as he came into the stern-gallery of the *Raisonable*, where Dr Maturin sat gazing wistfully at the land, 'what a capital fellow that Keating is! You might almost think he was a sailor. "When do you wish my men to be aboard?" says he. "Would six o'clock suit?" says I. "Perfectly, sir," says he; turns about, says to Major O'Neil, "Strike camp," and the tents vanish – the thing is done, with no more words bar a request that his Hindus should be given no salt beef and his Mahometans no salt pork. That is the kind of soldier I love! In three hours we shall be at sea! *Néréide* is preparing to receive them at this minute. Are you not delighted, Stephen?'

'Oh, excessively delighted; delighted beyond measure. But Jack, am I to understand that no shore-leave is to be allowed – that we are to be hurried from this place as we were hurried from the parturient whale off Cape Agulhas? I begged Mr Lloyd for a boat, a small boat, but he declared that it was as much as his skin was worth to suffer me to go without an order from you, adding, with an inhuman leer, that he thought the Commodore would have anchors atrip before the ebb. Yet surely it would be of immeasurable benefit to all hands, to be indulged in running about and frolicking, if no farther than the strand?'

'Bless you, Stephen,' said Jack, 'you shall have your boat, for what bugs you may gather in two hours and a half; for two hours and a half it is, mark you well, not a minute more; and I shall send Bonden with you.'

Stephen was making his laborious way down the stern-ladder, his searching foot was already poised over the boat itself, when the *Otter*'s yawl pulled alongside and a midshipman said, 'Dr Maturin, sir?'

Stephen writhed his neck round, directing a grim look at the young man: all his professional life ashore had been haunted by these vile messengers; innumerable concerts, theatres, operas, dinners, promised treats had been wrecked or interrupted by fools, mooncalves, who, to gain some private end, had broken a leg, had fits, or fallen into a catalepsy. 'Go and see my mate, Mr Carol,' he said.

'Dr McAdam's particular compliments to Dr Maturin,' went on the midshipman, 'and would be most grateful for his present advice.'

'Hell and death,' said Stephen. He crept up the ladder, flung some medical objects into a bag, and crept down again, holding the bag in his teeth.

A worried, perfectly sober McAdam received him aboard the *Otter*. 'You wished to see this case in its crisis, Doctor: pray step below,' he said in public; and in private, 'This is the crisis, God damn me, and a tear-my-guts-out crisis too. I am relieved to have you to consult with, colleague – am in three minds at the least.' He led him into the captain's cabin, and there, on the sofa, lay Lord Clonfert, doubled up with pain. He made a real attempt at mastering it to greet Stephen and to thank him for coming – 'Most benevolent – vastly obliged – désolé to receive him in these conditions' – but the strong gripes cut him very short.

Stephen examined him carefully, asked questions, examined him again, and the doctors withdrew. The attentive ears that hung about the neighbourhood could make precious little of their Latin, but it was understood that Dr Maturin would have nothing to do with Dr McAdam's iliac passion, still less his Lucatellus' balsam; that he slightly inclined to a clonic spasm; that he believed Dr McAdam might do well to exhibit *helleborns niger* in the heroic dose of twenty minims, together with forty drops of thebaic tincture and sixty of antimonial wine, accompanied, naturally, with a little Armenian bole, as a temporary expedient; he had known it answer in tormina of much the same kind (though less intense) that afflicted a purser, a wealthy purser who dreaded detection when the ship paid off; but this was a particularly difficult, interesting case, and one that called for a more prolonged consultation. Dr Maturin would send for the other lenitives he had mentioned, and when the enemata had had their effect, Dr McAdam might choose to walk on the island to discuss the matter at greater length: Dr Maturin always thought more clearly, when walking. The ears dispersed during the coming and going of the messenger; they made nothing of the administration of the drugs other than the fact that the groans in the cabin stopped; but they did catch some words about 'delighted to attend the opening of the body, in the event of a contrary result' that earned Dr Maturin some brooding glances as the two medical men went over the side, for the Otters loved their captain.

Up and down they strolled among the hurrying soldiers, then through the tortoise-park, where the disconsolate French superintendent stood thigh-deep among some hundreds of his charges, and so towards the interior, until at last the rollers crashing on the reef were no more than a continuous, half-heard thunder. Stephen had seen a flight of parrots that he could not identify, some francolins, a kind of banyan tree which, rooting from its branches, made dark arcades that sheltered countless fruit-bats the size of a moderate dove: and some promising caves; yet his professional mind had also followed McAdam's long and detailed account of his patient's habit of body, his diet, and his mind. He agreed with his colleague in rejecting physical causes. 'This is where the trouble lies,' repeated McAdam, striking the dome of his head, bald, naked and disagreeably blotched with ochre against the pallid, sweating scalp.

'You were not so sure of your diagnosis a little while ago, my friend, with your iliac passion and your strangulation,' said Stephen inwardly; and outwardly, 'You have known him a great while, I collect?'

'Sure, I knew him as a boy – I treated his father – and I have sailed with him these many years.'

'And *peccatum illud horribile inter Christianos non nominandum*, can you speak to that? I have known it produce strange sufferings, though mostly of a cutaneous nature; and none as extreme as this.'

'Buggery? No. I should certainly know it. There is repeated venereal commerce with the other sex, and always has been. Though indeed,' he said, standing while Stephen grubbed up a plant and wrapped it in his handkerchief, 'it is the wise man that can always separate male and female. Certainly men affect him far more than women; he has more women than he can do with – they pursue him in bands – they cause him much concern – but it is the men he really minds: I have seen it again and again. This crisis, now: I know it was brought on by your Captain Aubrey's checking him. Corbett is bad enough, but Aubrey . . . I had heard of him often and often, long before he ever came out to the Cape – every mention of him or of Cochrane in the Gazette, every piece of service gossip, analysed, diminished, magnified, praised, decried, compared with his own doings – cannot leave them alone, any more than a man can leave a wound in peace . . . Och, be damned to his whimsies – why does he have to be Alexander? Do you want a drink?' asked McAdam, in a different voice, pulling out a case-bottle.

'I do not,' said Stephen. Until now the decent conventions of medical conversation had restrained McAdam's language and even his harsh, barbarous dialect; but spirits worked very quickly upon his sodden frame, and Stephen found the liberated McAdam tedious. In any event, the sun was no more than a hand's-breadth above the horizon. He turned, walked quickly through the almost deserted camp, down the now empty beach with McAdam blundering after him, and into the boat.

'I beg you will take notice, Commodore,' he said, darting on to the poop, 'that I am come aboard seven minutes before my time, and desire it may be made up, whenever the requirements of the service next permit.'

For the time being the service required Stephen, his shipmates, and three hundred and sixty-eight soldiers to bowl along the twentieth parallel, and to cover the hundred leagues between Rodriguez and the rest of the squadron as briskly as ever the *Néréide*, with her heavy load, could be induced to pass through the sea. It would have been far more convenient to stow the troops in the spacious *Raisonable*, but here everything depended upon speed, and Jack dreaded the loss of time in transferring them to the *Néréide*, perhaps with the sea running high: for he had fixed upon Corbett's landing-place, and the *Néréide*, replete with local knowledge and drawing little water, was to set them ashore at the Pointe des Galets; she therefore ran westward horribly crowded and trailing a smell of Oriental cooking.

Cracking on as though yards, booms, gaffs and even top-masts were to be had for the asking in the nearest port, they ran off the distance in two days, and on the evening of the second they found the *Boadicea* and *Sirius* north-east of Mauritius, exact to the rendezvous and, as far as could be told, undetected from the land. This Jack learnt from the soaking Captain Pym, whom he summoned aboard the *Raisonable* in the most pitiless way through an ugly cross-sea, with a close-reef topsail wind sending warm green water over the waist of the two-decker. Pym had some solid intelligence, gained from two separate fishing-boats taken far off shore: the *Canonnière*, condemned by the surveyors as a man-of-war, had had all her guns but fourteen taken out and was refitting to carry a commercial cargo back to France in a month or so; on the other hand, only one of the powerful new frigates, the *Bellone*, was in Port-Louis, the *Manche* and the *Vénus* having sailed north-eastwards some time before, with six months provisions aboard.

The heavy sea, the increasing wind, the sudden tropical darkness made it impossible to gather a council of war; and having seen the half-drowned Pym regain his ship, Jack called the *Boadicea* under his lee and in a voice that carried loud and clear over the general roar he desired Captain Eliot to proceed to St Paul's with the utmost dispatch, *the utmost dispatch*, to lie there in the offing, and to 'bottle 'em up until

we join you – never mind about carrying away a spar or two.'
The *Boadicea*, with her fire-power, would hold them if there
was any attempt at getting away.

By the next day the squadron had left Saint-Louis far
astern; they were clear of the disturbed winds and currents to
the leeward of Mauritius, and in the moderate sea the
Marines and a hundred seamen went aboard the *Néréide* to
join the rest of the landing-party. The captains gathered with
the Colonel and his staff in the great cabin of the *Raisonable*,
and the Commodore ran over the plan of attack once more.
Stephen was there, and Jack presented him, as casually as
possible, as the political adviser to the governor-designate:
this earned him a broad stare from Corbett and a curiously
agreeable smile from Clonfert, but it aroused no emotion in
the others, taken up as they were with the coming event.
Lord Clonfert was looking pale and drawn, but much
stronger than Stephen had expected: before the conference
he had taken Dr Maturin aside and had thanked him for his
care with an obliging warmth that was evidently intended to
convey more than common civility. For most of the meeting
he sat silent: only towards the end, moved by some impulse
that Stephen could not make out, did he put forward the suggestion that he should lead the detachment of seamen – he
had some knowledge of the country, and he spoke French. It
made sense: Jack agreed, looked round the table, asked
whether anyone had any further point to make, caught
Stephen's eye, and said 'Dr Maturin?'

'Yes, sir,' said Stephen. 'I have only this to say: in the event
of the capture of St Paul's, it is of the first political consequence that the inhabitants should be well treated. Any loot-
ing, rape, or disorderly conduct would have the most
prejudicial effect upon the political ends in view.'

They all looked grave, murmuring a general agreement, and
shortly afterwards Jack stood up. He wished them all a very
good night's sleep, he said, 'for it will be a busy day tomorrow,

gentlemen; and if this blessed wind holds, it will start precious early. For my part I shall cut quarters and turn in the
minute hammocks are piped down.'

He turned in, but it was not to sleep. For the first time in
his sea-going life he lay awake, listening to the wind, watching the tell-tale compass over his cot, and going on deck every
hour or so to look at the sky. The blessed wind never faltered,
still less did it veer into the dreaded west; indeed it strengthened so much that early in the middle watch he reduced sail.

At the change of the watch he was on deck again. He could
feel the loom of the land somewhere on the larboard bow,
and as his eyes grew used to the darkness he could in fact see
the mountains of La Réunion clear against the starlit sky. He
looked at his watch by the binnacle lamp; paced up and down
the quarterdeck; called out 'Sharp the bowlines, there,' and
heard the answering 'One, two, three, belay oh!' 'Bowlines
hauled, sir,' said the officer of the watch, and the hands
returned to their cleaning of the decks. 'I wonder what Corbett will do about it,' he thought, 'with seven hundred people
aboard and not an inch to shove a swab.' He looked at his
watch again, stepped into the master's day-cabin to check it
with the chronometer, checked his reckoning once more, and
said, 'Signal *Néréide* carry on.' The coloured lanterns soared
up, *Néréide* acknowledged and a few moments later he saw
the dim form of the frigate shake out her reefs, set her topgallantsails, haul her wind two points, and stretch away for the
land, away from the squadron, trailing her string of boats.

According to the plan she was to go in alone to avoid suspicion: the landing-parties were to take the batteries commanding the roadstead, and the squadron was then to sail in and
deal with the men-of-war and the town. So far the timing was
perfect. Corbett would have just light enough to see: Jack
disliked the man, but he believed in his knowledge of the
coast. But the waiting was going to be hard and long, since
the troops had seven miles to march: he resumed his pacing.
Seven miles to march, and all he could do in the meantime

was to stand in quietly for St Paul's under topsails alone. He watched the sand in the half-hour glass: the top emptied, the glass was turned, the bell rang clear; again the sand began its busy journey, tumbling grain by grain, millions of grains. If all had gone well they should be on their way by now. The glass turned and turned again, and slowly the sky lightened in the east. Another turn, another bell: 'You may pipe the hands to breakfast, Mr Grant, and then clear the ship for action,' he said, and with a fair show of unconcern he walked into his cabin, into the smell of toast and coffee. How had Killick guessed?

Stephen was already up, sitting there clean, shaven and respectably dressed under the swinging lamp. He said, 'There is the strange look about you, brother?'

'A strange feeling, too,' said Jack. 'Do you know, Stephen, that in about one hour's time the dust will begin to fly, and what I shall do is just lie there in the road and give orders while the other men do the work? It has never happened to me before, and I don't relish it, I find. Though to be sure, Sophie would approve.'

'She would also beg you to drink your coffee while it is hot: and she would be in the right of it. There are few things more discouraging to the mind that likes to believe it is master in its own house, than the unquestionable effect of a full belly. Allow me to pour you a cup.'

The banging of the carpenters' mallets came closer as the bulk-heads went down and the cabins vanished to give a clean sweep fore and aft: not that the poor old *Raisonable* could do much, clean sweep or not; but even so the familiar sound, the coffee and the toast brought his heart back to something like a natural state. The carpenter himself appeared at the door, begged pardon, hesitated. 'Carry on, Mr Gill,' said Jack pleasantly. 'Don't mind us.'

'It is irregular, sir, I know,' said the carpenter, not carrying on at all but advancing towards the table, 'and I beg you will forgive the liberty. But I fair dread the notion of a battle, sir.

Man and boy I've been in the *Raisonable* these six and twenty
year; I know her timbers, and I know her butt-heads; and
with respect, sir, I make so bold as to say, the firing-off of they
old guns will start 'em.'

'Mr Gill,' said Jack, 'I promise you I will use her reasonable.
Reasonable, eh, you smoke it?' A ghost of his old merriment
showed for a moment; a ghost of a smile appeared on the carpenter's face; but not much conviction.

On deck again, and now the world was full of growing light.
The squadron was already right into the broad shallow bay:
on the larboard quarter the cape stretched out far westwards
into the sea; at the bottom of the bay stood the town of St
Paul's, now no more than five miles away; behind rose the
savage mountains of La Réunion, barring the eastern horizon;
and in the offing lay the *Boadicea*. The wind was steady in the
south-east out here, but the different patterns of the sea
inshore showed odd local breezes blowing. Jack took his
glass, searching for the *Néréide*: he swung it along the cape,
the Pointe des Galets – a moderate surf on the outer reef, far
less on the beach itself – and all at once he saw her, almost
becalmed in the lee of the headland, working slowly out from
behind an island against the scend of the sea. At the same
moment the signal-lieutenant caught sight of her, made out
her hoist, and reported, '*Néréide*, sir: *troops on shore*.'

'Very good, Mr – ' The young man's name escaped him. His
glass ran along the coast, along the causeway that traversed a
long stretch of flat watery ground, farther and farther along,
and there they were: three bodies of them: first an exact column of red; then the seamen in a smaller, irregular, but compact blueish mass; and then the sepoys. Already they were
much nearer to St Paul's than he had dared to hope: but
could they ever take the batteries by surprise? Viewed from
the sea, the red coats were horribly conspicuous.

'*Boadicea* signalling, sir,' said the lieutenant again. '*Enemy
in sight, bearing due east*.'

That meant that the *Caroline* had not slipped out. 'Thank

you, Mr Graham,' said Jack – the name came to him this time
– 'Reply *Stand in*: and to the squadron *Make more sail*.' As he
spoke a flaw in the wind shivered the *Raisonable*'s jib: he and
every other man on board glanced up at the clouds gathering
over the island: the dark masses had a look that none of them
much cared for. Was the wind going to come foul at last? But
in a moment the gust had passed, and the squadron, *Sirius*,
Raisonable and *Otter*, ran fast and true straight for St Paul's
and the powerful batteries guarding the port. And as they ran,
so every eye aboard, furtively or openly, watched that distant
progress on the land, for a long, long half hour.

The trim columns far over there were losing shape: they
were advancing at the double now, closer and closer to the
first battery guarding St Paul's, the Lambousière, closer and
closer until they were hidden from Jack by a screen of trees.
In a barely tolerable suspense he waited for the sound of the
heavy French guns sending grape into the close-packed companies; but what he heard was a remote crackle of musketry, a
faint wind-borne cheering. The red coats were swarming all
over the battery, and already the sailors were beyond it, racing
for the next, La Centière. Still in their dead silence the three
ships stood on, *Boadicea* converging upon them from the west,
Néréide tearing up from the north. In five minutes they would
be within the extreme range of the third battery, La Neuve,
right by the town, with its forty guns: now the harbour was
wide open; there lay the *Caroline*, and there lay the Indiamen;
and Jack could see boats plying between the frigate and the
shore. She was landing troops. Beyond her the two Indiamen,
a brig-of-war, several smaller vessels – total confusion there.
Confusion too just outside the town, where the musketry-fire
was spreading fast, two distinct lines of fire, as though the
French soldiers had formed at last, and were standing firm.
Musketry, and then Jack saw the *Caroline* begin to turn; there
had been some order amidst all that turmoil, for she had evidently laid out a spring: in his glass he could see the hands at
her capstan, slewing her; and as her guns bore so she fired at

the English troops, a steady, rapid independent fire. The brig
was firing too. Yet scarcely had her first guns spoken but there
was an answer from the Lambousière battery: the seamen had
turned the guns on the shipping in the port, and they had sent
up the union flag. Immediately afterwards the musket-fire
round the Centière reached a paroxysm; the British colours
ran up on the battery, and its guns joined in. The smoke
drifted wide, a cloud with flashes in its heart.

Jack glanced up and down his line. The *Boadicea* had
reached her station ahead: the *Néréide* was still half a mile
astern. He must stand on past the guns of the third battery,
tack and stand closer in. Although his guns would easily fetch
the town by now he dared not fire into the melee at this
range; even a broadside at the *Caroline* meant the risk of hitting his own people, directly behind. The inaction, the pas-
sive waiting, was extraordinarily painful, above all as the
English soldiers seemed to be falling back. Slowly, slowly on,
and silently; they were coming abreast of La Neuve. The
waiting would not last much longer: round-shot would be all
about their ears at any moment now. The battery glided by,
full on the beam, and he could see the mouths of the guns.
But not one spoke, and not a man was there to serve them:
the gunners had either run, or they had joined the defenders.
The confusion in the town now had a pattern, the French
line had broken, and they were retreating up the hill. Yet for
all that the round-shot came flying from the harbour. The
Caroline, still firing fast from her starboard broadside, now
gave the squadron her whole tier of larboard guns. She concentrated her fire on the pendant-ship, and at her first discharge she hulled the *Raisonable* three times and struck her
maintop. Wreckage, a studdingsail-boom, and some blocks
came hurtling down into the splinter-netting over the quarterdeck. The next sent a dozen hammocks flying amidships;
yet still the squadron could not reply.

'You have noted the time, Mr Peter?' asked Jack, knotting a
stray signal-halliard.

'Immediately, sir,' cried Peter. The secretary was a yellowish white, made all the more evident by his black clothes: his morning's beard showed strongly against his skin. 'Seventeen minutes after eight,' he said.

How the *Caroline* pasted them! She was completely shrouded in her own smoke, but still the twenty-four pound shot came crashing home. 'Admirable practice,' observed Jack to the secretary. Still another steady broadside, and the ship's bulwark of hammocks had great ragged gaps in it; three men were down. The glass turned; the bell struck one. 'Mr Woods,' said Jack to the master, as he stood conning the ship, 'as soon as the church and the tower are in line, we shall go about. Mr Graham, to the squadron: *Tack in succession at the gun.* And then *Close engagement.*' The minutes dropped by, then at last the signal-gun. The squadron went about as smoothly as a machine, *Boadicea, Sirius, Raisonable, Otter, Néréide*; smoothly, but slower, close-hauled on the failing inshore breeze, into the reach of the French guns again. Nearer still, and now the Indiamen let fly, together with the brig and every armed vessel in the port. But now in the town the situation was clear enough. Union flags were flying from all the batteries but one, and at this close range the squadron's guns could at last tell friend from foe. In succession their forward guns began to speak: *Boadicea* fired some deliberate sighting shots, *Sirius* her half-broadside, and the *Raisonable*, a moderate rolling fire; *Otter* and *Néréide* nothing but their bow-guns yet. Eliot had a fine notion of close engagement, observed Jack to himself. The *Boadicea* had stopped firing and she was standing straight in to cross the bows of the *Caroline* as she lay there within twenty-five yards of the shore. At this rate she would surely ground in the next few minutes.

'*Boadicea* signalling: *Permission to anchor, sir,*' said a voice in his ear.

'*Affirmative,*' said Jack, and he turned to the waiting carpenter.

'Five foot of water in the well, sir,' reported Mr Gill, 'and we sprung a butt-end, with them old guns.'

'Mr Woods, haul your wind,' said Jack, never moving his eye from the *Boadicea*. 'Ship the pumps.' He saw her small bower splash down, followed by her stream-anchor: there she lay, her sails clewed up, right athwart the *Caroline*, within pistol-shot of the shore. And now her crew's long training showed itself: in a furious eruption of fire and smoke she played with both broadsides on the frigate, the Indiamen, and the remaining battery. The *Sirius*, the *Otter*, and from some distance, the *Néréide* supported her: the *Raisonable*, lying to, said nothing apart from a few symbolic shots from her stern-chaser. But Jack's spirit was entirely aboard the *Boadicea*, in the true heart of the battle, approving her every stroke; and when, in less than half a glass, the *Caroline*'s colours came down, followed by those of all the other ships and of the last battery, his heart leapt as though she had struck to him. They came down, and a universal cheer went up from the entire squadron, echoed by a roaring from the land.

'My barge, Mr Warburton,' said Jack to the first lieutenant. 'And my compliments to Dr Maturin: we are going ashore.'

The town had suffered very little, and the square in which they met Colonel Keating, with a group of officers and civilians, might have been living in deep peace – windows open, stalls of bright fruit and vegetables displayed, the fountain played – but for the dead silence, all the heavier for the recent warlike thunder, and the total absence of inhabitants. 'Give you joy, Colonel,' said Jack in an unnaturally loud voice as they shook hands. 'You have done wonders, sir: I believe the place is ours.'

'For the moment we may say so, sir,' said Keating with a beaming smile, 'but they are rallying on the hills above, and Desbrusleys' column from Saint-Denis is likely to be here by nightfall. We must go to work at the double.' He laughed very cheerfully, and catching sight of Stephen he said, 'There you are, Doctor: a glorious good morning to you, sir. You politicoes will be pleased with us – we have behaved like lambs, sir, like Sunday-going lambs – not a maiden has been put to the blush, so far, and my men are all well in hand.'

'Might I beg for an officer and a few soldiers, Colonel?' said Stephen. 'I must find the mayor and the chief of police.'

'Certainly you may, sir. Captain Wilson will be delighted to accompany you. But please to remember, that we are likely to be bundled out in less than twelve hours' time; a couple of regiments, with their artillery playing on us from the heights, would make the place untenable.' He laughed again, and from some odd contagion the whole group laughed too: cautious faces peered at the mirth from behind window-curtains; a number of small black boys crept closer under the market stalls. 'Oh, Commodore,' he went on, 'where are my wits? Here are the captains of the Indiamen.'

'I am happy to see you, gentlemen,' said Jack, 'and beg you will go aboard your ships at once. We knocked them about a little, I fear, but I trust they will be ready for sea before . . .' His words were cut off by an earth-shaking explosion, the upward flight of dark lumps of masonry, their corresponding downward crash, as the Lambousière battery disintegrated.

'That will be your friend Lord Clonfert,' remarked the Colonel, chuckling. 'A very active officer. Now, Commodore, shall we attend to the public property?'

They attended to it, and to a great deal besides. Theirs was an enormously busy day, for not only had the more dangerous fortifications to be destroyed, a large number of English prisoners to be released, still more French prisoners to be secured, the wounded seamen from the *Caroline* – half the crew, headed by their captain – to be carried to the hospital, and committees of anxious citizens, clergy and merchants to be reassured, but the wind had fulfilled its earlier threat. It now lay somewhat to the west of south, and the surf was increasing every hour. The *Caroline*, the Indiamen, the *Grappler* brig, and several other vessels having cut their cables at the last moment, had to be heaved off; the *Raisonable* was

obliged to be laid in a mud berth at the ebb for the angry Mr
Gill to come at her sprung butt-end; while every officer, every
bosun and carpenter that could possibly be spared from a
thousand other urgent tasks was furiously busy in the French
naval yard, an undreamed-of Tom Tiddler's ground strewn
with cordage, sailcloth, and spars of every dimension.
Stephen had an equally strenuous time with the mayor, the
vicar-general, and the chief of police; while at the same time
he made a large number of private contacts. His was a less
physically active day than most, but at sunset, when the
senior officers gathered at Keating's headquarters, a carefully-
chosen cabaret by the port, and sat there refreshing themselves with white wine and an admirable local fish, he was as
tired as any of them. The weariness was apparent in their
drawn faces, the frequent yawns, the relaxed posture, but not
in their expressions, and their spirits: they were still a band of
grigs. Colonel Keating was as merry as ever when he passed
Jack his little spy-glass and pointed out the French soldiers
gathering on the heights above the town. 'They tell me the
main column is to be led by General Desbrusleys himself,' he
said, speaking loud to be heard above the surf. 'Yet I wonder a
man of such spirit has not placed his artillery before this;
there are some capital places up there, you know, for a plunging cross-fire. But no doubt he means to come by another
route.'

A frantic Company's supercargo darted by, in search of
hands to reload his precious silk. He plunged through the
gathering maidens lining the port and vanished with a low,
frustrated howl. The maidens resumed their vigil, clasping
one another and giggling: none had yet been caused to blush,
even by this late hour; but hope was not altogether dead,
though the last boats were putting off.

'Make the good woman understand we mean to pay, would
you, Stephen? She does not seem to understand French very
well,' said Jack privately; and aloud, 'I do not wish to hurry
you, gentlemen, but I believe it would be as well to go

aboard. Weather permitting, we shall come ashore tomorrow and finish our task. The hands will be rested, and' – nodding at Stephen – 'in daylight they will be out of temptation.'

The weather did not permit. The wind settled into the west, blowing right on the land, and although the squadron, together with its captures and recaptures, rode easily far beyond the breakers, with a fine holding-ground and two cables veered out on end, and although the swell did not prevent a numerous gathering for breakfast in the *Raisonable*, it seemed evident that the thunderous surf, a quarter of a mile deep along the shore as far as eye could reach, must prevent any communication with the town. It was an uncommonly cheerful breakfast, with yesterday's action on shore fought over point by point, with kind words from the soldiers about the Navy's versatility, discipline and enterprise, and it was a breakfast that made surprising inroads on Jack's mutton hams from the Cape and his soft tack from St Paul's; yet there was not an officer aboard who did not know that they had left a great deal undone in the town, partly from want of time and partly from want of an authoritative list of government as opposed to private property: Stephen had obtained the list a little before dark, but until that time he had strongly insisted that nothing but the most obvious military stores and equipment should be touched. Then again, all the sailors and most of the soldiers knew that if the wind kept in the west the squadron would be in a most uncomfortable position. Desbrusleys would bring his artillery from Saint-Denis under the cover of darkness and lob mortar-shells on to them from behind the nearest hill while they lay like sitting ducks, unable to beat out to sea: for the moment, however, the French seemed disinclined to move. Their forces could be seen on the mountain-ridge above St Paul's; but there they stayed, and their immobility contributed not a little to the gaiety of the meal.

It was not until well after dinner that a column was reported to be advancing over the causeway from Saint-

Denis. A remarkably large column, too, with artillery. 'He will never get his guns across the marsh without fascines, however,' observed Colonel Keating, 'because we destroyed the bridge; and it will take him the best part of the day to cut them. The most tedious, wearing task I know, getting guns across a marsh.'

'The surf is growing less,' said Captain Corbett. 'In my opinion we shall be able to land tomorrow – look at the westward sky. Soon come, soon go: that's my experience.'

'Earlier than that, I trust,' said Jack. 'I should never rest easy again, was we not to blow up at least the first three buildings in Dr Maturin's list.'

'And from the political point of view,' said Stephen, 'I should rejoice to see the archives go up in flames: such an invaluable confusion.'

'If I may speak, sir,' said Lord Clonfert, 'I believe it could be attempted now, or at least before the evening. I brought away a couple of surf-boats, and there are more alongside the *Sirius*, if I am not mistaken. My men are used to handling them, and I will undertake to put a party of Marines and seamen ashore.'

'Perhaps in two or three hours,' said Jack, staring at the sea. How much was this Clonfert's desire to outdo Corbett? Even after yesterday's joint action their relationship was obviously still as bad as ever: even worse, maybe. Yet there was the importance of the objective; and these surf-boats, well managed, could do surprising things. But was Clonfert merely showing away? What kind of capers would be cut on shore? On the other hand, he had certainly done well yesterday . . . Jack felt that Clonfert's mental processes were foreign to him: there was something about the man that he could not make out, either at this point or after some hours of reflection, when he came to his pragmatic decision, gave the order, and stood on the *Raisonable*'s poop, watching the surf-boats pull away. They were on the edge of the whiteness, waiting for the huge roller: it came, sweeping the sea, rose again black against the white water, and again they shot forward: again and again, and the last wave pitched them high on the beach.

Now they were busy. A tower to the left of the town gave a great jerk, its parapet flying bodily into the air: smoke and dust surrounded it, the whole building settled into a low shapeless heap, and the vast boom reached the ship. A long pause, and then smoke appeared behind the administrative buildings. 'Those are my tax-gatherer's records,' said Stephen, beside him. 'If that does not render us beloved, the Bourbonnais are hard to please. General Desbrusleys seems sadly bogged down,' he added, shifting his glass to the far-distant stationary column in the marsh.

They watched: they watched. At one time Jack remarked that the surf was certainly diminishing; and at another he said, 'You know, Stephen, I am growing almost used to being a spectator: yesterday I thought I should hang myself from mere misery . . . I suppose it is what you pay for command. Look at the smoke, over beyond the arsenal. What now, Mr Grant?'

'I beg pardon, sir, but Mr Dale of the *Streatham* Indiaman is in a great taking. He says they are burning his silk – begs you to see him.'

'Let him up, Mr Grant.'

'Sir, sir,' cried Mr Dale. 'They are burning our silk! Pray sir, signal them to stop. Our silk – our chief cargo – half a million pounds' worth of silk – the French stored it in that warehouse. Oh, pray, sir, signal them to . . . oh Lord, Lord' – clasping his hands – 'it is too late.' The smoke gave way to flame, to a great sheet of flame; and all the signals in the world would not put it out.

'Pray, Clonfert,' said Jack, when the captain came to report, 'why did you burn the store behind the arsenal?'

'Behind the arsenal, sir? I was assured it was government property. A most respectable man, a priest, assured me it was government property. Have I done wrong?'

'I am sure you acted with the best intentions, but it seems that the Indiamen's silk was there, to the tune of half a million.' Clonfert's face fell, he looked utterly wretched, and suddenly quite old. 'Never mind it,' said Jack. 'I dare say they exaggerate; and anyhow we have saved them three millions, as they themselves acknowledge. You have done nobly, nobly – how I envied you on shore! It was no doubt a necessary stroke, for if we are drove off, pretty foolish we should look, leaving all that in enemy hands. But come, you are soaking wet: should not you like to shift your clothes? I have plenty in my sleeping-cabin.'

It was no use. Clonfert retired, sad, cast down, his glory quite put out. Nor did he revive the next day, when, the sea almost calm again, the south-east wind re-established, and all the squadron's forces ready in the boats to oppose Desbrusleys, one of Stephen's new acquaintances put off from the shore with the news that the Saint-Denis column was retreating, and that Captain Saint-Michiel, the commandant of St Paul's, was willing to treat for a suspension of arms.

The news was visibly true: the column could be seen withdrawing. All hands turned to their ships, and presently the commandant's emissaries appeared. General Desbrusleys, it seemed, had blown out his brains; but whether this was the outcome of the unhappy gentleman's military or marital reverses, or of the two combined, did not appear. At all events, for the moment the French army command was in a state of hopeless confusion, and Saint-Michiel made no difficulty about signing an agreement that gave the British squadron a long, peaceful week in St Paul's. Peaceful, but active: they were able to destroy or take away a hundred and twenty-one guns and an immense quantity of powder and shot, to blow up the remaining fortifications, to reduce the naval yard to a mere desolation with not so much as a paint-pot in it, and to do wonders for that fine frigate the *Caroline*: while the Commodore and the Colonel had time to write their despatches, a most arduous and delicate undertaking.

When Jack's were finished at last, stripped of all humanity and copied fair in Mr Peter's hands, together with the very moderate casualty-list, an exact amount of the captured ships and vessels, a somewhat less exact account of the government stores and provisions taken, and many other documents, he came to his difficult decision.

He sent for Corbett and Clonfert, receiving them in some state with his secretary beside him. To the first he said, 'Captain Corbett, since we already have a *Caroline* in the service, I have provisionally renamed her the *Bourbonnaise*; but there is nothing provisional in my offering you the command of her, and at the same time desiring you to proceed forthwith to the Cape with my despatches. I have no doubt the Admiral will send you straight home with them, so I will burden you, if I may, with my own personal letters. I have manned her with something near her complement, barring Marines of course, from the merchant-seamen released at St Paul's, so I must ask you to be very moderate in the article of followers. Here is your order, and this is my private packet.'

Corbett's habitually angry face was ill-suited for the expression of pleasure, but even so it cracked and expanded with delight. The man who carried these despatches – the news of the neatest, completest little victory in his experience – would be much caressed at the Admiralty: would be certain of the next plum going.

'I shall be moderation incarnate, sir,' he said. 'And may I say, sir, that nothing could increase my sense of this command more than the obliging manner in which it has been given?'

To the second he said, 'Lord Clonfert, it gives me great pleasure to appoint you to the *Néréide*, vice Captain Corbett. Tomkinson, your first lieutenant, may have the *Otter*.' Clonfert too flushed bright at the news, the entirely unexpected news, of this decisive step in his career, the vital change from a sloop to a post-ship; he too made his acknowledgments, and more gracefully by far than Corbett; and for a while the full shining glory of the first day on La Réunion returned, indeed a greater glory. Yet it seemed to have some slight bitter aftertaste, for as he was taking his leave he said, with a smile not wholly of unmixed happiness, 'I never thought, sir, when we were lieutenants together, that it would be you that made me post.'

He is an odd fish, Clonfert,' said Jack to Stephen, between two peaceful duets. 'You might almost think I had done him an injury, giving him his step.'

'You did so advisedly, not from any sudden whim? It is the real expression of your sense of his deserts, and not an alms? He should in fact be made a post-captain?'

'Why,' said Jack, 'it is rather a case of *faute de mieux*, as you would say. I should not like to have to rely upon him at all times; but one of them had to go, and he is a better captain than Corbett. His men will follow him anywhere. Perhaps he may lay out popularity more than I think right, but whether or no, your foremast Jack dearly loves a lord; and I must take advantage of that just as I should take advantage of a tide or a shift in the wind; I shall let him take most of his *Otters* into the *Néréide*, and scatter the Néréides about the squadron. That was a damned unhealthy ship.' He shook his head, looking grave, and played a series of deep notes: they changed however, promising a happy development; but before he reached it his dry bow refused its duty, and he reached out for the rosin.

'When you have done with my rosin, Jack – *my* rosin, I say – would you be prepared to reveal our immediate destination?'

'It will please you, I believe. We must take Keating back to Rodriguez first, and you shall have a romp with your tortoises and your vampires; then, while the rest of the squadron is blockading Mauritius, down to the Cape to leave Eliot and the poor old *Raisonable*; then back in the *Boadicea*, which is taking the Indiamen south. Back to these waters, to see what can be done about the remaining frigates, unless you and Farquhar have further designs on La Réunion. I will not say I am sanguine, Stephen, because that might not be very clever; but I remember when you asked me how I should set the odds some weeks ago, I said three to five against us. Now I should say they are evens, or slightly in our favour.'

5

THE ADMIRAL WAS pleased with the Commodore, as well he might be, for not only had Jack captured one of the four powerful French frigates that so disturbed Mr Bertie's peace of mind, and retaken two Indiamen together with a useful eighteen-gun sloop, not only had he destroyed one of the strongest French bases in the Indian Ocean, doing so with such briskness that the Admiral's dispositions would be admired even in Whitehall, which always called for quick results, but he had also enriched Mr Bertie to the extent of several thousand pounds. Just how many thousand it was impossible to say until a tribe of officials six thousand miles away should have set a value on a prodigious number of objects such as the three hundred and twenty pikes, forty rammers and forty sponges taken at St Paul's; but in any case Admiral Bertie would eventually receive one twelfth of the total sum that they arrived at: without having stirred hand or foot, without having given any advice more valuable than a general exhortation to 'go in and win', he had acquired a considerable addition to his fortune; and ever since his first charming conference with Captain Corbett, the forerunner of the squadron, he had spent the chief of his time in drawing up detailed plans for new stabling and a pine-house at Langton Castle, where he lived, while in default of the coronet for which she longed, Mrs Bertie should have a suit of lace.

Yet although the Admiral was perhaps a little devious beneath his bonhomie he had a grateful heart a fairly grateful

heart; at least he was no gripe-farthing; and the moment the
Raisonable was signalled he began to lay on a feast, sending
two boats away to the westward for lobsters, his favourite
dish.

As he led the Commodore towards this glowing spread,
which was attended by almost all the eminent men and all
the beautiful women of Cape Town, so long as they were
white, he said, 'How happy I am to see you back so soon,
Aubrey, and how very well things have turned out! I sent Corbett straight home with your splendid news, as soon as I had
dashed off my covering letter: you will have a Gazette to yourself, I am sure. What a pretty ship she is, too, your *Bourbon-*
naise – fine narrow entry, and as stiff as a steeple. I wish our
yards could turn 'em out like that: yet after all, if you young
fellows take 'em ready made, it saves our shipwrights' time,
eh? Ha, ha. I confirmed her new name, by the by, and shall
confirm all your appointments: I am glad Clonfert is made
post, though that was a sad unlucky stroke with the Company's silk: I dare say you keel-hauled him for it at the time.
Still, 'tis of no use crying over spilt milk, as I always tell Mrs
Bertie; and all's well that ends well. Clonfert is made post,
and you have taken four thumping prizes and half a dozen little ones. You did not see anything else on your way down, I
suppose, just for the *bonne bouche*, as they say, ha, ha?'

'Well, sir, we sighted that Russian sloop *Diana* beating
about off Rodriguez; but I thought I should best fall in with
your views by disregarding her.'

The Admiral did not seem to hear. After a momentary
absence he went on, 'Well, and so you knocked their batteries
about their ears. I am glad of it, and Farquhar is cock-a-hoop,
as far as a dry stick of a man like that can be cock-a-hoop
drinks no wine, and the water has rotted all the joy out of him
I did not ask him to this dinner: in any case, he declines all
invitations. He is longing to see you, however, and your Dr
Maturin; for the next bite, once Rodriguez is reinforced, is

Bourbon for good and all. Or La Réunion, or Ile Buonaparte, as they call it. Damned fools: this chopping and changing is typical of your foreigner, don't you find, Aubrey? That should be with the next monsoon, as long as transports can be provided for three or four thousand men. What kind of man is this Dr Maturin, may I ask? Is he to be trusted? He looks something of the foreigner to me.'

'Oh, I believe he is quite trustworthy, sir,' said Jack, with an inward grin. 'Lord Keith has a great opinion of him: offered him to be physician of the fleet. And the Duke of Clarence called him in, when the whole faculty was at a stand. He thinks the world of Dr Maturin.'

'Oh, indeed?' cried the Admiral, deeply impressed. 'I shall have to take care of him, I find. Not that these clever politicoes can really be trusted, you know. You must take a long spoon to sup with the Devil, I always say. However, let us get to our lobsters. You can trust my lobsters, Aubrey, ha, ha. I sent a couple of boats to the westward for 'em, the moment you made your number.'

The lobsters were trustworthy, so were the oysters, so was the rest of the enormous meal, which carried on, remove after remove, until the cloth was drawn at last and the port appeared, when Admiral Bertie called out, 'Fill up, gentlemen. Bumpers all round. Here's to Lucky Jack Aubrey with three times three; and may he thump 'em again and again.'

A week later the Governor of the Cape also honoured the Commodore with a feast. It consisted of game – blauwbok, springbok, steinbok, klipspringer, hartebeest, wildebeest, the black and the blue no lobster at all, and it took even longer to eat; but this was as far as the Governor's originality could take him; once more the meal ended with cabinet pudding, and once more the guests drank their port wishing that Jack might thump them again and again.

At the time of this second toast Stephen was eating bread and cold meat with Mr Farquhar and Mr Prote, his secretary,

in an upper room of the government printing-house, a
secluded place from which the workmen had withdrawn.
They were all of them more or less black, for in the light of
Stephen's most recent intelligence they had been recasting a
proclamation to the people of La Réunion, as well as a number of handbills and broadsheets that painted, in glowing
colours and fluent French, the advantages of British rule,
promising respect for religion, laws, customs and property,
pointing out the inevitably disastrous consequences of resistance, and the rewards (perhaps a little imprecise and rhetorical) of cooperation. There were similar documents, though
in a less forward state of preparation, addressed to the inhabitants of Mauritius; and all these were to be printed as
secretly as possible, with the help of two confidential jour-
neymen. Yet since neither of these knew a word in French,
Farquhar and Prote had been perpetually in and out of the
house, and both had grown fascinated by the technical
processes of printing. In their eagerness to show Stephen
their proficiency they corrected three long texts in the galley,
reading by means of a little looking-glass that they tended to
snatch from one another, plucking out letters, inserting others, prating about upper case, lower case, formes, coigns and
composing-sticks, setting-rules and justification, and gradually smearing themselves, and him, with an unreasonable
quantity of printer's ink.

   They were no longer talking about the act of printing, however, not even about their insidious printed warfare: that,
together with Stephen's detailed report of the promising state
of public feeling on La Réunion and his account of the agents
he had acquired, was far behind them; and now, as they ate
their blotted meat, they discussed the poetry of the law, or
rather poetry in the law, a subject to which they had been led
by considerations on the inheritance of landed property in Mr
Farquhar's future kingdom.

   'The French system, their new French code, is very well on
paper,' observed Farquhar, 'very well for a parcel of logical

automata; but it quite overlooks the illogical, I might say almost supra-logical and poetic side of human nature. *Our* law, in its wisdom, has preserved much of this, and it is particularly remarkable in the customary tenure of land, and in petty serjeanty. Allow me to give you an example: in the manors of East and West Enbourne, in Berkshire, a widow shall have her free-bench – her *sedes libera*, or in barbarous law-Latin her *francus bancus* – in all her late husband's copyhold lands *dum sola et casta fuerit*; but if she be detected in amorous conversation with a person of the opposite sex – if she grant the last favours she loses all, unless she appears in the next manor-court, riding backwards on a black ram, and reciting the following words:

> 'Here I am
> Riding on a black ram
> Like a whore as I am;
> And for my crinkum-crankum
> Have lost my binkum-bankum;
> And for my tail's game
> Am brought to this worldly shame.
> Therefore good Mr Steward let me have my lands again.

'My uncle owns one of these manors, and I have attended the court. I cannot adequately describe the merriment, the amiable confusion of the personable young widow, the flood of rustic wit, and which is my real point the universal, contented acceptance of her reinstatement, which I attribute largely to the power of poetry.'

'There may be a significant statistical relationship between the number of black ram-lambs suffered to reach maturity,' said Prote, 'and that of personable young widows.'

'And 'tis no isolated case,' continued Farquhar. 'For in the manor of Kilmersdon in Somerset, for example, we find what is essentially the same purgation, though in an abbreviated form, since no more than this distich is required:

'*For mine arse's fault I take this pain.*
Therefore, my lord, give me my land again.

'Now is it not gratifying, gentlemen, to find our black rams – unprofitable creatures but for this interesting ceremony – so far apart as Berkshire and Somerset, with no record of a white ram's ever having been admitted? For your black ram, gentlemen, is, I am persuaded, intimately connected with the worship of the Druids . . .'

Mr Farquhar was a man with a good understanding and a great deal of information, but at the first mention of Druids, oak-groves or mistletoe a wild gleam came into his eye, a gleam so wild on this occasion that Stephen looked at his watch, rose to his feet, said that he must regretfully leave them, and gathered up his book.

'Should you not like to wash before you go?' asked Farquhar. 'You are somewhat mottled.'

'Thank you,' said Stephen. 'But the being upon whom I am about to wait, though eminent for precedence, does not stand on ceremony.'

'What can he have meant by eminent for precedence?' asked Mr Prote. 'Anyone who is anyone, apart from us, is at the Governor's.'

'He may well mean a black magus, or a potentate among the Hottentots. Now the Druids, I say . . .'

In fact the being's precedence was merely alphabetical: for in the gaiety of his heart Dr Maturin had referred to the aardvark. It stood before him now, a pale creature with a bulky hog-backed body close on five feet long, a broad tail, an immense elongated head ending in a disk-like snout, short stout legs and disproportionately long translucent ass's ears; it was partially covered with sparse yellowish hair that showed the unwholesome nightwalker's skin below; it blinked repeatedly. The aardvark was acutely conscious of its position and from time to time it licked its small tubular lips, for not only had it been measured and weighed, while a tuft of bristles that could ill be spared had been clipped from its flank, but now it was being looked at through a diminishing-glass and drawn. It was a meek, apologetic animal, incapable of biting and too shy to scratch; and it grew lower and lower in its spirits: its ears drooped until they obscured its weak, melancholy, long-lashed eyes.

'There, honey, it is done,' said Stephen, showing the aardvark its likeness: and calling upwards through the ceiling he said, 'Mr van der Poel, I am infinitely obliged to you, sir. Do not stir, I beg. I shall lock the door and leave the key under the mat: I am going back to the ship, and tomorrow you shall see the egg.'

Some hours later he beheld Simon's Town again, its inner anchorage scattered with Jack's prizes: it reminded him of Port Mahon long ago, when the *Sophie's* captured feluccas, trabacaloes and xebecs lined the quay. 'That was very well,' he said, 'and Minorca a delightful island; but even Minorca could never boast the aardvark.' The street was filled with liberty-men, a cheerful crew, for not only had Jack ordered a modest advance of prize-money – two dollars a nob paid down on the capstan-head – but Dr Maturin's words on loot had not been obeyed quite as strictly as he could have wished, and pieces of the finest Oriental silk, slightly charred, covered the lithe forms, the infinitely seductive bosoms of the sailors' companions. He was hailed on all sides; kind hands led his hired nag away; and a Boadicean midshipman, smelling strongly of patchouli, rowed him out to the *Raisonable*. At ease in his spacious cabin he opened his book and looked at the picture again. 'It is perhaps the most gratifying beast I have ever figured,' he said, 'and it displays a touching affection for the good Mr van der Poel; I believe I shall attempt to colour it.' He turned back through the pages. Most were covered with the small close-written text of his diary, but there were several drawings – the Rodriguez tortoise, the seals of False Bay – some washed with watercolour. 'Perhaps not,' he said, considering them. 'My talents scarcely seem to lie that way.' He converted the Dutch weight of the aardvark into avoirdupois, sharpened his pen to a finer point, reflected for a while, gazing out of the scuttle, and began to write in his personal cipher.

'I cannot trace the chain of thought or rather of associations that leads me to reflect upon Clonfert and Jack Aubrey. Conceivably the aardvark plays a part, so ill at ease: but the links are obscure. Clonfert's tormina exercise my mind; for by whatever private scale of pain one may measure them, they must come tolerably high. It seems ludicrously facile to regard them as the direct transposition of his state of mind; yet McAdam is no fool except to himself; and in some not dissimilar cases that Dupuytren and I dissected we were able to eliminate any direct physical cause. The vermiform appendix, so often the villain in these apparent strangulations, as pink as a healthy worm, the whole tract from the oesophagus downwards, devoid of lesion. Clonfert is more of an Irishman, with the exacerbated susceptibilities of a subject race, than I had supposed; more indeed than I gave Jack to understand. I find that as a boy he did not attend a great English public school, as did most of his kind I have known; nor did he go early to sea and thereby wash away the barrier: the first years of his nominal service were book-time, as they call the amiable cheat by which a complaisant captain places an absent child upon his muster-roll. Far from it: he was brought up almost entirely by the servants at Jenkinsville (a desolate region). Squireen foster-parents too for a while, his own being so mad or so disreputable: and he seems to have sucked in the worst of both sides. On the one hand he derived his notion of himself as a lord from people who have had to cringe these many generations to hold on to the odd patch of land that is their only living; and on the other, though half belonging to them, he has been bred up to despise their religion, their language, their poverty, their manners and traditions. A conquering race, in the place of that conquest, is rarely amiable; the conquerors pay less obviously than the conquered, but perhaps in time they pay even more heavily, in the loss of the humane qualities. Hard, arrogant, profit-seeking adventurers flock to the spoil, and the natives, though outwardly civil, contemplate them with a resentment mingled with contempt, while at the same time respecting the face of conquest – acknowledging their greater strength. And to be divided between the two must lead to a strange confusion of sentiment. In Clonfert's case the result of this and of other factors seems to me an uneasy awareness of his own distinction (he often mentions it), a profound uncertainty of its real value, and a conviction that to validate its claims he should be twice as tall as other men. In spite of his high heels, both literal and figurative, he is not twice as tall as other men: Jack, in particular, tops him by a head and more. He has surrounded himself with a strikingly inferior set of officers, which I do not remember to have seen done in the Navy, where the aristocratic captains are almost always accompanied by aristocratic officers and midshipmen, just as a Scotch commander will gather Scotchmen around him: no doubt they provide him with the approval he longs for; but how much can a man of his understanding value their approval? And if Lady Clonfert and Mrs Jennings are a fair example of his women, to what degree can their favours really gratify him?

'Upon this foundation, and upon what McAdam tells me, I could build up a moderately convincing Clonfert whose entire life is an unsatisfactory pretence: a puppet vainly striving to be another puppet, equally unreal – the antithesis of Jack, who has never played a part in his life, who has no need for any role. It would not satisfy me, however, for although it may have some truth in it and although it may go far towards pointing at the origin of the tormina and some other symptons I have noted (McAdam did not appreciate the significance of the asymmetric *sudor insignis*), it does not take into account the fact that he is *not* a puppet. Nor, which is far more important, does it take into account the affection of his men: Jack asserts that sailors love a lord and no doubt that is profoundly true (apart from anything else, the fancied difference diminishes the servitude); but they do not go on loving a lord if he is worthless. They did not go on loving Prince William. No: a continued affection over a long period must be based upon the recognition of real qualities in the man, for a ship at sea, particularly a small ship on a foreign station, is an enclosed village; and whoever heard of the long-matured judgment of a village being wrong? The communal mind, even where the community is largely made up of unthinking and illiterate men, is very nearly as infallible as a Council. And the qualities valued by a community of men are commonly good nature, generosity and courage. Courage: here I am on the most shifting ground in the world. For what is it? Men put different values on their lives at different times: different men value approval at different rates – for some it is the prime mover. Two men go through the same motions for widely different reasons; their conduct bears the same name. Yet if Clonfert has not performed these actions I am very sure that his men would not esteem him as they do. Farquhar's illogicality may well render their affection for Lord Clonfert greater than it would be for Mr Scroggs, but that is merely an addition; the esteem is already there, and so are the actions upon which it is founded. I saw him storm a battery at St Paul's; and in the result his outward gestures, his élan, and indeed his success were indistinguishable from Jack Aubrey's.

'Jack Aubrey. The lieutenant of long ago is still visible in the grave commodore, but there are times when he has to be looked for. One constant is that indubitable happy courage, the courage of the fabled lion – how I wish I may see a lion – which makes him go into action as some men might go to their marriage-bed. *Every man would be a coward if he durst*: it is true of most, I do believe, certainly of me, probably of Clonfert; but not of Jack Aubrey. Marriage has changed him, except in this: he had hoped for too much, poor sanguine creature (though indeed he is sick for news from home). And the weight of this new responsibility; he feels it extremely: responsibility and the years – his youth is going or indeed is gone. The change is evident, but it is difficult to name many particular alterations, apart from the comparative want of gaiety, of that appetence for mirth, of those infinitesimal jests that caused him at least such enormous merriment. I might mention his attitude towards those under his command, apart from those he has known for years: it is attentive, conscientious, and informed; but is far less personal; his mind rather than his heart is concerned, and the people are primarily instruments of war. And his attitude towards the ship itself: well do I remember his boundless delight in his first command, although the *Sophie* was a sad shabby little tub of a thing – the way he could not see enough of her meagre charms, bounding about the masts, the rigging, and the inner parts with an indefatigable zeal, like a great boy. Now he is the captain of a lordly two-decker, with these vast rooms and balconies, and he is little more than polite to her; she might be one set of furnished lodgings rather than another. Though here I may be mistaken: some aspects of the sailor's life I do not understand. Then again there is the diminution not only of his animal spirits but also of his appetites: I am no friend to adultery, which surely promises more than it can perform except in the article of destruction; but I could wish that Jack had at least some temptation to withstand. His more fiery emotions, except where war is concerned, have cooled; Clonfert, younger in this as in many other ways, has retained his capacity for the extremes of feeling, certainly the extremity of pain, perhaps that of delight. The loss is a natural process no doubt, and one that prevents a man from burning away altogether before his time; but I should be sorry if, in Jack Aubrey's case, it were to proceed so far as a general cool indifference; for then the man I have known and valued so long would be no more than the walking corpse of himself.'

The sound of the bosun's call, the clash of the Marines presenting arms, told him that Jack Aubrey's body, quick or dead, was at this moment walking about within a few yards of him. Stephen dusted sand upon his book, closed it, and waited for the door to open.

The officer who appeared did indeed resemble Commodore rather than Lieutenant Aubrey, even after he had flung his coat and with it the marks of rank on to a nearby locker. He was bloated with food and wine; his eyes were red and there were liverish circles under them; and he was obviously far too hot. But as well as the jaded look of a man who has been obliged to eat and drink far too much and then sit in an open carriage for twenty miles in a torrid dust-storm, wearing clothes calculated for the English Channel, his face had an expression of discouragement.

'Oh for some more soldiers like Keating,' he said wearily. 'I cannot get them to move. We had a council after dinner, and I represented to them, that with the regiments under their command we could take La Réunion out of hand: the *Raison-able* would serve as a troop-carrier. St Paul's is wide open, with not one stone of the batteries standing on another. They agreed, and groaned, and lamented – they could not move without an order from the Horse-Guards; it had always been understood that the necessary forces were to come from the Madras establishment, perhaps with the next monsoon if transports could be found; if not, with the monsoon after that. By the next monsoon, said I, La Réunion would be bristling with guns, whereas now the French had very few, and those few served by men with no appetite for a battle of any kind: by the next monsoon their spirits would have revived, and they would have been reinforced from the Mauritius. Very true, said the soldiers, wagging their heads; but they feared that the plan worked out by the staff must stand: should I like to go shooting warthogs with them on Saturday? And to crown all, the brig was not a packet but a merchantman from the Azores – no letters of any kind. We might as well be at the back of the moon.'

'It is very trying, indeed,' said Stephen. 'What say you to

some barley-water, with lime-juice in it? And then a swim? We could take a boat to the island where the seals live.'

To a cooler, fresher Jack he offered what comfort he could provide. He left the stolid torpor of the soldiers to one side – neither had really believed in the possibility of stirring them, after the dismal end of the unauthorized expedition to Buenos Aires from this very station not many years before – and concentrated on the changed perception of time during periods of activity; these busy weeks had assumed an importance unjustified by their sidereal, or as he might say their absolute measure; with regard to exterior events they still remained mere weeks; it had been unreasonable to expect anything on their return to the Cape; but now a ship might come in any day at all, loaded with mail.

'I hope you are right, Stephen,' said Jack, balancing on the gunwale and rubbing the long blue wound on his back. 'Sophie has been very much in my mind these last few days, and even the children. I dreamt of her last night, a huddled, uneasy dream; and I long to hear from her.' After a considering pause he said, 'I did bring back some more pleasant news, however: the Admiral is fairly confident of being able to add *lphigenia* and *Magicienne* to the squadron within the next few weeks; he had word from Sumatra. But of course they will be coming from the east – not the least possibility of anything from home. The old *Leopard*, too, though nobody wants *her*: iron-sick throughout, a real graveyard ship.'

'The packet will come in from one day to the next, and it will bring a budget of tax-demands, bills, and an account of the usual domestic catastrophes: news of mumps, chicken-pox, a leaking tap; my prophetic soul sees it beneath the horizon.'

The days dropped by while the *Boadicea*, her holds emptied and herself heaved down with purchase to bollards on the shore, had her foul bottom cleaned; Jack set up his telescope with a new counterbalance that worked perfectly on land; Stephen saw his lion, a pride of lions; and then, although it had mistaken the horizon, his prophetic soul was shown to have been right: news did come in. But it was not domestic news, nor from the west: the flying *Wasp* had turned about in mid-ocean and had come racing back to the Cape to report that the French had taken three more Indiamen, HM sloop *Victor*, and the powerful Portuguese frigate *Minerva*.

The *Vénus* and the *Manche*, already at sea when the squadron looked into Port-Louis, had captured the *Windham*, the *United Kingdom*, and the *Charlton*, all Indiamen of the highest value. The *Bellone*, slipping out past the blockade by night, had taken the eighteen-gun *Victor*, and then she and her prize had set about the *Minerva*, which mounted fifty-two guns, but which mounted them in vain against the fury of the French attack. The Portuguese, now *La Minerve*, was at present in Port-Louis, manned by seamen from the *Canonnière* and some deserters: the Indiamen, the *Vénus* and the *Manche* were probably there too, but of that the *Wasp* was not quite sure.

Before the turn of the tide Jack was at sea, the wart-hogs, the soldiers, and even his telescope left behind: he had shifted his pendant into the *Boadicea*, for the hurricane months were not far away, and the *Raisonable* could not face them. He was back in his own *Boadicea*, driving her through variable and sometimes contrary winds until they reached the steady south-east trade, when she layover with her lee-rail under white water, her deck sloping like the roof of Ashgrove Cottage, and began to tear off her two hundred and fifty and even three hundred nautical miles between one noon observation and the next; for there was some remote hope of catching the Frenchmen and their prizes, cutting them off before they reached Mauritius.

On the second Sunday after their departure, with church rigged, Jack was reading the Articles of War in a loud, official, comminatory voice by way of sermon and all hands were trying to keep upright (for not a sail might be attempted to be touched). He had just reached article XXIX, which dealt with sodomy by hanging the sodomite and which always made Spotted Dick and other midshipmen swell purple from suppressed giggling at every monthly repetition, when two ships heaved in sight. They were a great way off, and without interrupting her devotions, such as they might be with every mind fixed earnestly upon the mast-head, the *Boadicea* edged away to gain the weather-gage. But by the time Jack had reached *All crimes not capital* (there were precious few), and well before he cleared the ship for action, the windward stranger broke out the private signal. In answer to the *Boadicea*'s she made her number: the *Magicienne*; and her companion was the *Windham*.

The *Magicienne*, said Captain Curtis, coming aboard the Commodore, had retaken the Indiamen off the east coast of Mauritius. The *Windham* had been separated from her captor, the *Vénus*, during a tremendous sudden blow in seventeen degrees south; the *Magicienne* had snapped her up after something of a chase, beating to windward all day, and had then stood on all night in the hope of finding the French frigate. Curtis had found her at sunset, looking like a scarecrow with only her lower masts standing and a few scraps of canvas aboard, far away right under the land, creeping in with her tattered forecourse alone. But unhappily the land to which she was creeping was the entrance to Grand-Port; and when the land-breeze set in, blowing straight in her teeth, the *Magicienne* had the mortification of seeing the *Vénus* towed right under the guns of the Ile de la Passe, at the entrance to the haven.

'By the next morning, sir, when I could stand in,' said Curtis apologetically, 'she was half way up to the far end, and with my ammunition so low – only eleven rounds to a gun – and the Indiaman in such a state, I did not think it right to follow her.'

'Certainly not,' said Jack, thinking of that long inlet, guarded by the strongly fortified Ile de la Passe, by batteries on either side and at the bottom and even more by a tricky,

winding fairway fringed with reefs: the Navy called it Port
South-East, as opposed to Port-Louis in the north-west, and
he knew it well. 'Certainly not. It would have meant throwing
the *Magicienne* away; and I need her. Oh, yes, indeed, I need
her, now they have that thumping great *Minerva*. You will
dine with me, Curtis? Then we must bear away for Port-
Louis.' They passed the Indiaman a tow, and lugging their
heavy burden through the sea they stood on, the wind just
abaft the beam.

Stephen Maturin had been deeply mistaken in supposing
that Jack, older and more consequential, now looked upon
ships as lodgings, more or less comfortable: the *Raisonable*
had never been truly his; he was not wedded to her. The
Boadicea was essentially different; he entered into her; he
was one of her people. He knew them all, and with a few
exceptions he liked them all: he was delighted to be back,
and although Captain Eliot had been a perfectly unexceptionable officer, they were delighted to have him. They had in
fact led Eliot a sad life of it, opposing an elastic but effective
resistance to the slightest hint of change: 'The Commodore
had always liked it this way; the Commodore had always
liked it that; it was Captain Aubrey that had personally
ordered the brass bow-chasers to be painted brown.' Jack particularly valued Mr Fellowes, his bosun, who had clung even
more firmly than most to Captain Aubrey's sail-plan and his
huge, ugly snatch-blocks that allowed hawsers to be instantly
set up to the mastheads, there to withstand the strain of an
extraordinary spread of canvas; and now that the *Boadicea*'s
hold had been thoroughly restowed, her hull careened, and
her standing-rigging rerove with the spoils of St Paul's, she
answered their joint hopes entirely. In spite of her heavy burden she was now making nine knots at every heave of the log.

'She is making a steady nine knots,' said Jack, coming
below after quarters.

'How happy you make me, Jack,' said Stephen. 'And you
might make me even happier, should you so wish, by giving

me a hand with this. The unreasonable attitude, or lurch, of the ship caused me to overset the chest.'

'God help us,' cried Jack, gazing at the mass of gold coins lying in a deep curve along the leeward side of the cabin. 'What is this?'

'It is technically known as money,' said Stephen. 'And was you to help me pick it up, instead of leering upon it with a stunned concupiscence more worthy of Danae than a king's officer, we might conceivably save some few pieces before they all slip through the cracks in the floor. Come, come, bear a hand, there.'

They picked and shovelled busily, on all fours, and when the thick squat iron-bound box was full again, Stephen said, 'They are to go into these small little bags, if you please, by fifties: each to be tied with string. Will I tell you what it is, Jack?' he said, as the heavy bags piled up.

'If you please.'

'It is the vile corrupting British gold that Buonaparte and his newspapers do so perpetually call out against. Sometimes it exists, as you perceive. And, I may tell you, every louis, every napoleon, every ducat or doubloon is sound: the French sometimes buy services or intelligence with false coin or paper. That is the kind of thing that gives espionage a bad name.'

'If we pay real money, it is to be presumed we get better intelligence?' said Jack.

'Why, truly, it is much of a muchness: your paid agent and his information are rarely of much consequence. The real jewel, unpurchasable, beyond all price, is the man who hates tyranny as bitterly as I do: in this case the royalist or the true republican who will risk his life to bring down that Buonaparte. There are several of them on La Réunion, and I have every reason to believe there are more on the Mauritius. As for your common venal agents,' said Stephen, shrugging, 'most of these bags are for them; it may do some good; indeed it probably will, men rarely being all of a piece. Tell me, when

shall you be able to set me down? And how do you reckon the
odds at present?'

'As to the first,' said Jack, 'I cannot say until I have looked
into Port-Louis. The odds? I believe they are still about evens
for the moment. If they have gained the *Minerva*, we have
gained the *Magicienne*. You will tell me that the *Minerva* is
the heaviest of the two, and that the *Magicienne* only carries
twelve-pounders; but Lucius Curtis is a rare plucked 'un, a
damned good seaman. So let us say evens for the moment.
For the moment, I say, because the hurricane-season is coming, and if they lie snug in port and we outside, why, there is
no telling how we shall stand in a few weeks' time.'

During the night they brought the wind aft as they went
north about Mauritius, and when Stephen woke he found the
Boadicea on an even keel; she was pitching gently, and the
urgent music that had filled her between-decks these last
days was no longer to be heard. He washed his face perfunctorily, passed his hand over his beard, said 'It will do for
today,' and hurried into the day-cabin, eager for coffee and his
first little paper cigar of the day. Killick was there, gaping out
of the stern-window, with the coffee-pot in his hand.

'Good morning, Killick,' said Stephen. 'Where's himself?'

'Good morning, sir,' said Killick. 'Which he's still on deck.'

'Killick,' said Stephen, 'what's amiss? Have you seen the
ghost in the bread-room? Are you sick? Show me your tongue.'

When Killick had withdrawn his tongue, a flannelly object
of inordinate length, he said, paler still, 'Is there a ghost in
the bread-room, sir? Oh, oh, and I was there in the middle
watch. Oh, sir, I might a seen it.'

'There is always a ghost in the bread-room. Light along that
pot, will you now?'

'I durs'nt, sir, begging your pardon. There's worse news than
the ghost, even. Them wicked old rats got at the coffee, sir,
and I doubt there's another pot in the barky.'

'Preserved Killick, pass me that pot, or you will join the
ghost in the bread-room, and howl for evermore.'

With extreme unwillingness Killick put the pot on the very edge of the table, muttering, 'Oh, I'll cop it: oh, I'll cop it.'

Jack walked in, poured himself a cup as he bade Stephen good morning, and said, 'I am afraid they are all in.'

'All in what?'

'All the Frenchmen are in harbour, with their two Indiamen and the *Victor*. Have not you been on deck? We are lying off Port-Louis. The coffee has a damned odd taste.'

'This I attribute to the excrement of rats. Rats have eaten our entire stock; and I take the present brew to be a mixture of the scrapings at the bottom of the sack.'

'I thought it had a familiar tang,' said Jack. 'Killick, you may tell Mr Seymour, with my compliments, that you are to have a boat. And if you don't find at least a stone of beans among the squadron, you need not come back. It is no use trying *Néréide*; she don't drink any.'

When the pot had been jealously divided down to its ultimate dregs, dregs that might have been called dubious, had there been the least doubt of their nature, they went on deck. The *Boadicea* was lying in a splendid bay, with the rest of the squadron ahead and astern of her: *Sirius*, *Néréide*, *Otter*, the brig *Grappler* which they had retaken at St Paul's, and a couple of fore-and-aft-rigged avisoes, from the same source: to leeward the *Windham* Indiaman, with parties from each ship repairing the damage caused by the blow and the violence of the enemy, watched by the philosophical French prize-crew. At the bottom of the deep curve lay Port-Louis, the capital of Mauritius, with green hills rising behind and cloud-capped mountains beyond them.

'Shall you adventure to the maintop?' asked Jack. 'I could show you better from up there.'

'Certainly,' said Stephen. 'To the ultimate crosstrees, if you choose: I too am as nimble as an ape.'

Jack was moved to ask whether there were earthbound apes, as compact as lead, afflicted with vertigo, possessed of two left hands and no sense of balance; but he had seen the startling effect of a challenge upon his friend, and apart from grunting as he thrust Stephen up through the lubber's hole, he remained silent until they were comfortably installed among the studding-sails, with their glasses trained upon the town.

'You have the white building with the tricolour flying over it?' said Jack. 'That is General Decaen's headquarters. Now come down to the shore and a little to the right, and there is the *Bellone*: she is swaying up anew foretopmast. Another foot – he holds up his hand – he bangs home the fid: neatly done, most seamanlike. Inside her lies the *Victor*. Do you see the French colours over ours? The dogs; though indeed she was theirs before she was ours. Inside again, the French colours over the Portuguese: that is the *Minerva*. A very heavy frigate, Stephen; and no sign of her having been roughly handled that I can see. Then comes the *Vénus*, with the broad pendant, alongside the sheer-hulk. They are giving her a new mizzen. Now she has been handled rough – bowsprit gone in the gammoning, headrails all ahoo, not a dead-eye left this side, hardly; and very low in the water; pumps hard at it: I wonder they managed to bring her in. Yet it was early in the year for that kind of blow: she must have been in the heart of it, the Indiaman on the edge, and the *Magicienne* quite outside, for Curtis never even struck his top-gallant masts.'

'Your hurricano has a rotatory motion, I believe?'

'Exactly so. And you can be taken aback just when you think you have rode it out. Then over to the right you have the *Manche* and a corvette: the *Créole*, I believe. A very tidy squadron, once they have put the *Vénus* to rights. What a match it would be, was they to come out and fight their ships as well as that gallant fellow at St Paul's fought his. What was his name?'

'Feretier. Do you suppose they mean to come out?'

'Never in life,' said Jack. 'Not unless I can amuse them – not unless I can make their commodore believe we are no longer in the offing, or only one or two of us. No: it looks like

Brest or Toulon all over again: steady blockade until we are down to salt horse and Old Weevil's wedding-cake. We used to call it polishing Cape Sicié in the Mediterranean. But at least it means that I can send you down to La Réunion with the *Grappler*, if you really have to go: she can convoy the *Windham* that far, in case of the odd privateer, and be back the next day. It is barely thirty leagues, and with this steady wind . . . Forgive me, Stephen, it is time for my captains. There is Clonfert's gig putting off already, with his damn-fool boat's crew. Why does he have to make such a raree-show of himself?'

'Other captains dress their boat's crew in odd garments.'

'Still, there is such a thing as measure. I do not look forward to this meeting, Stephen. I shall have to call for an explanation – they will have to tell me how the *Bellone* got out. However, it will not be long. Shall you wait for me here?'

The conference was longer than Jack had expected, but Stephen, cradled in his top as it swung fore and aft on the long even swell, scarcely noticed the passage of time. He was warm through and through, so warm that he took off his neck-cloth; and while his eye dwelt on the motions of the seabirds (noddies, for the most part), the routine work on the deck below, the repairs carrying on aboard the *Windham*, and the boats moving to and fro, his mind was far away on La Réunion, following a large number of schemes designed to overcome the French reluctance to becoming British by means less forthright, and less murderous, than a yardarm-to-yardarm engagement with both broadsides roaring loud. He was therefore almost surprised to see the Commodore's large red face heave up over the edge of his capacious nest; while at the same time he was concerned to see its heavy, anxious expression, the comparative dullness of that bright blue eye.

'This is a damned awkward harbour for a close blockade,' observed the Commodore. 'Easy enough to slip out of, with the wind almost always in the south-east, but difficult to enter, without you are lucky with the sea-breeze and the tide

– that is why they use St Paul's so often – and difficult to bottle up tight in the dark of the moon. Still, come down into the cabin, if you would like a wet: Killick has discovered a few pale ancient beans that will just provide our elevenses.'

In the cabin he said, 'I do not blame them for letting the *Bellone* slip between them and the cape; and the *Canonnière* was gone before ever they reached their stations. But I do blame them for falling out over it. There they sat like a couple of cross dogs, answering short and glaring at one another. It was Pym's responsibility as the senior captain, of course; but whose fault it was in fact I could not make out. All I am sure of is that they are on wretched terms. Clonfert seems to have a genius that way, but I am surprised at Pym, such an easy, good-natured fellow. However, I have invited all captains to dine, and let us hope that will smooth things over. It is a miserable business, these rivalries in a squadron. I though I had got rid of them with Corbett.'

Although this dinner, whose main dishes were a four-hundred-pound turtle and a saddle of mutton from the Cape, was eaten in a humid ninety degrees, it did restore a semblance of civility, if not more. Pym was no man to keep up a resentment, and Clonfert could command the social graces; they drank wine together, and Jack saw with relief that his entertainment was going fairly well. Curtis of the *Magicienne* was a lively, conversable man, and he had much to tell them about the French squadron and its depredations in the Company's far eastern settlements: Hamelin, their commodore, was a savage, Jacobin fellow, it seemed, though a good seaman, while Duperré of the *Bellone* had a fine, swift-sailing ship, and he fought her with great determination; and the French crews were in a surprisingly high state of efficiency. Curtis's account carried the dinner over the first formal stage, and soon there was plenty of animated talk; although indeed Clonfert addressed almost all his conversation to his neighbour, Dr Maturin, and the two young commanders, Tomkinson of the *Otter* and Dent of the *Grappler*, did not feel it proper to open their mouths except to admit calipash and calipee, fat-tailed sheep and Cape Madeira.

'You and Clonfert got along very well together,' observed Jack, when his bloated guests had gone. 'What did you find to talk about? Is he a reading man?'

'He reads novels. But most of the time we spoke of his exploration of these coasts. He has charted many of the inlets, rowing in with his black pilot; and he has a surprising fund of information.'

'Yes. I know. He outdoes Corbett in that, I believe. He has real abilities, if only . . . What now?'

'All ready, sir,' said Bonden. 'Show me the pockets.'

'Number seven canvas, sir, double-sewn,' said Bonden, spreading his jacket and displaying an array of pouches. 'With flaps.'

'Very good. Now stow these away, and button 'em up tight.'

As he received the little heavy bags Bonden's visage took on a glassy, know-nothing look: he said no word; he extinguished the gleam of intelligence in his eye. 'There we are,' said Jack. 'And here is a chit for Captain Dent. He will ask you if you can make out the leading-marks for the cove where *Wasp* put the Doctor ashore, and if you can *not* —mark me, Bonden, if you are not dead certain of both marks and soundings – you are to say so, whether they think you a jack-pudden or no. And Bonden, you will take great care of the Doctor. Hammer his pistol-flints, d'ye hear me, and do not let him get his feet wet.'

'Aye, aye, sir,' said Bonden.

A few minutes later the boat pulled away; Bonden, though unnaturally stout in his close-buttoned jacket, sprang up the side of the *Grappler* and hauled Stephen aboard; and the brig headed south-west, followed by the Indiaman.

Jack watched them until they were hull-down, and then he turned his gaze to the shore, with its fortifications sharp and clear against the bright green of sugar-cane. He could almost feel the answering gaze of the French commanders training

their telescopes on the squadron, particularly that of
Hamelin, his equivalent on the other side; and as he gave the
orders that would set the long blockade in motion he turned
over the possibilities of amusing them and of bringing them
out to fight.

He had tried several before the *Grappler* came back, bearing Stephen, loaded with intelligence, a chest of the best coffee in the world, and a new machine for roasting it: he had
tried open provocation and lame-duck ruses, but Hamelin
would not bite, the cunning dog; the French lay there at their
ease, and the squadron was obliged to be content with its
steady routine of beating to and fro with only the prospect of
Christmas to encourage them.

By no means all the news that Stephen brought was good:
the frigate *Astrée* was expected from France; the disaffection
of the commandant of St Paul's had much diminished since
General Desbrusleys' death; and an important body of regulars with fervently Buonapartist officers had arrived. La Réunion would be much harder to take with the promised three
thousand troops from India than it would have been with half
that number from the Cape some weeks earlier. In the opinion of the French officers it could not be successfully
attacked, even with good weather for landing, by less than
five thousand men. On the other hand, he had learnt a great
deal about Mauritius, the more important island of the two
by far, with its splendid ports: among other things, a considerable part of the French garrison was made up of Irish troops,
prisoners of war or volunteers who still believed in Buonaparte. And Stephen had many contacts to make some that
might be of the greatest value. 'So,' said he, 'as soon as you
can let me have the *Néréide*, with Clonfert's local knowledge
and his black pilot, I should like to begin the work of preparation. Apart from other considerations, our broadsheets need
time to have their effect; and some well-chosen rumour,
some indiscretion in the proper place, might conceivably
bring your French frigates out.'

Jack freely admitted the importance of the task in hand. 'Yet do you think me weak, Stephen, when I say how I regret the days when we were of no account – when we cruised by ourselves, pretty busy at times, but often free for our hand of piquet in the evening and our music. You shall have *Néréide* tomorrow, if you choose, since *Vénus* has chosen this moment to heave down, and the *Manche* shows signs of doing much the same, so I can spare a ship; but at least let us have this evening to ourselves. While you were away I transposed the Corelli for violin and 'cello.'

The music tied them back to what seemed a very distant past, one in which no commodore's secretary with his heap of papers had to be kept away for a few hours' peace; a past where no susceptible captains had to have their feelings managed, and where what little administration the first lieutenant left to his captain could be settled out of hand, among people he knew intimately well. But the morning brought Mr Peter back with a score of documents; the *Magicienne* was very much afraid that she would have to ask for a court-martial upon her yeoman of the sheets for an almost unbelievable series of offences, starting with drunkenness and ending with a marlin-spike struck into the ship's corporal's belly; and the *Sirius* was running short of wood and water. Stephen crossed to the *Néréide* after no more than the briefest farewell.

He found Clonfert in high spirits, delighted to be away on his own, delighted to be away from the Commodore's rigid discipline: for although there were many things in which Jack and Lord St Vincent did not see eye to eye, including politics and free speech, they were at one in their notions on keeping station and on prompt, exact obedience to signals. They walked the quarterdeck in the forenoon, and as they strolled up and down the windward side, with the high wooded shore of Mauritius gliding by and shimmering in the heat, Stephen took in the atmosphere of the ship. There were few original *Néréide*'s left, since Clonfert had brought all his officers together with most of the *Otter*'s crew, and there was the same feeling in the frigate as there had been in the sloop. In many ways it was much like that in any man-of-war: that is to say, the hands' activities, the employment of their strictly-regulated time, the almost fanatical regard to neatness, were much the same as he had observed in other ships. Yet in none of Jack Aubrey's commands had he ever heard the captain's orders followed by suggestions that things might be better otherwise; and this as it were consultation appeared to be customary right down the hierarchy, from the officer of the watch to Jemmy Ducks, who looked after the poultry. With his limited experience, Stephen could not say that it was wrong: everybody seemed brisk and cheerful and when a manoeuvre was decided upon it was carried out promptly: but he had supposed this loquacity and tergiversation to be confined to the navy of the French, that lively, articulate nation.

The exception seemed to be the warrant-officers, the master, the bosun, the gunner and the carpenter, grave men who adhered to the Royal Navy's tradition as Stephen had seen it, particularly the magnificent granite-faced Mr Satterly, the elderly master, who appeared to regard his captain with a veiled affectionate indulgence and to run the ship with scarcely a word. The commissioned officers and the young gentlemen were far less mute; they obviously desired Clonfert's favour and attention, and they competed for it partly by activity and partly by a curious mixture of freedom and something not far from servility. The words 'my lord' were always in their mouths, and they pulled off their hats with a marked deference whenever they addressed him; yet they addressed him far more often than was usual in any ship that Stephen had known, crossing to his side of the quarterdeck unasked and volunteering remarks of no great consequence, unconnected with their duty.

Perhaps high spirits did not suit Clonfert quite so well as low. When he led Stephen to his cabin he showed its furnishings with a somewhat tiresome exultation, though insisting that this arrangement was merely temporary: 'not quite the thing for a post-captain – passable in a sloop, but a trifle shabby in a frigate.' The cabin, like most of those in rated ships, was a strikingly beautiful room: in Corbett's time it had been bare scrubbed wood, gleaming brass, shining windows, and little more; now that Spartan interior, rather too large for Clonfert's possessions, looked as though a brothel had moved into a monastery, and as though it had not yet settled down. The size of the room was increased by two large pier-glasses that Clonfert had brought with him from the *Otter*, one to port, the other to starboard: he strode to and fro between them telling Stephen the history of the hanging lamp in some detail; and Stephen, sitting cross-legged upon the sofa, noticed that at each turn Clonfert automatically glanced at his reflection with a look of inquiry, doubt, and complacence.

During dinner the Captain ran on about his Turkish and Syrian experiences with Sir Sydney Smith, and at some point Stephen became aware that for Clonfert he had ceased to be a table-companion and had turned into an audience. It was quite unlike their friendly discourse of some days before, and presently Stephen grew sadly bored: lies or half-lies, he reflected, had a certain value in that they gave a picture of what the man would wish to seem; but a very few were enough for that. And then they had a striving, aggressive quality, as though the listener had to be bludgeoned into admiration; they were the antithesis of conversation. 'They can also be embarrassing,' he thought, looking down at his plate, for Clonfert was now astride that unfortunate unicorn: it was a handsome plate, with the Scroggs crest engraved broad and fair upon the rim; but it was a Sheffield plate, and the copper was showing through. 'Embarrassing and hard work; since in common humanity one must keep the man in countenance, What a state of nervous excitement he is in, to be sure,'

Yet although Stephen kept Clonfert decently in countenance, mutely acquiescing in the unicorn and a variety of unlikely feats, he did not put such violence upon himself as to encourage a very long continuation; eventually Clonfert grew conscious that he had somehow missed the tone, that his audience was not impressed, was not with him, and an anxious look came into his eye. He laid himself out to be more agreeable, speaking once again of his gratitude for Stephen's care of him during his seizure. 'It is a wretched unmanly kind of disease,' he said, 'I have begged McAdam to use the knife, if it would do any good, but he seems to think it nervous, something like a fit of the mother, I do not suppose the Commodore ever suffers from anything of that kind?'

'If he did, I should certainly not speak of his disorder, nor the disorder of any other patient under my hands,' said Stephen. 'But,' he added more kindly, 'you are not to suppose that there is anything in the least discreditable in your malady. The degree of pain exceeds anything I have seen in any tormina, whatever their origin.' Clonfert looked pleased, and Stephen went on, 'It is a grave matter, indeed; and you are fortunate in having such an adviser as Dr McAdam in daily reach. I believe, with your leave, that I shall wait upon him presently.'

'Honest McAdam, yes,' said Clonfert, with a return to his former manner. 'Yes. He may be no Solomon, and we must overlook certain frailties and an unfortunate manner; but I believe he is sincerely devoted to me. He was somewhat indisposed this morning, or he would have paid his respects when you came aboard; but I believe he is up and about by now.'

McAdam was in his sick-bay, looking frail. Fortunately for the *Néréide*'s his mate, Mr Fenton, was a sound practical ship's surgeon, for McAdam had little interest in physical medicine. He showed Stephen his few cases, and they lingered a while over a seaman whose inoperable gummata were pressing on his brain in such a manner that his speech followed an inverted logic of its own. 'The sequence is not without its value,' said McAdam, 'though it is scarcely in my line.

For that matter there is little scope for my studies in a ship of war. Come away below, and we will take a drop.' Far below, in the smell of bilge-water and grog, he went on, 'Mighty little scope. The lower deck is kept far too busy for much to develop apart from the common perversions. Not that I would have you understand that I agree for a moment with the wicked old Bedlam chains and straw and cold water and whipping; but there may be some fancies that in the egg cannot stand a wee starting with a rope's end, nor close company. At any rate I have not had a decent melancholia from the lower deck this commission. Manias, yes; but they are two a penny. No: it is aft that you must look for your fine flower of derangement, not forgetting the pursers and clerks and schoolmasters, all mewed up more or less alone; but above all your captains – that is where the really interesting cases lie. How did you find our patient?'

'In a high flow of spirits. The helebore answers, I believe?'

For some time they discussed valerian, polypody of the oak, and stinking gladwin, their effects, and Stephen recommended the moderate use of coffee and tobacco; then McAdam branched off to ask, 'And did he speak of Captain Aubrey, at all?'

'Barely. In the circumstances it was an omission that I found remarkable.'

'Aye, and significant too, colleague, most significant. He has been on about Captain Aubrey these last days, and I took particular notice of the *sudor insignis* that you pointed out. It coincides within an hour or so. He was obliged to shift his coat after every bout: he has a chestful, and the right side of each one is pale from scrubbing away the salt, the right side alone.'

'It would be interesting to analyse that salt. Belladonna would suppress the sweat, of course. No more grog, I thank you. But it appears to me that for our patient truth is what he can persuade others to believe: yet at the same time he is a man of some parts, and I suspect that were you to attack him through his reason, were you to persuade him to abandon this self-defeating practice, with its anxiety, its probability of detection, and to seek only a more legitimate approval, then we should have no need for belladonna or any other anhidrotic.'

'You are coming into my way of thinking, I find: but you are not come far enough. The trouble lies much deeper, and it is through unreason that the whole nexus must be attacked. Your belladonna and your logic are pills from the same box: they only suppress the symptom.'

'How do you propose to attain this end?'

'Listen now, will you,' cried McAdam, slopping out a full tumbler and drawing his chair so near that his breath wafted in Stephen's face, 'and I will tell you.'

In his diary that night Stephen wrote, 'if he could carry out a reconstruction of the Irish political and social history for the last few ages which has formed our patient, and then a similar rebuilding of his mind from its foundation in early childhood to the present day, McAdam's scheme would be admirable. Yet even for the second part, what tools does he dispose of? A pickaxe is all. A pickaxe to repair a chronometer, and a pickaxe in drunken hands at that. For my part I have a higher opinion of Clonfert's understanding if not of his judgment than has my poor sodden colleague.'

This higher opinion was confirmed the next evening, when the *Néréide* made her way through a wicked series of reefs off Cape Brabant and the gig put Stephen and the captain ashore in a little creek; and the next, when the black pilot not only took them into a still lagoon but also guided them through the forest to a village where Stephen had a conversation with a second potential ally; and again some days later during a stroll behind Port South-East with a packet of subversive papers.

As he told Jack on rejoining the *Boadicea*, 'Clonfert may not be his own best friend in some ways, but he is capable of a steadiness and a resolution that surprised me; and I must observe that he perpetually took notes of the depth of the water and of the bearings in what I am persuaded you would call a seamanlike manner.'

'So much the better,' cried Jack, 'I am delighted to hear it, upon my word and honour. I have been doing something in that line myself, with young Richardson: he promises to be a capital hydrographer. We have laid down most of the nearby coast, with double angles and any number of soundings. And I have discovered a watering-place on Flat Island, a few leagues to the northwards; so we shall not have to be perpetually fagging out to Rodriguez.'

'No Rodriguez,' said Stephen in a low voice.

'Oh, you shall see Rodriguez again,' said Jack. 'We still have to put in there for stores, turn and turn about; but not quite so often.'

Turn and turn about they went, while the French remained obstinately at peace in their deep harbour, fitting themselves out anew to the last dump-bolt; and turn by turn, when he was not away in the *Néréide* down the coast, Stephen moved into each departing ship. His limestone caves on Rodriguez fulfilled all their golden promise; Colonel Keating was kindness itself, providing fatigue-parties and draining a small marsh; and by the third turn Stephen was able to report that from the bones found in the mud alone he could almost promise Jack the sight of a complete skeleton of the solitaire within the next two months, while at the same time he might partially clothe it with feathers and pieces of skin found in the caves.

For the rest of the time it was plain blockade, inshore at night, off the capes by day, but never far, lest a Frenchman should slip out on the land-breeze, go north about in the darkness and bear away for the rich waters of the Indian Ocean, leaving the squadron a great way to leeward. Up and down, up and down, and all the time their thin canvas grew thinner in the tropical sun and the sudden prodigious downpours, their running rigging, incessantly passing through the countless blocks as they trimmed sail, gradually wasted away in those wisps called shakings, and the weed accumulated on their bottoms, while through the gaps in their copper the teredos thrust their augers through the oak.

Christmas, and an immense feast on the upper deck of the *Boadicea*, with a barrel of providently salted penguins from off the Cape serving as geese or turkeys, according to the taste and fancy of the mess, and plum-duff blazing faint blue under the awnings spread against the fiercer blaze of the Mauritian sun. New Year, with a great deal of ship-visiting; Twelfth Night, and the midshipmen's berth regaled the gun-room with a two-hundred-pound turtle – an unfortunate experiment, for it was the wrong kind of turtle: the shell turned into glue, and all who had eaten of the creature pissed emerald green; and now Jack began to consult his barometer every watch.

It was a handsome, heavily-protected brass instrument hanging in gimbals by the table on which they breakfasted, and he was unscrewing its bottom when Stephen observed, 'I shall soon have to think of another trip to La Réunion. This Mauritius brew is sad stuff, in comparison.'

'Very true,' said Jack. 'But drink it while you may. Carpe diem, Stephen: you may not get another cup. I unscrewed this shield, because I thought the tube must have broke. But here is the quicksilver, do you see, lower than I have ever seen it in my life. You had better stow your bones in the safest place you can think of. We are in for an uncommon hearty blow.'

Stephen swept the vertebrae he had been sorting into his napkin and followed Jack on deck. The sky was pure and innocent, the swell rather less than usual: on the starboard bow the familiar landscape lay broad and green under the eastern sun. '*Magicienne* is at it already,' said Jack, glancing at the busy hands over the water, setting up double preventer-stays. '*Néréide* has been caught napping. Mr Johnson: *squadron make sail; course due west; prepare for heavy weather.*' He turned his glass to Port-Louis: yes, there was no fear of the French slipping out. They too could read a barometer, and they too were making all fast.

'Might this portend a hurricano?' asked Stephen privately in his ear.

'Yes,' said Jack, 'and we must have all the sea-room we can win. How I wish Madagascar were farther off.'

They won forty miles of sea-room; the boats on the booms could scarcely be seen for frappings; the guns were double-breeched, bowsed up against the side until they made it groan; topgallantmasts were down on deck; storm-canvas bent; spare gaskets, rolling-tackles, spritsailyard fore and aft – all that a great deal of activity and experienced seamanship could accomplish was done: and all under the same pure sun.

The swell increased long before a darkness gathered in the north. 'Mr Seymour,' said Jack, 'tarpaulins and battens for the hatchways. When it comes, it will blow across the sea.'

It came, a curved white line racing across the sea with inconceivable rapidity, a mile in front of the darkness. Just before it reached them the *Boadicea*'s close-reefed topsails sagged, losing all their roundness; then a tearing wall of air and water ripped them from their bolt-tops with an enormous shrieking howl. The ship was on her beam-ends, the darkness was upon them and the known world dissolved in a vast omnipresent noise. Air and water were intermingled; there was no surface to the sea; the sky vanished; and the distinction between up and down disappeared. Disappeared momentarily for those on deck, more durably for Dr Maturin, who, having pitched down two ladders, found himself lying on the ship's side. Presently, she righted and he slid down; but on her taking a most furious lee-lurch on wearing round, he shot across the deck, through all his remaining stock of Venice treacle, to land on hands and knees upon the other side, clinging to a suspended locker in the darkness, puzzled.

In time gravity reasserted itself; he climbed down, still mazed from the prodigious din and by his tumbles, and groped his way forward to the sick-bay. Here Carol, nominally his assistant but in fact the virtual surgeon of the frigate, and the loblolly-boy had preserved their lantern, by whose light they were disentangling their only patient, a poxed member of the afterguard, whose hammock, twirling in the violent motion, had enveloped him like a cocoon.

Here they remained, hooting lugubriously to one another for a while. Rank had little significance in this pandemonium, and the loblolly-boy, an ancient man once sailmaker's crew and still good at sewing, told them in his shrill, carrying voice that in Jamaica as a boy he had known seven ships of the line founder with all hands in a blow not half as hugeous as this here. Presently Stephen shouted, 'Come after, Mr Carol, and let us take all the lanterns we can find. The casualties will soon be coming down.'

They crept aft through the darkness – dead lights shipped long since, and the air that came blasting down was charged with shattered water, not light – and to them were brought the injured men: one from the wheel, his ribs cracked by the flying spokes; a small, light reefer dashed by the wind against the hances, and now limp, insensible; Mr Peter, who had made the same plunge as Stephen, though less luckily; more ribs, some broken limbs. Then, as lightning struck the ship, three men quite dazed and one with a shocking burn, dead before they brought him below.

Bandaging, splinting, operating in a space that heaved through forty-five degrees in all directions and on chests that shifted and slid beneath them, they worked on and on. At one point a messenger from the quarterdeck came with the Commodore's compliments and was all well, together with something about 'eight hours'; and then, much, much later, when the ship had been on a comparatively even keel for some time, with no new cases coming below and the last of the fractured clavicles reduced, there was the Commodore himself, streaming wet, in his shirt and breeches. He looked round, spoke to those casualties in any condition to hear him, and then in a hoarse voice he said to Stephen, 'If you have a moment at any time, Doctor, you will find a curious sight on deck.'

Stephen finished his bandage with a neat double turn and

made his way up through the small hole in the canvas-covered hatch. He stood blinking in the extraordinary orange-tawny light, bracing himself against the flying air, as solid as a wall. 'The lifeline, sir,' cried a seaman, putting it into his hand. 'Clap on to the lifeline for all love.'

'Thank you, friend,' said Stephen, gazing about him, and as he spoke he realized that the enormous universal roar had diminished: it was now slightly less than that of continuous battle at close quarters. The *Boadicea* was lying to under a scrap of mizzen staysail, riding the tremendous seas nobly, shouldering them aside with her bluff bows: her fore and main topmasts had gone by the board; wild ropes by the score stretched horizontally aft from the wrecked tops, sometimes cracking as loud as a gun; her remaining shrouds were packed with scraps of seaweed and pieces of terrestrial vegetation – a palm-frond was clearly recognizable. But this was not the curious sight. From the drowned forecastle aft, and particularly on the quarterdeck, wherever there was the slightest lee, there were birds. Seabirds for the most part, but right by him a little creature like a thrush. It did not move as he approached it, nor even when he touched its back. The others were the same, and he looked into the lustrous eye of a bosun-bird within a few inches. In this unearthly lurid glow it was hard to make out their true colours or their kind, but he did distinguish a white-headed noddy, scarcely to be seen within five thousand miles of the Mauritius. As he was struggling towards it a sort of growl in the orange clouds immediately above overcame the general roar, and in a second it was followed by a thunder so intolerably vast that it filled all the air about him; and with the thunder a blaze of lightning struck the ship again. He was flung down, and picking himself up with a confused recollection of a triple stroke, of a forward gun having gone off, blasting out its portlid, he crawled below to wait for the wounded.

There were no wounded. Instead there appeared a piece of jellied veal, brought by Killick with the message that 'the

thunderbolt had made hay of the best bower anchor, but otherwise all was well; that unless they were taken aback in the
next hour or so, the Commodore thought they might be
through the worst of it; and that he hoped Dr Maturin might
see better weather in the morning.'

Having slept like a corpse through the middle watch, and
having attended his urgent cases at first light, Dr Maturin did
indeed see better weather when he came on deck. The sky
was the most perfect blue, the sun delightfully warm, the
gentle south-east wind refreshing: there was an enormous
swell, but no white water, and apart from the desolation of
the deck, the steady gush of the pumps, and the worn look of
all hands, yesterday might have been a nightmare out of time.
Yet there were other proofs: Mr Trollope, the second lieutenant, limped up to him and pointed out two ships of the
squadron, far, far to leeward: the *Magicienne*, with her
mizzen gone, and the *Sirius*, with no topmast standing.

'Where is the Commodore?' asked Stephen.

'He turned in half a glass ago. I begged him to get some
sleep. But before he went below he told me to take care to
show you the best bower, a most amazing philosophical sight.'

Stephen considered the fused, distorted metal, and said,
'We seem to be heading south?'

'South-west as near as ever we can, with our compasses run
mad because of the lightning; south-west for the Cape to
refit. And don't we wish we may get there, ha, ha!'

6

THERE WERE NO banquets at the Cape for Jack Aubrey;
there were few kind words from the Admiral, either,
although the Commodore had brought in all his squadron
safe after one of the worst blows this last decade; and there
were less, if less were possible, when an American barque

arrived with the news that the *Bellone*, *Minerve*, and *Victor* were out —she had spoken them off the Cargados Garayos, standing north-east under a press of sail to cruise for Indiamen in the Bay of Bengal.

Not that Jack had any leisure for feasting in Cape Town or for comfortable chat with Admiral Bertie: it was an anxious, hurried time for him, with five ships to be refitted by a small yard with scarcely a spare frigate-topmast in it – supplies were expected from India – and no fit timber much nearer than Mossel Bay. A small, ill-furnished yard, and one governed by men of a rapacity that Jack had never seen equalled in all his long experience: the squadron was known to have done well for itself at St Paul's, and the yard was going to have a proper share come hell or high water, regardless of the fact that all this wealth depended on leisurely decisions to be taken far away at some future date —that the squadron had very little cash in hand, and could only take it up by bills at a usurious rate of interest. An anxious time, with the Frenchmen out; and one rendered more anxious still, as far as Jack was concerned, by a host of factors. By the steady obstruction of those in control of spars, cordage, paint, block, copper, iron-work, and the countless other objects the squadron cried out for. By the Admiral's apparent indifference to very gross corruption: Aubrey must be aware that dock-yard people were not plaster saints, observed Mr Bertie, nor yet choir-boys; these things should be settled as they were usually settled in the Navy; and for his part he did not give a straw how the Commodore set about it, so long as the squadron was ready for sea by Tuesday sennight at the latest. By the discovery that his own Mr Fellowes, seduced by the bosun of the *Sirius* and a desire to be rich now rather than at some later period when he might be dead, had not only looked upon the thunderstruck best bower as a perquisite, but had done the same by the kedge, fifty fathom of two-inch rope, and an unreasonable quantity of other stores – a court-martial quantity. By contention among his captains as to who should be

served first from the meagre supplies whose existence the
dock-yard could not conceal. And above all by the loss of one
vessel carrying mail and by the arrival of another so thoroughly soaked by rain-storms under the line that all letters
apart from those wrapped in waxed sailcloth had mouldered
and partly coalesced; Sophie had never learnt to use waxed
sailcloth, nor to number her letters, nor to send copies in
another bottom.

Immediately after the arrival of this blotting-paper packet,
Jack snatched an interval between visits to the master-attendant and the rope-walk and tried to disentangle the sequence
with the help of such dates as 'Friday' or 'after church'. But
this interval was also seized upon by Mr Peter, whose great
sheaf of documents reminded Jack of his duty as a commodore: all that he had told the Commander-in-chief by
word of mouth had to be cast into official, written form, carefully read over and considered. Very carefully, for although
Jack was the least suspicious creature afloat, Stephen was
not, and he had pointed out that it might be wise to regard
Mr Peter as a functionary with loyalties on land rather than as
a confidential ally. And then there was his duty as captain of
the *Boadicea*: although his first lieutenant saw to the daily
running of the ship, Mr Seymour was now exceedingly busy
with the refitting, and in any case there were several things
that necessarily fell to the captain. It was he who persuaded
Mr Collins, now at eighteen the senior master's mate, that he
was not absolutely required to marry the young lady who
alleged that, as a direct consequence of Mr Collins' attentions, all her girdles were now too tight; still less to marry her
at once. 'A fortnight is not enough, in these affairs,' he said.
'It may be only an indigestion, a pound or two of beefsteak
pudding. Wait until we come in from the next cruise. And
until then, Mr Collins, I desire you will not leave the ship.
Though indeed,' he added, 'was you to marry every girl you
play love-tokens with, when ashore, the place would very
soon come to look like Abraham's bosom.'

It was he who patiently listened to an indignant, rambling account of sharp practice far away, delivered by Matthew Bolton, forecastleman, starboard watch, in his own name and in that of three mute companions unnaturally shaved and scraped. Bolton had refused Mr Seymour's help, on the grounds that as the Commodore had pulled him out of the sea when they were shipmates in the *Polychrest*, it obviously fell to him to do the same throughout the length of Bolton's natural life.

This was a logic that seemed convincing to Bolton, the first lieutenant and the Commodore; and when Jack had extracted the facts from the circumstantial details, a description of the grass-combing bugger that had tried this guardo-move, and an account of Mrs Bolton's state of health, he reached for a pen, and, watched very closely indeed by the four seamen, wrote a letter, which he then read out to them in a harsh, all-hands-to-punishment voice that gave the utmost satisfaction:

> 'Boadicea,
> Simon's Town
>
> Sir,
> Conformably to the wishes of the men named in the margin, late of the *Néréide*, and now on board of his Majesty's ship under my command, I acquaint you that unless the prize-money due to them for Buenos Ayres and Monte Video, and received by you under their power of attorney, is forthwith paid, I shall state the case to the Lords Commissioners of the Admiralty, with a request that their solicitor may be directed to sue for the same.
>
> I am, etc.

There,' he said, 'that will clap a stopper over his antics. Now, Bolton, if the Doctor is aboard, I should like to see him when he is at leisure.'

As it happened the Doctor was not on board. He was half

way between Cape Town, where he had left Mr Farquhar, and False Bay, sitting in a sparse grove of proteas in a dust-storm, clasping a loose portfolio of plants to be dried for his herbal, and dividing what attention he had left between a small flock of crested mouse-birds and a troop of baboons. Presently he came down to the harbour, where he washed away some of the dust at his usual tavern and received from the landlord (an obliging African of Huguenot descent) the foetus of a porcupine: and here, as he had expected, he found McAdam, sitting in front of a bottle that would have pre-served the foetus almost indefinitely. Little of it had been drunk, however, and McAdam entertained him with a reason-able account of their patient's extraordinary activity and flow of spirits. Lord Clonfert, it appeared, was up well before dawn every day (a rare occurrence), inspiring all hands with a sense of extreme urgency; he had bleared Pym's eye over a couple of topgallant yards by means of a thumping bribe; and he was now negotiating with a known receiver of stolen goods for a gig. 'Sure it will break his heart if he is not the first that is ready for sea,' said McAdam. 'He has set his soul on outdo-ing the Commodore.'

'May we not in part attribute his activity to the roborative, stimulating use of coffee, and to the general soothing effect of mild tobacco, which has set his humours in equilibrio? Tobacco, divine, rare, superexcellent tobacco, which goes far beyond all their panaceas, potable gold, and philosopher's stones, a sovereign remedy to all diseases. A good vomit, I confess, a virtuous herb, if it be well qualified and oppor-tunely taken, and medicinally used, but as it is commonly abused by most men, which take it as tinkers do ale, 'tis a plague, a mischief, a violent purger of goods, lands, health; hellish, devilish and damned tobacco, the ruin and overthrow of body and soul. Here, however, it *is* medicinally taken; and I congratulate myself upon the fact, that in your hands there is no question of tinkers' abuse.'

The flying dust, the incessant wind, had made McAdam

more gross than usual; he had never cordially liked Stephen's prescription of coffee and tobacco; and from his wavering, red-rimmed eye it seemed that he was meditating a coarse remark. Indeed, he began 'A fig for . . .' but having belched at this point he reconsidered his words, fixed his gaze on the bottle, and continued, 'No, no: you do not have to be a conjuror to see it is all emulation. If the one is your dashing frigate-captain, t'other will be your dashing frigate-captain to the power of ten, whether or no. He will outdo the Commodore though he burst.'

It would not be difficult to outdo the Commodore in his present state, the creature, reflected Stephen as he walked into the cabin: not, at least, in the article of speed. Captain Aubrey was completely surrounded by papers, including those of the courts-martial that were to be held over the next few days – the usual offences of desertion and violence or disobedience or both when drunk: but time-consuming – and upon them all he had laid out the mildewed sheets of his private correspondence.

'There you are, Stephen,' he cried. 'How happy I am to see you. What have you there?'

'An unborn porcupine.'

'Well, there's glory for you. But Stephen, you are a rare one for making out a secret hand, I am sure. Would you help me try to find out the sequence of these letters, and perhaps even the sense?'

Together they pored over the sheets, using a magnifying-glass, intuition, crocus of antimony, and a little diluted copperas; but to small effect.

'I do make out that the Old Nonpareils we planted had three apples apiece, and that the strawberries failed,' said Jack, 'and she obviously heard from Ommaney, because here is the parlour chimney drawing fit to turn a mill, and a Jersey cow – the children have hair, and teeth, any number of teeth, poor little souls. Hair: with all my heart, though she does say it is straight. Straight or frizzled, 'tis all one: they will look far better with some hair – Lord, Stephen, it must have been their hair I blew away, thinking it was shakings that had got into the cover.' He crept about for some time and came up with a little wisp. 'Very little shakings, however,' he said, folding it into his pocket-book and returning to the letters. 'Neighbours most attentive: here is another brace of pheasants from Mr Beach last Thursday. But in this one she says she is well, surprisingly well, underlined twice: says it again in what I take to be the last. I am heartily glad of it, of course, yet why *surprisingly*? Has she been ill? And what is this about her mother? Could the second word be palsy? If Mrs Williams has been sick, with Sophie looking after her, that might explain the surprisingly.'

They pored again, and Stephen almost certainly deciphered a hare, a present from Captain Polixfen, eaten jugged on Saturday or Sunday or both; and something about the rain. All the rest was mere conjecture.

'I think old Jarvie was altogether wrong in saying that a sea-officer had no business to marry,' said Jack, carefully gathering the sheets. 'Yet I can see what he meant. I should not be unmarried for the world, you know; no, not for a flag; but you cannot conceive how my mind has been going back to Ashgrove Cottage these days, when I should be thinking about getting the squadron to sea.' He jerked his head over his shoulder and stared out of the scuttle for a while before adding, 'These God-damned courts-martial: and what to do about the land-sharks in the yard. To say nothing of the bosun and his infernal capers.'

During supper he picked at his mutton, setting out the difficulty of dealing with Mr Fellowes: disposing of His Majesty's property was an immemorial practice among His Majesty's servants – if the objects were damaged it was almost legitimate by length of custom – and in the Navy it went by the name of cappabar. Pursers, carpenters, and bosuns stole most, having more to steal, and better opportunities; but there were limits, and Fellowes had not confined himself to damaged goods, nor to those of slight value. He had carried cappabar too high by far – the thing was flagrant – and Jack could bring him before a court-martial and have him broke tomorrow. It was Jack's duty to have him broke. On the other hand, it was also his duty to keep his ship in the highest possible fighting-trim: for that he needed a first-rate bosun: and first-rate bosuns did not grow on trees, at the Cape. First-rate bosuns were not twelve a penny. He grew a little heated on the subject, cursing Fellowes for a half-witted zany, a mad lunatic, a fling-it-down-the-gutter sodomite; but his heart was not in it; his epithets lacked real warmth and inventiveness; and his mind was clearly still far away in Hampshire.

'Come,' said Stephen, 'if ever the Madras establishment fulfils its undertakings, and we move on La Réunion, which I begin to doubt, Mr Farquhar will be with us, and that will be an end to our music. Let us play my old lament for the Tir nan Og; I too am mighty low, and it will serve as a counter-irritant. Like will be cured by like.'

Jack said that he would be very happy to lament with Stephen until the moon went down, but with messengers expected from Cape Town and from every official in the yard, he did not expect they would reach any very high flow of soul before they were interrupted. In the event they had not even tuned their strings when Spotted Dick appeared, to state, with Mr Johnson's duty, that *Iphigenia* was off the point, had made her number, and was standing in.

With a brisk south-east wind and the making tide she had dropped anchor before moonrise, and the news that Captain Lambert brought drove all thoughts of England and of music from Jack Aubrey's head. The *Iphigenia*, that fine thirty-six-gun eighteen-pounder frigate, escorting a small fleet of transports, had reinforced Colonel Keating at Rodriguez to the extent of two regiments of European troops, two of Indian, and some auxiliaries: the numbers were fifteen hundred short of what had been hoped for, but the soldiers had done their

best: they had kept very nearly to their time, and the defini-
tive attack on La Réunion was now a possibility, though a
hazardous one, above all if the French had moved fresh
forces into the island. They would certainly have had time to
remount their batteries.

The first thing to do was to find out what ships Governor
Decaen had in Mauritius, and, if it could be done, to shut
them up in their harbours. 'Captain Lambert,' he said, 'what
is the state of the *Iphigenia?*'

He did not know Lambert at all, a recently-promoted young
man, but he liked the look of him – a small round jolly sailor
with a capable air – and he fairly loved him when he took a
paper from his pocket and said, 'These are my officers'
reports, sir, made as we were standing in. Purser: provisions
for nine weeks in full of all species, except rum: of that, only
thirty-nine days. Master: one hundred and thirteen tons of
water; beef very good, pork sometimes shrinks in the boiling;
the rest of the provisions very good. I should add, sir, that we
watered, wooded, and tortoised at Rodriguez. Gunner: eighteen rounds of powder filled; plenty of wads; forty rounds.
Carpenter: hull in good state; knees of the head supported by
two cheeks; masts and yards in good state; pretty well stored.
Surgeon: in the sick list, three men, objects for invaliding;
portable soup, fifty-seven pounds; other necessaries to the
19th of next month only. And as for my people, sir, we are
only sixteen short of complement.'

'Then I take it you can sail at once, Captain Lambert?'

'The moment we have won our anchors, sir, unless you
wish me to slip. Though I should be happy to take in a little
powder and shot, and some greenstuff: my surgeon is not
quite happy about his lime-juice.'

'Very good, very good, Captain Lambert,' said Jack, chuckling. 'You shall certainly have your powder and shot. Never
trouble with that damned yard at this time of night: I have
more than we can safely stow, from St Paul's, and my gunner
will have to disgorge the surplus. And you may have six of our

bullocks that are waiting on the beach. As for your greenstuff, my purser has an excellent unofficial man on shore, will rouse you out any quantity in half an hour. Mr Peter, be so good as to prepare a letter to the Admiral, to go at once: Mr Richardson is our best jockey, I believe – tell him to never mind the lions and tigers on the road; they are all gammon, for the most part. Then, an order for Captain Lambert – proceed to sea on the ebb, rendezvous off Port-Louis, copies of private signals, alternative rendezvous at Rodriguez after the – let me consider – the seventeenth. And let all captains come aboard. Killick, pass the word for the gunner, and bring a bottle of the Constantia with the yellow seal. The yellow seal, d'ye hear me?'

Between the signing of papers and the interview with the reluctant gunner they drank their bottle, the best bottle in the ship, and the captains began to arrive: their coxswains could be heard answering the sentry's hail in quick succession: '*Néréide*', '*Sirius*', '*Otter*', '*Magicienne*'.

'Now, gentlemen,' said the Commodore, when they were all assembled, 'when can your ships proceed to sea?'

If it were not for Pym's vile newfangled iron tanks, the *Sirius* could be ready in a couple of days: if it had not been for the yard's incomprehensible delay over the long-promised iron horse, the *Otter* might say the same. '*Néréide* will be ready for sea in thirty-six hours,' said Clonfert, smiling with intent at Captain Pym: but the smile changed to a look of surprised vexation when Curtis said, 'The *Magicienne* can sail this minute, sir, if I may have leave to water at Flat Island. We are no more than thirty ton shy.'

'I am delighted to hear it, Captain Curtis,' said Jack. 'Delighted. *Magicienne* and *Iphigenia* will proceed to Port-Louis with the utmost dispatch. Mr Peter will give you your orders; and with this wind you might be well advised to warp out into the fairway to catch the first minute of the ebb.'

They received their orders; they warped out into the fairway; and dawn saw the two frigates beating out of the bay, to vanish, close-hauled, round the Cape of Good Hope by the time the cabin's breakfast of eggs and mutton-ham came aft in a cloud of fragrance. Shortly afterwards Captain Eliot arrived with a formal order from the Admiral directing the Commodore to convene his court-martial, and a letter in which he congratulated Jack on this splendid accession of force at Rodriguez, from which the country might confidently expect wonders in a very short time indeed, particularly as for the next few weeks the squadron would have the use of the *Leopard*. The horrible old *Leopard*.

Jack changed into his full-dress uniform; the ominous union flag broke out at the *Boadicea's* peak; the captains gathered; and with Mr Peter acting as deputy judge-advocate they set about the unpleasant business of trying poor Captain Woolcombe for the loss of the *Laurel* of twenty-two guns, captured by the *Canonnière* – the Frenchman's last fight – off Port-Louis before Jack came to the Cape: for until this time a sufficient number of senior officers had never been in Simon's Town long enough for the court to be formed, and poor Woolcombe had been under nominal arrest ever since he had been exchanged. Everyone knew that in the circumstances, with the *Canonnière* in sight of her home port, carrying an enormous land-based crew and mounting more than twice the number of far heavier guns, no blame could be attached to the *Laurel's* captain; everyone knew that there must be an honourable acquittal – everybody except Woolcombe, for whom the issue was far too important for any certainty whatsoever and who sat throughout the long proceedings with a face of such anxiety that it made the members of the court very thoughtful indeed. Each of them might find himself in the same position, faced perhaps with ill-disposed judges, differing from him in politics or service loyalties or bearing him some long-nourished grudge: a court of amateur lawyers, from whose decision there was no appeal. Illogically, perhaps, since they themselves had framed the verdict, every member of the court shared in Woolcombe's glowing relief when the judge-advocate read it out, and when Jack handed back the captain's sword with an elegant if somewhat studied formal speech. They were happy with Captain Woolcombe, and the sentences for some of the desertions and embezzlements that followed were quite remarkably light. Yet for all that the sentences took a great while to reach: the stately process went on and on. In his own ship a captain could deal with any delinquent foremast hand so long as the offence did not carry the death-sentence, but he could not touch any officer holding a commission or a warrant; they had to come before the court; and at times it seemed to Jack, on the boil with impatience to get to sea, to make the most of the situation before the French knew of the forces on La Réunion, that no warrant officer in the squadron had found any better use for his time than getting drunk, overstaying his leave, disobeying, insulting, and even beating his superiors, and making away with the stores entrusted to his care. Indeed, a steady diet of courts-martial gave a most unpleasant impression of the Royal Navy: crime, oppression, complaints of illegal conduct, sometimes justified, sometimes fabricated or malicious (one master charged his captain with keeping false musters, on the grounds that he had a friend's son on the ship's books when in fact the young gentleman was at school in England, a perfectly normal practice, but one which would have wrecked the captain's career if the court had not performed some singular acrobatics to save him), brawling in the wardroom, against officers, evidence of long-standing ill-will; and all the bloody violence of the lower deck.

Between these grim sessions the presiding judge turned sailor again, and he drove on the refitting of his ships, fighting a most determined battle against obstruction and delay. But having all the time in the world, the dock-yard won hands down; they had gauged his needs and his impatience quite exactly, and he had not only to bleed borrowed gold at every vein, but even to thank his extortioners before the last sack of thirty-penny nails and ten-inch spikes came aboard. These actions took place at dawn and dusk, for at dinner-time the president of the court necessarily entertained the other members.

'Pray, Commodore, do you not find passing sentence of death cut your appetite?' asked Stephen, as he watched Jack carve a saddle of mutton.

'I cannot say I do,' said the Commodore, passing Captain Woolcombe a slice that dripped guiltless blood. 'I don't like it, to be sure; and if the court can possibly find a lesser offence, I think I should always give my vote for it. But when you have a straightforward case of cowardice or neglect of duty, why, then it seems to me plain enough: the man must be hanged, and the Lord have mercy on his soul, for the service will have none. I am sorry for it, but it don't affect my appetite. Captain Eliot, may I help you to a little of the undercut?'

'It seems to me perfectly barbarous,' observed Stephen.

'But surely, sir,' said Captain Pym, 'surely a medical man will cut off a gangrened limb to save the rest of the body?'

'A medical man does not cut off the limb in any spirit of corporate revenge, nor *in terrorem*; he does not make a solemn show of the amputation, nor is the peccant limb attended by all the marks of ignominy. No, sir: your analogy may be specious, but it is not sound. Furthermore, sir, you are to consider, that in making it you liken the surgeon to a common hangman, an infamous character held in universal contempt and detestation. And the infamy attaching to the executioner arises from what he does: the language of all nations condemns the man and *a fortiori* his act: which helps to make my point more forcibly.'

Captain Pym protested that he had not intended the least reflection upon surgeons – a capital body of men, essential in a ship, and on shore too, no doubt: he would not meddle with analogies any more; but still perhaps he might adventure to say that it was a hard service, and it needed a hard discipline.

'There was a man,' remarked Captain Eliot, 'who was sentenced to death for stealing a horse from a common. He said to the judge, that he thought it hard to be hanged for stealing a horse from a common; and the judge answered, "You are not to be hanged for stealing a horse from a common, but that others may not steal horses from commons." '

'And do you find,' asked Stephen, 'that in fact horses are not daily stolen from commons? You do not. Nor do I believe that you will make captains braver or wiser by hanging or shooting them for cowardice or erroneous judgment. It should join the ordeal of the ploughshare, floating or pricking to prove witchcraft, and judicial combat, among the relics of a Gothic past.'

'Dr Maturin is quite right,' cried Lord Clonfert. 'A capital execution seems to me a revolting spectacle. Surely a man could be . . .'

His words were drowned in the general flow of talk that Stephen's word 'shooting' had set going; for Admiral Byng had been shot to death on his own quarterdeck. Almost everybody was speaking, except for Captain Woolcombe, who ate in wolfish silence, his first meal without anxiety; and the names of Byng and Keppel flew about.

'Gentlemen, gentlemen,' cried Jack, who saw the far more recent Gambier and Hervey and the unfortunate engagement in the Basque roads looming ahead, 'let us for Heaven's sake keep to our humble level, and not meddle with admirals or any other god-like beings, or we shall presently run foul of politics, and that is the end of all comfortable talk.'

The noise diminished, but Clonfert's excited voice could be heard carrying on, '. . . the possibility of judicial error, and the value of human life – once it is gone, it cannot be brought back. There is nothing, nothing, so precious.'

He addressed himself to his neighbours and to those sitting opposite him; but none of the captains seemed eager to be the recipient, and there was the danger of an embarrassing silence, particularly as Stephen, convinced that two hundred years of talk would not shift his kind, bloody-minded companions an inch, had taken to rolling bread pills.

'As for the value of human life,' said Jack, 'I wonder whether you may not over-estimate it in theory; for in practice there is not one of us here, I believe, who would hesitate for a moment over pistoling a boarder, nor think twice about it afterwards. And for that matter, our ships are expressly made to blow as many people into kingdom come as possible.'

'It is a hard service, and it requires a hard discipline,' repeated Pym, peering through his claret at the enormous joint.

'Yes, it is a hard service,' said Jack, 'and we often call our uniform buttons the curse of God; but a man – an officer – enters it voluntarily, and if he don't like the terms he can leave it whenever he chooses. He takes it on himself – he knows that if he does certain things, or leaves them undone, he is to be cashiered or even hanged. If he has not the fortitude to accept that, then he is better out of the service. And as for the value of human life, why, it often seems to me that there are far too many people in the world as it is; and one man, even a post-captain, nay' – smiling – 'even a commodore or a jack-in-the-green, is not to be balanced against the good of the service.'

'I entirely disagree with you, sir,' said Clonfert.

'Well, my lord, I hope it is the only point upon which we shall ever differ,' said Jack.

'The Tory view of a human life . . .' began Clonfert.

'Lord Clonfert,' called Jack in a strong voice, 'the bottle stands by you.' And immediately afterwards, aiming at bawdy, in which all could share, and quickly attaining it, he spoke of the striking increase – the potential increase – in the population of the colony since the squadron's arrival: 'a single member of my midshipmen's berth has already contrived to get two girls with child: one brown, the other isabella-coloured.'

The others turned with equal relief to similar accounts, to reminiscences of burning wenches in Sumatra, at Port-au-Prince, in the Levantine ports; to rhymes, to conundrums; and the afternoon ended in general merriment.

The *Néréide*, her topgallantmasts and her new gig on board at last, left Simon's Town for Mauritius that evening: and as they stood watching her out of the bay, Stephen said to Jack, 'I am sorry I started that hare; it gave you some uneasiness, I am afraid. Had I recollected, I should not have asked it in public, for it was a private question – I asked for information sake. And now I do not know whether the public answer was that of the Commodore or of the plain, unpendanted Jack Aubrey.'

'It was something of both,' said Jack. 'I do in fact dislike hanging more than I said, though more for myself than for the hanged man: the first time I saw a man run up to the yardarm with a night cap over his eyes and his hands tied behind his back, when I was a little chap in the *Ramillies*, I was as sick as a dog. But as for the man himself, if he has deserved hanging, deserved it by our code, I find it don't signify so very much what happens to him. It seems to me that men are of different value, and that if some are knocked on the head, the world is not much the poorer.'

'Sure, it is a point of view.'

'Perhaps it sounds a little hard; and perhaps I came it a little over-strong and righteous, when I was speaking, speaking as a commodore, to Clonfert.'

'You certainly gave him an impression of unbending severity and perfect rectitude.'

'Yes, I was pompous: yet I did not speak far beyond my own mind. Though I must confess he vexed me with his tragic airs and his human life – he has a singular genius for hitting the wrong note; people will accept that kind of thing from a learned man, but not from him; yet he will be prating. I hope he did not resent my checking him: I had to, you know, once he got on to Whigs and Tories. But I did it pretty civil, if you remember. I have a regard for him – few men could have got the *Néréide* out so quickly. Look, she is going about to weather the point. Prettily done – stays as brisk as a cutter, stays in her own length – he has a very good officer in his master: and he would be one himself too, with a little more ballast – a very good officer, was he a little less flighty.'

'It is curious to reflect,' wrote Stephen in his diary that night, 'that Jack Aubrey, with so very much more to lose, should value life so very much more lightly than Clonfert, whose immaterial possessions are so pitifully small, and who is partly aware of it. This afternoon's exchange confirms all I have observed in my acquaintance with both. It is to be hoped, if only from a medical point of view, that some resounding action will soon give Clonfert a real basis – a sounder basis than his adventitious consequence. Nothing, as Milton observes, profits a man like proper self-esteem: I believe I have mangled the poor man; but here is Mr Farquhar, the all-knowing, who will set me right. If only there were another thousand men on Rodriguez, I might write Governor Farquhar with some confidence even now.'

MR FARQUHAR CAME aboard, but with no ceremony and with so small a train – one secretary, one servant – that it was clear he had been listening to the military men in Cape Town, who had little opinion of the sepoy in his own country and none at all of his fighting qualities elsewhere. Their considered opinion was that the French officers were right when they said that five regiments of European troops, supported by artillery, would be needed for a successful attack; that the hazards of landing on such a shore were so great that even five regiments were scarcely adequate, particularly as communication between the sea and the land might be cut off from one day to the next, and with it the troops' supplies; and that perhaps it would be better, all things considered, to wait for further reinforcements at the next monsoon.

'I wish I could share your sanguine outlook,' he said to

Stephen, when at last he was in a fit condition to say anything at all (the *Boadicea* had had heavy weather until she
reached the twenty-fifth parallel), 'but perhaps it is based
upon more information than I possess?'

'No: my reports were tolerably complete,' said Stephen.
'But I am not sure that you or the soldiers attach the same
weight to our present superiority in ships. If, as it appears
likely, two of their frigates are away from the scene of action,
our local advantage is five to two; a very great advantage, and
in this I do not count the *Leopard*, which is, I am told, only a
smaller *Raisonable*, the kind of vessel that is facetiously
termed a coffin-ship by the sailors, of questionable use even
as a transport. It was long before I came to appreciate the
prodigious force represented by a man-of-war of the larger
kind: we can all envisage the dreadful power of a battery, of a
fortress belching fire; but a ship seems so peaceful an object,
and to the untutored eye so very like the Holyhead packet
writ large, that perhaps one does not easily see it as a vast
battery in itself, and what is more a moveable battery that can
turn its resistless fire in various directions, and then, its work
of destruction completed, glide smoothly off to begin again
elsewhere. The three frigates, my dear sir, the three frigates
by which we presumably outnumber our adversaries, represent an enormous train of artillery, a train that is not painfully
dragged by innumerable horses, but is borne by the wind. I
have seen them in action upon this very coast, and I have
been amazed. There are also the enemy's lines of supply to be
considered: superiority at sea means that they may readily be
severed.'

'I take your point,' said Farquhar. 'But the decisive battle
must be fought on land; and the few regiments we possess
must be put down on that land.'

'Yes,' said Stephen. 'What you say is very true. And I admit
that these considerations would make me more doubtful of
the issue than in fact I am, were I not supported by what you
would perhaps term an illogical source of hope.'

'It would be benevolent in you to share your comfort.'

'As you may know, in the service our Commodore is known as Lucky Jack Aubrey. I am not prepared to enter into the concept of luck, as it is vulgarly called: philosophically it is indefensible; in daily experience we see it to exist. All I will say is, that Captain Aubrey seems to possess it in an eminent degree; and it is that which cheers my sometimes pensive nights.'

'How I hope you are right,' cried Farquhar. 'How sincerely I hope you are right.' After a pause he added, 'For countless reasons: among them the fact that I do not touch emolument or allowance until I enter into my functions.' He paused again, passed his hand over his eyes, and swallowed painfully.

'Let us take a turn on deck,' said Stephen. 'The greenish pallor is invading your face again, no doubt induced by melancholy thoughts as much as by the motion of the ship. The brisk trade-wind will blow them away.'

The brisk trade-wind instantly picked off Mr Farquhar's hat and wig. They flew forward, to be caught – a miracle of dexterity – by the bosun, who rose from the new best bower, seized the one in his right hand, the other in his left, and sent them aft by a midshipman. For his own part Mr Fellowes had preferred to keep the full length of the gangway between himself and the quarterdeck ever since a memorable day in Simon's Town, when the Commodore had had a private word with him, if private is quite the term for an explosion of honest rage that resounded from the after-cabin to the cutwater, filling the ship's company with mirth, glee, and apprehension, evenly mingled.

Covered once more, Mr Farquhar hooked himself into the rigging at Stephen's side; and as he gazed about him the corpse-like appearance faded from his face: the *Boadicea* was leaning over so that her lee chains were under the tearing white water and her weather side showed a broad streak of new copper; ahead of her the *Sirius*, under the same cloud of sail, kept as precisely to her station as though the two ships were joined by an iron bar; and together they were racing away to the north-east in the track of the *Néréide* to join the *Magicienne* and the *Iphigenia* off Port-Louis. They had already passed the *Leopard*, which had had two days' start (and which, since her captain was related to the Admiral, was strongly suspected of being present only to share in any prize money that might be going), and they were cracking on as though they meant to run off the two thousand miles and more in under a fortnight – a real possibility, they having picked up the powerful trade so soon. 'Celerity is everything, in these operations,' he said, 'and here we have celerity given form. How we fly! It is exhilarating! It is like a race for a thousand pound! It is like wrestling with a handsome woman!'

Stephen frowned; he disliked Mr Farquhar's warmer similes. 'Sure celerity is all,' he said. 'Yet a great deal also depends upon our finding the other ships at the rendezvous. The sea is so uncommonly vast, the elements so capricious, the instruments for finding the latitude so imperfect, or so imperfectly used, that I have known a vessel cruise ten days and more without finding her consorts.'

'Let us put our trust in the Commodore's mathematical powers,' said Mr Farquhar. 'Or his luck: or both. I believe, Dr Maturin, that if you would so far indulge me, I could relish a little, a very little, of your portable soup again, with just a sippet of toast; and I promise that if ever I come to govern my island, my first care, after the new constitution, shall be to repay you in turtle.'

Their trust was not misplaced. The day after they had seen the mountains of La Réunion piercing the white trade-clouds far to the leeward the two frigates went north about Mauritius, and there, true to the appointed coordinates, they found the rest of the squadron. Lambert, the senior captain, came aboard at once: the position in Port-Louis was just what they had expected, with the *Vénus*, the *Manche*, and the *Entreprenant* corvette lying snug in port and the *Bellone* and *Minerve* still far away; but on the other hand Clonfert, sent to cruise off the south-east of the island, had discovered a new French frigate, the 38-gun *Astrée*, moored under the batteries of the Rivière Noire in an impregnable position, obviously aware of the blockade of Port-Louis and unwilling to emerge. He had also cut out a four-hundred-ton merchantman from Jacotet, spiking the guns of the little batteries and taking some officers prisoner. It was true that the ship had proved to be a neutral, an American, one of the many Americans who used these seas, almost the only neutrals and almost the only source of casual information available to either side: but even so, said Lambert, it was a most dashing affair.

'This is a damned unfortunate object for dashing at and a damned odd moment to choose for dashing,' said Jack afterwards. 'If the *Néréide* had been knocked about in this cutting-out lark (for it was no more), we should have been put to our shifts to cover the landing, above all now that they have the *Astrée*. I wonder at Lambert, sending him off alone: though indeed it is plain that he knows these waters, and that he don't want conduct. Jacotet is a hellish awkward anchorage to get into. However, I think we must take Clonfert with us to Rodriguez as soon as we have watered, to keep his ardent spirits out of the way of temptation until there is a proper scope for 'em. He may dash till he goes blue in the face, once the real battle is engaged.'

They watered at Flat Island, and the *Boadicea* and the *Néréide* stretched away to the east for Rodriguez, leaving Pym in command with orders to fade imperceptibly away by night with the *Iphigenia* and *Magicienne*, leaving the *Leopard* and two avisoes off Port-Louis to bring instant warning if the *Bellone* and *Minerve* should return from the Bay of Bengal. 'For there's the rub,' said Jack. 'If those two heavy frigates, together with *Vénus*, *Manche* and *Astrée* were to fall on our rear at the wrong moment, with the troops half on shore and half off, we should be like Jackson, hard up in a clinch, and no knife to cut the seizing.'

Ordinarily Rodriguez presented the appearance of a desert

island; perhaps somewhat larger than the ideal desert island, being a good ten miles long, and perhaps somewhat greyer and more sterile inland than might have been wished, though pleasant enough after a long voyage with no sight of land; but now the bay was crowded with shipping, and on the shore exactly squared streets of tents stretched away in all directions, while in these streets hundreds and even thousands of men moved about, their red coats visible from a great way off.

Jack was first ashore, taking Stephen and Farquhar with him: to his intense relief he found that Keating was still in command – no glum, over-cautious general had superseded him. The two commanders instantly and with great goodwill plunged into the details of moving soldiers, ammunition, stores, provisions, arms, and even some howitzers in due order to the scene of action, and Stephen slipped silently away. 'The solitaire could never have borne this,' he reflected as he made his way through the crowded camp. 'And even the tortoise-park is sadly diminished.'

He had not gone a hundred yards before a voice behind him called out, 'Doctor! Doctor!'

'Not again?' he muttered angrily, walking faster among the screw-pines and drawing his head down between his shoulders. But he was pursued, run down; and in his overtaker he instantly recognized the tall, lank, and still very boyish form of Thomas Pullings, a shipmate from his first day at sea. 'Thomas Pullings,' he cried, with a look of real pleasure replacing the first malignant glare. 'Lieutenant Pullings, upon my word and honour. How do you do, sir?'

They shook hands, and having inquired tenderly after the Doctor's health and the Commodore's, Pullings said, 'I remember you was the first that ever called me Lieutenant P, sir, back in dear old Pompey. Well, now, if you chose to tip it the most uncommon civil, you could say Captain.'

'You do not tell me so? And are you indeed a captain already?'

'Not by land, sir; I am not Captain P by land. But at sea I am the captain of the *Groper* transport. You can see her from here, if you stand from behind the tree. Hey, you, the lobster there,' he called to an intervening soldier, 'your dad worn't no glazier. We can't see through you. There, sir: the brig just beyond the snow. She's only a transport, but did you ever see such lovely lines?'

Stephen had seen just such lines in a Dutch herring-buss, but he did not mention the fact, saying no more than 'Elegant, elegant'.

When her captain had gloated over the squat, thick object for a while he said, 'She's my first command, sir. A wonderful brig on a bowline; and she draws so amazing little water, she can run up the smallest creek. Will you honour us with a visit?'

'I should be very happy, Captain,' said Stephen. 'And since you are in command, might I beg the favour of a shovel, a crowbar, and a stout man of fair average understanding?'

The Commodore and the Colonel worked on their plan of campaign; the staff-officers worked on their lists; the soldiers polished their buttons, formed in squares, formed in fours, and marched off by the right into the boats, filling the transports and the frigates until the harassed sailors could scarcely holystone the decks, let alone come at the rigging; and Dr Maturin, with two Gropers of fair average understanding dug out the remains of the solitaire from the caves into which she had retired from hurricanes, only to be overwhelmed by the ensuing deluge of now rock-like mud.

The last soldier left the beach, a crimson major in charge of the operation; and as he set his weary foot on the *Boadicea's* quarterdeck he looked at his watch and cried, 'One minute fifty-three seconds a man, sir: that beats Wellington by a full two seconds!' A single gun to windward from the Commodore, the signal *Make sail*, and the fourteen transports began to file through the narrow opening in the reef to join the men-of-war.

By the evening they had sunk the island. They were sailing towards the setting sun with a fine topgallantsail breeze on the larboard quarter; and nothing but open sea lay between them and the beaches of La Réunion. The enterprise was now in train. Jack was far too busy with Colonel Keating and his maps for anything but the living present, but Stephen felt the long hours of gliding towards the inevitable future more than he had expected. He had been intimately concerned in matters of greater moment, but none in which the issue would be so clear-cut – total success, or total failure with a shocking loss of life – in a matter of hours.

He was not altogether happy about the plan to attack, which assumed that they would be expected at St Paul's, a restored, strengthened St Paul's, and which required a feint and then a landing at two points, the one east and the other south-west of Saint-Denis, the capital, the second being designed to cut off communication between Saint-Denis and St Paul's; nor was Jack, who feared the surf. But since Colonel Keating, a man in whom they had great confidence, and one who had fought over some of the terrain, strongly urged its strategic importance, and since he was supported by the other colonels, the Commodore had yielded, neither Stephen nor Farquhar saying anything, except when they stressed the importance of respect for civilian and ecclesiastical property.

The hours dropped by. At every heave of the log La Réunion was seven or eight miles nearer. Mr Farquhar was busy with his proclamation, and Stephen paced the quarterdeck, silently hating Buonaparte and all the evil he had brought into the world. 'Good only for destruction – has destroyed all that was valuable in the republic, all that was valuable in the monarchy – is destroying France with daemonic energy – this tawdry, theatrical empire – a deeply vulgar man – nothing French about him – insane ambition – the whole world one squalid tyranny. His infamous treatment of the Pope! Of this Pope and the last. And when I think of what

he has done to Switzerland and to Venice, and to God
knows how many other states, and what he might have done
to Ireland – the Hibernian Republic, divided into departments – one half secret police, the other informers – con-
scription – the country bled white – ' A subaltern of the
86th caught his pale wicked glare full in the eye and backed
away, quite shocked.

In the afternoon of the day after the council three ships
were sighted from the masthead: *Sirius*, *Iphigenia* and *Magicienne*, exact to the rendezvous, having seen no sign of the
Bellone or *Minerve*, nor any hint of movement in Port-Louis.
That evening they began to take chosen troops aboard over an
easy, gentle sea: and Jack summoned the captains to explain
the course of action. While the main force made a demonstration before Sainte-Marie, the *Sirius* was to land Colonel
Fraser's brigade and the howitzers at Grande-Chaloupe, a
beach on the leeward side of the island between Saint-Denis
and St Paul's. At the same time part of the brigades under
Colonel Keating were to be landed at the Rivière des Pluies,
thus placing Saint-Denis between two fires; and here the
other troops should also be landed as the transports came in;
for the frigates were now to press on alone under all the sail
they could bear.

They pressed on, still over this long easy swell, in a gentle
breeze with studding-sails aloft and alow: a magnificent sight
in their perfect line stretching over a mile of sea, the only
white in that incomparable blue. They pressed on, never
touching a sail except to make it draw better, from sunset
until the morning watch; and all the time the Commodore
took his sights on the great lambent stars hanging there in the
velvet sky, checking his position again and again with the real
help of Richardson and the nominal help of Mr Buchan the
master, calling for the log at every glass, and perpetually sending below for the readings of the chronometers and the
barometer. At two bells in the morning watch he gave orders

to reduce sail; and coloured lanterns, with a leeward gun, bade the squadron do the same.

Dawn found him still on deck, looking yellow and unshaved and more withdrawn than Stephen cared to see. La Réunion lay clear on the larboard bow, and the soldiers, coming sleepily on deck, were delighted to see it: they clustered on the forecastle, looking at the land with telescopes; and more than one cried out that he could find no surf upon the reefs, nothing but a little line of white. 'They may not be so pleased in twelve hours' time,' said Jack in a low voice, answering Stephen's inquiring look. 'The glass has been sinking all through the night: still, we may be in before it comes on to blow.' As he spoke he took off his coat and shirt, and then, having given his orders to Trollope, the officer of the watch, his breeches: from the rail he pitched head-first into the sea, rose snorting, swam along the line of boats that each frigate towed behind her, made his way back along them, and so went dripping below: the Boadiceas were perfectly used to this, but it shocked the redcoats, as savouring of levity. Once below and free of good mornings right and left, he went straight to sleep, with barely a pause between laying his long wet hair on the pillow and unconsciousness; and fast asleep he remained, in spite of the rumbling boots of a regiment of soldiers and the din inseparable from working the ship, until the faint tinkle of a teaspoon told some layer of his mind that coffee was ready. He sprang up, looked at the barometer, shook his head, dipped his face into a kid of tepid water, shaved, ate a hearty breakfast, and appeared on deck, fresh, pink, and ten years younger.

The squadron was coasting along just outside the reef, a reef upon which the sea broke mildly: three lines of rollers that a well-handled boat could manage easily enough.

'Upon my word, Commodore, the weather seems to serve our turn,' said Colonel Keating; and then in a louder voice and waving his hat to a young woman who was gathering clams on the reef, 'Bonjour, Mademoiselle.' The young woman, who had already been greeted by the three leading frigates, turned her back, and the Colonel went on, 'How do you think it will stay?'

'It may hold up,' said Jack. 'But then again it may come on to blow. We must move smartly: you will not object to a very early dinner, at the same time as the men?'

'Never in life, sir. Should be very happy – indeed I am sharp-set even now.'

Sharp-set he might be, reflected Jack, but he was also nervous. Keating set about his very early dinner with a decent appearance of phlegm, yet precious little went down his gullet. He had never had such an important command; nor had Jack; and in this waiting period they both felt the responsibility to a degree that neither of them would have thought possible. It affected them differently, however; for whereas Keating ate very little and talked a good deal, Jack devoured the best part of a duck and followed it with figgy-dowdy, gazing thoughtfully out of the stern-window as the not very distant landscape slipped by: far off, the harsh, precipitous mountains; nearer to, cultivated land, the occasional house: forest, plantations, a hamlet, and some carts creeping against the green. Their dinner did not last long: it was first interrupted by the report of two sail bearing east a half south – they later proved to be the leading transports, *Kite* and *Groper* – and then cut short entirely by the appearance of the little town of Sainte-Marie before Jack had quite finished his first attack upon the figgy-dowdy.

Here the reef trended in towards the coast, and the squadron turned with it, heaving to at the Commodore's signal. Already the town was in a state of turmoil: people were running about in all directions, pointing, screeching audibly, putting up their shutters, loading carts. They had plenty to screech about, for there, right off their anchorage, where the fresh water of the stream made gaps in the coral, and well within gunshot, lay five ships, broadside on, with their ports open and a frightful array of cannon pointing straight at Sainte-Marie. Even worse, large numbers of boats with soldiers in them were rowing about, evidently determined to land, to take, bum, rase, and sack the town. The sergeant's guard from the little post was lined up on the beach, but they did not seem to know what to do, and every man who could command a horse had long since galloped off to Saint-Denis to give the alarm and to implore instant succour from the military there.

'This is going very well,' said Colonel Keating some time later, as he watched the vanguard of the succour through his telescope. 'Once their field-pieces are across the stream, they will have a devil of a time getting them back again. Their horses are quite done up already. See the company of infantry at the double! They will be pooped, sir, pooped entirely.'

'Aye,' said Jack. 'It is very well.' But his mind was more on the sea than on the land, and it appeared to him that the surf was growing: the rollers, perhaps from some blow far to the east, were coming in with more conviction. He looked at his watch, and although it wanted forty minutes of the stated time he said, 'Make *Sirius*'s signal to carryon.'

The *Sirius*'s paid off heavily, filled, and bore away for Grande-Chaloupe, carrying close on a thousand men and the howitzers. As she moved off, her place was taken by the *Kite*, the *Groper*, and two other transports, increasing the alarm on shore.

The plan had been unable to allot any precise interval between the two landings, since obviously that must depend on the time the *Sirius* should take to pass Saint-Denis and reach the agreed point between that town and St Paul's; but they had hoped for something in the nature of two hours. With the failing breeze, however, it now looked as though at least three would be required: and all the while the surf was growing. The waiting was hard, and it would have been harder still if the newly-arrived French field-pieces, drawn up on a hill behind the post, had not seen fit to open fire. They threw no more than four-pound balls, but they threw them with striking accuracy, and after the first sighting shots one passed so close to Colonel Keating's head that he cried out indignantly, 'Did you see that, sir? It was perfectly deliberate. Infernal scrubs! They must know I am the commanding officer.'

'Do you not shoot at commanding officers in the army, Colonel?'

'Of course not, sir. Never, except in a melee. If I were on land, I should send a galloper directly. There they go again. What unprincipled conduct: Jacobins.'

'Well, I believe we can put a stop to it. Pass the word for the gunner. Mr Webber, you may fire at the field-pieces by divisions: but you must point all the guns yourself, and you must not damage any civilian or ecclesiastical property. Pitch them well up beyond the town.'

With the great guns going off one after another in a leisurely, deliberate fire, and the heady smell of powder swirling about the deck, tension slackened. The soldiers cheered as Mr Webber sent his eighteen-pound balls skimming among the Frenchmen on their knoll, and they roared again when he hit a limber full on, so that one wheel sprang high into the air, turning like a penny tossed for heads or tails. But such an unequal contest could not last long, and presently the French guns were silenced: and all the time the swell increased, sending white water high on the reef and surging through the gap to break in great measured rollers on the strand.

Yet after the lull the breeze had strengthened too, with every sign of blowing hard before the night, and at length Jack said, '*Sirius* should be at Grande-Chaloupe by now. I think we may move on.'

Their move took them briskly past another shallow gap in the reef, where more fresh water broke the coral, and to another anchorage (though still indifferent) off the mouth of the Rivière des Pluies.

'This is it,' said Colonel Keating, map in hand. 'If we can go ashore here, the landing will be unopposed. It will be at least an hour before they can get round: probably more.'

'My God,' thought Jack, looking at the broad belt of surf, the steep-to beach of rounded boulders. He stepped to the taffrail and hailed, '*Néréide*, ahoy. Come under my stern.' The *Néréide* shot up, backed her foretopsail, and lay pitching on the swell: there was Lord Clonfert on her quarterdeck; and Stephen noticed that he was wearing full-dress uniform – no unusual thing in a fleet-action, but rare for a skirmish.

'Lord Clonfert,' called Jack, 'do you know the deep-water channel?'

'Yes, sir.'

'Is a landing practicable?'

'Perfectly practicable at present, sir. I will undertake to put a party ashore this minute.'

'Carry on, Lord Clonfert,' said Jack. The *Néréide* had a little captured schooner among her boats, a local craft; and into this and some of her boats she poured an eager party of soldiers and seamen. The squadron watched the schooner run down to the edge of the surf, followed by the boats. Here she took to her sweeps, backing water and waiting for the master-wave: it came, and she shot in through the breaking water, on and on, and they thought she was through until at the very last she struck, ten yards from the shore, slewed round, and was thrown on to the beach, broadside on. As the wave receded all the men leapt ashore, but the backdraught took her into the very curl of the next, which lifted her high and flung her down so hard that it broke her back at once and shattered her timbers. Most of the other craft fared the same: the boats beaten to pieces, the men safe. Only four bodies were to be seen, dark in the white water, drifting westwards along the shore.

'It is essential to carry on,' cried Colonel Keating in a harsh voice. 'We must take Saint-Denis between two fires, whatever the cost.'

Jack said to Mr Johnson, 'Make *Groper*'s signal.'

While the transport was coming up he stared at the beach and the floating wreckage: as he had thought, it was only the last stretch that was mortal at this stage. Anything of a break-water would allow boats to land; and the Groper was the only vessel with a draught shallow enough to go in so far. When she was under the *Boadicea*'s lee he called, 'Mr Pullings, you must shelter the boats: take your brig in, drop your stern-anchor at the last moment, and run her ashore as near as you can heading south-west.'

'Aye, aye, sir,' said Pullings.

The *Groper* bore up in a volley of orders, made her way slowly towards the land while her people were busy below, rousing a cable out of a stern-port, and then much faster: into the surf, on and on through it. In his glass Jack saw the anchor drop, and a moment later the *Groper* ran hard aground right by the shore. Her foretopmast went by the board with the shock, but the hands at the capstan took no notice: they were furiously heaving the cable in, forcing her stern round so that she lay just south-west, braced against the seas and creating a zone of quiet water right in by the shore.

'Well done, Tom Pullings, well done indeed: but how long will your anchor hold?' muttered Jack, and aloud, 'First division away.'

The boats ran in, landed and hauled up, half-swamped in most cases but rarely overset: the beach was filling with red-coats, forming neatly in line as they came ashore. Some, with Colonel McLeod, had taken up position a few hundred yards inland. Then the *Groper*'s cable parted. A tall comber took her stern, wrenched it round, and flung her on that unforgiv-ing beach: and since her bows were already stove, she went to pieces at once, leaving the surf the full sweep of the shore. The wave that broke her was the first of a growing series; and presently the belt of surf grew wider and wider, thundering louder still.

'Can another ship be sent in, Commodore?' asked Keating.

'No, sir,' said Jack.

On the road that led from Sainte-Marie to Saint-Denis, and that here curved inland from the coast to avoid a swamp, three separate bodies of French troops could be seen, moving slowly from east to west, towards Saint- Denis. Colonel McLeod's party on shore had already thrown up dry-stone breastworks between the beach and the road, and had formed behind them in good order. To the left of their line the seamen and the Marines had done much the same; but being on wetter ground they had made a broad turf wall, upon which stood Lord Clonfert, conspicuous with his star and his gold-laced hat.

The first body came abreast of the landing-party at a distance of two hundred yards: they halted, loaded, levelled their pieces, and fired. Clonfert waved his sword at them, reached behind him for a Marine's musket, and returned the fire. It was almost the only shot in reply to the French discharge: clearly the landing-party had spoilt nearly all its powder.

As the squadron watched, too far for accurate fire on this heaving sea but near enough for telescopes to show every detail, two cavalrymen came galloping down the road from Saint-Denis, spoke to an officer and rode on. The troops shouldered their muskets, reformed, and set off towards Saint-Denis at the double. The second and third bodies, also given orders by the horsemen, came fast along the road: each halted long enough for a volley or two, and each was saluted by Clonfert from the top of his wall. He was eating a biscuit, and each time he put it down on his handkerchief to shoot. Once he hit an officer's horse, but most of the time his musket missed fire.

Still more horsemen came riding fast from Saint-Denis, one of them probably a field-officer, urging the troops to hurry. The inference was as clear as the day: Colonel Fraser had landed in force from the *Sirius*, and these men were being called back to protect the capital.

'*Magicienne* and the *Kite* and *Solebay* transports must go and support him at once,' said Jack. 'The rest of the squadron will stay here, in case the sea goes down by the morning.' Colonel Keating agreed: he seemed glad of the authoritative statement, and Stephen had the impression that he had lost his sense of being in control of the situation – that this impossibility of communicating with the visible shore was something outside his experience.

Throughout this time Stephen and Farquhar had stood by the hances, out of the way, two figures as unregarded as they had been at the time of the military councils, where they sat virtually mute, dim among the splendid uniforms; but now, after a hurried consultation with Farquhar, Stephen said to Jack, 'We are agreed that if Colonel Fraser has a firm footing on the other side of the island, I should be put ashore there.'

'Very well,' said Jack. 'Mr Fellowes, a bosun's chair, there. Pass the word for my coxswain. Bonden, you go aboard *Magicienne* with the Doctor.'

What remained of this anxious day off the Rivière des Pluies was taken up with watching the surf. A little before sunset half an hour's downpour of a violence rare even for those latitudes deadened the white water of the breakers so that the channel was a little clearer, and a subaltern of the 56th, born in the West Indies and accustomed to surf from his childhood, volunteered to swim ashore with Colonel Keating's orders to Colonel McLeod. He launched himself into the rollers with the confidence of a seal, vanished, and reappeared on the crest of a wave that set him neatly on his feet at high-water-mark: shortly afterwards McLeod, covering the subaltern's nakedness with a plaid, marched off at the head of his men to seize the little post at Sainte-Marie, deserted by its occupants, to hoist the British colours, and to regale upon the stores left by the sergeant's guard.

Yet darkness fell with its usual suddenness in the tropics, and it was impossible to send boats in through the reviving turmoil. The ships stood off and on all night, and in the morning the combers were still roaring up the beach. There might, Jack agreed, be a slight improvement, but it was nothing like enough; and his strongly-held opinion was that they should proceed at once to Grande-Chaloupe to reinforce the troops landed from the *Sirius* and *Magicienne*, leaving the *Iphigenia* and some transports to land at the Rivière des Pluies later in the day if the sea went down. Happily Colonel Keating shared this opinion to the full, and the *Boadicea* made sail, passed Saint-Denis, where the soldiers swore they could distinguish gunfire on the far side of the town, rounded Cape Bernard, and stretched south-south-west under a cloud of canvas for the beach of Grande-Chaloupe, obvious from miles away by the congregation of shipping and the now unmistakeable gunfire in the hills above.

They stood in, and here, on the leeward side of the island, what a different state of things was seen! Calm beaches, lapping billows, boats plying to and fro: and up in the hills companies of redcoats regularly formed; companies of turbans; guns at work, and still more guns being dragged up by ant-like lines of seamen.

The Colonel and his staff raced ashore, all weariness forgotten; troops, guns, heavy equipment began to pour from the frigate. Jack's duty bound him to the ship, however, and he stood watching through his telescope. 'This is a damned poor way of being present at a battle,' he said to Mr Farquhar. 'How I envy Keating.'

Colonel Keating, provided with a captured horse on the beach itself, spurred his mount up the paths to Colonel Fraser's forward post, where they both surveyed the scene. 'You have a charmingly regular attack here,' said Keating with great satisfaction, directing his spy-glass right and left. 'And a most judicious defence: the French have made a very proper disposition of their forces.'

'Yes, sir. It is as regular as one could wish, except for the blue-jackets. They will rush forward and take out works before they are due to fall: though I must confess, they have done wonders in getting the howitzers up. But on the whole it *is* pretty regular: over on the right, sir, beyond the signal-post, Campbell and his sepoys have made the prettiest set of approaches. They are only waiting for the word to charge: that will carry us two hundred yards nearer their demi-lune.'

'Then why don't you give it, Mother of God? They have clearly outflanked the enemy already. Where is your galloper?'

'He is just behind you, sir. But if you will forgive me, there is a parley in train. The political gentleman from the ship came up with a clergyman and a party of tars and said he must speak to the French commanding officer. So knowing he was the governor's adviser, we beat a chamade and sent him across with a flag of truce. It seemed to me proper; and yet now I half regret it . . . Can he be quite right in the head, sir? He desired me to keep this bone for him, saying he would not trust it to the French for the world.'

'Oh, these politicoes, you know, Fraser . . .' said Colonel Keating. 'It will come to nothing, however. They are very strongly entrenched on the hill; and even if McLeod comes up from the east, it will take us a good week of regular approaches to press them to their main works.'

They were studying the main works with great attention through their telescopes when an aide-de-camp said, 'I beg your pardon, sir, but Dr Maturin is approaching with a French officer and a couple of civilians.'

Colonel Keating walked forward to meet them. Stephen said, 'Colonel Keating, this is Colonel Saint-Susanne, who commands the French forces on the island. These gentlemen represent the civil administration.' The two soldiers saluted one another: the civilians bowed. Stephen went on, 'From a desire to avert the effusion of human blood, they wish to know the terms upon which you will grant a capitulation covering the whole island: and I have taken it upon myself to assure them that the terms will be honourable.'

'Certainly, sir,' said Colonel Keating, with an icy glare at Stephen. 'Gentlemen, pray step this way.'

Jack and Farquhar, prosaically eating an early elevenses and wondering vaguely, repetitively, why there was no longer any firing in the hills, were interrupted first by cheering on the shore and then by an ensign bearing a scribbled note. 'Forgive me, sir,' said Jack; and he read, 'My dear Commodore – Your friend has disappointed us – he has *done us out* of our battle, as neat a battle as you could wish to see. We had driven in their piquets – outflanked their right wing – and then quite out of order a capitulation is proposed, *to avert the effusion of human blood* forsooth – they accept the usual terms – honours of war, side-arms and baggage, personal effects and so on – so if you are satisfied, please come ashore to sign together with your obliged humble servant, H. Keating, Lieut.-Col.'

The Commodore laughed aloud, beat his massive thigh, held out his hand and said, 'Governor, I give you joy. They have surrendered, and your kingdom awaits you. Or this island of it, at the least.'

7

His Excellency the Governor of La Réunion sat at the head of his council table: he now wore a uniform as splendid as that of the gold and scarlet colonels on his left hand, more splendid by far than the weather-worn blue of the sea-officers on his right; and now there was no question of his sitting mute. Yet there was no trace of hauteur to be seen on his eager, intelligent face as he tried to guide the meeting towards a unanimous approval of the Commodore's revolutionary scheme, his plan of an instant attack upon Mauritius, with simultaneous landings from Flat Island off Port-Louis and in the neighbourhood of Port South-East at the other end of the island. Colonel Keating had been with him from the first; but a distinct inclination to enjoy the fruits of victory for a while, 'to allow the men a little rest', and, more creditably, a

desire to prepare the campaign with due deliberation, so that
mortars for example did not arrive without their shells, had
yet to be overcome; for if so ambitious and risky an operation
as this were to fail, the attempt could be justified only by a
unanimous vote.

'I shall echo the Commodore's words, gentlemen,' said Mr
Farquhar, 'and cry "Lose not a moment". This is the moment
at which we have a superiority of five to three in frigates,
when we possess a fleet of transports, troops in the first flush
of victory, and exact intelligence of the enemy's strength and
dispositions on the Mauritius, supplied by their own records
here.'

'Hear him, hear him,' said Colonel Keating. 'With command of the sea we may concentrate our forces wherever we
choose. Furthermore, my colleague' – bowing to Stephen at
the far end of the table – 'assures me that at this juncture,
this very favourable juncture, our efforts at sapping the
enemy's morale are more than likely to be crowned with success; and we are all aware of Dr Maturin's powers in that
direction.' It was not the most fortunate stroke: some of the
colonels who had toiled and sweated extremely in the hope of
glory turned a sombre gaze upon Dr Maturin. Feeling this,
Mr Farquhar hurried on, 'And perhaps even more important,
this is the moment at which our hands are free. The *Leopard*
has taken our despatches to the Cape: she will not return. No
orders from any authority unacquainted with the exact state
of local conditions can take the guidance of operations from
the hands of those who *are* acquainted with them – no new
set of staff-officers can, for the moment, arrive with a plan of
campaign matured in Bombay, Fort William, or Whitehall.
This is a state of affairs that cannot last.'

'Hear him, hear him,' said Colonel Keating, Colonel
McLeod and Colonel Fraser; and the fatter, more cautious
staff-officers exchanged uneasy glances.

'Far be it from me to decry patient laborious staff-work,'
said the Governor. 'We have seen its gratifying results on this

island: but, gentlemen, time and tide wait for no man; and I must remind you that Fortune is bald behind.'

Walking away from the Residence through streets placarded with the Governor's proclamation, Jack said to Stephen, 'What is this that Farquhar tells us about Fortune? Is she supposed to have the mange?'

'I conceive he was referring to the old tag – his meaning was, that she must be seized by the forelock, since once she is passed there is no clapping on to her hair, at all. In the figure she ships none abaft the ears, if you follow me.'

'Oh, I see. Rather well put: though I doubt those heavy-sided lobsters will smoke the simile.' He paused, considering, and said, 'It don't sound very eligible, bald behind; but, however, it is all figurative, all figurative . . .' He gazed with benign approval at a strikingly elegant woman accompanied by an even more willowy black slave-girl, stepped into the gutter to let them pass, they looked haughty, unconscious, a thousand miles away, and continued, 'Still, I am glad they have come to see reason. But Lord, Stephen, what an infernal waste of time these councils are! If it had dragged on another day the squadron would have been dispersed – *Sirius* is gone already – and I should have had to follow my own scheme. My first duty is to the sea, and I must get at Hamelin before the *Bellone* and *Minerve* are back. But as it is, I can combine the two. Pullings!' he exclaimed.

On the other side of the street Pullings cast off the girl at his side and crossed, blushing a reddish mahogany yet beaming too. 'Did you find anything you liked, Pullings?' asked Jack. 'I mean, in the professional line?'

'Oh, yes, sir – I was only looking after her for a minute, for Mr – for another officer, sir – but I don't suppose you will let me have her, sir – far too pretty, except for a trifle of worm in her futtocks, her ground futtocks.' Pullings had been sent to St Paul's in the *Sirius* when the frigate tore down immediately after the capitulation to snap up all the shipping in the road; he had been told to make his own choice of a replacement for

the *Groper*, and he had done himself as proud as Pontius
Pilate. They watched the young woman attach herself to the
arm of Mr Joyce of the *Kite* transport, and as they walked
along, Pullings, more coherent now that he was relieved of a
sense of guilt – for very strangely his officers looked upon
Jack Aubrey as a moral figure, in spite of all proofs to the contrary – expatiated on the merits of his prize, a privateer
schooner, copper-fastened, wonderfully well-found.

At the gates of the government stable-yard they parted, and
while Bonden led forth a powerful black horse, once the
pride of the French garrison, Stephen said, 'This is not the
moment to ask how you mean to combine the two schemes;
yet I admit that I am curious to know. Bonden, I advise you,
in your own best interest, not to stand behind that creature's
heels.'

'If you will ride over to St Paul's with me,' said Jack, 'I will
tell you.'

'Alas, I have an audience of the Bishop in half an hour, and
then an appointment at the printing-shop.'

'Maybe it is just as well. Things will be clearer in the morning. Bonden, cast off afore.'

Things were indeed clearer in the morning: the Commodore had seen all the officers concerned; he had all the
facts distinctly arranged; and he received Stephen in a room
filled with charts and maps.

'Here, do you see,' he said, pointing to an island three or
four miles off Port South-East, 'is the Ile de la Passe. It lies on
the reef at the very edge of the only deep-water channel into
the port: a devilish channel, narrow, with a double dog-leg
and any number of banks and rocks in its bed. The island is
pretty strongly held – it mounts about twenty heavy guns –
but the town is not. They expect us in the north, where we
have been blockading all this while, and most of their forces
are around Port-Louis: so if we knock out the Ile de la Passe –
and a couple of frigates should be able to manage it – '

'In spite of the intricate navigation? These are very alarming shoals, brother. I see two and three fathoms marked for a couple of miles inside the reef; and here is a vast area with the words *Canoe-passage at high-tide*; while your channel is a mere serpent; a lean serpent at the best. But I am not to be teaching you your business.'

'It can be done. Clonfert and his black pilot know these waters perfectly. Look, here is the Jacotet anchorage just at hand, where he cut out the American. Yes, they should manage it well enough; though of course it must be done by boats and in the night; ships could not stand in against that fire, without being sadly mauled. Then once the island is seized, the French cannot easily retake it: their batteries cannot reach across the inner bay and since they have no ship of force in Port South-East, nor even gun-boats, they have no means of getting their artillery any nearer. Nor can they starve it out, so long as we victual it from the sea. So if we hold the Ile de la Passe we deny the French their best harbour after Port-Louis; we have a base for our landing; and we open up all the country out of range of the batteries for your handing-out of broadsheets and culling simples. For their little garrisons in the town and along the coast will scarcely stir outside the reach of their own guns.'

'This is a very beautiful plan,' said Stephen.

'Ain't it?' said Jack. 'Keating has already sent some Bombay gunners and European troops into the *Néréide*, to garrison the place when we have taken it: for obviously the *Néréide* possesses more local knowledge than all the rest of the squadron put together.'

'You do not feel that Clonfert's oversetting of the little ship off the Rivière des Pluies throws a certain shade on his qualifications?'

'No, I do not. It could have happened to anyone in those circumstances, with the soldiers ready to call us shy. I should have tried it myself. But I am not going to give him his head at the Ile de la Passe; I do not want him to be coming it the Cochrane: Pym shall command. Pym may not be very wise, but he is a good, sound man, as regular as a clock; so *Néréide*, *Iphigenia* and perhaps *Staunch* – '

'What is this *Staunch*?'

'She is a brig: came in last night from Bombay. A useful little brig, and in excellent order. Narborough has her, a most officer-like cove: you remember Narborough, Stephen?' Stephen shook his head. 'Of course you do,' cried Jack. 'Lord Narborough, a big black man with a Newfoundland dog, third of the *Surprise*.'

'You mean Garron,' said Stephen.

'Garron, of course: you are quite right. Garron he was then, but his father died last year, and now he is called Narborough. So *Néréide*, *Iphigenia*, and perhaps *Staunch* if she can get her water in quick enough, are to run up to Port-Louis, where Pym is watching Hamelin's motions. *Iphigenia* will stay, and *Sirius* and *Néréide* will come south for the Ile de la Passe.'

'The *Néréide* is not to come back here, so?'

'To wait for the dark of the moon, you mean? No; we cannot afford the time.'

'Then in that case I had better go aboard her now. There is a great deal to be done in the Mauritius, and the sooner I get there the better. For I tell you, my dear, that though they are less lethal, my broadsheets are as effective as your – as your roundshot.'

'Stephen,' said Jack, 'I am convinced of it.'

'I had almost said, as effective as your broad*sides*, but I was afraid the miserable play upon words might offend an embryonic baronet; for Farquhar tells me that if this second campaign should succeed as well as the first the happy commander will certainly be so honoured. Should you not like to be a baronet, Jack?'

'Why, as to that,' said Jack, 'I don't know that I should much care for it. The Jack Aubrey of King James's time paid a thumping fine not to be a baronet, you know. Not that I mean the least fling against men who have won a great fleet action

– it is right and proper that *they* should be peers – but when you look at the mass of titles, tradesmen, dirty politicians, moneylenders . . . why, I had as soon be plain Jack Aubrey – Captain Jack Aubrey, for I am as proud as Nebuchadnezzar of my service rank, and if ever I hoist my flag, I shall paint *here lives Admiral Aubrey* on the front of Ashgrove Cottage in huge letters. Do not think I am one of your wild democratical Jacobins, Stephen – do not run away with that notion – but different people look at these things in different lights.' He paused, and said with a grin, 'I'll tell you of one chap who would give his eye-teeth to be a baronet, and this is Admiral Bertie. He puts it down to Mrs Bertie, but the whole service knows how he plotted and planned for the Bath. Lord,' he said, laughing heartily, 'to think of crawling about St James's for a ribbon when you are an ancient man, past sixty. Though to be sure, perhaps I might think differently if I had a son: but I doubt it.'

In the afternoon of the next day, Dr Maturin, preceded by two bales of hand-bills, proclamations and broadsheets, some printed in Cape Town and others so recently struck off in Saint-Denis that they were still damp from the press, came alongside the *Néréide*, six hours late. But the Néréides were not used to his ways; they were in a fuming hurry to be off in pursuit of the *Iphigenia*, which had sailed at crack of dawn; and they let him drop between the boat and the ship's side. In his fall he struck his head and back on the boat's gunwale, cracking two ribs and sinking stunned down through the warm clear water: the frigate was already under way, and although she heaved to at once not a man aboard did anything more valuable than run about shouting for some minutes, and by the time she had dropped her stern-boat Stephen would have been dead if one of the bale-carrying black men had not dived in and fetched him out.

He had had a shrewd knock, and although the weather was so kind, the sun so warm, an inflammation of the lungs kept him pinned to his cot for days. Or rather to the captain's cot, for Lord Clonfert moved from his own sleeping-cabin and slung a hammock in the coach.

Stephen therefore missed their rapid voyage north, the meeting of the ships off Port-Louis, and their return south-wards through heavy seas to carry out the Commodore's plan of attack on the Ile de la Passe; he missed all but the sounds of their first abortive attempt at gathering the boats for the assault in a pitch-black night with the wind blowing a close-reef topsail gale, when even the *Néréide*'s pilot could not find the channel and when the weather forced them back to Port-Louis; but on the other hand, in these circumstances of par-ticular intimacy he did grow more closely acquainted with Clonfert and McAdam.

The captain spent many hours at Stephen's bedside: their conversation was desultory and for most part of no great con-sequence; but Clonfert was capable of an almost female deli-cacy – he could be quiet without constraint, and he always knew when Stephen would like a cooling drink or the skylight opened – and they talked about novels, the more recent romantic poetry, and Jack Aubrey, or rather Jack Aubrey's actions, in a most companionable way; and at times Stephen saw, among the various persons that made up his host, a gen-tle, vulnerable creature, one that excited his affection. 'His intuition, however,' reflected Stephen, 'though so nice in a tête-à-tête, does not serve him when three or more are gath-ered in a room, nor when he is anxious. Jack has never seen him in his quasi-domestic character. His women have, no doubt; and it may be this that accounts for his notorious suc-cess among them.'

These reflections were prompted by the visit of his old shipmate Narborough, before whom Clonfert pranced away, monopolizing the talk with anecdotes of Sir Sydney Smith, and to whom he behaved with such an aggressive affectation of superiority that the commander of the *Staunch* soon returned aboard her, thoroughly displeased. Yet that same evening, as the *Néréide* and *Staunch* approached the Ile de la

Passe once more, coming south about while the *Sirius* took the northern route, to avoid suspicion, Clonfert was as quiet and agreeable and well-bred as ever he had been: particularly conciliating, indeed, as though he were aware of his lapse. And when, at his request, Stephen had once again related Jack's taking of the *Cacafuego*, shot by shot, Clonfert said with a sigh, 'Well, I honour him for it, upon my word. I should die happy, with such a victory behind me.'

With McAdam Stephen's relationship was by no means so pleasant. Like most medical men Stephen was an indifferent patient; and like most medical men McAdam had an authoritative attitude towards those under his care. As soon as the patient had recovered his wits they fell out over the advisability of a cingulum, a black draught, and phlebotomy, all of which Stephen rejected in a weak, hoarse, but passionate voice as 'utterly exploded, fit for Paracelsus, or a quicksalver at the fair of Ballinasloe,' together with a fling about McAdam's fondness for a strait-waistcoat. Yet this, even when it was coupled with Stephen's recovery without any treatment but bark administered by himself, would not have caused real animosity if McAdam had not also taken to resenting Clonfert's attention to Stephen, Stephen's ascendancy over Clonfert, and their pleasure in one another's company.

He came into the cabin, only half-drunk, the evening before the *Néréide* and the *Staunch*, though delayed by headwinds, hoped to rendezvous with the *Sirius* off the Ile de la Passe for the assault, took Stephen's pulse, said, 'There is still a wee smidgeon of fever that bleeding would certainly have cured before this; but I shall allow you to take the air on deck again tomorrow, if the action leaves you any deck to take it upon,' drew his case-bottle from his pocket, poured himself a liberal dram in Stephen's physic-glass, and bending, picked up a paper that had slipped beneath the cot, a single printed sheet. 'What language is this?' he asked, holding it to the light.

'It is Irish,' said Stephen calmly: he was extremely vexed

with himself for letting it be seen, for although there was no kind of remaining secrecy about his activities, his ingrained sense of caution was deeply wounded: he was determined not to let this appear, however.

'Tis not the Irish character,' said McAdam.

'Irish type is rarely to be found in the French colonies, I believe.'

'I suppose it is meant for those papisher blackguards on the Mauritius,' said McAdam, referring to the Irishmen who were known to have enlisted in the French service. Stephen made no reply, and McAdam went on, 'What does it say?'

'Do you not understand Irish?'

'Of course not. What would a civilized man want with Irish?'

'Perhaps that depends upon your idea of a civilized man.'

'I'll just give you my idea of a civilized man: it is one thot makes croppies lie down, thot drinks to King Billy, and thot cries – the Pope.' With this McAdam began to sing *Croppies lie down*, and the grating, triumphant noise wounded Stephen's still fevered and over-acute hearing. Stephen was fairly sure that McAdam did not know he was a Catholic, but even so his irritation, increased by the heat, the din, the smell, and his present inability to smoke, rose to such a pitch that against all his principles he said, 'It is the pity of the world, Dr McAdam, to see a man of your parts obnubilate his mind with the juice of the grape.'

McAdam instantly collected his faculties and replied, 'It is the pity of the world, Dr Maturin, to see a man of your parts obnubilate his mind with the juice of the poppy.'

In his journal that night Stephen wrote '. . . and his blotched face clearing on a sudden, he checked me with my laudanum. I am amazed at his perspicacity. Yet do I indeed obnubilate my mind? Surely not: looking back in this very book, I detect no diminution of activity, mental or physical. The pamphlet on Buonaparte's real conduct towards this Pope and the last is as good as anything I have ever written: I wish it may be as well translated. I rarely take a thousand drops, a trifle compared with your true opium-eater's dose or with my own in Diana's day: I can refrain whenever I choose: and I take it only when my disgust is so great that it threatens to impede my work. One day, when he is sober, I shall ask McAdam whether disgust for oneself, for one's fellows, and for the whole process of living was common among his patients in Belfast – whether it incapacitated them. My own seems to grow; and it is perhaps significant that I can feel no gratitude towards the man who took me from the water: I make the gestures that humanity requires but I feel no real kindness for him: surely this is inhuman? Humanity drained away by disgust? It grows; and although my loathing for Buonaparte and his evil system is an efficient stimulant, hatred alone is a poor sterile kind of a basis. And, laudanum or not, the disgust seems to persist even through my sleep, since frequently it is there, ready to envelop me when I wake.'

The next morning was not one of those occasions, frequent though they were. Having listened in vain at intervals throughout the night for sounds that might herald an action or even a meeting with the other ships, Stephen awoke from a long comfortable dozing state, a wholly relaxed well-being, aware that his fever was gone and that he was being looked at through the crack of the partly open door. 'Hola,' he cried, and a nervous midshipman, opening wider, said, 'The Captain's compliments to Dr Maturin, and should he be awake and well enough, there is a mermaid on the starboard bow.'

She was abaft the beam before Stephen reached the rail, a vast greyish creature with a round snout and thick lips, upright in the sea, staring at the ship with her minute beady eyes. If she was indeed a maid, then she must have had a friend who was none, for in her left flipper she held a huge grey baby. She was going fast astern, staring steadily, but he had time to see her opulent bosom, her absence of neck, hair, and external ears, and to estimate her weight at forty stone, before she dived, showing her broad tail above the wave. He made the fullest acknowledgments for such a treat – had always longed to see one – had searched the Rodriguez lagoons and those of an island near Sumatra but had always been disappointed until this happy moment – and now he found the realization of his wishes even more gratifying than he had hoped.

'I am glad you was pleased,' said Lord Clonfert, 'and I hope it may be some lay-off against my wretched news. *Sirius* has queered our pitch: see where she lays.'

Stephen took his bearings. Four or five miles away on his right hand rose the south-east coast of Mauritius, with the Pointe du Diable running into the sea: also on his right hand, but within a hundred yards, the long reef stretched out fore and aft, sometimes dry, sometimes buried under the white rollers, with the occasional island standing on it or rising from the paler shallow water inside; and at the far end, where Clonfert was pointing, there lay the *Sirius*, close to a fortified island from whose walls, clear in the telescope, flew the union jack.

In spite of his pleasure at Stephen's delight, it was clear that Clonfert was profoundly disappointed and put out. 'They must have gained twenty leagues on us, while we were beating up off the cape,' he said: 'But if Pym had had any bowels he would have waited for tonight: after all, I did lend him my pilot.' However, as an attentive host he checked any bitter reflections that might have occurred to him, and asked Stephen whether he would like his breakfast.

'You are very good, my lord,' said Stephen, 'but I believe I shall stay here in the hope of seeing another siren. They are usually found in the shallow water by a reef, I am told; and I should not miss one for a dozen breakfasts.'

'Clarges will bring it to you here, if you are quite sure you are strong enough,' said Clonfert. 'But I must send for McAdam to survey you first.'

McAdam looked singularly unappetizing in the morning

light, ill-conditioned and surly: apprehensive too, for he had some confused recollection of harsh words having passed the night before. But, having beheld the mermaid, Stephen was in charity with all men, and he called out, 'You missed the mermaid, my dear colleague; but perhaps, if we sit quietly here, we may see another.'

'I did not,' said McAdam, 'I saw the brute out of the quarter-gallery scuttle; and it was only a manatee.'

Stephen mused for a while, and then he said, 'A dugong, surely. The dentition of the dugong is quite distinct from that of the manatee: the manatee, as I recall, has no incisors. Furthermore, the whole breadth of Africa separates their respective realms.'

'Manatee or dugong, 'tis all one,' said McAdam. 'As far as my studies are concerned, the brute is of consequence only in that it is the perfect illustration of the strength, the irresistible strength, of suggestion. Have you been listening to their gab, down there in the waist?'

'Not I,' said Stephen. There had been much talk among the men working just out of sight forward of the quarterdeck rail, cross, contentious talk; but the *Néréide* was always a surprisingly chatty ship, and apart from putting this outburst down to vexation at their late arrival, he had not attended to it. 'They seem displeased, however,' he added.

'Of course they are displeased: everyone knows the ill-luck a mermaid brings. But that is not the point. Listen now, will you? That is John Matthews, a truthful, sober, well-judging man; and the other is old Lemon, was bred a lawyer's clerk, and understands evidence.'

Stephen listened, sorted out the voices, caught the thread of the argument: the dispute between Matthews and Lemon, the spokesmen of two rival factions, turned upon the question of whether the mermaid had held a comb in her hand or a glass.

'They saw the flash of that wet flipper,' said McAdam, 'and have translated it, with total Gospel-oath conviction, into one or other of these objects. Matthews offers to fight Lemon and any two of his followers over a chest in support of his belief.'

'Men have gone to the stake for less,' said Stephen: and walking forward to the rail he called down, 'You are both of you out entirely: it was a hairbrush.'

Dead silence in the waist. The seamen looked at one another doubtfully, and moved quietly away among the boats on the booms with many a backward glance, thoroughly disturbed by this new element.

'*Sirius* signalling, sir, if you please,' said a midshipman to the officer of the watch, who had been picking his teeth with a pertinacity so great that it had rendered him deaf to the dispute. '*Captain to come aboard.*'

'I am anxious to see whether the *Sirius* has any prisoners,' said Stephen, when the Captain appeared, 'and if I may, I will accompany you.'

Pym welcomed them with less than his usual cheerfulness: it had been a bloody little action, one in which he had lost a young cousin, and although the frigate's decks were now as trim as though she were lying at St Helen's, there was a row of hammocks awaiting burial at sea, while her boats still lay about her in disorder, all more or less battered and one with a dismounted carronade lying in a red pool. The anxiety of the night had told on Pym and now that the stimulus of the victory was dying he looked very tired. Furthermore, the *Iphigenia* had sent an aviso with word that the three frigates in Port-Louis were ready for sea, and the *Sirius* was extremely busy, preparing her return. Her captain found time to be affable to Stephen, but his preoccupation made his words to Clonfert seem particularly curt and official. When Clonfert, having offered his congratulations, began to say that the *Néréide* felt she might have been allowed to take part, Pym cut him short: 'I really cannot go into all that now. First come first served is the rule in these matters. Here are the French commandant's signals; he did not have time to destroy them. As for your orders, they are very simple: you will garrison the island with a suitable force – the French had about a hundred men and two officers – and hold it until you receive further instructions; and in the meantime you will carry out such operations ashore as seem appropriate after consultation with Dr Maturin, whose advice is to be followed in all political matters. Doctor, if you choose to see the French commandant, my dining-cabin is at your disposition.'

When Stephen returned after questioning poor Captain Duvallier, he gained the impression that Clonfert had been rebuked for his tardiness or for some professional fault to do with the *Néréide*'s sailing; and this impression was strengthened as they pulled back in the barge, together with the black Mauritian pilot; for Clonfert was silent, his handsome face ugly with resentment.

Yet Clonfert's moods were as changeable as a weatherglass, and very shortly after the *Sirius* and *Staunch* had vanished over the western horizon, with Pym flying back to blockade the French frigates in Port-Louis, he blossomed out in a fine flow of spirits. They had cleared up the bloody mess in the fort, blasting holes in the coral rock for the dead soldiers; they had installed the Bombay gunners and fifty grenadiers of the 69th, reordering the heavy guns so that one battery commanded the narrow channel and the other all the inner anchorage that was within their range; they had taken the *Néréide* through the narrow channel into a snug berth behind the fort; and now he was a free man, his own master, with the whole of the nearby coast upon which to distinguish himself. No doubt he was directed to advise with Dr Maturin; but Dr Maturin, having required him to harangue the men on the absolute necessity for good relations with all civilians, black or white, male or female, was quite happy to fall in with his military views, such as an assault upon the battery on the Pointe du Diable and indeed upon any other batteries that might catch his fancy. Dr Maturin's attitude towards these forays was so far remote from the killjoy disapproval Clonfert had at one time feared that he even accompanied the flotilla which crossed the wide lagoon by night to carry the Pointe du Diable in great style at dawn, without the loss of a man. He watched the destruction of the guns, the carrying-off of a beautiful brass mortar, and the prodigious jet of fire as the powder-magazine blew up, with evident complacency, and then walked off into the country to make a variety of contacts and to spread his subversive literature.

Day after day the raids on military installations continued, in spite of the opposition of the French regulars and of the far more numerous militia; for the French had no cavalry, and boats guided by a pilot who knew every creek and passage could reach their goal far sooner than the infantry. Moreover, as Stephen's printed sheets attained a wider circulation, it became apparent that the militia was growing less and less inclined to fight: in fact, after about a week in which the Néréides had traversed the country in all directions, doing no harm to private property, paying for whatever they needed, treating the private Mauritians civilly, and routing all the meagre troops that the southern commander could bring against them, the attitude of the militia came more to resemble a neutrality, and a benevolent neutrality at that. Day after day the soldiers, Marines, and seamen went ashore: the frigate grew steadily more infested with monkeys and parrots, bought in the villages or captured in the woods; and Stephen, though busy with his own warfare, had an interview with an ancient gentlewoman whose grandfather had not only seen, run down and devoured a dodo, perhaps the last dodo to tread the earth, but had stuffed a bolster with its feathers.

Although there was no loot, this was a pleasant interval for all hands, with plenty of excitement and charming weather to say nothing of fresh fruit, fresh vegetables, fresh meat and soft tack: yet Clonfert exultant was a less agreeable companion than Clonfert oppressed. Stephen found his boisterous energy wearisome, his appetite for destruction distasteful, and his continual dashing about the country, often in full dress with his diamond-hilted sword and his foolish star, as tedious as the dinners he gave to celebrate the sometimes important, sometimes trivial conquests of his little force. They were conquests in which Stephen could detect no coherent plan: to him they seemed no more than a series of raids determined by the whim of the day; though on the other hand their want of logical sequence puzzled the French commander extremely.

These feasts were attended by Clonfert's officers, and once again Stephen noted the curiously vulgar tone of the Néréide's gunroom and midshipmen's berth, the open flattery of the Captain, and the Captain's appetite for this flattery, however gross. Not a dinner passed without Webber, the second lieutenant, comparing Clonfert with Cochrane, to Clonfert's advantage: the word 'dashing' was in daily use: and once the purser, with a sideways look at Stephen, offered a comparison with Commodore Aubrey – a comparison that Clonfert, with an affectation of modesty, declined to allow. Stephen also observed that when McAdam was invited, which was not always the case, he was encouraged to drink and then openly derided: it grieved him to see a grey-haired man so used by young fellows who, whatever their seamanship and courage might be – and there was little doubt of either – could make no claim to any intellectual powers nor yet to common good-breeding. And he found it still more painful to see that Clonfert never checked their merriment: the Captain seemed more concerned with gaining the approval – even the worship – of his young men than with protecting an old, diminished friend.

It was in the mornings that Stephen found Clonfert's boisterousness more than usually tiresome: and he particularly regretted his company one forenoon, when, in an interval between political activities, he was negotiating with his old lady for the bolster. Clonfert spoke quite good French and he meant to help, but he hit a false note from the beginning. His noisy facetiousness offended and confused her; she began to show signs of incomprehension and alarm and to repeat that 'one never slept so well as upon dodo – sleep was the greatest blessing that God sent to the old – the gentlemen were young, and could do very well on booby-down.' Stephen had almost abandoned hope when Clonfert was called away; but once he was out of the room she reconsidered his argument, and he was paying down the price when the door burst open, a voice shouted 'Run, run for the boats. The enemy is in sight,' and the village was filled with pounding feet. He laid down the last broad piece, caught the bolster to his bosom, and joined the rout.

Far out at sea, to windward, five ships were standing in towards the Ile de la Passe. Steadying himself in the gig, with his spy-glass to his eye, Clonfert read them off. 'Victor, the corvette, leading. Then their big frigate, the Minerve. I can't make out the next. Then, by God, the Bellone. I could almost swear the last is the Windham Indiaman again. Stretch out, stretch out, there; pull strong.'

The gig's crew pulled strong, so strong they left the two other boats that had been launched far behind – three more in a farther creek had not yet even gathered their men. But it was a long, long pull, the whole length of the two spreading anchorages between the shore and the island, four miles and more against the wind.

'I shall lure them in,' said Clonfert to Stephen. And then, having glanced impatiently back towards the distant boats, he added, 'Besides, if they go round to Port-Louis, Sirius and Iphigenia will be no match for them, with Hamelin bringing his three frigates out.' Stephen made no reply.

The exhausted crew ran the gig alongside the Néréide. Clonfert told the coxswain to stay there and ran aboard; a few moments later the frigate displayed a French ensign and pendant and Clonfert dropped down into the boat, crying, 'The fort, and stretch out for all you are worth.'

Now the fort too showed French colours, and after a short pause the French signal ran up the flagstaff on the island: 'Enemy cruising north of Port-Louis'. The leading frigate replied with the French private signal; the island answered it correctly; and each ship made her number. Clonfert had been right: *Victor, Minerve, Bellone*; and the two others were Indiamen, outward-bound Indiamen taken in the Mozambique channel, the Ceylon and the unlucky *Windham* again.

On nearing the reef the French squadron reduced sail; it was clear that they were coming in, but they were coming slowly now, and there would be time to make ready for them. Stephen chose a high, remote corner of the fort from which he could survey the whole scene and sat there on his bolster. Above him the white trade-clouds passed steadily over the pure sky; in the warm sunlight the breeze cooled his cheek; and overhead a bosun-bird wheeled in perfect curves: but within the ramparts below he saw far more confusion than he had expected. Aboard the *Néréide*, which had warped in closer to the island and which was now anchored with a spring on her cable, everything seemed to be in order, although so many of her hands were away in the boats; she was clearing for action, her guns were run out already, and her old standing officers had the process well in hand. But in the fort people were running hither and thither; there was a great deal of shouting; and the Indian gunners, whose officer was somewhere in the boats or perhaps on shore, were arguing passionately among themselves. Soldiers and sailors were at cross purposes: and even among the seamen there was none of that quiet, efficient cheerfulness that marked the actions Stephen had seen with Jack Aubrey – no impression of a machine moving smoothly into place. No food was served out, either: a small point, but one that Jack had always insisted upon. And the remaining boats, with at least a hundred and fifty soldiers and seamen in them, were still a great way off: as far as he could make out, the launch had run aground on the horn of a bank, and since the tide was on the ebb the others were having great difficulty hauling it off.

In the fort and on the lagoon time seemed to stagnate, in spite of the strenuous activity: out at sea it flowed steadily, perhaps faster than its natural pace, and Stephen felt a large, ill-defined apprehension fill the back of his mind, like that which accompanies a nightmare. Now men could be distinguished aboard the ships: now their faces were becoming visible, and orders came clear upon the wind. The French ships had formed a line to enter the channel, the *Victor* first, then the *Minerve*, then the *Ceylon*. The corvette steadied, hauled up her courses, and led in under topsails alone, the lead going in the chains on either side. The noise in the fort had given place to dead silence, with the smell of slow-match wafting on the breeze, drifting from the spare tubs and those beside each gun. The corvette entered the narrows, glided nearer and nearer, her bell flashing in the sun; came abreast of the fort, where the turbanned gunners crouched behind the parapet, and passed it, still in this dead silence. Her master's order to the helmsman brought her round in a tight curve behind the fort, into the deep water, and within twenty yards of the *Néréide*. The *Néréide*'s French ensign came down, the English colours ran up with a cheer, and her side vanished in a great cloud of smoke as her broadside roared out in a single vast prolonged explosion. Another and another, with incessant cheering: the corvette dropped her anchor under the *Néréide*'s starboard quarter, still under her full traversing fire, and an officer ran aft along her shattered deck, calling out that she had struck.

At this point the powerful *Minerve* was already in the channel, well within the channel, with the *Ceylon* close behind her: now they were right under the heavy guns of the fort; they could not turn nor bear away nor move any faster. This was the deadly moment, and every man was poised for the order. At the flagstaff the tricolour raced down to make place for the union flag; but the cheering fool who hauled it down flung it wide on to a tub of burning match near the upper magazine. Flame leapt across and with a crash far louder than a broadside and more blinding than the sun a hundred charges exploded all together. At the same second the Bombay artillerymen, still without an officer to stop them over-loading, set off their ill-pointed guns, bursting or dismounting six of them and killing a man in the *Néréide*'s gig as it was going to take possession of the *Victor*.

Stephen picked himself up in the clearing smoke, realized that shrieks were piercing through his deafness, and hurried to the dead and wounded men scattered all about the flagstaff and the dismounted guns. McAdam's assistant was there and his loblolly-boy, and with the help of a few clear-headed seamen they carried them to the shelter of a rampart. By the time they had done what little they could, dressing horrible burns with their torn-up shirts and handkerchiefs, the scene had changed. The *Victor*, having hoisted her colours again, had cut her cable, and she was following the *Minerve* and the *Ceylon* in towards Port South-East. The *Bellone* and *Windham*, just far enough out to sea, far enough from the narrows, to be able to turn, had hauled their wind. The French ships in the lagoon were standing straight for the narrow pass where the *Néréide*'s other boats were advancing in a confused heap, and it seemed that they must take them in the next few minutes. The *Minerve* showed no obvious damage at all.

Clonfert hailed the fort from the *Néréide*, calling for all the soldiers to come aboard: he was going to attack the *Minerve*, and he needed every man to work his guns. It was not an impossible contest in spite of the *Néréide*'s lighter metal; the *Minerve* was not yet cleared for action, she was approaching the second dog-leg off the Horseshoe bank, where she could not turn, whereas the *Néréide* would still have room in the nearer anchorage to luff up and rake her; and neither the *Victor* nor the *Ceylon* could give her much support. But while the soldiers were in the act of going aboard, the *Bellone* changed her mind. She let fall her topgallantsails and headed for the channel and the island. The moment she was engaged in the narrows there was no doubt of what she meant to do: she must come on. And she did come on, with great determination. As she came, handled no doubt by a man who knew the passage perfectly, for she threw an extraordinary bow-wave for such a dangerous piece of navigation, Stephen looked round to see what Clonfert was at, and to his astonishment he saw that the launch and the cutters were passing, had passed, the French men-of-war without being touched – had passed them in the narrows within a biscuit-toss. It was inexplicable. But in any case there they were, with their men pouring into the *Néréide*, and cheering as they came. The *Néréide* had not yet slipped her cables.

The *Bellone* stood on. She had already cleared her starboard broadside and as she approached the island she fired her forward guns: the smoke, sweeping before her, veiled the fort, and through this veil she fired her full array as she swept by, sending eighteen-pound ball and countless lethal fragments of stone flying among the small remaining garrison. Swinging round into the *Néréide*'s anchorage she sent in another broadside against the other face of the battery: and to all this the demoralized Bombay gunners, deprived of support from small-arms men, unofficered, unused to ships, returned no more than a ragged, ineffectual fire. The *Bellone* went straight for the *Néréide*, as though to run her aboard; but just before they touched the *Bellone* put her helm hard down and shot by. For a moment the two frigates were yardarm to yardarm, almost touching: both broadsides crashed out together, and when the smoke cleared the *Bel/one* was well beyond the *Néréide*, running on, still under her topgallant-sails, for the second sharp turn in the channel, apparently undamaged. The *Néréide* had lost her driver-boom and a couple of upper yards, but her turn and a sudden gust had laid the *Bellone* over so that her fire was too high to hurt the *Néréide*'s hull or to kill many of her crew: it had cut the spring to her cable, however, and she slewed round so far and so fast that she could not fire into the Frenchman's stern.

Now the silence fell again. The four French ships – for the *Windham*, shying at the entrance and the fort, had stood out along the coast – moved smoothly down to anchor in twenty fathom water off the Olive bank, half way to Port South-East, and Clonfert returned to the island with a strong party of soldiers. He was in excellent spirits, hurrying about with the army officers to put the fort into such order that it could withstand an attack by the French squadron. Catching sight of Stephen he called out, 'How did you like that, Dr Maturin? We have them in the bag!'

A little later, when the armourers had set up the dismounted guns and spare carronades had replaced those that had burst, he said, 'If it had not been for that infernal luck with the flag, we should have sunk the *Minerve*. But it was just as well – the *Bellone* would have hauled her wind, and as it is we have both of them hard up in a clinch. I am sending Webber in the launch to tell Pym that if he can spare me just one frigate – *Iphigenia*, or *Magicienne* if she has joined – I will lead in and destroy the whole shooting-match. We have them finely in the bag! They can never get out except on the land-wind just before sunrise. How Cochrane will envy us!'

Stephen looked at him: did Clonfert, in his euphoria or his leaping excitement, really believe that he had done well, that his position was tenable? 'You do not intend sailing away yourself in the *Néréide* to bring down the reinforcements, I collect?' he said.

'Certainly not. Pym ordered me to hold this fort, and I shall hold it to the last. To the last,' he repeated, throwing up his head with a look of pride. At the next word his expression changed. 'And did you see that dog?' he cried. 'The *Victor* struck her colours to me and then hoisted them again and made off like a scrub, a contemptible sneaking little God-damned scrub. I shall send a flag of truce to demand her. See where she lays!'

She lay between the two heavy frigates, and from the fort her crew could be seen busily repairing the damage the *Néréide* had inflicted: the French colours flew at her peak.

'They are too close by far,' said Clonfert. He turned to the artillery officer, haggard and quite wretched at having been separated from his men, at having lost the finest opportunity of his professional career, and said, 'Captain Newnham, will the brass mortar fetch them, do you think?'

'I shall try it, my lord,' said Newnham. He loaded the piece himself with a thirteen-inch bomb-shell, laid it – a long and delicate operation – set the fuse just so, and fired. The shell soared high in the clean air, a rapidly-diminishing black ball, and burst right over the *Bellone*. A delighted cheer went up: the French ships slipped their cables and stood farther in, to anchor out of range. The last shell, fired at extreme elevation, fell short: and it was the last shot of the day.

The remaining hours of light saw all the precautions taken that should have been taken the day before: by the next morning the Ile de la Passe was capable of sinking any ship that attempted the passage. The *Néréide* had crossed new topgallant yards, had repaired her boom and fished her wounded foremast; and she sent in a boat to demand the surrender of the corvette.

'I hope to God Webber has found the *Sirius*,' said Clonfert, gazing eagerly out to sea. But the day passed, and no sail showed beyond the cape. The night passed too, with boats rowing guard: before sunrise the perilous land-breeze began to blow – perilous because it might bring the powerful ships and a swarm of boats across the lagoon in the darkness, but the French never stirred, and at dawn the reviving south-easter kept them where they lay. So two days went by, with no incident apart from the French commodore's refusal to give up the *Victor*. The soldiers drilled and polished their equipment; the artillerymen exercised their pieces; the master-gunner filled cartridge and checked his stores. Clonfert remained as cheerful and active as ever, and his spirits reached a new height on the third day, when the French ships were seen to move down to the far end of the harbour, right down among the shoals and under the batteries of Port South-East, mooring in a curved line that stretched from one end of the sunken reef that guarded the port's entrance to the other; for this, said he, must mean that Webber had found the *Sirius*. At least some of the blockading force must have disappeared from off Port-Louis, and Governor Decaen, fearing an attack upon the *Minerve* and *Bellone*, had surely sent the news overland to Port South-East. Clonfert was right. Some hours later the *Sirius* herself rounded the cape under a great press of sail.

'Look sharp with the signal,' said Clonfert, when they had exchanged numbers. The prepared hoist broke out, and he laughed aloud.

'What does it signify?' asked Stephen.

'*Ready for action* and *Enemy of inferior force*,' replied Clonfert with a slightly conscious look; and immediately afterwards, 'Look alive with the book, Briggs. What is she saying?'

The signal-yeoman muttered the answer, and the midshipman spoke up: '*Send Néréide's master aboard*, my lord.'

'Gig's crew,' cried Clonfert. 'Mr Satterly, bring her in as quick as ever you can.'

In she came, and her last signal before she entered the channel told the *Néréide* to get under way. The *Sirius* passed the fort almost as fast as the *Bellone*, and still under her topsails and courses swept by the *Néréide*, Pym leaning over the rail and hailing Clonfert to follow him. Down the long winding channel they went, more cautiously now, but the *Sirius* still with her topsails set, for there was not much daylight left. In the *Néréide* her black pilot was at the con; he had her under staysails, no more, arid he was muttering to himself, for after the Horseshoe bank their course would lead them into a region of the inner harbour that they did not know well – a region that they had avoided, it being swept by the guns of Port South-East. Past the Noddy shoal, with the lead going fast: past the Three Brothers, and a four-point turn to larboard. The leadsman's calls came sharp, quick and clear: 'By the mark ten; and a half ten; by the deep eleven; by the deep eleven; by the mark fifteen.' A good depth of water, a clear channel one would have sworn: yet at the last call the *Sirius*, only just ahead, struck hard on the tail of a bank and ran far up on to the submerged coral.

Yet if she had to go aground at least she had chosen a good place for doing so. The shore-batteries could not reach her, and the wind, blowing right on to the land, pinned the French frigates to their moorings. The *Sirius* and the *Néréide* carried out their warps undisturbed as the sun set over Mauritius, and they settled down to heaving her off in a seaman-like manner. But she would not come off at the first heave, nor in the first hour of heaving, during which the tide began to ebb: however, tomorrow's flood would be higher and there were great hopes of floating her at about eight in the morning; and in the meantime there was nothing to be done except to ensure that no French boat-attack could succeed.

'What have you to say to our patient's present state of exaltation?' said Stephen to McAdam. 'In these circumstances, does it pass the limits of reasonable conduct? Do you find it morbid?'

'I am at a loss,' said McAdam. 'I have never seen him like this, at all. He may know what he is about, but he may be bent on wiping your friend's eye, and damn the whole world, so he does it. Have you ever seen a man look so beautiful?'

Dawn, and still the French had not moved. For once no holystone was heard aboard the *Sirius* or the *Néréide*; no swabs beat the decks, littered as they were with cables, hawsers, heavy tackles, all the resources of the bosun's art. The tide rose, the capstans turned, slower and slower as the full strain came on and as all hands who could find a place at the bars heaved her grinding off into deep water, where she anchored by the *Néréide* and all the carpenters crowded about her bows, cut deep by the sharp and jagged coral. The exhausted hands were piped to their late breakfast, and they were beginning to set the still-encumbered deck into some kind of fighting-trim when the *Iphigenia* and *Magicienne* were seen in the offing.

Clonfert sent his master to bring them in, for Mr Satterly, though harassed and ashamed, now certainly knew the channel up to this point very well; but he had grown so cautious that it was not until after dinner that they dropped anchor and all captains gathered aboard the *Sirius* to hear Pym's plan of attack. It was clear: it made good plain sense. *Néréide*, with her black pilot, was to lead in and anchor between the *Victor* and the *Bellone* at the northern end of the French line; *Sirius* with her eighteen-pounders was to anchor abreast of the *Bellone*; *Magicienne* between the *Ceylon* and the powerful *Minerve*; and *Iphigenia*, who also carried eighteen- pounders, abreast of the *Minerve*, closing the line on the south.

The captains turned to their ships. Clonfert, who did in fact look extraordinarily gay, young, and lighthearted, as though possessed by some happy spirit, went below to put on a new coat and fresh white breeches; coming on deck again he said to Stephen, with a particularly sweet and affectionate smile, 'Dr Maturin, I believe we may show you something to be compared to what you have seen with Commodore Aubrey.'

The *Sirius* made her signal, and the *Néréide*, slipping her cable, led in under staysails, her pilot conning the ship from the foretopmast yard. The *Sirius* followed her, then the *Magicienne*, then the *Iphigenia*, each falling into line at. intervals of a cable's length. On through the winding channel with the steady breeze, the shore coming closer and closer: with successive turns in the channel the intervals grew wider, and the *Sirius*, hurrying to close the gap and misjudging her swing, struck hard and grounded on the rocky edge. At the same moment the French frigates and the shore-batteries opened fire.

Pym hailed his ships to carry on. In five minutes the *Néréide* was out of the narrow pass. The *Magicienne* and the *Iphigenia*, judging the channel by the stranded *Sirius*, pressed on after her but now at a somewhat greater distance; and in the last wind, four hundred yards from the French line, the *Magicienne* took the ground. By now the French broadsides were sweeping high over the *Néréide*'s deck from stem to stern to disable her as she ran down, making for the *Victor*'s bow. 'Warm work, Dr Maturin,' said Clonfert, and then, glancing over the taffrail, '*Sirius* has not backed off; she is hard and fast,' he said. 'We must tackle the *Bellone* for her. Mr Satterly, lay me alongside the *Bellone*. Lay me alongside the *Bellone*,' he said louder, to be heard above the din; for now the bow guns were answering the French. 'Aye, aye, sir,' said the master. For another cable's length she held on, straight through the French fire: another fifty yards, and the master, waving his hand to the watchful bosun, ordered the helm put up.

The *Néréide* swung round, dropped her anchor, and lay there broadside to broadside, abeam of the big Frenchman, and her twelve-pounders roared out at point-blank range. She was firing fast: the Marines and soldiers packed tight on the quarterdeck and forecastle were blazing away over the hammocks with steady pertinacity: stray ropes and blocks fell on to the splinter-netting overhead: smoke hung thick between the ships, continually renewed as it blew away, and through the smoke the *Bellone*'s guns flashed orange – flashes from the *Victor* too, on the *Néréide*'s starboard quarter.

Stephen walked across to the other side: the *Magicienne*, hard aground on her sharp piercing reef with her figurehead pointing at the French line, could nevertheless bring her forward guns to bear and she was hitting the enemy as hard as she could, while her boats worked furiously to get her off: the *Iphigenia* was close alongside the *Minerve*; they were separated by a long narrow shoal but they were not a stone's throw apart and they were hammering one another with appalling ferocity. The volume of noise was greater than anything Stephen had ever experienced: yet through it all there was a sound familiar to him – the cry of the wounded. The *Bellone*'s heavy guns were mauling the *Néréide* most terribly, tearing gaps in her hammocks, dismounting guns: presently she would use grape. He was a little uncertain of his position. In all previous engagements his place as a surgeon had been below, in the orlop; here it was perhaps his duty to stand and be shot at, to stand with nothing to do, like the army officers: it did not move him unduly, he found, though by now grape was screeching overhead. Yet at the same time men were carrying below in increasing numbers, and there at least he could be of some use. 'I shall stay for the present, however,' he reflected. 'It is something, after all, to view an action from such a vantage-point.' The glass turned, the bell rang: again and again. 'Six bells,' he said, counting. 'Is it possible we have been at it so long?' And it seemed to him that the *Bellone* was now firing with far less conviction, far less accuracy – that her ragged broadsides had far longer intervals between them.

A confused cheering forward, and from the *Iphigenia* too: a gap in the cloud of smoke showed him the weakly manned and weakly armed *Ceylon*, battered by the grounded *Magicienne* and by the *Iphigenia* quarter-guns, in the act of striking her colours; and in one of those strange momentary pauses without a gun he heard the captain of the *Iphigenia* hail the *Magicienne* in a voice of thunder, desiring her to take possession of the Indiaman. But as the *Magicienne*'s boat neared her, pulling fast through water whipped white with small shot and great, the *Ceylon* dropped her topsails and ran for the shore behind the *Bellone*. The boat was still pursuing her and roaring out when the *Minerve*, either cutting her cable or having it cut for her by the *Iphigenia*'s murderous and continual fire, swung round, got under way, and ran straight before the wind, following the *Ceylon*. She steered better than the *Ceylon* however, for the Indiaman blundered right into the *Bellone*, forcing her too to cut. They all three drifted on shore – a heap of ships ashore, with the *Minerve* lying directly behind the *Bellone* and so near that she could not fire. But the *Bellone*'s broadside still lay square to the *Néréide*, and now men were pouring into her from the land and from the *Minerve* and the *Ceylon*: her fire, which had slackened, now redoubled and grew more furious still, the broadsides now coming fast and true. The *Iphigenia*, directly to the windward of her shoal and only a pistol-shot from it, could not stir, and it was clear that in these last few minutes the face of the battle had totally changed. There was no more cheering aboard the *Néréide*. The gun-crews, for all their spirit, were growing very tired, and the rate of fire fell off. By now the sun had almost gone: and the shore-batteries, which had hitherto played on the *Iphigenia* and the *Magicienne*, now concentrated their fire on the *Néréide*.

'Why do we swing so?' wondered Stephen, and then he realized that a shot had cut the spring on the *Néréide*'s cable, the spring that held her broadside-on to the *Bellone*. Round she came, and farther yet, until her stern took the ground, thumping gently with the swell and pointing towards the enemy, who poured in a steady raking fire. She still fired her quarter-guns and her stern-chaser, but now men were falling fast. The first lieutenant and three of the army officers were dead: blood ran over her quarterdeck not in streams but in a sheet. Clonfert was giving the bosun orders about a warp when a messenger from below, a little terrified boy, ran up to him, pointing at Dr Maturin as he spoke: Clonfert crossed the deck and said, 'Dr Maturin, may I beg you to give a hand in the orlop? McAdam has had an accident. I should be most infinitely obliged.'

McAdam's accident was an alcoholic coma, and his assistant, who had never been in action before, was completely overwhelmed. Stephen threw off his coat, and in the darkness, weakly lit by a lantern, he set to work: tourniquet, saw, knife, sutures, forceps, probe, retractor, dressings, case after case, with the sometimes perilously delicate operations continually interrupted by the huge, all-pervading, sonorous jar of heavy shot smashing into the frigate's hull. And still the wounded came, until it seemed that half and even more than half of the *Néréide*'s company had passed through his bloody hands as she lay there, quite unsupported, her fire reduced to half a dozen guns.

'Make a lane there, make a lane for the Captain,' he heard, and here was Clonfert on the chest before him, under the lantern. One eye was torn out and dangling: maxilla shattered: neck ripped open and the carotid artery laid bare, pulsing in the dim light, its wall shaved almost to the bursting-point. A typical splinter-wound. And the frightful gash across his face was grape. He was conscious, perfectly clear in his mind, and at present he felt no pain, a far from uncommon phenomenon in wounds of this kind and at such a time. He was not even aware of the scalpel, probe and needle, except to say that they were oddly cold; and as Stephen worked over him he spoke, sensibly though in a voice altered by his shattered teeth, he told Stephen that he had sent to ask Pym whether he judged the ship could be towed out or whether the wounded should be put into the squadron's boats and the *Néréide* set on fire. 'She might wreck the *Bellone*, when she blows up,' he added.

His wounds were still being dressed when Webber came back from the *Sirius* with one of her officers and a message from Pym, a message that had to be shouted above the crash of the *Bellone*'s guns. Pym suggested that Clonfert should come aboard the *Sirius*. The *Iphigenia* could not possibly warp off from behind her shoal until daylight and in the meantime the *Néréide* lay between her and the French ships; she could not fire upon them; Lord Clonfert might certainly come aboard the *Sirius*.

'Abandon my men?' cried Clonfert in that strange new voice. 'I'll see him damned first. Tell him I have struck.' And when the officer had gone and the dressing was finished he said to Stephen, 'Is it done, Doctor? I am most truly grateful to you,' and made as though to rise.

'You will never get up?' asked Stephen.

'Yes,' he said. 'My legs are sound enough. I am going on deck. I must do this properly, not like a scrub.'

He stood up and Stephen said, 'Take care of the bandage on your neck. Do not pluck at it, or you may die within the minute.'

Shortly afterwards most of the remaining men carne below, sent by the Captain: the routine of the ship was gone – there had been no bells this hour and more – and her life was going. Some clustered in the orlop, and from their low, muted talk and from those who carne and went their shipmates learnt what was going on: a boat had come from the *Iphigenia* to ask why the *Néréide* was no longer firing, and would the Captain come aboard of her – told, had struck, and the Captain would not stir – Captain had sent to *Bellone* to tell her to stop firing, because why? Because he had struck; but the boat could not reach her nor make her hear. Then there was the cry of fire on deck and several men ran up to put it out: and shortly after the mainmast went by the board.

Lord Clonfert came below again, and sat for a while in the orlop. Although Stephen was still working hard he took a look at him between patients and formed the impression that he was in a state of walking unconsciousness; but after some time Clonfert got up and began moving about among the wounded, calling them by name.

It was long past midnight. The French fire was slackening; the British fire had stopped long since; and now after a few random shots the night fell silent. Men slept where they had chanced to sit or throw themselves down. Stephen took Clonfert by the arm, guided him to the dead purser's cot, well under the water-line, directed him how to rest his head so that he should not endanger his wound, and returned to his patients. There were more than a hundred and fifty of them: twenty-seven had already died below, but he had hopes for about a hundred of the rest: the Dear knew how many had been killed outright on deck and thrown overboard. Seventy or so, he thought. He roused Mr Fenton, who was sleeping with his head on his arms, leaning on the chest that formed their operating-table, and together they looked to their dressings.

They were still busy when the sun rose and the *Bellone* began to fire at the *Néréide* again: on and on, in spite of repeated hails. The gunner came below with a gushing splinter-wound in his forearm, and while Stephen applied the tourniquet and tied the artery the gunner told him that the Néréide's colours had not in fact been struck: they were flying still, and they could not be hauled down. There was a rumour that they had been nailed to the mast, but the gunner knew nothing of it, and the bosun, who would have had the true word, he was dead. 'And not a scrap of rigging to come at them,' he said. 'So his lordship's told the carpenter to cut the mizzen away. Thank you kindly, sir: that's a right tidy job. I'm much obliged. And, Doctor,' he said in a low rumble behind his hand, 'if you don't much care for a French prison, there's some of us topping our boom in the cutter, going aboard of Sirius.'

Stephen nodded, looked over his worst cases, and made his way through the wreckage to the cabin. Clonfert was not there. He found him on the quarterdeck, sitting on an upturned match-tub and watching the carpenters ply their axes. The mizzenmast fell, carrying the colours with it, and the Bellone's fire ceased. 'There, I have done it properly,' said Clonfert in a barely intelligible murmur, out of the side of his ruined, bandaged face. Stephen looked at his most dangerous wound, found him sensible, though by now at a far remove, and said, 'I wish to go to the Sirius, my lord: the remaining boat is fit to leave, and I beg you will give an order to that effect.'

'Make it so, Doctor Maturin,' said Clonfert. 'I wish you may get away. Thank you again.' They shook hands. Stephen took some papers from his cabin, destroyed others, and made his way to the boat. It was no great climb down, for the Néréide had settled on the sea-bed.

ALTHOUGH PYM received him kindly aboard the stranded Sirius, his conduct did not raise Stephen's opinion of him as a commander or as a man of sense. The Iphigenia, having at last warped herself free of the long shoal that had stood between her and the *Minerve*, sent to ask permission to stand in, to attack the immobilized French ships, boarding them with extra hands from *Sirius* and *Magicienne*, and not only taking them but rescuing the *Néréide* too. No, said Pym, who needed her help to heave his own ship off, she must go on warping towards the *Sirius*. Twice he sent back this categorical reply, each time as a direct order. With the *Iphigenia* warping out, the French fire concentrated on the *Magicienne*, hard and fast on her reef, badly holed, with nine foot of water in her hold and only a few guns that could be brought to bear. The French shot poured in upon her, and sometimes upon the other ships, and upon the frantically busy, exhausted hands in the remaining boats all that long, appalling, bloody day. It was impossible to get her off; it was impossible that she should swim if she were got off. Her men were ordered into the *Iphigenia*, and after sunset she was set on fire, blowing up in doleful splendour about midnight.

The next day the French had a new battery ready on shore, closer to, and the battery and the ships began to fire on the Iphigenia and the *Sirius* as they strove to heave Pym's frigate off her reef. At last, after incessant labour all in vain, and after some ugly scenes with the captain of the Iphigenia, who was utterly convinced (and Stephen, together with many better-qualified observers, agreed with him) that his plan would have meant a total victory and who could barely bring himself to speak civilly to the man who had forbidden it, Pym realized that the *Sirius* could not be saved. Her ship's company were taken into the *Iphigenia* and the *Sirius* too was set on fire, Pym thereby relinquishing his command, twenty-four hours too late; and the now solitary *Iphigenia* returned to her warping.

She was obliged to warp – to carry out an anchor on the end of a cable, drop it, and wind herself up to it by the capstan – because never in the daylight did the wind cease blowing dead on shore. She could make no progress whatsoever in any other way, for when the land-breeze got up before dawn she dared not attempt the dark and unseen channel, and it always died with the rising of the sun. So hour after hour her boats, carrying the ponderous great anchors, dragged out the sodden nine-inch hawsers; and if the anchors held, if the ground was not foul, she then crept a very little way, rarely more than fifty yards, because of the turns. But often the ground was foul, and sometimes the anchors came home or were broken or were lost altogether; and all this exhausting labour had to be carried out in the blazing sun by a dispirited crew. Meanwhile the French ships in Port South-East had been heaved off, and a French brig was sighted beyond the Ile de la Passe, probably the forerunner of Hamelin's squadron from Port-Louis.

However, there was nothing for it, and the *Iphigenia* warped on and on towards the fort, fifty yards by fifty yards with long pauses for the recovery of fouled anchors, the whole length of that vast lagoon. It was two full days before she reached a point about three quarters of a mile from the island, and here she anchored for the night. The next day, when the *Bellone* and *Minerve* had profited by the land-breeze to advance fair into the lagoon whose channels they knew so well, and had there anchored, she set to again; and by eight o'clock, when she was within a thousand feet of the fort, of the open sea and the infinite delight of sailing free, she saw three ships join the French brig outside the reef: the *Vénus*, *Manche* and *Astrée*. They were exchanging signals with the *Bellone* and *Minerve*; and the wind, still right in the Iphigenia's teeth, was bearing them fast towards the lie de la Passe, where they would lie to, just out of range.

The *Iphigenia* at once sent the soldiers and many of the seamen to the fort and cleared for action. She had little ammunition, however: even before the end of the Port South-East battle she had had to send to the *Sirius* for more, and since then she had fired away so much that half an hour's engagement would see her locker bare. The clearing was therefore largely symbolic, and it was carried out, as her captain told Stephen privately, to let the French see that he would not surrender unconditionally, that he still had teeth, and that if he could not get decent terms he would use them.

'That being so,' said Stephen, 'I must ask you for a sailing-boat before the *Vénus* and her consorts close the entrance to the channel.'

'For Réunion, you mean? Yes, certainly. You shall have the launch and my own coxswain, an old whaling hand, and young Craddock to navigate her: though I should not carry the news that you must take, no, not for a thousand pound.' He gave orders for the preparation of the launch – stores, instruments, charts, water – and returning he said, 'You would oblige me extremely, Dr Maturin, by carrying a letter for my wife: I doubt I shall see her again this war.'

The launch pulled along the wicked channel in the darkness, touching twice for all their care; pulled out well beyond the reef, set her lugsail and bore away south-west. She carried ten days' provisions, but although she had many of the *Iphigenia*'s hungry young gentlemen and ship's boys aboard – their captain could not see them spend those years in a prison – the stores were almost intact when, after a perfect voyage, Stephen made his laborious way up the *Boadicea*'s side as she lay at single anchor in the road of St Paul's, close by the *Windham* and the Bombay transport.

'Why, Stephen, there you are!' cried Jack, springing from behind a mass of papers as Stephen walked into the cabin. 'How happy I am to see you – another couple of hours and I should have been off to Flat Island with Keating and his men – Stephen, what's amiss?'

'I must tell you what's amiss, my dear,' said Stephen: but he sat down and paused a while before going on. 'The attack on Port South-East has failed. The *Néréide* is taken; the *Sirius* and *Magicienne* are burnt; and by now the *Iphigenia* and the Ile de la Passe will almost certainly have surrendered.'

'Well,' said Jack, considering, '*Minerve, Bellone, Astrée, Vénus, Manche*; together with *Néréide* and *Iphigenia*: that makes seven to one. But we have seen longer odds, I believe.'

8

'ALL HANDS unmoor ship,' said Jack. The bosun's calls wailed and twittered; the *Boadicea*s ran to their stations; the fife began its thin piercing tune; 'Stamp and go, stamp and go,' cried the bosun's mates; and in the midst of the familiar din of proceeding to sea Stephen turned from the rail, where he had been staring under his shading hand at the ship lying within the frigate. 'I could almost swear I had see that vessel before,' he said.

'Oh, not above a hundred times,' said Jack. 'She is the *Windham*. The *Windham* Indiaman again. This time she was outward-bound, and they took her in the Mozambique channel. *Sirius* very neatly retook her when she shied away from Port South-East. Did not Pym tell you?'

'Faith, we had little conversation, Captain Pym and I.'

'No: I suppose not. But, however, Pullings snapped her up in his little schooner just as she was running under the guns of Rivière Noire: a good, seamanlike officer, Tom Pullings . . .'

'Up and down, sir,' called the bosun.

'Thick and dry,' came Jack's answer, as automatic as a response in church; and he continued '. . . and he brought her in, cracking on regardless. That was the first I knew of the affair. Let fall, there,' he cried, directing his voice upwards.

The topsails flashed out, the frigate's head swung to the north-east and steadied: she heeled, steeper and steeper as the courses, topgallants and staysails were sheeted home in smooth succession and the way came on her, the water slipping fast and faster still along her side. She shaved the cruel reef off Saint-Denis, altered course two points to eastward, and setting a flying-jib she stretched for the Ile de la Passe, making her ten knots watch after watch, her wake a straight green line of phosphorescence in the dark.

Every minute counted. Stephen's voyage had taken so little time that there was a possibility the fort had not yet surrendered, and that the *Iphigenia* still lay under its protection, within the reef. Every minute counted, and although sailcloth and spars were so precious they drove her through the sea as though they had a Spanish galleon in chase: with an even greater zeal indeed; so great that they raised the island before the light of day.

When he had two peaks of the Bamboo Mountain in a line and the Pointe du Diable bearing N 17 W Jack reduced sail, carried a night-glass up to the foretop, and took the ship in, ghosting along under topsails on the edge of the land-breeze. His eyes were used to the night, helped as it was by the stars and the sickle-moon: he had made out a good deal of what lay inshore and out to sea, and when the first dawn came up before the sun he was not surprised to see the *Manche* and *Vénus* – but not the *Astrée* – lying two miles off the reef to leeward, the Iphigenia just inside it, the *Bellone*, *Minerve*, *Néréide* and *Ceylon* Indiaman far over by Port South-East, and the charred wrecks of the *Sirius* and *Magicienne* in the lagoon. But what did give him a shock was the sight of a fifth ship down there, just astern of the shattered *Néréide*. Leaning his telescope on the rim and focusing with care he discovered what she was: the *Ranger* from Bombay. She was only a transport, but she would have been a treasure-ship to the remnant of his squadron, for she carried spare yards and topmasts, besides three hundred tons of invaluable stores, and he had been looking for her arrival at St Paul's these many days – the *Otter*, quite unfit for sea, was heaved down in expectation of what she should bring; the *Staunch* lacked almost everything; and if the *Boadicea* carried away a spar, she would have to whistle for it. And here was the *Ranger* fitting out the enemy. The *Bellone*, which must have suffered terribly in the long action, already had her topgallant yards across. His face took on a harder look.

No colours were flying yet from either the fort or the *Iphigenia*: had they surrendered? If not, conceivably his boats might tow the *Iphigenia* through the channel, covered by the

Boadicea and the fort, and with even a battered consort he could set about the *Vénus* and the *Manche*; for although he was short of stores, he was rich in men and ammunition. And this was no time for timid defensive measures. He came down on deck, gave orders for the ensign, the private signal, and a hoist stating his intention. The *Boadicea* stood in as the sun came up, signals flying, one eye on the French frigates, the other on the fort and the *Iphigenia*. Farther and farther in, and still no colours, though the sun was now a hand's-breadth over the horizon. Another few minutes and the *Boadicea* would be within random shot.

'A gun to windward, Mr Seymour,' said Jack. 'And shiver the foretopsail.'

In reply the British colours ran up the not so distant flagstaff: yet still the *Boadicea* hung off. Then after a pause in which hoists jerked up and down without the flags breaking out but with a crafty pretence of the halliard's jamming, the private signal.

'Hands about ship,' said Jack, for the island's private signal was ten days out of date.

Not one of the *Boadicea*s was unprepared for this, and she came about on to the larboard tack as briskly as a smuggling schooner, staying in her own length. The fort's seaward guns sent plumes of white water leaping from the swell two hundred yards short of her; a derisive cheer floated after them, and a little later a line of boats, carrying prisoners, put off the island for the *Manche*.

The *Manche* took them aboard and stood after the *Vénus*, which was already beating up under easy sail as though to get to the windward of the *Boadicea*. As soon as the *Manche* was up, both French frigates set their topgallants. They could be seen clearing for action, and they came on as though they meant it. Jack gazed at them with the utmost intensity, his eye hard to his glass, examining their captains' handling of their ships, gauging their sailing qualities, watching for ruses designed to mask their speed; and all the while he kept the

Boadicea a little ahead, just out of range. By the time the watch had changed he knew he had the legs of them: he also knew that the *Vénus* could outsail the *Manche* and that if he could induce them to separate . . . but while his mind was running on to the possible consequences of this separation – to a night-engagement – to a boat-landing on the reef behind the fort – the French gave over the chase.

The *Boadicea* wore and pursued them, setting her royals to bring them within the extreme range of her brass bow-chaser, perched on the forecastle, and firing at the *Vénus*, which wore Hamelin's broad pendant. The *Vénus* and the *Manche* replied with guns run out of their gunroom ports, so low as to be ineffectual at this distance; and so the three ships ran, neither side doing the other any damage, until a lucky shot from the *Boadicea*, skipping three times over on the smooth swell, came aboard the *Vénus*. The midshipman high on the foremast jack reported a commotion on the *Vénus*'s quarterdeck: immediately afterwards the French ships went about, and once more the *Boadicea* ran south and west.

All day she ran, trying every kind of ruse and lame-duck trick to lure the faster-sailing *Vénus* ahead of the *Manche*: but nothing would serve. Hamelin had no romantic notions of single combat, and he was determined to fight at an advantage. The two Frenchmen kept within half a mile of one another, doggedly chasing the *Boadicea* over the whole stretch of sea between Mauritius arid La Réunion.

'At least we are tolerably well acquainted with our enemies,' said Jack to Seymour and the quarterdeck in general, when the lights of Saint-Denis bore south-west two miles, and all hope was gone.

'Yes, sir,' said Seymour. 'We could have given them topgallants at any time. Dirty bottoms, no sort of doubt.'

'*Manche* was precious slow, shifting her sheets over the stays,' said Trollope. 'I remarked it twice.'

'Surely, sir, they are not what you would call enterprising?' said Johnson.

'Slowbellies,' said an unidentified voice in the darkness.

In the cabin, over a late supper, Jack said to Stephen, 'Here is Fellowes' list of our requirements. May I beg you to go to Farquhar, tell him how things lie, and ask him to rouse out all that can possibly be found and have 'em down by the water-side at St Paul's in the morning? Make no excuses – I have a thousand things to do – he will understand.' Before Stephen could answer, Spotted Dick walked in and said, 'You sent for me, sir?'

'Yes. Mr Richardson, you will take the *Pearl* aviso with four good hands and run up to Port-Louis, find the *Staunch*, and bring her down. Mr Peter has her orders ready for you to take.'

'So much responsibility for that pimply lad,' observed Stephen, through his Welsh rabbit.

'Aye,' said Jack, who had brought a prize hermaphrodite into Plymouth from far off Finisterre before his voice had broken. 'We must depend on our small-fry now, men and ships. If we had had the *Otter* or even the *Staunch* with us today, we could have made a dash at that unhandy *Manche*, you know.'

'Could we, indeed?'

'Lord, yes,' said Jack. 'And I trust we shall tomorrow. I have sent Seymour galloping over to St Paul's to bid Tomkinson leave the *Otter* where she lies, shift all his people into the *Windham*, and join me in the roadstead. With this wind get-ting up, Hamelin will stand off and on tonight, I am very sure.'

Hamelin was more off than on in the light of dawn when the *Boadicea* ran down to St Paul's, and the *Vénus* and the *Manche* were a mere flash of topsails against the western sky. But they were there, and once he had settled that fact beyond any hint of a doubt, Jack Aubrey turned his glass to the dis-tant shipping in the road.

'What in Hell's name is the *Windham* thinking of?' he cried. 'She has not even crossed her yards. Mr Collins: *Windham proceed to sea immediately*, with a gun; and give her another gun every minute until she weighs. God rot the . . .' He clapped his mouth shut, and clenching his hands behind his back he paced up and down. 'His face is darker than I have ever seen it,' observed Stephen, looking at him from the taffrail. 'Up until now, he has borne these reverses with a singular magnanimity, greater by far than I had looked for. Not a word about Clonfert's disastrous folly; nothing but sympathy for his wounds, and a hope that the French hospital may set him up. No reflection upon Pym's dogged stupidity. Yet there is no greatness of mind without its limits: is this breaking-point?'

'Shoot the next gun,' said Jack, stopping short in his stride, with a furious glare at the far-off Hamelin.

'Sir,' said Trollope timidly, 'a transport is rounding the point. The *Emma*, I believe. Yes, sir, the *Emma*.'

The *Emma* she was, and quite apart from her signal it was evident that she wished to speak the *Boadicea* as she hovered there, backing and filling in a black fury of impatience; for the slab-sided transport had already spread a great press of sail.

'*Captain come aboard pendant*, Mr Collins,' said Jack.

The *Emma*'s stem-boat splashed down, pulled across, hooked on, and Pullings came up the side. 'Mr Pullings,' said Jack, 'what is this caper?'

'I beg pardon, sir,' said Pullings, pale with emotion. 'I have *Windham*'s guns aboard: Captain Tomkinson declined the command.'

'Come below and explain yourself,' said Jack. 'Mr Seymour, carry on: course nor'-nor'-west.'

In the cabin it appeared, from Pullings' nervous, involved, embarrassed statement that Tomkinson, having looked into the Indiaman's condition, had refused to take her to sea until she should be made seaworthy, and had returned to the immobilized *Otter*. Pullings, a witness of this, had come to an agreement with the *Emma*'s captain, sick ashore; had moved

his men and a score of volunteers into her, she being in a better state than the Indiaman, and by inhuman labour all
through the night had shifted the *Windham*'s guns and his
own carronades across, helped by Colonel Keating, who had
also given him gunners and small-arms men.

'This Tomkinson,' cried Stephen, who could speak openly
before Pullings, 'must he not be hanged, or flogged, or at least
dismissed the service, the infamous whore?'

'No,' said Jack. 'He is a poor creature, God help him, but he
is within his rights. A captain can refuse a command, on
those grounds. Tom,' he said, shaking Pullings' hand, 'you are
a right sea-officer; I am obliged to you. If you can get eight
knots out of your *Emma*, we shall have a touch of those
Frenchmen out there, before long.'

The two ships bore away in company, steering a course that
would give them the weather-gage in a couple of hours, well
north of the island, where the wind came more easterly. But
in far less time than that it became apparent to all hands that
the *Emma* could not keep up. Six or at the most seven knots
was her utmost limit, even with the wind abaft the beam –
studdingsails aloft and alow, and even kites, strange sails
without a name, all set and drawing – and once they had
hauled their wind three points, even six was beyond her
power, driven though she was with all the resources of seamanship and an able, willing crew. The *Boadicea* had to take
in her topgallants to keep the *Emma* in sight at all; while on
the other hand, Hamelin, the necessary complement of a
quarrel, kept steadily ahead, with never a sign of reducing
sail, still less of heaving-to to wait for them.

Yet for all that, Hamelin had now run so far to the westward that he would have to go up to Port-Louis rather than
Port South-East, which was something gained, since it would
allow Jack to look into the Ile de la Passe again: and the
Emma was there to perform a most important task that
should have fallen to the *Otter*.

'Back the foretopsail, Mr Johnson, if you please,' said Jack, just before the hands were piped to dinner; and when the *Emma* had come labouring up he hailed Pullings, directing him to make for Rodriguez, acquaint the military with the situation, and then to cruise between that island and 57° East to warn any King's or Company's ships he saw, at the same time taking all appropriate measures. 'And Mr Pullings,' he added, in his strong voice, 'I shall not object to your taking one of their frigates, or even two: that will still leave plenty for me.'

The joke was limp enough, in all conscience; but the tone in which it was said, or rather roared, caused Pullings' distressed, tired face to spread in an answering grin.

The *Boadicea* looked at the Ile de la Passe, which greeted her with a roar of heavy guns: she looked beyond it, over the billowing smoke, into Port South-East, and there she saw the *Bellone*, new-rigged and ready for sea. The *Minerve* now had jury topmasts and the *Néréide* something in the way of a main and a mizzen, while caulkers and carpenters were busy about them both: the *Iphigenia* had already sailed. There was nothing to be done, and the *Boadicea* turned about for La Réunion.

'Mr Seymour,' said Jack, in that curiously detached, impersonal tone that had come on him since the news of the defeat, 'when did we last exercise the guns?'

'Several days ago, sir. Much longer than usual,' said Seymour, searching wildly in his mind for the exact date; for this new and somewhat inhuman commodore, though neither fault-finding nor severe, put the fear of God into the quarterdeck. 'It was last Saturday, I believe.'

'Then we will advance quarters by half an hour, and rattle them in and out. We can afford two – no, three – rounds a gun; and I believe we may fire upon targets.'

If Hamelin was the man Jack thought him to be, he would surely have *Astrée* and one or two of his corvettes cruising between Mauritius and Réunion by now, and the sound of gunfire might bring them down: so late that afternoon the sky echoed to *Boadicea*'s thunder. The gun-crews, stripped to the waist and gleaming with sweat, plied the massive cannon with even more than their usual diligence, for they too had long since caught their commander's mood: he watched them with a grave satisfaction, a remarkably healthy crew, well fed on fresh meat and garden-stuff, in fine fettle and high training. Good men; a rapid, accurate fire, surpassing anything the *Boadicea* had yet achieved by a clear eight seconds. Although the *Boadicea* was not and never could be an outstanding sailer, he need not fear any single French ship afloat in these waters; nor any two, if only he had the support of a well-handled sloop and if only he could bring them to that perilous thing, an engagement in the darkness, when high discipline and true aim counted for so much. Yet when the guns were housed and cool again the sea remained as empty as it had been before, a vast disk of unbroken blue, now fast darkening to deep sapphire: there was to be no action that night.

Nor the next day either, in the twenty miles of sea before the frigate dropped anchor at St Paul's again. No action at sea, but enormous activity on shore. Jack flung himself into the task of getting the *Otter* and the *Windham* into fighting-trim. He took little notice of Captain Tomkinson, now perhaps the unhappiest man on La Réunion, but directed the work himself: with the Governor's total, intelligent support, he had a sovereign hand in the yards of St Paul's and Saint-Denis, and there, labouring through the night by flares, every artificer in the island did all that could conceivably be done to turn a sixteen-gun sloop and a decayed, cruelly battered Indiaman with no guns but what the soldiers could afford her into honorary frigates, or at least into something that might have some remote chance of standing the enemy's fire, of holding him long enough for the *Boadicea* to run alongside and board.

On the Sunday morning, with the *Otter* in her final stage of refitting but with the *Windham* still heaved down, he was taking a very late breakfast after four hours of the deepest sleep he had known, taking it in the company of Stephen Maturin, whom he saw but rarely these days: he had resolutely dismissed the problems of the dock-yard from his mind for twenty minutes, when Stephen involuntarily brought them back by asking the significance of the devil, among those that followed the sea, as in the devil to pay, a phrase he had often heard, particularly of late – was it a form of propitiation, a Manichaean remnant, so understandable (though erroneous) upon the unbridled elements?

'Why, the devil, do you see,' said Jack, 'is the seam between the deck-planking and the timbers, and we call it the devil, because it is the *devil* for the caulkers to come at: in full we say, the devil to pay and no pitch hot; and what we mean is, that there is something hell-fire difficult to be done – must be done – and nothing to do it with. It is a figure.'

'A very elegant figure, too.'

'Was you a weak, superficial cove, and feeling low, you might say it described our situation at the moment,' said Jack. 'But you would be wrong. With *Staunch*, and *Otter* and *Windham*, in a day or two . . .' he cocked his ear, and called out, 'Killick, who is that coming aboard?'

'Only an army officer, sir.'

The clash of Marines presenting arms on the quarterdeck: a midshipman to ask whether the Commodore would receive Colonel Fraser, and then the Colonel himself, his face as scarlet as his coat from galloping under the torrid sun.

'Good morning, Colonel,' said Jack. 'Sit down and take a cup.'

'Good morning, sir. Doctor, how d'ye do?'

'Colonel Fraser should instantly drink something cool, and throw off his stock,' said Stephen. 'Your servant, sir.'

'Happy to do so, sir, in one minute; but first I must deliver my despatch – verbal, sir: no time to can for pen and ink. Colonel Keating's compliments to Commodore Aubrey, and HMS *Africaine* is in Saint-Denis. Captain Corbett – '

'Corbett? Robert Corbett?'

'I believe so, sir: a little man, looks rather black and cross when put out – the same that was here before – splendid disciplinarian. Captain Corbett, sir, proceeding to Madras, learnt of the state of affairs here from one of your ships when he was putting in to water at Rodriguez, so he turned off to La Réunion. He had some kind of a small engagement with a schooner on the coast of the Mauritius on the way and he is now landing his wounded: Colonel Keating has given him twenty-five men and an officer to take their place, because, sir, two French frigates and a brig are coming in after him. And Captain Corbett charges me to say, with his duty, that he has taken the liberty of hoisting your broad pendant, to amuse 'em, that he is clearing for action, and will put to sea the moment all his wounded are ashore.'

'Colonel,' said Jack, 'I am infinitely obliged to you. Killick, light along a jug of something cool for Colonel Fraser – sandwiches – mangoes.' These words he called backwards as he ran on to the quarterdeck. 'Mr Trollope, all hands from the yard immediately, and prepare to slip the moment they are aboard. Mr Collins, to *Otter* and *Staunch*: *proceed to sea immediately and enemy cruising east-north-east.* Pass the word for the gunner.' The gunner came running, for the news was spreading fast. 'Mr Webber,' said Jack, how much have you filled?'

'Thirty rounds a gun, sir,' said the gunner, 'and twenty-three for the carronades: we been at it all this forenoon.' And then, encouraged by old acquaintance and by the glowing change in the Commodore, 'May I hope to fill some more, sir, for the right true end?'

'Yes, Mr Webber,' said Jack. 'And none of your white letter stuff. Let it all be our very best red large grain.'

ROUNDING THE POINTE des Galets at noon, the *Boadicea*, followed by the *Otter* and the *Staunch*, made out the French ships in the offing: two frigates. The French brig was already

topsails down to the northwards, no doubt hurrying off to tell
Hamelin what was afoot. There was a general hum of satisfaction, tempered by the fact that the Frenchmen were no
longer standing in, but had gone about on the starboard tack,
and by the sight of long white lines far out, which meant that
the wind, south or south-east to the leeward of La Réunion,
was blowing from the east to the north of it, so that the
enemy would have the weather-gage. They also saw the
Africaine, and the actual sight of her raised Jack's heart still
higher: she was a thirty-six-gun eighteen-pounder frigate,
French-built of course, and one of the finest sailers in the
Royal Navy, particularly on a wind. She must have been the
plum with which Corbett was rewarded when he brought
home the St Paul's despatches. 'He will certainly handle her
well,' reflected Jack. 'A capital seaman. Let us hope he has
taught his men how to point their guns this time, and that he
has made himself more amiable aboard her.' A plum sometimes had that effect upon a disappointed man; and Corbett
had often been disappointed.

When he caught sight of her, the *Africaine* was also on the
starboard tack, under a press of sail, about eight miles south
of the enemy. The two ships exchanged numbers, no more.
Jack had no intention of worrying the *Africaine* with signals:
Corbett was a fighting captain; he knew very well what to do;
there was no doubt that he would do it; and in the meantime
he must be left free to concentrate on making up at least
seven of those eight miles. The same applied with even
greater force to the *Boadicea*: although she could hit harder
than the *Africaine*, she could not rival her in speed. Happily
one of the Frenchmen was their old *Iphigenia*, now the
Iphigénie once more, and she was no flyer: the other was
probably the *Astrée*, whose qualities he did not know.

He would soon find them out, however, he said, smiling, as
he took his glass into the foretop and the six ships settled
down to the long chase. An hour later he knew that she had
an able captain, that she was faster than the *Iphigenia*, but

not faster than the *Boadicea*, while the *Africaine* could give her topgallantsails at least. If the wind held true, the *Africaine* should be up with them before sunset, and the *Boadicea* not long after dark. If the wind held true: that was his chief concern. For were it to back more easterly or even a little north of east as it sometimes did by night, then the *Boadicea* would be dead to leeward of the Frenchmen, and they might be able to run up to Port-Louis before that leeway could be made up. For the *Boadicea* was not at her best on a bowline: and although he would not have it generally known, she could not come up so close to the wind as some other ships, not by half a point, in spite of all his care.

Yet taking thought would neither keep the wind south of east nor improve the *Boadicea*'s sailing: he came down, glanced at the now distant *Staunch* and *Otter*, he told Seymour that he was to be called in case the position changed, and went fast to sleep in a hammock slung in the desolate clean sweep fore and aft that had once been his array of cabins, knowing that his officers would sail the ship admirably well and that he must keep his wits as sharp as they could be for what might well be a difficult night-engagement, calling for instant decision.

When he came on deck again the *Otter* and the *Staunch* were barely in sight from the masthead: the *Africaine* was something better than two leagues ahead and she was gaining visibly on the Frenchmen. At his second hail the lookout replied, after a studying pause, that *Staunch* and *Otter* had vanished now: and while the lookout was answering, an unpleasant rattle accompanied his voice: the wind had come too far forward for the studdingsails to set, and they were shivering, in spite of fiddle-taut bowlines. The *Boadicea* took them in: she lost way at once, and presently the *Africaine* was a full eight miles away, pursuing the now invisible French towards the coming night.

A dirty night, though warm, with sudden squalls and a mounting cross-sea that kept forcing the *Boadicea*'s head northwards. The best helmsmen in the ship were at the wheel, with Jack behind them, standing by the master at the con. For some little while after full darkness he saw the rockets and the blue lights that showed the *Africaine*'s position. Then nothing. Hour after hour of low driving cloud, very heavy showers of rain, the seas breaking over her starboard bow, the wind in the rigging as she stood on and on; but never the sound that the silent, listening men were waiting for.

Nothing until seven bells in the middle watch, when the breeze turned gusty before dropping to something near a calm: at seven bells and again at the changing of the watch flashes were seen under the cloud to windward, and remote gunfire followed them. 'God send he has not engaged close without me,' murmured Jack, altering course for the flash. That fear had occurred to him in these hours of waiting, together with others, equally wild: but he had put it away – Corbett was no Clonfert; and in any case Corbett knew the *Boadicea*'s rate of sailing perfectly.

The gunfire was louder every glass; but at every glass the breeze grew less; and at last the *Boadicea* had scarcely steerage-way. The short twilight before dawn was veiled by a last sheet of tepid rain. It faded slowly in the still air as the sun rose up; and all at once there was the whole stretch of sea, brilliantly lit, and upon it, four miles away, the *Africaine* with one French ship within pistol-shot on her bow, another on her quarter. She was firing an occasional gun: the enemy answered with full broadsides: then she fell silent.

Four miles away: clear in his telescope Jack saw her colours waver at the peak and come slowly down, down, right down on deck; and still the French kept firing. For a quarter of an hour they kept firing into her silent hull.

Never had he had to master himself with such force: the sight was so horrible that if the breeze had not got up while he was watching it seemed that his heart must break with grief and rage. The royals took it first. The *Boadicea* gave a gentle heave against the sea and the water began to whisper

along her side. Jack gave his orders automatically; said, 'Mr
Seymour, the slow-match needs renewing,' and took the
Boadicea down towards the Frenchmen as they lay about
their prize, the boats coming and going. 'Masthead, there,' he
called. 'What do you see of *Staunch* and *Otter*?'

'Nothing, sir,' came the reply. 'Nothing to windward, nothing to leeward.'

Jack nodded. The breeze was freshening; he could feel it
on his cheek, coming beautifully though soft from the south-
east and even south of that – the breeze that would have
brought him up. The *Boadicea* stood on; and as they watched
the *Africaine*'s masts went by the board; first her foremast,
then the mizzen, then the main. The *Astrée* and the *Iphigenia*
did not appear to have suffered at all.

Whatever it cost, he must resist the temptation to run down
and engage them: it would be criminal folly. But the temptation to set the *Boadicea* right between the two, firing both
sides, was terribly strong; and with the wind as it lay he might
be able to yield just so far and still regard his duty – a quick
hard strike and away was allowable: it was even called for.

'Mr Seymour,' said he, 'I am going to run down to within
musket-shot of the windward ship. When I give the order, let
the starboard guns fire, starting from forwards: deliberate fire
at her stern, the smoke to clear between each shot. When the
last gun has fired, about ship, and then the larboard broadside as we go about to come up as near as she will lie. Mr
Buchan, lay me for the *Iphigenia*.'

The *Boadicea* was bringing up the wind. The Frenchmen
had steerage-way, but little more, while she was moving at
three knots; and the *Astrée*, behind the *Africaine*, had not run
clear before Jack said 'Fire.' The guns went off in steady, even
succession, undisturbed by the ragged broadsides from the
Iphigenia, the first two wild, the third deadly enough: the
Boadicea's was a deliberate fire, aimed with hatred, and hammocks and splinters of rail leapt from the *Iphigenia*'s stern;
one fine shot from number twelve struck her between wind

and water very near her rudder and a cheer went up. Then
the cry 'Helm's a-lee,' and the *Boadicea* came up into the
wind. She was in stays when the *Astrée*, clear of the *Iphigenia*
and the *Africaine* at last, let fly. She hit the *Boadicea* very
hard, shattering the stern-boat on its davits and giving her
such a blow that for a moment Jack thought she was going to
fall off – that he had risked her just that hair's-breadth too far.
'Flat in forward, there,' he cried, felt the fine balance change,
and with infinite relief called, 'Mainsail haul.' Round she
came and filled, the way still on her: round, round, till her larboard ports stared full at the *Iphigenia*. With one great rippling crash her broadside went off, and she sailed clear of her
smoke. At the same moment a shot from the *Astrée* struck the
master in the back, cutting him in two at Jack's side. Jack saw
his astonished, indignant face jerk forward, knocking the starboard helmsman down. He took the man's place for a
moment, bringing the frigate still farther round until her
headsails shivered and a quartermaster seized the spokes;
then stepping over the body he walked to the taffrail. The
Iphigenia's stern had suffered, but her rudder had not gone,
nor yet her mizzenmast. She had dropped her foresail and
was now before the wind, moving down towards the *Astrée*,
masking her fire again: he heard the master's body splash into
the sea as he considered her: a scratch crew, no doubt, with
not much sense and still less appetite for a close engagement
with the *Boadicea*. And as the *Boadicea* stretched away close-
hauled and the distance widened, he saw the *Iphigenia* put
up her helm and fall foul of the *Astrée*, just as the *Astrée* tried
to slip through the gap between her and the *Africaine* to rake
the *Boadicea* at extreme range.

He took the frigate some way to windward and there
heaved to. In the brilliant sunlight he could see the French
ships perfectly, the people on their decks, even the state of
their rigging. Sitting on the slide of the aftermost carronade
he contemplated the scene; for this was a time for contemplation. No sudden decisions were called for at this point, nor

would they be required for some considerable time. The *Astrée* was a formidable ship; she was undamaged; she had disentangled herself from the *Iphigenia* and had worn clear at last; the sea between her and the *Boadicea* was clear. Yet she did not come on. Her shivering foretopsail – her deliberately shivering foretopsail – told him a great deal about her commander, and a score of less obvious details told him more: a competent seaman, no doubt, but he did not mean to fight. He no more meant to fight than Hamelin, at an even greater advantage, had meant to fight; neither this man nor his commodore chose to risk the throw. The conviction, growing stronger as he watched, filled him with grave joy.

On the other hand, said his reason as it compelled his heart to be quiet, the *Astrée* carried a great broadside weight of metal, her gunnery was accurate, and although she was not faster than the *Boadicea* she could haul closer to the wind: then again, attack and defence were two different things; in a close action the *Astrée* would do tolerably well, and although the *Iphigenia* was handled by a nincompoop, tackling the two of them together by daylight would be unjustifiable in the present balance. Yet he must necessarily retake the the *Africaine* . . .

'On deck, there,' hailed the lookout. 'Two sail right to windward, sir. I think it's *Staunch* and *Otter*.' Some minutes later, 'Yes, sir: *Staunch* and *Otter*.' With this wind it would take them two or three hours to reach him: very well. He stood up smiling and looked across to the lee side, where his first lieutenant, the carpenter and the bosun were waiting to report.

'Three wounded, sir,' said Seymour, 'and of course poor Mr Buchan.' The carpenter had only four shot-holes and eight inches of water in the well: Fellowes gave an account of a fair amount of damage to the sails and rigging forward. 'I reckon an hour will see it to rights, sir,' he added.

'As smartly as ever you can, Mr Fellowes, said Jack. 'Mr Seymour, let the hands go to breakfast; and the watch below must have: some rest.'

He went down into the orlop, where he found Stephen reading in a small book, holding it up to the lantern.

'Are you hurt?' asked Stephen.

'No, not at all, I thank you: I am come down to look at the wounded. How are they coming along?'

'Colley, the depressed cranial fracture, I will not answer for: he is comatose, as you see. We must operate as soon as we have peace and quiet and light – the sooner the better. The two splinter-wounds will do very well. Your breeches are covered with blood.'

'It is the master's. He lost the number of his mess right by me, poor fellow.' Jack went over to the patients, asked them how they felt, told them that things looked very well on deck, that *Staunch* and *Otter* were coming up hand over fist, and that presently the Frenchmen might be served out for what they did to the *Africaine*. Returning to Stephen he said, 'Killick has a little spirit-stove on the go, if you could fancy breakfast.'

And standing by the stern-window while the coffee flowed into them by the pint, he explained the situation, pointing out just how the French lay now and how they had lain at different stages. 'I know you will think it illogical,' he said, his hand firmly gripping the wooden frame, 'and maybe even superstitious, but I have a feeling that the tide has turned. I do not mean to tempt fate, God forbid, but I believe that when the *Staunch* and *Otter* join, we shall retake the *Africaine*. We might even snap up the *Iphigenia*: she is shy; I think we may have hit her hard – look at the people over her side; and the captain of the *Astrée* don't trust her. But I will not go so far as that: the *Africaine* will be enough.'

On deck once more, and a surprisingly respectable deck, with the knotting and splicing almost finished, the swabbers of the afterguard washing the last pale smears from by the wheel, the davits righted, a new foretopsail bent: over the water the French boats were still removing prisoners from the *Africaine*, the *Iphigenia*'s pumps were going hard, and from the look of the feverish activity among the parties inboard and outboard of her, she would be in no way to get under sail for some time. The *Astrée* had moved into a better position to cover her and the *Africaine*: her captain might be no fire-eater, but clearly he meant to cling to his prize if he possibly could. But now from the deck the *Staunch* and *Otter* could be seen hull up; and the breeze was blowing fresher.

An early dinner, cold; and the grog cut by half; yet there was no grumbling. The Commodore's look of contained pleasure, his certainty, the indefinable change that had come over him, had spread a feeling of total confidence throughout the ship. The hands ate their good biscuit and their execrable cheese, wetted with more watered lime-juice than rum, and they looked at him, they looked at the Frenchmen in their uneasy heap to leeward, they looked at the two ships coming closer every minute, and they talked in low cheerful voices: there was a good deal of quiet laughter in the waist and on the forecastle.

WITH A PIECE of chalk the Commodore drew his plan of attack on the deck: the captains of the sloop and the brig watched attentively. The three were to run down in line abreast, the *Boadicea* in the middle, and they were to endeavour to separate the two French frigates; there were many possibilities, depending on the movements of the *Astrée*, and Jack explained them clearly. 'But at all events, gentlemen,' he said, 'in case of the unforeseen, you will not go far wrong by closing with the *Iphigenia*, ahead and astern, and leaving the *Astrée* to me.'

With the wind three points abaft the beam, and under topsails alone for freedom of manoeuvre, they bore down, the brig looking pitifully small on the *Boadicea*'s starboard beam and the sloop a mere wisp to port. Jack had given them plenty of time to feed and rest their hands; he knew that they were thoroughly prepared and well manned, and that their commanders understood his intentions beyond any sort of doubt.

He had foreseen a great many possibilities, and he stood on with a confidence that he had rarely felt so strongly before, a steady rising of his heart; but he had not foreseen what in fact took place. They were still a mile and a half away when the *Astrée* passed the *Iphigenia* a towline and both frigates made sail. Abandoning the *Africaine*, they gathered away, packed on more sail and still more, hauled their wind and stretched to the eastwards as fast as they could go, the fine-sailing *Astrée* keeping the *Iphigenia*'s head right up to the wind, closer than ever the *Boadicea* could lie.

By coming to instantly it was conceivable that since she was somewhat to windward the *Boadicea* might bring them to action at the end of a very long converging chase, in spite of the *Astrée*'s superiority on a bowline; but neither the *Otter* nor the *Staunch* could possibly keep up, and in the meanwhile it was probable that Hamelin's reinforcement, brought by the French brig, would be down for the *Africaine*. No: this, alas, was a time for discretion, and the *Boadicea* stood quietly on for the sad dismantled hulk, which lay wallowing on the swell with no more than her ensign-staff to show the French colours.

The *Boadicea* came alongside: the *Africaine* fired two guns to leeward and the French colours came down, to the sound of immense cheering from the prisoners still aboard her. 'Mr Seymour,' said Jack, with a feeling of anticlimax, yet with a deep glowing satisfaction beneath it, 'be so good as to take possession. What the devil is this?'

This was the sight of a score of Africaines plunging into the sea, swimming across, and swarming up the side of the *Boadicea*. They were in a state of wild enthusiasm, joy and rage strangely mingled: nearly all sense of discipline was gone and they crowded dripping on the quarterdeck, begging the Commodore to renew the action – they would fight his guns for him – they would be happy to serve under Captain Aubrey – not like under some brass-bound buggers – they knew him – and they knew he could serve those French farts out for

swarming up the *Boadicea*'s side, using his powerful arms
alone and trailing his withered leg. Once aboard he shipped
his half-crutch, saluted the quarterdeck, brushed an officious
bosun's mate aside, and stumped aft. Everything was ready:
under an awning that spread the brilliant light stood an
upright chair, made fast to cleats, and in it sat Colley the
patient, lead-coloured, snoring still, and so tightly lashed by
his friends that he was as incapable of independent movement as the ship's figurehead. The deck and the tops were
strangely crowded with men, many of them feigning busyness, for the old Sophies had told their present shipmates of
that memorable day in the year two, when, in much the same
light, Dr Maturin had sawed off the top of the gunner's head,
had roused out his brains, had set them to rights, and had
clapped a silver dome over all, so that the gunner, on coming
back to life, was better than new: this they had been told, and
they were not going to miss a moment of the instructive and
even edifying spectacle. From under the forecastle came the
sound of the armourer at his forge, beating a three-shilling
piece into a flat and gleaming pancake.

'I have desired him to await our instructions for the final
shape,' said Stephen, 'but he has already sharpened and
retempered my largest trephine.' He held up the circular saw,
still gleaming from its bath, and suggested that Mr Cotton
might like to make the first incision. The medical civilities
that followed, the polite insistence and refusal, made the
audience impatient but presently their most morbid hopes
were gratified. The patient's shaved scalp, neatly divided from
ear to ear and flensed away, hung over his unshaved livid
snorting face, and now the doctors, poised above the flayed,
shattered skull, were talking in Latin.

'Whenever they start talking foreign,' observed John Harris,
forecastleman, starboard watch, 'you know they are at a
stand, and that all is, as you might say, in a manner of speaking, up.'

'You ain't seen nothing, John Harris,' said Davis, the old

Sophie. 'Our doctor is only tipping the civil to the one-legged cove; just you wait until he starts dashing away with his boring-iron.'

'Such a remarkable thickness of bone, and yet the metopic suture has not united,' said Mr Cotton. 'I have never seen the like, and am deeply gratified. 'But, as you say, it confronts us with a perplexing situation: a dilemma, as one might say.'

'The answer, as I conceive it, lies in a double perforation,' said Stephen. 'And here the strength and steadiness of your left forearm will prove invaluable. If you would have the goodness to support the parietal here, while I begin my first cut at this point, and if then we change hands, why, there is a real likelihood that we may lift out the whole in one triumphant piece.'

Had it not been for the need to preserve the appearance of professional infallibility and god-like calm, Mr Cotton would have pursed his lips and shaken his head: as it was he muttered, 'The Lord be with us,' and slid in his flattened probe. Stephen turned back his cuffs, spat on his hands, waited for the roll, placed his point and began his determined cut, the white bone skipping from the eager teeth and Carol swabbing the sawdust away. In the silence the ship's company grew still more intent: the midshipmen's berth, ghouls to a man, craned forward, unchid by their officers. But as the steel bit down into the living head, more than one grew pale, more than one looked away into the rigging; and even Jack, who had seen this grisly performance before, turned his eyes to the horizon, where the distant *Astrée* and *Iphigenia* flashed white in the sun.

He heard Stephen call out the measurements to the armourer as the second cut began; he heard a renewed hammering on the anvil forward; but as he listened a movement far over there to windward seized upon the whole of his attention. Both the Frenchmen were filling: did they mean to edge down at last? He clapped his glass to his eye, saw them come right before the wind, and shut his telescope with a smile: from the busy way they were passing their sheets it was obvious that they were merely wearing once again, as they had done five times since dawn. Yes, they had hauled their wind. Although they had the weather-gage they did not choose to bring him and the crippled *Africaine* to action; and if he was not very much mistaken, this last manoeuvre had put it out of their power, now that the mountains of La Réunion were looming on the larboard bow and the breeze was likely to veer two points inshore. To be sure, the *Africaine* still had all her teeth intact, and the *Staunch* and the *Otter* could give a shrewd nip in a melee; but even so . . . He laughed aloud, and at the same moment he heard Mr Cotton cry, 'Oh, pretty. Oh, very prettily done, sir.'

Stephen raised the piece of skull entire and held it up to peer at its underside with a look of sober triumph – a moment during which the audience might gaze with fascinated horror into the awful gulf, where Mr Cotton was now fishing for splinters with a pair of whalebone tongs. As he fished, and as a long transverse splinter stirred the depths, an awful voice, deep, slow, thick-tongued and as it were drunk, but recognizable as Colley's, spoke from behind the hanging skin and said, 'Jo. Pass that fucking gasket, Jo.' By this time the audience had dwindled, and many of the remaining ghouls were as wan as Colley himself; they revived, however, when the surgeons placed the silver cover on the hole, fastened it down, restored the patient's scalp to its usual place, sewed it up, washed their hands in the scuttle-butt, and dismissed him below. A pleased murmur ran round the ship, and Jack, stepping forward, said, 'I believe I may congratulate you, gentlemen, upon a very delicate manoeuvre?'

They bridled and said it was nothing so extraordinary – any competent surgeon could have done as much – and in any case, they added, with a sincerity that would have caused Mrs Colley a dreadful pang, there was no call for congratulation until the inevitable crisis had declared itself: after all, it could not be said that any operation was wholly successful unless the patient at least outlived the crisis. After that the cause of death might reasonably be assigned to a host of other factors.

'Oh, how I hope he lives,' said Jack, his eye still on the distant enemy. 'Colley is a prime seaman, a capital, steady hand, and can point his gun as well as any man in the ship. Has a large number of children, too, as I recall.'

All this was very true: Tom Colley, when sober, was a valuable though pugnacious member of his division; he had been bred to the sea and he could hand, reef and steer without having to take thought, and it was a joy to see him dance a hornpipe: the ship would not be the same without him. But beneath this valid reasoning lay a region that the kind observer might have called a sort of mysticism and that others, perhaps more enlightened, would have described as brutish superstition. Jack would not have had it known for the world, but he equated the seamart's recovery with the success of his campaign: and from the behaviour of the *Astrée* and *Iphigenia* over there, Colley was in a fair way to resurrection. If Hamelin had been present, flying his broad pendant aboard the *Astrée* rather than the *Vénus*, would the French attitude have been more determined? Would those two ships have risked the battle, to destroy all his hopes, whatever the cost to themselves? From what he knew of the French commodore, he doubted it.

'AN IMPRESSIVE DOCUMENT,' said Governor Farquhar, handing back the copy of Pius VII's excommunication of Buonaparte, the hitherto unpromulgated but effective personal, greater excommunication, authenticated by the bishop's seal, 'and although some of the expressions are perhaps not quite Ciceronian, the whole amounts to the most tremendous damnation that I have ever seen. Were I a Catholic, it would make me extremely uneasy in my mind, if I were obliged to have anything to do with the wretch. The Bishop made no difficulty, I presume?' Stephen smiled, and

Farquhar went on, 'How I regret your scruples. This would be of the greatest value to the ministry. Surely we should make another copy?'

'Never concern yourself about the ministry, my dear sir,' said Stephen. 'They know of its existence. They know very well; it is a tolerably open secret, I assure you. But in any event, I must not imperil my source of information: and I have given an undertaking that only three men on the Mauritius shall see it, and that I shall then commit it to the flames.' He lapped the document, heavy with curses, in his handkerchief, and thrust it into his bosom: Farquhar looked wistfully at the bulge, but he only said, 'Ah, if you have given an undertaking . . .' and they both glanced at the slips of paper upon which they had noted the subjects they were to discuss.

Stephen's were all crossed off: one remained on Farquhar's list, but he seemed to find it difficult to broach. He paused, and laughed, and said, 'The form in which I have written this will never do. You would find it offensive. I reminded myself – very unnecessarily, I may add – to beg you to give me an explanation – oh, not in any way an *official* explanation, you understand – for the Commodore's abounding sanguine activity. He really seems to assume that our plans for invading the Mauritius can go forward in spite of this appalling disaster at the Ile de la Passe: he has thoroughly infected or perhaps I should say *convinced* Keating, and the two of them dart from point to point, day and night, flying in the face of the clearest evidence. Naturally I second him with all my power – I scarcely dare do otherwise, now that he has taken on his present heroic Jovian stature. He runs into this room, says, "Farquhar, my good fellow, be so good as to cut all the tallest trees on the island and set all carpenters to work directly. The *Africaine* must have masts by dawn on Thursday at the latest," and runs out again. I tremble and obey: but when I reflect that the French possess seven frigates to our one and a pitiful wreck, and when I reckon up the guns at their disposal as opposed to ours, why, I am seized with an amazement.' He stared out of the window, seized with retro-spective stupor; and to fill the gap Stephen observed that the number of guns counted for less than the accuracy with which they were pointed and the zeal with which they were served, adding that although the *Africaine* was not yet fit for battle, her guns were available for the other vessels, such as they were.

'Very true,' said the Governor. 'But I will confess that a per-haps unworthy explanation of the Commodore's eagerness thrust itself into my mind: it occurred to me that he might possibly have some encouraging intelligence that I did not share. Do not take my words amiss, Dr Maturin, I beg.'

'Never in life, my dear sir,' said Stephen. 'No: I have told him nothing that I have not told you. The answer lies on another plane entirely. As I understand it, Commodore Aubrey has arrived at an intimate conviction that we have a moral superiority over our opponents; that the initiative has changed sides; and that, as he puts it himself, although they want neither ships nor seamanship nor conduct, they do lack spirit. They lack an earnest desire to engage, to risk every-thing on one throw; and he is of the opinion that Hamelin also lacks the sense of the decisive moment in the ebb and flow of a campaign. Furthermore, it is his view that Com-modore Hamelin is more interested in snapping up Indiamen than in gathering laurels at the one moment when they lie ready to his hand. He quoted your remark about Fortune with great approval, declaring that Hamelin would find the wench's forelock hellfire hard to grapple, now that she had forged ahead.'

'I made that remark in a very different context,' said Far-quhar; but Stephen, carrying on with his thought, continued, 'I am no strategist, but I know Jack Aubrey well: I respect his judgment in naval matters, and I find his conviction, his mili-tary intuition, wholly persuasive. There may also be some illogical factors,' he added, being perfectly aware of the rea-son for Jack's frequent hurried visits to the hospital and his immoderate delight in Colley's recovery, 'such as seamen's omens and the like, that need not detain a rational mind.'

'So you are persuaded,' said the Governor doubtfully. 'Well then, I too am persuaded; though at one remove. But at least there is no prospect of his stirring until the *Africaine* is ready for sea? No prospect, in this extremely dangerous situation, of his dashing out like a sea-borne Bayard to engage at seven to one?'

'I imagine not, but I would scarcely answer for it. Now, sir,' said Stephen, standing up, 'I must beg to take my leave: the boat is no doubt waiting, and I shall have harsh words if I do not hurry.'

'I shall see you again very shortly?' asked Farquhar. 'Yes, with the blessing. This journey takes me no farther than the south-west tip of the Mauritius, the Morne Brabant, where I see two officers of the Irish troops and another gentleman; and I think I can promise that the Commodore and Colonel Keating will have little trouble with the more Catholic members of General Decaen's garrison, when they come face to face.' As they walked through the hall he said in an undertone, tapping his chest, 'This is so very much more portable than a hundredweight of gold, and so very, very much more effective.'

The great door opened, and in the entrance they were very nearly run down by Mr Trollope, who came bounding up the steps of the Residence four at a time. He recovered himself, cast a reproachful look at Stephen, plucked off his hat, and said, 'I beg your pardon, your Excellency, but I am charged with the Commodore's respectful compliments and might he have seven hundred and fifty blacks before the evening gun? I was also to remind Dr Maturin that he asked for the aviso at five and twenty minutes past four o'clock precisely.'

Stephen looked at his watch, uttered a low howl, and set off at a shambling run for the harbour, where the *Pearl of the Mascarenes*, the fastest aviso in the island, lay champing at her buoy.

AT DAWN on Sunday the two quartermasters at the signal-station high above Saint-Denis were weighing the probabilities of duff today: last Sunday they, like all the Boadiceas and all the Africaines, Staunches and Otters, had been deprived of their duff, on account of the furious pace of work in the dockyards; and it looked very much as though the same might happen today. As they leaned out to peer at the yard below the strong land-breeze whipped their pigtails forward, obscuring their view: automatically they grasped them with their teeth and peered on: judging by the feverish activity down there, the parties of blacks and seamen and artificers and soldiers already toiling like so many ants, Sunday duff seemed as remote as wedding-cake. Even beef was by no means certain.

'Some foreign mess again,' said William Jenkins, 'and ate cold, no doubt. How Goldilocks does crack on. Slave-driving ain't in it, when you consider two weeks of no duff; and it was much the same in Simon's Town. Hurry, hurry, hurry, and don't you dare sweat the glass.'

Goldilocks was Jack Aubrey's nickname in the service, and the other quartermaster, Henry Trecothick, had sailed with him when the locks were indeed golden, rather than their present dull sun-bleached yellow. He felt that Jenkins was coming it a little high, and he said coldly, 'He's got a job of work to do, ain't he? And dogged does it. Though I must say a man likes a hot dinner, as being more natural and – Bill, what do you make of that craft out there?'

'Where away?'

'Nor-nor-east: just coming round the point. Behind the islands. She's dowsed her mainsail.'

'I can't see nothing.'

'What a wall-eyed slab-sided Dutch-built bugger you are, to be sure, Bill Jenkins. Behind the islands.'

'Behind the islands? Why didn't you say so? She's a fisherman, that's what she is. Can't you see they're a-pulling? Ain't you got no eyes?'

'Light along the glass, Bill,' said Trecothick. And having

stared fixedly he said, 'She ain't no fisherman. They're pulling like Dogget's coat and badge; pulling right into the wind's eye like it was a race for a thousand pound. No fisherman ever pulled like that.' A pause. 'I tell you what, Bill Jenkins, she's that little old aviso, *Pearl* by name.'

'You and your fancies, Henry. *Pearl* ain't due back this tide, no, nor the next. Was that thunder? A drop of rain would – '

'Christ, she's broke out a signal. Get your fat arse out of the way. *Enemy in sight* – what's red white chequer? – *due north*. Bill, jump down and rouse out Mr Ballocks. I'll fix the hoist. Bear a hand, mate, bear a hand.'

Up flew the signal, out banged the gun: the station above St Paul's repeated within a matter of seconds, and into the dining-cabin of the *Boadicea* darted the midshipman of the watch, who found the Commodore pink and cheerful, surrounded by papers and already dictating to his blear-eyed, unshaved secretary as he devoured his first, or sunrise, breakfast, 'Mr Johnson's duty, sir,' he cried, St Paul's repeating from Saint-Denis *enemy in sight, bearing due north.*'

'Thank you, Mr Bates,' said Jack. 'I shall be on deck directly. '

There he found the whole quarterdeck motionless, all faces turned towards the distant flagstaff: he said, 'Prepare to slip, Mr Johnson,' and then he too fixed his eyes on the hill. Two full minutes passed with no further hoist, and he said to the signal-midshipman, 'Repeat to Saint-Denis, *Staunch and Otter proceed to sea immediately: attend to pendant's motions.*' Then stepping to the taffrail he hailed the *Africaine*. 'Mr Tullidge, I have room for fifty volunteers, no more.'

The Africaines were less remarkable for their discipline than their ferocious eagerness to serve the Frenchmen out, and now began a disorderly savage jostling race, whose fifty winners, headed by a powerful master's mate with a face like a baboon, came aboard the *Boadicea* by boat or strong swimming as her buoyed cable ran smoking from her hawse and she cast to the fine land-breeze.

The sails came crowding on; she gathered way, and the good breeze carried them up towards Cape Bernard, the high land that barred out all the ocean due north of Saint-Denis as well as the town itself. With studdingsails on either side, the *Boadicea* threw a bow-wave that came creaming down to the mainchains, but even so the cape moved tediously slow, and Jack found it something of a relief to have his impatience distracted by the ugly scene that developed when it was rumoured that the Africaines were to take over the forward starboard guns. Loud angry voices, rarely raised aboard the *Boadicea*, could be heard on the forecastle, disturbing the holy calm of a well-run man-of-war: the bosun came hurrying aft, spoke to the first lieutenant, and Seymour, crossing the quarterdeck to the rail where Jack was staring at the station in the hope of some more definite signal, coughed and said, 'I beg your pardon, sir, but the men of Mr Richardson's division believe that their guns are to be taken from them, and with the utmost respect they wish to represent that they would find this a little hard.'

'Let the hands come aft, Mr Seymour,' said Jack, with his telescope still trained on the flagstaff, now at the far limit of his view. When he clapped the glass to and turned there they were before him, the whole waist of the ship crowded with men, whose utmost respect (though genuine) was for the moment scarcely discernible beneath their rage at injustice.

'What a precious set of old women you are, upon my word,' he said testily. 'You clap on to a silly buzz with no truth in it and set about one another like a parcel of fish-fags. Look at Eames there, with a bloody nose and on a Sunday too, for shame. And all this before we know whether the enemy is anything more than some stray sloop, or whether he will be so polite as to stay until you have stopped clawing one another. Now I tell you what it is: if we have the good fortune to come into action, every team is going to fight the gun it's used to. That's justice. But if any Boadicea is hurt, then an Africaine takes his place: and if we board, then the Africaines board first. That's flat and that's fair all round. Mr Seymour, be so good as to have cutlasses and boarding-axes served out to the Africaines.'

The general opinion was that this was fair enough: and although for the present the Boadiceas could not be brought to love the Africaines, they did at least treat their guests with a distant civility – no oaths, no blows, little more than a covert kick or nudge, accidental done a-purpose.

Cape Bernard at last, and the frigate rounded it, shaving the reef so close that a lobbed biscuit might have reached the wicked breakers. And as she rounded it, opening new skies, so her people heard the sound of gunfire, the growling of heavy guns a great way off in the north.

'Jump up to the masthead, Mr Richardson,' said Jack, 'and tell me what you see.'

As the midshipman vanished aloft Saint-Denis came into sight: the *Staunch* was still working out of the harbour, and the *Otter* was only a mile ahead of her. Jack frowned; he was about to call the signal-midshipman when he saw fresh canvas break out aboard both of them. It was true that neither had been ready for action, ready to slip at a moment's notice, as the *Boadicea* had been these last twenty-four hours; it was true that they must have had most of their hands ashore or in the yard; but even so he was not pleased, and he meditated a rebuke. 'Am I growing pompous?' he wondered, and the answer 'Probably' had taken disagreeable form in his mind when Spotted Dick, after a scrupulous examination of the distant northern sea, hailed him. 'On deck, there. Sir, I believe I can make out three ships hull-down two points on the larboard bow.' And as if to confirm his words, the distant thunder growled again. Every man aboard listened with all his might, strained ears trying to pierce through the song of the rigging and the slap of the sea to the underlying silence; and every man aboard heard the popping of a musket, weak, but nothing near so remote as the great guns.

Again the masthead hailed the deck, reporting, perhaps a

little late, the presence of the aviso a couple of miles away, almost invisible against the reef. She was still pulling strongly against the wind, still announcing that the enemy was in sight, with a musket-shot to underline the signal.

'Close the aviso, Mr Seymour,' said Jack.

As the *Boadicea* swept down the *Pearl* set her jib and mainsail, spun about and ran quartering before the wind, clear of the reef and its islands, so that when the two vessels converged they were both running fast on almost parallel courses – Dr Maturin could be restored to the frigate without the loss of a moment.

His standard of seamanship being tolerably well-known aboard the *Boadicea*, no orders were required for his reception: there was not time for a bosun's chair, but a whip appeared at the mainyardarm; and now, as they tore along together with no more than a few feet of foaming, heaving sea between them, Bonden, poised on the rail of the *Pearl*, seized the line, made Stephen fast, adjured him 'to take it easy', called out 'Heave away, there: cheerly now', sprang across the gulf and ran up the frigate's side like a cat to receive the Doctor as he came aboard. He: had timed the roll exactly, and all would have gone well if Stephen, with some notion of steadying himself, had not grasped at the *Pearl*'s rigging. A slack slabline at once took a turn about his dangling legs and jerked him into a maze of cordage that he could neither name nor disentangle. A fairly heavy swell was running, and for a moment it seemed that Stephen must come aboard in two pieces. A nimble Pearl raced aloft and at great cost to the aviso's rigging cut him free; but this he did at the very moment when the Boadiceas, realizing that they were tearing their surgeon apart, let go; and Stephen therefore swung in a sickening downward curve to strike the frigate's side a little below the waterline. Now, urged by cries, they heaved again, but he stuck under the chains, and the ship's next roll plunged him deep. Unfortunately for Stephen he counted none but friends aboard, and a large proportion of these sprang to his rescue; powerful hands pulled him in different directions by the arms, legs and hair, and only the violent intervention of the Commodore preserved him. He reached the deck at last, more dead than alive, oozing blood from scratches inflicted by the barnacles; they emptied some of the water out of him, carried him below, and plucked off his clothes.

'There, there, take it easy,' said Jack, looking anxiously into his face and speaking in that compassionate protective voice which has vexed so many invalids into the tomb.

'There is not a moment to lose,' cried Stephen, starting up.

Jack pressed him back into the cot with irresistible force, and still in the same soothing voice he said, 'We are not losing any time at all, old Stephen. Not a moment. Do not grow agitated. All is well. You are all right now.'

'Oh, your soul to the devil, Jack Aubrey,' said Stephen, and in an even stronger tone, 'Killick, Killick, you mumping villain, bring in the coffee, will you now, for the love of God. And a bowl of sweet oil. Listen, Jack' – writhing from beneath his hand and sitting up – 'you must press on, crack on, clap on, as fast as ever you can go. There are two frigates out there battering one of ours. And one of them, the *Vénus*, has lost masts, rigging – Bonden will tell you the details – and you may catch her, if only you will make haste, and not sit there leering like a mole with the palsy.'

'Pass the word for my coxswain,' called Jack, and to Stephen he said, 'We are already making haste, you know.' He named the sails that were now urging the *Boadicea* towards the distant battle, and he assured Stephen that the moment she cleared the land-breeze and entered the region of the south-easter offshore, he would let fall his maincourse and set his staysails, for then they would have the wind on the quarter, rather than right aft; and Stephen was to take notice that the presence of the captain on deck was not essential to the progress of the ship, once he was blessed with a seamanlike set of officers. The appearance of Bonden and of Killick bearing the sweet oil cut off Stephen's reply: he groped among the heap of wet clothes, brought out his watch and dipped it in the oil, observing, 'It has survived several grave immersions; let us hope it may survive this. Now, Barret Bonden, I shall give the Commodore a succinct account of the position, and you will supply the technical details.' He collected his mind, and went on, 'Yesterday evening, you must understand, I was standing on the most elevated point of the Morne Brabant, where it overlooks the sea, and conversing with some gentlemen who among other things told me, and this I must not omit, that the *Bellone*, *Minerve* and *Iphigenia* are undergoing heavy repairs, with their guns all out, and will not be fit for sea this fortnight and more: Bonden was at a certain distance – '

'A cable's length, sir,' said Bonden.

' – when I perceived a ship sailing down from Port-Louis in the direction of La Réunion. One of the gentlemen, who had followed the sea for many years, asserted that she was an Indiaman. He pointed out her general mercantile appearance, and the presence of a subsidiary posterior deck, or platform – '

'Poop,' muttered Bonden.

' – the infallible mark of your Indiaman; and he remarked that it would be strange indeed if Monsieur Hamelin, then in Port-Louis, should let such a prize escape him. And in fact shortly afterwards we descried the *Vénus* and a smaller frigate – '

'Pardon me, sir,' said Bonden, *Wenus* and a *sloop*.'

'The little one had three masts,' said Stephen sharply. 'I counted them.'

'Yes, sir; but she was only a sloop.' And addressing Jack, Bonden went on, 'Sixteen-gun corvette *Victor*, sir.'

'Well, never mind. They pursued the alleged Indiaman, the *Vénus* outsailing her companion: and then to our surprise the Indiaman turned out to be no Indiaman, at all. She took down or folded a number of sails, allowed the *Vénus* to come close, and discharged a number of guns upon her, at the same time displaying a banner indicating she was a man-of-war.'

Jack looked at Bonden, who said, 'Bombay, sir; a country-built Indiaman bought into the service in the year five. My cousin George, he sailed in her one commission, gunner's mate; said she was a good sea-boat, but mortal slow. Twenty-four eighteen-pounders, two long nines, and fourteen twenty-four-pounder carronades.'

'At this,' said Stephen, 'the Vénus drew back, waiting for her consort, and the Bombay pressed on. The sun had set: we descended the cliff, made our way to the aviso, and there I resigned the conduct of affairs into Bonden's hands.'

'Well, sir,' said Bonden, 'I knew you would be wishful to know as soon as ever could be, so we nipped through the Dutchman's Passage with barely a scrape, though the tide was out, fetched the Victor's wake, crossed under her stern in the dark just before moonrise, and worked up to windward with all she could wear and well-nigh more. We was well ahead, running nine-ten knots by the time the moon was well up, and we see Wenus coming up on the Bombay hand over hand, seven knots to her six, maybe; and at the beginning of the middle watch, when we had sunk the land long since, she ranged up alongside and they set to hammer and tongs. I ought to of said, sir, that Bombay had a tidy packet of redcoats aboard, and there seemed to be plenty of soldiers in Wenus too, her decks were that crowded with men. Well now, Wenus didn't care for it overmuch, and presently she wore out of range, new-gammoning her bowsprit, as far as I could judge. Howsoever, in a couple of glasses she perked her spirits up again, and the wind having backed two points she set her stuns'ls and bore down. The action started again in the morning watch, a running fight, with both on 'em under royals and larboard stuns'ls; but by now we was so far ahead I couldn't rightly see how it went. I did see Wenus lose her foretopmast and her gaff, and Bombay, she lost her main and mizzen topmasts, and her courses were chawed up something cruel; but

she was standing on for Saint-Denis and giving as good as she
got when last we see her plain, and the sloop was still a
league and more astern.'

While he was speaking the *Boadicea* began to heel to larboard; she had run beyond the land-breeze, which came from
aft, and she was now in the south-easter, a gentle wind today,
untimely gentle. In spite of his words about seamanlike officers Jack went on deck the moment Bonden's account was
done. He automatically checked the spread of canvas against
the force of the wind, and found something of a dispropor-
tion: like so many others, young Johnson still entertained the
delusion that more sail meant more speed, and in his eagerness he was pressing her down by the head. Jack did not wish
the change to have the appearance of a check, however, and
first he hailed the masthead. 'Masthead, there. What do you
see?'

'They are hull-up now, sir,' called the lookout. 'Heavy
frigate, Indiaman, and a ship-rigged sloop or maybe a jackass
frigate, all wearing French colours; pendant aboard the big
frigate. No firing since four bells. Frigate's lost her topmasts,
all three of them. Indiaman too. Sloop unwounded, I believe.'

Jack nodded, took a turn or so, told Johnson that he might
find her labour less with the flying-jib hauled down, slung his
glass, set his hands to the shrouds, and swung himself up: up
and up, through the maintop, up again to the crosstrees,
slower than he would have climbed twenty years before, but
still at a respectable pace.

All that the lookout had told him was true; but what the
lookout had not been able to tell him was the spirit of the
scene far over there to the north, so far over that the shimmering air sometimes gave the distant ships their masts and
sometimes took them away; and it was that he had climbed
his airy pinnacle to make out. After a backward glance at the
Staunch and the *Otter*, both of them a couple of miles astern
and losing steadily, he settled down to a prolonged study of
the position. Between them the *Vénus* and the *Victor* had cer-

tainly taken the *Bombay*, having reduced her to her lower masts alone: the *Vénus* had paid heavily, however, losing not only her fore and main topmasts but the greater part of her mizzen too. The sloop had not suffered at all. There was great activity aboard the *Vénus*, and it appeared to him that they were preparing to send up a new foretopmast: they had certainly fished a fine great spar of some kind to the stump of the mizzen. Boats were passing between the ships. The distance was too great for any certainty, but it looked as though bodies of men were moving in both directions: as though it were not merely a shifting of prisoners. Did Hamelin intend to man his prize? It was by no means impossible: sailing from his home port he might very well have doubled his crew with seamen drafted from his other ships, to say nothing of all the soldiers in Port-Louis. If he could spare enough men to serve the *Bombay*'s forty guns, and if he had the hardihood to do so, that would change the situation.

Within himself Jack had not the slightest doubt of victory, but it would never do to let this conviction take the form of even unspoken words; it must remain in the state of that inward glow which had inhabited him ever since the retaking of the *Africaine* and which had now increased to fill the whole of his heart – a glow that he believed to be his most private secret, although in fact it was evident to everyone aboard from Stephen Maturin to the adenoidal third-class boy who closed the muster-book. So leaving that to one side he set himself to a cold, professional, objective examination of the factors that might delay or even prevent it.

The first was the wind. The south-easter was slackening; already there were glassy patches of sea on the starboard bow, forerunners of the usual midday lull, which might leave him without steerage-way or compel a very slow advance, head-on, into the combined broadside fire of the *Vénus* and *Bombay*, and which might allow Hamelin time to set up a jury-rig that would at least give him twice his present power of manoeuvring.

The second was the arrival of reinforcements. He had no very high opinion of the French commodore's enterprise, but Hamelin was no halfwit. On finding himself in such a position at dawn, with La Réunion looming large on the south horizon, he would certainly have sent his best cutter racing back to Mauritius for support. In Hamelin's place he would have done so the moment the *Bombay* struck.

While he turned these things over in his mind, the pattern to the northward grew clearer. The boats had been hoisted in; the *Victor*, all sails abroad, had taken the *Bombay* in tow; the *Vénus*, cropping her fore and main courses, had put before the wind. And now a foresail appeared aboard the *Bombay*. They still had a fresh breeze out there, and presently they were moving at about three knots, while the *Boadicea*, with all her noble spread of canvas, was making little better than five and a half. 'However,' he reflected, 'there is nothing much I can do about that.'

What little he could do, he did. Having finished 'Plymouth Point,' the surest of tunes for a wind, he was whistling at random when he became aware that Sophie was in his mind, present with an extraordinary clarity. 'Was I a superstitious cove,' he said, smiling with singular sweetness in the direction of England, 'I should swear she was thinking of me.'

The smile was still lingering on his face when he reached the deck, and this encouraged Seymour to ask whether he might start to clear the ship for action.

'As to that, Mr Seymour,' said Jack, looking at the log-board, 'it might be a little premature. We must not tempt fate, you know. Mr Bates, be so good as to heave the log.'

'Heave the log it is, sir,' said the midshipman, darting to the lee-rail with his attendant boy and quartermaster. The boy held the reel, the quartermaster the thirty-second sand-glass; Bates threw the log, watched the mark go clear, called 'Turn' and the quartermaster held the glass to his eye, while the boy held up the reel with a hieratic solemnity. The log went

astern, the knots in the line passing smoothly through Bates'
fingers. 'Nip,' cried the quartermaster. The midshipman
nipped, then jerked the line; the boy reeled in, and Bates
crossed the deck to announce, 'Just on the five, sir, if you
please.'

Jack nodded, glanced up at the frigate's towering array of
canvas, at the fire-hose in the tops wetting all the jet could
reach, at the buckets hoisting to the crosstrees to damp the
topgallants so that they should catch every last ounce of
thrust, and said, 'No, Mr Seymour. Without the gods are
kind, we have more time on our hands than I could wish. It
would be a pity to dowse the galley fires so soon; so let the
men be piped to dinner at six bells, and since they went without their duff last Sunday, let there be a double ration of
plums today. On the other hand, only half the grog will be
served out this spell: and no plush allowed.' The faces of the
men at the wheel, the quartermaster conning the ship, the
yeoman of the signals and the nearer members of the afterguard took on a stony look. Jack paced fore and aft and continued, 'The rest will be kept for supper, wind, weather and
the enemy permitting. And Mr Seymour, since we shall be
pinched for time, dinner being so early, church will not be
rigged today; however, I believe we may proceed to divisions.
Mr Kiernan,' he added, nodding towards the baboon-faced
officer, 'will muster his Africaines on the forecastle.'

From this moment on time raced by aboard the frigate.
Every man, with little notice and even less expectation of this
solemn event (practised on every peaceful Sunday, but never,
never when bearing down on the enemy), had to present himself, an hour earlier than usual, washed, shaved, and in a
clean shirt for inspection by his particular midshipman and
officer and then by the Commodore himself. Furthermore,
there was a general determination to wipe the Africaines' collective eye by a brilliantly striking appearance. All along the
gangway and on the forecastle the tie-for-tie pairs swiftly and

silently combed and plaited one another's pigtails, while impatient groups clustered round the barber's tubs, urging him to even greater speed, whatever it might cost; and anxious Marines pipeclayed and polished in the blazing sun.

The inspection itself was a creditable affair, with the officers, in full dress and wearing their swords, accompanying the Commodore in his slow progress along the lines of trim seamen in their best; and the hairy Africaines in their dirty shirts were brought suitably low. But the ceremony was marred by an extraordinary degree of distraction: remarkable things were happening in the north – the *Bombay's* towline had parted, the *Victor* was having a devilish time passing another, the *Vénus* had first sheered off and had then come up into what wind there was to lend a hand, and above all the vast stretch of ocean between the *Boadicea* and the French had narrowed surprisingly. Even while the Commodore was on deck, few men apart from the rigid Marines could resist glancing northwards and passing remarks; and when he was exploring the galley and the berth-deck with the first lieutenant, Mr Trollope was obliged to call out 'Silence, fore and aft' several times, and to take the names of the more loquacious, for future punishment.

The moment divisions was over, the bosun and his mates piped loud and shrill to dinner. Every man aboard knew that the order *clear for action* would follow in a very short time indeed, for the wind had freshened markedly this last half hour, and that he must make up his mind at once between fighting the ship in his best clothes and missing if not his beef then his double-shotted duff. Most plumped for the duff, which they ate on deck, by their guns, holding it carefully away from their snowy shirts, their silk neckerchiefs, and trousers beribboned at the seams. Scarcely was the last crumb down when the expected order carne. Mess-kids vanished and the men, some still chewing, set about the familiar task of making a clean sweep fore and aft: they had done so, and they were standing at their action-stations staring now at the enemy, not far from extreme range, and now astern at the distant *Staunch* and *Otter*, when Stephen appeared on the quarterdeck, bearing a plate of sandwiches.

Doctor Maturin was a God-send to the Boadiceas: not only would he accost the Commodore with a freedom impossible to any other man aboard, but he would ask questions that none but he might propound, and receive civil answers rather than a severe set-down. Any gentlemanly reluctance to over-hear private conversation had long since died away, and casual chat on the quarterdeck fell silent, in case any word between the Commodore and the Doctor should be lost.

He did not disappoint them now. 'Why, sir,' said he, looking about him, 'what splendour I see: gold lace, breeches, cocked hats. Allow me to recommend a sandwich. And would you be contemplating an attack, at all?'

'It had crossed my mind, I must admit,' said Jack. 'Indeed, I may go so far as to say, that I am afraid a conflict is now virtu-ally inevitable. Did you notice we have cleared for action?'

'Certainly I did. I have not ploughed the ocean all these weary years without learning the significance of this wild dis-order, the cabins vanishing, my papers, my specimens, flung upside-down into the nearest recess. That is why I am come out here, for a little peace. Dear me, how close they are! It would be indiscreet, perhaps, to ask what happens next?'

'To tell you the truth, Doctor,' said Jack, 'for the moment I am in two minds. The corvette, do you see, has cast off her tow for good and all, and she is bearing away for the Mauri-tius under all sail, no doubt on her commodore's orders, while he is corning down towards the *Bombay*. Now if he has manned his prize, if he has sent enough men aboard the *Bombay* to serve her guns, then his plan will be to fight us with both ships in close support; and in that case we must run between 'em, firing both sides. But if he has not manned her, and if he is only covering the *Victor*'s retreat by this manoeuvre, why, then he means to meet us alone. And in that case we must run down on his bow, or his quarter if he wears, and carry him by boarding, so as not to damage his hull nor those precious spars I see on his deck. Another ten minutes will tell us what he means to do. If he don't back his foresail just before reaching the *Bombay*, so as to heave to beside her, you understand, that will mean she is not manned and that he must fight us by himself. Masthead,' he cried, 'what do you see in the north?'

'Nothing, sir, bar the sloop,' replied the masthead. 'A clear horizon all round. Sloop's carried away a kite on the main: is setting another.'

After this there was a prolonged silence aboard the *Boadicea*: the men stationed at the guns stared over the barricade of hammocks or out through the open ports at the *Vénus*; the splinter-netting over their heads sent a strange shifting rectangular pattern down on the deck; the wind hummed and sighed through the rigging.

The minutes passed; ten minutes passed; and then a general murmur ran through the ship. The *Vénus* had not backed her foresail and now she was well beyond the *Bombay*. She was ugly, with her stumpy masts, but she was dangerous, determined, and her gun ports were all open; she carried heavy metal, and her decks were crowded with men.

'Mr Seymour,' said Jack, 'topsails and forecourse alone, and draw the guns. Reload with grape. Not a shot is to touch her hull. Sweep her decks, but do not touch her hull. D'ye hear me, there?' he cried, raising his voice. 'Any gun-crew that wounds her hull will be flogged. Mr Hall, lay me for the bow.'

Closer and closer. Jack's opinion of Hamelin rose: the Frenchman was staking everything on coming so close before he yawed that his broadside must do the *Boadicea* irreparable damage – staking everything, because after that one turn the *Vénus*, with no more sail than she could spread, would never come up into the wind again, but must lie there to be battered to death.

Closer still in the silence: they were within pistol-shot. The *Vénus*' bow guns cracked out; the turn began, and the moment before her side came into full view Jack said, 'Hard a-port.' The *Boadicea* moved fast, heeling abruptly, and the thundering broadside from the *Vénus* cut no mast away. The foretopsail yard was wounded, two studdingsail booms had gone, some rigging hung loose; the starboard cathead was shattered and the best bower swung free; but Hamelin had lost his bet.

'Duck up forward,' said Jack, and at once the foresail puckered, checking the frigate's speed as she swept through the enemy's smoke. The *Vénus* turned, turned until she was almost before the wind and stern-on to the *Boadicea*. 'Bear a hand with the clew-line,' said Jack. 'Mr Hall, clear her starboard quarter, and bump me her bows.' The *Boadicea* shot forward, and it was clear that she would range up on the *Vénus* before the Frenchmen had had time to reload. 'Africaines stand by to board over her bow,' he cried. 'Boadiceas, come aft: we go for her quarterdeck. And we give the Africaines one minute's law, mark what I say. Steady there by the guns,' he said, loosening his sword. 'Bonden, where are my pistols?'

There was Killick at his side, holding an old pair of shoes and a coat over his arm. 'You can't go in your best silver-buckled shoes, your honour, nor in your number one coat,' he kept saying in an angry whine. 'It won't take you a minute to change.'

'Nonsense,' said Jack. 'Everyone else is going in his best, so why should I be left out?'

The *Vénus*' soldiers were firing from her stern, but it was too late. The *Boadicea* ranged alongside, Jack said 'Fire,' and the *Boadicea*'s grape swept the *Vénus*'s deck at head-height and in the smoke grapnels flew over the side; topmen ran out and lashed the Frenchman's yardarms tight; their bows ground together, and Jack roared 'Africaines away.' A moment later their sterns swung in, and the two ships lay side by side.

For a full minute he stood at the head of his boarders, while the Marines behind him plied their muskets as though

they were on parade and the small-arms men in the tops kept
up a fire on the guns. A full minute of vast din and shouting
forward, the crackle of pistols and the bellow of a carronade
that the Africaines had turned into the waist of the *Vénus*.
Then he cried, 'Boadiceas, come along with me,' vaulted on to
the torn hammocks, leapt sword in hand across to the
shrouds of the mainmast, slashed the boarding-netting,
slashed at a head below him, and so down to the *Vénus'* quarterdeck, followed by a cheering mass of seamen.

Before him stood a line of soldiers – the seamen were in
the waist, facing the Africaines' furious attack – and in the
second before the wave of Boadiceas broke over them a little
terrified corporal lunged at Jack with his bayonet. Bonden
caught the muzzle, wrenched the musket free, flogged three
men flat with the butt and broke the line. On the deck
behind the soldiers lay several bodies – officers – and in the
momentary pause Jack thought he saw a French captain's
uniform. Then the aftermost group on the larboard gangway,
led by a young officer, turned and came for the Boadiceas
with such a rush that they were swept back to the wheel, and
the next few minutes were a furious confusion of violence,
cut and parry, duck the pistol, kick and thrust and hack.

But the Vénuses were no match for the boarders; they were
oppressed and hemmed in by their own numbers; they were
worn out by their long night's battle and the toil that had followed it; their spirits were crushed by the sight of the *Otter* and
the *Staunch* coming up fast, and by the certainty of eventual
defeat. A body of Croatian soldiers, who had no real concern
with the quarrel, leapt down the now unguarded main hatchway; others followed them, seeking safety below. The remaining Frenchmen on the gangway made a last desperate charge,
and a short, broadshouldered seaman with a knife grappled
Jack round the waist. Jack dashed his hilt into the seaman's
face, trampled him down, broke free; and there in the clear
space by the fife-rail stood an officer, offering his sword and
pointing aft, where a boy was hauling down the colours.

Through the enormous cheering that spread from the *Vénus'* quarterdeck to the *Boadicea*, Jack roared out, ' 'Vast fighting, there. Forward there, Africaines, 'vast fighting. She's struck.'

Men fell apart, stared impersonally at one another, and moved slowly away. The extreme tension died with extraordinary speed and within moments a new relationship had established itself, a kind of primitive social contract – men could no longer hit one another.

Jack accepted the officer's sword with a civil bend of his head and passed it to Bonden. The man he had trampled upon got to his feet without looking at him and stumbled away to his shipmates, who were standing where the battle had It left them or who had gathered in little groups by the lee-rail, silent, as though the act of surrender had drained their spirit away, leaving them quite numb.

Still the *Boadicea* was cheering, and the exultant din was echoed by the *Bombay*, a quarter of a mile away: she had rehoisted her ensign, and her crew was skipping and waving and roaring all along her side and in her tops.

'Commodore Hamelin?' said Jack to the officer, and the officer pointed to one of the bodies close by the wheel.

'I WAS SORRY about Hamelin, however,' said Jack, as he and Stephen sat over a late dinner. 'Though when you come to think of it, a man could hardly ask better.'

'For my part,' said Stephen, 'I could ask for very much better. A grapeshot in the heart is not my idea of bliss, and I should do my utmost to avoid it. Yet your grief does not affect your appetite, I find: that is the eighth chop you have eaten. Nor, which strikes me with peculiar force, do I find that this battle has produced the melancholy reaction I have so often noticed in you.'

'That is true,' said Jack. 'An action clears your mind amazingly, for the moment; but afterwards the black dog comes down. The butcher's bill, the funerals, the men's widows to write to, the mess to be cleared up, the knotting and splicing, the pumping – you feel done up, hipped, as flat as ditch-water; though there is more to it than that. But this time it is different. To be sure, we have come off scot-free or very near, but that is not the point. The point is that this dust-up is only the beginning of the real action. *Africaine* will be ready for sea on Tuesday: with the spars preparing at St Paul's and what we have captured today, *Vénus* and *Bombay* will not take much longer, working double tides – their hulls would already pass a survey, you know. That is four capital frigates, plus the *Windham*, three good sloops, and all our armed transports: while on their side they have only *Astrée* and *Manche* ready for sea. *Bellone* and *Minerve* must certainly be heaved down; and *Iphigenia* and *Néréide* are little use to man or beast even when they are repaired. They have lost their commodore; and the captain of the *Astrée* at least is a booby. And where is their spirit? No: I tell you what, Stephen, by the end of the week Keating and I will carry out our plan – that will be the real action, what I call the real action; and I don't care how glum I grow after it.'

'Well, my dear,' said Stephen, 'politically Mauritius was ready to fall like a ripe plum, or mango, even before the Ile de la Passe; and now that you have repaired the disaster and more, I believe you may install Governor Farquhar at Port-Louis within a week of landing your troops.'

10

'**YOU HAVE BEEN** very much in my mind these days, sweetheart, even more than usual,' wrote Jack, continuing his serial letter to Sophie, a letter that he been building up to its present bulk ever since the *Leopard* had sailed from St Paul's for the Cape, his last contact with the flag, 'and I should certainly have wrote, had we not been so uncommon busy. Since Monday morning we have been on the run, with all hands turning to, to make the squadron ready for sea; and such a sawing of carpenters, a thumping of caulkers, and a busyness of bosuns you never heard in your life. Poor Trollope, an active officer but of a bilious turn, was overcome with a sunstroke, while a black blacksmith, that had wrought eighteen hours on a stretch, was carried off in a dead swoon, quite grey. But now it is done. Now we are at sea, sinking the land as the sun comes up' – he looked, smiling, out of the *Boadicea*'s stern-window, and there in her wake, two cable-lengths away, he saw the *Vénus*, her sails pearly in the growing light; beyond her he could make out the *Africaine*, and far to leeward the last three transports. As the pendant-ship, the *Boadicea* was sailing in the middle of the squadron with the *Bombay* and the *Windham* ahead of her, the *Staunch*, the *Otter* and the *Grappler* far up to windward, and under her lee the transports, comfortably full of soldiers – 'and a very respectable body we are. It is true some of our masts would make the dock-yard mateys stare, but they will serve: they may not be very pretty, but they will serve. We took many of the spars out of *Bombay* and *Vénus*, and the Devil's own job we had to bring them home: I had promised the men the other half of their grog should be served out with their ration for supper, which might have been well enough if they had not found their way into the enemy's spirit-room, too. Lord, Sophie, we rolled back that night like a whole herd of Davey's sows, with seven Boadiceas and seven Africaines in irons, and most of the rest not fit to go aloft. Fortunately the *Otter* had *Bombay* in tow, or I doubt we should ever have brought them both in. As it was, any French brig in her right wits could have snapped us up.

'By the morning most of the hands were sober, and I harangued them on the beastly vice of inebriation; but I am afraid the effect of my words (and thundering good words they were) were quite lost because of the welcome they gave us ashore. Rockets, Bengal lights you could hardly see

because of the sun though kindly intended, salvoes from all
the fortifications, and three times three all round the port:
the Governor, a capital determined fellow, with a good head
on his shoulders, and thoroughly understands cooperation,
was so pleased at the sight of two frigates bringing in that he
would, though a tea-drinker himself, have made the men
drunk again directly, if I had not represented to him, that *we
must make hay while the sun shone.* Colonel Keating was positively overjoyed, and expressed himself in the most obliging
manner; and he too thoroughly agreed that *we must strike
while the iron is hot.*

'Nothing could exceed his zeal in harrying his staff-officers
and other slow-bellies and in getting his men aboard with all
their proper accoutrements and in the right order: for I will
tell you, my dear (since no eye but yours will see this letter,
and that only after the event), that we mean to invade the
Mauritius the day after tomorrow; and we have a very fair
hope of a happy outcome.' He cast a furtive glance at
Stephen Maturin as he wrote these words, so offensive to all
his friend's principles and so contrary to all his repeated
injunctions, and Stephen, catching his eye, said, 'Should you
like some encouragement, joy?'

'If you please,' said Jack.

'Then you must know that the captain of the ship the *Jeffer-
son B. Lowell* –'

'The barque, Stephen. The American was a barque; and an
amazing fine sailer, too.'

'Bah. Was so good as to tell me of the various rates he and
his colleagues trading to St Louis have placed on Mauritius
paper money. Before our arrival it was very nearly at par with
cash; then it dropped to twenty-two per centum below, and
so rose and fell according to the fortunes of the campaign,
rising to ninety-three after the Ile de la Passe. But now it is
not admitted upon any discount at all, and gold is absolutely
insisted upon. There is cool, objective testimony for you.'

'I am delighted to hear it, Stephen: thank you very much,'

said Jack. He returned to his letter, and Stephen to his 'cello.

'Keating would, I am sure, have been as busy as a bee in any event, out of zeal for our joint campaign (and never did army and navy work so well together, I believe, since ships were first found out); but in this case he was as busy as two or even more, from an uneasiness in his mind at what he had heard from the army officers we released from the *Vénus*. They spoke of a General Abercrombie, who was to command them and a very considerable force gathered from all parts of India: it is difficult to make much sense of what they said, for their colonel was killed in the action, and the junior officers had only fag-ends of gossip; but the general notion is that they were to rendezvous at Rodriguez with several regiments from Fort William and some troops from the Cape and that they were then to make a descent on La Réunion; which, when you come to think of it, is absurd. Even so, Keating was much concerned: "If any gouty old fool of a general comes along to snatch the bread out of my mouth again the very moment it is buttered," cries he in a great passion, "I shall sell my commission to the highest bidder, and be d—d to the service: to be choused out of the glory when we have done all the work, would be more than flesh and blood can bear." And he told me again of the siege of some Indian city whose name I forget, where he had carried the approaches right up to the walls, had repelled sorties by the score, had made a practicable breach, and was on the eve of storming the place when a general appeared in a palanquin, took over, gave the order to attack, wrote a despatch giving himself all the credit for the victory, was promoted and given the Bath, with an augmentation to his coat of arms. Keating added some pretty severe reflections on the Bath and old men who would do anything for a trumpery piece of ribbon, which I will not repeat, they being somewhat too warm.' Jack paused, meditating a witticism in which *hot water* should combine with *Bath* to produce a brilliant effect, but his genius did not lie that way, and having chewed his pen for some time, he carried on: 'For my own part, I could not make much more sense out of poor Graham of the *Bombay*, either. He had had a cruise after pirates in the Persian Gulf, and when he put in, precious short-handed, he was at once ordered to take a whole heap of soldiers aboard and to rendezvous with the *Illustrious*, 74, just south of the Eight Degree Channel – had nothing but ill-luck all the way – sprang a leak low down under his fore-peak ten days out, had to put back, beating up with the wind in his teeth, pumping hard and his men falling sick – endless delays in the yard – missed his first rendezvous, missed the next, so bore away, sick himself with a low fever, for Port-Louis, where he expected to find us blockading – and was taken, after a long and tolerably bloody running fight. I am afraid the heat and the wear and the anxiety and the action may have sent his wits astray, for the unfortunate wight absolutely struck to a sloop, which he took for a second frigate in the darkness. (It is true she was ship-rigged: our old sixteen-gun *Victor*, but a very mere cockle in fact.) Stephen was of my opinion about his intellects, filled him to the hatches with opium-draughts, shaving and blistering his head just before we left. But in any case, I cannot find that he ever had orders for Rodriguez; so it is a hundred to one that Keating was nourishing a chimaera, as they say. But since it made him so desperate eager to present any lurking general, hungry for honours, with a fait accompli, viz. a conquered island with HM Governor already installed, and since his eagerness chimed in with my eagerness to get to sea before the French had the *Minerve* and *Bellone* afloat (there is a rumour that someone, a Royalist or Papist or both, damaged their bottoms with an infernal machine: but I find it hard to believe that even a foreigner could be so wicked) – why, I fairly caressed the chimaera of his. Stephen,' he called, over the growling 'cello, 'how do you spell chimaera?'

'Many people start with ch, I believe. Have you told her about my stink-pot petrel?'

'Is not stink-pot a hellish low expression for a letter, Stephen?'

'Bless you, my dear, a mother that tends her own babies will not boggle at stink-pot. But you may put thalassodrome, if you find it more genteel.'

The pen scratched on; the 'cello sang deep; a midshipman tapped on the door. He reported a sail on the starboard quarter, adding that from a curious patch in her foretopsail she was thought to be the *Emma*.

'Aye, no doubt,' said Jack. 'She has made amazing good time. Thank you, Mr Penn.' The *Emma* had been called in by aviso from her station off Rodriguez, but he had not looked for her sooner than Thursday. 'Tom Pullings will be aboard presently,' he said to Stephen. 'We must keep him for dinner. After all this to and fro-ing off Rodriguez he will be glad of a bite of fresh mutton.' He called out to Killick: the saddle of yesterday's sheep was to be ready at five bells precisely, together with half a dozen of the red Constantia and a drowned baby. They discussed Thomas Pullings, his indifferent prospects, his real deserts, his probable appetite; and the midshipman reappeared, breathless and staring: *Staunch* had just signalled four sail, bearing north-east.

'What says *Emma*?' asked Jack.

'I don't know, sir,' said the midshipman.

'Then be so good as to find out,' said the Commodore, with some asperity.

The *Emma*, it appeared, had nothing to say, *No enemy in sight* flew from her fore; no gun called for her pendant's attention; yet the *Emma*, with a seamanlike captain aboard, was nearer those four sail than the *Staunch*. The conclusion was obvious: the four sails were Indiamen . . . unless, he reflected, with a cold grip in his heart, they were English men-of-war.

Stepping thoughtfully out of the cabin, he took over the deck, hailed the *Africaine* that he was leaving the line, and hauled up to close the *Emma*. Hitherto the *Boadicea* had been proceeding under easy sail, at a pace suited to that of the transports, but now topgallants broke out, and with the fine breeze two points free she began to move like a thoroughbred. Her wake stretched white and long; her bow-wave rose to the bridle-ports and the spray came sweeping aft from her forecastle, making rainbows in the sun. Spirits rose high, and the boys and the younger topmen laughed aloud as they raced aloft to loose the royals: but a few sharp, unusually vehement orders from the quarterdeck did away with their more obvious mirth. The afterguard and the waisters moved as mute as mice, ludicrously tiptoeing when they could not be seen; those forward exchanged covert winks and nudges; and those high above murmured, 'Watch out for squalls, mate' with a knowing grin. Little passes unnoticed in a man-of-war, and although only the Marine sentry and one or two members of the anchor-watch had seen Jack and Colonel Keating come aboard after Governor Farquhar's farewell dinner, the whole ship's company knew that the skipper 'had taken a glass', that he had been 'as pissed as old Noah', that he had been 'brought down in a barrow, roaring for a woman – for a black girl in his cot', and they smiled indulgently, whispering quotations from his homily on the beastly vice of inebriation, as he called out to know whether that tack was to be brought to the chesstrees this watch or not.

Now the *Boadicea* was really lying down to her work, shouldering the long swell aside with a fine living motion and making her ten knots with no effort, so that for all those untormented by vile premonitions it was a pleasure to feel her sail.

'This is what I had imagined life at sea to be like,' said Mr Peter, a rare visitor to the quarterdeck – he spent most of his days in an airless paper-lined hole beneath the waterline, dividing his time between seasickness and work. 'Do you not find it exhilarating, sir?'

'Sure, it is like a glass of champagne,' replied Stephen; and

Mr Peter smiled, looking significantly at Colonel Keating, greyish-yellow and blinking in the sun. It was in fact the Colonel who had been brought down in a wheelbarrow; it was he who had so often cried 'Let copulation thrive.'

The *Boadicea* and the *Emma* were approaching at a combined rate of sixteen knots, and every few minutes pushed the eastward horizon back another mile. Soon the lookout told the deck of the four sail reported by the *Staunch*: then came another hail – two ships bearing east-north-east, and a hint of topgallantsails beyond them.

Six ships at least: it was almost impossible that so many should be Indiamen. Jack took a few turns, and his face grew more forbidding: he tossed off his coat, borrowed Seymour's telescope, and made his way up to the foretopgallant masthead. He was nearly there, with the shrouds creaking under his weight and the wind sweeping his long hair away to the north-west, when he heard the lookout mutter 'Sixteen, seventeen . . . 'tis a bleeding armada. An invincible bleeding armada. On deck, there . . .'

'Never mind, Lee,' said Jack, 'I can see 'em myself. Shift over.' He settled himself into the crosstrees and trained his glass east and north-east. There they lay, the greatest concentration of men-of-war he had ever seen in the Indian Ocean. And presently, to knock any lingering ghost of hope on the head, he made out the *Illustrious*, a two-decker wearing a vice-admiral's flag at the fore.

By this time the *Emma* was well within range. They had long since exchanged signals, and now the *Emma* was coming under the *Boadicea*'s lee in her heavy wallowing fashion, while the frigate backed her foretopsail and lay to.

Jack took a last long look at the fleet, men-of-war and transports, and then lowered himself heavily down through the rigging, much as another man might have walked heavily down the stairs in his house, thinking not of the steps but of his own problems. He reached the deck and put on his coat as Pullings came up the side; and the contrast between the lieutenant's beaming face, white teeth flashing in the deep ruddy tan, and the Commodore's sombre look would have struck an eye far less observant than Stephen's. However, the mere force of Pullings's grin, his evident pleasure, brought an answering smile; and the smile grew a little more lively at the sight of a large bag hoisting up from the *Emma*'s boat, the much-loved familiar mail-sack.

'There is no one so welcome as the postman, Mr Pullings,' said Jack, inviting him into the cabin. 'Whence come ye, Tom?' he asked, once they were there.

'Straight from the Admiral, sir,' said Pullings, as though this were the best news that could ever be brought.

'From Mr Bertie?' asked Jack, whose protesting mind had faintly offered a hypothetical force bound for Java, perhaps, under a different vice-admiral, one with no responsibility for the Cape – an admiral who was merely passing by.

'That's right, sir,' said Pullings cheerfully. 'And he gave me this for you.' He took a dog-eared Naval Chronicle from his pocket and plucked an official letter from among its pages, marking the place with his thumb; but holding the letter aloft, not quite delivering it, he said, 'So no post, sir, since I last saw you?'

'Not a word, Tom,' said Jack. 'Not a word since the Cape; and that was out of order. Not a word for the best part of a year.'

'Then I am the first,' cried Pullings with infinite satisfaction. 'Let me wish you and Mrs Aubrey all the joy in the world.' He grasped Jack's limp, wondering hand, wrung it numb, and showed the printed page, reading aloud, 'At Ashgrove Cottage, Chilton Admiral, in Hants, the lady of Captain Aubrey, of the *Boadicea*, of a son and heir,' following the words with his finger.

'Give it here,' said Jack. He grasped the magazine, sloped the page to the light and pored over it intently. ' "At Ashgrove Cottage, Chilton Admiral, in Hants, the lady of Captain Aubrey, of the *Boadicea*, of a son . . ." Well, I'll be damned.

God bless me. Lord, Lord . . . upon my word and honour . . .
I'll be damned to Hell and back again . . . strike me down.
Killick, Killick, rouse out a bottle of champagne – pass the
word for the Doctor – here, Killick, there's for you – God love
us all – ha, ha, ha.'

Killick took the handful of money, put it slowly into his
pocket with a look of extreme suspicion and walked out of
the cabin, his lips pursed in disapproval. Jack leapt from his
seat, took several turns fore and aft, chuckling from time to
time, his mind filled with mingled love, happiness, fulfil-
ment, and a most piercing nostalgia. 'I thank you, Pullings, I
thank you with all my heart for your news,' he said.

'I thought you would be pleased, sir,' said Pullings. 'We
always knew, Mrs P. and I, how you wanted a boy. Girls are
very well, in course, but they are not quite the same; you
could not wish them about all the time. And then you never
know what they will be at. But a boy! – Our nipper, sir, if ever
I get a settled command of my own, shall come to sea the
minute he is out of coats, and properly breeched.'

'I trust Mrs Pullings and young John are quite well?' said
Jack; but before he could learn much of them, Stephen
walked in, followed by the sack of mail. 'Stephen,' said Jack,
'Sophie is brought to bed of a boy.'

'Aye? I dare say,' said Stephen. 'Poor thing. But it must be a
great relief to your mind.'

'Why,' said Jack, with a blush, 'I never had wind of it, you
know.' Calculation had already established the fact that the
distant nameless wonder was conceived the night of his leaving, and this made him bashful, even confused.

'Well, I give you joy of your son,' said Stephen. 'And I hope
with all my heart that dear Sophie does well? At least,' he
observed, as he watched Jack busy with the mail-sack, 'this
will make a baronetcy more welcome: will give it more point.

'Lord, what am I at?' cried Jack. 'Orders come first.' He
dropped the sack, broke the seal of the Admiral's letter, found
the expected words directing and requiring him to proceed

with all possible dispatch to the flag at or off Rodriguez immediately upon receipt of these orders. He laughed, and said, 'If there is any baronetcy in the wind, it don't come this way. I am superseded.'

He went on deck, gave one order for the signal that should set the squadron on its new course, away from Mauritius, and another to splice the mainbrace. To Seymour's astonished expression he replied, in a voice as offhand as he could make it, that he had just learnt of the birth of a son. He received the congratulations of the quarterdeck and many a kind look from the seamen nearby, invited Colonel Keating to take a glass in the cabin, and so returned. The bottle was soon out, the letters distributed; and Jack, giving Keating his packet, said, 'I hope, Colonel, that your news may be as pleasant as mine, to offset the rest; because you were too good a prophet by half, and I fear there may be a general waiting for you at Rodriguez, just as there is an admiral waiting for me.' With these words he retired with his letters to the quarter-gallery, his own private place of ease, leaving the soldier transfixed, pale and even trembling, with indignation.

A little before dinner he came out and found Stephen alone in the great cabin. Pullings had now, for the first time, learnt of the squadron's destination; and realizing that a little tactful delay on his part would have allowed the Commodore to carry out his plans and to reap honour and glory, had withdrawn to the taffrail, where he stood by the ensign-staff, cursing his untimely zeal. 'I wish you too may have had very good news, Stephen?' said Jack, nodding at the pile of open letters at Stephen's side.

'Tolerably so in parts, I thank you; but nothing that causes me a joy comparable with yours. You are still in a glow, brother, a roseate glow. Pray tell me of Sophie's condition.'

'She says she has never felt better in her life – swears it passed off as easy as a letter in the post – finds the little chap a great comfort, and excellent company. Now I know you are about as partial to children as old Herod, Stephen, but – '

'No, no. I am not doggedly, mechanically set against them, though I freely admit I find most babies superfluous, and unnecessary.'

'Without there were babies, we should have no next generation.'

'So much the better, when you consider the state to which we have reduced the world they must live in, the bloody-minded wolfish stock from which they spring, and the wicked, inhuman society that will form them. Yet I do admit of exceptions: the replication of such a creature as Sophie, and even I may say of yourself, can be seen as a good. But I am afraid I interrupt you.'

'I was only going to say, that you might like to hear Sophie's description of him. It appears that he is a most unusual, exceptional child.'

Stephen listened with a decent show of complaisance: the smell of roasting meat drifted aft, and that of fried onions; he heard the drum beat 'Heart of Oak' for the gunroom's dinner; his stomach called out for his own; and still the tale ran on.

'You cannot conceive, Stephen, how it extends a man's future, having a son,' said Jack. 'Now it is worth while planting a walnut-tree! Why, I may even lay down a whole plantation of oaks.'

'The girls would have gathered your walnuts. The girls would have sported under the oaks; and their grandchildren would have felled them.'

'No, no. It is not the same thing at all. Now, thank God, they have portions; and so eventually they will marry some greasy fellow called Snooks – you must admit, Stephen, that it is not the same thing at all.'

Just before five bells Jack was cut short by the arrival of Pullings, still sadly reduced, and of the Colonel, still trembling with rage; and at five bells itself Killick announced, 'Wittles is up,' with a courtly jerk of his thumb, and they moved into the dining-cabin.

Pullings ate his mutton silently, with little appetite;

Colonel Keating, though allowed by convention to speak freely at the Commodore's table, remained almost equally mute, not wishing to spoil a happy occasion by giving vent to the words he longed to utter; Stephen was lost in reflection, though from time to time he did respond to pauses in Jack's cheerful flow. When the long meal was over, when the King, Mrs Aubrey and young Stupor Mundi had been drunk in bumpers of luke-warm port, and when the guests had moved into the open air to dissipate the fumes of their wine, he said to Jack, 'I scarcely know which I most admire, the strength of your philoprogenitive instinct, or your magnanimity in the face of this disappointment. Not many years ago you would have clapped your telescope to your blind eye; you would have evaded these orders; and you would have taken the Mauritius before Mr Bertie knew what you were at.'

'Well, I *am* disappointed,' said Jack, 'I must confess; and when first I smoked the Admiral's intentions I had a month's mind to steer due west for a while. But it would not do, you know. Orders is orders, bar one case in a million; and this is not one of those cases. The Mauritius must fall in the next week or so, whoever is in command, or whoever takes the glory.'

'Keating does not take it so philosophically.' 'Keating has not just heard he has a son. Ha, ha, ha: there's for you, Stephen.'

'Keating already has five, and a sad expense they are to him, as well as a grave disappointment. The news of a sixth boy would not have mollified his indignation, unless indeed it had been a daughter, the one thing he longs for. Strange, strange: it is a passion to which I cannot find the least echo, when I peer into my bosom.'

Colonel Keating's indignation was shared throughout the *Boadicea* and her companions. It was universally held that the Commodore had been done out of his rights, cheated of his due, and wiped in the eye if not stabbed in the back: and there was not a man in the squadron who did not know that two captured Indiamen lay in Port-Louis, together with a large number of only slightly less magnificent prizes, and that the appearance – the totally unnecessary appearance – of a seventy-four, eight frigates, four sloops, and maybe a dozen regiments of lobsters, would reduce the share of all who had done the real work to half a pint of small beer, if that.

The indignation increased with brooding, and as the two bodies slowly converged, meeting at Rodriguez, it grew to such a pitch that when the *Boadicea*'s salute to the flag roared out, the gunner said, 'And I wish they was loaded with grape, you old – ' without a word of reproach from the officers near at hand. When the last gun had been fired, and before the flagship began her reply, Jack said, 'Strike the pendant. Hoist out my barge.' Then, a mere post-captain again, he stepped into the cabin and called for his breeches, cocked hat and number one coat to go aboard the Admiral. It had been a hard moment, the striking of his pendant – for a pendant could not fly in the presence of a flag without the unusual compliment of a direct invitation – but little comfort did he meet with below. Killick's sense of injustice had been inflamed by the extra ration of grog served out to all hands. It now overflowed on to the principal victim, and in his old shrewish voice he said, 'You ain't got no number one coat, sir. All bloody and mucked up, with figuring away aboard the *Vénus*, when two minutes would of changed it. The scraper will pass with a shove' – spitting on the lace of the cocked hat and rubbing it with his sleeve – 'but you'll have to wear it athwartships, on account of the rats. As for coats and breeches, this is the best I can do – I've shipped the old epaulettes – and if any jumped-up new-come son of a Gosport fart don't like it, he may – '

'Bear a hand, bear a hand,' cried Jack. 'Give me my stockings and that packet, and don't stand muttering there all day.'

The same sullen resentment was obvious in the barge-men who pulled Captain Aubrey across to the *Illustrious*; it was evident in his coxswain's rigour, in the vicious stab of the boathook that clamped on to the two-decker's chains, removing a good hand's-breadth of paint, and in the expressionless reserve that met the friendly advances of the seamen peering out of her lowerdeck ports.

Admiral Bertie expected it; he knew very well what he was doing, and he was fully armoured against all reaction except cheerfulness. From the outset he adopted an attitude of jovial bonhomie, with a good deal of laughter: he spoke as though it were the most natural thing in the world to find a ready and willing compliance, no trace of ill-feeling or resentment; and to his astonishment he did find it. The Naval Instructions clearly laid down that he must find it, and that anything less than total abnegation, total perfection of conduct, would render a subordinate liable to punishment; but his whole service life had proved that there was a world of difference between the Navy in print and the Navy in practice, and that although in theory a senior post-captain must be as submissive to an admiral as a newly-joined midshipman, in fact an oppressed commodore, growing froward under ill-usage, might make things extremely awkward for his oppressor and still keep the right side of the law: he had himself used obstruction in all its refinements often enough to know what it could accomplish. He had been prepared to meet the cunningest ploys or the most violent expressions of dissent (his secretary was there to note down any choleric word): none appeared: he was taken aback, rendered uneasy. He probed a little deeper, asking whether Aubrey was not surprised to see so many ships coming to queer his pitch? And when Jack, with equal joviality, replied that he was not, that the greater the number the less the bloodshed (so repugnant to him, as to all right-feeling men), and that the more the merrier was his motto, the Admiral glanced at his secretary, to see whether Mr Shepherd shared his suspicion that Captain Aubrey was somewhat disguised, cheerfully disguised, in wine.

The suspicion could not be maintained. As soon as the captains of the fleet were assembled aboard the flagship, at the Admiral's request Jack Aubrey delivered to them a singularly lucid, cogent account of the situation, with all the facts, all the figures at instant command. To the anxious words about the notorious difficulty of the reefs surrounding Mauritius, the wicked surf that beat upon them, and the paucity of harbours, he replied with a chart, a little masterpiece of hydrography, showing Flat Island and the Grande Baie, exactly surveyed by himself, with triple-sextant-bearings and doubled-checked soundings showing plenty of room and clean anchorage for seventy ships, as well as sheltered beaches for a very great number of men. He ended his exposition by observing that in view of the lateness of the season he would respectfully suggest an immediate descent.

The Admiral was by no means so sure of that: long before Captain Aubrey was born the Admiral's old nurse had told him 'The more hurry, the less speed.' He would take the matter under consideration – urgent consideration – and advise with General Abercrombie and the gentlemen of his staff.

When the meeting broke up he kept Jack for a while, by way of plumbing his mind: for Aubrey was either a nonpareil of docility (and that was not his reputation at all), or he had something up his sleeve. It made the Admiral uneasy. It seemed to him that beneath all his proper deference Jack regarded him with a certain detachment and something not far from a secret amused contempt; and since the Admiral was not altogether a scrub he found this extremely disagreeable. Then again, Mr Bertie had invariably met with hostility from those he had over-reached, a hostility that gave him a retrospective justification; and here there was none – continuing cheerfulness, even benignity. It made him feel nervous, and on parting with Jack he said, 'By the way, Aubrey, it was quite right to strike your pendant, of course; but you must hoist it again the moment you set foot aboard the *Boadicea*.'

Admiral Bertie was more uneasy still by the time he reached his cot. In the interval, as the fleet lay at anchor in the road of Rodriguez and the visiting boats passed to and fro, Mr Peter had called upon his near relation Mr Shepherd. Mr

Peter had seen a good deal of Dr Maturin, a simpler, more penetrable man than he had been led to suppose, particularly since this last flood of letters and information from home: and from Maturin's casual remarks, some of them really far from discreet, Peter had formed the conviction that General Aubrey, the Commodore's father and a member of parliament, was probably playing a very deep game, that he might be about to change sides, that he was secretly very well with the ministry, and that it was by no means impossible that he might shortly appear in an office connected with honours and patronage, if not on the Board of Admiralty itself. Stephen had poisoned too many sources of intelligence to derive much satisfaction from this elementary exercise; but in fact the sneaking underhand little tale was admirably suited to the ears that received it a few minutes after Peter's departure. It explained Aubrey's disconcerting nonchalance: a man with such allies must be handled with care.

In the morning a council, attended by the captains and the senior army officers, considered the plan of attack worked out by Jack and Colonel Keating. General Abercombie's plea for delay, strongly supported by his staff, was brushed aside with even greater strength by the Admiral himself. The General looked surprised and even injured: he was a stout old gentleman, and he stared across the table at nothing in particular, with a look of hostile stupidity in his protuberant eyes, as though he did not quite understand what had happened. But having repeated himself for the space of about three quarters of an hour he yielded to the Admiral's insistence; and the plan, scarcely mangled in any important respect, was agreed to, though with very little grace. Half an hour later the flagship stood out to sea, with a fine topgallant breeze to send her north about Mauritius for Flat Island and the beaches up the coast from Port-Louis.

THE CONQUEST OF Mauritius ran its leisurely course, with the regiments marching and countermarching in a scientific manner that pleased the generals on either side. The infantrymen sweated, but few of them bled. They had been landed smoothly, without opposition, and they presented General Decaen with an insuperable problem. His numerous militia was no use to him at all: most of its members had read Stephen's broadsheets, many of them had already seen copies of Governor Farquhar's proposed proclamation, all of them were more concerned with the revival of their strangled trade than with the welfare of Buonaparte's empire. His Irish troops were clearly disaffected; his French regulars were out-numbered by well over five to one; and his navy was block-aded by an overwhelming force of ships. His only concern was to delay General Abercrombie's advance until his surren-der should meet certain arcane military requirements, so that he should be able to justify his conduct at home and obtain honourable terms at Port-Louis for himself and his men.

He succeeded to admiration, and Abercrombie particular praised his orderly retreat on the night of Thursday, when his flanking battalions fell back from Terre Rouge and the Long Mountain, changing face at the double in the most profes-sional way. 'That is real soldiering,' said the General.

While these rural gestures were being made the emissaries passed to and fro, and although Port-Louis was still nominally French Stephen Maturin walked up to the military hospital without his usual detour; and there he found McAdam on the verandah. 'How is our patient this morning?' he asked.

"Och, the night was good enough, with your draught,' said McAdam, though with no great satisfaction. 'And the eye shows some wee improvement. It is the neck that keeps me so anxious – slough, slough and slough again, and this morn-ing it looked as ugly as ever. He will pluck at the dressing in his sleep. Dr Martin suggests sewing flaps of healthy skin across the whole morbid area.'

'Martin is a fool,' said Stephen. 'What we are concerned with is the artery-wall itself, not the gross exfoliation. Rest is the answer, clean dressings, lenitives and peace of mind:

there is physical strength in galore. How is the agitation?'

'Fair enough this morning; and he has been sleeping since my early rounds.'

'Very good, very good. Then we must certainly not disturb him; there is nothing like sleep for repair. I shall come back about noon, bringing the Commodore. He has a letter from Lady Clonfert at the Cape; he wishes to deliver it himself, and to tell Clonfert how the fleet praises his noble defence of the *Néréide*.' McAdam whistled and screwed up his face. 'Do you think it imprudent?' asked Stephen.

McAdam scratched himself: he could not say – Clonfert had been very strange these days – did not talk to him – no longer opened his mind – remained silent, listening for gunfire hour after hour. 'Maybe it would be best if you was to come a few minutes ahead. We can sound him out, and if we judge the excitement would not be too much, the Commodore can see him. It might do him a world of good. He liked seeing you,' said McAdam with a burst of generosity that he instantly balanced by asking in a sneering voice, 'I suppose your Big Buck Aubrey is prancing about on shore, the lord of creation? How are things going along down there, will you tell me?'

'Much as we had expected. Mr Farquhar has landed from the *Otter*, and I dare say the capitulation will be signed before dinner.'

They talked about other wounded Néréides: some were doing well, some were at death's door. Young Hobson, a master's mate emasculated late in the battle, had passed through it that night, thankful to go. Stephen nodded, and for a while he watched two geckoes on the wall, paying some attention to McAdam's account of the French surgeon's words about the impossibility of saving patients when the vital spring was gone. After a long pause he said, 'McAdam, you know more about this aspect of medicine than I do: what do you say to a patient with no physical injury, no tangible lesion, who loses all real concern with his life? Who takes a disgust to the world? A scholar, say, who has edited Livy, Livy his sole study and his delight: he stumbles on the lost books, carries them home, and finds he has not the courage, the spirit, to open even the first. He does not care about Livy's lost books, nor about his books that are known, nor about any books or authors at all. They do not interest him. He will not lift the cover; and he sees that very soon his own animal functions will not interest him either. Do you understand me? Have you seen cases of this sort in your practice?'

'Certainly I have. And they are not so rare, neither, even in men that are kept busy.'

'What is the prognosis? How do you see the nature of the malady?'

'I take it that here we are to leave grace to one side?'

'Just so.'

'As to the nature, why, I believe he perceives the void that has always surrounded him, and in doing so he falls straight into a pit. Sometimes his perception of the void is intermittent; but where it is not, then in my experience spiritual death ensues, preceding physical death sometimes by ten years and more. Occasionally he may be pulled out by his prick.'

'You mean he may remain capable of love?'

As between men and women I use the term lust: but call it what you like: desire, a burning desire for some slut may answer, if only he burns hard enough. In the early stages, however,' said McAdam, leering at the geckoes, 'he may tide himself over with opium, for a while.'

'Good day to you, now, Dr McAdam.'

On his way down through the growing heat Stephen overtook two crippled boys, the one with his leg taken off at the knee, the other with an empty sleeve pinned over his breast, midshipmen of the *Néréide*. 'Mr Lomax,' he cried, 'sit down at once. This is madness: your stitches will burst, Sit down at once on that stone: elevate your limb.'

Pale young wraithlike Lomax, propped by his crutch and

his companion, hopped to the stone, the mounting-stone outside a rich-looking house, and sat upon it. 'It is only another hundred yards, sir,' he said. 'All the Néréides are there. You can see the ship from the corner; and we are to go aboard the minute her colours go up.'

'Nonsense,' said Stephen. But having considered for a while he knocked at the door: a little later he came out with a chair, a cushion, and two stout anxious care-worn black men. He put Lomax into the chair, properly padded, and the black men carried it down to the turn in the road where the little group of mobile survivors looked down on their frigate, tight-packed among the Indiamen, the merchant ships and the men-of-war in Port-Louis harbour. Some of their eager life seeped into him. 'Mr Yeo,' he said to a lieutenant with a great bandage covering most of his face, 'you may do me an essential service, if you will be so kind. I was obliged to leave a valuable bolster in your ship, and I should be most grateful if you would order the strictest search when you go aboard. I have already mentioned it to the Admiral and the Commodore, but – ' His words were cut off by cheering away to the right, a cheering that spread as the French colours came down on the citadel, and that redoubled when the union flag replaced them. The Néréides cheered too, thin and piping, a poor volume of sound that was lost in the salvoes of artillery and then in a deep rolling thunder from the guns of the fleet.

'I shall not forget, sir,' said Yeo, shaking Stephen by the hand. 'Pass it on, there: the Doctor's bolster to be preserved.'

Stephen walked on, now quite through the town, where the closed shutters gave an impression of death, and where the few white people in the streets looked oppressed, as though the plague were abroad; only the blacks, whose lot could scarcely change for the worse, showed any liveliness or curiosity. He attended to various points of business, and met Jack at their appointed place. 'The capitulation is signed, I collect?' he said.

'Yes,' said Jack. 'Uncommon handsome terms, too: they march out with colours flying, match burning, drum beating – all the honours of war – and they are not to be prisoners. Tell me, how did you find Clonfert? I have his wife's letter here in my pocket.'

'I did not see him this morning: he was asleep. McAdam seems to think his general state to be much the same. He should come through, I believe, barring accidents: but of course he will be horribly disfigured. That will have a bearing on his state of mind, and in these cases the patient's mind is of great importance. I propose leaving you under the trees near the gate, while I attend to his dressings with McAdam. He may be in no state to receive you.'

They made their way up the hill, talking of the ceremony. 'Farquhar was astonished you had not been invited,' said Jack. 'He checked the Admiral so hard we all looked away – said your work had saved innumerable lives and that the slight must be repaired: you should be given the place of honour at his official dinner. The Admiral looked concerned, and salaamed, and said he would instantly do everything in his power – would mention you with the greatest respect in his despatch; and then he ran off like a boy to start writing it – had been itching to do so since dawn. And a precious document it will be, I am sure, ha, ha, ha. Much the same as most of 'em, only more so; but it will certainly have a whole Gazette to itself.'

'Who is to carry it?'

'Oh, his nephew, I dare say, or one of his favourite captains: it is the greatest plum to carry these last five years and more – attendance at court, kind words and a tip from the King, dinner at Guildhall, freedom of this and that: promotion of course or a damned good billet. I shall give the lucky man my letters to Sophie – he will go like the wind, cracking on regardless, homeward bound with such welcome news, the dog.'

Jack's mind flew off to Hampshire, and it was still there when Stephen said in a louder tone, 'I repeat, what do you think is our next destination?'

'Eh? Oh, Java, no doubt, to have a crack at the Dutchmen.'

'Java: oh, indeed. Listen, now: here are your trees. There is a bench. I shall be with you directly.'

The hospital courtyard was in a strange state of disorder: not only the confusion of a defeat, with people making the most of a vacation of power to carry off everything portable, but something quite out of the common. Stephen walked faster when he heard McAdam's raucous northern voice calling out, and he pushed through a knot of attendants staring up at the verandah. McAdam was drunk, but not so drunk that he could not stand, not so drunk that he did not recognize Stephen. ,'Make a lane, there,' he cried. 'Make a lane for the great Dublin physician. Come and see your patient, Dr Maturin, you whore.'

In the low-ceilinged room the shutters drawn against the noonday sun made Clonfert's blood show almost black: no great pool, but all there was in his small, wasted body. He lay on his back, arms spread out and dangling, the unshattered side of his face looking beautiful and perfectly grave, even severe. The bandage had been torn from his neck.

Stephen bent to listen for any trace of a heart-beat, straightened, closed Clonfert's eyes, and pulled up the sheet. McAdam sat on the side of the bed, weeping now, his fury gone with his shouting; and between his sobs he said, 'It was the cheering that woke him. What are they cheering for? says he, and I said the French have surrendered. Aubrey will be here and you shall have your *Néréide* back. Never, by God, says he, not from Jack Aubrey: run out McAdam and see are they coming. And when I stepped out of the door so he did it, and so bloody Christ he did it.' A long silence, and he said, 'Your Jack Aubrey destroyed him. Jack Aubrey destroyed him.'

Stephen crossed the blazing courtyard again, and under the trees Jack stood up, expectant. His smile vanished when

Stephen said, 'He is dead,' and they paced down in silence through the town. A town busier now, with the shops opening, men posting up the proclamation, large numbers of people walking about, companies of soldiers marching, parties of bluejackets, queues forming outside the brothels, several French officers who saluted punctiliously, putting the best face they could on defeat. Stephen stopped to kneel as the Sacrament passed by to a deathbed, a single priest and a boy with a bell.

'I trust he went easy?' said Jack in a low voice, at last. Stephen nodded, and he looked at Jack with his pale, expressionless eyes, looking objectively at his friend, tall, sanguine, almost beefy, full of health, rich, and under his kindly though moderate concern happy and even triumphant. He thought, 'You cannot blame the bull because the frog burst: the bull has no comprehension of the affair,' but even so he said, 'Listen, Jack: I do not much care for the taste of this victory. Nor any victory, if it comes to that. I shall see you at dinner.'

THE DINNER WAS NOTHING in comparison with those usually eaten at Government House under the rule of General Decaen: many of his cooks and all of his plate had vanished in the brief interregnum, and a stray mortar-bomb had destroyed part of the wall. But even so the creole dishes made a pleasant contrast with the hard fare of recent days, and above all the ceremony provided an ideal occasion for speeches.

Something, reflected Jack, something came over officers who reached flag-rank or the equivalent, something that made them love to get up on their hind legs and produce long measured periods with even longer pauses between them. Several gentlemen had already risen to utter slow compliments to themselves, their fellows, and their nation, and now General Abercrombie was struggling to his feet, with a sheaf of notes in his hand. 'Your Excellency, my lords, Admiral Bertie, and gentlemen. We are met here together,' two bars of silence, 'on this happy, eh, *occasion*,' two more bars, 'to celebrate what I may perhaps be permitted to call, an unparalleled feat, of *combined* operations, of *combination*, valour, organization, and I may say, of indomitable will.' Pause. 'I take no credit to myself.' Cries of No, no; and cheers. 'No. It is all due,' pause, 'to a young lady in Madras.'

'Sir, sir,' hissed his aide-de-camp, 'you have turned over two pages. You have come to the joke.'

It took some time to get the General back to his eulogy of Abercrombie and all present, and in the interval Jack looked anxiously at his friend, one of the few black coats present, sitting on the Governor's right. Stephen loathed speeches, but though paler than usual he seemed to be bearing up, and Jack noticed with pleasure that as well as his own he was secretly drinking the wine poured into the abstinent Governor's glass.

The General boomed on, came to a close, a false close, rallied and began again, and at last sank into his chair, glared round in surly triumph and drank like a camel with a broad desert before it.

A broad desert threatened, to be sure, for here was Admiral Bertie, fresh and spry, game for a good half hour: and his first words about his inability to match the gallant General's eloquence struck a chill to Jack's heart. His mind wandered during the Admiral's compliments to the various corps that made up the force, and he was in the act of building an observatory-dome of superior design on the top of Ashgrove hill – he had of course purchased the hill and felled the trees on the summit – when he heard Mr Bertie's voice take on a new and unctuous tone.

'In the course of my long career,' said the Admiral, 'I have been compelled to give many orders, which, though always for the good of the service, have sometimes been repugnant to my finer feelings. For even an Admiral retains finer feelings, gentlemen.' Dutiful laughter, pretty thin. 'But now, with His Excellency's permission, I shall indulge myself by giving one that is more congenial to the spirit of a plain British

sailor.' He paused and coughed in a suddenly hushed atmosphere of genuine suspense, and then in an even louder voice
he went on, 'I hereby request and require Captain Aubrey to
repair aboard the *Boadicea* as soon as he has finished his dinner, there to receive my despatches for the Lords Commissioners of the Admiralty and to convey them to Whitehall
with all the diligence in his power. And to this, gentlemen' –
raising his glass – 'I will append a toast: let us all fill up to the
brim, gunwales under, and drink to England, home and
beauty, and may Lucky Jack Aubrey reach 'em with fair winds
and flowing sheets every mile of the way.'

The music room in the Governor's Ho
octagonal ~~room~~ with gilt pilasters. ~~n~~
climax ~~of the first movement~~ of Locatel
Italians penned in against the far wo
chairs. played with passionate convic
intensity towards towards the penulti
final ~~note~~ chord ⊙ And on the little gilt c
were following the rise with equal con
hand side. there were two of these, them
one another.   The one was a man
form overflowed his chair. leaving on
& there; he was wearing his best u
& silk stockings of a lieutenant in
buttoned cuff of his sleeve beat the t
                    face